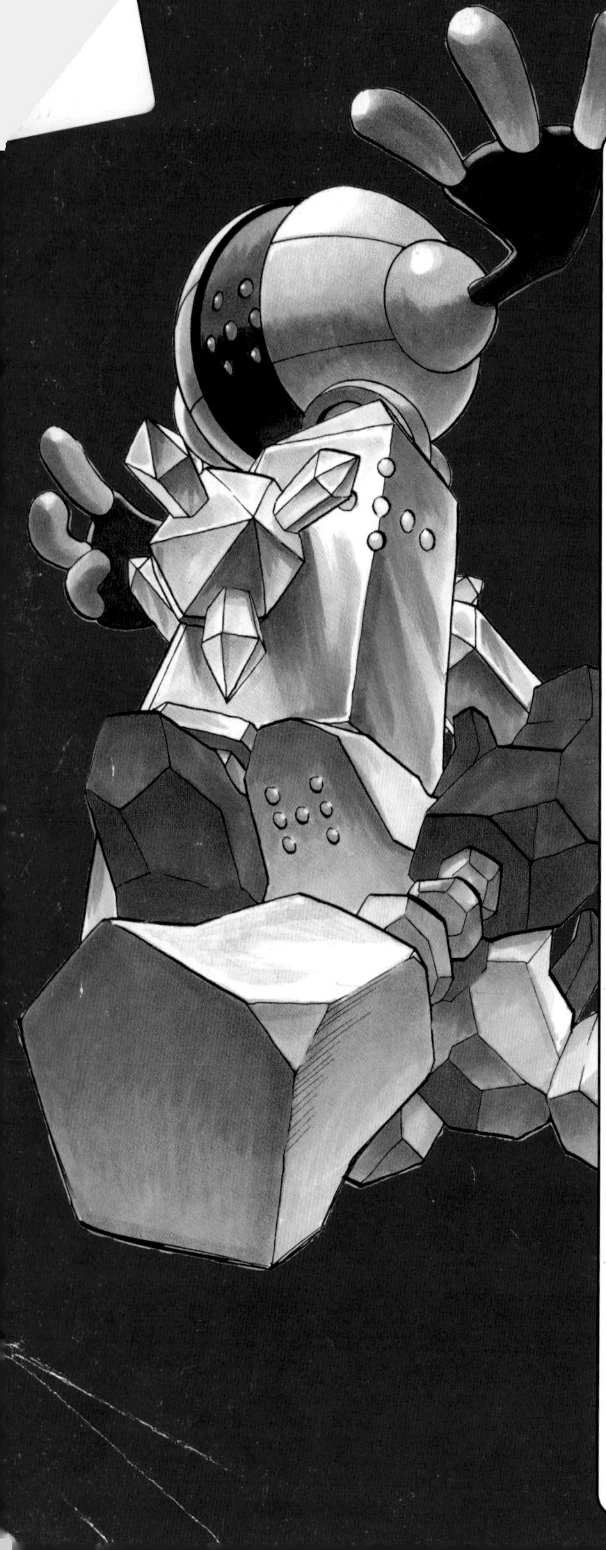

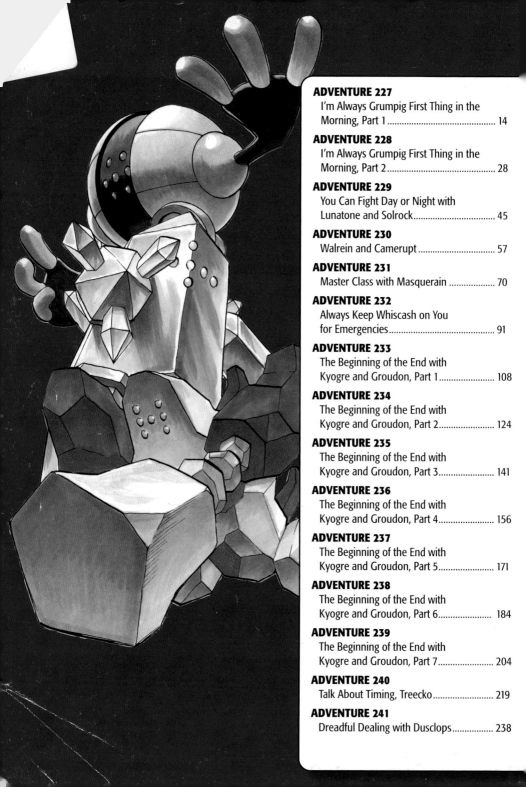

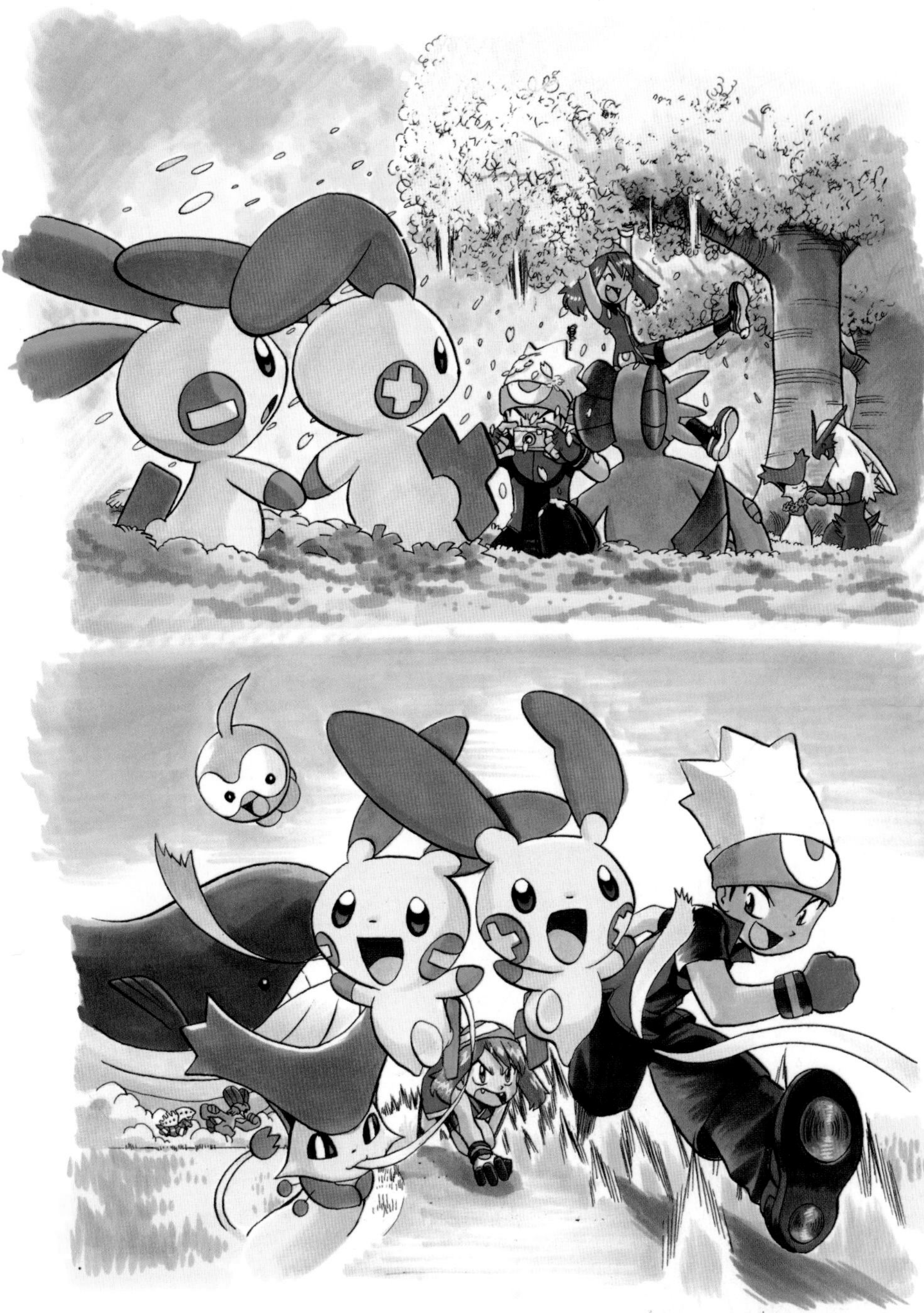

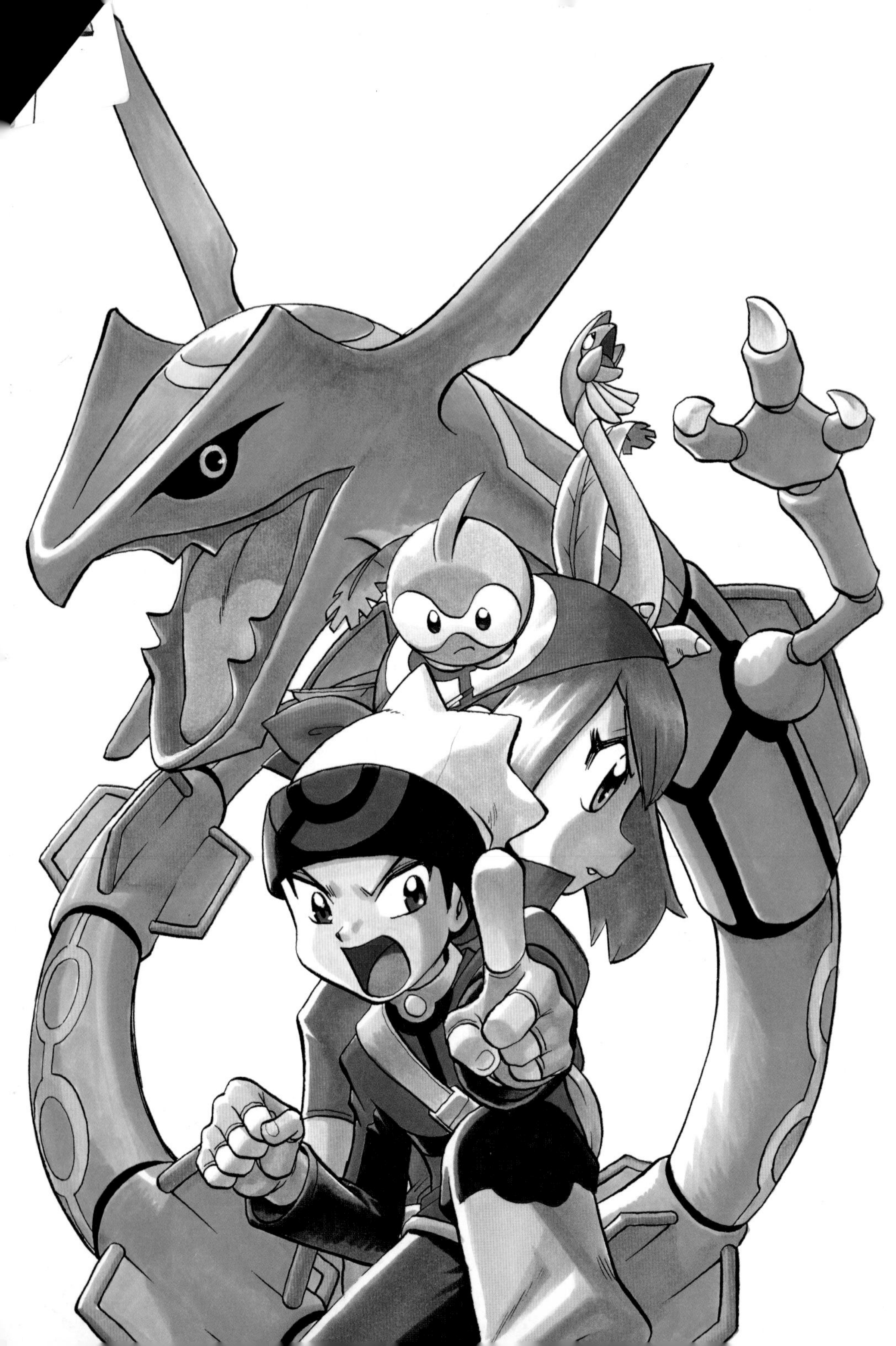

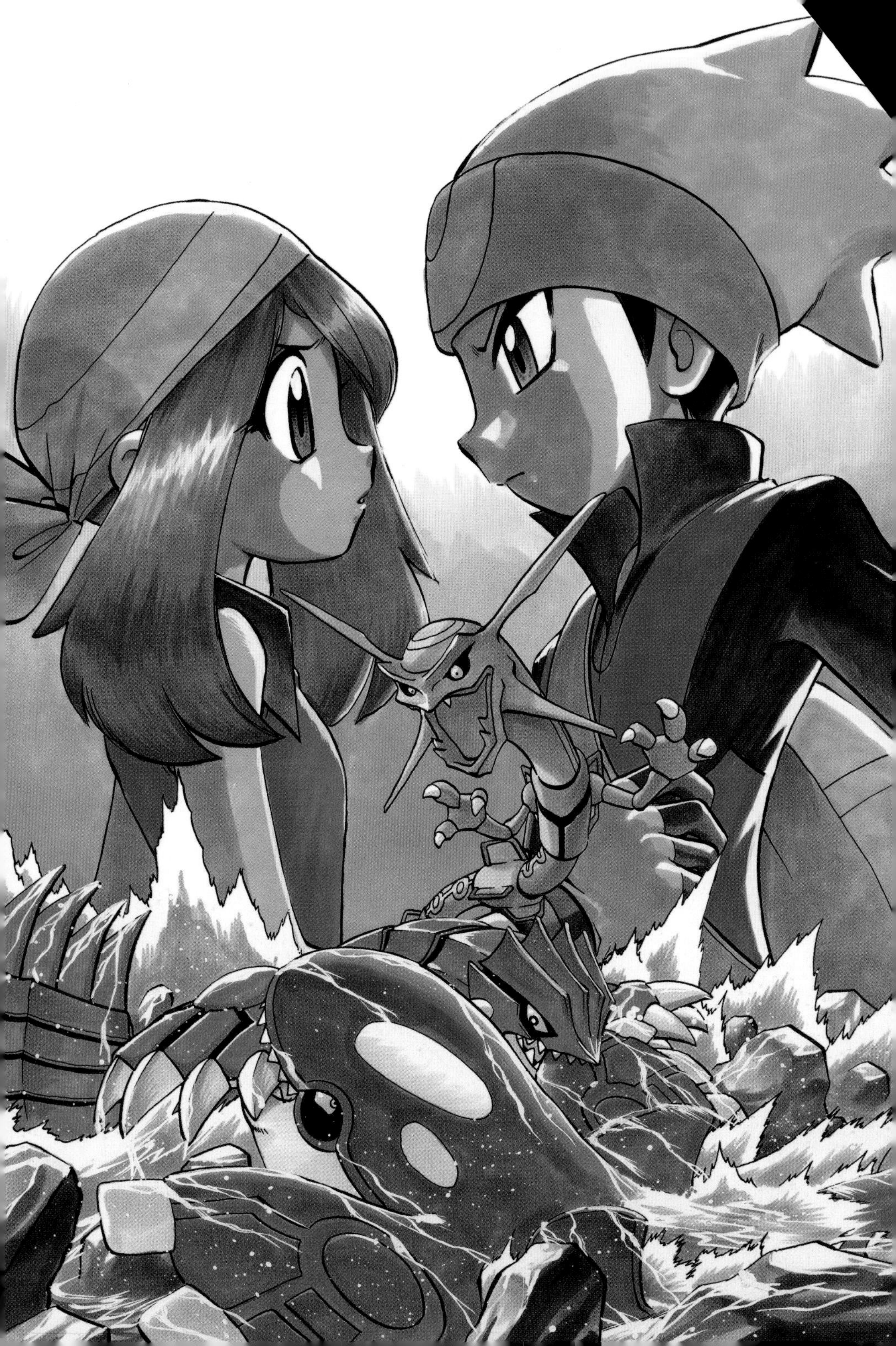

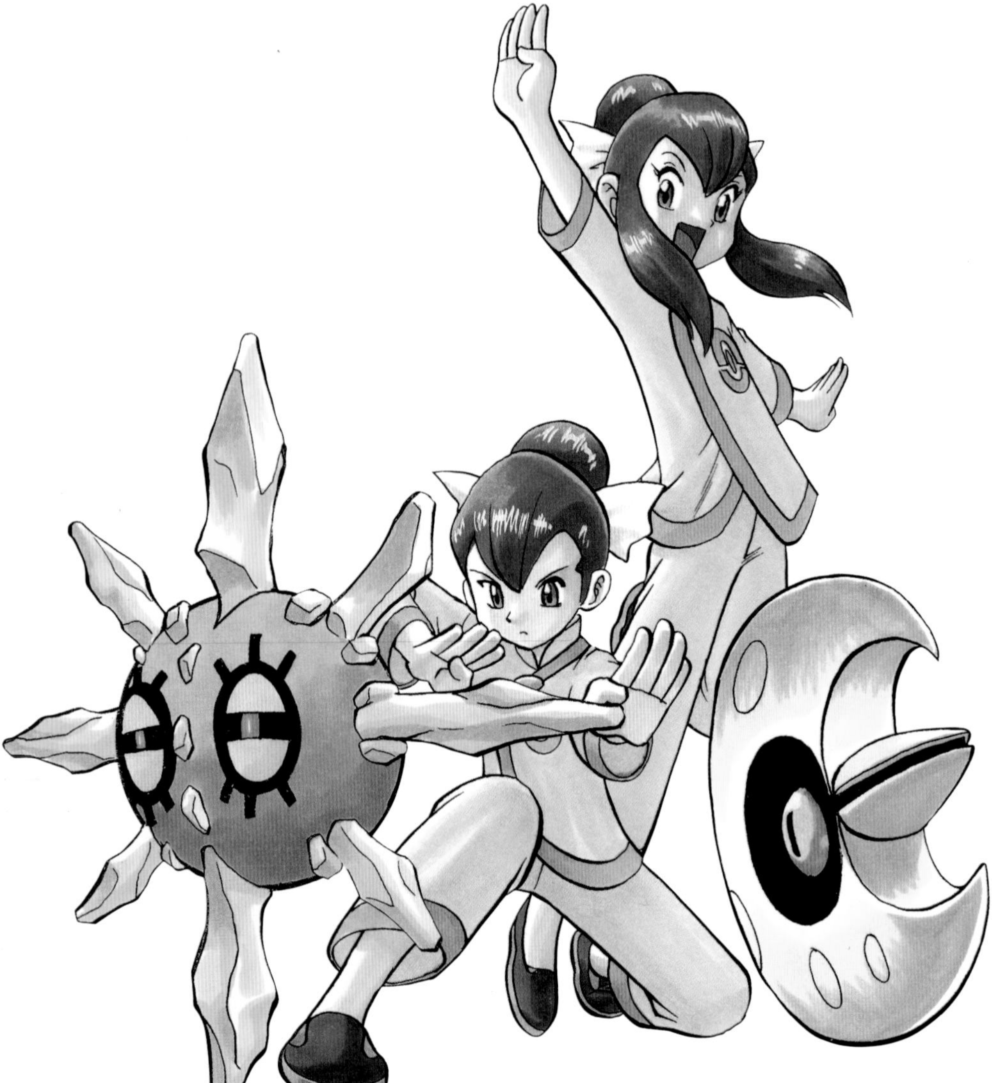

COLLECTOR'S EDITION

07

Story by **HIDENORI KUSAKA**   Art by **SATOSHI YAMAMOTO**

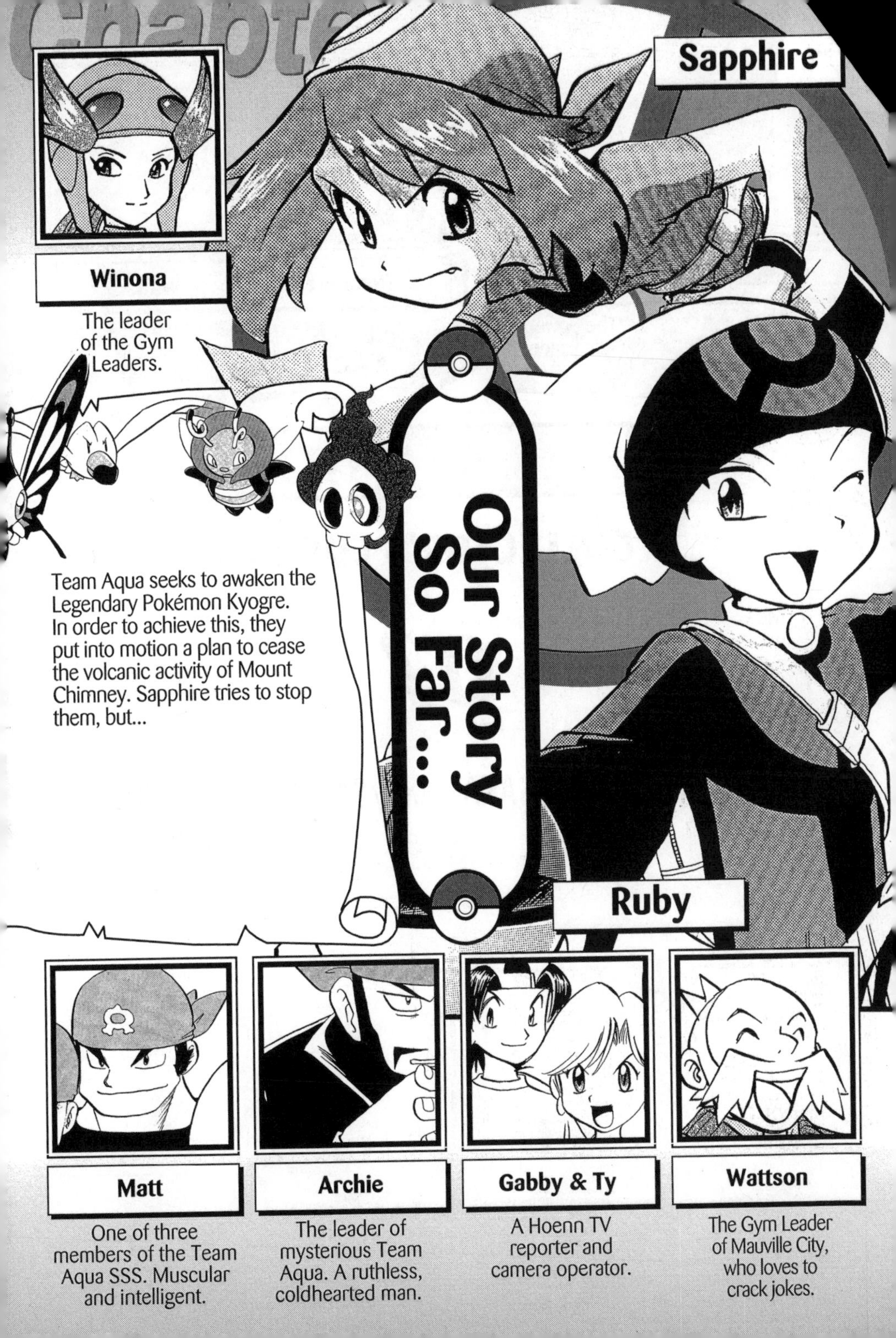
Chapter
Our Story So Far...
Sapphire
Ruby
Winona
The leader of the Gym Leaders.
Team Aqua seeks to awaken the Legendary Pokémon Kyogre. In order to achieve this, they put into motion a plan to cease the volcanic activity of Mount Chimney. Sapphire tries to stop them, but...
Wattson
The Gym Leader of Mauville City, who loves to crack jokes.
Gabby & Ty
A Hoenn TV reporter and camera operator.
Archie
The leader of mysterious Team Aqua. A ruthless, coldhearted man.
Matt
One of three members of the Team Aqua SSS. Muscular and intelligent.

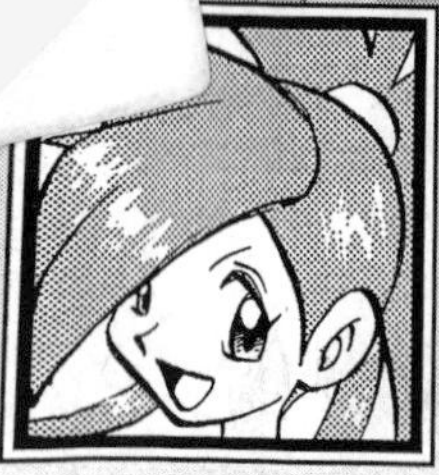

Flannery

The hot-tempered Gym Leader of Lavaridge Town.

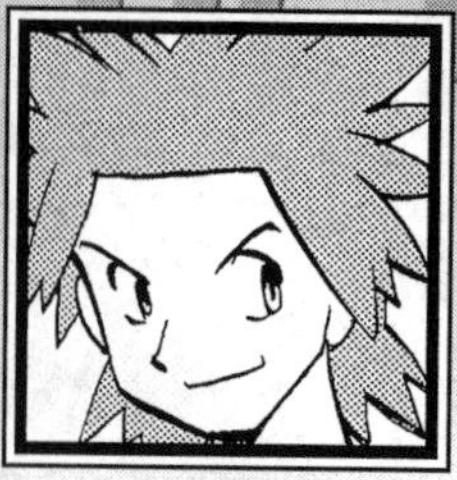

Brawly

The powerful Gym Leader of Dewford Gym.

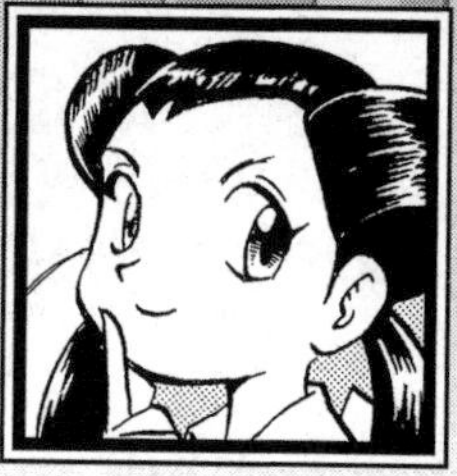

Roxanne

The Gym Leader of Rustboro City. She can be quite emotional.

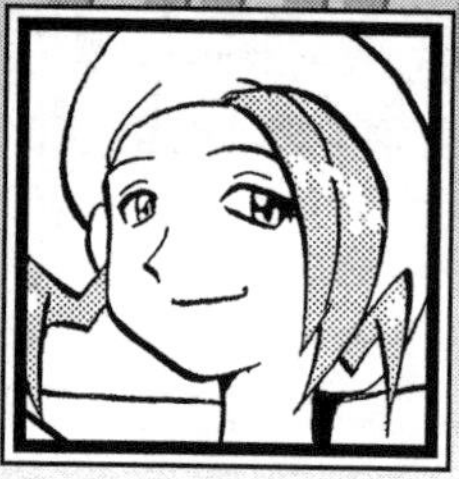

Wallace

The Gym Leader of Sootopolis City. Ruby considers him to be his master trainer!

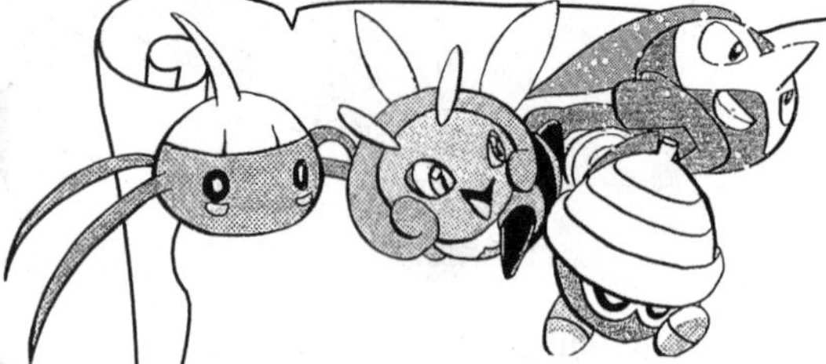

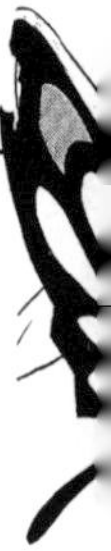

...is unsuccessful. Frustrated, Sapphire heads down to Fortree City from Lavaridge Town.

Meanwhile, Ruby helps trapped workers when Team Magma causes a Rusturf Tunnel collapse. Then, Ruby manages to win all the categories at the Normal Rank Pokémon Contest. But while at Fallarbor Town, Ruby meets Wallace, the Gym Leader of Sootopolis, whose Pokémon are far more “beautiful” than Ruby's. Ruby insists on becoming Wallace’s pupil.

Later, Ruby and Sapphire are reunited on Route 109 at Fortree City, where the Gym Leaders have gathered for an urgent meeting...

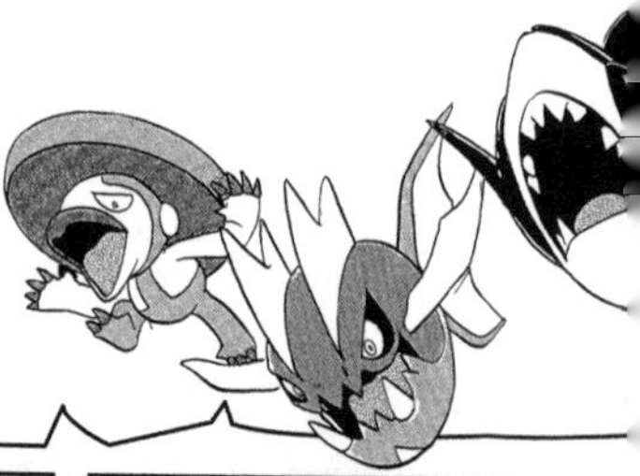

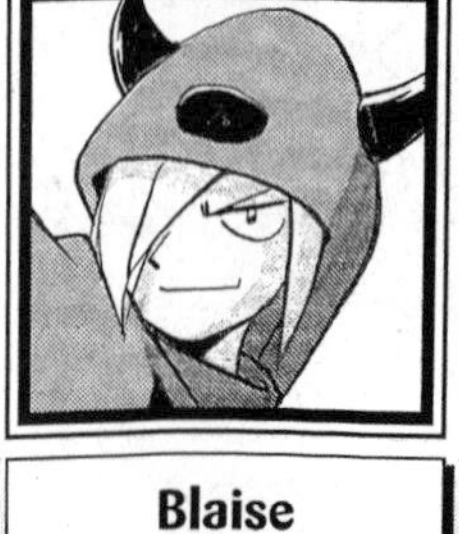

Blaise

One of the Three Fires of Team Magma. He creates illusions with flame to deceive people.

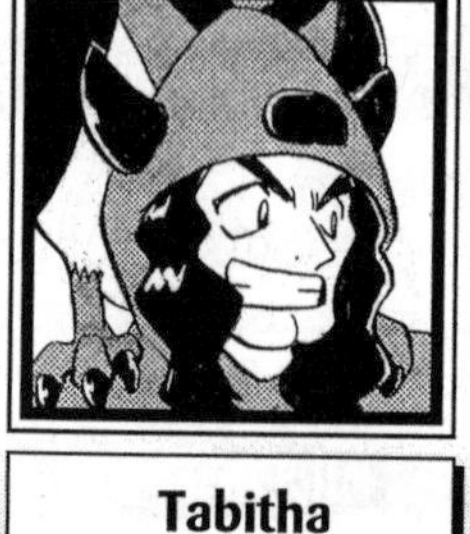

Tabitha

One of the Three Fires of Team Magma. He has a Torkoal.

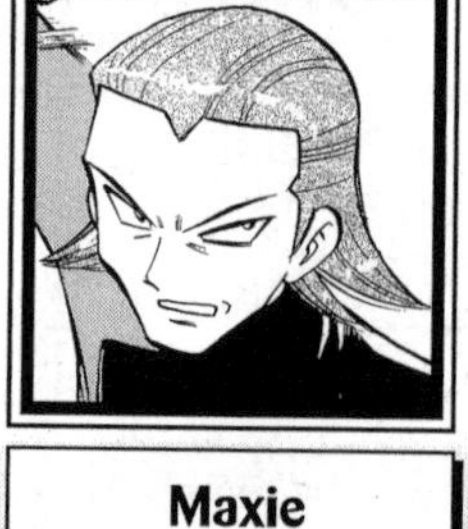

Maxie

The leader of Team Magma.

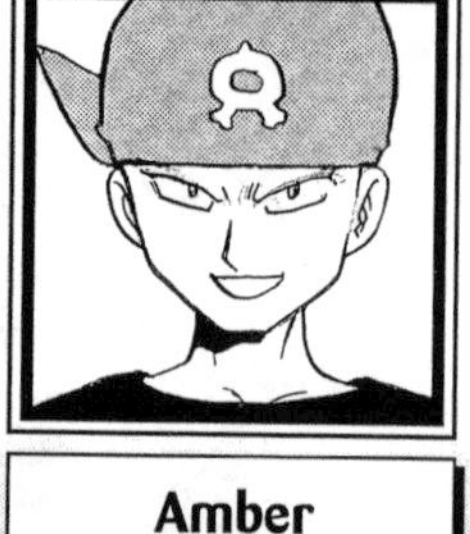

Amber

Archie's most trusted follower. He has a Carvanha.

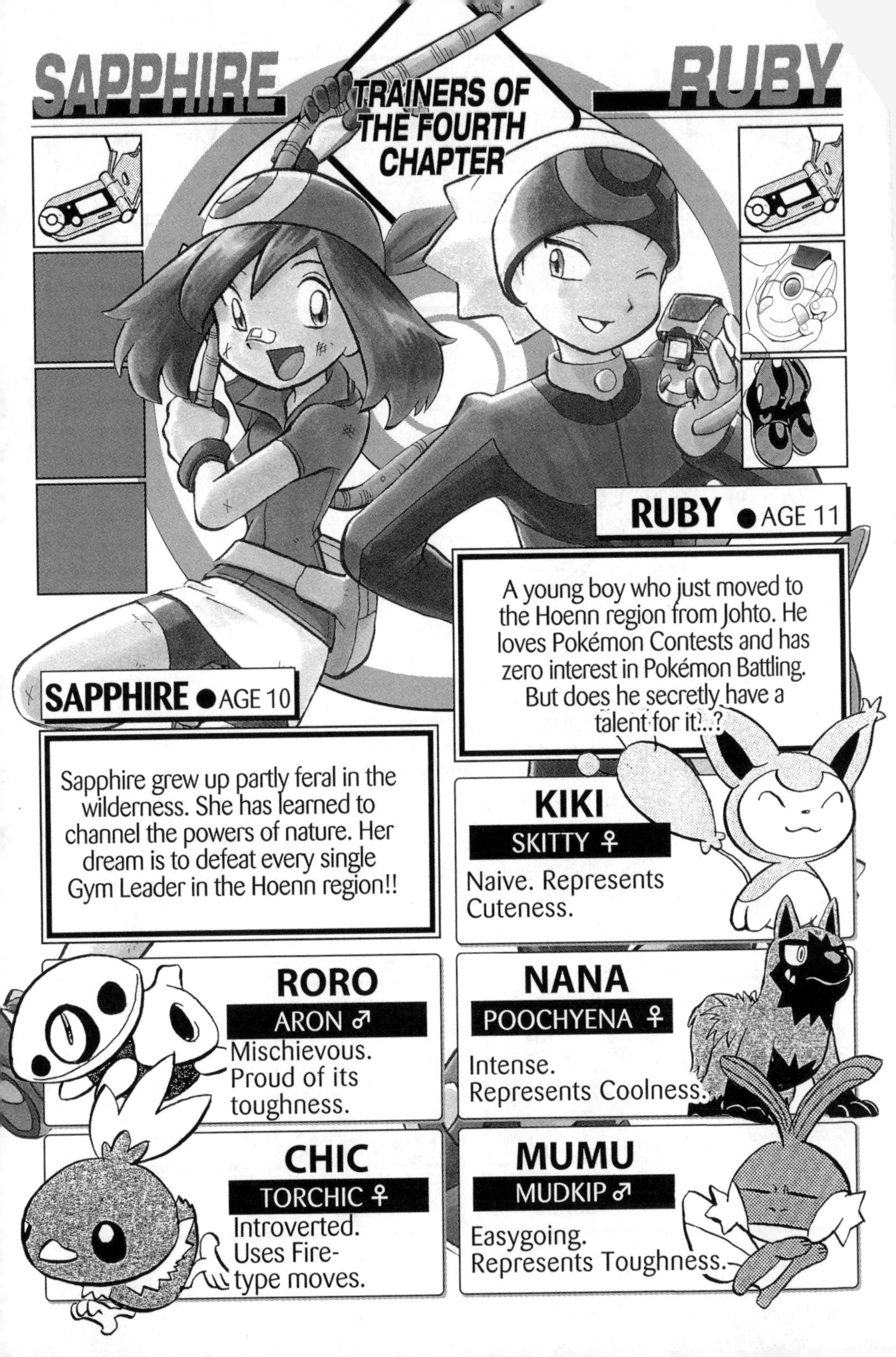
SAPPHIRE
TRAINERS OF THE FOURTH CHAPTER
RUBY
RUBY ●AGE 11
A young boy who just moved to the Hoenn region from Johto. He loves Pokémon Contests and has zero interest in Pokémon Battling. But does he secretly have a talent for it...?
SAPPHIRE ●AGE 10
Sapphire grew up partly feral in the wilderness. She has learned to channel the powers of nature. Her dream is to defeat every single Gym Leader in the Hoenn region!!
KIKI
SKITTY ♀
Naive. Represents Cuteness.
RORO
ARON ♂
Mischievous. Proud of its toughness.
NANA
POOCHYENA ♀
Intense. Represents Coolness.
CHIC
TORCHIC ♀
Introverted. Uses Fire-type moves.
MUMU
MUDKIP ♂
Easygoing. Represents Toughness.

Message from
Hidenori Kusaka

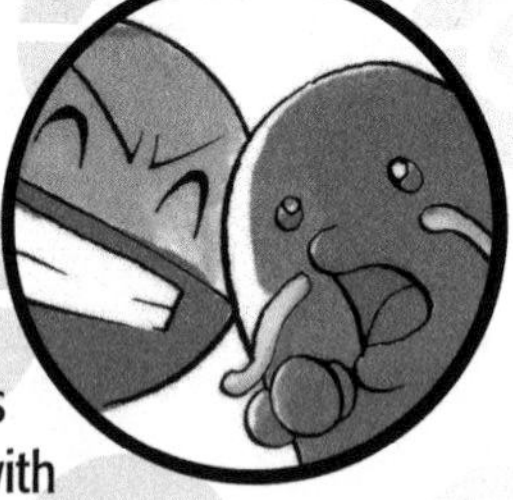

Not one, but *two* evil organizations—Team Aqua and Team Magma—appear in the Ruby and Sapphire story arc. Plus, the story is filled with all sorts of exciting new characters, starting with the bosses of the teams and their six admins. I tried to make a clear distinction between the two organizations when working on these episodes. I really like volume 19 because it depicts the failure and comeback of a major character. I hope you enjoy it too...!

—2004

Message from
Satoshi Yamamoto

The awakening of Kyogre and Groudon and the ensuing natural disasters that tear the Hoenn region apart... I've put a lot of effort into drawing these two Legendary Pokémon. I'm trying to emulate the style of my favorite monster movies and disaster movies. And then there are the misunderstandings and the bonds in the student and master relationships of Ruby and Wallace, Sapphire and Winona... I hope you enjoy all the ups and downs, the joys and sorrows!

—2004

● Adventure 227 ●
I'm Always Grumpig First Thing in the Morning, Part 1

The Fourth Chapter

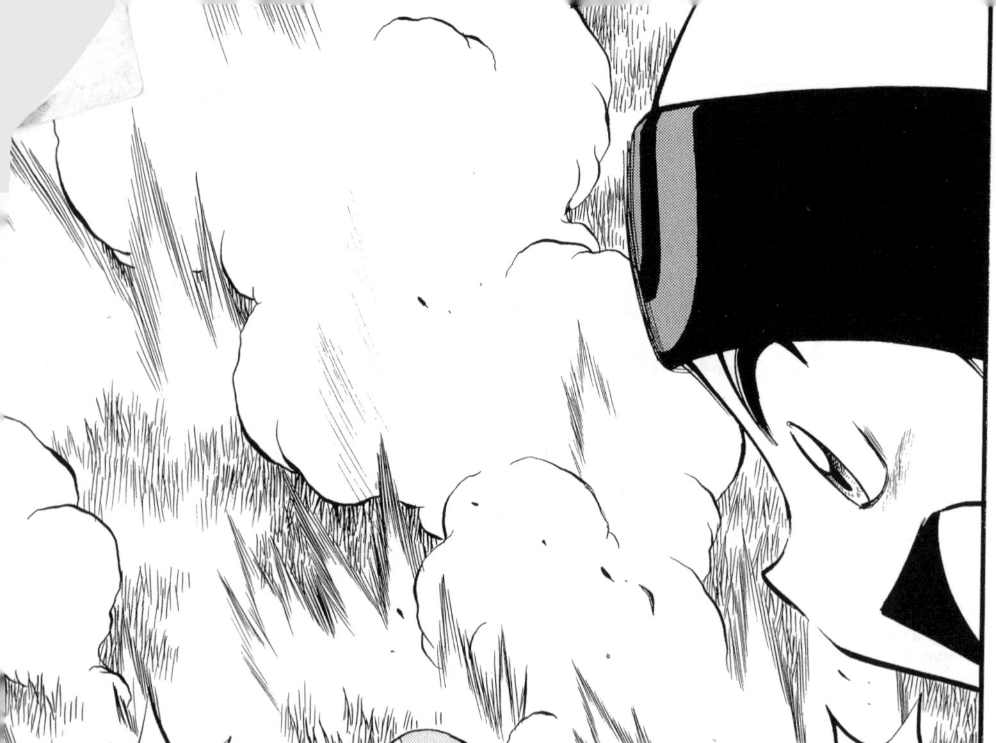
YOU !!
YOU !!
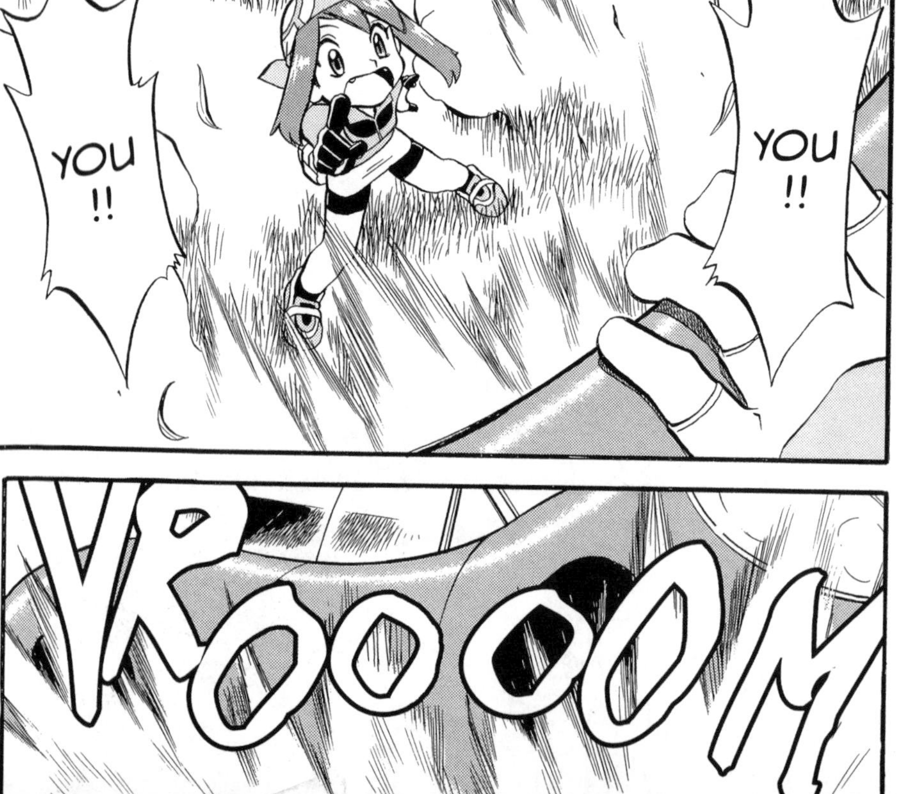
VROOOOM

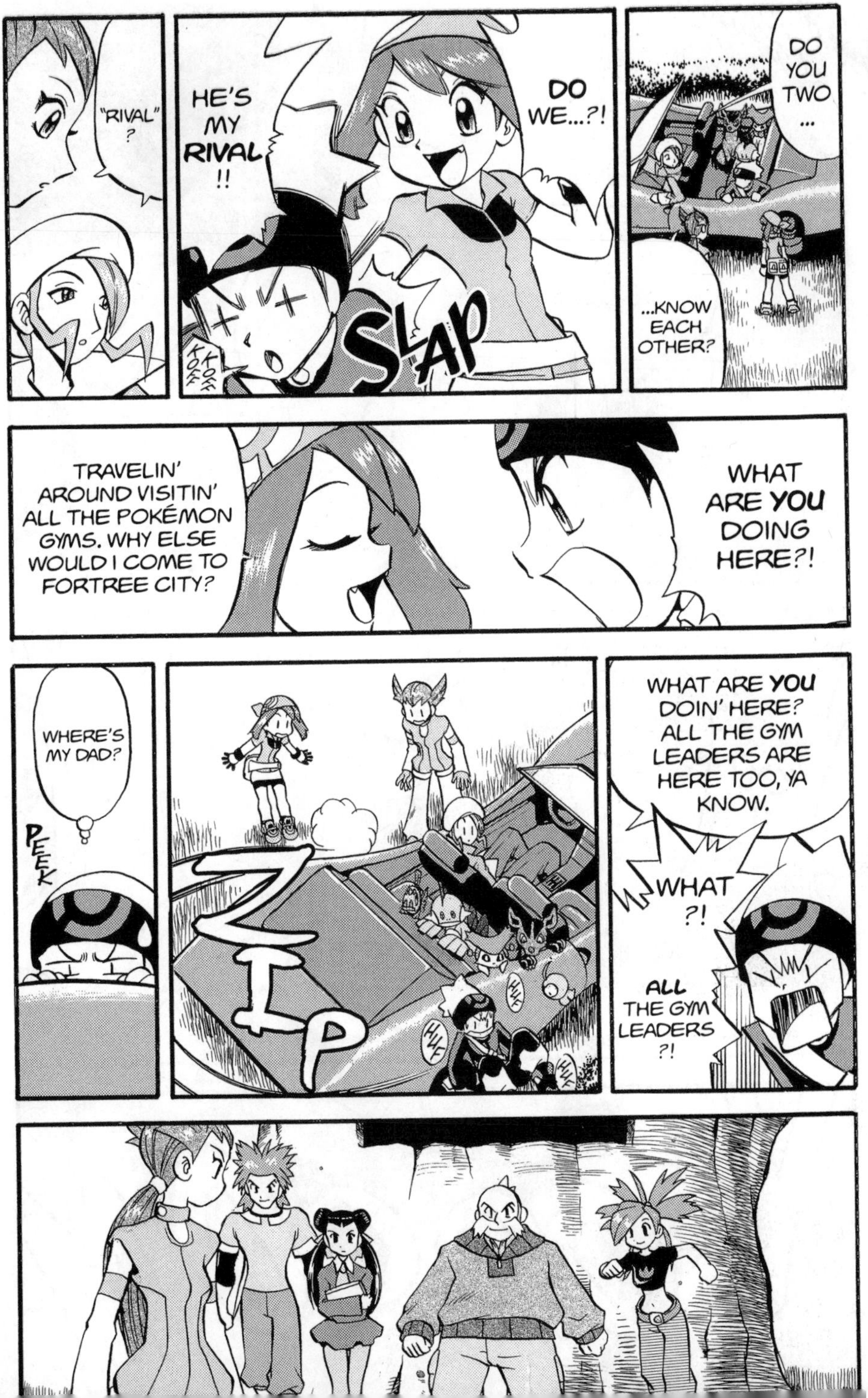
DO YOU TWO ...
...KNOW EACH OTHER?
DO WE...?!
HE'S MY RIVAL!!
SLAP
KOFF KOFF
"RIVAL"?
WHAT ARE YOU DOING HERE?!
TRAVELIN' AROUND VISITIN' ALL THE POKÉMON GYMS. WHY ELSE WOULD I COME TO FORTREE CITY?
WHAT ARE YOU DOIN' HERE? ALL THE GYM LEADERS ARE HERE TOO, YA KNOW.
WHAT?!
ALL THE GYM LEADERS?!
ZIP
HUF
HUF
HUF
WHERE'S MY DAD?
PEEK

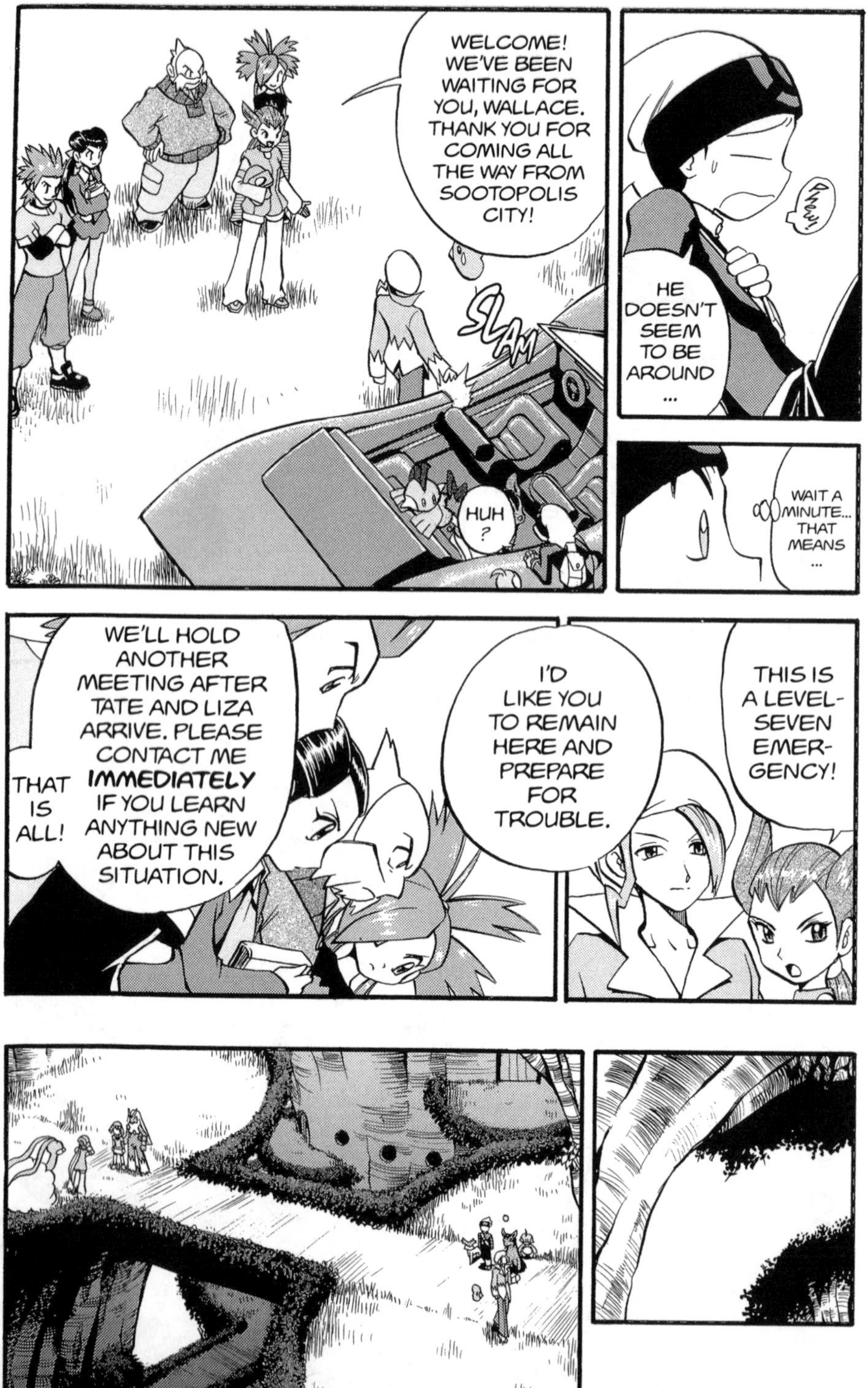
Phew!
HE DOESN'T SEEM TO BE AROUND...
WAIT A MINUTE... THAT MEANS...
WELCOME! WE'VE BEEN WAITING FOR YOU, WALLACE. THANK YOU FOR COMING ALL THE WAY FROM SOOTOPOLIS CITY!
SLAM
HUH?
THIS IS A LEVEL-SEVEN EMERGENCY!
I'D LIKE YOU TO REMAIN HERE AND PREPARE FOR TROUBLE.
WE'LL HOLD ANOTHER MEETING AFTER TATE AND LIZA ARRIVE. PLEASE CONTACT ME **IMMEDIATELY** IF YOU LEARN ANYTHING NEW ABOUT THIS SITUATION.
THAT IS ALL!

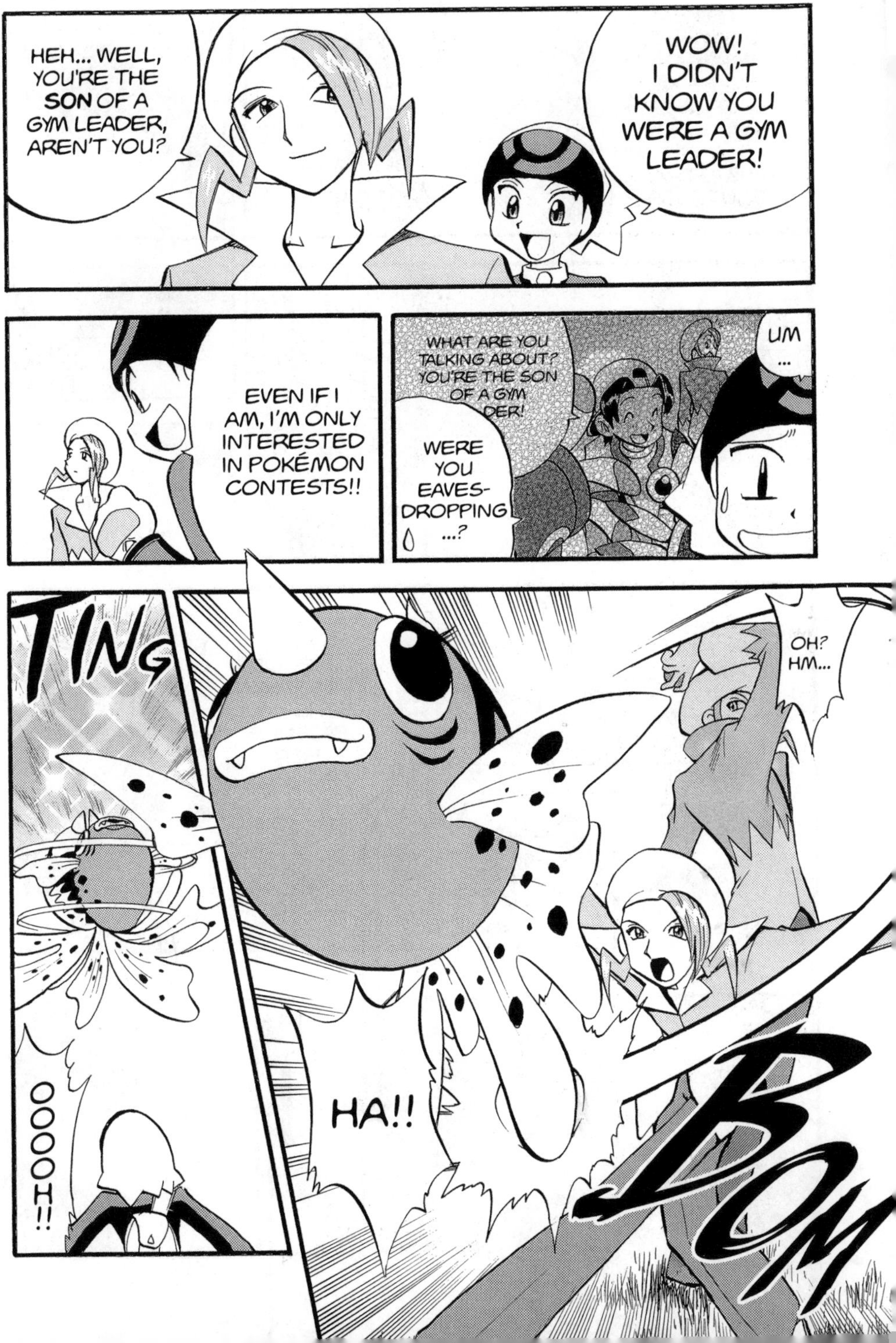
WOW! I DIDN'T KNOW YOU WERE A GYM LEADER!
HEH... WELL, YOU'RE THE **SON** OF A GYM LEADER, AREN'T YOU?
UM ...
WHAT ARE YOU TALKING ABOUT? YOU'RE THE SON OF A GYM DER!
WERE YOU EAVES-DROPPING ...?
EVEN IF I AM, I'M ONLY INTERESTED IN POKÉMON CONTESTS!!
OH? HM...
HA!!
BOM
TING
OOOOOH!!

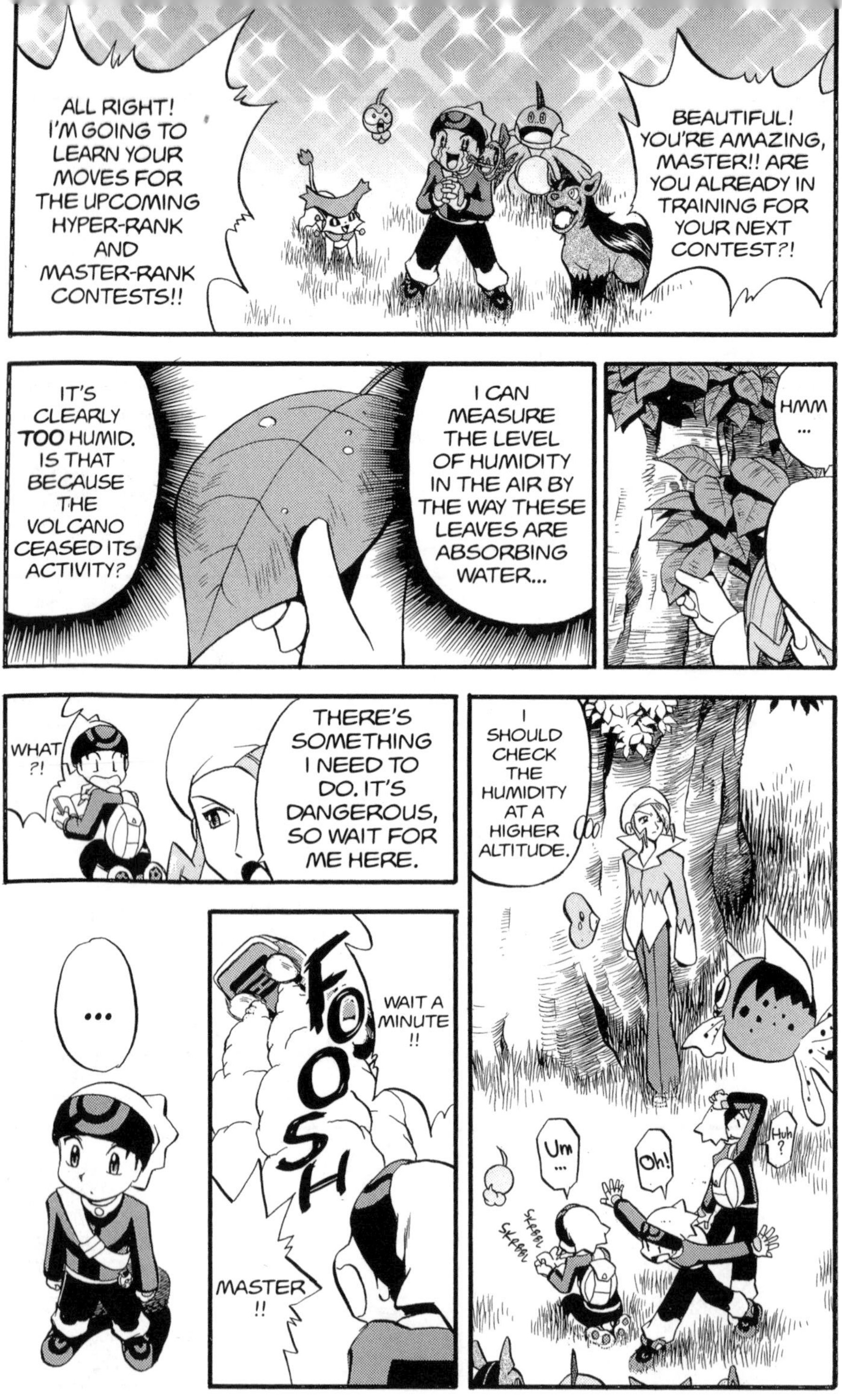
BEAUTIFUL! YOU'RE AMAZING, MASTER!! ARE YOU ALREADY IN TRAINING FOR YOUR NEXT CONTEST?!
ALL RIGHT! I'M GOING TO LEARN YOUR MOVES FOR THE UPCOMING HYPER-RANK AND MASTER-RANK CONTESTS!!
HMM ...
I CAN MEASURE THE LEVEL OF HUMIDITY IN THE AIR BY THE WAY THESE LEAVES ARE ABSORBING WATER...
IT'S CLEARLY **TOO** HUMID. IS THAT BECAUSE THE VOLCANO CEASED ITS ACTIVITY?
I SHOULD CHECK THE HUMIDITY AT A HIGHER ALTITUDE.
Huh?
Oh!
Um ...
THERE'S SOMETHING I NEED TO DO. IT'S DANGEROUS, SO WAIT FOR ME HERE.
WHAT?!
WAIT A MINUTE!!
FOOSH
MASTER!!
...

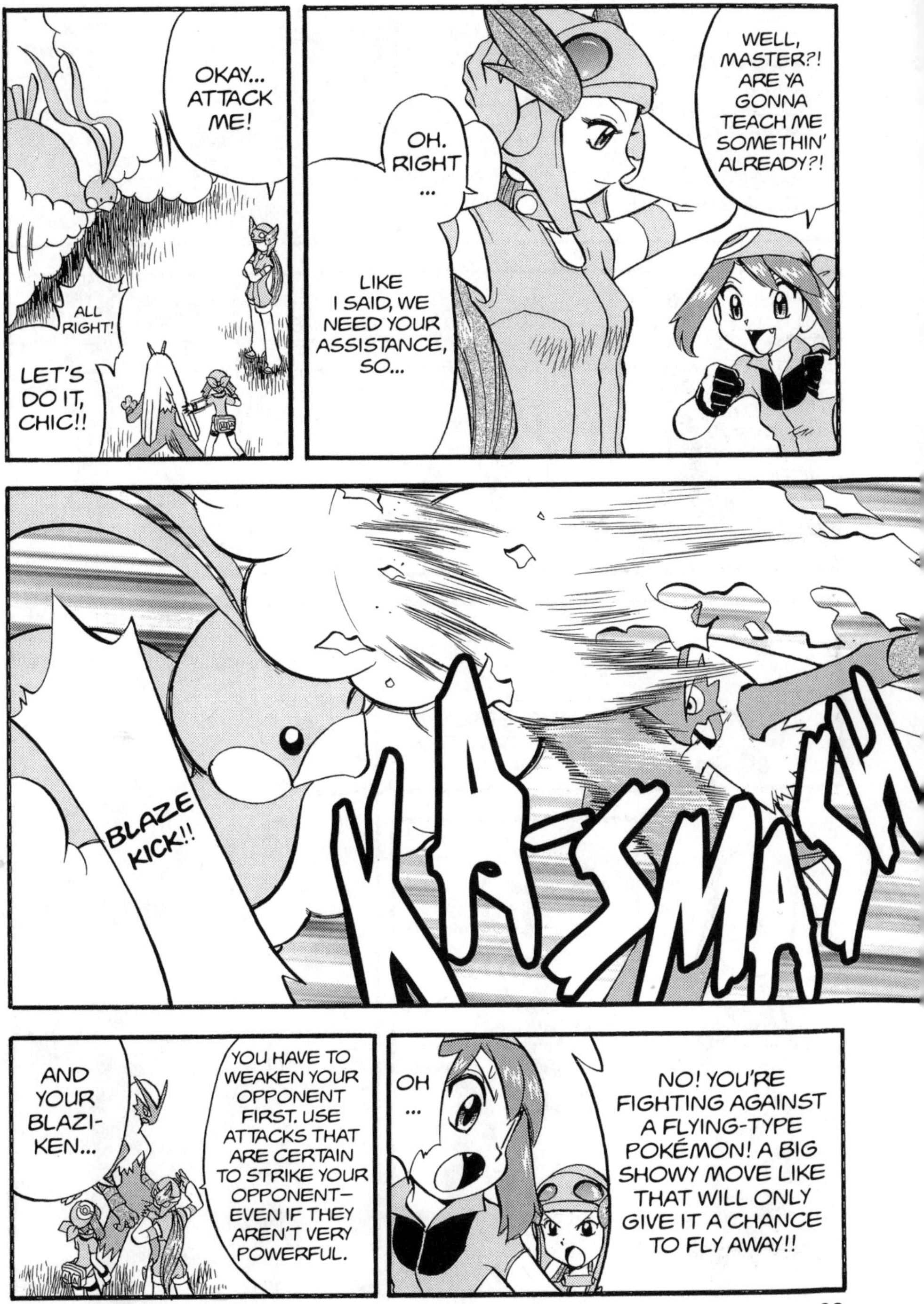
WELL, MASTER?! ARE YA GONNA TEACH ME SOMETHIN' ALREADY?!
OH. RIGHT ...
LIKE I SAID, WE NEED YOUR ASSISTANCE, SO...
OKAY... ATTACK ME!
ALL RIGHT!
LET'S DO IT, CHIC!!
BLAZE KICK!!
KA-SMASH
NO! YOU'RE FIGHTING AGAINST A FLYING-TYPE POKÉMON! A BIG SHOWY MOVE LIKE THAT WILL ONLY GIVE IT A CHANCE TO FLY AWAY!!
OH ...
YOU HAVE TO WEAKEN YOUR OPPONENT FIRST. USE ATTACKS THAT ARE CERTAIN TO STRIKE YOUR OPPONENT—EVEN IF THEY AREN'T VERY POWERFUL.
AND YOUR BLAZI-KEN...

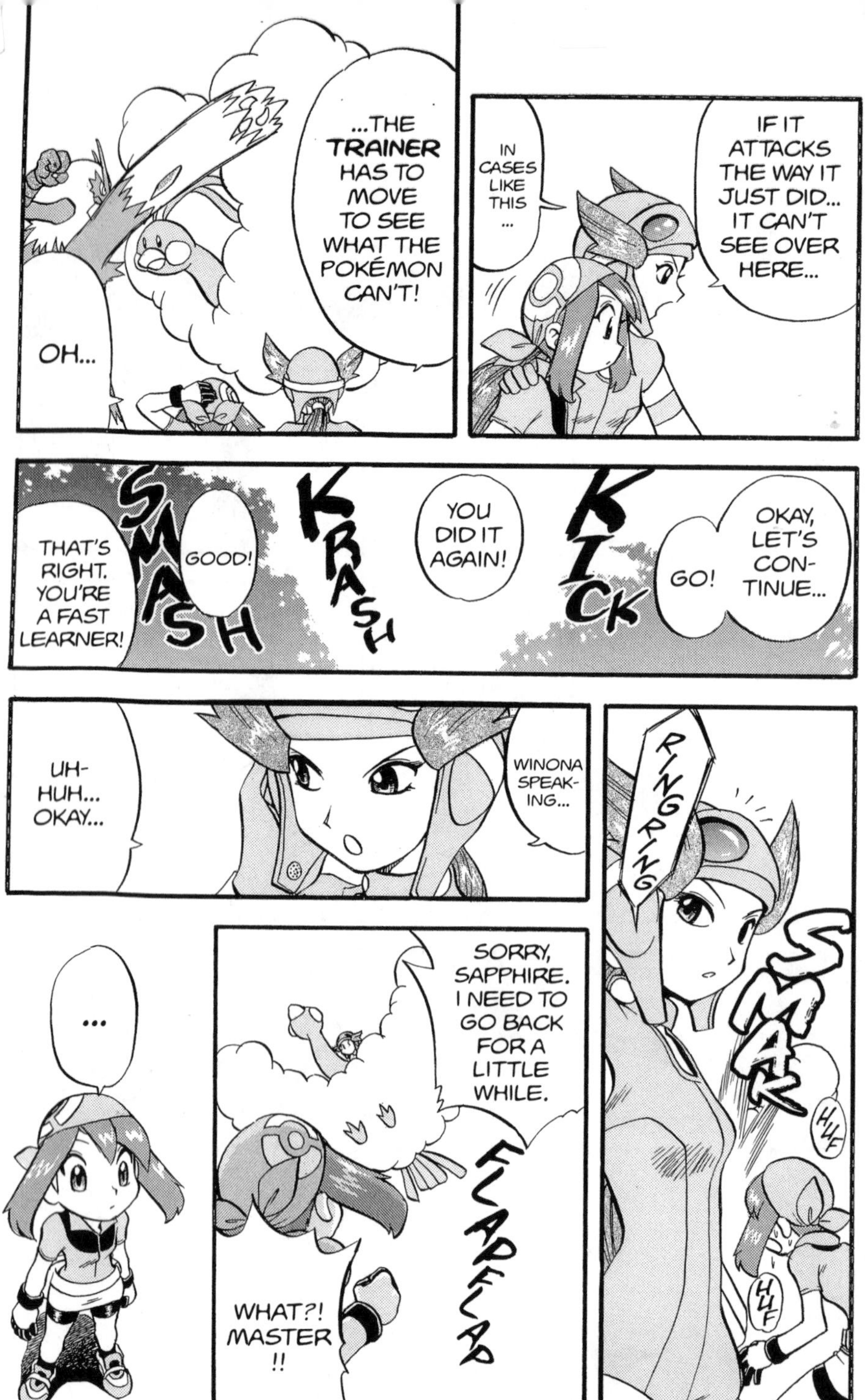
IF IT ATTACKS THE WAY IT JUST DID... IT CAN'T SEE OVER HERE...
IN CASES LIKE THIS ...
...THE TRAINER HAS TO MOVE TO SEE WHAT THE POKÉMON CAN'T!
OH...
OKAY, LET'S CON-TINUE...
GO!
KICK
YOU DID IT AGAIN!
KRASH
GOOD!
SMASH
THAT'S RIGHT. YOU'RE A FAST LEARNER!
RINGRING
SMAK
HUF
HUF
WINONA SPEAK-ING...
UH-HUH... OKAY...
SORRY, SAPPHIRE. I NEED TO GO BACK FOR A LITTLE WHILE.
FLAPFLAP
WHAT?! MASTER !!
...

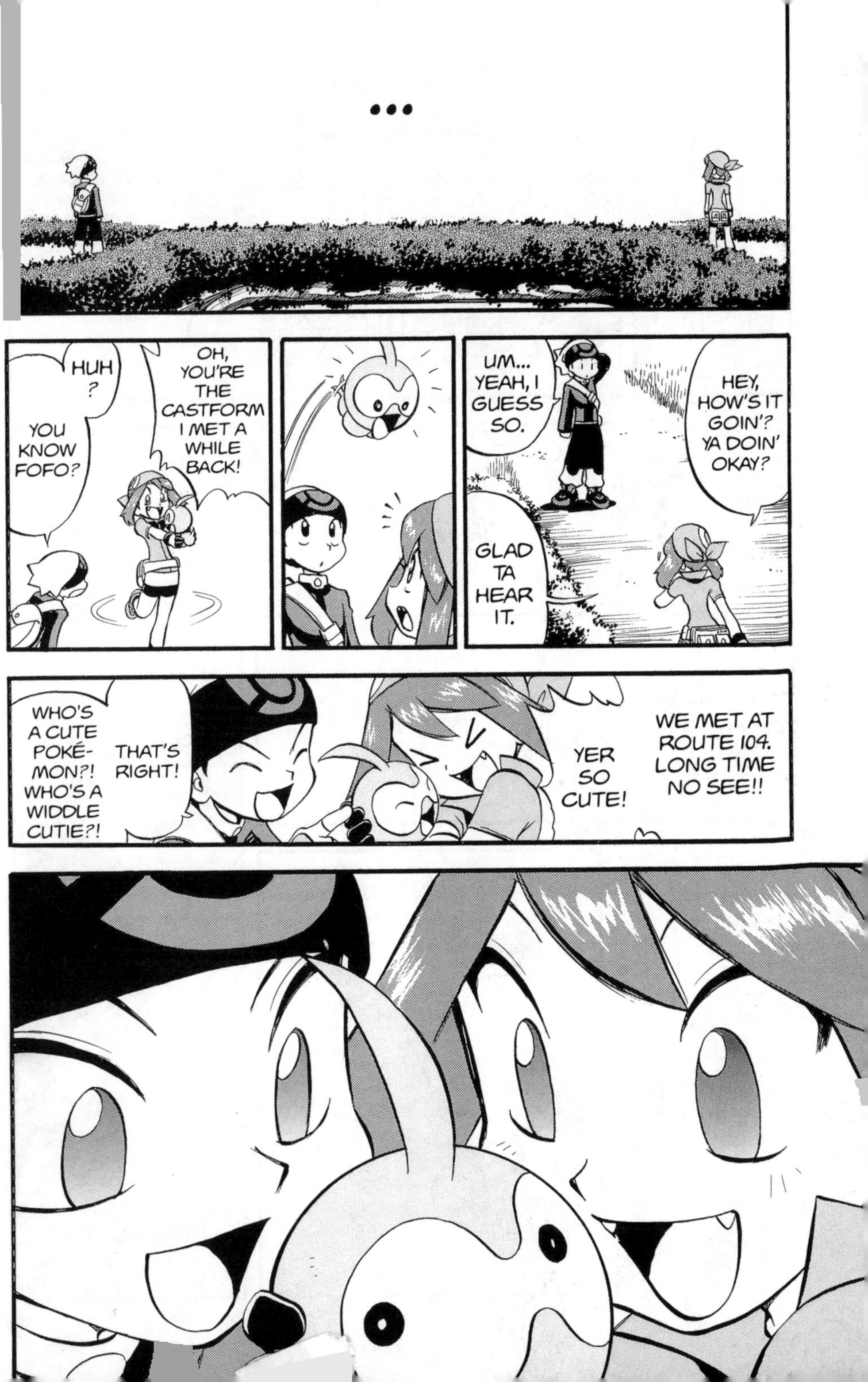
...
HEY, HOW'S IT GOIN'? YA DOIN' OKAY?
UM... YEAH, I GUESS SO.
GLAD TA HEAR IT.
OH, YOU'RE THE CASTFORM I MET A WHILE BACK!
HUH?
YOU KNOW FOFO?
WE MET AT ROUTE 104. LONG TIME NO SEE!!
YER SO CUTE!
THAT'S RIGHT!
WHO'S A CUTE POKÉ-MON?! WHO'S A WIDDLE CUTIE?!

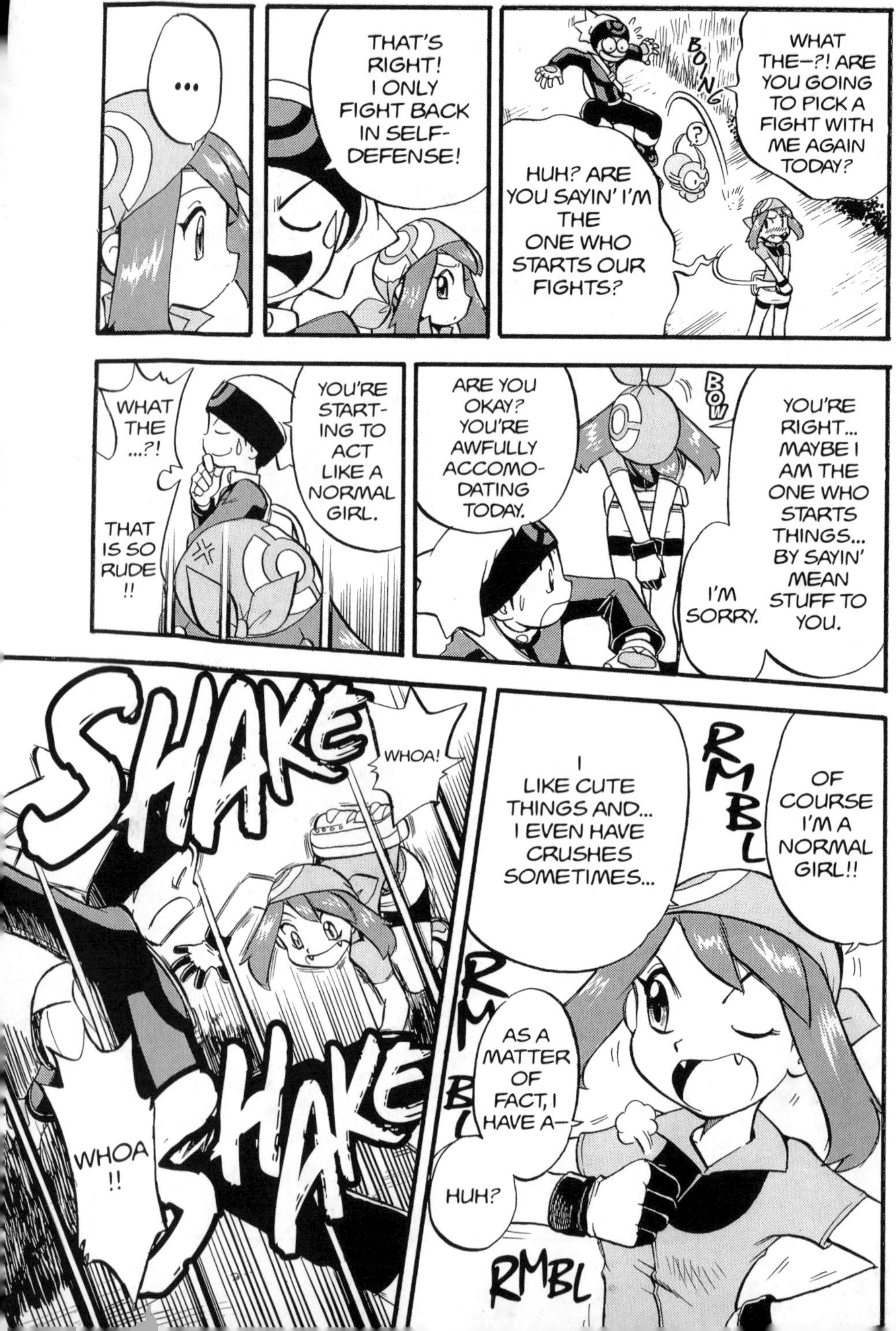
WHAT THE—?! ARE YOU GOING TO PICK A FIGHT WITH ME AGAIN TODAY?
BOING
?
HUH? ARE YOU SAYIN' I'M THE ONE WHO STARTS OUR FIGHTS?
THAT'S RIGHT! I ONLY FIGHT BACK IN SELF-DEFENSE!
...
BOW
YOU'RE RIGHT... MAYBE I AM THE ONE WHO STARTS THINGS... BY SAYIN' MEAN STUFF TO YOU.
I'M SORRY.
ARE YOU OKAY? YOU'RE AWFULLY ACCOMODATING TODAY.
YOU'RE START-ING TO ACT LIKE A NORMAL GIRL.
WHAT THE ...?!
THAT IS SO RUDE !!
OF COURSE I'M A NORMAL GIRL!!
RMBL
I LIKE CUTE THINGS AND... I EVEN HAVE CRUSHES SOMETIMES...
RMBL
AS A MATTER OF FACT, I HAVE A—
HUH?
RMBL
SHAKE
WHOA!
SHAKE
WHOA !!

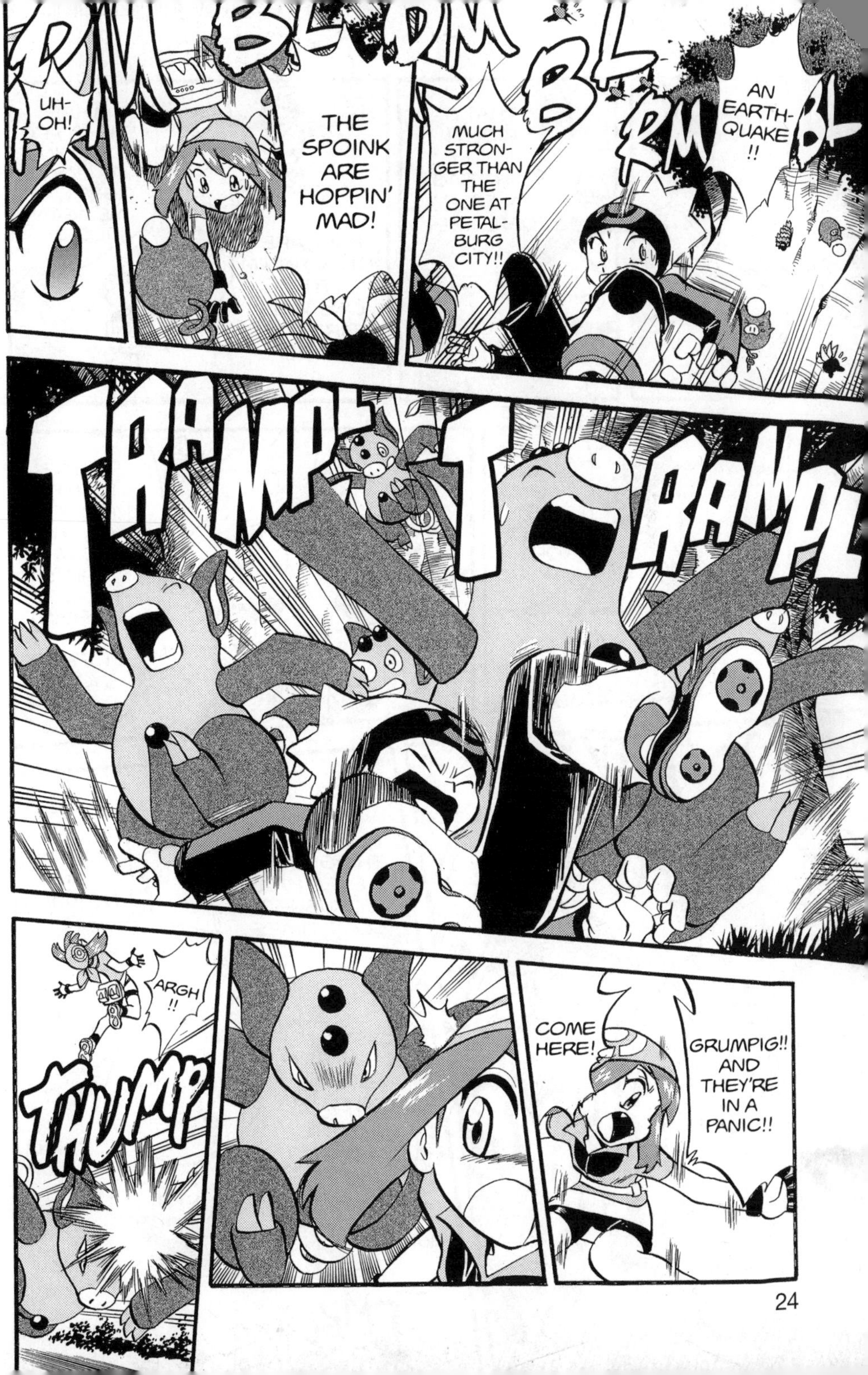

AN EARTHQUAKE!!
RM BL
MUCH STRONGER THAN THE ONE AT PETALBURG CITY!!
BL
BLOOM
THE SPOINK ARE HOPPIN' MAD!
RM
UH-OH!
RAMPL
TRAMPL
GRUMPIG!! AND THEY'RE IN A PANIC!!
COME HERE!
ARGH!!
THUMP

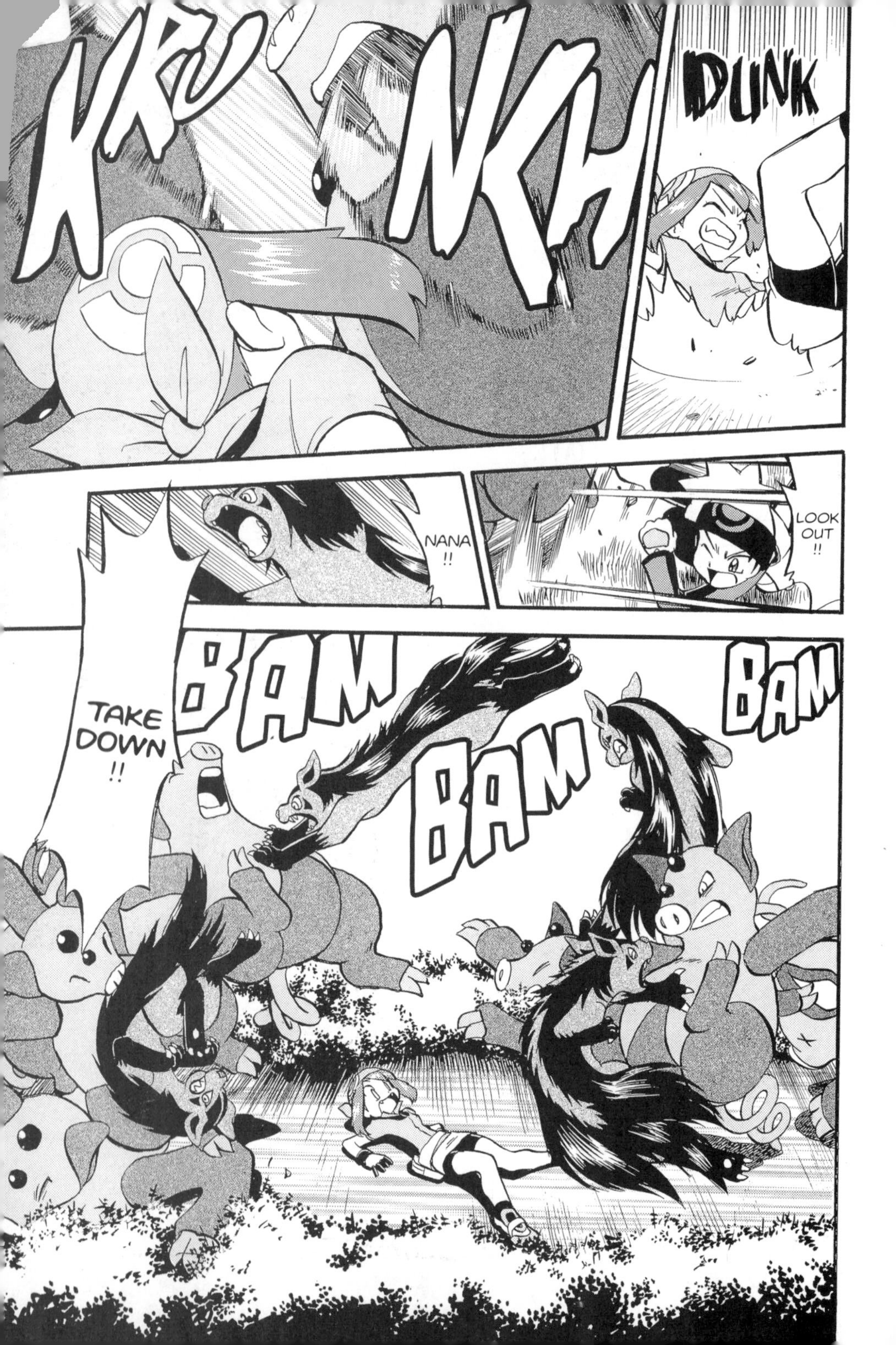

DUNK
KRUNKH
LOOK OUT !!
NANA !!
BAM
BAM
BAM
TAKE DOWN !!

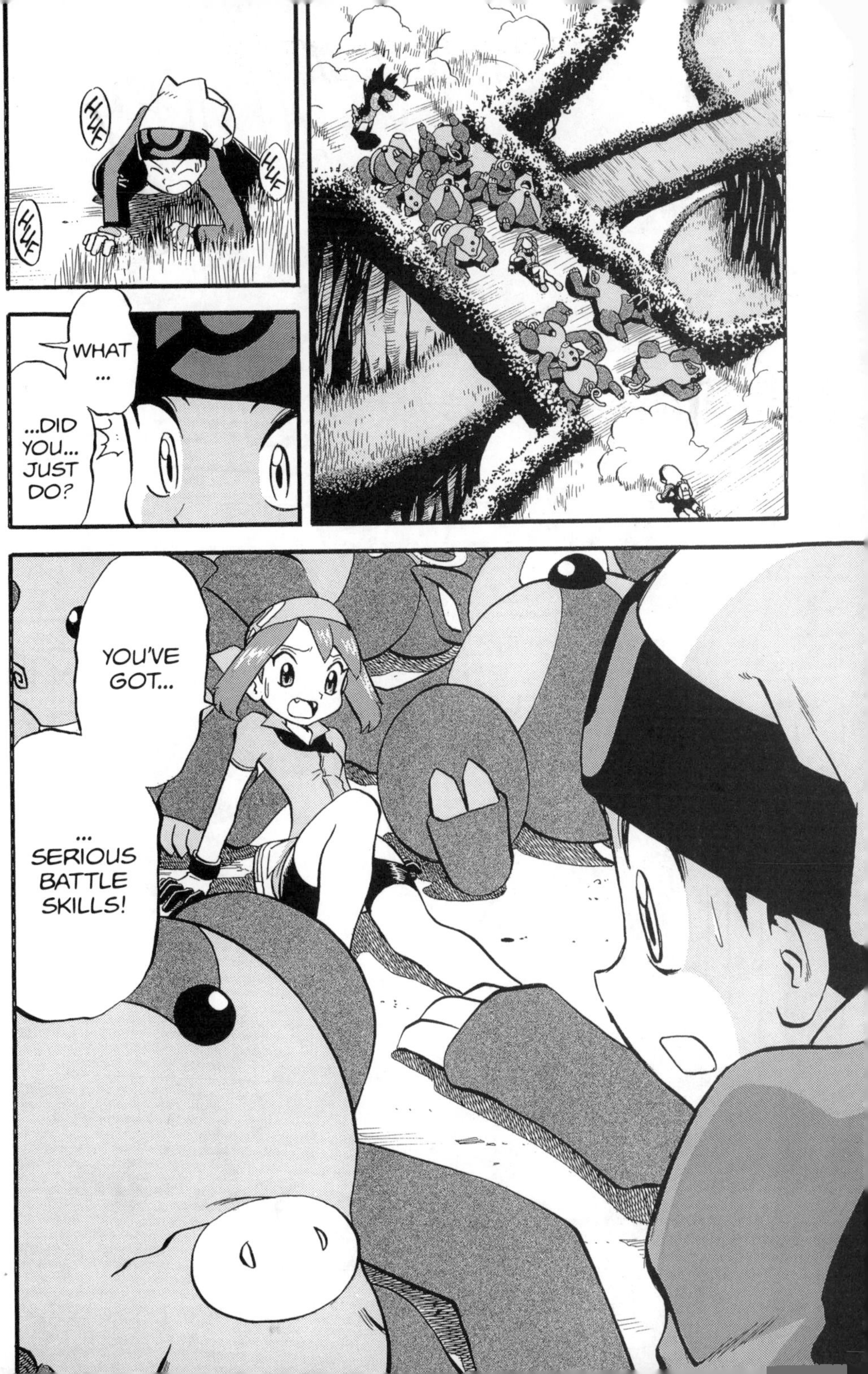
HUF
HUF
HUF
WHAT ...
...DID YOU... JUST DO?
YOU'VE GOT...
... SERIOUS BATTLE SKILLS!

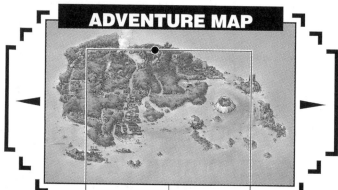

ADVENTURE MAP

SAPPHIRE		RUBY
Jagged Pass		Fallarbor Town
Route 111		Route 111
Fortree City		Fortree City

SAPPHIRE

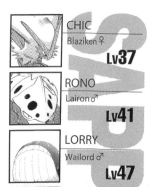

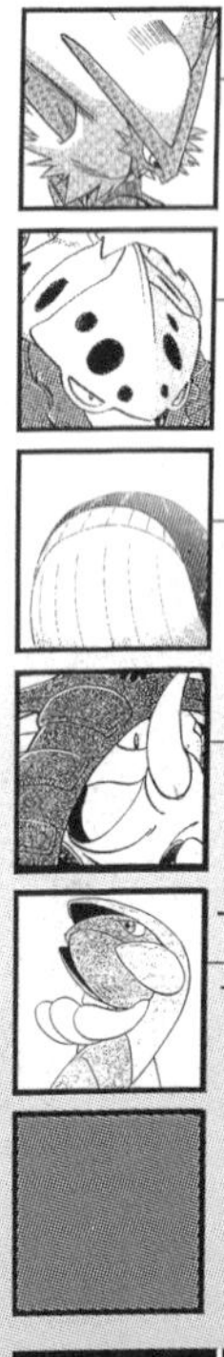

CHIC
Blaziken ♀
Lv37

RONO
Lairon ♂
Lv41

LORRY
Wailord ♂
Lv47

PHADO
Donphan ♂
Lv46

TROPPY
Tropius ♂
Lv45

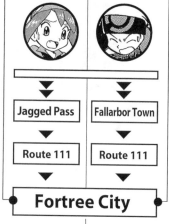

RUBY

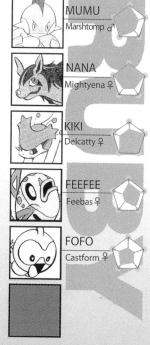

MUMU
Marshtomp ♂

NANA
Mightyena ♀

KIKI
Delcatty ♀

FEEFEE
Feebas ♀

FOFO
Castform ♀

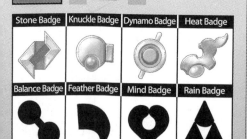

Stone Badge	Knuckle Badge	Dynamo Badge	Heat Badge
Balance Badge	Feather Badge	Mind Badge	Rain Badge

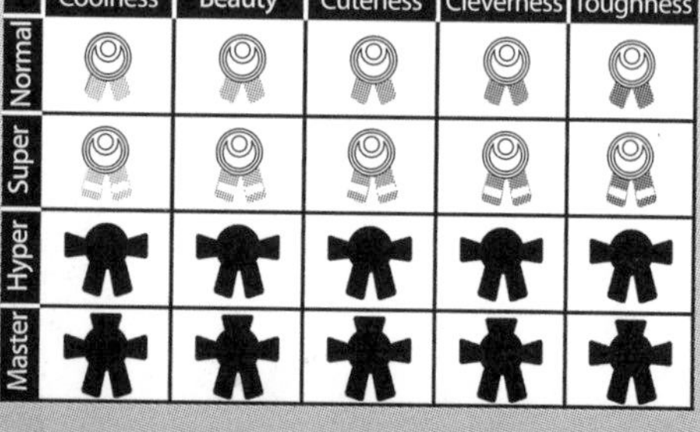

	Coolness	Beauty	Cuteness	Cleverness	Toughness
Normal					
Super					
Hyper					
Master					

● Adventure 228 ●

I'm Always Grumpig First Thing in the Morning, Part 2

Pokémon™ Adventures Ruby & Sapphire

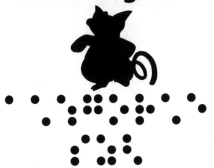

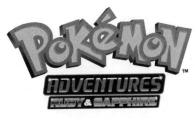

The Fourth Chapter

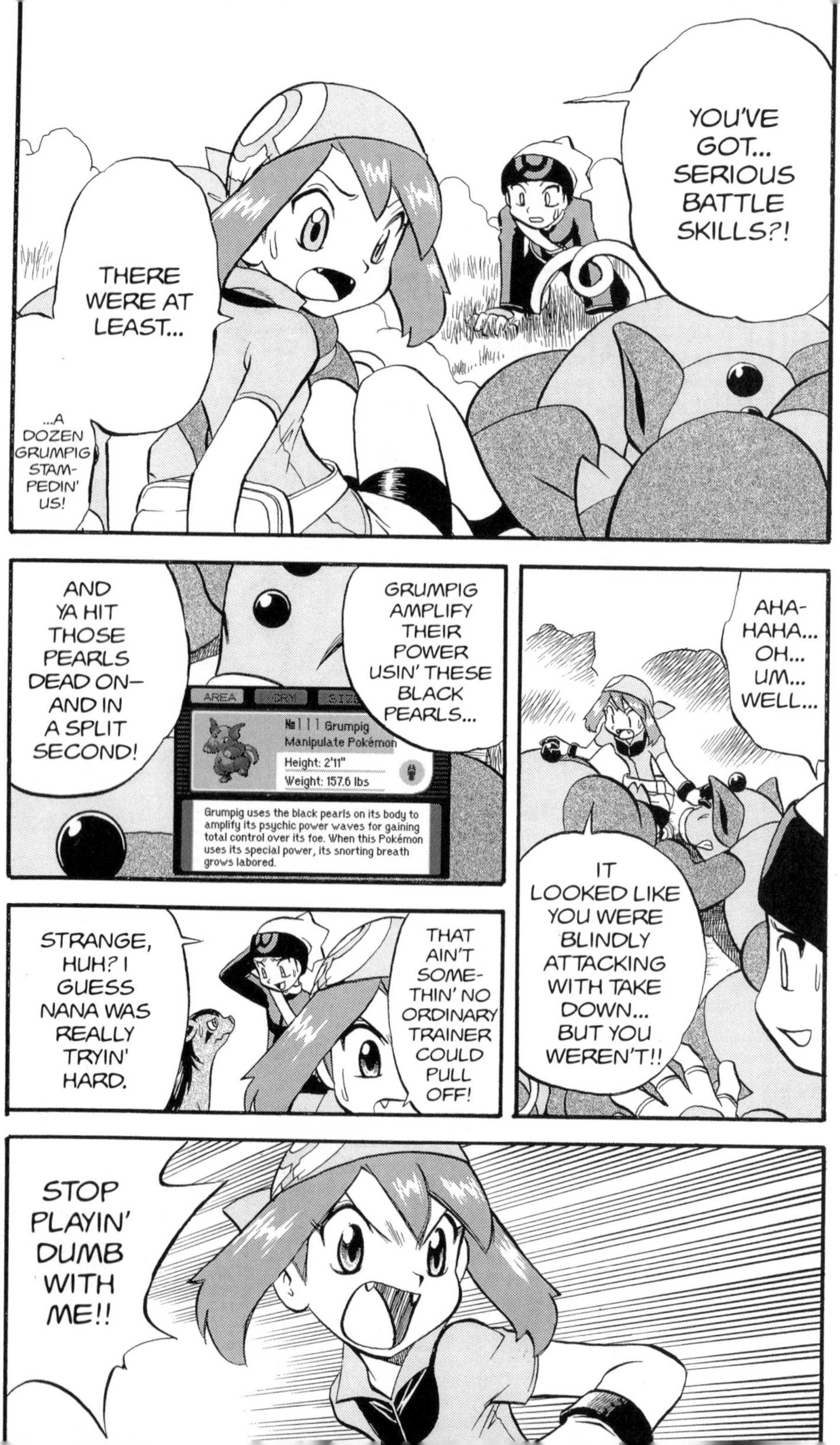
YOU'VE GOT... SERIOUS BATTLE SKILLS?!
THERE WERE AT LEAST...
...A DOZEN GRUMPIG STAMPEDIN' US!
AHA-HAHA... OH... UM... WELL...
IT LOOKED LIKE YOU WERE BLINDLY ATTACKING WITH TAKE DOWN... BUT YOU WEREN'T!!
GRUMPIG AMPLIFY THEIR POWER USIN' THESE BLACK PEARLS...
AND YA HIT THOSE PEARLS DEAD ON—AND IN A SPLIT SECOND!
AREA
CRY
SIZE
№111 Grumpig
Manipulate Pokémon
Height: 2'11"
Weight: 157.6 lbs
Grumpig uses the black pearls on its body to amplify its psychic power waves for gaining total control over its foe. When this Pokémon uses its special power, its snorting breath grows labored.
THAT AIN'T SOMETHIN' NO ORDINARY TRAINER COULD PULL OFF!
STRANGE, HUH? I GUESS NANA WAS REALLY TRYIN' HARD.
STOP PLAYIN' DUMB WITH ME!!

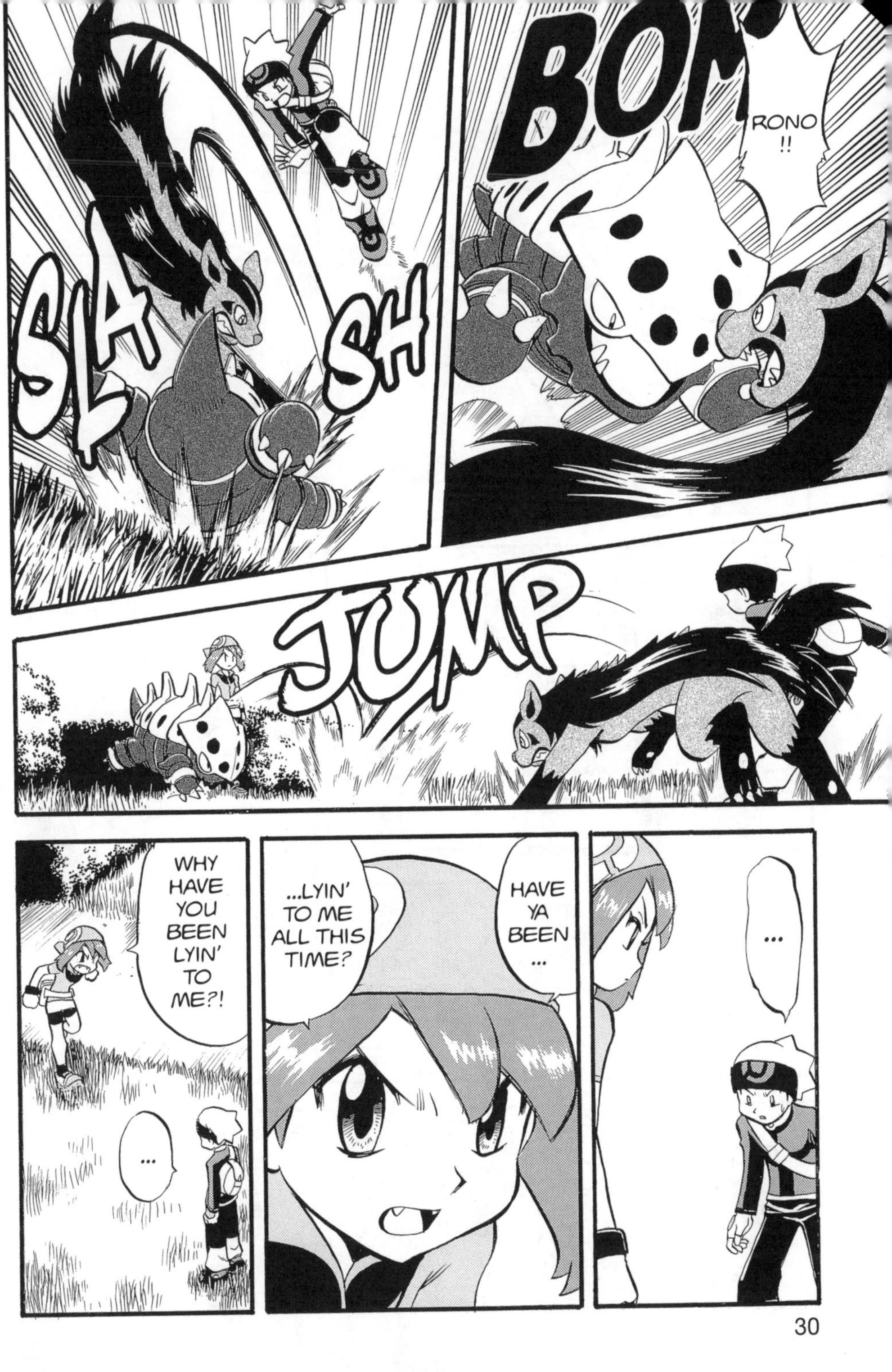
BOM
RONO !!
SLASH
JUMP
...
HAVE YA BEEN ...
...LYIN' TO ME ALL THIS TIME?
WHY HAVE YOU BEEN LYIN' TO ME?!
...

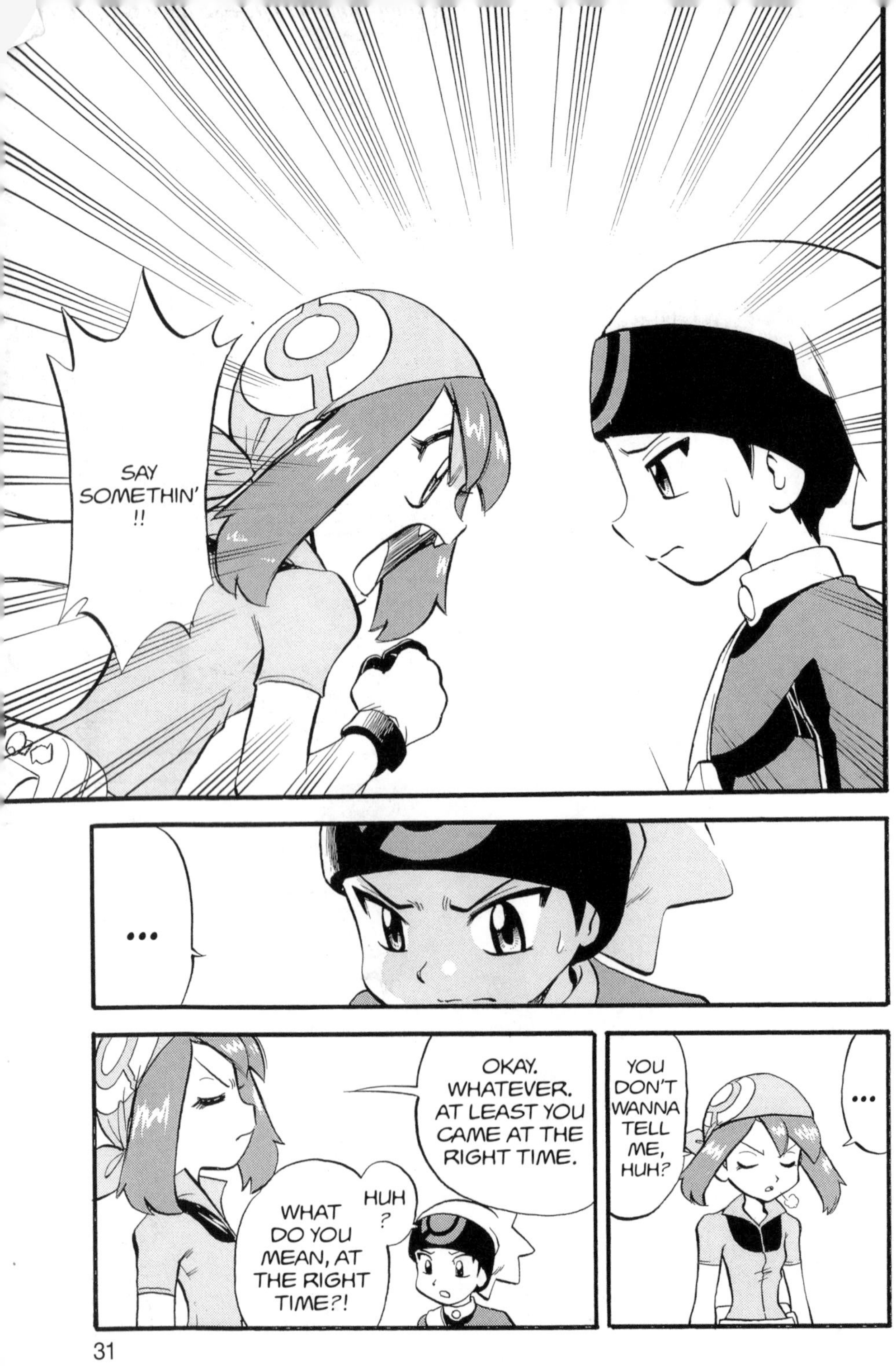
SAY SOMETHIN' !!
...
...
YOU DON'T WANNA TELL ME, HUH?
OKAY. WHATEVER. AT LEAST YOU CAME AT THE RIGHT TIME.
HUH?
WHAT DO YOU MEAN, AT THE RIGHT TIME?!

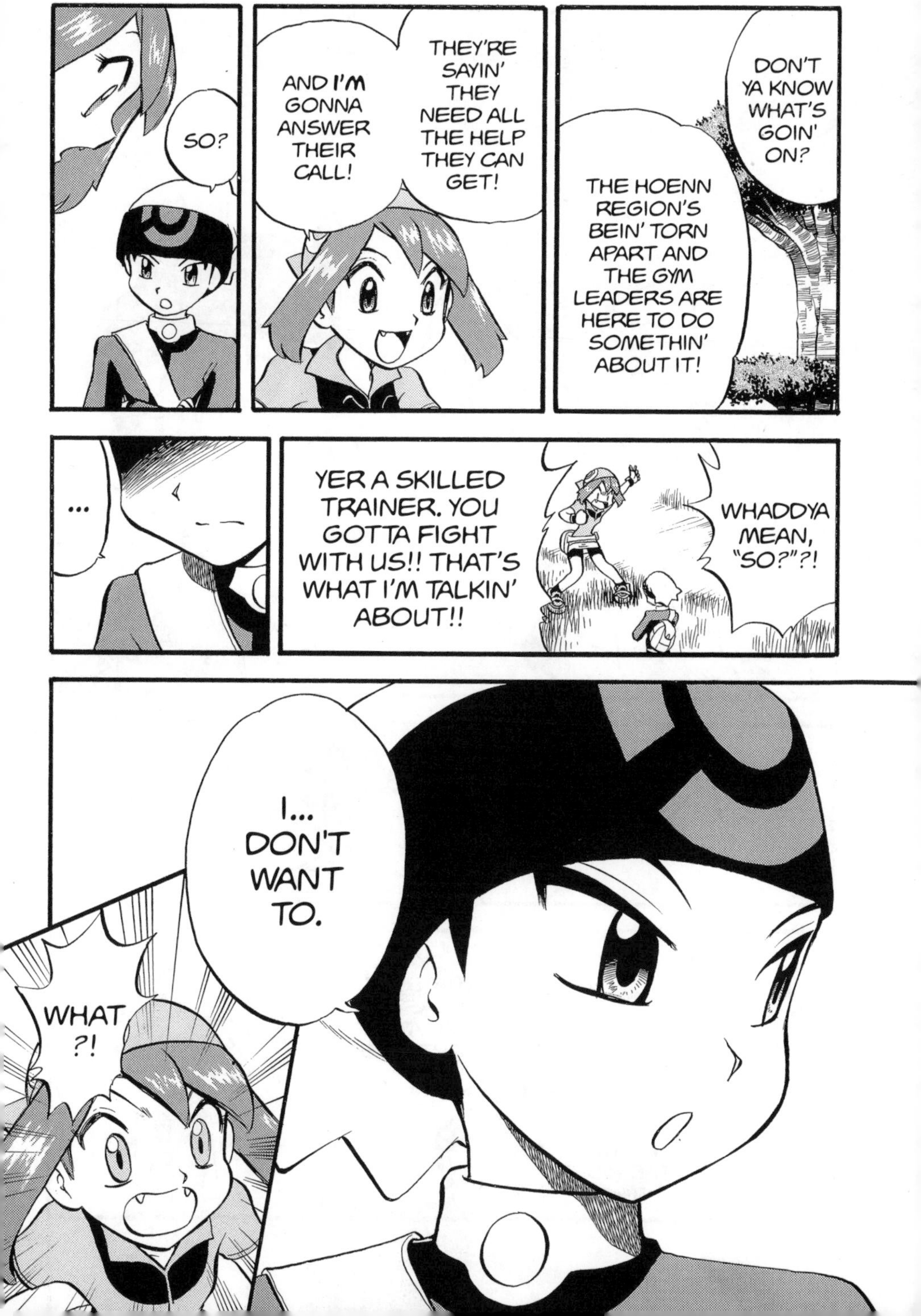
DON'T YA KNOW WHAT'S GOIN' ON?
THE HOENN REGION'S BEIN' TORN APART AND THE GYM LEADERS ARE HERE TO DO SOMETHIN' ABOUT IT!
THEY'RE SAYIN' THEY NEED ALL THE HELP THEY CAN GET!
AND **I'M** GONNA ANSWER THEIR CALL!
SO?
WHADDYA MEAN, "SO?"?!
YER A SKILLED TRAINER. YOU GOTTA FIGHT WITH US!! THAT'S WHAT I'M TALKIN' ABOUT!!
...
I... DON'T WANT TO.
WHAT ?!

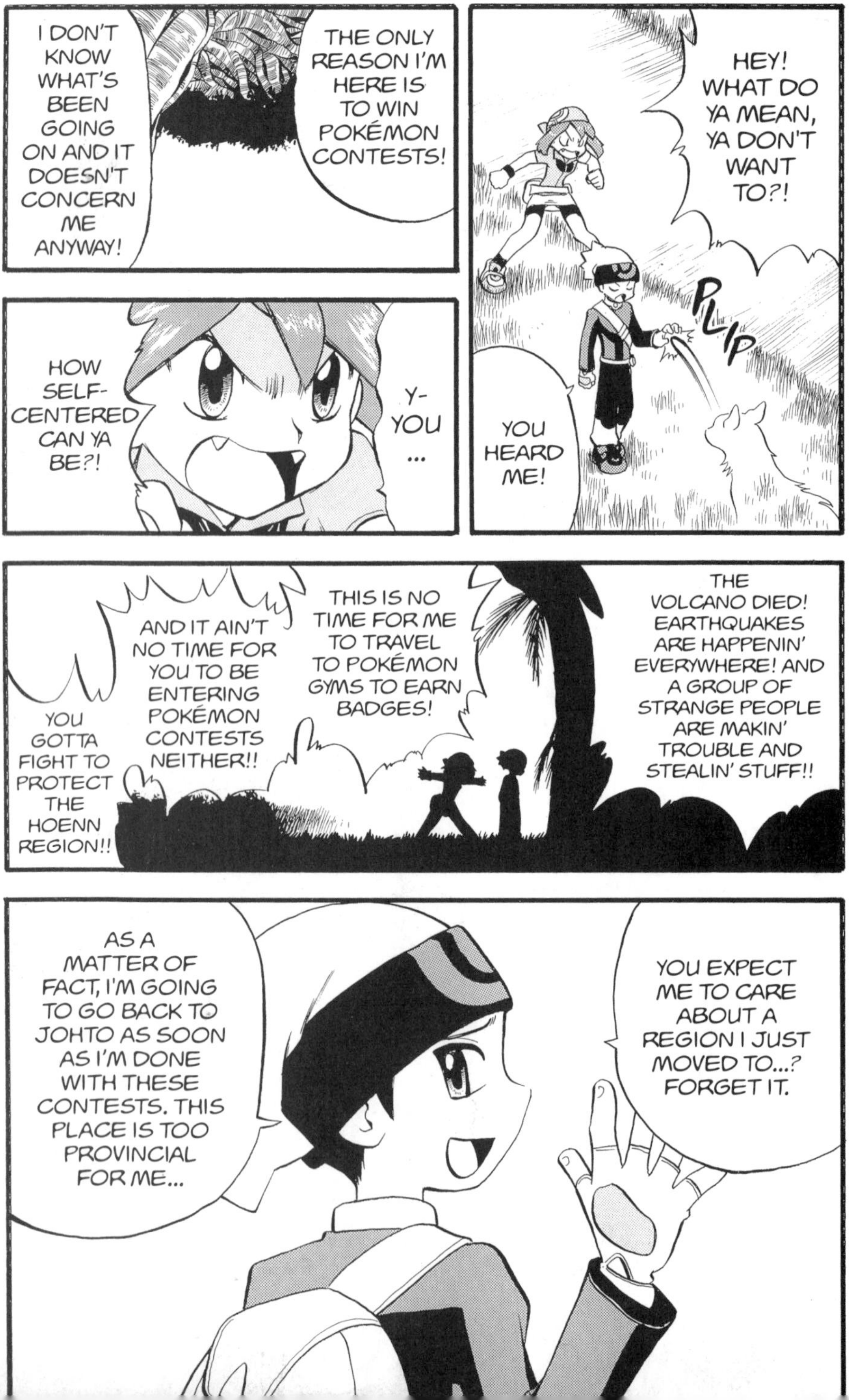
HEY! WHAT DO YA MEAN, YA DON'T WANT TO?!
PLIP
YOU HEARD ME!
THE ONLY REASON I'M HERE IS TO WIN POKÉMON CONTESTS!
I DON'T KNOW WHAT'S BEEN GOING ON AND IT DOESN'T CONCERN ME ANYWAY!
Y-YOU...
HOW SELF-CENTERED CAN YA BE?!
THE VOLCANO DIED! EARTHQUAKES ARE HAPPENIN' EVERYWHERE! AND A GROUP OF STRANGE PEOPLE ARE MAKIN' TROUBLE AND STEALIN' STUFF!!
THIS IS NO TIME FOR ME TO TRAVEL TO POKÉMON GYMS TO EARN BADGES!
AND IT AIN'T NO TIME FOR YOU TO BE ENTERING POKÉMON CONTESTS NEITHER!!
YOU GOTTA FIGHT TO PROTECT THE HOENN REGION!!
YOU EXPECT ME TO CARE ABOUT A REGION I JUST MOVED TO...? FORGET IT.
AS A MATTER OF FACT, I'M GOING TO GO BACK TO JOHTO AS SOON AS I'M DONE WITH THESE CONTESTS. THIS PLACE IS TOO PROVINCIAL FOR ME...

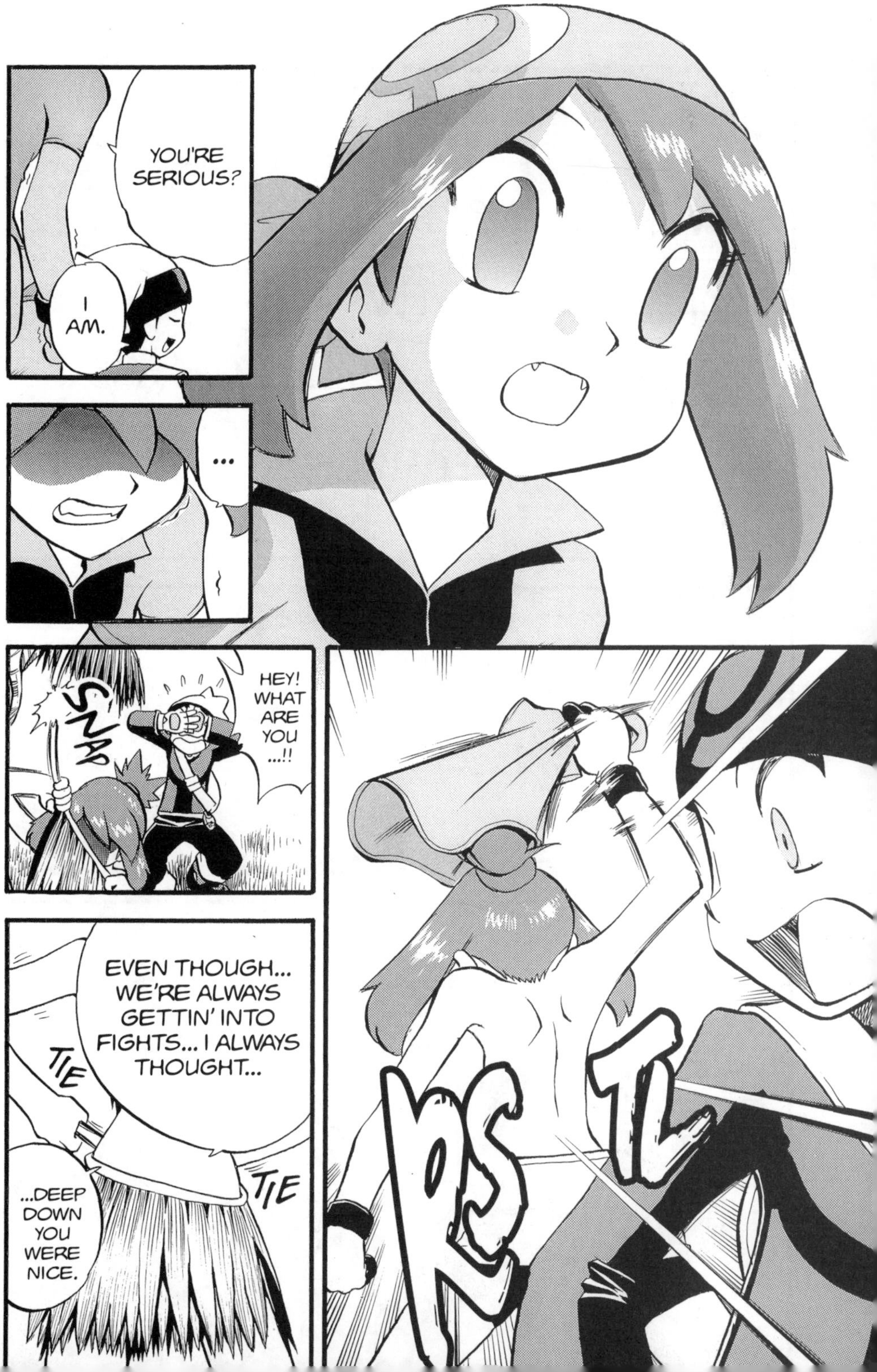
YOU'RE SERIOUS?
I AM.
...
HEY! WHAT ARE YOU ...!!
SNAP
EVEN THOUGH... WE'RE ALWAYS GETTIN' INTO FIGHTS... I ALWAYS THOUGHT...
TIE
TIE
...DEEP DOWN YOU WERE NICE.

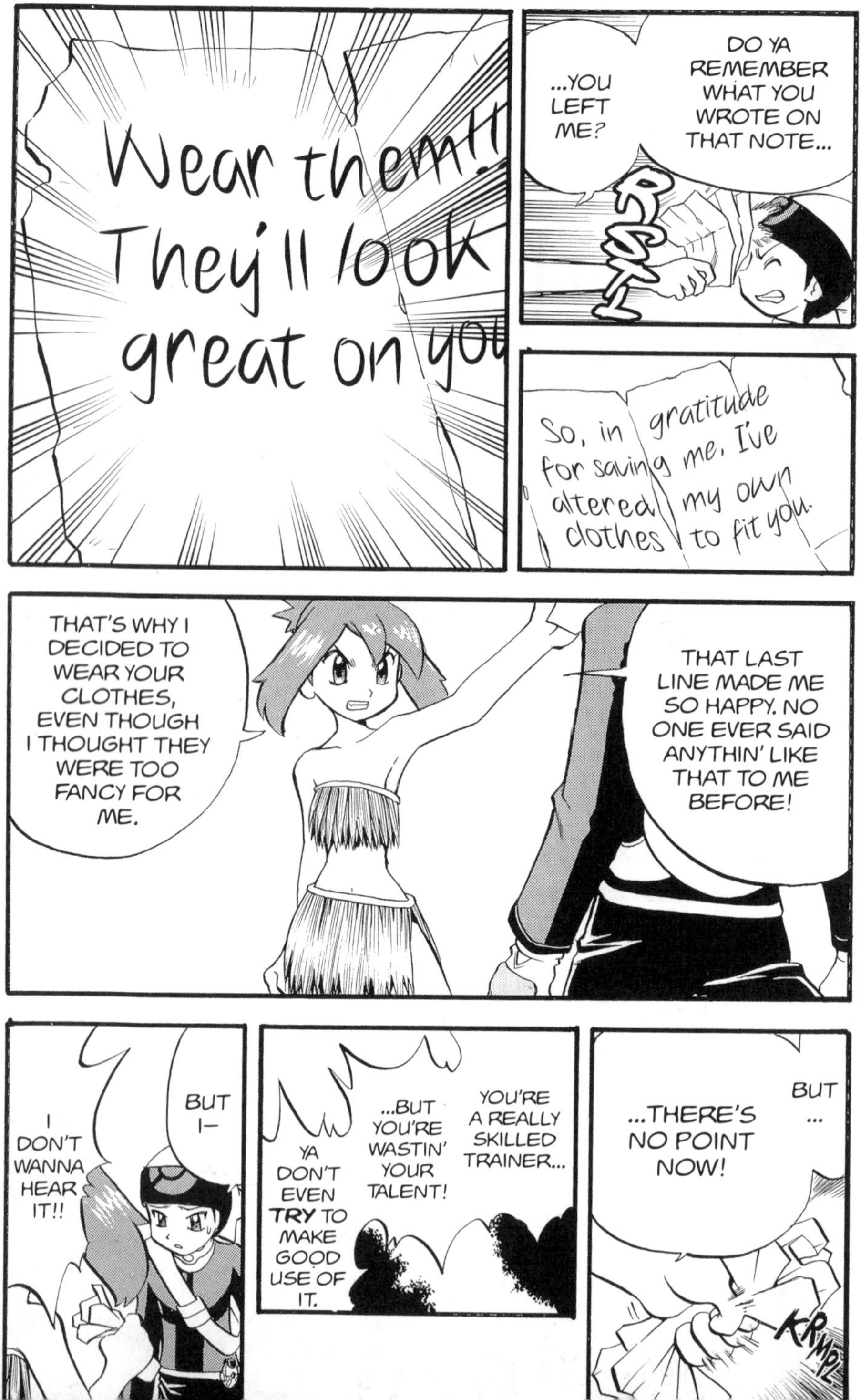
DO YA REMEMBER WHAT YOU WROTE ON THAT NOTE...
...YOU LEFT ME?
So, in gratitude for saving me, I've altered my own clothes to fit you.
Wear them!! They'll look great on you
THAT LAST LINE MADE ME SO HAPPY. NO ONE EVER SAID ANYTHIN' LIKE THAT TO ME BEFORE!
THAT'S WHY I DECIDED TO WEAR YOUR CLOTHES, EVEN THOUGH I THOUGHT THEY WERE TOO FANCY FOR ME.
BUT ...
...THERE'S NO POINT NOW!
KRMPL
YOU'RE A REALLY SKILLED TRAINER...
...BUT YOU'RE WASTIN' YOUR TALENT!
YA DON'T EVEN **TRY** TO MAKE GOOD USE OF IT.
BUT I—
I DON'T WANNA HEAR IT!!

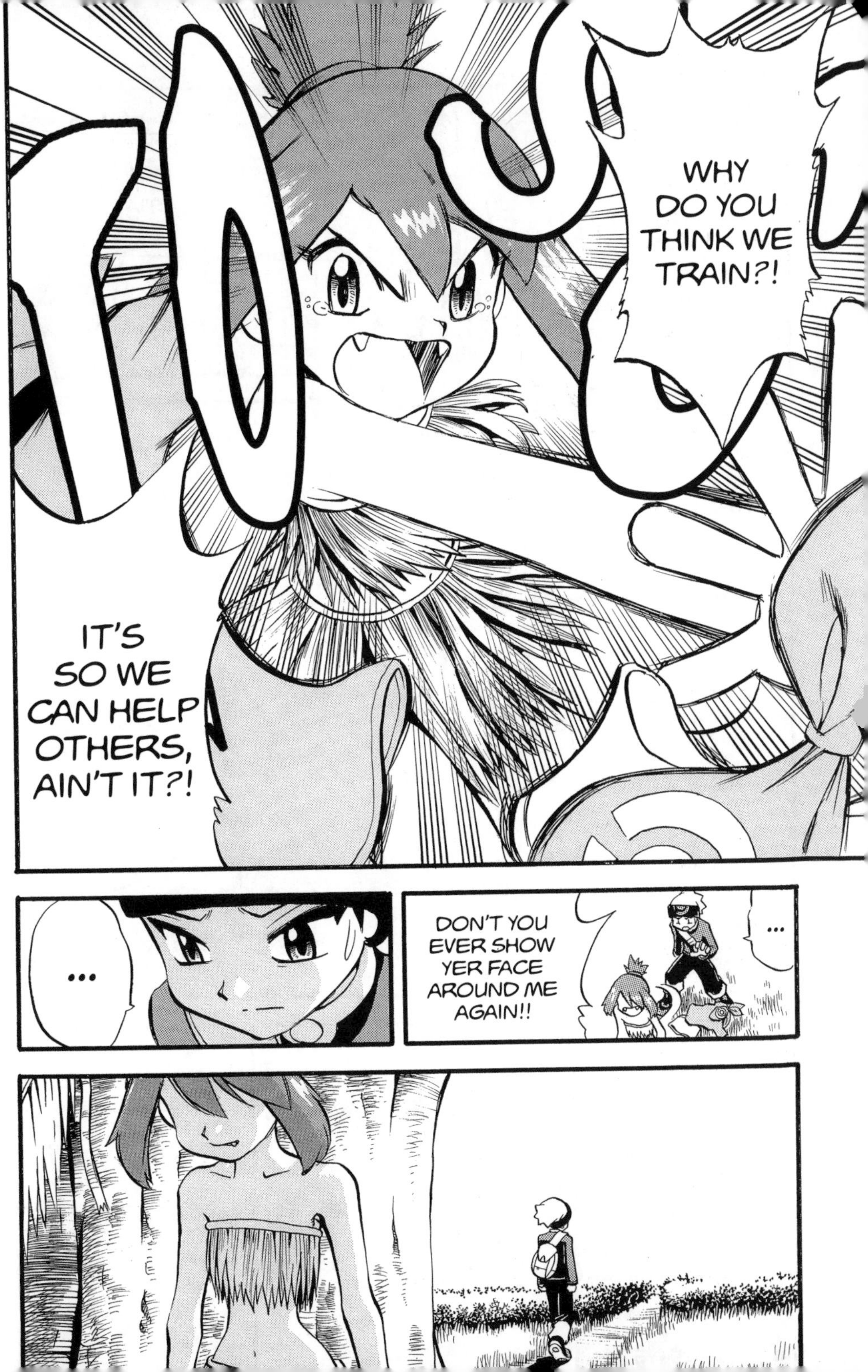
WHY DO YOU THINK WE TRAIN?!
IT'S SO WE CAN HELP OTHERS, AIN'T IT?!
...
DON'T YOU EVER SHOW YER FACE AROUND ME AGAIN!!
...

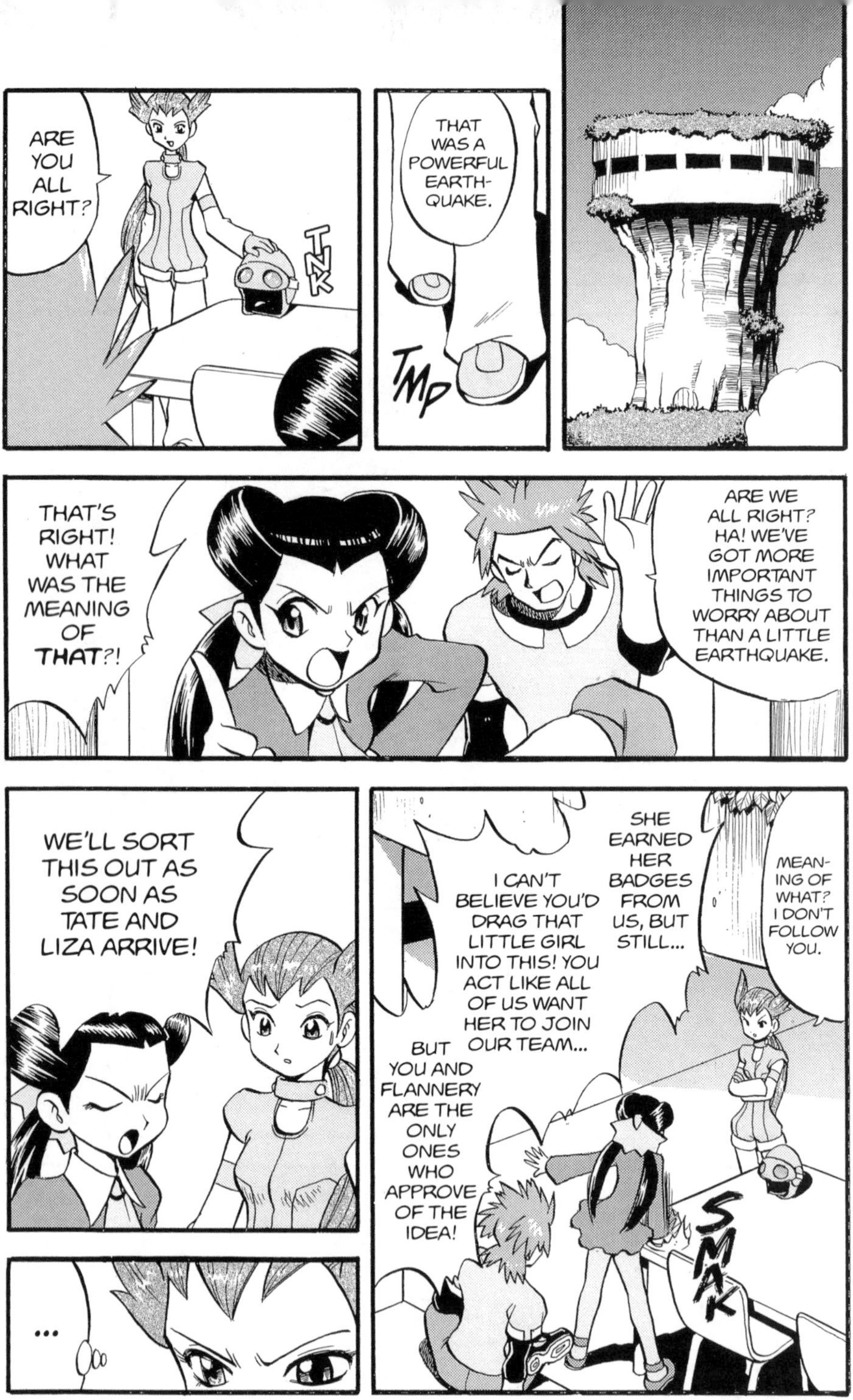
THAT WAS A POWERFUL EARTH-QUAKE.
TMP
ARE YOU ALL RIGHT?
TNK
ARE WE ALL RIGHT? HA! WE'VE GOT MORE IMPORTANT THINGS TO WORRY ABOUT THAN A LITTLE EARTHQUAKE.
THAT'S RIGHT! WHAT WAS THE MEANING OF **THAT**?!
MEAN-ING OF WHAT? I DON'T FOLLOW YOU.
SHE EARNED HER BADGES FROM US, BUT STILL...
I CAN'T BELIEVE YOU'D DRAG THAT LITTLE GIRL INTO THIS! YOU ACT LIKE ALL OF US WANT HER TO JOIN OUR TEAM...
BUT YOU AND FLANNERY ARE THE ONLY ONES WHO APPROVE OF THE IDEA!
SMAK
WE'LL SORT THIS OUT AS SOON AS TATE AND LIZA ARRIVE!
...

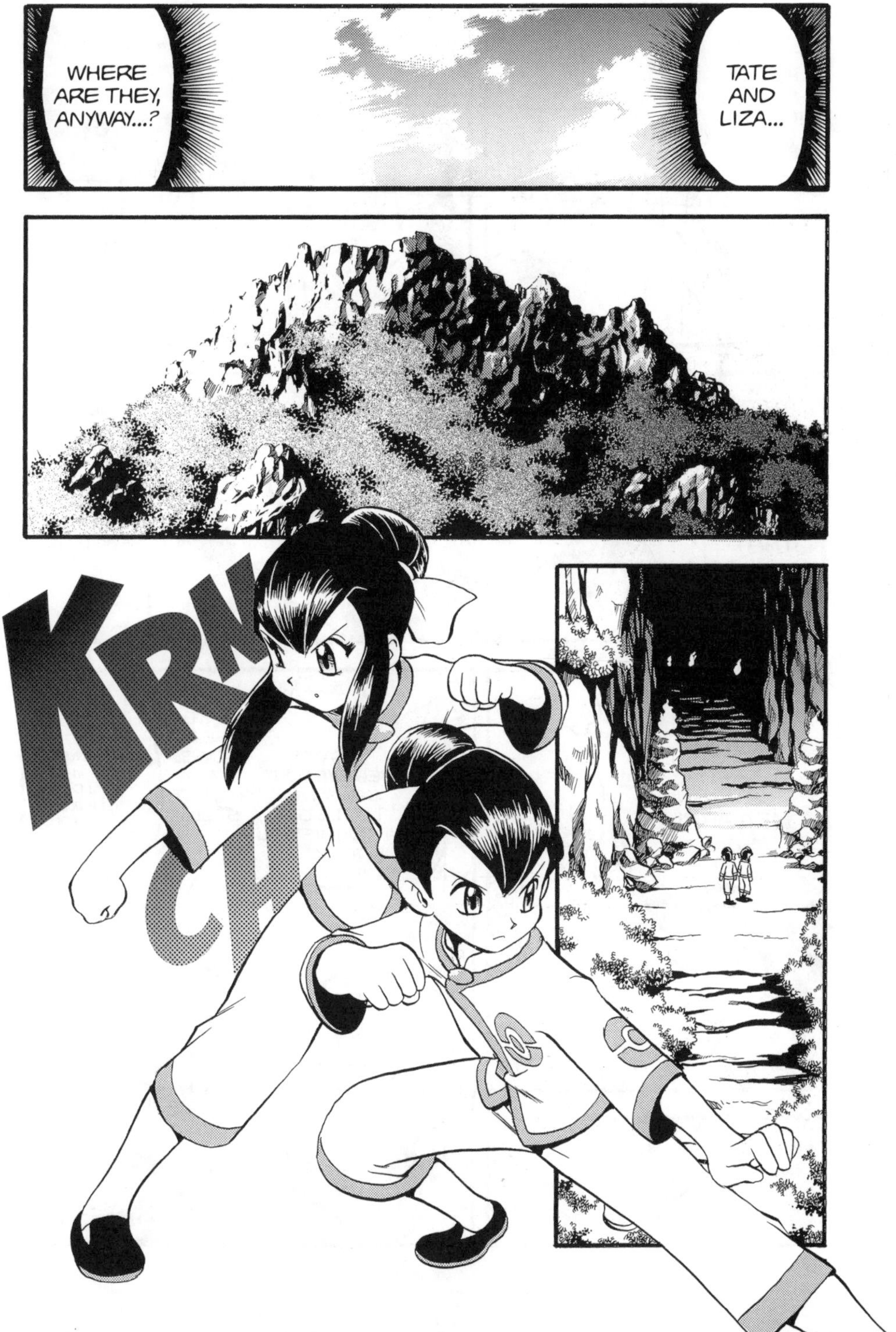

TATE AND LIZA...
WHERE ARE THEY, ANYWAY...?
KRN
CH

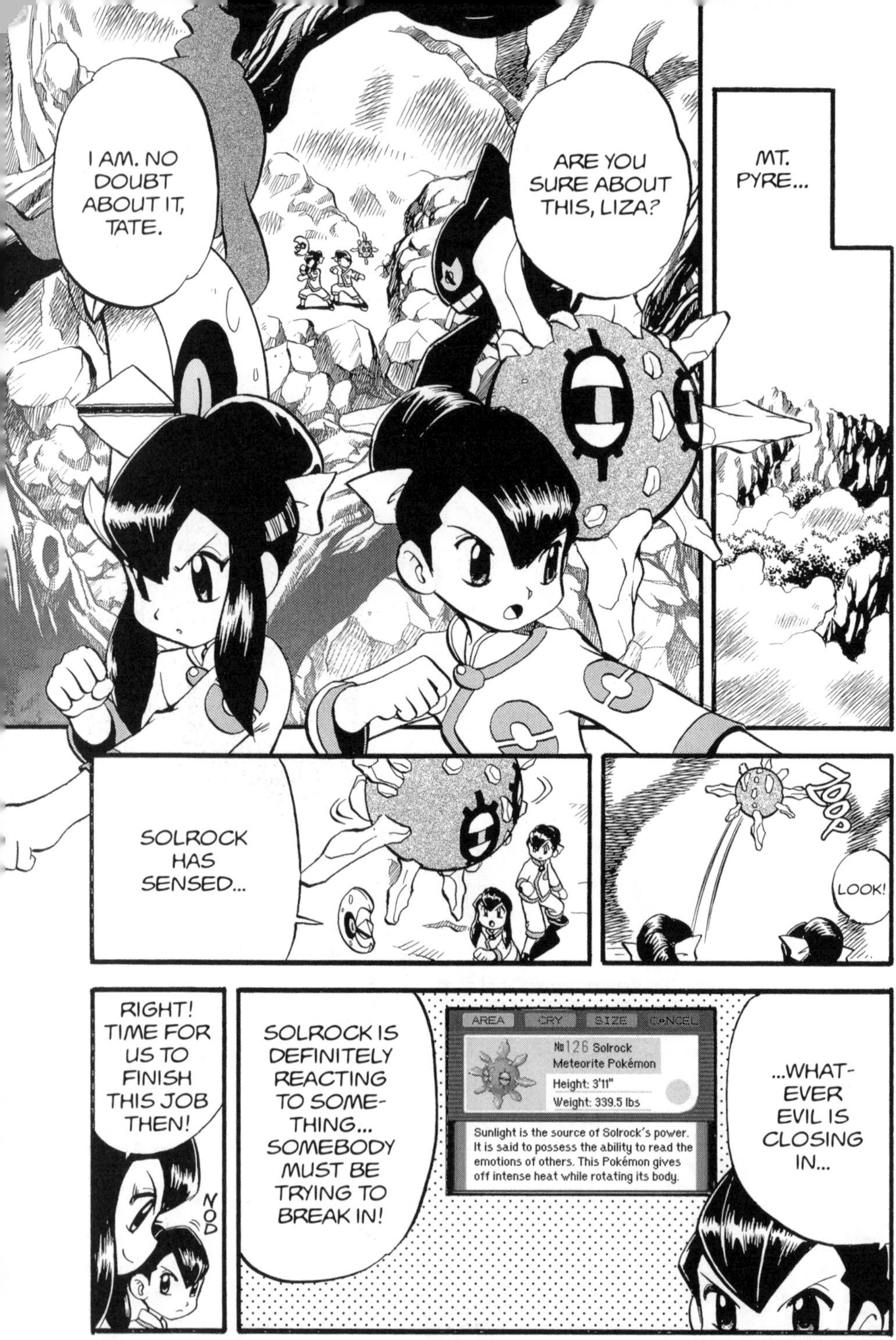
MT. PYRE...
ARE YOU SURE ABOUT THIS, LIZA?
I AM. NO DOUBT ABOUT IT, TATE.
ZOOP
LOOK!
SOLROCK HAS SENSED...
...WHAT-EVER EVIL IS CLOSING IN...
AREA CRY SIZE CANCEL
№126 Solrock
Meteorite Pokémon
Height: 3'11"
Weight: 339.5 lbs
Sunlight is the source of Solrock's power. It is said to possess the ability to read the emotions of others. This Pokémon gives off intense heat while rotating its body.
SOLROCK IS DEFINITELY REACTING TO SOME-THING... SOMEBODY MUST BE TRYING TO BREAK IN!
RIGHT! TIME FOR US TO FINISH THIS JOB THEN!
NOD

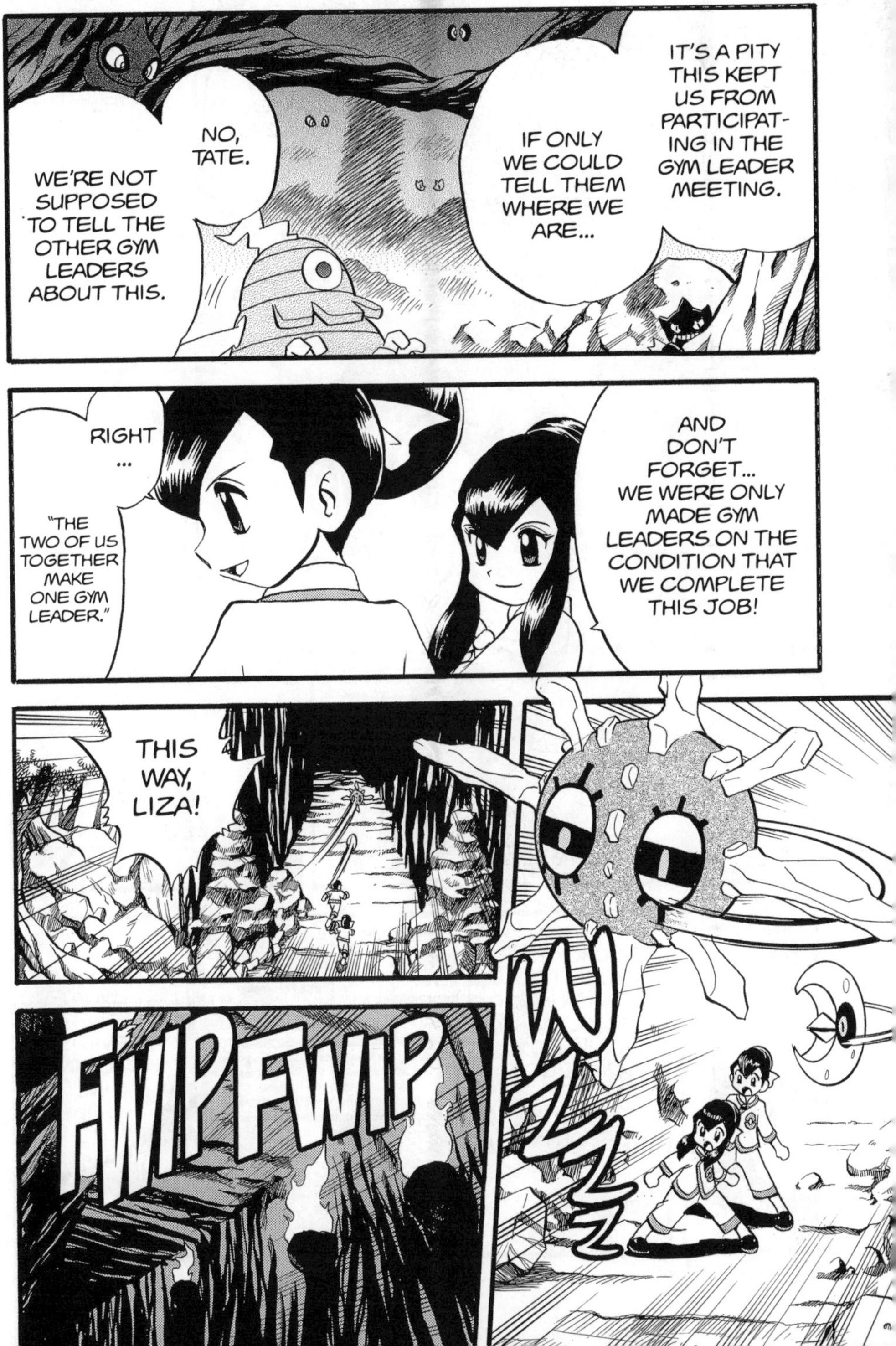
IT'S A PITY THIS KEPT US FROM PARTICIPAT-ING IN THE GYM LEADER MEETING.
IF ONLY WE COULD TELL THEM WHERE WE ARE...
NO, TATE.
WE'RE NOT SUPPOSED TO TELL THE OTHER GYM LEADERS ABOUT THIS.
AND DON'T FORGET... WE WERE ONLY MADE GYM LEADERS ON THE CONDITION THAT WE COMPLETE THIS JOB!
RIGHT ...
"THE TWO OF US TOGETHER MAKE ONE GYM LEADER."
WUZZ
THIS WAY, LIZA!
FWIP FWIP

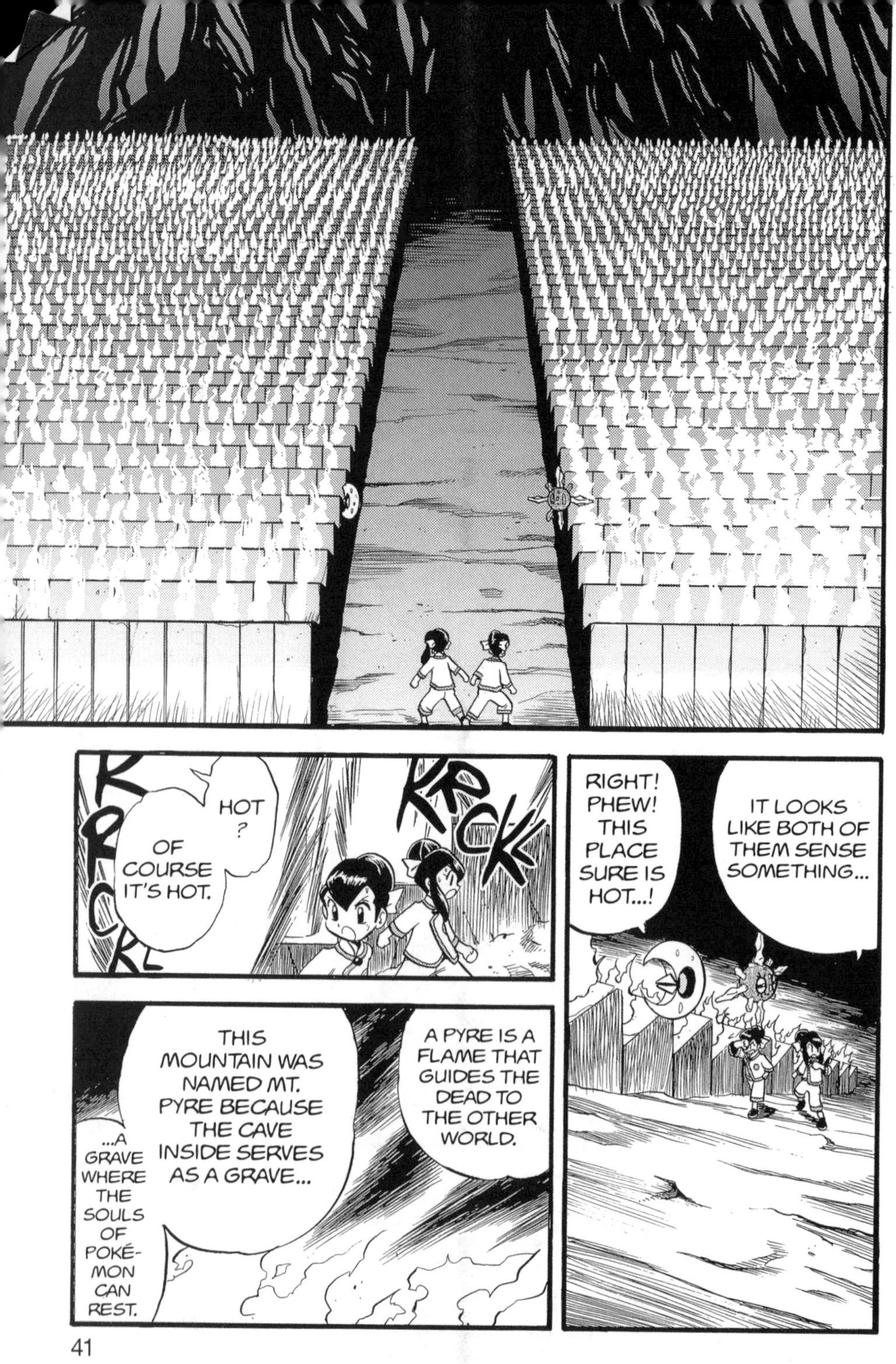
IT LOOKS LIKE BOTH OF THEM SENSE SOMETHING...
RIGHT! PHEW! THIS PLACE SURE IS HOT...!
KRCKL
HOT?
OF COURSE IT'S HOT.
KRCKL
A PYRE IS A FLAME THAT GUIDES THE DEAD TO THE OTHER WORLD.
THIS MOUNTAIN WAS NAMED MT. PYRE BECAUSE THE CAVE INSIDE SERVES AS A GRAVE...
...A GRAVE WHERE THE SOULS OF POKÉMON CAN REST.

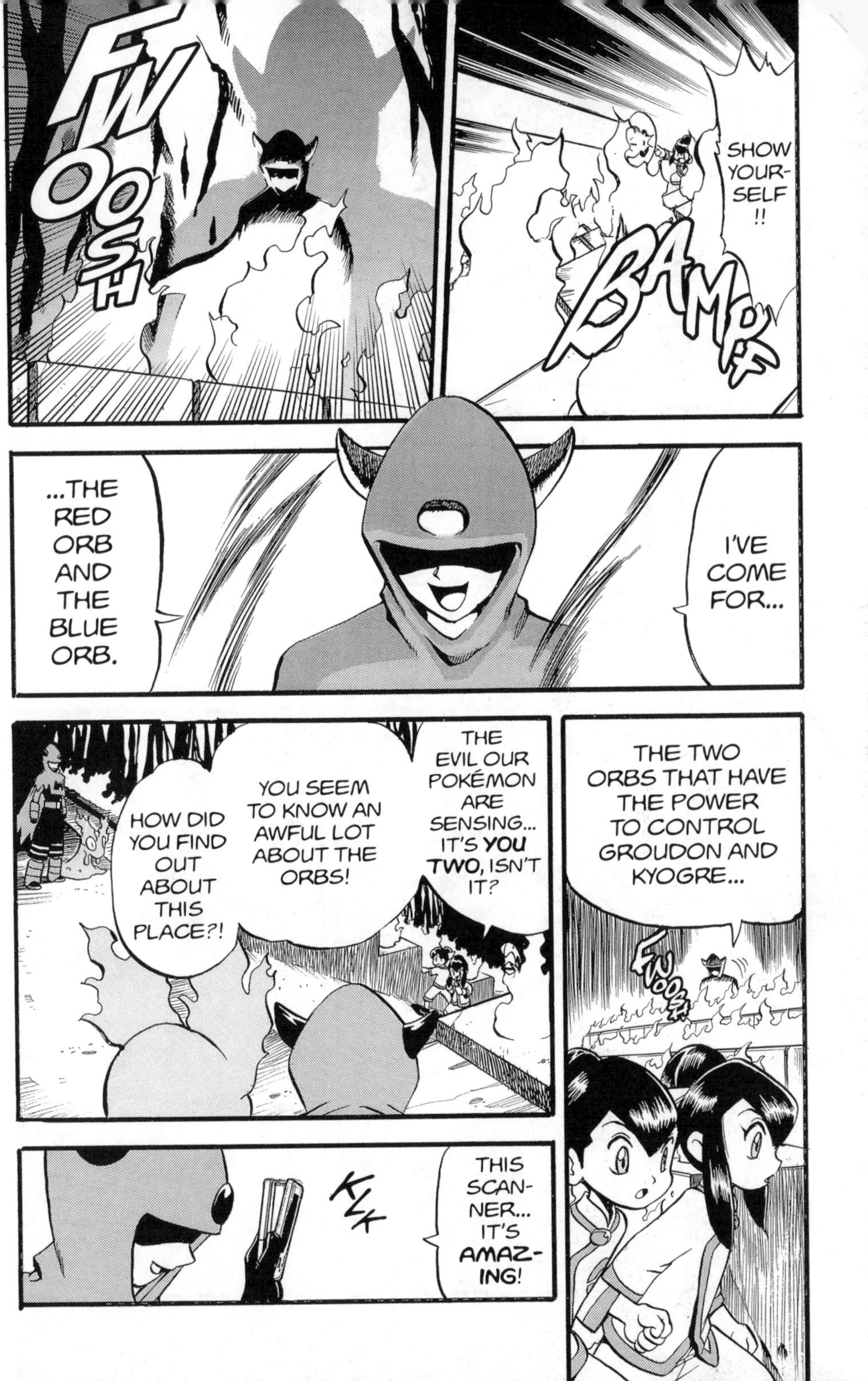
SHOW YOURSELF!!
BAMPF
FWOOOSH
I'VE COME FOR...
...THE RED ORB AND THE BLUE ORB.
THE TWO ORBS THAT HAVE THE POWER TO CONTROL GROUDON AND KYOGRE...
FWOOSH
THE EVIL OUR POKÉMON ARE SENSING... IT'S **YOU TWO,** ISN'T IT?
YOU SEEM TO KNOW AN AWFUL LOT ABOUT THE ORBS!
HOW DID YOU FIND OUT ABOUT THIS PLACE?!
THIS SCANNER... IT'S **AMAZING!**
KLIK

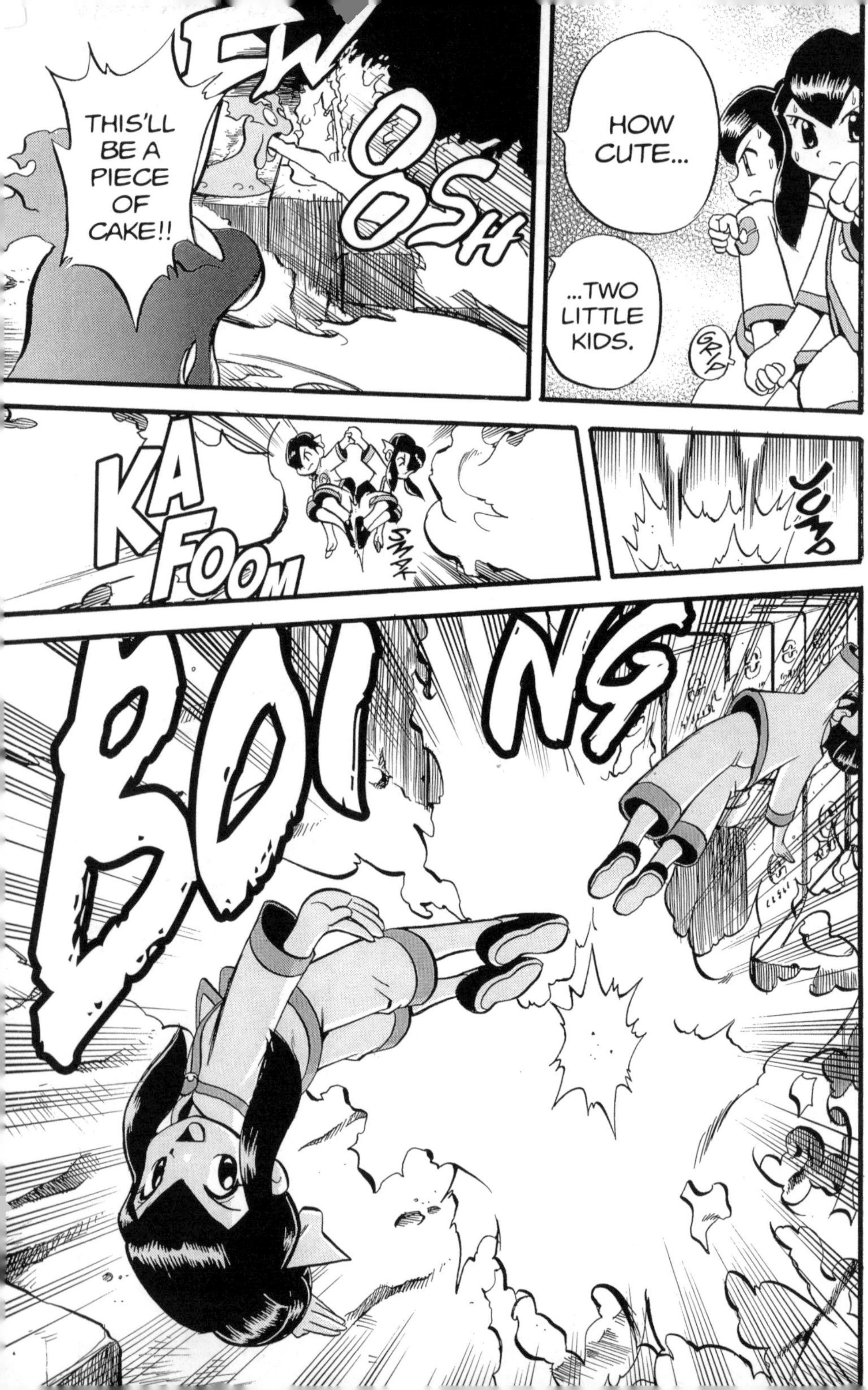
HOW CUTE...
...TWO LITTLE KIDS.
GRIP
THIS'LL BE A PIECE OF CAKE!!
SWOOSH
JUMP
KA FOOM
SMAK
BOING

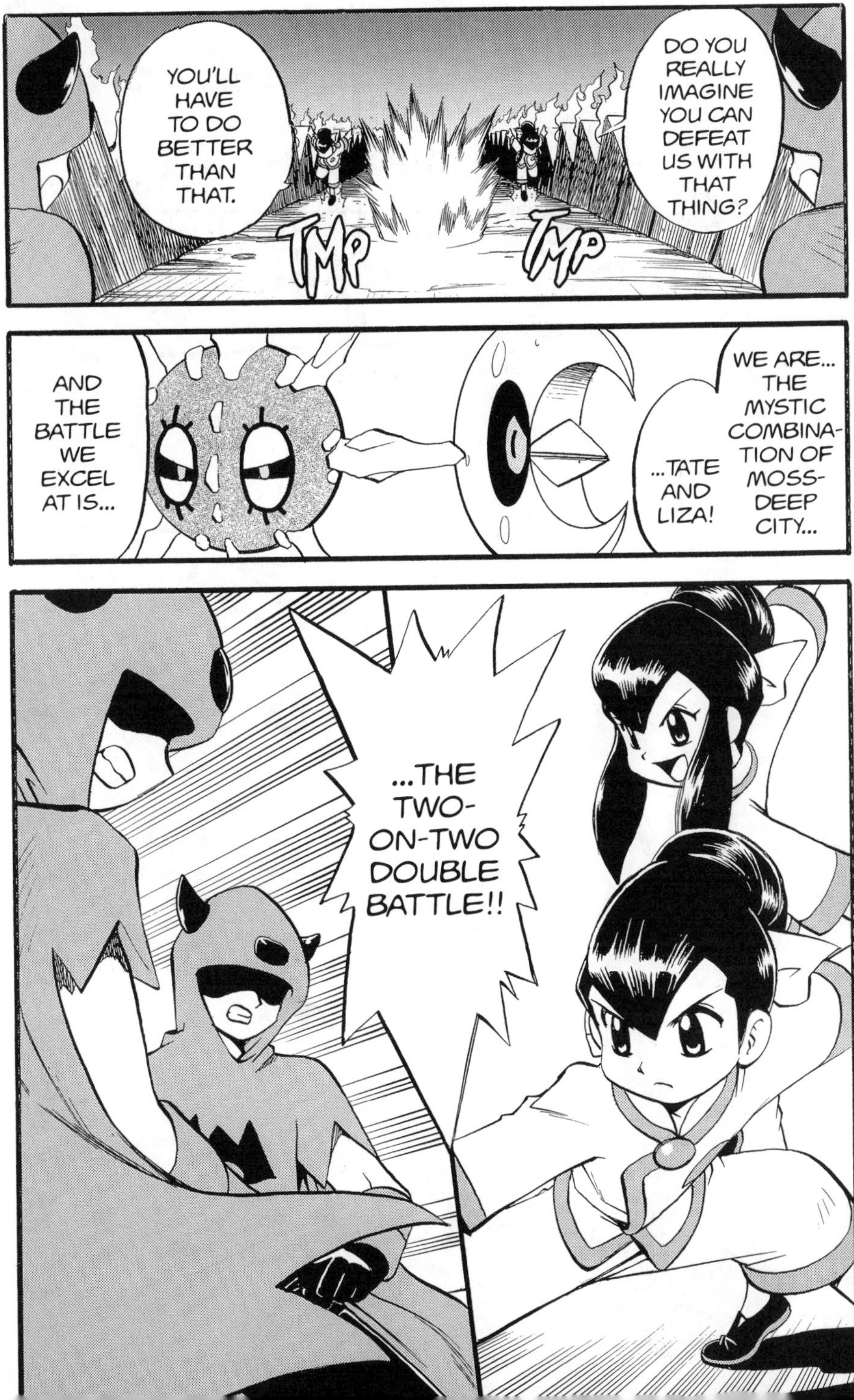
DO YOU REALLY IMAGINE YOU CAN DEFEAT US WITH THAT THING?
YOU'LL HAVE TO DO BETTER THAN THAT.
TMP
TMP
WE ARE... THE MYSTIC COMBINATION OF MOSSDEEP CITY...
...TATE AND LIZA!
AND THE BATTLE WE EXCEL AT IS...
...THE TWO-ON-TWO DOUBLE BATTLE!!

● Adventure 229 ●

You Can Fight Day or Night with Lunatone and Solrock

POKÉMON ADVENTURES RUBY & SAPPHIRE

The Fourth Chapter

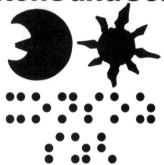

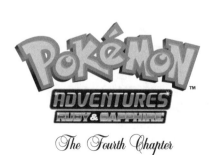

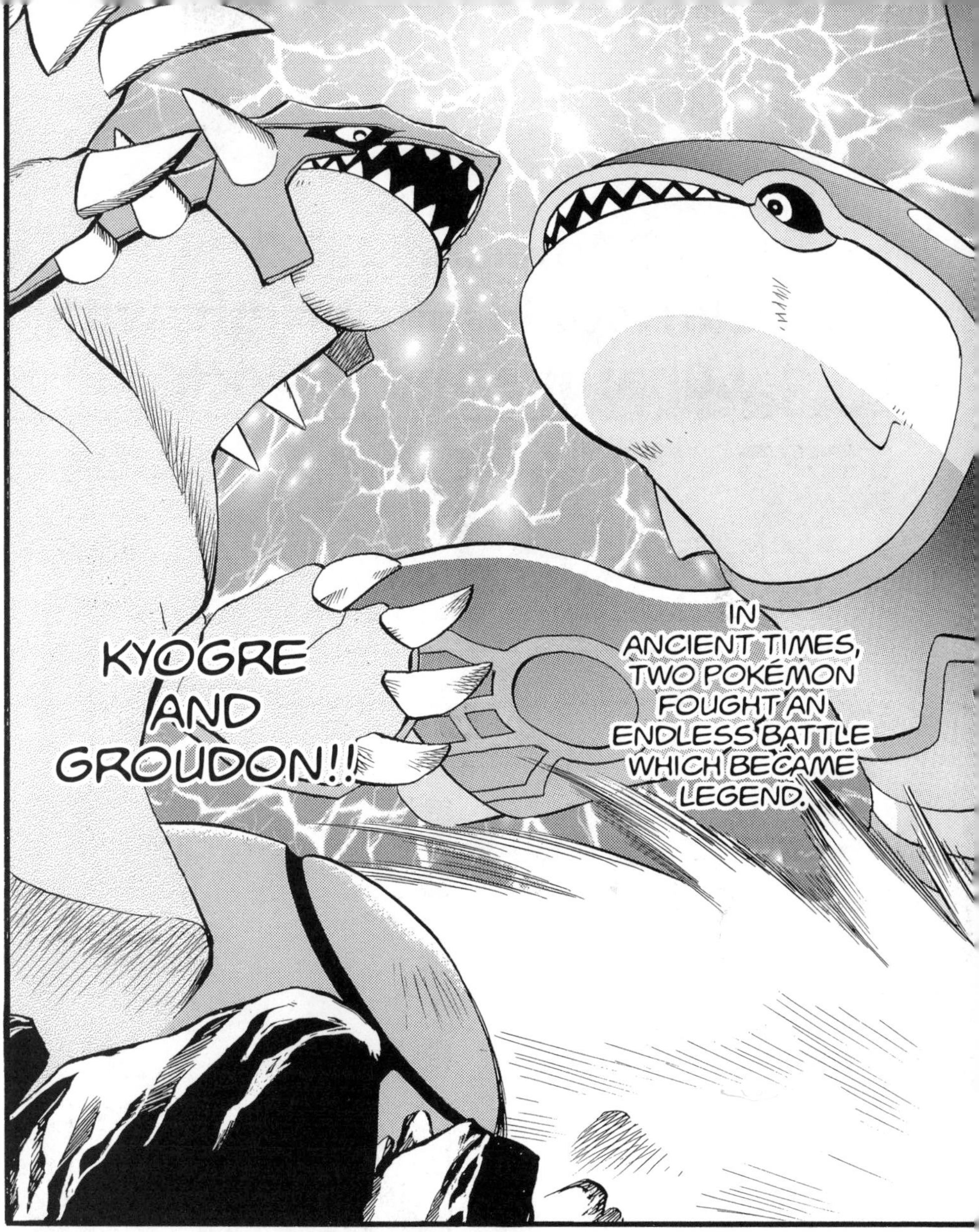
IN ANCIENT TIMES, TWO POKÉMON FOUGHT AN ENDLESS BATTLE WHICH BECAME LEGEND.
KYOGRE AND GROUDON!!

BUT IT WAS THE PRESENCE OF TWO SPECIAL ORBS THAT BROUGHT THEIR BATTLE TO AN END...

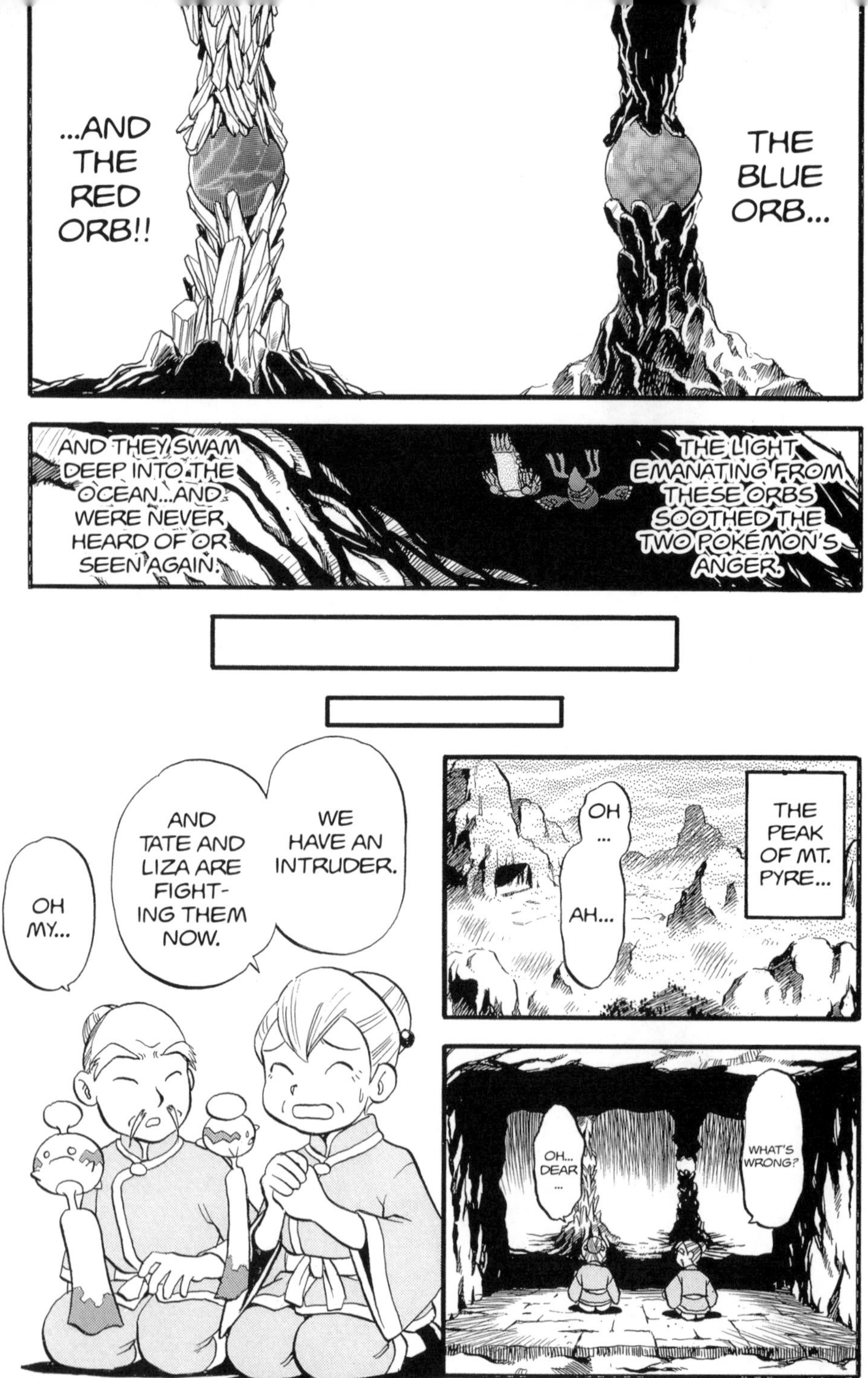
THE BLUE ORB...
...AND THE RED ORB!!
THE LIGHT EMANATING FROM THESE ORBS SOOTHED THE TWO POKÉMON'S ANGER.
AND THEY SWAM DEEP INTO THE OCEAN...AND WERE NEVER HEARD OF OR SEEN AGAIN.
THE PEAK OF MT. PYRE...
OH ...
AH...
WHAT'S WRONG?
OH... DEAR ...
WE HAVE AN INTRUDER.
AND TATE AND LIZA ARE FIGHT-ING THEM NOW.
OH MY...

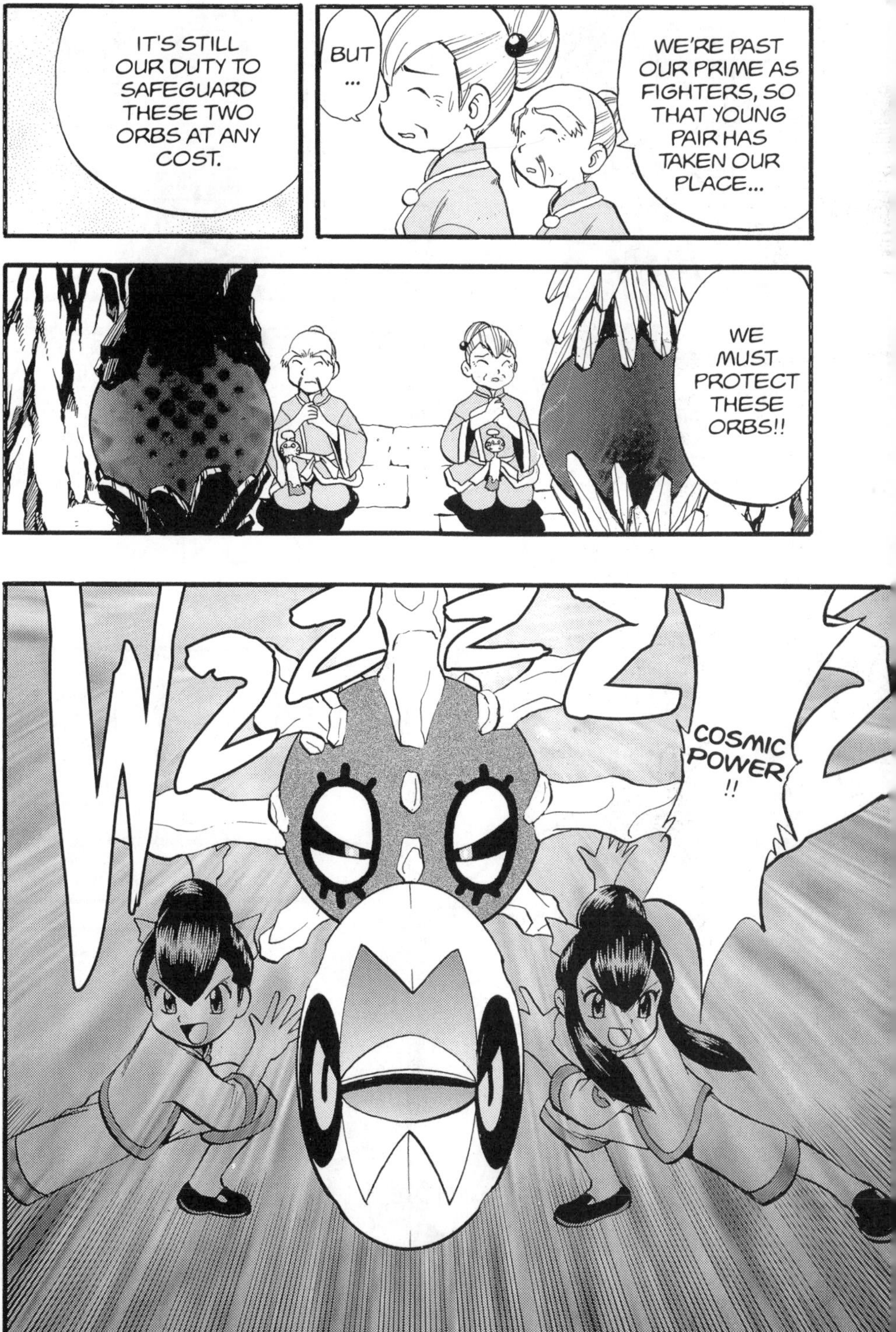
WE'RE PAST OUR PRIME AS FIGHTERS, SO THAT YOUNG PAIR HAS TAKEN OUR PLACE...
BUT ...
IT'S STILL OUR DUTY TO SAFEGUARD THESE TWO ORBS AT ANY COST.
WE MUST PROTECT THESE ORBS!!
COSMIC POWER!!
WZZZZZ

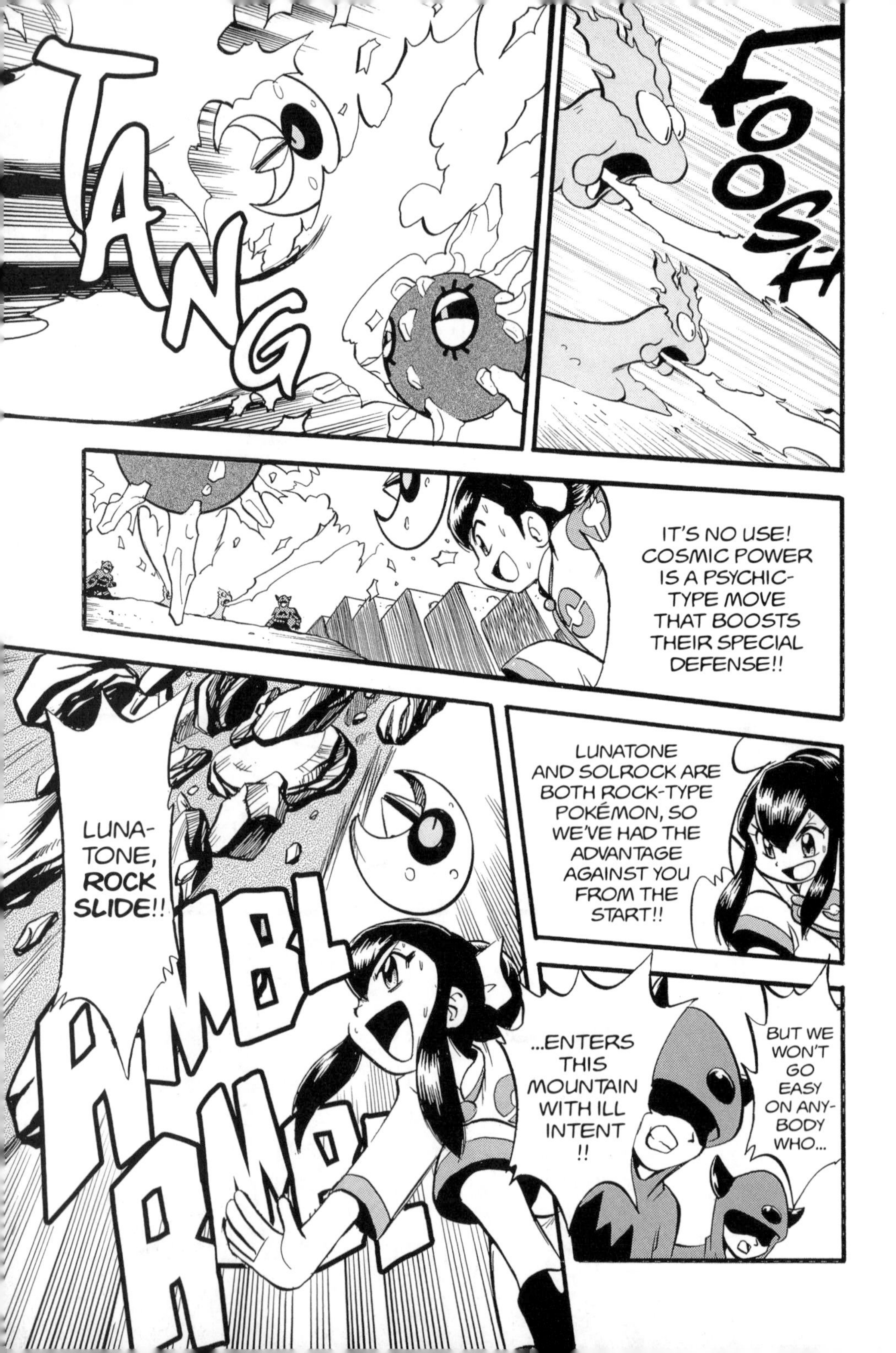
FOOSH
TANG
IT'S NO USE! COSMIC POWER IS A PSYCHIC-TYPE MOVE THAT BOOSTS THEIR SPECIAL DEFENSE!!
LUNATONE AND SOLROCK ARE BOTH ROCK-TYPE POKÉMON, SO WE'VE HAD THE ADVANTAGE AGAINST YOU FROM THE START!!
BUT WE WON'T GO EASY ON ANY-BODY WHO...
...ENTERS THIS MOUNTAIN WITH ILL INTENT!!
LUNA-TONE, ROCK SLIDE!!
AMBL
AMBL

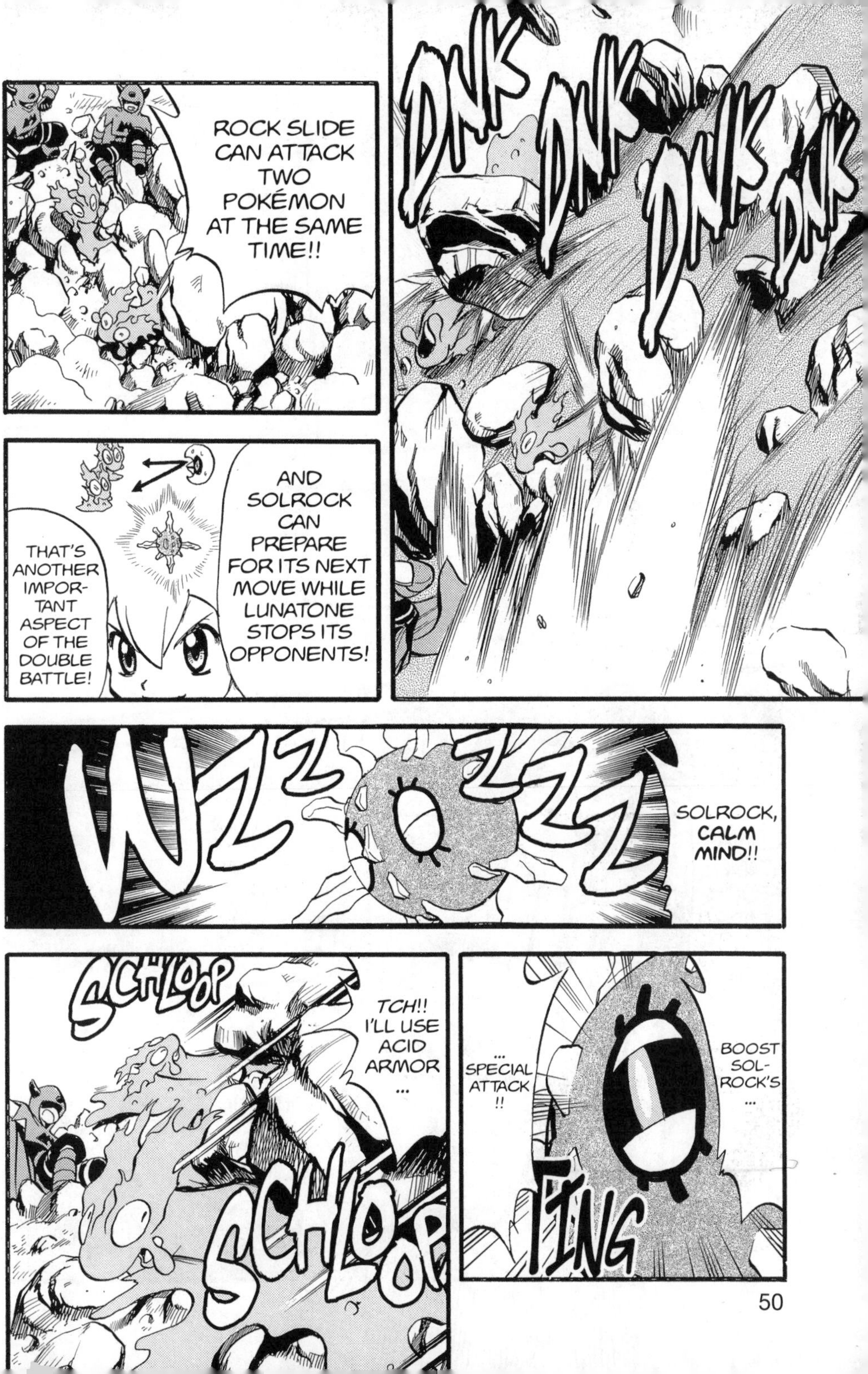
DNK DNK DNK DNK
ROCK SLIDE CAN ATTACK TWO POKÉMON AT THE SAME TIME!!
AND SOLROCK CAN PREPARE FOR ITS NEXT MOVE WHILE LUNATONE STOPS ITS OPPONENTS!
THAT'S ANOTHER IMPOR-TANT ASPECT OF THE DOUBLE BATTLE!
SOLROCK, CALM MIND!!
WZZZZZ
BOOST SOL-ROCK'S ...
... SPECIAL ATTACK !!
TING
TCH!! I'LL USE ACID ARMOR ...
SCHLOOP
SCHLOOP

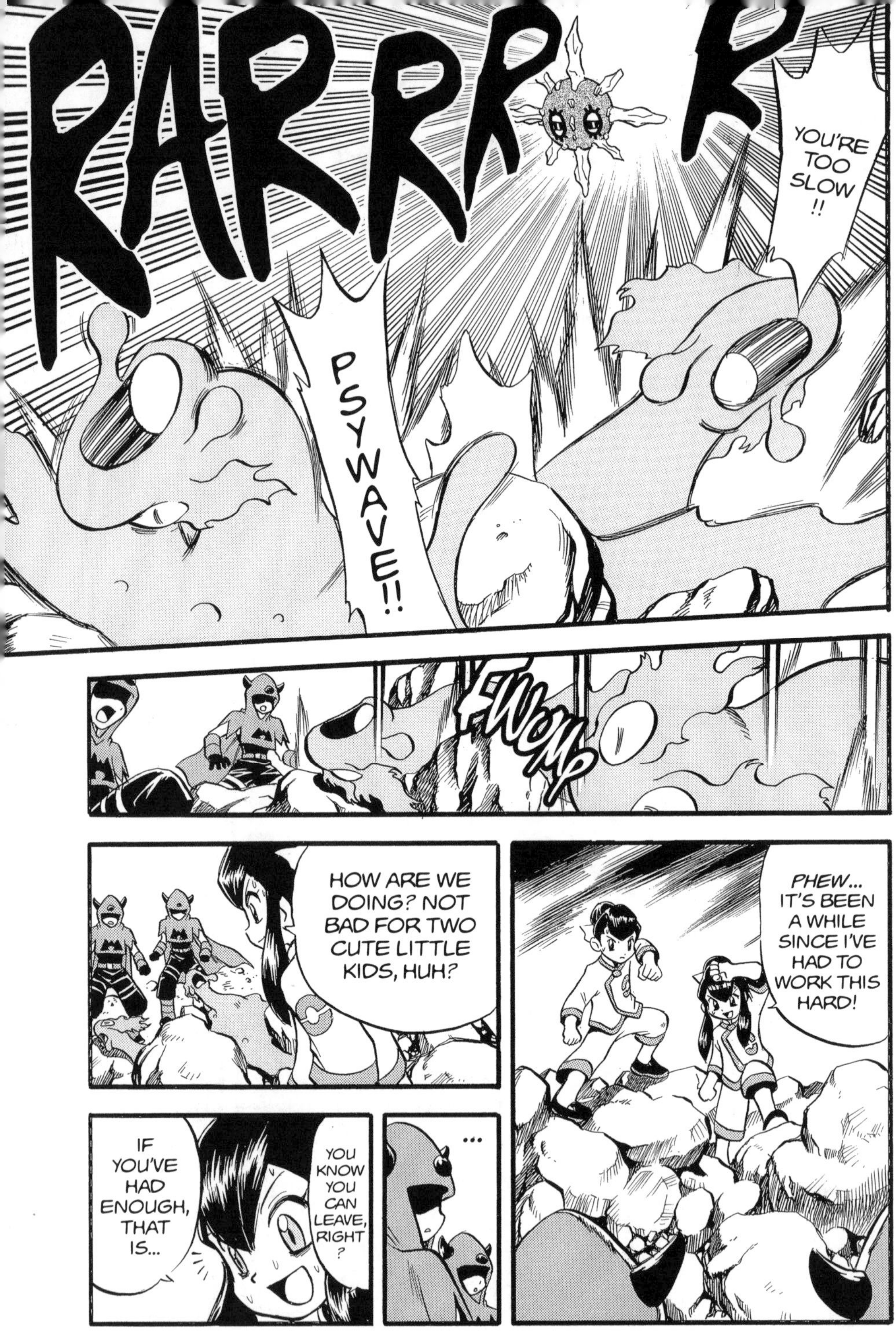
RARRRRR
YOU'RE TOO SLOW!!
PSYWAVE!!
FWOMP
PHEW... IT'S BEEN A WHILE SINCE I'VE HAD TO WORK THIS HARD!
HOW ARE WE DOING? NOT BAD FOR TWO CUTE LITTLE KIDS, HUH?
...
YOU KNOW YOU CAN LEAVE, RIGHT?
IF YOU'VE HAD ENOUGH, THAT IS...

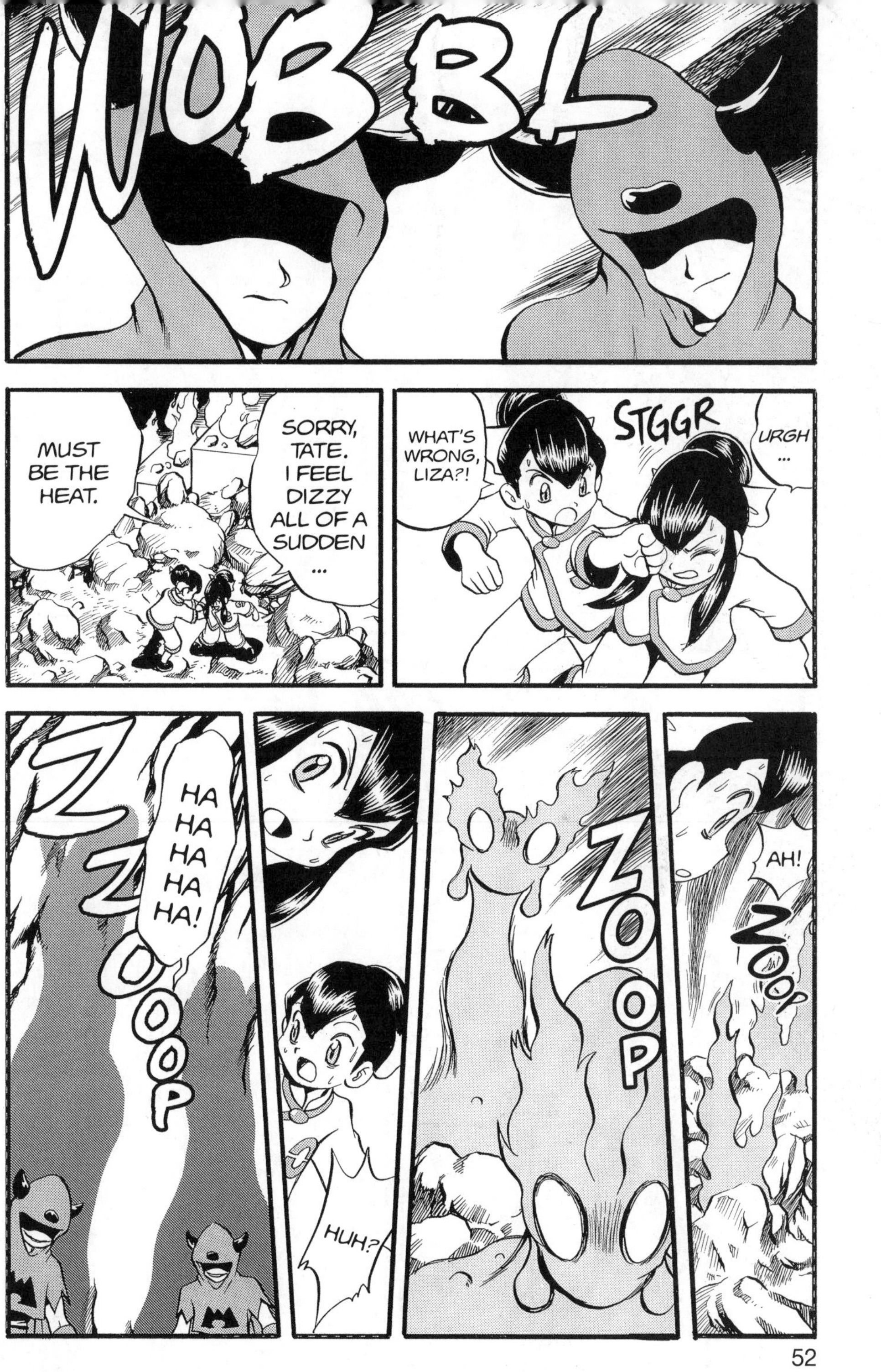
WOBBL
URGH ...
STGGR
WHAT'S WRONG, LIZA?!
SORRY, TATE. I FEEL DIZZY ALL OF A SUDDEN ...
MUST BE THE HEAT.
AH!
ZOOOP
ZOOP
HUH?
HA HA HA HA HA!
ZZOOOOP

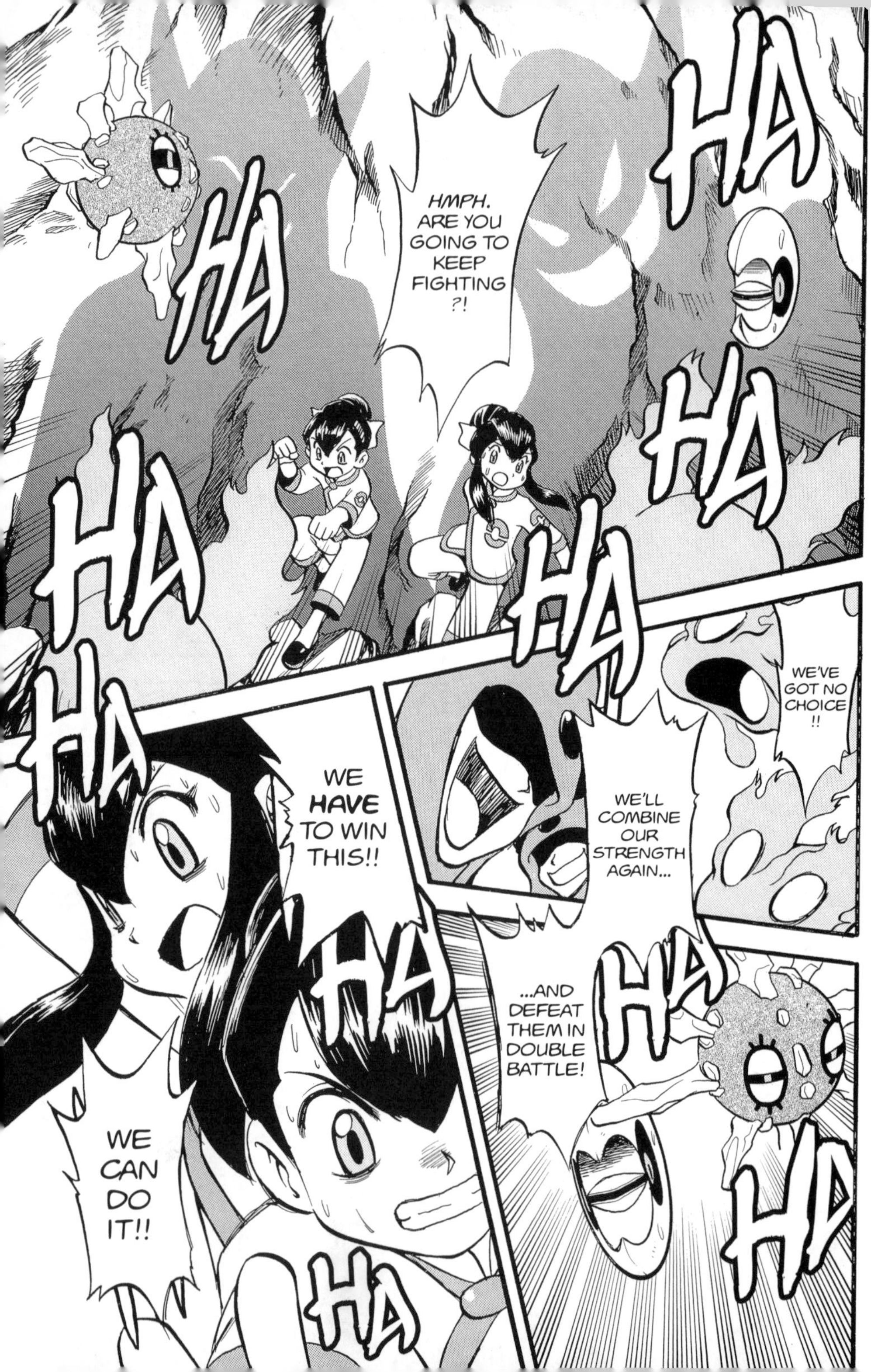
HA HA
HMPH. ARE YOU GOING TO KEEP FIGHTING ?!
HA HA
HA HA
HA HA
HA HA
WE'VE GOT NO CHOICE!!
WE'LL COMBINE OUR STRENGTH AGAIN...
WE HAVE TO WIN THIS!!
HA HA
...AND DEFEAT THEM IN DOUBLE BATTLE!
HA HA
HA HA
WE CAN DO IT!!

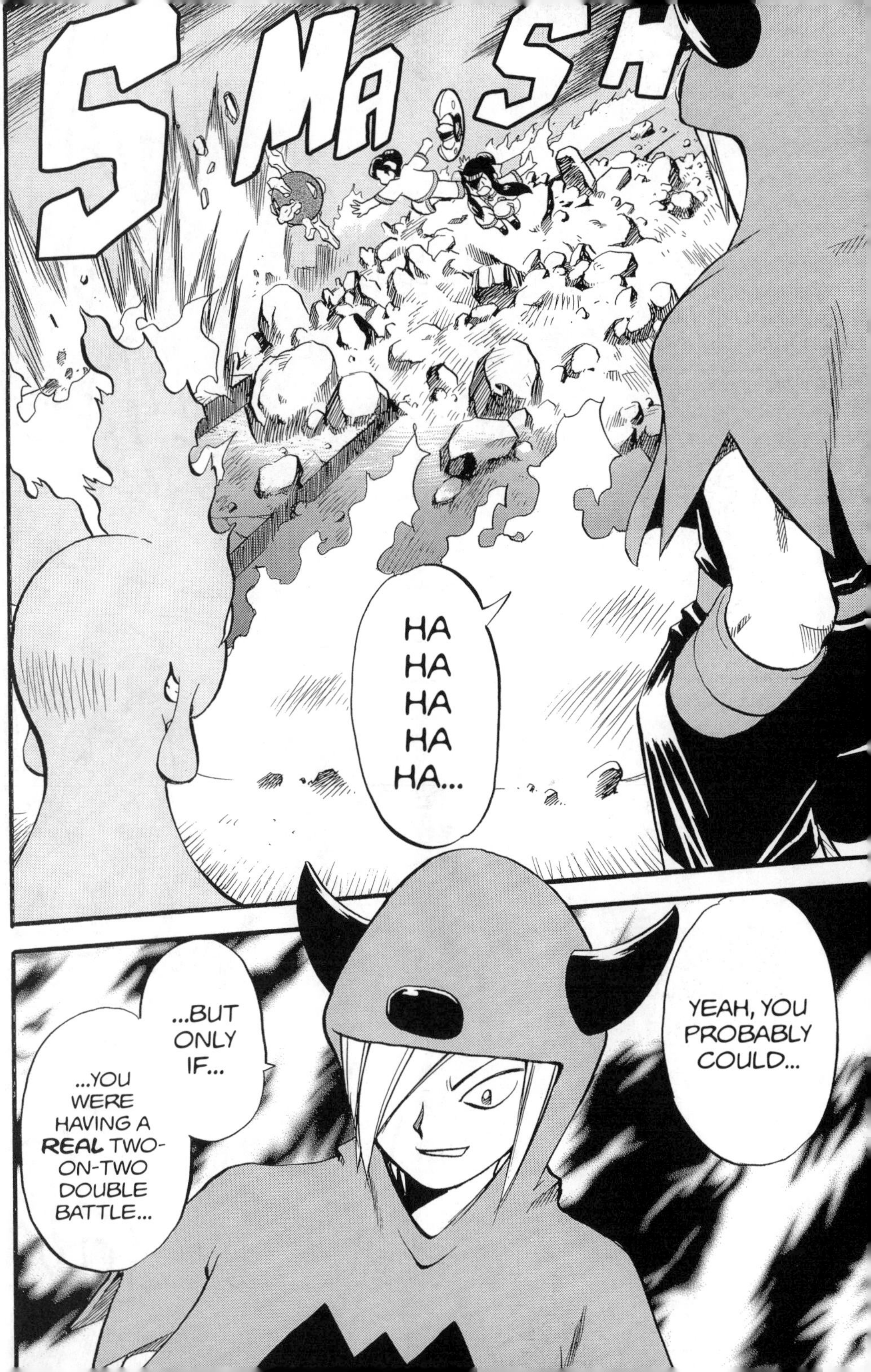
SMASH
HA HA HA HA HA...
YEAH, YOU PROBABLY COULD...
...BUT ONLY IF...
...YOU WERE HAVING A **REAL** TWO-ON-TWO DOUBLE BATTLE...

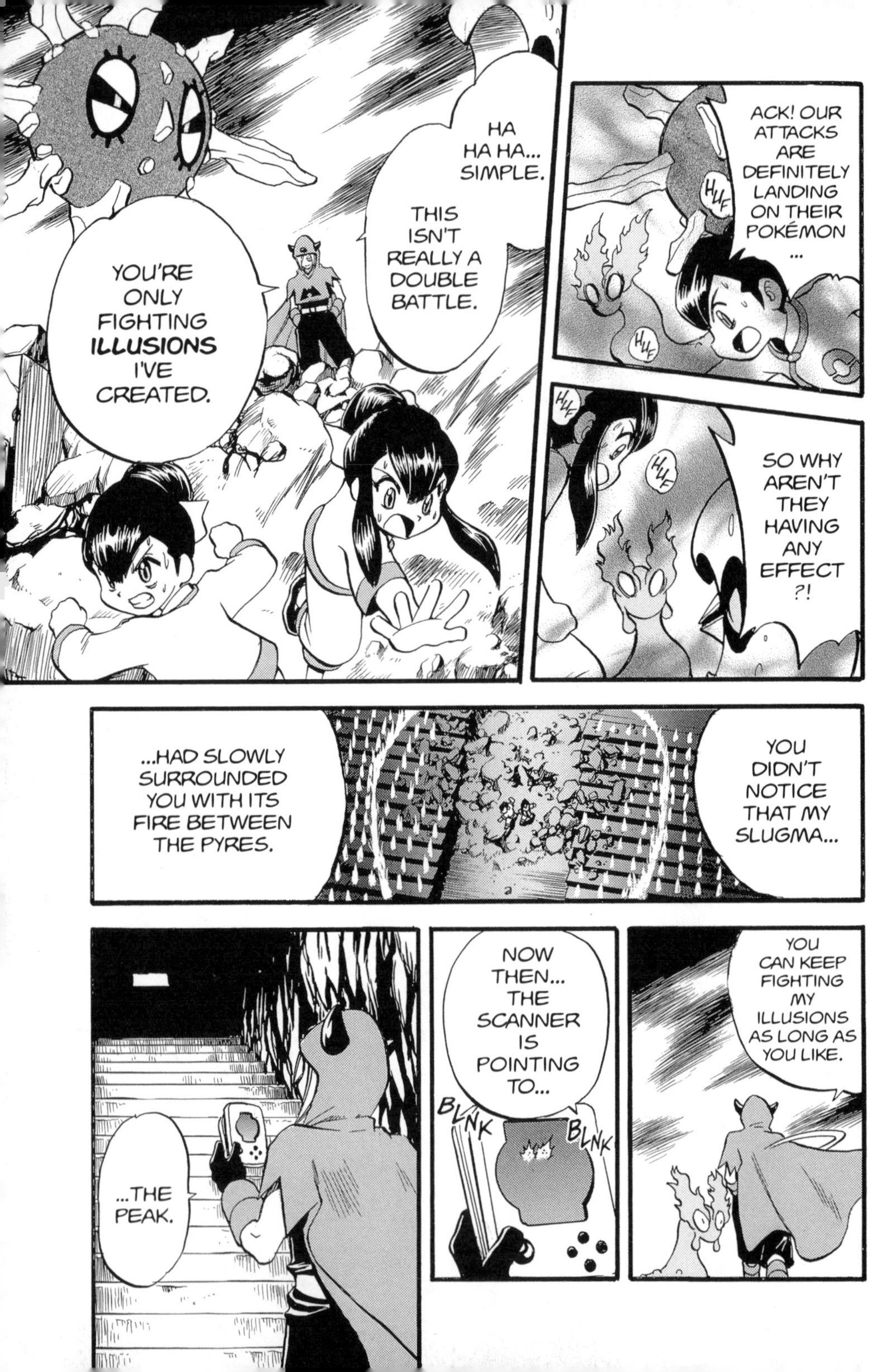
ACK! OUR ATTACKS ARE DEFINITELY LANDING ON THEIR POKÉMON ...
HUF
HUF
HUF
HUF
SO WHY AREN'T THEY HAVING ANY EFFECT ?!
HA HA HA... SIMPLE.
THIS ISN'T REALLY A DOUBLE BATTLE.
YOU'RE ONLY FIGHTING **ILLUSIONS** I'VE CREATED.
YOU DIDN'T NOTICE THAT MY SLUGMA...
...HAD SLOWLY SURROUNDED YOU WITH ITS FIRE BETWEEN THE PYRES.
YOU CAN KEEP FIGHTING MY ILLUSIONS AS LONG AS YOU LIKE.
NOW THEN... THE SCANNER IS POINTING TO...
BLNK
BLNK
...THE PEAK.

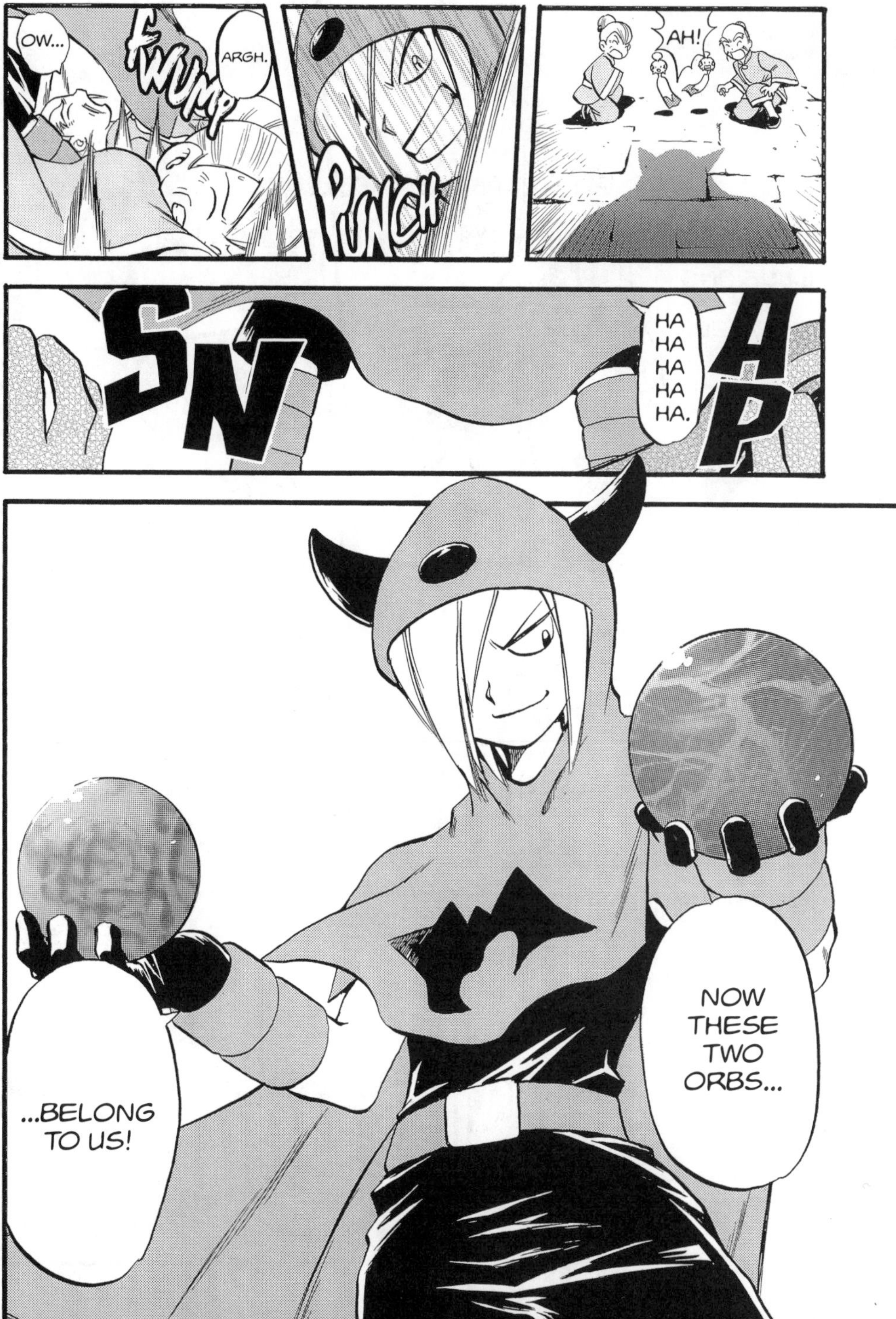
AH!
PUNCH
ARGH.
FWUMP
OW...
SNAP
HA HA HA HA HA.
NOW THESE TWO ORBS...
...BELONG TO US!

● Adventure 230 ●
Walrein and Camerupt

Pokémon™ Adventures Ruby & Sapphire
The Fourth Chapter

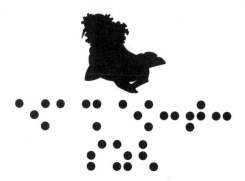

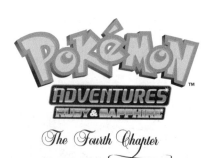

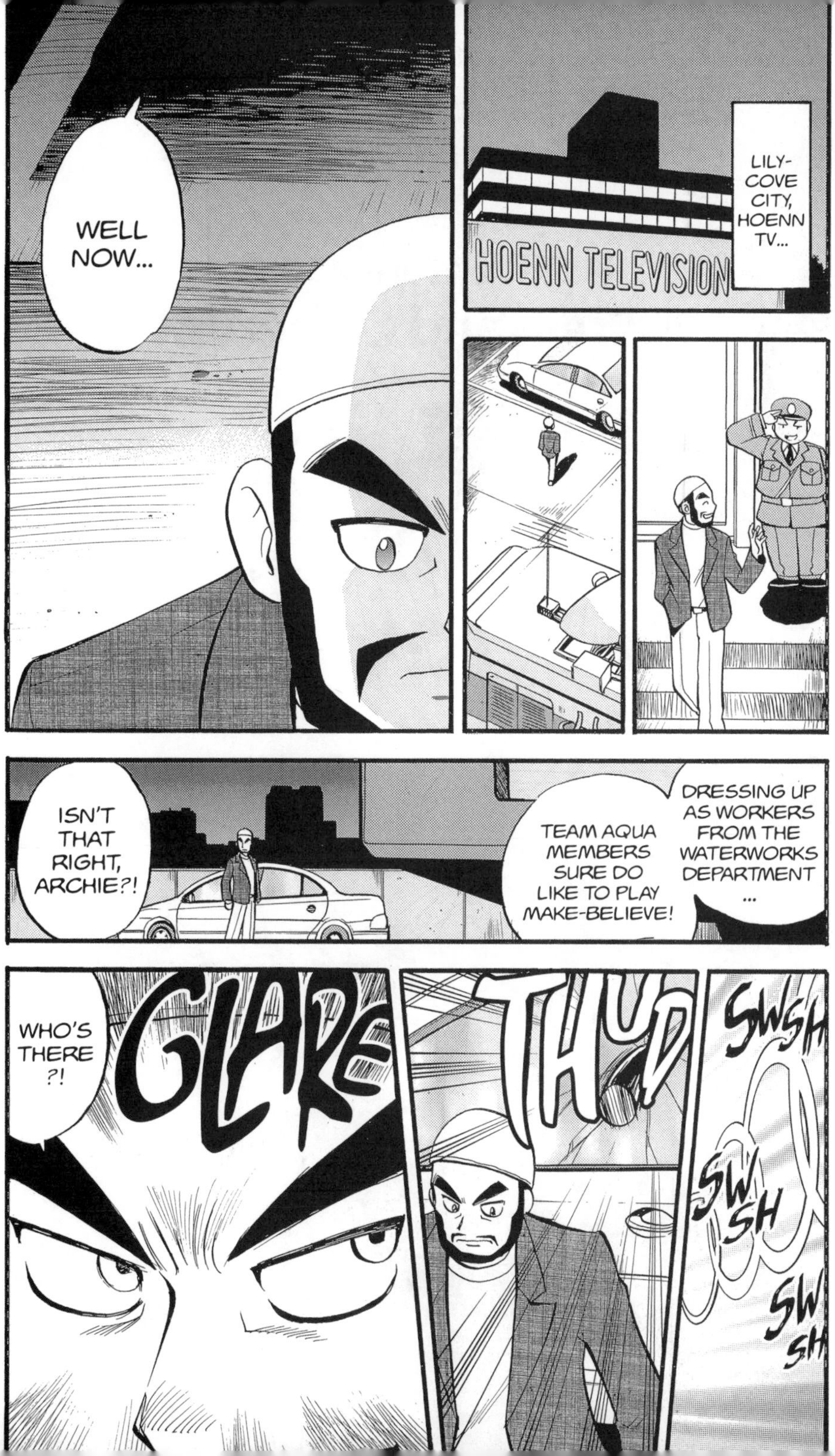

HOENN TELEVISION
LILY-COVE CITY, HOENN TV...
WELL NOW...
DRESSING UP AS WORKERS FROM THE WATERWORKS DEPARTMENT ...
TEAM AQUA MEMBERS SURE DO LIKE TO PLAY MAKE-BELIEVE!
ISN'T THAT RIGHT, ARCHIE?!
SWSH
SWSH
SWSH
THUD
GLARE
WHO'S THERE ?!

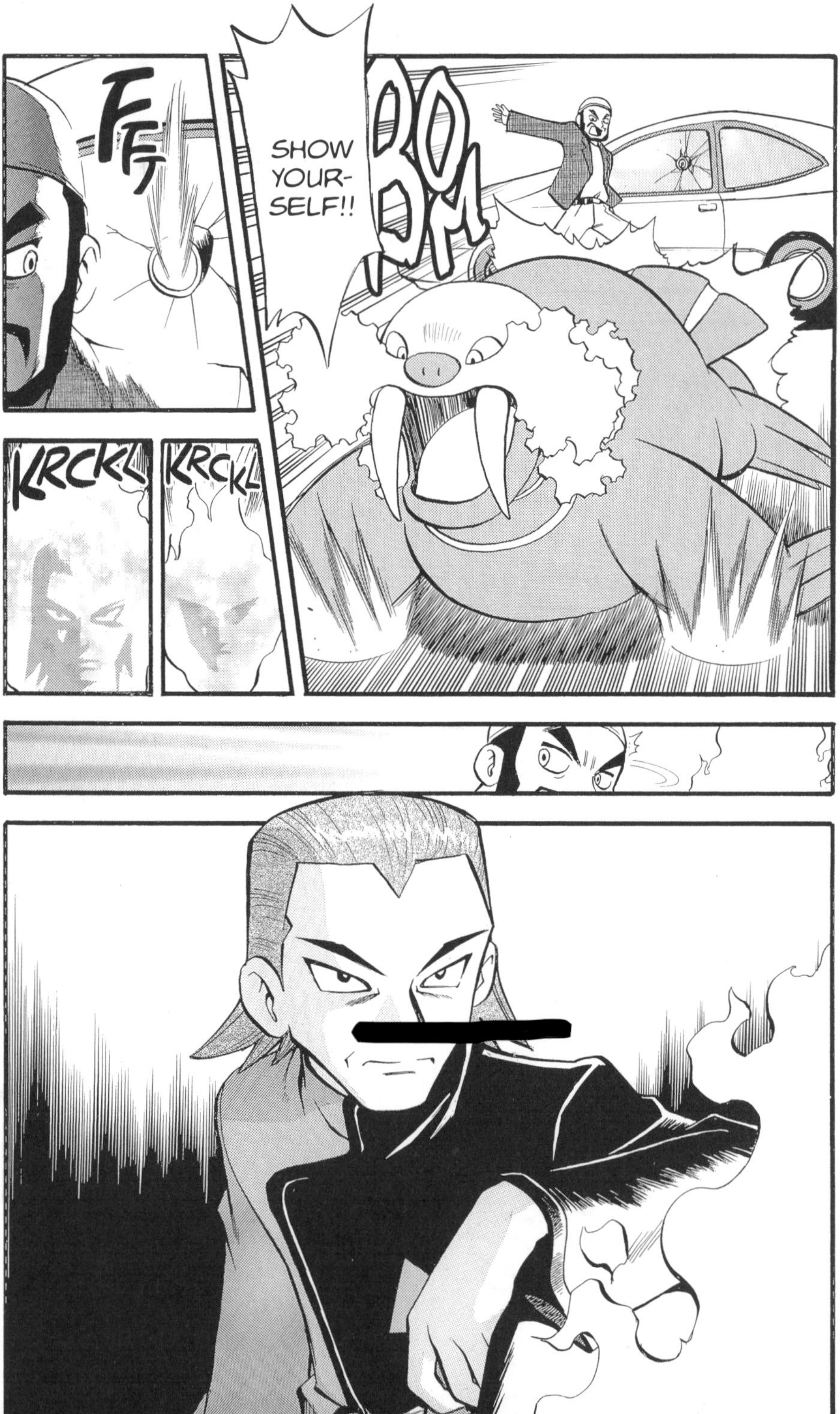
SHOW YOUR-SELF!!
BOOM
FFT
KRCKL
KRCKL

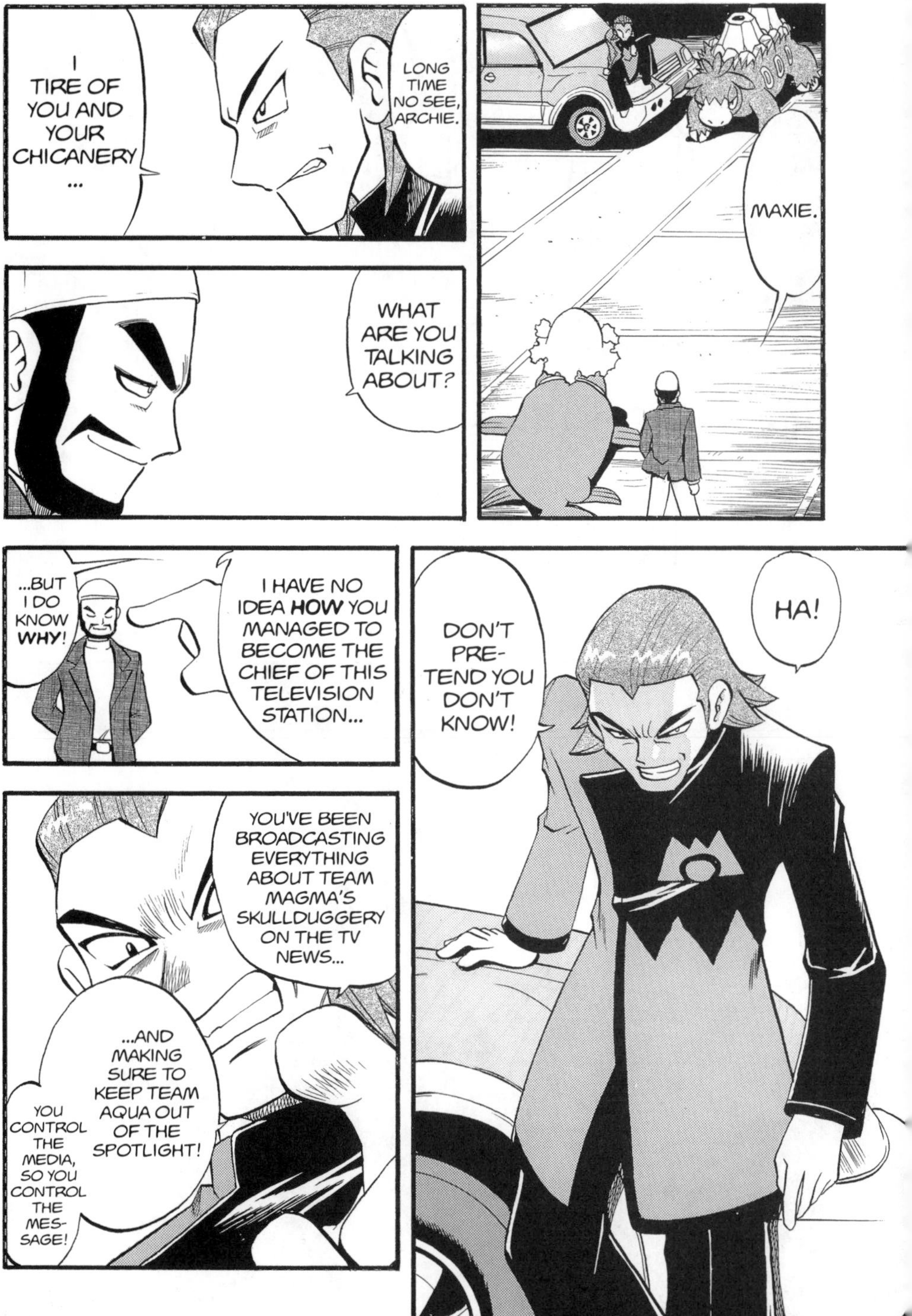
MAXIE.
LONG TIME NO SEE, ARCHIE.
I TIRE OF YOU AND YOUR CHICANERY...
WHAT ARE YOU TALKING ABOUT?
HA!
DON'T PRETEND YOU DON'T KNOW!
I HAVE NO IDEA **HOW** YOU MANAGED TO BECOME THE CHIEF OF THIS TELEVISION STATION...
...BUT I DO KNOW **WHY**!
YOU'VE BEEN BROADCASTING EVERYTHING ABOUT TEAM MAGMA'S SKULLDUGGERY ON THE TV NEWS...
...AND MAKING SURE TO KEEP TEAM AQUA OUT OF THE SPOTLIGHT!
YOU CONTROL THE MEDIA, SO YOU CONTROL THE MESSAGE!

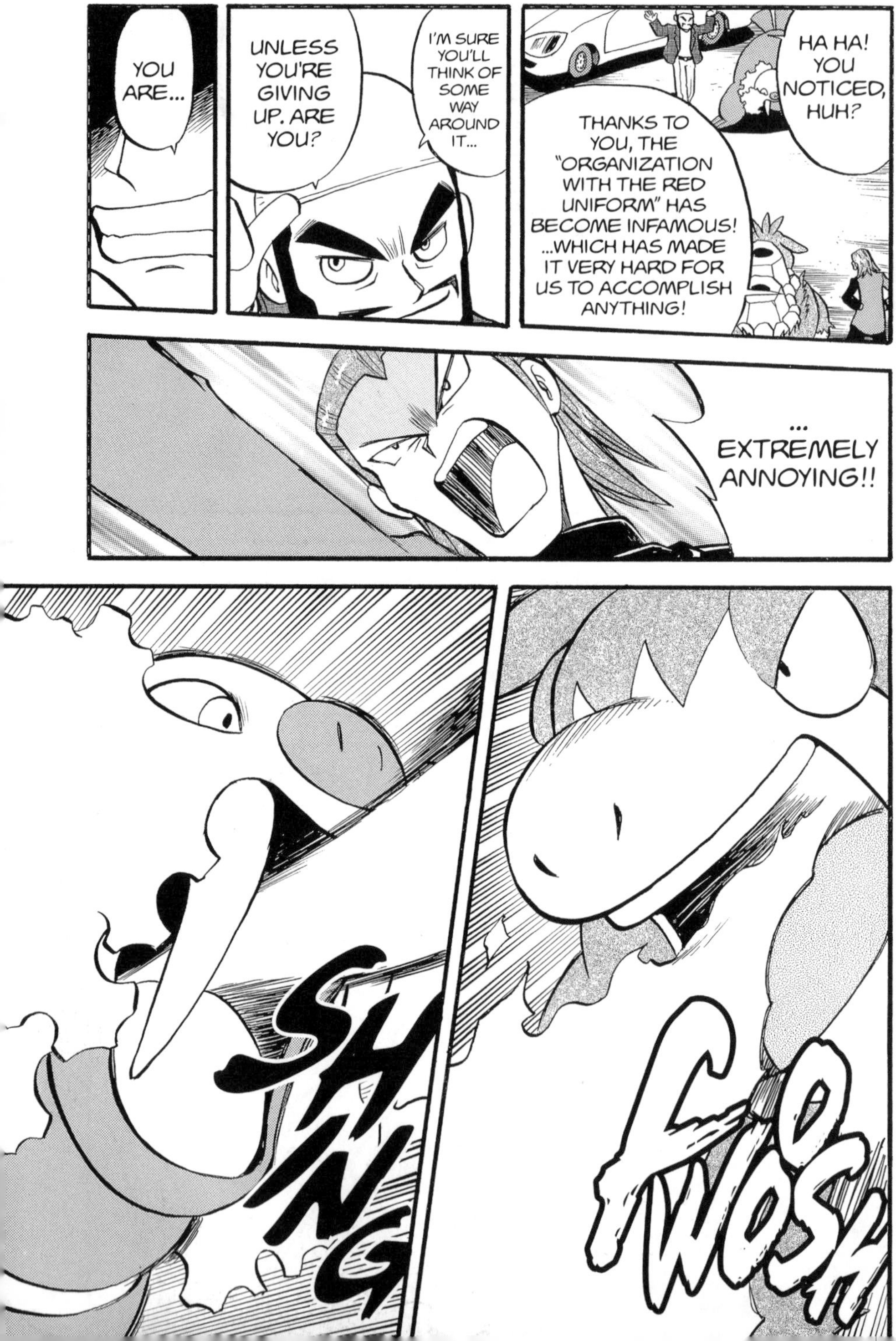
HA HA! YOU NOTICED, HUH?
THANKS TO YOU, THE "ORGANIZATION WITH THE RED UNIFORM" HAS BECOME INFAMOUS! ...WHICH HAS MADE IT VERY HARD FOR US TO ACCOMPLISH ANYTHING!
I'M SURE YOU'LL THINK OF SOME WAY AROUND IT...
UNLESS YOU'RE GIVING UP. ARE YOU?
YOU ARE...
... EXTREMELY ANNOYING!!
FWOOSH
SHING

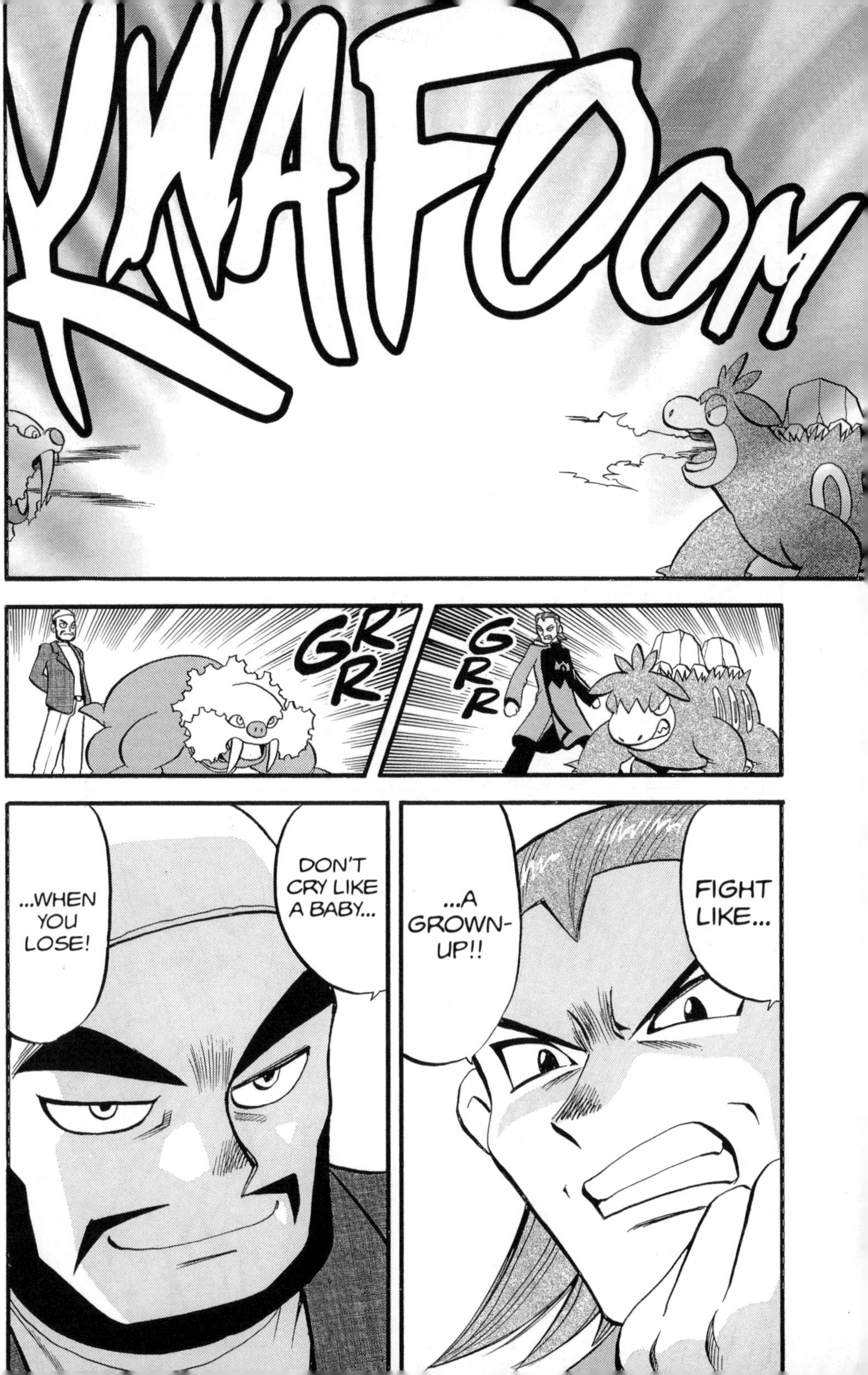
KWAFOOM
GRR
GKR
FIGHT LIKE...
...A GROWN-UP!!
DON'T CRY LIKE A BABY...
...WHEN YOU LOSE!

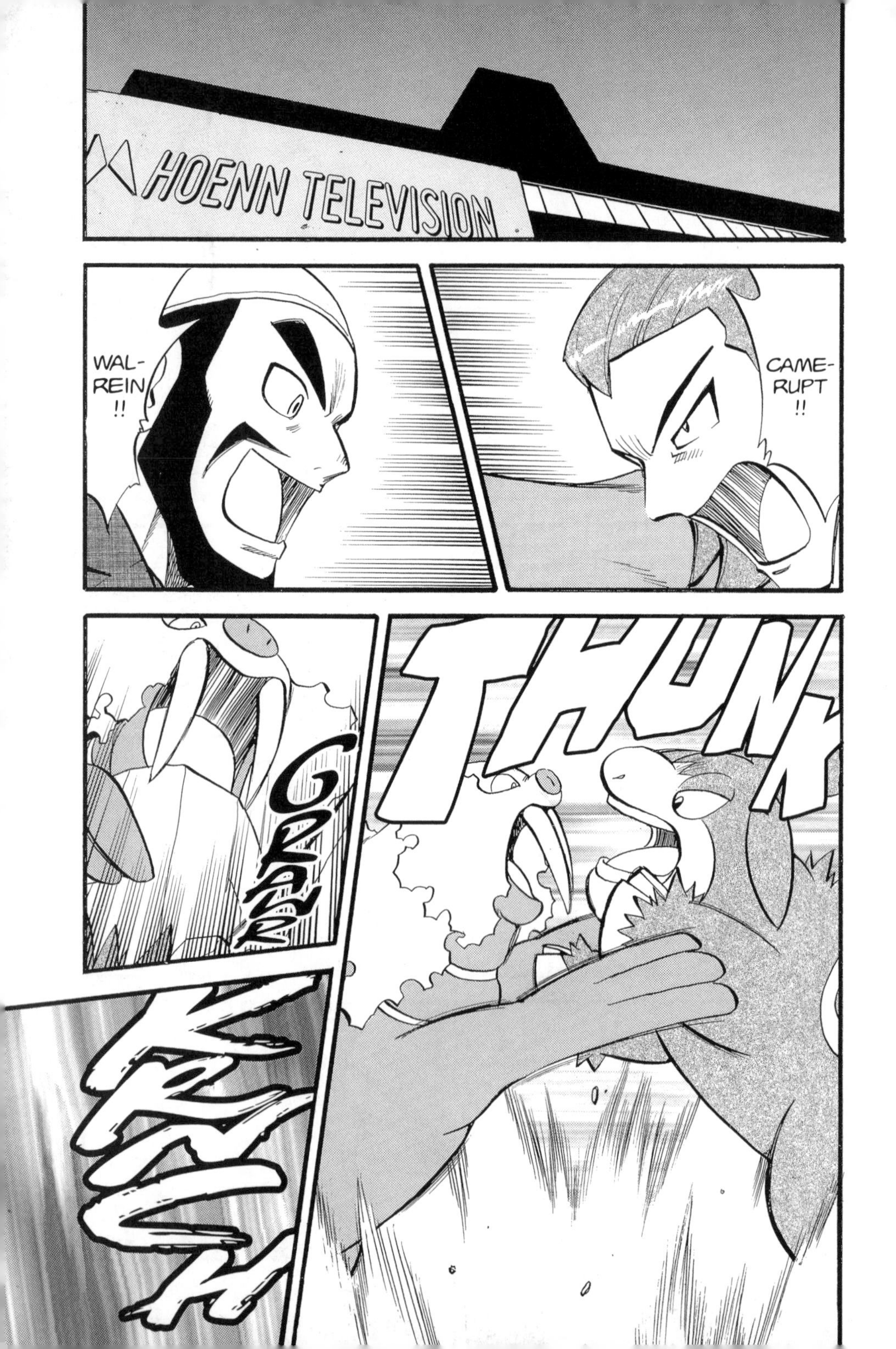
HOENN TELEVISION
CAME-RUPT !!
WAL-REIN !!
THUNK

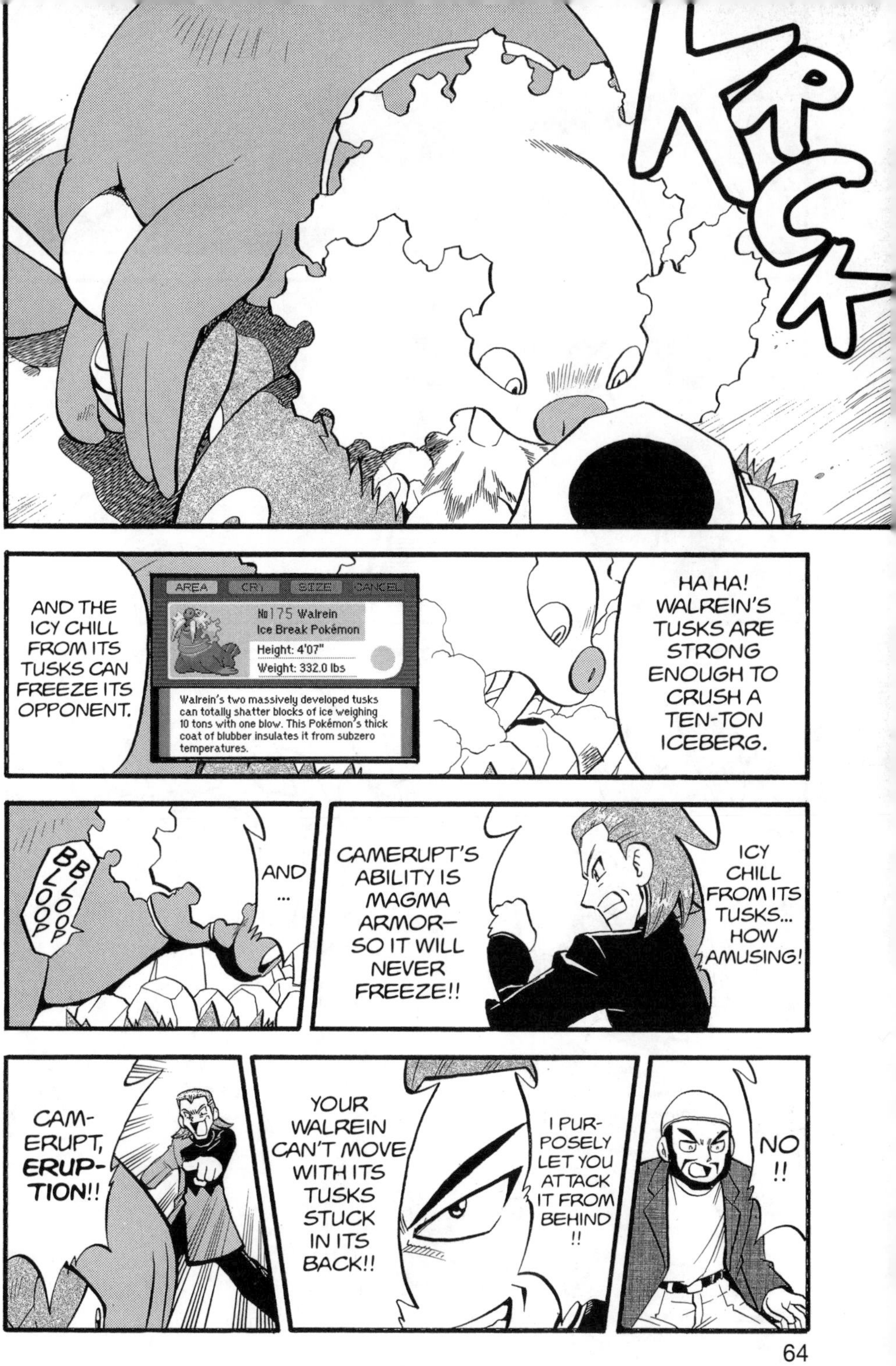
KRRCK
HA HA! WALREIN'S TUSKS ARE STRONG ENOUGH TO CRUSH A TEN-TON ICEBERG.
AREA CRY SIZE CANCEL
No175 Walrein
Ice Break Pokémon
Height: 4'07"
Weight: 332.0 lbs
Walrein's two massively developed tusks can totally shatter blocks of ice weighing 10 tons with one blow. This Pokémon's thick coat of blubber insulates it from subzero temperatures.
AND THE ICY CHILL FROM ITS TUSKS CAN FREEZE ITS OPPONENT.
ICY CHILL FROM ITS TUSKS... HOW AMUSING!
CAMERUPT'S ABILITY IS MAGMA ARMOR— SO IT WILL NEVER FREEZE!!
AND ...
BBLOOP BLOOP
NO !!
I PURPOSELY LET YOU ATTACK IT FROM BEHIND !!
YOUR WALREIN CAN'T MOVE WITH ITS TUSKS STUCK IN ITS BACK!!
CAMERUPT, **ERUPTION**!!

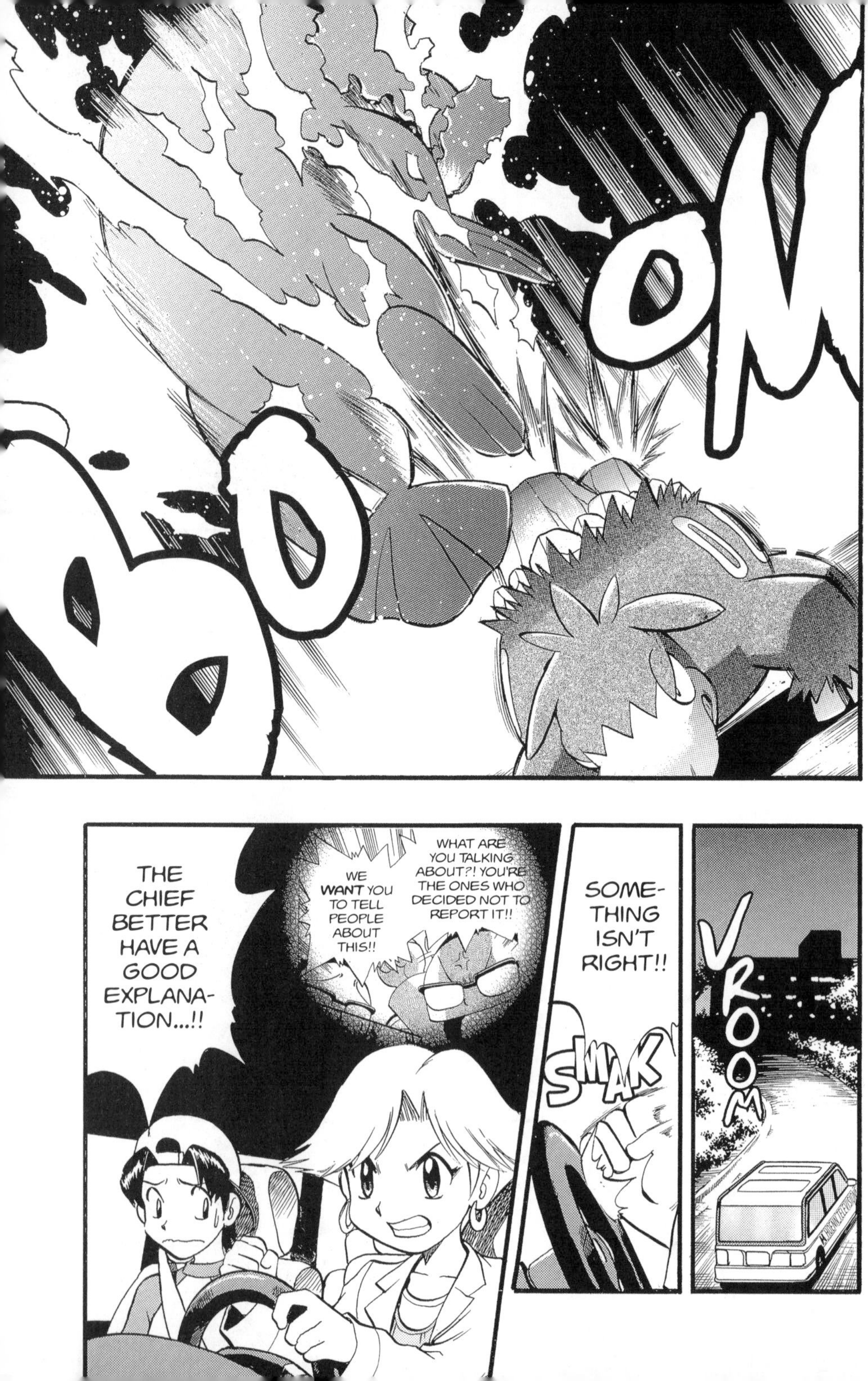
BOOOM
VROOM
SOME-THING ISN'T RIGHT!!
SMAK
WHAT ARE YOU TALKING ABOUT?! YOU'RE THE ONES WHO DECIDED NOT TO REPORT IT!!
WE WANT YOU TO TELL PEOPLE ABOUT THIS!!
THE CHIEF BETTER HAVE A GOOD EXPLANA-TION...!!

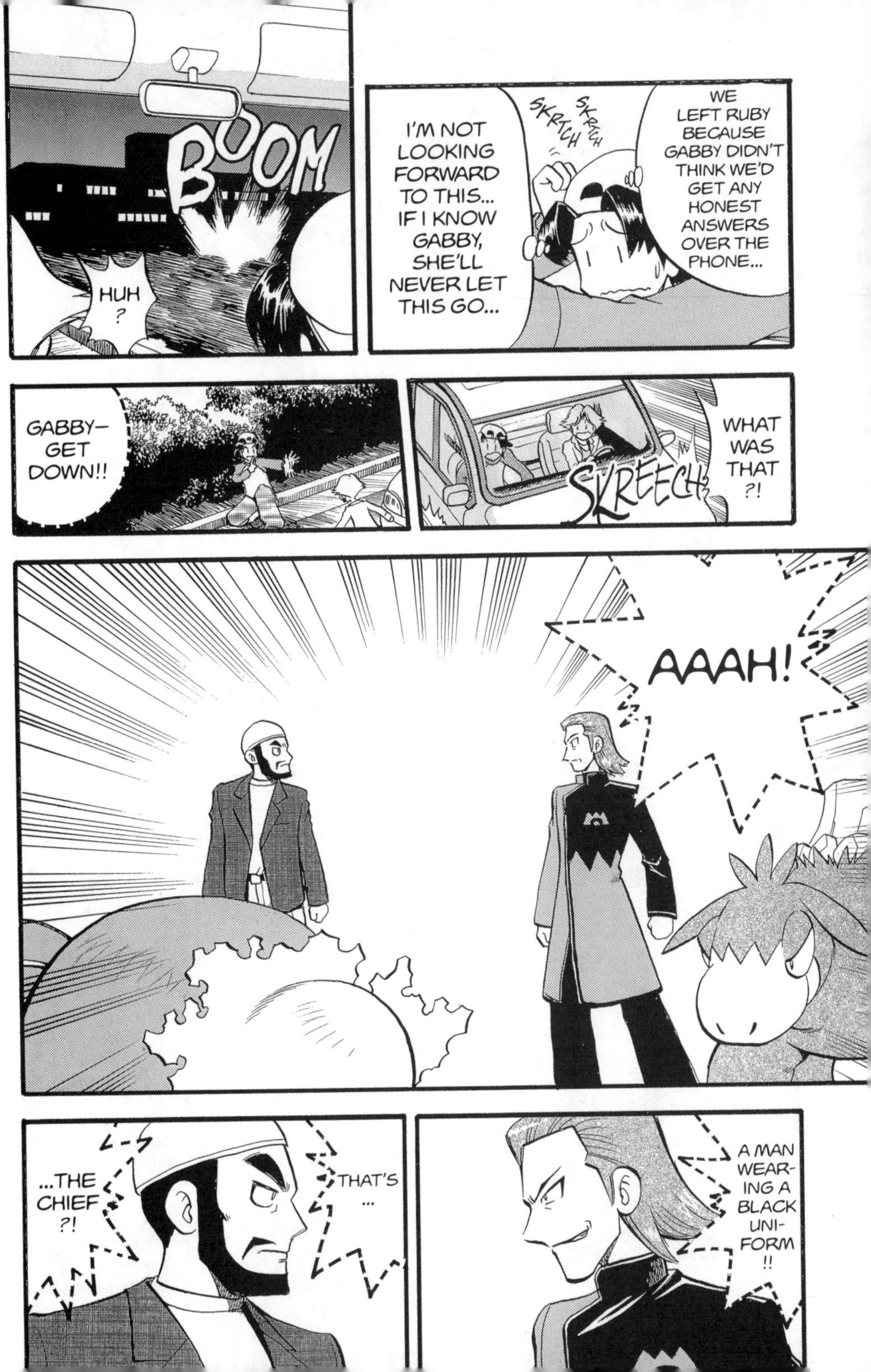
WE LEFT RUBY BECAUSE GABBY DIDN'T THINK WE'D GET ANY HONEST ANSWERS OVER THE PHONE...
SKRTCH
SKRTCH
I'M NOT LOOKING FORWARD TO THIS... IF I KNOW GABBY, SHE'LL NEVER LET THIS GO...
BOOM
HUH?
WHAT WAS THAT?!
SKREECH
GABBY—GET DOWN!!
AAAH!
A MAN WEARING A BLACK UNIFORM!!
THAT'S...
...THE CHIEF?!

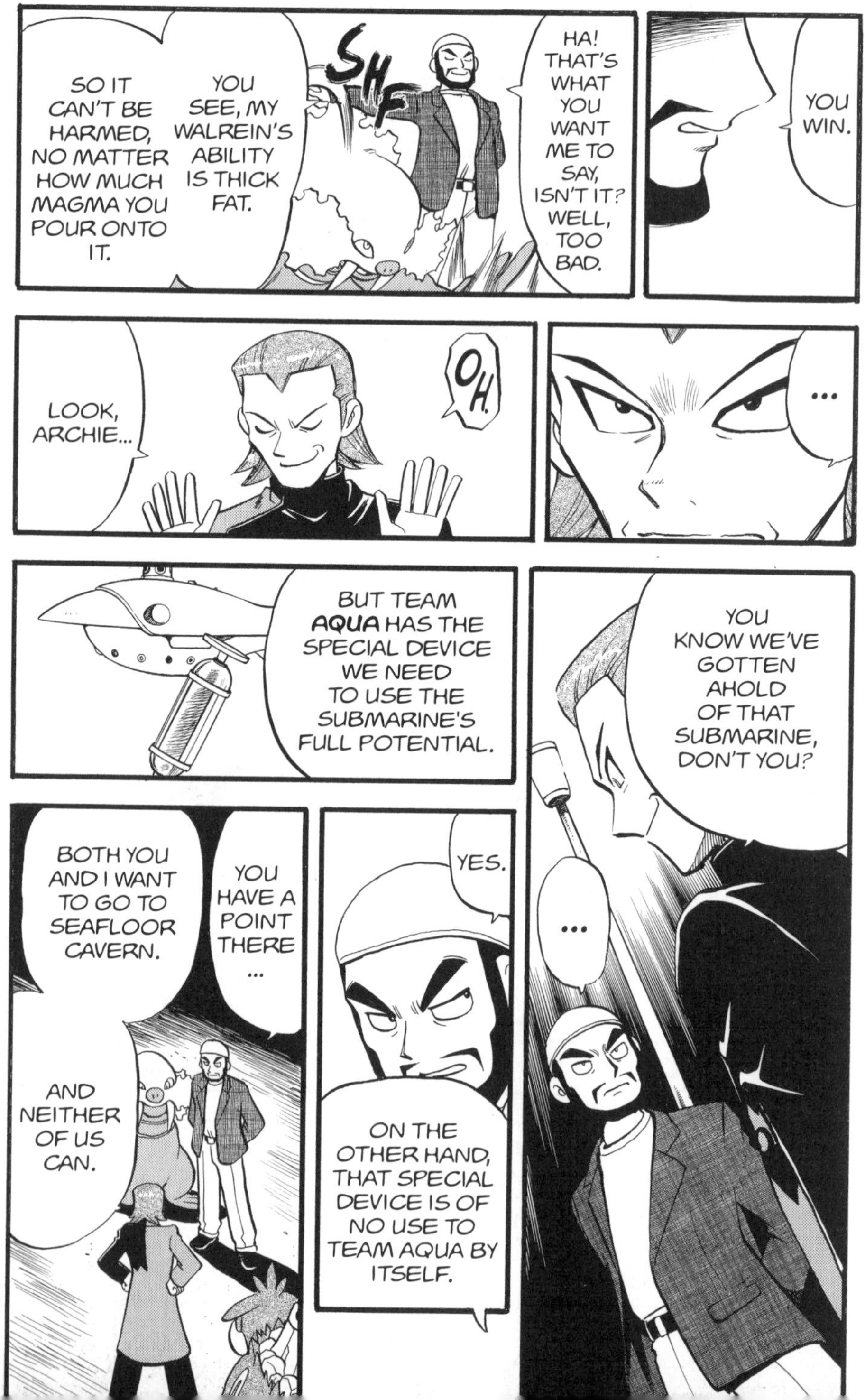
YOU WIN.
HA! THAT'S WHAT YOU WANT ME TO SAY, ISN'T IT? WELL, TOO BAD.
SHF
YOU SEE, MY WALREIN'S ABILITY IS THICK FAT.
SO IT CAN'T BE HARMED, NO MATTER HOW MUCH MAGMA YOU POUR ONTO IT.
...
OH.
LOOK, ARCHIE...
YOU KNOW WE'VE GOTTEN AHOLD OF THAT SUBMARINE, DON'T YOU?
...
BUT TEAM AQUA HAS THE SPECIAL DEVICE WE NEED TO USE THE SUBMARINE'S FULL POTENTIAL.
YES.
ON THE OTHER HAND, THAT SPECIAL DEVICE IS OF NO USE TO TEAM AQUA BY ITSELF.
YOU HAVE A POINT THERE ...
BOTH YOU AND I WANT TO GO TO SEAFLOOR CAVERN.
AND NEITHER OF US CAN.

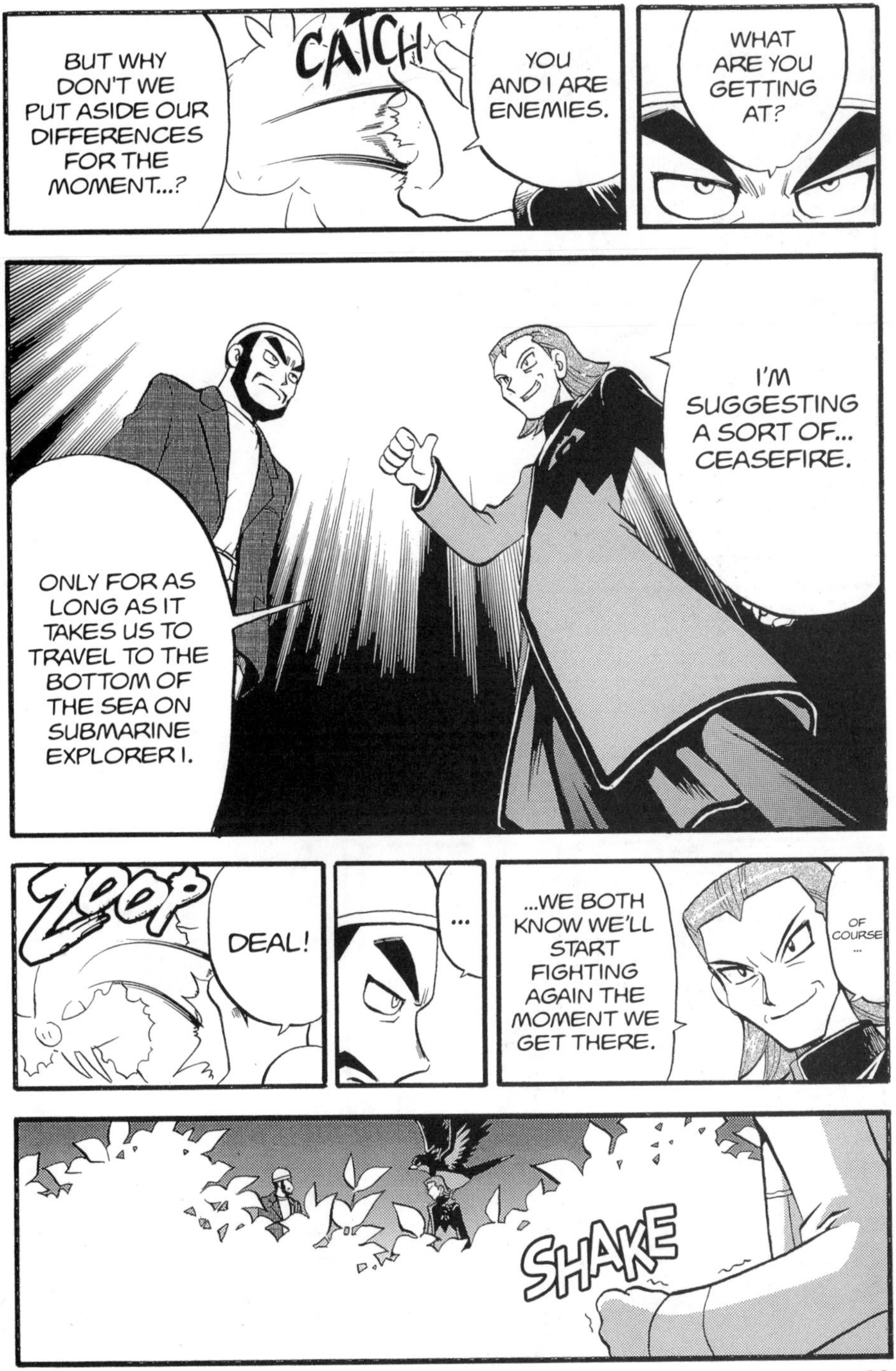
WHAT ARE YOU GETTING AT?
YOU AND I ARE ENEMIES.
CATCH
BUT WHY DON'T WE PUT ASIDE OUR DIFFERENCES FOR THE MOMENT...?
I'M SUGGESTING A SORT OF... CEASEFIRE.
ONLY FOR AS LONG AS IT TAKES US TO TRAVEL TO THE BOTTOM OF THE SEA ON SUBMARINE EXPLORER 1.
OF COURSE...
...WE BOTH KNOW WE'LL START FIGHTING AGAIN THE MOMENT WE GET THERE.
...
DEAL!
ZOOP
SHAKE

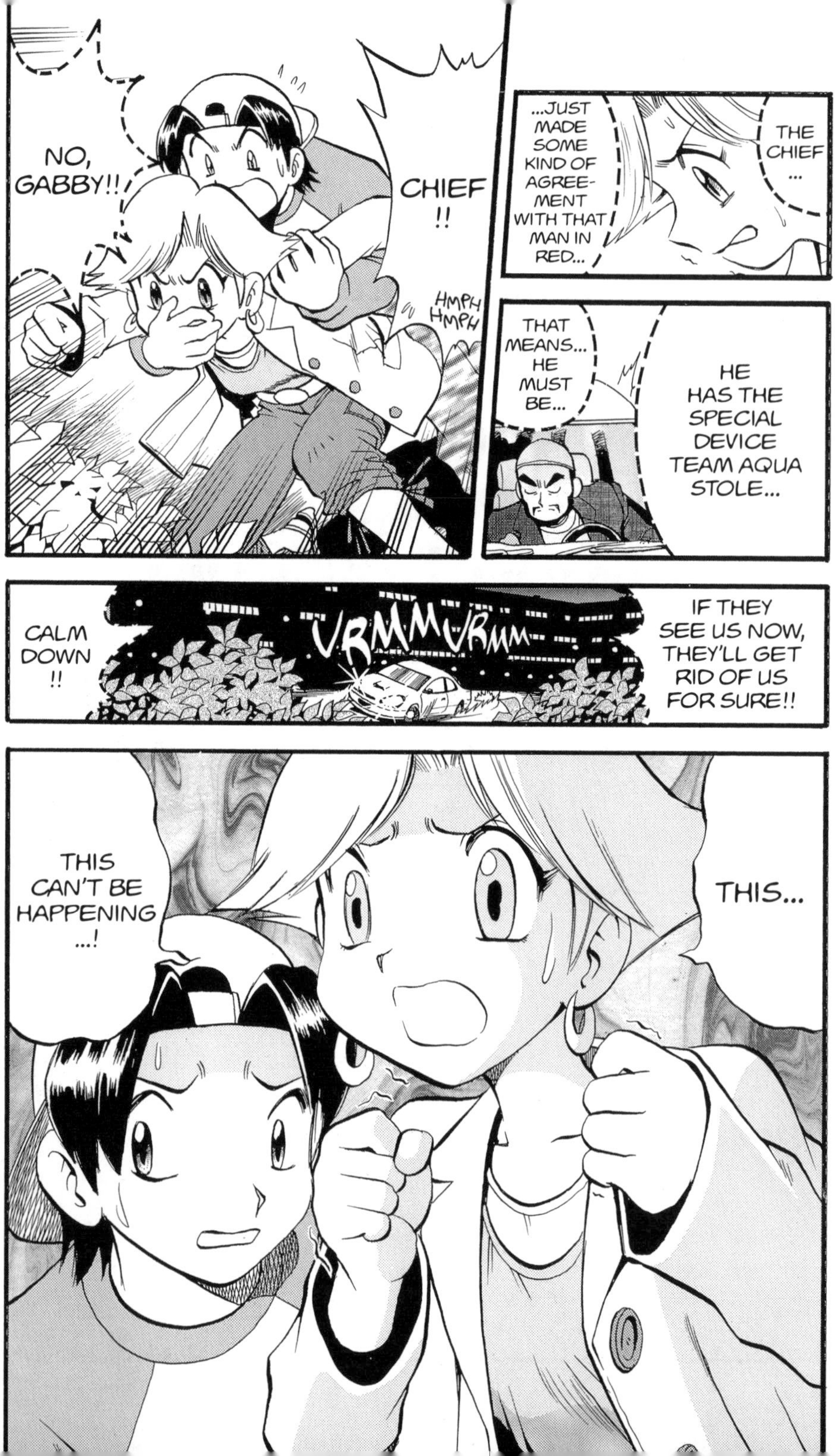
THE CHIEF ...
...JUST MADE SOME KIND OF AGREEMENT WITH THAT MAN IN RED...
HE HAS THE SPECIAL DEVICE TEAM AQUA STOLE...
THAT MEANS... HE MUST BE...
CHIEF !!
HMPH HMPH
NO, GABBY!!
IF THEY SEE US NOW, THEY'LL GET RID OF US FOR SURE!!
VRMM VRMM
CALM DOWN !!
THIS...
THIS CAN'T BE HAPPENING ...!

● Adventure 231 ●
Master Class with Masquerain

Pokémon™ Adventures Ruby & Sapphire

The Fourth Chapter

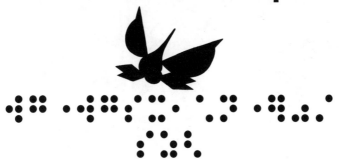

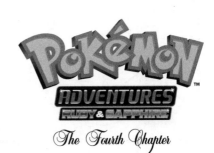

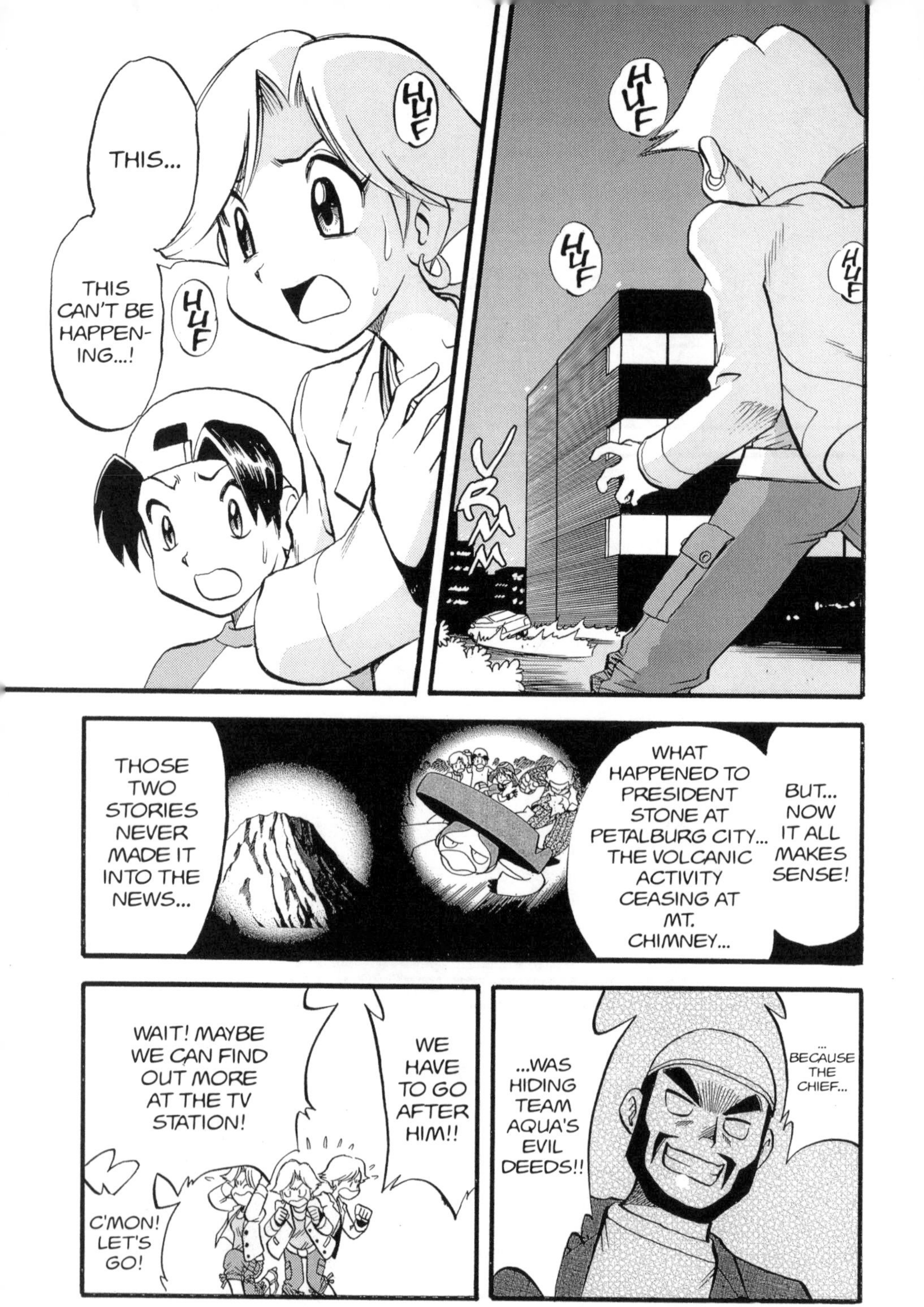
HUF
HUF
HUF
VRMM
THIS...
THIS CAN'T BE HAPPENING...!
HUF
BUT... NOW IT ALL MAKES SENSE!
WHAT HAPPENED TO PRESIDENT STONE AT PETALBURG CITY... THE VOLCANIC ACTIVITY CEASING AT MT. CHIMNEY...
THOSE TWO STORIES NEVER MADE IT INTO THE NEWS...
...BECAUSE THE CHIEF...
...WAS HIDING TEAM AQUA'S EVIL DEEDS!!
WE HAVE TO GO AFTER HIM!!
WAIT! MAYBE WE CAN FIND OUT MORE AT THE TV STATION!
C'MON! LET'S GO!

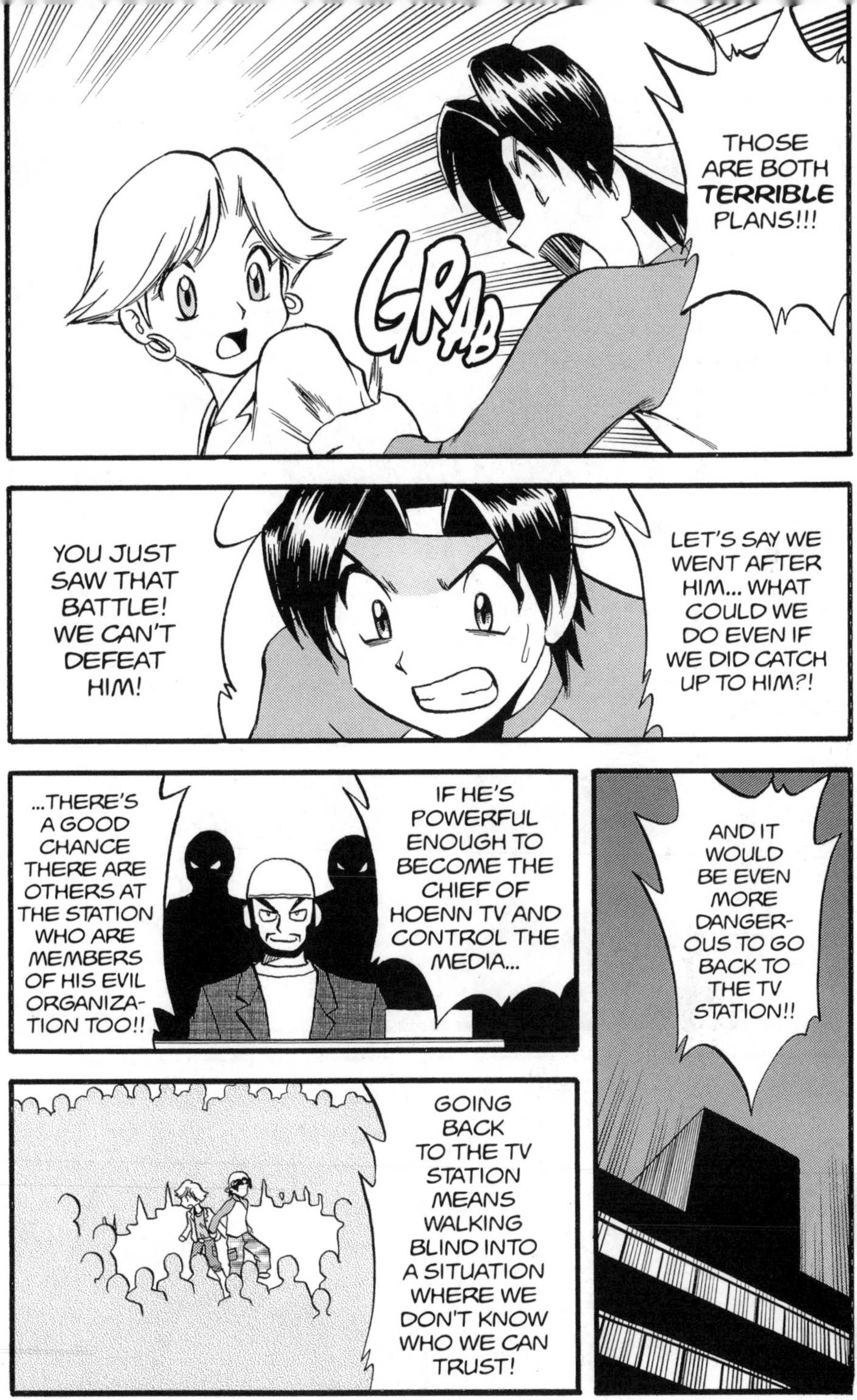
THOSE ARE BOTH **TERRIBLE** PLANS!!!
GRAB
LET'S SAY WE WENT AFTER HIM... WHAT COULD WE DO EVEN IF WE DID CATCH UP TO HIM?!
YOU JUST SAW THAT BATTLE! WE CAN'T DEFEAT HIM!
AND IT WOULD BE EVEN MORE DANGER-OUS TO GO BACK TO THE TV STATION!!
IF HE'S POWERFUL ENOUGH TO BECOME THE CHIEF OF HOENN TV AND CONTROL THE MEDIA...
...THERE'S A GOOD CHANCE THERE ARE OTHERS AT THE STATION WHO ARE MEMBERS OF HIS EVIL ORGANIZA-TION TOO!!
GOING BACK TO THE TV STATION MEANS WALKING BLIND INTO A SITUATION WHERE WE DON'T KNOW WHO WE CAN TRUST!

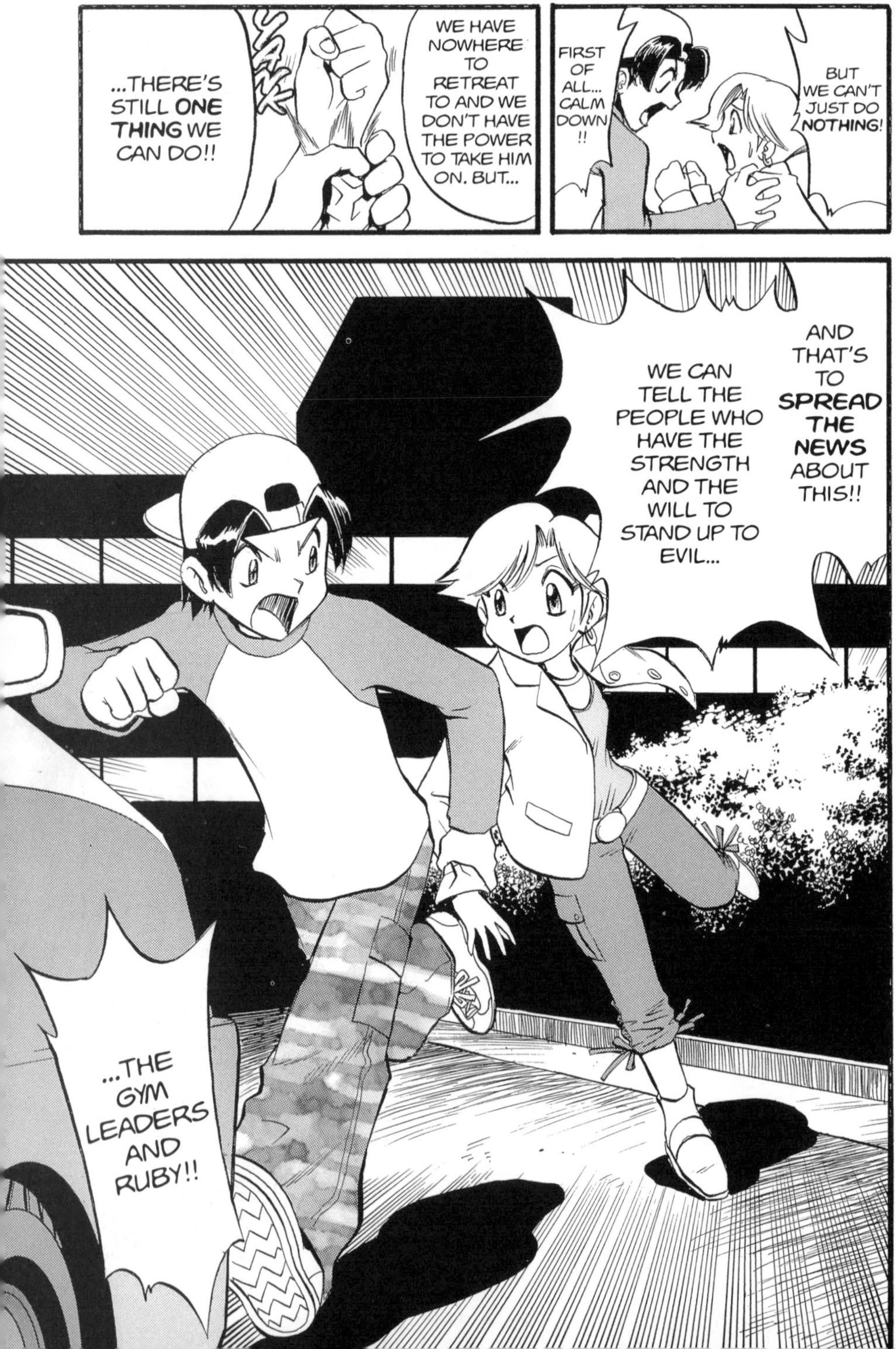
BUT WE CAN'T JUST DO NOTHING!
FIRST OF ALL... CALM DOWN!!
WE HAVE NOWHERE TO RETREAT TO AND WE DON'T HAVE THE POWER TO TAKE HIM ON. BUT...
...THERE'S STILL ONE THING WE CAN DO!!
AND THAT'S TO SPREAD THE NEWS ABOUT THIS!!
WE CAN TELL THE PEOPLE WHO HAVE THE STRENGTH AND THE WILL TO STAND UP TO EVIL...
...THE GYM LEADERS AND RUBY!!

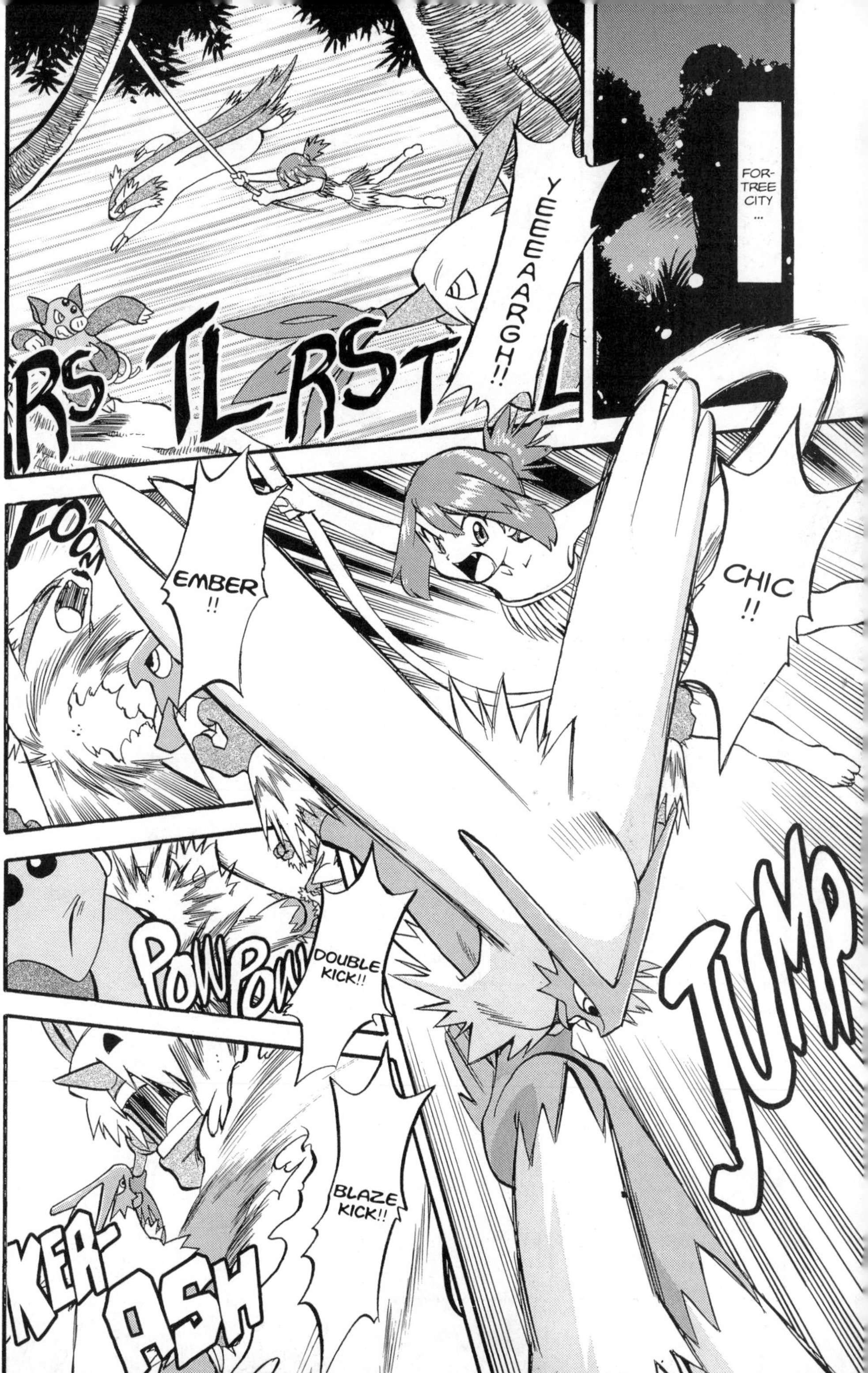
FOR-TREE CITY ...
YEEEAARGH!!
RSTLRSTL
CHIC!!
EMBER!!
DOUBLE KICK!!
POW POW
TUMP
BLAZE KICK!!
KER-ASH

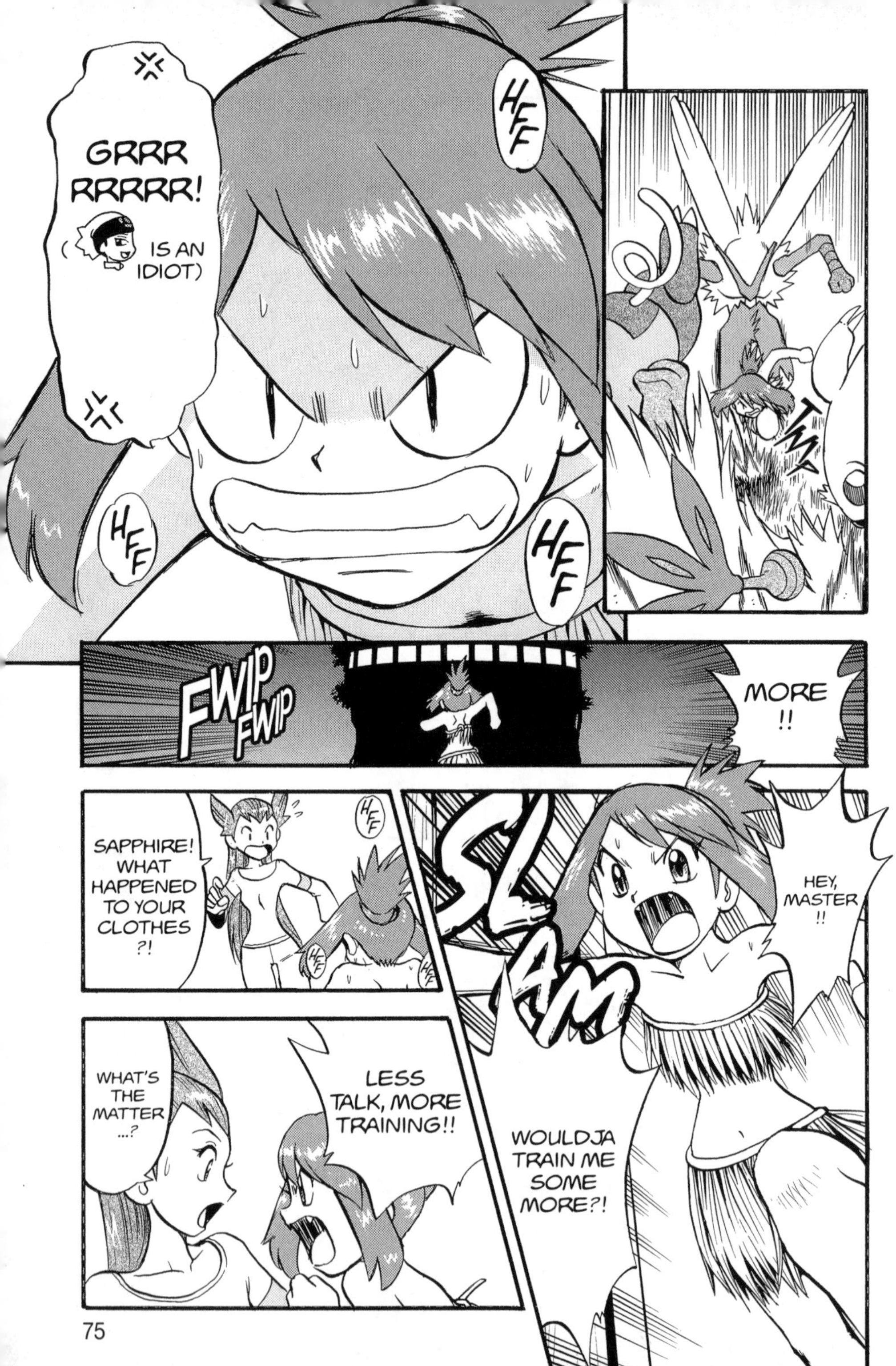
HFF
GRRR RRRRR!
(IS AN IDIOT)
HFF
HFF
MORE!!
FWIP FWIP
HEY, MASTER!!
SLAM
WOULDJA TRAIN ME SOME MORE?!
HFF
SAPPHIRE! WHAT HAPPENED TO YOUR CLOTHES?!
HFF
HFF
LESS TALK, MORE TRAINING!!
WHAT'S THE MATTER...?

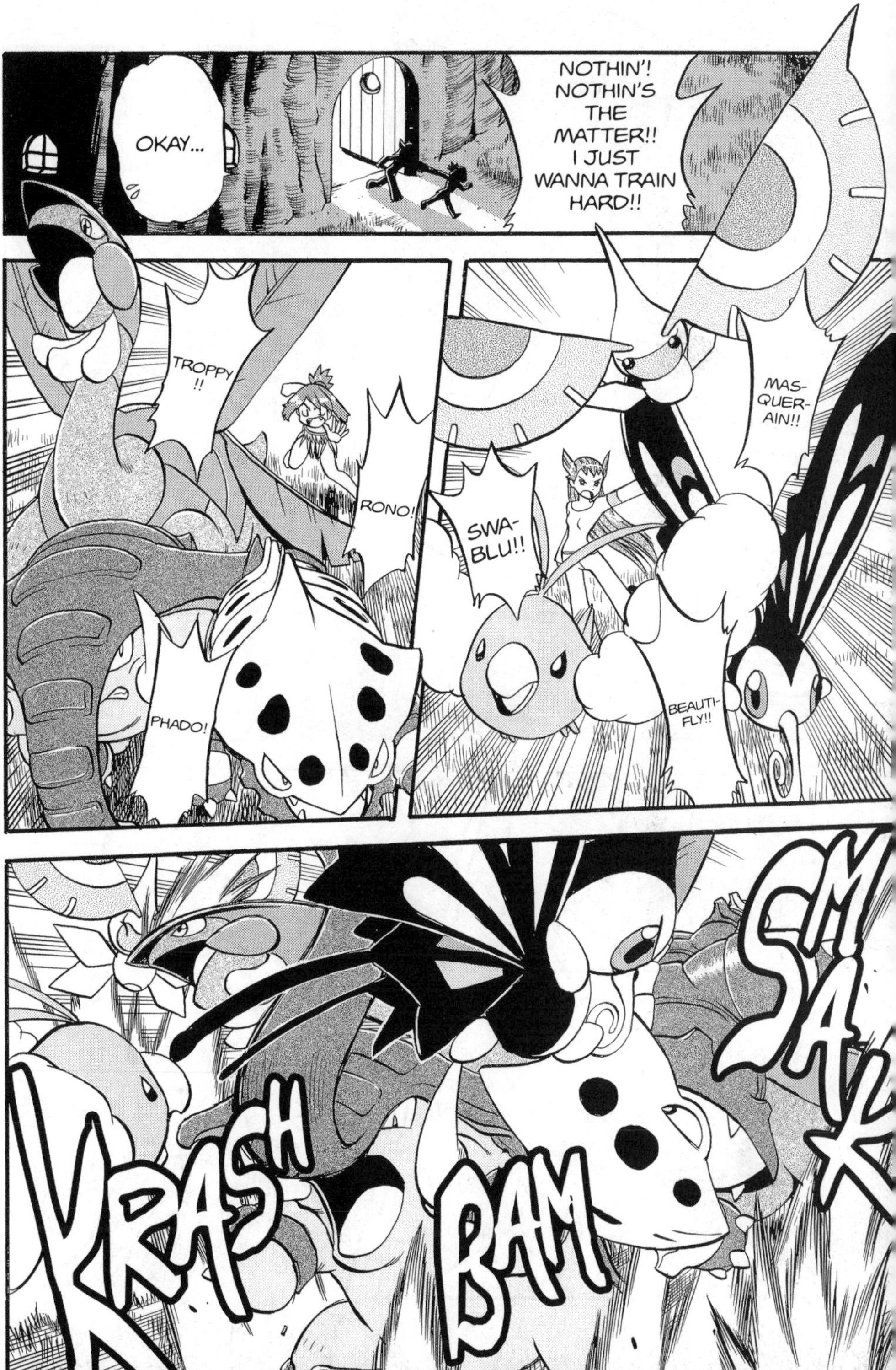
NOTHIN'! NOTHIN'S THE MATTER!! I JUST WANNA TRAIN HARD!!
OKAY...
MAS-QUER-AIN!!
SWA-BLU!!
BEAUTI-FLY!!
TROPPY!!
RONO!
PHADO!
BAM
KRASH

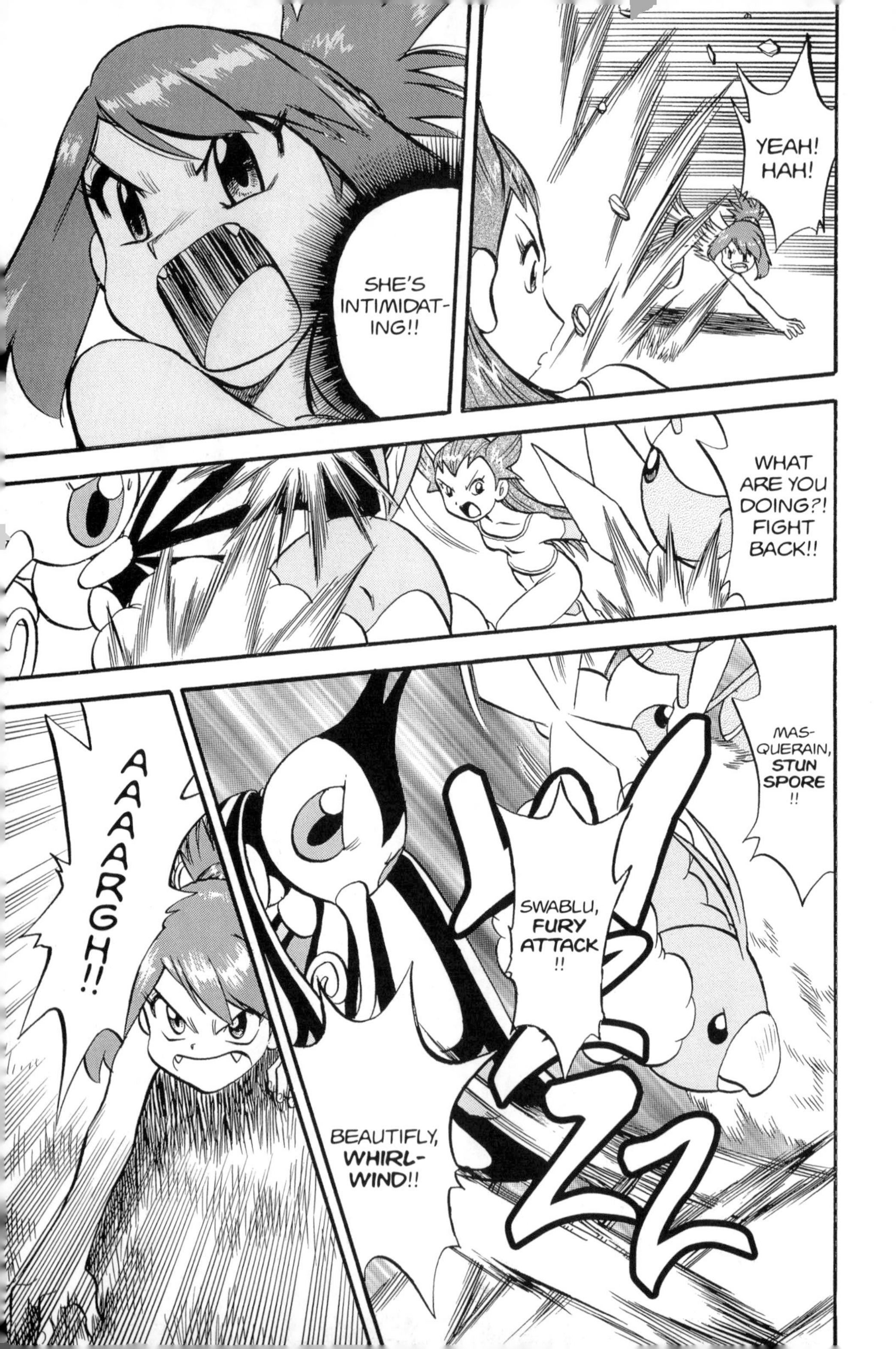
YEAH! HAH!
SHE'S INTIMIDATING!!
WHAT ARE YOU DOING?! FIGHT BACK!!
MASQUERAIN, **STUN SPORE**!!
SWABLU, **FURY ATTACK**!!
BEAUTIFLY, **WHIRLWIND**!!
AAAAARGH!!

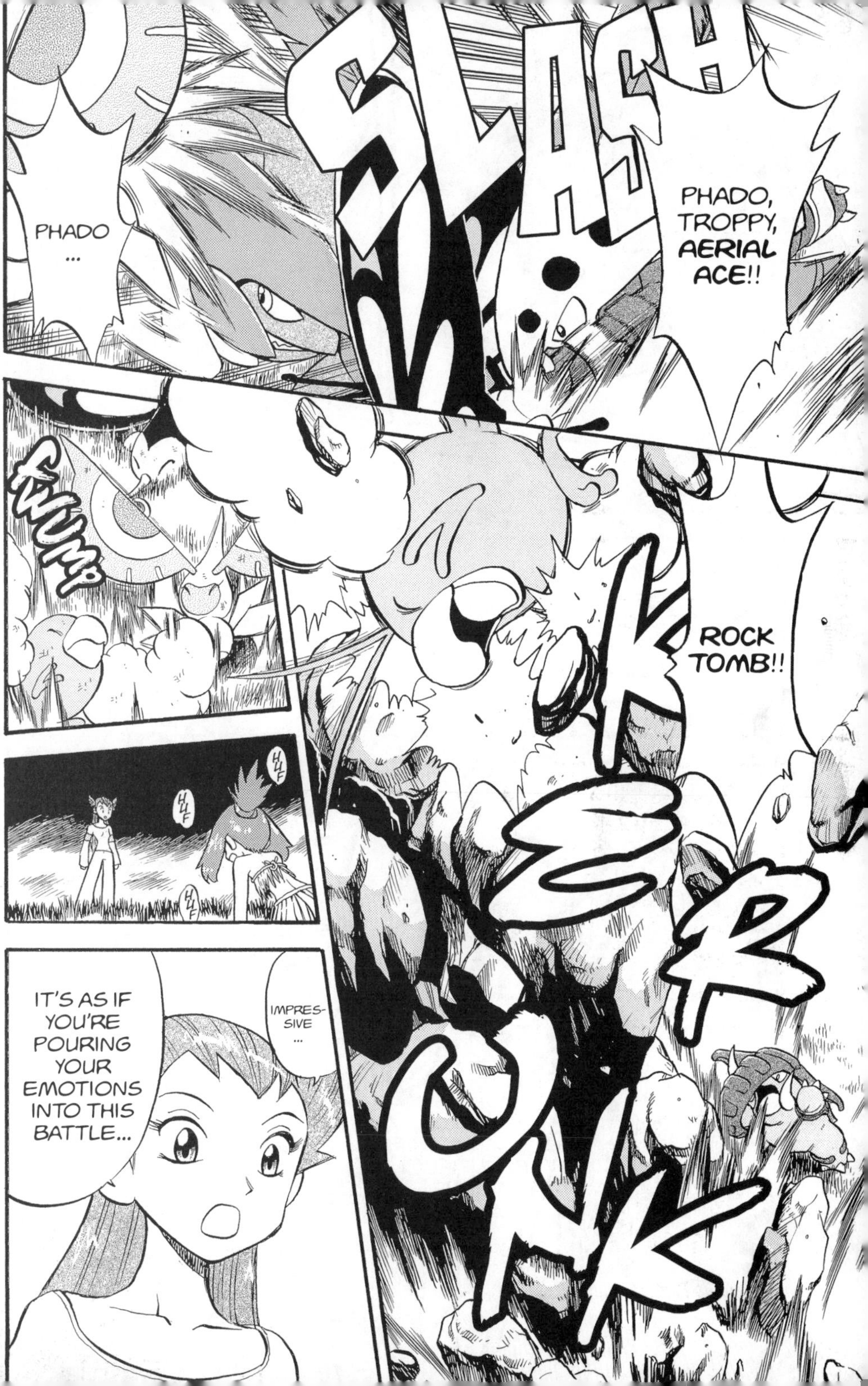
PHADO, TROPPY, AERIAL ACE!!
SLASH
PHADO ...
ROCK TOMB!!
FWUMP
HUF
HUF
HUF
IMPRES-
SIVE
...
IT'S AS IF YOU'RE POURING YOUR EMOTIONS INTO THIS BATTLE...

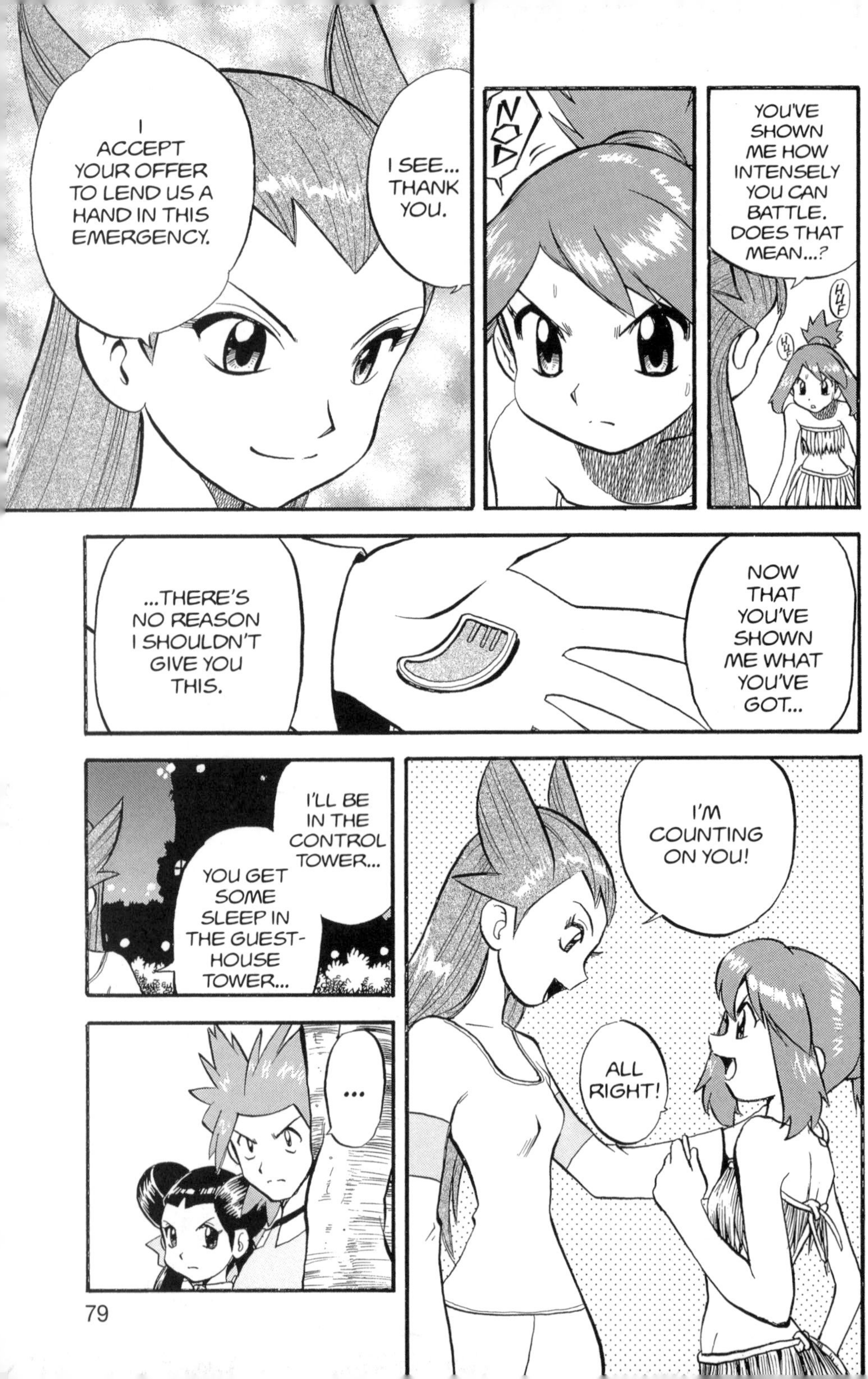
YOU'VE SHOWN ME HOW INTENSELY YOU CAN BATTLE. DOES THAT MEAN...?
HUF
HUF
NOD
I SEE... THANK YOU.
I ACCEPT YOUR OFFER TO LEND US A HAND IN THIS EMERGENCY.
NOW THAT YOU'VE SHOWN ME WHAT YOU'VE GOT...
...THERE'S NO REASON I SHOULDN'T GIVE YOU THIS.
I'M COUNTING ON YOU!
ALL RIGHT!
I'LL BE IN THE CONTROL TOWER...
YOU GET SOME SLEEP IN THE GUEST-HOUSE TOWER...
...

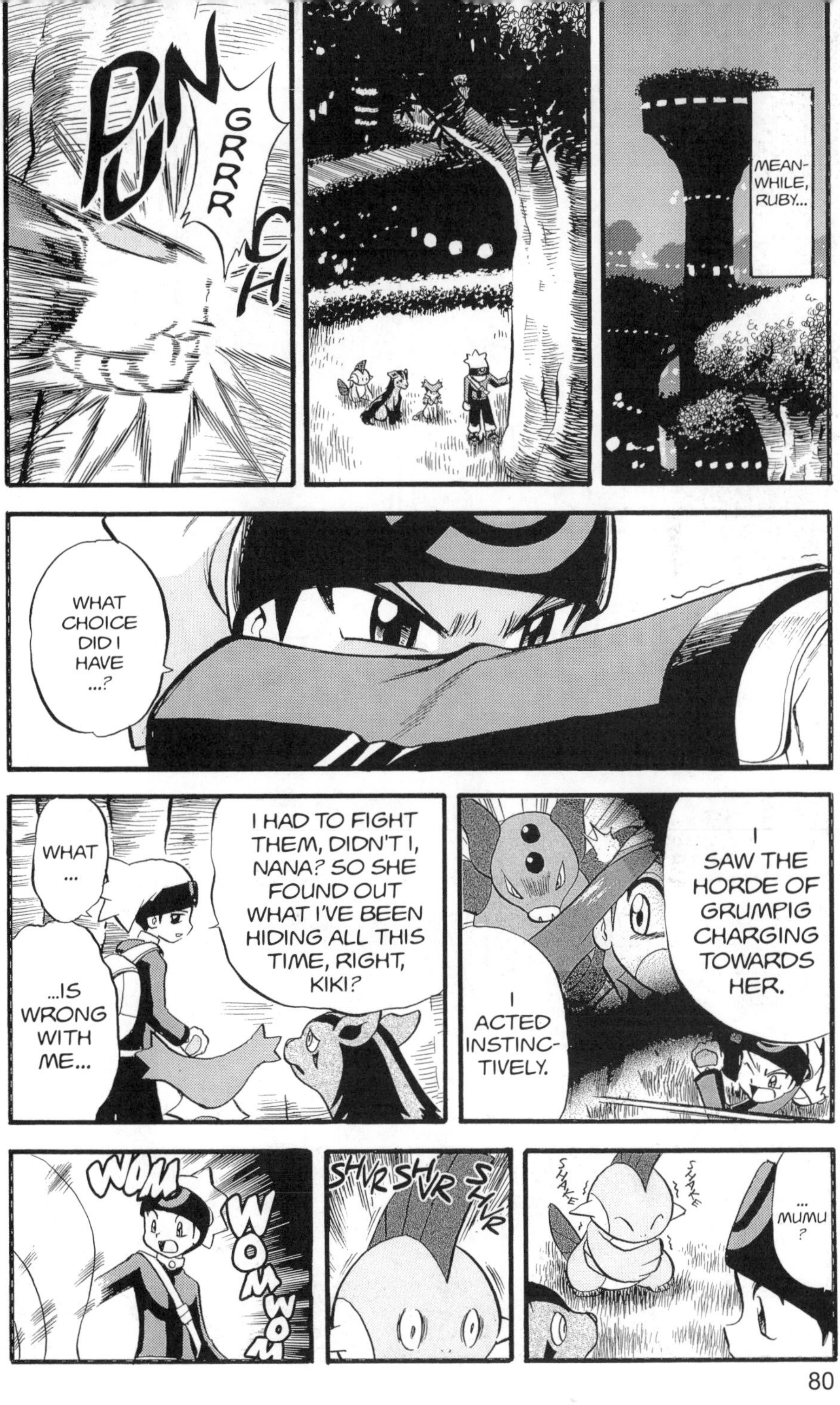
MEAN-WHILE, RUBY...
GRRR
PUNCH
WHAT CHOICE DID I HAVE ...?
I SAW THE HORDE OF GRUMPIG CHARGING TOWARDS HER.
I ACTED INSTINC-TIVELY.
I HAD TO FIGHT THEM, DIDN'T I, NANA? SO SHE FOUND OUT WHAT I'VE BEEN HIDING ALL THIS TIME, RIGHT, KIKI?
WHAT ...
...IS WRONG WITH ME...
... MUMU ?
SHAKE
SHAKE
SHVR SHVR SHVR
WOM
WOMWOMWOM

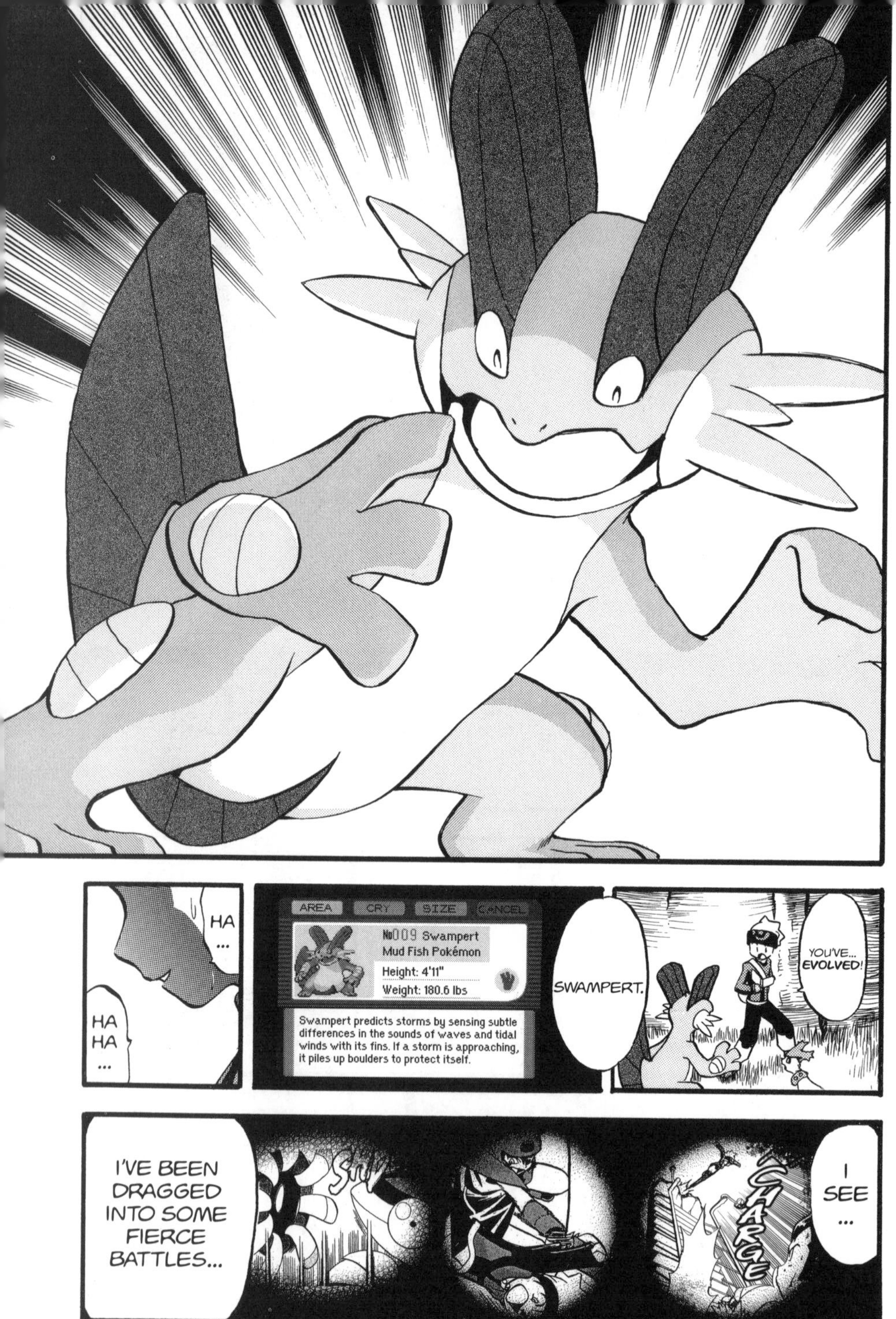
YOU'VE... EVOLVED!
SWAMPERT.
AREA
CRY
SIZE
CANCEL
No009 Swampert
Mud Fish Pokémon
Height: 4'11"
Weight: 180.6 lbs
Swampert predicts storms by sensing subtle differences in the sounds of waves and tidal winds with its fins. If a storm is approaching, it piles up boulders to protect itself.
HA ...
HA HA ...
I SEE ...
CHARGE
I'VE BEEN DRAGGED INTO SOME FIERCE BATTLES...

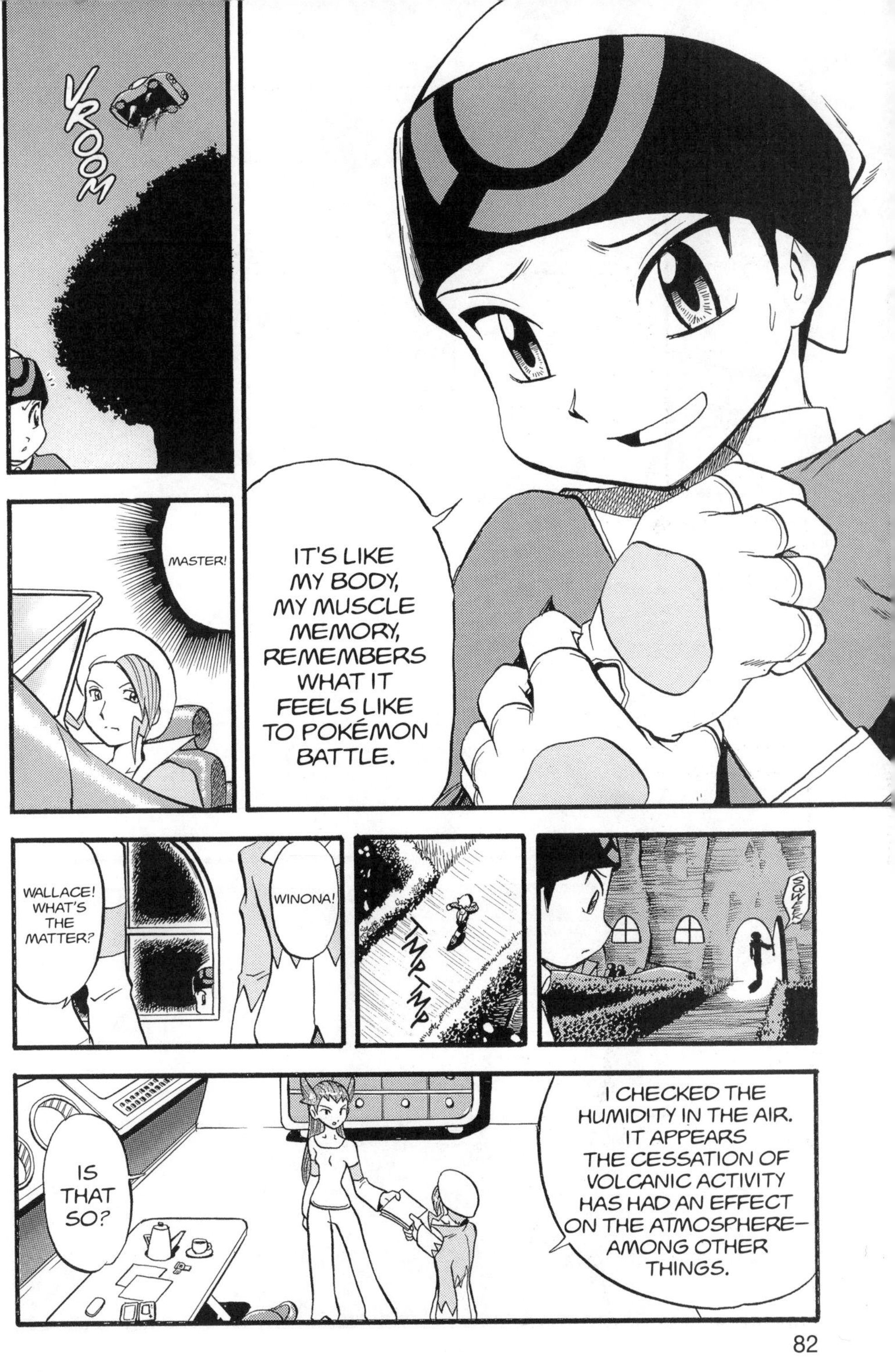
IT'S LIKE MY BODY, MY MUSCLE MEMORY, REMEMBERS WHAT IT FEELS LIKE TO POKÉMON BATTLE.
VROOM
MASTER!
SQWEEK
TMP TMP
WINONA!
WALLACE! WHAT'S THE MATTER?
I CHECKED THE HUMIDITY IN THE AIR. IT APPEARS THE CESSATION OF VOLCANIC ACTIVITY HAS HAD AN EFFECT ON THE ATMOSPHERE—AMONG OTHER THINGS.
IS THAT SO?

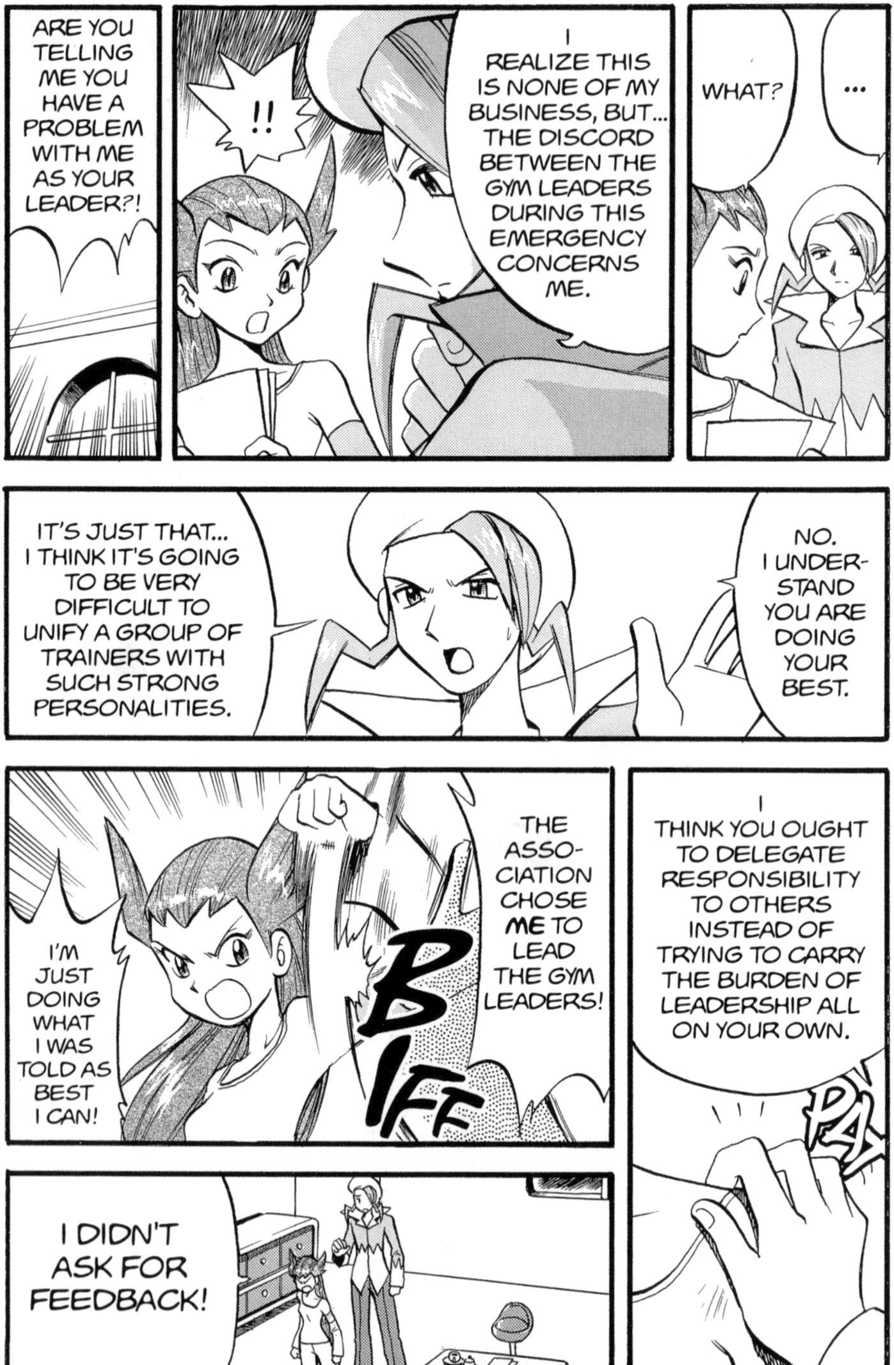
...
WHAT?
I REALIZE THIS IS NONE OF MY BUSINESS, BUT... THE DISCORD BETWEEN THE GYM LEADERS DURING THIS EMERGENCY CONCERNS ME.
!!
ARE YOU TELLING ME YOU HAVE A PROBLEM WITH ME AS YOUR LEADER?!
NO. I UNDER-STAND YOU ARE DOING YOUR BEST.
IT'S JUST THAT... I THINK IT'S GOING TO BE VERY DIFFICULT TO UNIFY A GROUP OF TRAINERS WITH SUCH STRONG PERSONALITIES.
I THINK YOU OUGHT TO DELEGATE RESPONSIBILITY TO OTHERS INSTEAD OF TRYING TO CARRY THE BURDEN OF LEADERSHIP ALL ON YOUR OWN.
THE ASSO-CIATION CHOSE ME TO LEAD THE GYM LEADERS!
I'M JUST DOING WHAT I WAS TOLD AS BEST I CAN!
BIFF
I DIDN'T ASK FOR FEEDBACK!

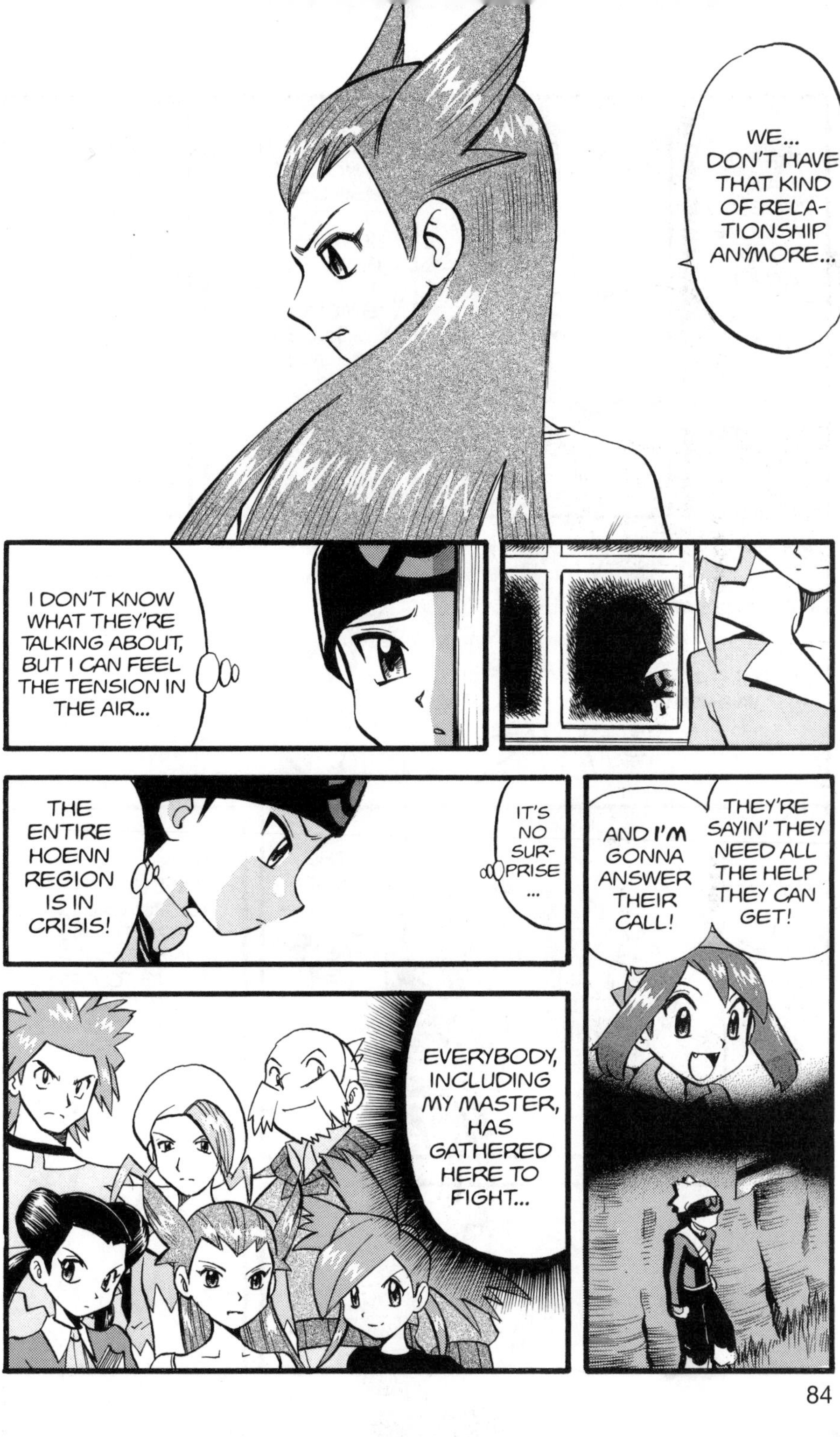
WE... DON'T HAVE THAT KIND OF RELA-TIONSHIP ANYMORE...
I DON'T KNOW WHAT THEY'RE TALKING ABOUT, BUT I CAN FEEL THE TENSION IN THE AIR...
THEY'RE SAYIN' THEY NEED ALL THE HELP THEY CAN GET!
AND **I'M** GONNA ANSWER THEIR CALL!
IT'S NO SUR-PRISE ...
THE ENTIRE HOENN REGION IS IN CRISIS!
EVERYBODY, INCLUDING MY MASTER, HAS GATHERED HERE TO FIGHT...

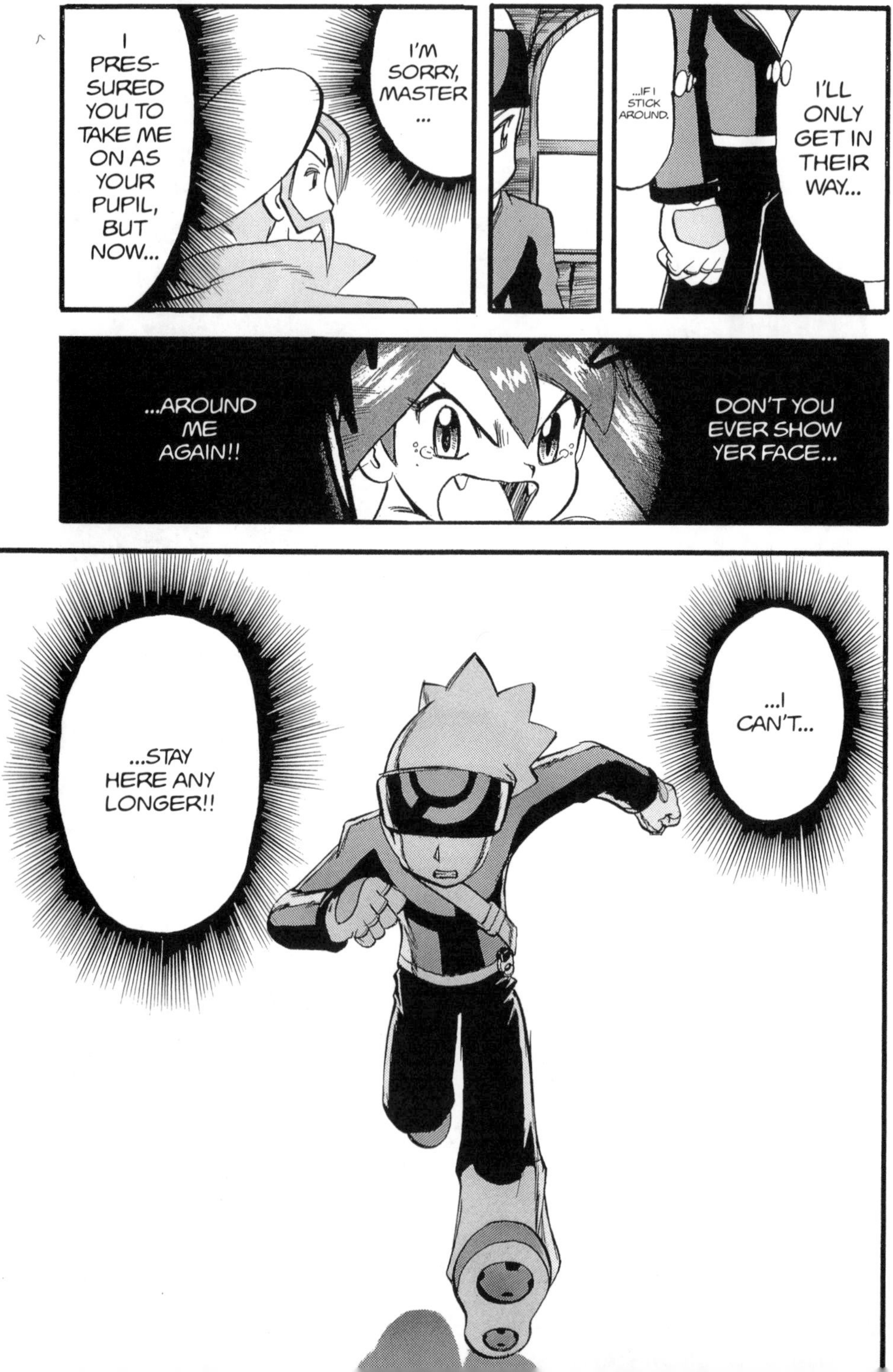
I'LL ONLY GET IN THEIR WAY...
...IF I STICK AROUND.
I'M SORRY, MASTER...
I PRES-SURED YOU TO TAKE ME ON AS YOUR PUPIL, BUT NOW...
DON'T YOU EVER SHOW YER FACE...
...AROUND ME AGAIN!!
...I CAN'T...
...STAY HERE ANY LONGER!!

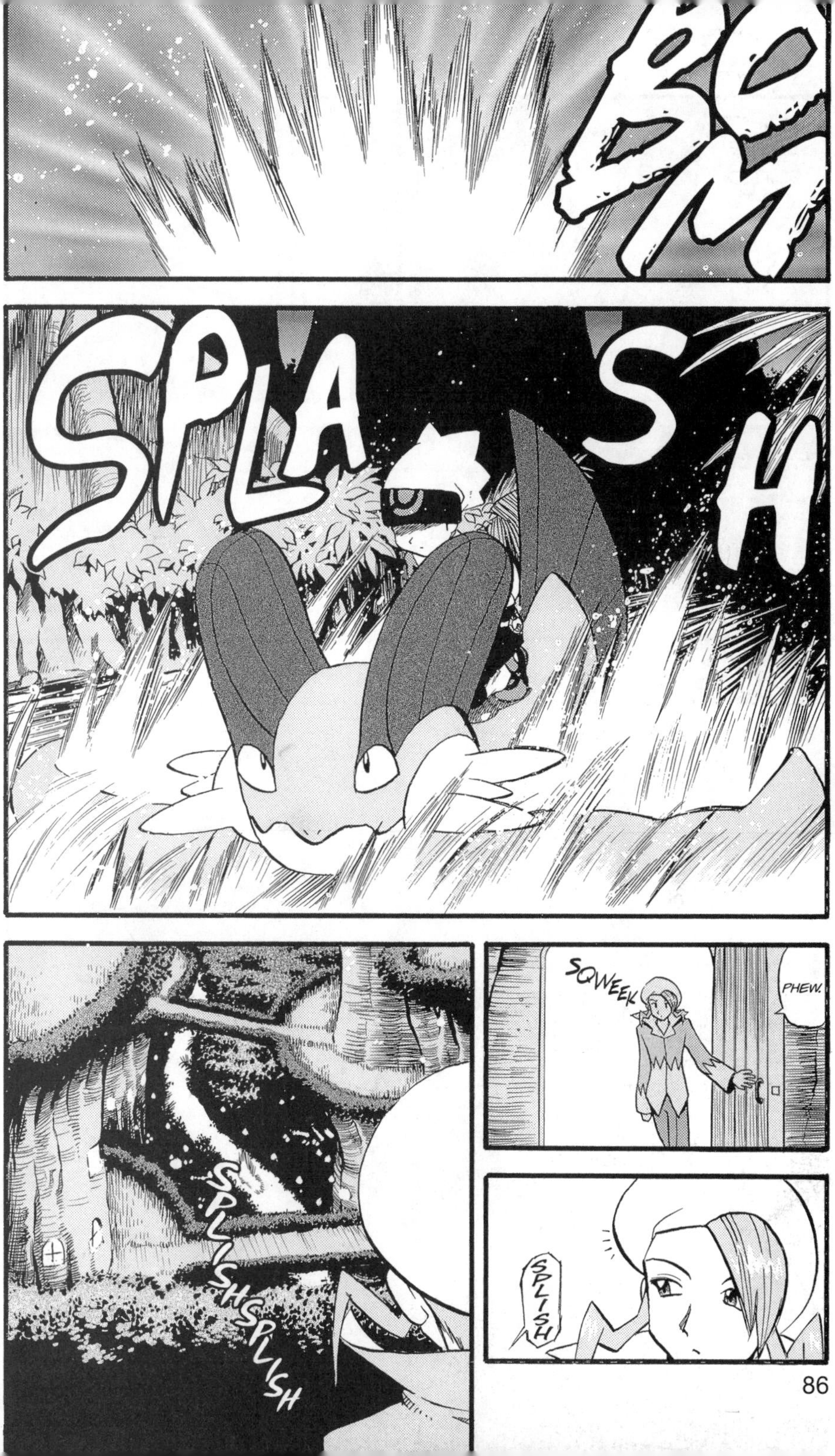
BOOM
SPLASH
SQWEEK
PHEW.
SPLISH
SPLISHSPLISH

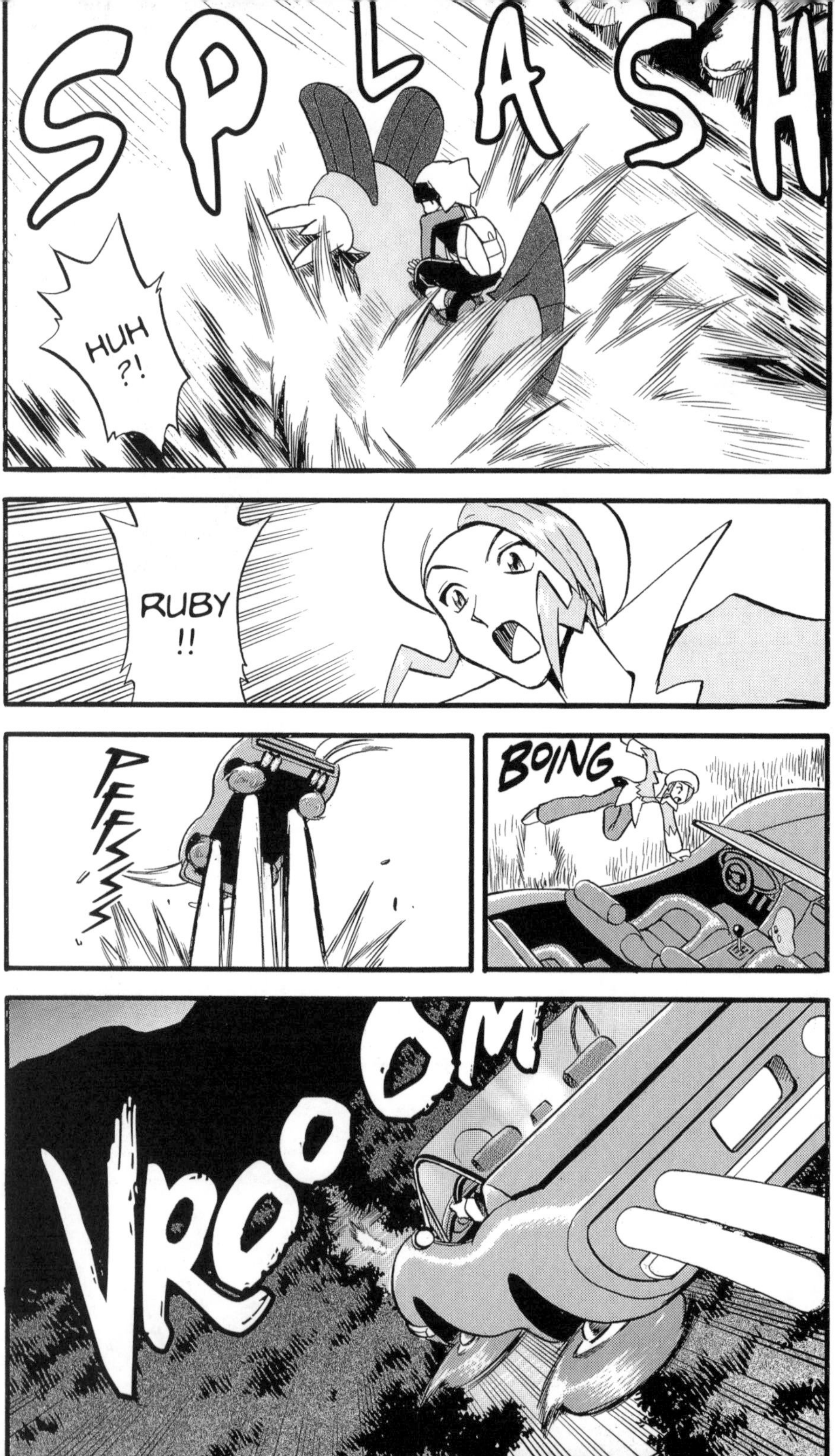
SPLASH
HUH ?!
RUBY !!
BOING
PFFSSSS
VROOOM

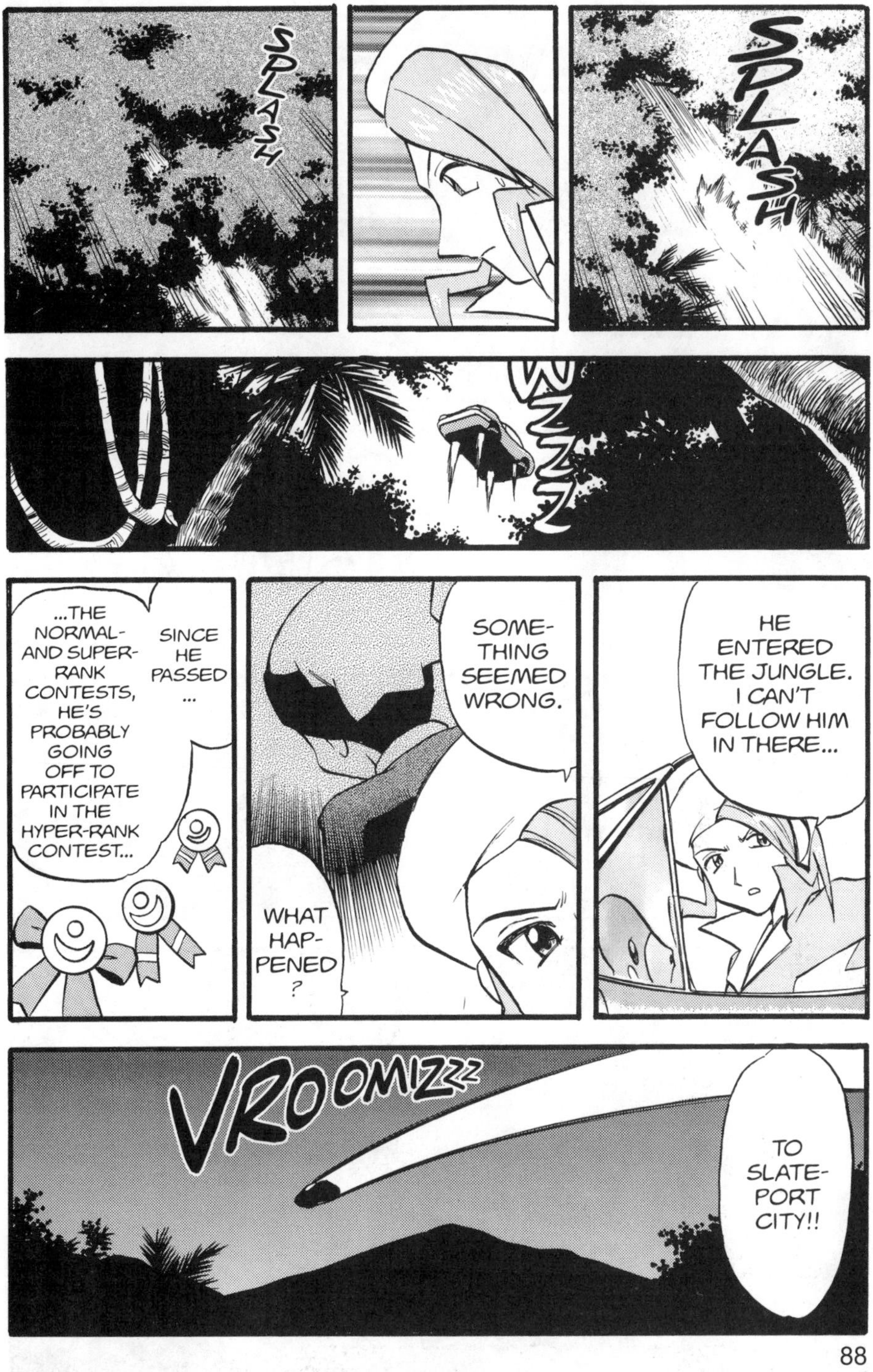
SPLASH
SPLASH
WZZZ
HE ENTERED THE JUNGLE. I CAN'T FOLLOW HIM IN THERE...
SOMETHING SEEMED WRONG.
WHAT HAPPENED?
SINCE HE PASSED...
...THE NORMAL- AND SUPER-RANK CONTESTS, HE'S PROBABLY GOING OFF TO PARTICIPATE IN THE HYPER-RANK CONTEST...
TO SLATEPORT CITY!!
VROOMIZZZ

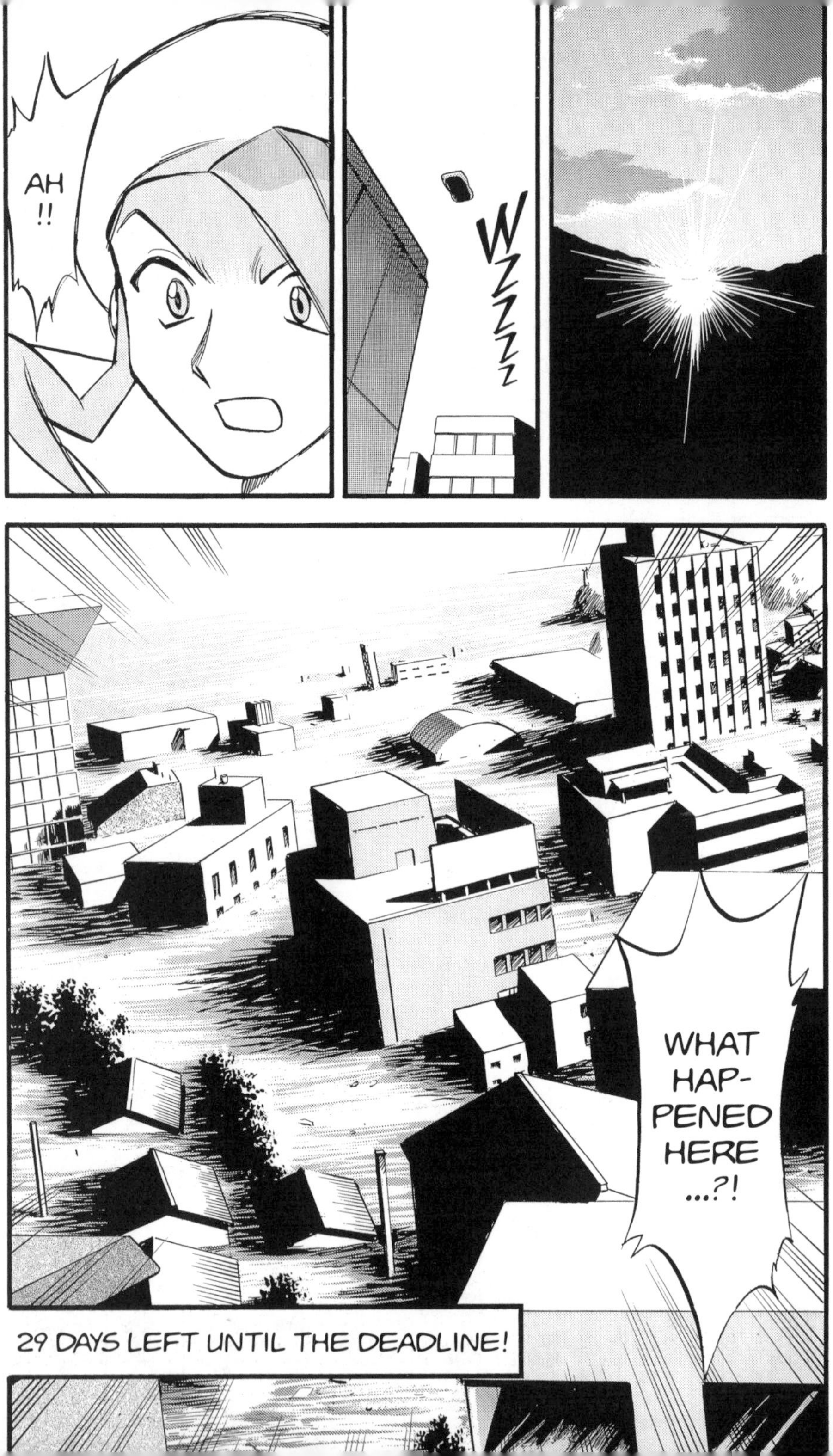
WZZZZ
AH !!
WHAT HAP-PENED HERE ...?!
29 DAYS LEFT UNTIL THE DEADLINE!

ADVENTURE MAP

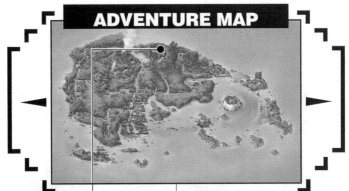

SAPPHIRE

Jagged Pass

Route 111

Fortree City

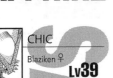

CHIC
Blaziken ♀
Lv39

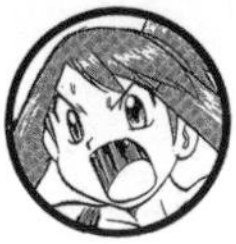

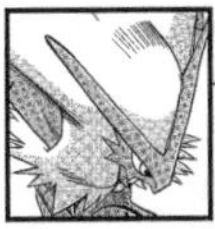

RONO
Lairon ♂
Lv41

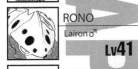

LORRY
Wailord ♂
Lv47

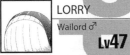

PHADO
Donphan ♂
Lv47

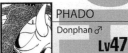

TROPPY
Tropius ♂
Lv46

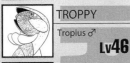

Stone Badge	Knuckle Badge	Dynamo Badge	Heat Badge
Balance Badge	**Feather Badge**	**Mind Badge**	**Rain Badge**

RUBY

Fallarbor Town

Route 111

Fortree City

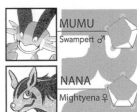

MUMU
Swampert ♂

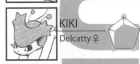

NANA
Mightyena ♀

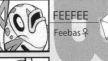

KIKI
Delcatty ♀

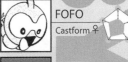

FEEFEE
Feebas ♀

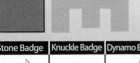

FOFO
Castform ♀

	Coolness	Beauty	Cuteness	Cleverness	Toughness
Normal					
Super					
Hyper					
Master					

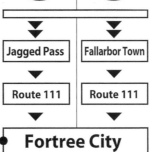

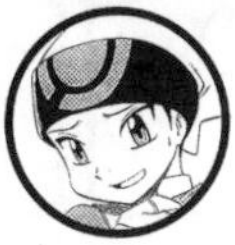

● Adventure 232 ●
Always Keep Whiscash on You for Emergencies

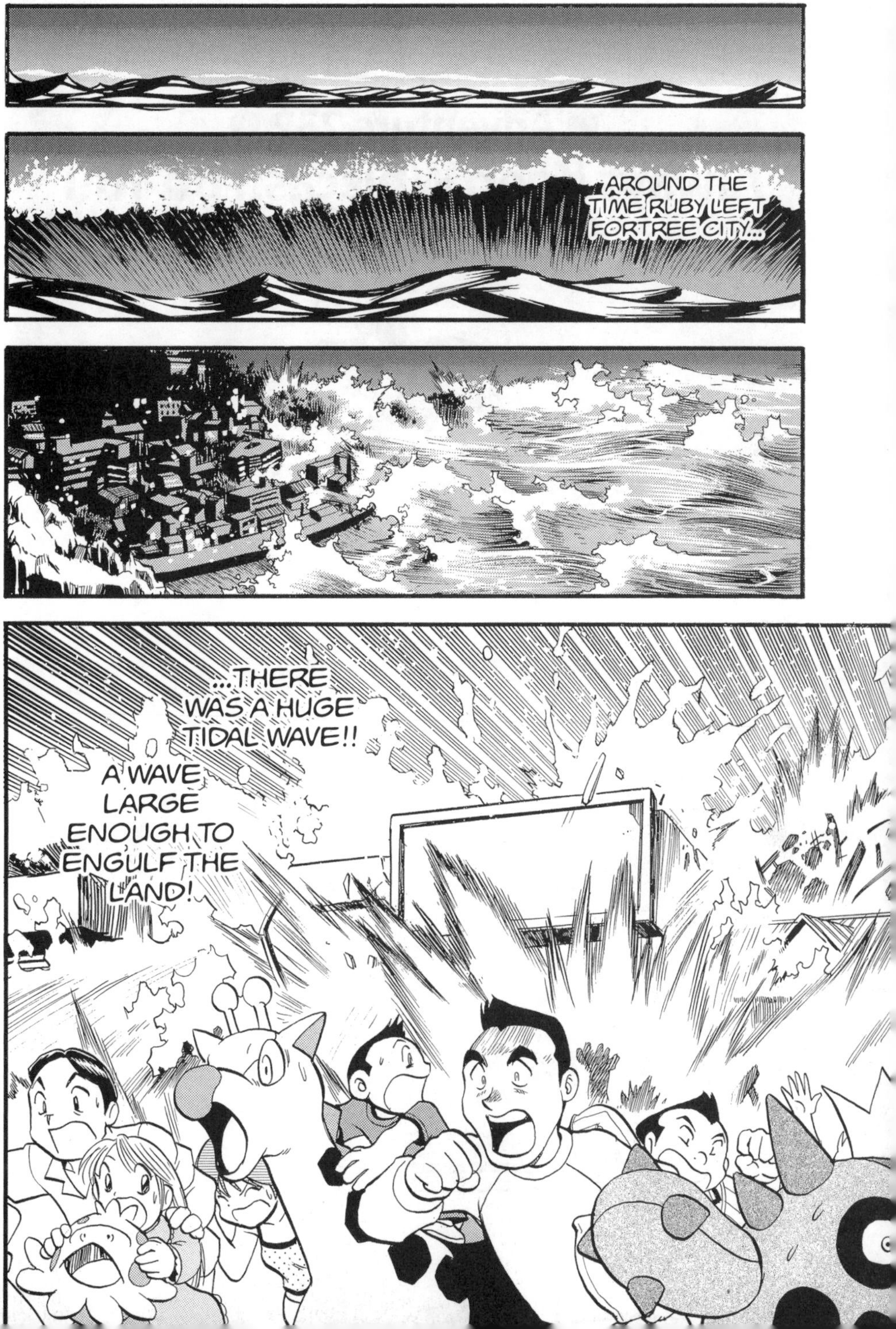
AROUND THE TIME RUBY LEFT FORTREE CITY...
...THERE WAS A HUGE TIDAL WAVE!!
A WAVE LARGE ENOUGH TO ENGULF THE LAND!

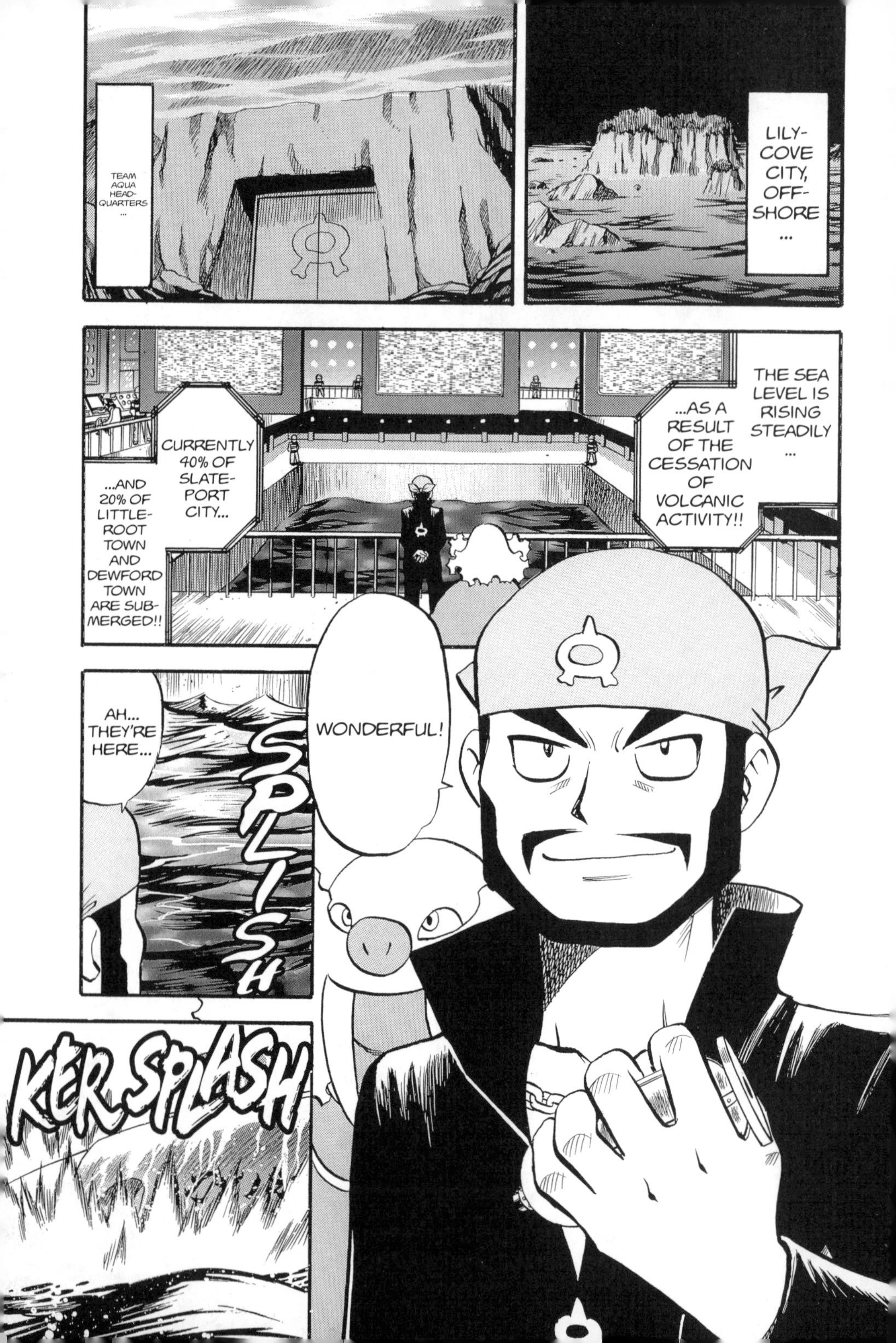

LILY-COVE CITY, OFF-SHORE ...
TEAM AQUA HEAD-QUARTERS ...
THE SEA LEVEL IS RISING STEADILY ...
...AS A RESULT OF THE CESSATION OF VOLCANIC ACTIVITY!!
CURRENTLY 40% OF SLATE-PORT CITY...
...AND 20% OF LITTLE-ROOT TOWN AND DEWFORD TOWN ARE SUB-MERGED!!
WONDERFUL!
AH... THEY'RE HERE...
SPLISH
KER SPLASH

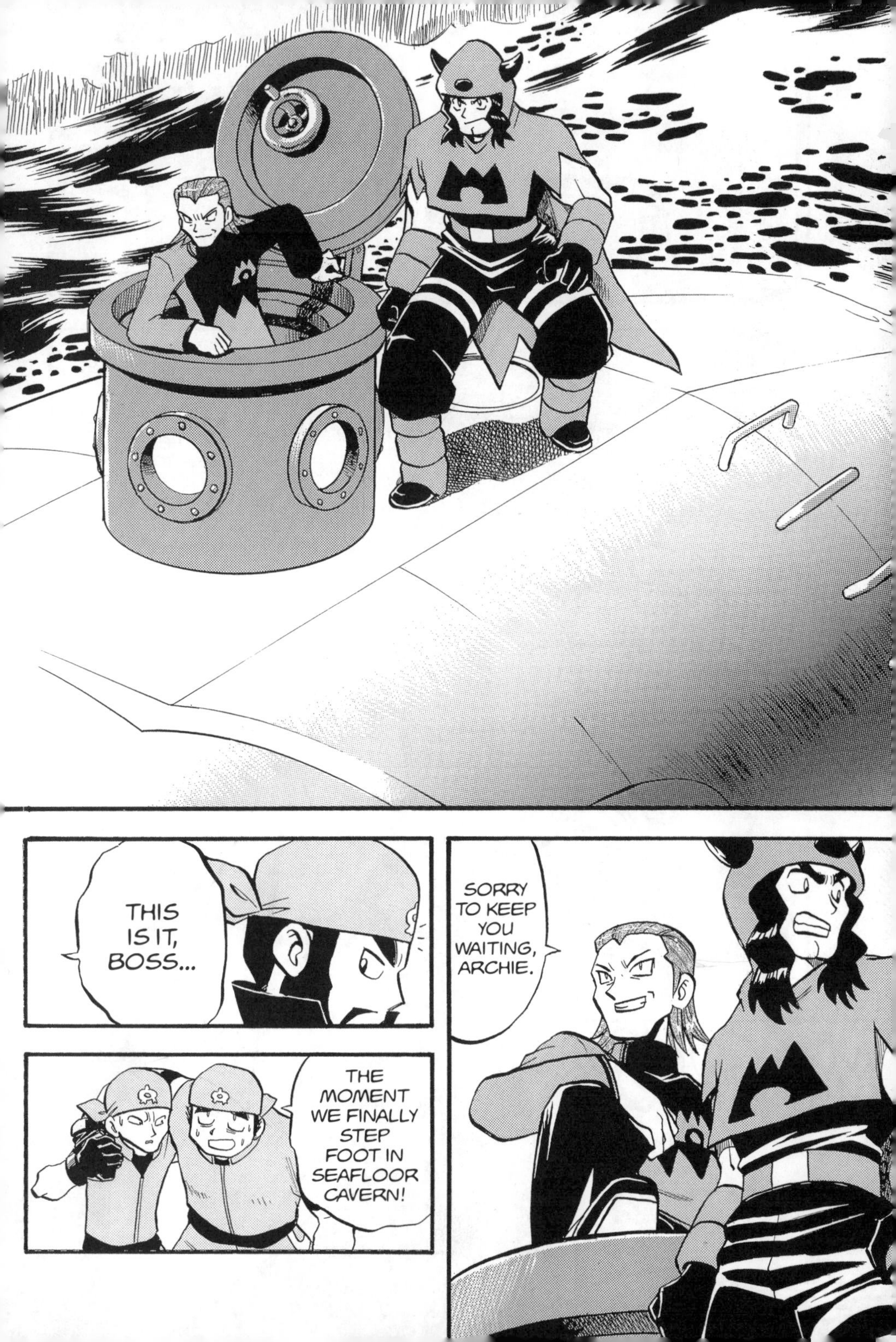
SORRY TO KEEP YOU WAITING, ARCHIE.
THIS IS IT, BOSS...
THE MOMENT WE FINALLY STEP FOOT IN SEAFLOOR CAVERN!

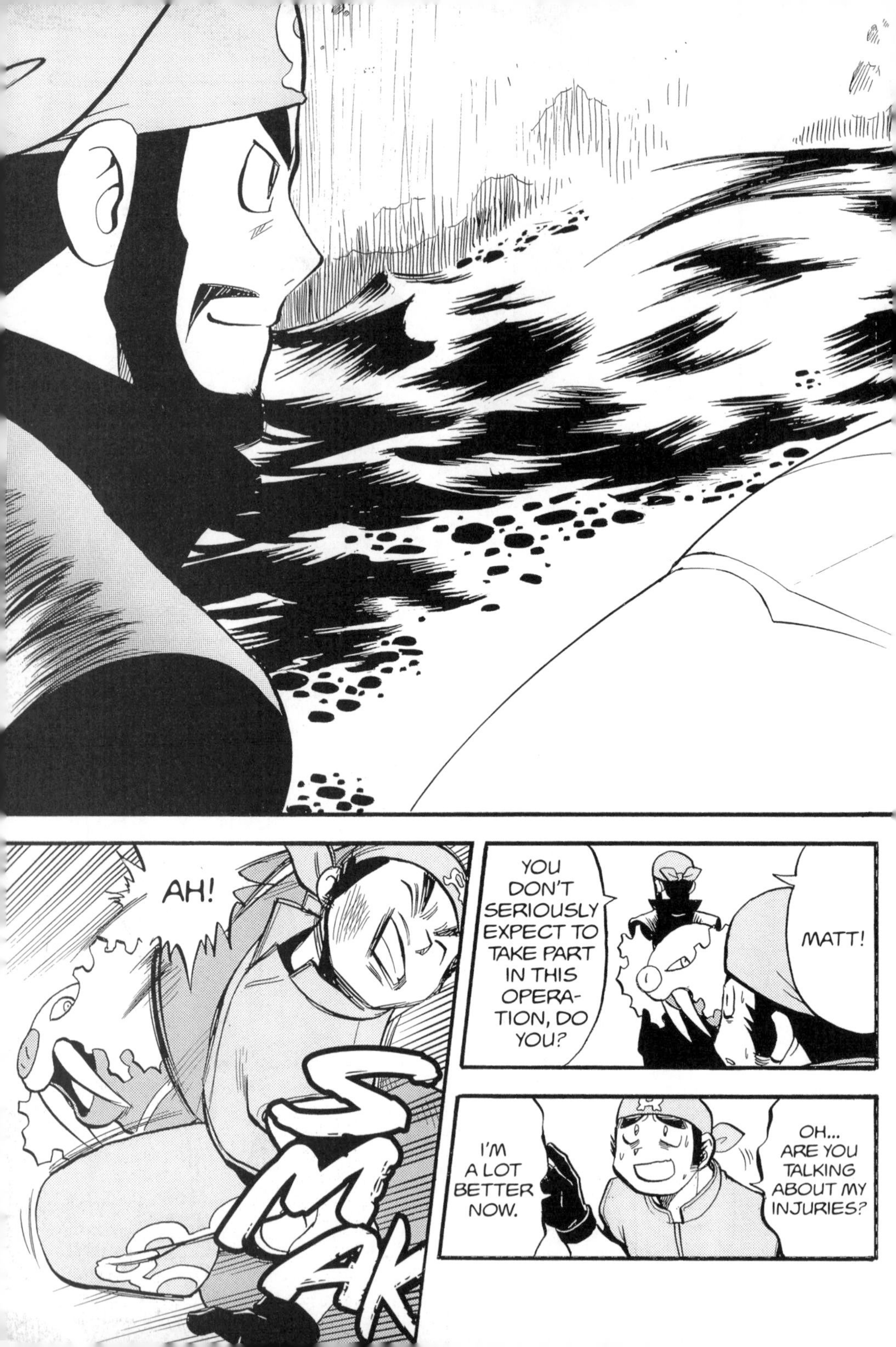
MATT!
YOU DON'T SERIOUSLY EXPECT TO TAKE PART IN THIS OPERATION, DO YOU?
OH... ARE YOU TALKING ABOUT MY INJURIES?
I'M A LOT BETTER NOW.
AH!
SMAK

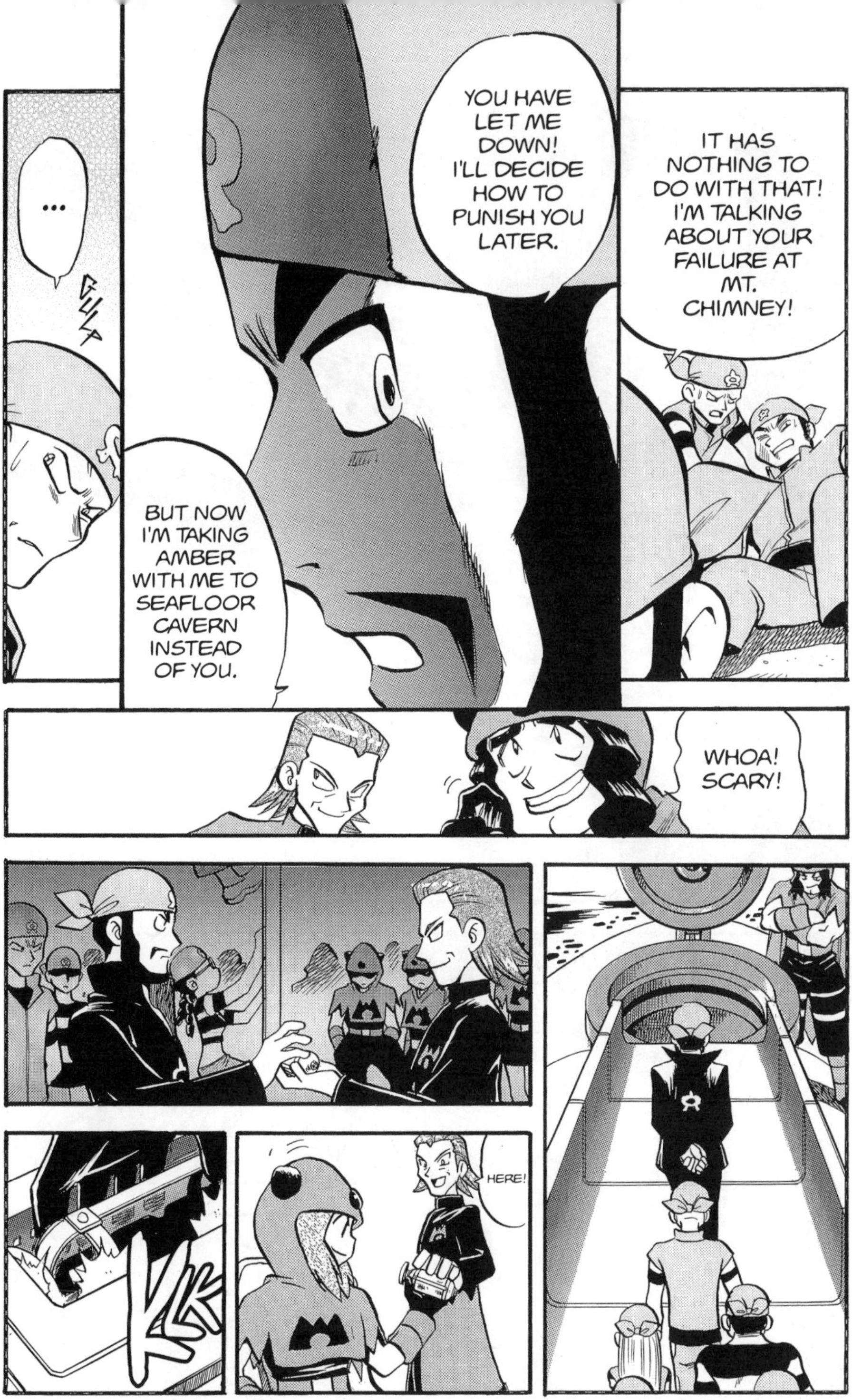
IT HAS NOTHING TO DO WITH THAT! I'M TALKING ABOUT YOUR FAILURE AT MT. CHIMNEY!
YOU HAVE LET ME DOWN! I'LL DECIDE HOW TO PUNISH YOU LATER.
BUT NOW I'M TAKING AMBER WITH ME TO SEAFLOOR CAVERN INSTEAD OF YOU.
...
GULP
WHOA! SCARY!
HERE!
KLK

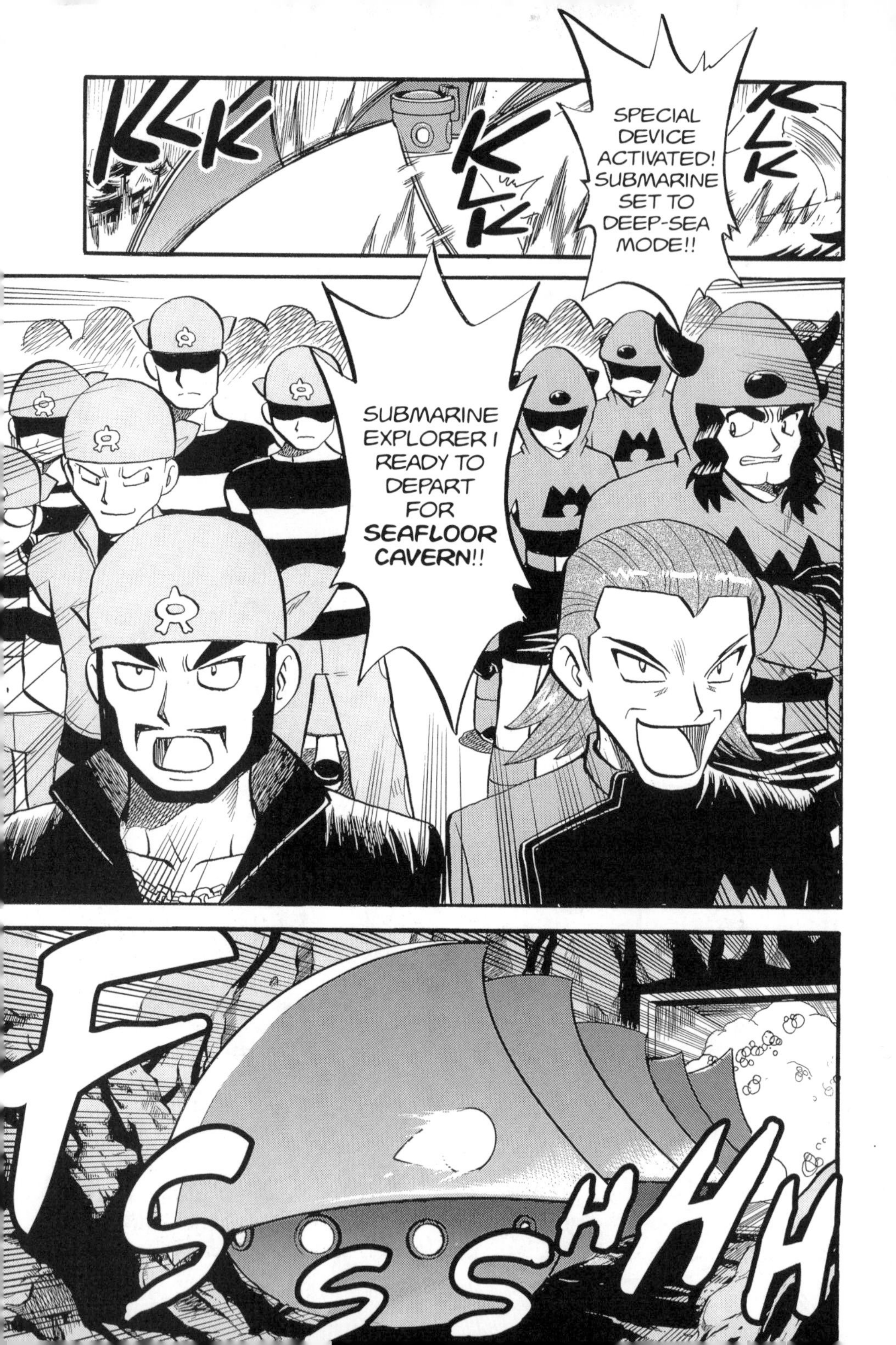
KLK
SPECIAL DEVICE ACTIVATED! SUBMARINE SET TO DEEP-SEA MODE!!
KLK
KSK
SUBMARINE EXPLORER I READY TO DEPART FOR **SEAFLOOR CAVERN**!!
FSSSHHH

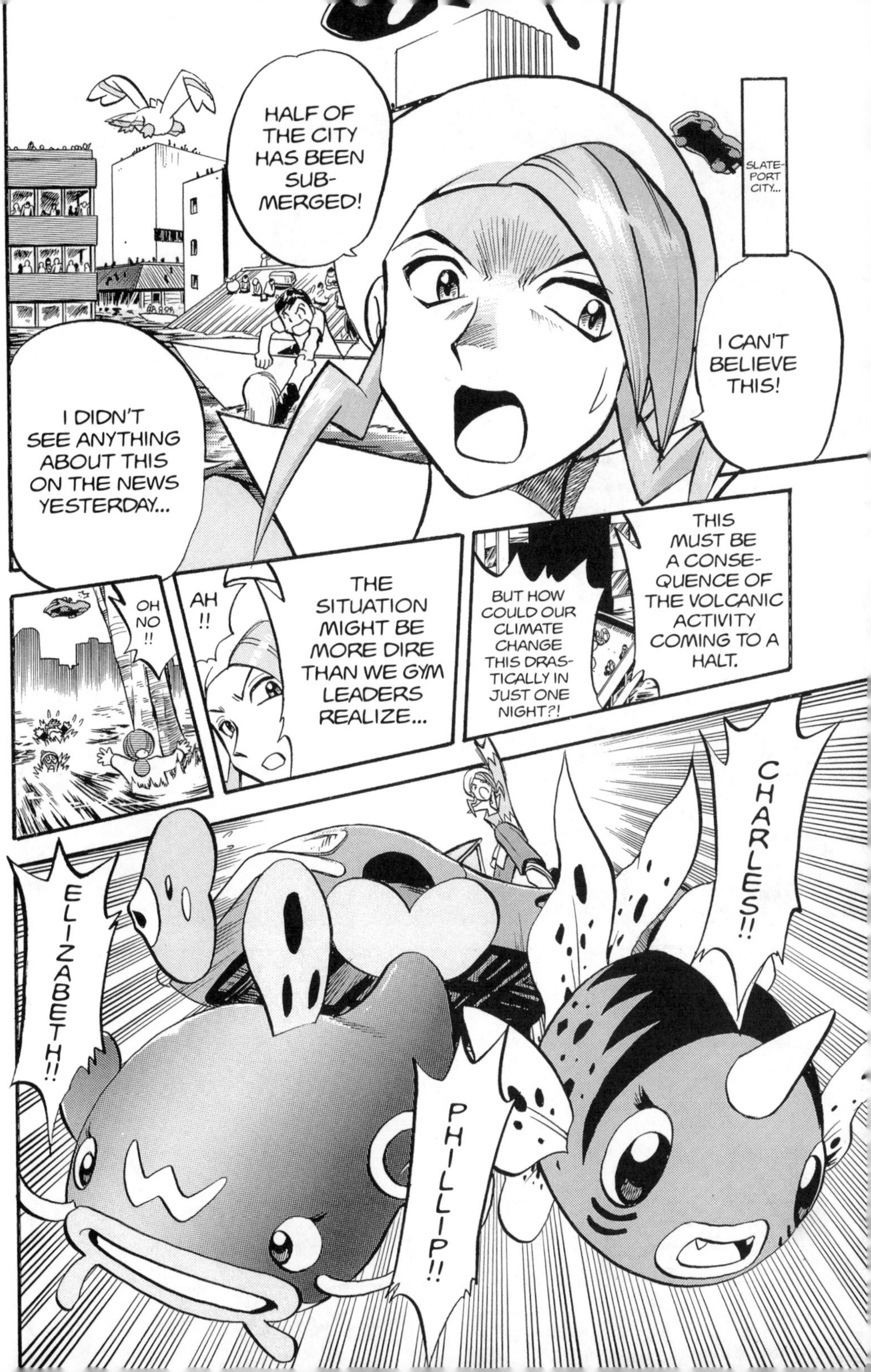
SLATE-PORT CITY...
I CAN'T BELIEVE THIS!
HALF OF THE CITY HAS BEEN SUB-MERGED!
I DIDN'T SEE ANYTHING ABOUT THIS ON THE NEWS YESTERDAY...
THIS MUST BE A CONSE-QUENCE OF THE VOLCANIC ACTIVITY COMING TO A HALT.
BUT HOW COULD OUR CLIMATE CHANGE THIS DRAS-TICALLY IN JUST ONE NIGHT?!
THE SITUATION MIGHT BE MORE DIRE THAN WE GYM LEADERS REALIZE...
AH !!
OH NO !!
CHARLES!!
PHILLIP!!
ELIZABETH!!

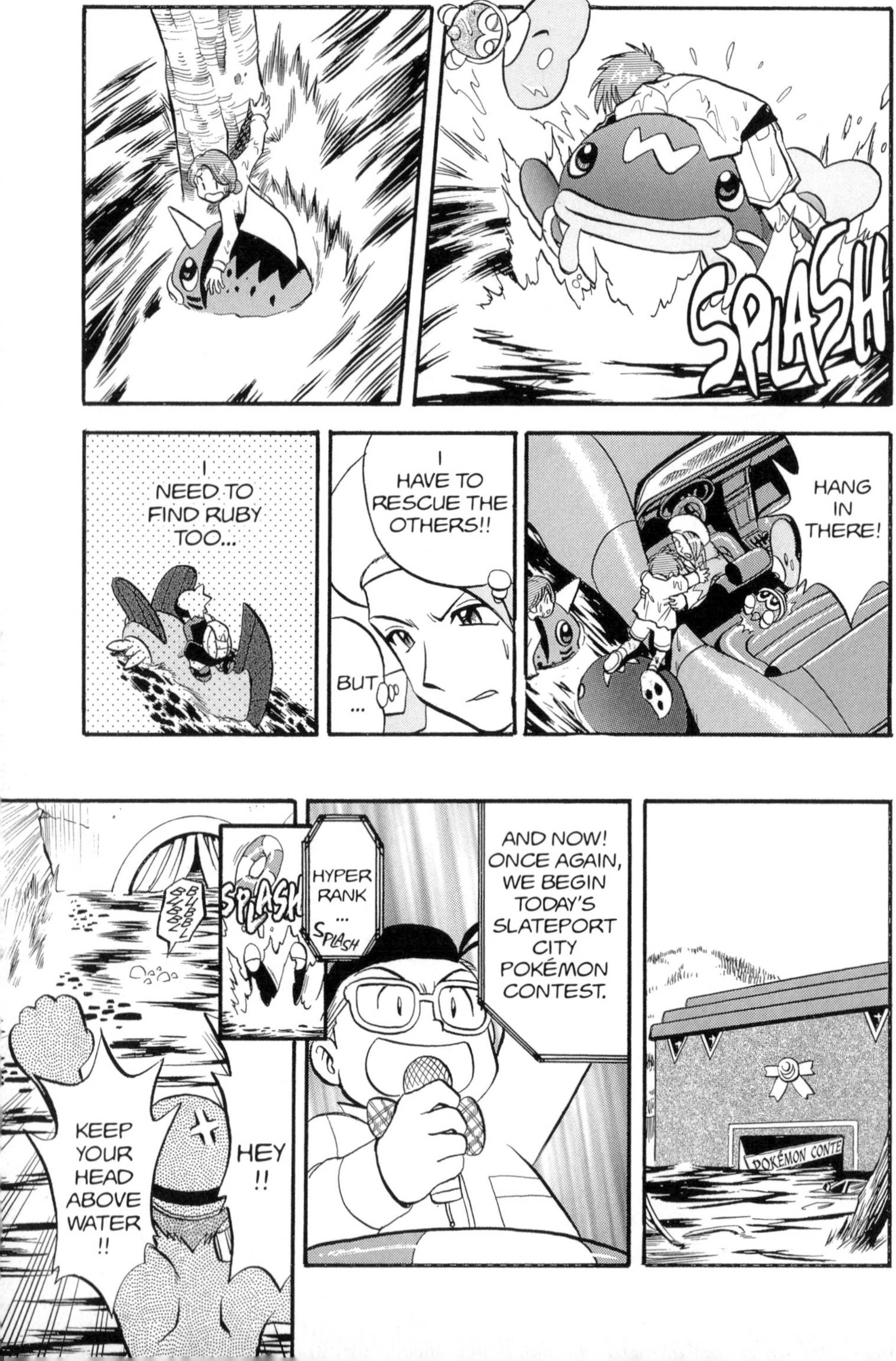
SPLASH
HANG IN THERE!
I HAVE TO RESCUE THE OTHERS!!
BUT ...
I NEED TO FIND RUBY TOO...
POKÉMON CONTE
AND NOW! ONCE AGAIN, WE BEGIN TODAY'S SLATEPORT CITY POKÉMON CONTEST.
HYPER RANK ...
SPLASH
SPLASH
BUBBL BUBBL
HEY !!
KEEP YOUR HEAD ABOVE WATER !!

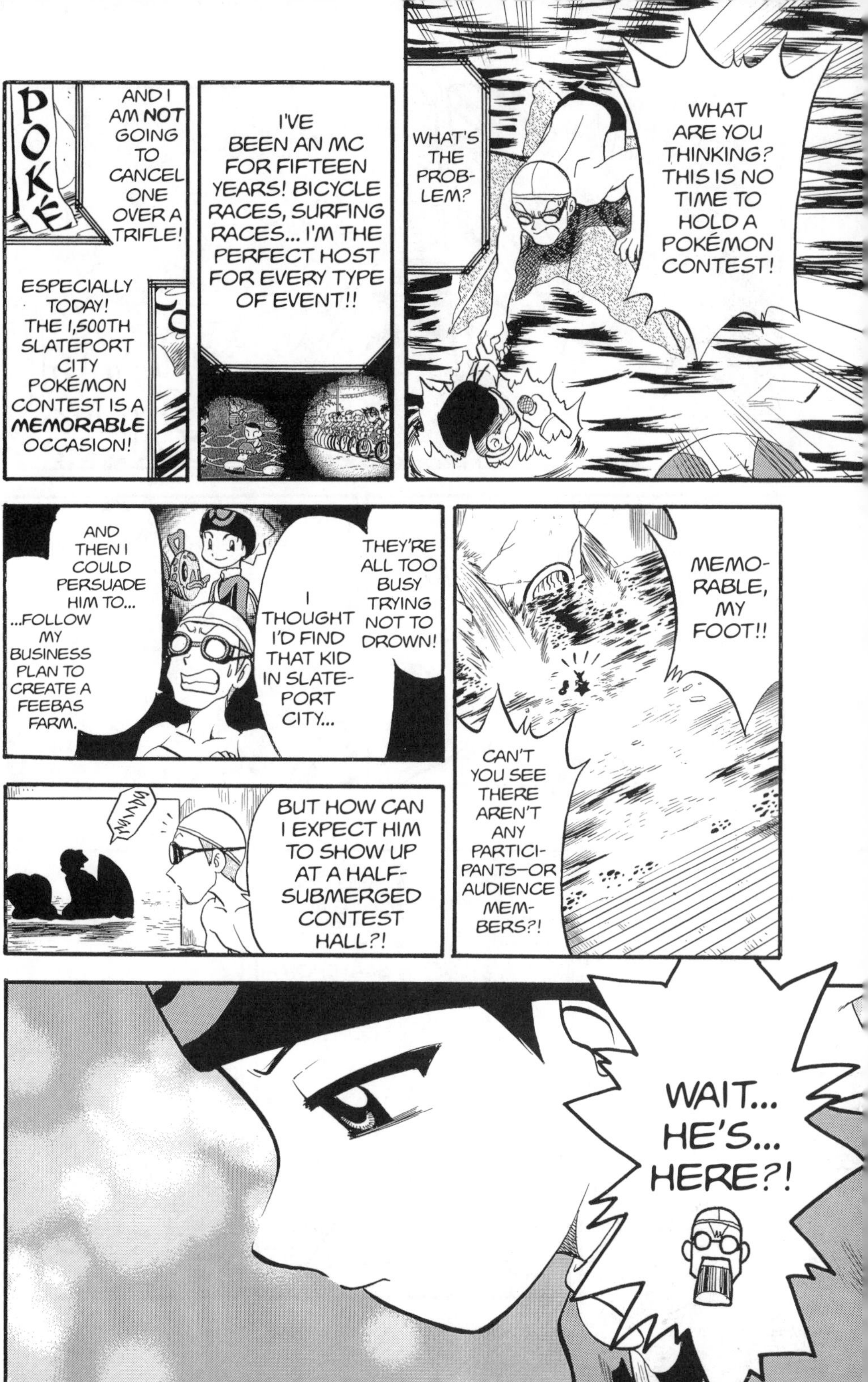
WHAT ARE YOU THINKING? THIS IS NO TIME TO HOLD A POKÉMON CONTEST!
WHAT'S THE PROBLEM?
I'VE BEEN AN MC FOR FIFTEEN YEARS! BICYCLE RACES, SURFING RACES... I'M THE PERFECT HOST FOR EVERY TYPE OF EVENT!!
AND I AM **NOT** GOING TO CANCEL ONE OVER A TRIFLE!
POKÉ
ESPECIALLY TODAY! THE 1,500TH SLATEPORT CITY POKÉMON CONTEST IS A **MEMORABLE** OCCASION!
MEMORABLE, MY FOOT!!
CAN'T YOU SEE THERE AREN'T ANY PARTICIPANTS—OR AUDIENCE MEMBERS?!
THEY'RE ALL TOO BUSY TRYING NOT TO DROWN!
I THOUGHT I'D FIND THAT KID IN SLATEPORT CITY...
AND THEN I COULD PERSUADE HIM TO...
...FOLLOW MY BUSINESS PLAN TO CREATE A FEEBAS FARM.
BUT HOW CAN I EXPECT HIM TO SHOW UP AT A HALF-SUBMERGED CONTEST HALL?!
WAIT... HE'S... HERE?!

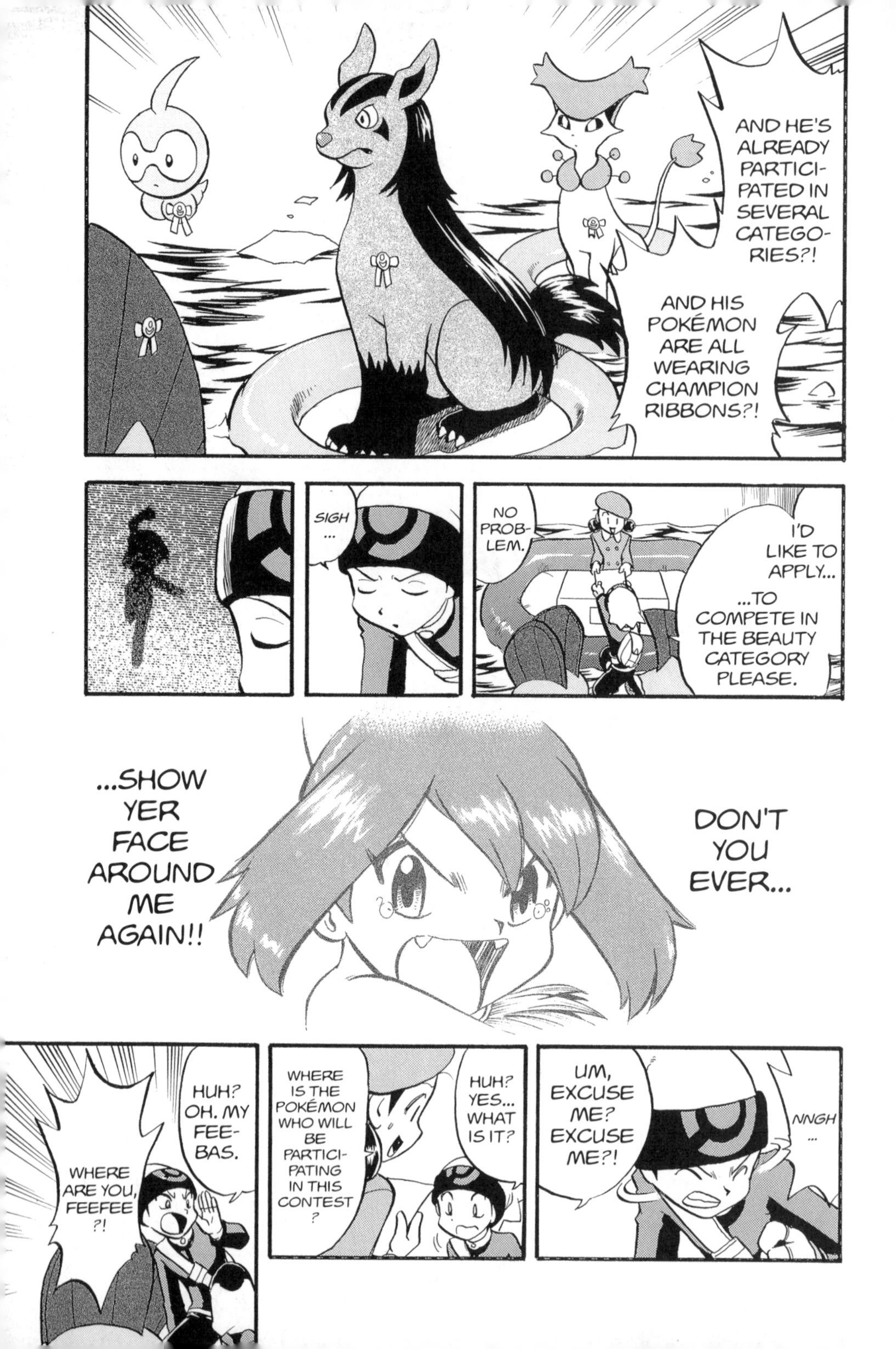
AND HE'S ALREADY PARTICIPATED IN SEVERAL CATEGORIES?!
AND HIS POKÉMON ARE ALL WEARING CHAMPION RIBBONS?!
I'D LIKE TO APPLY...
...TO COMPETE IN THE BEAUTY CATEGORY PLEASE.
NO PROBLEM.
SIGH...
DON'T YOU EVER...
...SHOW YER FACE AROUND ME AGAIN!!
NNGH...
UM, EXCUSE ME? EXCUSE ME?!
HUH? YES... WHAT IS IT?
WHERE IS THE POKÉMON WHO WILL BE PARTICIPATING IN THIS CONTEST?
HUH? OH. MY FEEBAS.
WHERE ARE YOU, FEEFEE?!

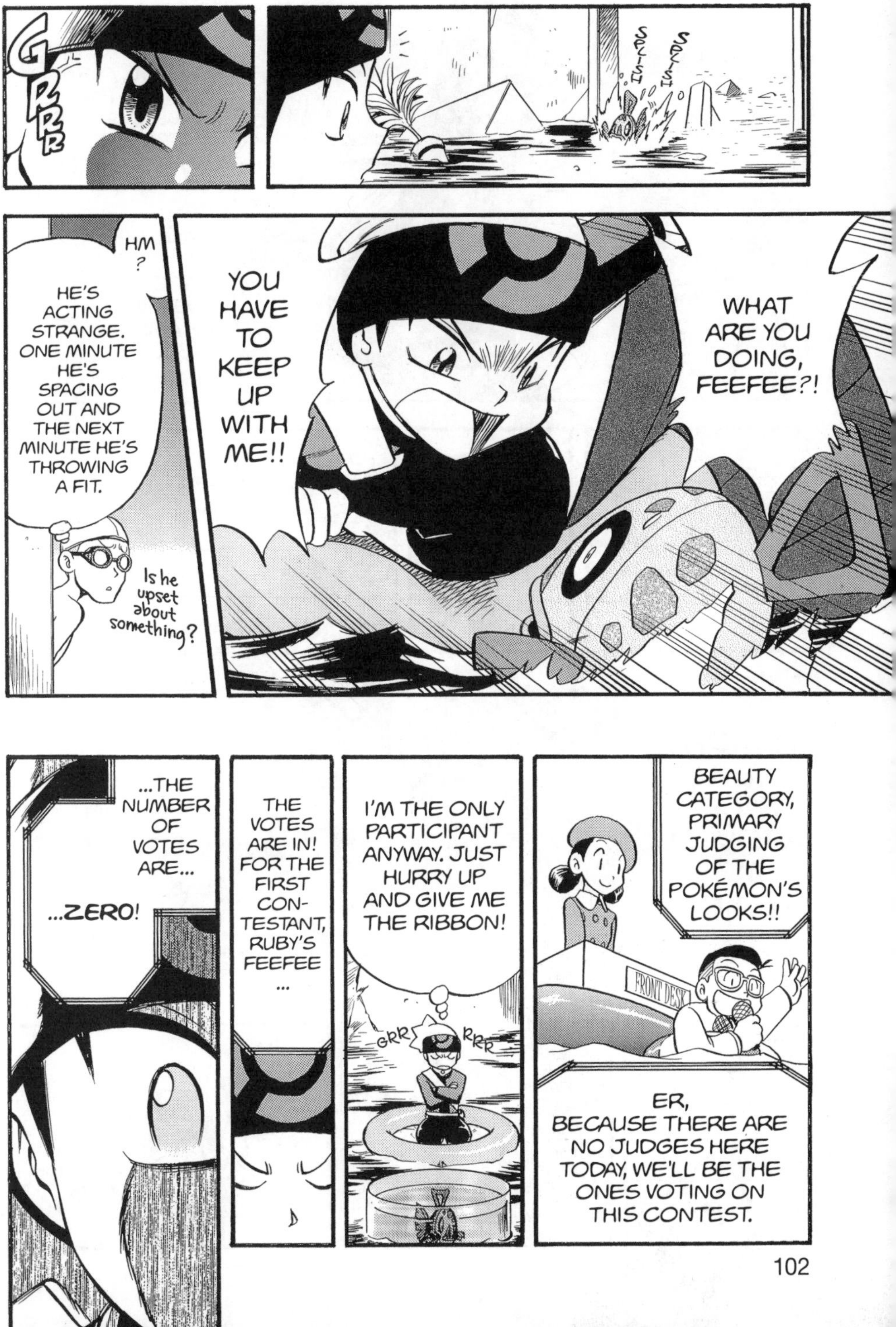

SPLISH
SPLISH
GRRR
WHAT ARE YOU DOING, FEEFEE?!
YOU HAVE TO KEEP UP WITH ME!!
HM?
HE'S ACTING STRANGE. ONE MINUTE HE'S SPACING OUT AND THE NEXT MINUTE HE'S THROWING A FIT.
Is he upset about something?
BEAUTY CATEGORY, PRIMARY JUDGING OF THE POKÉMON'S LOOKS!!
FRONT DESK
ER, BECAUSE THERE ARE NO JUDGES HERE TODAY, WE'LL BE THE ONES VOTING ON THIS CONTEST.
I'M THE ONLY PARTICIPANT ANYWAY. JUST HURRY UP AND GIVE ME THE RIBBON!
GRR
RRR
THE VOTES ARE IN! FOR THE FIRST CON-TESTANT, RUBY'S FEEFEE ...
...THE NUMBER OF VOTES ARE...
...ZERO!

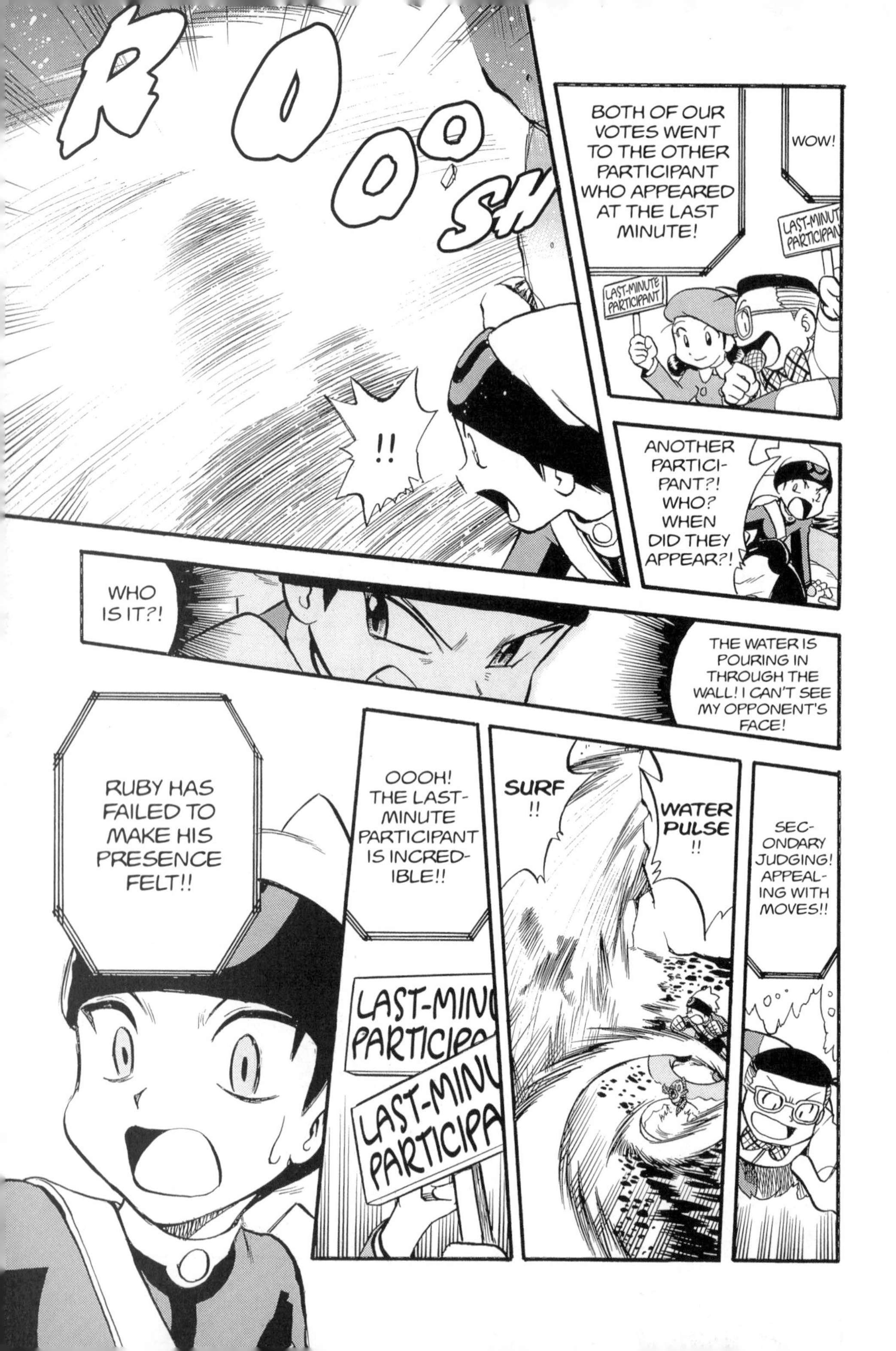

BOTH OF OUR VOTES WENT TO THE OTHER PARTICIPANT WHO APPEARED AT THE LAST MINUTE!
WOW!
LAST-MINUTE PARTICIPANT
LAST-MINUT PARTICIPAN
ANOTHER PARTICI-PANT?! WHO? WHEN DID THEY APPEAR?!
ROOOSH
!!
WHO IS IT?!
THE WATER IS POURING IN THROUGH THE WALL! I CAN'T SEE MY OPPONENT'S FACE!
SEC-ONDARY JUDGING! APPEAL-ING WITH MOVES!!
SURF!!
WATER PULSE!!
OOOH! THE LAST-MINUTE PARTICIPANT IS INCRED-IBLE!!
LAST-MINU PARTICIPA
LAST-MINU PARTICIPA
RUBY HAS FAILED TO MAKE HIS PRESENCE FELT!!

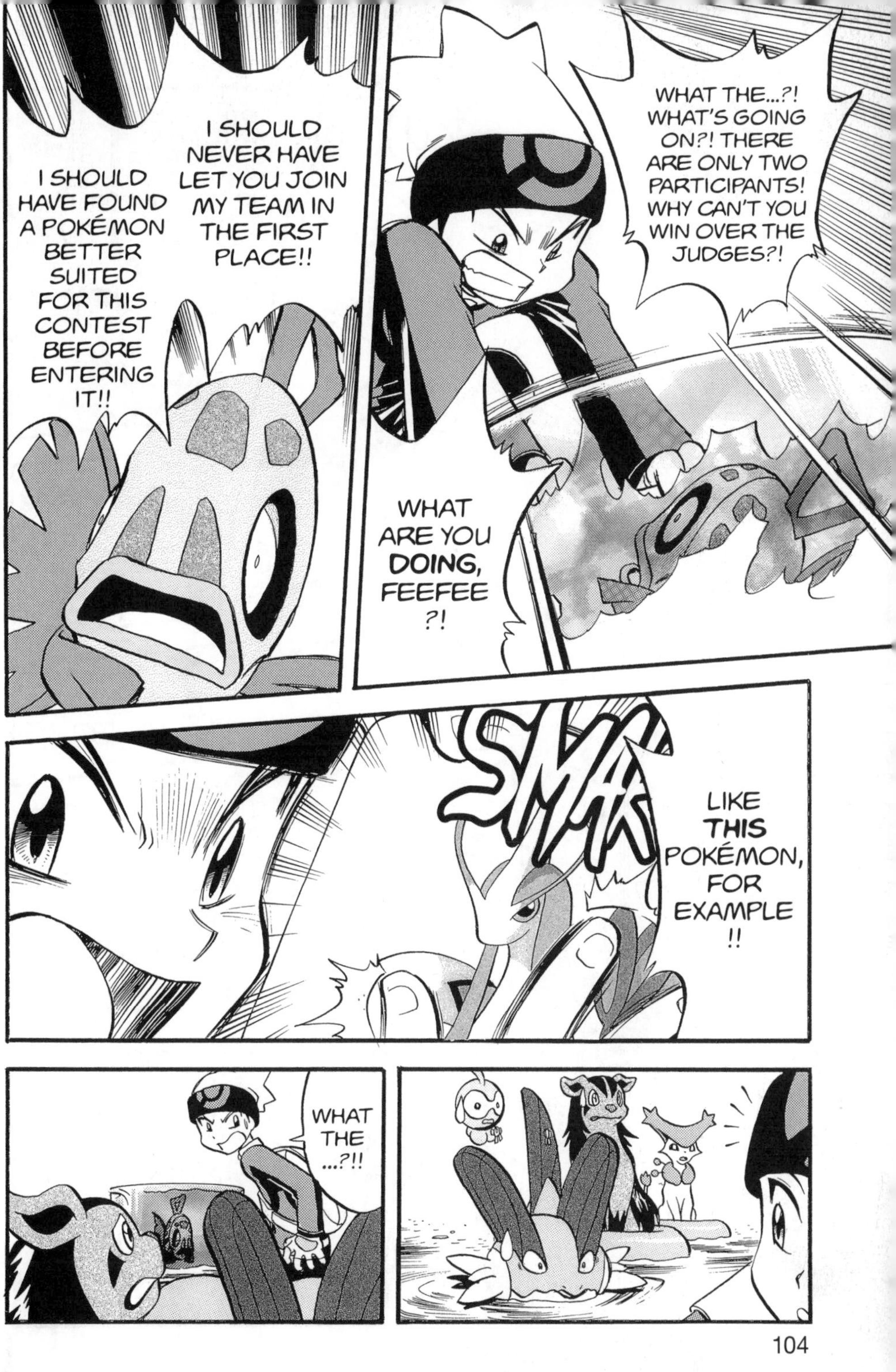
WHAT THE...?! WHAT'S GOING ON?! THERE ARE ONLY TWO PARTICIPANTS! WHY CAN'T YOU WIN OVER THE JUDGES?!
WHAT ARE YOU **DOING**, FEEFEE?!
I SHOULD NEVER HAVE LET YOU JOIN MY TEAM IN THE FIRST PLACE!!
I SHOULD HAVE FOUND A POKÉMON BETTER SUITED FOR THIS CONTEST BEFORE ENTERING IT!!
SMA
LIKE **THIS** POKÉMON, FOR EXAMPLE!!
WHAT THE...?!!

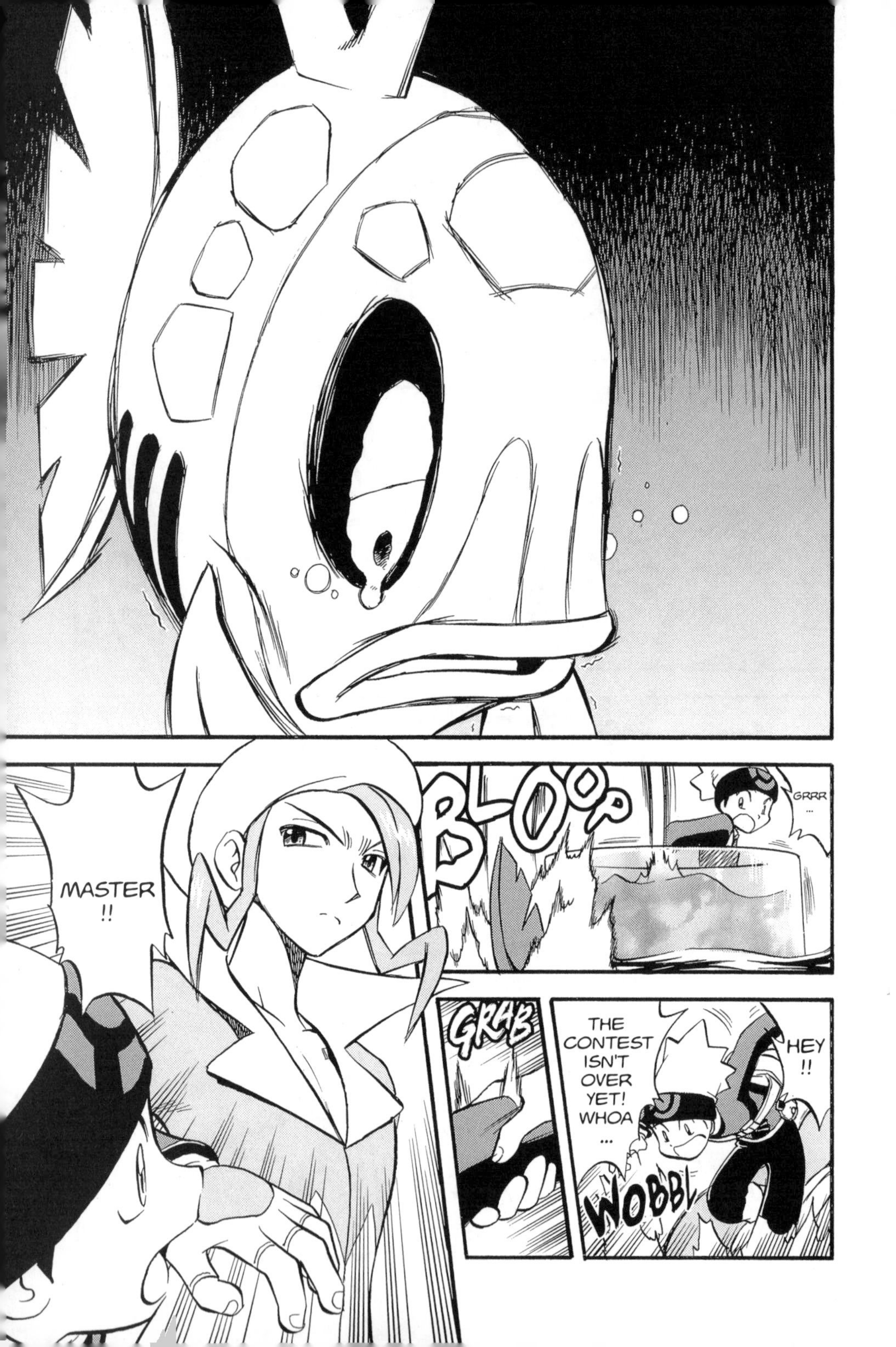
BLOOP
GRRR...
HEY!!
THE CONTEST ISN'T OVER YET! WHOA...
WOBBL
GRAB
MASTER!!

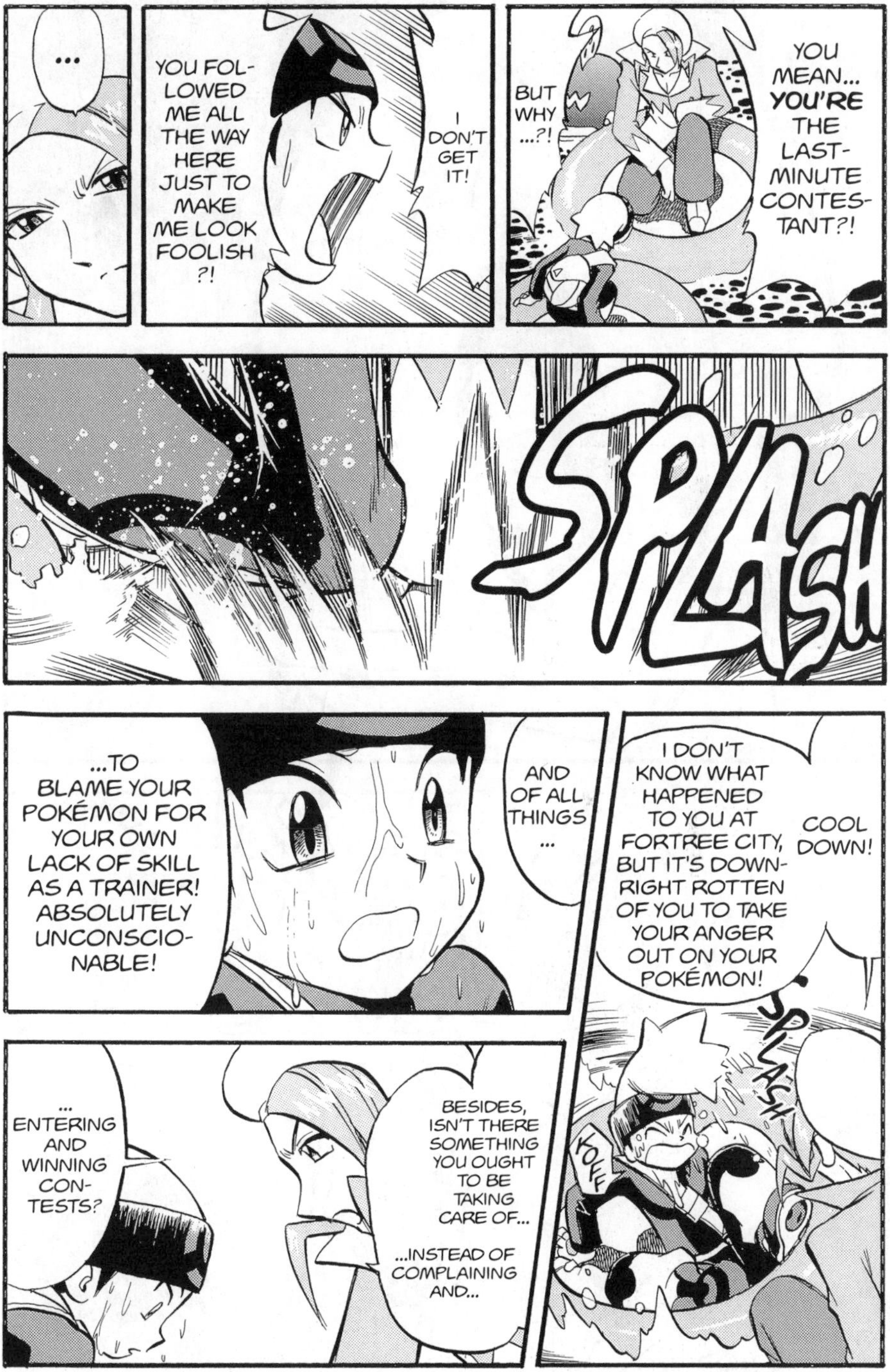
YOU MEAN... YOU'RE THE LAST-MINUTE CONTESTANT?!
BUT WHY ...?!
I DON'T GET IT!
YOU FOLLOWED ME ALL THE WAY HERE JUST TO MAKE ME LOOK FOOLISH ?!
...
SPLASH
COOL DOWN!
I DON'T KNOW WHAT HAPPENED TO YOU AT FORTREE CITY, BUT IT'S DOWNRIGHT ROTTEN OF YOU TO TAKE YOUR ANGER OUT ON YOUR POKÉMON!
SPLASH
KOFF
AND OF ALL THINGS ...
...TO BLAME YOUR POKÉMON FOR YOUR OWN LACK OF SKILL AS A TRAINER! ABSOLUTELY UNCONSCIONABLE!
BESIDES, ISN'T THERE SOMETHING YOU OUGHT TO BE TAKING CARE OF...
...INSTEAD OF COMPLAINING AND...
... ENTERING AND WINNING CONTESTS?

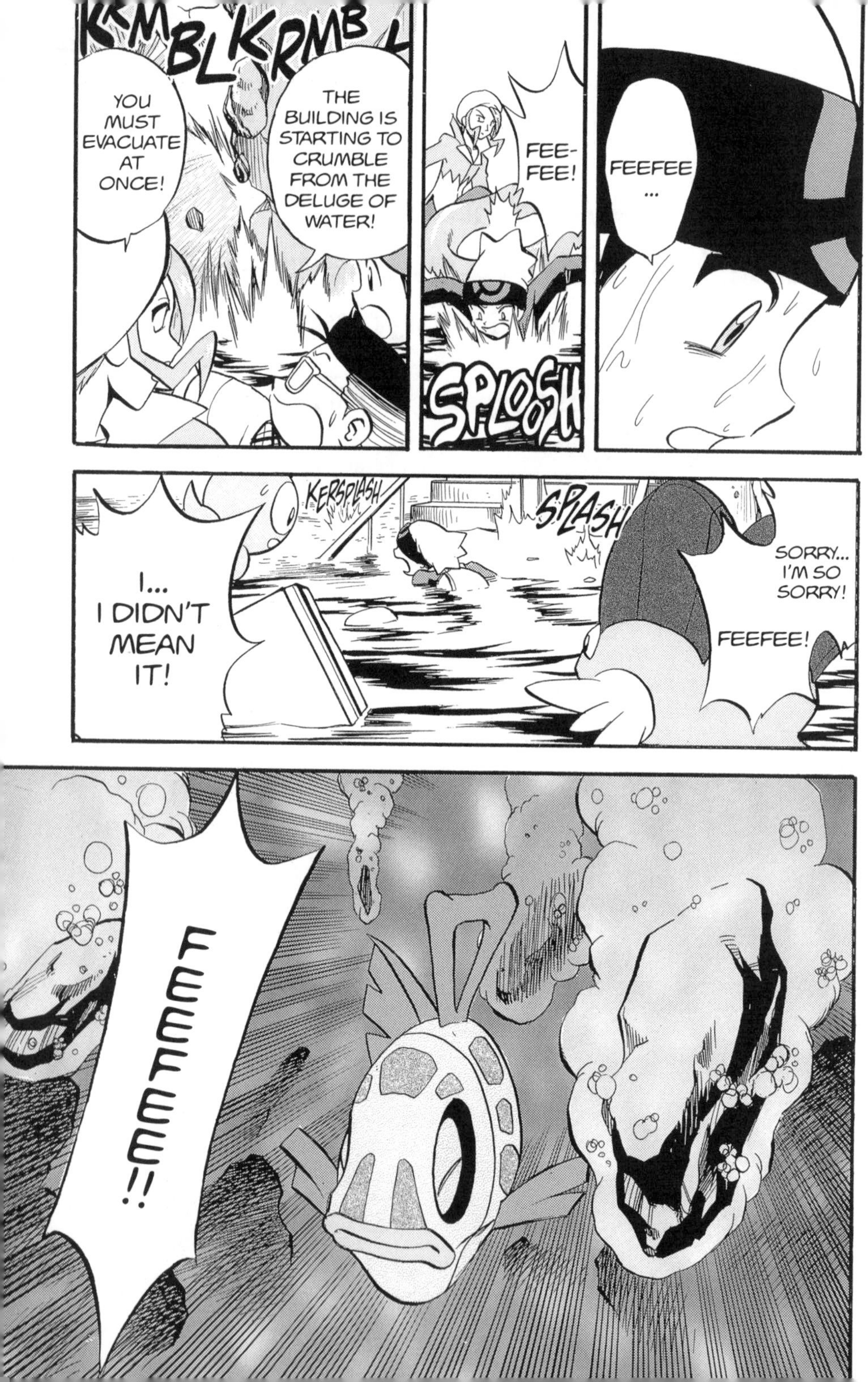
FEEFEE ...
FEE-FEE!
SPLOSH
KRMBL KRMBL
THE BUILDING IS STARTING TO CRUMBLE FROM THE DELUGE OF WATER!
YOU MUST EVACUATE AT ONCE!
SORRY... I'M SO SORRY!
FEEFEE!
SPLASH
KERSPLASH
I... I DIDN'T MEAN IT!
FEEFEE!!

● Adventure 233 ●

The Beginning of the End with Kyogre and Groudon, Part 1

Pokémon Adventures Ruby & Sapphire

The Fourth Chapter

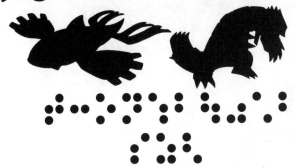

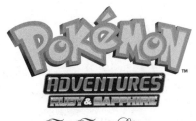

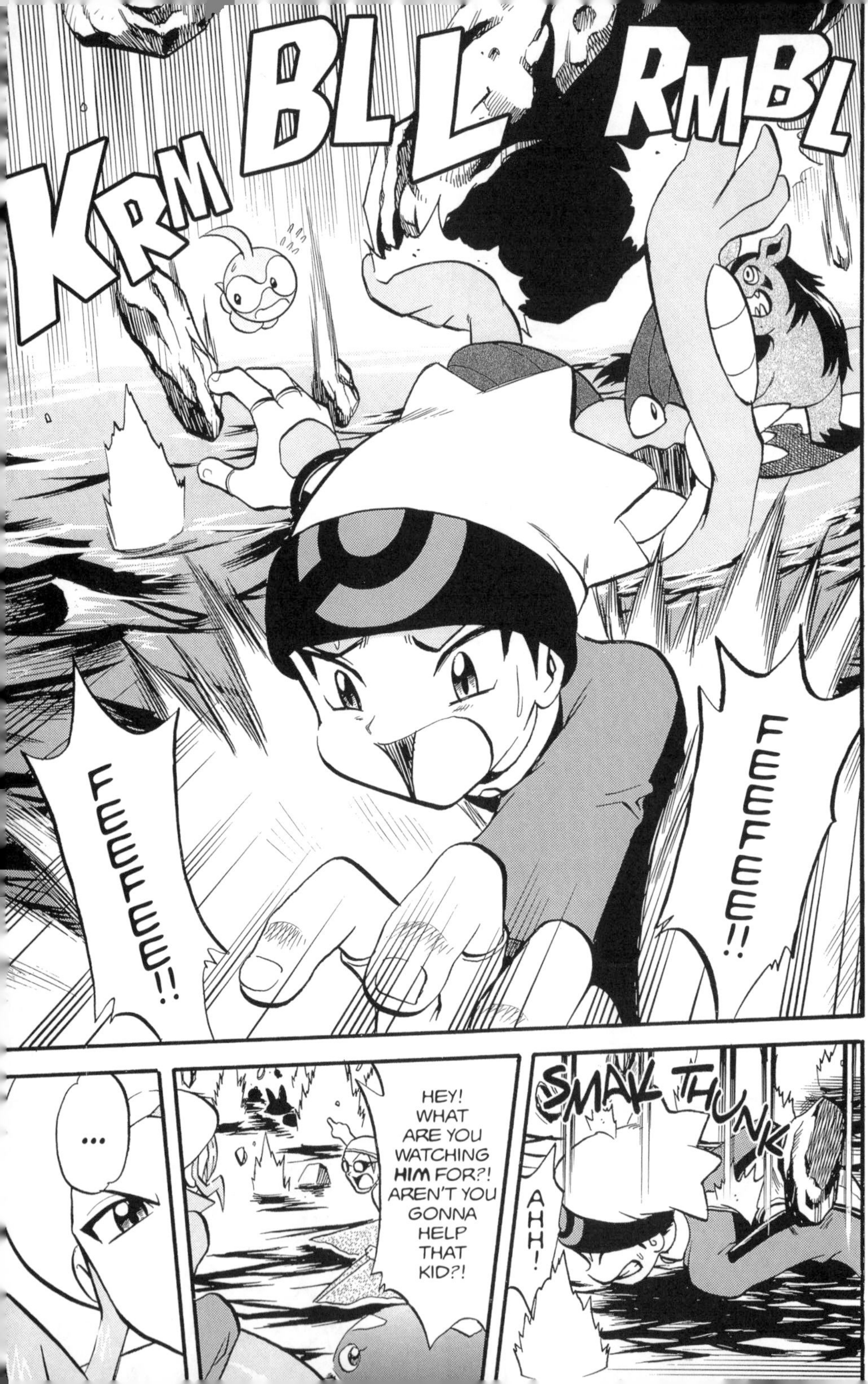
KRMBLL RMBL
FEEFEE!!
FEEFEE!!
SMAK THUNK
AHH!
HEY! WHAT ARE YOU WATCHING **HIM** FOR?! AREN'T YOU GONNA HELP THAT KID?!
...

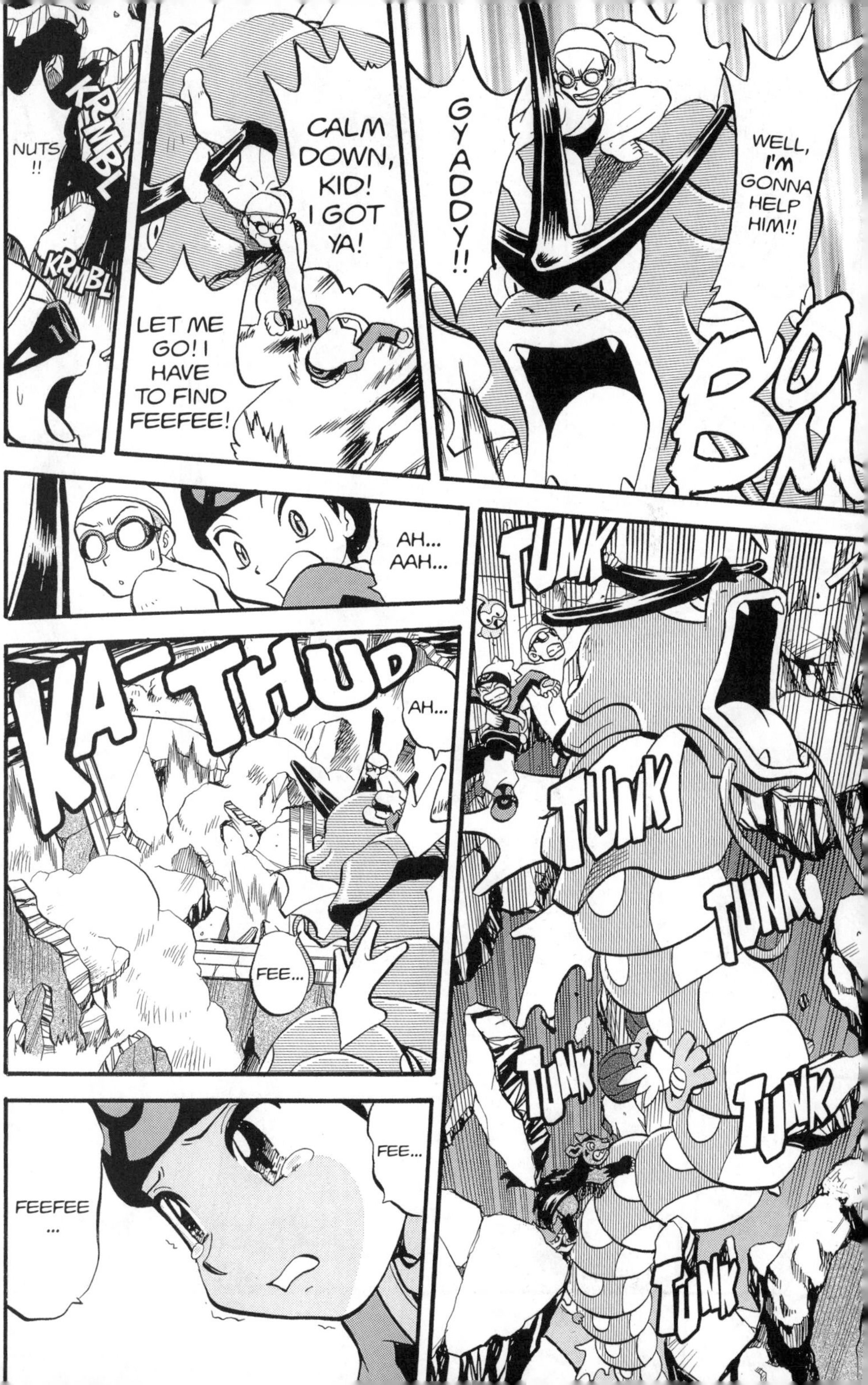
WELL, I'M GONNA HELP HIM!!
GYADDY!!
CALM DOWN, KID! I GOT YA!
LET ME GO!! I HAVE TO FIND FEEFEE!
NUTS!!
KRMBL
KRMBL
TUNK
TUNK
TUNK
TUNK
TUNK
TUNK
AH... AAH...
KA-THUD
AH...
FEE...
FEE...
FEEFEE ...

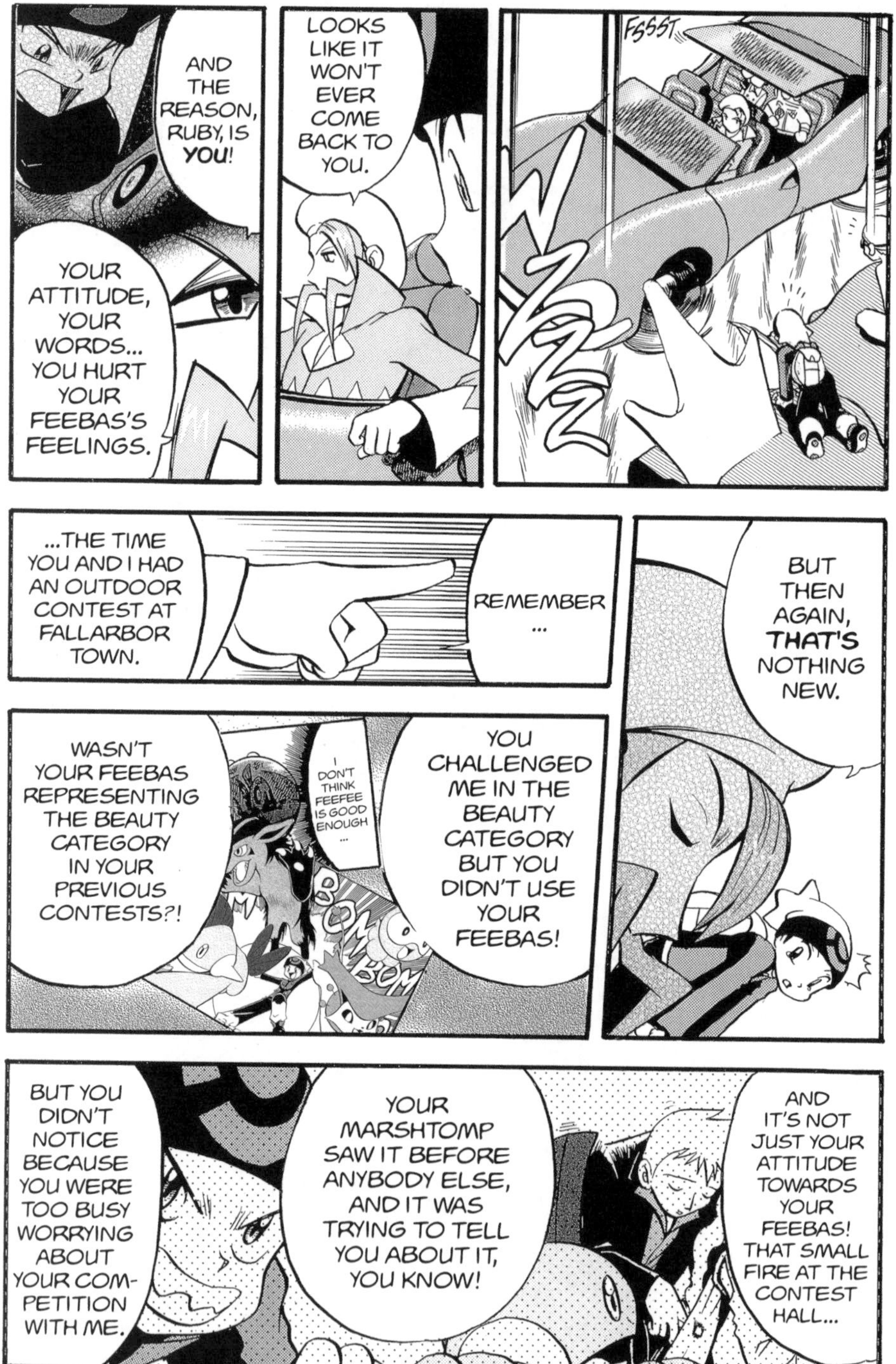
FSSST
LOOKS LIKE IT WON'T EVER COME BACK TO YOU.
AND THE REASON, RUBY, IS **YOU**!
YOUR ATTITUDE, YOUR WORDS... YOU HURT YOUR FEEBAS'S FEELINGS.
BUT THEN AGAIN, **THAT'S** NOTHING NEW.
REMEMBER...
...THE TIME YOU AND I HAD AN OUTDOOR CONTEST AT FALLARBOR TOWN.
YOU CHALLENGED ME IN THE BEAUTY CATEGORY BUT YOU DIDN'T USE YOUR FEEBAS!
I DON'T THINK FEEFEE IS GOOD ENOUGH...
WASN'T YOUR FEEBAS REPRESENTING THE BEAUTY CATEGORY IN YOUR PREVIOUS CONTESTS?!
AND IT'S NOT JUST YOUR ATTITUDE TOWARDS YOUR FEEBAS! THAT SMALL FIRE AT THE CONTEST HALL...
YOUR MARSHTOMP SAW IT BEFORE ANYBODY ELSE, AND IT WAS TRYING TO TELL YOU ABOUT IT, YOU KNOW!
BUT YOU DIDN'T NOTICE BECAUSE YOU WERE TOO BUSY WORRYING ABOUT YOUR COM-PETITION WITH ME.

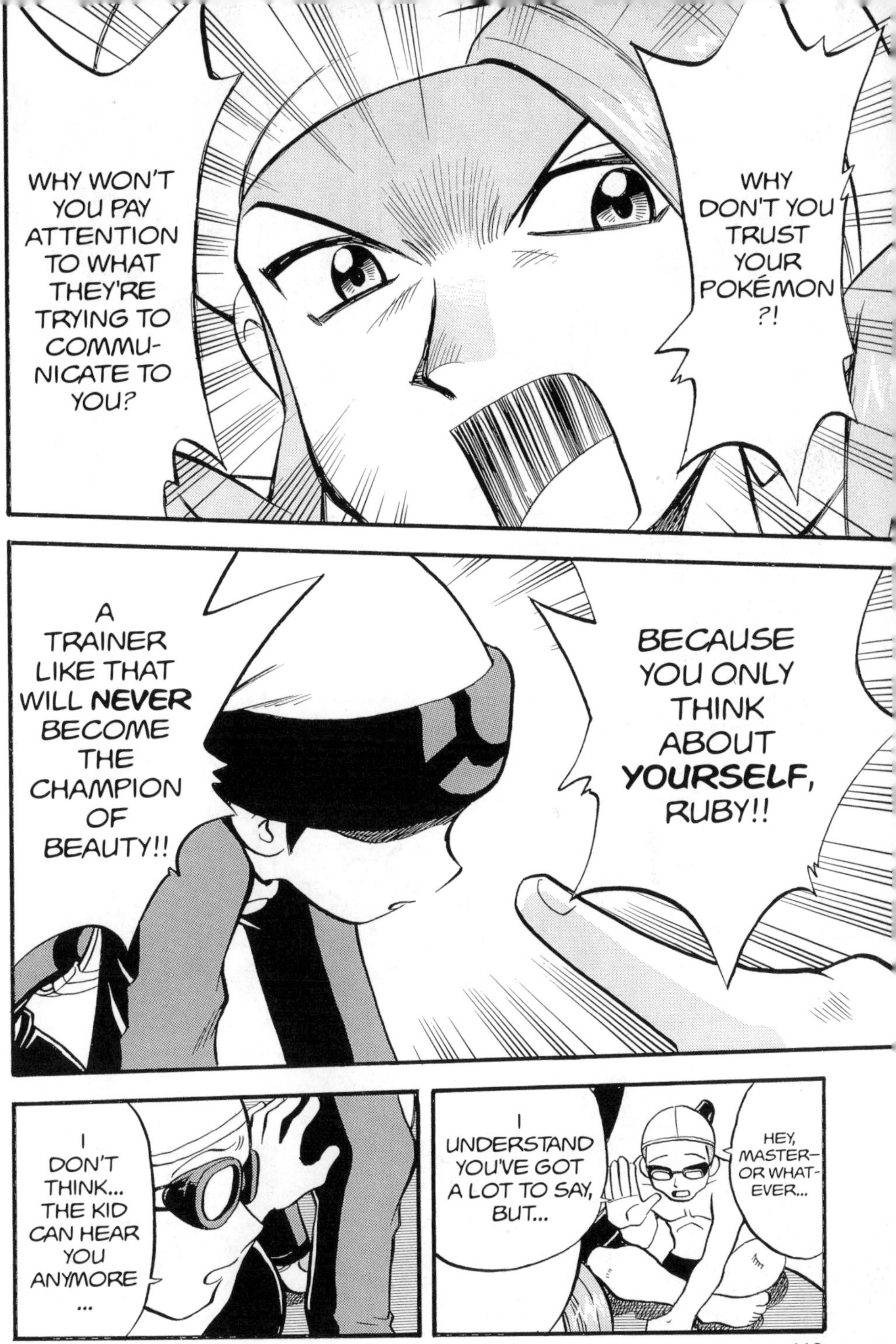
WHY DON'T YOU TRUST YOUR POKÉMON ?!
WHY WON'T YOU PAY ATTENTION TO WHAT THEY'RE TRYING TO COMMUNICATE TO YOU?
BECAUSE YOU ONLY THINK ABOUT **YOURSELF**, RUBY!!
A TRAINER LIKE THAT WILL **NEVER** BECOME THE CHAMPION OF BEAUTY!!
HEY, MASTER— OR WHATEVER...
I UNDERSTAND YOU'VE GOT A LOT TO SAY, BUT...
I DON'T THINK... THE KID CAN HEAR YOU ANYMORE ...

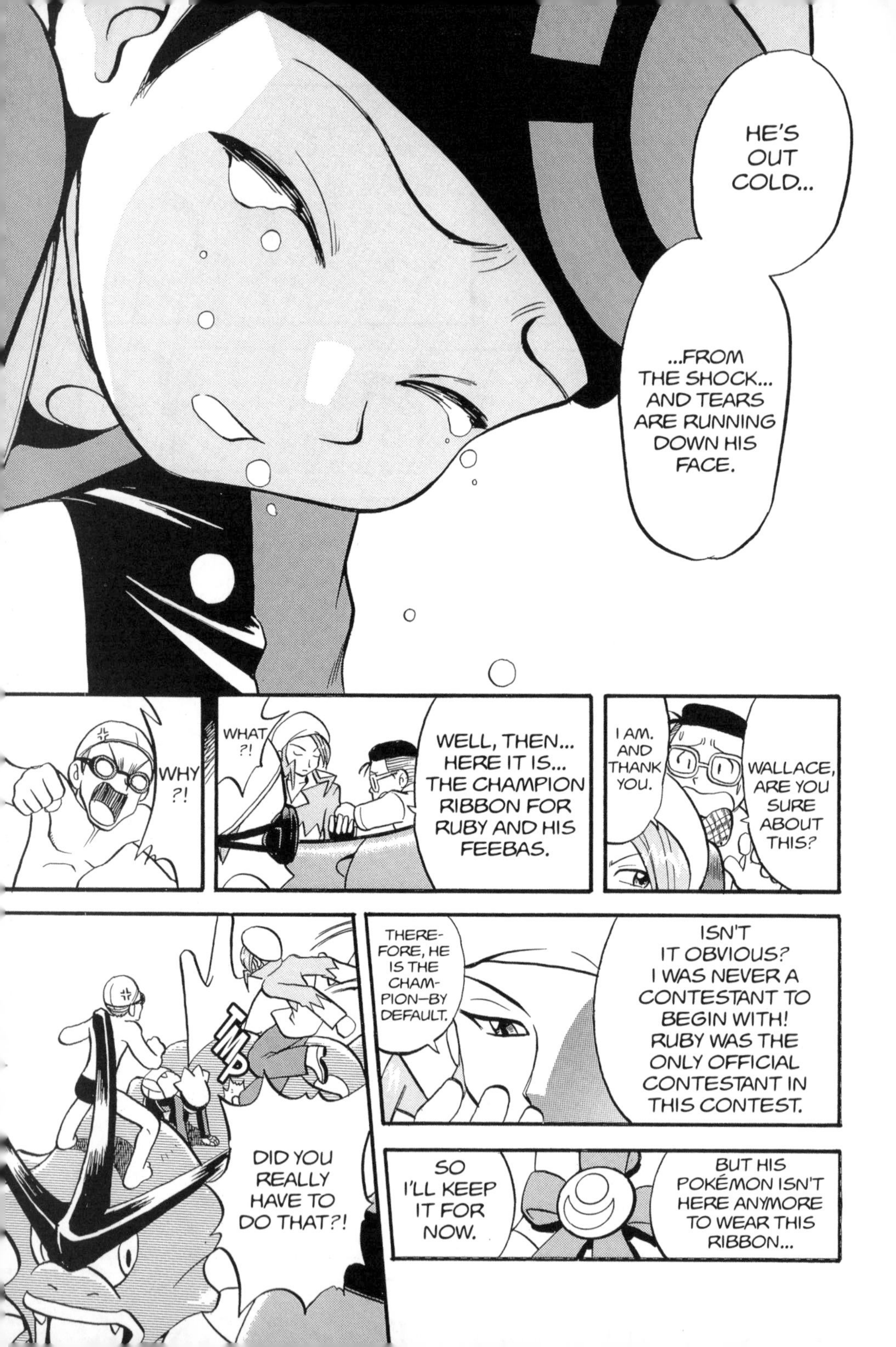
HE'S OUT COLD...
...FROM THE SHOCK... AND TEARS ARE RUNNING DOWN HIS FACE.
WALLACE, ARE YOU SURE ABOUT THIS?
I AM. AND THANK YOU.
WELL, THEN... HERE IT IS... THE CHAMPION RIBBON FOR RUBY AND HIS FEEBAS.
WHAT?!
WHY?!
ISN'T IT OBVIOUS? I WAS NEVER A CONTESTANT TO BEGIN WITH! RUBY WAS THE ONLY OFFICIAL CONTESTANT IN THIS CONTEST.
THEREFORE, HE IS THE CHAMPION—BY DEFAULT.
BUT HIS POKÉMON ISN'T HERE ANYMORE TO WEAR THIS RIBBON...
SO I'LL KEEP IT FOR NOW.
TMP
DID YOU REALLY HAVE TO DO THAT?!

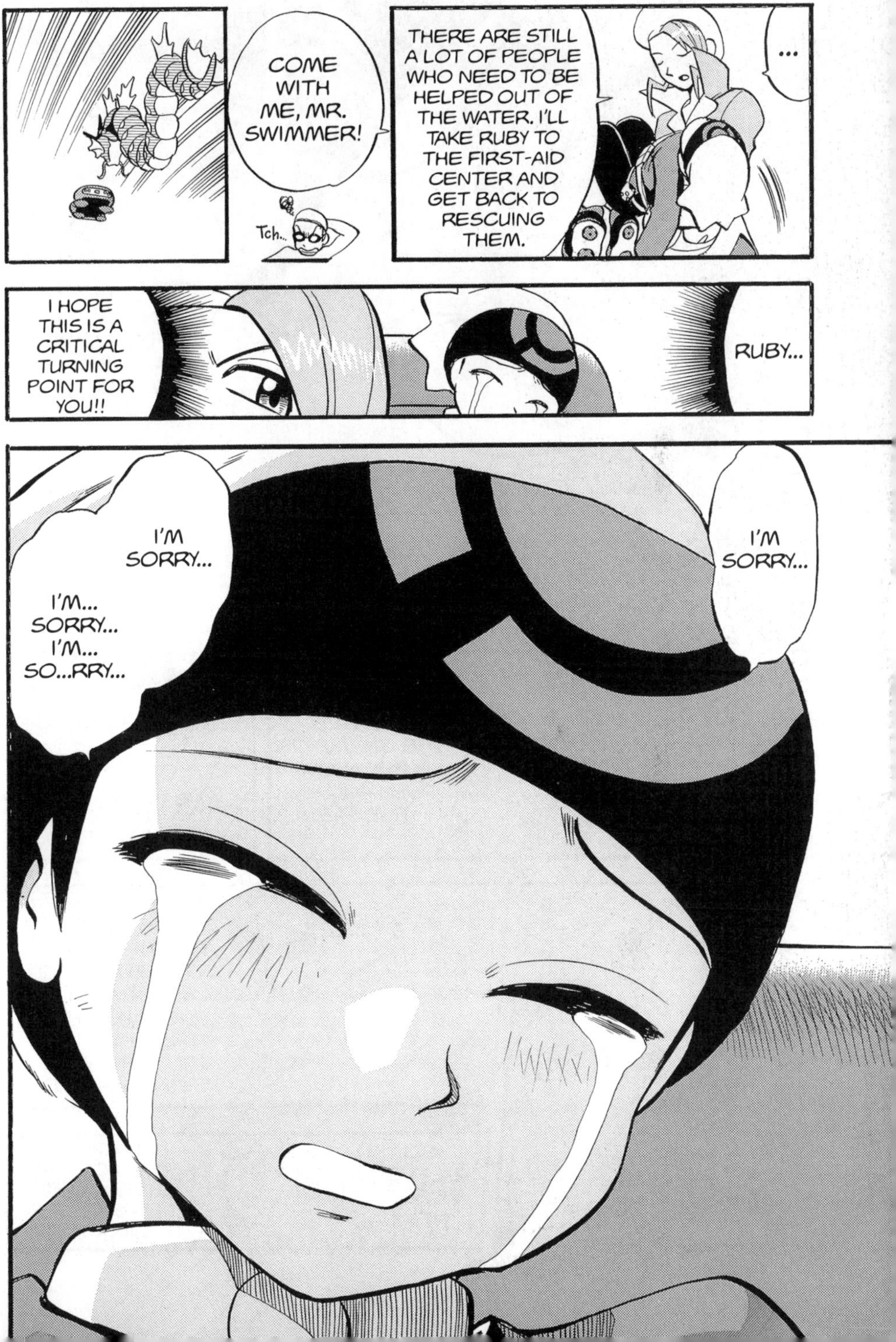
...
THERE ARE STILL A LOT OF PEOPLE WHO NEED TO BE HELPED OUT OF THE WATER. I'LL TAKE RUBY TO THE FIRST-AID CENTER AND GET BACK TO RESCUING THEM.
COME WITH ME, MR. SWIMMER!
Tch...
RUBY...
I HOPE THIS IS A CRITICAL TURNING POINT FOR YOU!!
I'M SORRY...
I'M SORRY...
I'M... SORRY... I'M... SO...RRY...

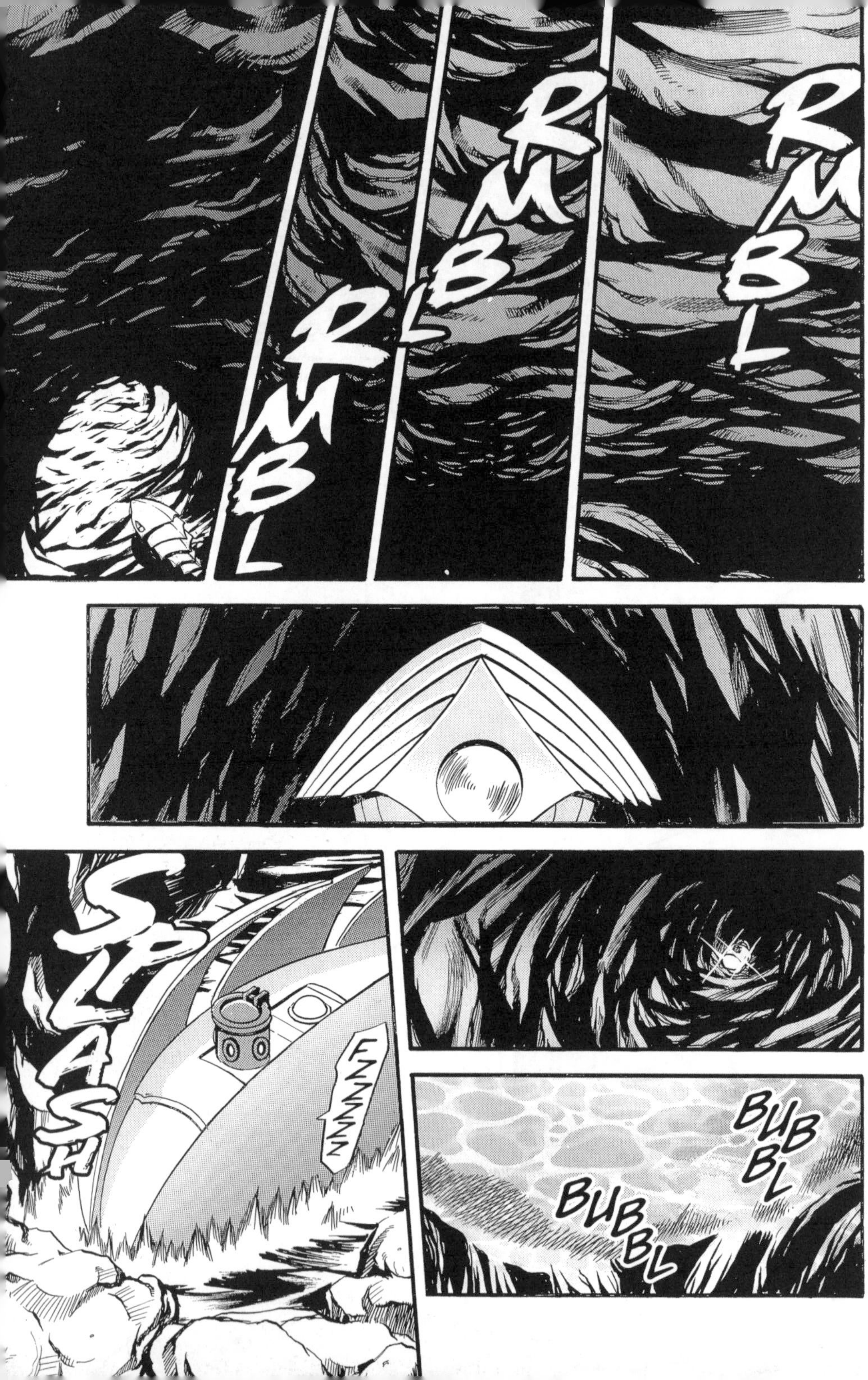
RMBL
RMBL
RMBL
BUBBL
BUBBL
SPLASH
FZZZZZZ

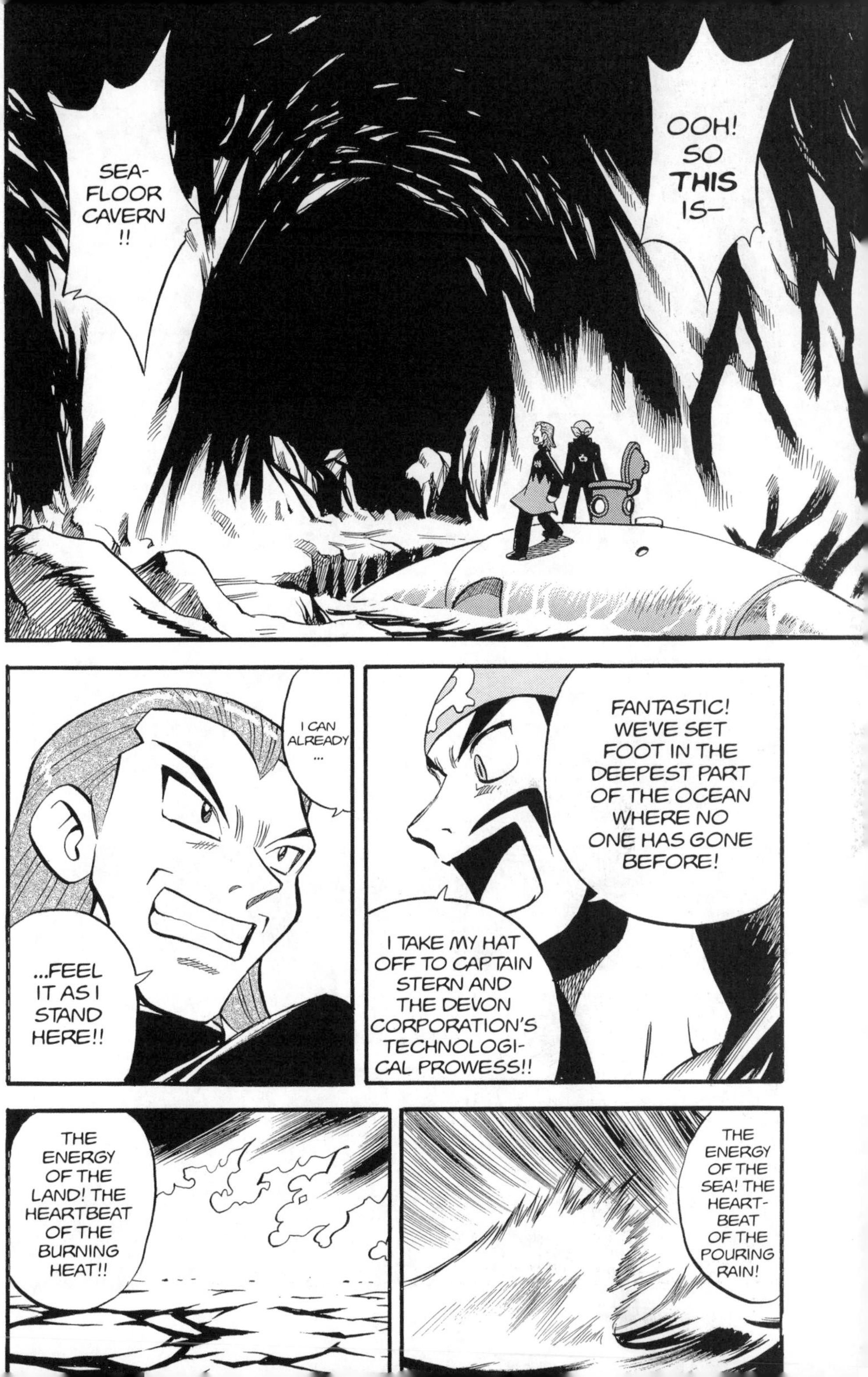
OOH! SO THIS IS—
SEA-FLOOR CAVERN!!
FANTASTIC! WE'VE SET FOOT IN THE DEEPEST PART OF THE OCEAN WHERE NO ONE HAS GONE BEFORE!
I TAKE MY HAT OFF TO CAPTAIN STERN AND THE DEVON CORPORATION'S TECHNOLOGICAL PROWESS!!
I CAN ALREADY ...
...FEEL IT AS I STAND HERE!!
THE ENERGY OF THE SEA! THE HEART-BEAT OF THE POURING RAIN!
THE ENERGY OF THE LAND! THE HEARTBEAT OF THE BURNING HEAT!!

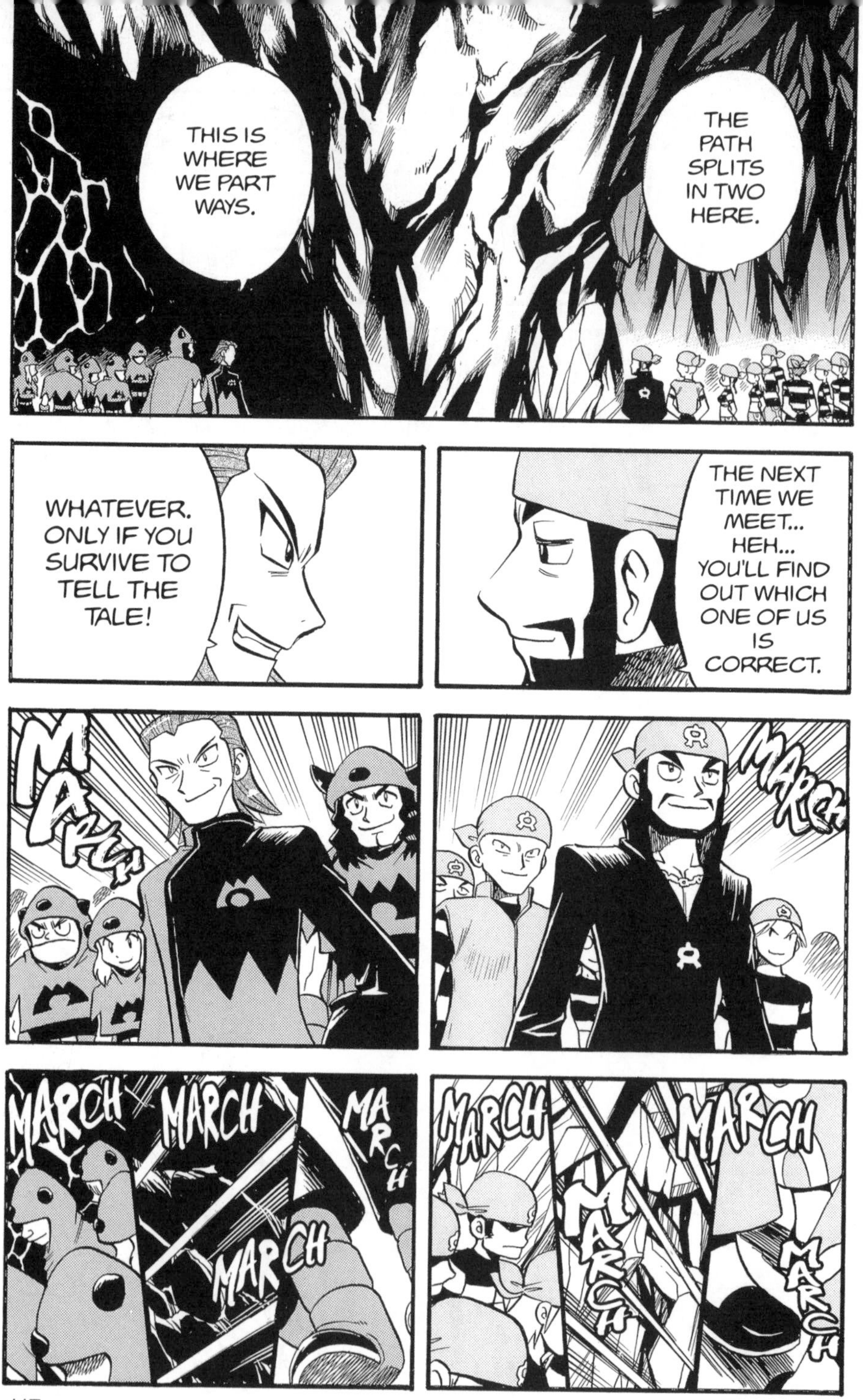
THE PATH SPLITS IN TWO HERE.
THIS IS WHERE WE PART WAYS.
THE NEXT TIME WE MEET... HEH... YOU'LL FIND OUT WHICH ONE OF US IS CORRECT.
WHATEVER. ONLY IF YOU SURVIVE TO TELL THE TALE!
MARCH
MARCH
MARCH
MARCH
MARCH
MARCH
MARCH
MARCH
MARCH
MARCH

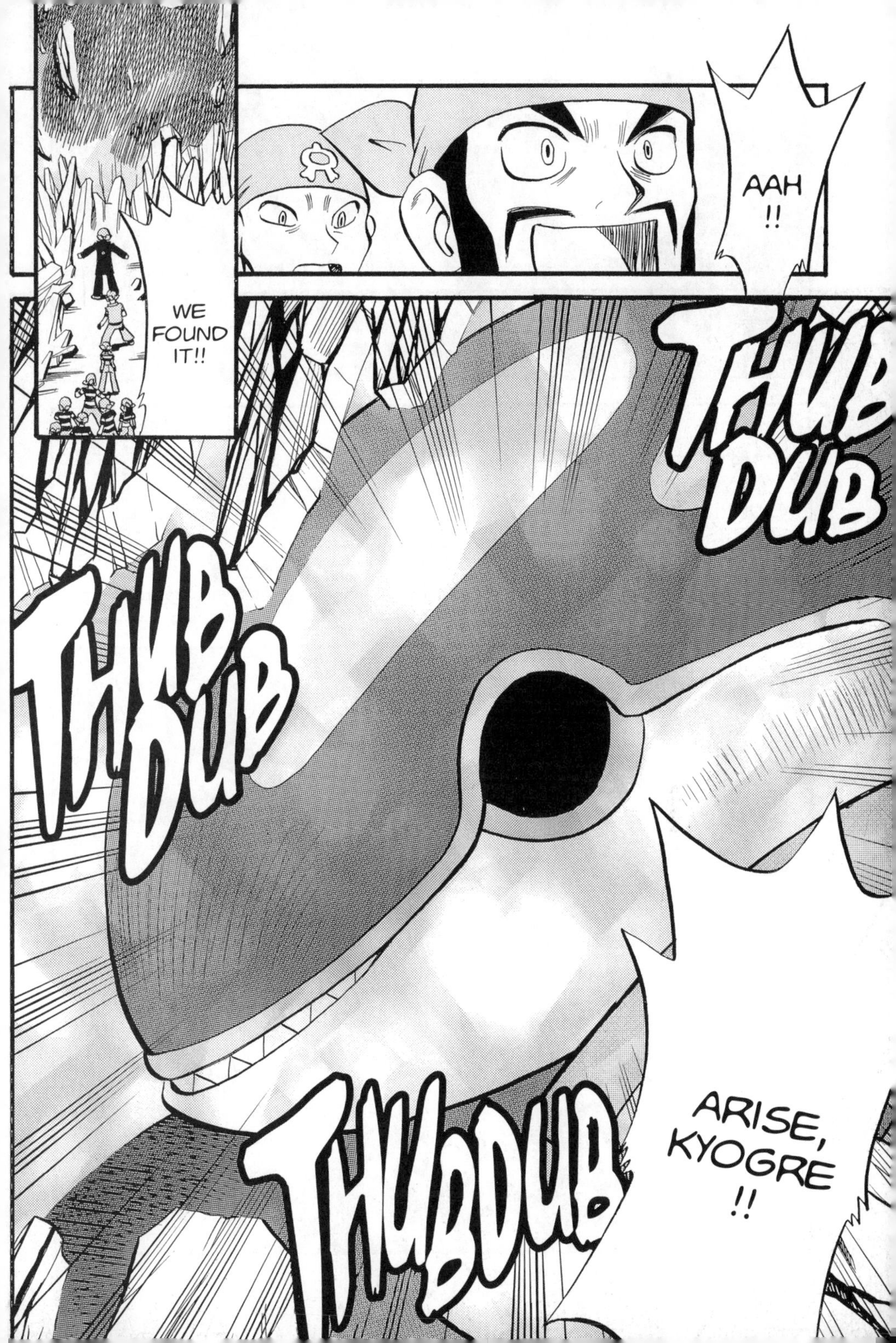
AAH!!
WE FOUND IT!!
THUB DUB
THUB DUB
ARISE, KYOGRE!!
THUBDUB

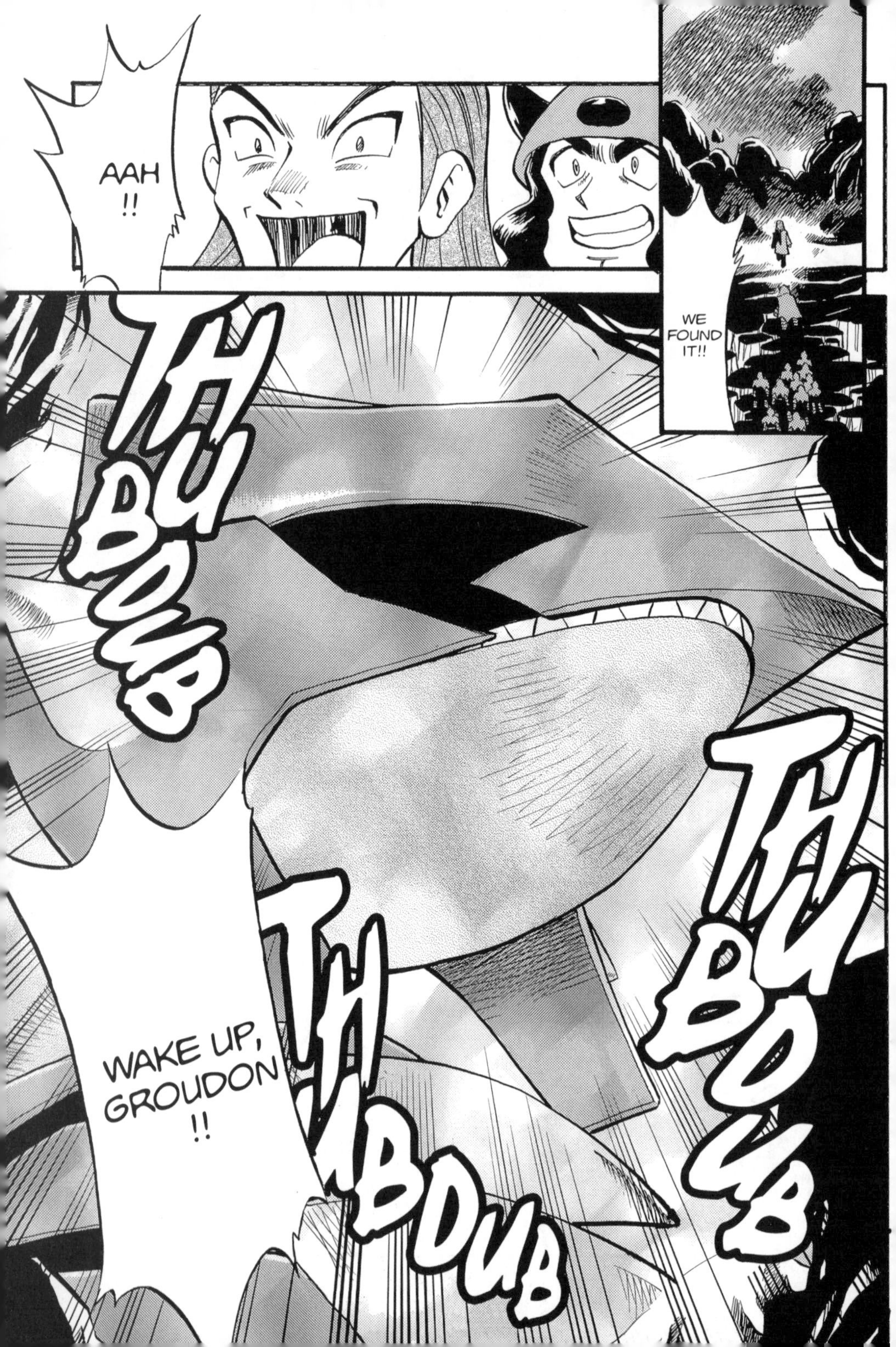
WE FOUND IT!!
AAH!!
THUBOUB
THUBOUB
WAKE UP, GROUDON!!
THUBOUB

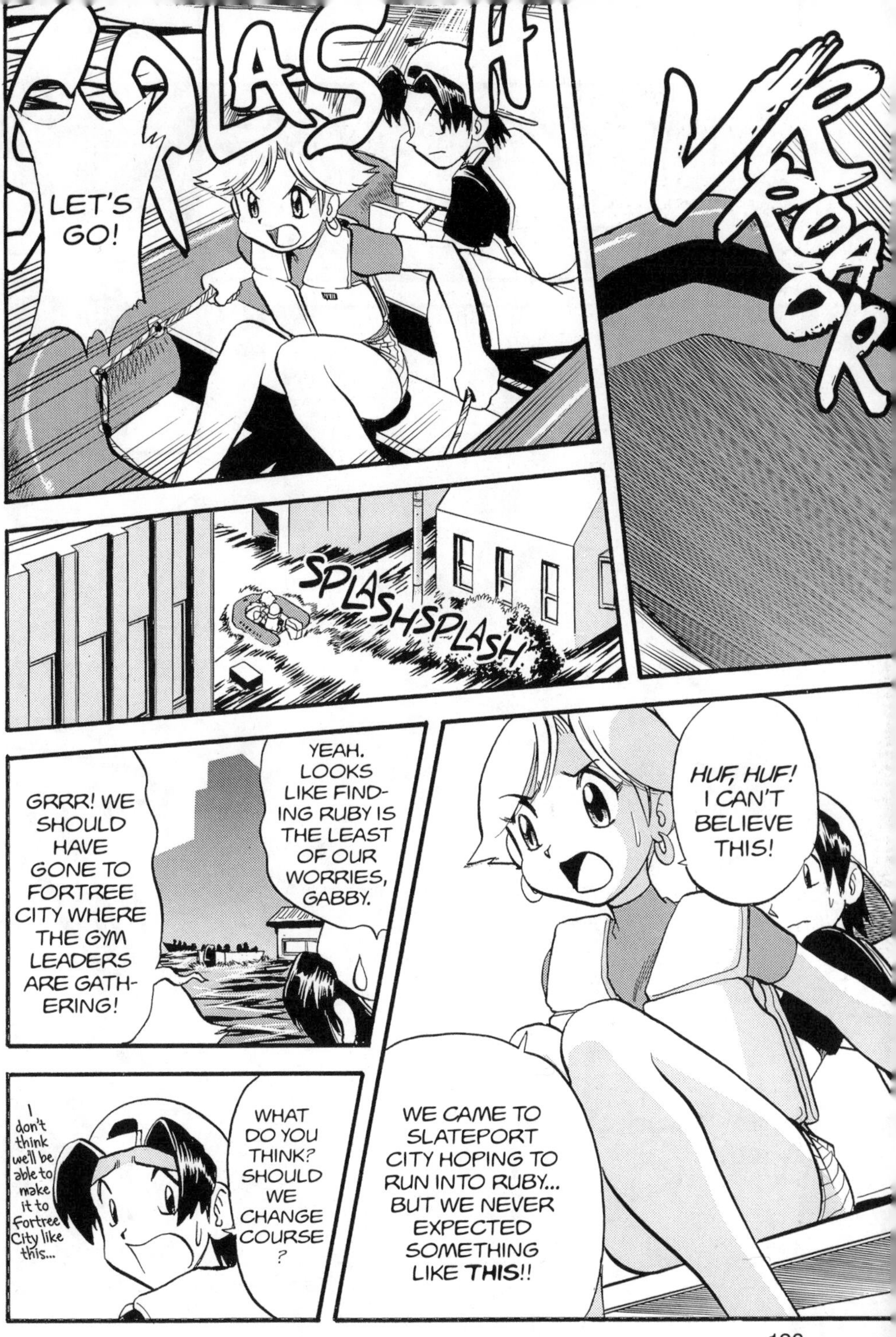
SPLASH
LET'S GO!
SPLASHSPLASH
HUF, HUF! I CAN'T BELIEVE THIS!
WE CAME TO SLATEPORT CITY HOPING TO RUN INTO RUBY... BUT WE NEVER EXPECTED SOMETHING LIKE **THIS**!!
YEAH. LOOKS LIKE FINDING RUBY IS THE LEAST OF OUR WORRIES, GABBY.
GRRR! WE SHOULD HAVE GONE TO FORTREE CITY WHERE THE GYM LEADERS ARE GATHERING!
WHAT DO YOU THINK? SHOULD WE CHANGE COURSE?
I don't think we'll be able to make it to Fortree City like this...

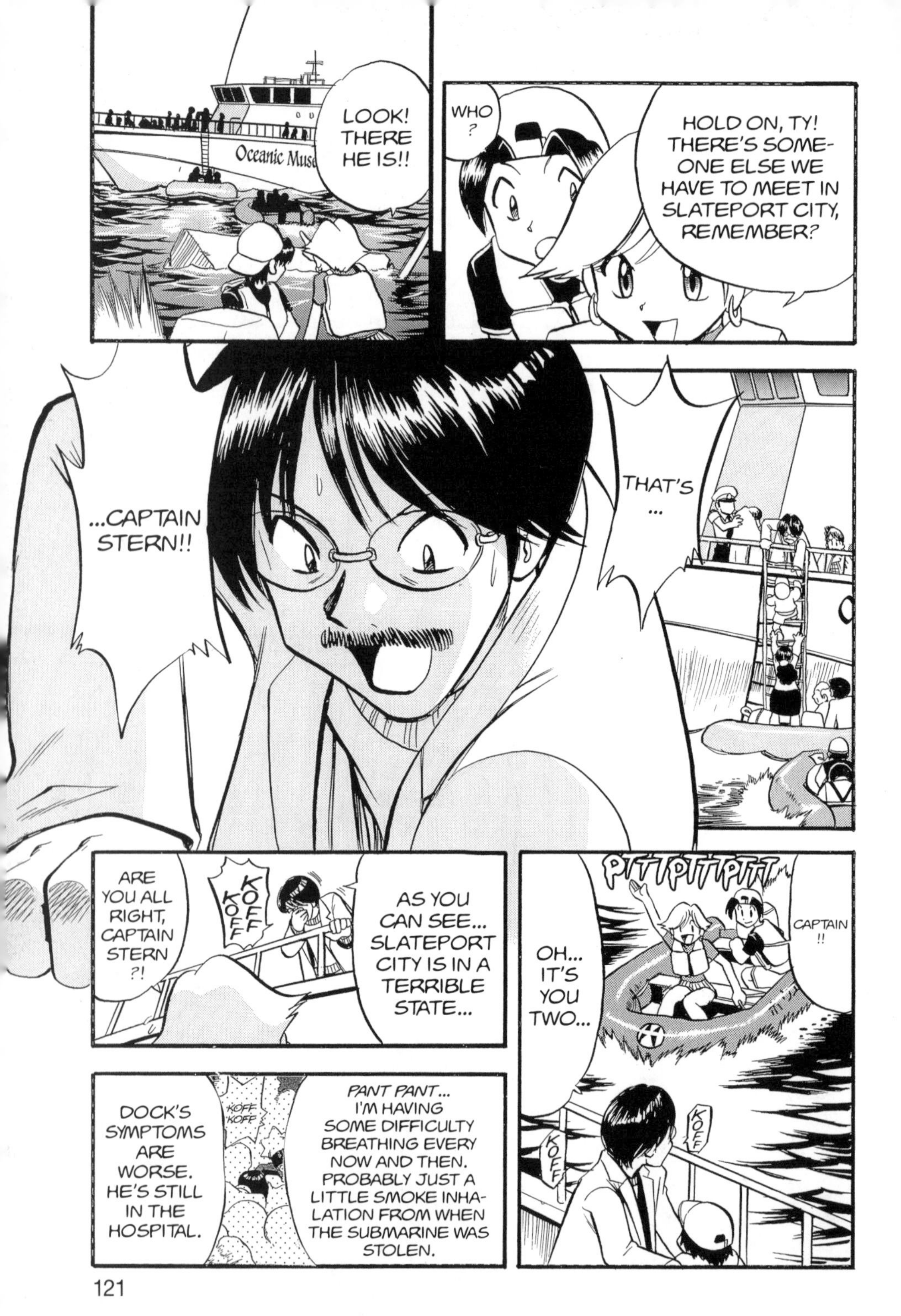
HOLD ON, TY! THERE'S SOME-ONE ELSE WE HAVE TO MEET IN SLATEPORT CITY, REMEMBER?
WHO ?
LOOK! THERE HE IS!!
Oceanic Muse
THAT'S ...
...CAPTAIN STERN!!
PTTTPTTTPTTT
CAPTAIN !!
OH... IT'S YOU TWO...
KOFF
KOFF
AS YOU CAN SEE... SLATEPORT CITY IS IN A TERRIBLE STATE...
KOFF KOFF
ARE YOU ALL RIGHT, CAPTAIN STERN ?!
PANT PANT... I'M HAVING SOME DIFFICULTY BREATHING EVERY NOW AND THEN. PROBABLY JUST A LITTLE SMOKE INHA-LATION FROM WHEN THE SUBMARINE WAS STOLEN.
KOFF KOFF
DOCK'S SYMPTOMS ARE WORSE. HE'S STILL IN THE HOSPITAL.

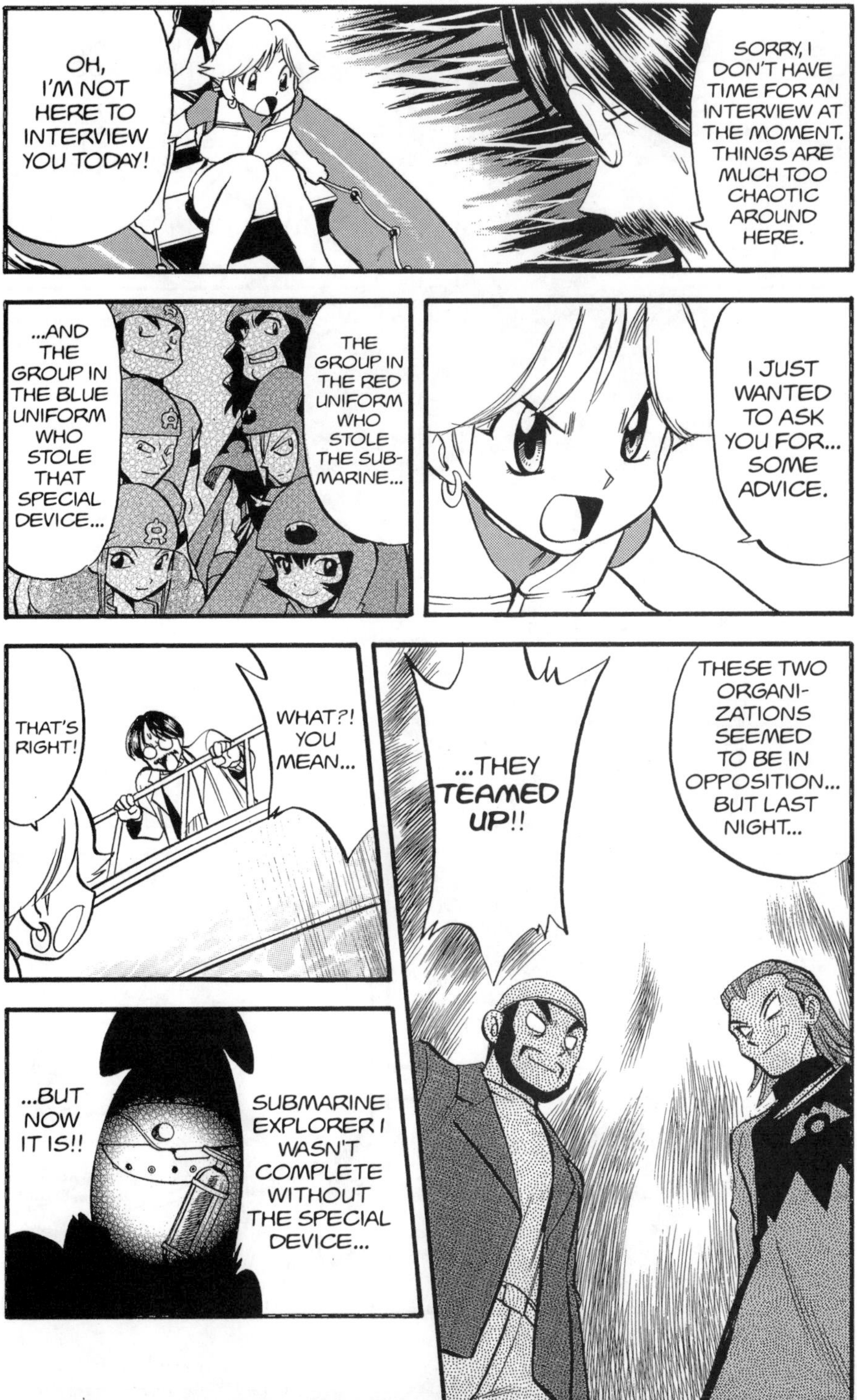
SORRY, I DON'T HAVE TIME FOR AN INTERVIEW AT THE MOMENT. THINGS ARE MUCH TOO CHAOTIC AROUND HERE.
OH, I'M NOT HERE TO INTERVIEW YOU TODAY!
I JUST WANTED TO ASK YOU FOR... SOME ADVICE.
THE GROUP IN THE RED UNIFORM WHO STOLE THE SUB-MARINE...
...AND THE GROUP IN THE BLUE UNIFORM WHO STOLE THAT SPECIAL DEVICE...
THESE TWO ORGANI-ZATIONS SEEMED TO BE IN OPPOSITION... BUT LAST NIGHT...
...THEY **TEAMED UP**!!
WHAT?! YOU MEAN...
THAT'S RIGHT!
SUBMARINE EXPLORER 1 WASN'T COMPLETE WITHOUT THE SPECIAL DEVICE...
...BUT NOW IT IS!!

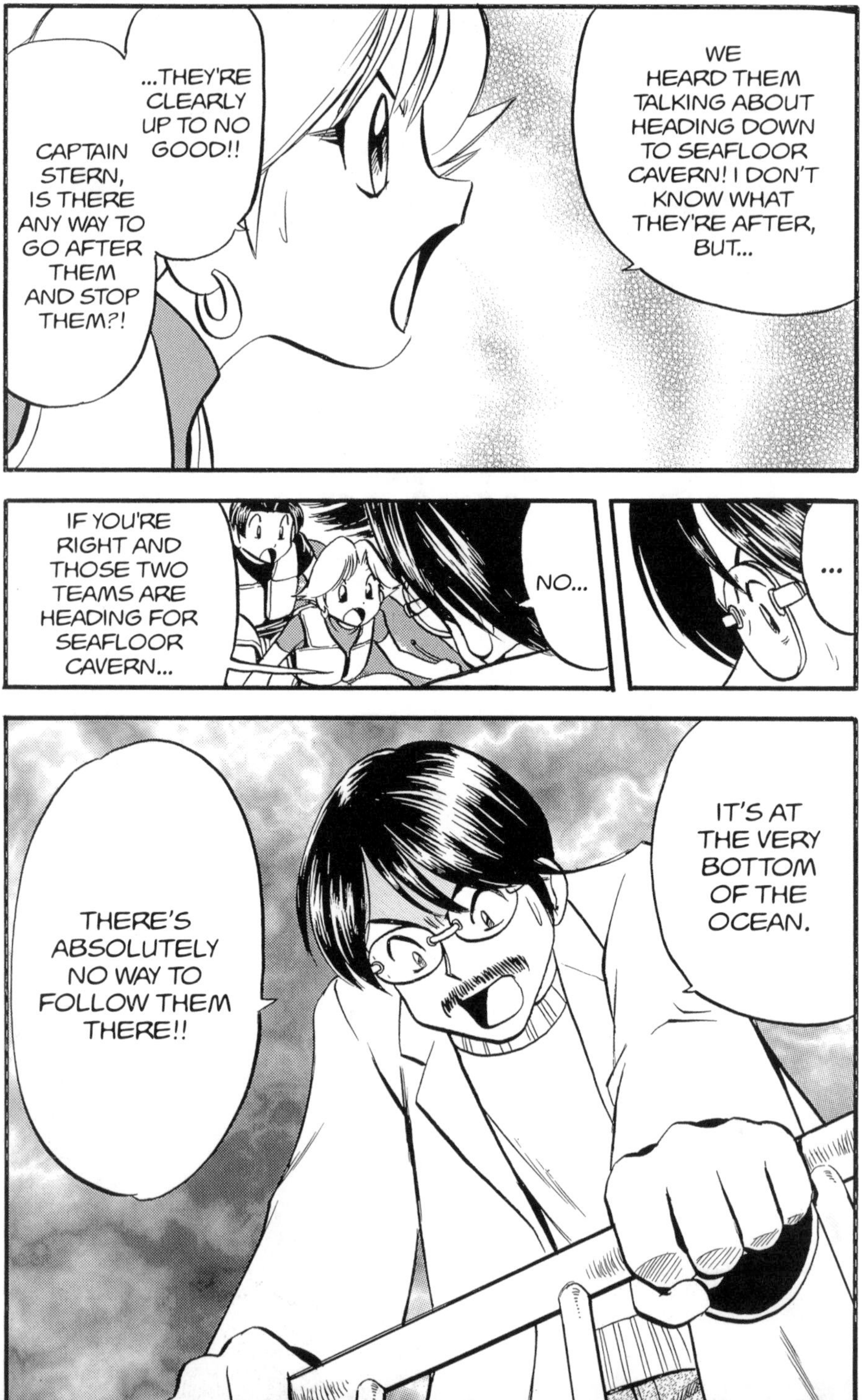
WE HEARD THEM TALKING ABOUT HEADING DOWN TO SEAFLOOR CAVERN! I DON'T KNOW WHAT THEY'RE AFTER, BUT...
...THEY'RE CLEARLY UP TO NO GOOD!!
CAPTAIN STERN, IS THERE ANY WAY TO GO AFTER THEM AND STOP THEM?!
...
NO...
IF YOU'RE RIGHT AND THOSE TWO TEAMS ARE HEADING FOR SEAFLOOR CAVERN...
IT'S AT THE VERY BOTTOM OF THE OCEAN.
THERE'S ABSOLUTELY NO WAY TO FOLLOW THEM THERE!!

● Adventure 234 ●
The Beginning of the End with Kyogre and Groudon, Part 2

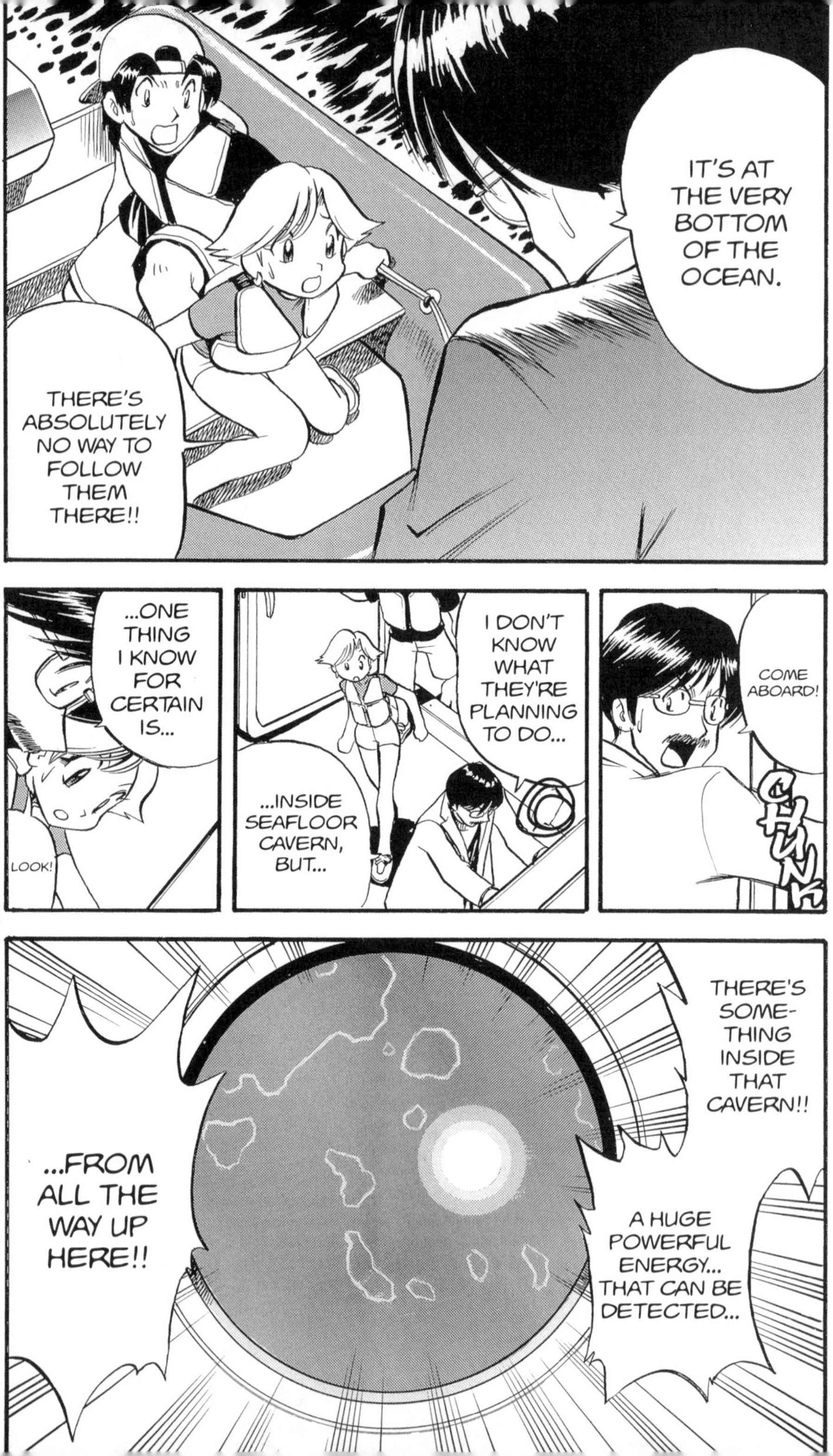
IT'S AT THE VERY BOTTOM OF THE OCEAN.
THERE'S ABSOLUTELY NO WAY TO FOLLOW THEM THERE!!
COME ABOARD!
CHUNK
I DON'T KNOW WHAT THEY'RE PLANNING TO DO...
...INSIDE SEAFLOOR CAVERN, BUT...
...ONE THING I KNOW FOR CERTAIN IS...
LOOK!
THERE'S SOME-THING INSIDE THAT CAVERN!!
A HUGE POWERFUL ENERGY... THAT CAN BE DETECTED...
...FROM ALL THE WAY UP HERE!!

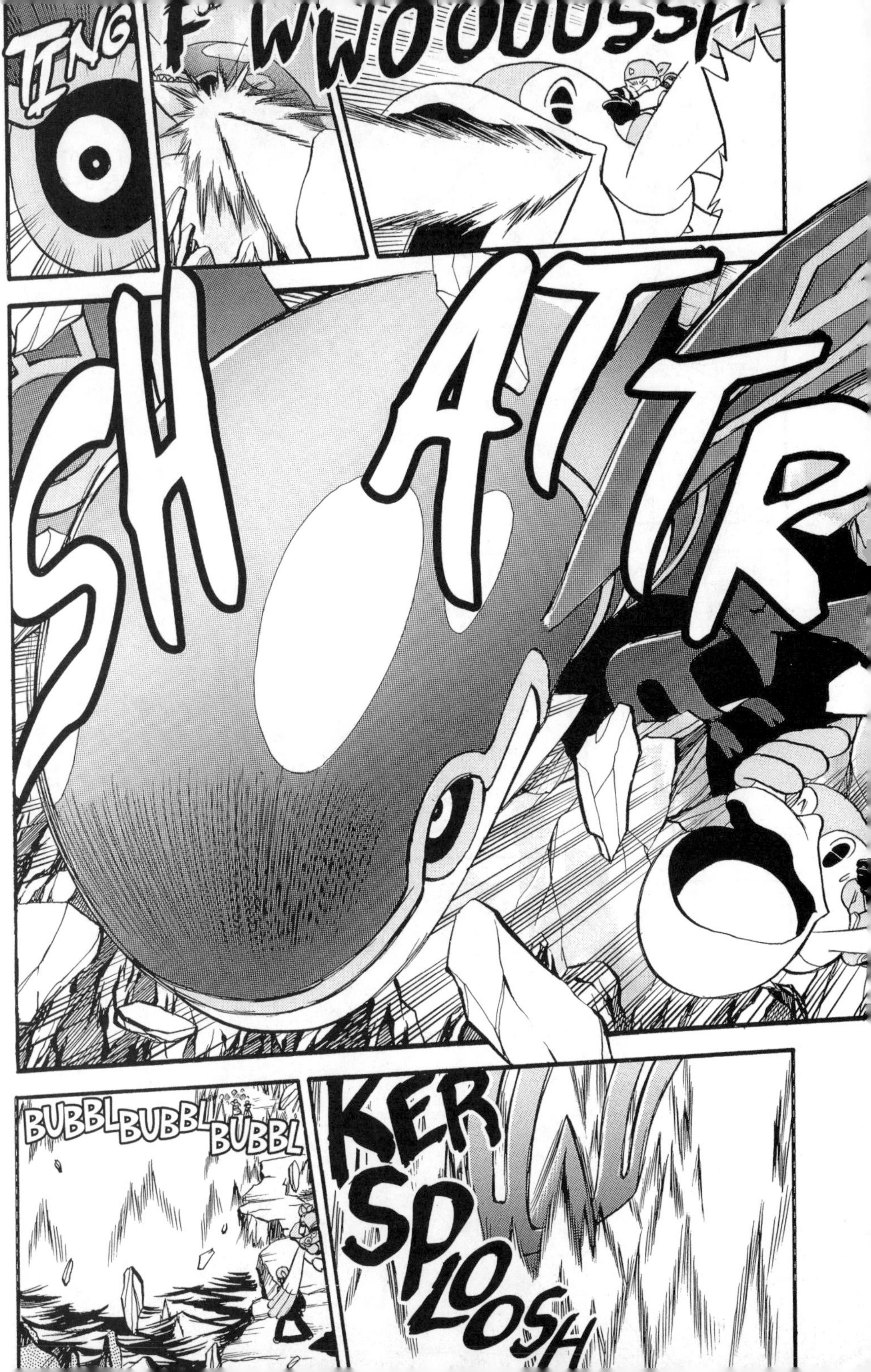
FWWOOUUSSH
TING
SHATTR
KER
SPLOOSH
BUBBL BUBBL BUBBL

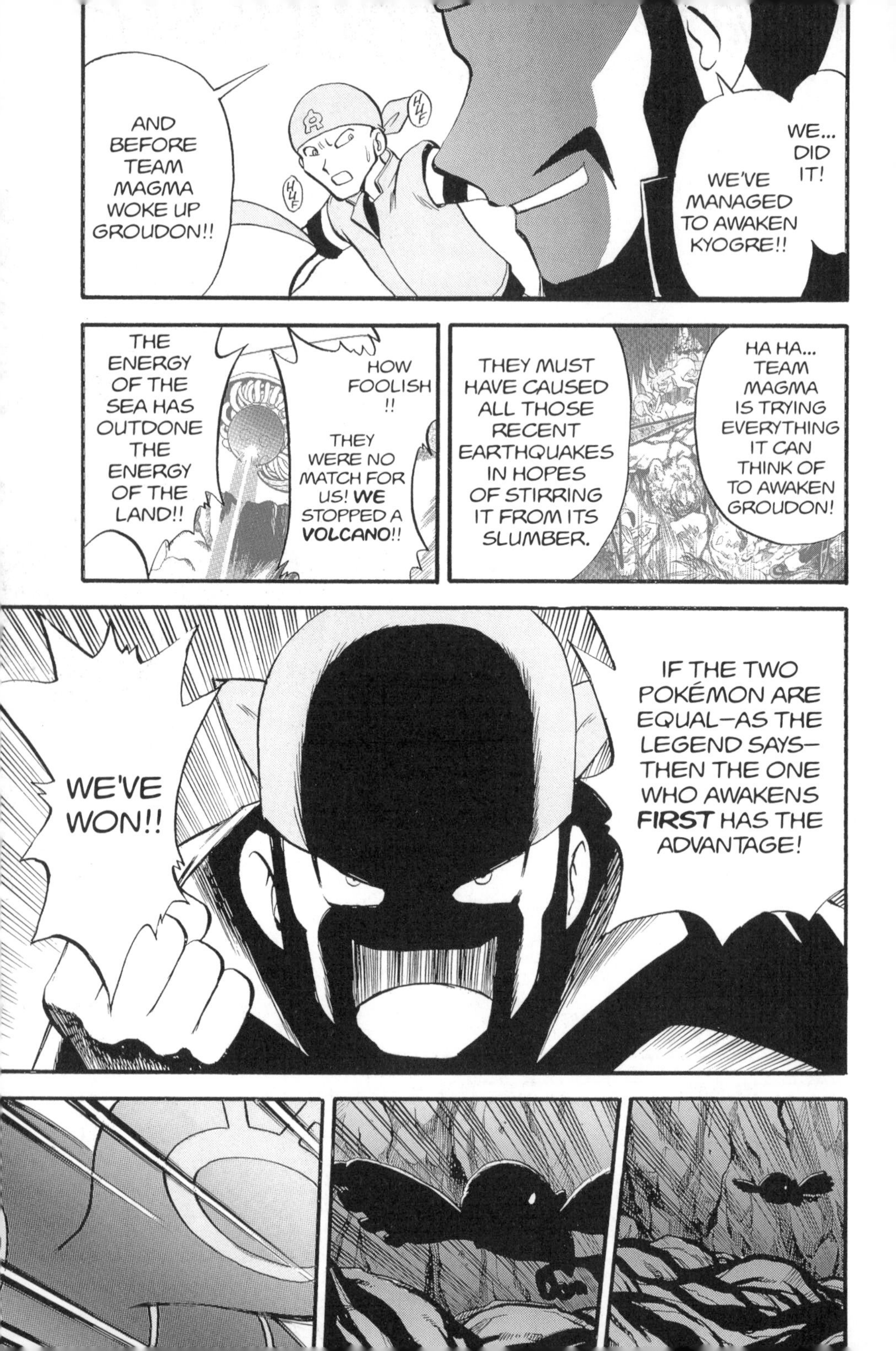
WE... DID IT!
WE'VE MANAGED TO AWAKEN KYOGRE!!
HUF
HUF
AND BEFORE TEAM MAGMA WOKE UP GROUDON!!
HA HA... TEAM MAGMA IS TRYING EVERYTHING IT CAN THINK OF TO AWAKEN GROUDON!
THEY MUST HAVE CAUSED ALL THOSE RECENT EARTHQUAKES IN HOPES OF STIRRING IT FROM ITS SLUMBER.
HOW FOOLISH!!
THEY WERE NO MATCH FOR US! **WE** STOPPED A **VOLCANO**!!
THE ENERGY OF THE SEA HAS OUTDONE THE ENERGY OF THE LAND!!
IF THE TWO POKÉMON ARE EQUAL—AS THE LEGEND SAYS—THEN THE ONE WHO AWAKENS **FIRST** HAS THE ADVANTAGE!
WE'VE WON!!

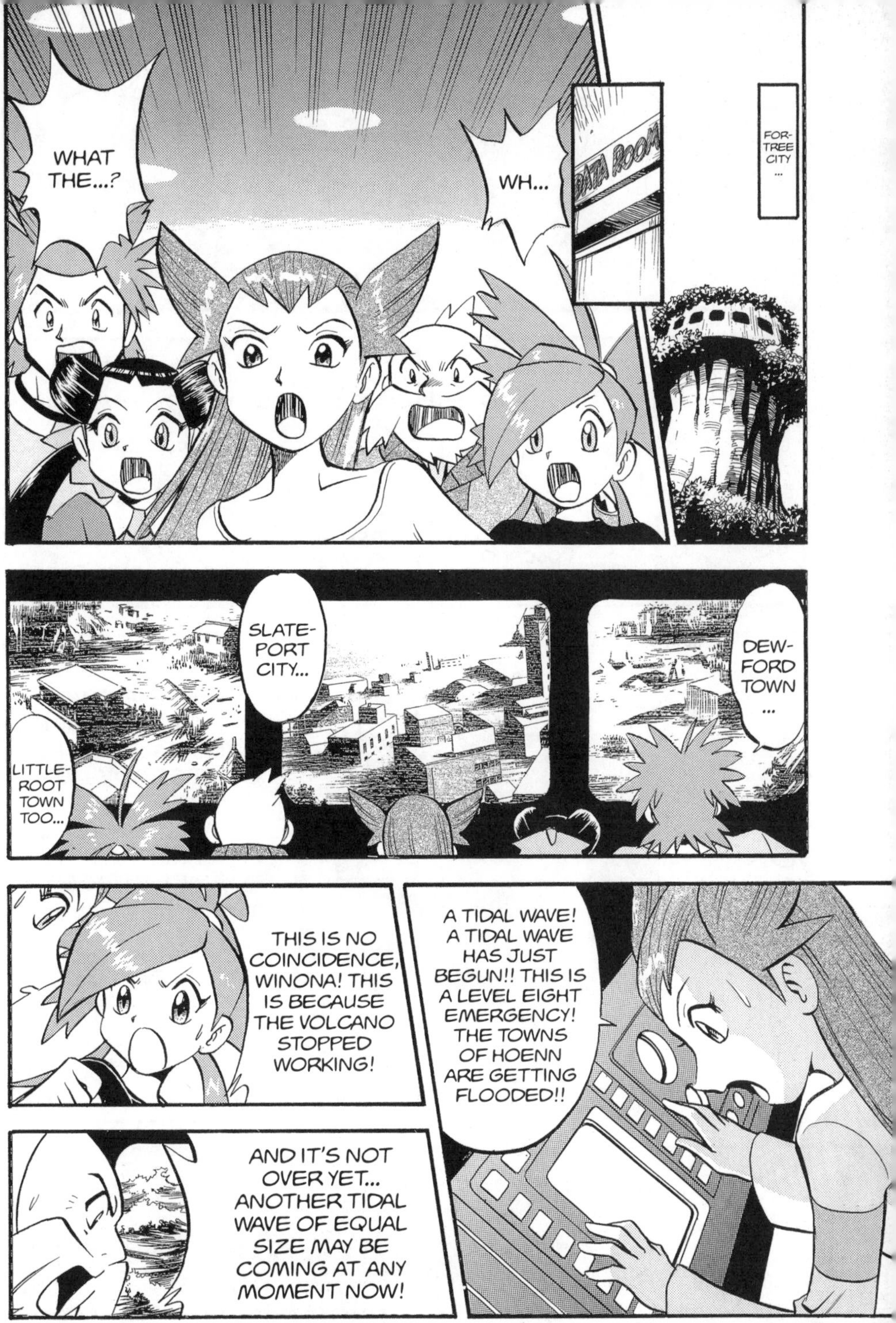
FORTREE CITY...
DATA ROOM
WH...
WHAT THE...?
DEWFORD TOWN...
SLATEPORT CITY...
LITTLEROOT TOWN TOO...
A TIDAL WAVE! A TIDAL WAVE HAS JUST BEGUN!! THIS IS A LEVEL EIGHT EMERGENCY! THE TOWNS OF HOENN ARE GETTING FLOODED!!
THIS IS NO COINCIDENCE, WINONA! THIS IS BECAUSE THE VOLCANO STOPPED WORKING!
AND IT'S NOT OVER YET... ANOTHER TIDAL WAVE OF EQUAL SIZE MAY BE COMING AT ANY MOMENT NOW!

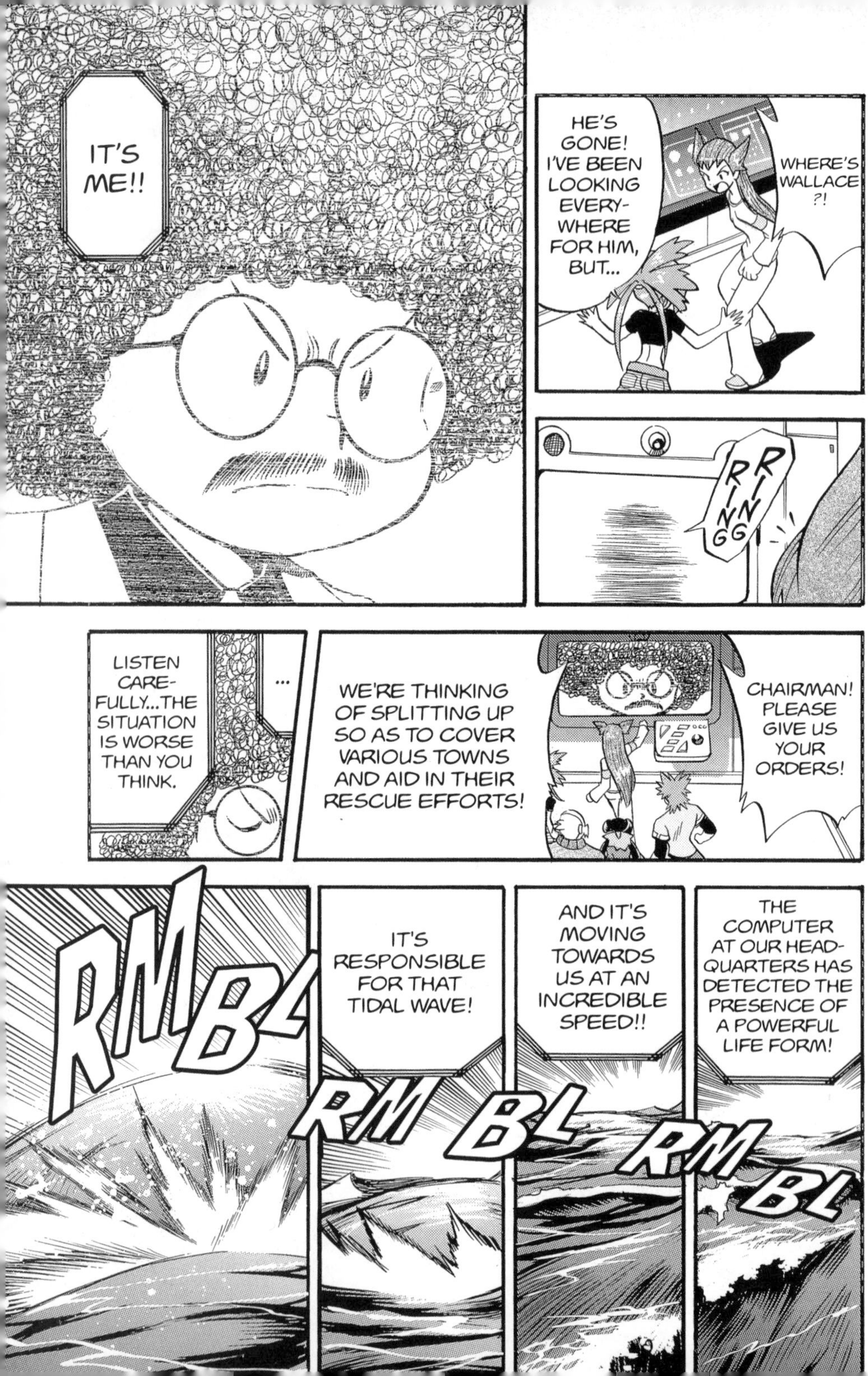

WHERE'S WALLACE ?!
HE'S GONE! I'VE BEEN LOOKING EVERY-WHERE FOR HIM, BUT...
RING RING
IT'S ME!!
CHAIRMAN! PLEASE GIVE US YOUR ORDERS!
WE'RE THINKING OF SPLITTING UP SO AS TO COVER VARIOUS TOWNS AND AID IN THEIR RESCUE EFFORTS!
...
LISTEN CARE-FULLY...THE SITUATION IS WORSE THAN YOU THINK.
THE COMPUTER AT OUR HEAD-QUARTERS HAS DETECTED THE PRESENCE OF A POWERFUL LIFE FORM!
AND IT'S MOVING TOWARDS US AT AN INCREDIBLE SPEED!!
IT'S RESPONSIBLE FOR THAT TIDAL WAVE!
RMBL
RM BL RM BL

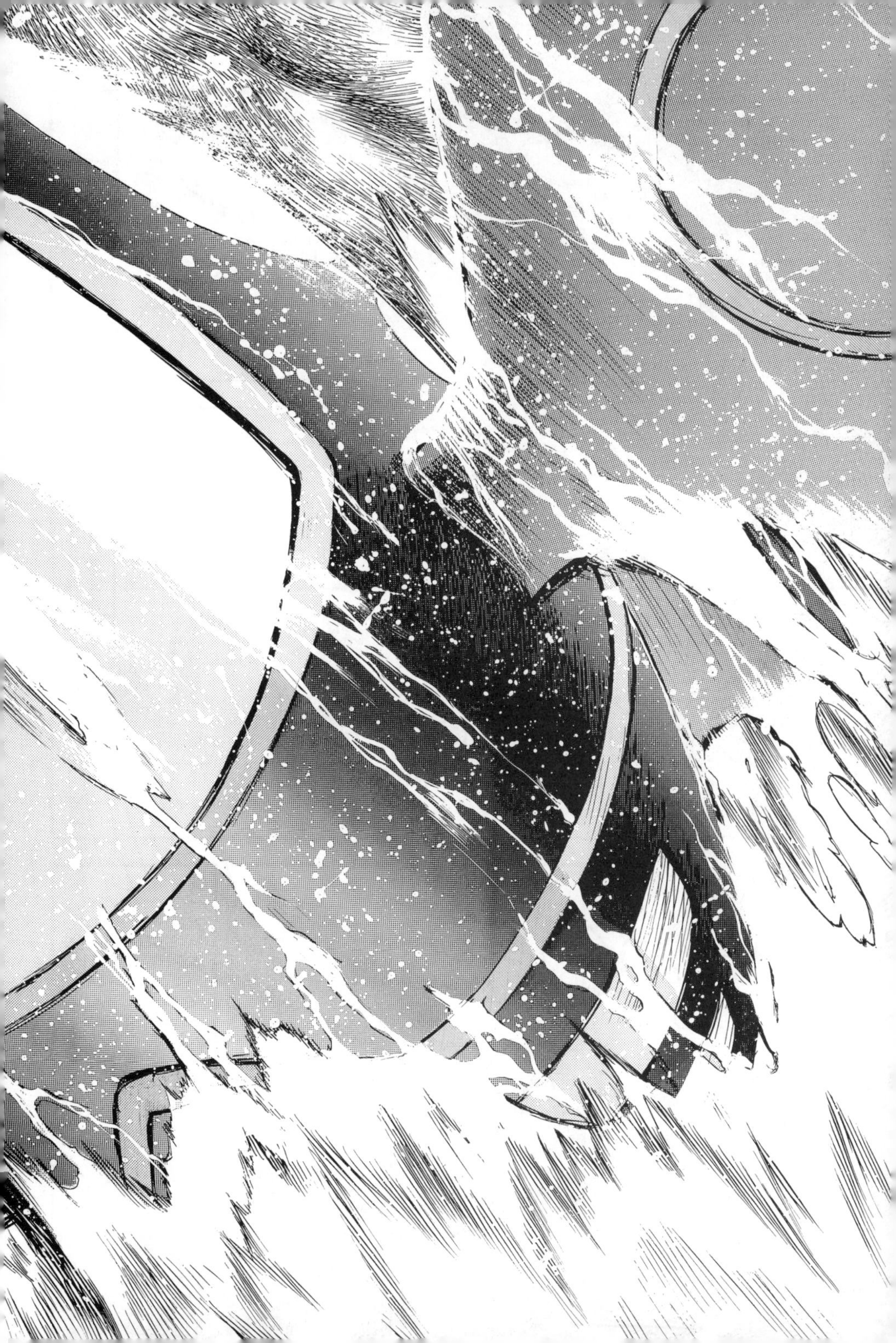

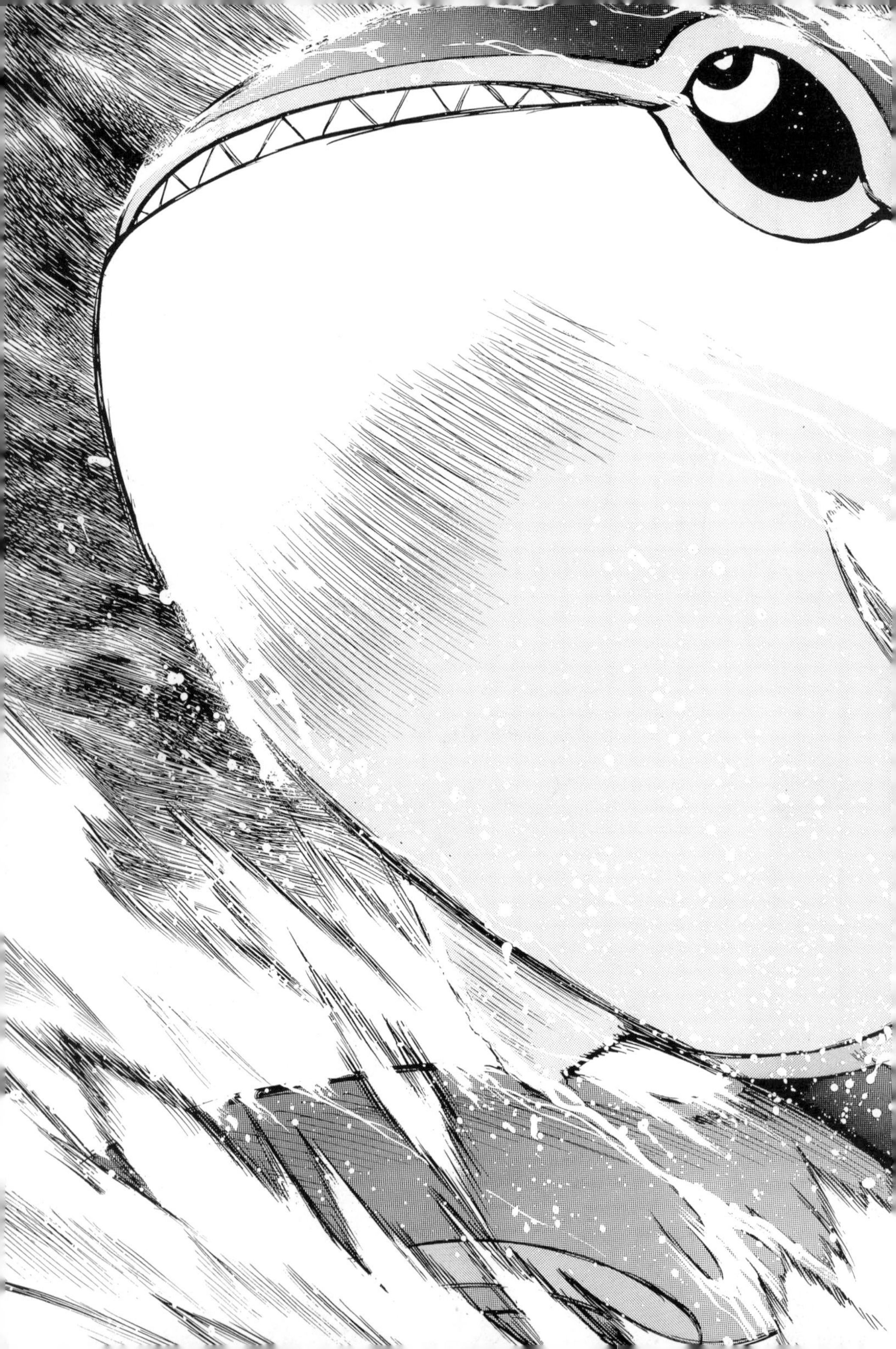

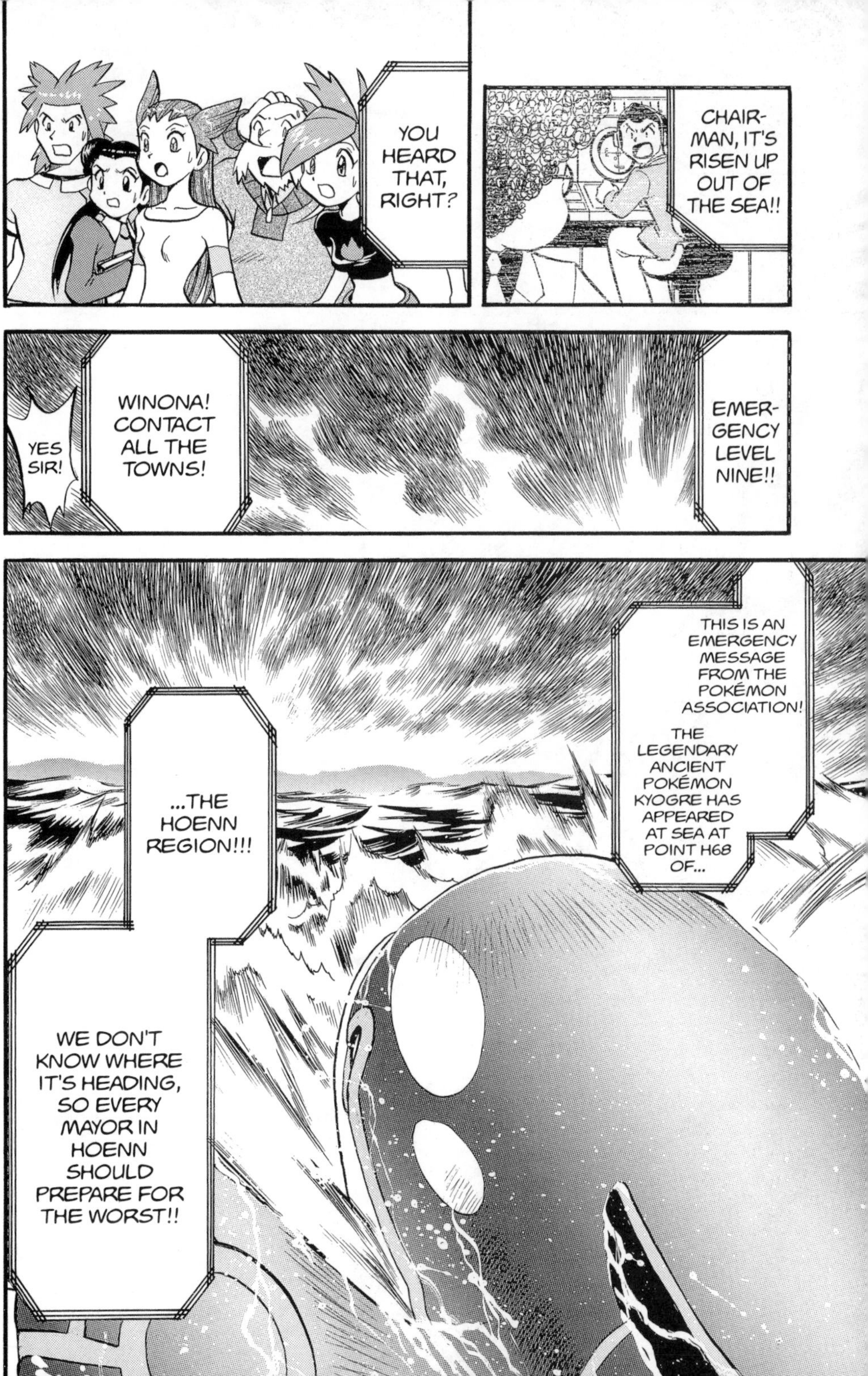
CHAIRMAN, IT'S RISEN UP OUT OF THE SEA!!
YOU HEARD THAT, RIGHT?
EMERGENCY LEVEL NINE!!
WINONA! CONTACT ALL THE TOWNS!
YES SIR!
THIS IS AN EMERGENCY MESSAGE FROM THE POKÉMON ASSOCIATION!
THE LEGENDARY ANCIENT POKÉMON KYOGRE HAS APPEARED AT SEA AT POINT H68 OF...
...THE HOENN REGION!!!
WE DON'T KNOW WHERE IT'S HEADING, SO EVERY MAYOR IN HOENN SHOULD PREPARE FOR THE WORST!!

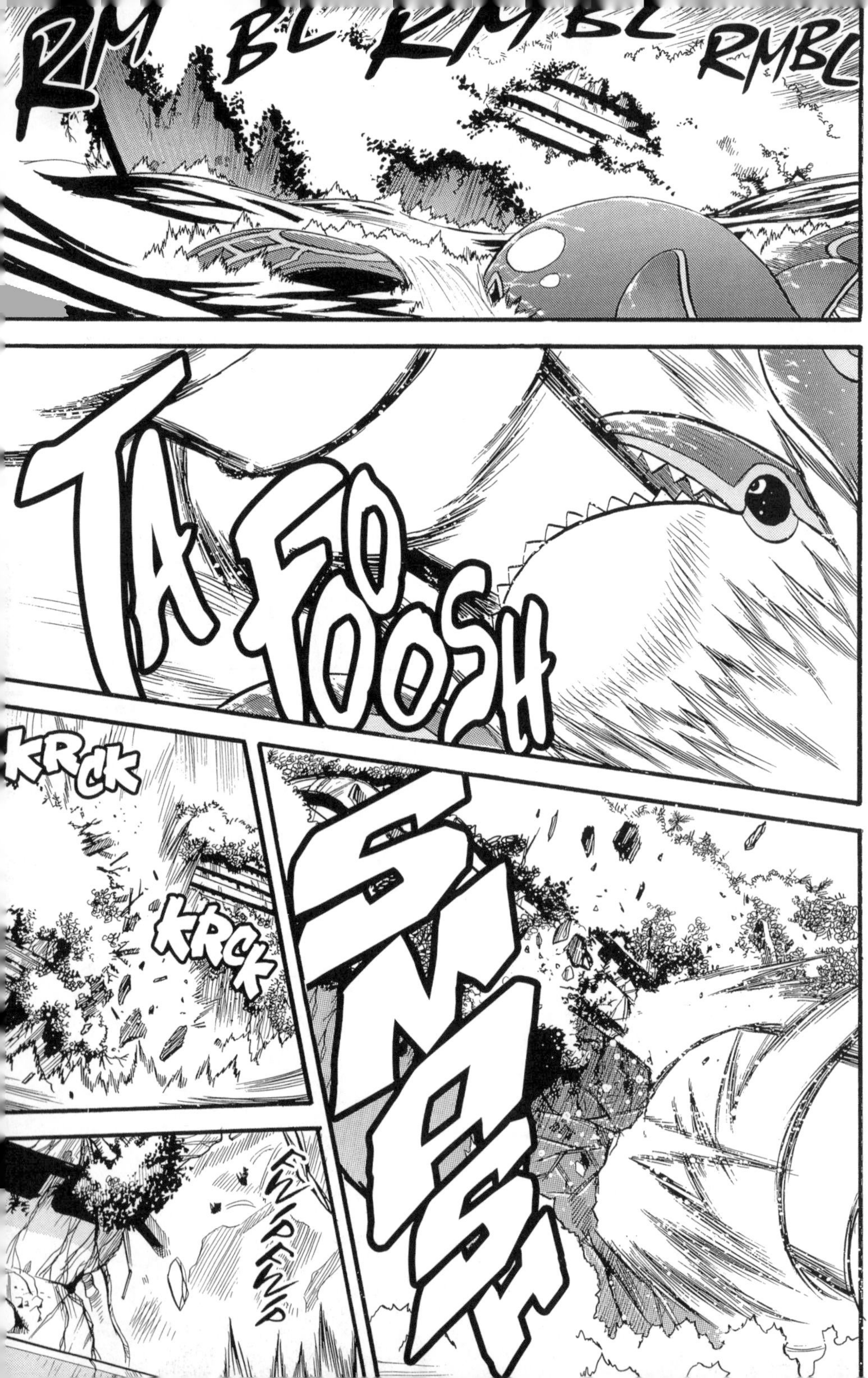
RM BL RM BL
RMBL
TA
FO
FOOSH
SMASH
KRCK
KRCK
FWIP FWIP

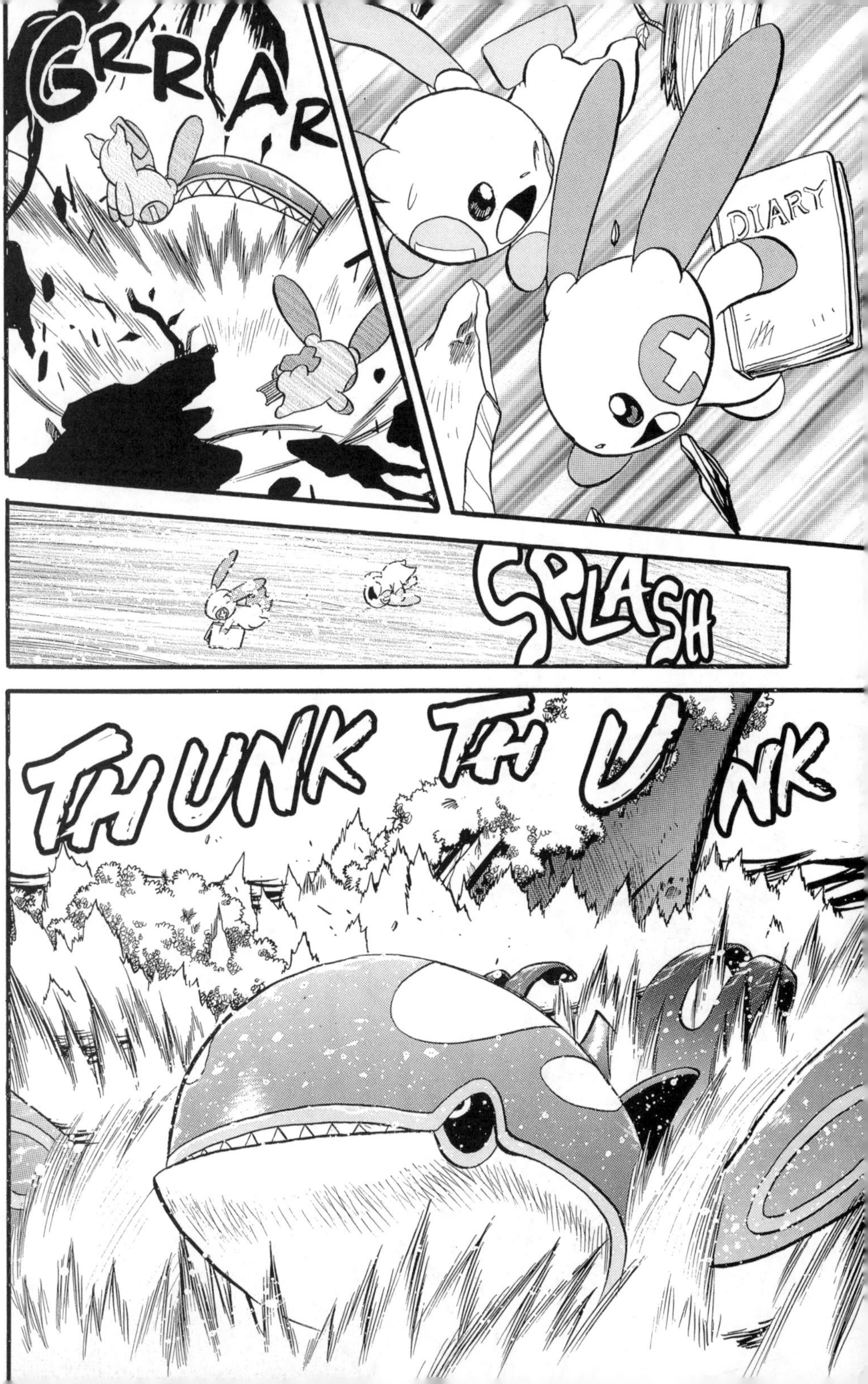
DIARY
GRRAR
SPLASH
THUNK THUNK

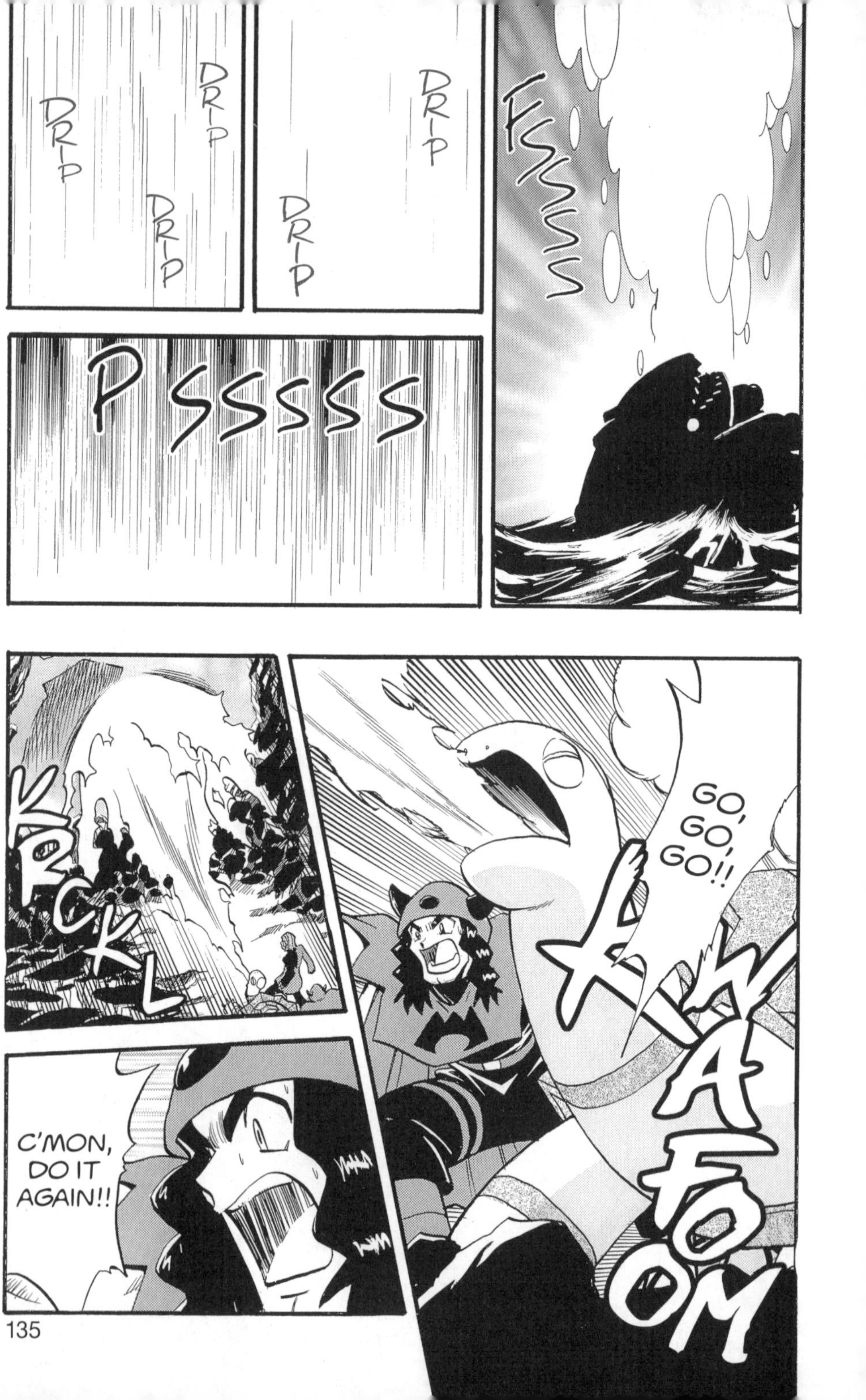
FSSSSSS
DRIP
DRIP
DRIP
DRIP
DRIP
PSSSSSS
GO, GO, GO!!
KWAFOOM
KRCKL
C'MON, DO IT AGAIN!!

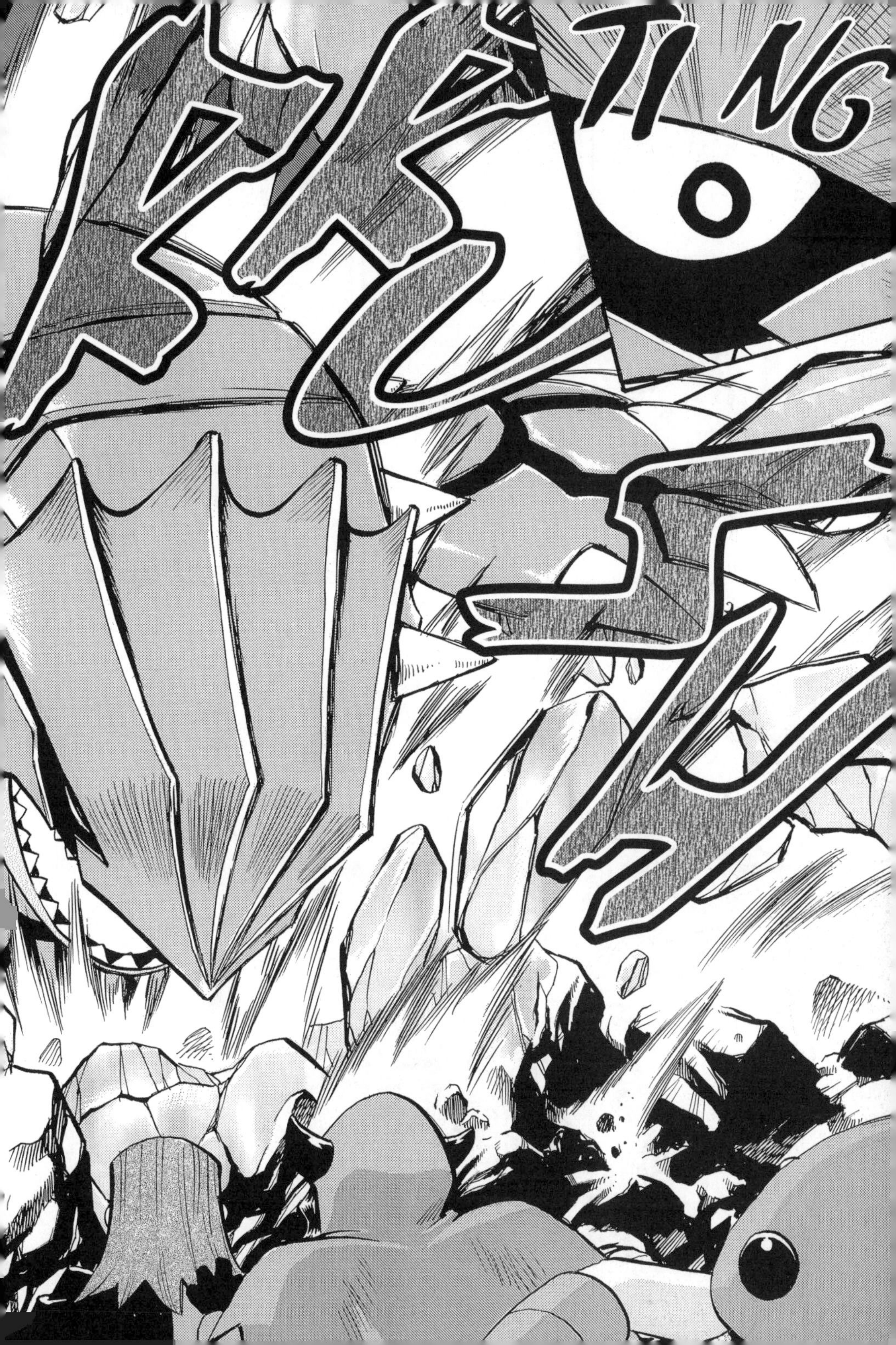
TING

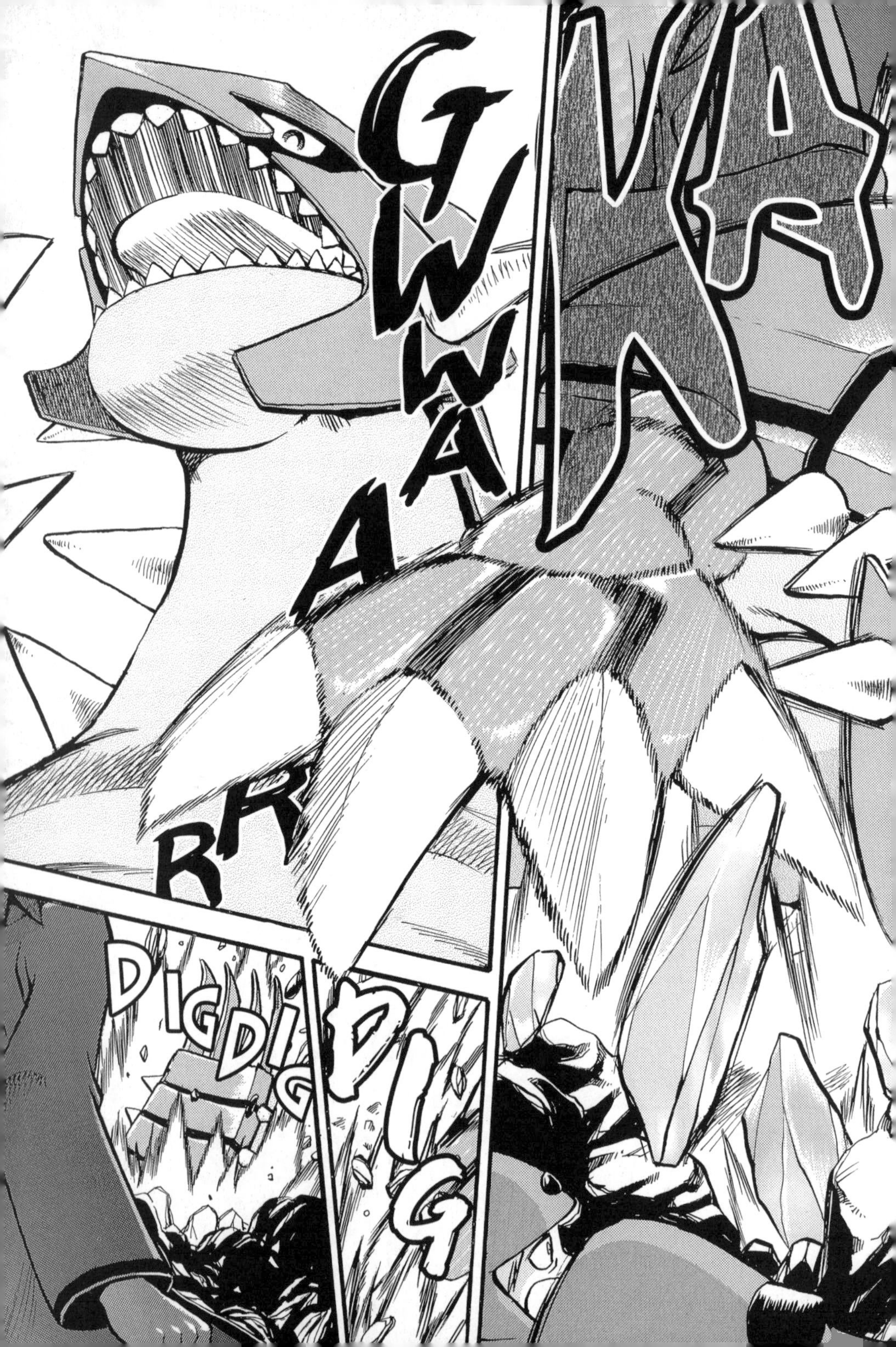
GWWAA
DIGDIG
DIG

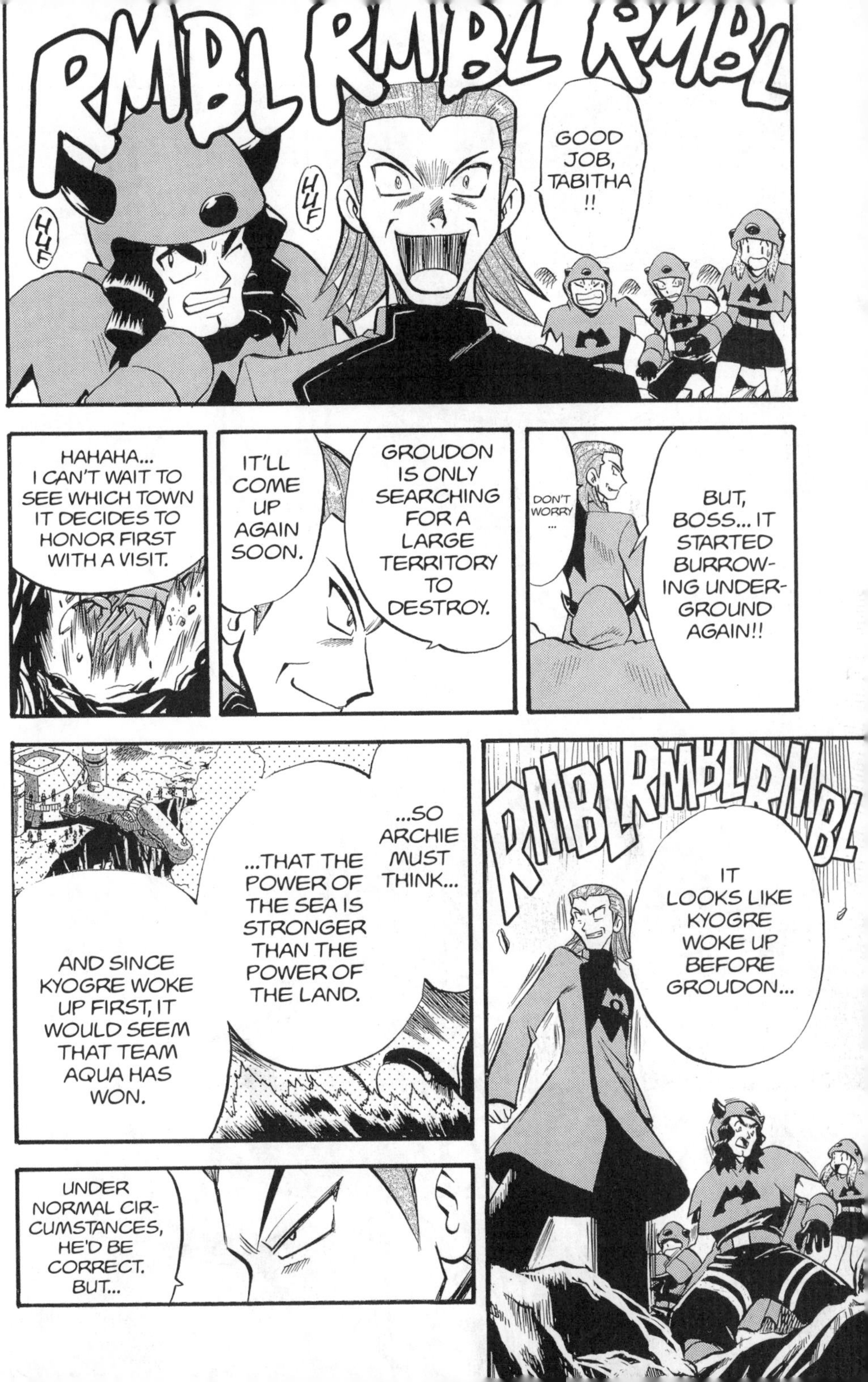
RMBL RMBL RMBL
GOOD JOB, TABITHA!!
HUF
HUF
BUT, BOSS... IT STARTED BURROW-ING UNDER-GROUND AGAIN!!
DON'T WORRY...
GROUDON IS ONLY SEARCHING FOR A LARGE TERRITORY TO DESTROY.
IT'LL COME UP AGAIN SOON.
HAHAHA... I CAN'T WAIT TO SEE WHICH TOWN IT DECIDES TO HONOR FIRST WITH A VISIT.
RMBLRMBLRMBL
IT LOOKS LIKE KYOGRE WOKE UP BEFORE GROUDON...
...SO ARCHIE MUST THINK...
...THAT THE POWER OF THE SEA IS STRONGER THAN THE POWER OF THE LAND.
AND SINCE KYOGRE WOKE UP FIRST, IT WOULD SEEM THAT TEAM AQUA HAS WON.
UNDER NORMAL CIR-CUMSTANCES, HE'D BE CORRECT. BUT...

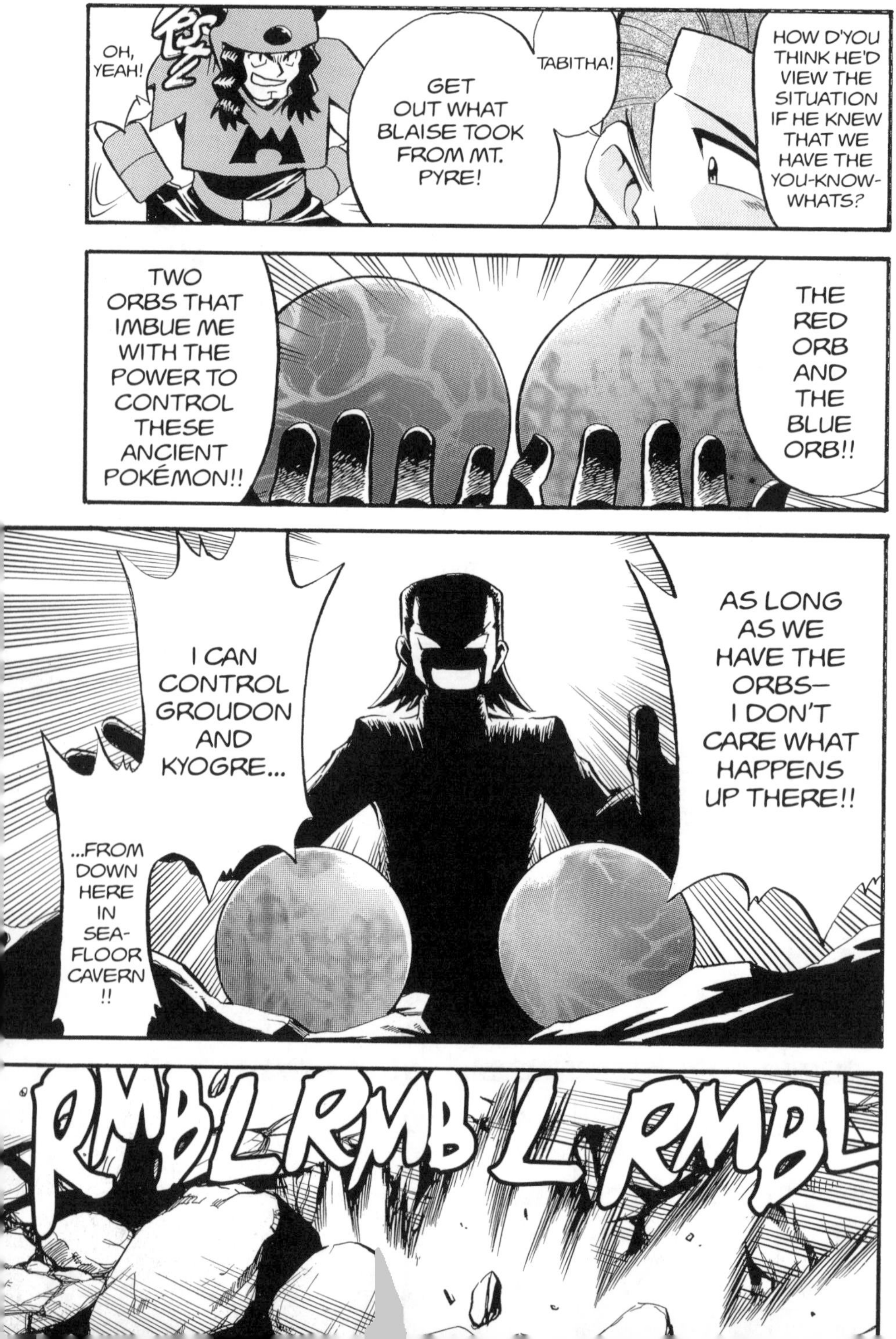
HOW D'YOU THINK HE'D VIEW THE SITUATION IF HE KNEW THAT WE HAVE THE YOU-KNOW-WHATS?
TABITHA!
GET OUT WHAT BLAISE TOOK FROM MT. PYRE!
OH, YEAH!
THE RED ORB AND THE BLUE ORB!!
TWO ORBS THAT IMBUE ME WITH THE POWER TO CONTROL THESE ANCIENT POKÉMON!!
AS LONG AS WE HAVE THE ORBS— I DON'T CARE WHAT HAPPENS UP THERE!!
I CAN CONTROL GROUDON AND KYOGRE...
...FROM DOWN HERE IN SEA-FLOOR CAVERN!!
RMBL RMBL RMBL

ADVENTURE MAP

SAPPHIRE

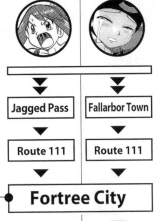

CHIC
Blaziken ♀
Lv40

RONO
Lairon ♂
Lv41

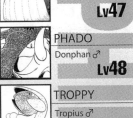
LORRY
Wailord ♂
Lv47

PHADO
Donphan ♂
Lv48

TROPPY
Tropius ♂
Lv46

RUBY

▼	▼
Jagged Pass	**Fallarbor Town**
▼	▼
Route 111	**Route 111**
▼	▼

Fortree City

▼▼

Slateport City ●

MUMU
Swampert ♂

NANA
Mightyena ♀

KIKI
Delcatty ♀

FEEFEE
Feebas ♀

FOFO
Castform ♀

Stone Badge	Knuckle Badge	Dynamo Badge	Heat Badge
Balance Badge	Feather Badge	Mind Badge	Rain Badge

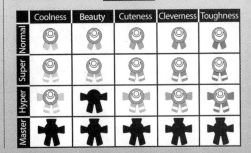

		Coolness	Beauty	Cuteness	Cleverness	Toughness
Normal		◎	◎	◎	◎	◎
Super		◎	◎	◎	◎	◎
Hyper		◎	★	◎	◎	◎
Master		★	★	★	★	★

● Adventure 235 ●

The Beginning of the End with Kyogre and Groudon, Part 3

Pokémon Adventures Ruby & Sapphire

The Fourth Chapter

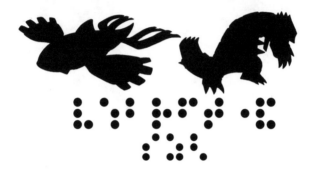

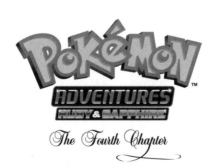

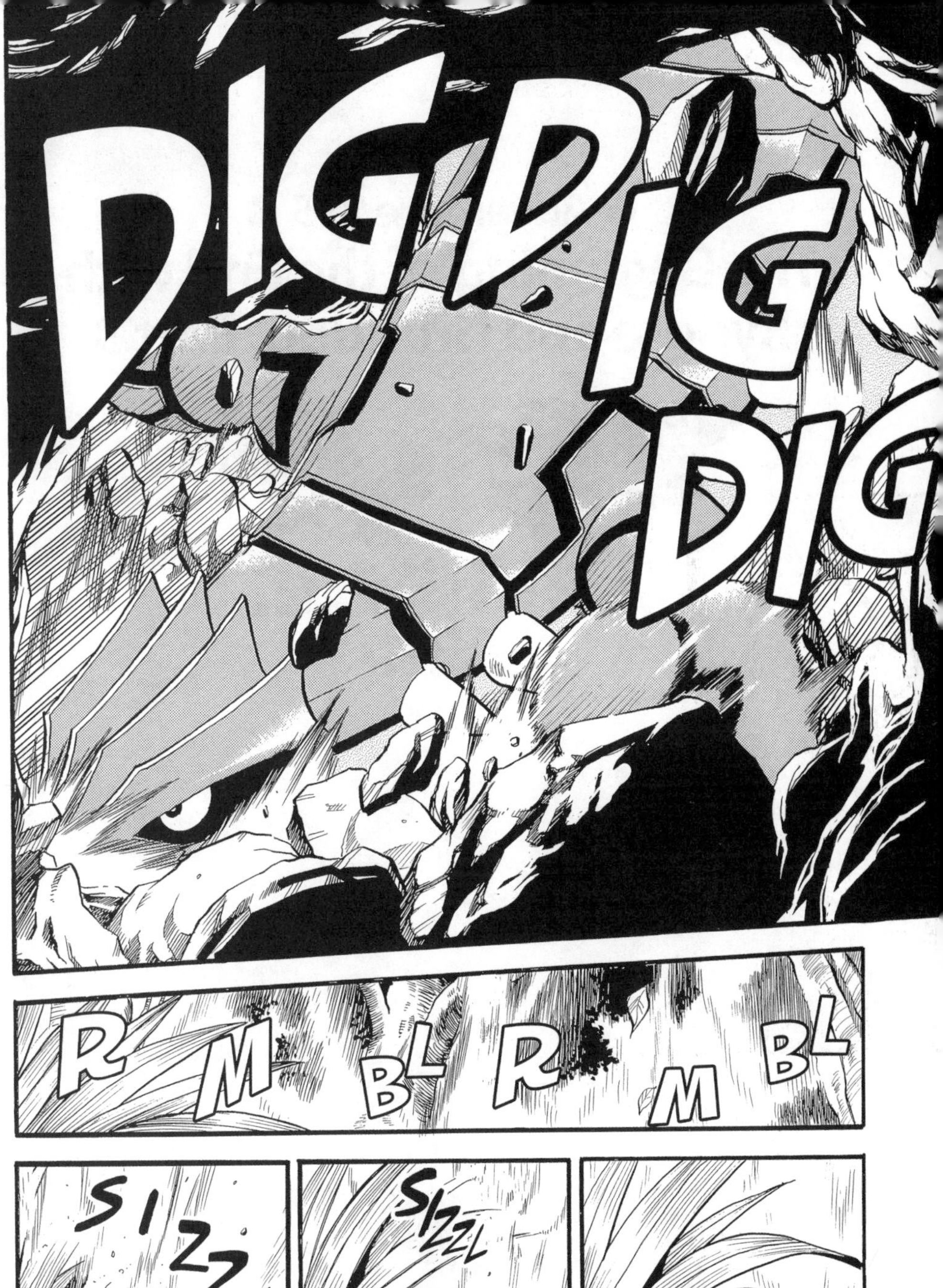
DIG
DIG
DIG
RMBL
RMBL
SIZZL
SIZZL

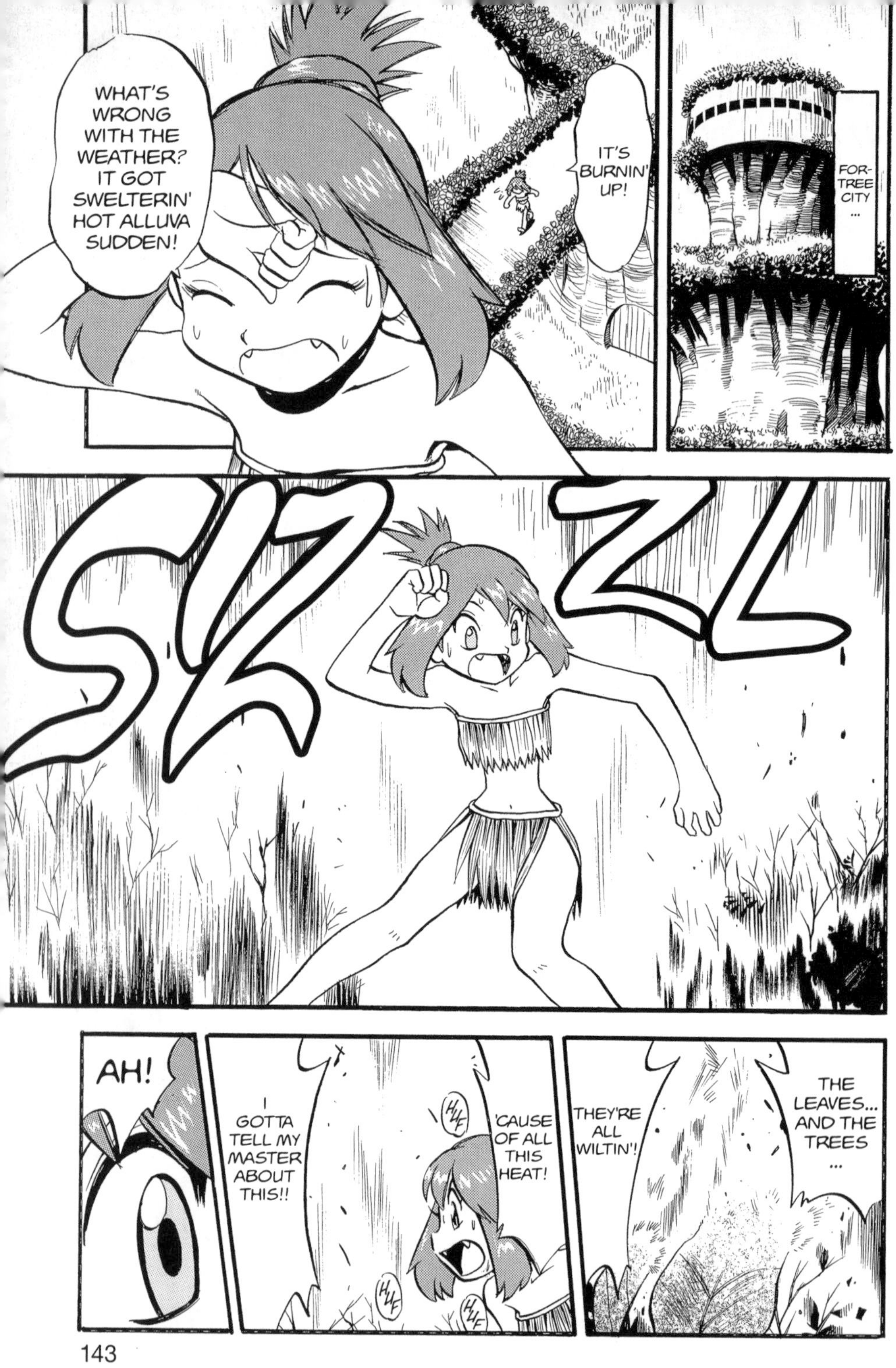
FOR-TREE CITY ...
IT'S BURNIN' UP!
WHAT'S WRONG WITH THE WEATHER? IT GOT SWELTERIN' HOT ALLUVA SUDDEN!
SIZZL
THE LEAVES... AND THE TREES ...
THEY'RE ALL WILTIN'!
'CAUSE OF ALL THIS HEAT!
HUF
I GOTTA TELL MY MASTER ABOUT THIS!!
HUF
HUF
AH!

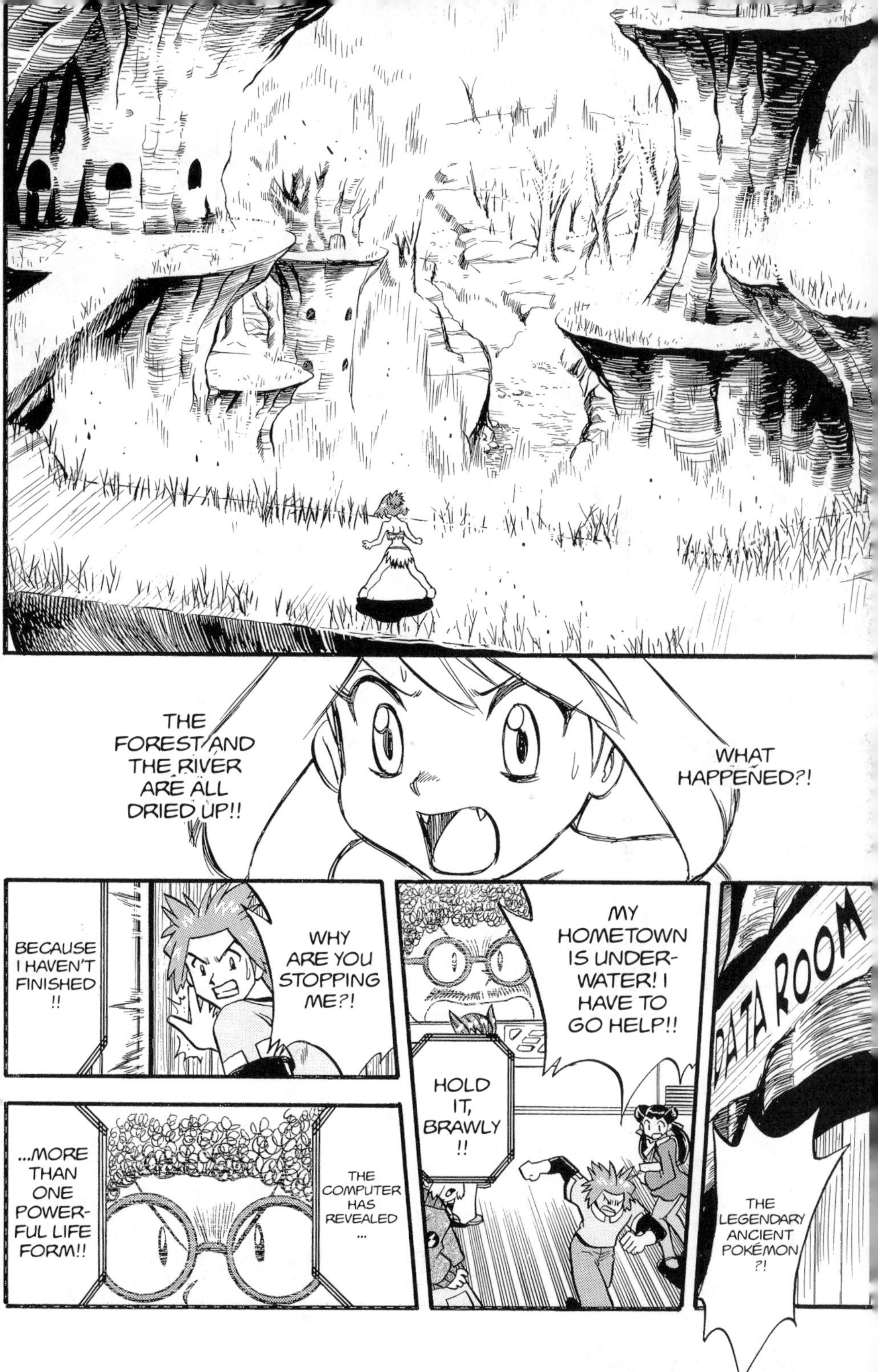
WHAT HAPPENED?!
THE FOREST AND THE RIVER ARE ALL DRIED UP!!
DATA ROOM
THE LEGENDARY ANCIENT POKÉMON?!
MY HOMETOWN IS UNDER-WATER! I HAVE TO GO HELP!!
HOLD IT, BRAWLY!!
WHY ARE YOU STOPPING ME?!
BECAUSE I HAVEN'T FINISHED!!
THE COMPUTER HAS REVEALED...
...MORE THAN ONE POWER-FUL LIFE FORM!!

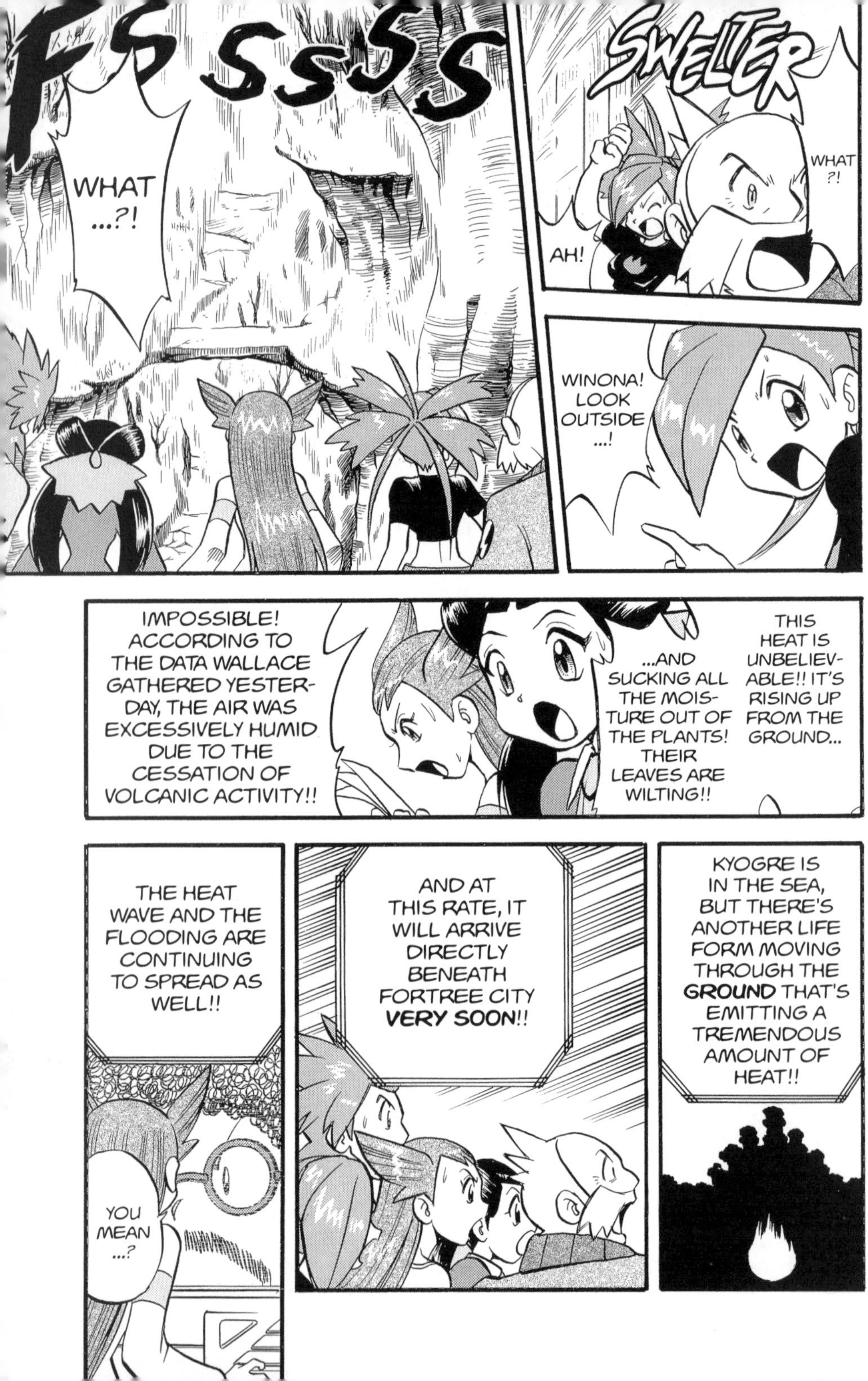
SWELTER
WHAT?!
AH!
WINONA! LOOK OUTSIDE...!
FSSSSS
WHAT...?!
THIS HEAT IS UNBELIEVABLE!! IT'S RISING UP FROM THE GROUND...
...AND SUCKING ALL THE MOISTURE OUT OF THE PLANTS! THEIR LEAVES ARE WILTING!!
IMPOSSIBLE! ACCORDING TO THE DATA WALLACE GATHERED YESTERDAY, THE AIR WAS EXCESSIVELY HUMID DUE TO THE CESSATION OF VOLCANIC ACTIVITY!!
KYOGRE IS IN THE SEA, BUT THERE'S ANOTHER LIFE FORM MOVING THROUGH THE **GROUND** THAT'S EMITTING A TREMENDOUS AMOUNT OF HEAT!!
AND AT THIS RATE, IT WILL ARRIVE DIRECTLY BENEATH FORTREE CITY **VERY SOON**!!
THE HEAT WAVE AND THE FLOODING ARE CONTINUING TO SPREAD AS WELL!!
YOU MEAN...?

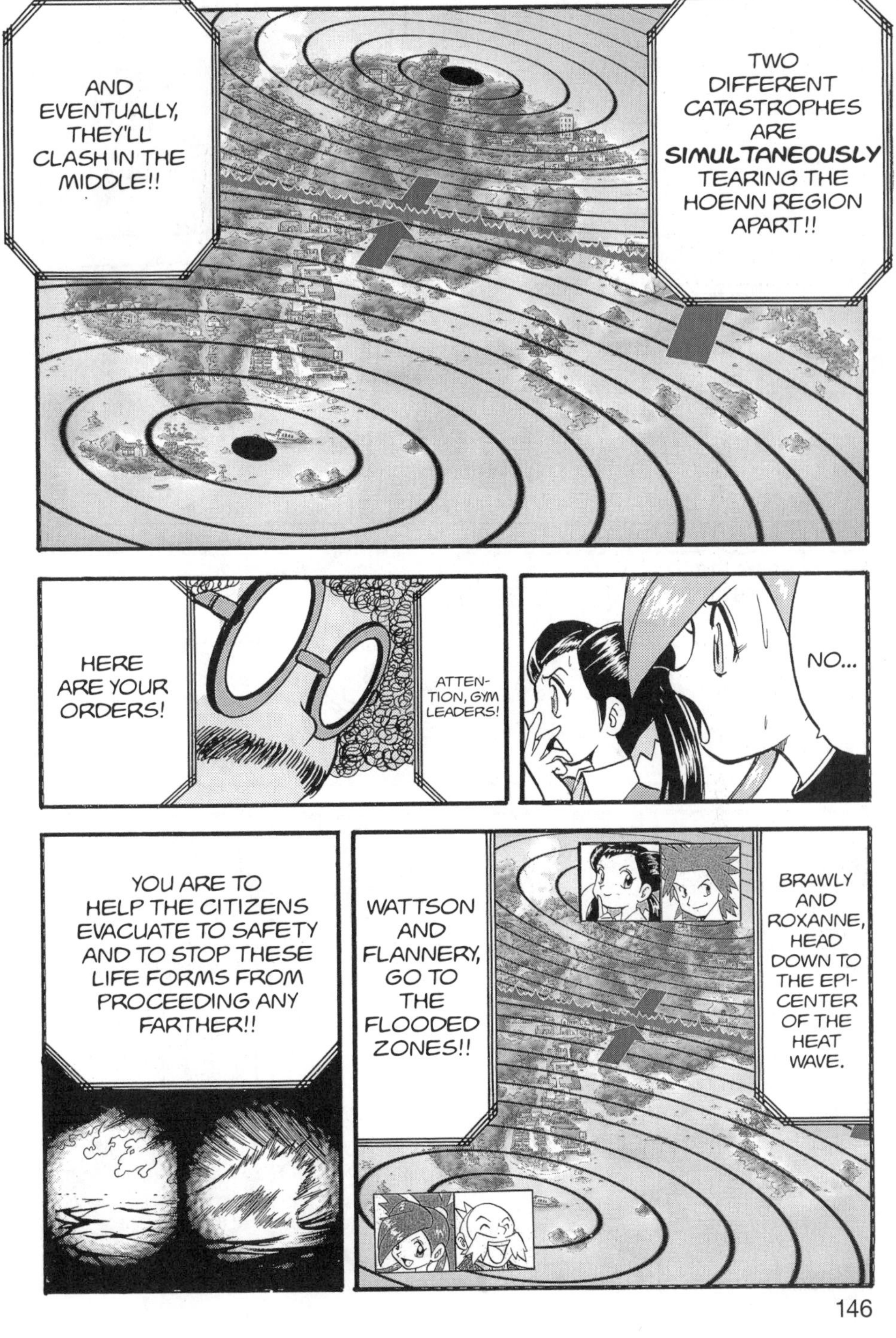
TWO DIFFERENT CATASTROPHES ARE **SIMULTANEOUSLY** TEARING THE HOENN REGION APART!!
AND EVENTUALLY, THEY'LL CLASH IN THE MIDDLE!!
NO...
ATTEN-TION, GYM LEADERS!
HERE ARE YOUR ORDERS!
BRAWLY AND ROXANNE, HEAD DOWN TO THE EPI-CENTER OF THE HEAT WAVE.
WATTSON AND FLANNERY, GO TO THE FLOODED ZONES!!
YOU ARE TO HELP THE CITIZENS EVACUATE TO SAFETY AND TO STOP THESE LIFE FORMS FROM PROCEEDING ANY FARTHER!!

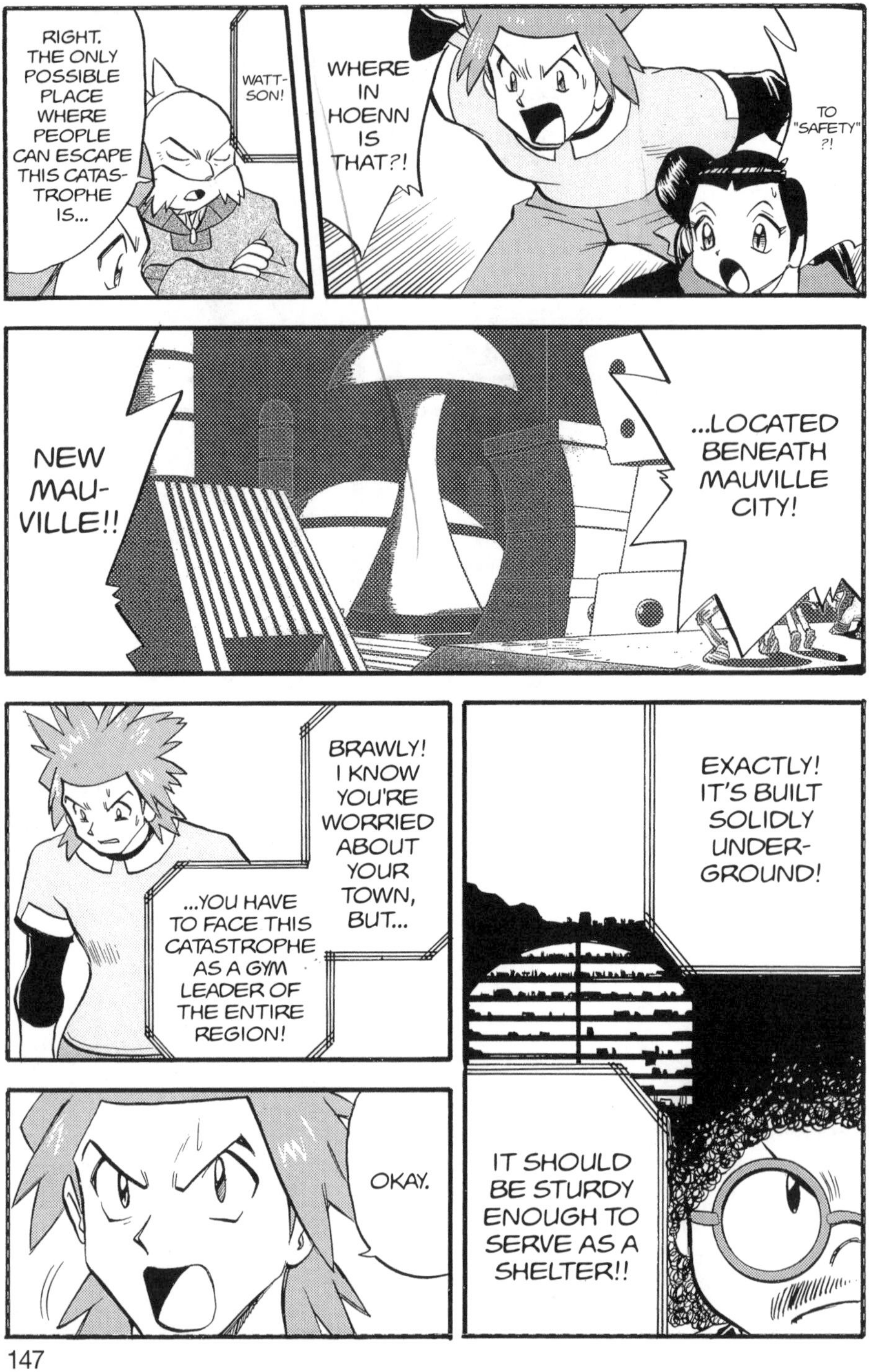

TO "SAFETY"?!
WHERE IN HOENN IS THAT?!
WATT-SON!
RIGHT. THE ONLY POSSIBLE PLACE WHERE PEOPLE CAN ESCAPE THIS CATAS-TROPHE IS...
...LOCATED BENEATH MAUVILLE CITY!
NEW MAU-VILLE!!
EXACTLY! IT'S BUILT SOLIDLY UNDER-GROUND!
BRAWLY! I KNOW YOU'RE WORRIED ABOUT YOUR TOWN, BUT...
...YOU HAVE TO FACE THIS CATASTROPHE AS A GYM LEADER OF THE ENTIRE REGION!
IT SHOULD BE STURDY ENOUGH TO SERVE AS A SHELTER!!
OKAY.

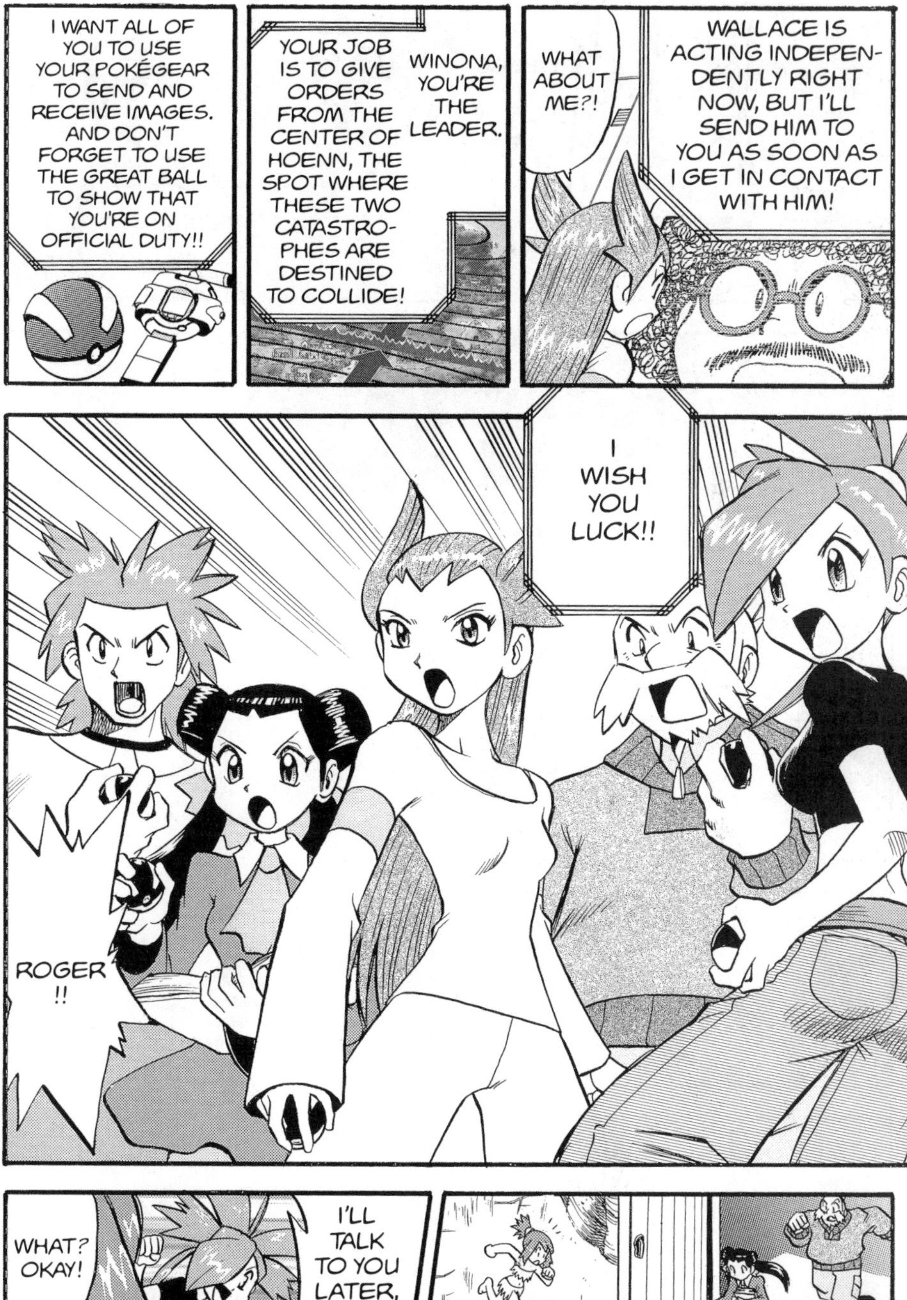
WALLACE IS ACTING INDEPENDENTLY RIGHT NOW, BUT I'LL SEND HIM TO YOU AS SOON AS I GET IN CONTACT WITH HIM!
WHAT ABOUT ME?!
WINONA, YOU'RE THE LEADER.
YOUR JOB IS TO GIVE ORDERS FROM THE CENTER OF HOENN, THE SPOT WHERE THESE TWO CATASTROPHES ARE DESTINED TO COLLIDE!
I WANT ALL OF YOU TO USE YOUR POKÉGEAR TO SEND AND RECEIVE IMAGES. AND DON'T FORGET TO USE THE GREAT BALL TO SHOW THAT YOU'RE ON OFFICIAL DUTY!!
I WISH YOU LUCK!!
ROGER!!
I'LL TALK TO YOU LATER, SAPPHIRE!!
WHAT? OKAY!

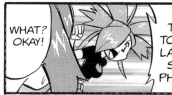

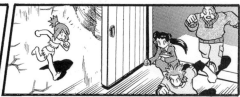

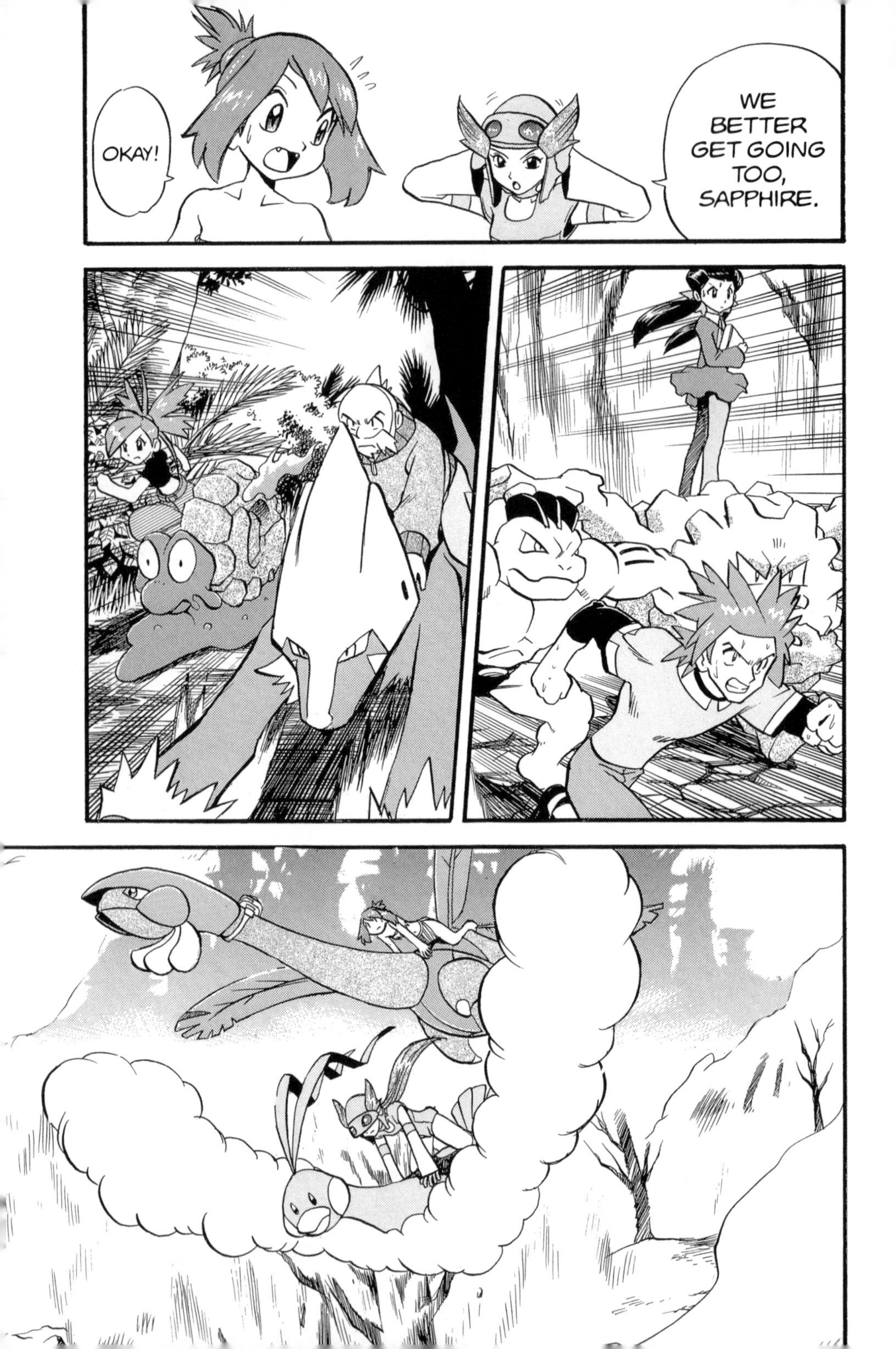
WE BETTER GET GOING TOO, SAPPHIRE.
OKAY!

THIS IS A MESSAGE FROM THE POKÉMON ASSOCIATION TO ALL TOWNS AND CITIES. YOU MUST EVACUATE!

WE HAVE A LEVEL NINE EMERGENCY. EVERY CITIZEN IS TO EVACUATE TO NEW MAUVILLE AS SOON AS POSSIBLE!

EMERGENCY EVACUATION SHELTER: NEW MAUVILLE

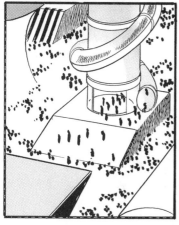

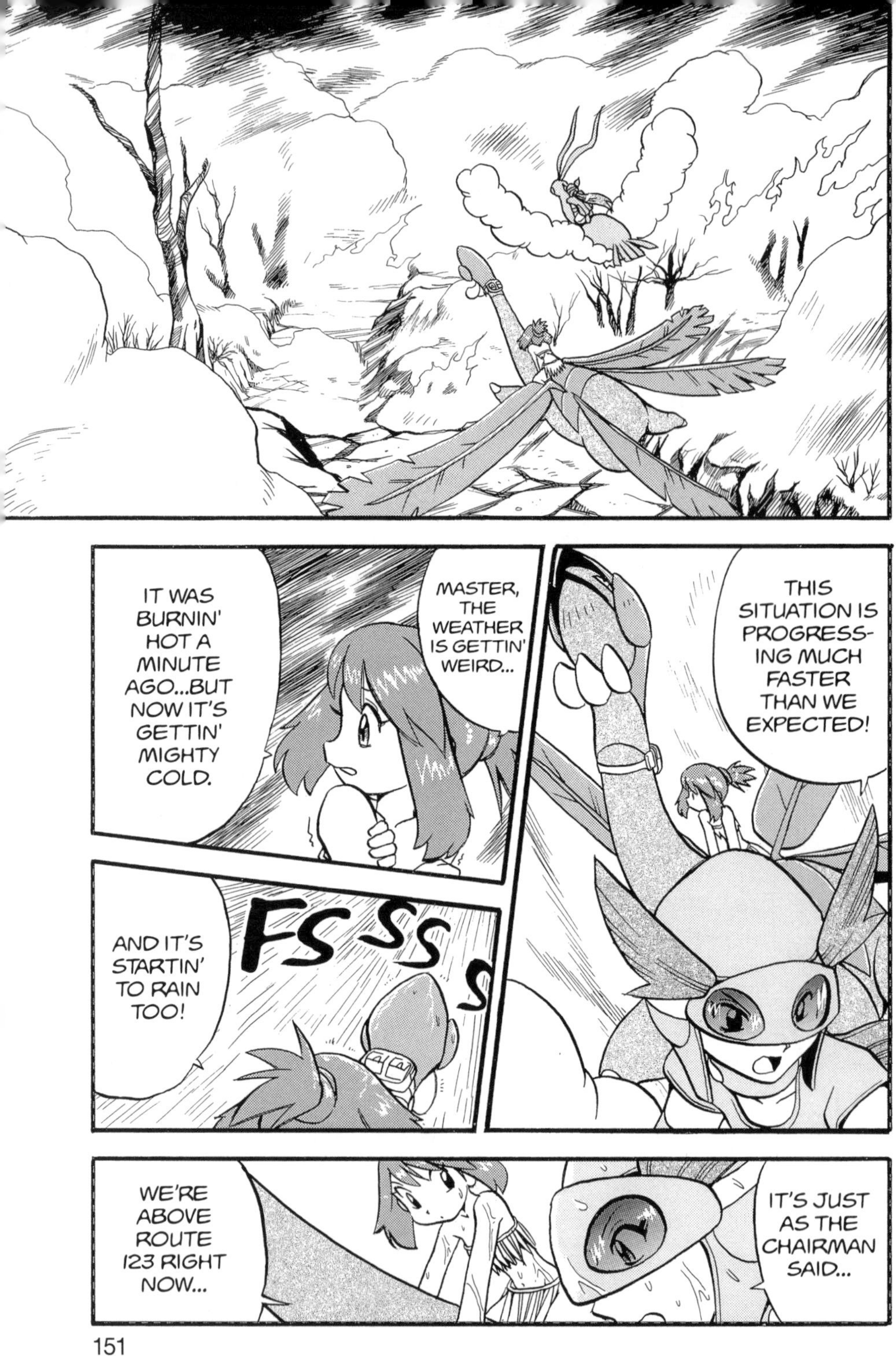

THIS SITUATION IS PROGRESS-ING MUCH FASTER THAN WE EXPECTED!
MASTER, THE WEATHER IS GETTIN' WEIRD...
IT WAS BURNIN' HOT A MINUTE AGO...BUT NOW IT'S GETTIN' MIGHTY COLD.
FSSSS
AND IT'S STARTIN' TO RAIN TOO!
IT'S JUST AS THE CHAIRMAN SAID...
WE'RE ABOVE ROUTE 123 RIGHT NOW...

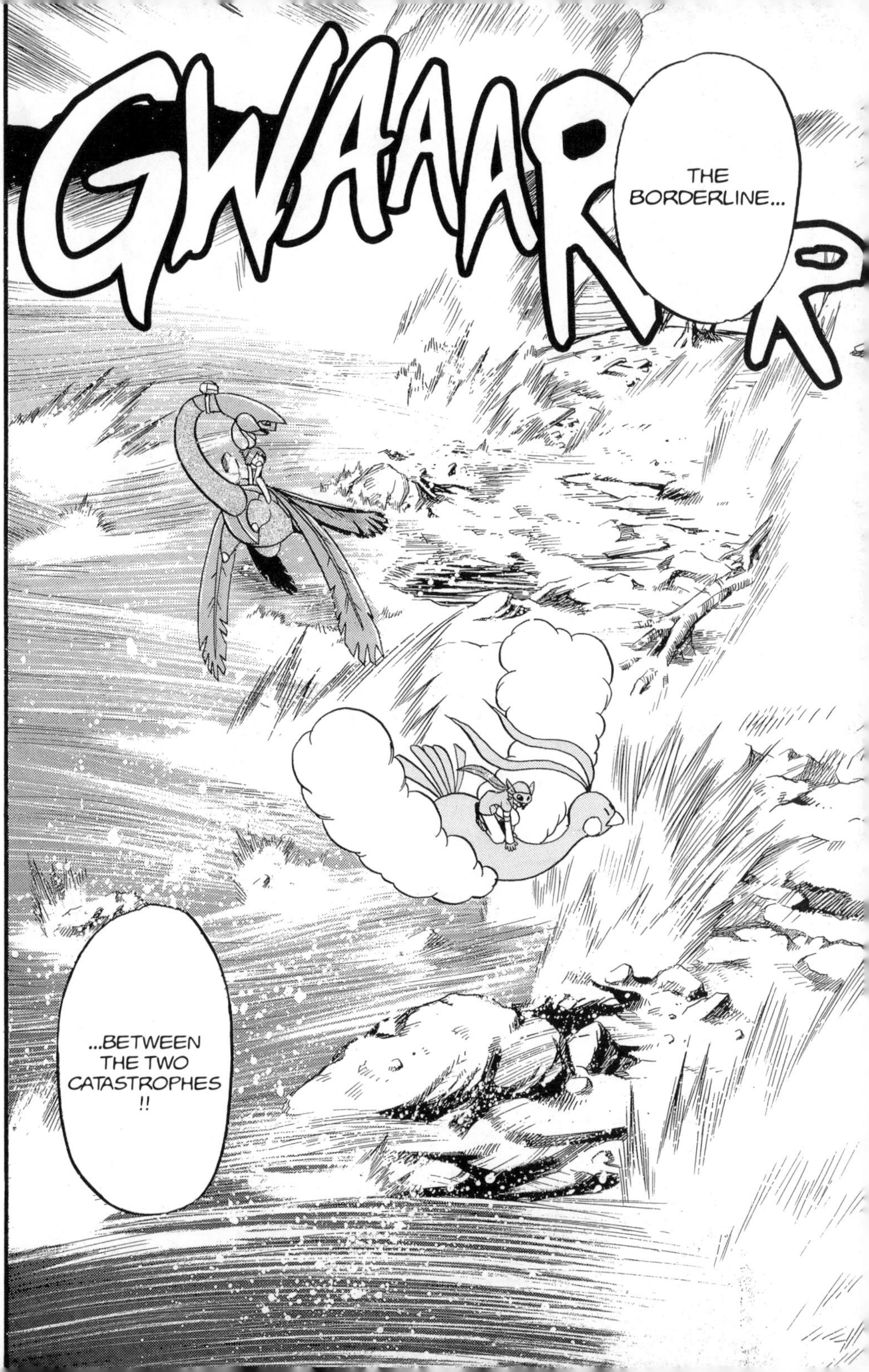
GWAAAROOR
THE BORDERLINE...
...BETWEEN THE TWO CATASTROPHES !!

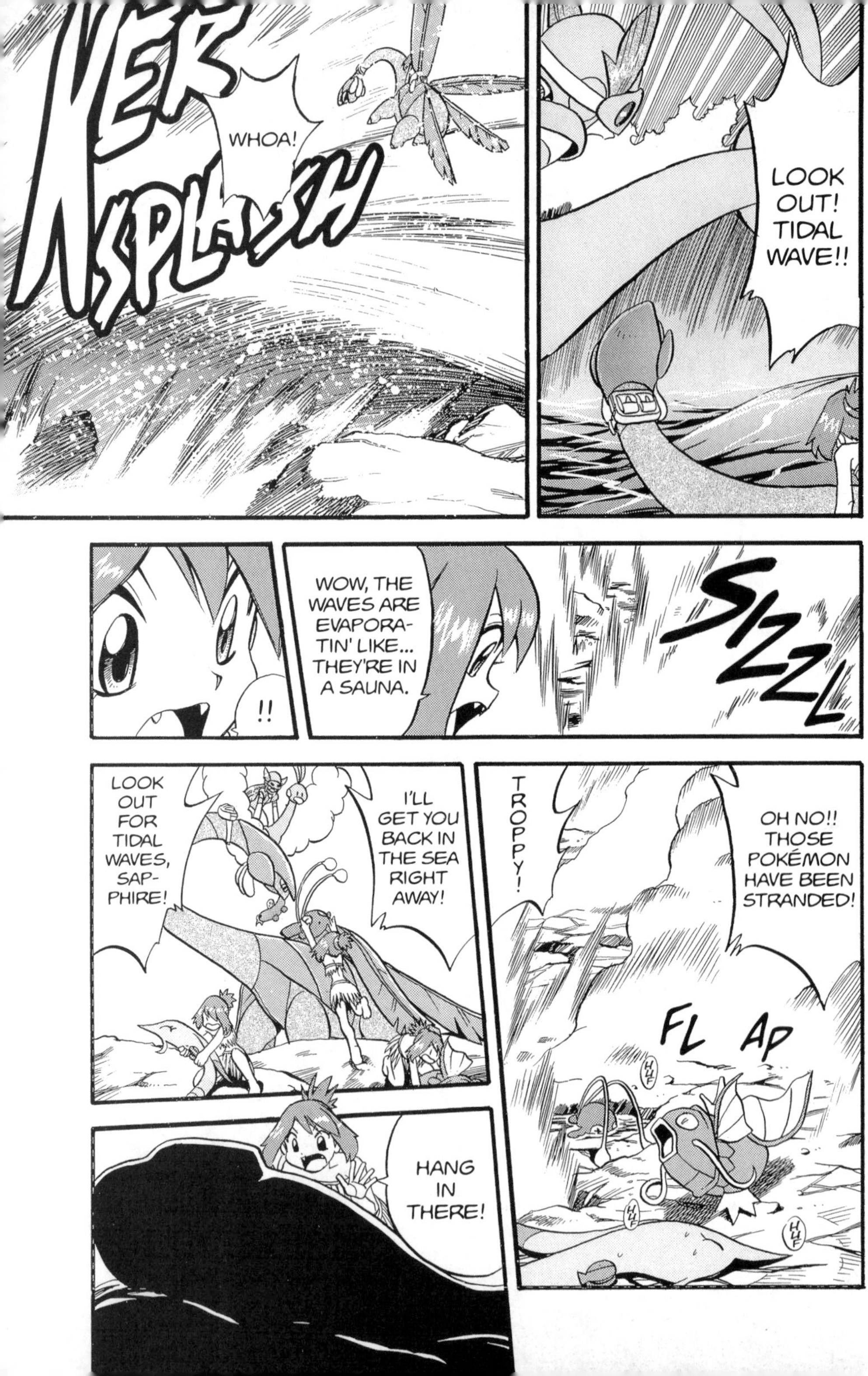
LOOK OUT! TIDAL WAVE!!
WHOA!
WOW, THE WAVES ARE EVAPORATIN' LIKE... THEY'RE IN A SAUNA.
SIZZZL
!!
OH NO!! THOSE POKÉMON HAVE BEEN STRANDED!
TROPPY!
FLAP
HUF
HUF
HUF
I'LL GET YOU BACK IN THE SEA RIGHT AWAY!
LOOK OUT FOR TIDAL WAVES, SAPPHIRE!
HANG IN THERE!

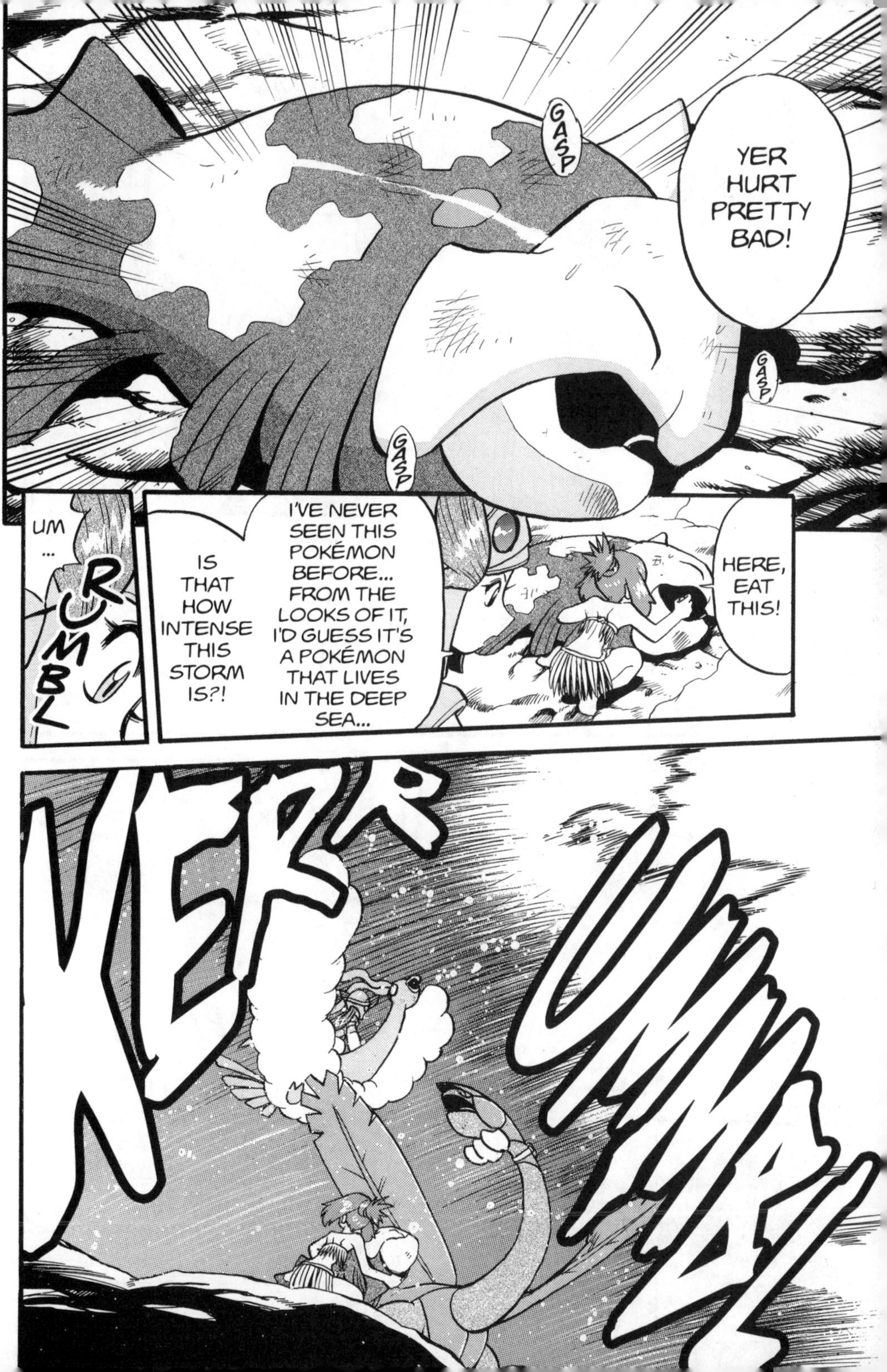
YER HURT PRETTY BAD!
GASP
GASP
GASP
HERE, EAT THIS!
I'VE NEVER SEEN THIS POKÉMON BEFORE... FROM THE LOOKS OF IT, I'D GUESS IT'S A POKÉMON THAT LIVES IN THE DEEP SEA...
IS THAT HOW INTENSE THIS STORM IS?!
UM ...
RUMBL

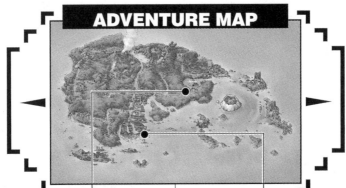

ADVENTURE MAP

SAPPHIRE

RUBY

SAPPHIRE	RUBY
Jagged Pass	Fallarbor Town
Route 111	Route 111
Verdanturf Town	Verdanturf Town
Route 123	Slateport City

SAPPHIRE

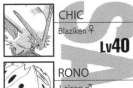

- CHIC — Blaziken ♀ — Lv40
- RONO — Lairon ♂ — Lv41
- LORRY — Wailord ♂ — Lv47
- PHADO — Donphan ♂ — Lv48
- TROPPY — Tropius ♂ — Lv46
- .... — ?

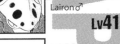

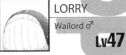

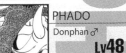

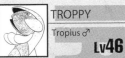

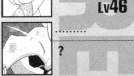

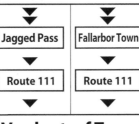

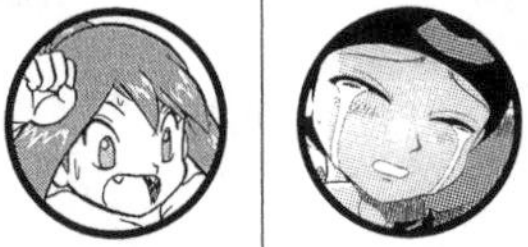

RUBY

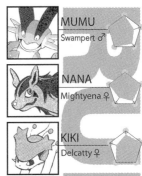

- MUMU — Swampert ♂
- NANA — Mightyena ♀
- KIKI — Delcatty ♀
- FEEFEE — Feebas ♀
- FOFO — Castform ♀

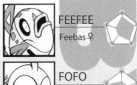

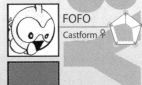

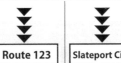

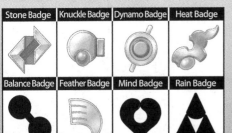

Stone Badge	Knuckle Badge	Dynamo Badge	Heat Badge
Balance Badge	Feather Badge	Mind Badge	Rain Badge

	Coolness	Beauty	Cuteness	Cleverness	Toughness
Normal					
Super					
Hyper					
Master					

● Adventure 236 ●
The Beginning of the End with Kyogre and Groudon, Part 4

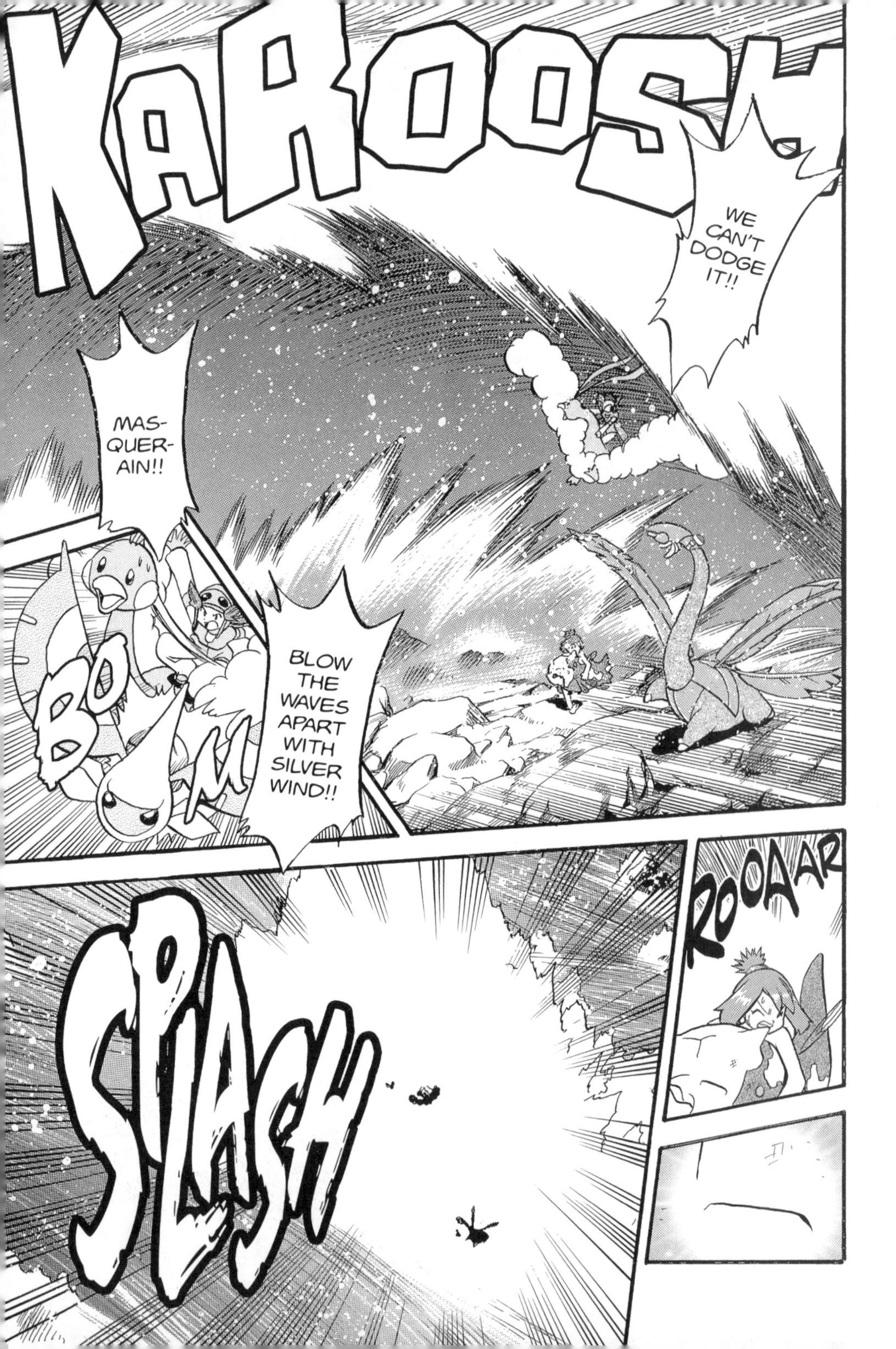
KAROOSH
WE CAN'T DODGE IT!!
MAS-QUER-AIN!!
BLOW THE WAVES APART WITH SILVER WIND!!
BOOM
ROOAAR
SPLASH

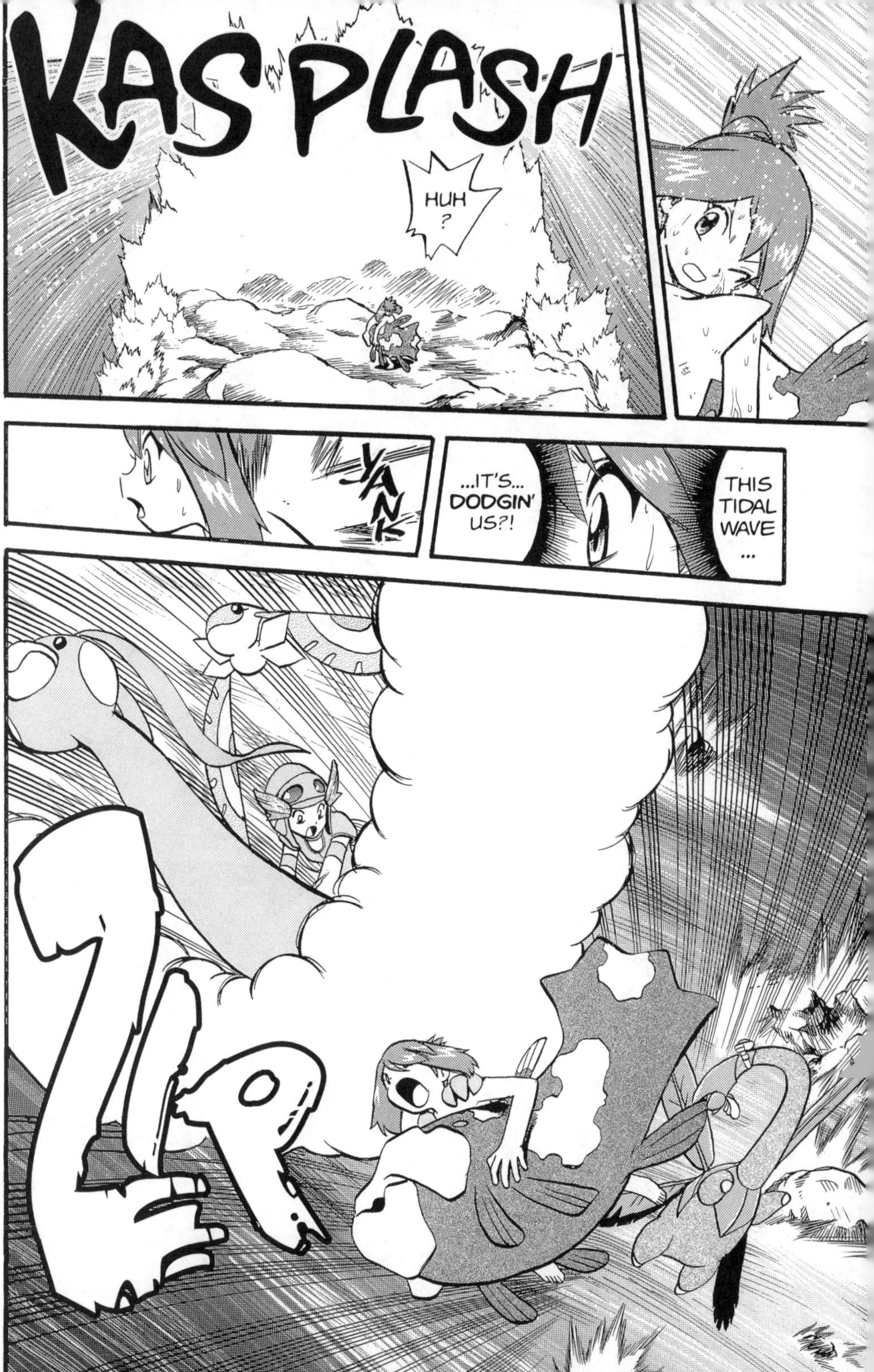
KASPLASH
HUH ?
THIS TIDAL WAVE ...
...IT'S... DODGIN' US?!
YANK

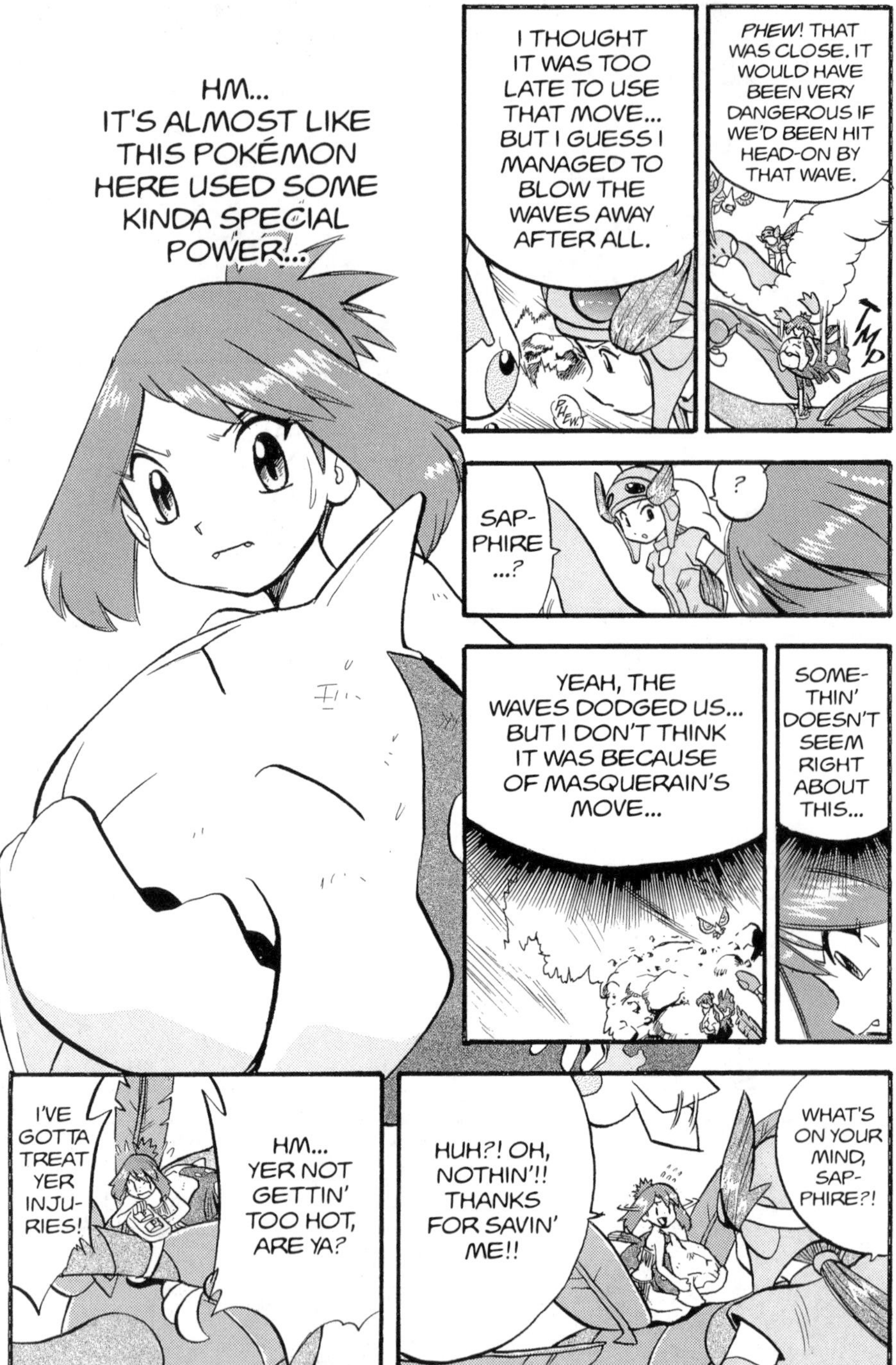
PHEW! THAT WAS CLOSE. IT WOULD HAVE BEEN VERY DANGEROUS IF WE'D BEEN HIT HEAD-ON BY THAT WAVE.
TMP
I THOUGHT IT WAS TOO LATE TO USE THAT MOVE... BUT I GUESS I MANAGED TO BLOW THE WAVES AWAY AFTER ALL.
PHEW.
?
SAP-PHIRE ...?
SOME-THIN' DOESN'T SEEM RIGHT ABOUT THIS...
YEAH, THE WAVES DODGED US... BUT I DON'T THINK IT WAS BECAUSE OF MASQUERAIN'S MOVE...
HM... IT'S ALMOST LIKE THIS POKÉMON HERE USED SOME KINDA SPECIAL POWER!...
WHAT'S ON YOUR MIND, SAP-PHIRE?!
HUH?! OH, NOTHIN'!! THANKS FOR SAVIN' ME!!
HM... YER NOT GETTIN' TOO HOT, ARE YA?
I'VE GOTTA TREAT YER INJU-RIES!

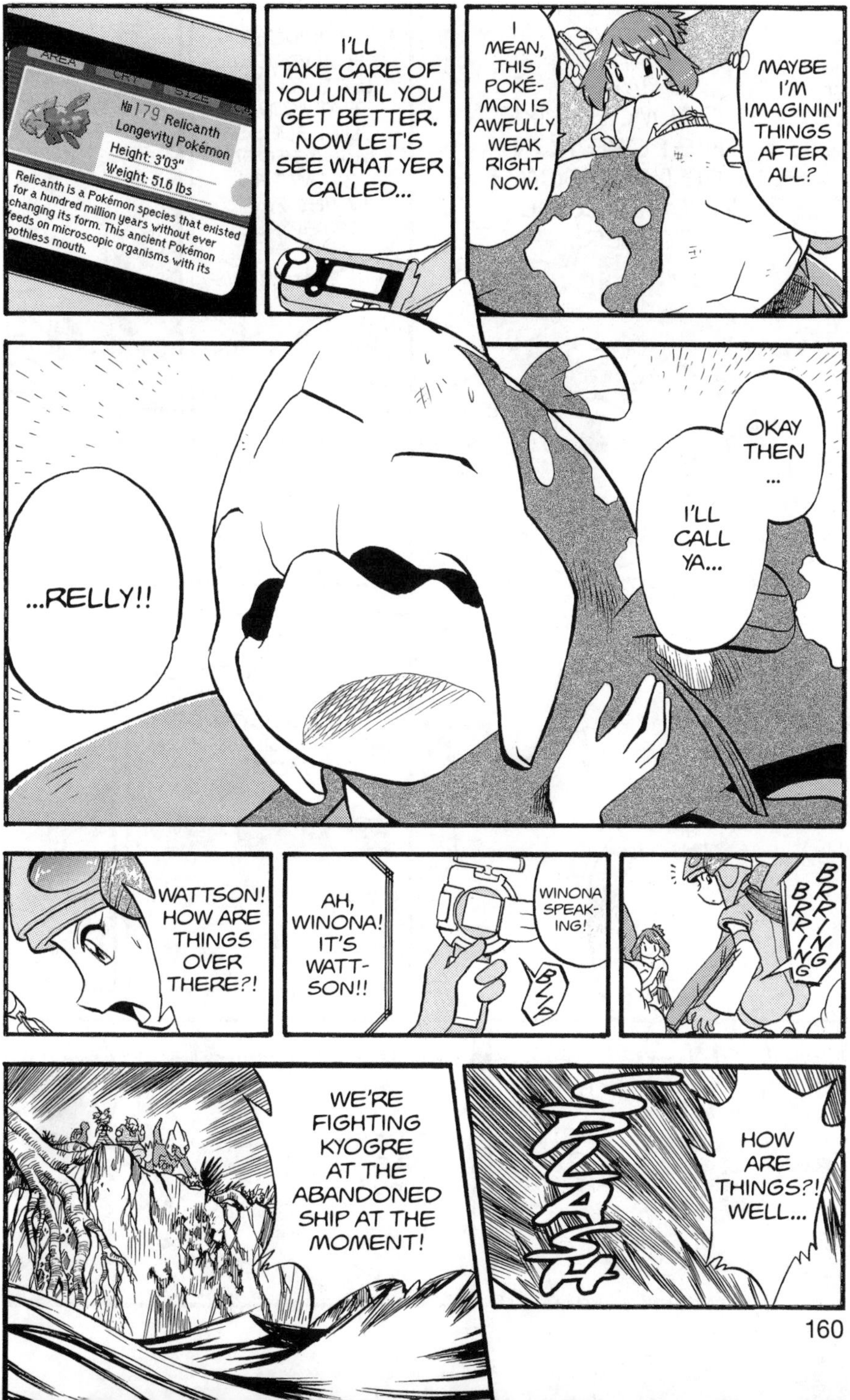

MAYBE I'M IMAGININ' THINGS AFTER ALL?
I MEAN, THIS POKÉ-MON IS AWFULLY WEAK RIGHT NOW.
I'LL TAKE CARE OF YOU UNTIL YOU GET BETTER. NOW LET'S SEE WHAT YER CALLED...
AREA
CRY
SIZE
№179 Relicanth
Longevity Pokémon
Height: 3'03"
Weight: 51.6 lbs
Relicanth is a Pokémon species that existed for a hundred million years without ever changing its form. This ancient Pokémon feeds on microscopic organisms with its othless mouth.
OKAY THEN ...
I'LL CALL YA...
...RELLY!!
BRRING BRRING
WINONA SPEAK-ING!
AH, WINONA! IT'S WATT-SON!!
WATTSON! HOW ARE THINGS OVER THERE?!
HOW ARE THINGS?! WELL...
SPLASH
WE'RE FIGHTING KYOGRE AT THE ABANDONED SHIP AT THE MOMENT!

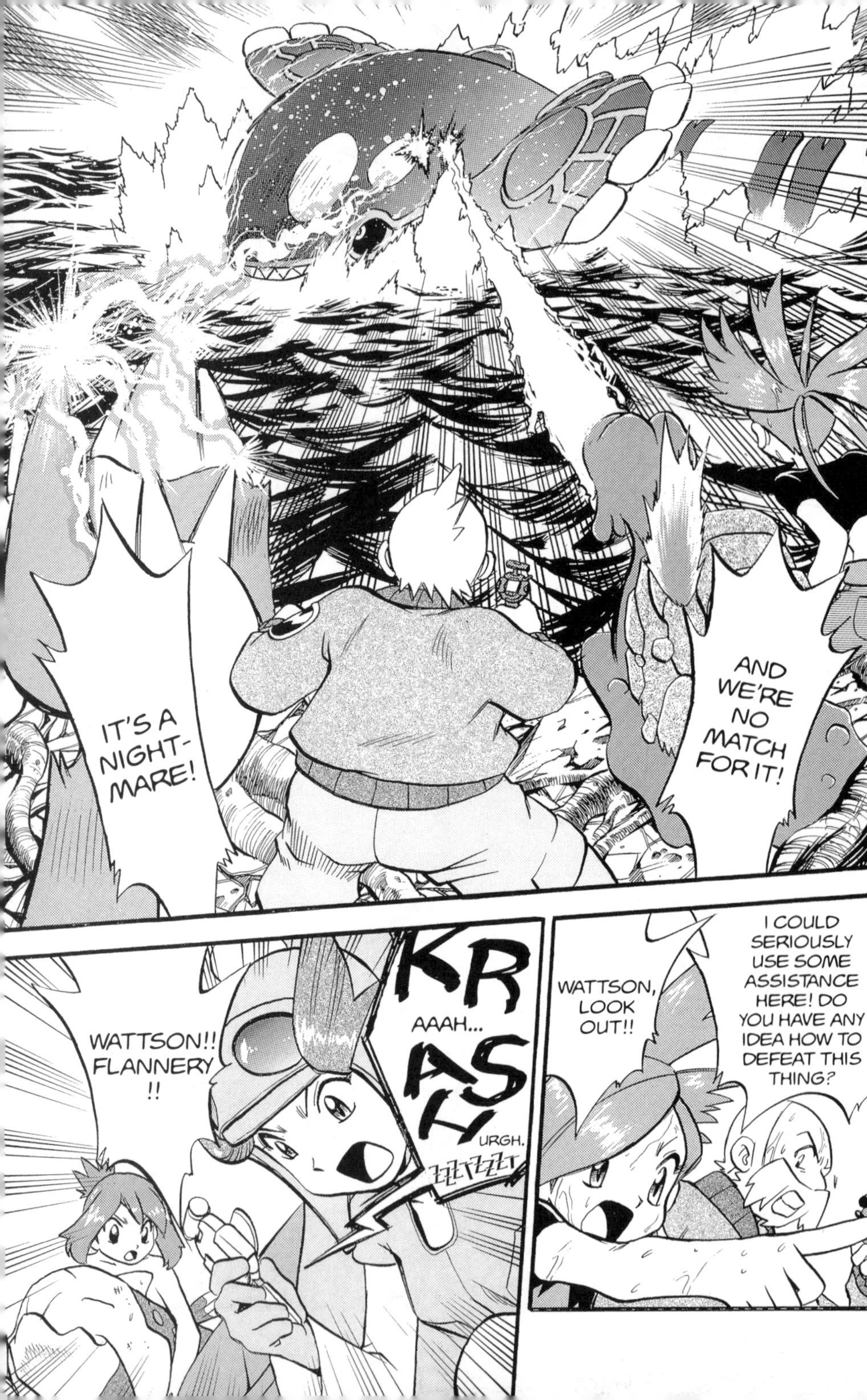
AND WE'RE NO MATCH FOR IT!
IT'S A NIGHT-MARE!
I COULD SERIOUSLY USE SOME ASSISTANCE HERE! DO YOU HAVE ANY IDEA HOW TO DEFEAT THIS THING?
WATTSON, LOOK OUT!!
KRASH
AAAH...
URGH.
ZZZT ZZZT
WATTSON!! FLANNERY!!

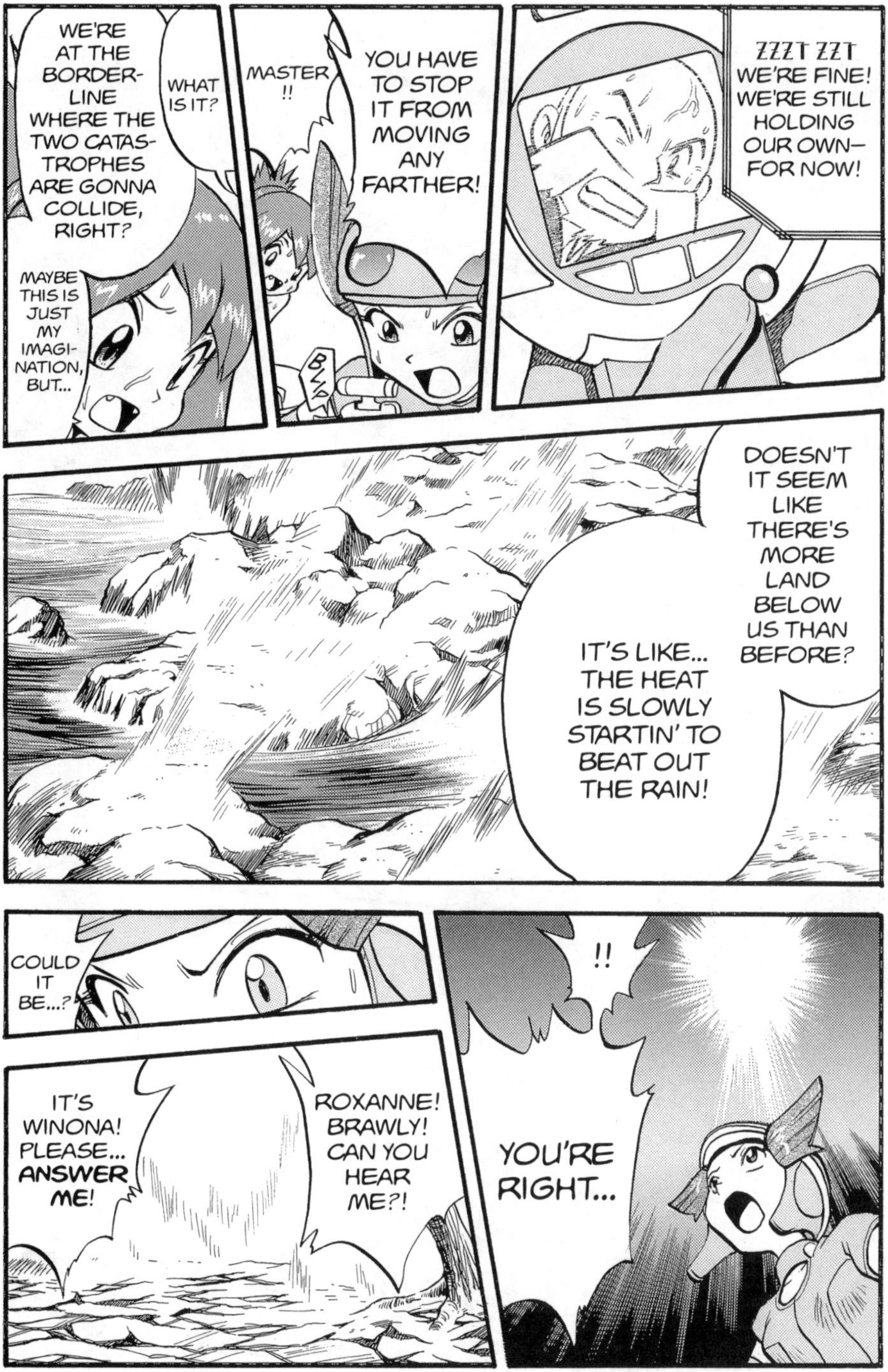

ZZZT ZZT WE'RE FINE! WE'RE STILL HOLDING OUR OWN— FOR NOW!
YOU HAVE TO STOP IT FROM MOVING ANY FARTHER!
MASTER !!
WHAT IS IT?
WE'RE AT THE BORDER-LINE WHERE THE TWO CATAS-TROPHES ARE GONNA COLLIDE, RIGHT?
MAYBE THIS IS JUST MY IMAGI-NATION, BUT...
DOESN'T IT SEEM LIKE THERE'S MORE LAND BELOW US THAN BEFORE?
IT'S LIKE... THE HEAT IS SLOWLY STARTIN' TO BEAT OUT THE RAIN!
!!
YOU'RE RIGHT...
COULD IT BE...?
ROXANNE! BRAWLY! CAN YOU HEAR ME?!
IT'S WINONA! PLEASE... **ANSWER ME!**

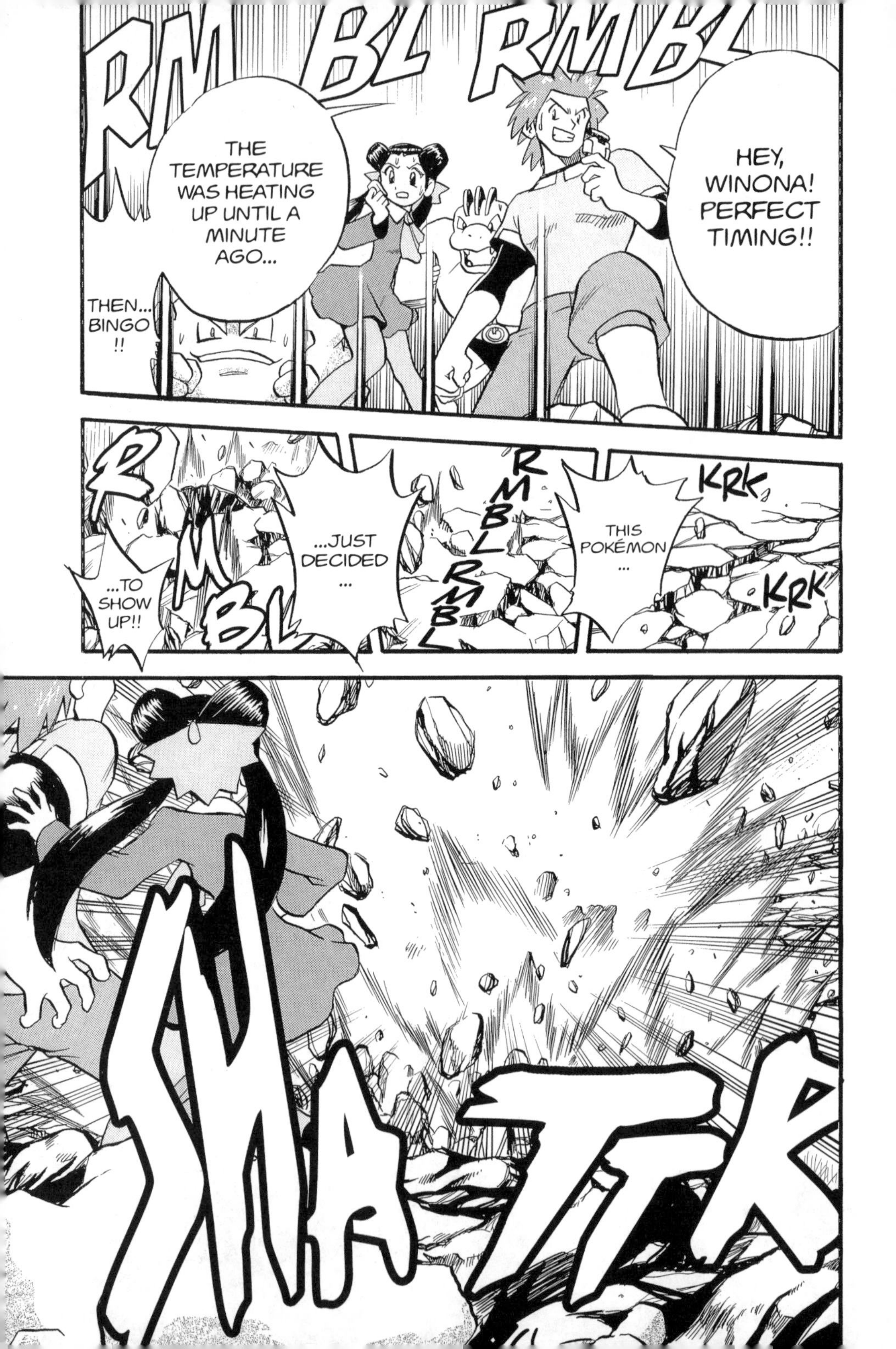
RMBL RMBL
HEY, WINONA! PERFECT TIMING!!
THE TEMPERATURE WAS HEATING UP UNTIL A MINUTE AGO...
THEN... BINGO!!
KRK KRK
THIS POKÉMON...
RMBL RMBL
...JUST DECIDED...
RMBL
...TO SHOW UP!!
SMATTK

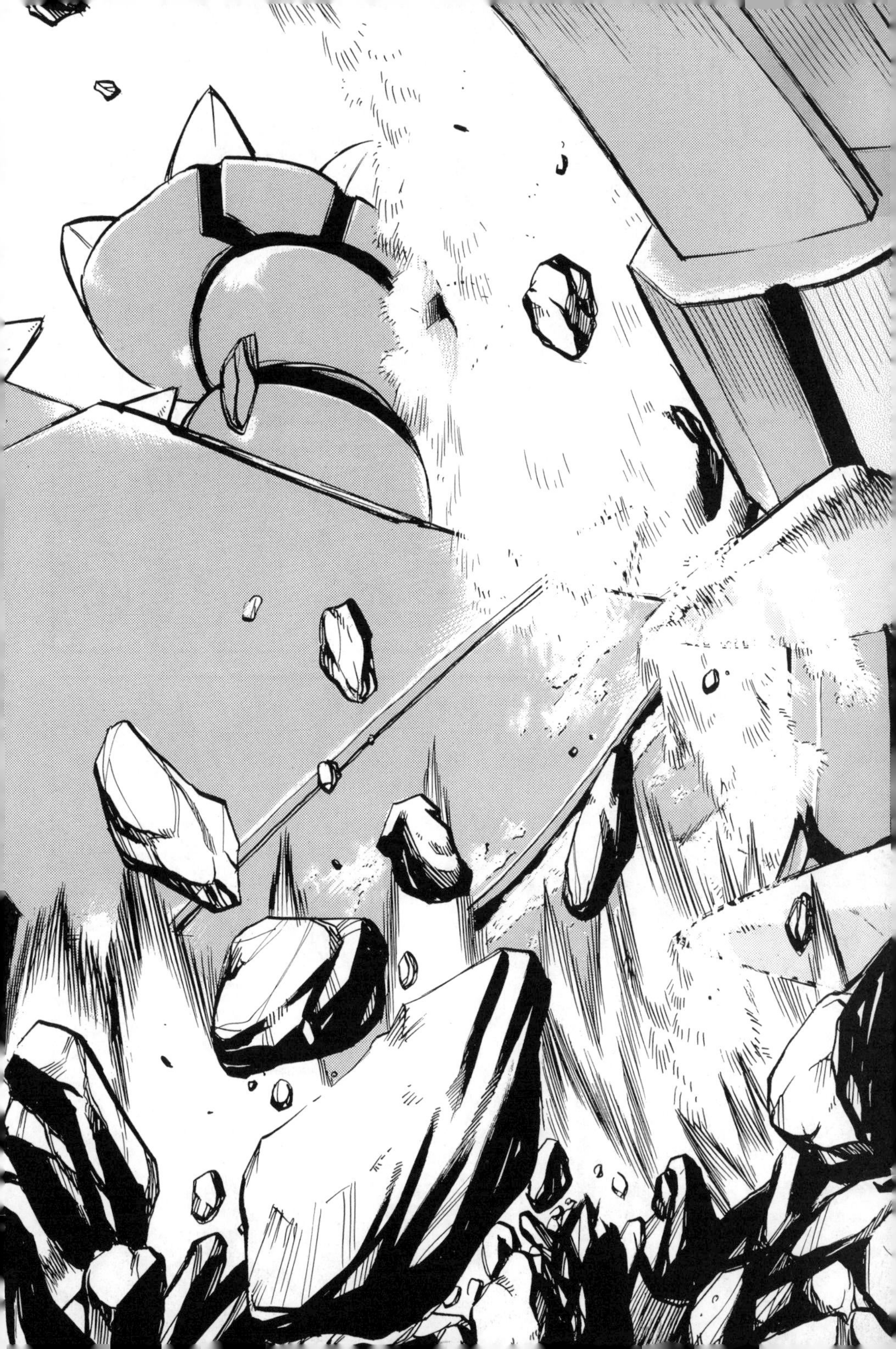

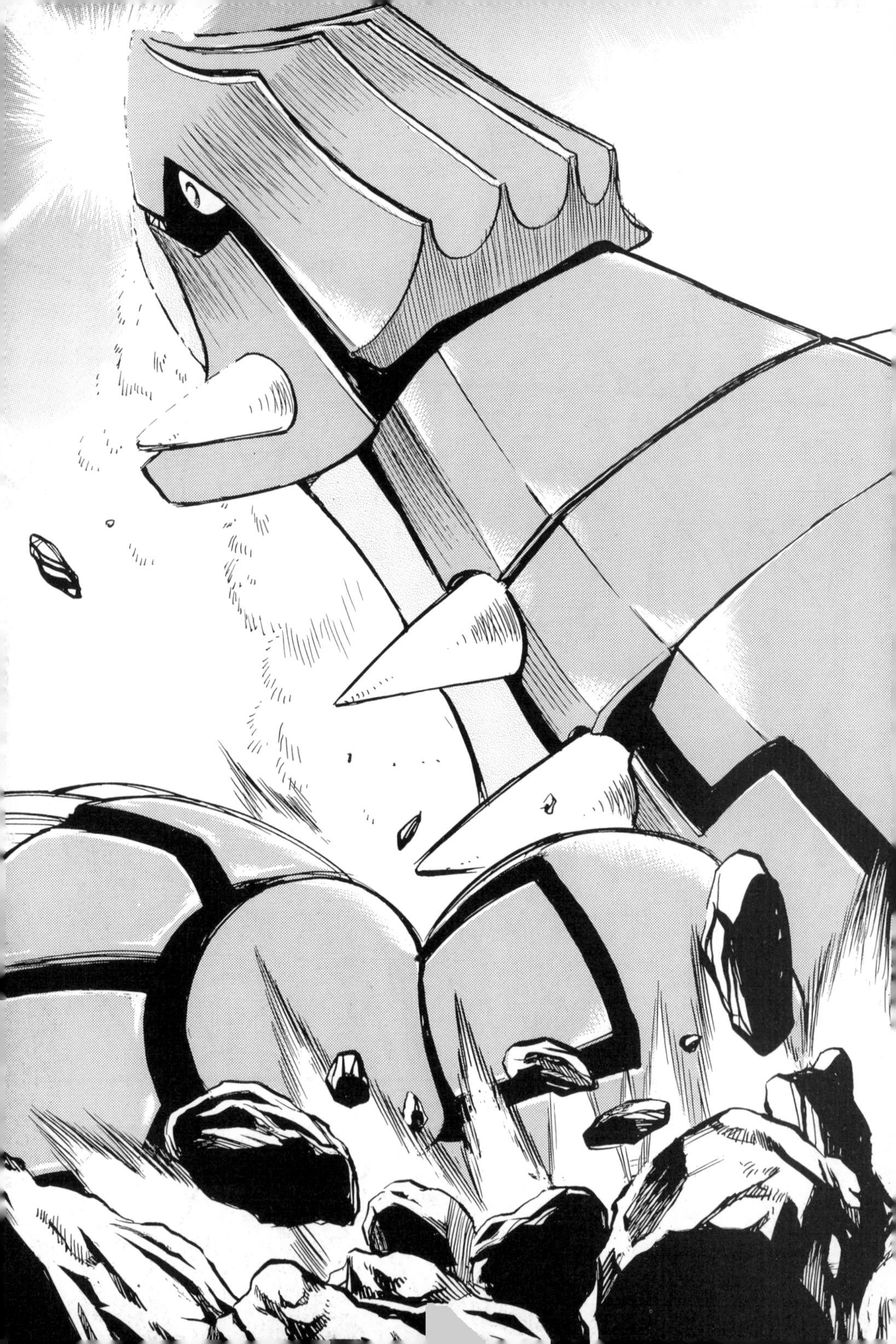

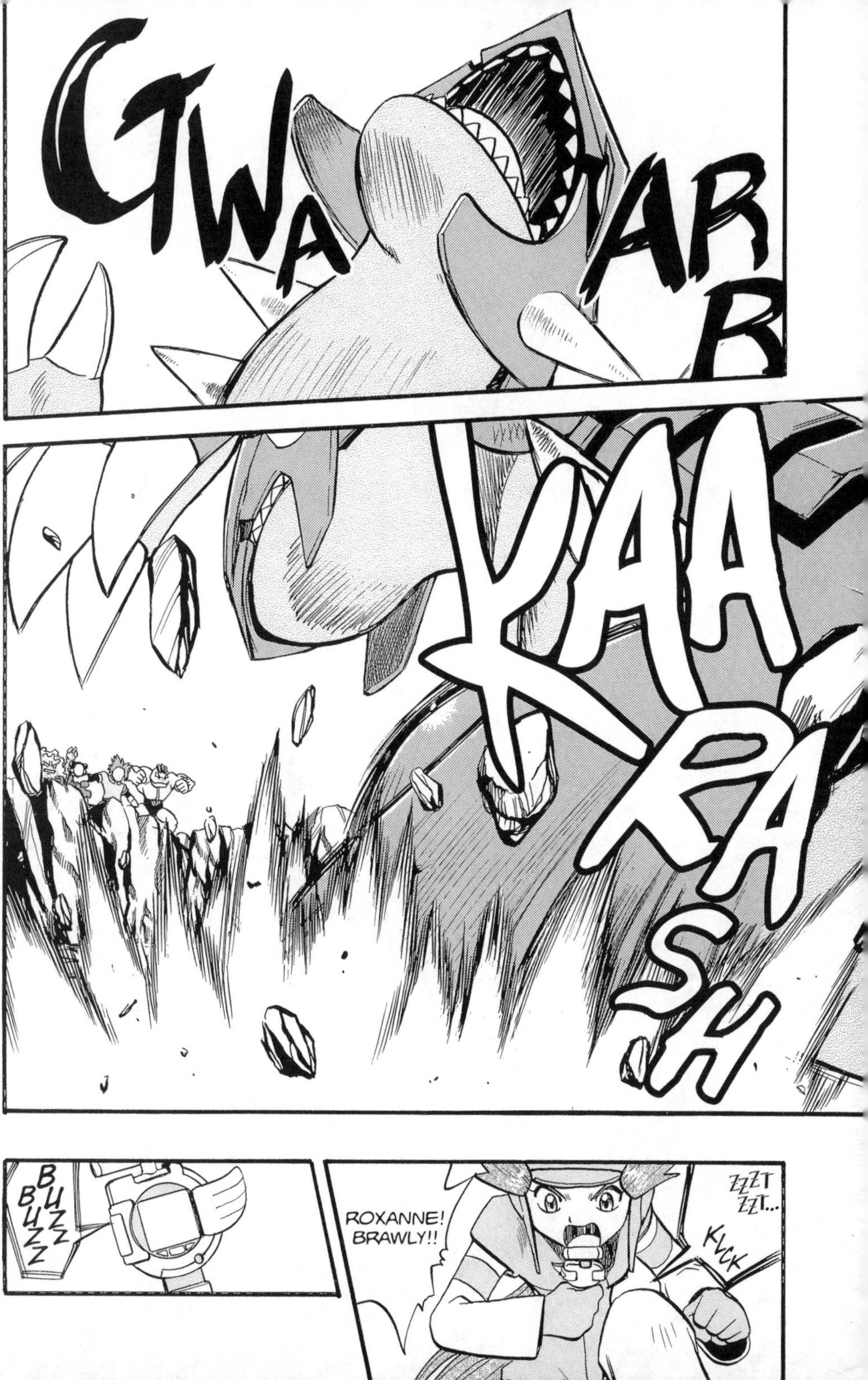
GWAARR
KAARAASH
ZZZT
ZZT...
ROXANNE! BRAWLY!!
KLICK
BUZZ
BUZZ

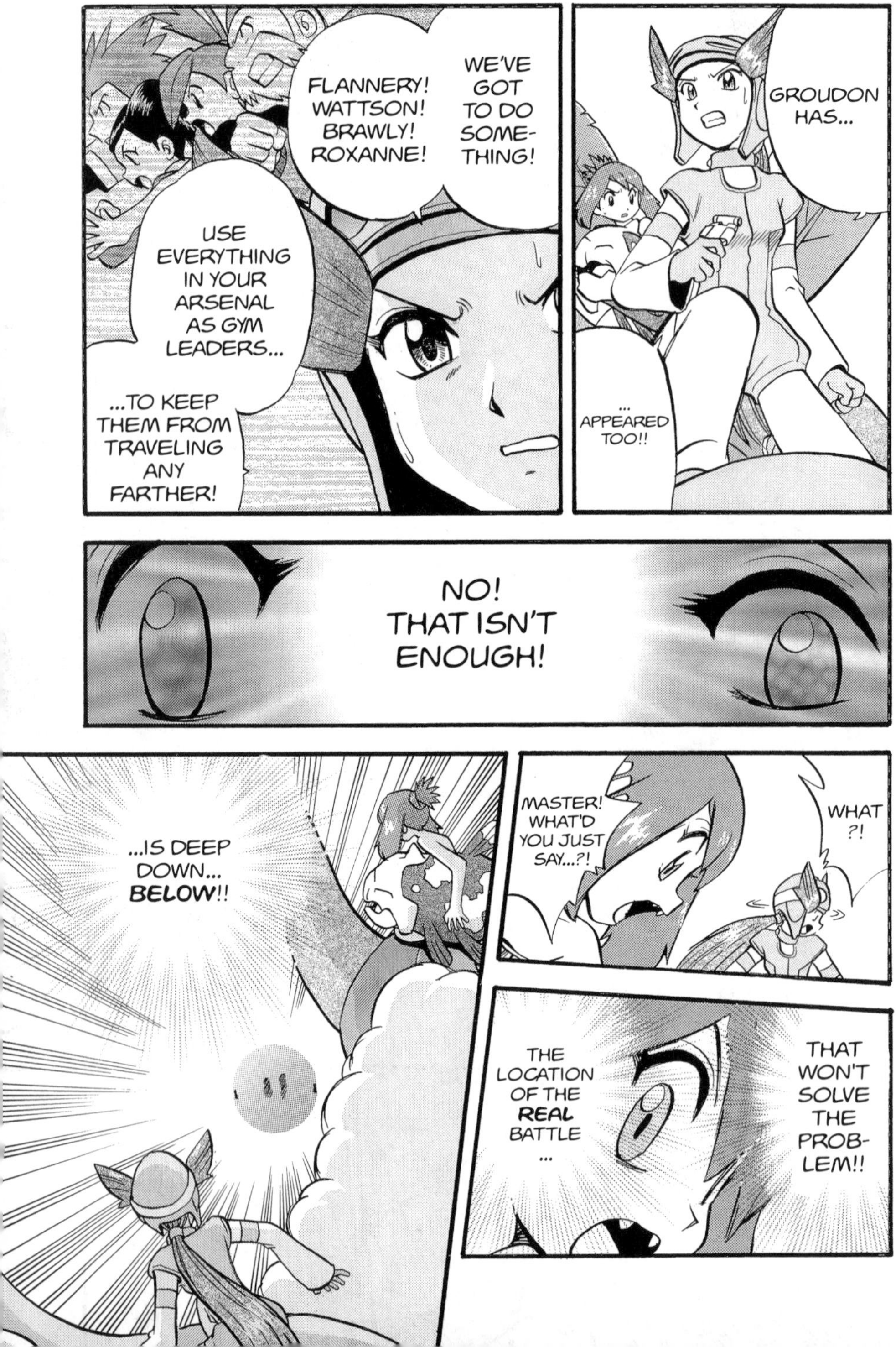
GROUDON HAS...
...APPEARED TOO!!
WE'VE GOT TO DO SOME-THING!
FLANNERY! WATTSON! BRAWLY! ROXANNE!
USE EVERYTHING IN YOUR ARSENAL AS GYM LEADERS...
...TO KEEP THEM FROM TRAVELING ANY FARTHER!
NO! THAT ISN'T ENOUGH!
WHAT?!
MASTER! WHAT'D YOU JUST SAY...?!
THAT WON'T SOLVE THE PROB-LEM!!
THE LOCATION OF THE **REAL** BATTLE...
...IS DEEP DOWN... **BELOW**!!

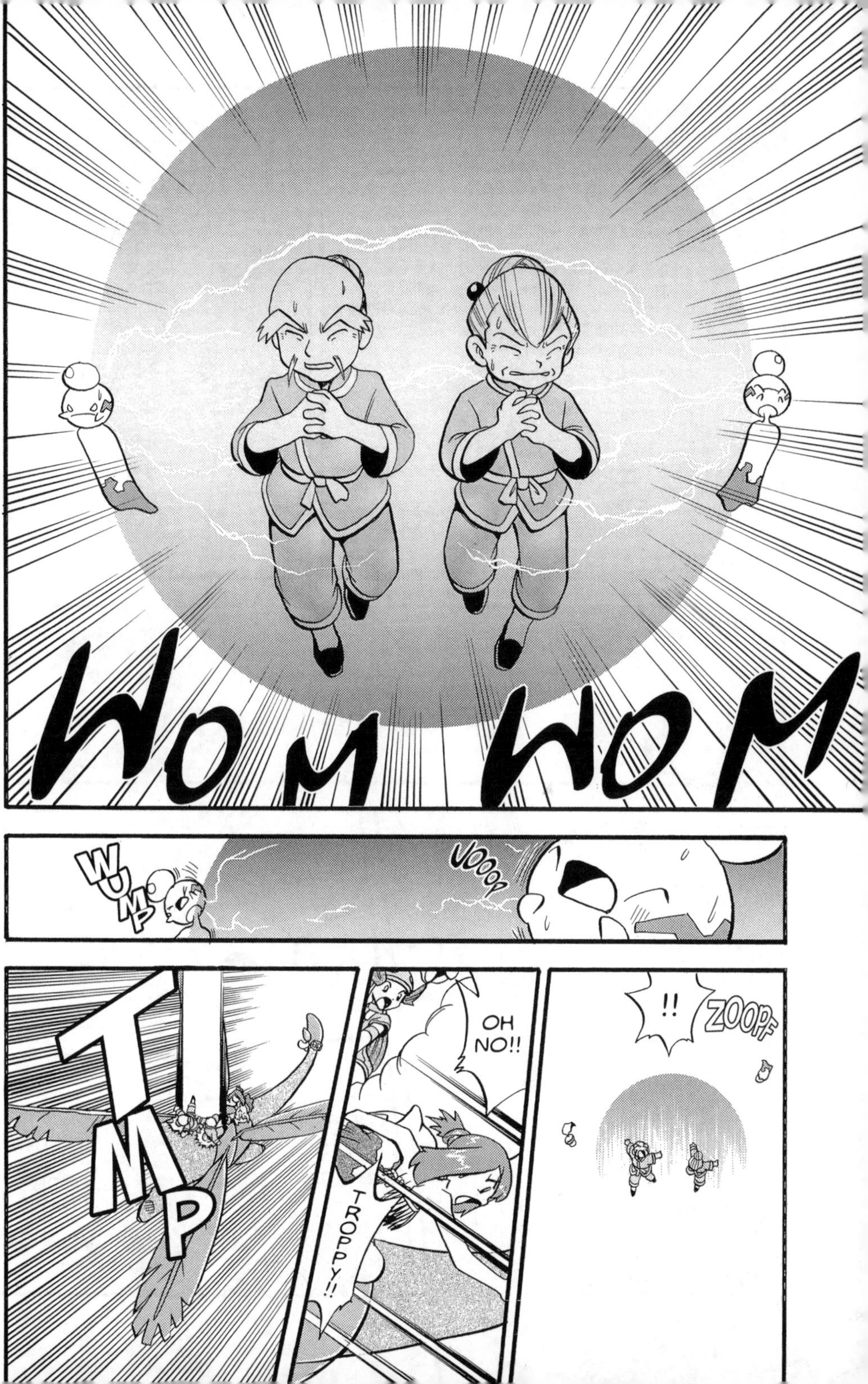
WOM WOM
VOOOP
WUMP
!!
ZOOPF
OH NO!!
TROPPY!!
TIMP

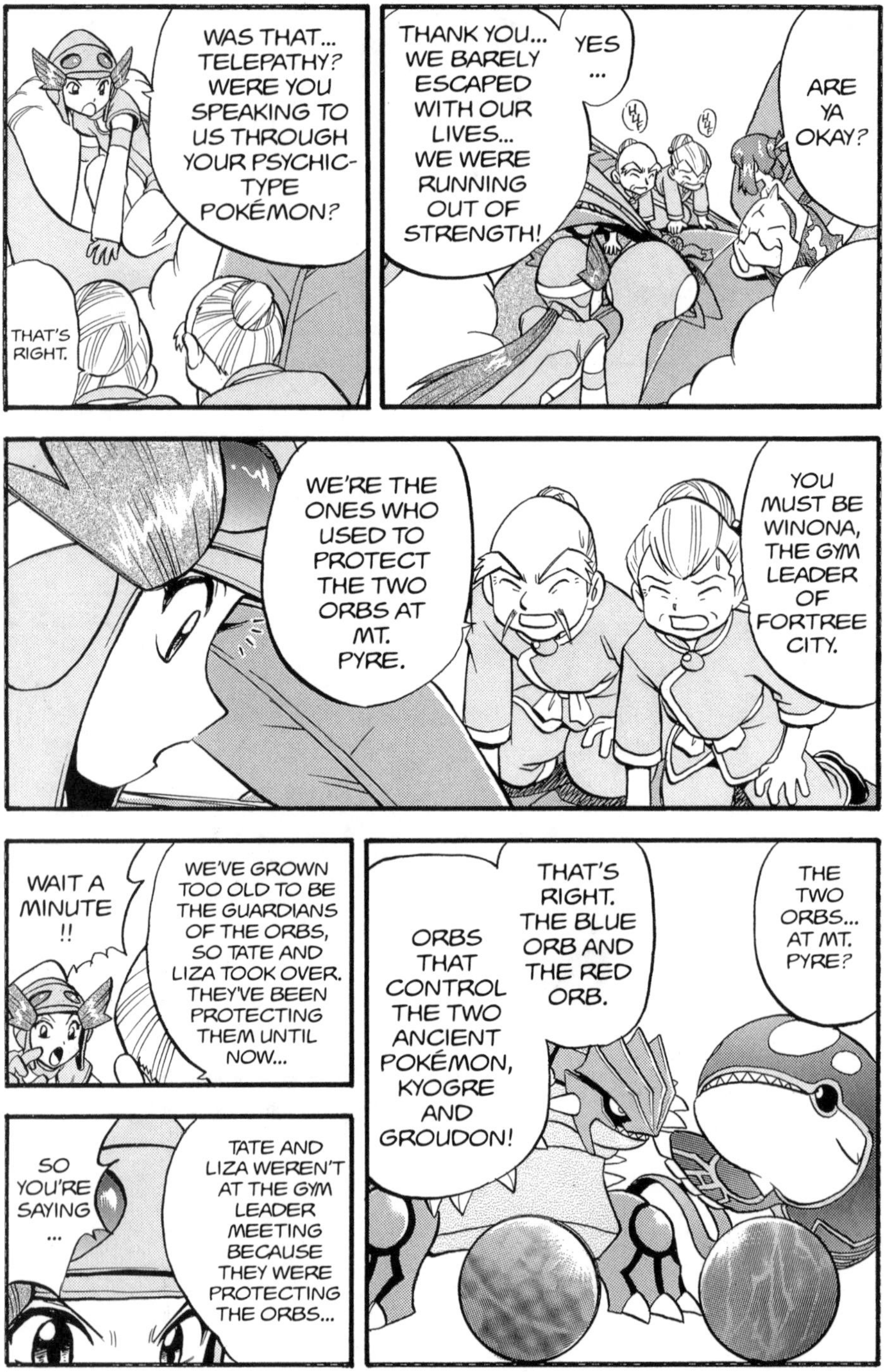
ARE YA OKAY?
YES ...
THANK YOU... WE BARELY ESCAPED WITH OUR LIVES... WE WERE RUNNING OUT OF STRENGTH!
WAS THAT... TELEPATHY? WERE YOU SPEAKING TO US THROUGH YOUR PSYCHIC-TYPE POKÉMON?
THAT'S RIGHT.
YOU MUST BE WINONA, THE GYM LEADER OF FORTREE CITY.
WE'RE THE ONES WHO USED TO PROTECT THE TWO ORBS AT MT. PYRE.
THE TWO ORBS... AT MT. PYRE?
THAT'S RIGHT. THE BLUE ORB AND THE RED ORB.
ORBS THAT CONTROL THE TWO ANCIENT POKÉMON, KYOGRE AND GROUDON!
WE'VE GROWN TOO OLD TO BE THE GUARDIANS OF THE ORBS, SO TATE AND LIZA TOOK OVER. THEY'VE BEEN PROTECTING THEM UNTIL NOW...
WAIT A MINUTE !!
TATE AND LIZA WEREN'T AT THE GYM LEADER MEETING BECAUSE THEY WERE PROTECTING THE ORBS...
SO YOU'RE SAYING ...

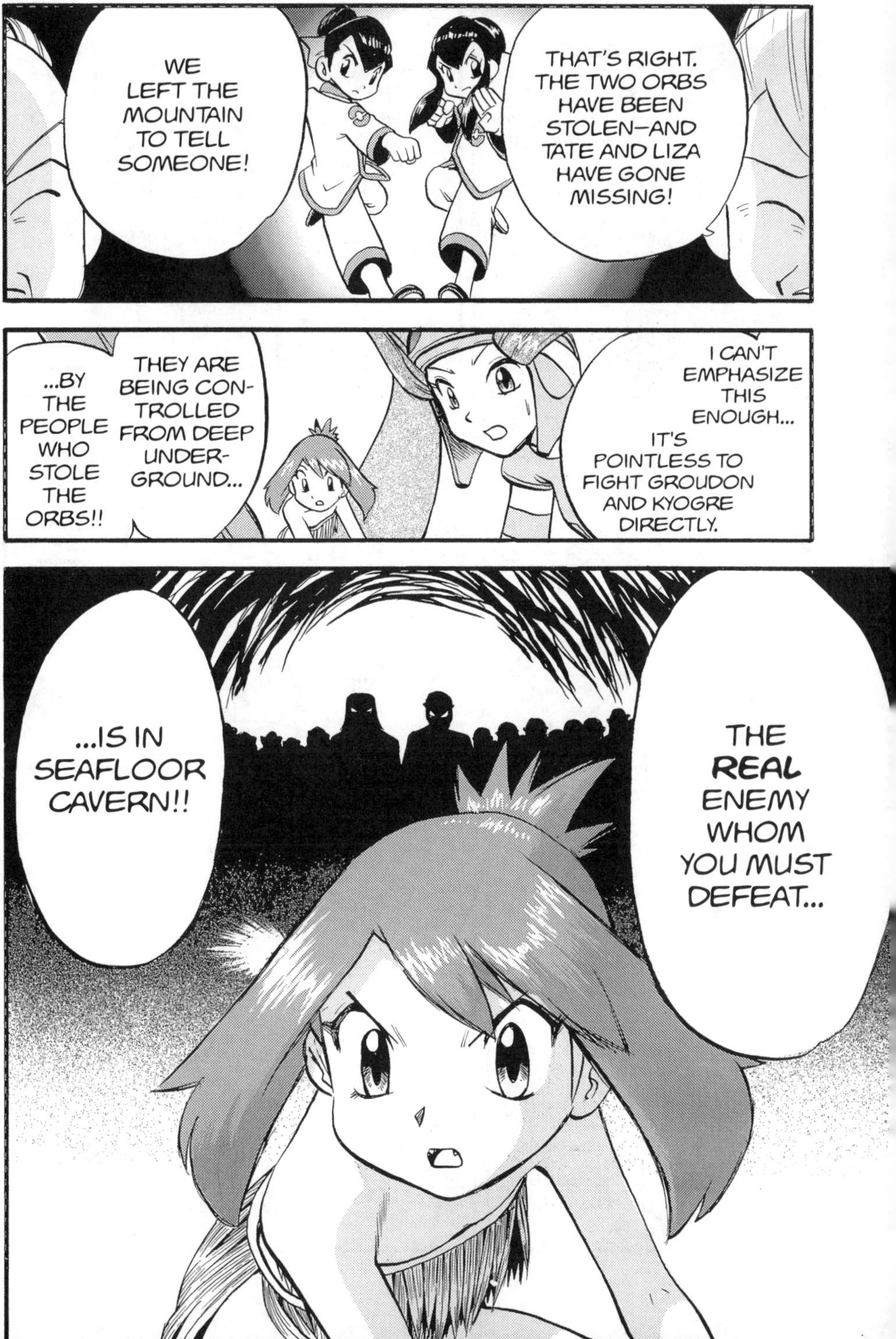
THAT'S RIGHT. THE TWO ORBS HAVE BEEN STOLEN—AND TATE AND LIZA HAVE GONE MISSING!
WE LEFT THE MOUNTAIN TO TELL SOMEONE!
I CAN'T EMPHASIZE THIS ENOUGH...
IT'S POINTLESS TO FIGHT GROUDON AND KYOGRE DIRECTLY.
THEY ARE BEING CON-TROLLED FROM DEEP UNDER-GROUND...
...BY THE PEOPLE WHO STOLE THE ORBS!!
THE **REAL** ENEMY WHOM YOU MUST DEFEAT...
...IS IN SEAFLOOR CAVERN!!

Adventure 237
The Beginning of the End with Kyogre and Groudon, Part 5

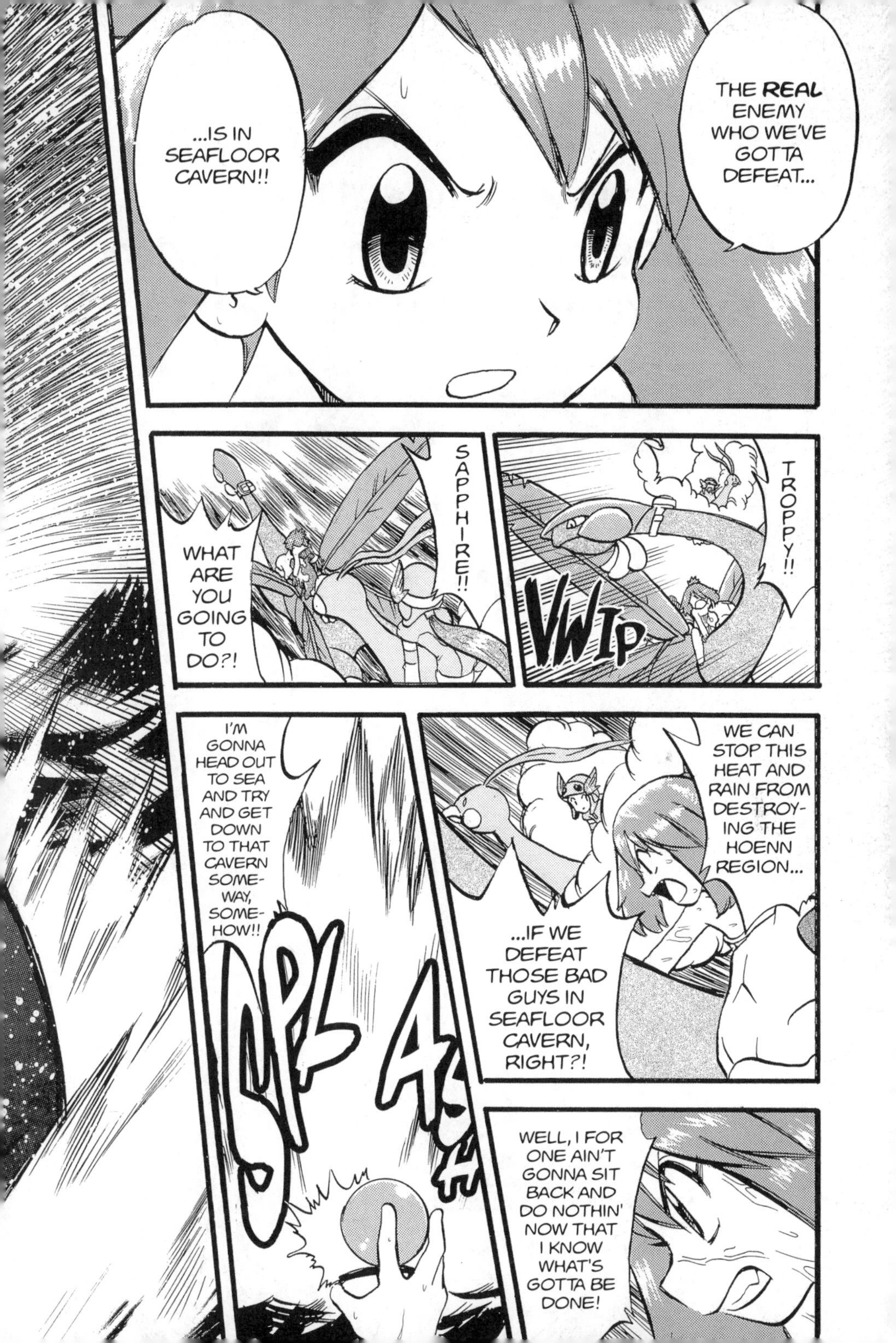
THE REAL ENEMY WHO WE'VE GOTTA DEFEAT...
...IS IN SEAFLOOR CAVERN!!
TROPPY!!
VWIP
SAPPHIRE!!
WHAT ARE YOU GOING TO DO?!
WE CAN STOP THIS HEAT AND RAIN FROM DESTROYING THE HOENN REGION...
...IF WE DEFEAT THOSE BAD GUYS IN SEAFLOOR CAVERN, RIGHT?!
WELL, I FOR ONE AIN'T GONNA SIT BACK AND DO NOTHIN' NOW THAT I KNOW WHAT'S GOTTA BE DONE!
I'M GONNA HEAD OUT TO SEA AND TRY AND GET DOWN TO THAT CAVERN SOMEWAY, SOMEHOW!!

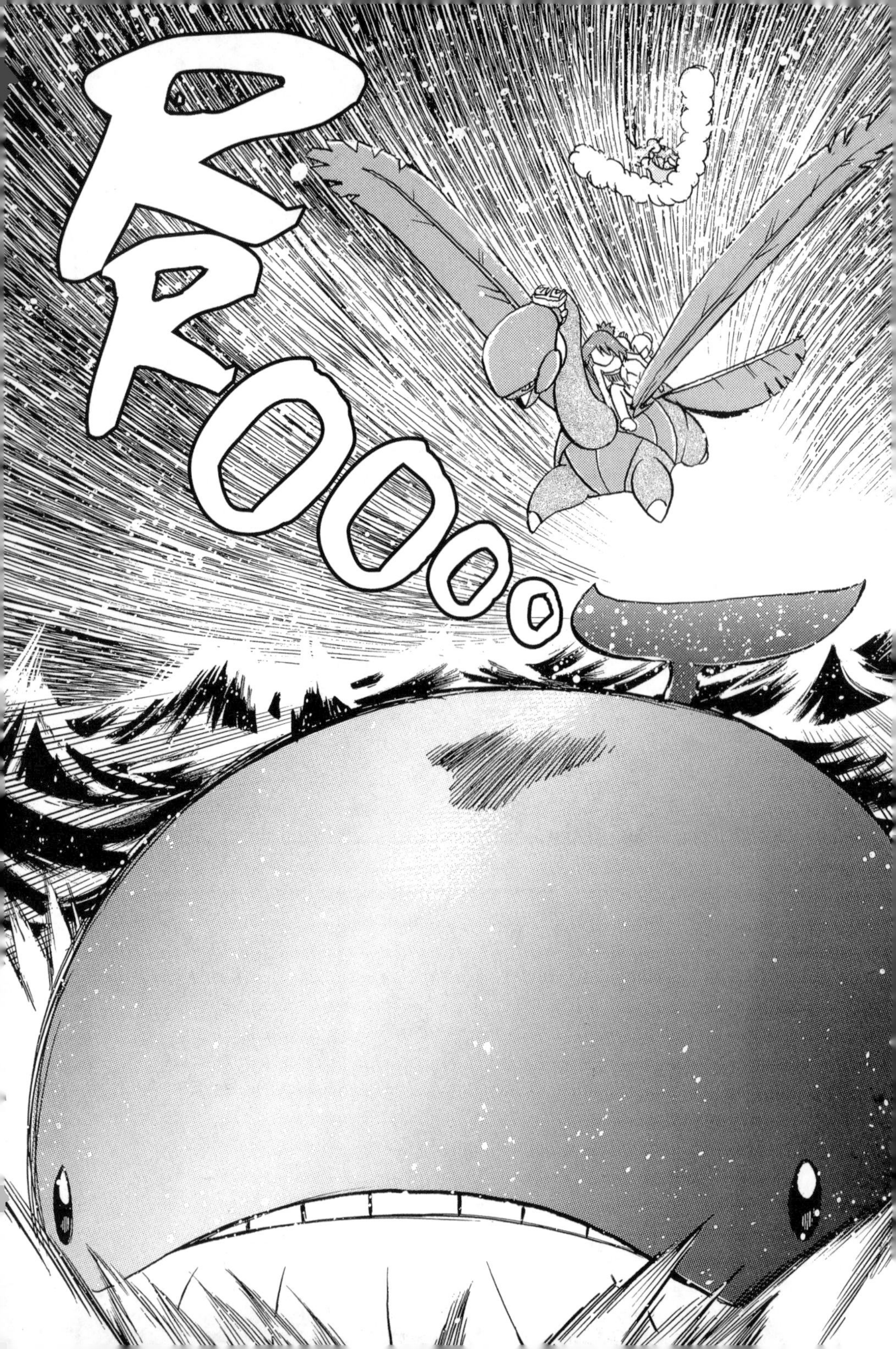
RROOOOO

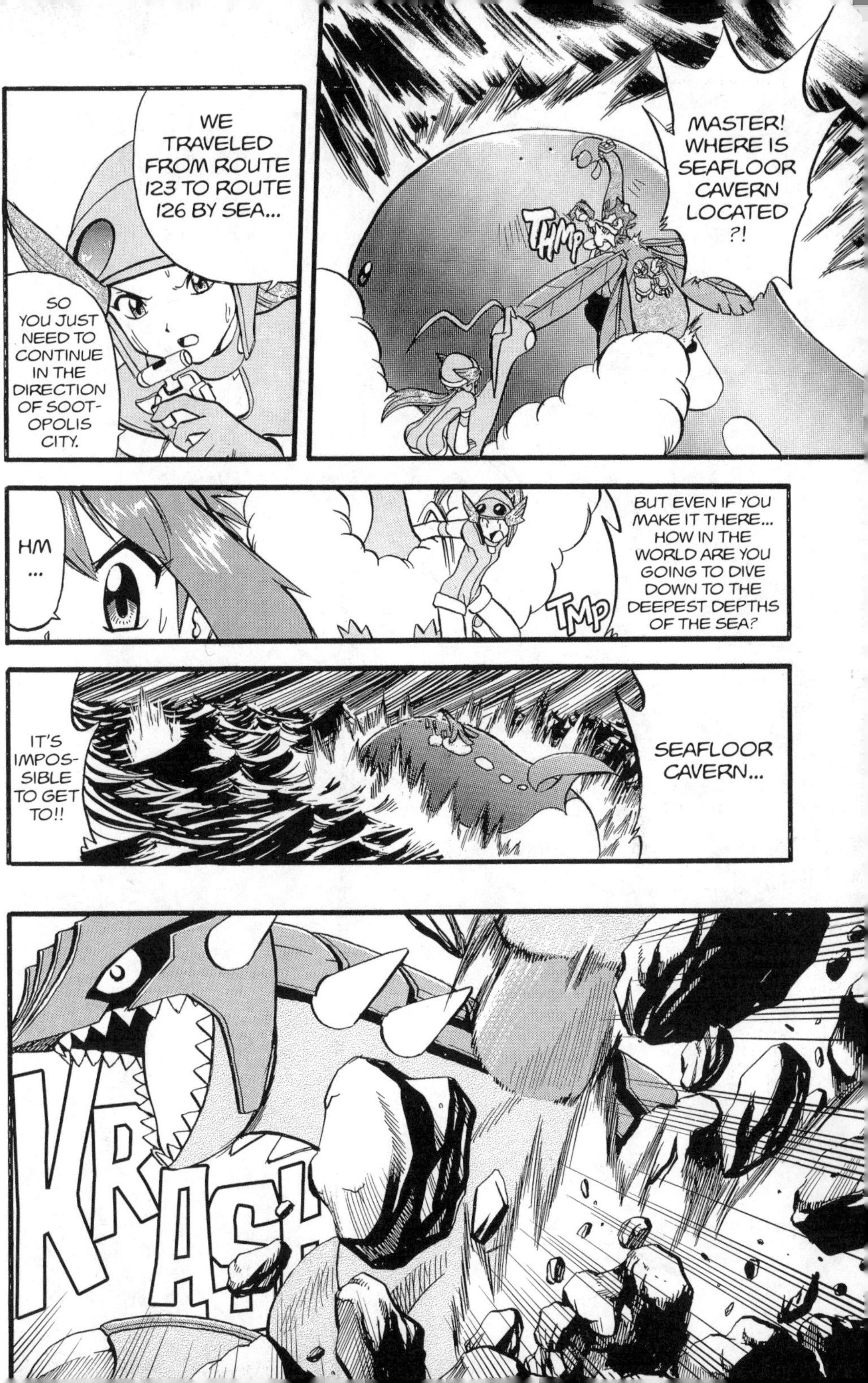
MASTER! WHERE IS SEAFLOOR CAVERN LOCATED?!
THMP
WE TRAVELED FROM ROUTE 123 TO ROUTE 126 BY SEA...
SO YOU JUST NEED TO CONTINUE IN THE DIRECTION OF SOOT-OPOLIS CITY.
BUT EVEN IF YOU MAKE IT THERE... HOW IN THE WORLD ARE YOU GOING TO DIVE DOWN TO THE DEEPEST DEPTHS OF THE SEA?
TMP
HM...
SEAFLOOR CAVERN...
IT'S IMPOS-SIBLE TO GET TO!!
KRASH

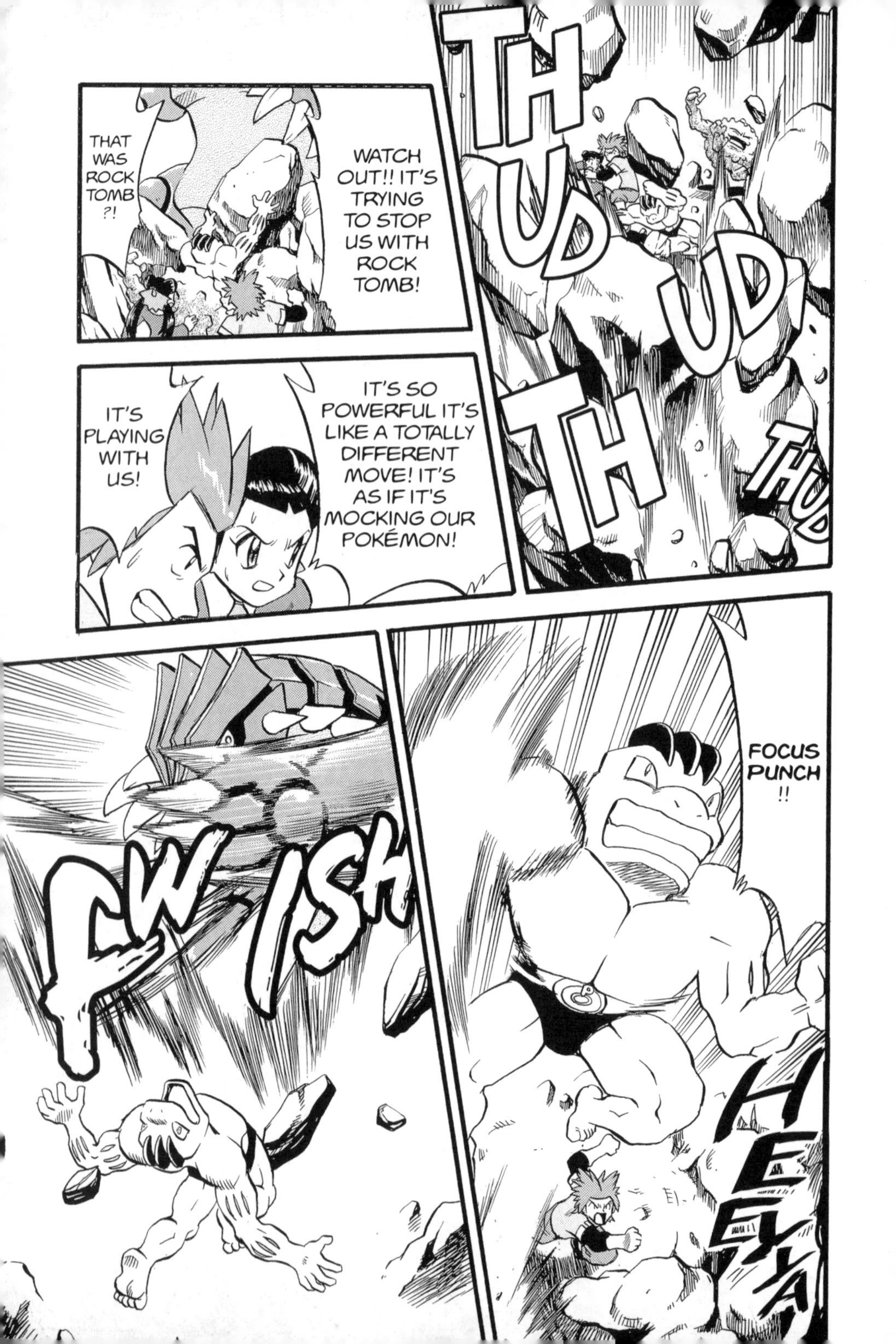
THUD
THUD
THUD
WATCH OUT!! IT'S TRYING TO STOP US WITH ROCK TOMB!
THAT WAS ROCK TOMB ?!
IT'S SO POWERFUL IT'S LIKE A TOTALLY DIFFERENT MOVE! IT'S AS IF IT'S MOCKING OUR POKÉMON!
IT'S PLAYING WITH US!
FOCUS PUNCH !!
FWISH

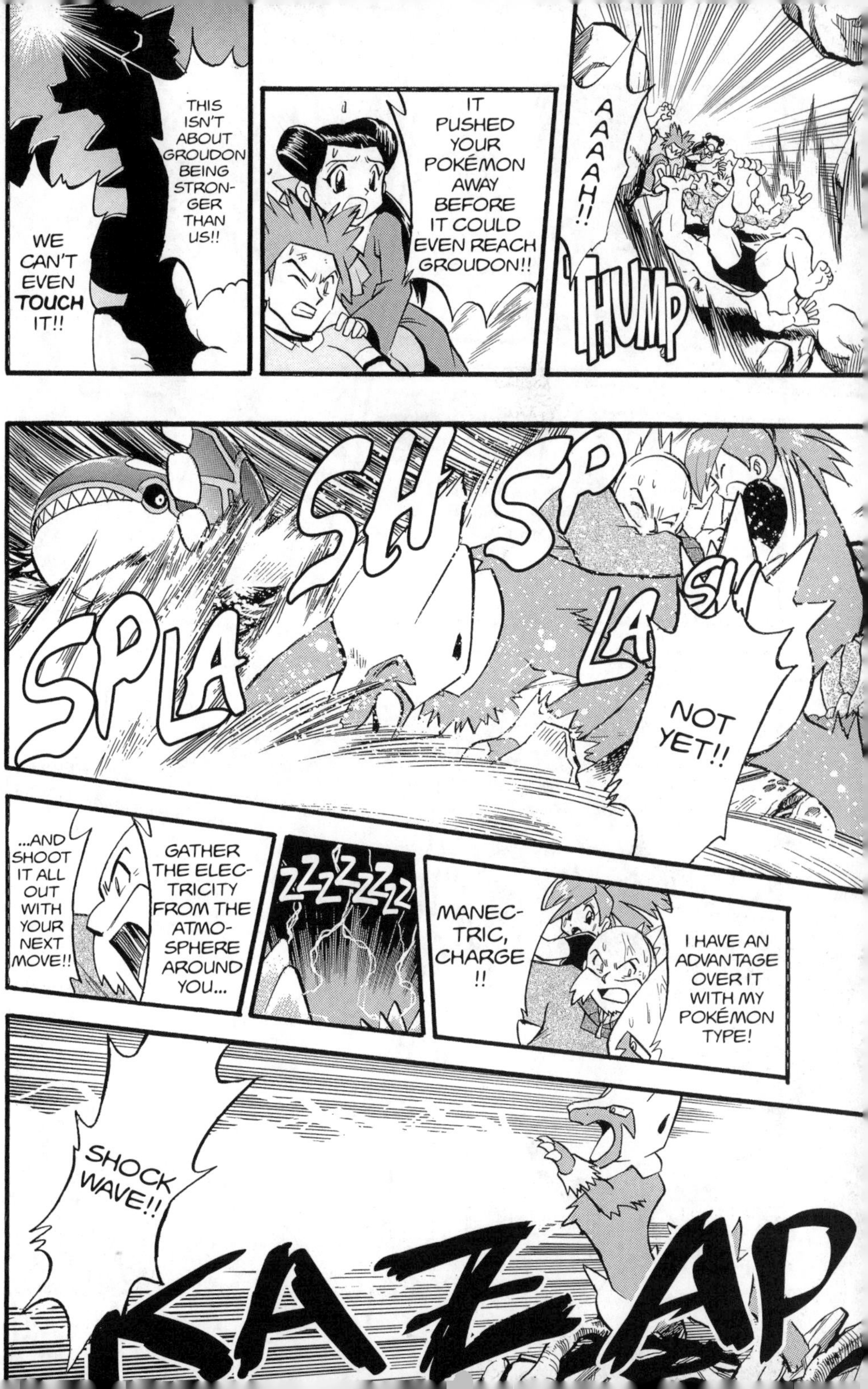
AAAAAH!!
THUMP
IT PUSHED YOUR POKÉMON AWAY BEFORE IT COULD EVEN REACH GROUDON!!
THIS ISN'T ABOUT GROUDON BEING STRON-GER THAN US!!
WE CAN'T EVEN **TOUCH** IT!!
SP LA SH
NOT YET!!
SPLA SH
I HAVE AN ADVANTAGE OVER IT WITH MY POKÉMON TYPE!
MANEC-TRIC, CHARGE!!
ZZZZZZZZ
GATHER THE ELEC-TRICITY FROM THE ATMO-SPHERE AROUND YOU...
...AND SHOOT IT ALL OUT WITH YOUR NEXT MOVE!!
SHOCK WAVE!!
KA-ZAP

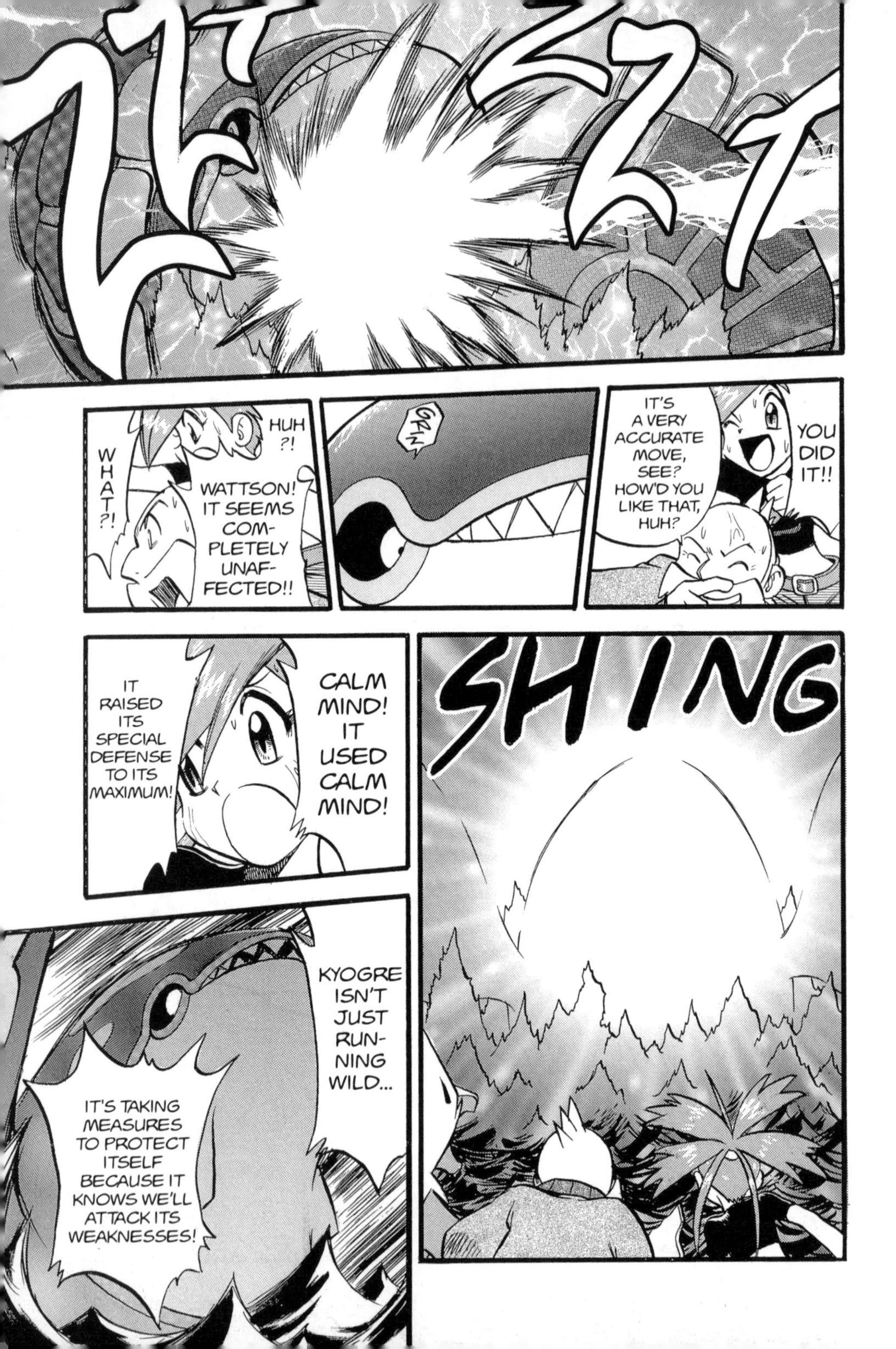
YOU DID IT!!
IT'S A VERY ACCURATE MOVE, SEE? HOW'D YOU LIKE THAT, HUH?
GRIN
HUH?!
WATTSON! IT SEEMS COMPLETELY UNAFFECTED!!
WHAT?!
SHING
CALM MIND! IT USED CALM MIND!
IT RAISED ITS SPECIAL DEFENSE TO ITS MAXIMUM!
KYOGRE ISN'T JUST RUNNING WILD...
IT'S TAKING MEASURES TO PROTECT ITSELF BECAUSE IT KNOWS WE'LL ATTACK ITS WEAKNESSES!

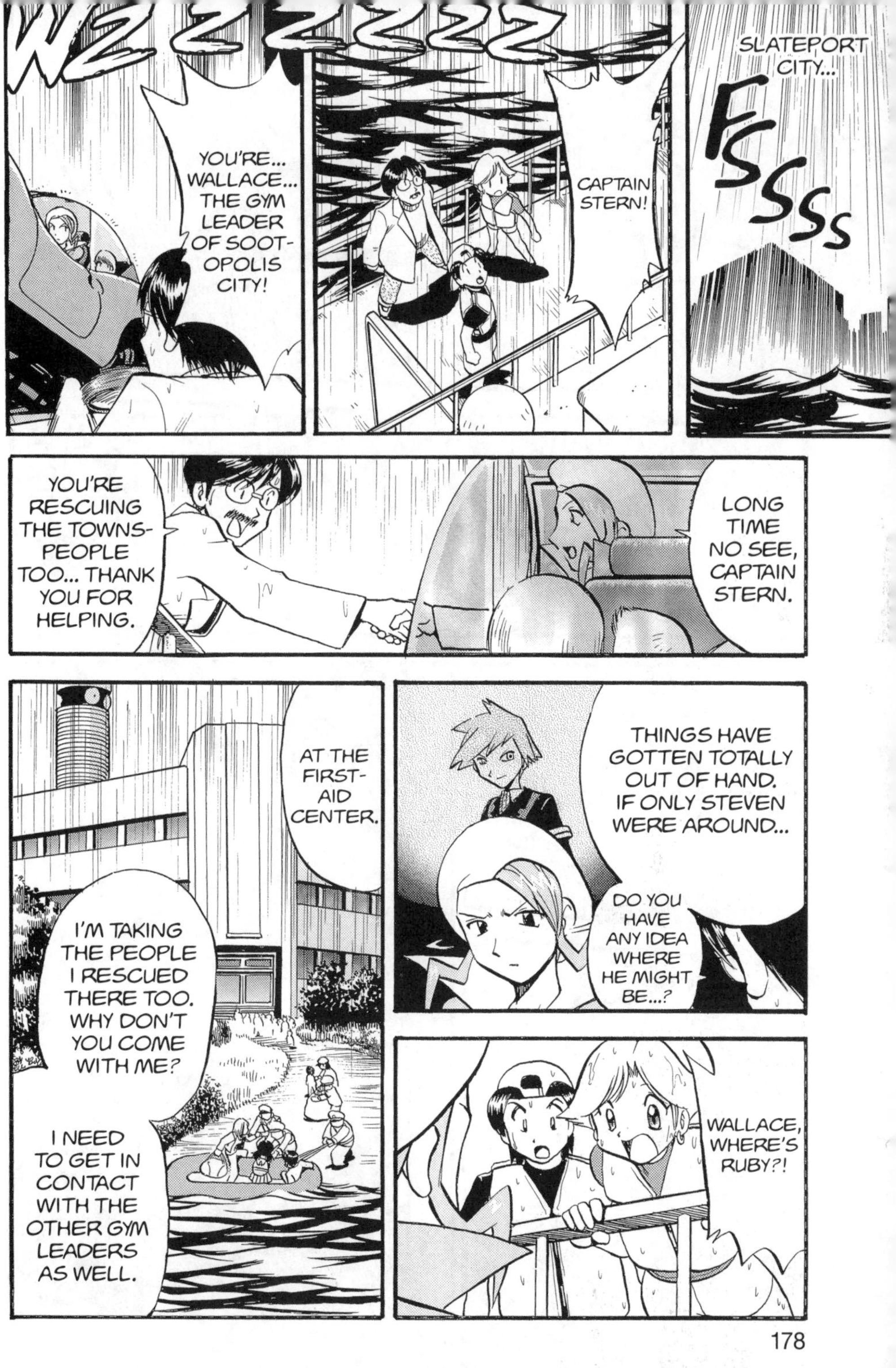
SLATEPORT CITY...
FSSSS
CAPTAIN STERN!
WZZZZZZZ
YOU'RE... WALLACE... THE GYM LEADER OF SOOTOPOLIS CITY!
LONG TIME NO SEE, CAPTAIN STERN.
YOU'RE RESCUING THE TOWNSPEOPLE TOO... THANK YOU FOR HELPING.
THINGS HAVE GOTTEN TOTALLY OUT OF HAND. IF ONLY STEVEN WERE AROUND...
DO YOU HAVE ANY IDEA WHERE HE MIGHT BE...?
WALLACE, WHERE'S RUBY?!
AT THE FIRST-AID CENTER.
I'M TAKING THE PEOPLE I RESCUED THERE TOO. WHY DON'T YOU COME WITH ME?
I NEED TO GET IN CONTACT WITH THE OTHER GYM LEADERS AS WELL.

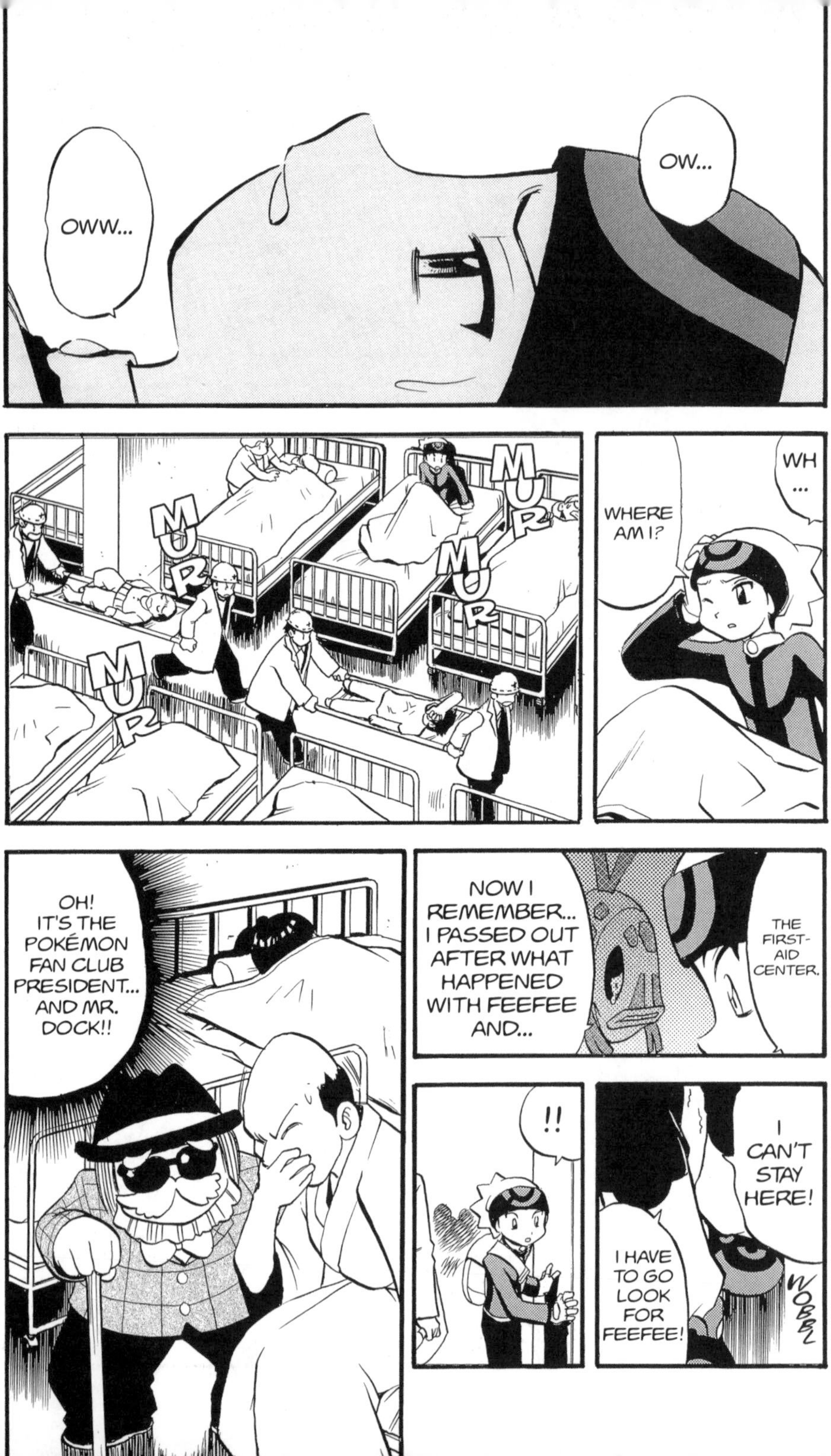

OW...
OWW...
WH ...
WHERE AM I?
MUR
MUR
MUR
MUR
THE FIRST-AID CENTER.
NOW I REMEMBER... I PASSED OUT AFTER WHAT HAPPENED WITH FEEFEE AND...
I CAN'T STAY HERE!
I HAVE TO GO LOOK FOR FEEFEE!
WOBBL
!!
OH! IT'S THE POKÉMON FAN CLUB PRESIDENT... AND MR. DOCK!!

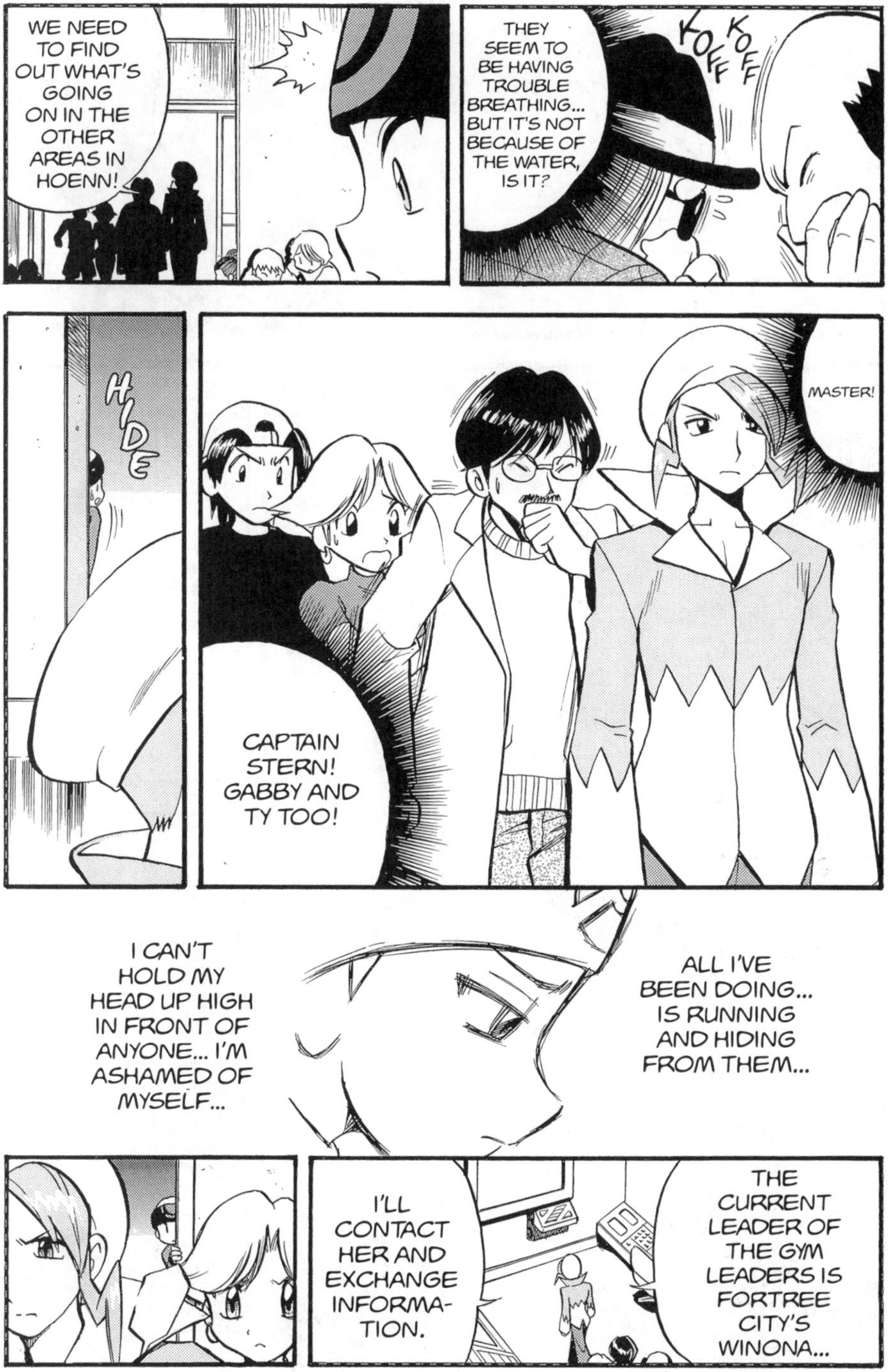
THEY SEEM TO BE HAVING TROUBLE BREATHING... BUT IT'S NOT BECAUSE OF THE WATER, IS IT?
KOFF KOFF
WE NEED TO FIND OUT WHAT'S GOING ON IN THE OTHER AREAS IN HOENN!
MASTER!
CAPTAIN STERN! GABBY AND TY TOO!
HIDE
ALL I'VE BEEN DOING... IS RUNNING AND HIDING FROM THEM...
I CAN'T HOLD MY HEAD UP HIGH IN FRONT OF ANYONE... I'M ASHAMED OF MYSELF...
THE CURRENT LEADER OF THE GYM LEADERS IS FORTREE CITY'S WINONA...
I'LL CONTACT HER AND EXCHANGE INFORMATION.

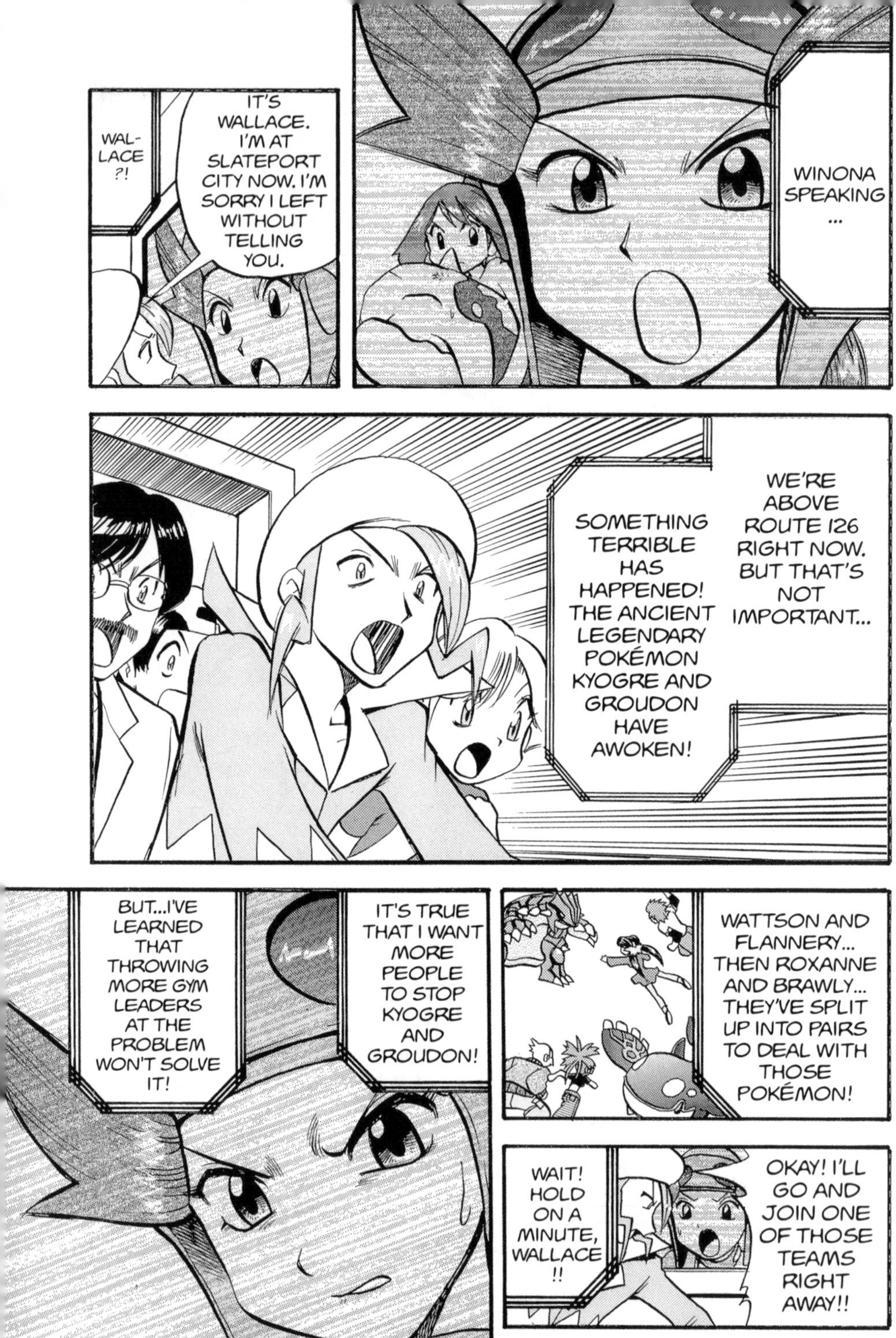
WINONA SPEAKING ...
IT'S WALLACE. I'M AT SLATEPORT CITY NOW. I'M SORRY I LEFT WITHOUT TELLING YOU.
WAL-LACE ?!
WE'RE ABOVE ROUTE 126 RIGHT NOW. BUT THAT'S NOT IMPORTANT...
SOMETHING TERRIBLE HAS HAPPENED! THE ANCIENT LEGENDARY POKÉMON KYOGRE AND GROUDON HAVE AWOKEN!
WATTSON AND FLANNERY... THEN ROXANNE AND BRAWLY... THEY'VE SPLIT UP INTO PAIRS TO DEAL WITH THOSE POKÉMON!
OKAY! I'LL GO AND JOIN ONE OF THOSE TEAMS RIGHT AWAY!!
WAIT! HOLD ON A MINUTE, WALLACE !!
IT'S TRUE THAT I WANT MORE PEOPLE TO STOP KYOGRE AND GROUDON!
BUT...I'VE LEARNED THAT THROWING MORE GYM LEADERS AT THE PROBLEM WON'T SOLVE IT!

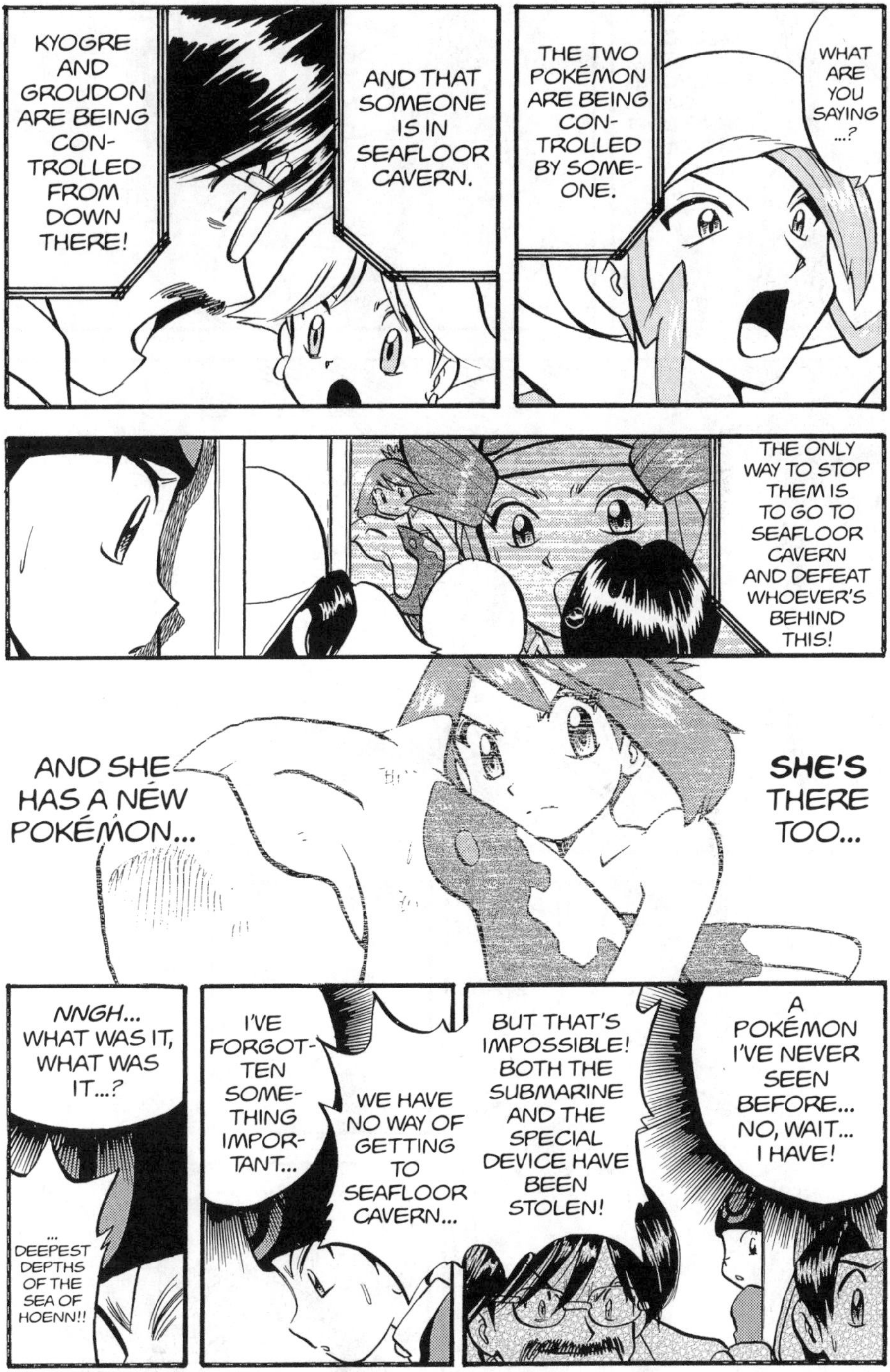
WHAT ARE YOU SAYING ...?
THE TWO POKÉMON ARE BEING CON-TROLLED BY SOME-ONE.
AND THAT SOMEONE IS IN SEAFLOOR CAVERN.
KYOGRE AND GROUDON ARE BEING CON-TROLLED FROM DOWN THERE!
THE ONLY WAY TO STOP THEM IS TO GO TO SEAFLOOR CAVERN AND DEFEAT WHOEVER'S BEHIND THIS!
SHE'S THERE TOO...
AND SHE HAS A NEW POKÉMON...
A POKÉMON I'VE NEVER SEEN BEFORE... NO, WAIT... I HAVE!
BUT THAT'S IMPOSSIBLE! BOTH THE SUBMARINE AND THE SPECIAL DEVICE HAVE BEEN STOLEN!
WE HAVE NO WAY OF GETTING TO SEAFLOOR CAVERN...
I'VE FORGOT-TEN SOME-THING IMPOR-TANT...
NNGH... WHAT WAS IT, WHAT WAS IT...?
... DEEPEST DEPTHS OF THE SEA OF HOENN!!

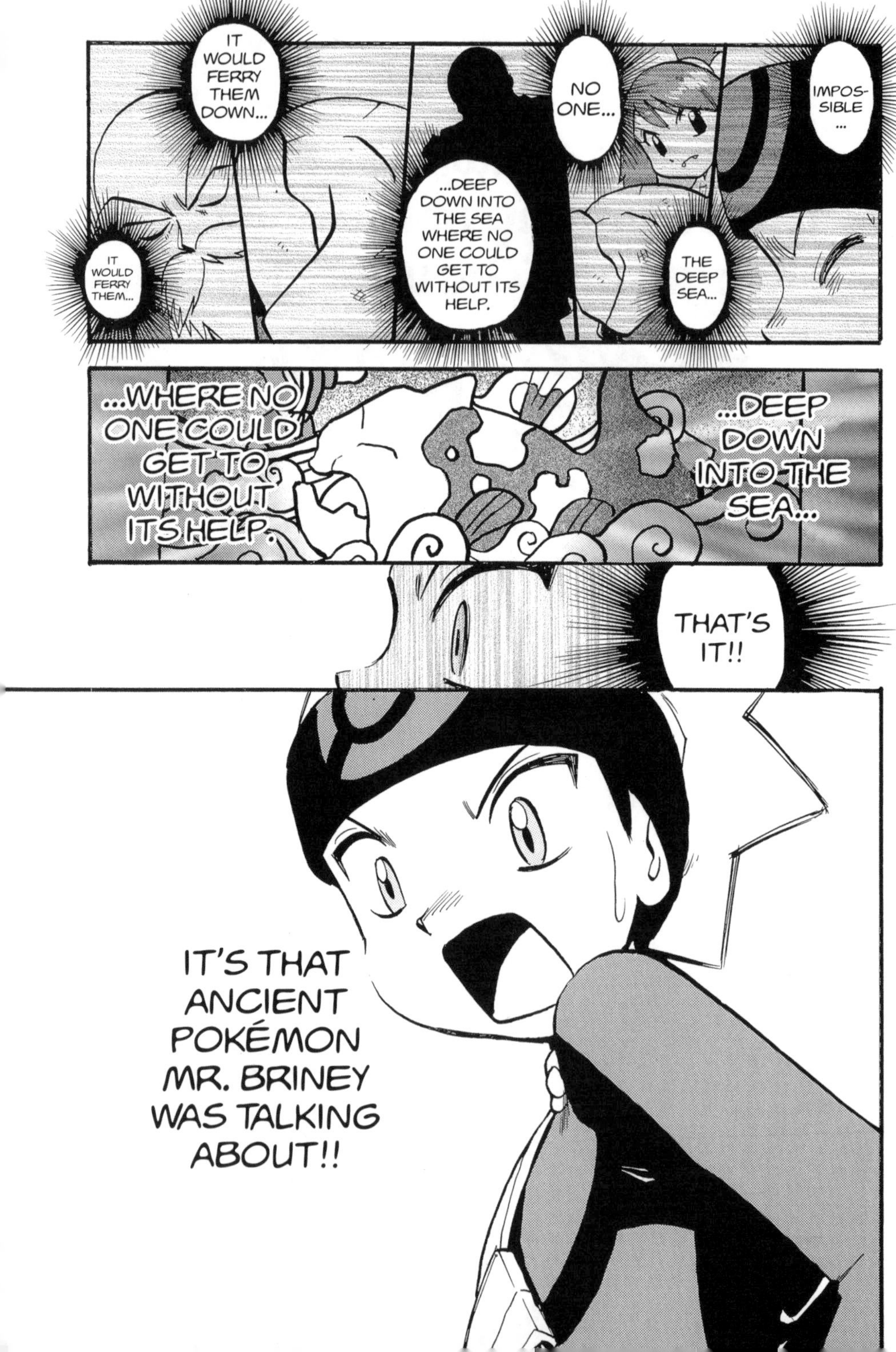
IMPOS-SIBLE...
THE DEEP SEA...
NO ONE...
...DEEP DOWN INTO THE SEA WHERE NO ONE COULD GET TO WITHOUT ITS HELP.
IT WOULD FERRY THEM DOWN...
IT WOULD FERRY THEM...
...DEEP DOWN INTO THE SEA...
...WHERE NO ONE COULD GET TO WITHOUT ITS HELP.
THAT'S IT!!
IT'S THAT ANCIENT POKÉMON MR. BRINEY WAS TALKING ABOUT!!

● Adventure 238 ●
The Beginning of the End with Kyogre and Groudon, Part 6

THAT'S IT!

IT'S THAT ANCIENT POKÉMON MR. BRINEY WAS TALKING ABOUT!

THE ONLY WAY TO STOP THEM IS TO GO TO SEAFLOOR CAVERN AND DEFEAT WHOEVER'S

BUT THAT'S IMPOSSIBLE! BOTH THE SUBMARINE AND THE SPECIAL DEVICE HAVE BEEN STOLEN!

WE HAVE NO WAY OF GETTING TO SEAFLOOR CAVERN...

JUDGING FROM THEIR CONVERSATION, THEY DON'T KNOW ABOUT THIS POKÉMON'S SPECIAL POWER...

EVEN **SHE** DOESN'T KNOW...

WE'RE ALL IN DANGER... AND I'M THE ONLY ONE...WHO KNOWS... WHAT TO DO!

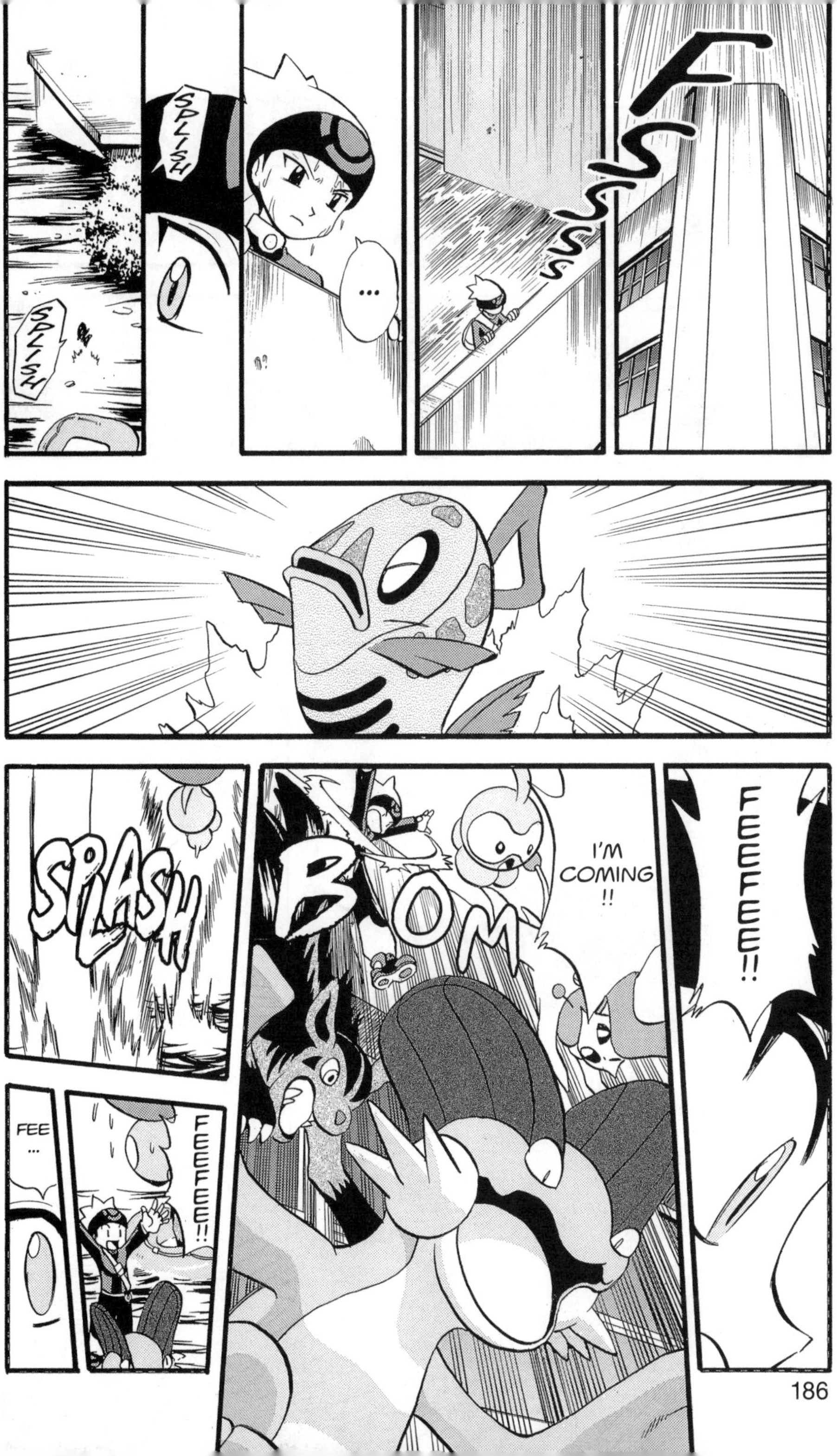
FSSSSS
...
SPLISH
SPLISH
FEEFEE!!
I'M COMING!!
BOOM
SPLASH
FEEFEE!!
FEE...

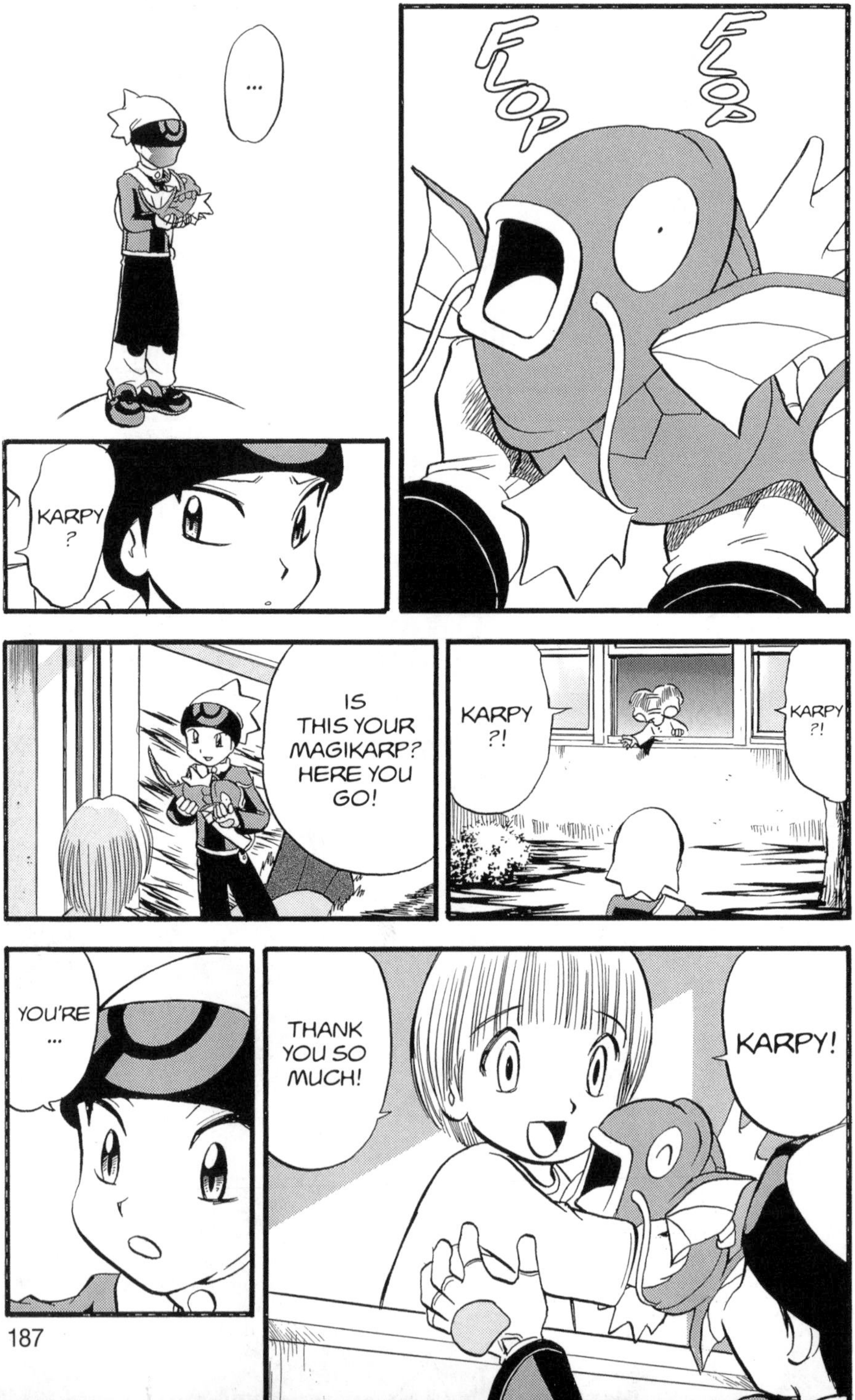
FLOP
FLOP
...
KARPY ?
KARPY ?!
KARPY ?!
IS THIS YOUR MAGIKARP? HERE YOU GO!
KARPY!
THANK YOU SO MUCH!
YOU'RE ...

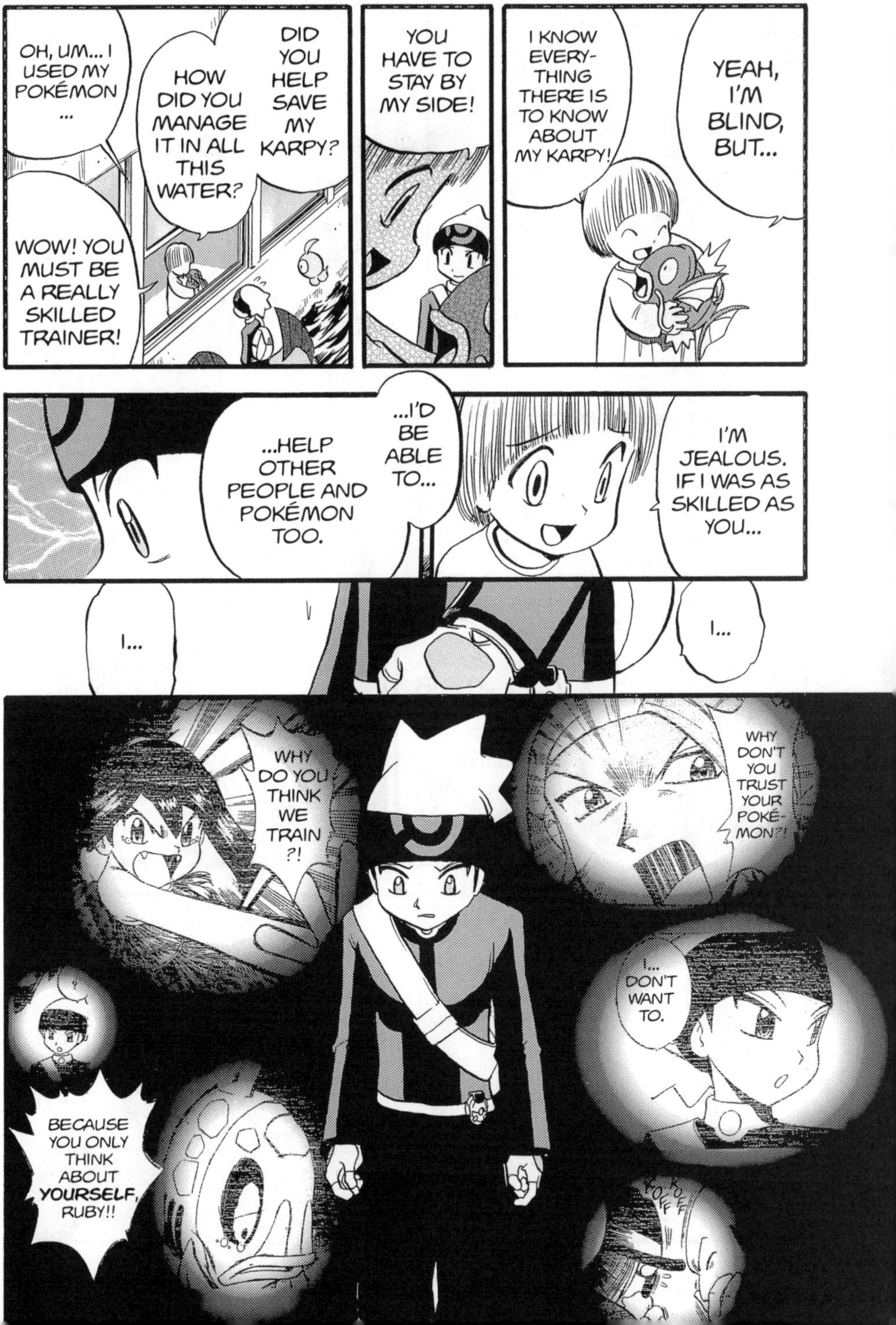
YEAH, I'M BLIND, BUT...
I KNOW EVERYTHING THERE IS TO KNOW ABOUT MY KARPY!
YOU HAVE TO STAY BY MY SIDE!
DID YOU HELP SAVE MY KARPY?
HOW DID YOU MANAGE IT IN ALL THIS WATER?
OH, UM... I USED MY POKÉMON ...
WOW! YOU MUST BE A REALLY SKILLED TRAINER!
I'M JEALOUS. IF I WAS AS SKILLED AS YOU...
...I'D BE ABLE TO...
...HELP OTHER PEOPLE AND POKÉMON TOO.
I...
I...
WHY DON'T YOU TRUST YOUR POKÉMON?!
WHY DO YOU THINK WE TRAIN?!
I... DON'T WANT TO.
BECAUSE YOU ONLY THINK ABOUT **YOURSELF**, RUBY!!

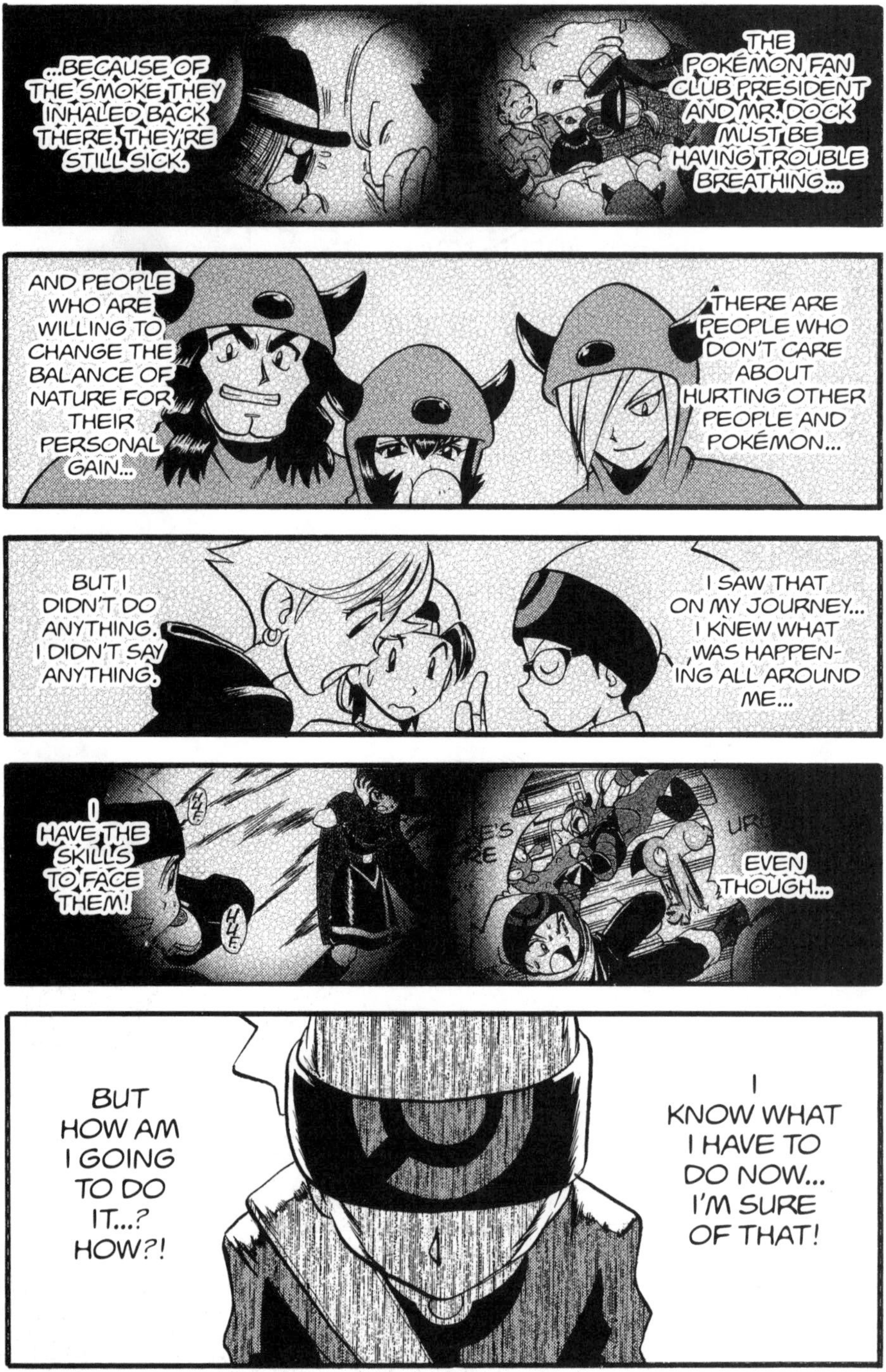
THE POKÉMON FAN CLUB PRESIDENT AND MR. DOCK MUST BE HAVING TROUBLE BREATHING...
...BECAUSE OF THE SMOKE THEY INHALED BACK THERE, THEY'RE STILL SICK.
THERE ARE PEOPLE WHO DON'T CARE ABOUT HURTING OTHER PEOPLE AND POKÉMON...
AND PEOPLE WHO ARE WILLING TO CHANGE THE BALANCE OF NATURE FOR THEIR PERSONAL GAIN...
I SAW THAT ON MY JOURNEY... I KNEW WHAT WAS HAPPENING ALL AROUND ME...
BUT I DIDN'T DO ANYTHING. I DIDN'T SAY ANYTHING.
EVEN THOUGH...
I HAVE THE SKILLS TO FACE THEM!
I KNOW WHAT I HAVE TO DO NOW... I'M SURE OF THAT!
BUT HOW AM I GOING TO DO IT...? HOW?!

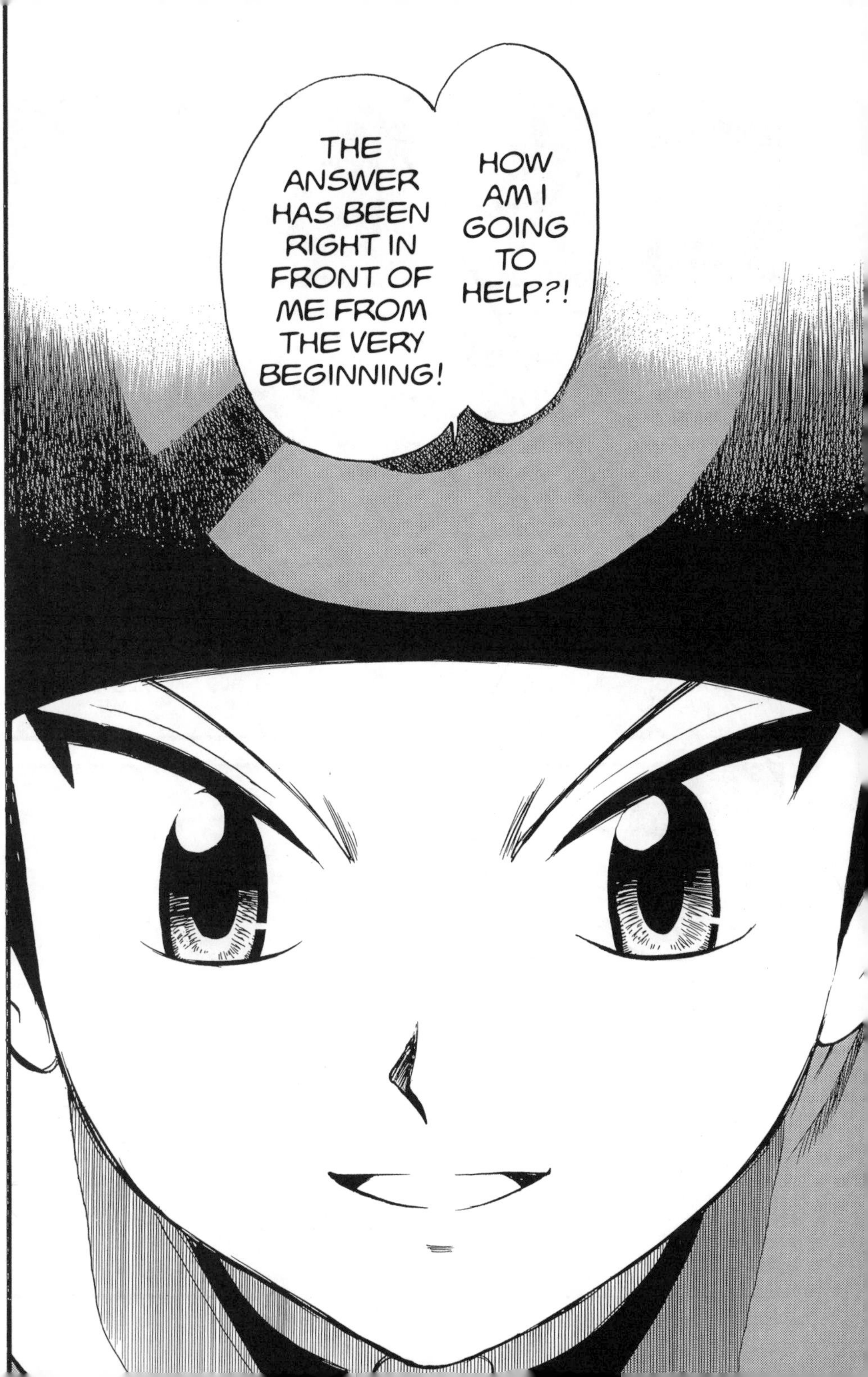
HOW AM I GOING TO HELP?!
THE ANSWER HAS BEEN RIGHT IN FRONT OF ME FROM THE VERY BEGINNING!

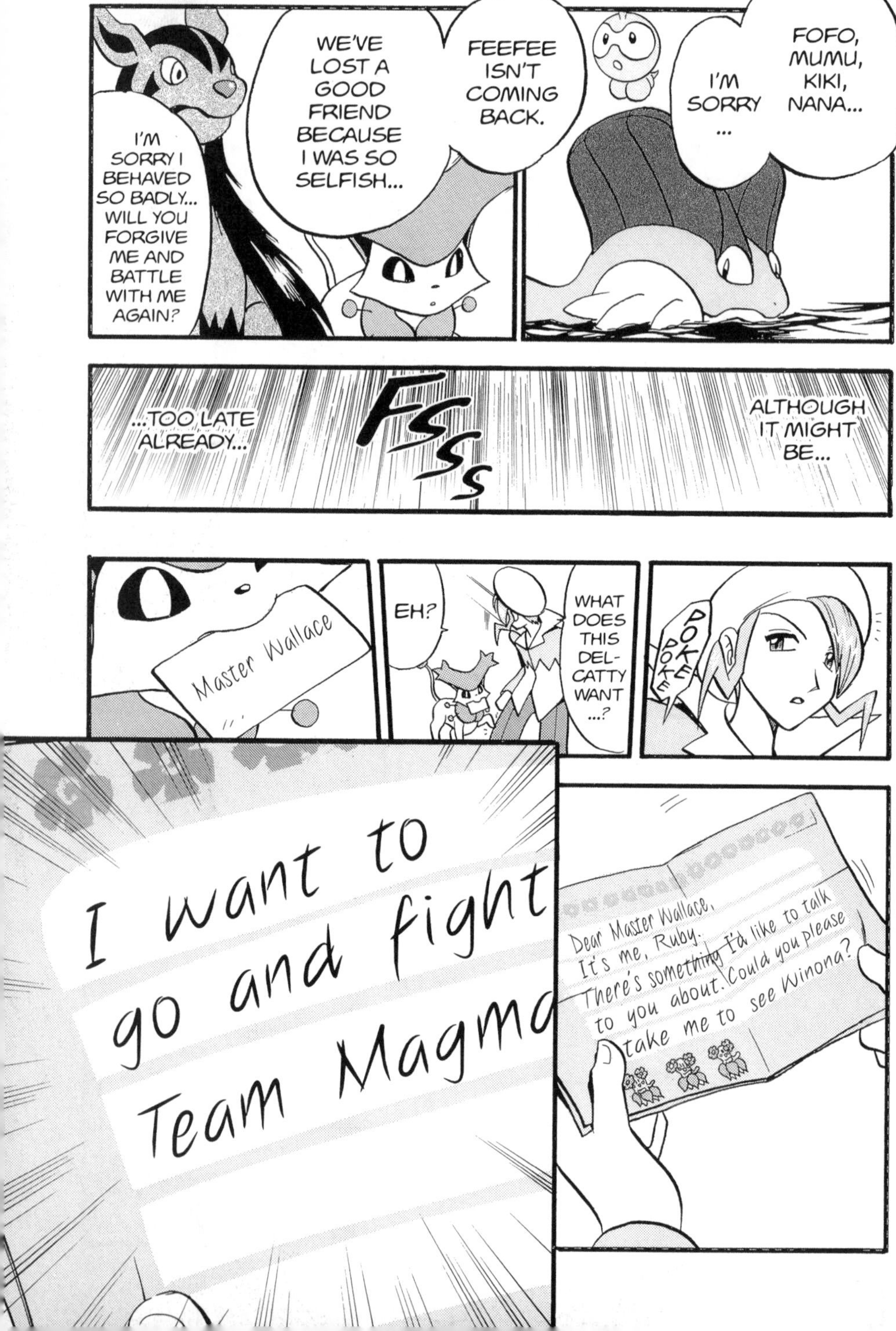
FOFO, MUMU, KIKI, NANA...
I'M SORRY...
FEEFEE ISN'T COMING BACK.
WE'VE LOST A GOOD FRIEND BECAUSE I WAS SO SELFISH...
I'M SORRY I BEHAVED SO BADLY... WILL YOU FORGIVE ME AND BATTLE WITH ME AGAIN?
ALTHOUGH IT MIGHT BE...
FSSS
...TOO LATE ALREADY...
POKE POKE
WHAT DOES THIS DEL-CATTY WANT...?
EH?
Master Wallace
Dear Master Wallace,
It's me, Ruby.
There's something I'd like to talk to you about. Could you please take me to see Winona?
I want to go and fight Team Magma

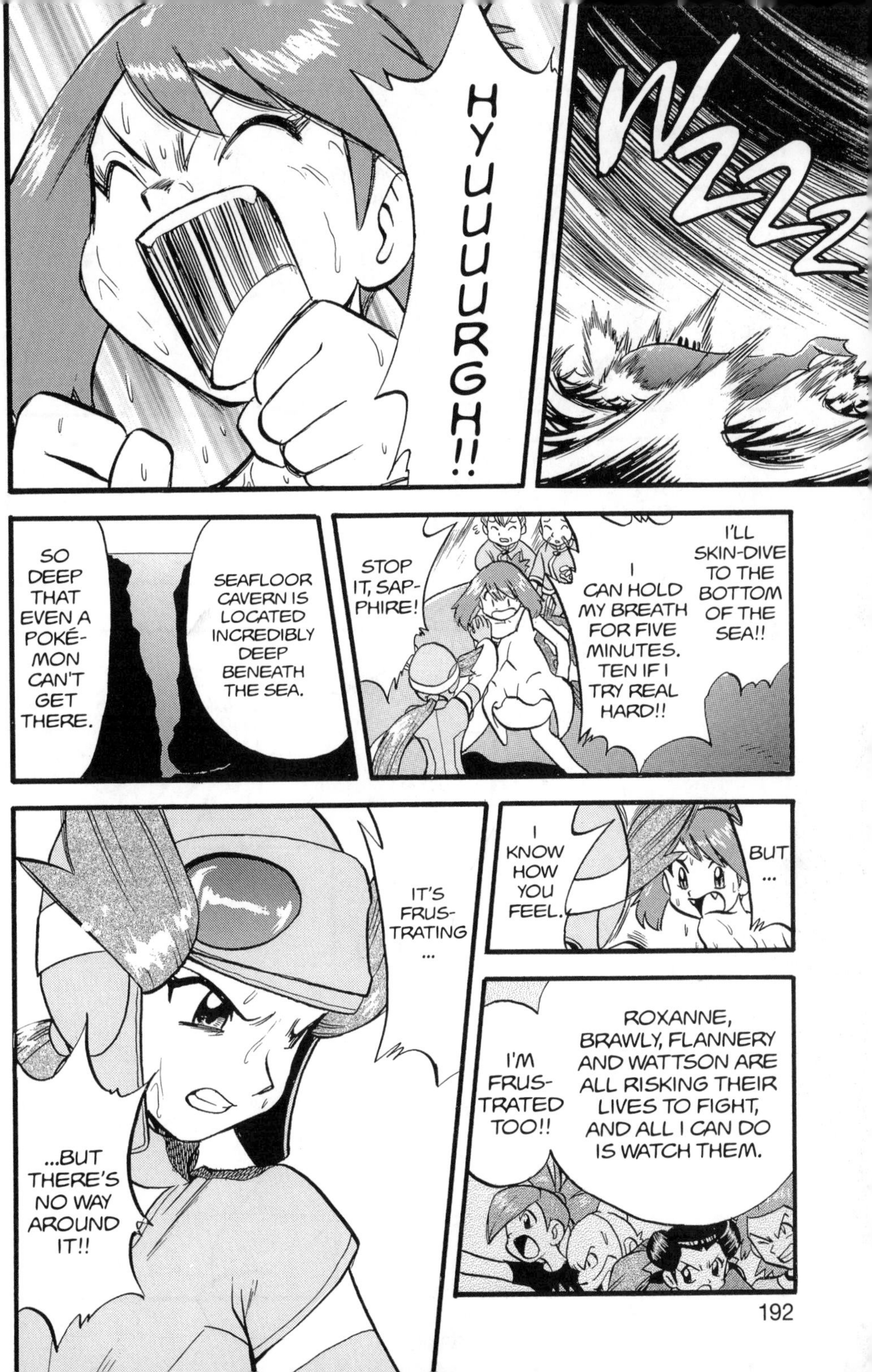
WZZZZ
HYUUUURGH!!
I'LL SKIN-DIVE TO THE BOTTOM OF THE SEA!!
I CAN HOLD MY BREATH FOR FIVE MINUTES. TEN IF I TRY REAL HARD!!
STOP IT, SAPPHIRE!
SEAFLOOR CAVERN IS LOCATED INCREDIBLY DEEP BENEATH THE SEA.
SO DEEP THAT EVEN A POKÉMON CAN'T GET THERE.
BUT...
I KNOW HOW YOU FEEL.
ROXANNE, BRAWLY, FLANNERY AND WATTSON ARE ALL RISKING THEIR LIVES TO FIGHT, AND ALL I CAN DO IS WATCH THEM.
I'M FRUSTRATED TOO!!
IT'S FRUSTRATING...
...BUT THERE'S NO WAY AROUND IT!!

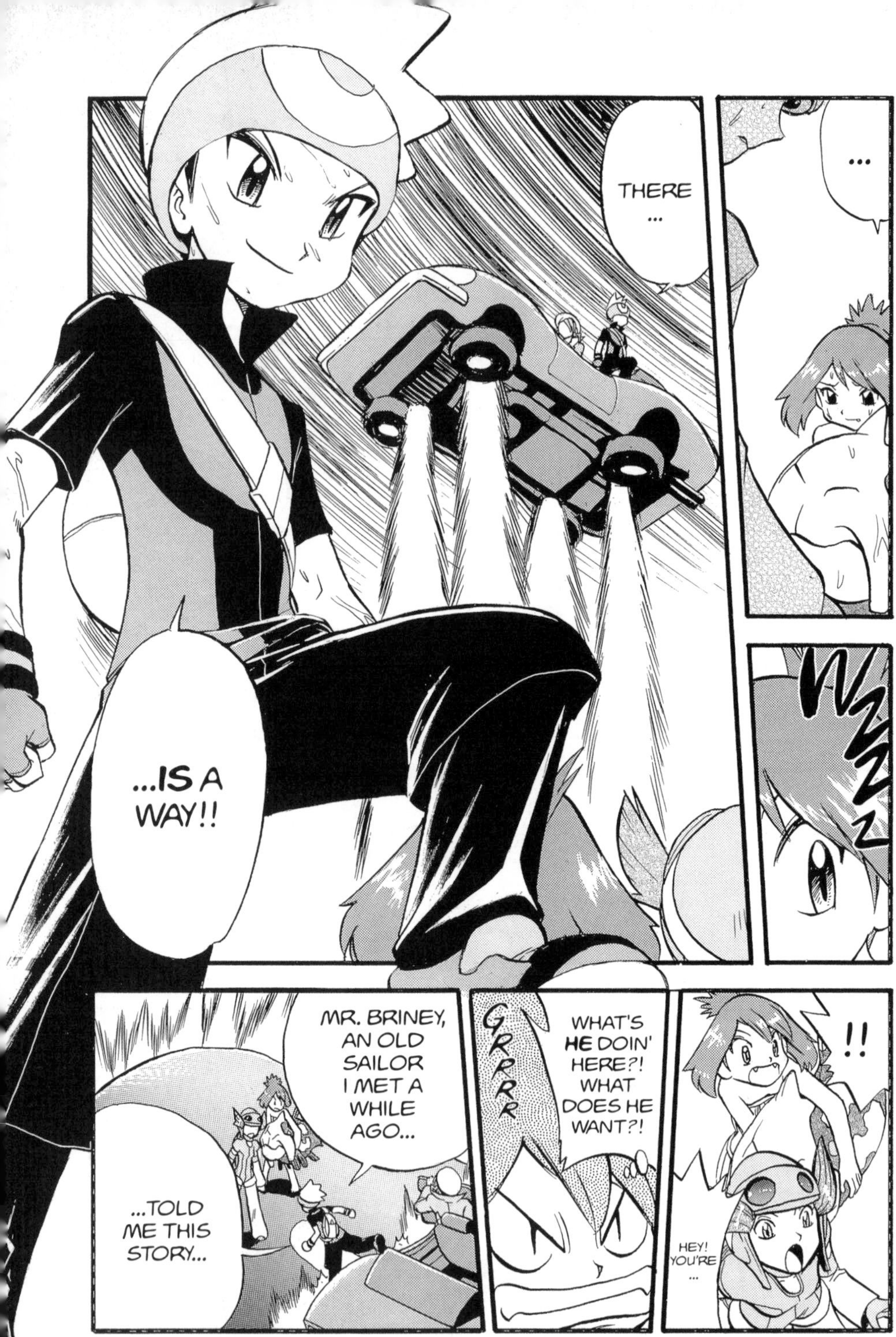
...
WZZZ
THERE ...
...IS A WAY!!
!!
HEY! YOU'RE ...
WHAT'S HE DOIN' HERE?! WHAT DOES HE WANT?!
GRRRR
MR. BRINEY, AN OLD SAILOR I MET A WHILE AGO...
...TOLD ME THIS STORY...

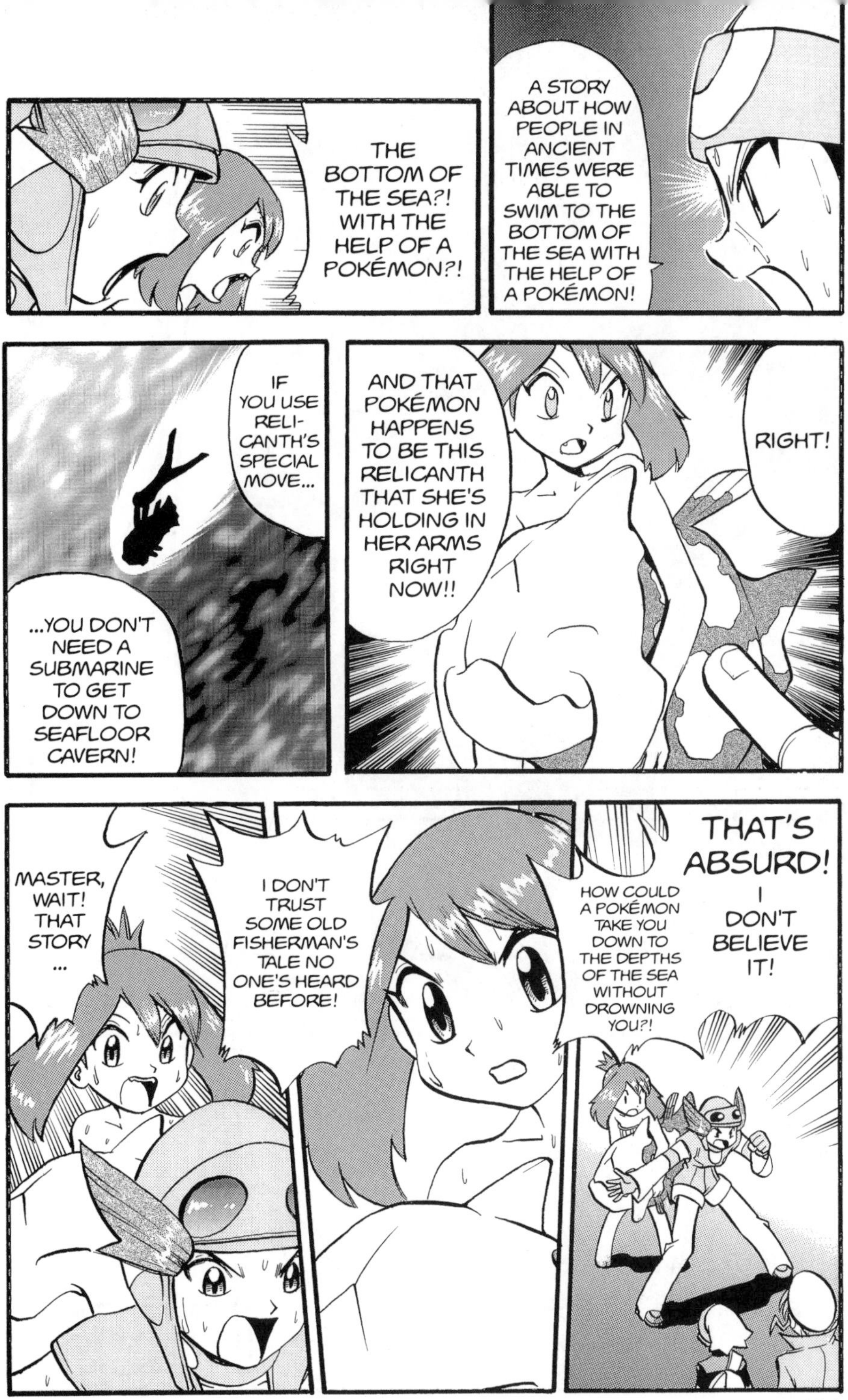
A STORY ABOUT HOW PEOPLE IN ANCIENT TIMES WERE ABLE TO SWIM TO THE BOTTOM OF THE SEA WITH THE HELP OF A POKÉMON!
THE BOTTOM OF THE SEA?! WITH THE HELP OF A POKÉMON?!
RIGHT!
AND THAT POKÉMON HAPPENS TO BE THIS RELICANTH THAT SHE'S HOLDING IN HER ARMS RIGHT NOW!!
IF YOU USE RELI-CANTH'S SPECIAL MOVE...
...YOU DON'T NEED A SUBMARINE TO GET DOWN TO SEAFLOOR CAVERN!
THAT'S ABSURD!
I DON'T BELIEVE IT!
HOW COULD A POKÉMON TAKE YOU DOWN TO THE DEPTHS OF THE SEA WITHOUT DROWNING YOU?!
I DON'T TRUST SOME OLD FISHERMAN'S TALE NO ONE'S HEARD BEFORE!
MASTER, WAIT! THAT STORY ...

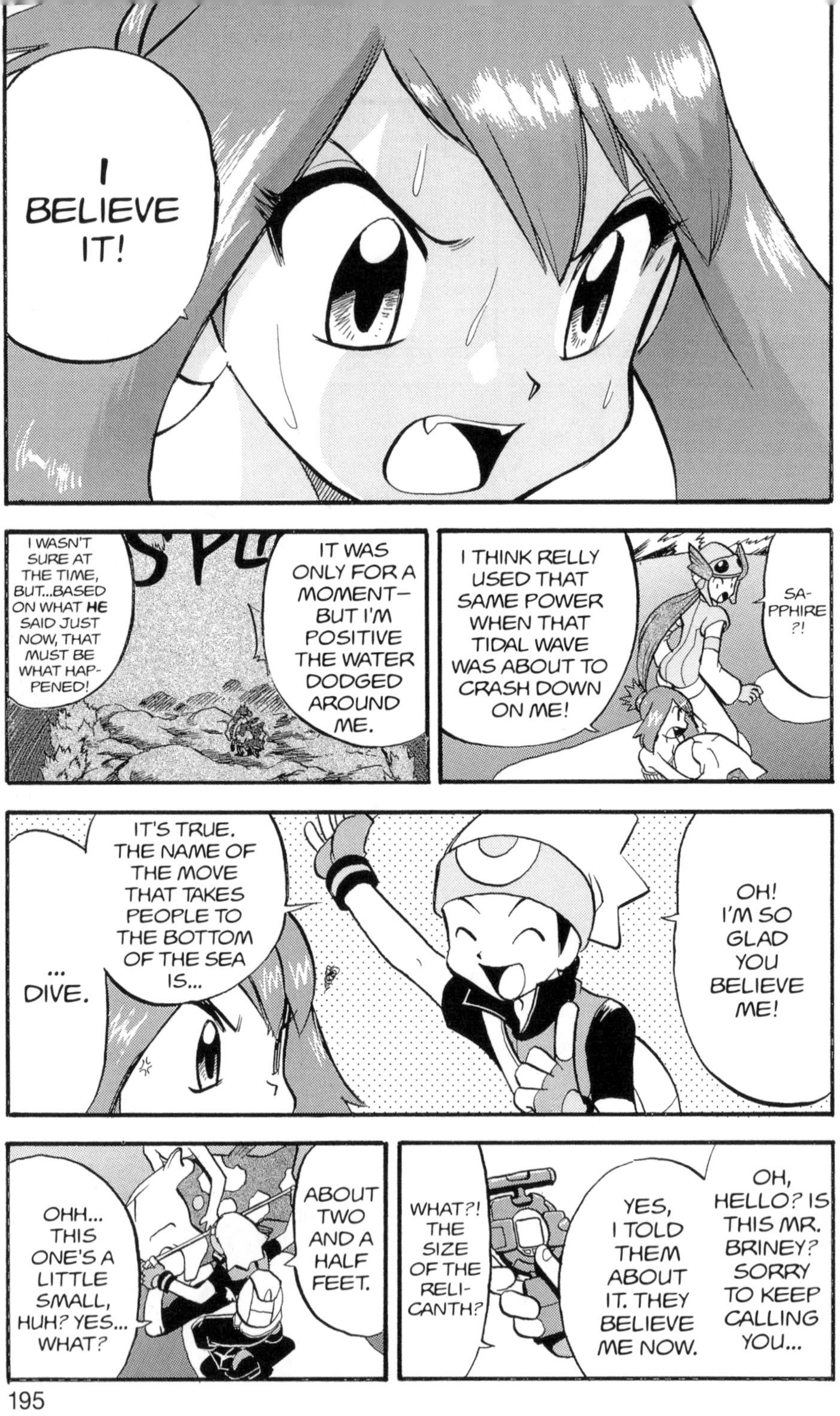
I BELIEVE IT!
SA-PPHIRE?!
I THINK RELLY USED THAT SAME POWER WHEN THAT TIDAL WAVE WAS ABOUT TO CRASH DOWN ON ME!
IT WAS ONLY FOR A MOMENT—BUT I'M POSITIVE THE WATER DODGED AROUND ME.
I WASN'T SURE AT THE TIME, BUT...BASED ON WHAT **HE** SAID JUST NOW, THAT MUST BE WHAT HAP-PENED!
OH! I'M SO GLAD YOU BELIEVE ME!
IT'S TRUE. THE NAME OF THE MOVE THAT TAKES PEOPLE TO THE BOTTOM OF THE SEA IS...
... DIVE.
OH, HELLO? IS THIS MR. BRINEY? SORRY TO KEEP CALLING YOU...
YES, I TOLD THEM ABOUT IT. THEY BELIEVE ME NOW.
WHAT?! THE SIZE OF THE RELI-CANTH?
ABOUT TWO AND A HALF FEET.
OHH... THIS ONE'S A LITTLE SMALL, HUH? YES... WHAT?

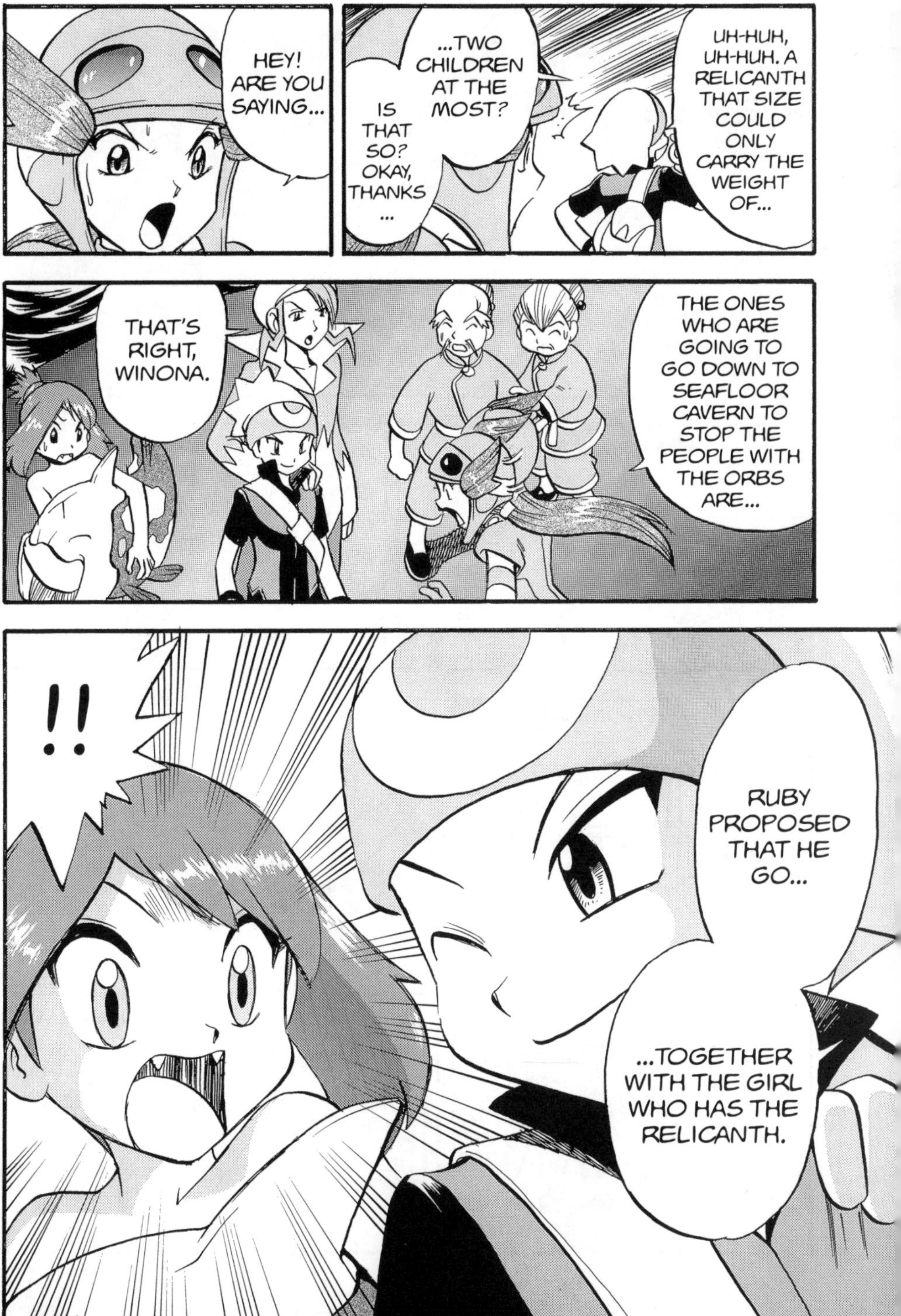
UH-HUH, UH-HUH. A RELICANTH THAT SIZE COULD ONLY CARRY THE WEIGHT OF...
...TWO CHILDREN AT THE MOST?
IS THAT SO? OKAY, THANKS...
HEY! ARE YOU SAYING...
THE ONES WHO ARE GOING TO GO DOWN TO SEAFLOOR CAVERN TO STOP THE PEOPLE WITH THE ORBS ARE...
THAT'S RIGHT, WINONA.
RUBY PROPOSED THAT HE GO...
...TOGETHER WITH THE GIRL WHO HAS THE RELICANTH.
!!

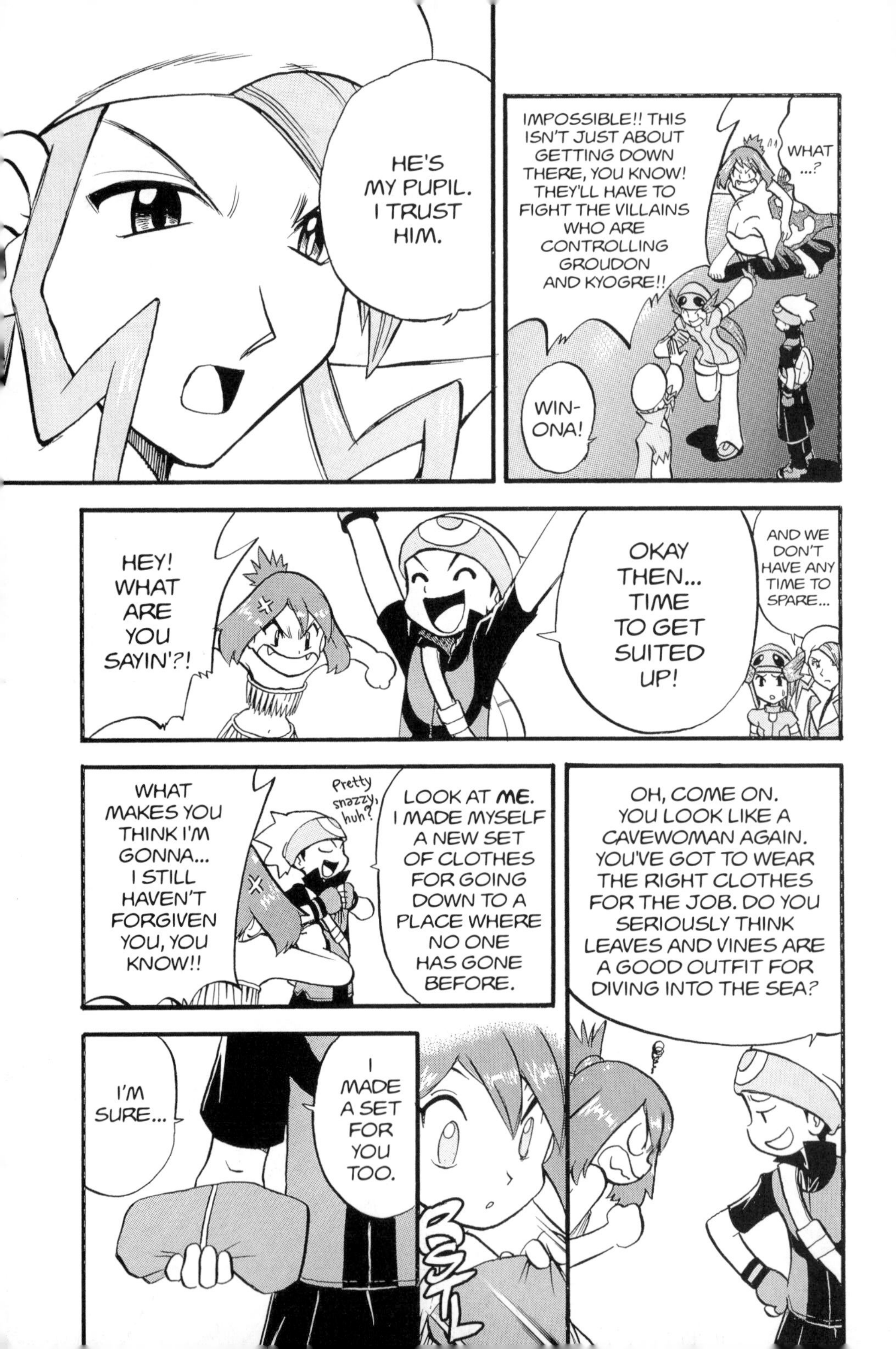
WHAT ...?
IMPOSSIBLE!! THIS ISN'T JUST ABOUT GETTING DOWN THERE, YOU KNOW! THEY'LL HAVE TO FIGHT THE VILLAINS WHO ARE CONTROLLING GROUDON AND KYOGRE!!
WIN-ONA!
HE'S MY PUPIL. I TRUST HIM.
AND WE DON'T HAVE ANY TIME TO SPARE...
OKAY THEN... TIME TO GET SUITED UP!
HEY! WHAT ARE YOU SAYIN'?!
OH, COME ON. YOU LOOK LIKE A CAVEWOMAN AGAIN. YOU'VE GOT TO WEAR THE RIGHT CLOTHES FOR THE JOB. DO YOU SERIOUSLY THINK LEAVES AND VINES ARE A GOOD OUTFIT FOR DIVING INTO THE SEA?
LOOK AT **ME**. I MADE MYSELF A NEW SET OF CLOTHES FOR GOING DOWN TO A PLACE WHERE NO ONE HAS GONE BEFORE.
Pretty snazzy, huh?
WHAT MAKES YOU THINK I'M GONNA... I STILL HAVEN'T FORGIVEN YOU, YOU KNOW!!
I MADE A SET FOR YOU TOO.
I'M SURE...

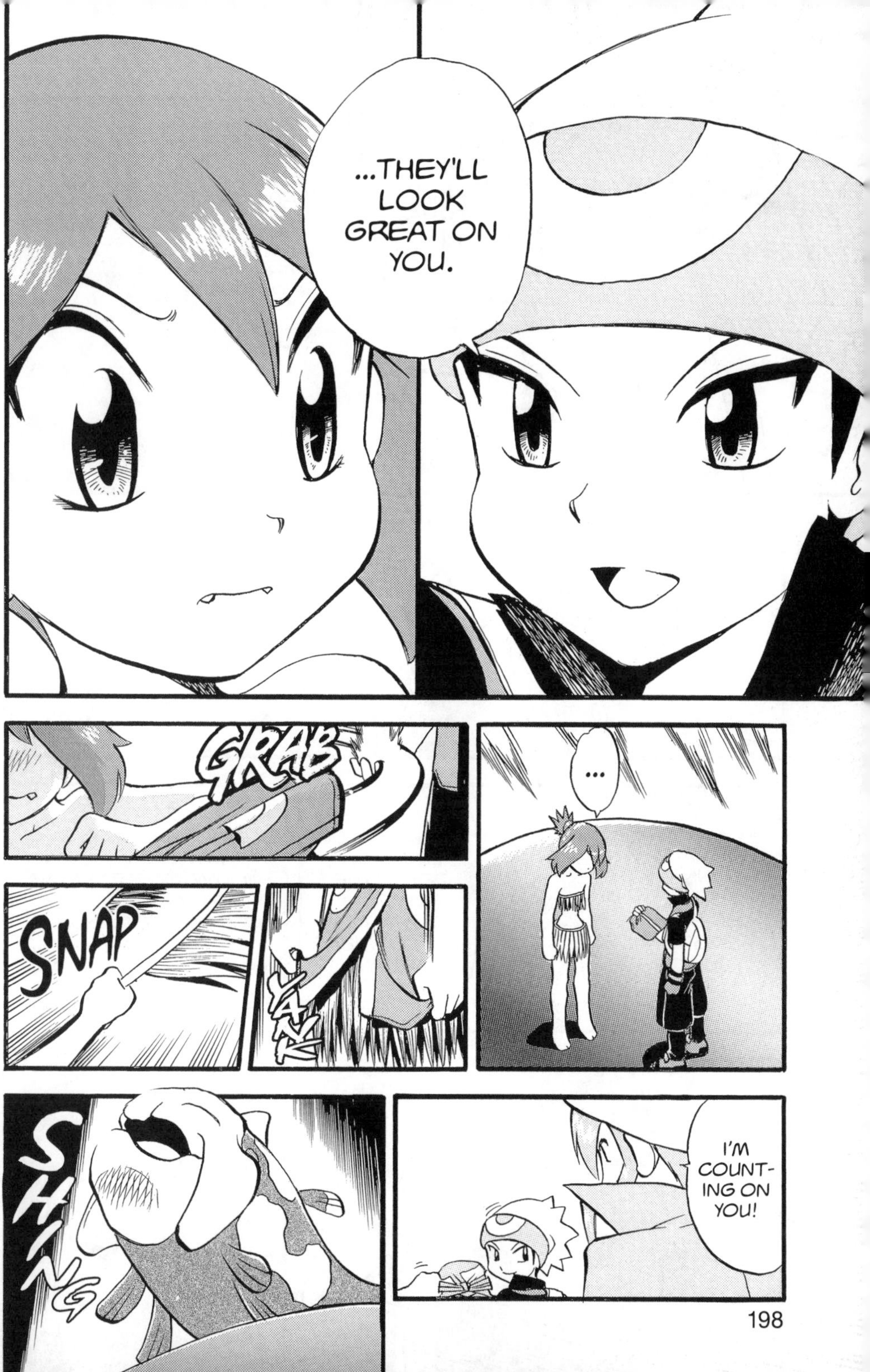
...THEY'LL LOOK GREAT ON YOU.
...
GRAB
YANK
SNAP
I'M COUNTING-ING ON YOU!
SHING

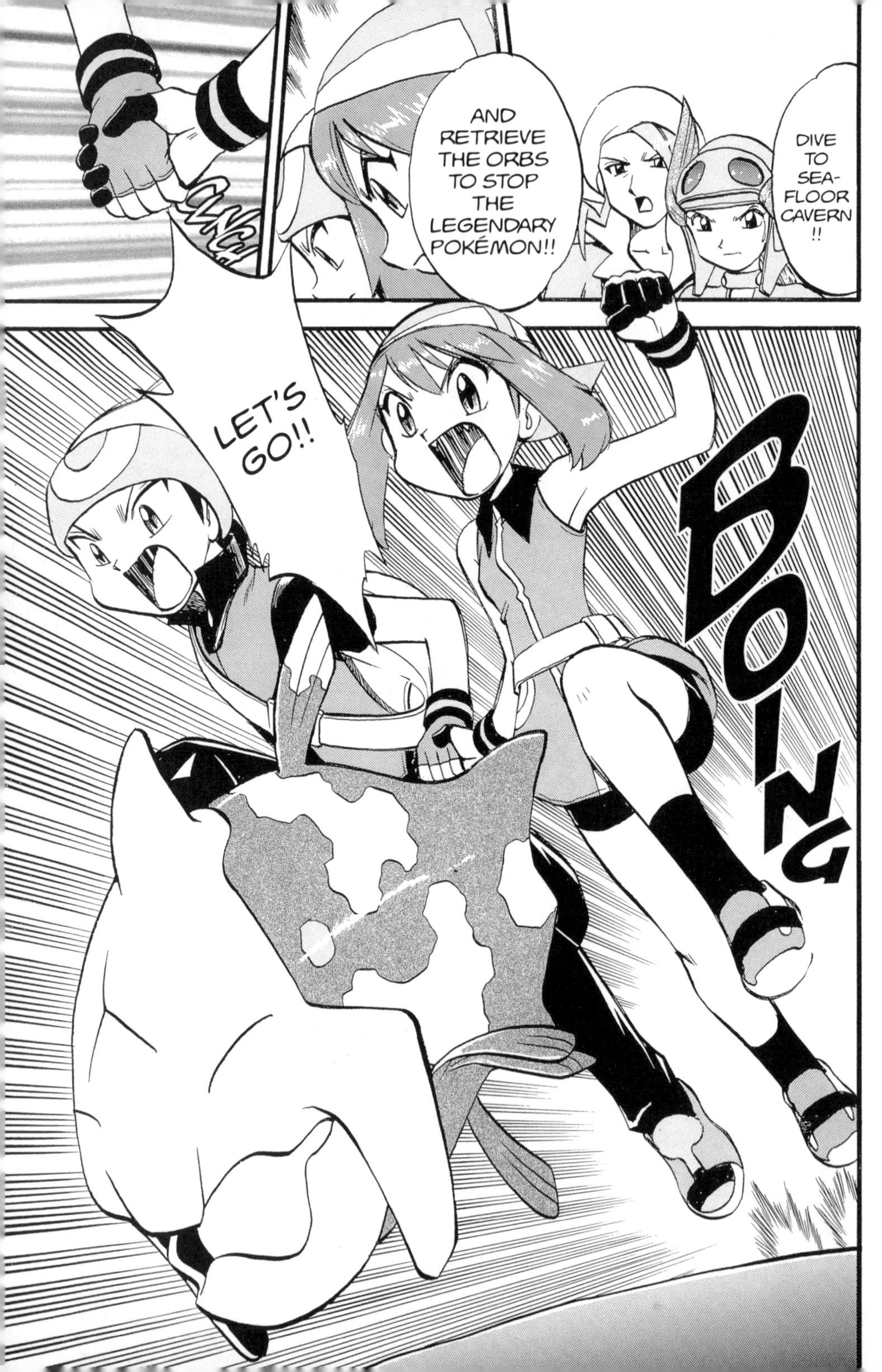
DIVE TO SEA-FLOOR CAVERN!!
AND RETRIEVE THE ORBS TO STOP THE LEGENDARY POKÉMON!!
CLNCH
BOING
LET'S GO!!

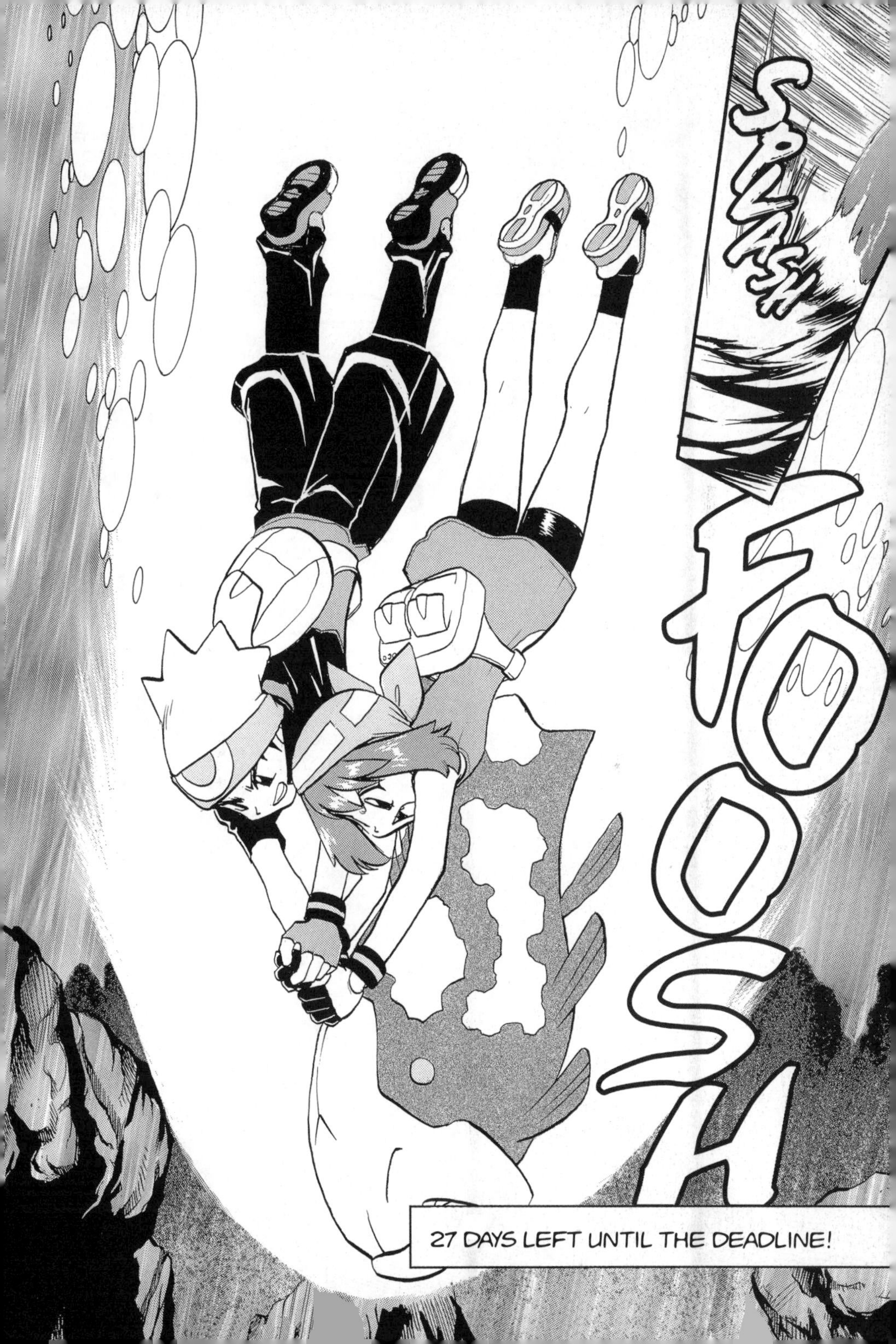
SPLASH
FOOOSH
27 DAYS LEFT UNTIL THE DEADLINE!

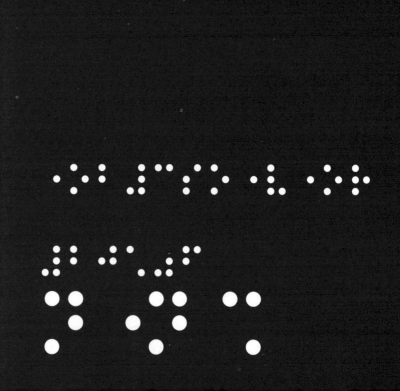

Message from
Hidenori Kusaka

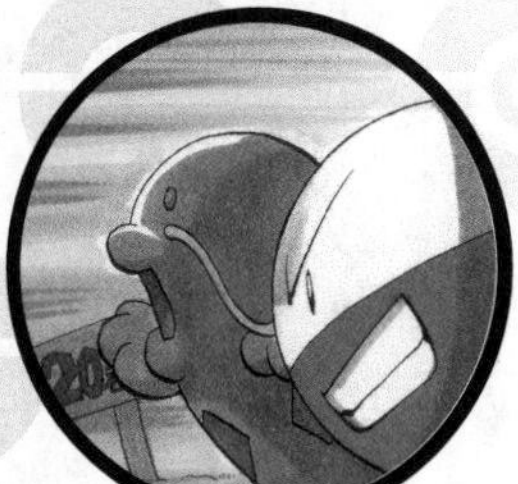

The two main characters in this story arc, Ruby and Sapphire, change their clothes a couple of times during the story. Their change of outfit before they head for Seafloor Cavern is part of a particularly memorable episode for me, especially because Ruby's change of heart coincides symbolically with his change of clothes. Even I am touched when I read over that episode! Most of this volume consists of the fight against the bosses of the two evil organizations. It's such a heated final battle! I hope your blood boils when you read it...!

–2005

Message from
Satoshi Yamamoto

The father-son battle between Ruby and Norman, Ruby's maturing and new resolve... There are all sorts of core episodes in each volume. But volume 20 is a parade of battle after battle!! Battles occur up high in the air at the Sky Pillar as well as down low under the sea in Seafloor Cavern. I hope you enjoy these battles in which sometimes you can barely tell friend from foe.

–2005

● Adventure 239 ●

The Beginning of the End with Kyogre and Groudon, Part 7

Pokémon Adventures Ruby & Sapphire

The Fourth Chapter

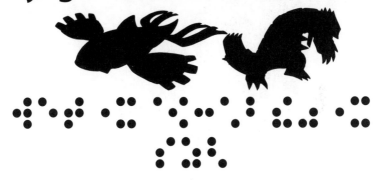

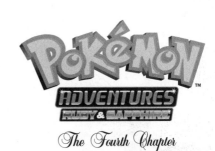

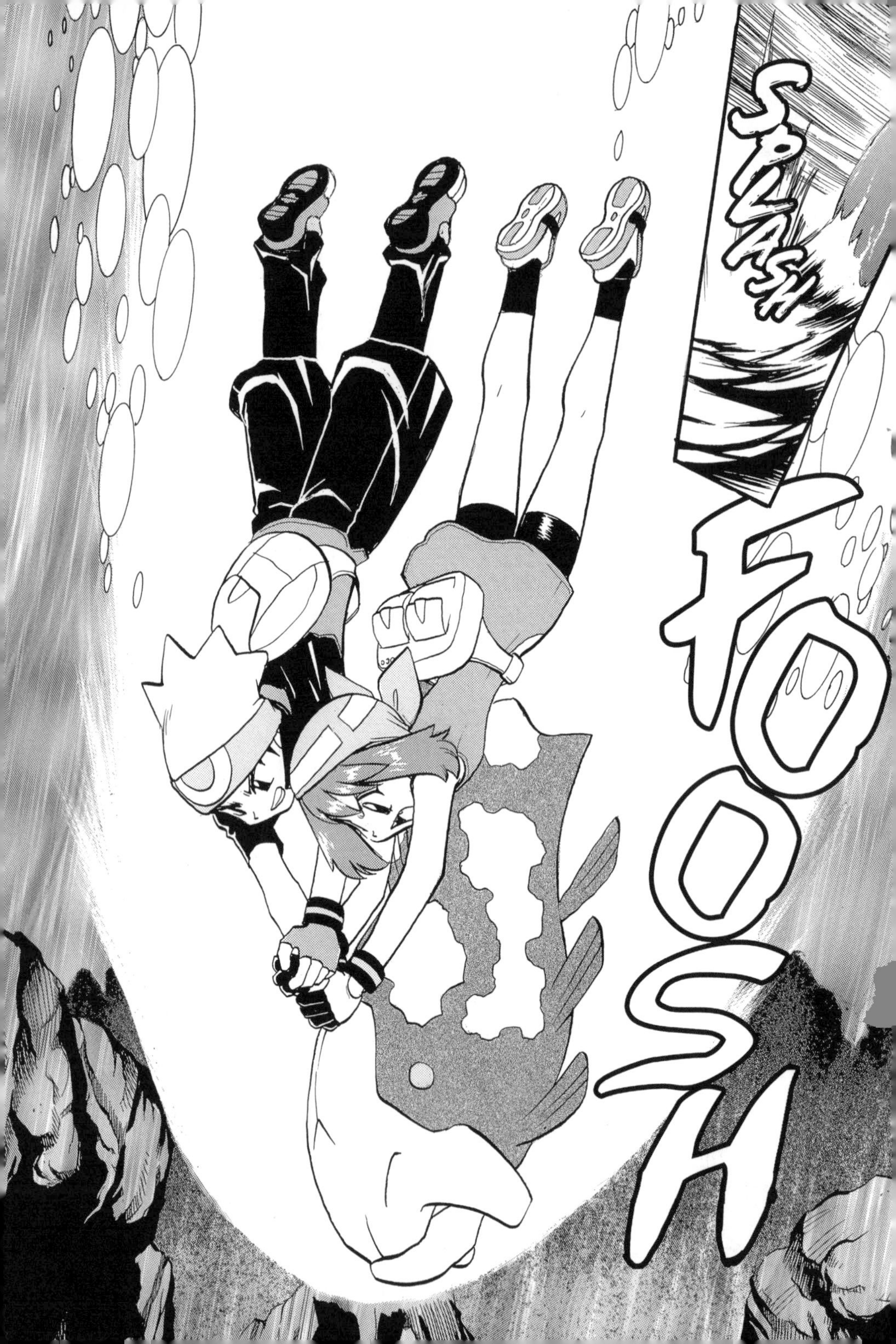
SPLASH
FOOSH

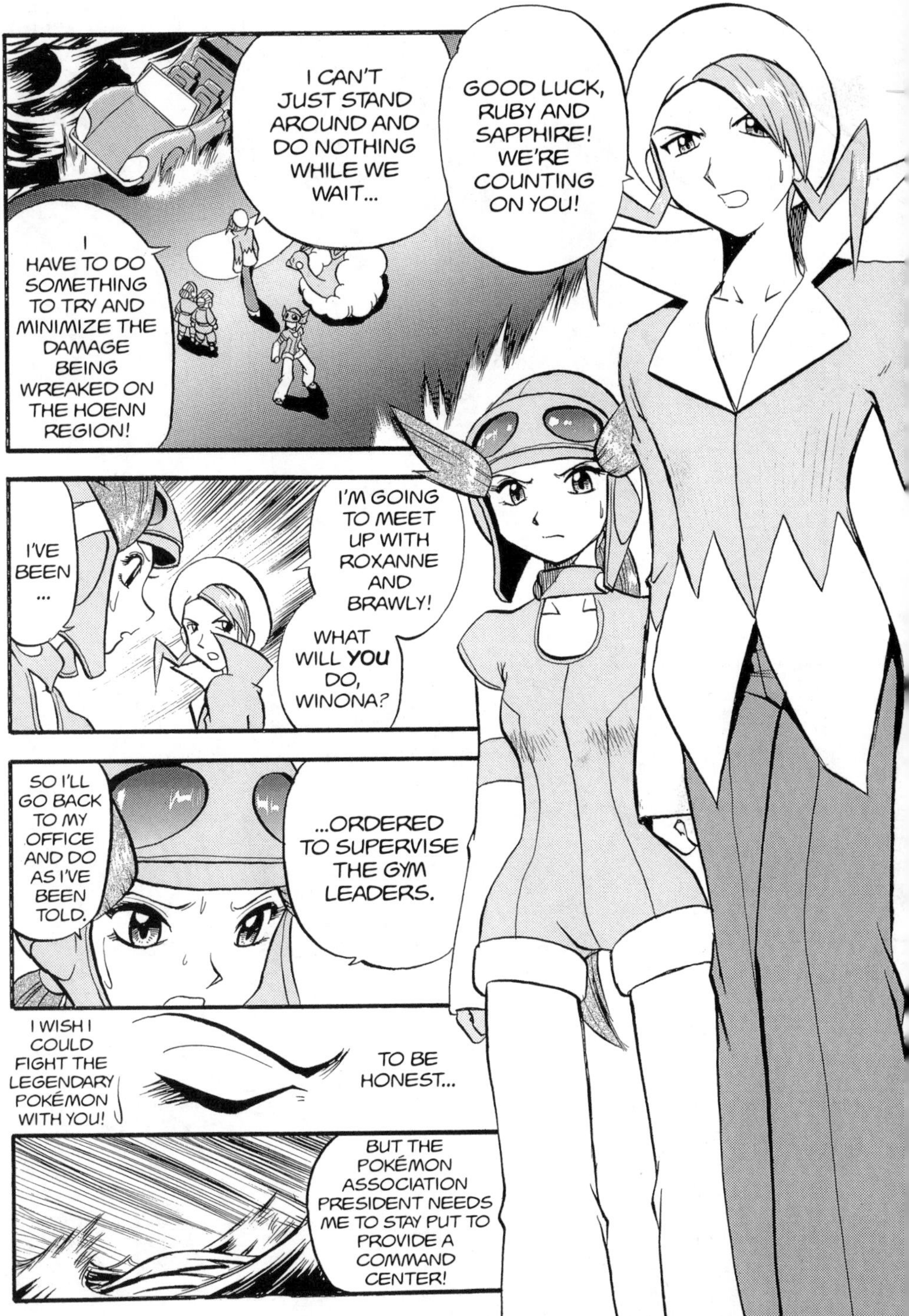
GOOD LUCK, RUBY AND SAPPHIRE! WE'RE COUNTING ON YOU!
I CAN'T JUST STAND AROUND AND DO NOTHING WHILE WE WAIT...
I HAVE TO DO SOMETHING TO TRY AND MINIMIZE THE DAMAGE BEING WREAKED ON THE HOENN REGION!
I'M GOING TO MEET UP WITH ROXANNE AND BRAWLY!
WHAT WILL **YOU** DO, WINONA?
I'VE BEEN ...
...ORDERED TO SUPERVISE THE GYM LEADERS.
SO I'LL GO BACK TO MY OFFICE AND DO AS I'VE BEEN TOLD.
TO BE HONEST...
I WISH I COULD FIGHT THE LEGENDARY POKÉMON WITH YOU!
BUT THE POKÉMON ASSOCIATION PRESIDENT NEEDS ME TO STAY PUT TO PROVIDE A COMMAND CENTER!

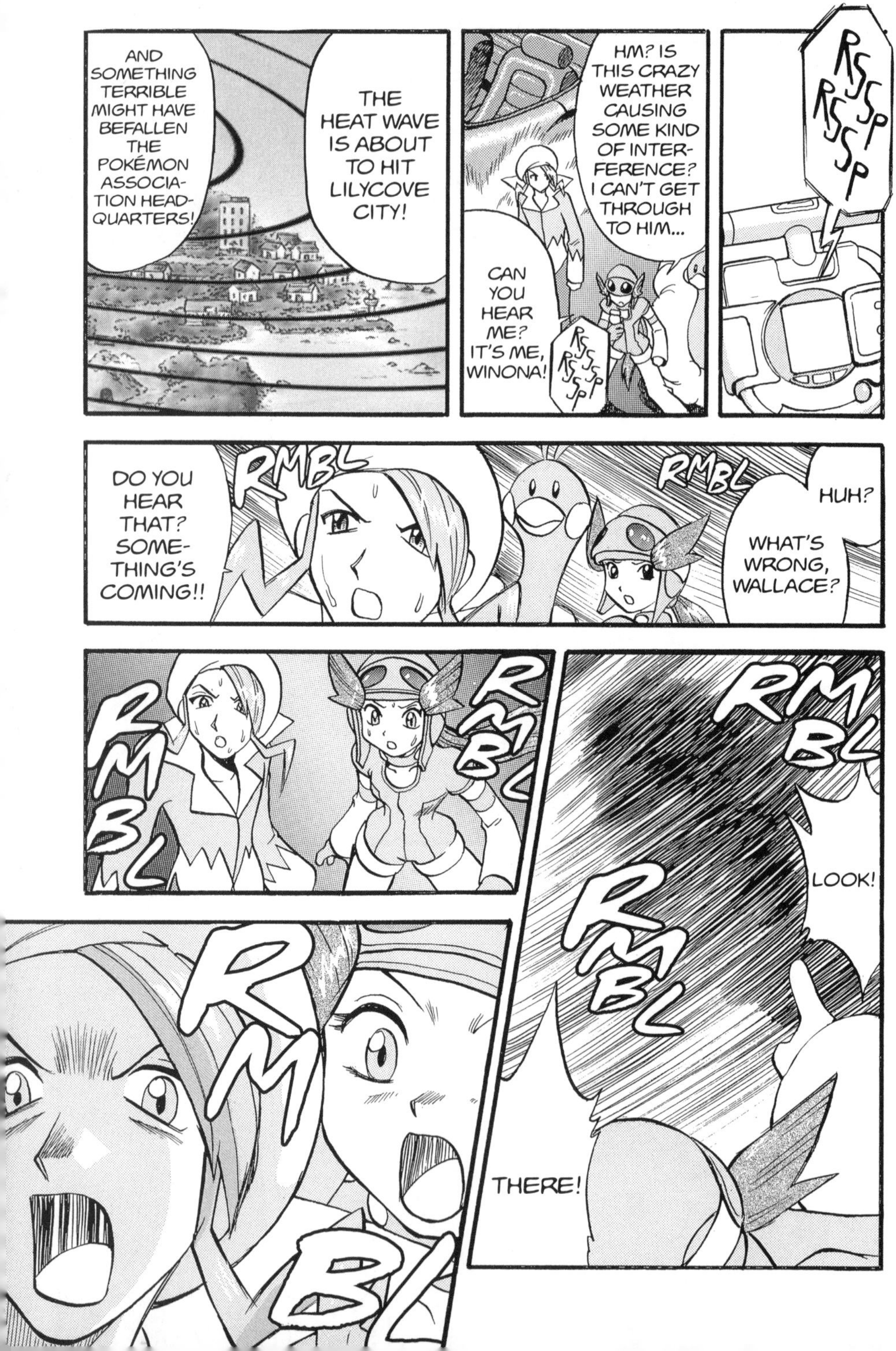

RSSSP RSSP
HM? IS THIS CRAZY WEATHER CAUSING SOME KIND OF INTER-FERENCE? I CAN'T GET THROUGH TO HIM...
CAN YOU HEAR ME? IT'S ME, WINONA!
RSSSP RSSSP
THE HEAT WAVE IS ABOUT TO HIT LILYCOVE CITY!
AND SOMETHING TERRIBLE MIGHT HAVE BEFALLEN THE POKÉMON ASSOCIA-TION HEAD-QUARTERS!
HUH?
WHAT'S WRONG, WALLACE?
RMBL
RMBL
DO YOU HEAR THAT? SOME-THING'S COMING!!
RMBL
LOOK!
RMBL
THERE!
RMBL
RMBL
RMBL

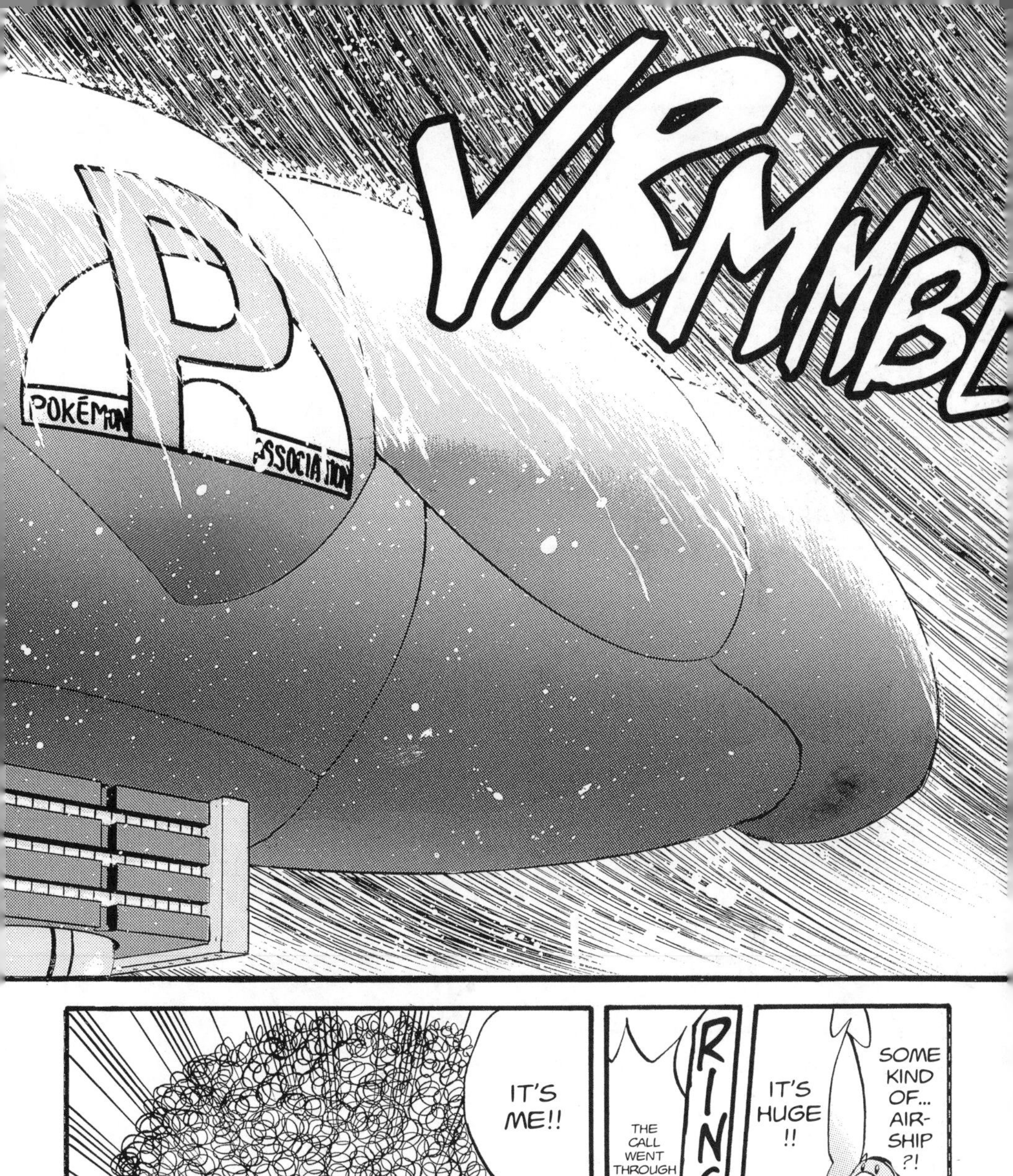
VRMMBL
POKÉMON ASSOCIATION

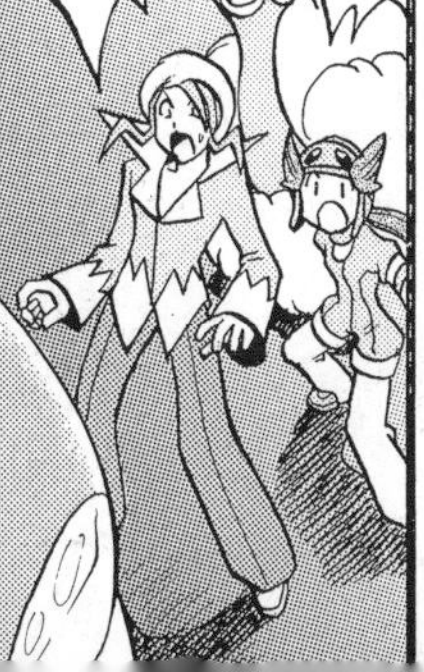
SOME KIND OF... AIR-SHIP?!
IT'S HUGE!!

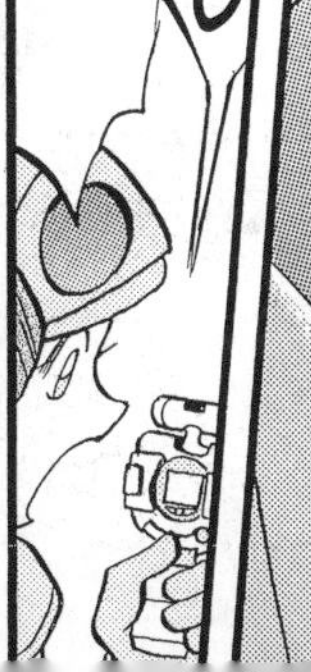
RING
THE CALL WENT THROUGH!!

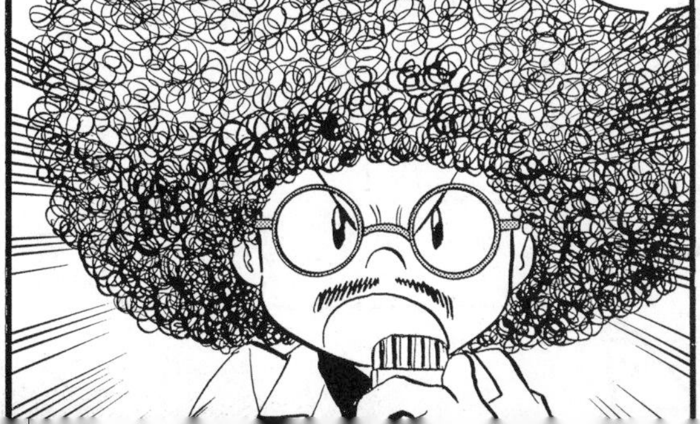
IT'S ME!!

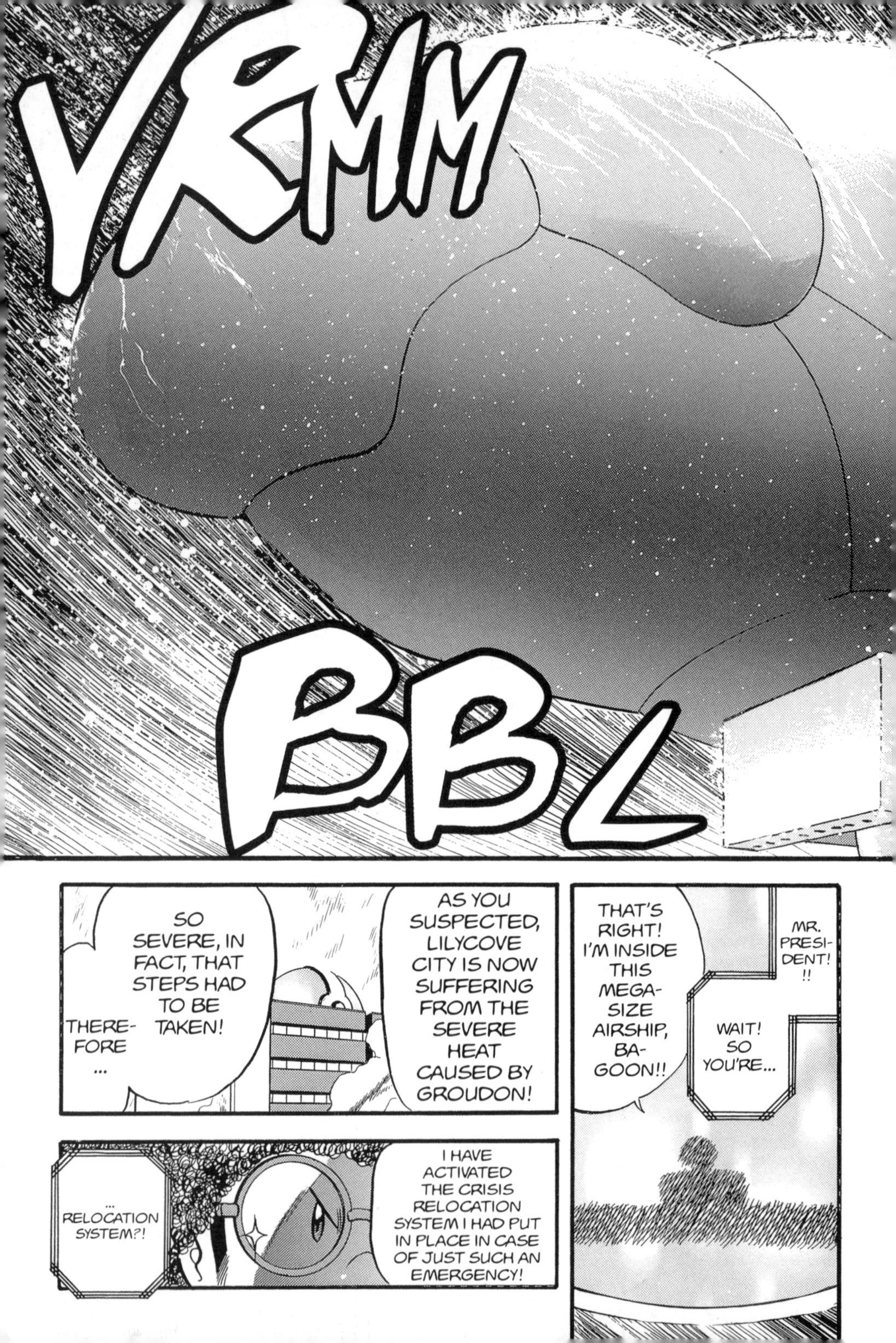
VRMM
BBL
MR. PRESIDENT!!!
THAT'S RIGHT! I'M INSIDE THIS MEGA-SIZE AIRSHIP, BAGOON!!
WAIT! SO YOU'RE...
AS YOU SUSPECTED, LILYCOVE CITY IS NOW SUFFERING FROM THE SEVERE HEAT CAUSED BY GROUDON!
SO SEVERE, IN FACT, THAT STEPS HAD TO BE TAKEN!
THEREFORE...
I HAVE ACTIVATED THE CRISIS RELOCATION SYSTEM I HAD PUT IN PLACE IN CASE OF JUST SUCH AN EMERGENCY!
...RELOCATION SYSTEM?!

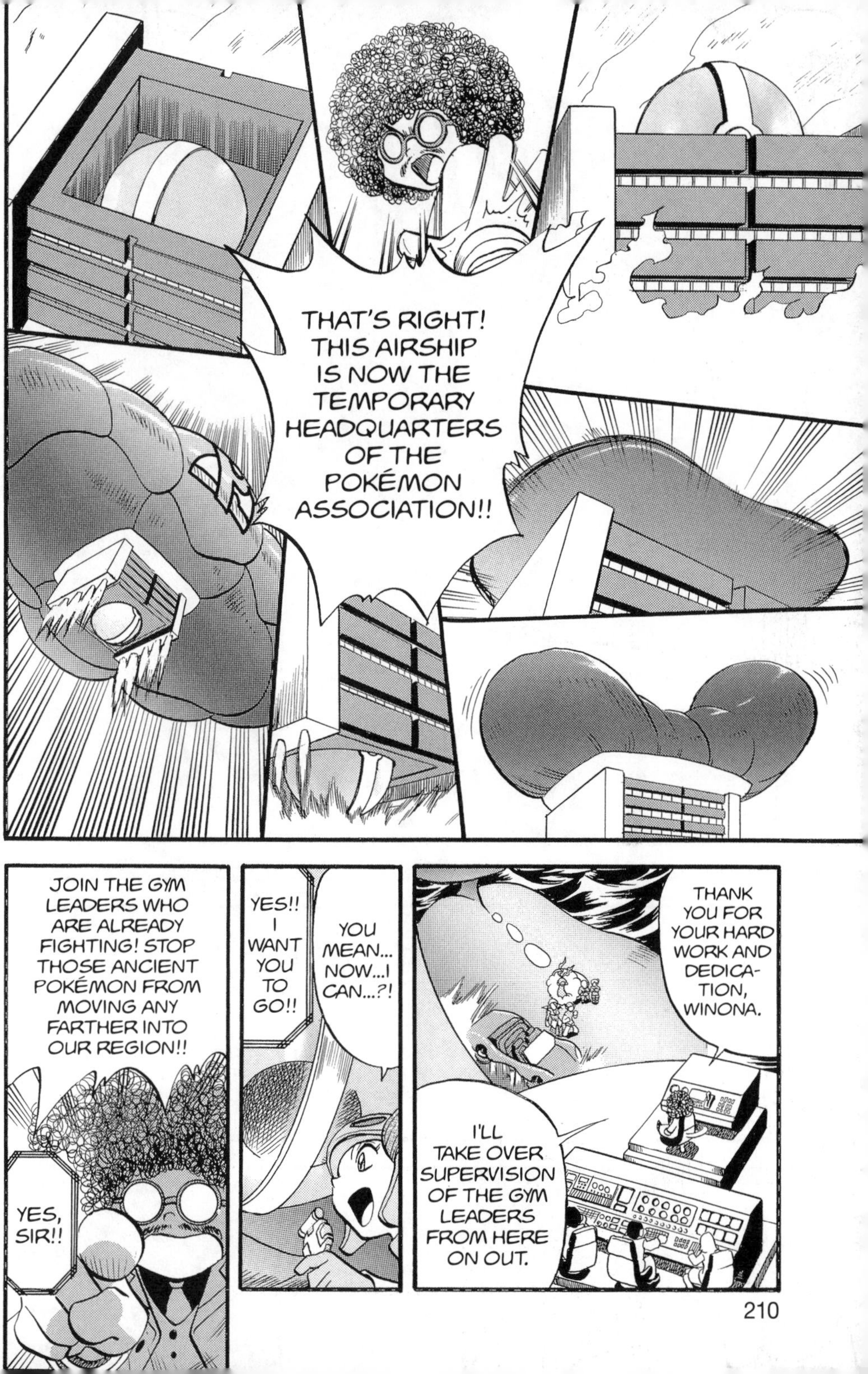
THAT'S RIGHT! THIS AIRSHIP IS NOW THE TEMPORARY HEADQUARTERS OF THE POKÉMON ASSOCIATION!!
THANK YOU FOR YOUR HARD WORK AND DEDICA-TION, WINONA.
I'LL TAKE OVER SUPERVISION OF THE GYM LEADERS FROM HERE ON OUT.
YOU MEAN... NOW...I CAN...?!
YES!! I WANT YOU TO GO!!
JOIN THE GYM LEADERS WHO ARE ALREADY FIGHTING! STOP THOSE ANCIENT POKÉMON FROM MOVING ANY FARTHER INTO OUR REGION!!
YES, SIR!!

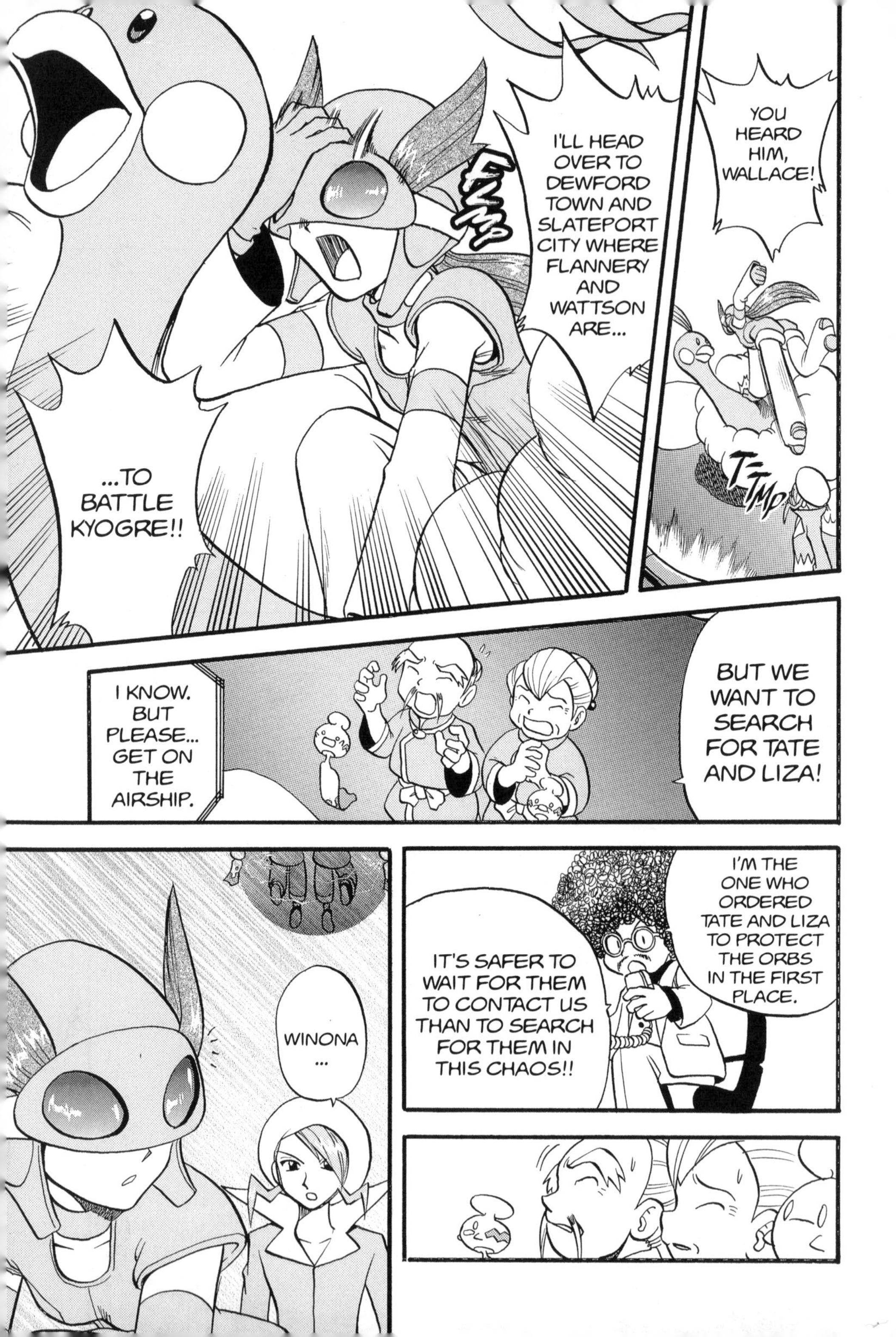
YOU HEARD HIM, WALLACE!
T-TMP
I'LL HEAD OVER TO DEWFORD TOWN AND SLATEPORT CITY WHERE FLANNERY AND WATTSON ARE...
FLMP
...TO BATTLE KYOGRE!!
BUT WE WANT TO SEARCH FOR TATE AND LIZA!
I KNOW. BUT PLEASE... GET ON THE AIRSHIP.
I'M THE ONE WHO ORDERED TATE AND LIZA TO PROTECT THE ORBS IN THE FIRST PLACE.
IT'S SAFER TO WAIT FOR THEM TO CONTACT US THAN TO SEARCH FOR THEM IN THIS CHAOS!!
WINONA ...

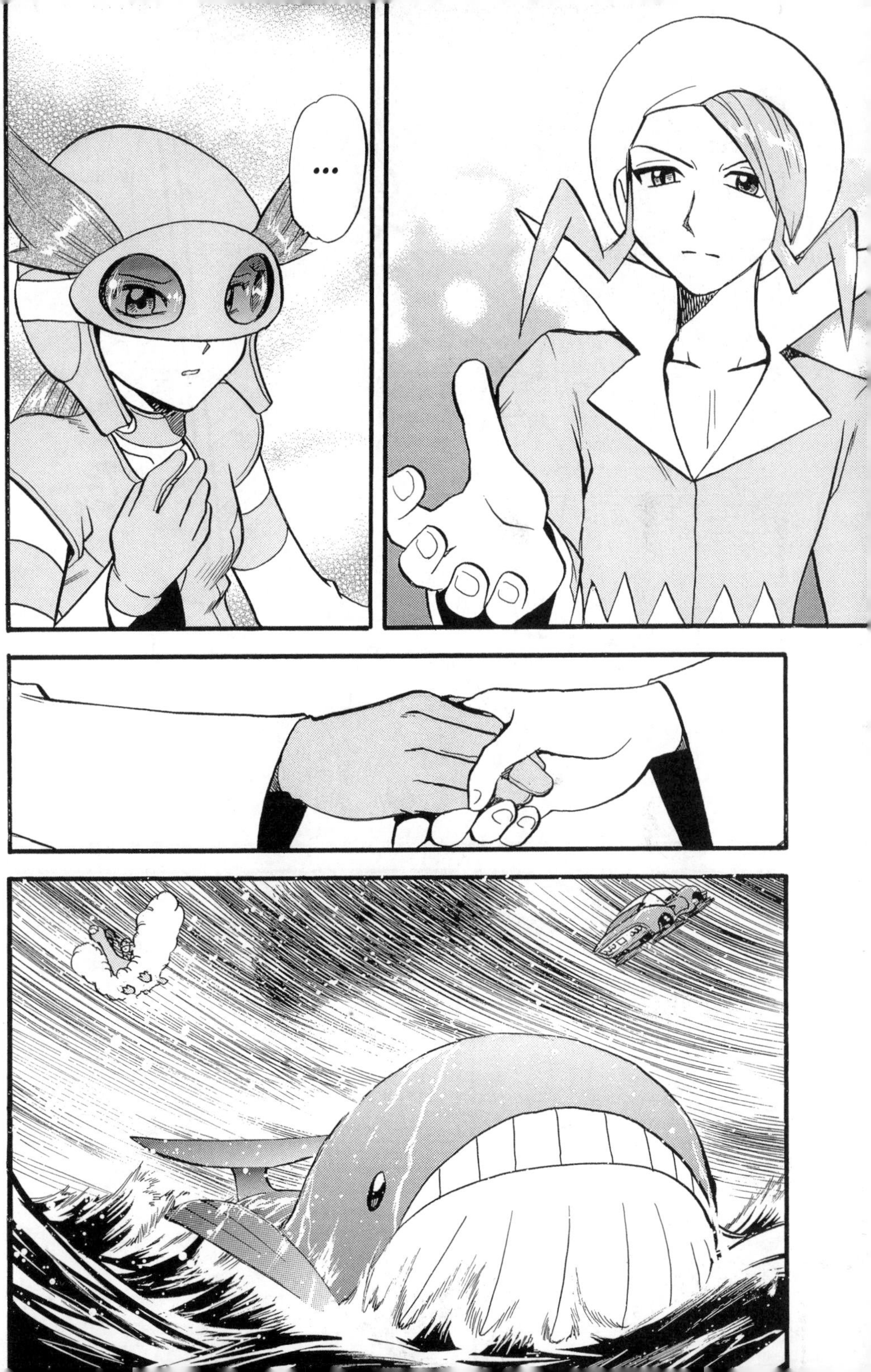
...

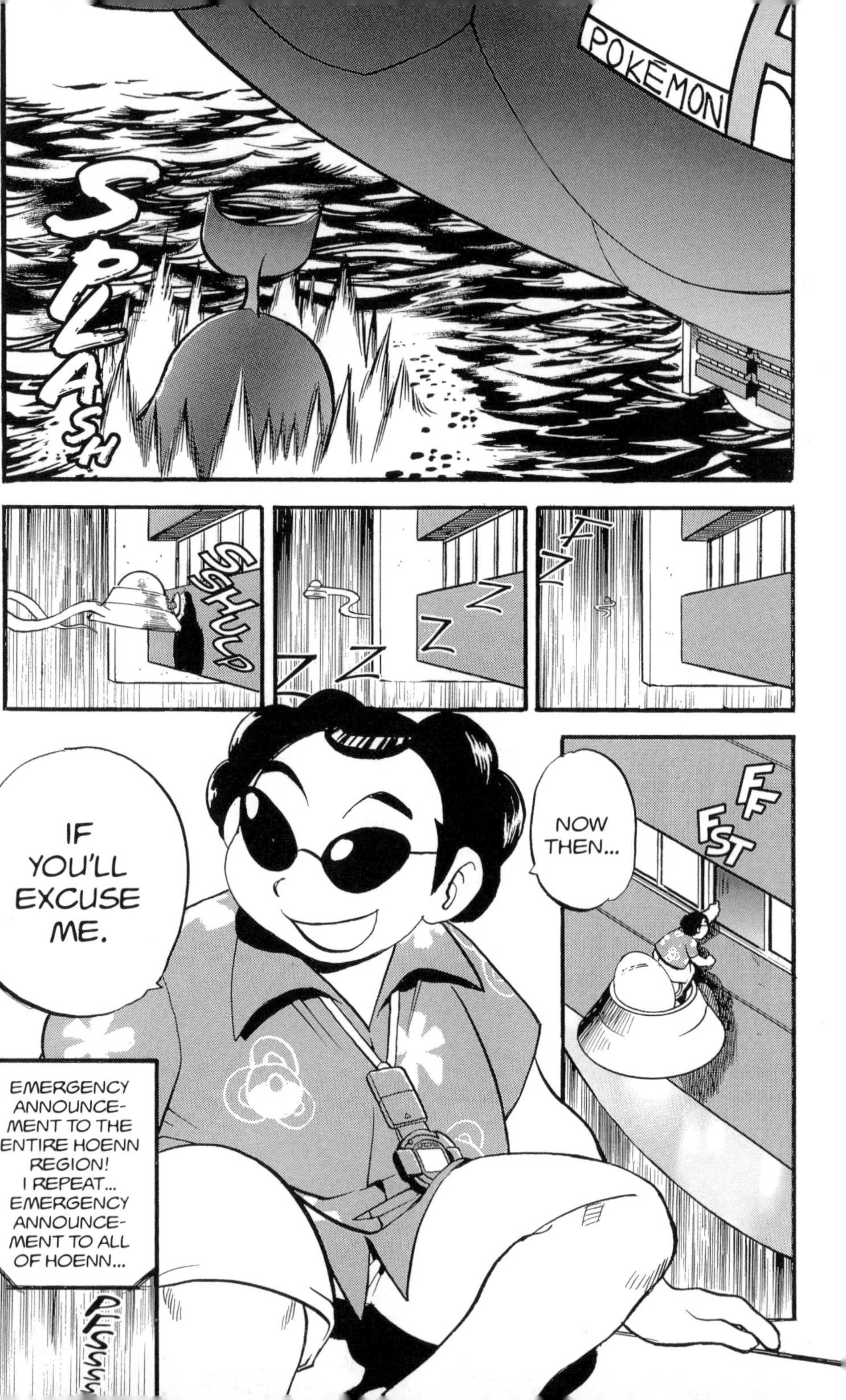
POKéMON
SPLASH
FZ
ZZZZ
SSHUP
NOW THEN...
FFFST
IF YOU'LL EXCUSE ME.
EMERGENCY ANNOUNCEMENT TO THE ENTIRE HOENN REGION! I REPEAT... EMERGENCY ANNOUNCEMENT TO ALL OF HOENN...
PFSSSS

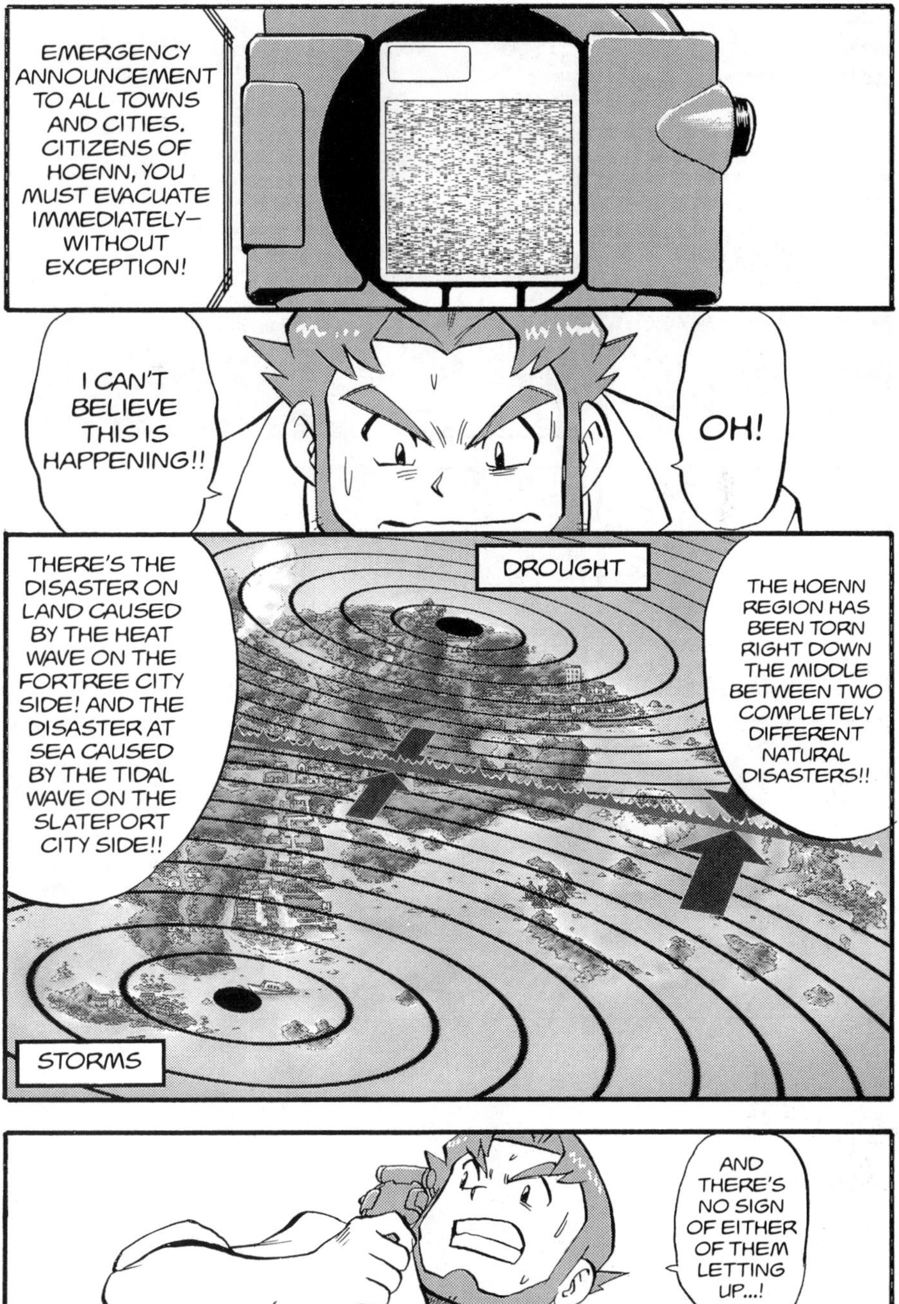
EMERGENCY ANNOUNCEMENT TO ALL TOWNS AND CITIES. CITIZENS OF HOENN, YOU MUST EVACUATE IMMEDIATELY—WITHOUT EXCEPTION!
OH!
I CAN'T BELIEVE THIS IS HAPPENING!!
THE HOENN REGION HAS BEEN TORN RIGHT DOWN THE MIDDLE BETWEEN TWO COMPLETELY DIFFERENT NATURAL DISASTERS!!
DROUGHT
THERE'S THE DISASTER ON LAND CAUSED BY THE HEAT WAVE ON THE FORTREE CITY SIDE! AND THE DISASTER AT SEA CAUSED BY THE TIDAL WAVE ON THE SLATEPORT CITY SIDE!!
STORMS
AND THERE'S NO SIGN OF EITHER OF THEM LETTING UP...!

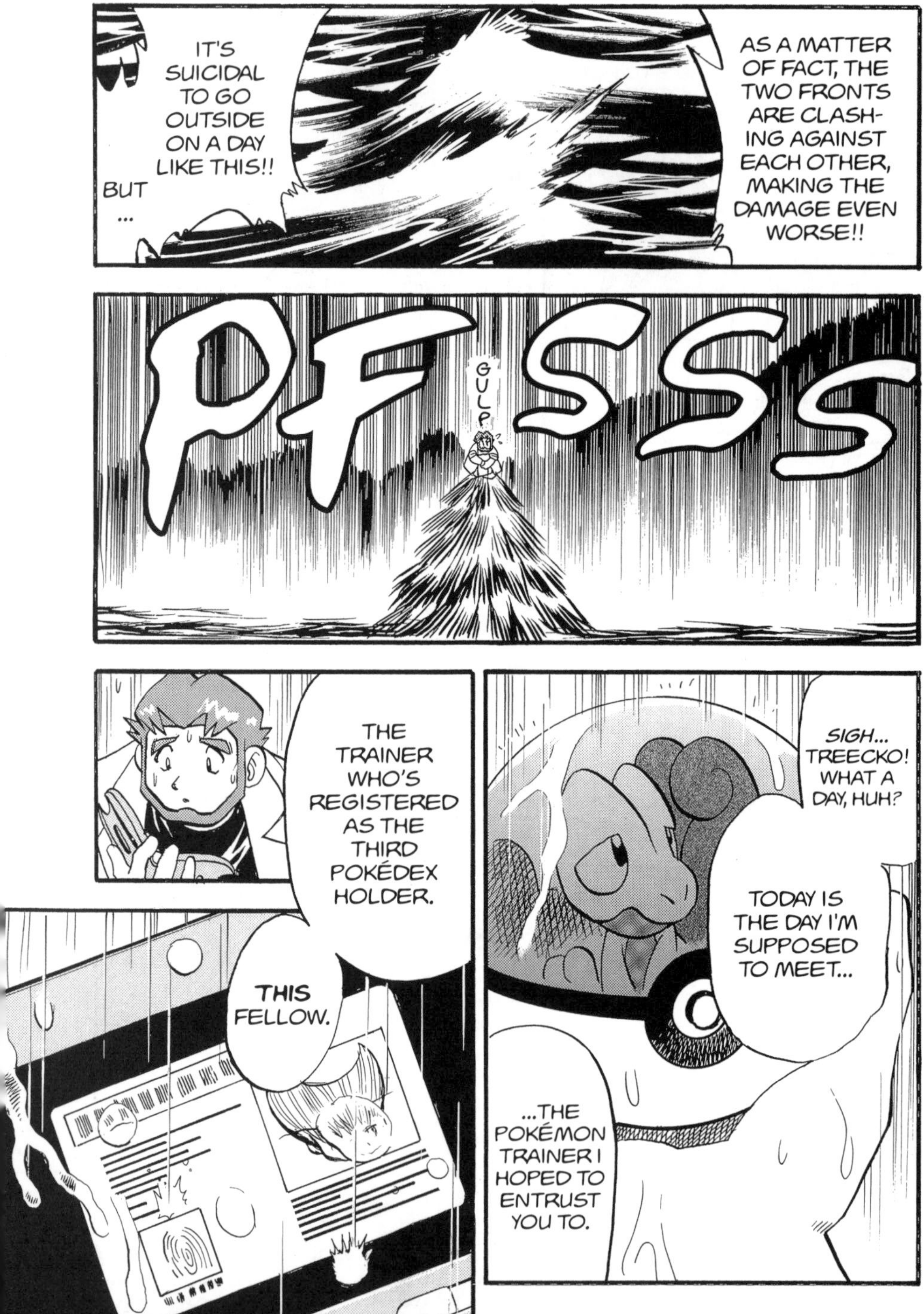

AS A MATTER OF FACT, THE TWO FRONTS ARE CLASHING AGAINST EACH OTHER, MAKING THE DAMAGE EVEN WORSE!!
IT'S SUICIDAL TO GO OUTSIDE ON A DAY LIKE THIS!!
BUT ...
PFSSS
GULP
SIGH... TREECKO! WHAT A DAY, HUH?
TODAY IS THE DAY I'M SUPPOSED TO MEET...
...THE POKÉMON TRAINER I HOPED TO ENTRUST YOU TO.
THE TRAINER WHO'S REGISTERED AS THE THIRD POKÉDEX HOLDER.
THIS FELLOW.

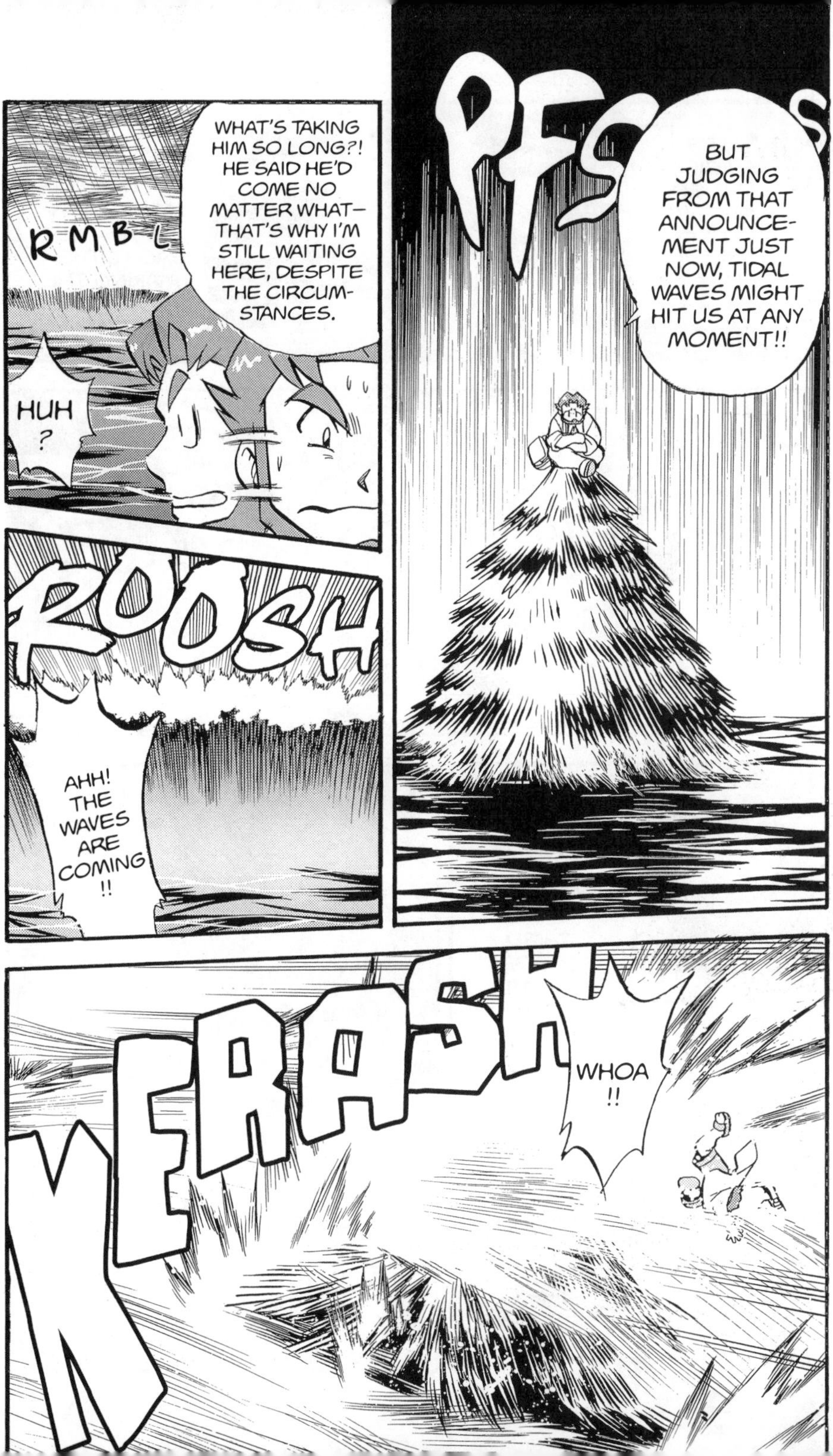
PFS
BUT JUDGING FROM THAT ANNOUNCEMENT JUST NOW, TIDAL WAVES MIGHT HIT US AT ANY MOMENT!!
RMBL
WHAT'S TAKING HIM SO LONG?! HE SAID HE'D COME NO MATTER WHAT—THAT'S WHY I'M STILL WAITING HERE, DESPITE THE CIRCUMSTANCES.
HUH?
ROOSH
AHH! THE WAVES ARE COMING!!
KERASH
WHOA!!

MY BAG ...!!

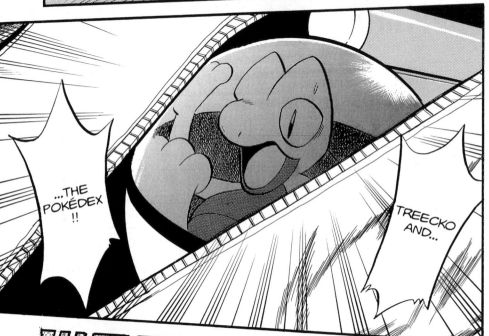

...THE POKÉDEX !!

TREECKO AND...

GLUG GLUG

SPLASH

217

ADVENTURE MAP

SAPPHIRE

CHIC
Blaziken ♀
Lv40

RONO
Lairon ♂
Lv41

RELLY
Relicanth ♂
Lv47

PHADO
Donphan ♂
Lv48

TROPPY
Tropius ♂
Lv46

LORRY
Wailord ♂
Lv48

RUBY

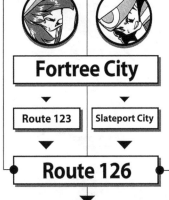

Fortree City

| Route 123 | Slateport City |

Route 126

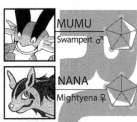
MUMU
Swampert ♂

NANA
Mightyena ♀

KIKI
Delcatty ♀

FOFO
Castform ♀

| Stone Badge | Knuckle Badge | Dynamo Badge | Heat Badge |
| Balance Badge | Feather Badge | Mind Badge | Rain Badge |

	Coolness	Beauty	Cuteness	Cleverness	Toughness
Normal					
Super					
Hyper					
Master					

● Adventure 240 ●
Talk About Timing, Treecko

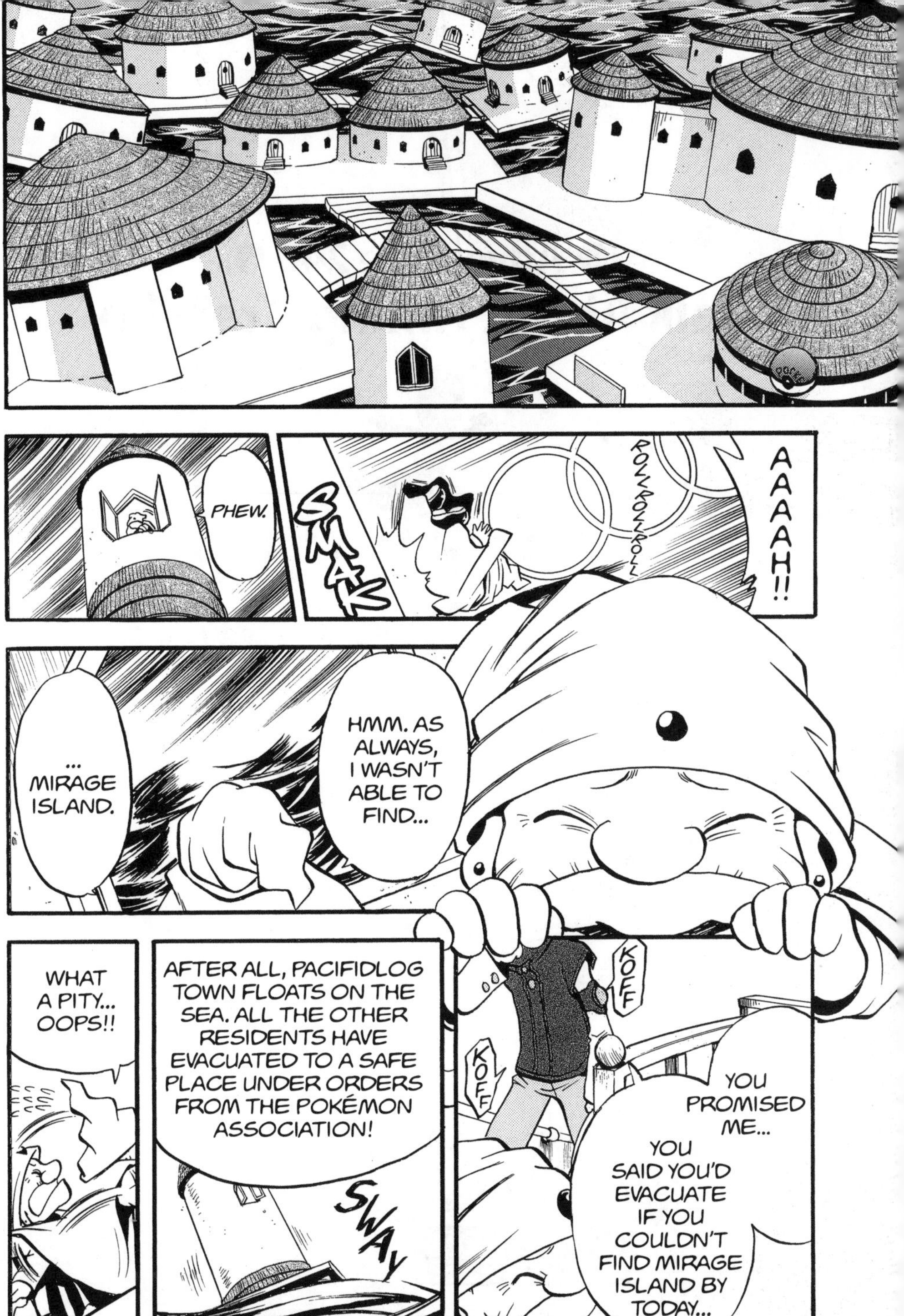
AAAAAH!!
ROLLROLLROLL
SMAK
PHEW.
HMM. AS ALWAYS, I WASN'T ABLE TO FIND...
... MIRAGE ISLAND.
KOFF
KOFF
YOU PROMISED ME...
YOU SAID YOU'D EVACUATE IF YOU COULDN'T FIND MIRAGE ISLAND BY TODAY...
AFTER ALL, PACIFIDLOG TOWN FLOATS ON THE SEA. ALL THE OTHER RESIDENTS HAVE EVACUATED TO A SAFE PLACE UNDER ORDERS FROM THE POKÉMON ASSOCIATION!
SWAY
WHAT A PITY... OOPS!!

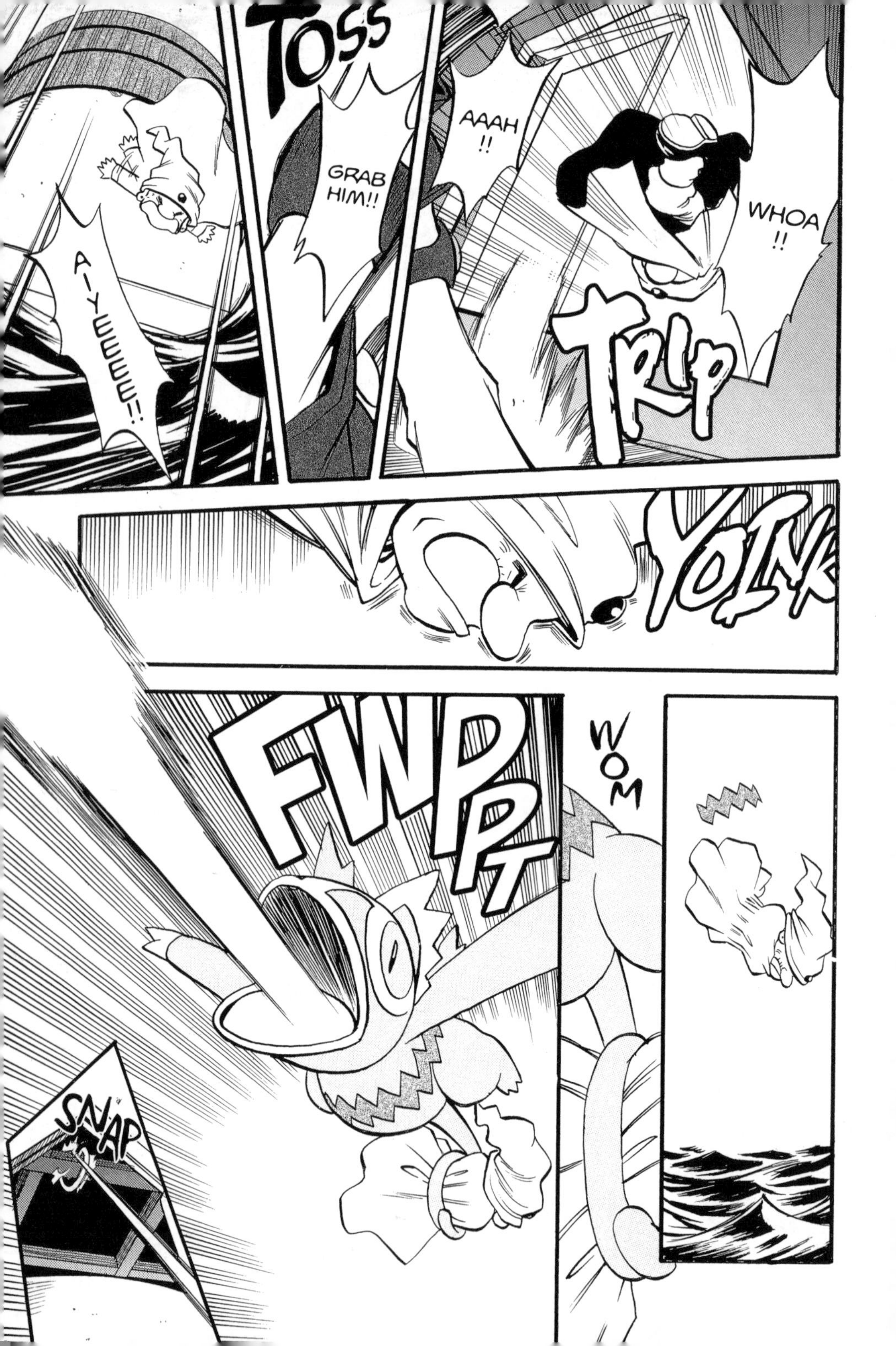
AAAH!!
WHOA!!
TRIP
TOSS
GRAB HIM!!
AIYEEEEE!!
YOINK
WOM
FWPPT
SNAP

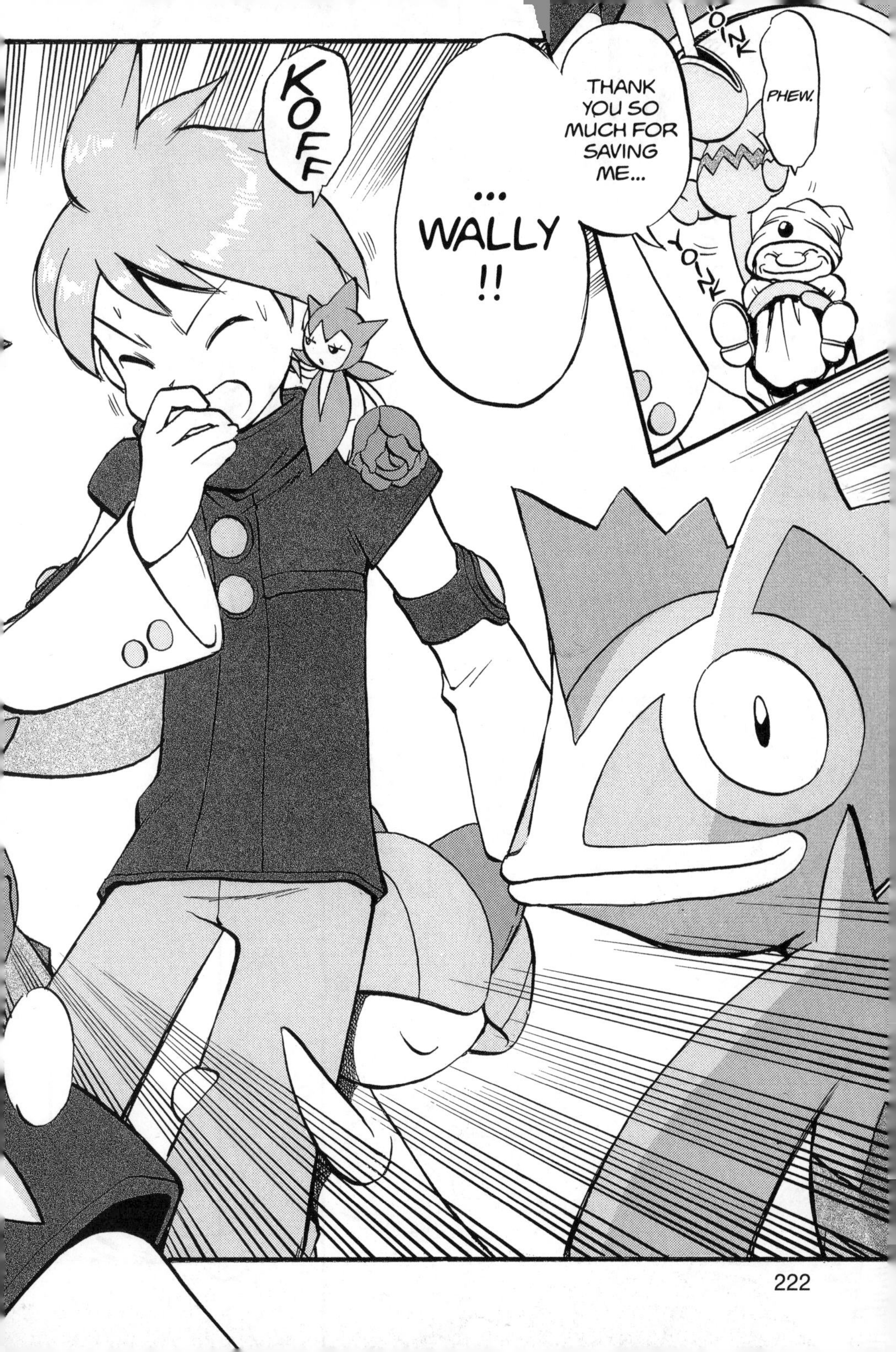
YOINK
PHEW.
THANK YOU SO MUCH FOR SAVING ME...
YOINK
... WALLY !!
KOFF

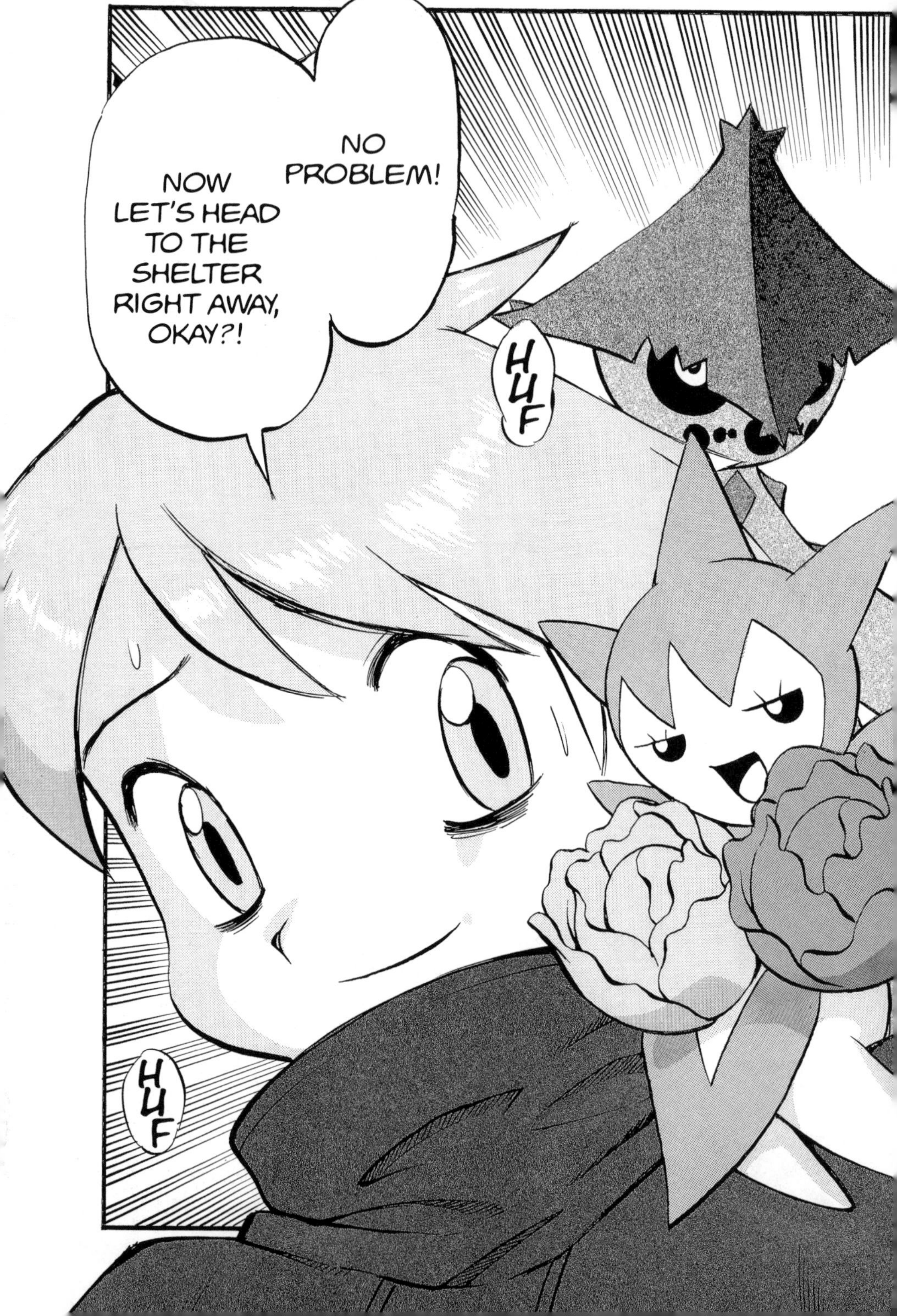
NO PROBLEM!
NOW LET'S HEAD TO THE SHELTER RIGHT AWAY, OKAY?!
HUF
HUF

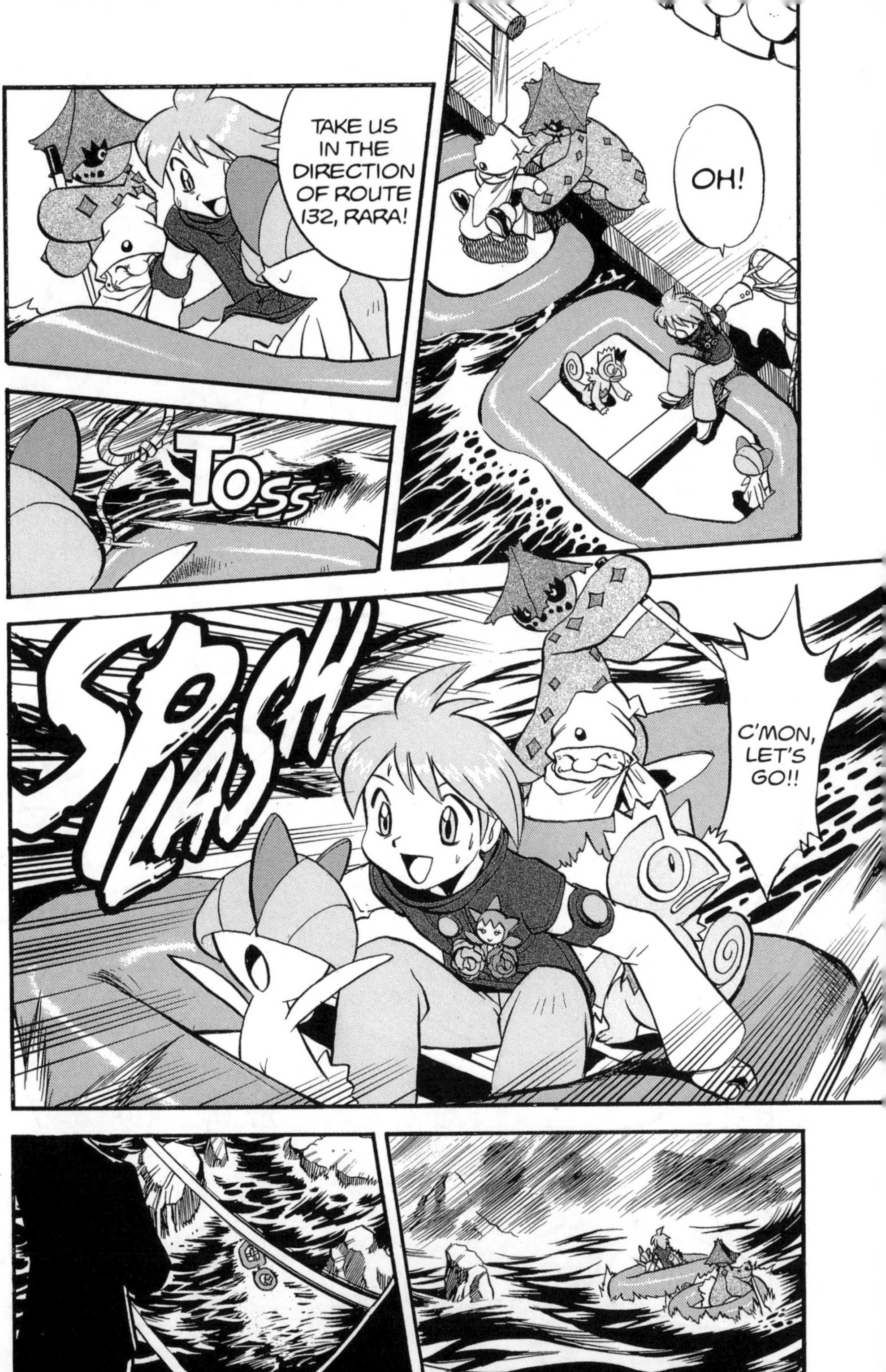
OH!
TAKE US IN THE DIRECTION OF ROUTE 132, RARA!
TOSS
C'MON, LET'S GO!!
SPLASH

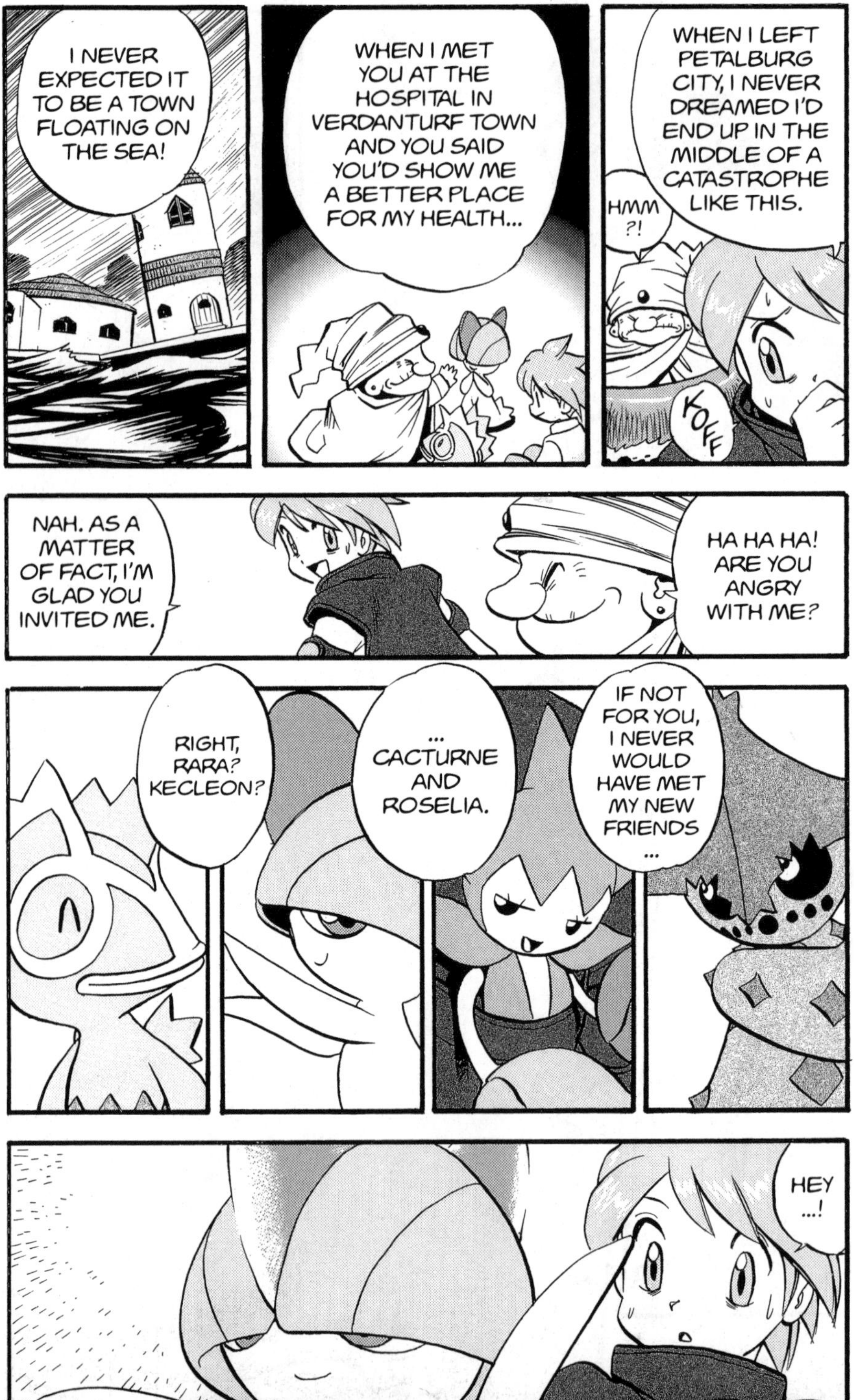
WHEN I LEFT PETALBURG CITY, I NEVER DREAMED I'D END UP IN THE MIDDLE OF A CATASTROPHE LIKE THIS.
HMM ?!
KOFF
WHEN I MET YOU AT THE HOSPITAL IN VERDANTURF TOWN AND YOU SAID YOU'D SHOW ME A BETTER PLACE FOR MY HEALTH...
I NEVER EXPECTED IT TO BE A TOWN FLOATING ON THE SEA!
HA HA HA! ARE YOU ANGRY WITH ME?
NAH. AS A MATTER OF FACT, I'M GLAD YOU INVITED ME.
IF NOT FOR YOU, I NEVER WOULD HAVE MET MY NEW FRIENDS ...
... CACTURNE AND ROSELIA.
RIGHT, RARA? KECLEON?
HEY ...!

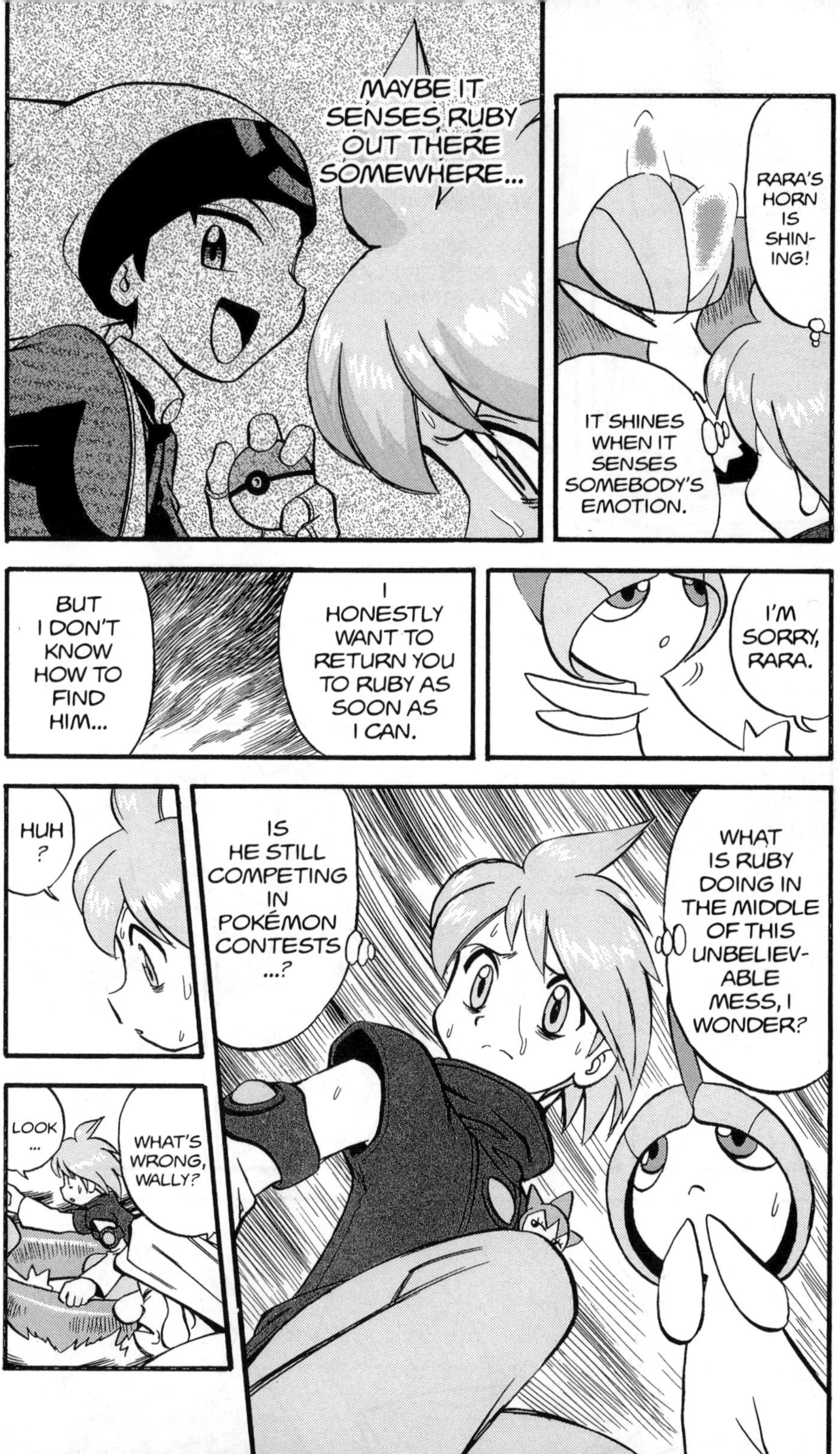
RARA'S HORN IS SHINING!
IT SHINES WHEN IT SENSES SOMEBODY'S EMOTION.
MAYBE IT SENSES RUBY OUT THERE SOMEWHERE...
I'M SORRY, RARA.
I HONESTLY WANT TO RETURN YOU TO RUBY AS SOON AS I CAN.
BUT I DON'T KNOW HOW TO FIND HIM...
WHAT IS RUBY DOING IN THE MIDDLE OF THIS UNBELIEVABLE MESS, I WONDER?
IS HE STILL COMPETING IN POKÉMON CONTESTS...?
HUH?
WHAT'S WRONG, WALLY?
LOOK...

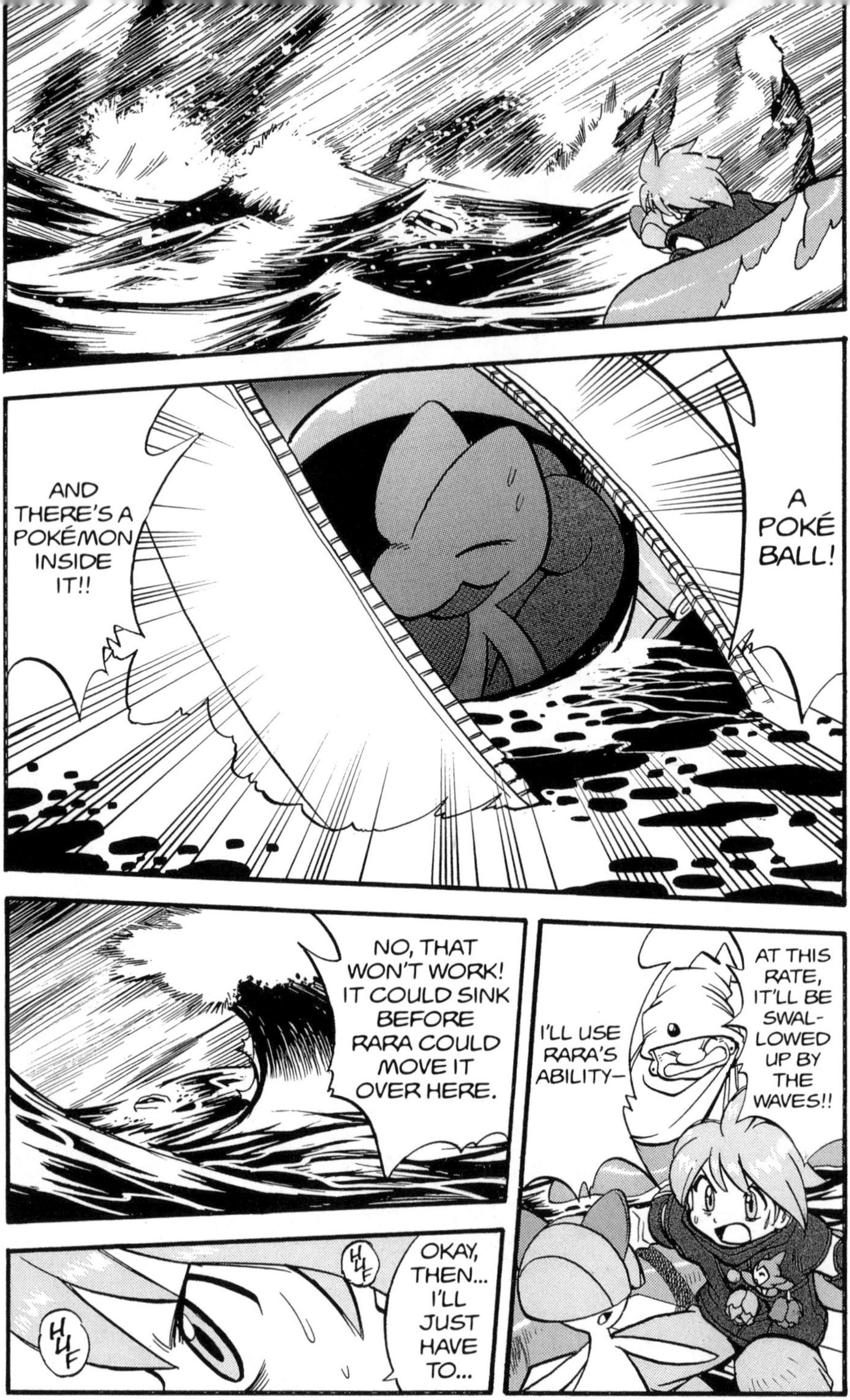
A POKÉ BALL!
AND THERE'S A POKÉMON INSIDE IT!!
AT THIS RATE, IT'LL BE SWAL-LOWED UP BY THE WAVES!!
I'LL USE RARA'S ABILITY—
NO, THAT WON'T WORK! IT COULD SINK BEFORE RARA COULD MOVE IT OVER HERE.
OKAY, THEN... I'LL JUST HAVE TO...
HUF
HUF

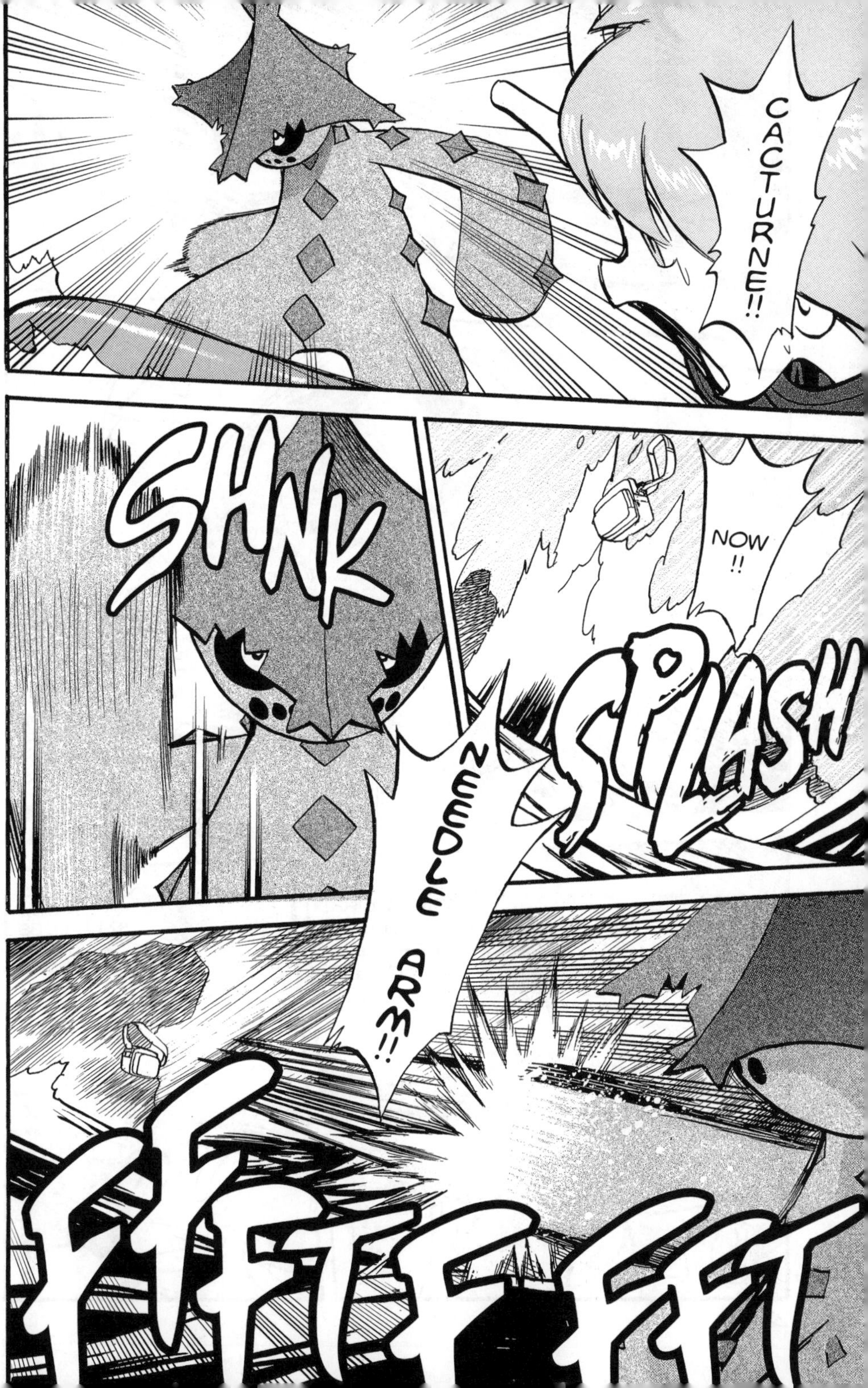
CACTURNE!!
SHNK
NOW!!
SPLASH
NEEDLE ARM!!
FFFTFFFT

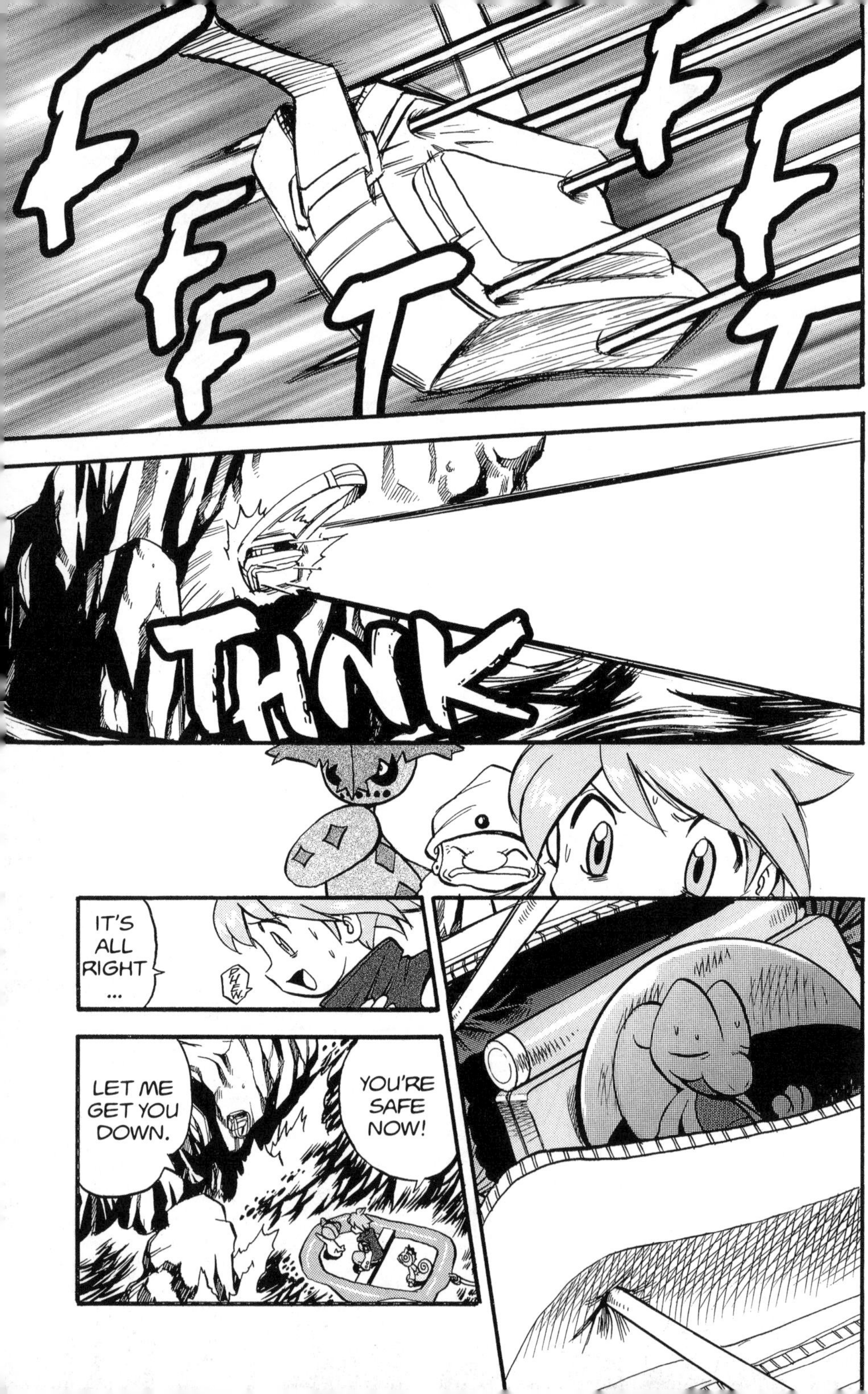
FFT
FFFT
THNK
PHEW.
IT'S ALL RIGHT...
YOU'RE SAFE NOW!
LET ME GET YOU DOWN.

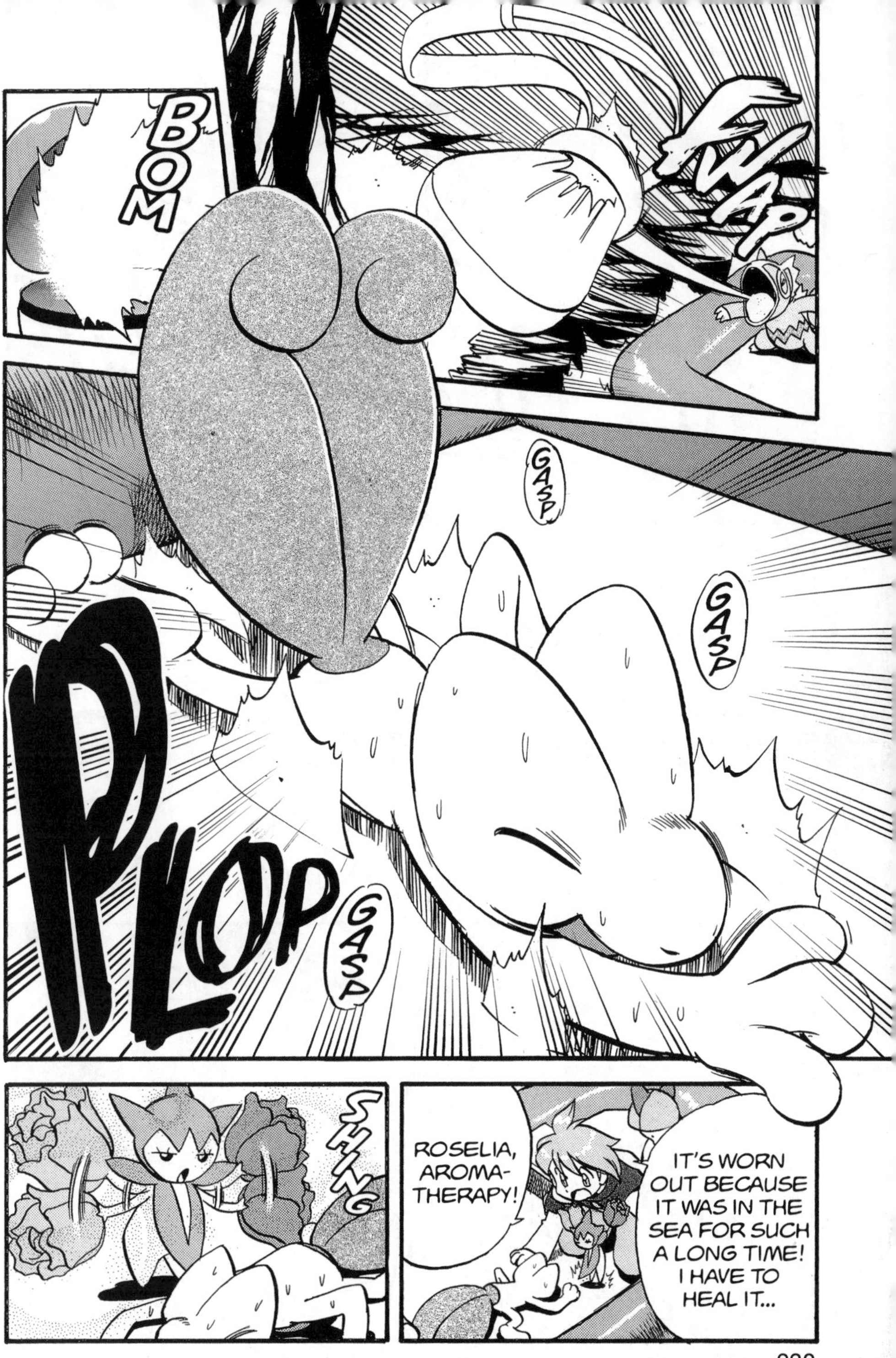
FWAP
BOM
GASP
GASP
PLOP
GASP
IT'S WORN OUT BECAUSE IT WAS IN THE SEA FOR SUCH A LONG TIME! I HAVE TO HEAL IT...
ROSELIA, AROMA-THERAPY!
SHING

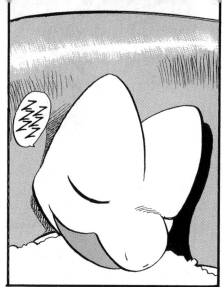

ZZZ

ITS BREATH HAS STARTED TO STABILIZE. LET'S LET IT SLEEP.

ROSELIA, GRASS-WHISTLE.

HMM! NOT BAD. NOT BAD AT ALL.

KLAP KLAP KLAP KLAP

TMP

FLAP

HWOOOSH

THAT WAS AN IMPRESSIVE USE OF YOUR POKÉMON.

BUT I HAVE ONE QUESTION ...

WHY DID YOU CHOOSE TO USE NEEDLE ARM...?

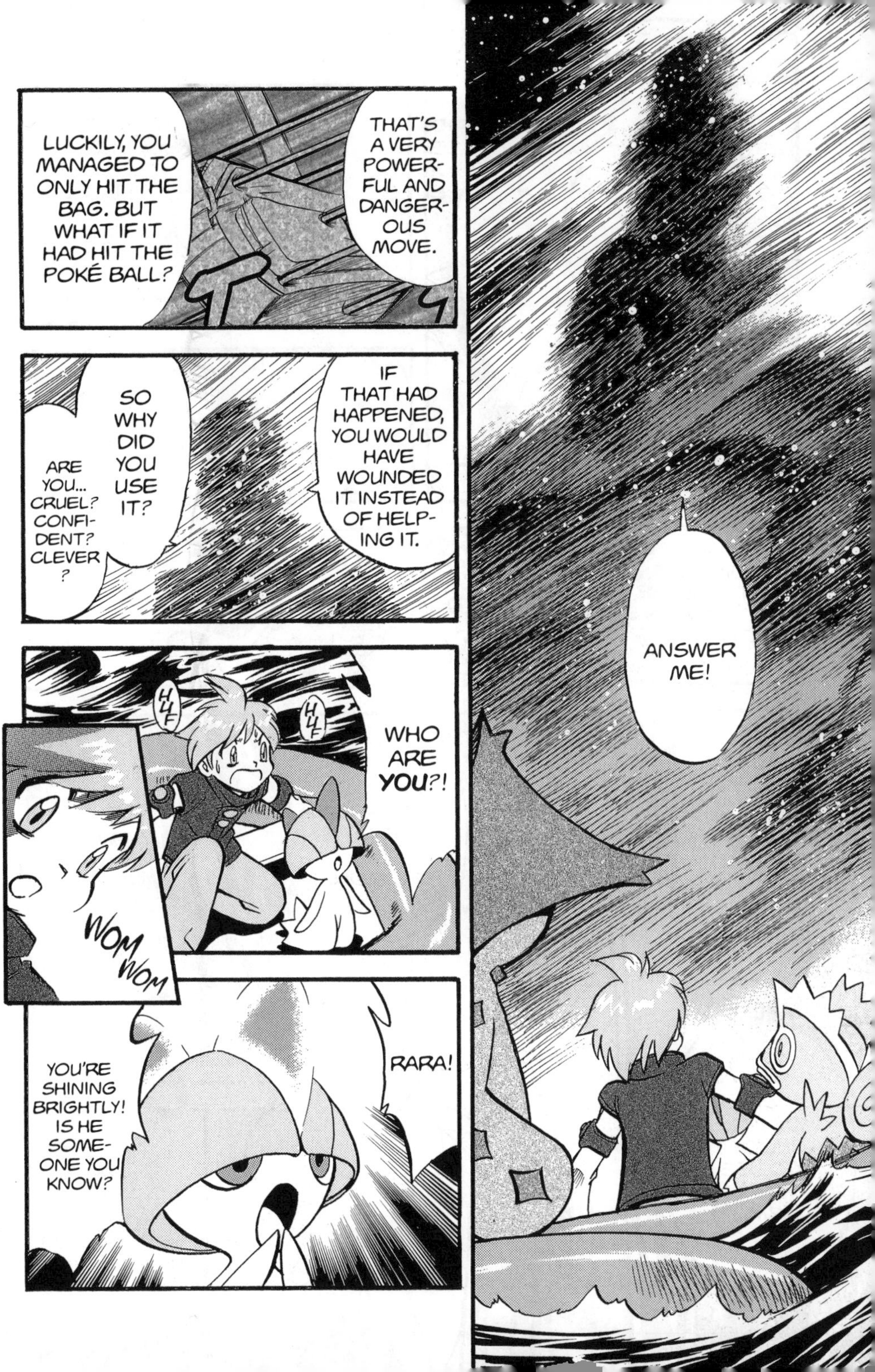
ANSWER ME!
THAT'S A VERY POWER-FUL AND DANGER-OUS MOVE.
LUCKILY, YOU MANAGED TO ONLY HIT THE BAG. BUT WHAT IF IT HAD HIT THE POKÉ BALL?
IF THAT HAD HAPPENED, YOU WOULD HAVE WOUNDED IT INSTEAD OF HELP-ING IT.
SO WHY DID YOU USE IT?
ARE YOU... CRUEL? CONFI-DENT? CLEVER?
HUF
HUF
WHO ARE YOU?!
WOM WOM
RARA!
YOU'RE SHINING BRIGHTLY! IS HE SOME-ONE YOU KNOW?

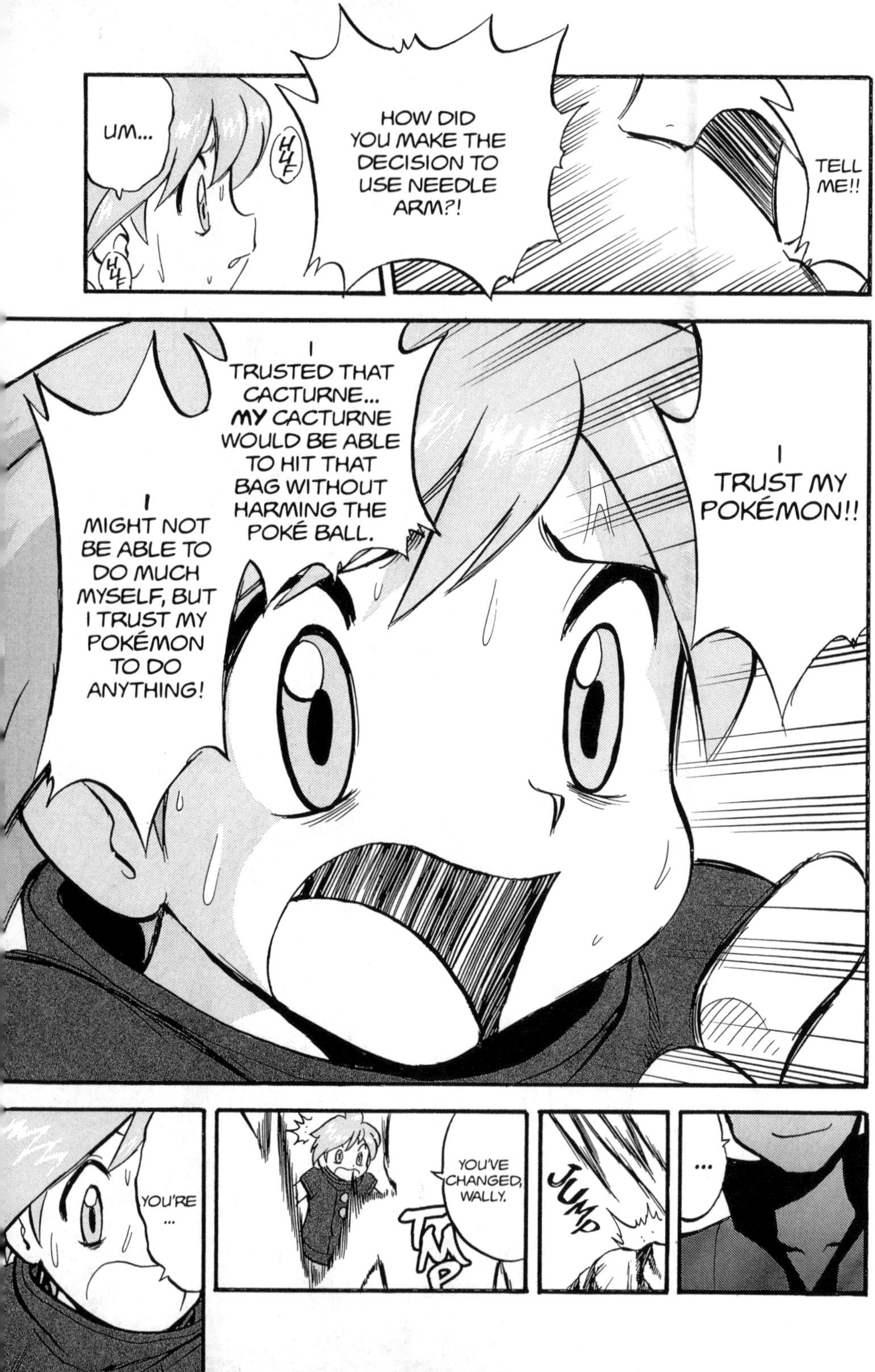
TELL ME!!
HOW DID YOU MAKE THE DECISION TO USE NEEDLE ARM?!
HUF
HUF
UM...
I TRUST MY POKÉMON!!
I TRUSTED THAT CACTURNE... **MY** CACTURNE WOULD BE ABLE TO HIT THAT BAG WITHOUT HARMING THE POKÉ BALL.
I MIGHT NOT BE ABLE TO DO MUCH MYSELF, BUT I TRUST MY POKÉMON TO DO ANYTHING!
...
JUMP
YOU'VE CHANGED, WALLY.
TMP
YOU'RE ...

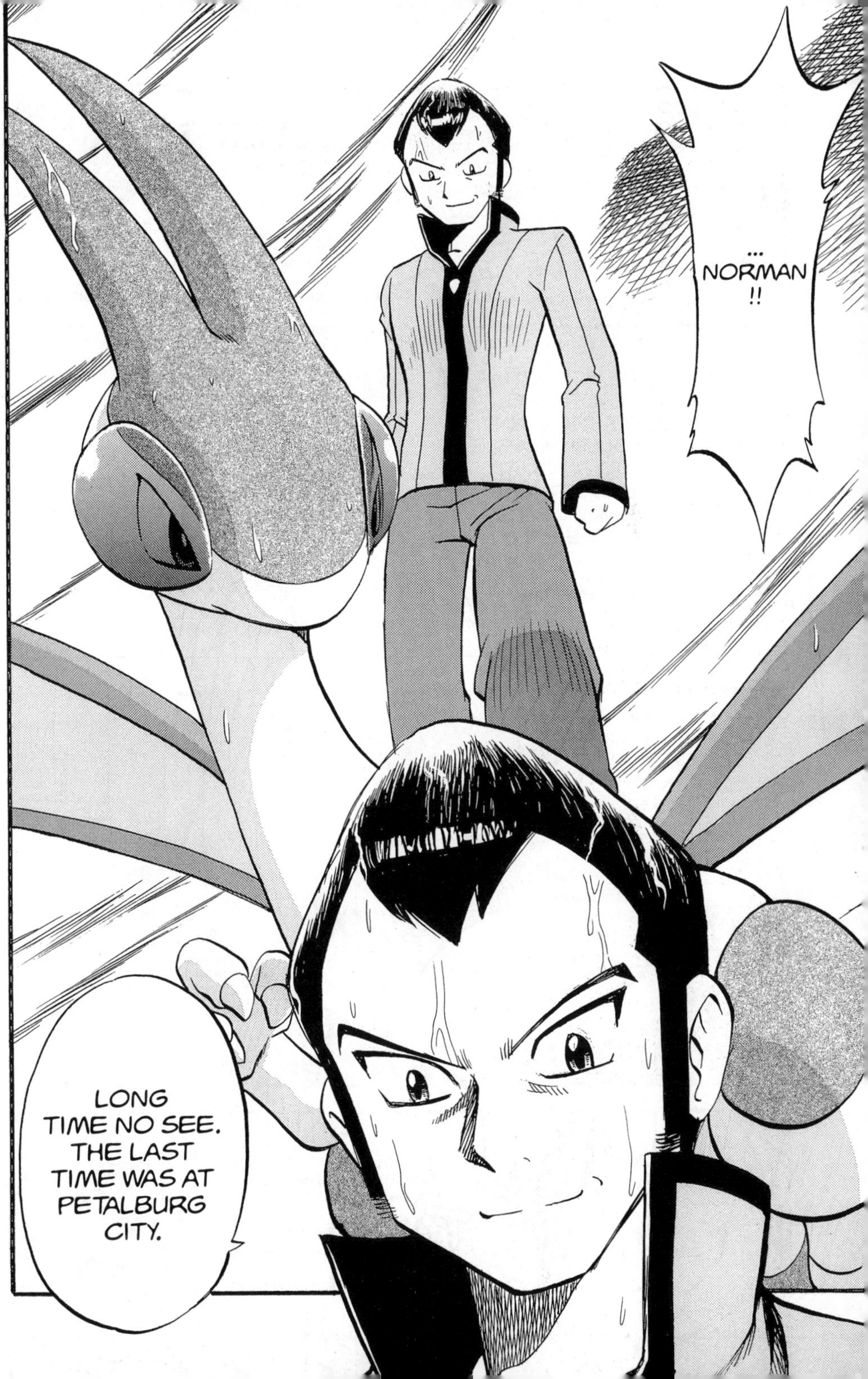
...NORMAN!!
LONG TIME NO SEE. THE LAST TIME WAS AT PETALBURG CITY.

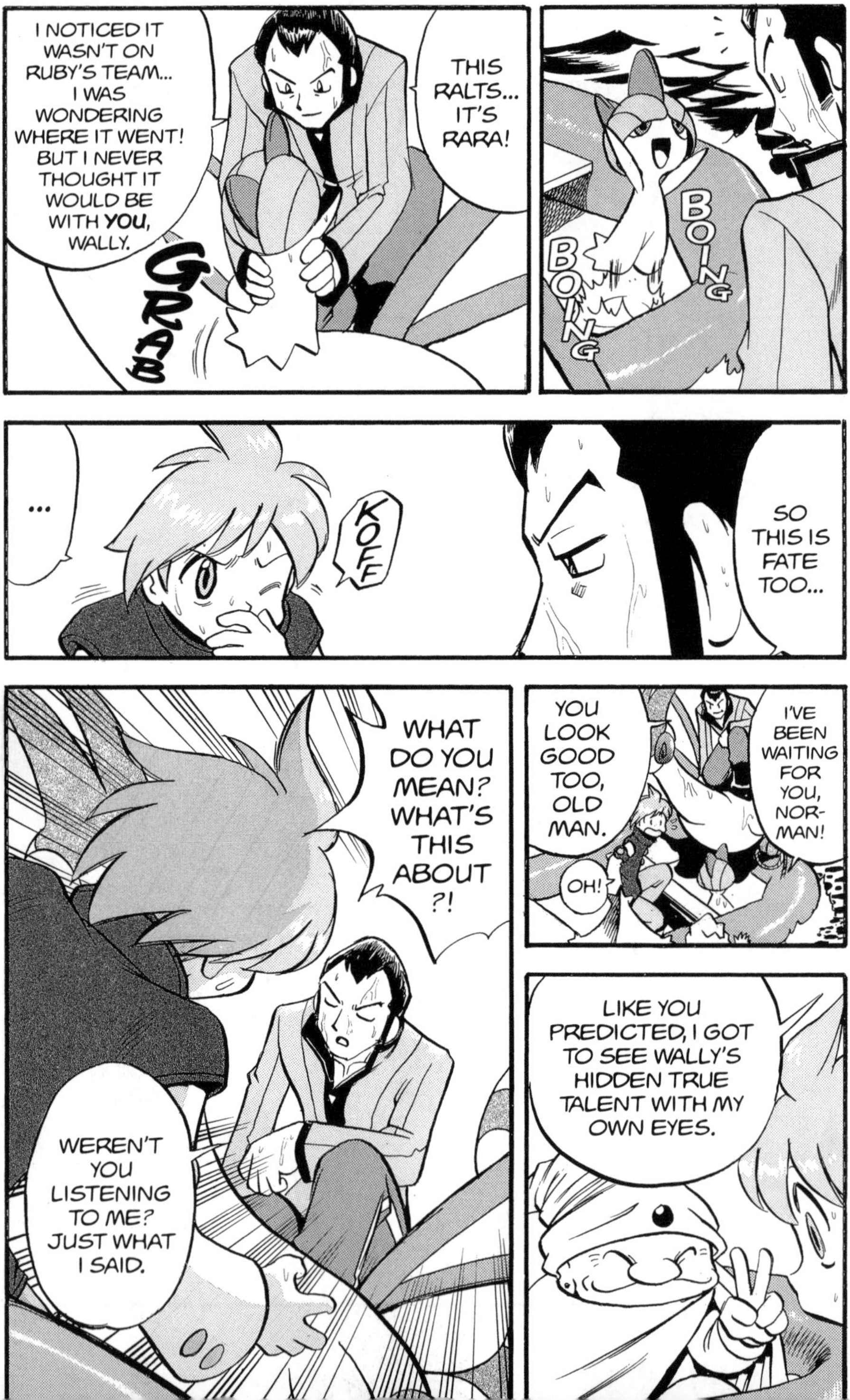
BOING
BOING
BOING
THIS RALTS... IT'S RARA!
I NOTICED IT WASN'T ON RUBY'S TEAM... I WAS WONDERING WHERE IT WENT! BUT I NEVER THOUGHT IT WOULD BE WITH **YOU**, WALLY.
GRAB
SO THIS IS FATE TOO...
KOFF
...
I'VE BEEN WAITING FOR YOU, NOR-MAN!
YOU LOOK GOOD TOO, OLD MAN.
OH!
LIKE YOU PREDICTED, I GOT TO SEE WALLY'S HIDDEN TRUE TALENT WITH MY OWN EYES.
WHAT DO YOU MEAN? WHAT'S THIS ABOUT ?!
WEREN'T YOU LISTENING TO ME? JUST WHAT I SAID.

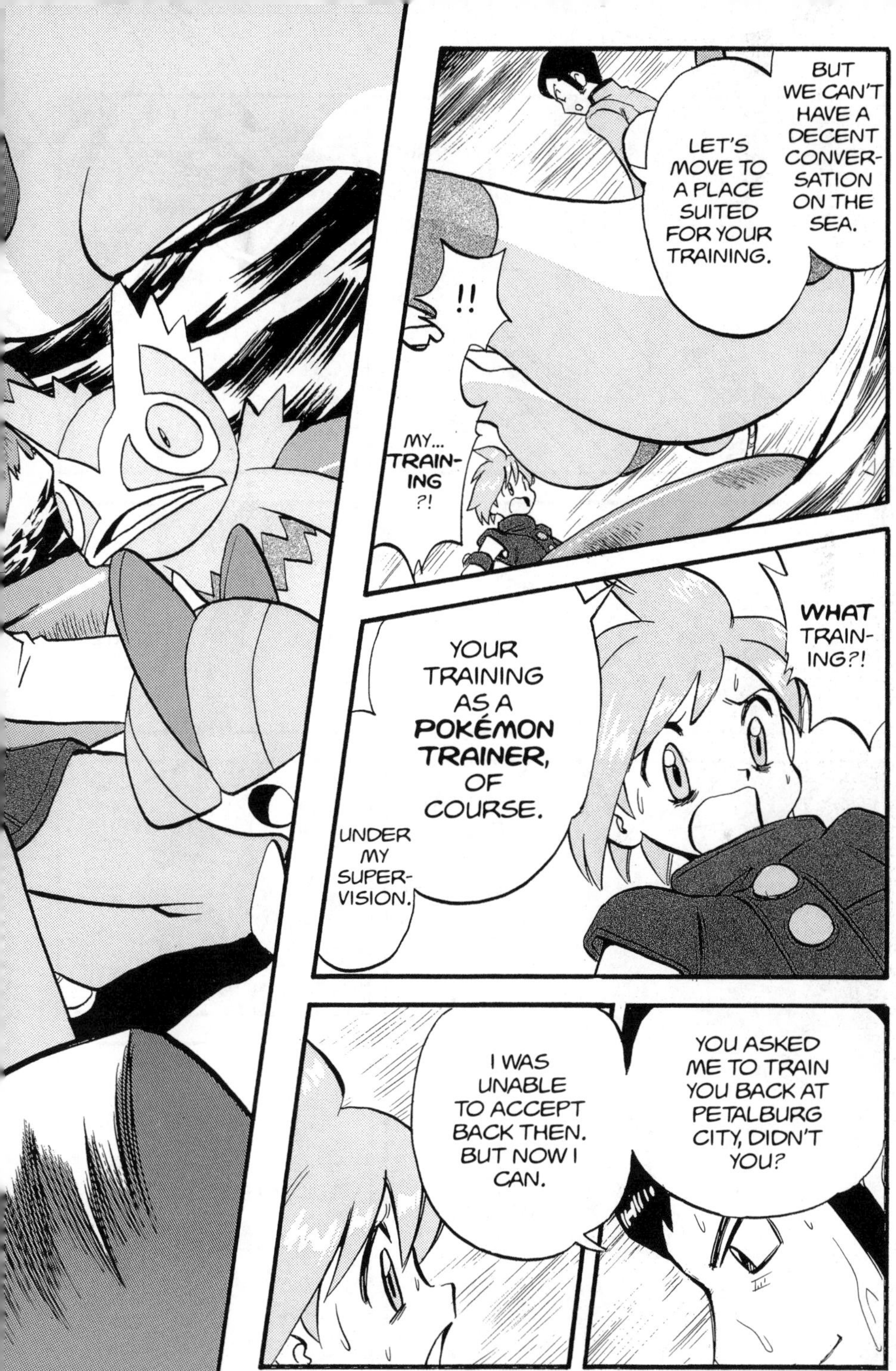
BUT WE CAN'T HAVE A DECENT CONVERSATION ON THE SEA.
LET'S MOVE TO A PLACE SUITED FOR YOUR TRAINING.
!!
MY... TRAINING?!
WHAT TRAINING?!
YOUR TRAINING AS A POKÉMON TRAINER, OF COURSE.
UNDER MY SUPERVISION.
YOU ASKED ME TO TRAIN YOU BACK AT PETALBURG CITY, DIDN'T YOU?
I WAS UNABLE TO ACCEPT BACK THEN. BUT NOW I CAN.

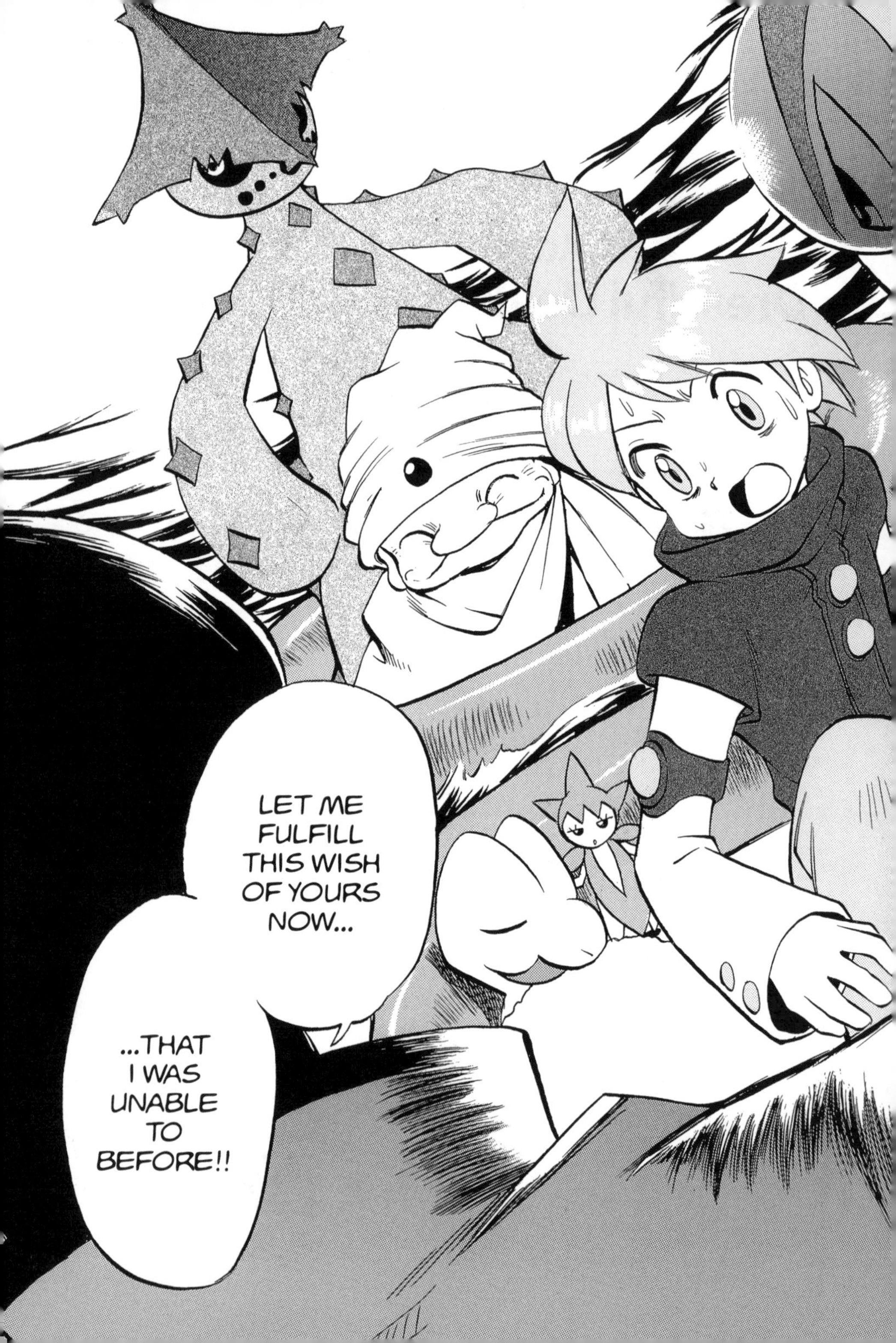
LET ME FULFILL THIS WISH OF YOURS NOW...
...THAT I WAS UNABLE TO BEFORE!!

● Adventure 241 ●
Dreadful Dealing with Dusclops

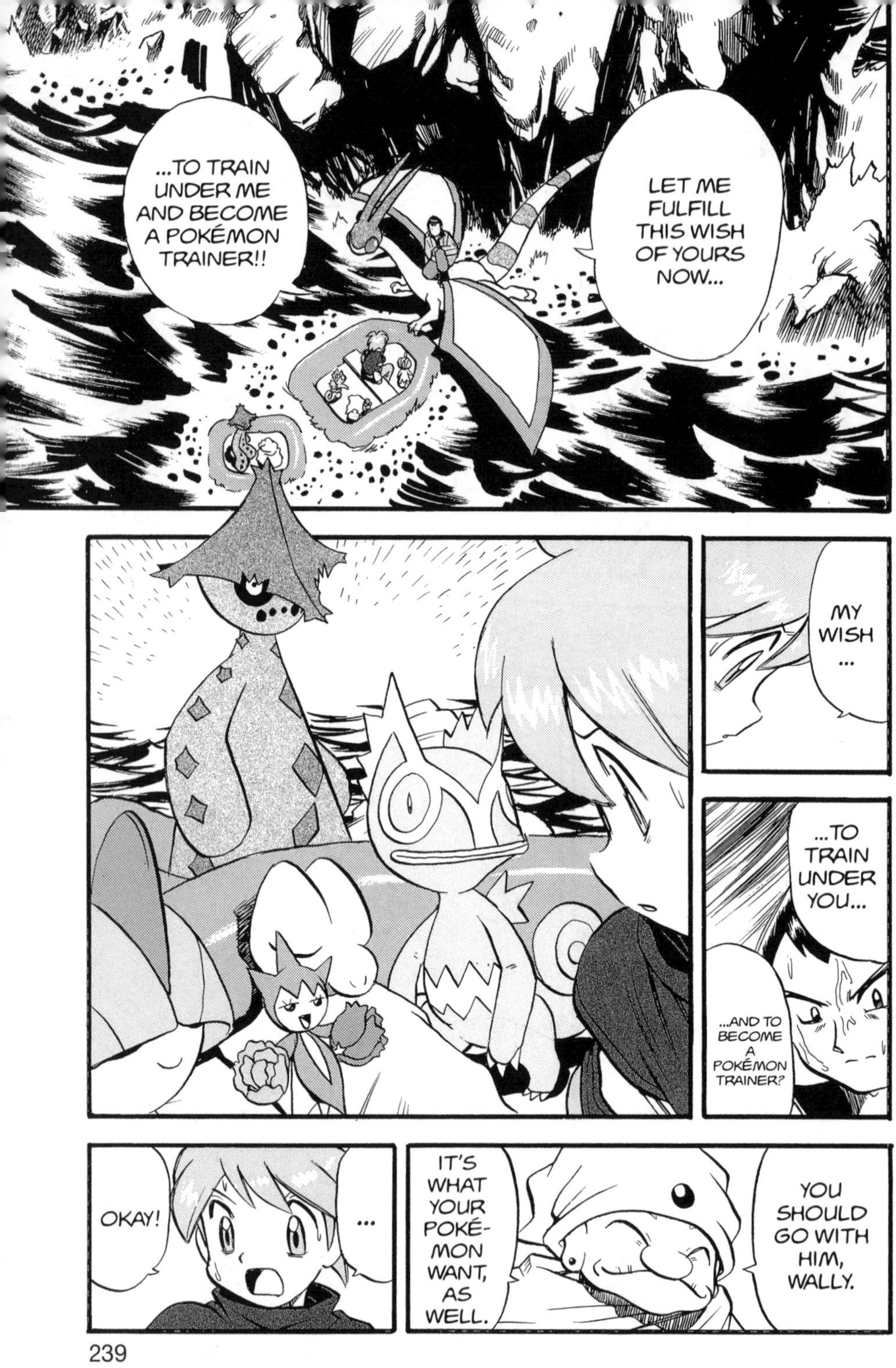
LET ME FULFILL THIS WISH OF YOURS NOW...
...TO TRAIN UNDER ME AND BECOME A POKÉMON TRAINER!!
MY WISH ...
...TO TRAIN UNDER YOU...
...AND TO BECOME A POKÉMON TRAINER?
YOU SHOULD GO WITH HIM, WALLY.
IT'S WHAT YOUR POKÉ-MON WANT, AS WELL.
...
OKAY!

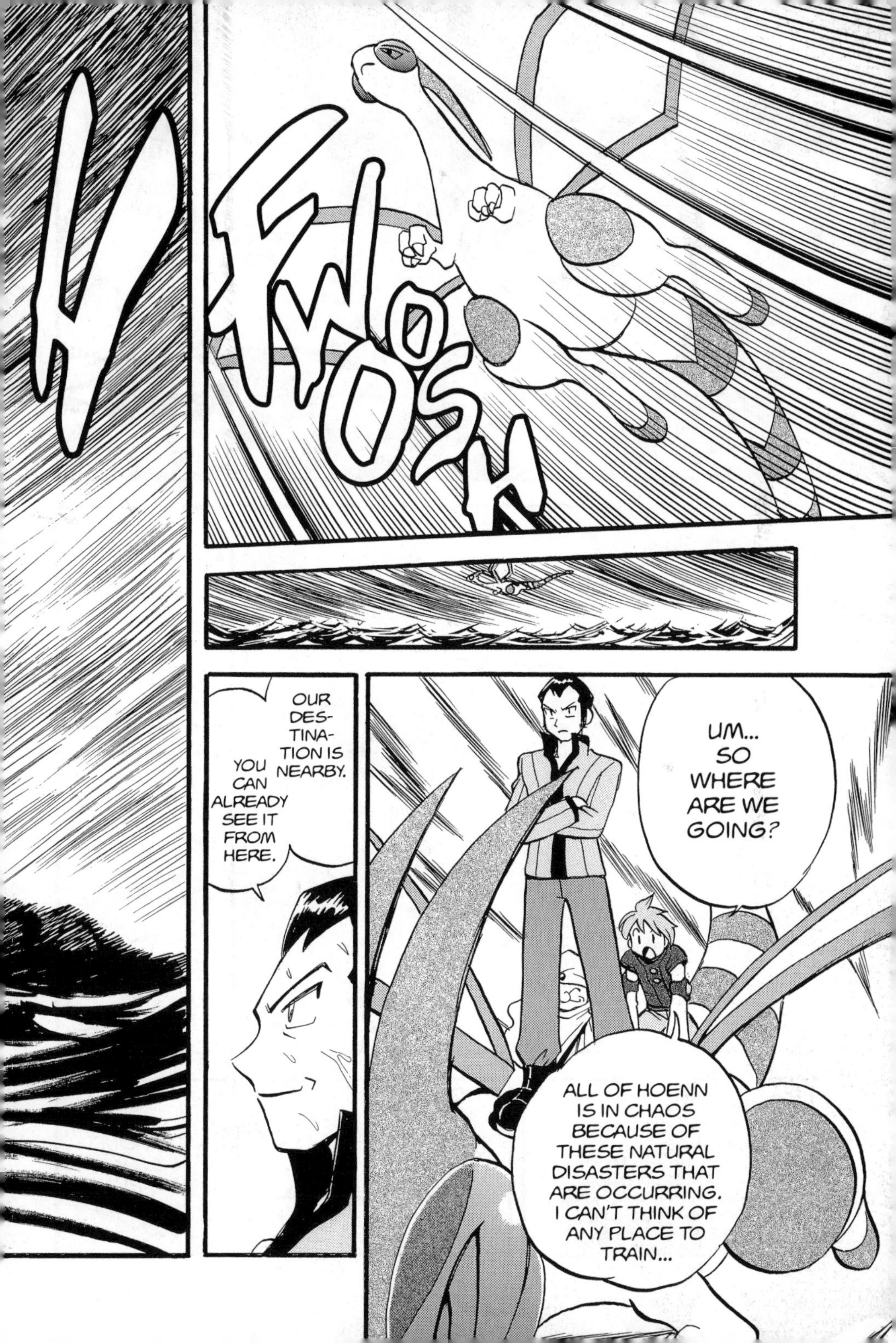
FWOOSH
UM... SO WHERE ARE WE GOING?
ALL OF HOENN IS IN CHAOS BECAUSE OF THESE NATURAL DISASTERS THAT ARE OCCURRING. I CAN'T THINK OF ANY PLACE TO TRAIN...
OUR DESTINATION IS NEARBY.
YOU CAN ALREADY SEE IT FROM HERE.
!!

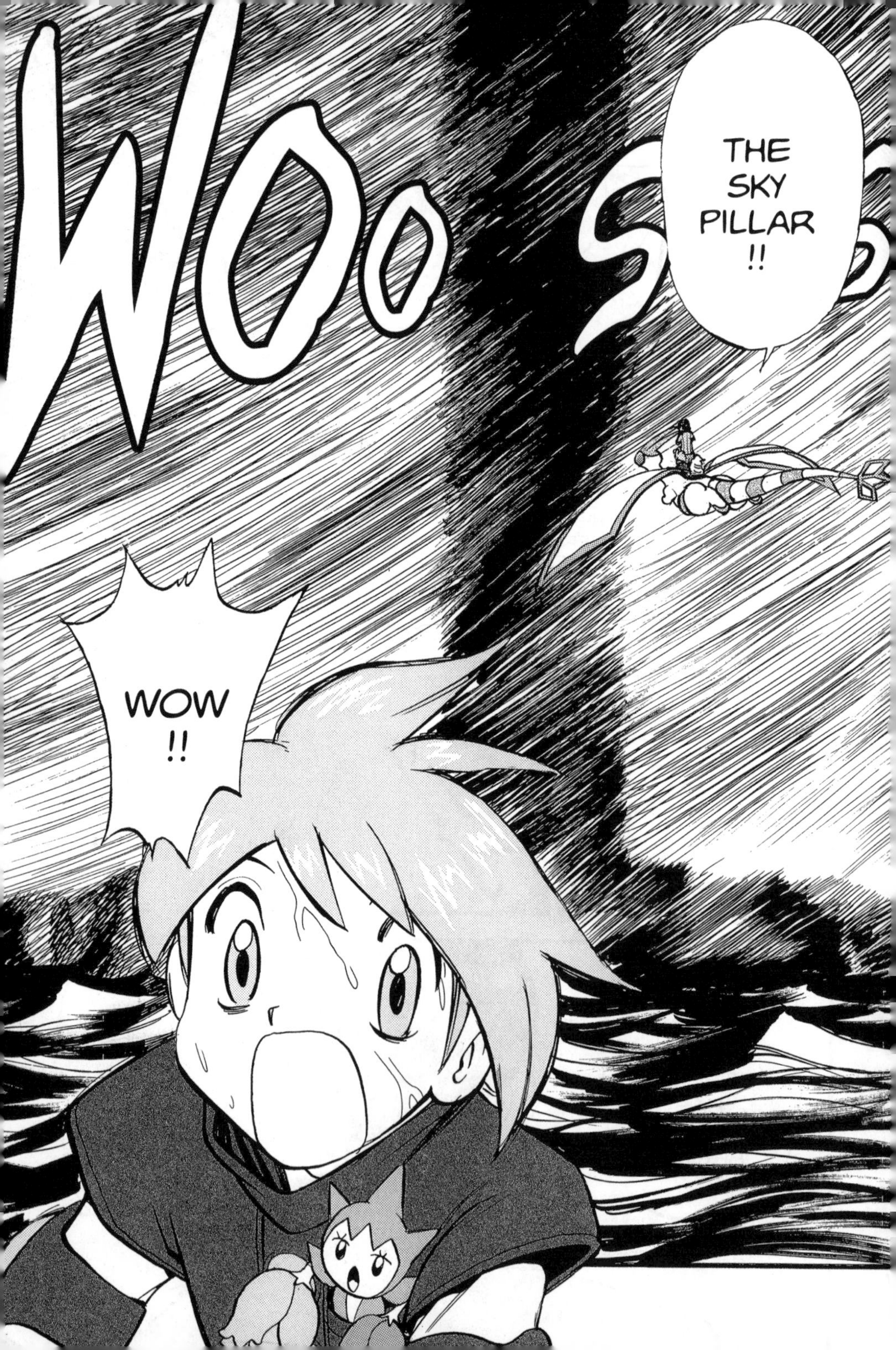
THE SKY PILLAR !!
WOW !!

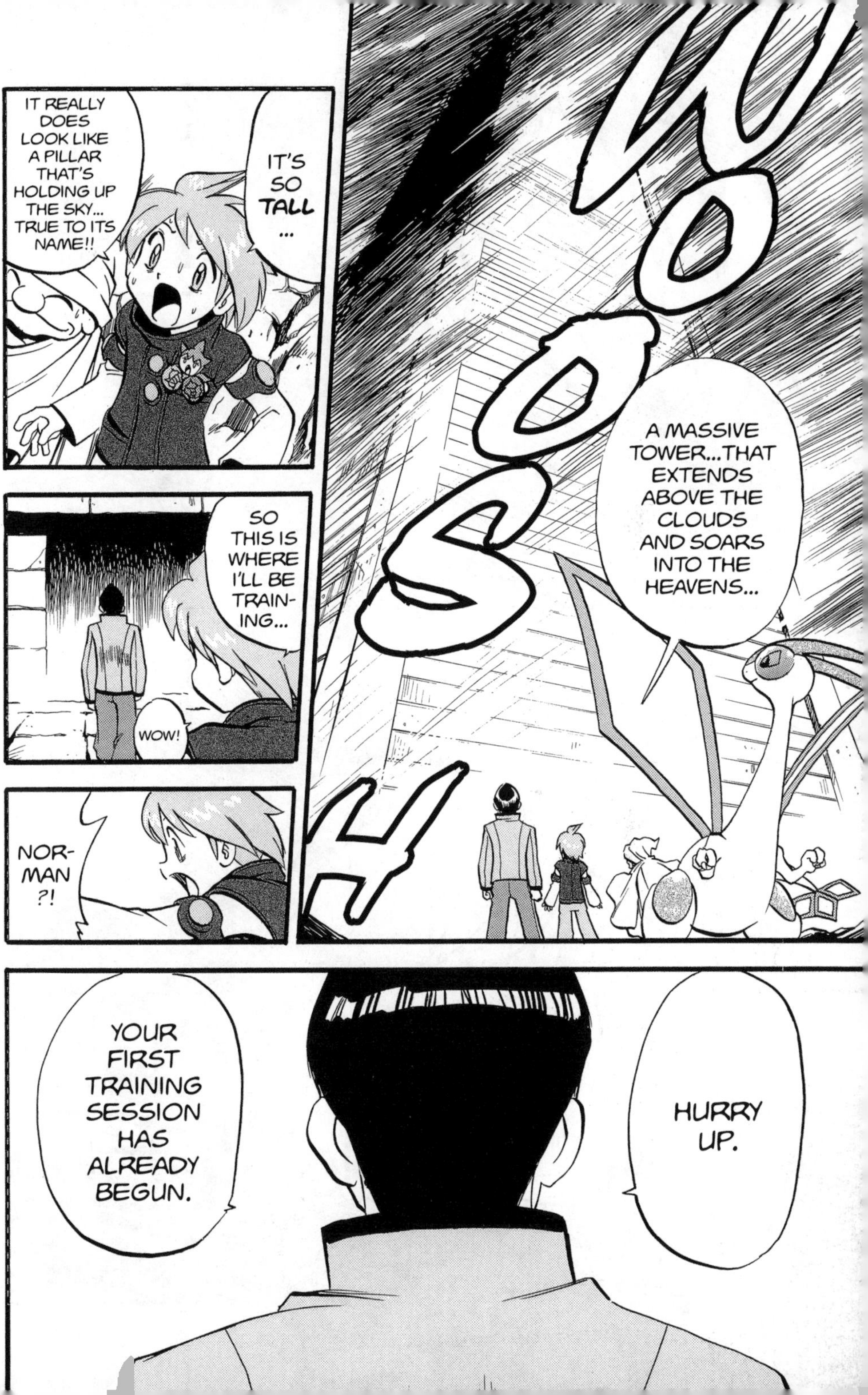
WOOSH
A MASSIVE TOWER...THAT EXTENDS ABOVE THE CLOUDS AND SOARS INTO THE HEAVENS...
IT'S SO TALL...
IT REALLY DOES LOOK LIKE A PILLAR THAT'S HOLDING UP THE SKY... TRUE TO ITS NAME!!
SO THIS IS WHERE I'LL BE TRAINING...
WOW!
NORMAN?!
HURRY UP.
YOUR FIRST TRAINING SESSION HAS ALREADY BEGUN.

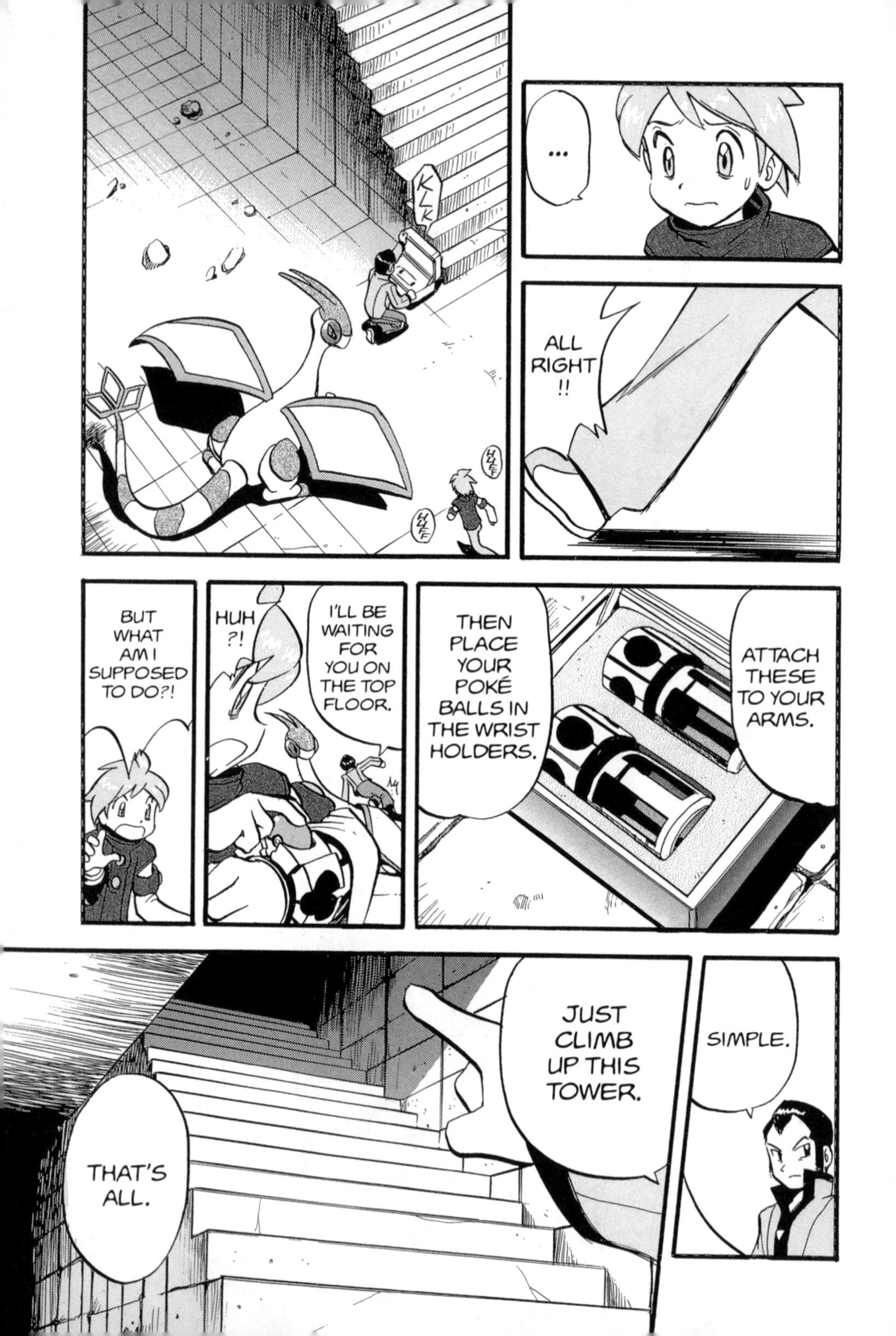
...
ALL RIGHT !!
HUFF
HUFF
ATTACH THESE TO YOUR ARMS.
THEN PLACE YOUR POKÉ BALLS IN THE WRIST HOLDERS.
I'LL BE WAITING FOR YOU ON THE TOP FLOOR.
HUH ?!
BUT WHAT AM I SUPPOSED TO DO?!
SIMPLE.
JUST CLIMB UP THIS TOWER.
THAT'S ALL.

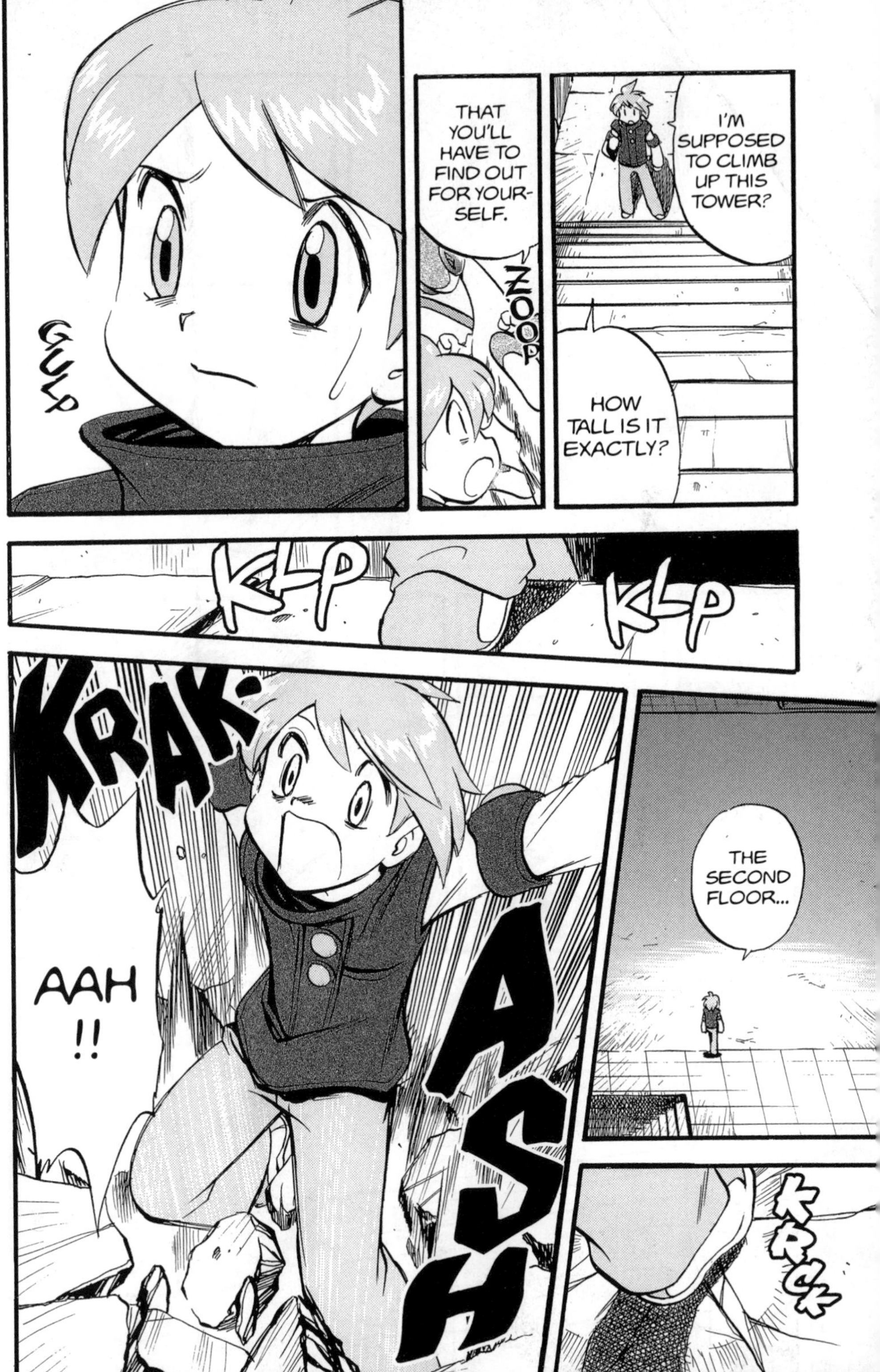
I'M SUPPOSED TO CLIMB UP THIS TOWER?
HOW TALL IS IT EXACTLY?
THAT YOU'LL HAVE TO FIND OUT FOR YOUR-SELF.
ZOOP
GULP
KLP
KLP
THE SECOND FLOOR...
KRCK
KRAK-
AAH !!
ASH

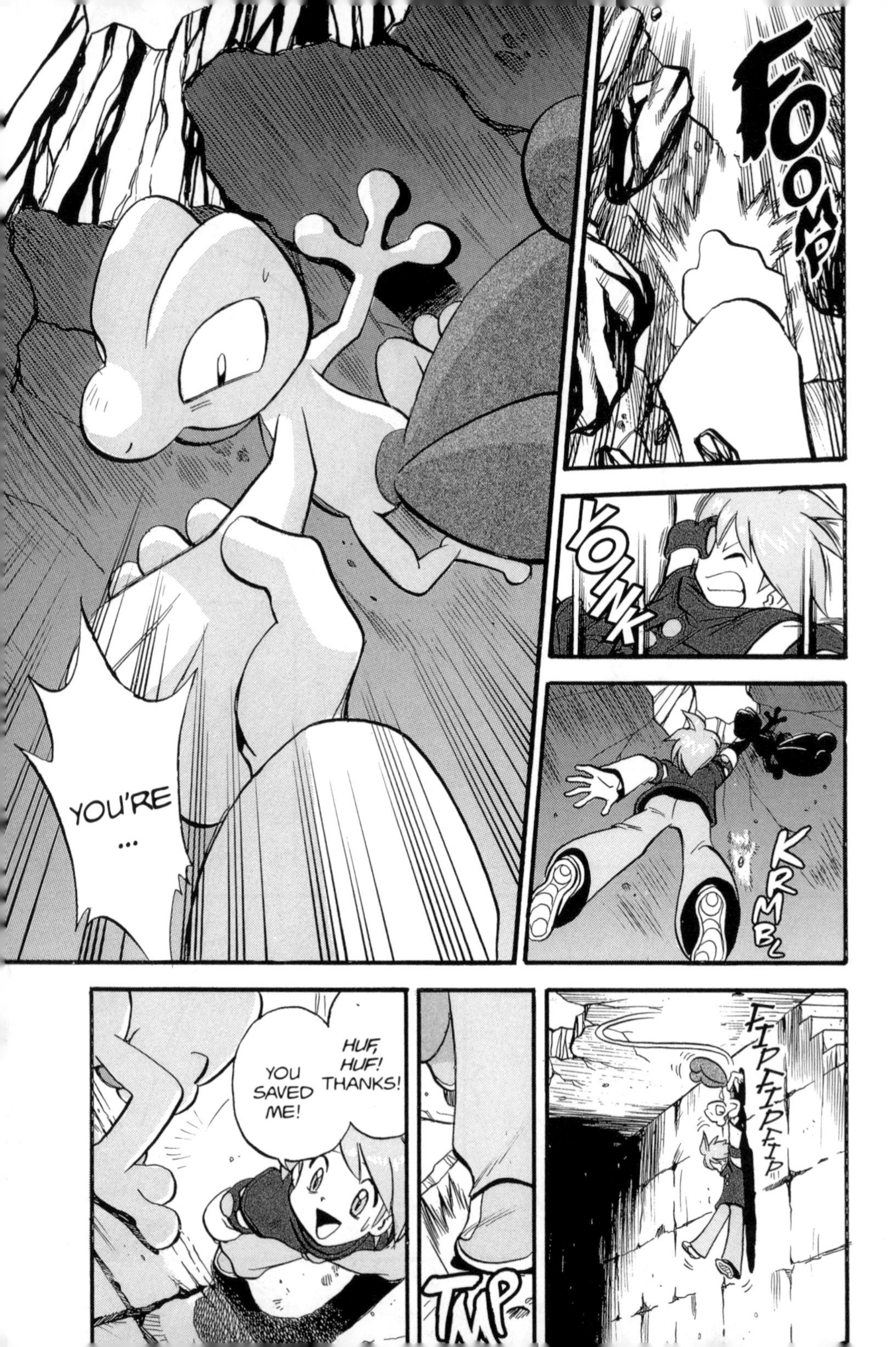
FOOMP
YOINK
KRMBL
YOU'RE ...
FIPFIPFIP
TMP
HUF, HUF! THANKS!
YOU SAVED ME!

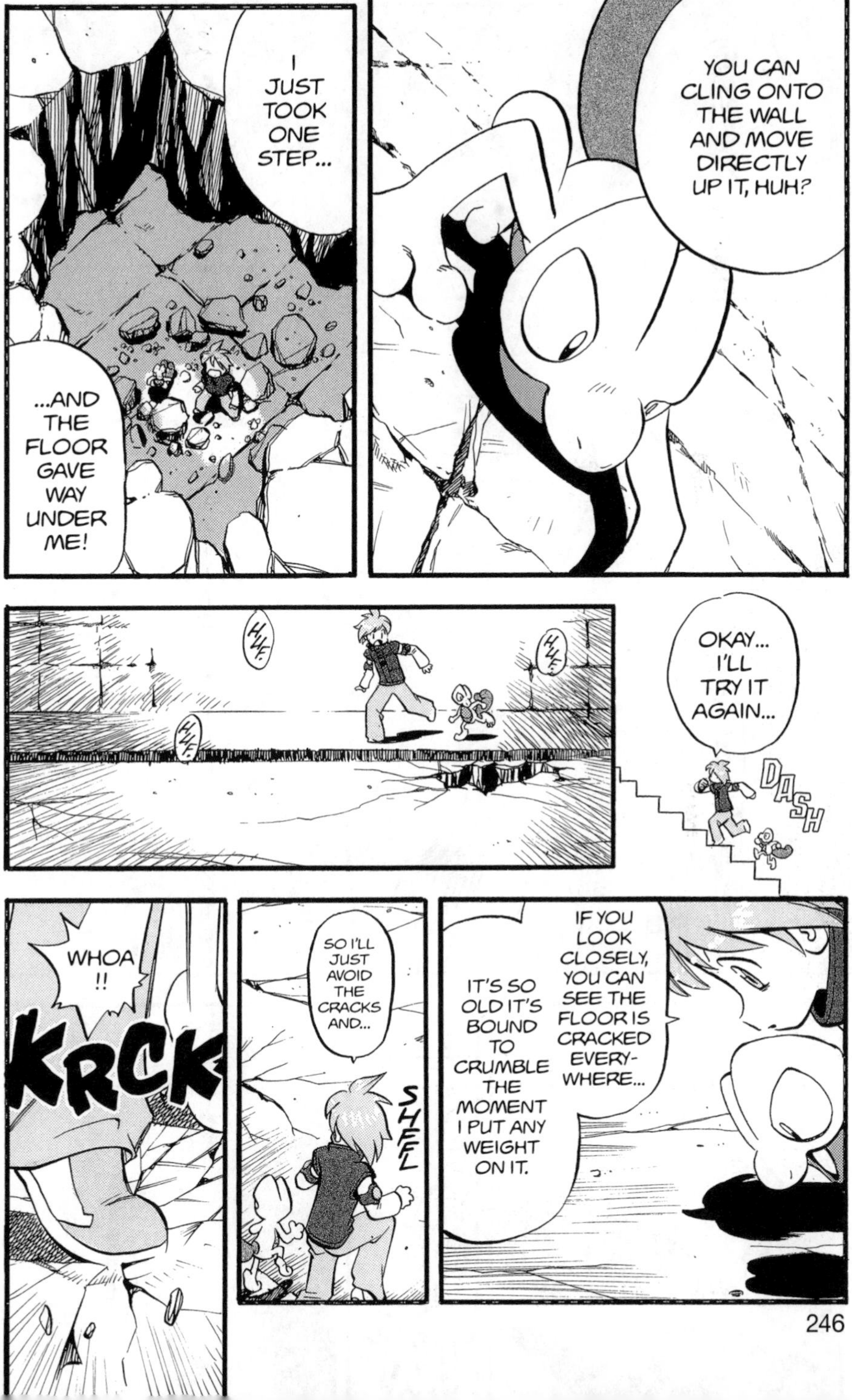
YOU CAN CLING ONTO THE WALL AND MOVE DIRECTLY UP IT, HUH?
I JUST TOOK ONE STEP...
...AND THE FLOOR GAVE WAY UNDER ME!
OKAY... I'LL TRY IT AGAIN...
DASH
HUF
HUF
HUF
IF YOU LOOK CLOSELY, YOU CAN SEE THE FLOOR IS CRACKED EVERY-WHERE...
IT'S SO OLD IT'S BOUND TO CRUMBLE THE MOMENT I PUT ANY WEIGHT ON IT.
SO I'LL JUST AVOID THE CRACKS AND...
SHFFL
WHOA !!
KRCK

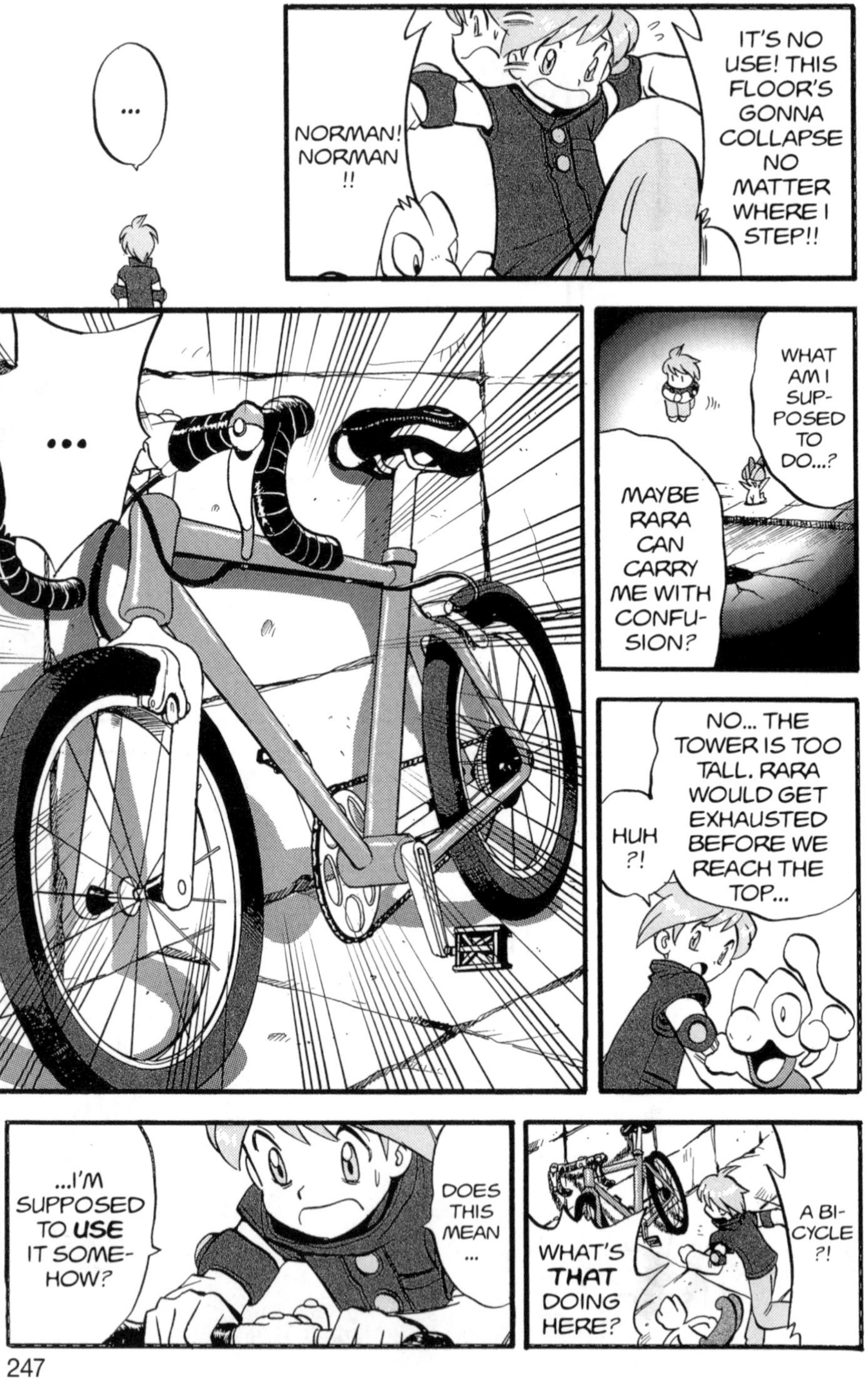
IT'S NO USE! THIS FLOOR'S GONNA COLLAPSE NO MATTER WHERE I STEP!!
NORMAN! NORMAN !!
...
WHAT AM I SUP-POSED TO DO...?
MAYBE RARA CAN CARRY ME WITH CONFU-SION?
NO... THE TOWER IS TOO TALL. RARA WOULD GET EXHAUSTED BEFORE WE REACH THE TOP...
HUH ?!
...
A BI-CYCLE ?!
WHAT'S **THAT** DOING HERE?
DOES THIS MEAN ...
...I'M SUPPOSED TO **USE** IT SOME-HOW?

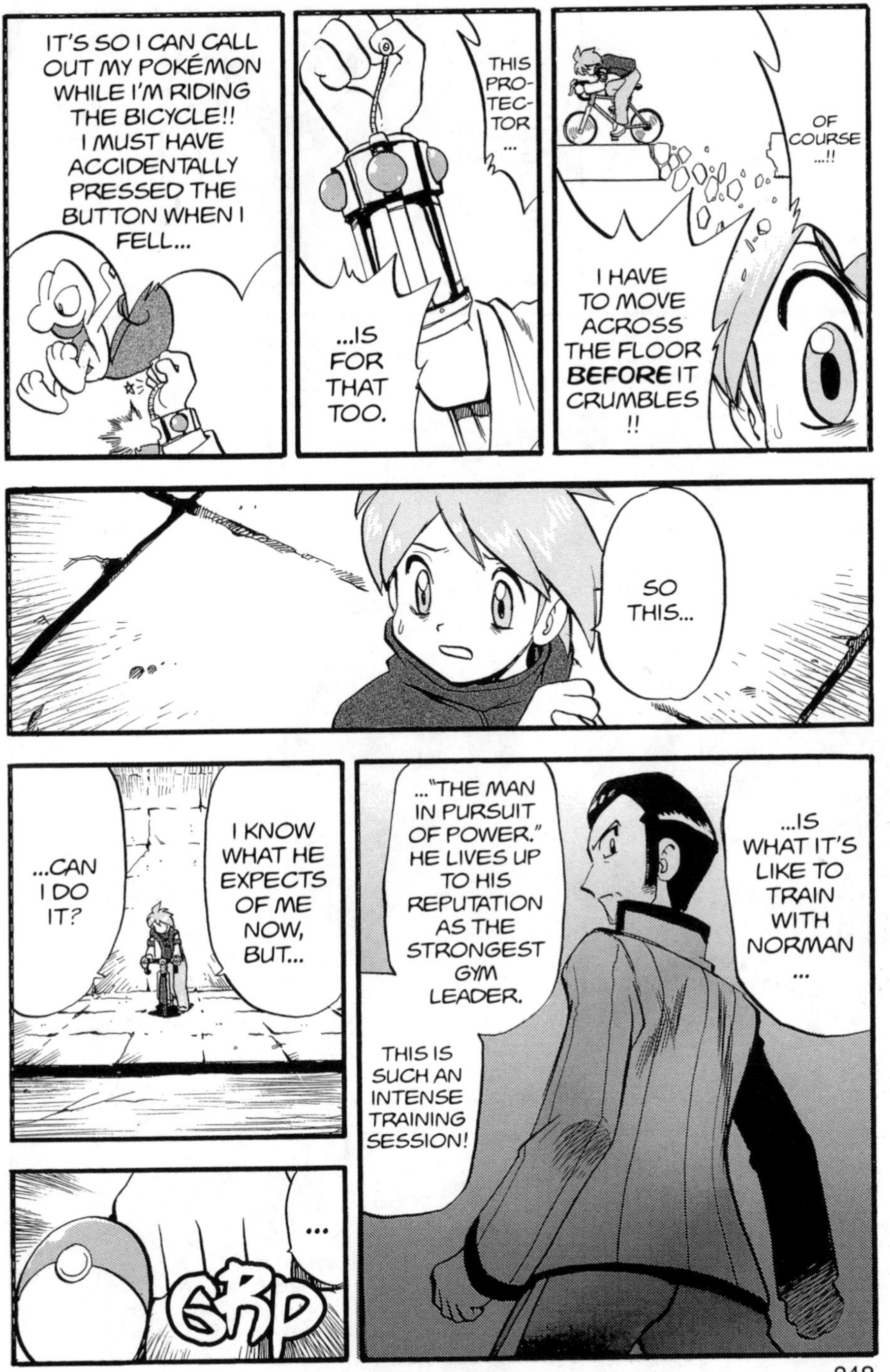

OF COURSE ...!!
I HAVE TO MOVE ACROSS THE FLOOR **BEFORE** IT CRUMBLES !!
THIS PROTECTOR ...
...IS FOR THAT TOO.
IT'S SO I CAN CALL OUT MY POKÉMON WHILE I'M RIDING THE BICYCLE!! I MUST HAVE ACCIDENTALLY PRESSED THE BUTTON WHEN I FELL...
SO THIS...
...IS WHAT IT'S LIKE TO TRAIN WITH NORMAN ...
..."THE MAN IN PURSUIT OF POWER." HE LIVES UP TO HIS REPUTATION AS THE STRONGEST GYM LEADER.
THIS IS SUCH AN INTENSE TRAINING SESSION!
I KNOW WHAT HE EXPECTS OF ME NOW, BUT...
...CAN I DO IT?
...
GRP

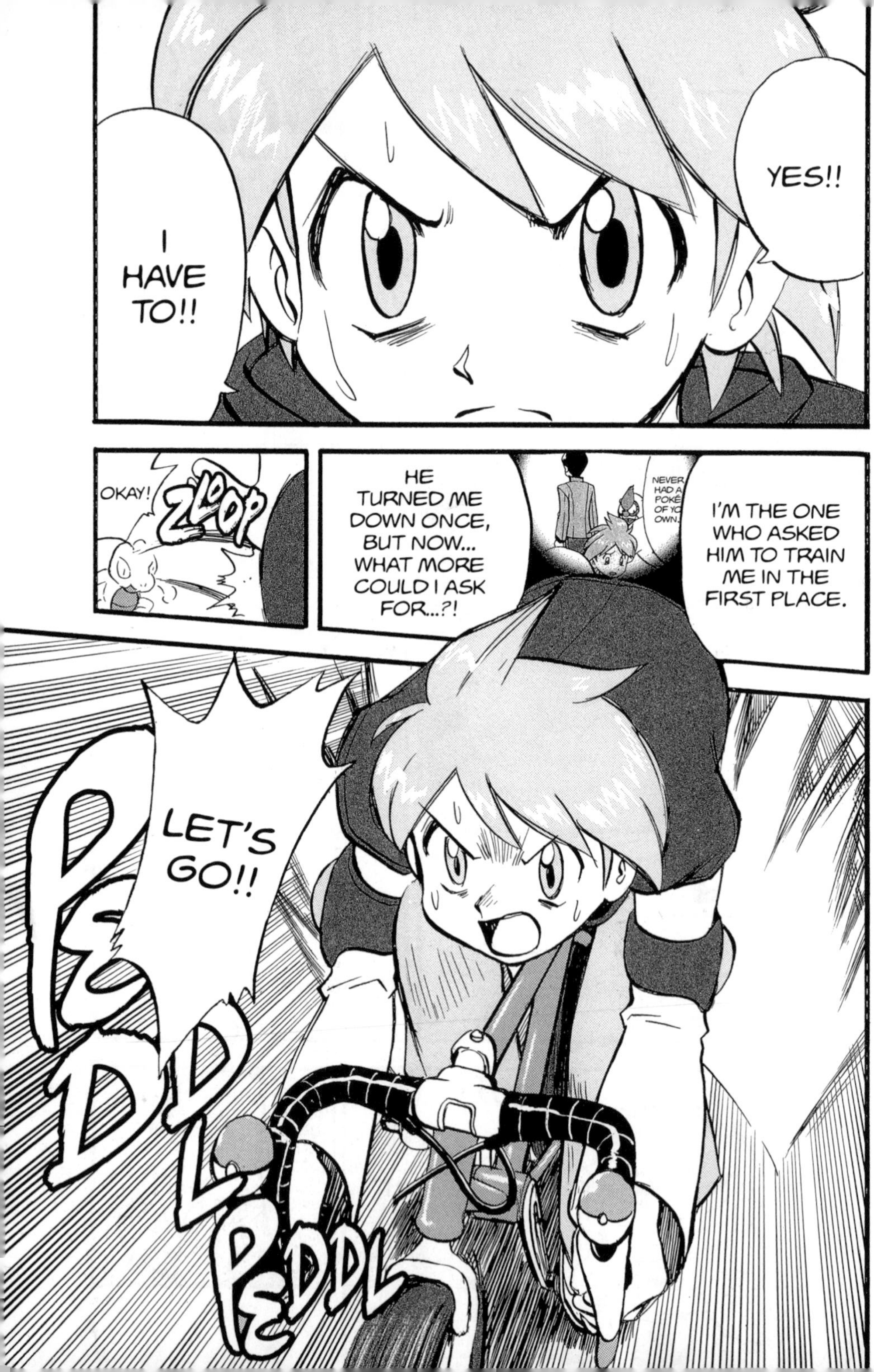
YES!!
I HAVE TO!!
I'M THE ONE WHO ASKED HIM TO TRAIN ME IN THE FIRST PLACE.
HE TURNED ME DOWN ONCE, BUT NOW... WHAT MORE COULD I ASK FOR...?!
OKAY!
ZLOOP
LET'S GO!!
PEDDL
PEDDL

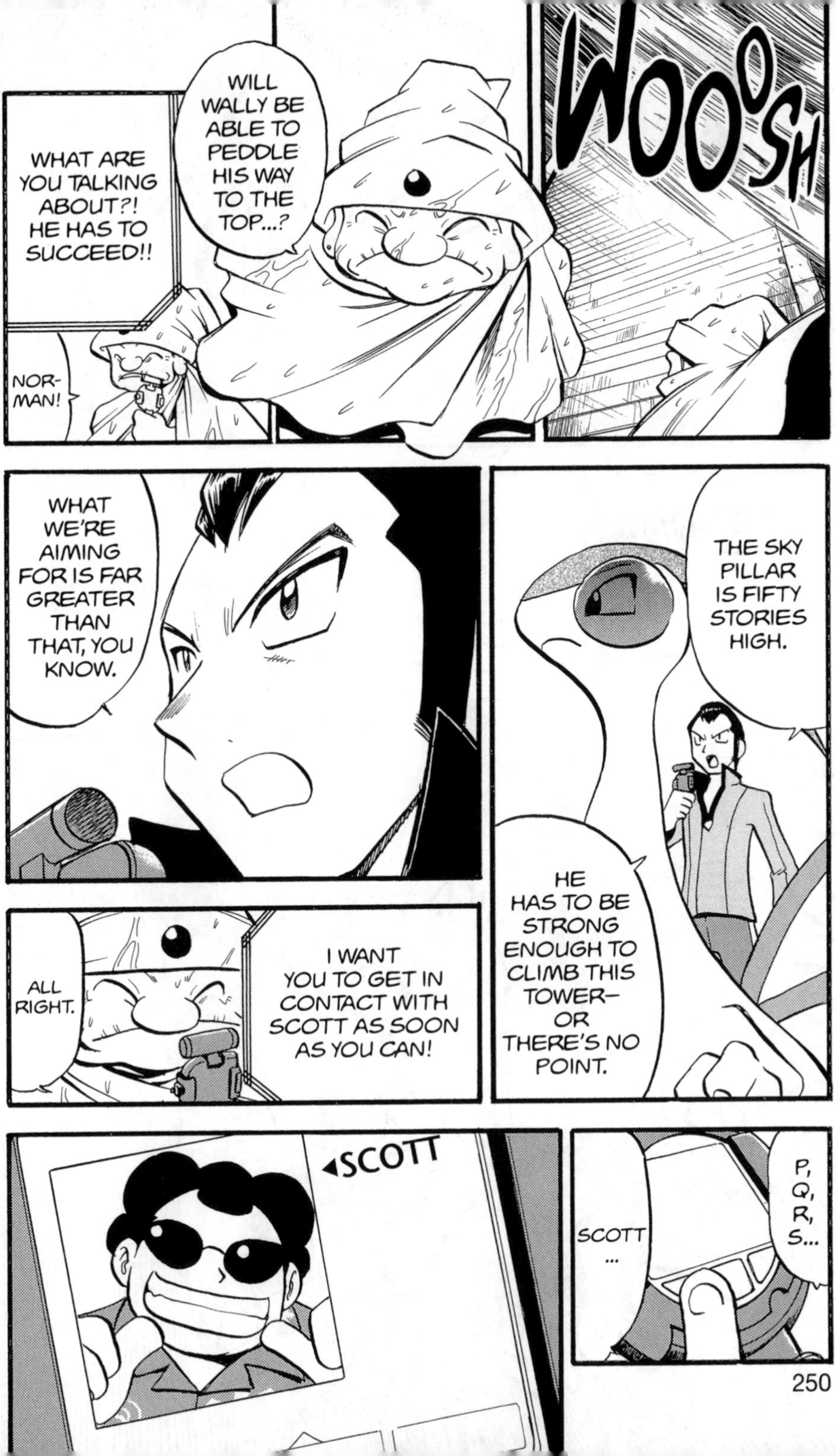
WOOOSH
WILL WALLY BE ABLE TO PEDDLE HIS WAY TO THE TOP...?
WHAT ARE YOU TALKING ABOUT?! HE HAS TO SUCCEED!!
NOR-MAN!
THE SKY PILLAR IS FIFTY STORIES HIGH.
HE HAS TO BE STRONG ENOUGH TO CLIMB THIS TOWER—OR THERE'S NO POINT.
WHAT WE'RE AIMING FOR IS FAR GREATER THAN THAT, YOU KNOW.
I WANT YOU TO GET IN CONTACT WITH SCOTT AS SOON AS YOU CAN!
ALL RIGHT.
P, Q, R, S...
SCOTT...
◂SCOTT

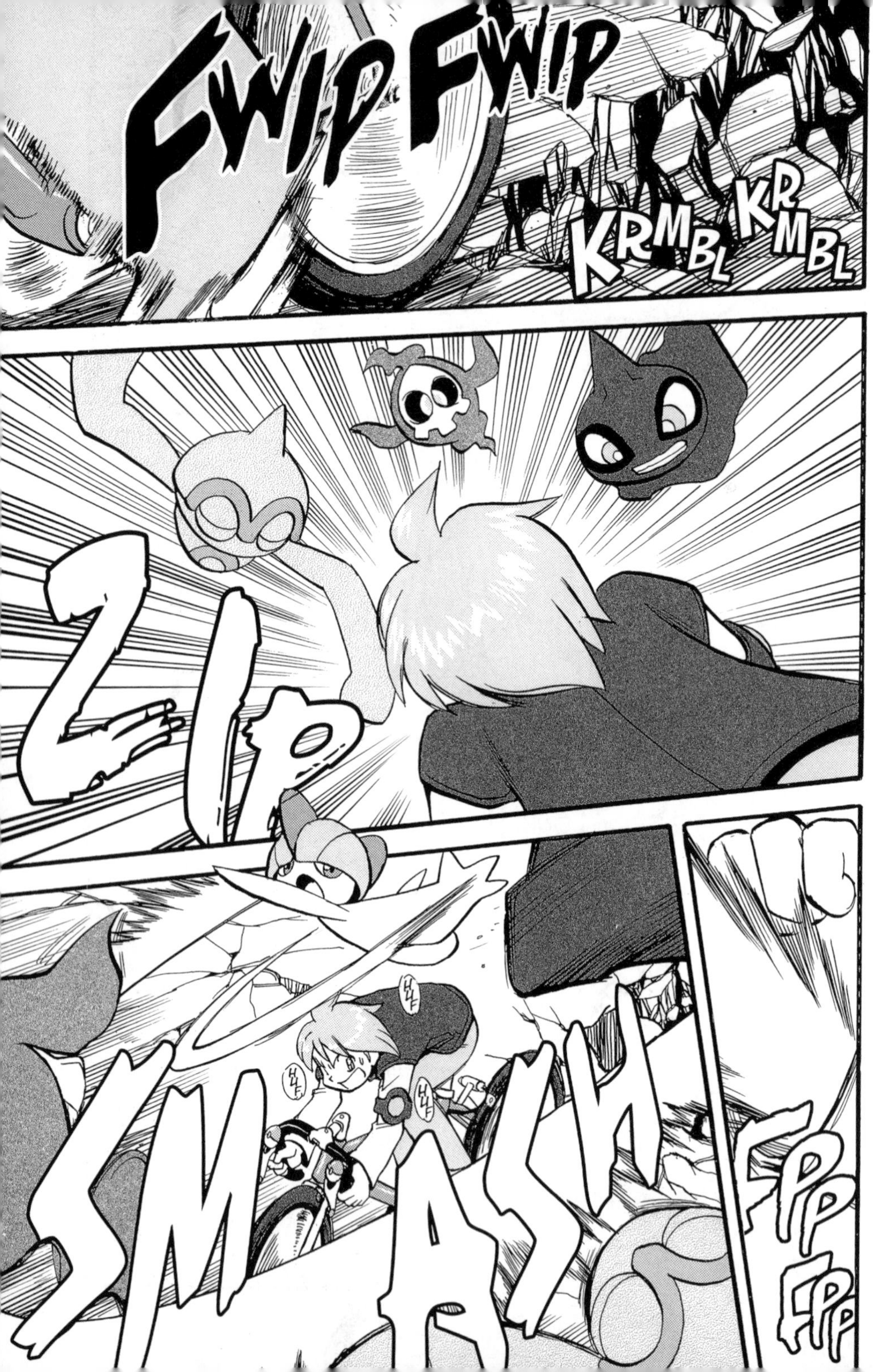
FWIP FWIP
KRMBL KRMBL
ZIP
FPP FPP
SMASH
HUF
HUF
HUF

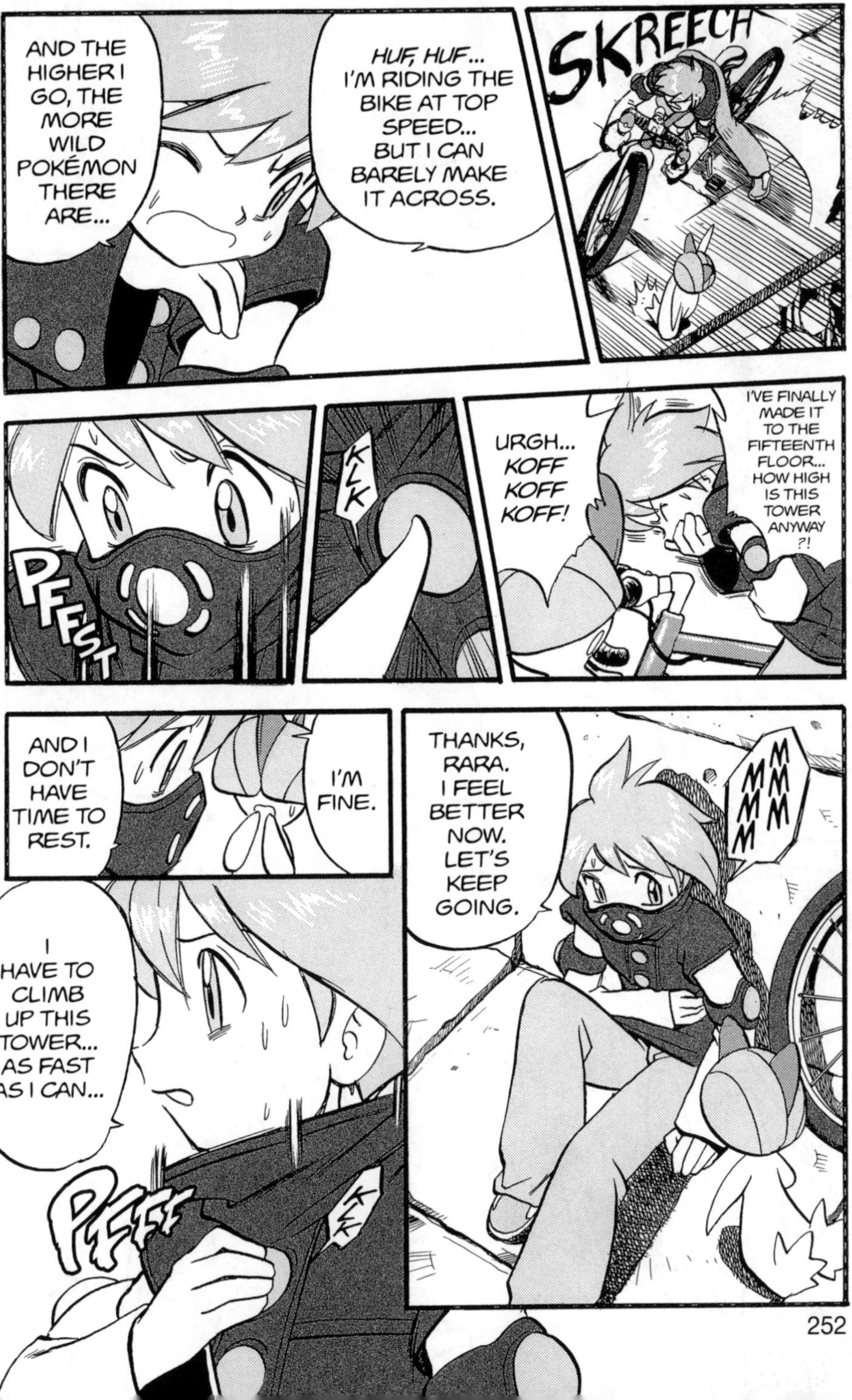
SKREECH
HUF, HUF... I'M RIDING THE BIKE AT TOP SPEED... BUT I CAN BARELY MAKE IT ACROSS.
AND THE HIGHER I GO, THE MORE WILD POKÉMON THERE ARE...
I'VE FINALLY MADE IT TO THE FIFTEENTH FLOOR... HOW HIGH IS THIS TOWER ANYWAY ?!
URGH... KOFF KOFF KOFF!
KLK
PFFST
MMMMMMMMM
THANKS, RARA. I FEEL BETTER NOW. LET'S KEEP GOING.
I'M FINE.
AND I DON'T HAVE TIME TO REST.
I HAVE TO CLIMB UP THIS TOWER... AS FAST AS I CAN...
PFFFF
KLK

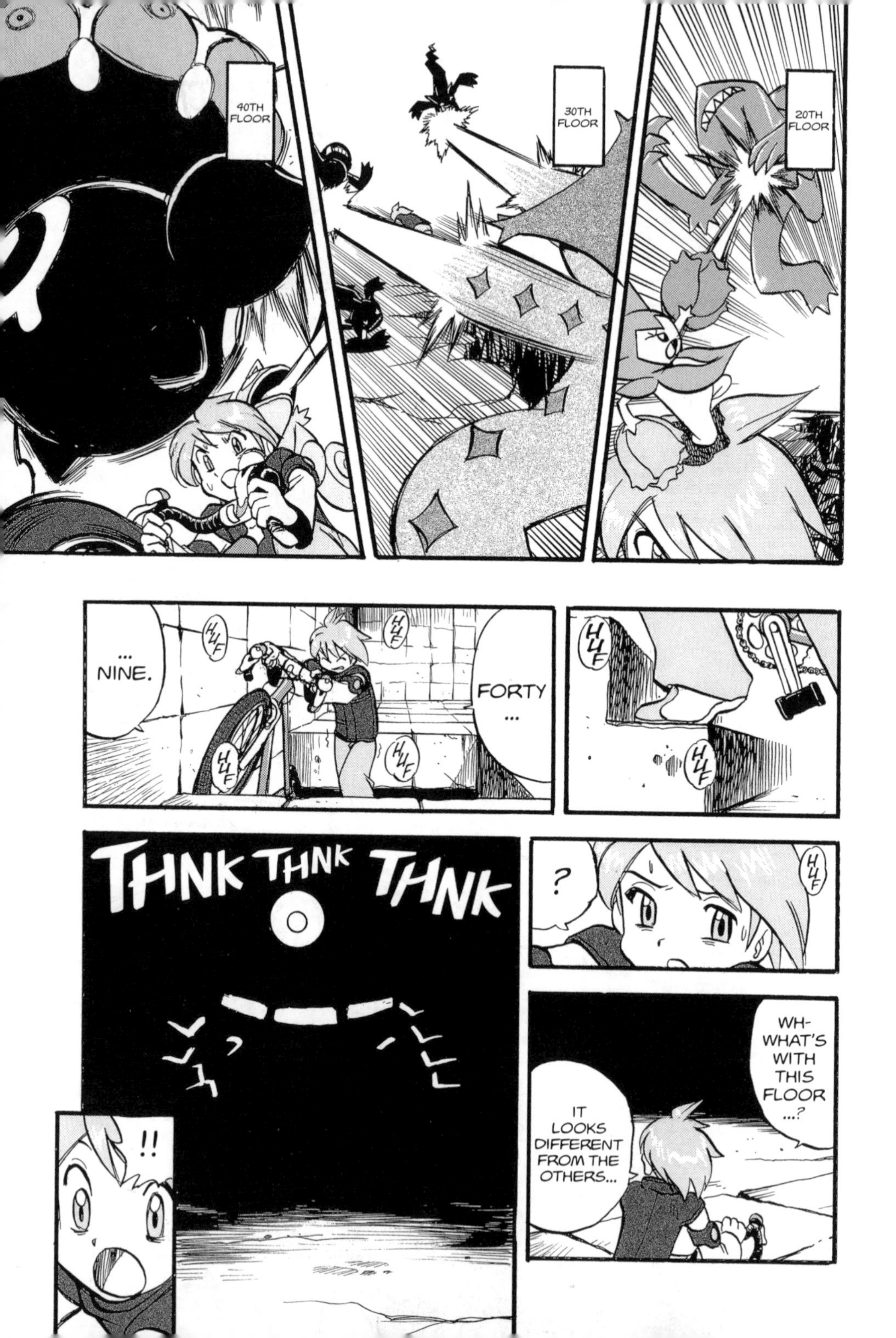
20TH FLOOR
30TH FLOOR
40TH FLOOR
HUF
HUF
HUF
FORTY ...
HUF
... NINE.
HUF
HUF
?
WH- WHAT'S WITH THIS FLOOR ...?
IT LOOKS DIFFERENT FROM THE OTHERS...
THNK THNK THNK
!!

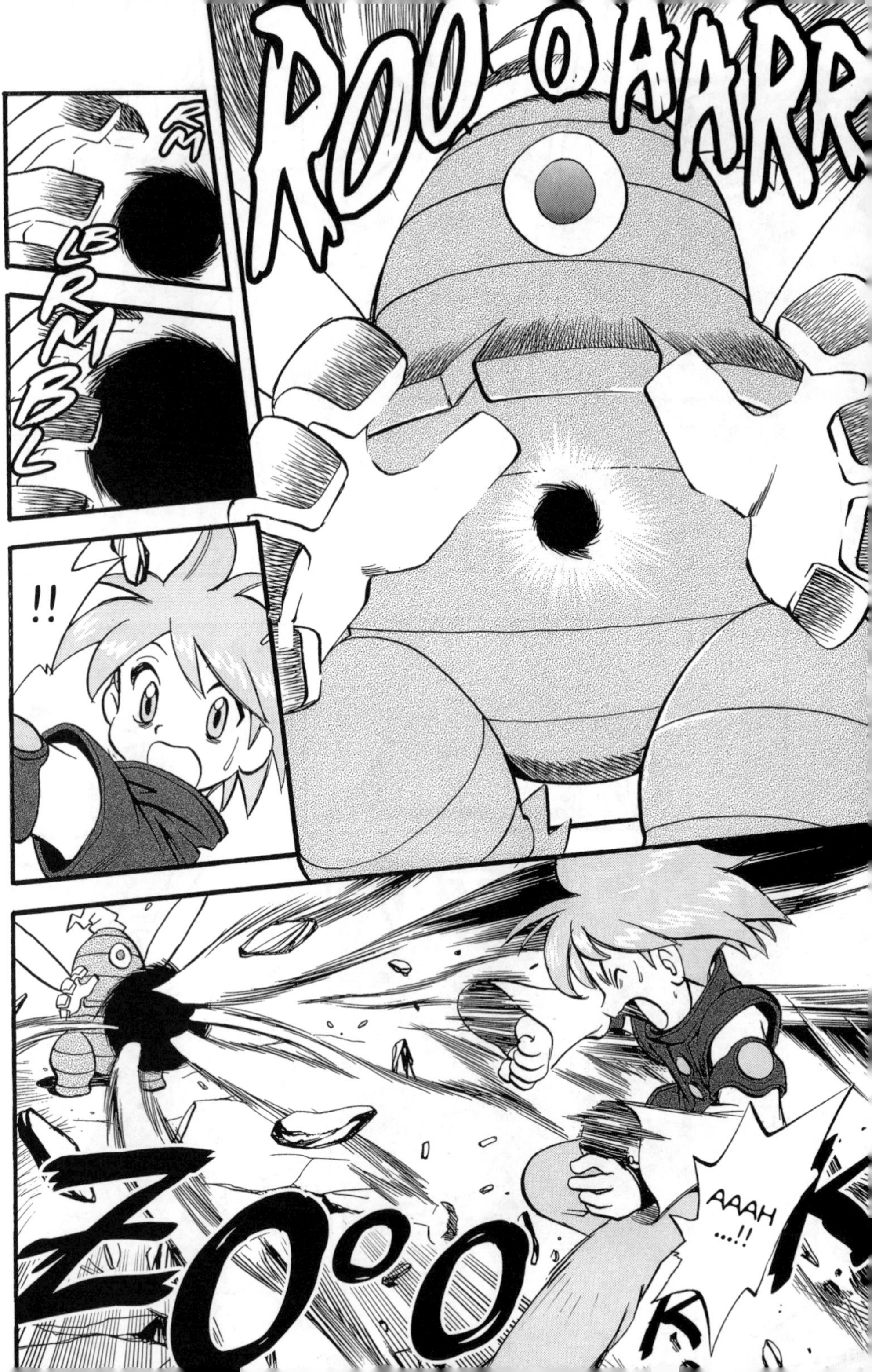
ROO OAARR
RM
BLRMBL
!!
AAAH ...!!
K
K
ZOOO

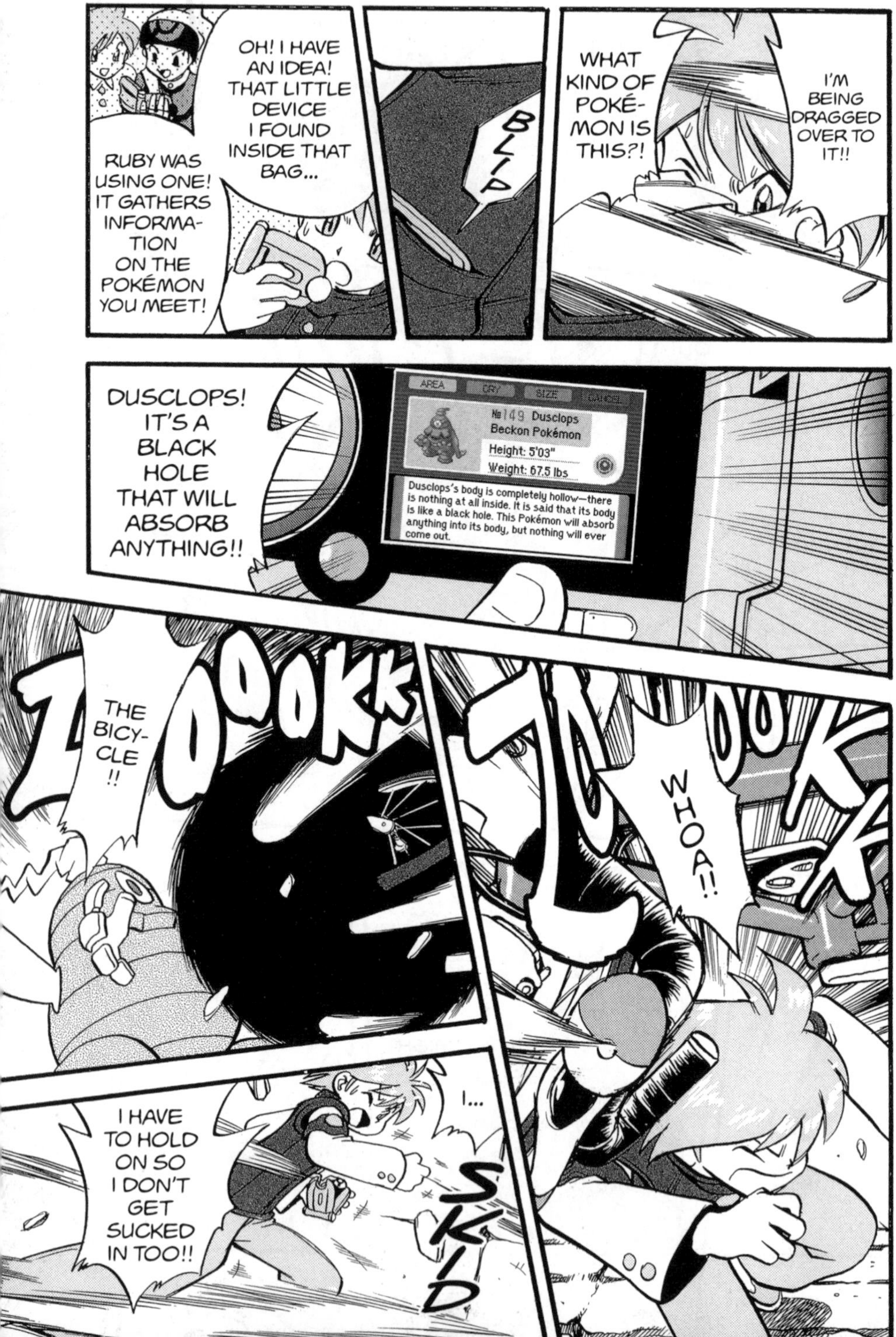
I'M BEING DRAGGED OVER TO IT!!
WHAT KIND OF POKÉMON IS THIS?!
BLIP
OH! I HAVE AN IDEA! THAT LITTLE DEVICE I FOUND INSIDE THAT BAG...
RUBY WAS USING ONE! IT GATHERS INFORMATION ON THE POKÉMON YOU MEET!
DUSCLOPS! IT'S A BLACK HOLE THAT WILL ABSORB ANYTHING!!
AREA CRY SIZE CANCEL
№149 Dusclops
Beckon Pokémon
Height: 5'03"
Weight: 67.5 lbs
Dusclops's body is completely hollow—there is nothing at all inside. It is said that its body is like a black hole. This Pokémon will absorb anything into its body, but nothing will ever come out.
WHOA!!
ZOOOKK
THE BICYCLE!!
I...
I HAVE TO HOLD ON SO I DON'T GET SUCKED IN TOO!!
SKID

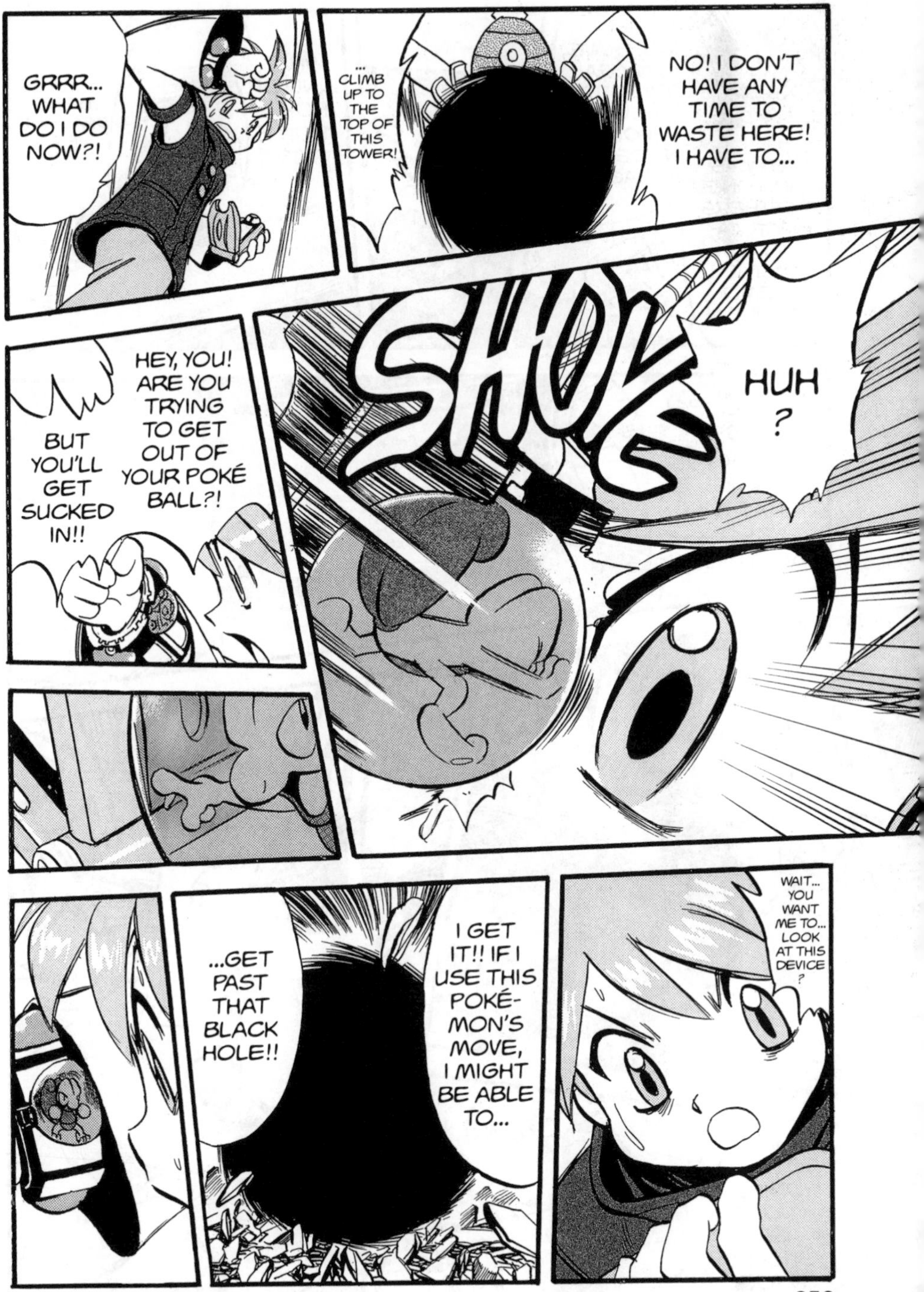
NO! I DON'T HAVE ANY TIME TO WASTE HERE! I HAVE TO...
...CLIMB UP TO THE TOP OF THIS TOWER!
GRRR... WHAT DO I DO NOW?!
SHOV
HUH?
HEY, YOU! ARE YOU TRYING TO GET OUT OF YOUR POKÉ BALL?!
BUT YOU'LL GET SUCKED IN!!
WAIT... YOU WANT ME TO... LOOK AT THIS DEVICE?
I GET IT!! IF I USE THIS POKÉ-MON'S MOVE, I MIGHT BE ABLE TO...
...GET PAST THAT BLACK HOLE!!

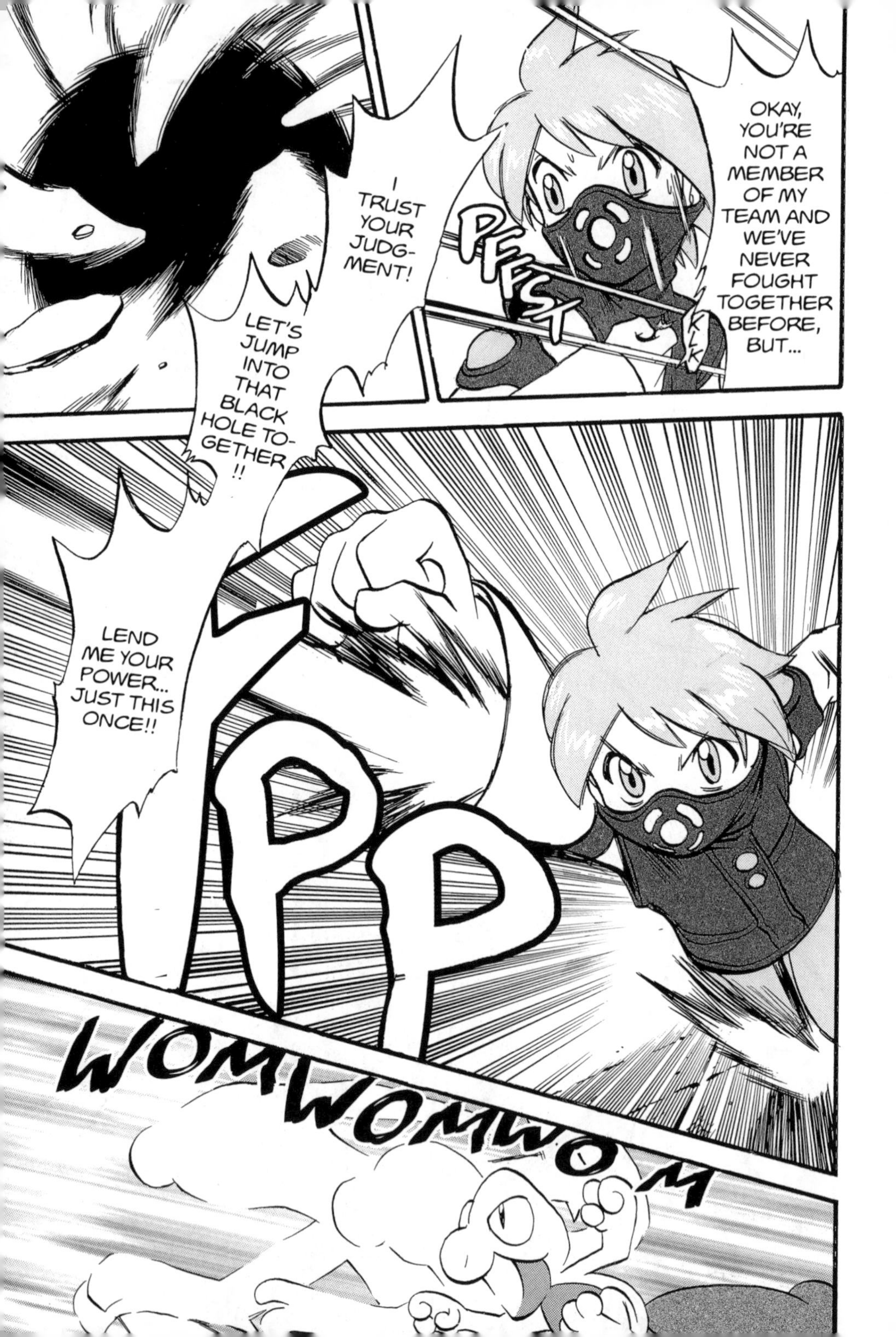
OKAY, YOU'RE NOT A MEMBER OF MY TEAM AND WE'VE NEVER FOUGHT TOGETHER BEFORE, BUT...
KLK
PFFSK
I TRUST YOUR JUDG-MENT!
LET'S JUMP INTO THAT BLACK HOLE TO-GETHER!!
LEND ME YOUR POWER... JUST THIS ONCE!!
PP
WOMWOMWOM

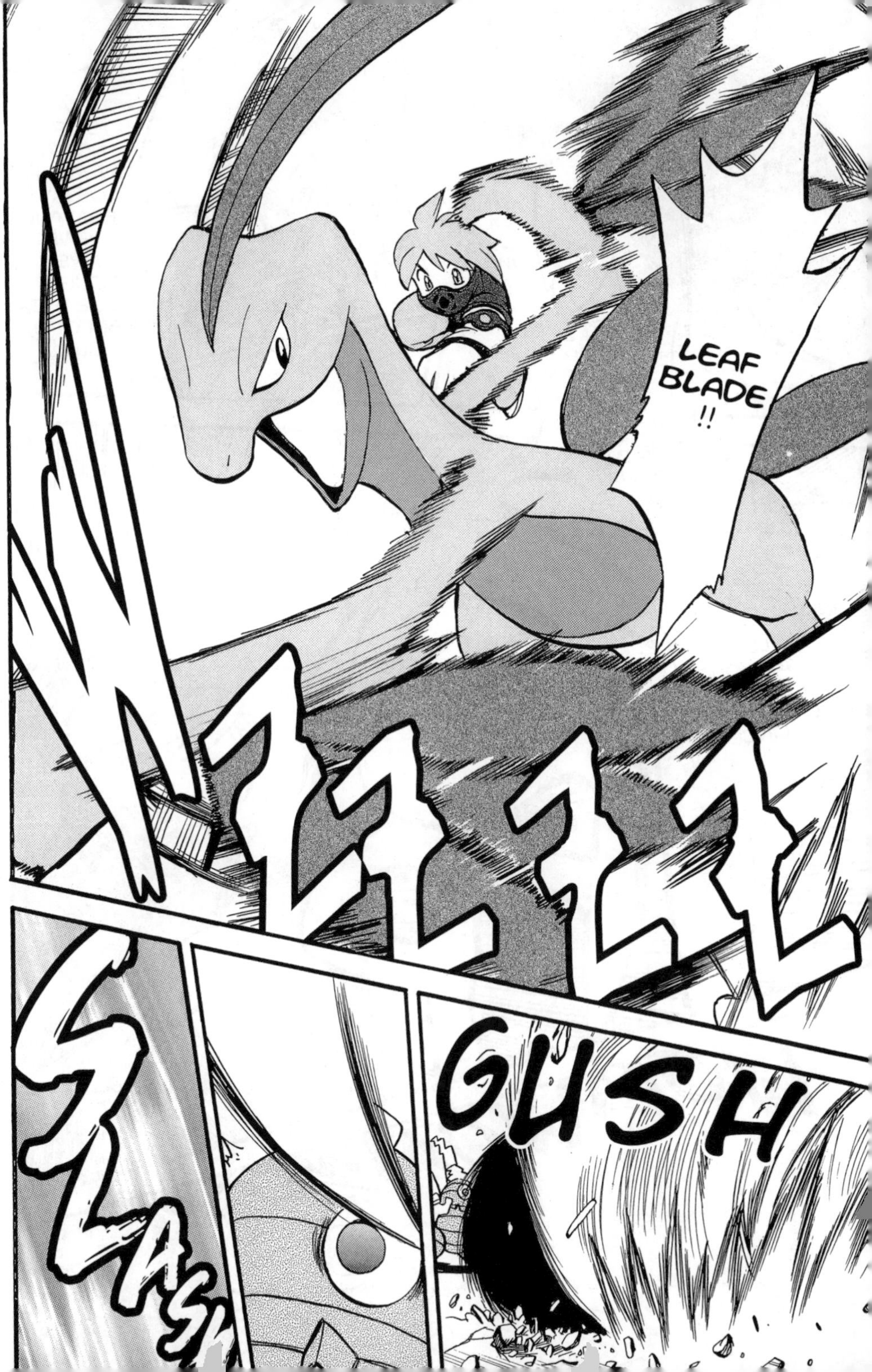
LEAF BLADE !!
GUSH
SLAS

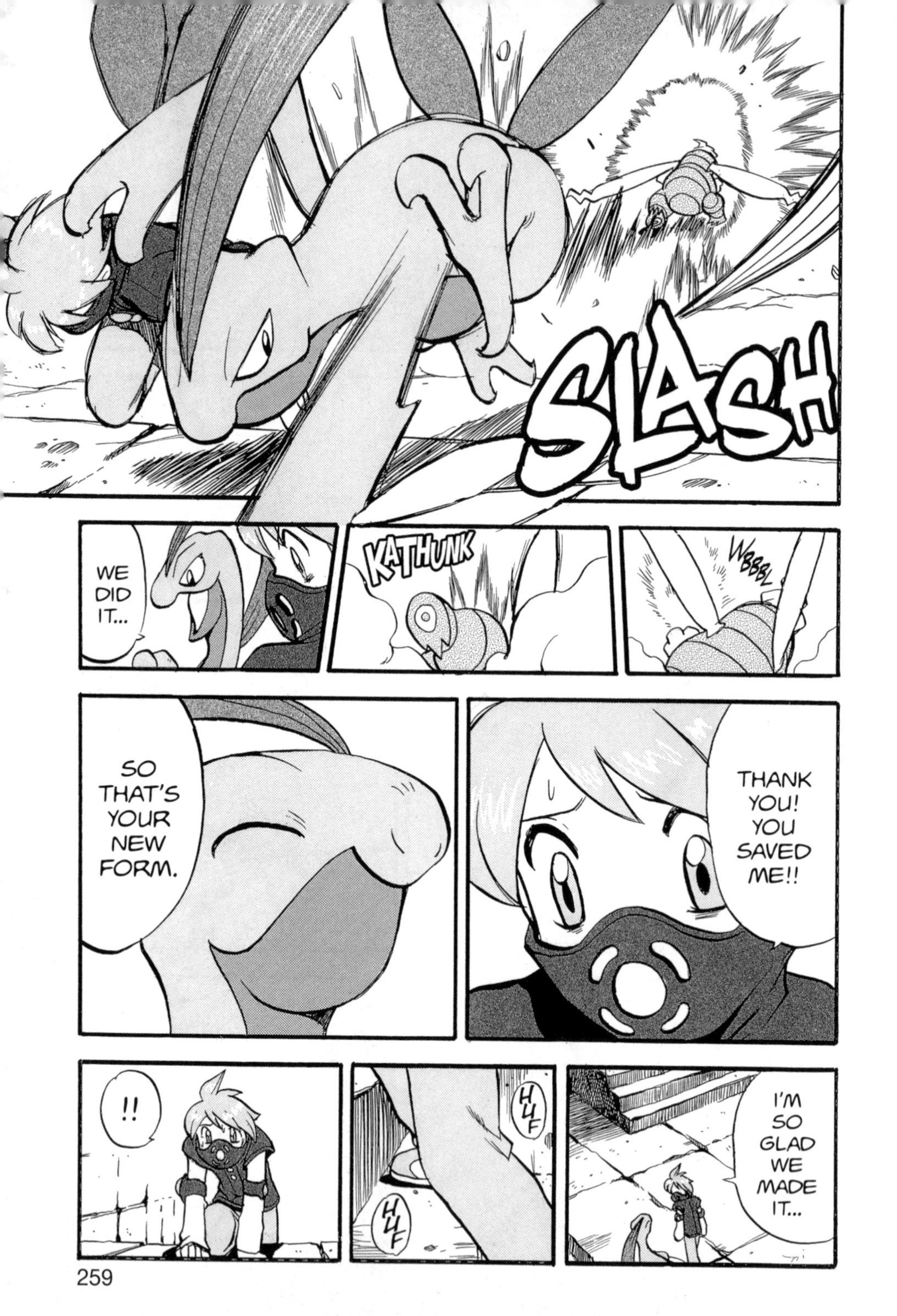
SLASH
WBBBL
KATHUNK
WE DID IT...
THANK YOU! YOU SAVED ME!!
SO THAT'S YOUR NEW FORM.
I'M SO GLAD WE MADE IT...
HUF
HUF
!!

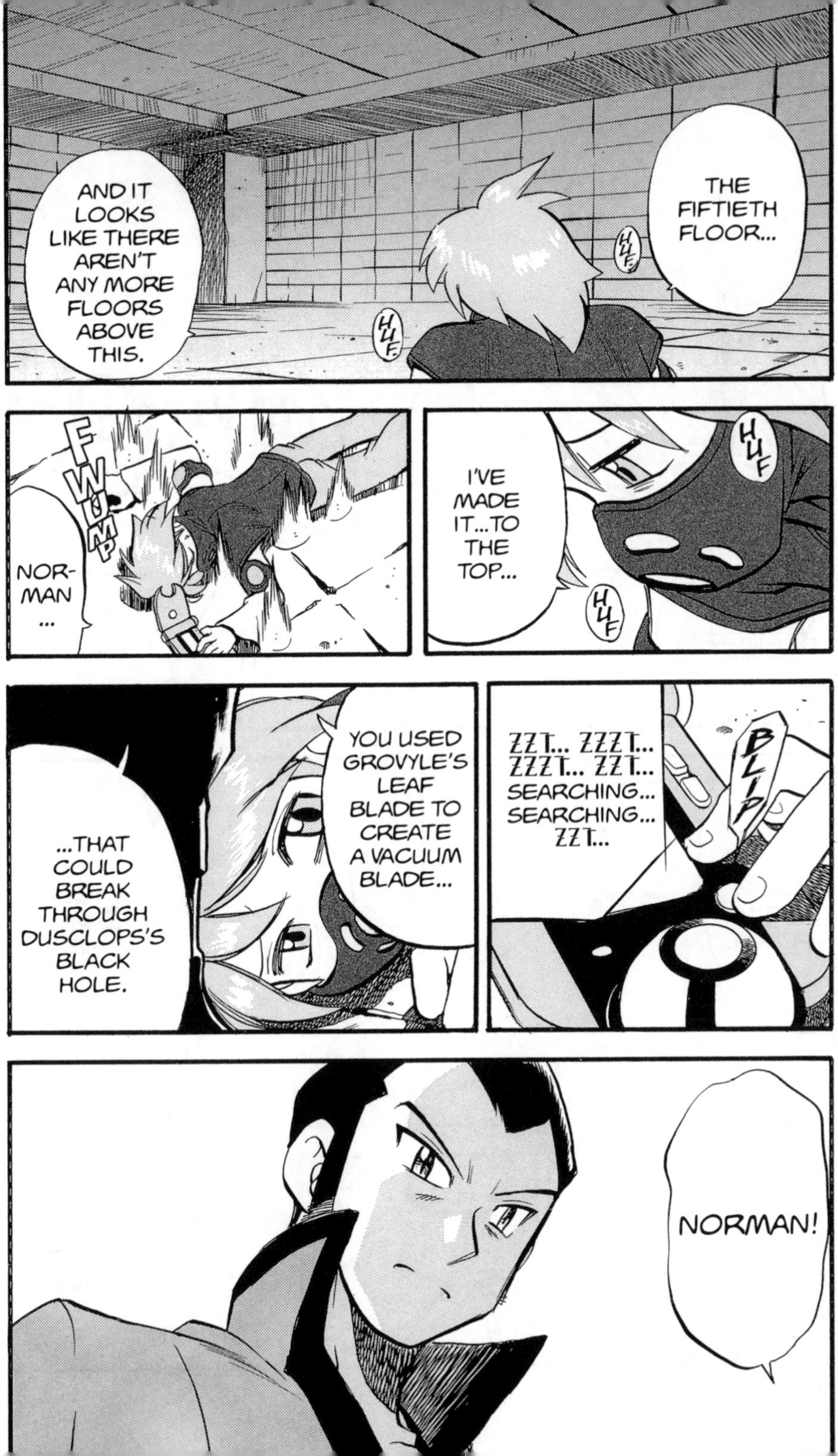
THE FIFTIETH FLOOR...
HUF
HUF
AND IT LOOKS LIKE THERE AREN'T ANY MORE FLOORS ABOVE THIS.
HUF
I'VE MADE IT...TO THE TOP...
HUF
FWUMP
NOR-MAN ...
BLIP
ZZT... ZZZT... ZZZT... ZZT... SEARCHING... SEARCHING... ZZT...
YOU USED GROVYLE'S LEAF BLADE TO CREATE A VACUUM BLADE...
...THAT COULD BREAK THROUGH DUSCLOPS'S BLACK HOLE.
NORMAN!

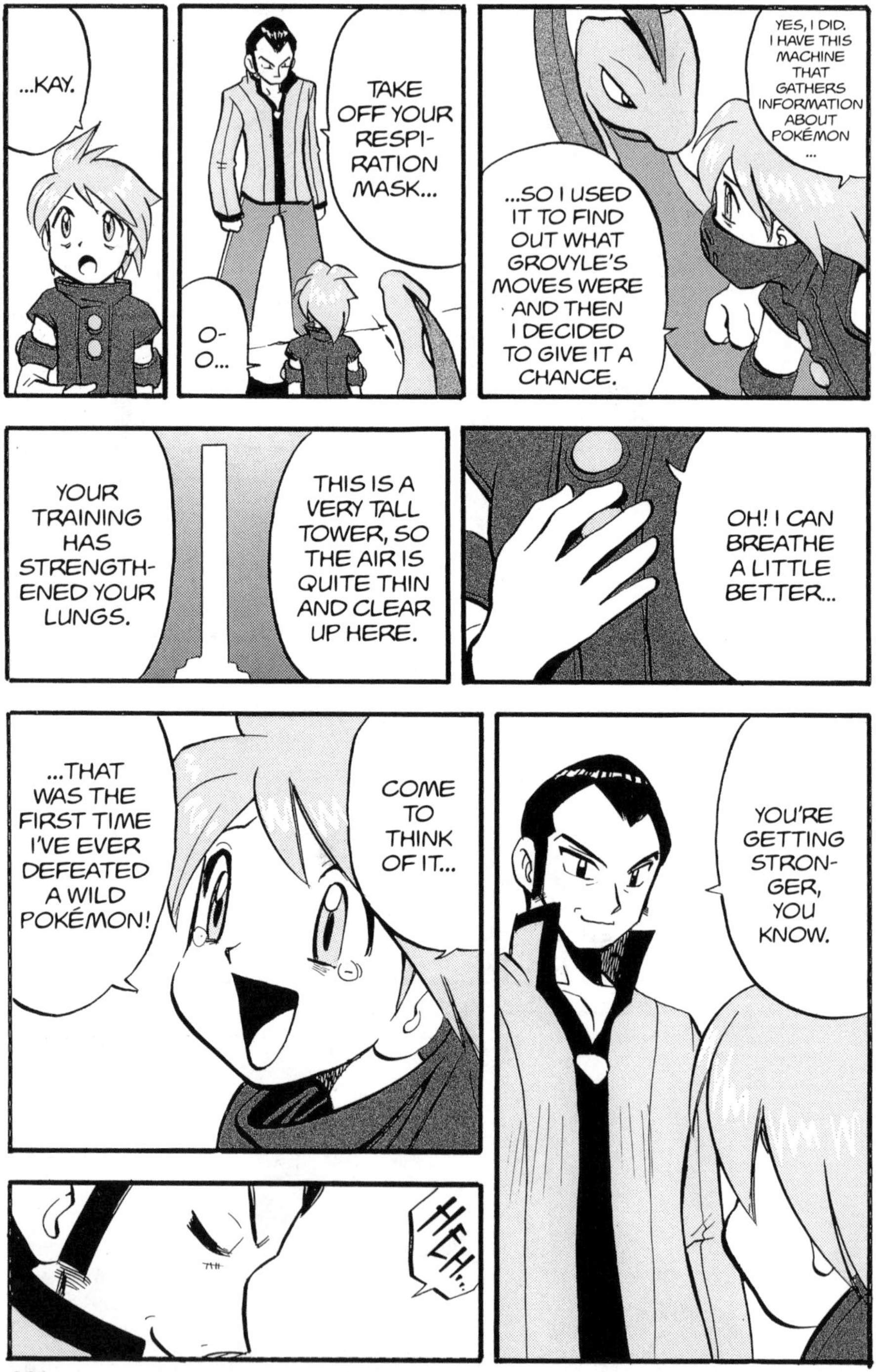
YES, I DID. I HAVE THIS MACHINE THAT GATHERS INFORMATION ABOUT POKÉMON ...
...SO I USED IT TO FIND OUT WHAT GROVYLE'S MOVES WERE AND THEN I DECIDED TO GIVE IT A CHANCE.
TAKE OFF YOUR RESPI-RATION MASK...
O-O...
...KAY.
OH! I CAN BREATHE A LITTLE BETTER...
THIS IS A VERY TALL TOWER, SO THE AIR IS QUITE THIN AND CLEAR UP HERE.
YOUR TRAINING HAS STRENGTH-ENED YOUR LUNGS.
YOU'RE GETTING STRON-GER, YOU KNOW.
COME TO THINK OF IT...
...THAT WAS THE FIRST TIME I'VE EVER DEFEATED A WILD POKÉMON!
HEH...

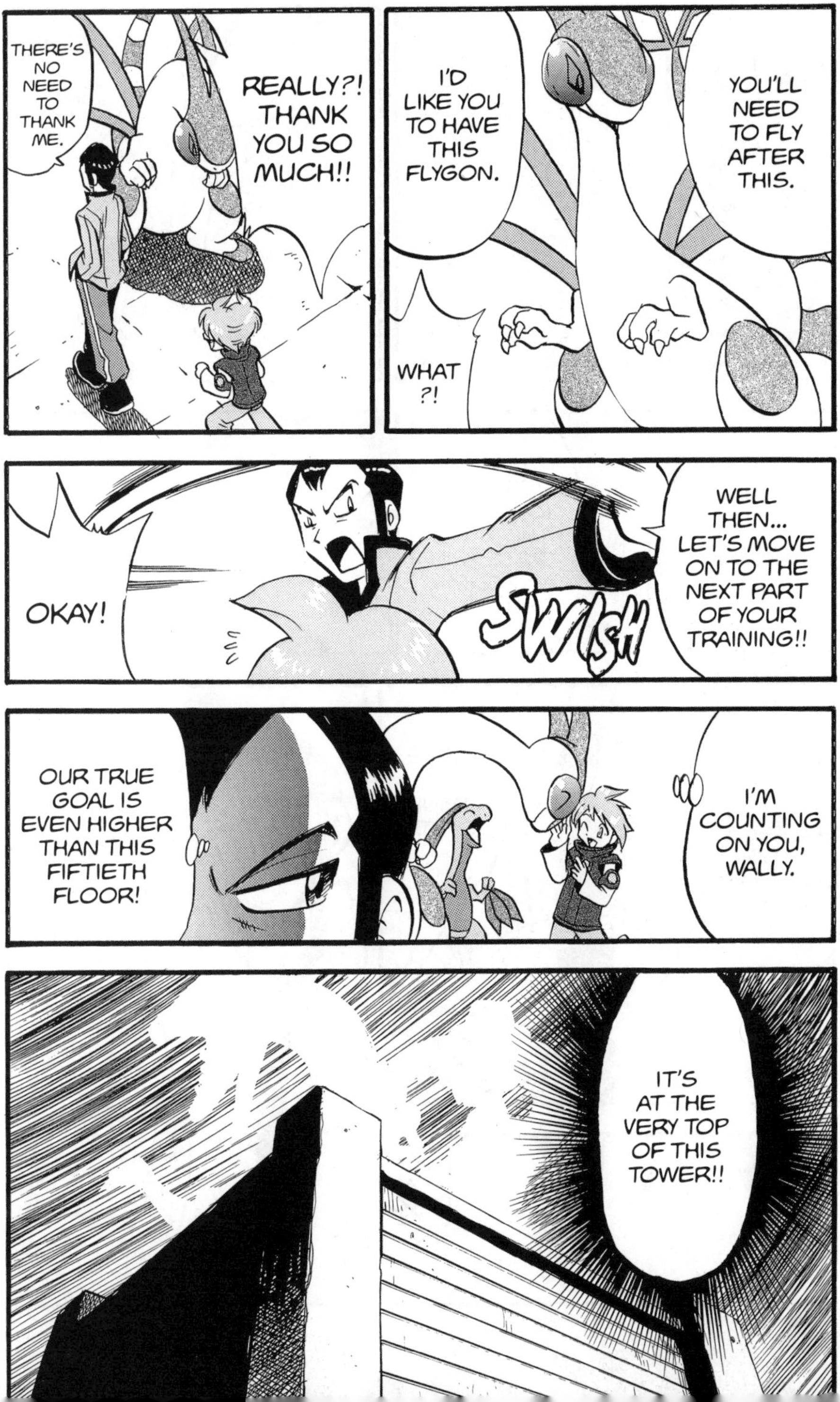
YOU'LL NEED TO FLY AFTER THIS.
I'D LIKE YOU TO HAVE THIS FLYGON.
WHAT?!
REALLY?! THANK YOU SO MUCH!!
THERE'S NO NEED TO THANK ME.
WELL THEN... LET'S MOVE ON TO THE NEXT PART OF YOUR TRAINING!!
SWISH
OKAY!
I'M COUNTING ON YOU, WALLY.
OUR TRUE GOAL IS EVEN HIGHER THAN THIS FIFTIETH FLOOR!
IT'S AT THE VERY TOP OF THIS TOWER!!

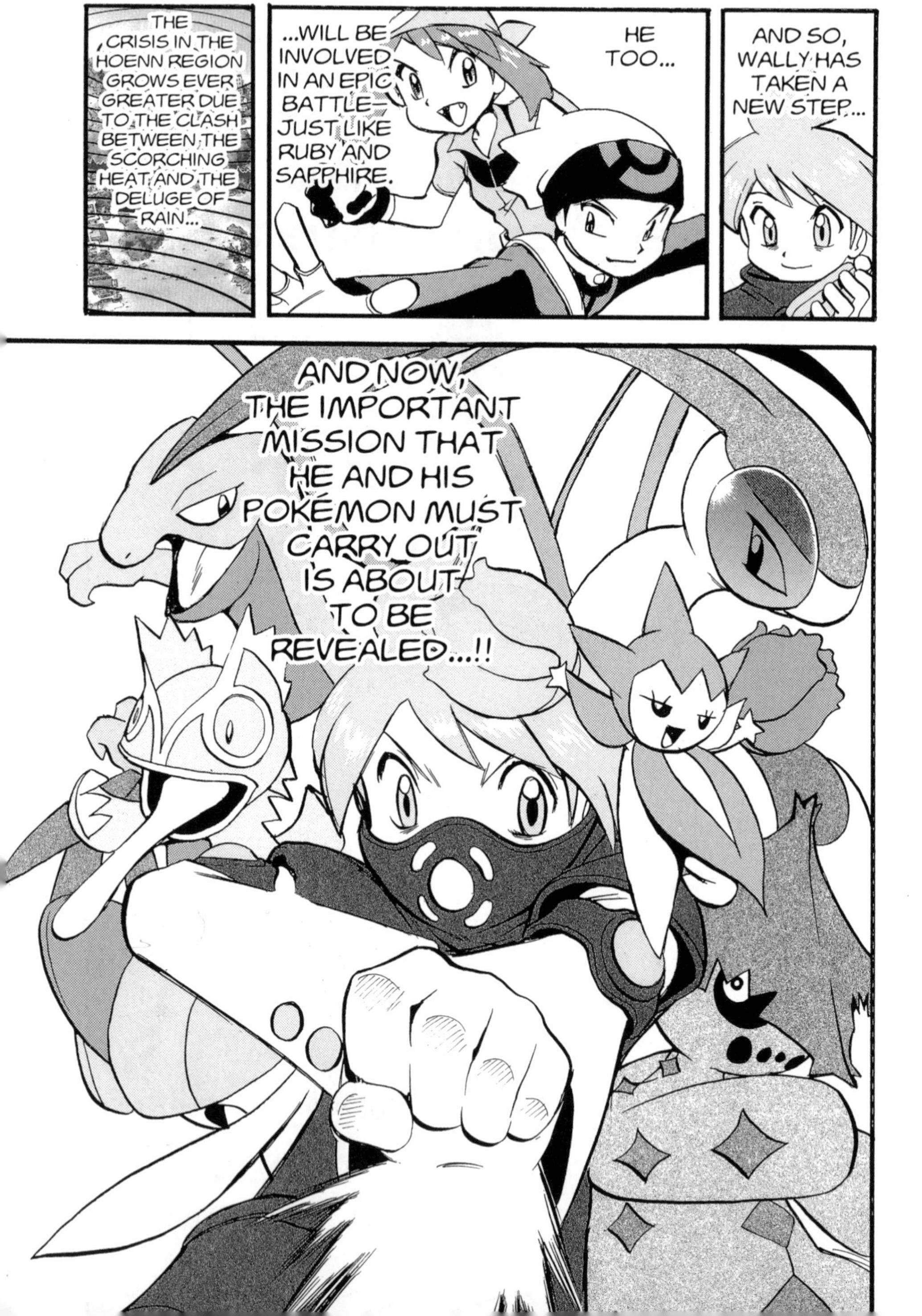
AND SO, WALLY HAS TAKEN A NEW STEP...
HE TOO...
...WILL BE INVOLVED IN AN EPIC BATTLE— JUST LIKE RUBY AND SAPPHIRE.
THE CRISIS IN THE HOENN REGION GROWS EVER GREATER DUE TO THE CLASH BETWEEN THE SCORCHING HEAT AND THE DELUGE OF RAIN...
AND NOW, THE IMPORTANT MISSION THAT HE AND HIS POKéMON MUST CARRY OUT IS ABOUT TO BE REVEALED...!!

● Adventure 242 ●
Very Vexing Volbeat

Pokémon™ Adventures Ruby & Sapphire

The Fourth Chapter

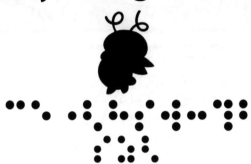

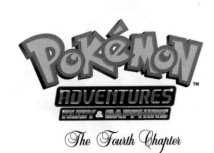

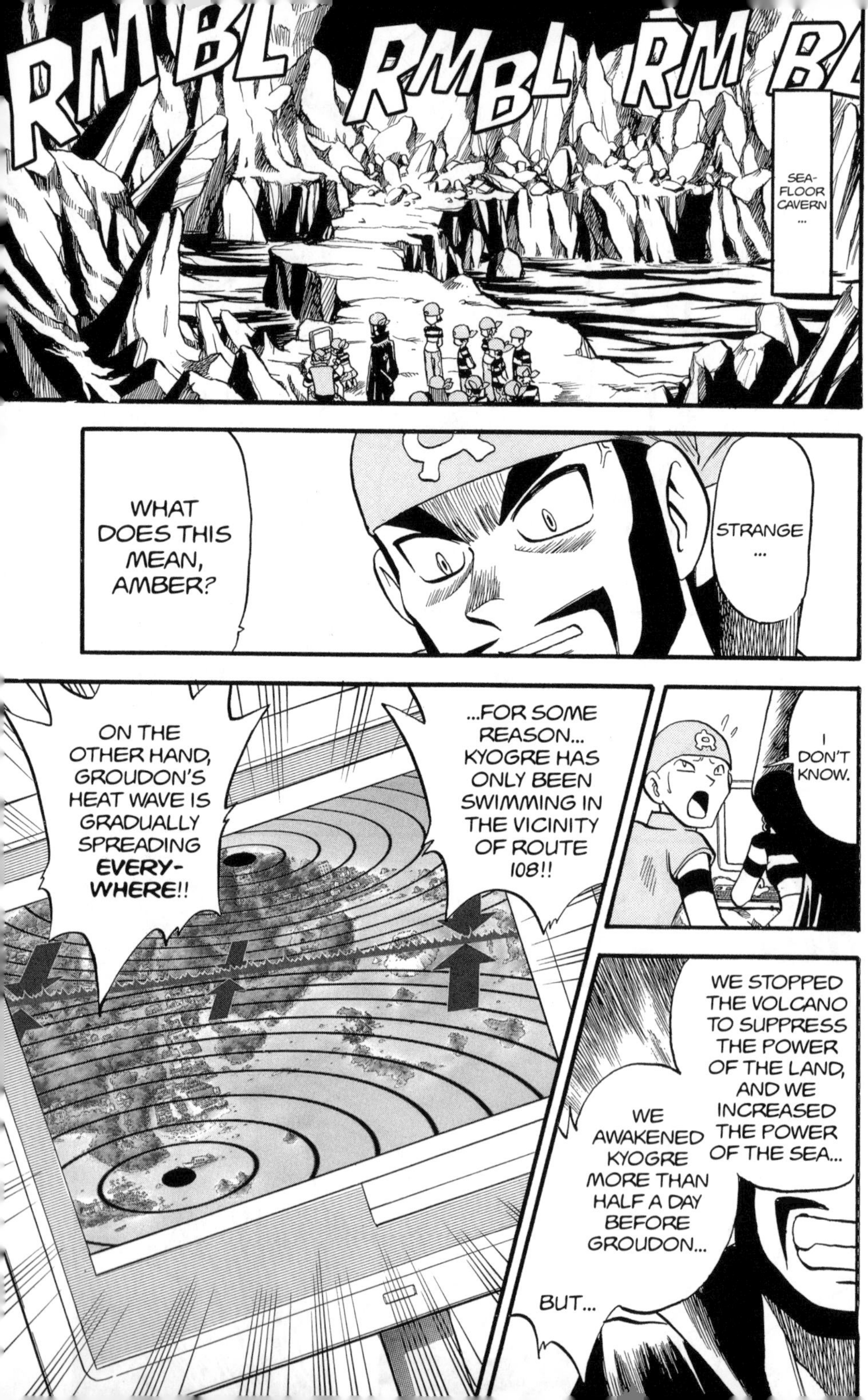
RMBL RMBL RM BL
SEA-FLOOR CAVERN ...
STRANGE ...
WHAT DOES THIS MEAN, AMBER?
I DON'T KNOW.
WE STOPPED THE VOLCANO TO SUPPRESS THE POWER OF THE LAND, AND WE INCREASED THE POWER OF THE SEA...
WE AWAKENED KYOGRE MORE THAN HALF A DAY BEFORE GROUDON...
BUT...
...FOR SOME REASON... KYOGRE HAS ONLY BEEN SWIMMING IN THE VICINITY OF ROUTE 108!!
ON THE OTHER HAND, GROUDON'S HEAT WAVE IS GRADUALLY SPREADING **EVERYWHERE**!!

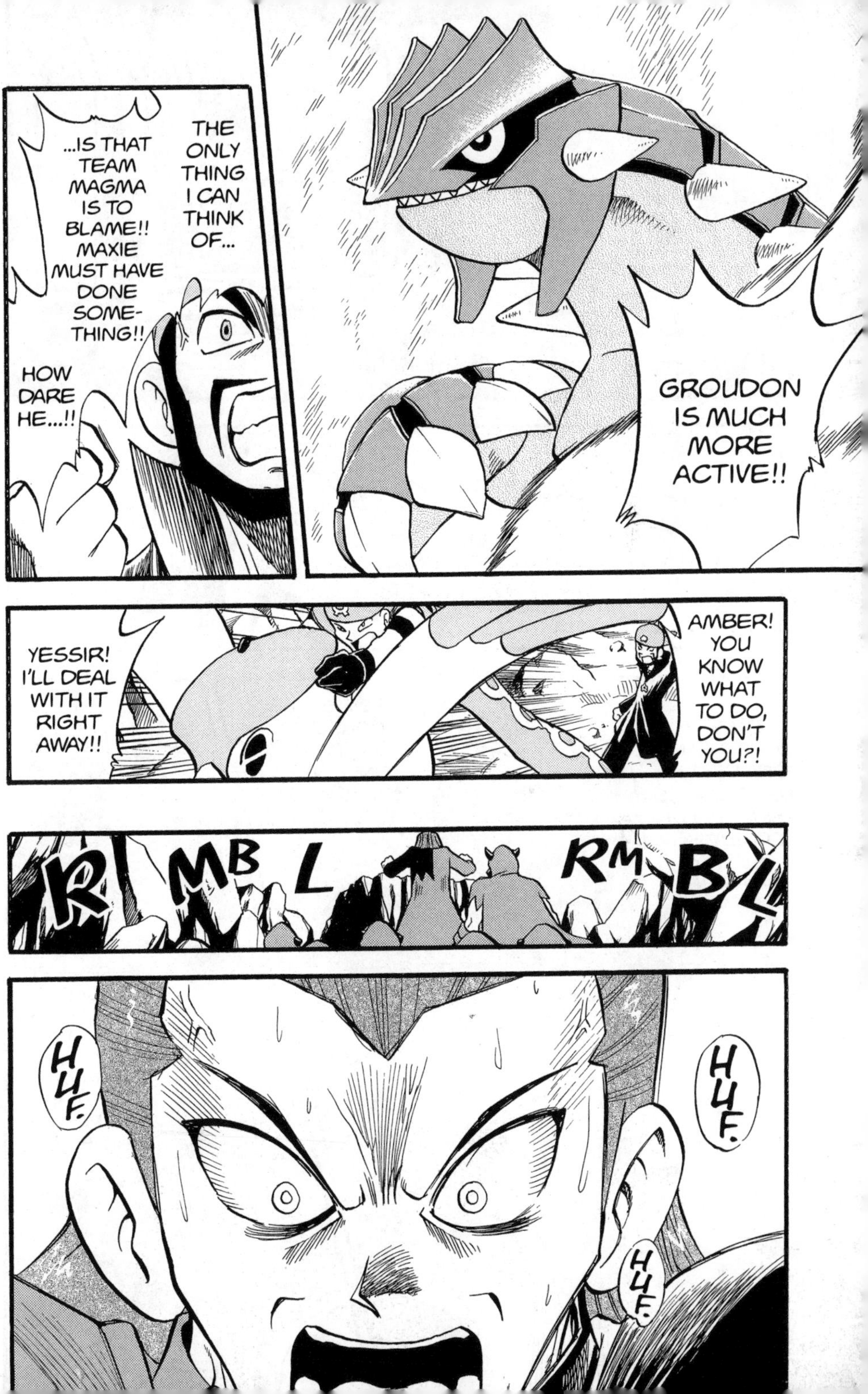
GROUDON IS MUCH MORE ACTIVE!!
THE ONLY THING I CAN THINK OF...
...IS THAT TEAM MAGMA IS TO BLAME!! MAXIE MUST HAVE DONE SOME-THING!!
HOW DARE HE...!!
AMBER! YOU KNOW WHAT TO DO, DON'T YOU?!
YESSIR! I'LL DEAL WITH IT RIGHT AWAY!!
RMBL
RMBL
HUF.
HUF.
HUF.

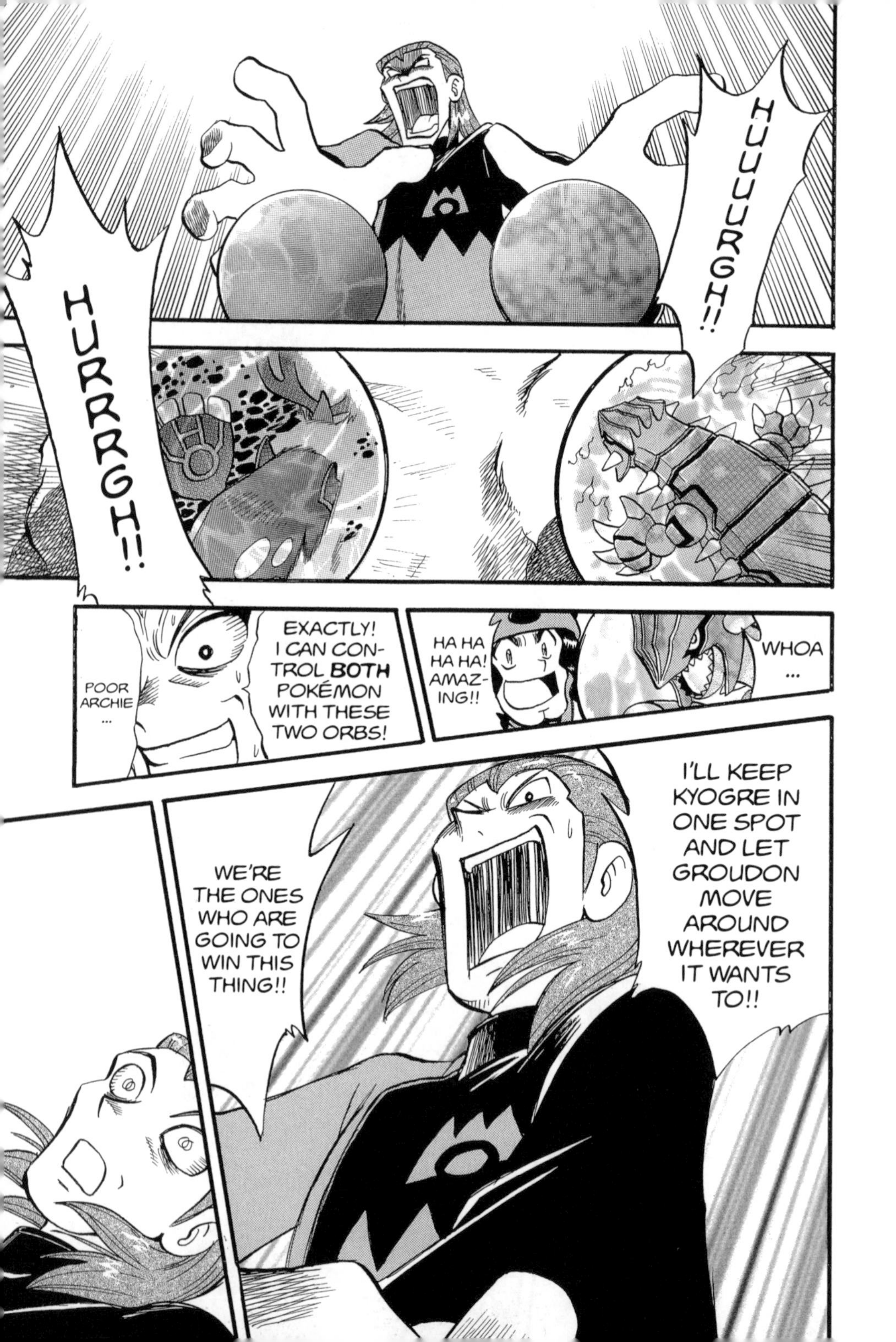
HUUUURGH!!
HURRRGH!!
WHOA ...
HA HA HA HA! AMAZING!!
EXACTLY! I CAN CONTROL BOTH POKÉMON WITH THESE TWO ORBS!
POOR ARCHIE ...
I'LL KEEP KYOGRE IN ONE SPOT AND LET GROUDON MOVE AROUND WHEREVER IT WANTS TO!!
WE'RE THE ONES WHO ARE GOING TO WIN THIS THING!!

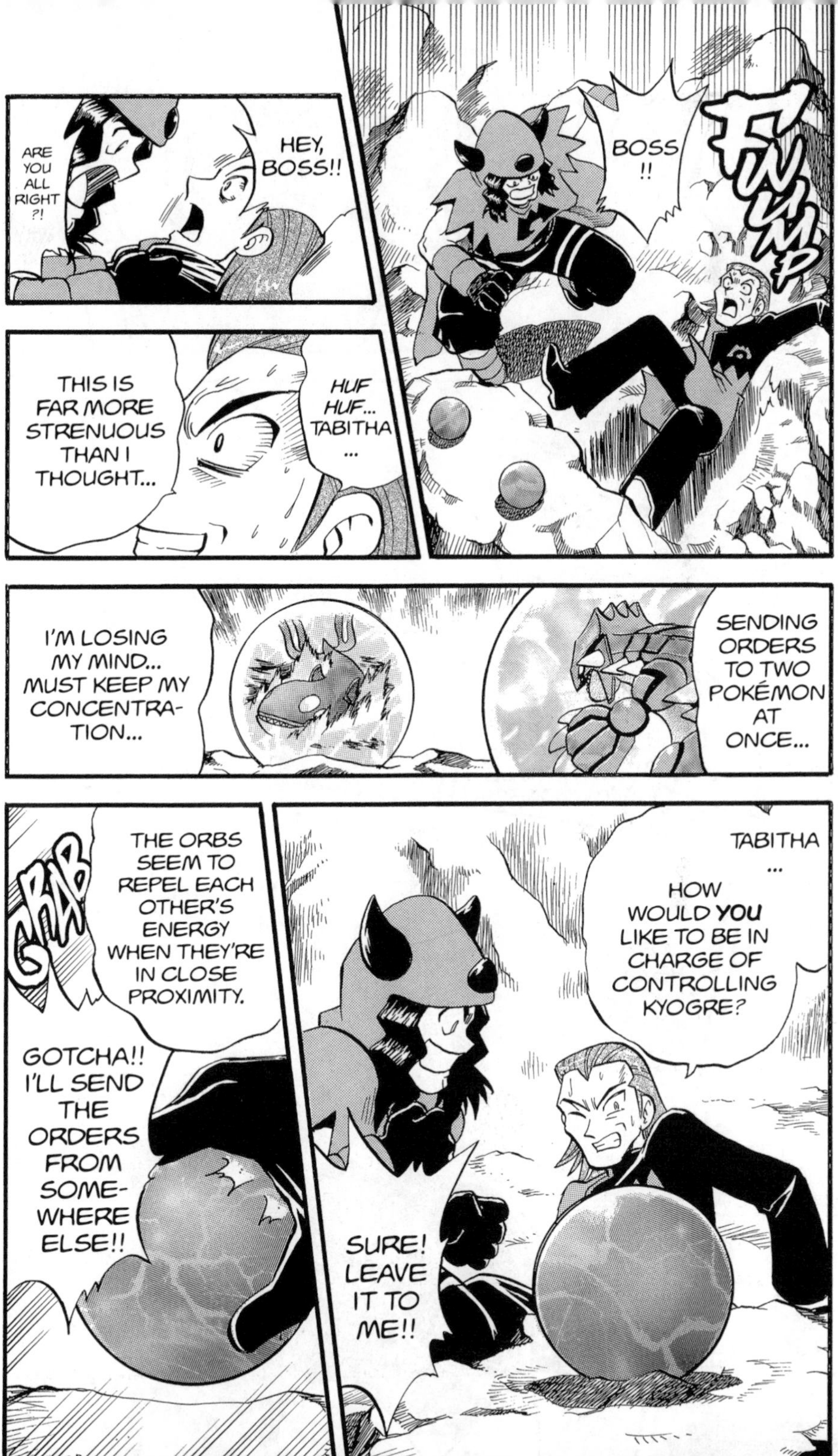
BOSS!!
FWUMP
HEY, BOSS!!
ARE YOU ALL RIGHT?!
HUF HUF... TABITHA...
THIS IS FAR MORE STRENUOUS THAN I THOUGHT...
SENDING ORDERS TO TWO POKÉMON AT ONCE...
I'M LOSING MY MIND... MUST KEEP MY CONCENTRATION...
TABITHA...
HOW WOULD **YOU** LIKE TO BE IN CHARGE OF CONTROLLING KYOGRE?
SURE! LEAVE IT TO ME!!
GRAB
THE ORBS SEEM TO REPEL EACH OTHER'S ENERGY WHEN THEY'RE IN CLOSE PROXIMITY.
GOTCHA!! I'LL SEND THE ORDERS FROM SOMEWHERE ELSE!!

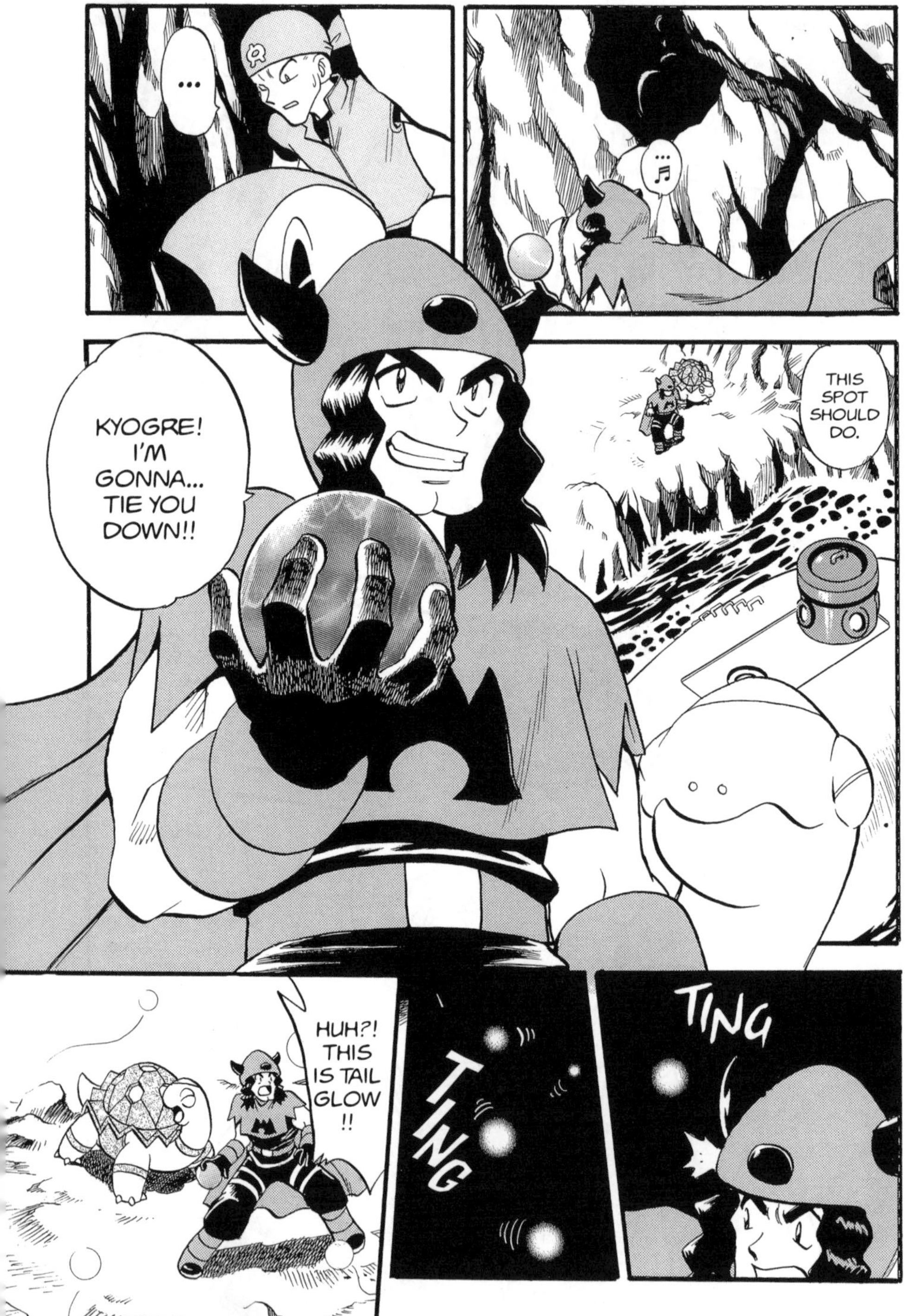

...♪
...
THIS SPOT SHOULD DO.
KYOGRE! I'M GONNA... TIE YOU DOWN!!
TING
TING
HUH?! THIS IS TAIL GLOW !!

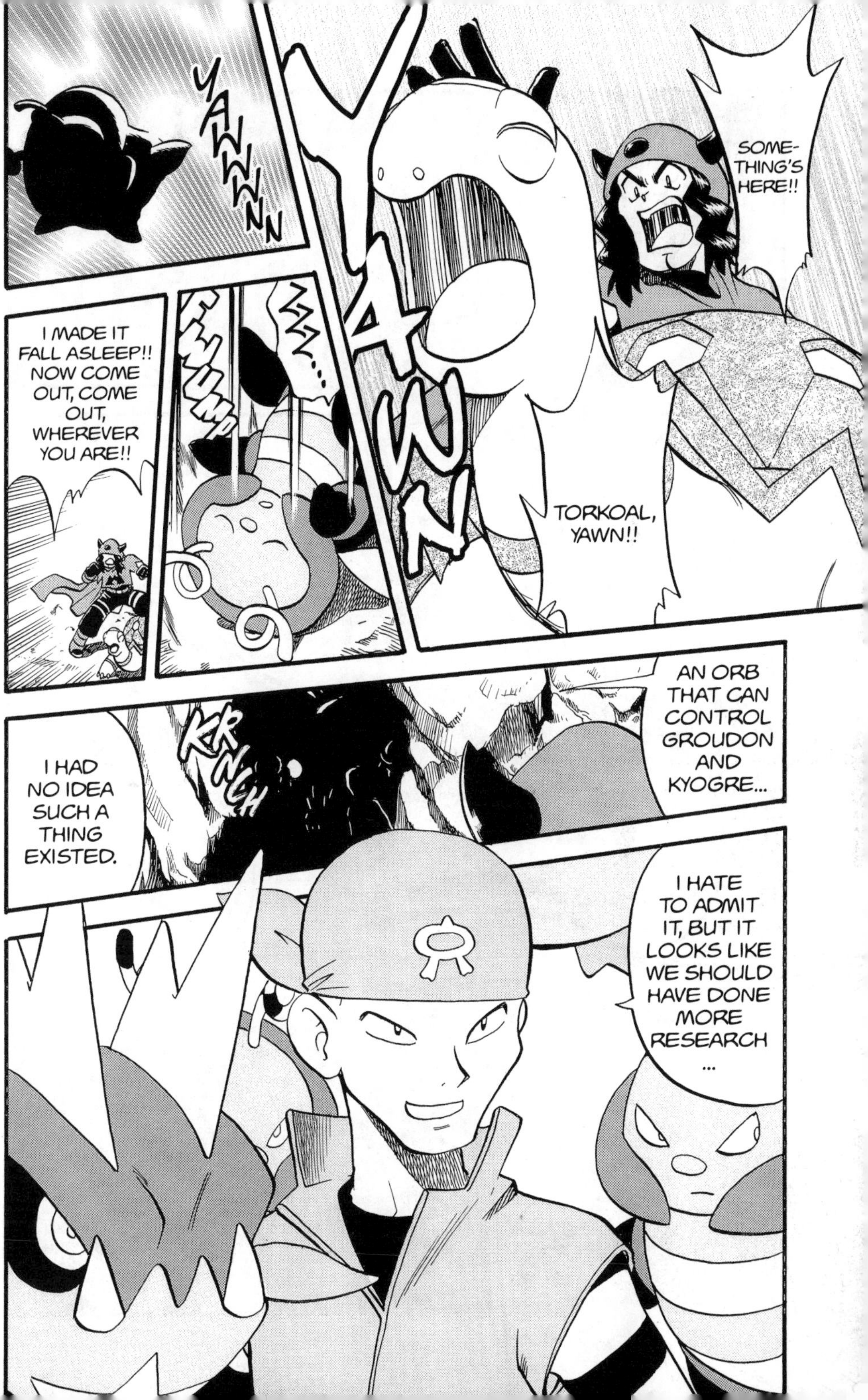
SOME-
THING'S
HERE!!
YAWN
TORKOAL, YAWN!!
YAWWWNN
ZZZ...
FWUMP
I MADE IT FALL ASLEEP!! NOW COME OUT, COME OUT, WHEREVER YOU ARE!!
AN ORB THAT CAN CONTROL GROUDON AND KYOGRE...
KRNCH
I HAD NO IDEA SUCH A THING EXISTED.
I HATE TO ADMIT IT, BUT IT LOOKS LIKE WE SHOULD HAVE DONE MORE RESEARCH...

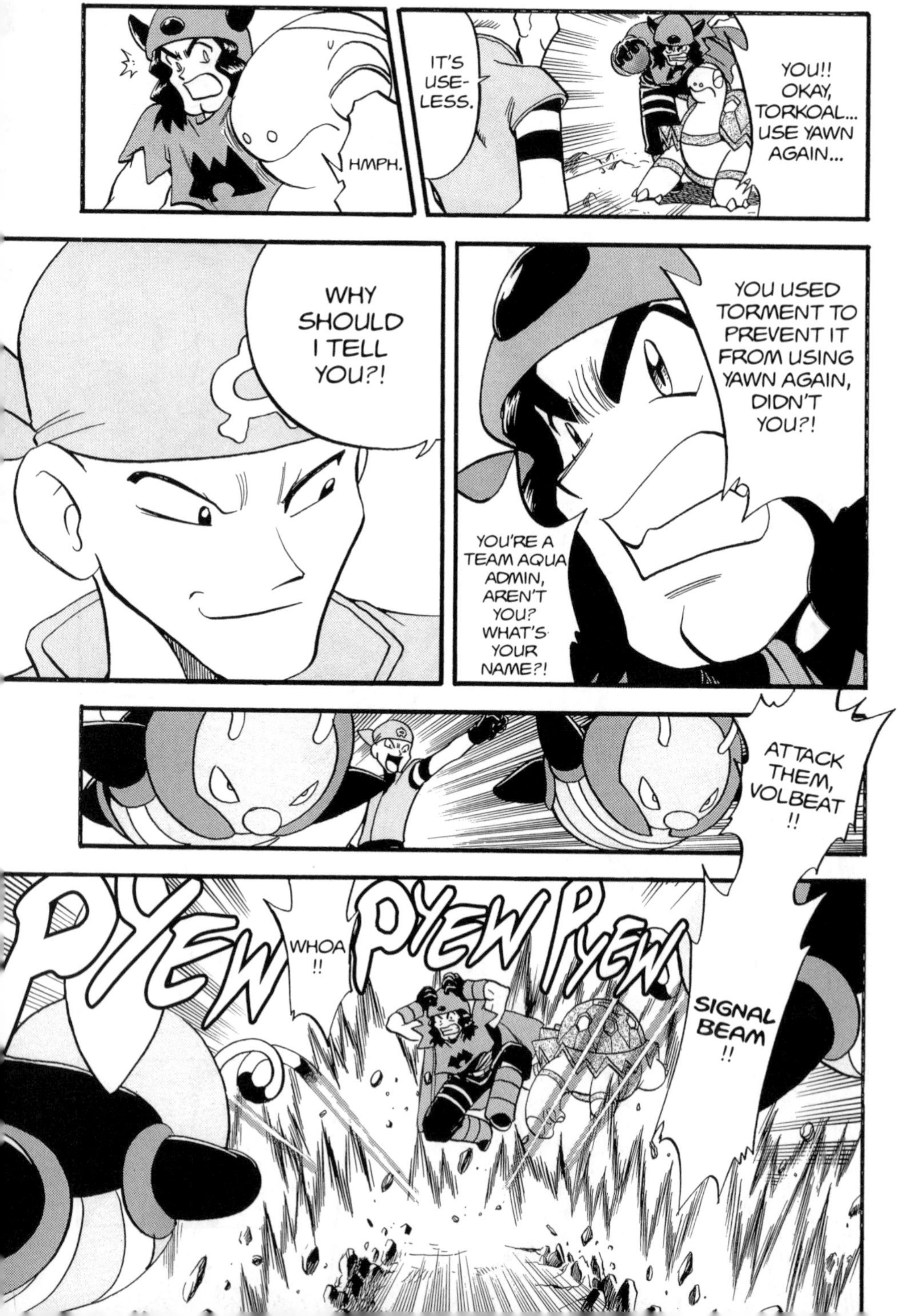
YOU!! OKAY, TORKOAL... USE YAWN AGAIN...
IT'S USE-LESS.
HMPH.
YOU USED TORMENT TO PREVENT IT FROM USING YAWN AGAIN, DIDN'T YOU?!
YOU'RE A TEAM AQUA ADMIN, AREN'T YOU? WHAT'S YOUR NAME?!
WHY SHOULD I TELL YOU?!
ATTACK THEM, VOLBEAT!!
PYEW PYEW
SIGNAL BEAM!!
WHOA!!
PYEW

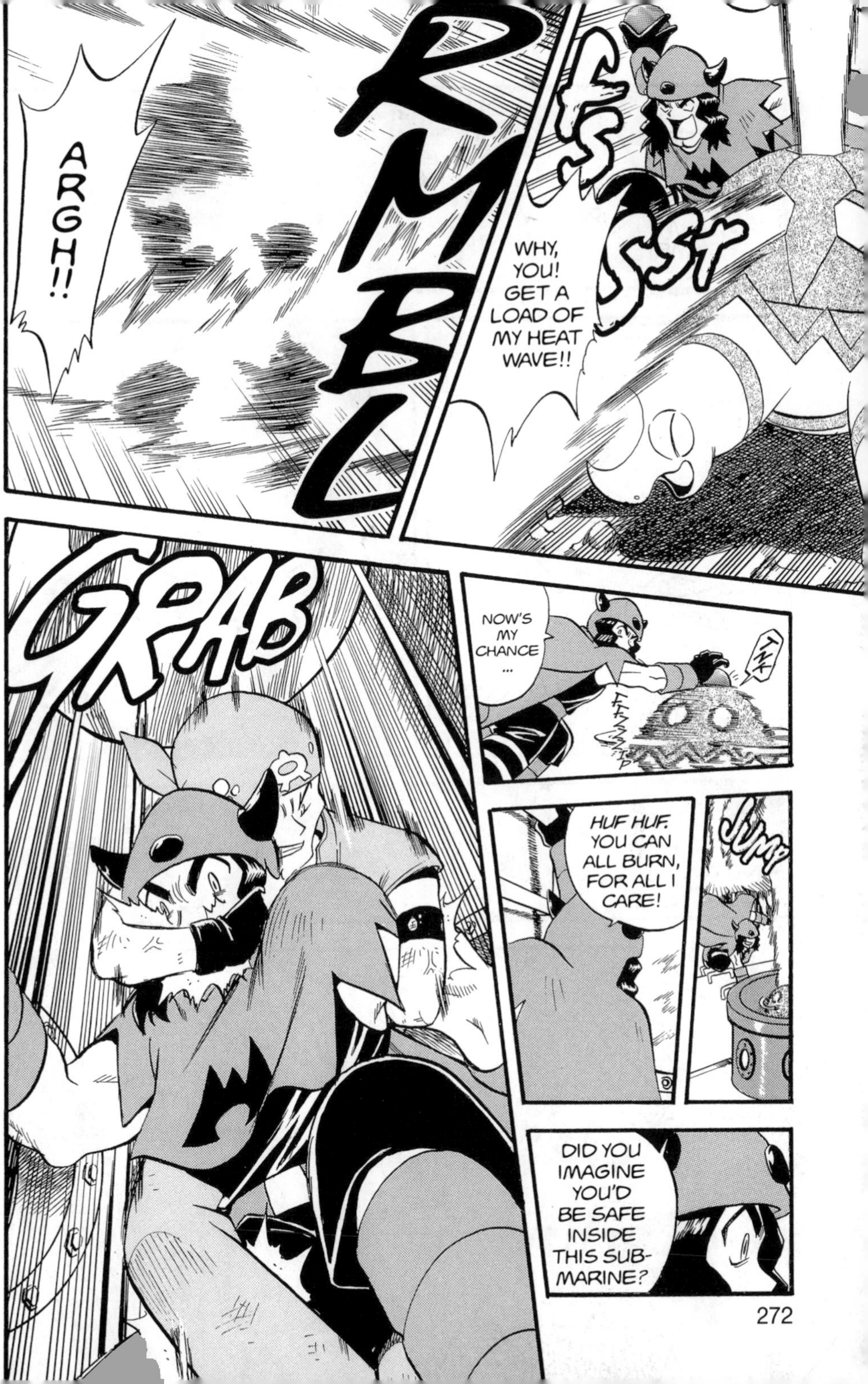
RFS
SSST
WHY, YOU! GET A LOAD OF MY HEAT WAVE!!
RMBL
ARGH!!
NOW'S MY CHANCE ...
TNK
FFZZZZIP
JUMP
HUF HUF. YOU CAN ALL BURN, FOR ALL I CARE!
DID YOU IMAGINE YOU'D BE SAFE INSIDE THIS SUB-MARINE?
GRAB

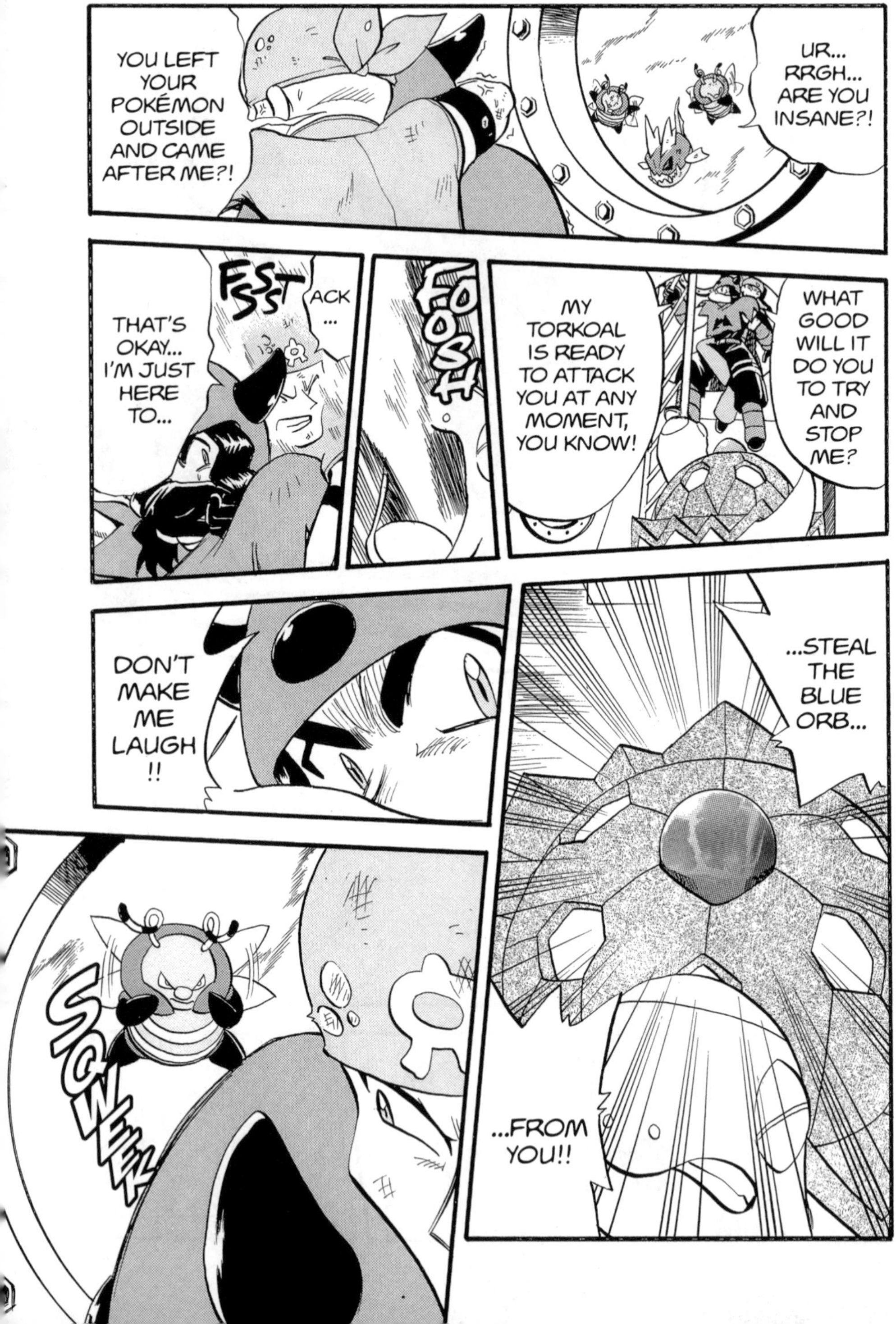
UR... RRGH... ARE YOU INSANE?!
YOU LEFT YOUR POKÉMON OUTSIDE AND CAME AFTER ME?!
WHAT GOOD WILL IT DO YOU TO TRY AND STOP ME?
MY TORKOAL IS READY TO ATTACK YOU AT ANY MOMENT, YOU KNOW!
FOOSH
ACK...
FSSST
THAT'S OKAY... I'M JUST HERE TO...
...STEAL THE BLUE ORB...
...FROM YOU!!
DON'T MAKE ME LAUGH!!
SQWEEK

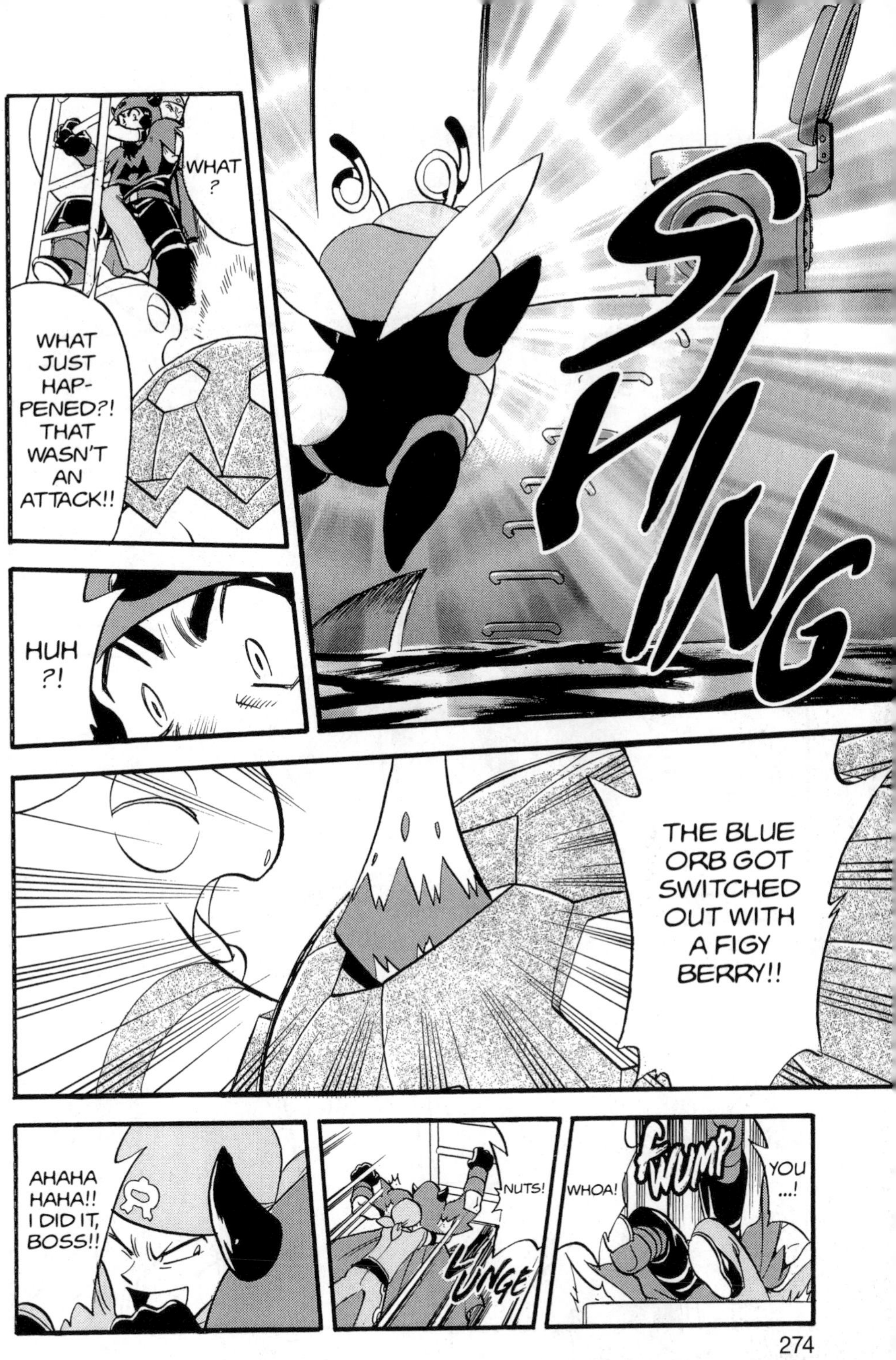
SHING
WHAT ?
WHAT JUST HAP-PENED?! THAT WASN'T AN ATTACK!!
HUH ?!
THE BLUE ORB GOT SWITCHED OUT WITH A FIGY BERRY!!
YOU ...!
FWUMP
WHOA!
NUTS!
LUNGE
AHAHA HAHA!! I DID IT, BOSS!!

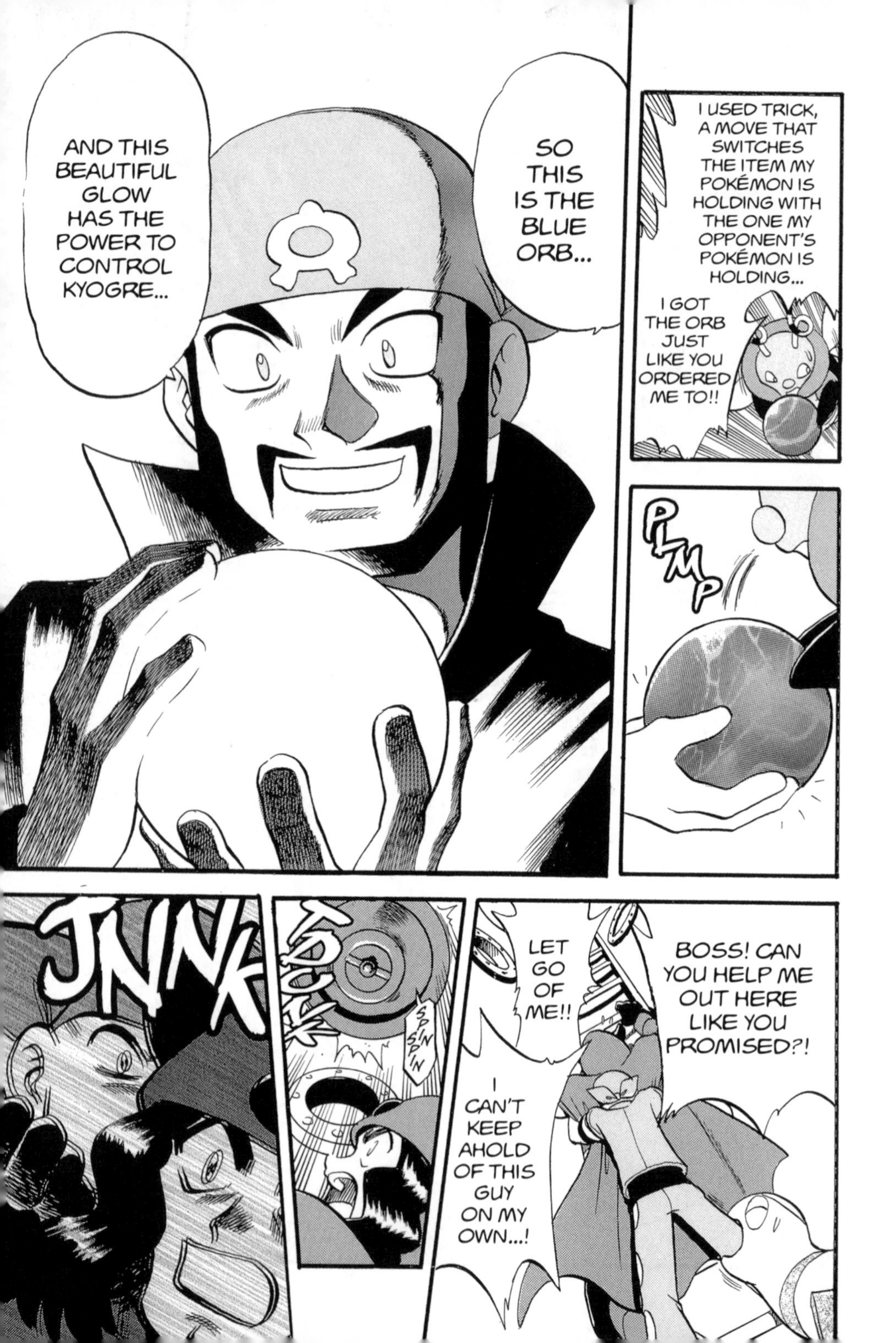
I USED TRICK, A MOVE THAT SWITCHES THE ITEM MY POKÉMON IS HOLDING WITH THE ONE MY OPPONENT'S POKÉMON IS HOLDING...
I GOT THE ORB JUST LIKE YOU ORDERED ME TO!!
PLMP
SO THIS IS THE BLUE ORB...
AND THIS BEAUTIFUL GLOW HAS THE POWER TO CONTROL KYOGRE...
BOSS! CAN YOU HELP ME OUT HERE LIKE YOU PROMISED?!
LET GO OF ME!!
I CAN'T KEEP AHOLD OF THIS GUY ON MY OWN...!
SPIN SPIN
JINK

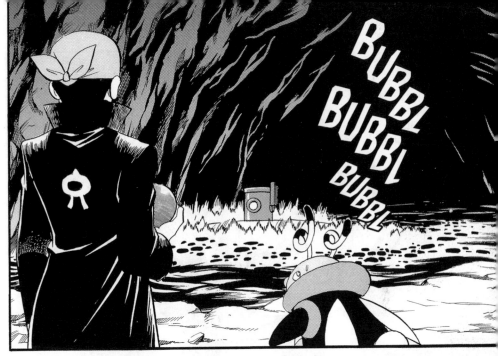

BUBBL
BUBBL
BUBBL
THANK YOU SO MUCH FOR ALL YOUR HARD WORK, AMBER.
HAVE A NICE TRIP! ENJOY YOUR DEEP SEA TOUR!
AUTOMATIC PILO
BUT YOU'LL NOTICE ...
...THAT I'VE TAKEN THE LIBERTY OF REMOVING THE SPECIAL CORE.
KLK
I'M AFRAID THE SUBMARINE MIGHT NOT BE ABLE TO WITHSTAND THE PRESSURE AT THIS DEPTH ANYMORE. I GUESS YOU'LL FIND OUT...
AHA HAHA HAHA!
NOW MAXIE AND I ARE ON EQUAL TERMS!!

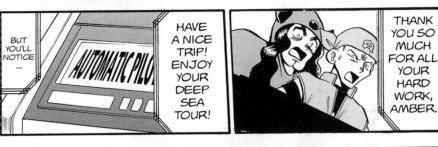

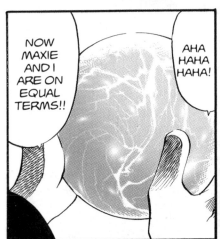

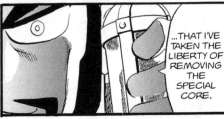

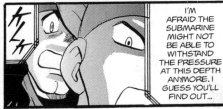

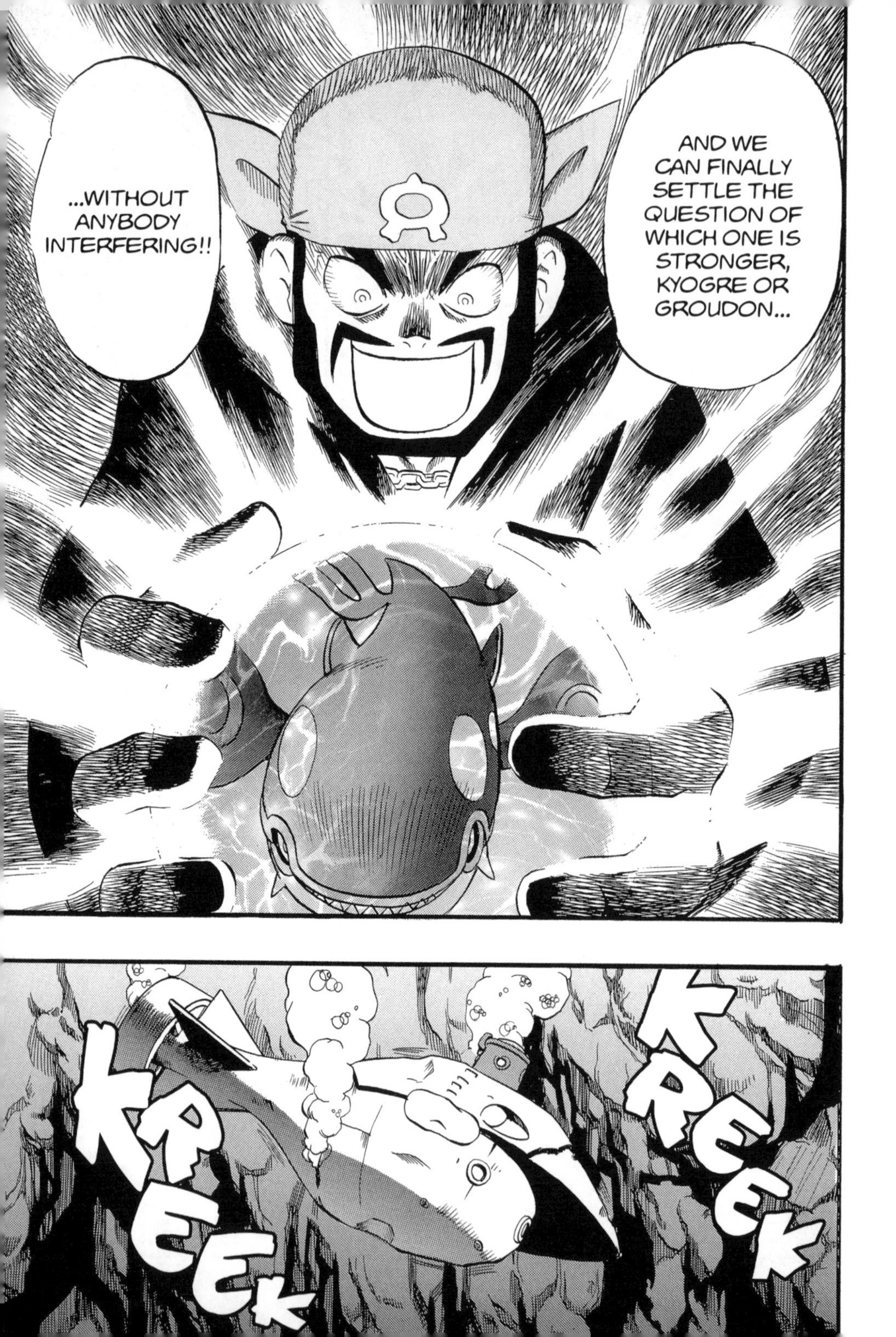
AND WE CAN FINALLY SETTLE THE QUESTION OF WHICH ONE IS STRONGER, KYOGRE OR GROUDON...
...WITHOUT ANYBODY INTERFERING!!
KREEK
KREEK

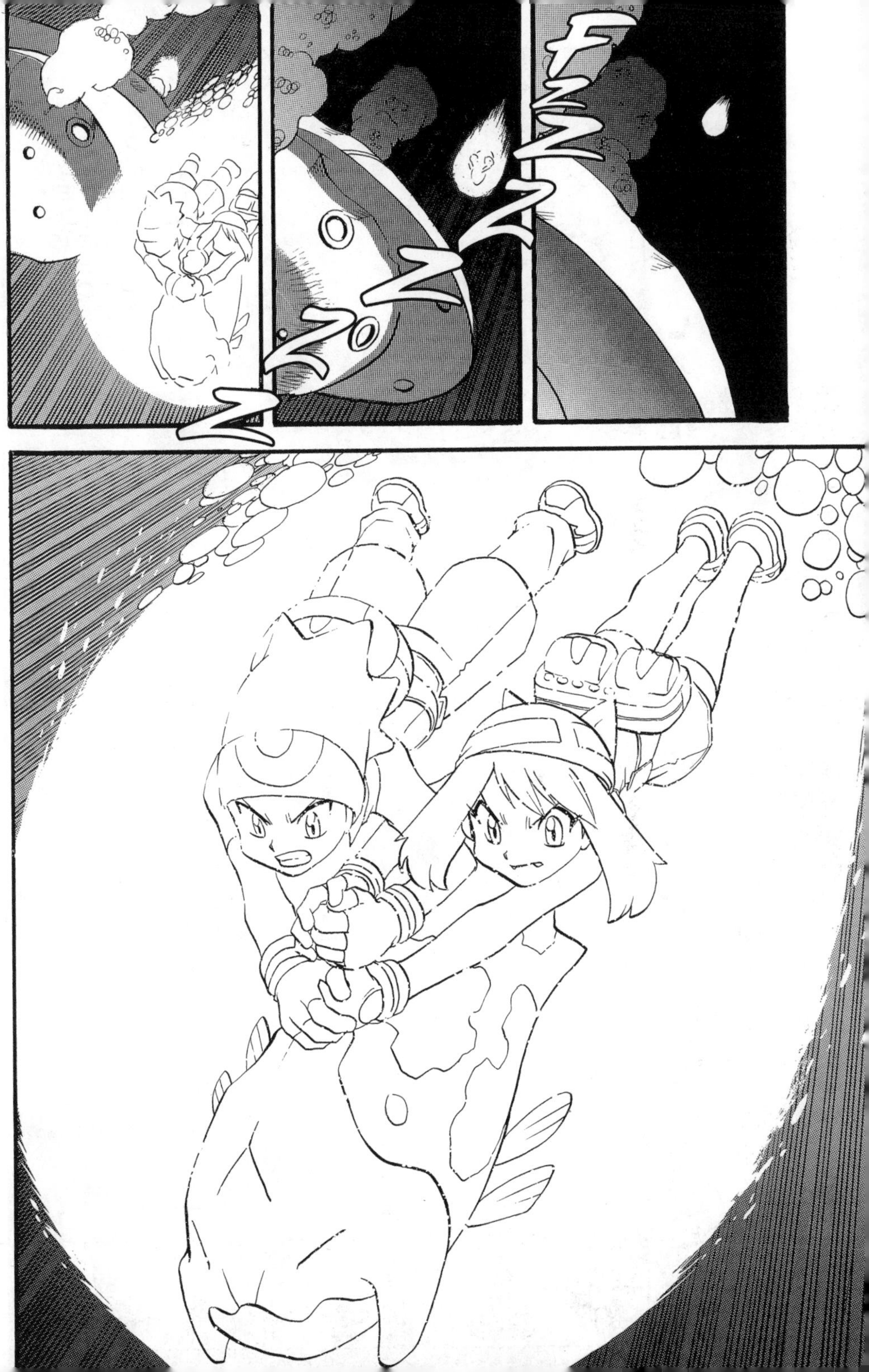

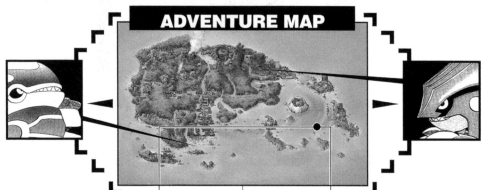

ADVENTURE MAP

SAPPHIRE

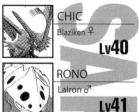

Name	Pokémon	Level
CHIC	Blaziken ♀	Lv40
RONO	Lairon ♂	Lv41
RELLY	Relicanth ♂	Lv48
PHADO	Donphan ♂	Lv48
TROPPY	Tropius ♂	Lv46
LORRY	Wailord ♂	Lv48

RUBY

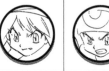

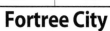

Name	Pokémon
MUMU	Swampert ♂
NANA	Mightyena ♀
KIKI	Delcatty ♀
FOFO	Castform ♀

Fortree City

▼ Sapphire: Route 123 | Ruby: Slateport City

▼

Route 126

▼

Seafloor Cavern

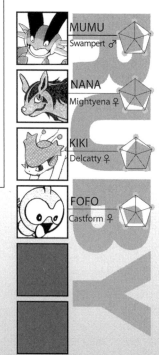

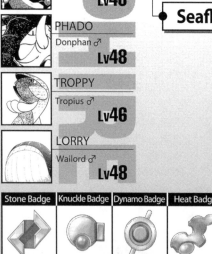

Stone Badge	Knuckle Badge	Dynamo Badge	Heat Badge
Balance Badge	Feather Badge	Mind Badge	Rain Badge

	Coolness	Beauty	Cuteness	Cleverness	Toughness
Normal					
Super					
Hyper					
Master					

● Adventure 243 ●
No Armaldo Is an Island

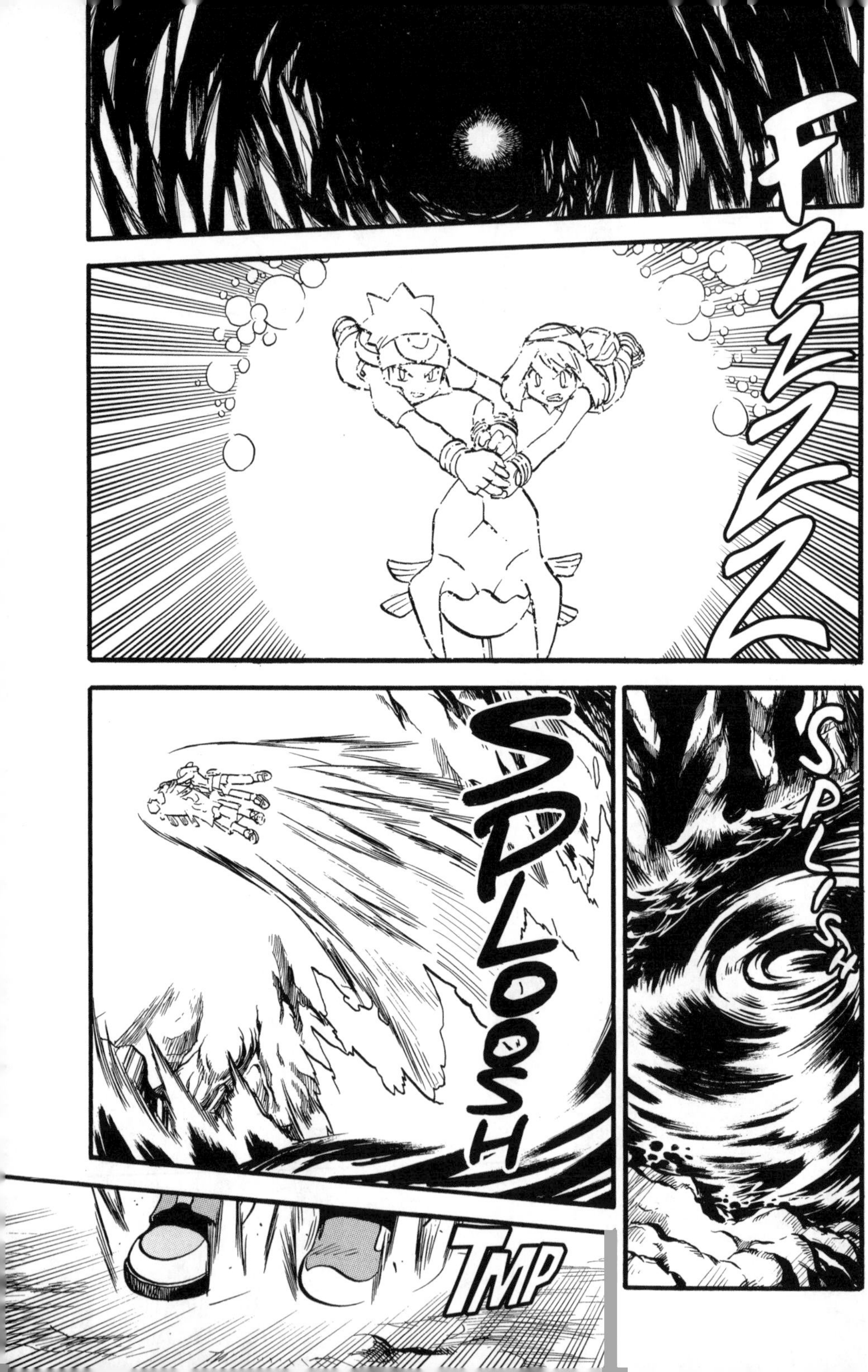
FZZZZZ
SPLISH
SPLOOSH
TMP

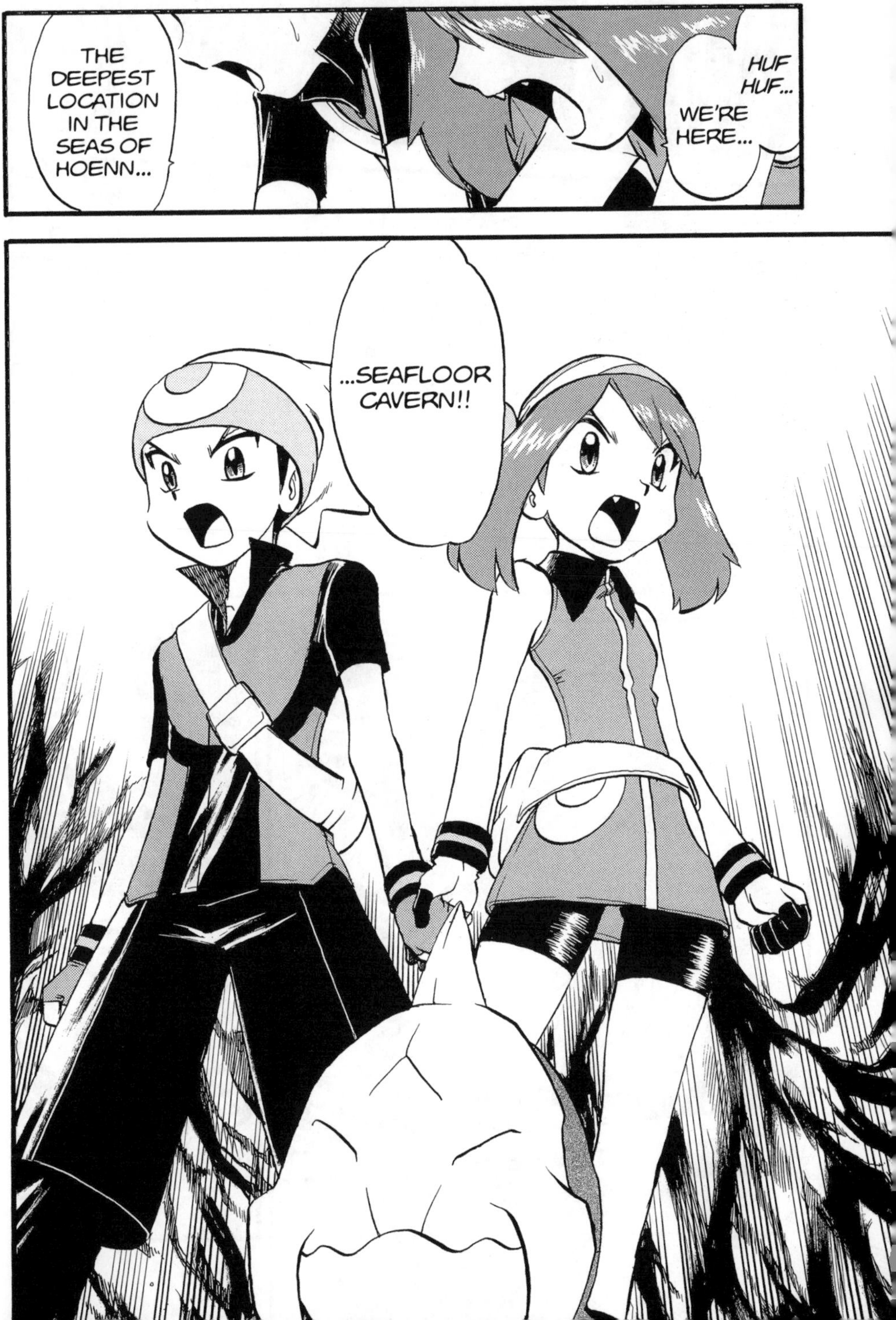
HUF HUF... WE'RE HERE...
THE DEEPEST LOCATION IN THE SEAS OF HOENN...
...SEAFLOOR CAVERN!!

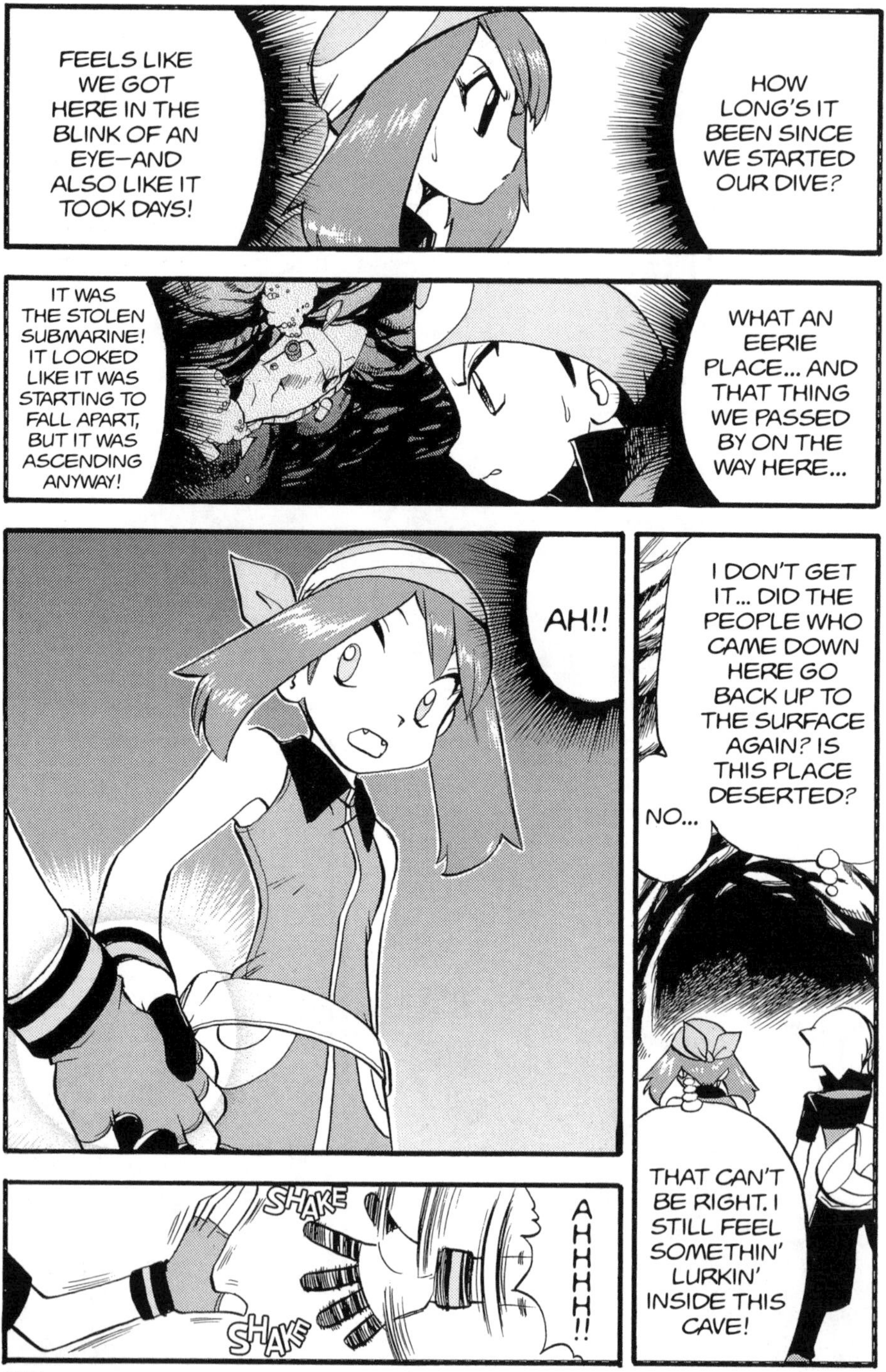
HOW LONG'S IT BEEN SINCE WE STARTED OUR DIVE?
FEELS LIKE WE GOT HERE IN THE BLINK OF AN EYE—AND ALSO LIKE IT TOOK DAYS!
WHAT AN EERIE PLACE... AND THAT THING WE PASSED BY ON THE WAY HERE...
IT WAS THE STOLEN SUBMARINE! IT LOOKED LIKE IT WAS STARTING TO FALL APART, BUT IT WAS ASCENDING ANYWAY!
I DON'T GET IT... DID THE PEOPLE WHO CAME DOWN HERE GO BACK UP TO THE SURFACE AGAIN? IS THIS PLACE DESERTED?
NO...
THAT CAN'T BE RIGHT. I STILL FEEL SOMETHIN' LURKIN' INSIDE THIS CAVE!
AH!!
AHHHHH!!
SHAKE
SHAKE

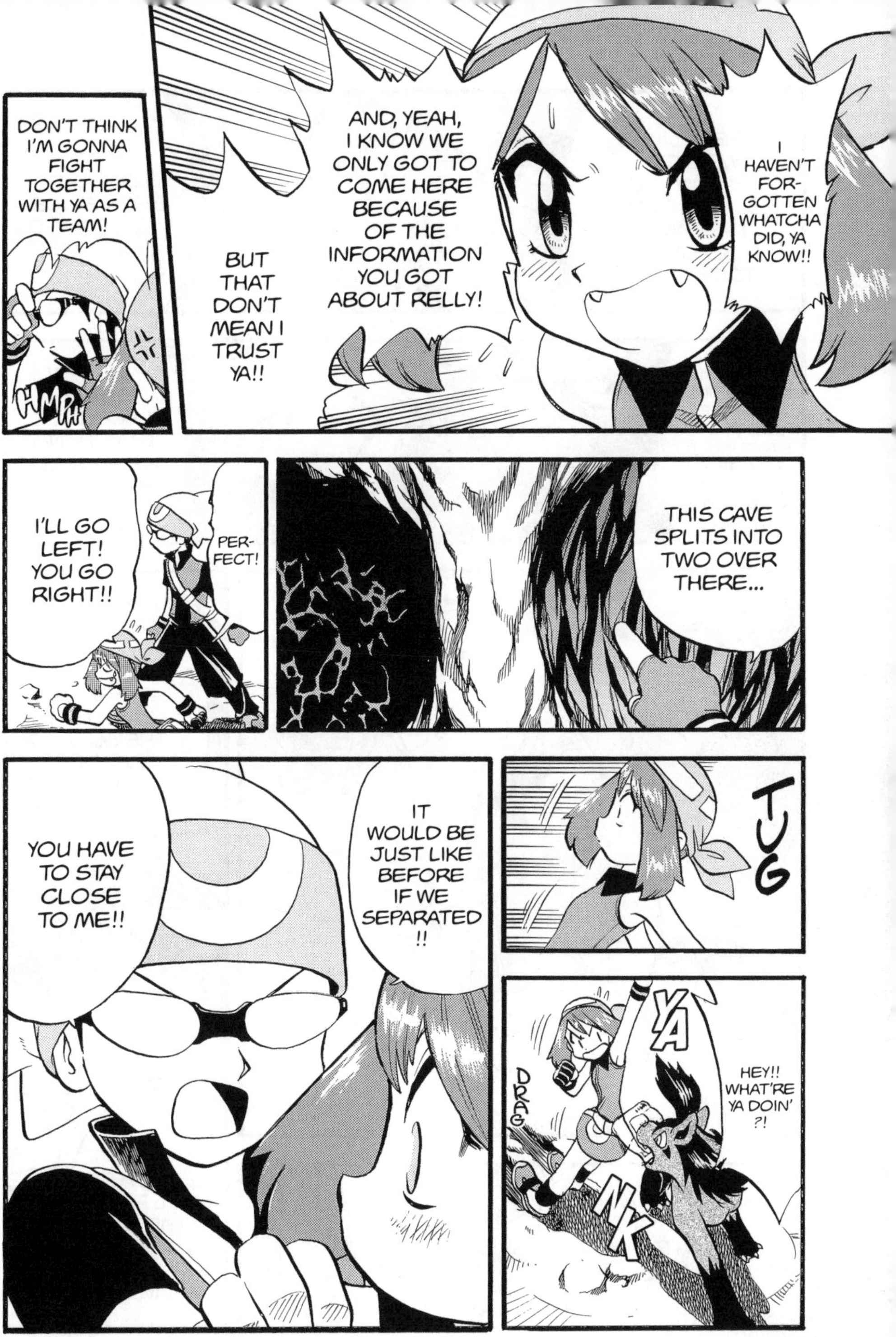
I HAVEN'T FOR-GOTTEN WHATCHA DID, YA KNOW!!
AND, YEAH, I KNOW WE ONLY GOT TO COME HERE BECAUSE OF THE INFORMATION YOU GOT ABOUT RELLY!
BUT THAT DON'T MEAN I TRUST YA!!
DON'T THINK I'M GONNA FIGHT TOGETHER WITH YA AS A TEAM!
HMPH
THIS CAVE SPLITS INTO TWO OVER THERE...
PER-FECT!
I'LL GO LEFT! YOU GO RIGHT!!
TUG
YANK
DRAG
HEY!! WHAT'RE YA DOIN' ?!
IT WOULD BE JUST LIKE BEFORE IF WE SEPARATED !!
YOU HAVE TO STAY CLOSE TO ME!!

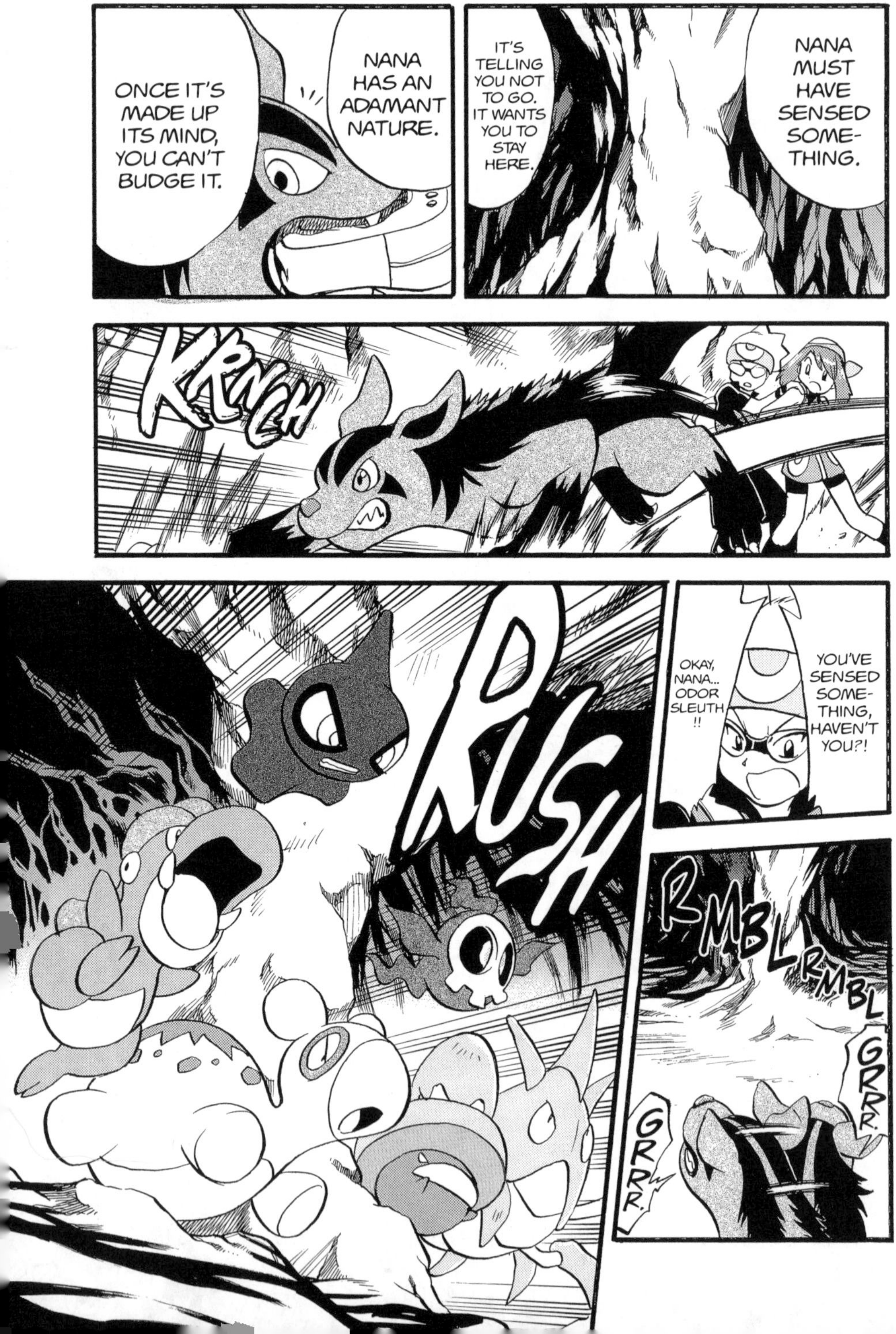
NANA MUST HAVE SENSED SOMETHING.
IT'S TELLING YOU NOT TO GO. IT WANTS YOU TO STAY HERE.
NANA HAS AN ADAMANT NATURE.
ONCE IT'S MADE UP ITS MIND, YOU CAN'T BUDGE IT.
KRNCH
YOU'VE SENSED SOMETHING, HAVEN'T YOU?!
OKAY, NANA... ODOR SLEUTH!!
RMBL RMBL
GRRR.
GRRR.
RUSH

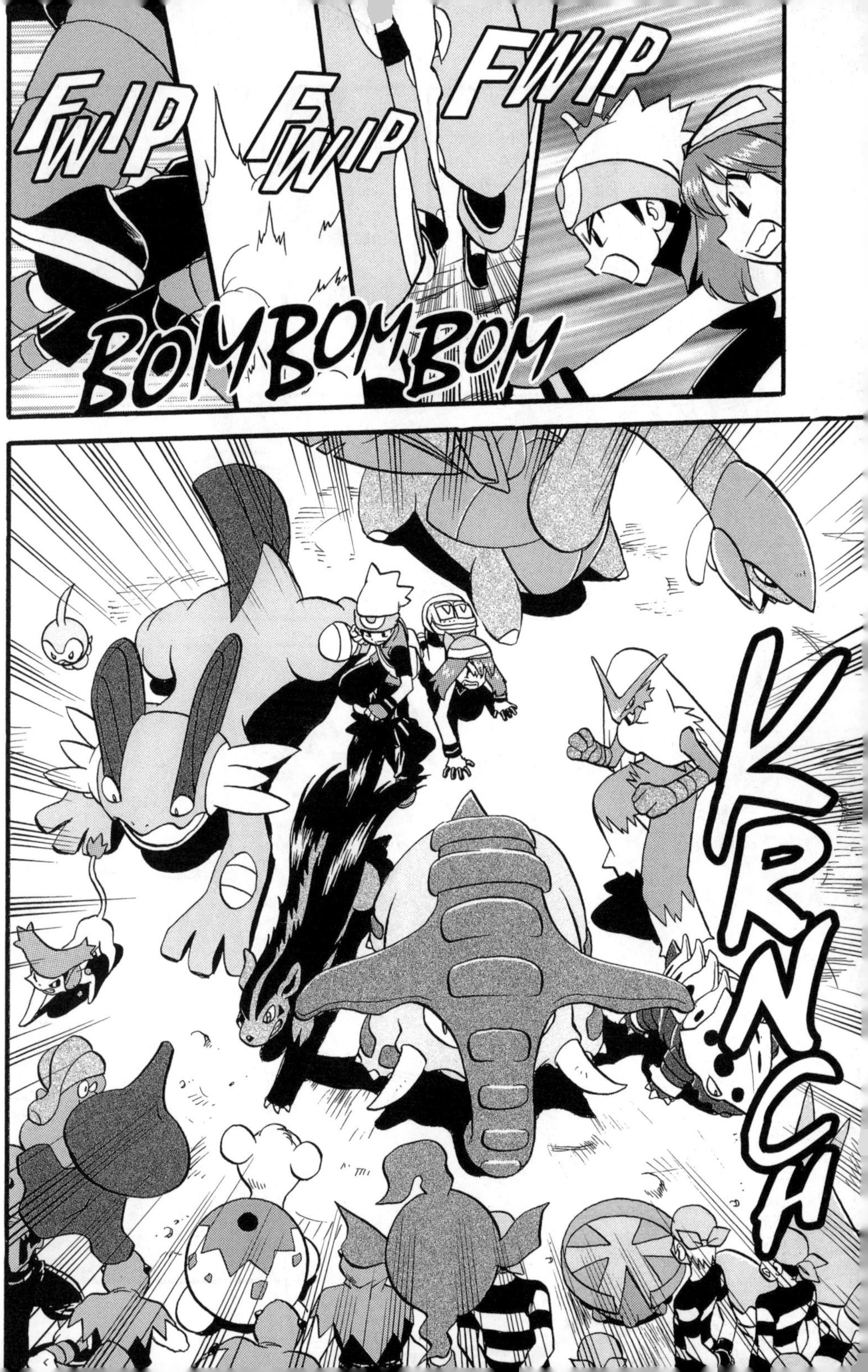
FWIP
FWIP
FWIP
BOMBOMBOM
KRNCH

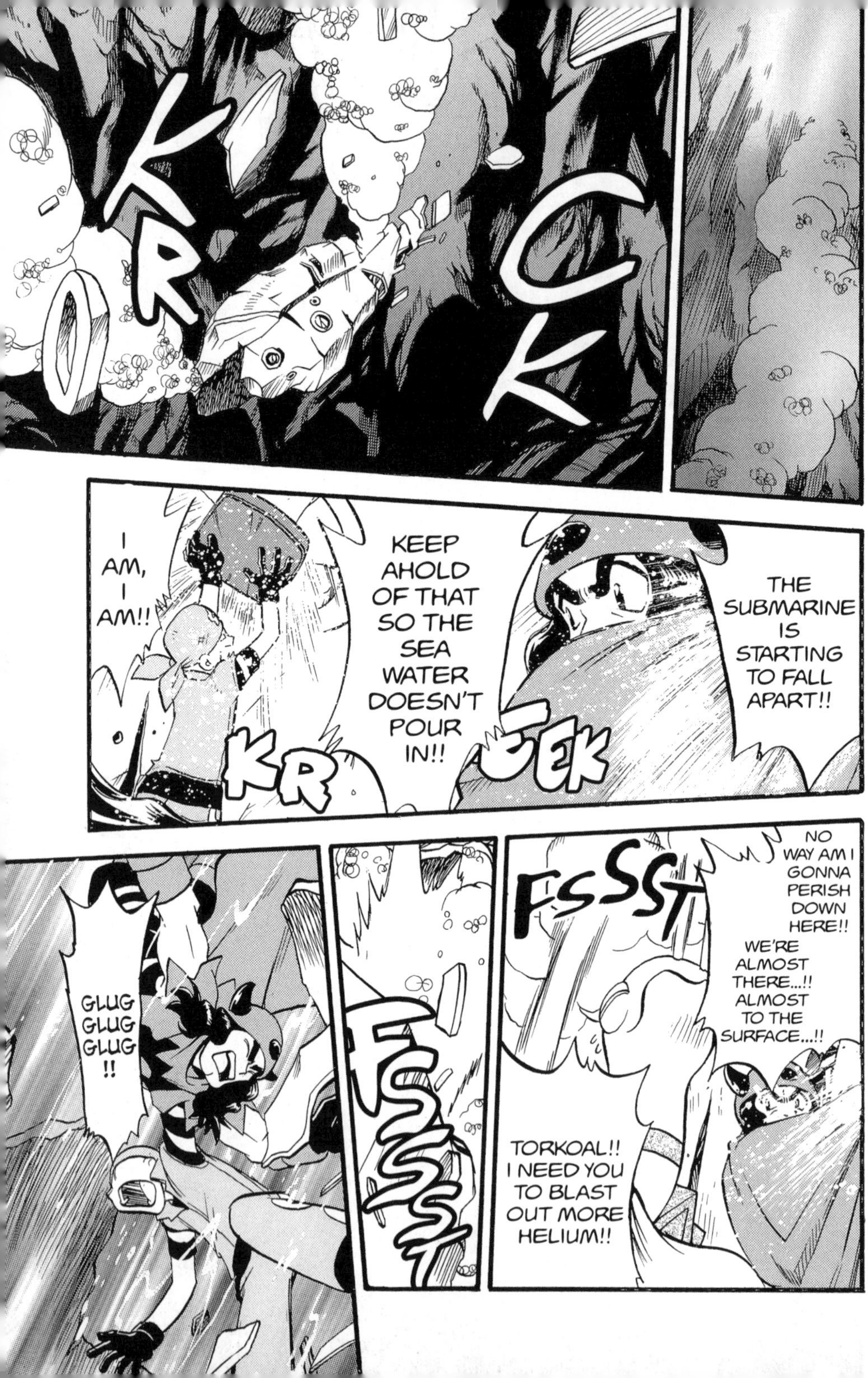
KROCK
THE SUBMARINE IS STARTING TO FALL APART!!
KEEP AHOLD OF THAT SO THE SEA WATER DOESN'T POUR IN!!
I AM, I AM!!
KR EK
NO WAY AM I GONNA PERISH DOWN HERE!!
WE'RE ALMOST THERE...!! ALMOST TO THE SURFACE...!!
FSSST
TORKOAL!! I NEED YOU TO BLAST OUT MORE HELIUM!!
FSSSST
GLUG GLUG GLUG!!

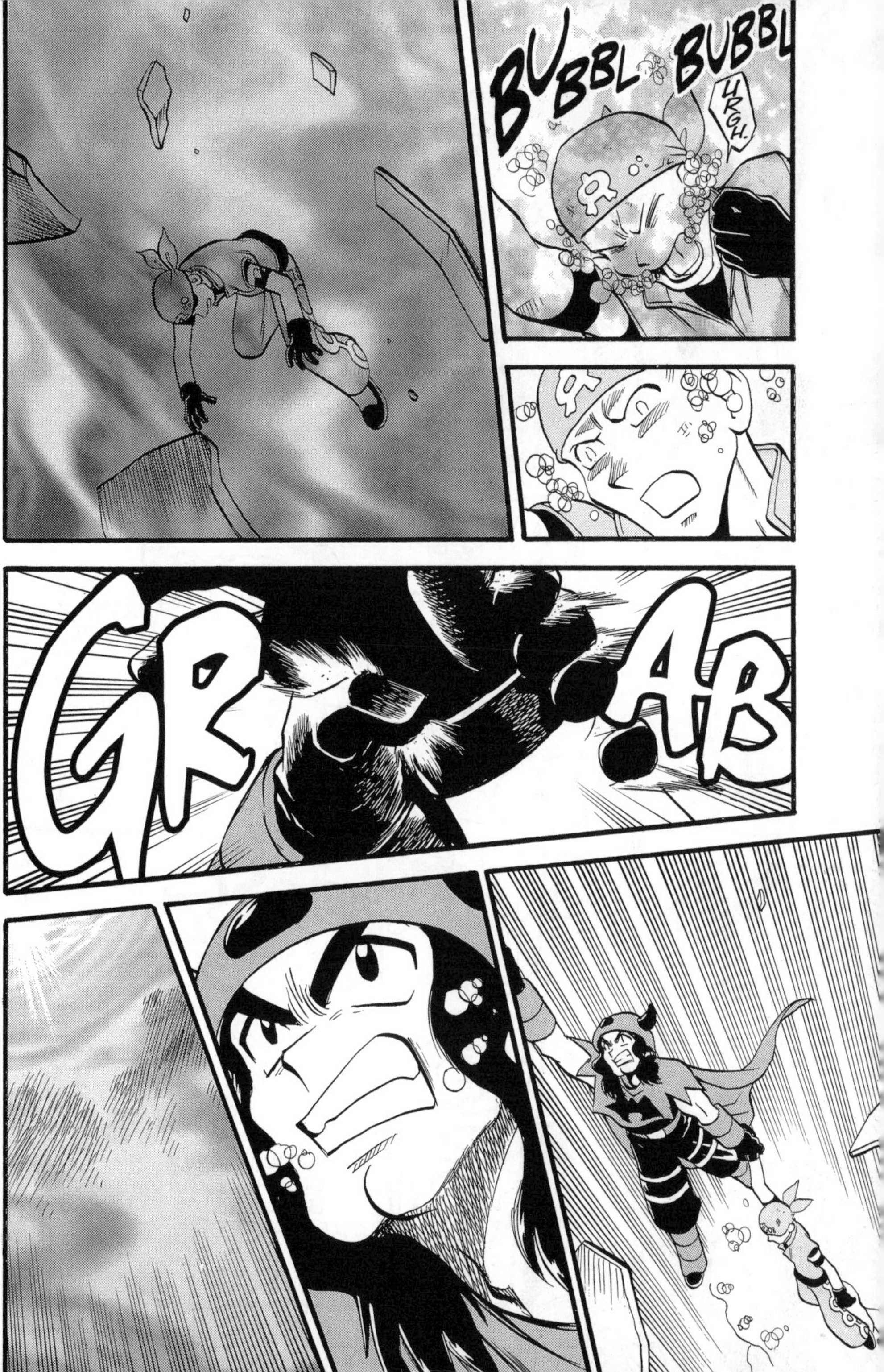
BUBBL BUBBL
URGH.
GRAB

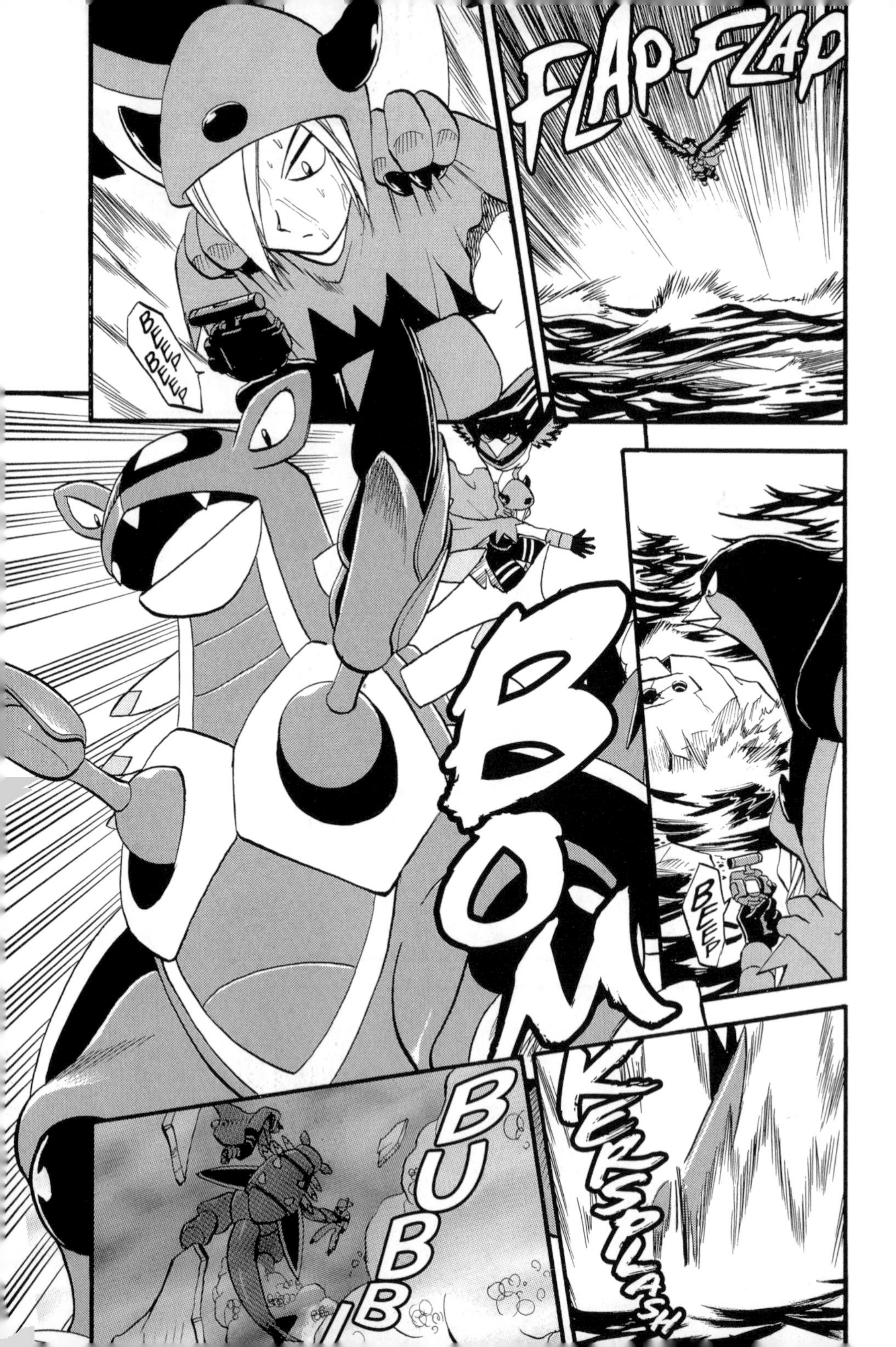
FLAP FLAP
BWWA BWWA
BEEP
BOOM
KERSPLASH
BUBB

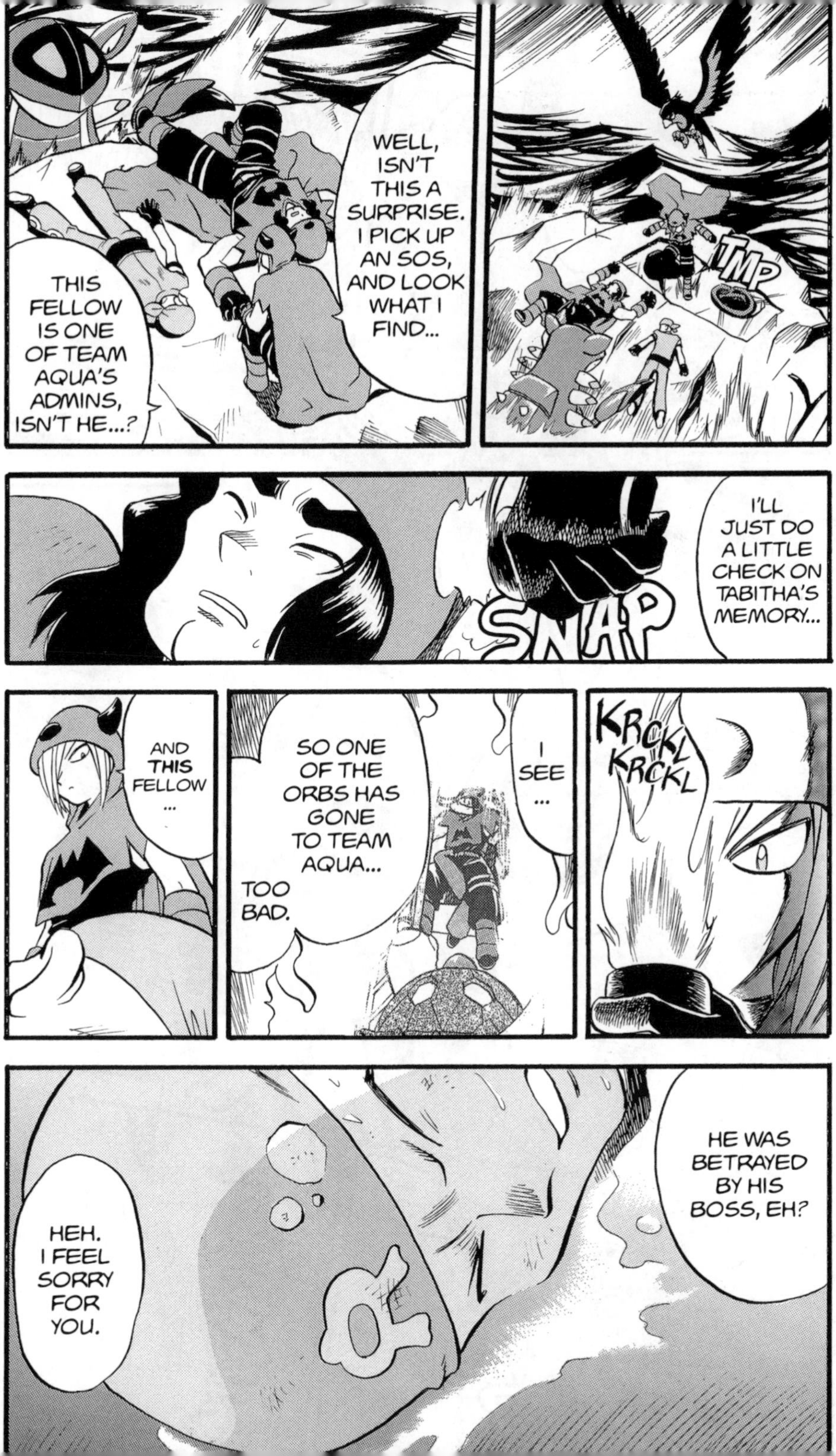
TMP
WELL, ISN'T THIS A SURPRISE. I PICK UP AN SOS, AND LOOK WHAT I FIND...
THIS FELLOW IS ONE OF TEAM AQUA'S ADMINS, ISN'T HE...?
I'LL JUST DO A LITTLE CHECK ON TABITHA'S MEMORY...
SNAP
KRCKL KRCKL
I SEE...
SO ONE OF THE ORBS HAS GONE TO TEAM AQUA...
TOO BAD.
AND THIS FELLOW...
HE WAS BETRAYED BY HIS BOSS, EH?
HEH. I FEEL SORRY FOR YOU.

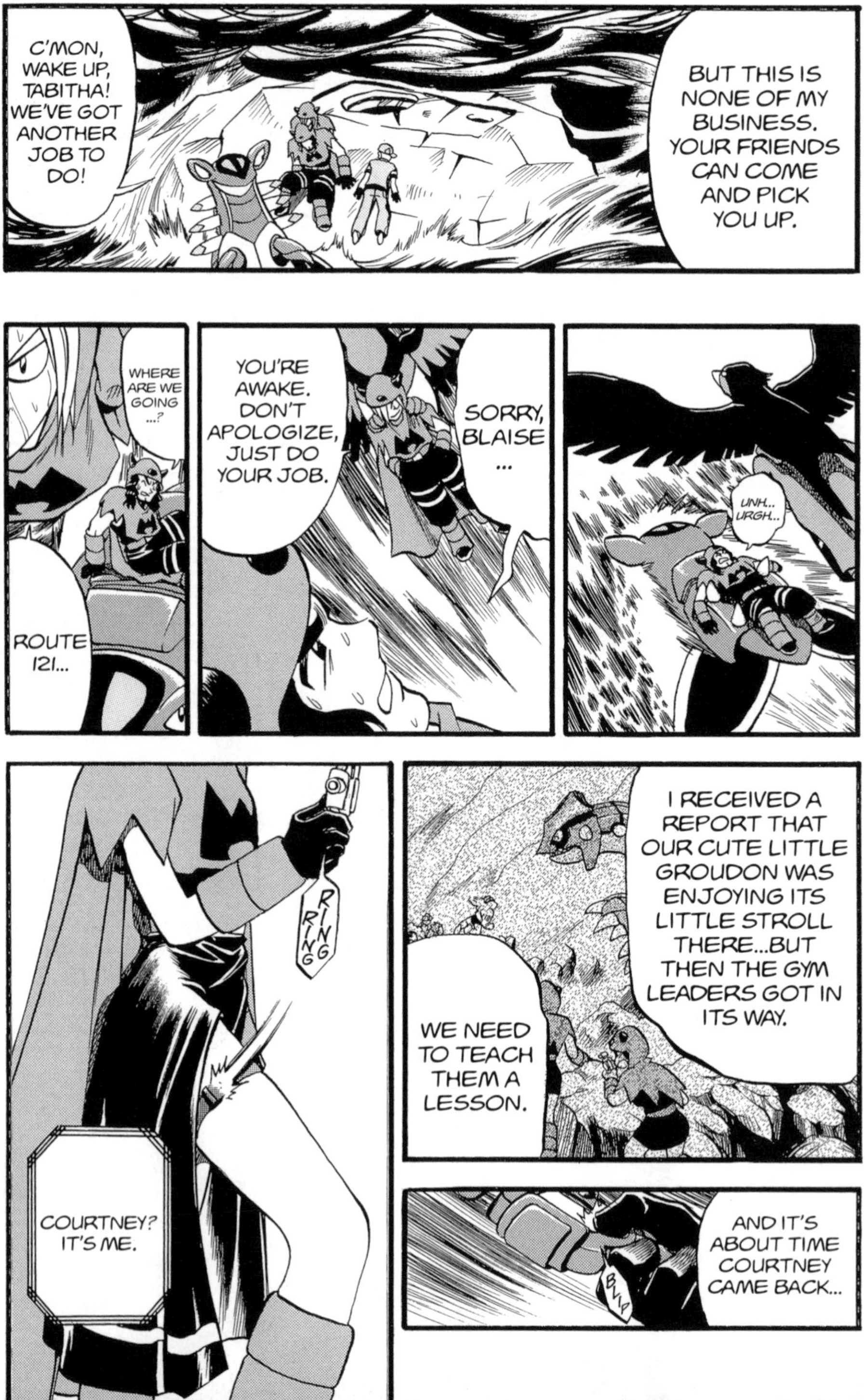
BUT THIS IS NONE OF MY BUSINESS. YOUR FRIENDS CAN COME AND PICK YOU UP.
C'MON, WAKE UP, TABITHA! WE'VE GOT ANOTHER JOB TO DO!
UNH... URGH...
SORRY, BLAISE ...
YOU'RE AWAKE. DON'T APOLOGIZE, JUST DO YOUR JOB.
WHERE ARE WE GOING ...?
ROUTE 121...
I RECEIVED A REPORT THAT OUR CUTE LITTLE GROUDON WAS ENJOYING ITS LITTLE STROLL THERE...BUT THEN THE GYM LEADERS GOT IN ITS WAY.
WE NEED TO TEACH THEM A LESSON.
AND IT'S ABOUT TIME COURTNEY CAME BACK...
BLIP
RING RING
COURTNEY? IT'S ME.

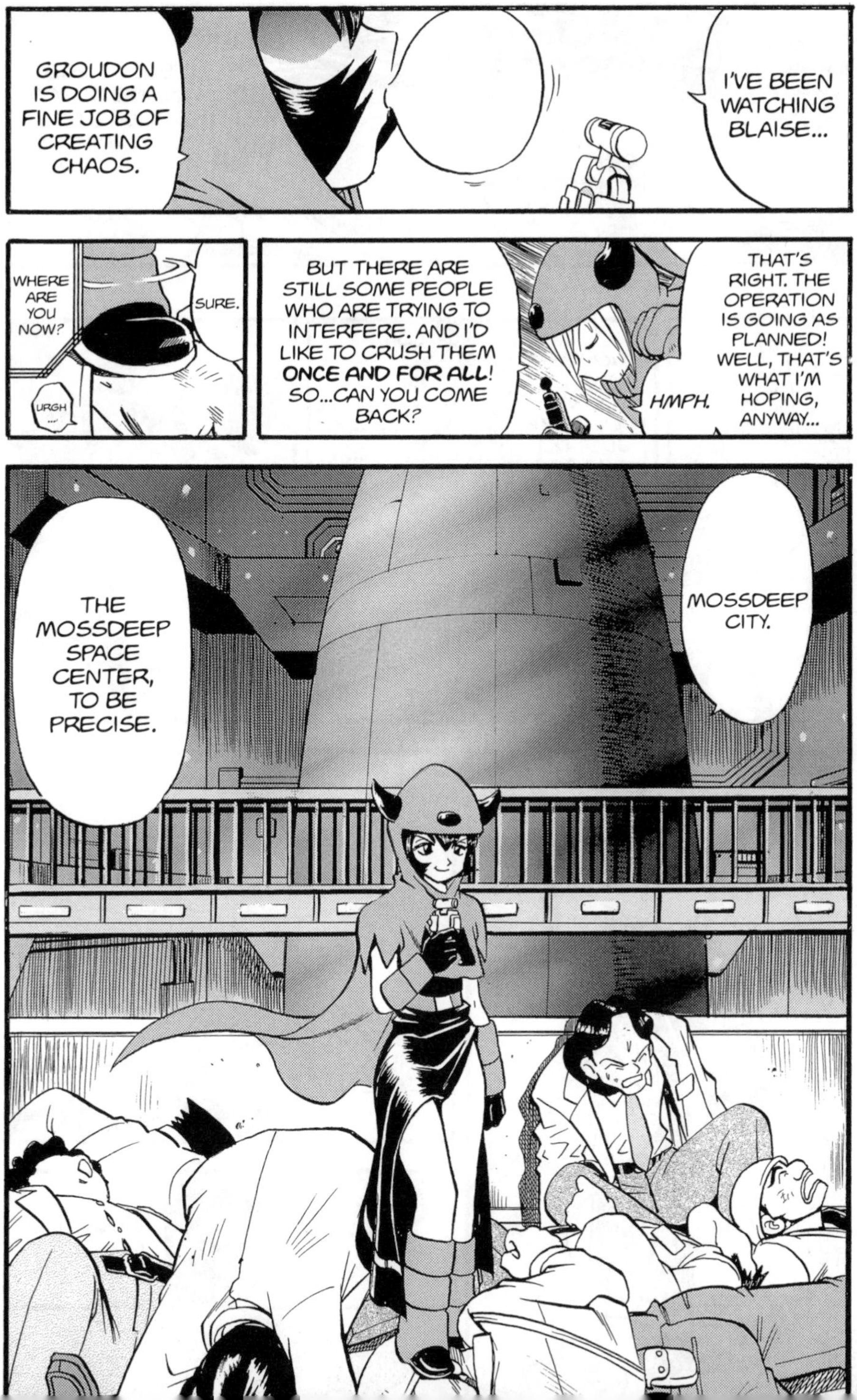

I'VE BEEN WATCHING BLAISE...
GROUDON IS DOING A FINE JOB OF CREATING CHAOS.
THAT'S RIGHT. THE OPERATION IS GOING AS PLANNED! WELL, THAT'S WHAT I'M HOPING, ANYWAY...
HMPH.
BUT THERE ARE STILL SOME PEOPLE WHO ARE TRYING TO INTERFERE. AND I'D LIKE TO CRUSH THEM **ONCE AND FOR ALL**! SO...CAN YOU COME BACK?
SURE.
WHERE ARE YOU NOW?
URGH...
MOSSDEEP CITY.
THE MOSSDEEP SPACE CENTER, TO BE PRECISE.

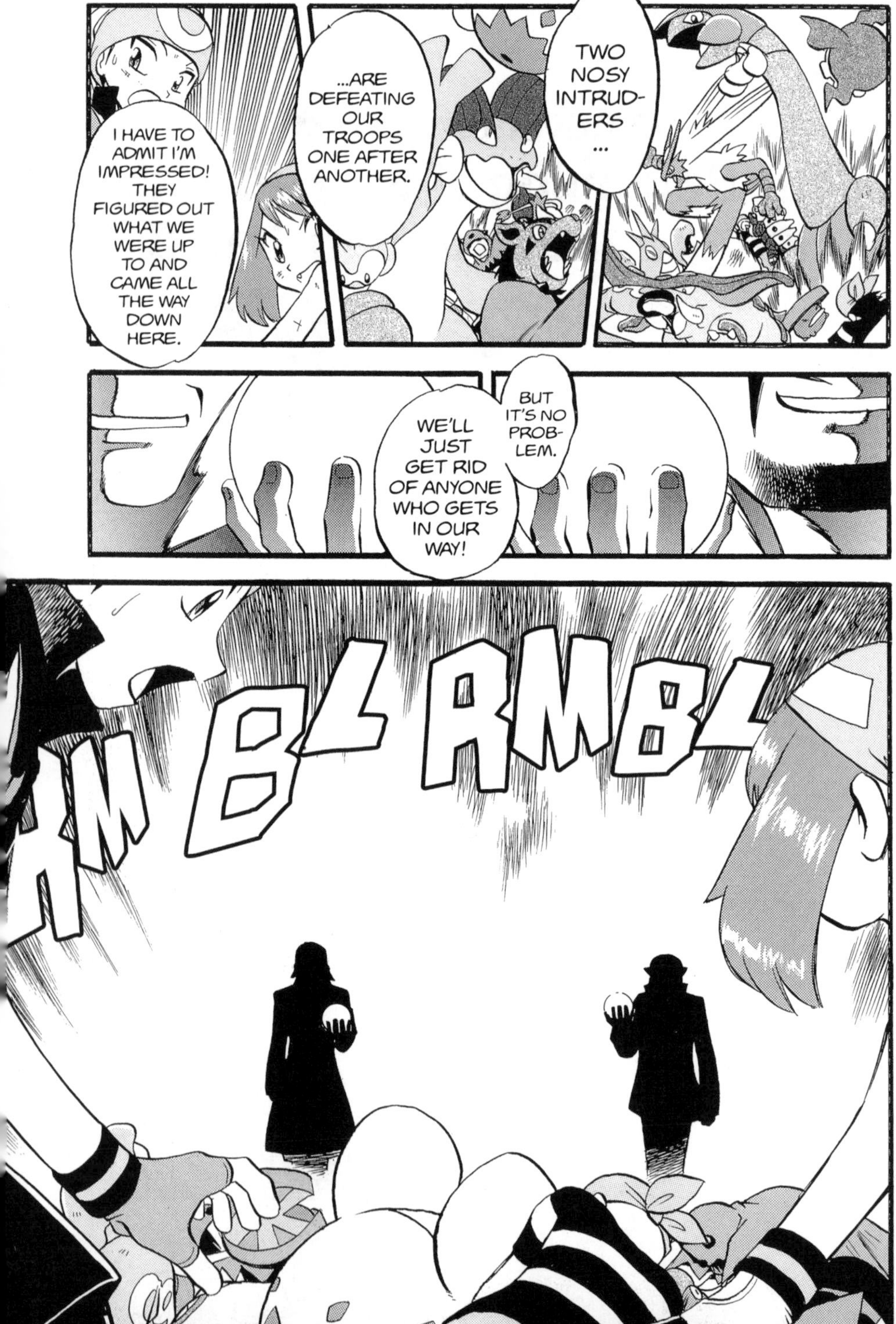
TWO NOSY INTRUDERS...
...ARE DEFEATING OUR TROOPS ONE AFTER ANOTHER.
I HAVE TO ADMIT I'M IMPRESSED! THEY FIGURED OUT WHAT WE WERE UP TO AND CAME ALL THE WAY DOWN HERE.
BUT IT'S NO PROBLEM.
WE'LL JUST GET RID OF ANYONE WHO GETS IN OUR WAY!
RMBL

● Adventure 244 ●
The Beginning of the End with Kyogre and Groudon, Part 8

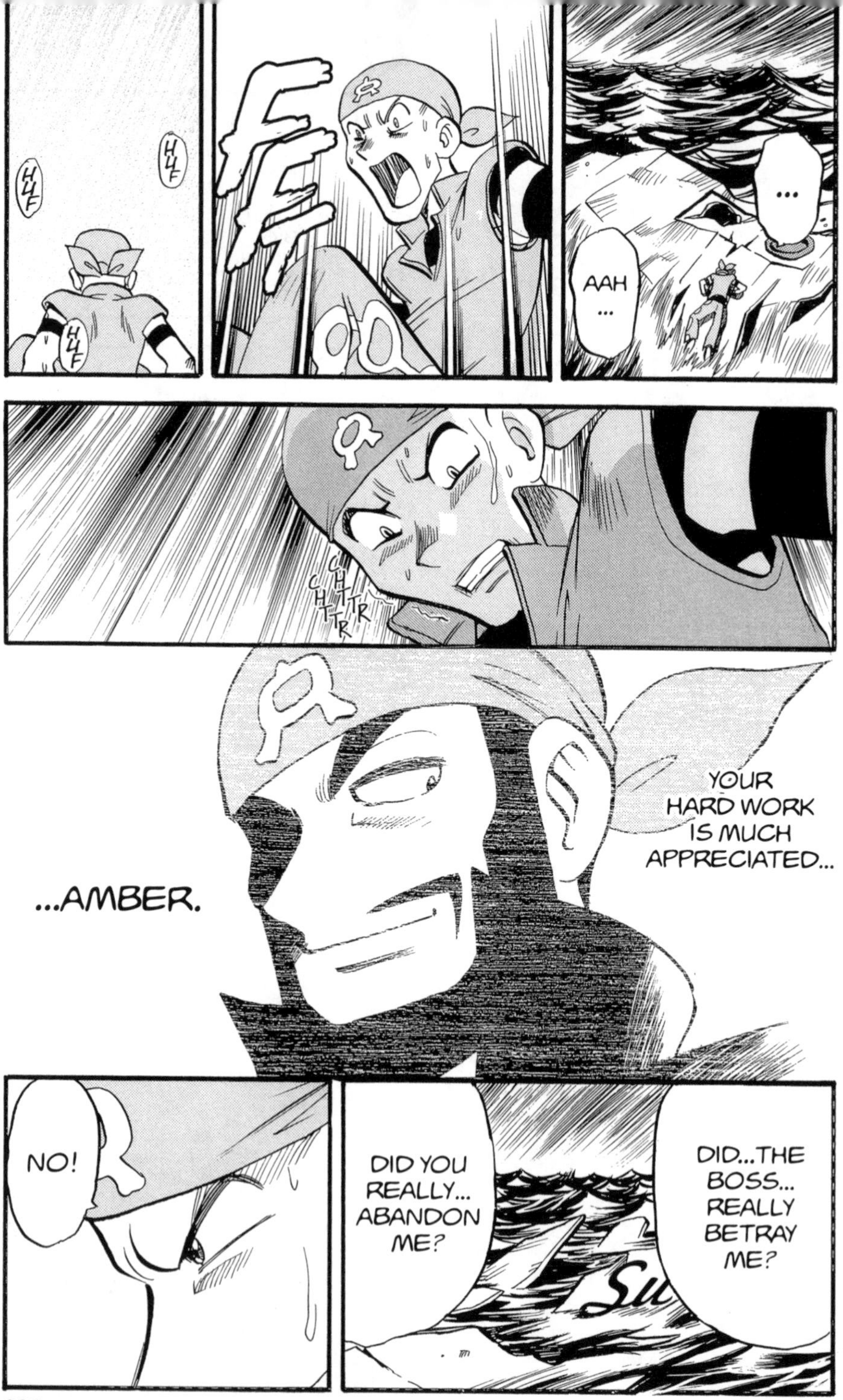
...
AAH ...
HUF
HUF
HUF
CHTTR
CHTTR
YOUR HARD WORK IS MUCH APPRECIATED...
...AMBER.
DID...THE BOSS... REALLY BETRAY ME?
DID YOU REALLY... ABANDON ME?
SU
NO!

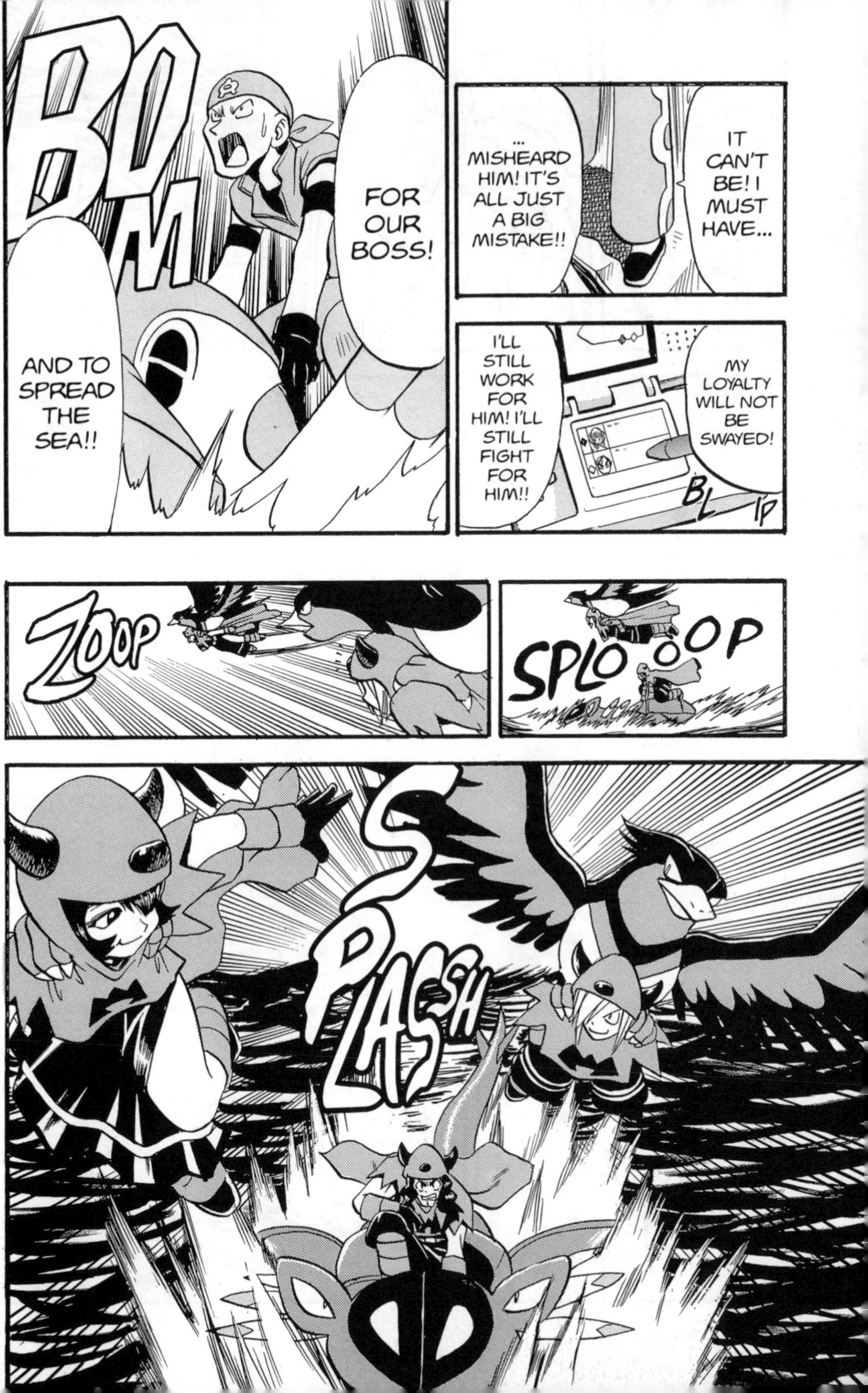
IT CAN'T BE!! I MUST HAVE...
...MISHEARD HIM! IT'S ALL JUST A BIG MISTAKE!!
MY LOYALTY WILL NOT BE SWAYED!
I'LL STILL WORK FOR HIM! I'LL STILL FIGHT FOR HIM!!
BLIP
FOR OUR BOSS!
BOOM
AND TO SPREAD THE SEA!!
SPLOOOP
ZOOP
SPLASH

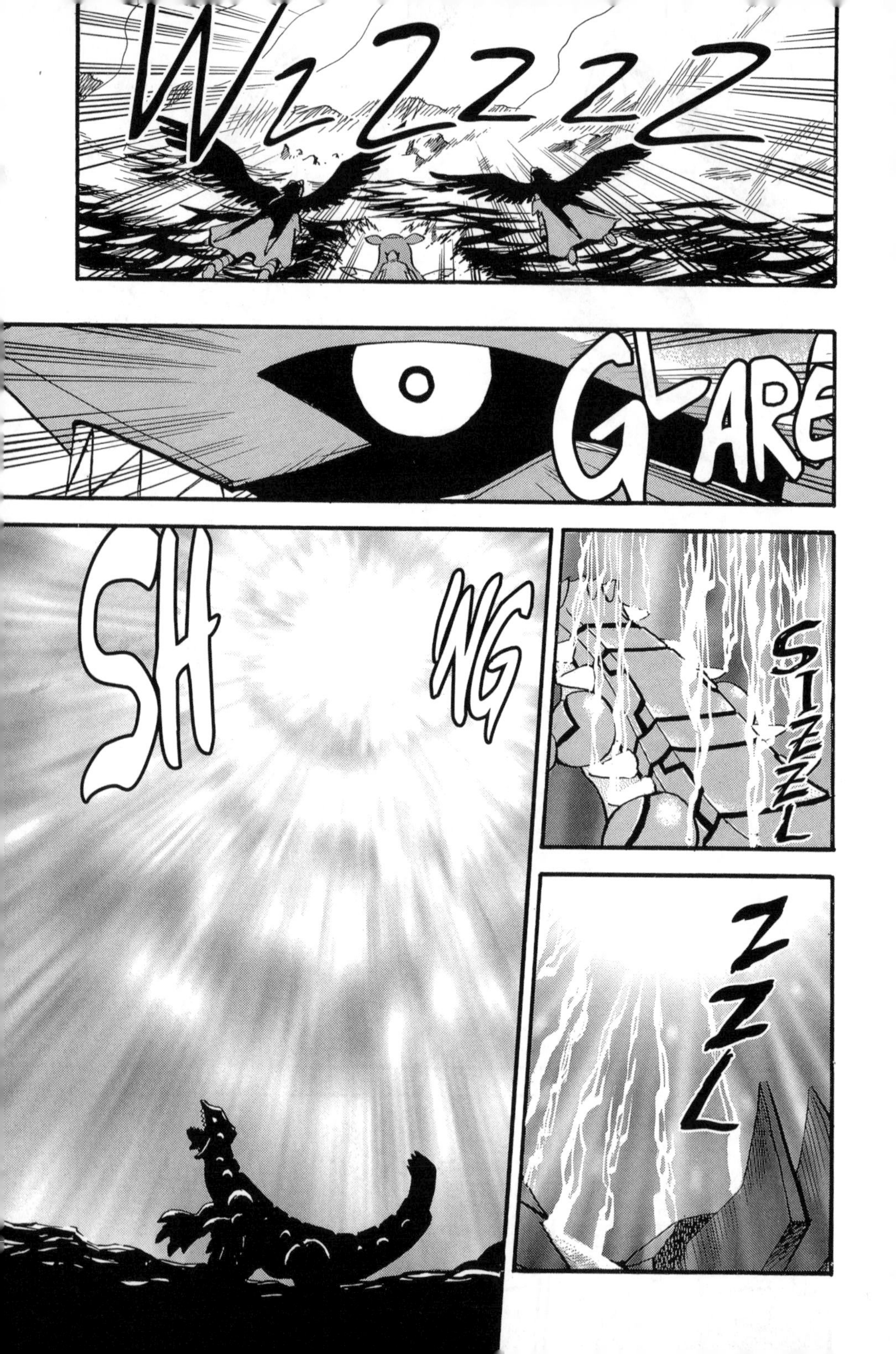
WZZZZZ
GLARE
SIZZL
ZZL
SHING

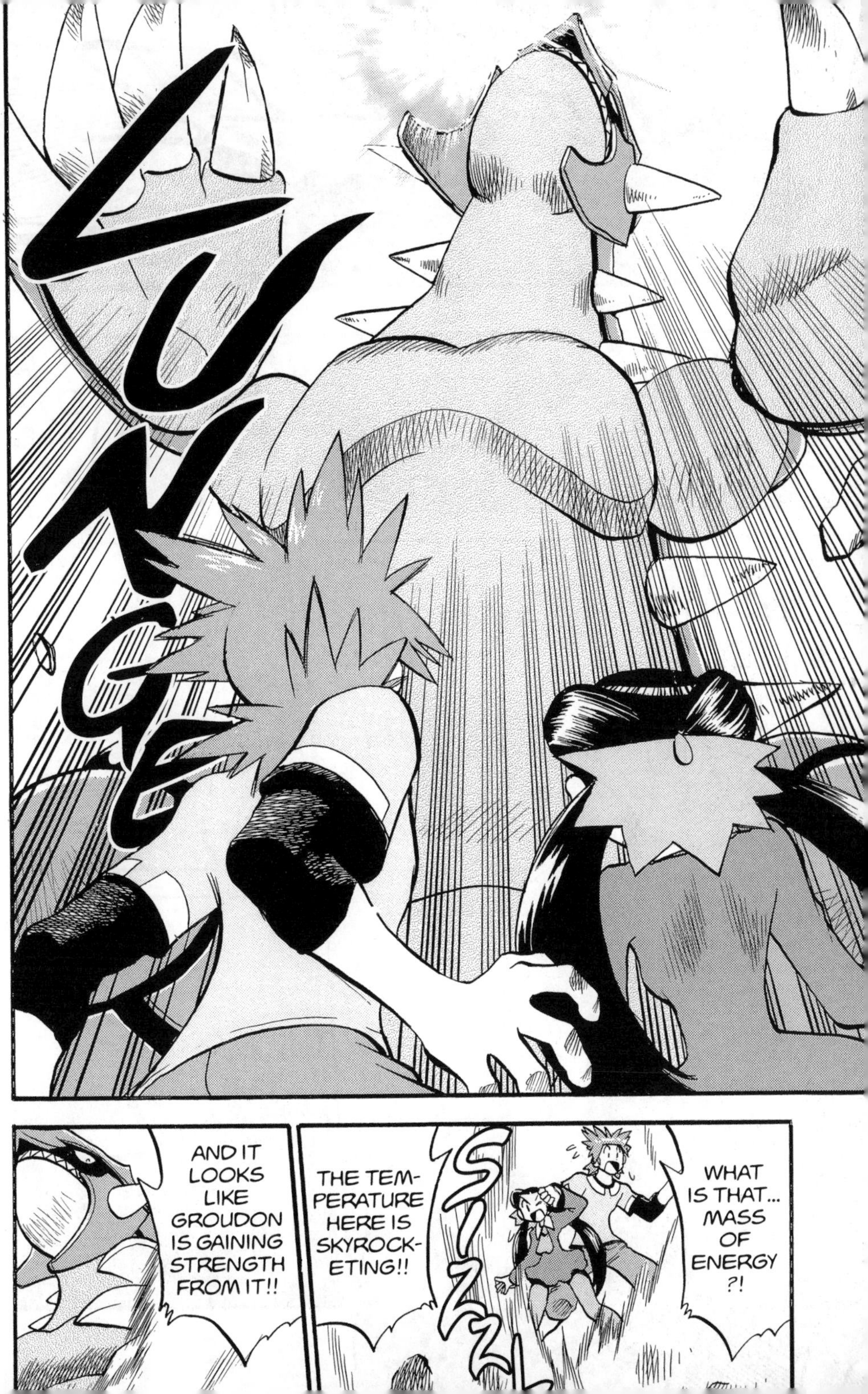
LUNGE
WHAT IS THAT... MASS OF ENERGY?!
SIZZZL
THE TEM-PERATURE HERE IS SKYROCK-ETING!!
AND IT LOOKS LIKE GROUDON IS GAINING STRENGTH FROM IT!!

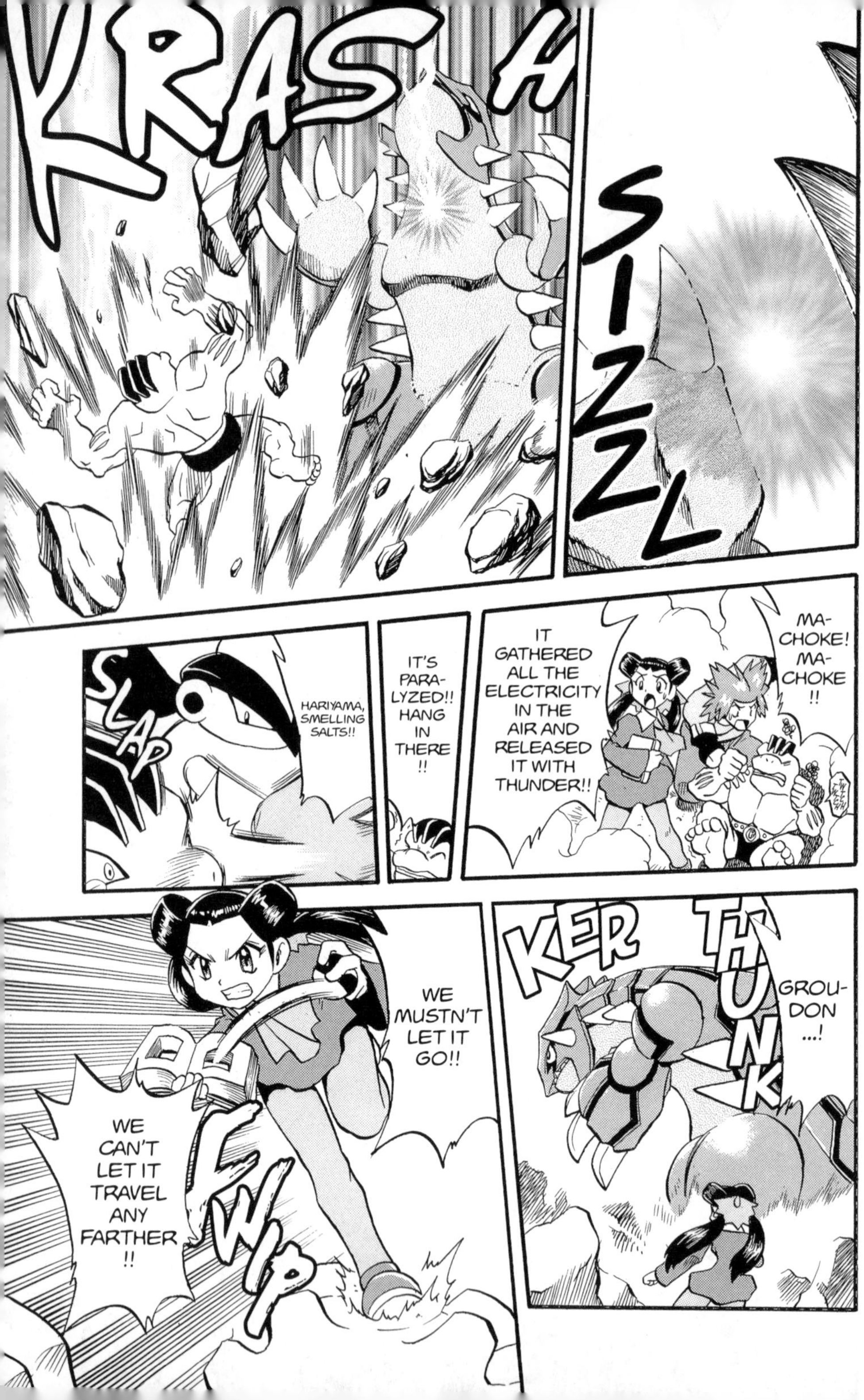
SIZZLE
KRASH
MA-CHOKE! MA-CHOKE!!
IT GATHERED ALL THE ELECTRICITY IN THE AIR AND RELEASED IT WITH THUNDER!!
IT'S PARALYZED!! HANG IN THERE!!
HARIYAMA, SMELLING SALTS!!
SLAP
KER THUNK
GROUDON...!
WE MUSTN'T LET IT GO!!
WE CAN'T LET IT TRAVEL ANY FARTHER!!
WHIP

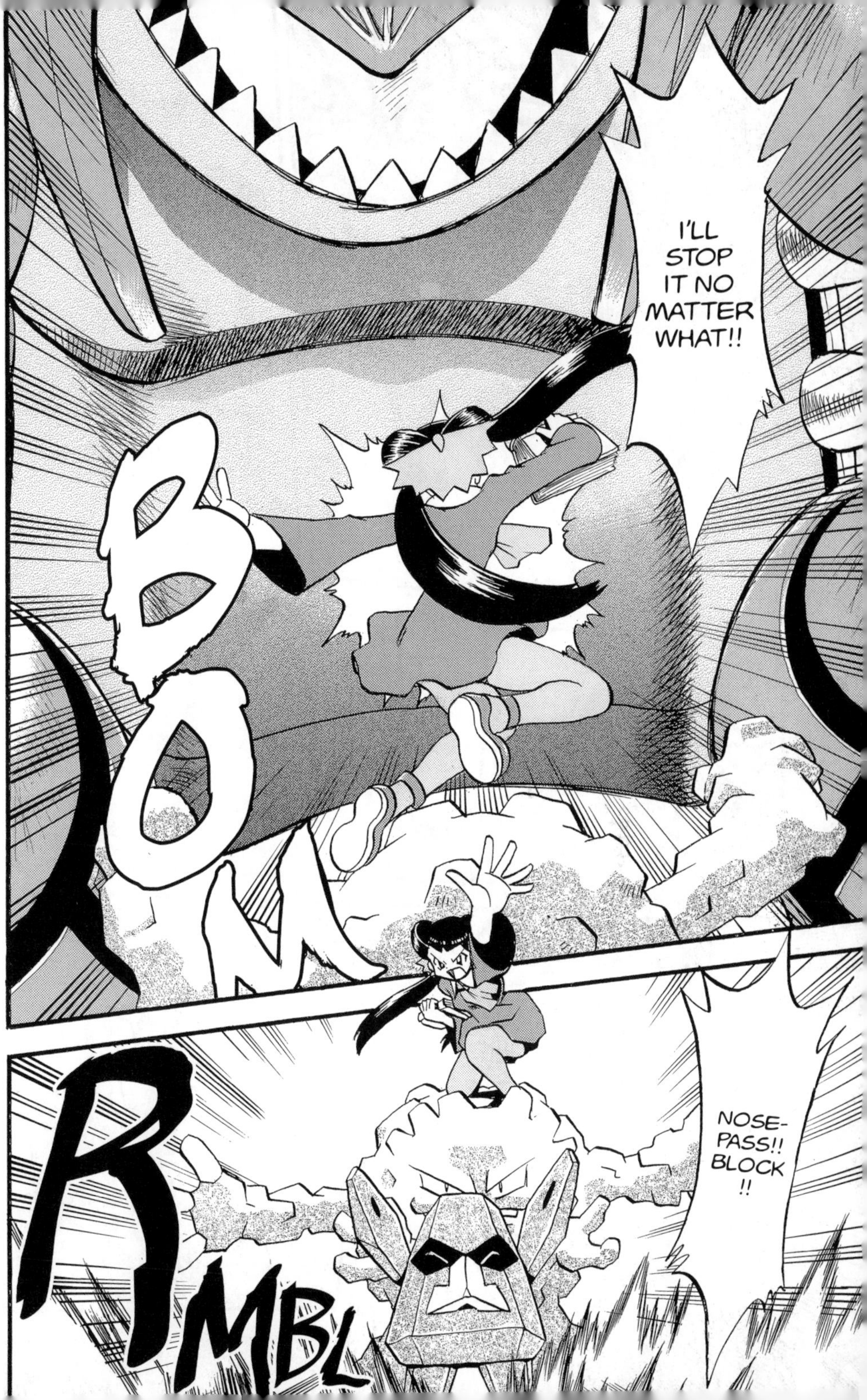
I'LL STOP IT NO MATTER WHAT!!
BOM
NOSE-PASS!! BLOCK!!
RMBL

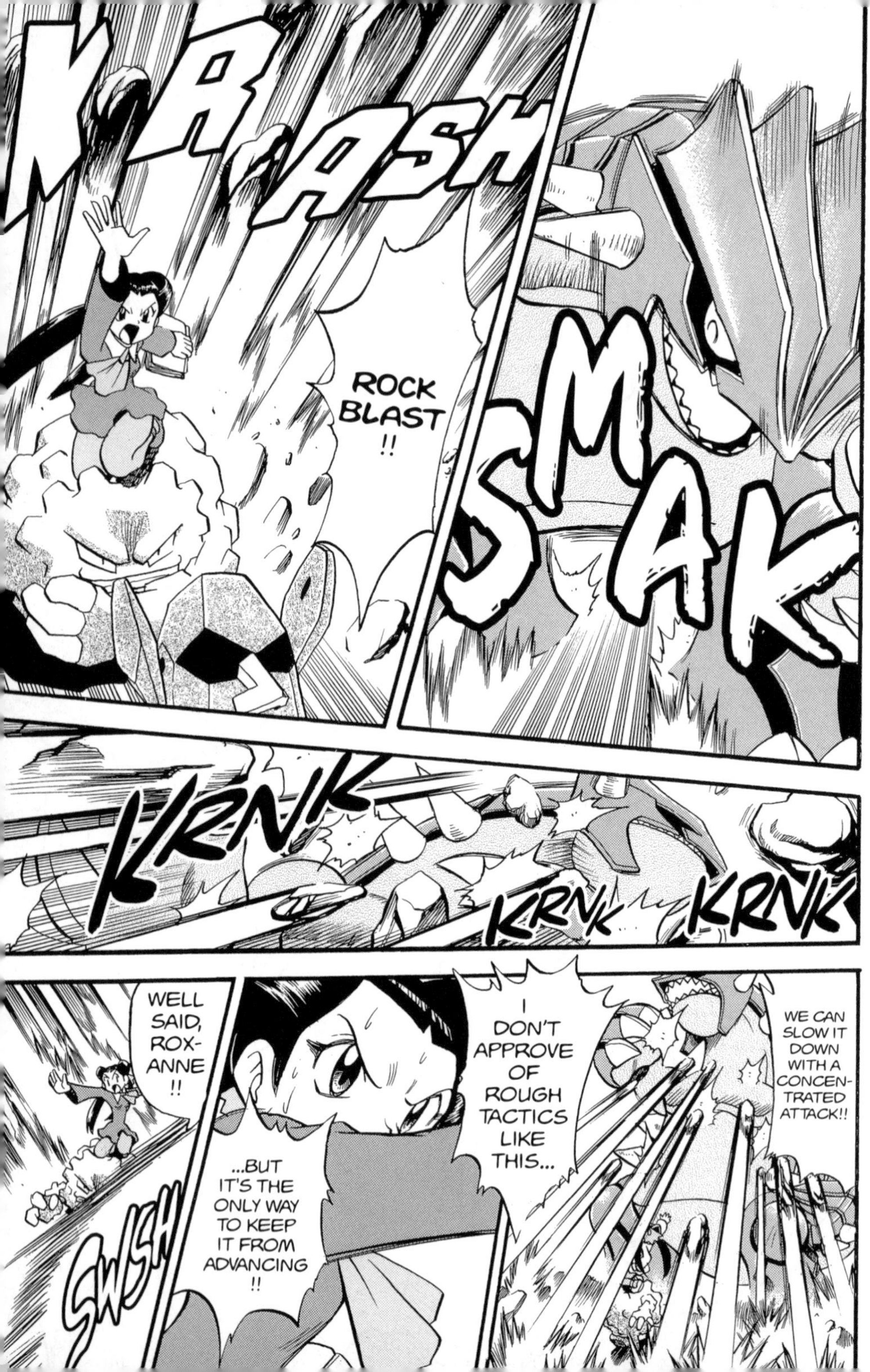
SMAK
KRASH
ROCK BLAST !!
KRNK
KRNK
KRNK
WE CAN SLOW IT DOWN WITH A CONCEN-TRATED ATTACK!!
I DON'T APPROVE OF ROUGH TACTICS LIKE THIS...
...BUT IT'S THE ONLY WAY TO KEEP IT FROM ADVANCING !!
WELL SAID, ROX-ANNE !!
SWISH

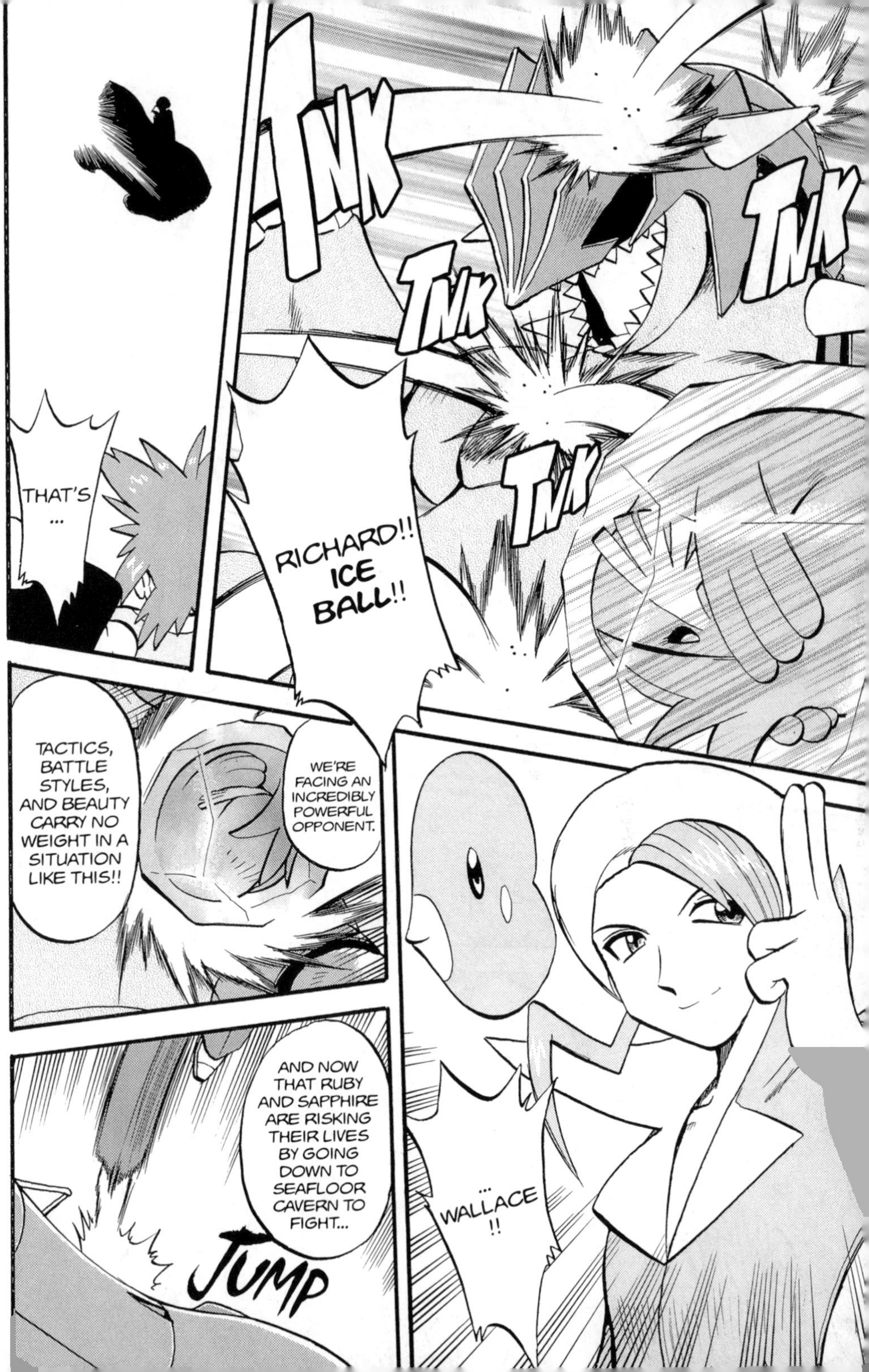
TNK
TNK
TNK
TNK
RICHARD!! ICE BALL!!
THAT'S ...
... WALLACE !!
WE'RE FACING AN INCREDIBLY POWERFUL OPPONENT.
TACTICS, BATTLE STYLES, AND BEAUTY CARRY NO WEIGHT IN A SITUATION LIKE THIS!!
AND NOW THAT RUBY AND SAPPHIRE ARE RISKING THEIR LIVES BY GOING DOWN TO SEAFLOOR CAVERN TO FIGHT...
JUMP

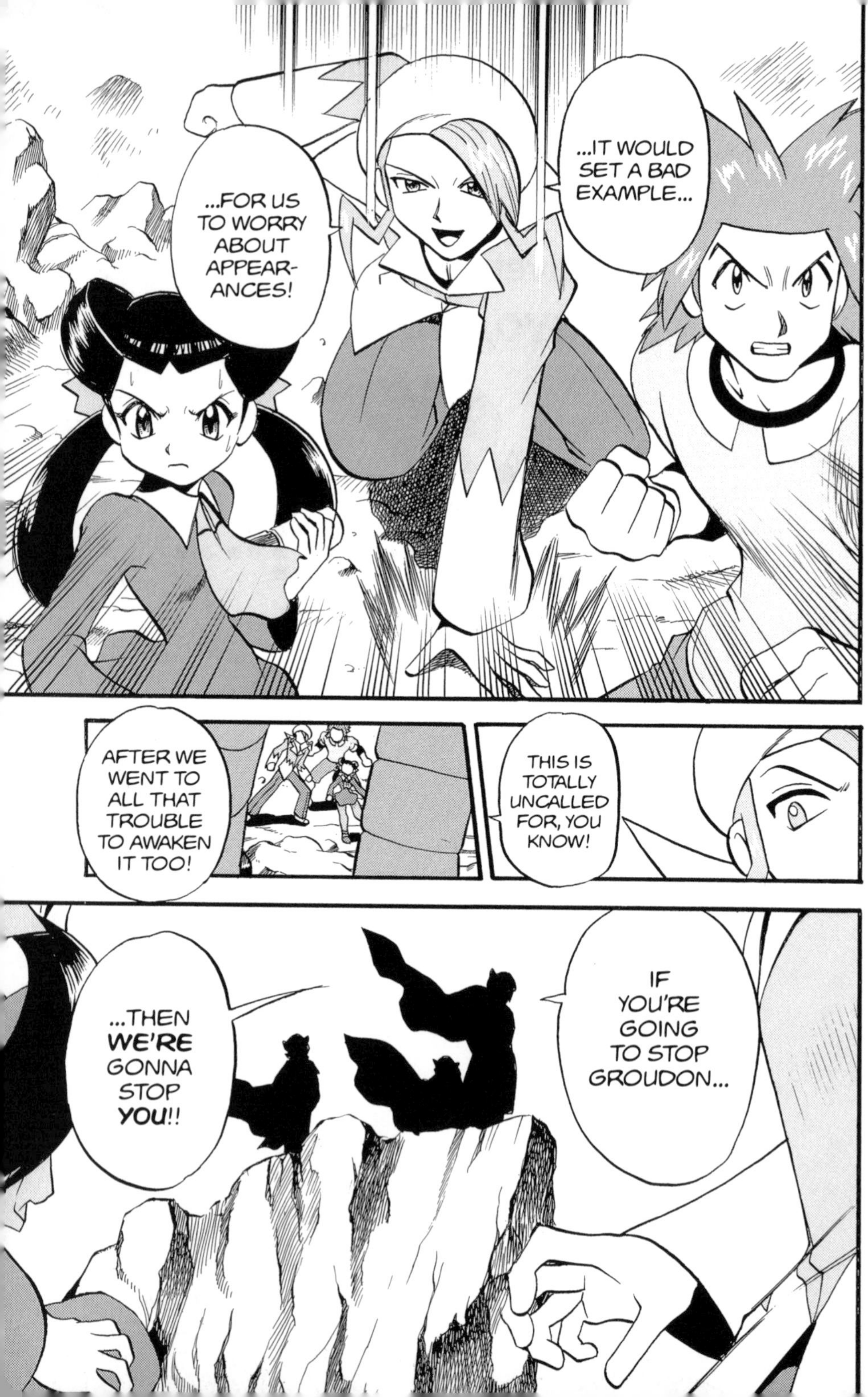
...IT WOULD SET A BAD EXAMPLE...
...FOR US TO WORRY ABOUT APPEARANCES!
THIS IS TOTALLY UNCALLED FOR, YOU KNOW!
AFTER WE WENT TO ALL THAT TROUBLE TO AWAKEN IT TOO!
IF YOU'RE GOING TO STOP GROUDON...
...THEN **WE'RE** GONNA STOP **YOU**!!

● Adventure 245 ●
Bravo, Vibrava

Pokémon™ Adventures Ruby & Sapphire

The Fourth Chapter

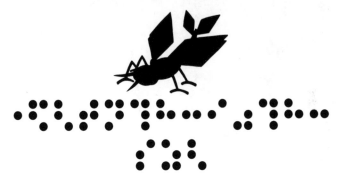

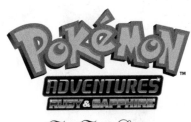

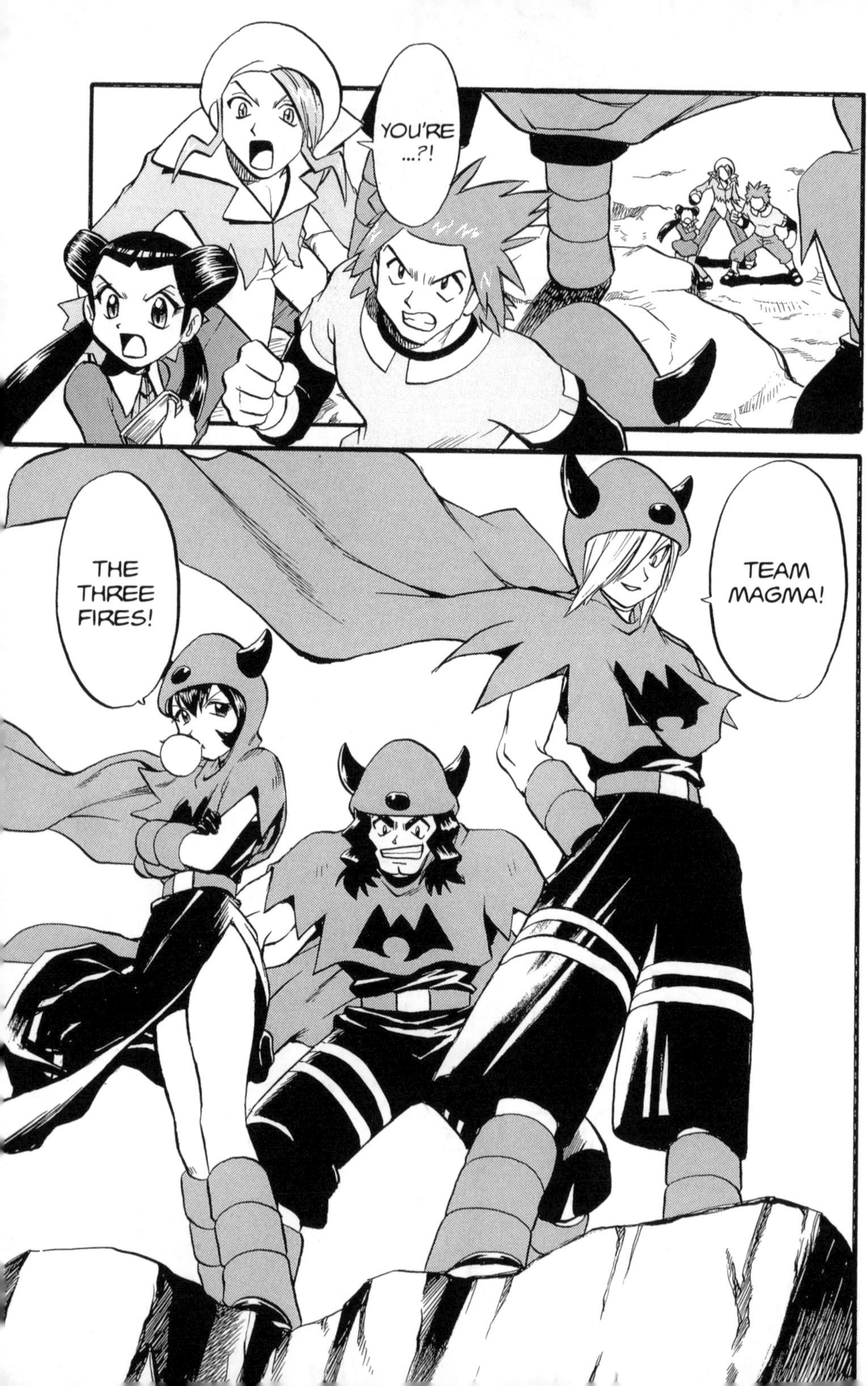
YOU'RE ...?!
TEAM MAGMA!
THE THREE FIRES!

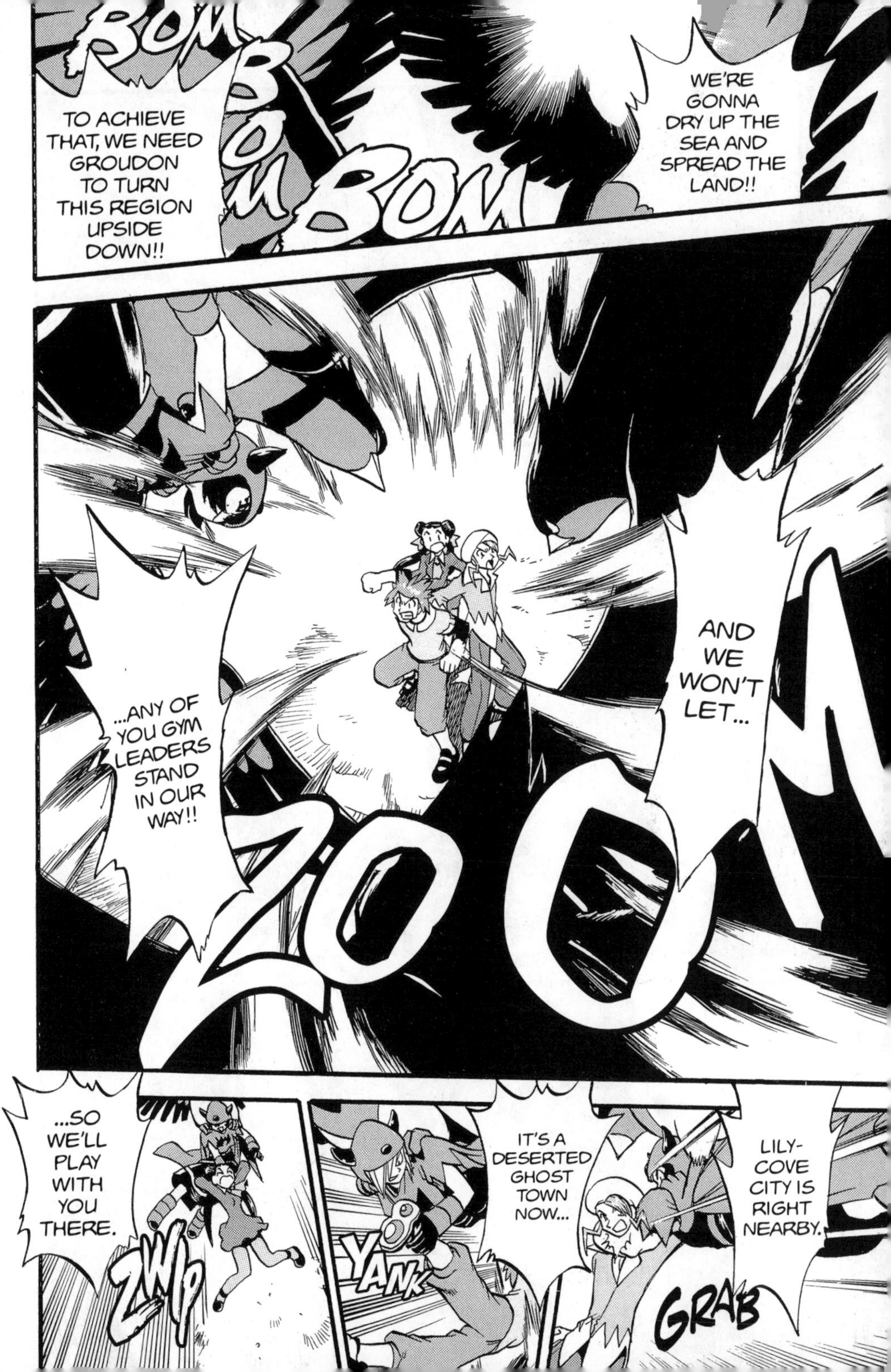
WE'RE GONNA DRY UP THE SEA AND SPREAD THE LAND!!
BOM BOM BOM
TO ACHIEVE THAT, WE NEED GROUDON TO TURN THIS REGION UPSIDE DOWN!!
AND WE WON'T LET...
...ANY OF YOU GYM LEADERS STAND IN OUR WAY!!
ZOOM
LILY-COVE CITY IS RIGHT NEARBY.
GRAB
IT'S A DESERTED GHOST TOWN NOW...
YANK
...SO WE'LL PLAY WITH YOU THERE.
ZWIP

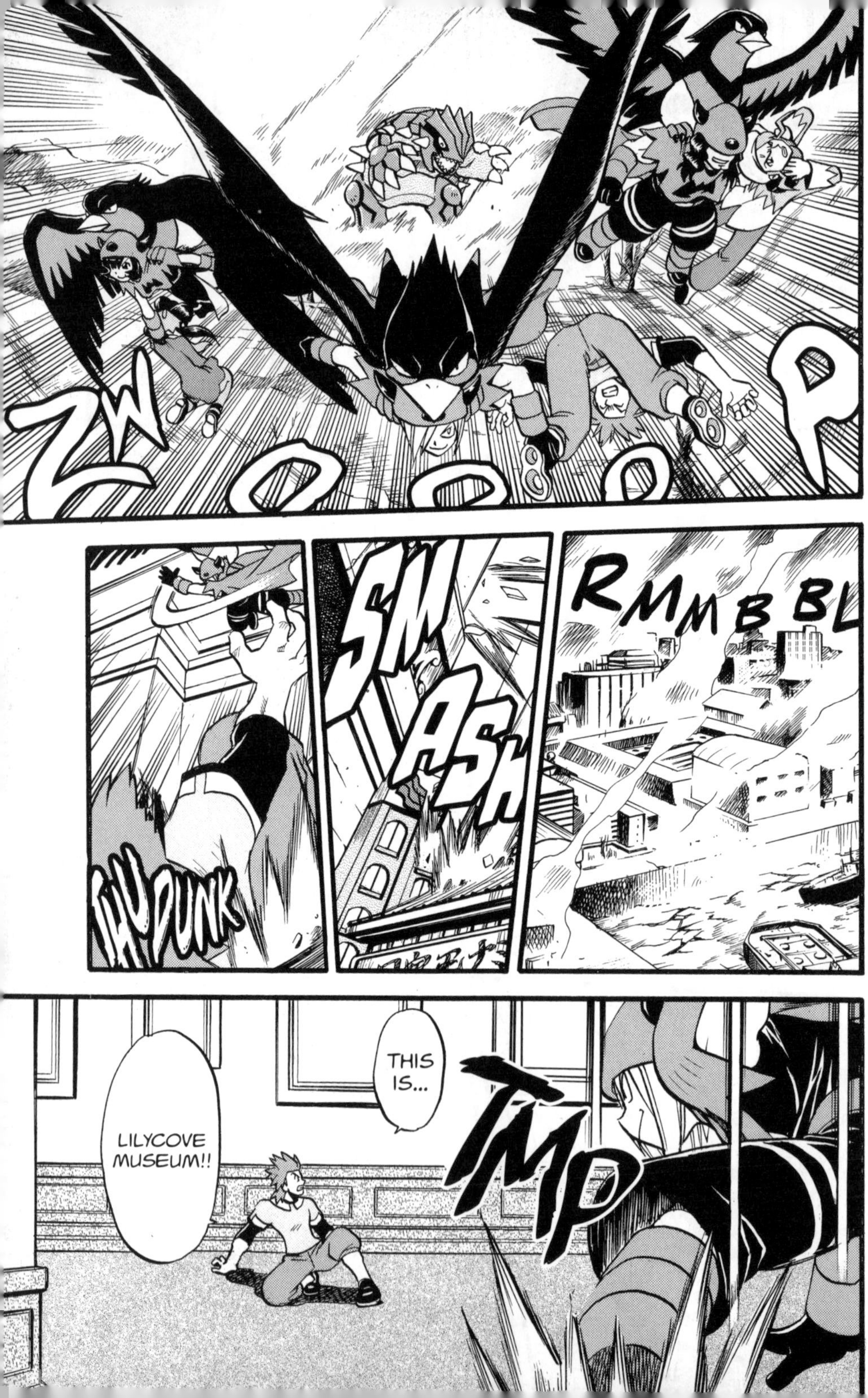
ZWOOOP
RMMBBL
SMASH
THUDUNK
TMP
THIS IS...
LILYCOVE MUSEUM!!

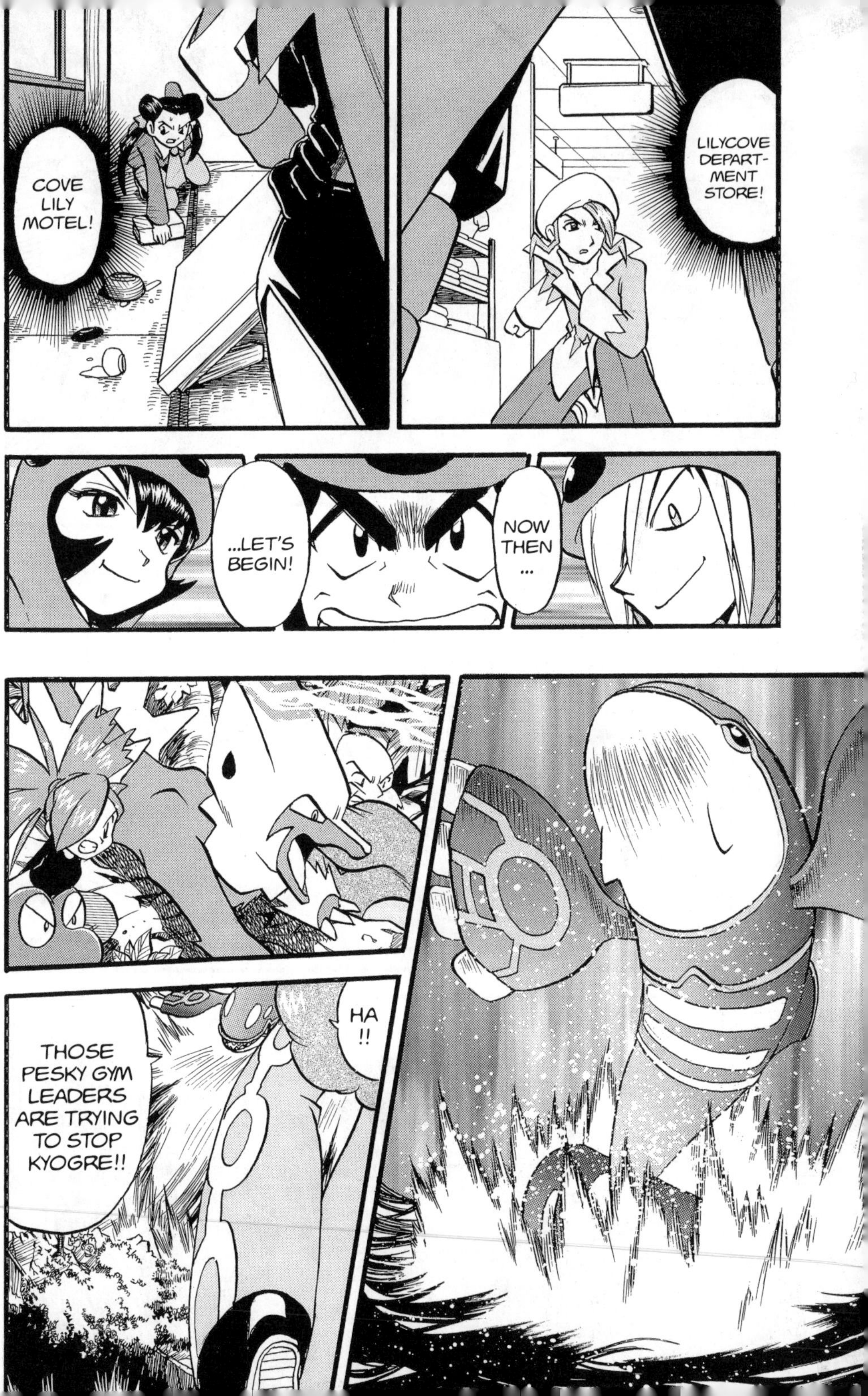

LILYCOVE DEPARTMENT STORE!
COVE LILY MOTEL!
NOW THEN ...
...LET'S BEGIN!
HA !!
THOSE PESKY GYM LEADERS ARE TRYING TO STOP KYOGRE!!

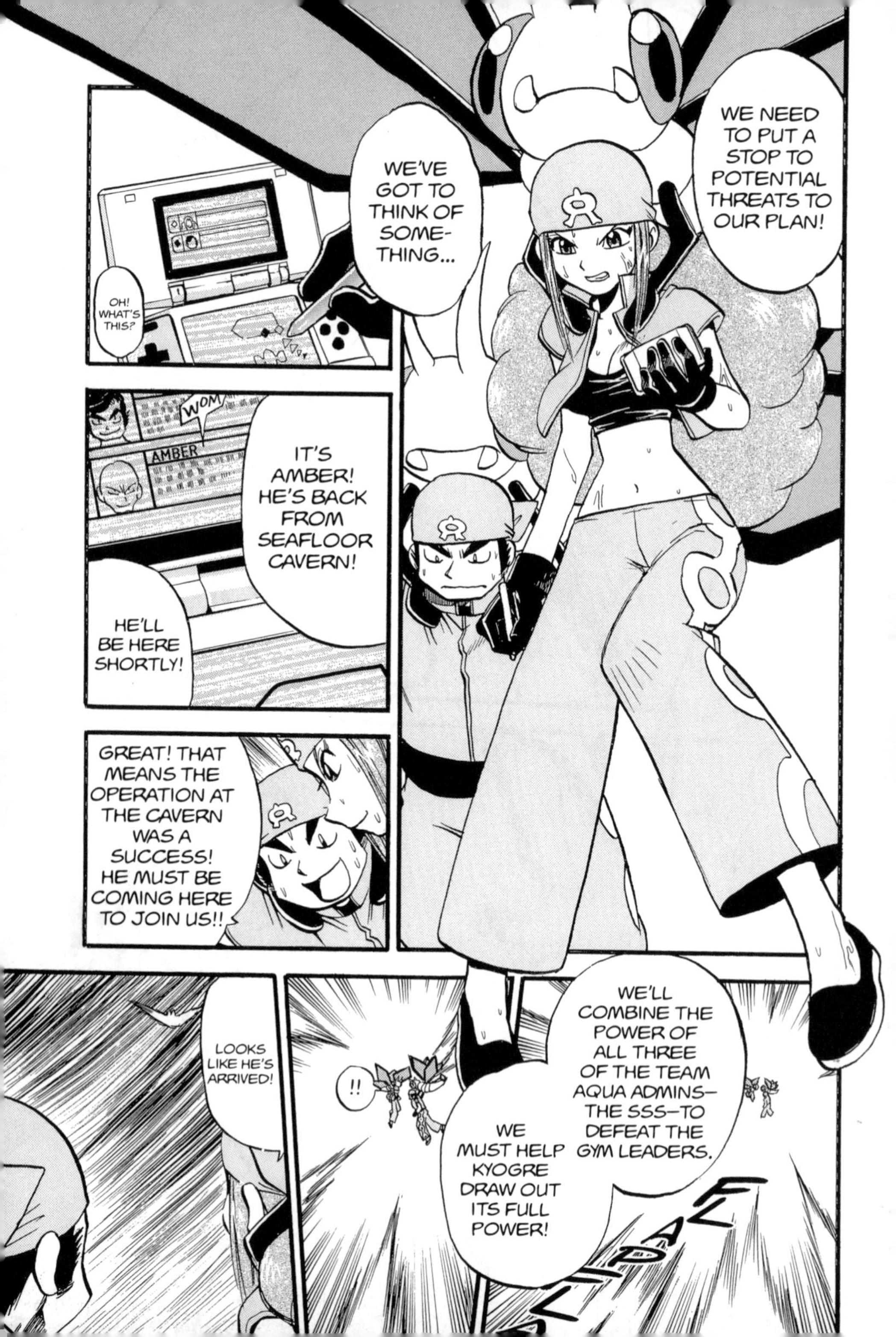
WE NEED TO PUT A STOP TO POTENTIAL THREATS TO OUR PLAN!
WE'VE GOT TO THINK OF SOME-THING...
OH! WHAT'S THIS?
WOM
AMBER
IT'S AMBER! HE'S BACK FROM SEAFLOOR CAVERN!
HE'LL BE HERE SHORTLY!
GREAT! THAT MEANS THE OPERATION AT THE CAVERN WAS A SUCCESS! HE MUST BE COMING HERE TO JOIN US!!
WE'LL COMBINE THE POWER OF ALL THREE OF THE TEAM AQUA ADMINS—THE SSS—TO DEFEAT THE GYM LEADERS.
WE MUST HELP KYOGRE DRAW OUT ITS FULL POWER!
!!
FLAP
LOOKS LIKE HE'S ARRIVED!

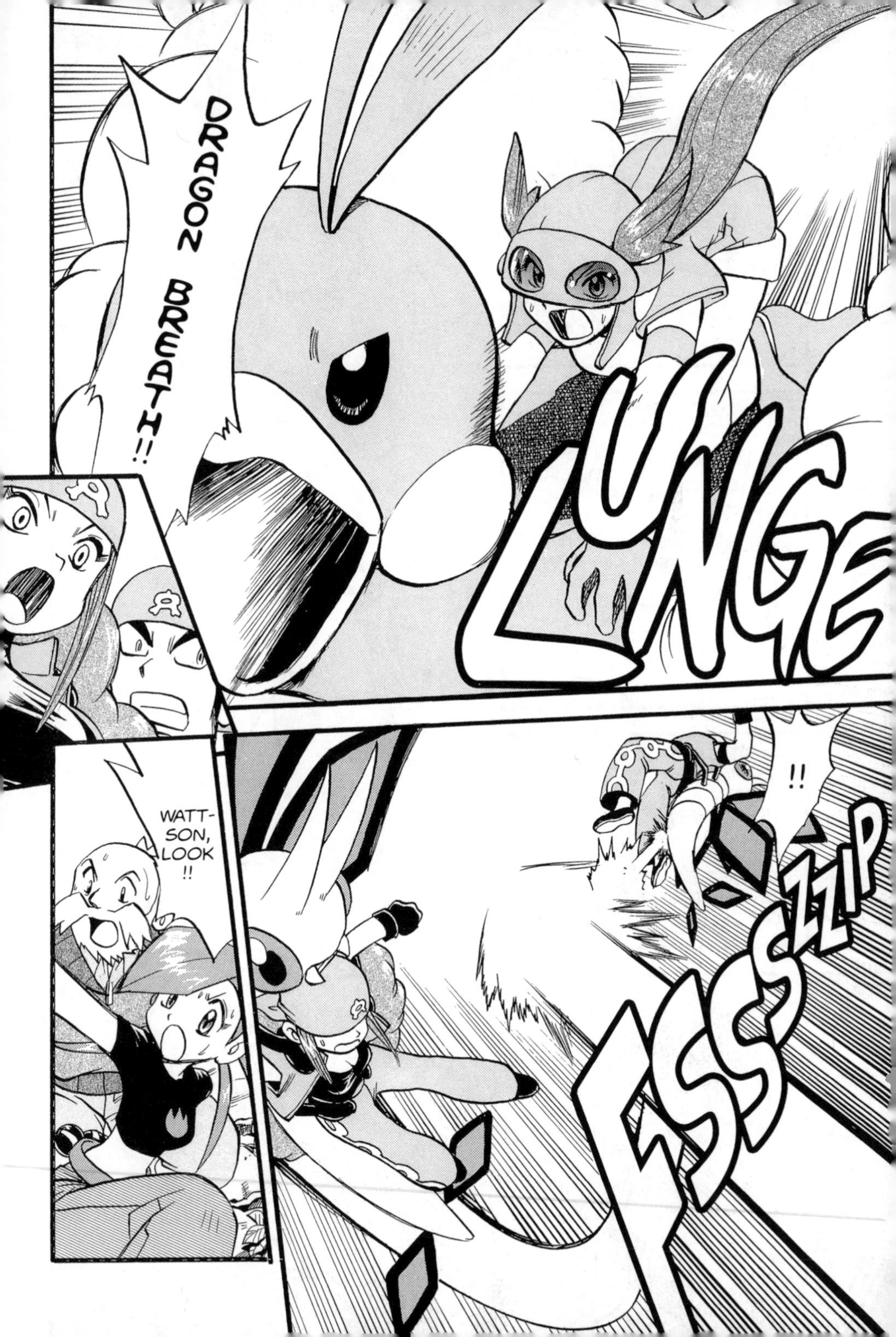
DRAGON BREATH!!
LUNGE
!!
FSSSZZIP
WATTSON, LOOK!!

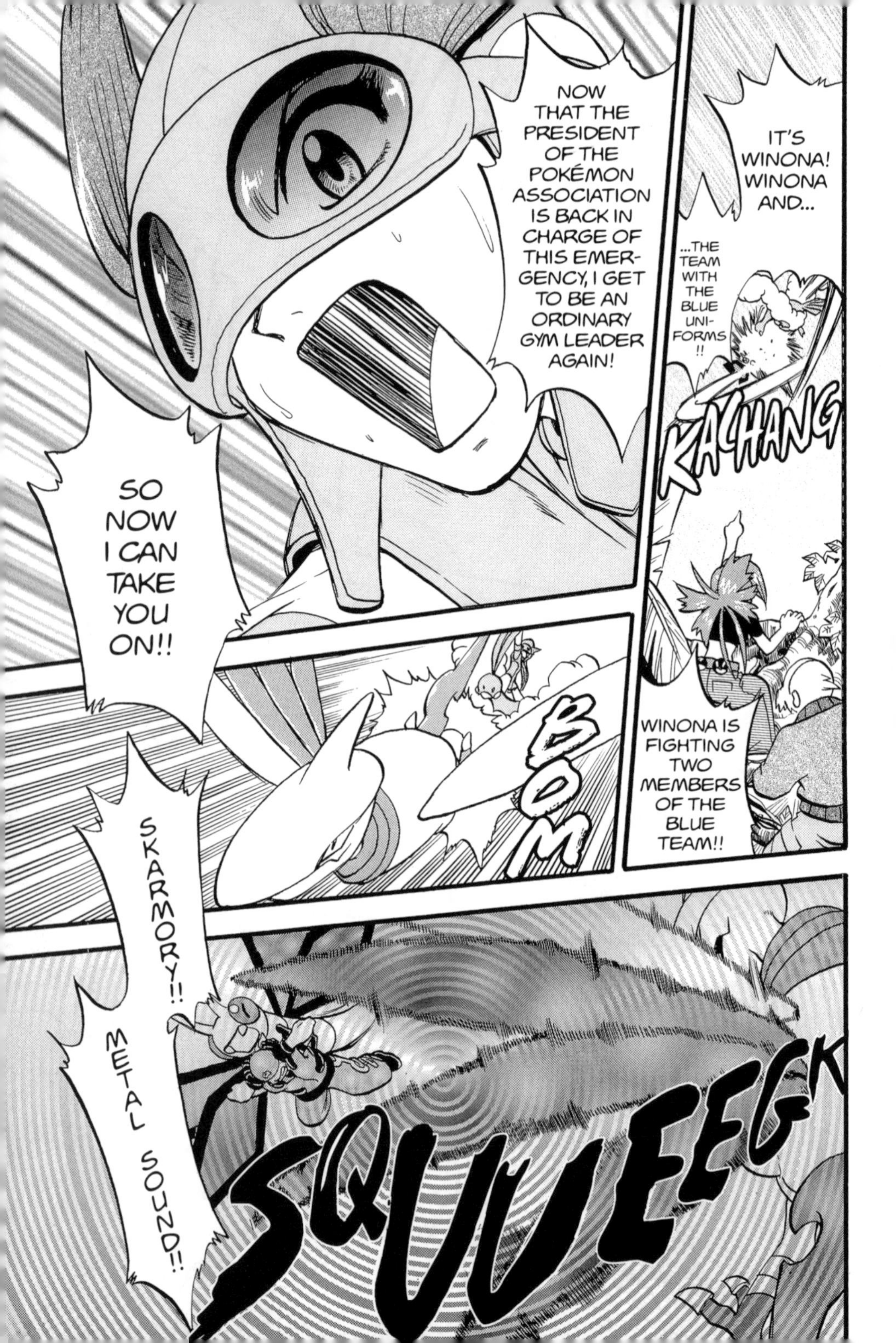
IT'S WINONA! WINONA AND...
...THE TEAM WITH THE BLUE UNI-FORMS!!
KACHANG
WINONA IS FIGHTING TWO MEMBERS OF THE BLUE TEAM!!
NOW THAT THE PRESIDENT OF THE POKÉMON ASSOCIATION IS BACK IN CHARGE OF THIS EMER-GENCY, I GET TO BE AN ORDINARY GYM LEADER AGAIN!
SO NOW I CAN TAKE YOU ON!!
BOOM
SKARMORY!!
METAL SOUND!!
SQUEEEGK

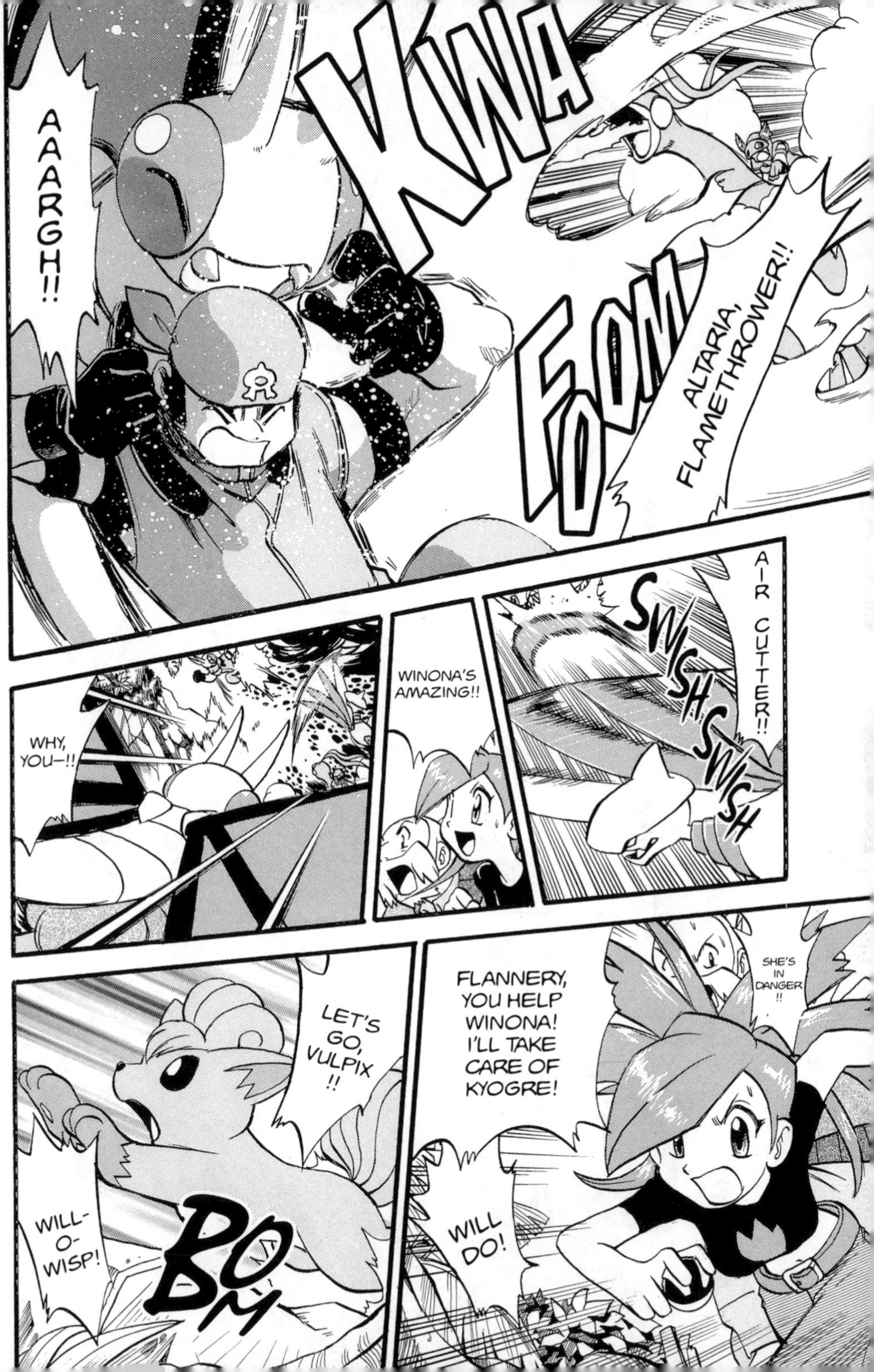
KWA
ALTARIA, FLAMETHROWER!!
FOOM
AAAARGH!!
AIR CUTTER!!
SWISH SWISH SWISH
WINONA'S AMAZING!!
WHY, YOU—!!
SHE'S IN DANGER!!
FLANNERY, YOU HELP WINONA! I'LL TAKE CARE OF KYOGRE!
WILL DO!
LET'S GO, VULPIX!!
WILL-O-WISP!
BOOM

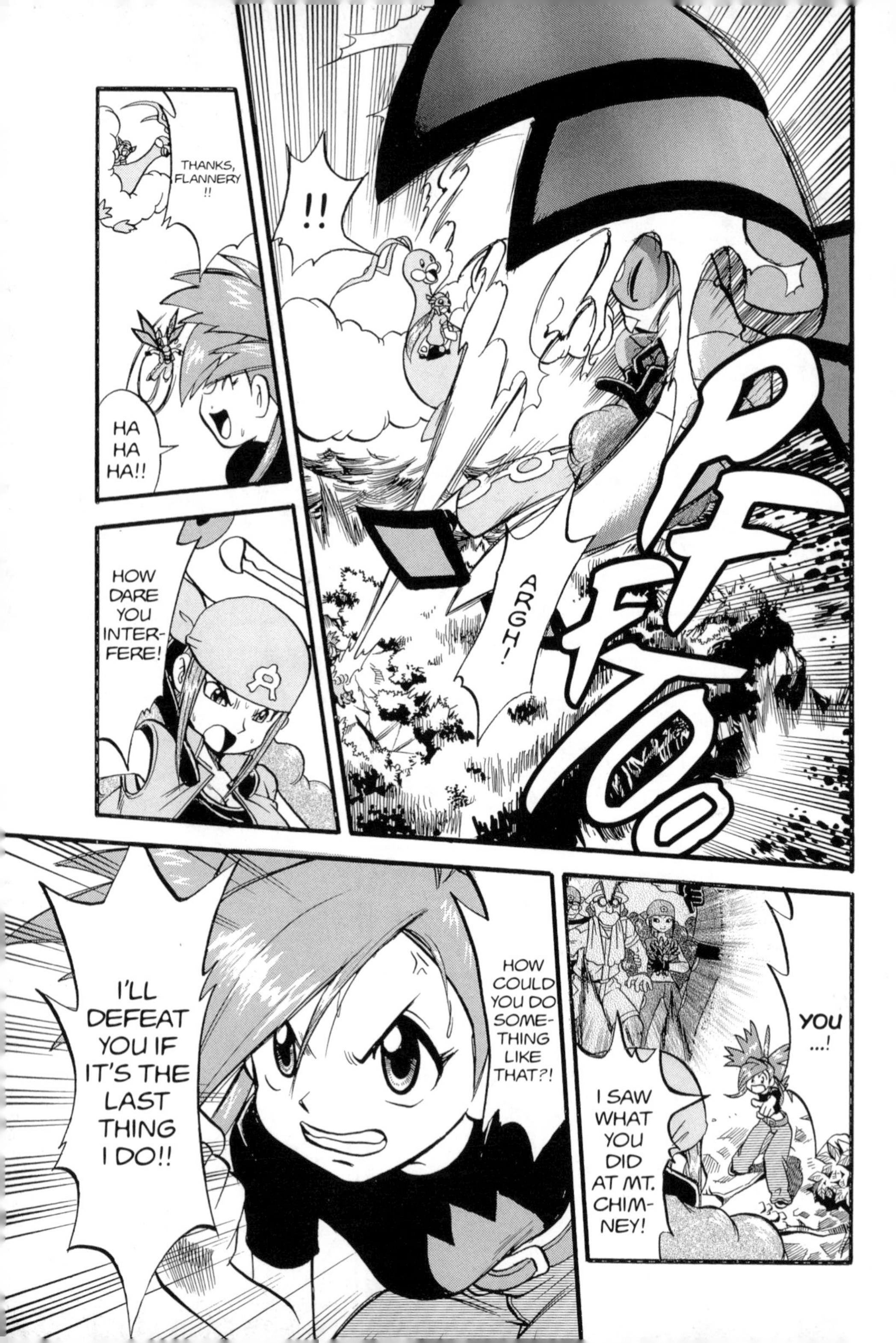
!!
ARGH!
PFFZOO
THANKS, FLANNERY!!
HA HA HA!!
HOW DARE YOU INTERFERE!
YOU...!
I SAW WHAT YOU DID AT MT. CHIMNEY!
HOW COULD YOU DO SOMETHING LIKE THAT?!
I'LL DEFEAT YOU IF IT'S THE LAST THING I DO!!

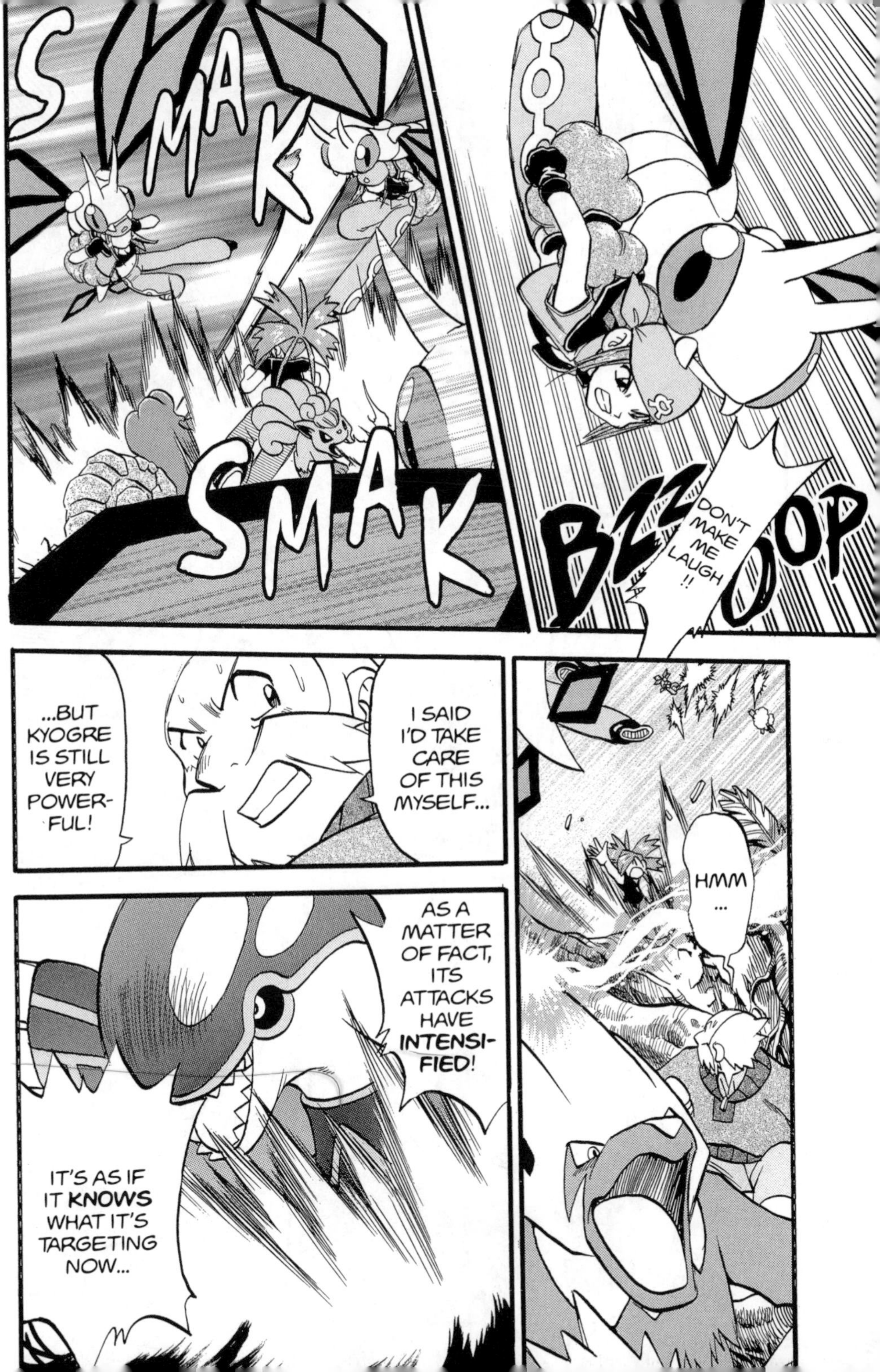
BZZOOP
DON'T MAKE ME LAUGH!!
SMAK
SMAK
HMM...
I SAID I'D TAKE CARE OF THIS MYSELF...
...BUT KYOGRE IS STILL VERY POWER-FUL!
AS A MATTER OF FACT, ITS ATTACKS HAVE **INTENSI-FIED**!
IT'S AS IF IT **KNOWS** WHAT IT'S TARGETING NOW...

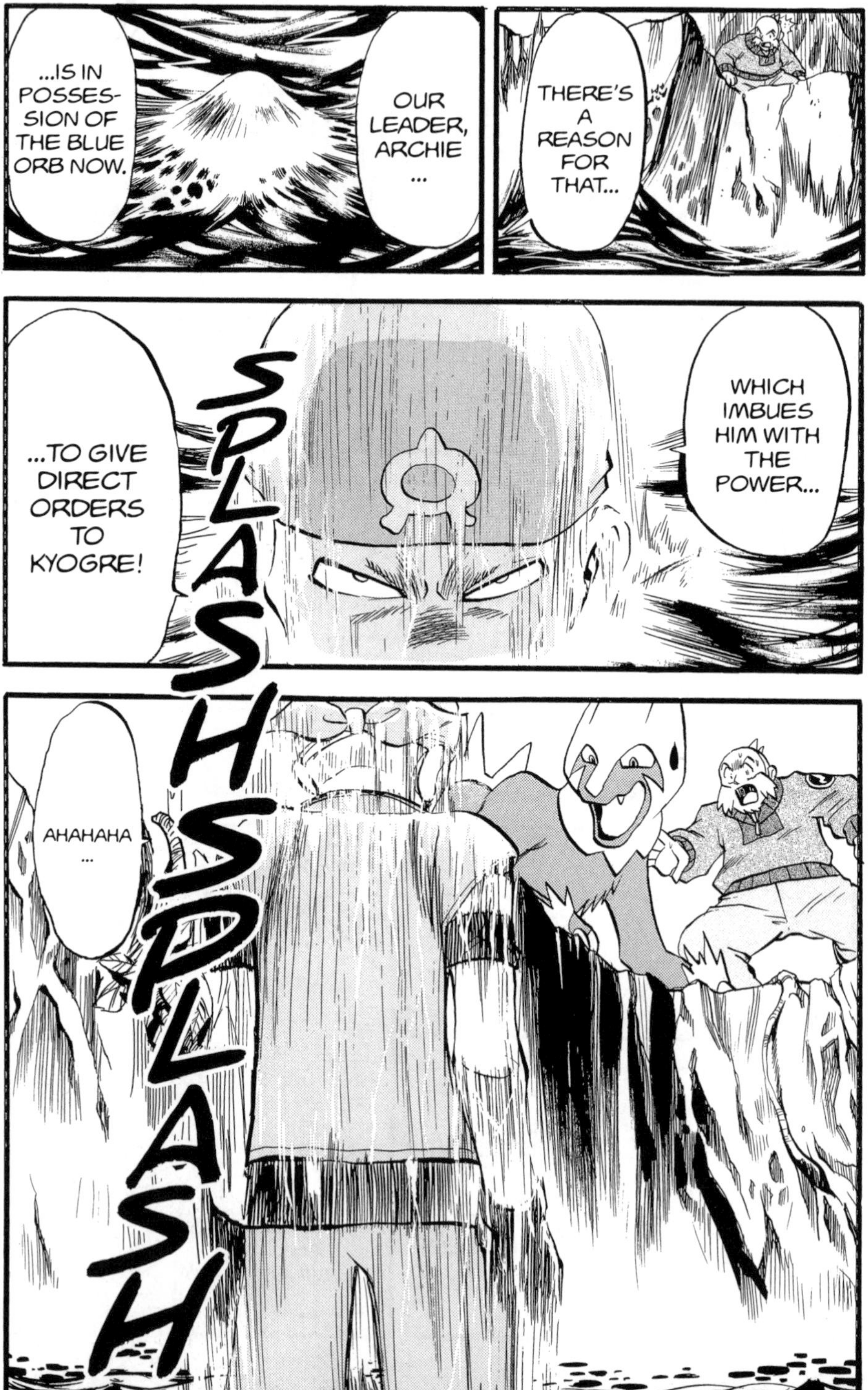
THERE'S A REASON FOR THAT...
OUR LEADER, ARCHIE...
...IS IN POSSESSION OF THE BLUE ORB NOW.
WHICH IMBUES HIM WITH THE POWER...
...TO GIVE DIRECT ORDERS TO KYOGRE!
SPLASH
SPLASH
AHAHAHA...

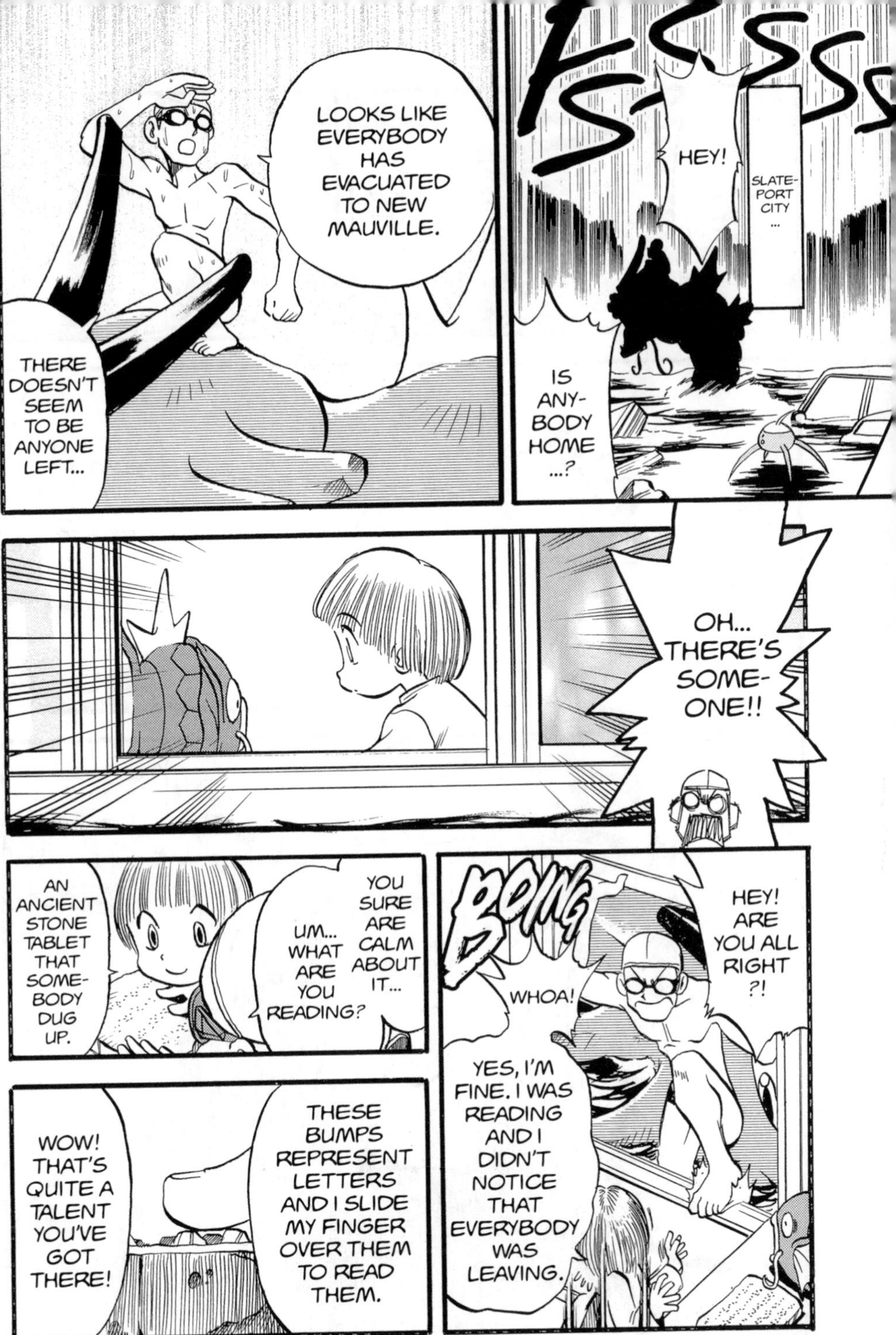
SLATEPORT CITY ...
HEY!
IS ANYBODY HOME ...?
LOOKS LIKE EVERYBODY HAS EVACUATED TO NEW MAUVILLE.
THERE DOESN'T SEEM TO BE ANYONE LEFT...
OH... THERE'S SOMEONE!!
HEY! ARE YOU ALL RIGHT ?!
BOING
WHOA!
YES, I'M FINE. I WAS READING AND I DIDN'T NOTICE THAT EVERYBODY WAS LEAVING.
YOU SURE ARE CALM ABOUT IT...
UM... WHAT ARE YOU READING?
AN ANCIENT STONE TABLET THAT SOMEBODY DUG UP.
THESE BUMPS REPRESENT LETTERS AND I SLIDE MY FINGER OVER THEM TO READ THEM.
WOW! THAT'S QUITE A TALENT YOU'VE GOT THERE!

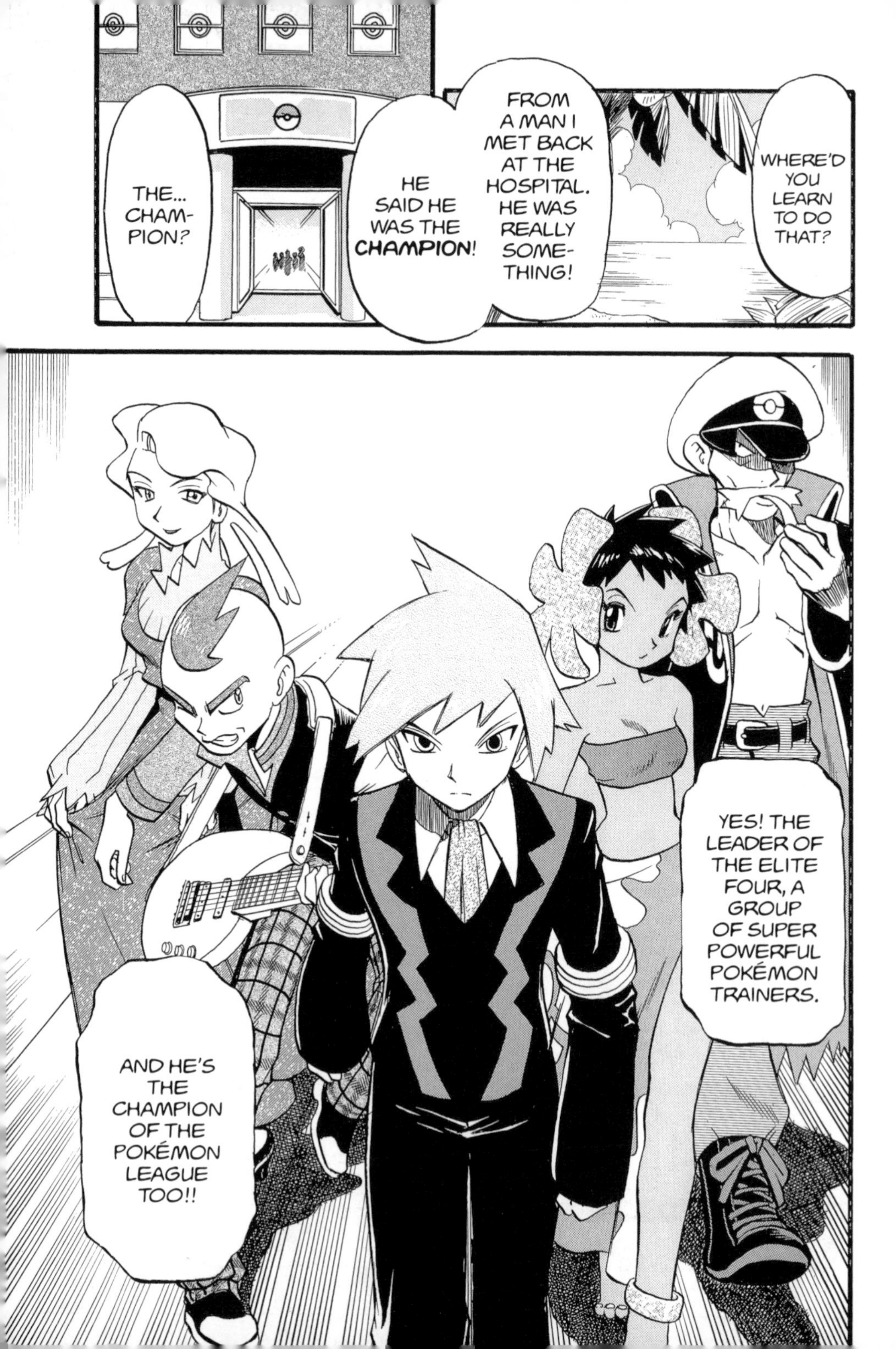
WHERE'D YOU LEARN TO DO THAT?
FROM A MAN I MET BACK AT THE HOSPITAL. HE WAS REALLY SOME-THING!
HE SAID HE WAS THE **CHAMPION**!
THE... CHAM-PION?
YES! THE LEADER OF THE ELITE FOUR, A GROUP OF SUPER POWERFUL POKÉMON TRAINERS.
AND HE'S THE CHAMPION OF THE POKÉMON LEAGUE TOO!!

ADVENTURE MAP

SAPPHIRE

RUBY

Fortree City

→ **Route 123** | **Slateport City**

→ **Route 126**

Seafloor Cavern

CHIC
Blaziken ♀
Lv40

RONO
Lairon ♂
Lv41

RELLY
Relicanth ♂
Lv47

PHADO
Donphan ♂
Lv48

TROPPY
Tropius ♂
Lv46

LORRY
Wailord ♂
Lv48

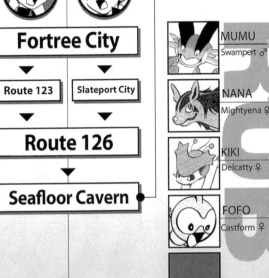

MUMU
Swampert ♂

NANA
Mightyena ♀

KIKI
Delcatty ♀

FOFO
Castform ♀

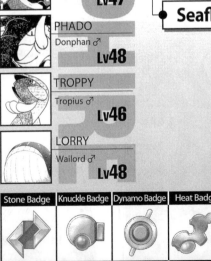

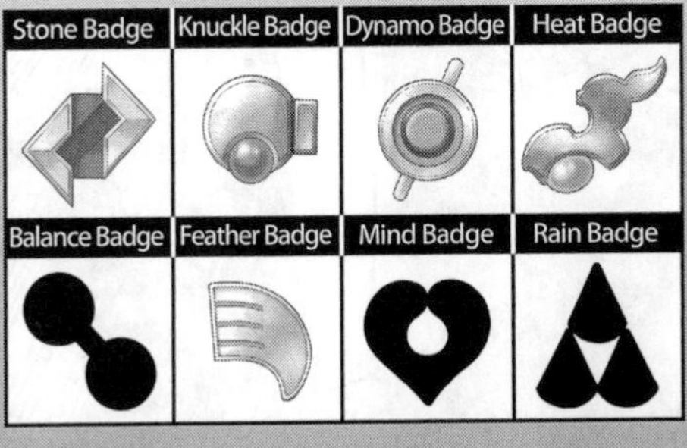

Stone Badge	Knuckle Badge	Dynamo Badge	Heat Badge
Balance Badge	Feather Badge	Mind Badge	Rain Badge

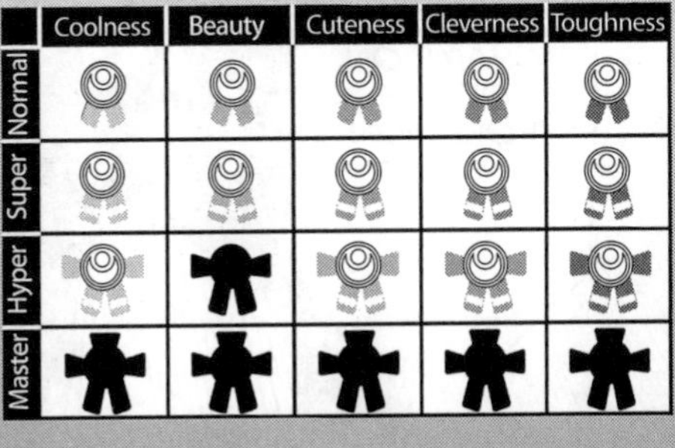

		Coolness	Beauty	Cuteness	Cleverness	Toughness
Normal		◎	◎	◎	◎	◎
Super		◎	◎	◎	◎	◎
Hyper		◎	★	◎	◎	◎
Master		✖	✖	✖	✖	✖

● Adventure 246 ●

Can I Ninjask You a Question?

Pokémon™ Adventures Ruby & Sapphire

The Fourth Chapter

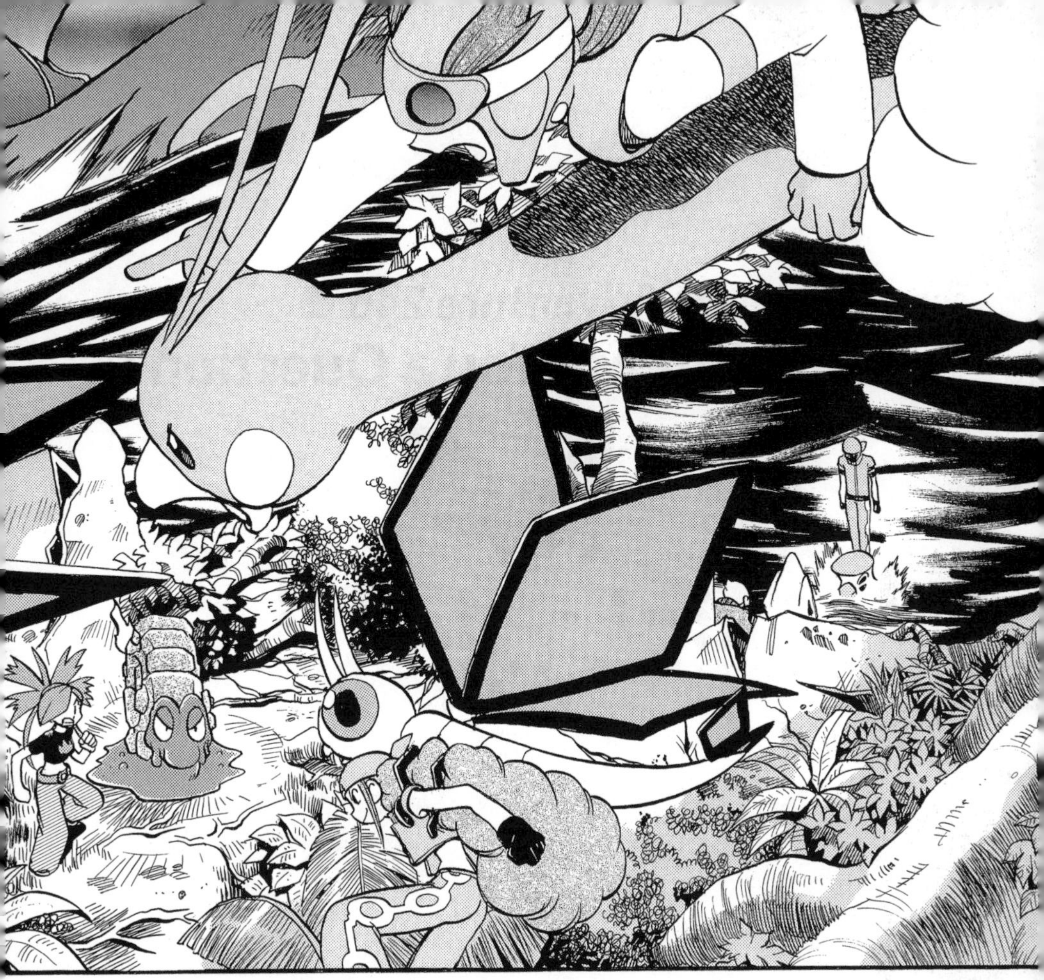

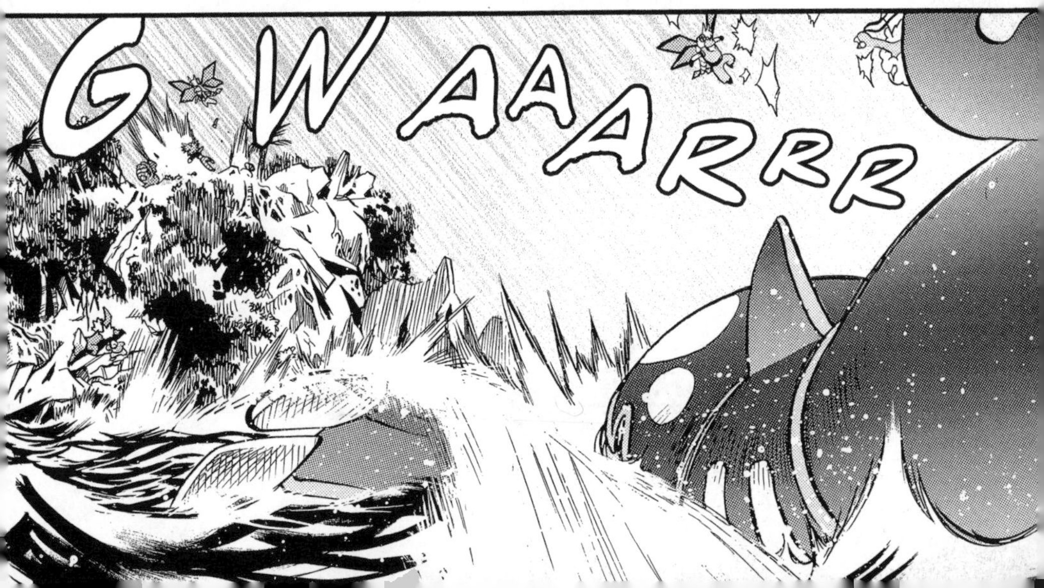
GWAAARRR

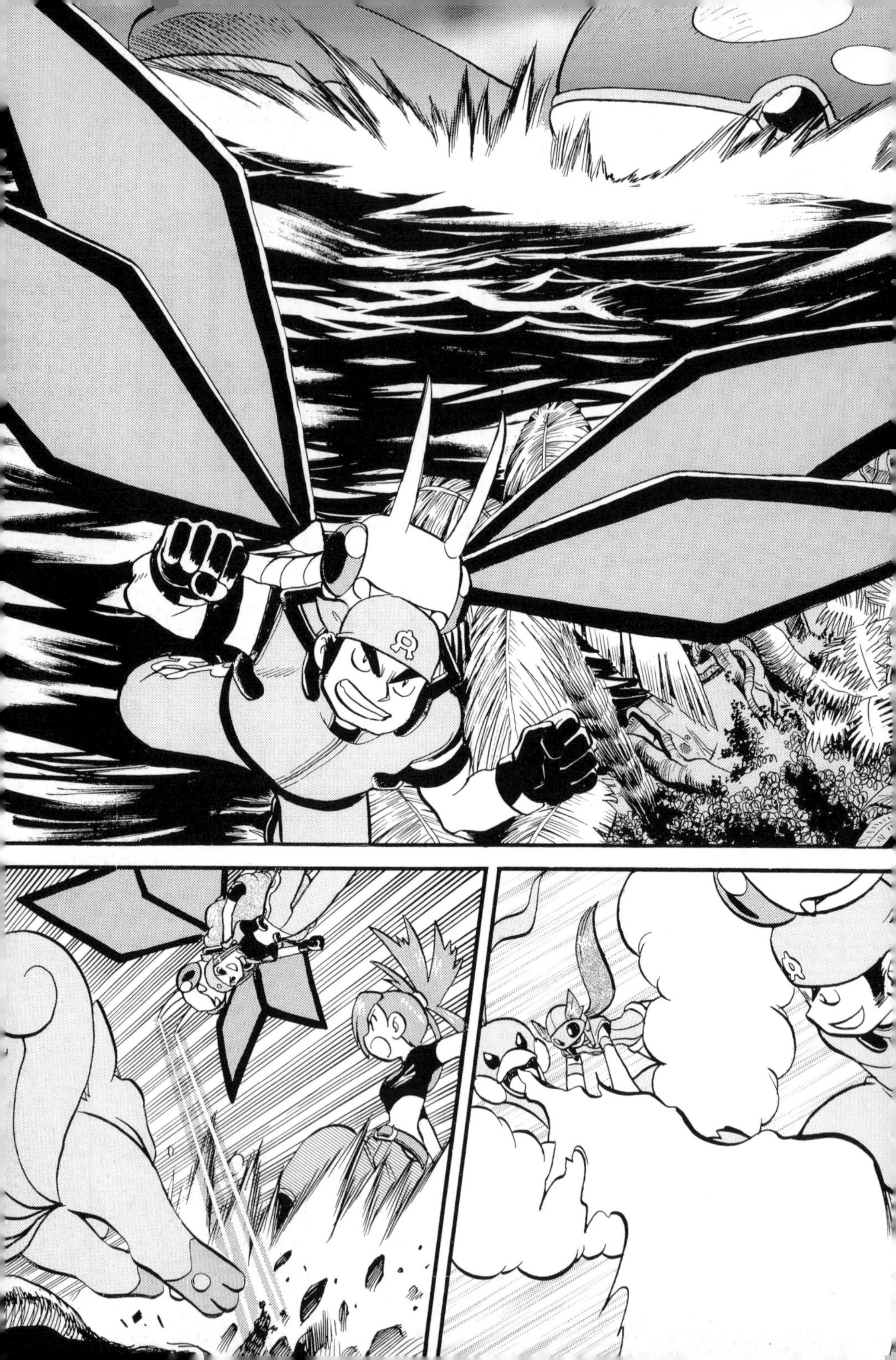

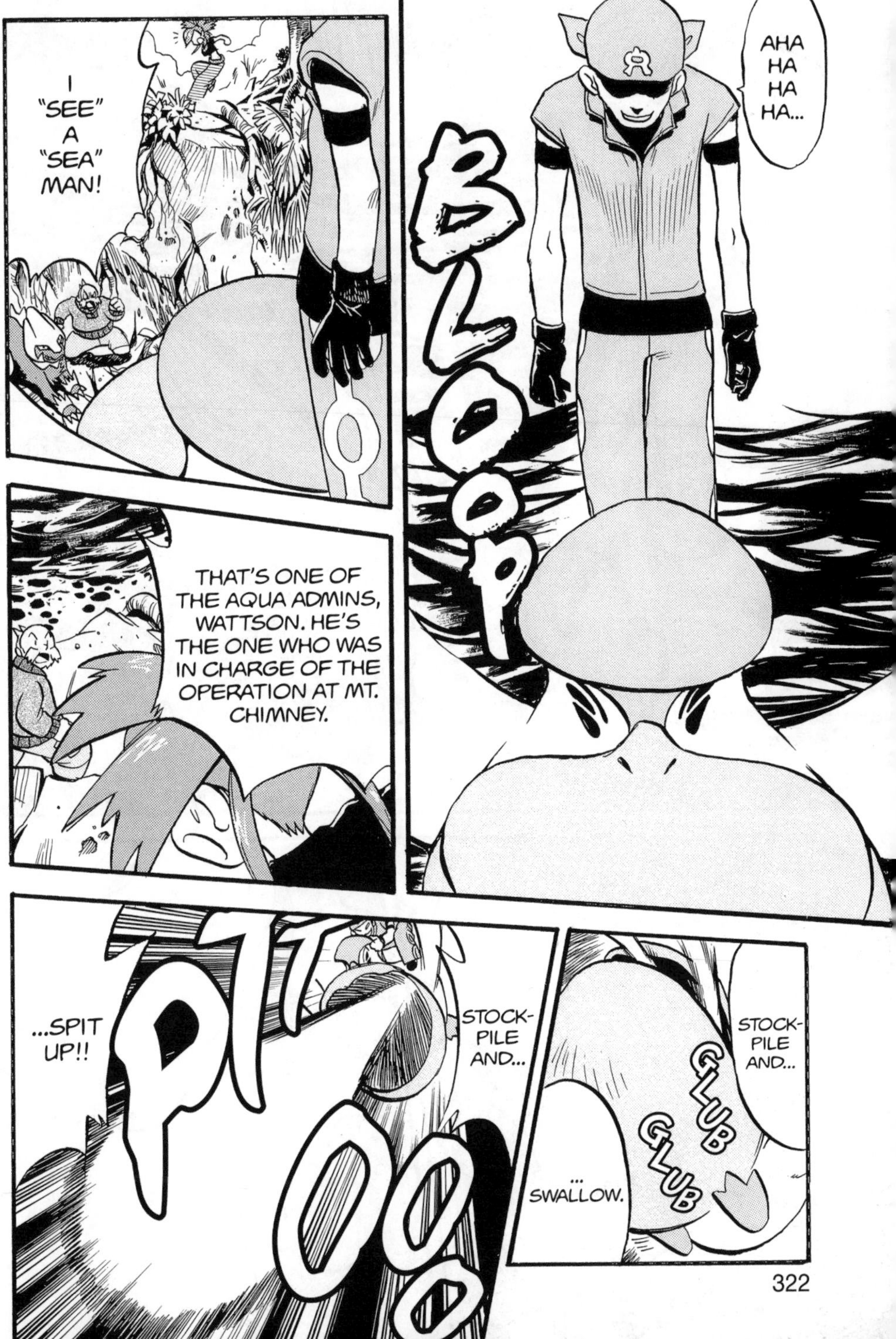
AHA HA HA HA...
BLOOOP
I "SEE" A "SEA" MAN!
THAT'S ONE OF THE AQUA ADMINS, WATTSON. HE'S THE ONE WHO WAS IN CHARGE OF THE OPERATION AT MT. CHIMNEY.
STOCK-PILE AND...
GLUB GLUB
... SWALLOW.
STOCK-PILE AND...
...SPIT UP!!
PTOOOO

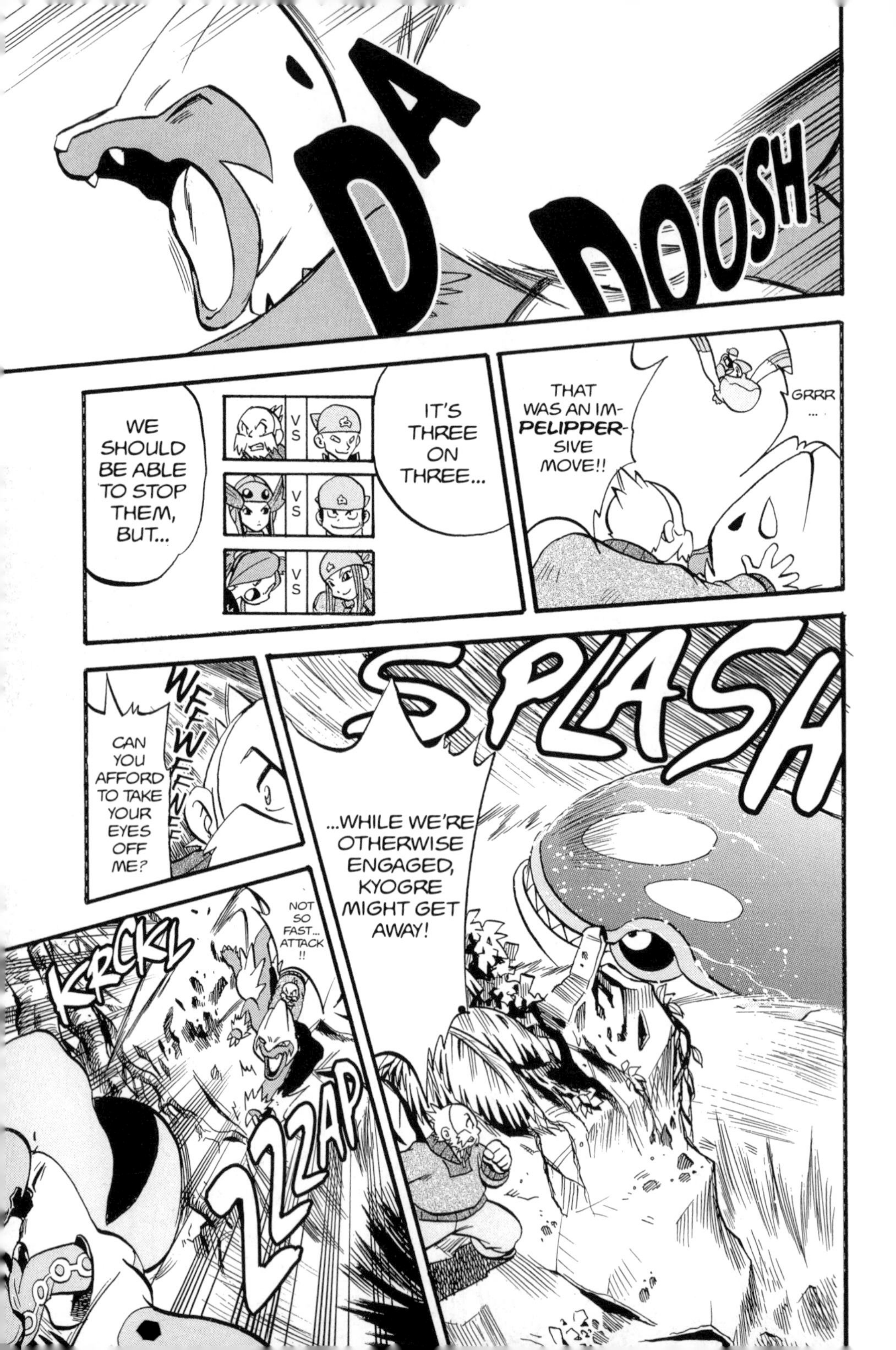

DA
DOOSH
GRRR ...
THAT WAS AN IM-PELIPPER-SIVE MOVE!!
IT'S THREE ON THREE...
VS
VS
VS
WE SHOULD BE ABLE TO STOP THEM, BUT...
SPLASH
...WHILE WE'RE OTHERWISE ENGAGED, KYOGRE MIGHT GET AWAY!
WFF WFF
CAN YOU AFFORD TO TAKE YOUR EYES OFF ME?
NOT SO FAST... ATTACK!!
KRCKL
ZZZAP

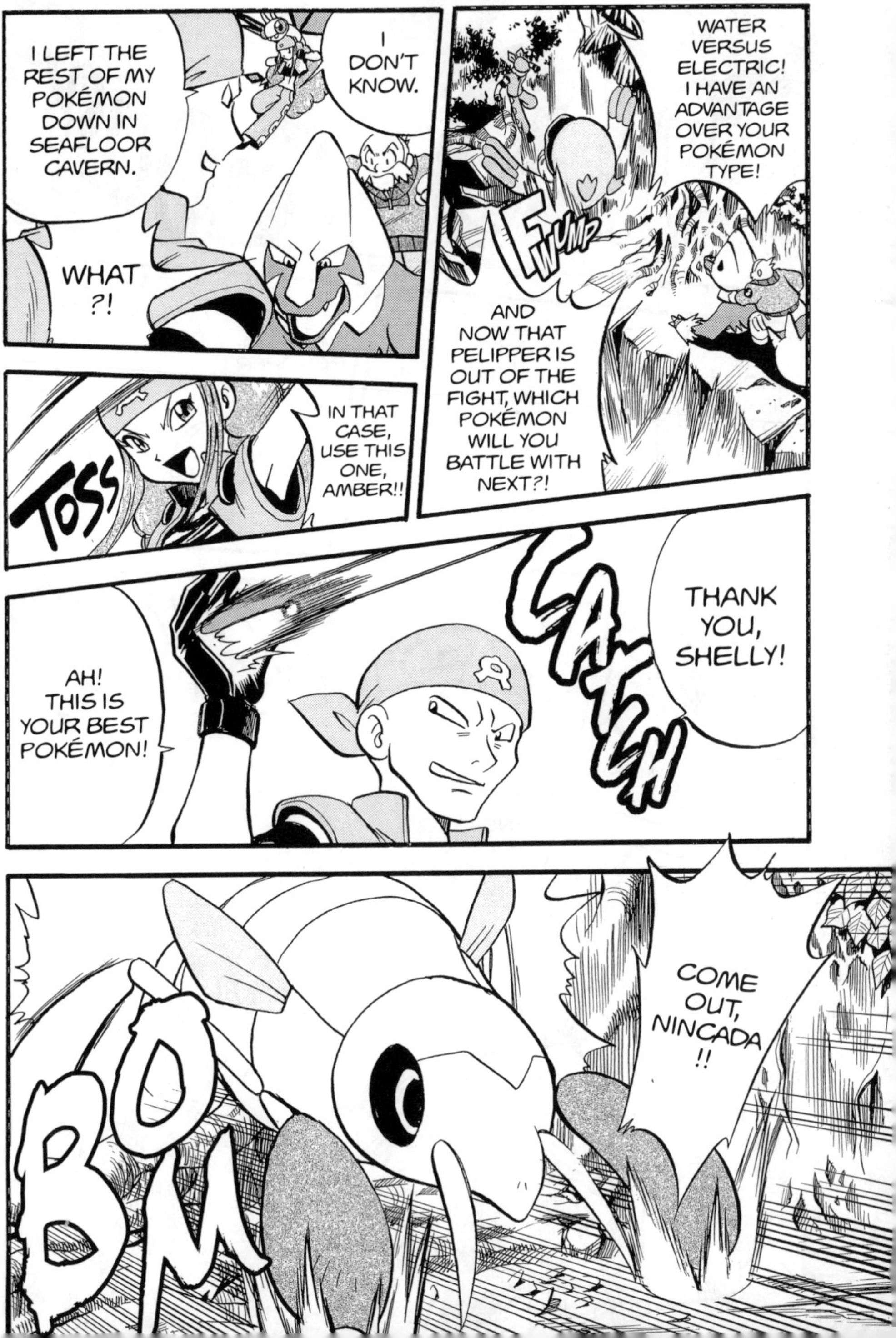
WATER VERSUS ELECTRIC! I HAVE AN ADVANTAGE OVER YOUR POKéMON TYPE!
FWUMP
AND NOW THAT PELIPPER IS OUT OF THE FIGHT, WHICH POKéMON WILL YOU BATTLE WITH NEXT?!
I DON'T KNOW.
I LEFT THE REST OF MY POKéMON DOWN IN SEAFLOOR CAVERN.
WHAT ?!
IN THAT CASE, USE THIS ONE, AMBER!!
TOSS
THANK YOU, SHELLY!
CATCH
AH! THIS IS YOUR BEST POKéMON!
COME OUT, NINCADA !!
BOOM

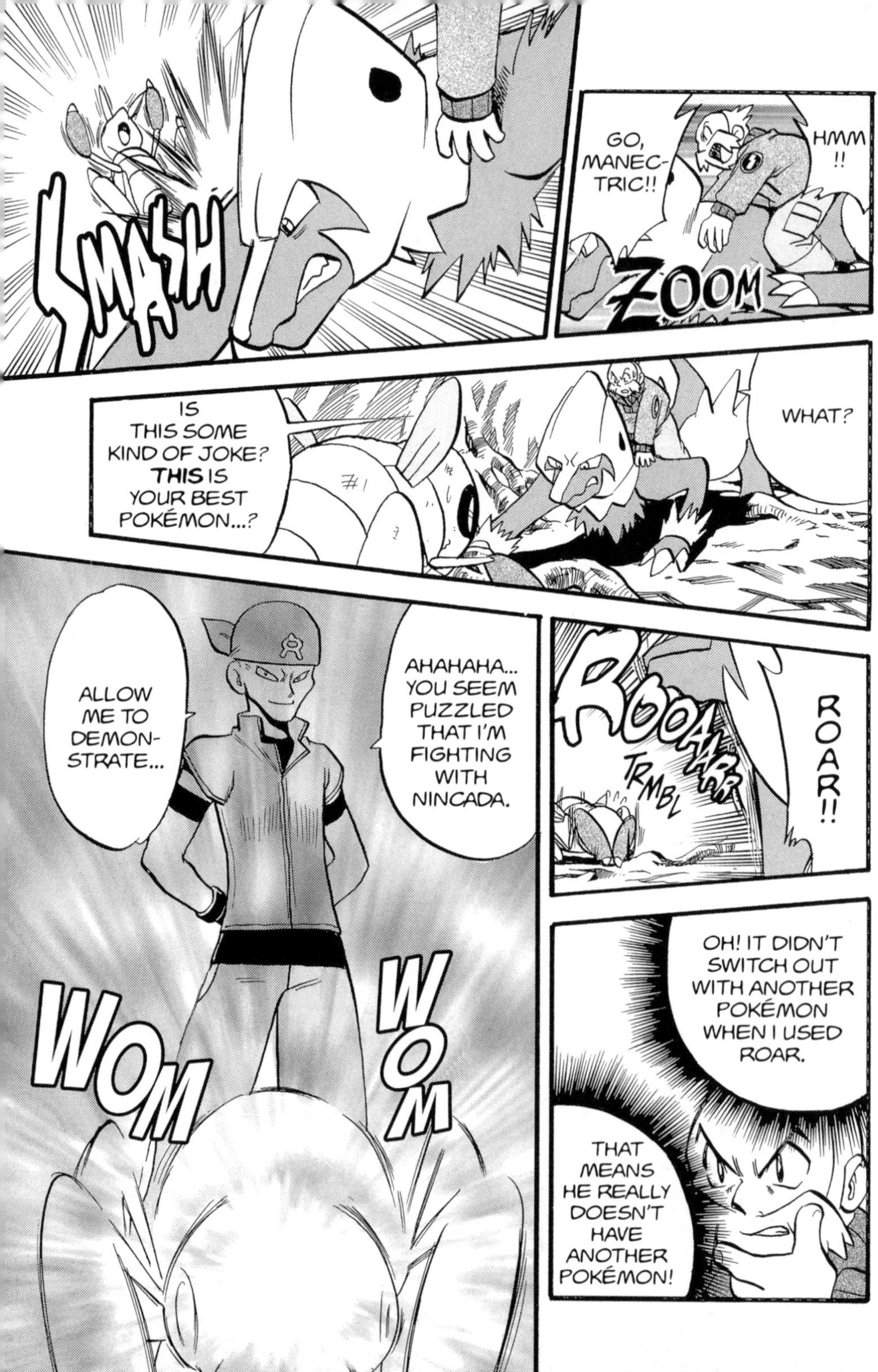
HMM !!
GO, MANEC-TRIC!!
ZOOM
SMASH
WHAT?
IS THIS SOME KIND OF JOKE? **THIS** IS YOUR BEST POKÉMON...?
ROAR!!
ROOAARR
TRMBL
OH! IT DIDN'T SWITCH OUT WITH ANOTHER POKÉMON WHEN I USED ROAR.
THAT MEANS HE REALLY DOESN'T HAVE ANOTHER POKÉMON!
AHAHAHA... YOU SEEM PUZZLED THAT I'M FIGHTING WITH NINCADA.
ALLOW ME TO DEMON-STRATE...
WOM
WOM

IT EVOLVED!!

HUH?!

TING

...WHY THIS IS THE BEST POKÉMON!!

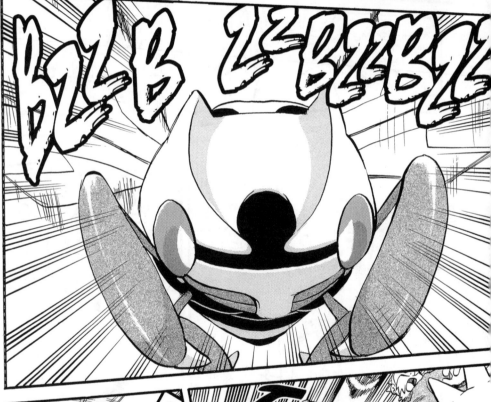

BZZB ZZ BZZBZ

ZZZZ

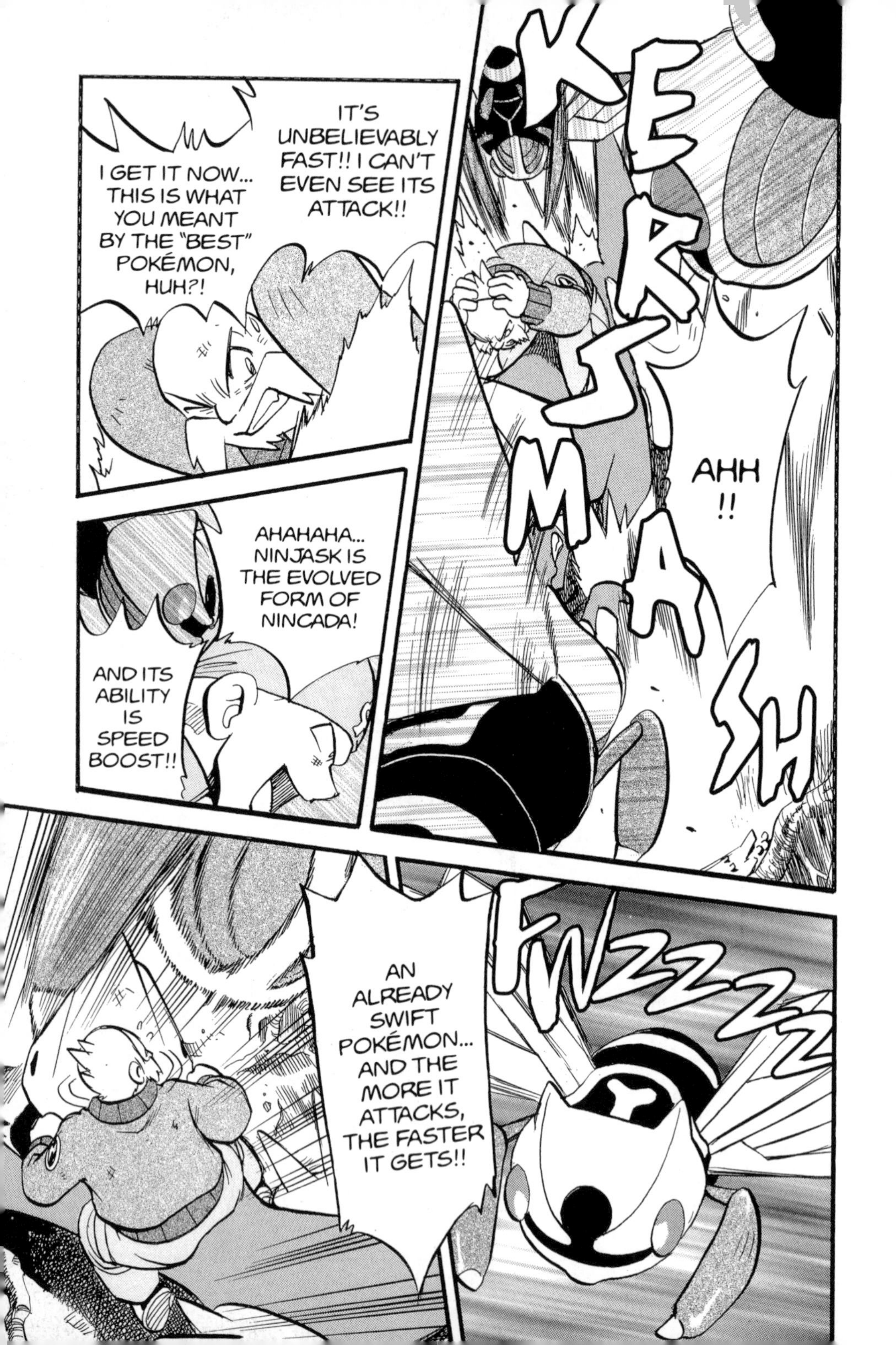
KERSMASH
AHH!!
IT'S UNBELIEVABLY FAST!! I CAN'T EVEN SEE ITS ATTACK!!
I GET IT NOW... THIS IS WHAT YOU MEANT BY THE "BEST" POKÉMON, HUH?!
AHAHAHA... NINJASK IS THE EVOLVED FORM OF NINCADA!
AND ITS ABILITY IS SPEED BOOST!!
FWZZZZZ
AN ALREADY SWIFT POKÉMON... AND THE MORE IT ATTACKS, THE FASTER IT GETS!!

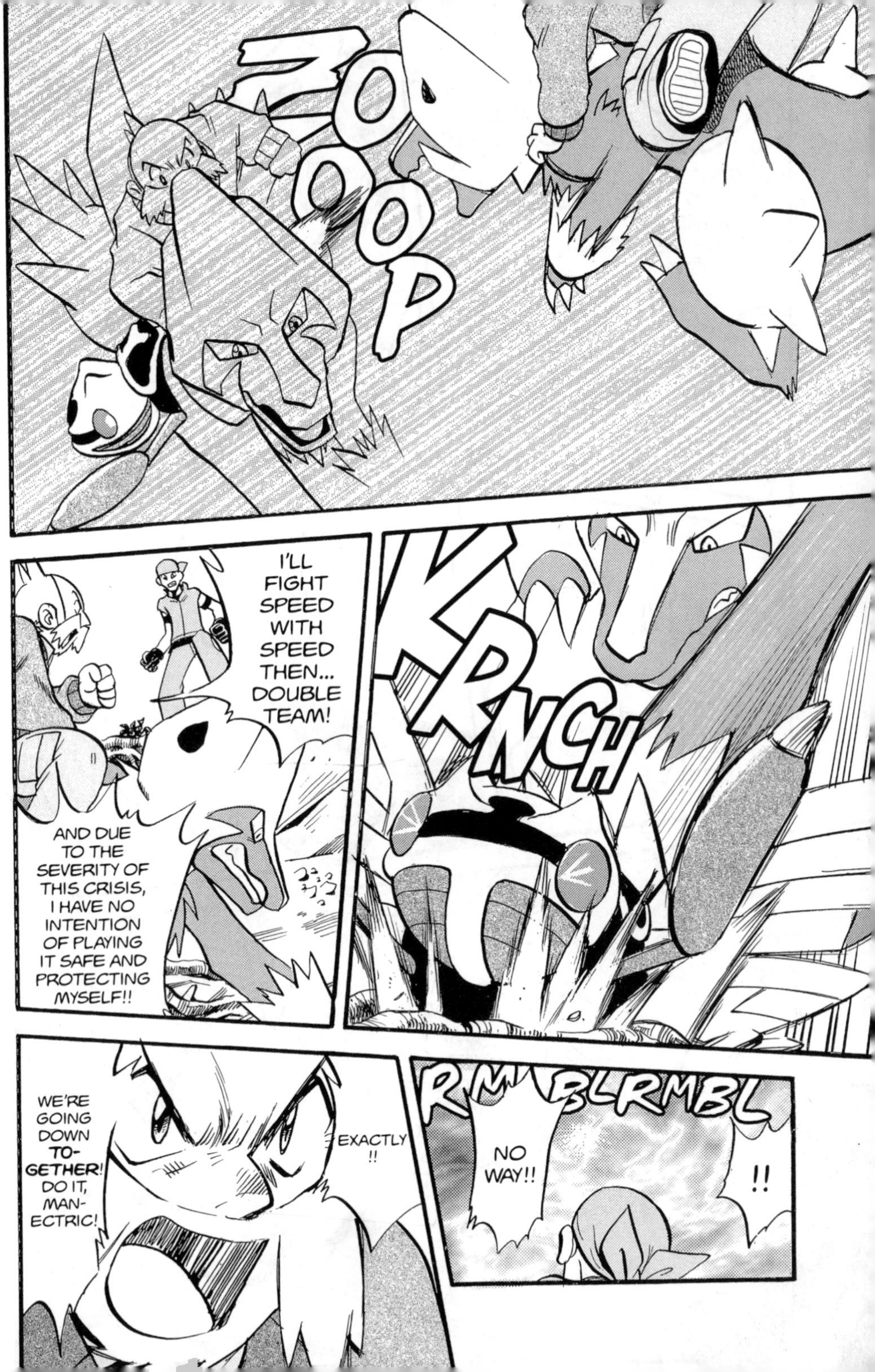
ZOOOOP
KRNCH
I'LL FIGHT SPEED WITH SPEED THEN... DOUBLE TEAM!
AND DUE TO THE SEVERITY OF THIS CRISIS, I HAVE NO INTENTION OF PLAYING IT SAFE AND PROTECTING MYSELF!!
RMBLRMBL
!!
NO WAY!!
EXACTLY!!
WE'RE GOING DOWN **TO-GETHER**! DO IT, MAN-ECTRIC!

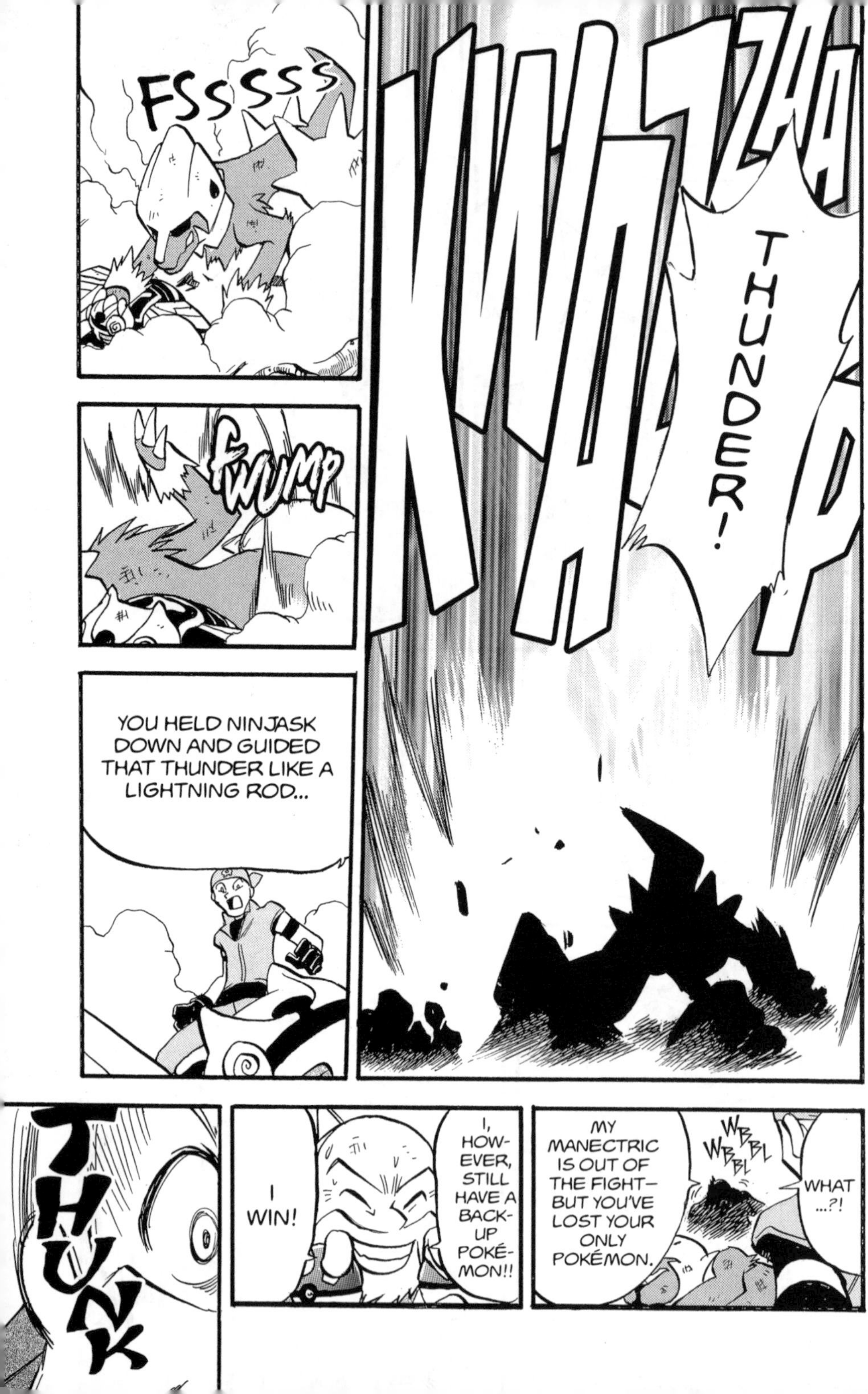
KWAZHAP
THUNDER!
FSSSSS
fwump
YOU HELD NINJASK DOWN AND GUIDED THAT THUNDER LIKE A LIGHTNING ROD...
WBBL WBBL
WHAT ...?!
MY MANECTRIC IS OUT OF THE FIGHT—BUT YOU'VE LOST YOUR ONLY POKÉMON.
I, HOW-EVER, STILL HAVE A BACK-UP POKÉ-MON!!
I WIN!
THUNK

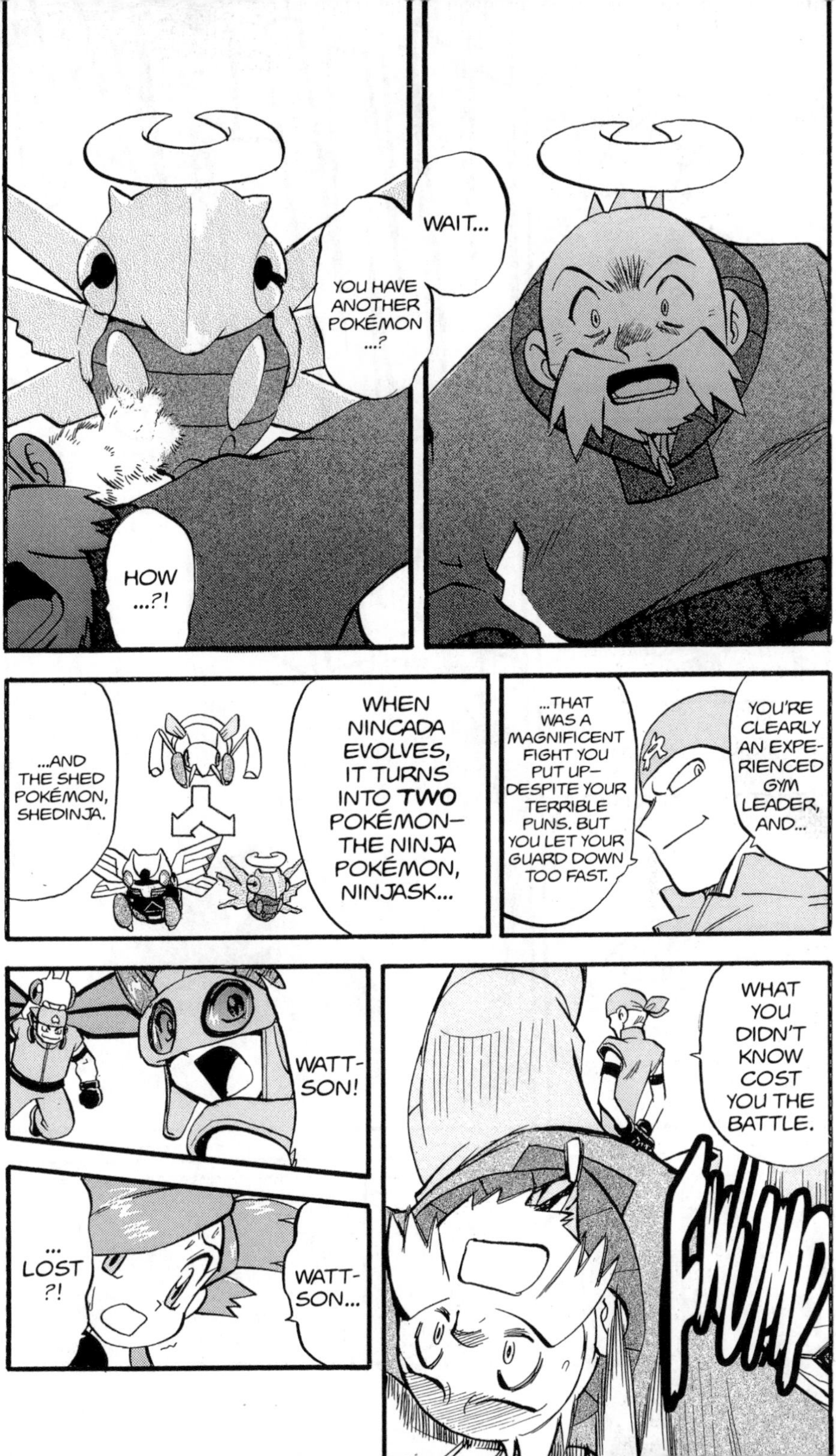
WAIT...
YOU HAVE ANOTHER POKÉMON ...?
HOW ...?!
YOU'RE CLEARLY AN EXPE-RIENCED GYM LEADER, AND...
...THAT WAS A MAGNIFICENT FIGHT YOU PUT UP—DESPITE YOUR TERRIBLE PUNS. BUT YOU LET YOUR GUARD DOWN TOO FAST.
WHEN NINCADA EVOLVES, IT TURNS INTO **TWO** POKÉMON—THE NINJA POKÉMON, NINJASK...
...AND THE SHED POKÉMON, SHEDINJA.
WHAT YOU DIDN'T KNOW COST YOU THE BATTLE.
WATT-SON!
WATT-SON...
... LOST ?!

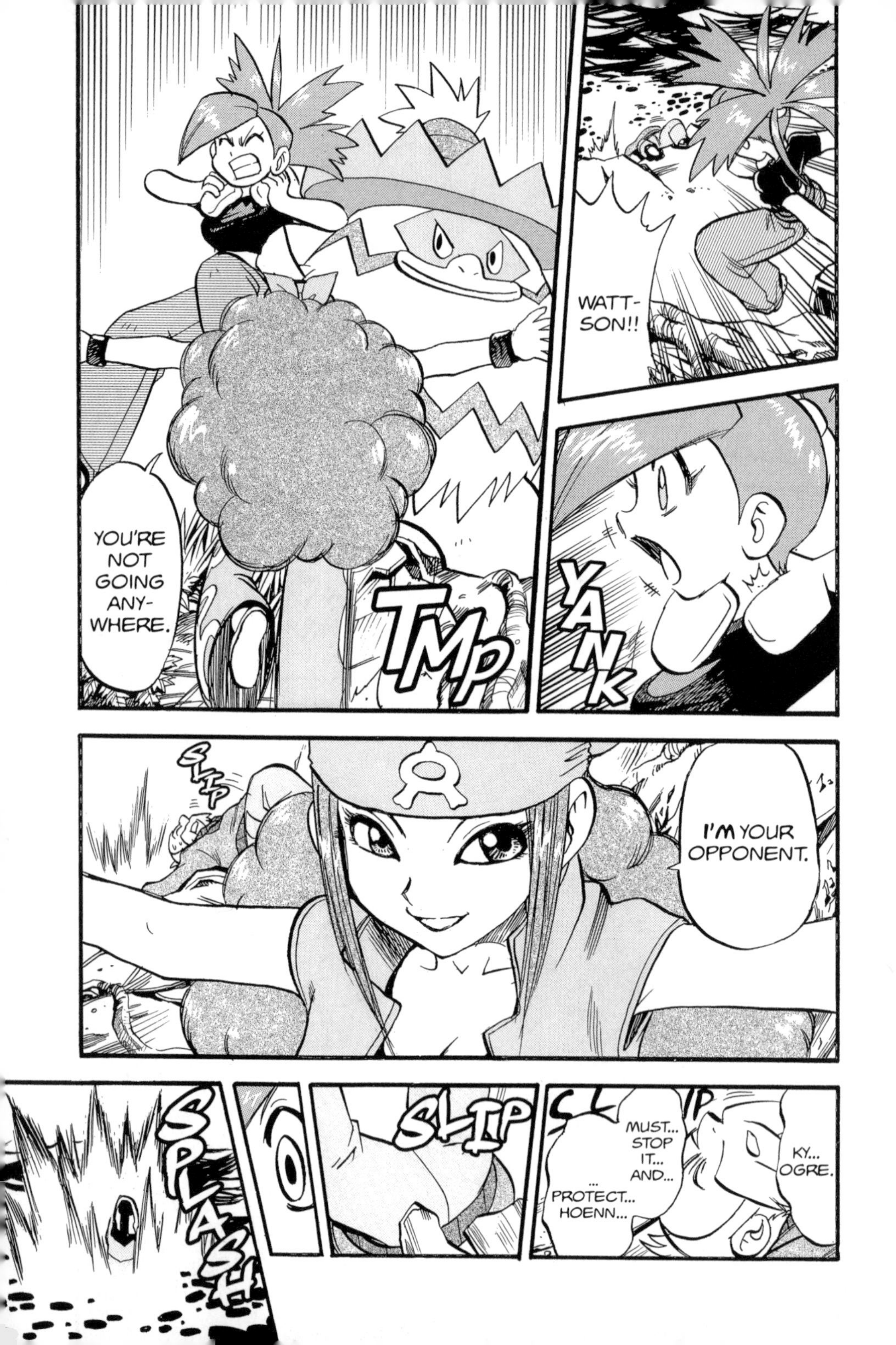
WATT-SON!!
YANK
YOU'RE NOT GOING ANY-WHERE.
TMP
I'M YOUR OPPONENT.
SLIP
SLIP
KY... OGRE.
MUST... STOP IT... AND...
... PROTECT... HOENN...
SLIP
SPLASH

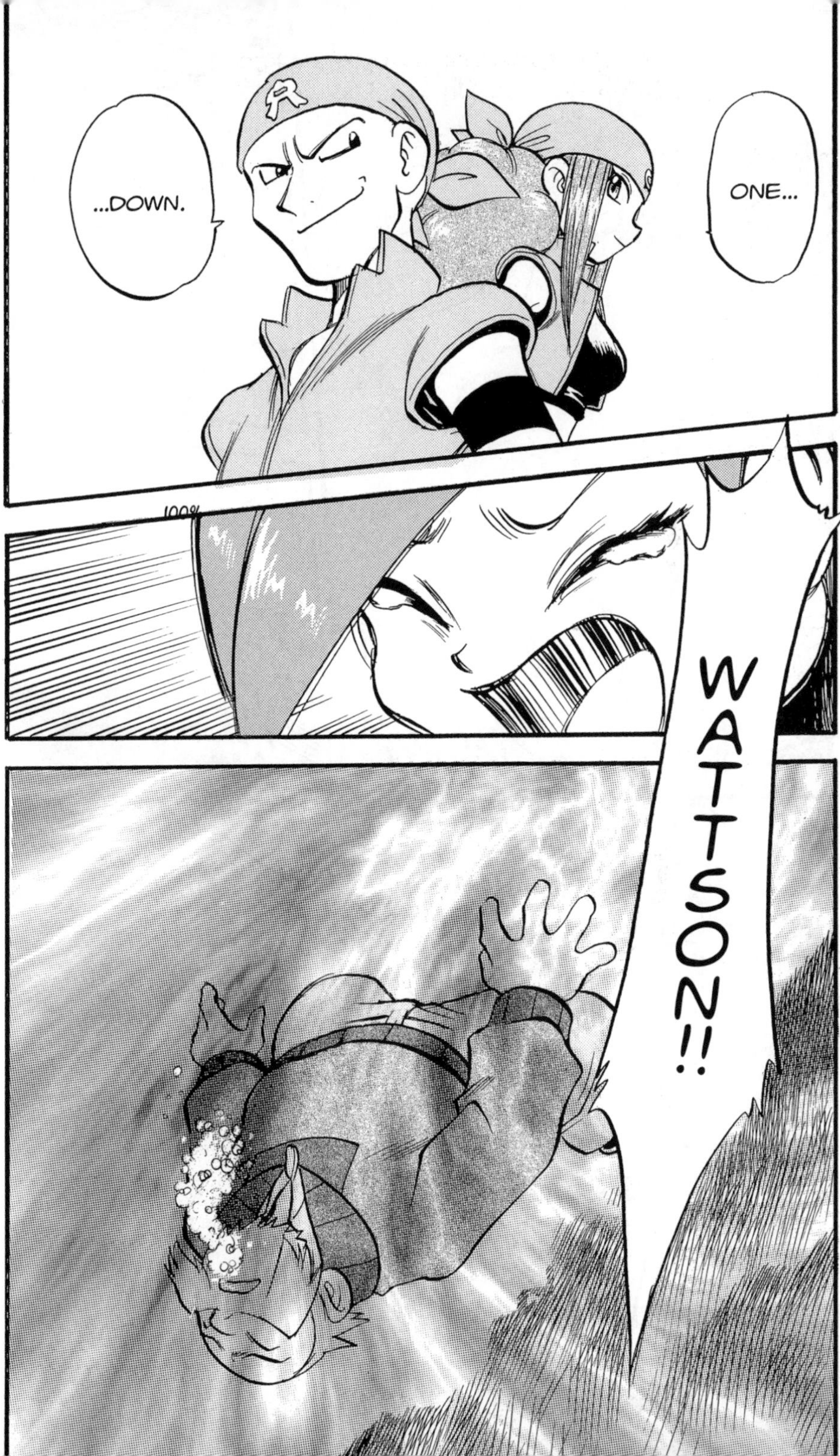
ONE...
...DOWN.
WATTSON!!

ADVENTURE MAP

SAPPHIRE

Name	Pokémon	Level
CHIC	Blaziken ♀	Lv42
RONO	Lairon ♂	Lv41
RELLY	Relicanth ♂	Lv49
PHADO	Donphan ♂	Lv50
TROPPY	Tropius ♂	Lv48
LORRY	Wailord ♂	Lv48

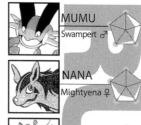

Fortree City

▼ Route 123 (Sapphire) / ▼ Slateport City (Ruby)

▼

Route 126

▼

Seafloor Cavern

RUBY

Name	Pokémon
MUMU	Swampert ♂
NANA	Mightyena ♀
KIKI	Delcatty ♀
FOFO	Castform ♀

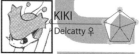

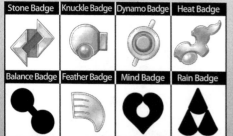

Stone Badge	Knuckle Badge	Dynamo Badge	Heat Badge
Balance Badge	Feather Badge	Mind Badge	Rain Badge

	Coolness	Beauty	Cuteness	Cleverness	Toughness
Normal					
Super					
Hyper					
Master					

● Adventure 247 ●
The Beginning of the End with Kyogre and Groudon, Part 9

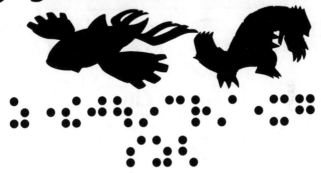

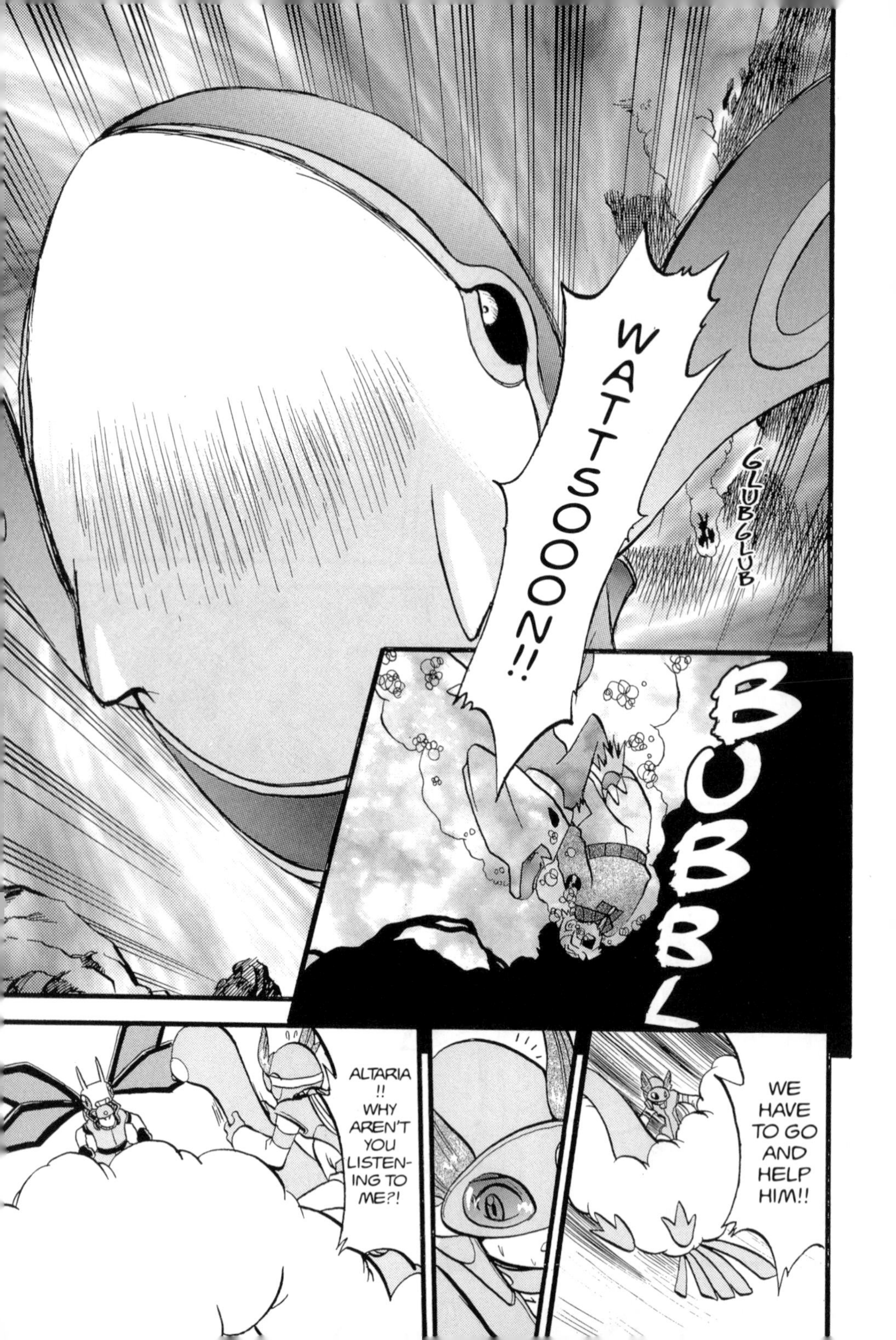
WATTSOOON!!
GLUBGLUB
BUBBL
WE HAVE TO GO AND HELP HIM!!
ALTARIA!! WHY AREN'T YOU LISTENING TO ME?!

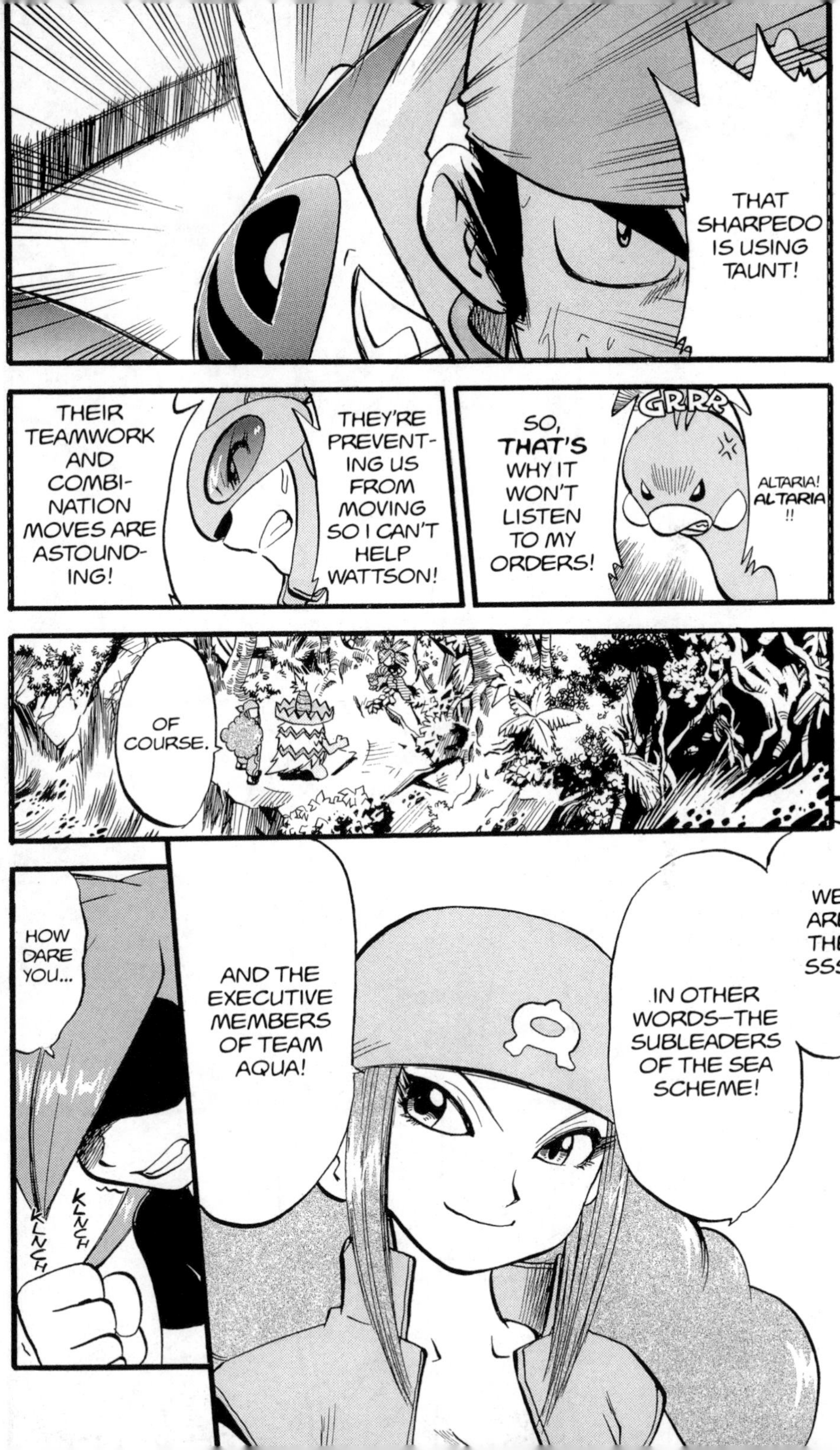
THAT SHARPEDO IS USING TAUNT!
GRRR
ALTARIA! **ALTARIA** !!
SO, **THAT'S** WHY IT WON'T LISTEN TO MY ORDERS!
THEY'RE PREVENTING US FROM MOVING SO I CAN'T HELP WATTSON!
THEIR TEAMWORK AND COMBINATION MOVES ARE ASTOUNDING!
OF COURSE.
WE ARE THE SSS.
IN OTHER WORDS—THE SUBLEADERS OF THE SEA SCHEME!
AND THE EXECUTIVE MEMBERS OF TEAM AQUA!
HOW DARE YOU...
KLNCH
KLNCH

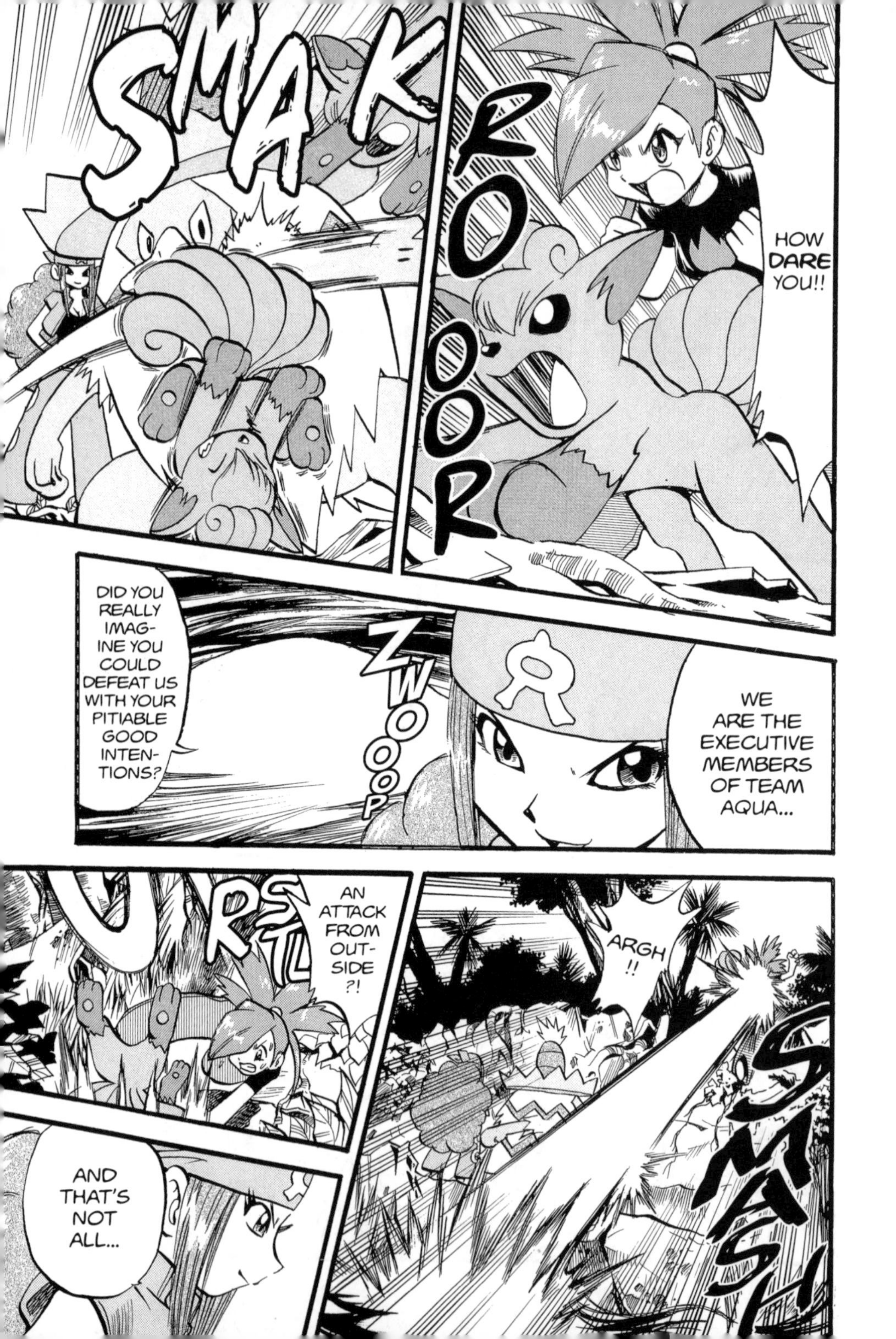
ROOOOR
HOW DARE YOU!!
SMAK
WE ARE THE EXECUTIVE MEMBERS OF TEAM AQUA...
ZWOOOOP
DID YOU REALLY IMAG-INE YOU COULD DEFEAT US WITH YOUR PITIABLE GOOD INTEN-TIONS?
ARGH!!
SMASH
RSTL
AN ATTACK FROM OUT-SIDE?!
AND THAT'S NOT ALL...

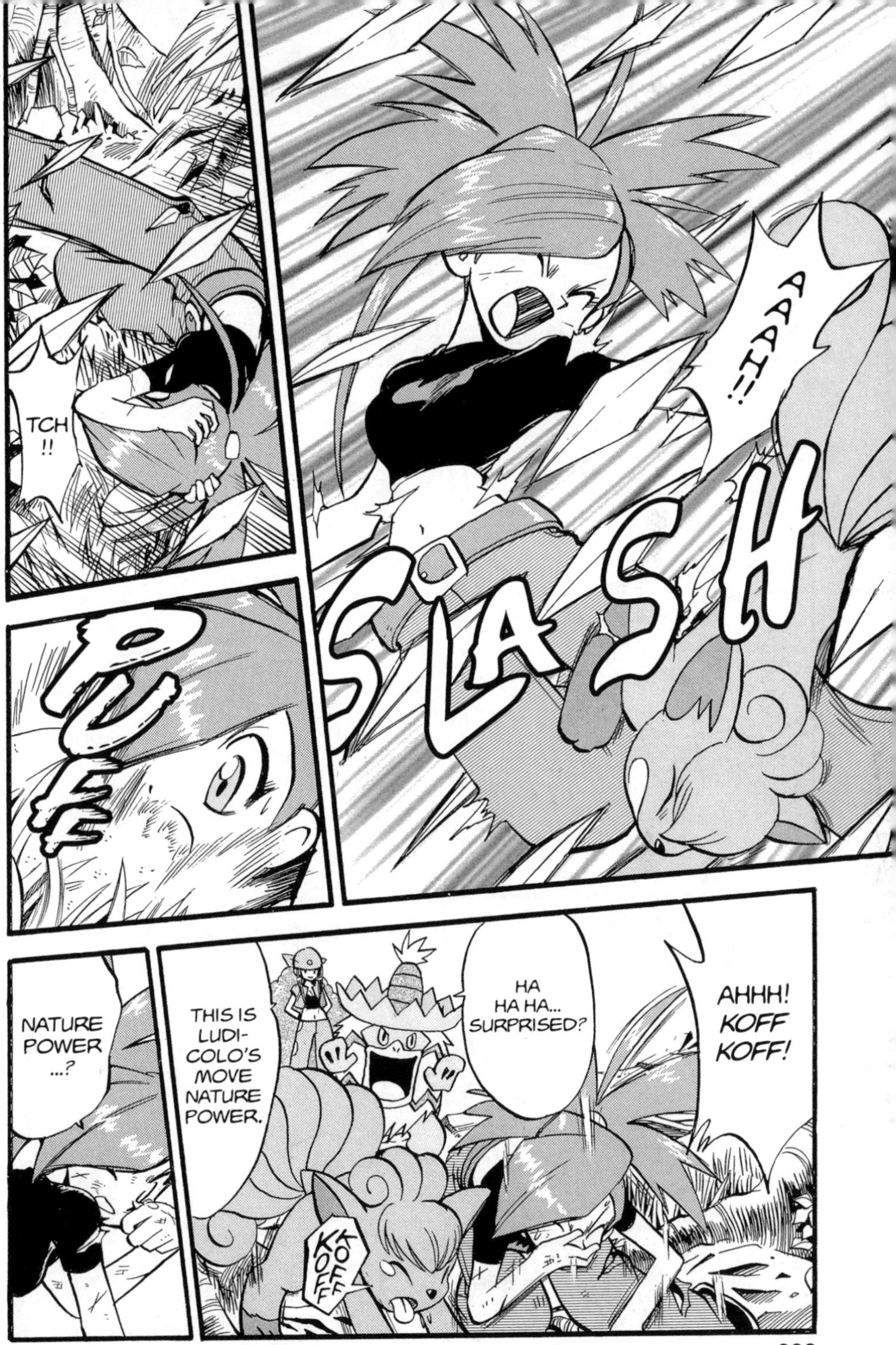
AAAAH!!
SLASH
TCH!!
PUFF
AHHH! KOFF KOFF!
HA HA HA... SURPRISED?
THIS IS LUDI-COLO'S MOVE NATURE POWER.
KOFF KOFF
NATURE POWER ...?

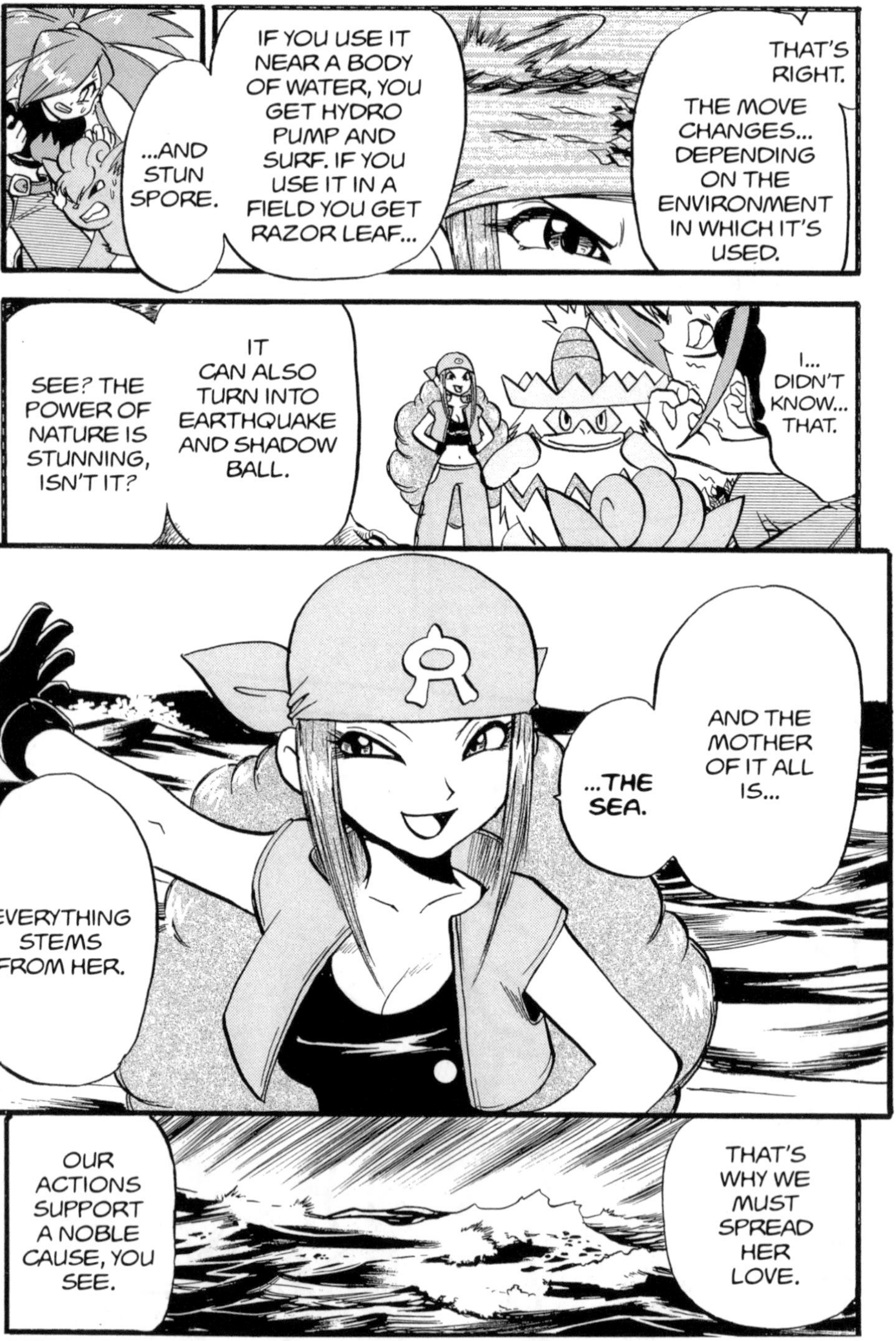
THAT'S RIGHT.
THE MOVE CHANGES... DEPENDING ON THE ENVIRONMENT IN WHICH IT'S USED.
IF YOU USE IT NEAR A BODY OF WATER, YOU GET HYDRO PUMP AND SURF. IF YOU USE IT IN A FIELD YOU GET RAZOR LEAF...
...AND STUN SPORE.
I... DIDN'T KNOW... THAT.
IT CAN ALSO TURN INTO EARTHQUAKE AND SHADOW BALL.
SEE? THE POWER OF NATURE IS STUNNING, ISN'T IT?
AND THE MOTHER OF IT ALL IS...
...THE SEA.
EVERYTHING STEMS FROM HER.
THAT'S WHY WE MUST SPREAD HER LOVE.
OUR ACTIONS SUPPORT A NOBLE CAUSE, YOU SEE.

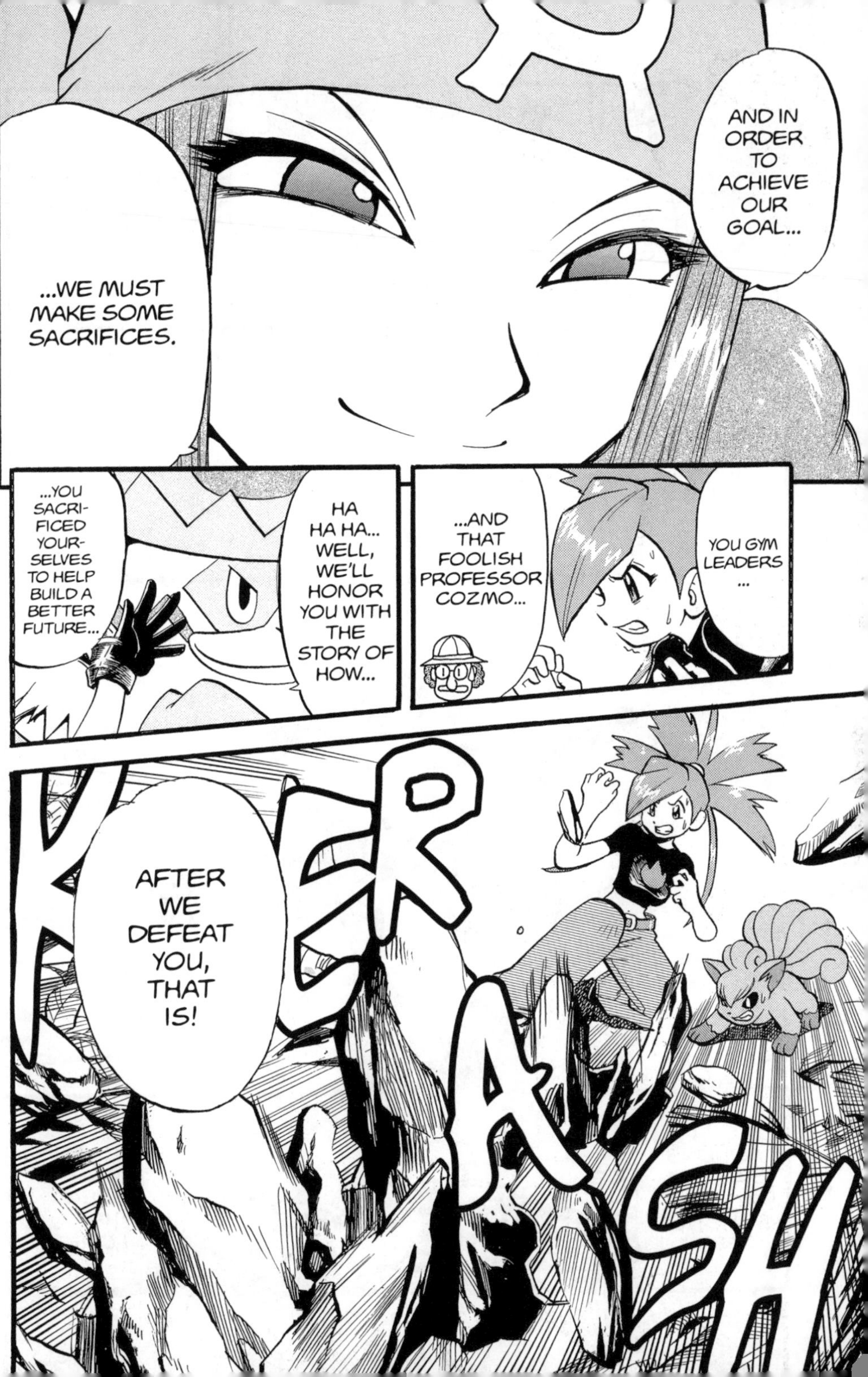
AND IN ORDER TO ACHIEVE OUR GOAL...
...WE MUST MAKE SOME SACRIFICES.
YOU GYM LEADERS ...
...AND THAT FOOLISH PROFESSOR COZMO...
HA HA HA... WELL, WE'LL HONOR YOU WITH THE STORY OF HOW...
...YOU SACRIFICED YOURSELVES TO HELP BUILD A BETTER FUTURE...
AFTER WE DEFEAT YOU, THAT IS!
KRASH

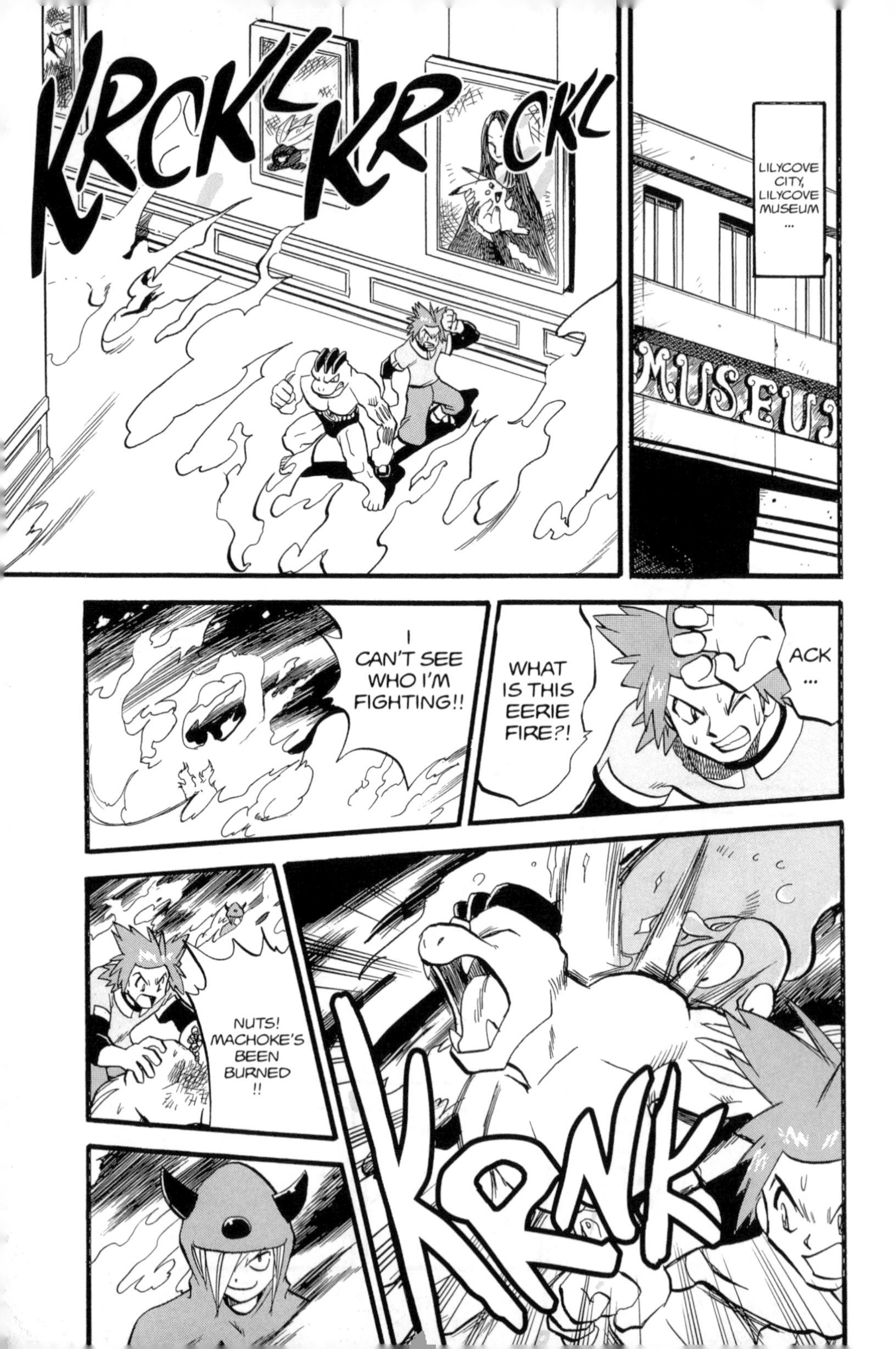
LILYCOVE CITY, LILYCOVE MUSEUM ...
KRCKL KRCKL
ACK ...
WHAT IS THIS EERIE FIRE?!
I CAN'T SEE WHO I'M FIGHTING!!
KRNK
NUTS! MACHOKE'S BEEN BURNED !!

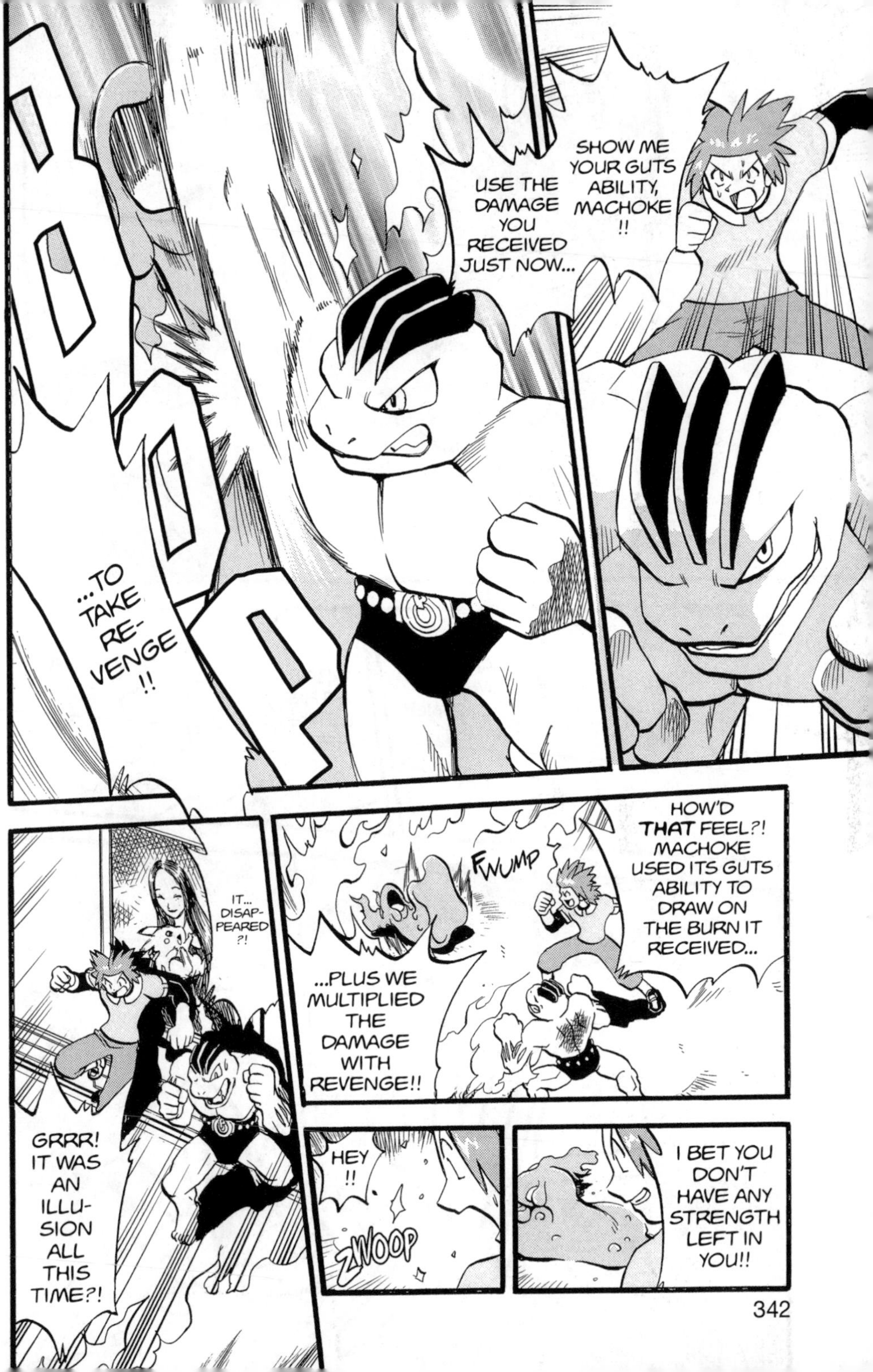

SHOW ME YOUR GUTS ABILITY, MACHOKE!!
USE THE DAMAGE YOU RECEIVED JUST NOW...
...TO TAKE RE-VENGE!!
HOW'D **THAT** FEEL?! MACHOKE USED ITS GUTS ABILITY TO DRAW ON THE BURN IT RECEIVED...
FWUMP
...PLUS WE MULTIPLIED THE DAMAGE WITH REVENGE!!
I BET YOU DON'T HAVE ANY STRENGTH LEFT IN YOU!!
HEY!!
ZWOOP
IT... DISAP-PEARED?!
GRRR! IT WAS AN ILLU-SION ALL THIS TIME?!

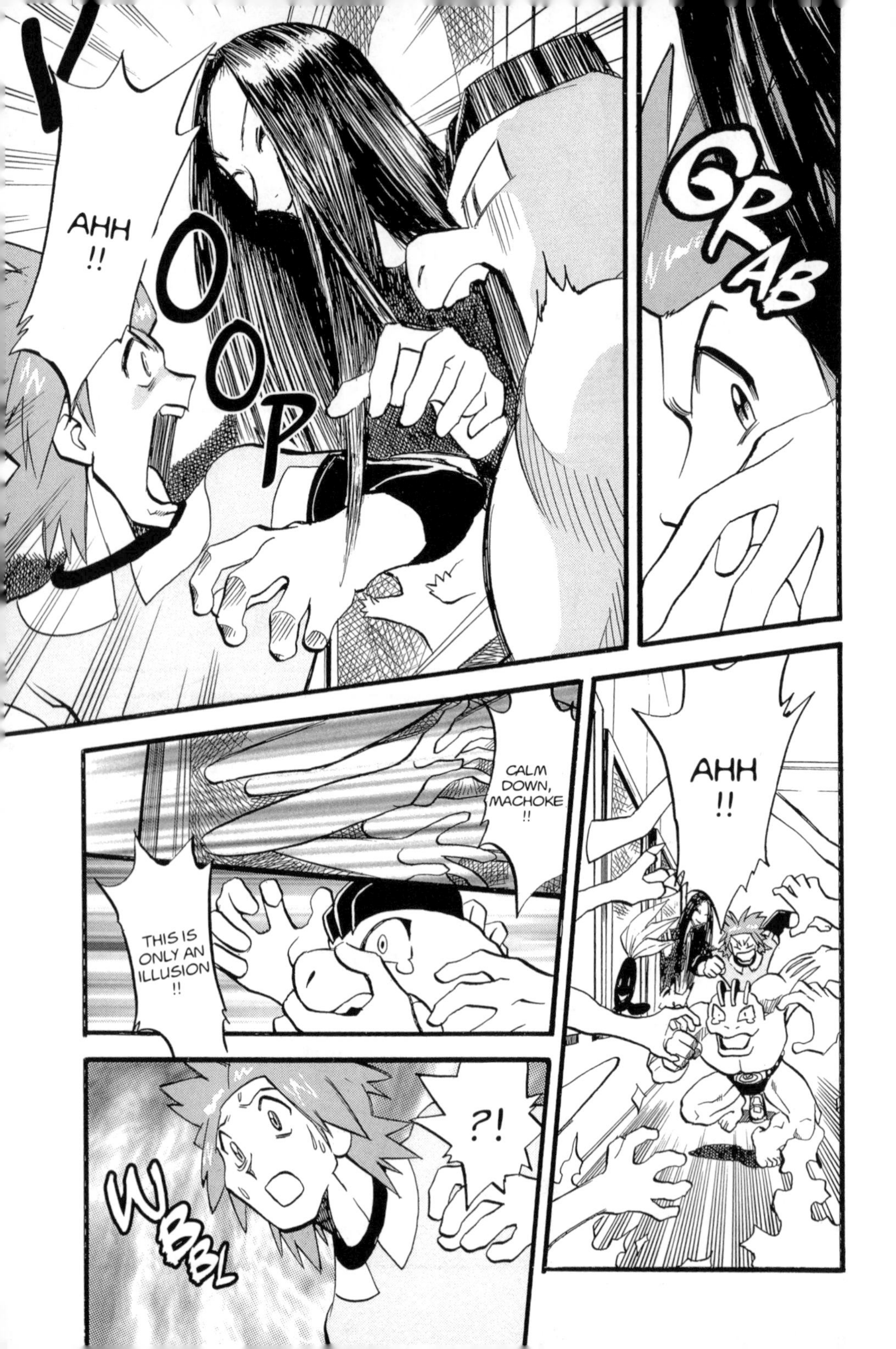

GRAB
WOOP
AHH !!
AHH !!
CALM DOWN, MACHOKE !!
THIS IS ONLY AN ILLUSION !!
?!
WBBL

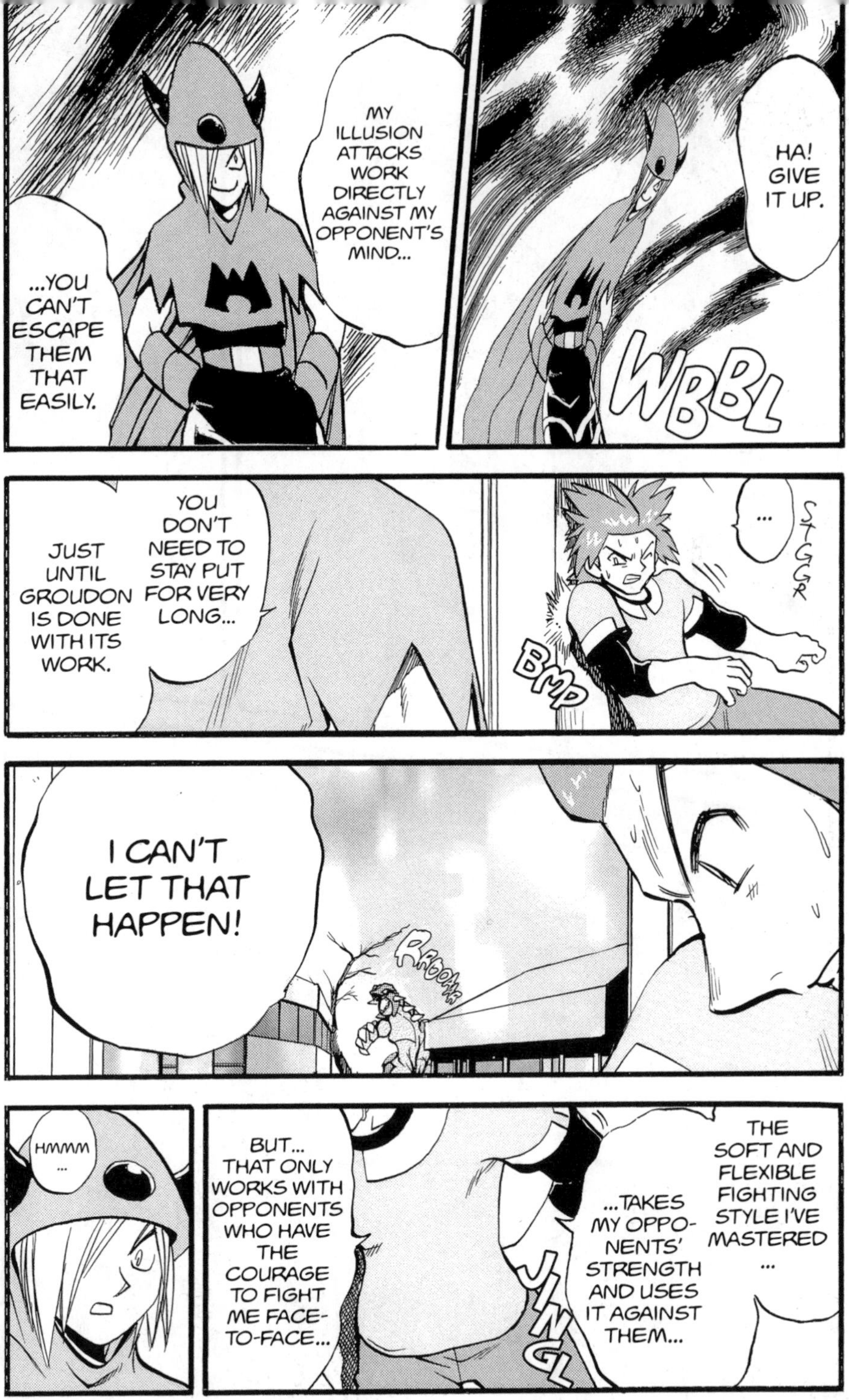
HA! GIVE IT UP.
WBBL
MY ILLUSION ATTACKS WORK DIRECTLY AGAINST MY OPPONENT'S MIND...
...YOU CAN'T ESCAPE THEM THAT EASILY.
...
STGGR
BMP
YOU DON'T NEED TO STAY PUT FOR VERY LONG...
JUST UNTIL GROUDON IS DONE WITH ITS WORK.
I CAN'T LET THAT HAPPEN!
THE SOFT AND FLEXIBLE FIGHTING STYLE I'VE MASTERED ...
...TAKES MY OPPO-NENTS' STRENGTH AND USES IT AGAINST THEM...
JINGL
BUT... THAT ONLY WORKS WITH OPPONENTS WHO HAVE THE COURAGE TO FIGHT ME FACE-TO-FACE...
HMMM ...

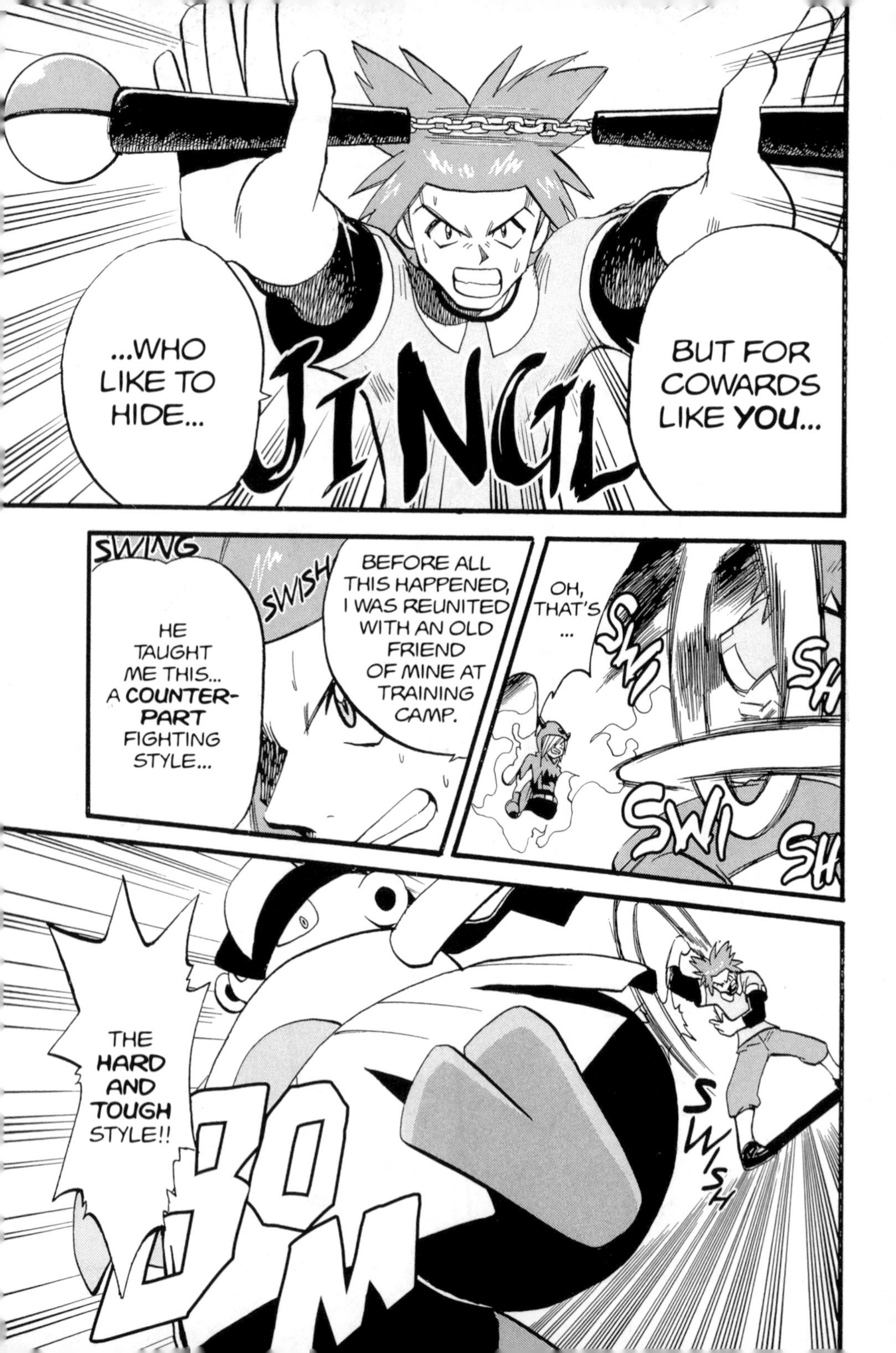
BUT FOR COWARDS LIKE YOU...
...WHO LIKE TO HIDE...
JINGL
OH, THAT'S ...
SWI SH
SWI SH
BEFORE ALL THIS HAPPENED, I WAS REUNITED WITH AN OLD FRIEND OF MINE AT TRAINING CAMP.
SWISH
SWING
HE TAUGHT ME THIS... A COUNTER-PART FIGHTING STYLE...
SWISH
THE HARD AND TOUGH STYLE!!
BOOM

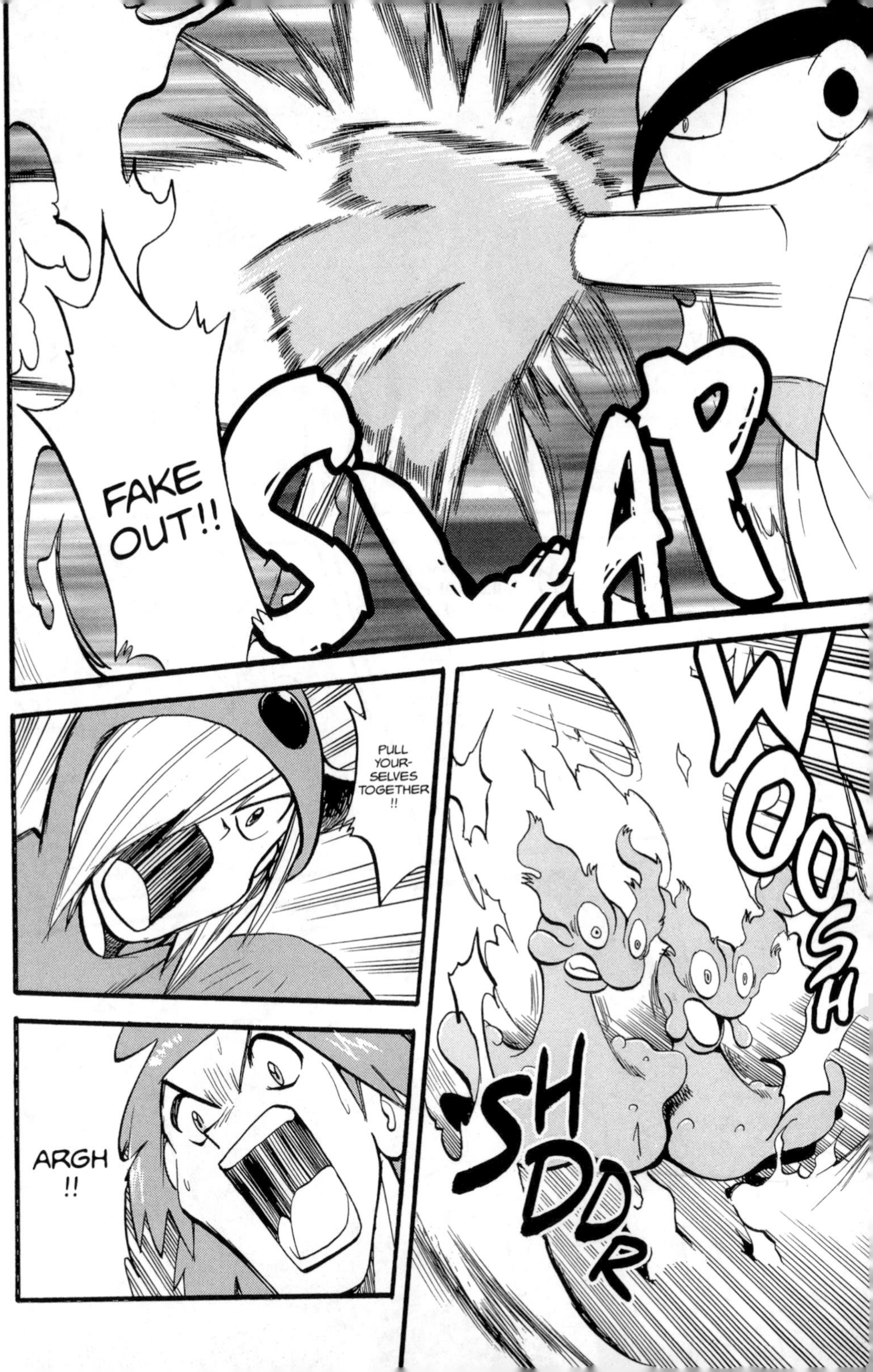
SLAP
FAKE OUT!!
WOOOSH
SHDDR
PULL YOUR-SELVES TOGETHER!!
ARGH!!

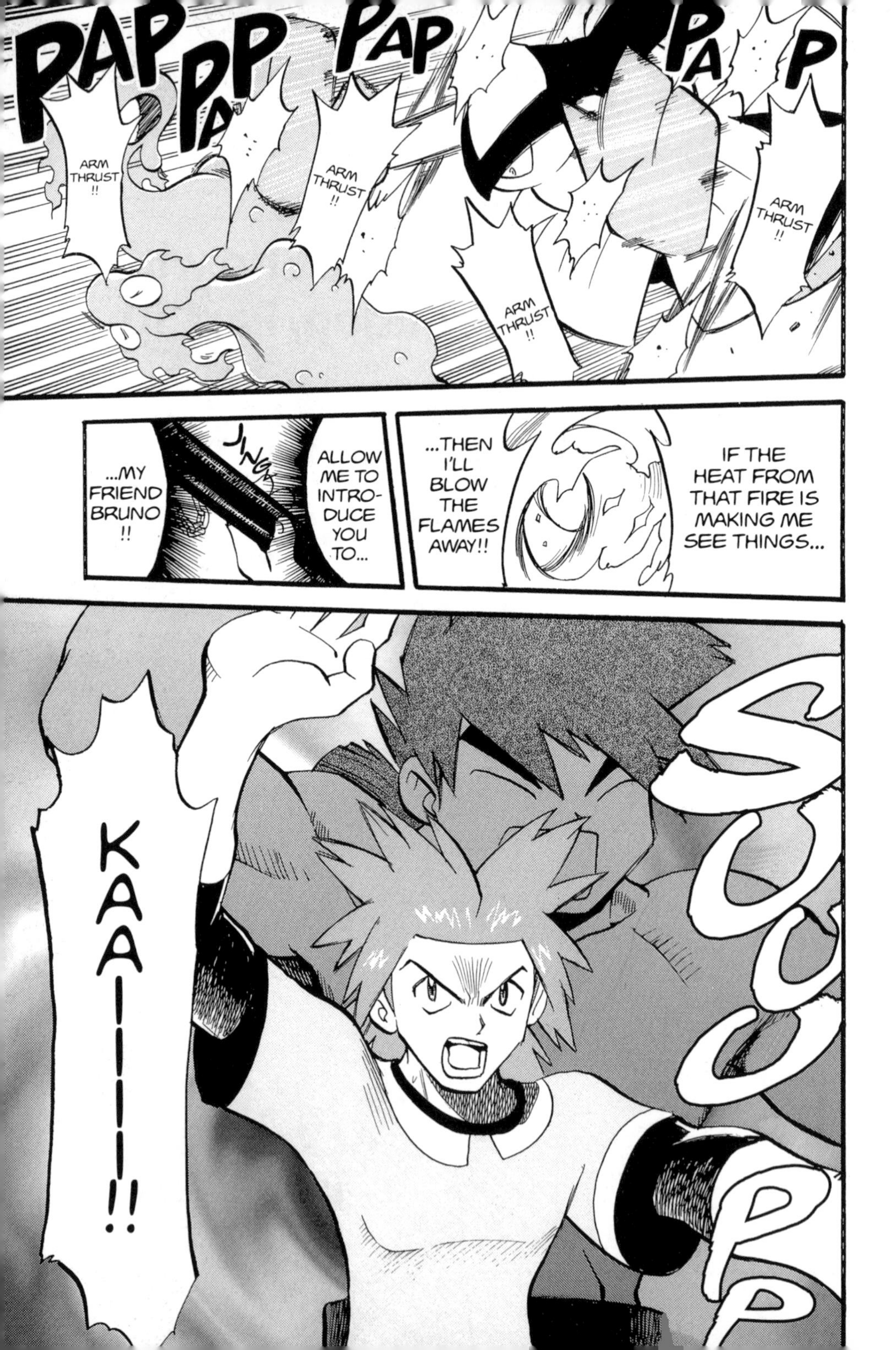
PAP
ARM THRUST!!
ARM THRUST!!
PAP
ARM THRUST!!
PAP PA
PAP
ARM THRUST!!
IF THE HEAT FROM THAT FIRE IS MAKING ME SEE THINGS...
...THEN I'LL BLOW THE FLAMES AWAY!!
ALLOW ME TO INTRO-DUCE YOU TO...
JING
...MY FRIEND BRUNO!!
KAAIIIII!!

● Adventure 248 ●

The Beginning of the End with Kyogre and Groudon, Part 10

Pokémon™ Adventures Ruby & Sapphire

The Fourth Chapter

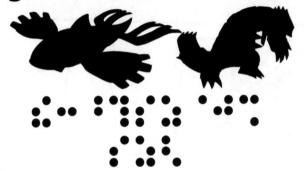

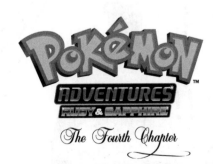

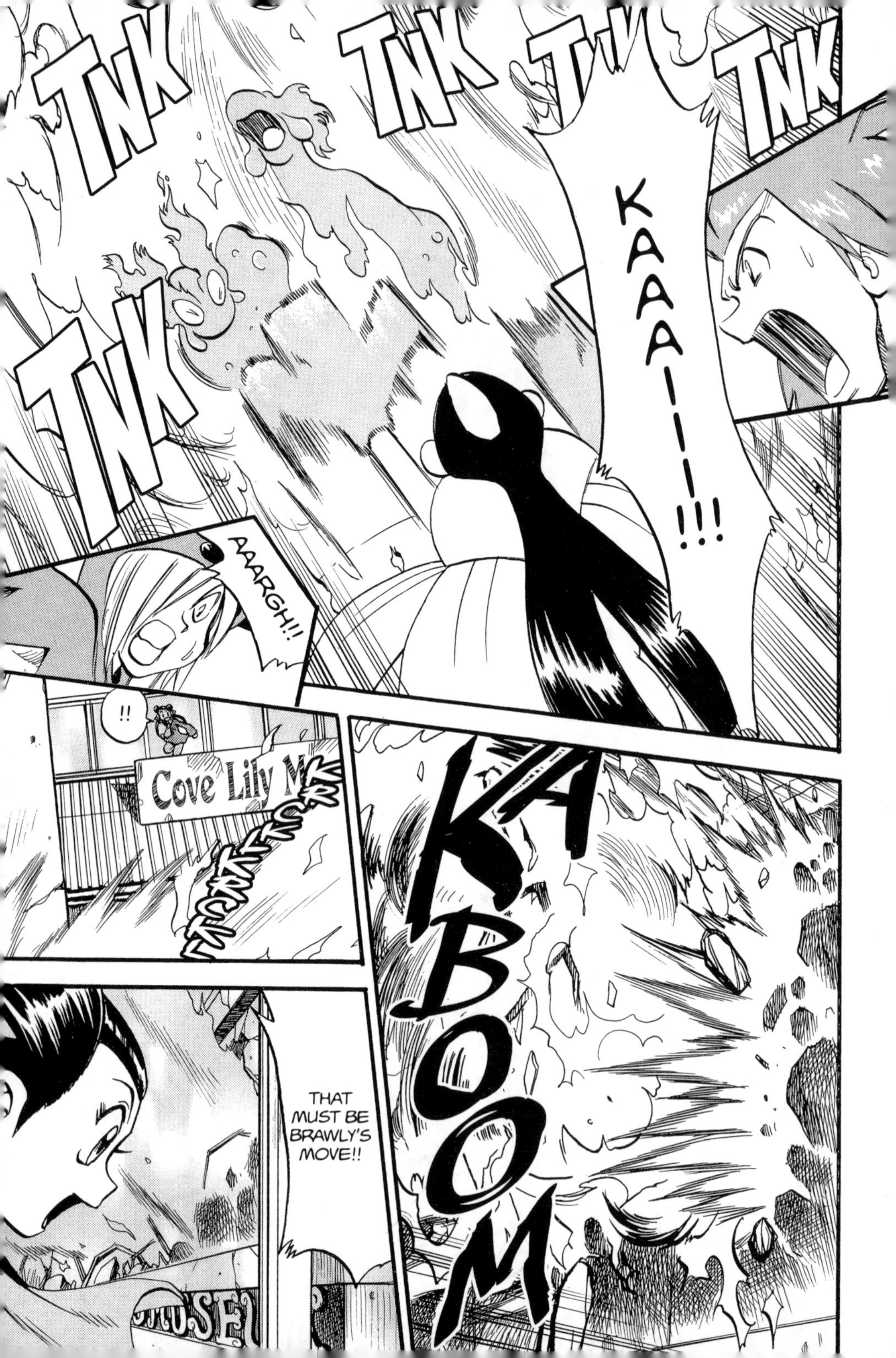
TNK
TNK
TNK
TNK
TNK
KAAAIIII!!!!
AAARGH!!
KABOOM
!!
Cove Lily M
KRCKL KRCKL
THAT MUST BE BRAWLY'S MOVE!!

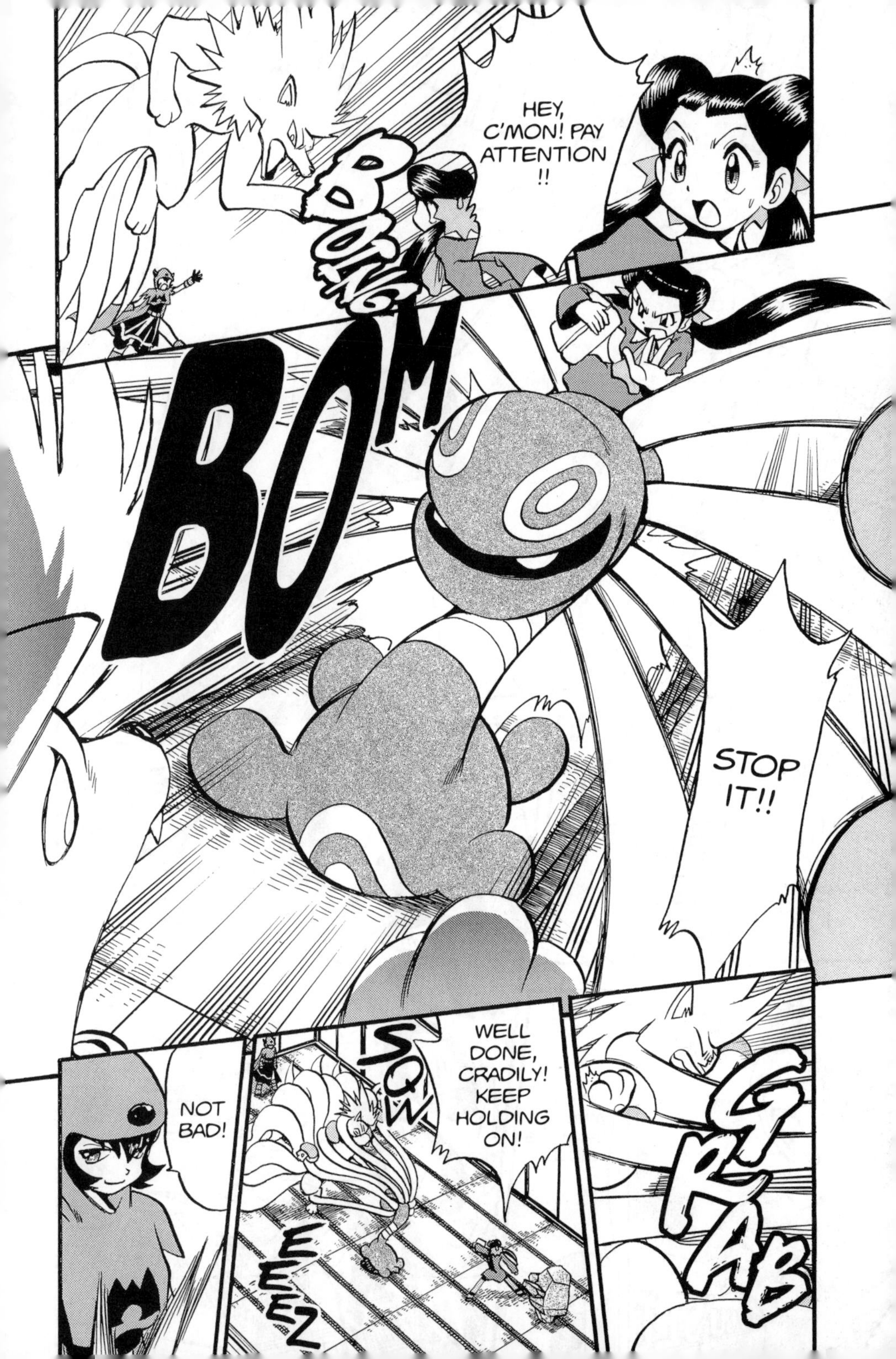
HEY, C'MON! PAY ATTENTION !!
BOING
BOOM
STOP IT!!
GRAB
SQW
EEEZ
WELL DONE, CRADILY! KEEP HOLDING ON!
NOT BAD!

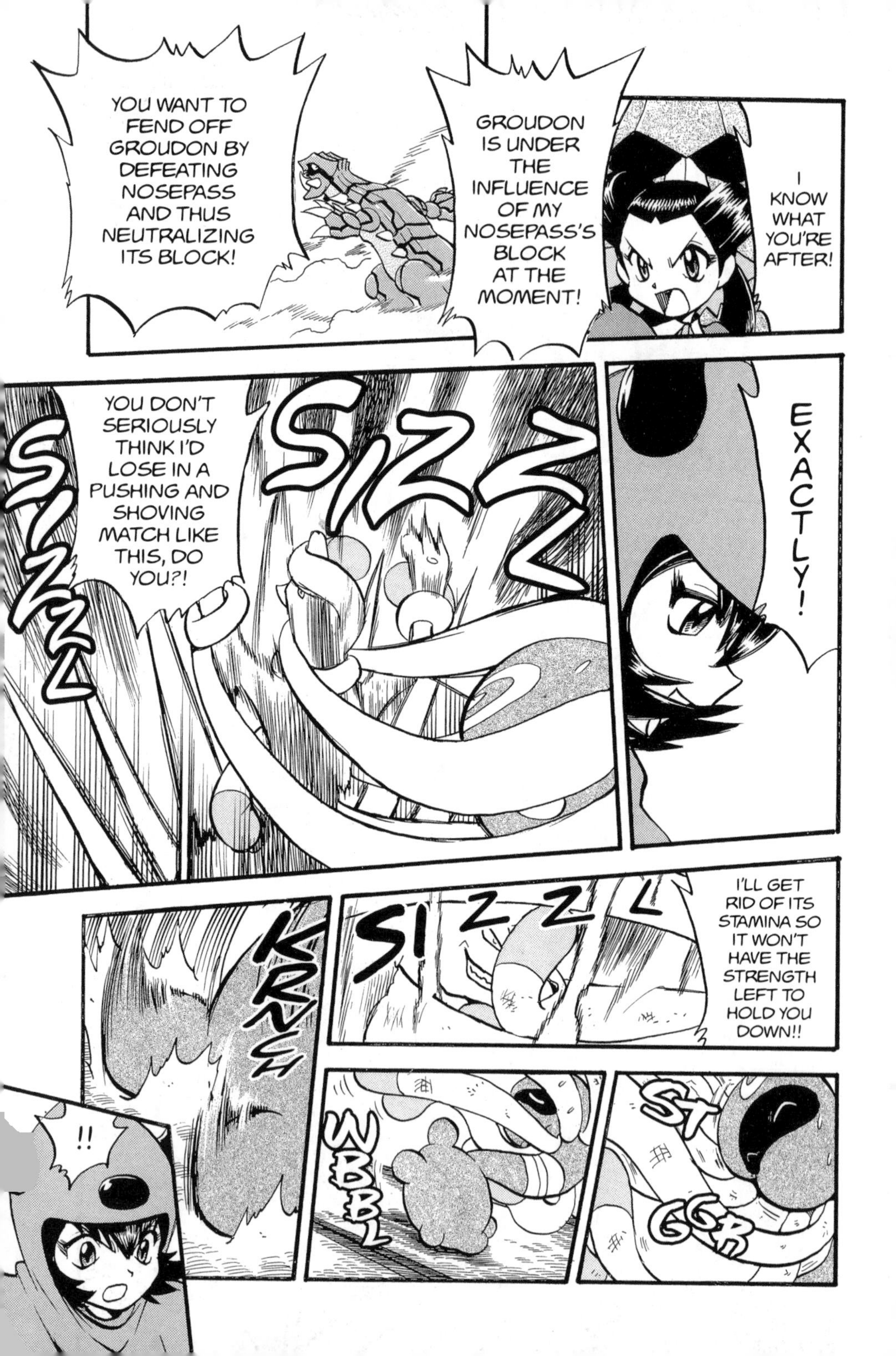
I KNOW WHAT YOU'RE AFTER!
GROUDON IS UNDER THE INFLUENCE OF MY NOSEPASS'S BLOCK AT THE MOMENT!
YOU WANT TO FEND OFF GROUDON BY DEFEATING NOSEPASS AND THUS NEUTRALIZING ITS BLOCK!
EXACTLY!
SIZZZL
YOU DON'T SERIOUSLY THINK I'D LOSE IN A PUSHING AND SHOVING MATCH LIKE THIS, DO YOU?!
SIZZZL
I'LL GET RID OF ITS STAMINA SO IT WON'T HAVE THE STRENGTH LEFT TO HOLD YOU DOWN!!
SIZZZL
KRNCH
ST
GGR
WBBL
!!

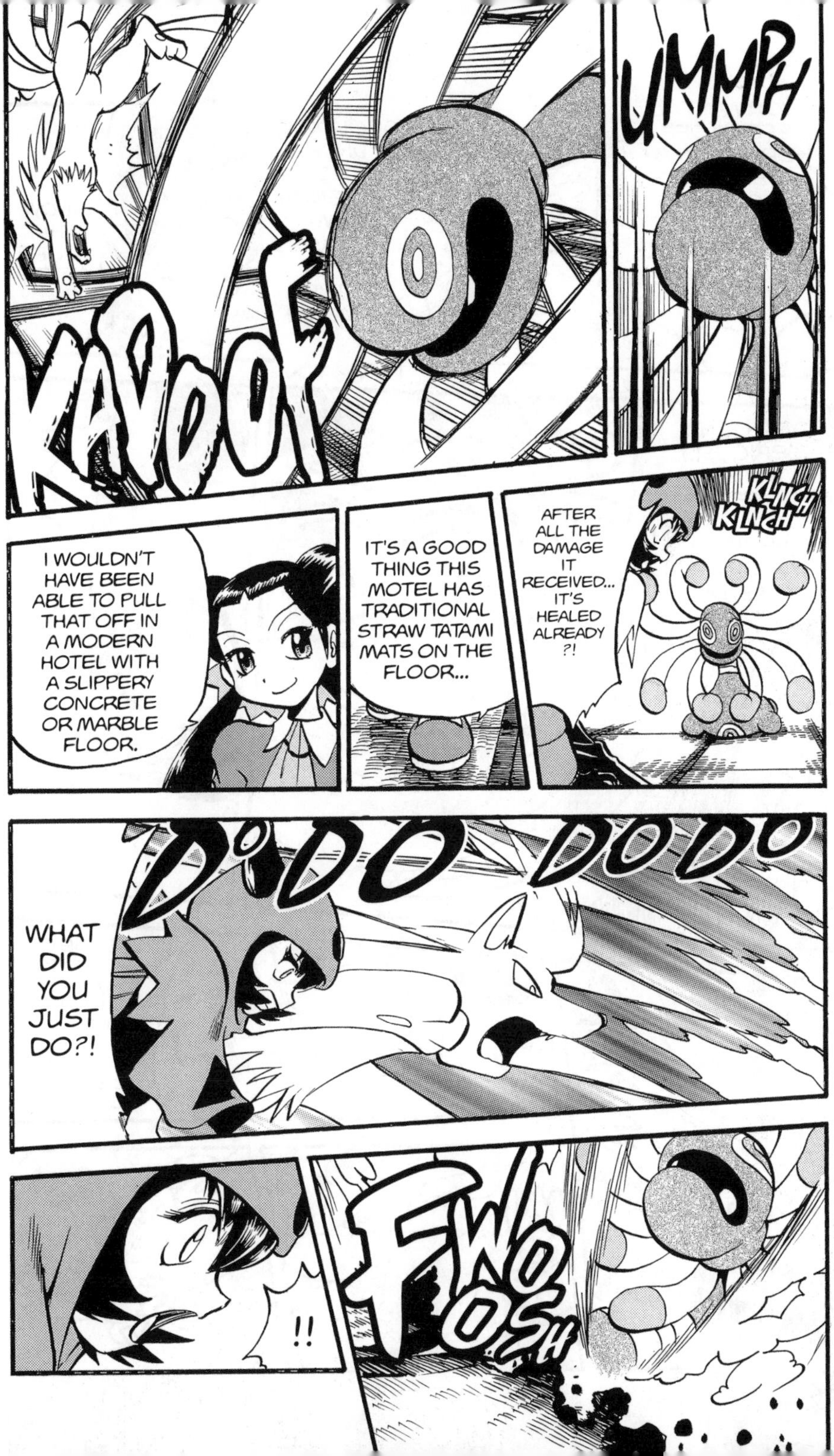
UMMPH
KAPOOF
KLNCH KLNCH
AFTER ALL THE DAMAGE IT RECEIVED... IT'S HEALED ALREADY?!
IT'S A GOOD THING THIS MOTEL HAS TRADITIONAL STRAW TATAMI MATS ON THE FLOOR...
I WOULDN'T HAVE BEEN ABLE TO PULL THAT OFF IN A MODERN HOTEL WITH A SLIPPERY CONCRETE OR MARBLE FLOOR.
DO DO DO DO
WHAT DID YOU JUST DO?!
FWOOSH
!!

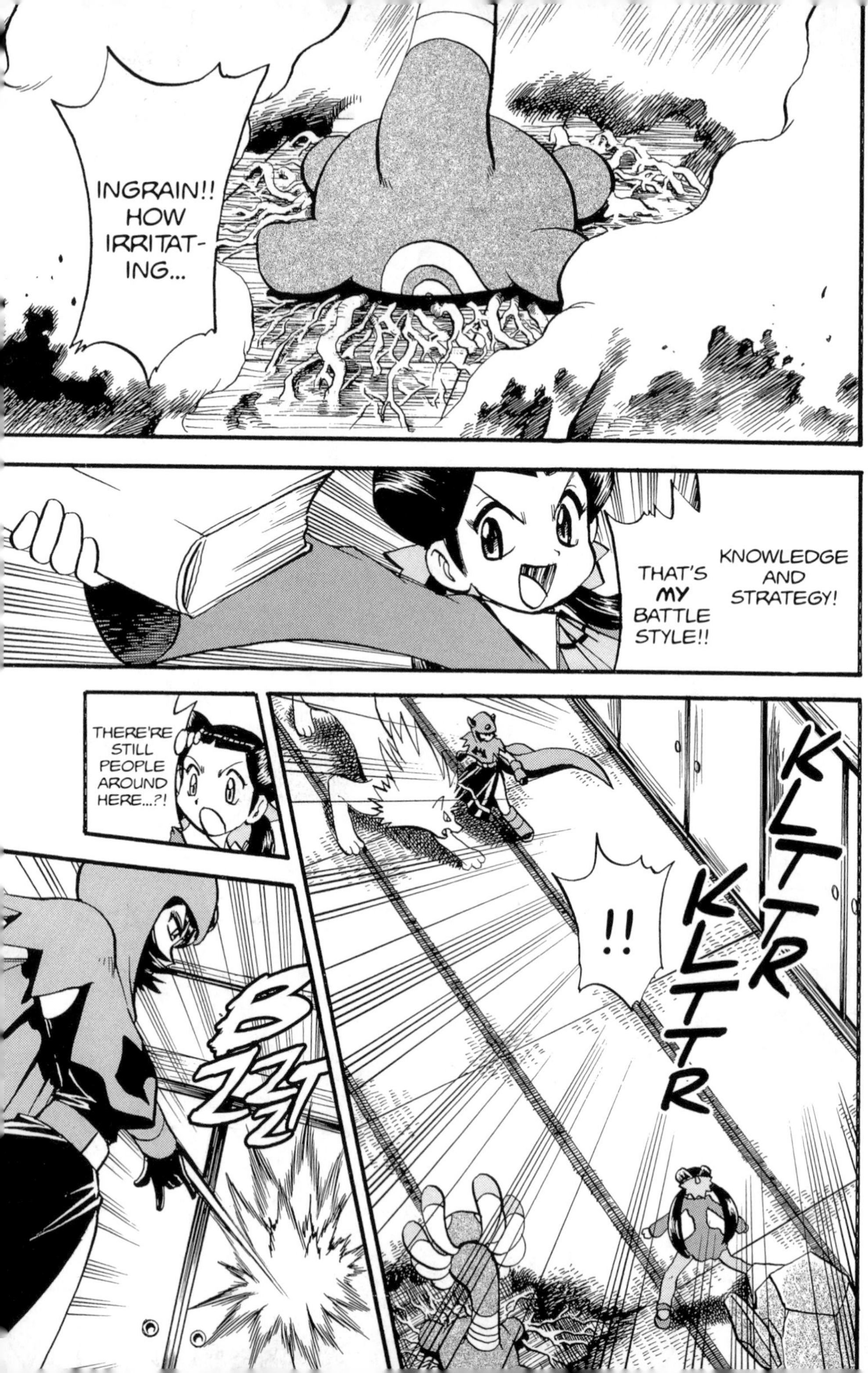
INGRAIN!! HOW IRRITAT-ING...
KNOWLEDGE AND STRATEGY!
THAT'S MY BATTLE STYLE!!
KLTTR KLTTR
!!
THERE'RE STILL PEOPLE AROUND HERE...?!
BZZT

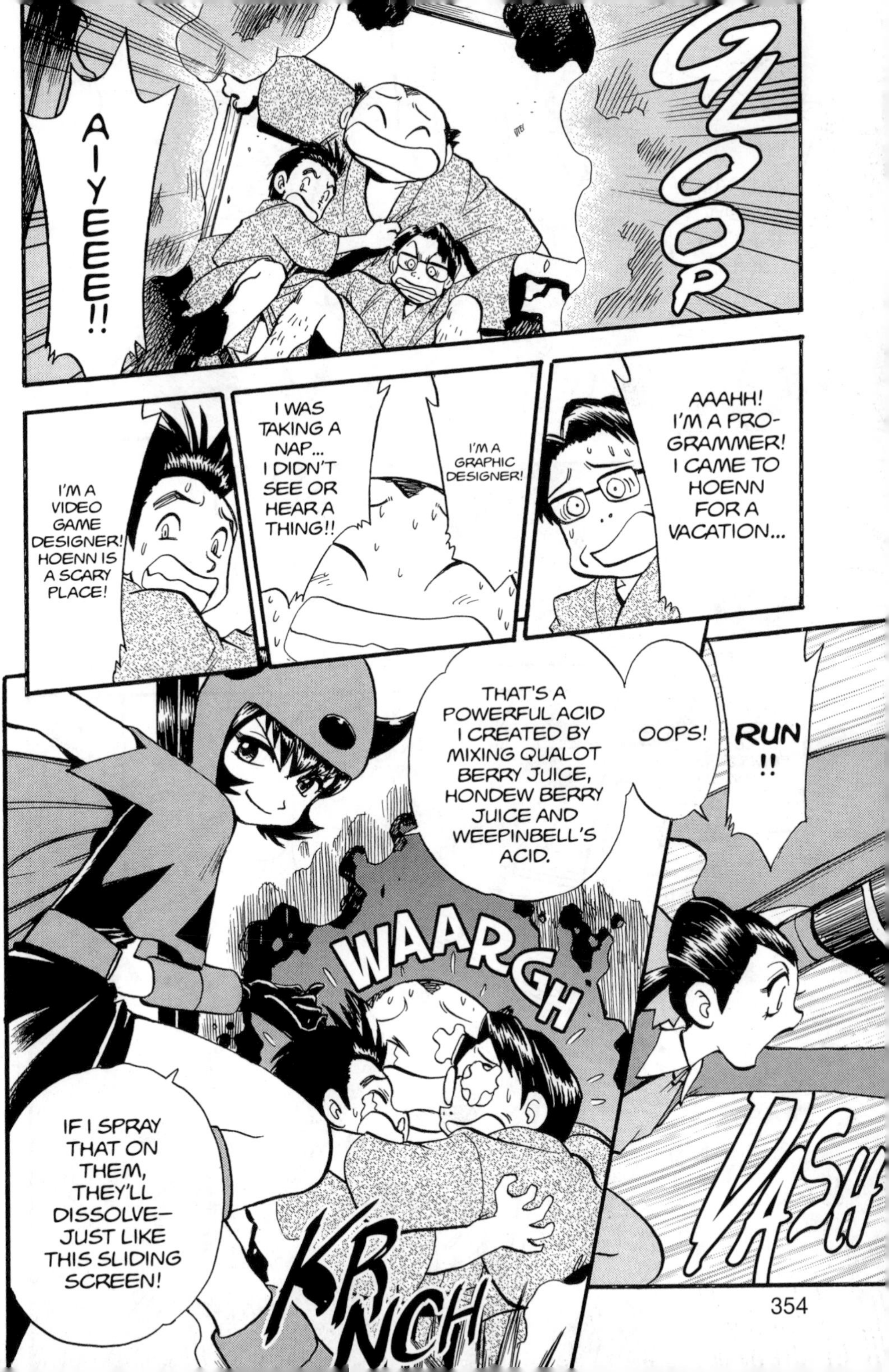

GLOOOP
AIYEEEE!!
AAAHH! I'M A PRO-GRAMMER! I CAME TO HOENN FOR A VACATION...
I'M A GRAPHIC DESIGNER!
I WAS TAKING A NAP... I DIDN'T SEE OR HEAR A THING!!
I'M A VIDEO GAME DESIGNER! HOENN IS A SCARY PLACE!
RUN !!
OOPS!
THAT'S A POWERFUL ACID I CREATED BY MIXING QUALOT BERRY JUICE, HONDEW BERRY JUICE AND WEEPINBELL'S ACID.
WAARGH
DASH
IF I SPRAY THAT ON THEM, THEY'LL DISSOLVE—JUST LIKE THIS SLIDING SCREEN!
KRNCH

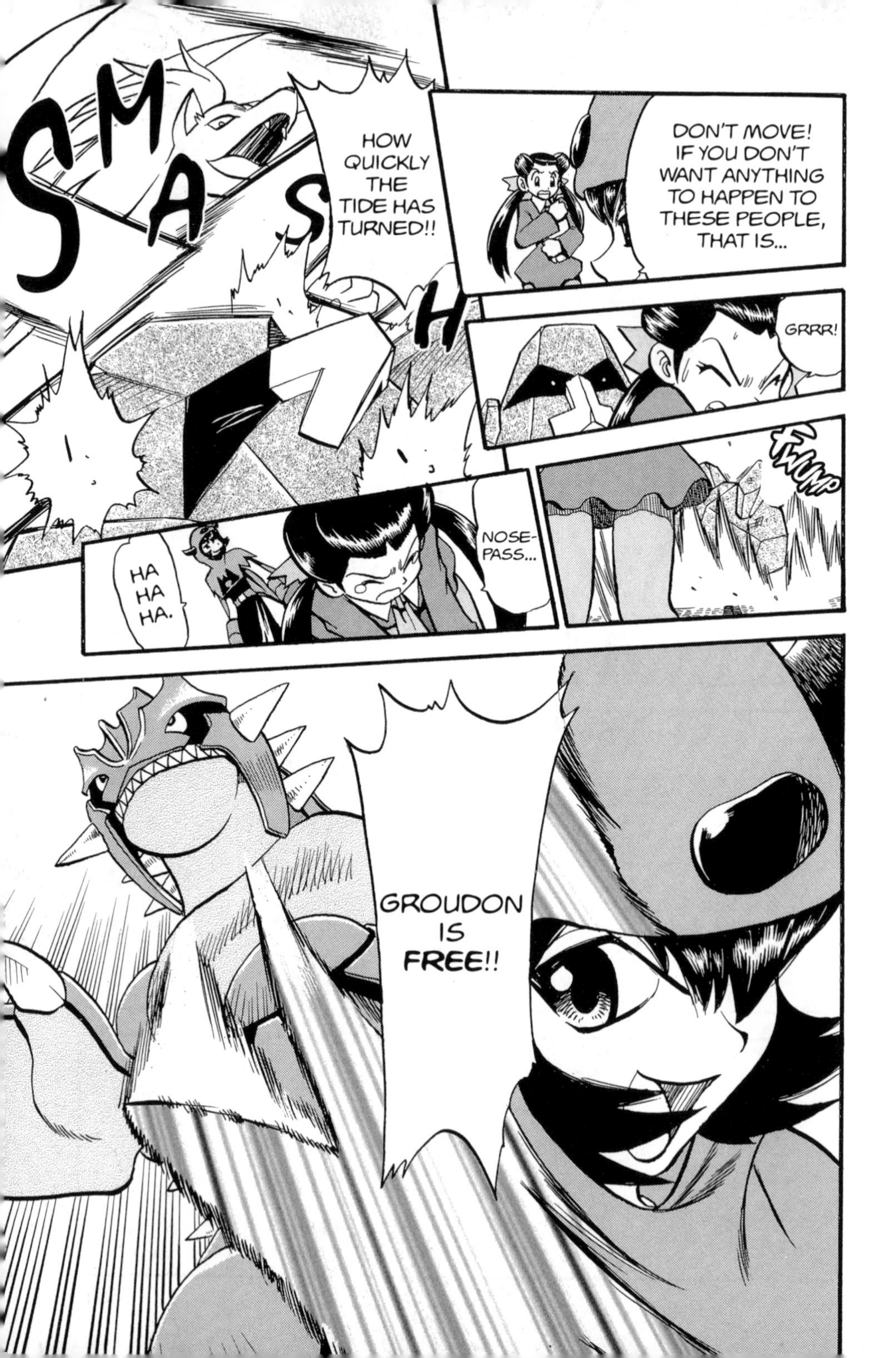
SMASH
HOW QUICKLY THE TIDE HAS TURNED!!
DON'T MOVE! IF YOU DON'T WANT ANYTHING TO HAPPEN TO THESE PEOPLE, THAT IS...
GRRR!
FWUMP
NOSE-PASS...
HA HA HA.
GROUDON IS **FREE**!!

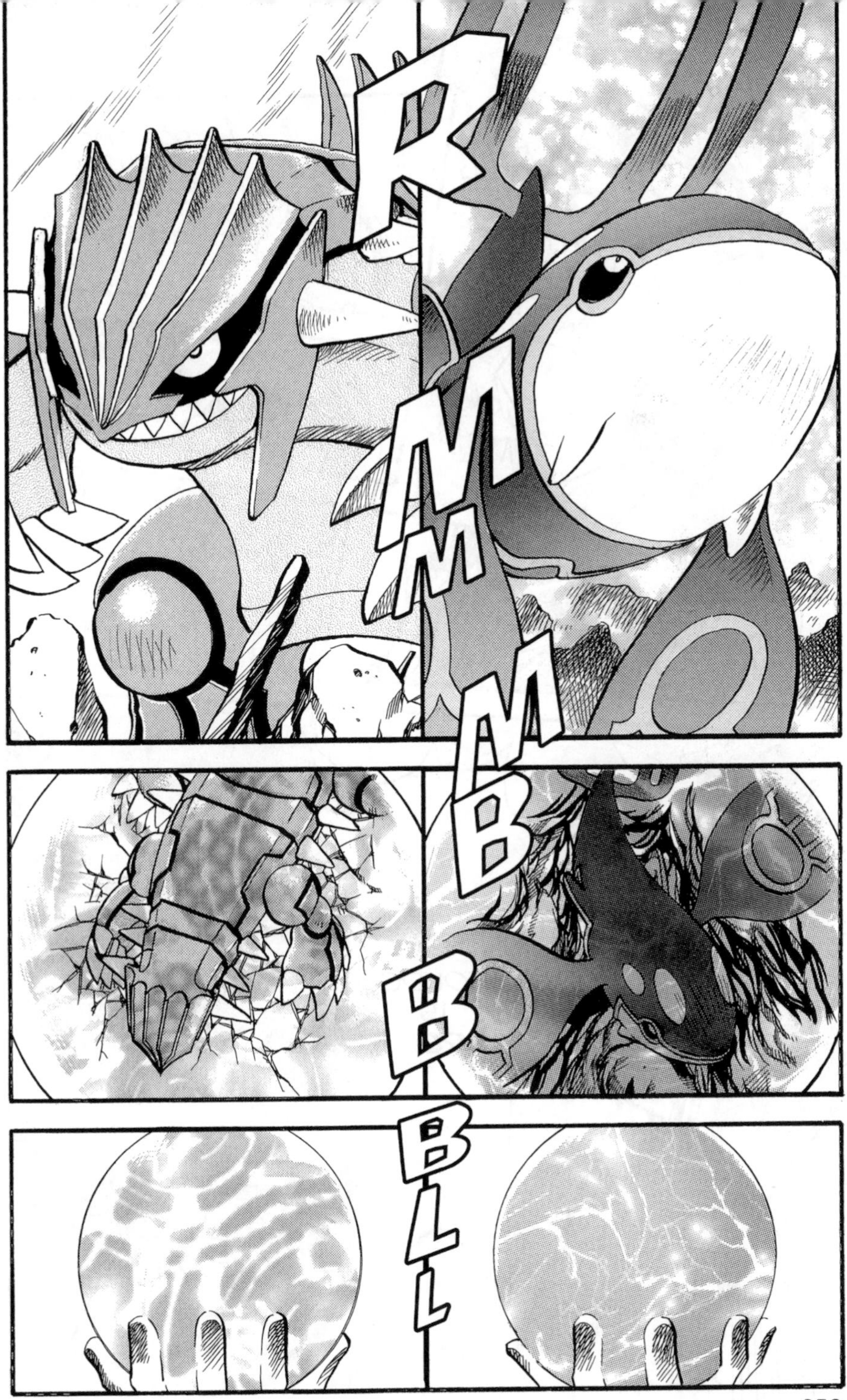
RMMMBBBLL

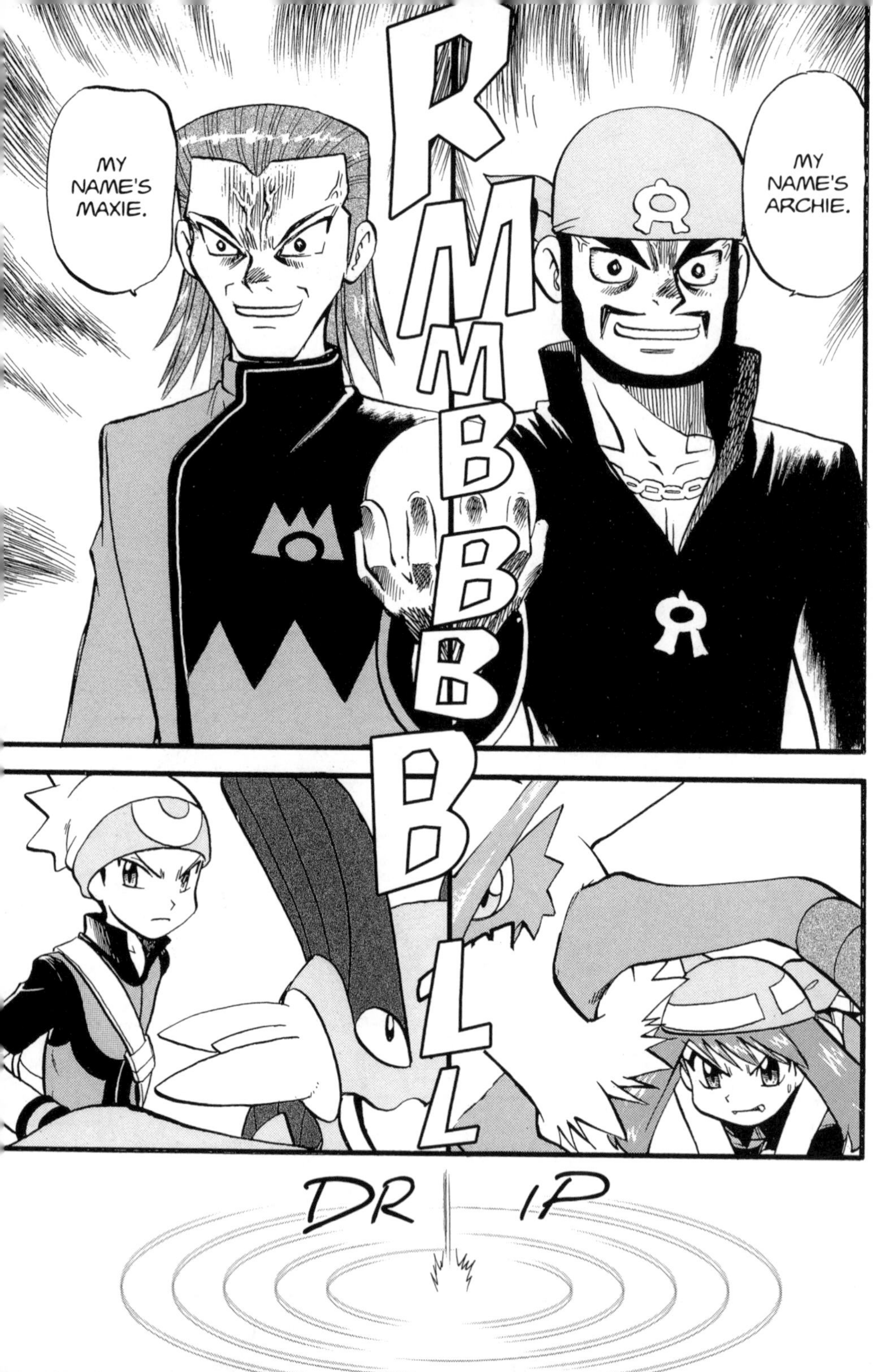
MY NAME'S ARCHIE.
MY NAME'S MAXIE.
RMMBBBBLL
DR IP

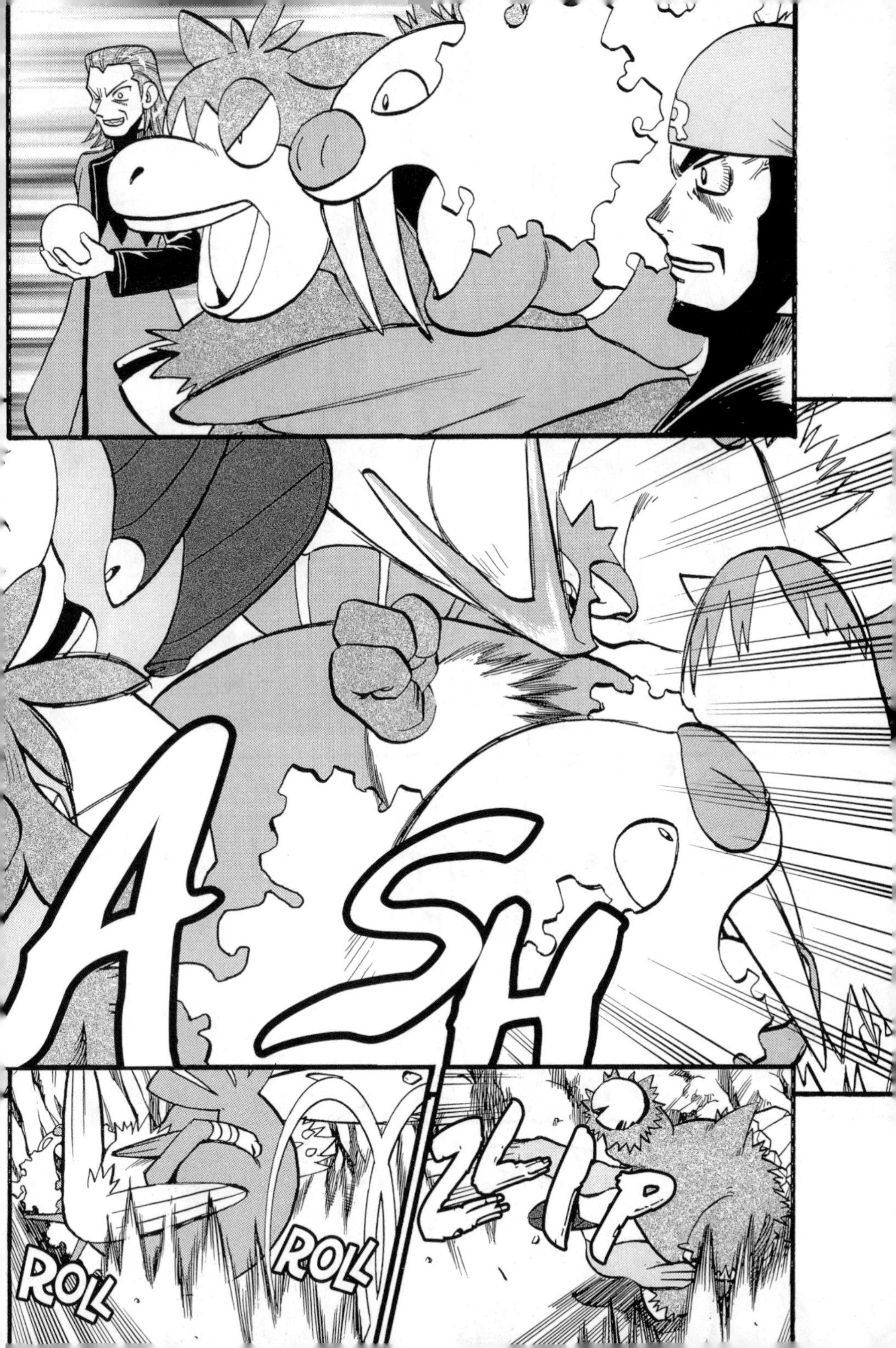
ASH
ZLIP
ROLL
ROLL

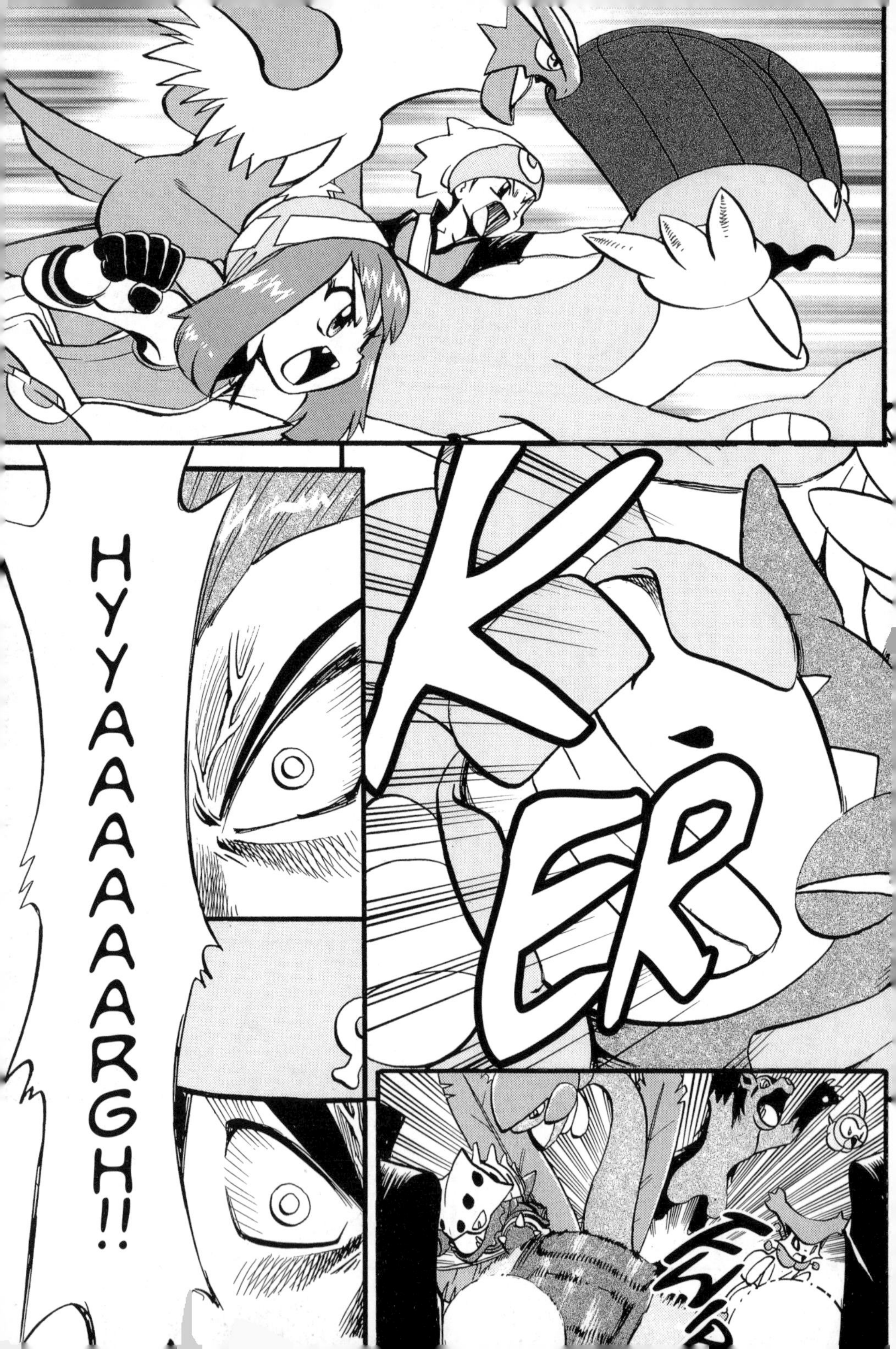
KER
TWIP
HYYAAAAAARGH!!

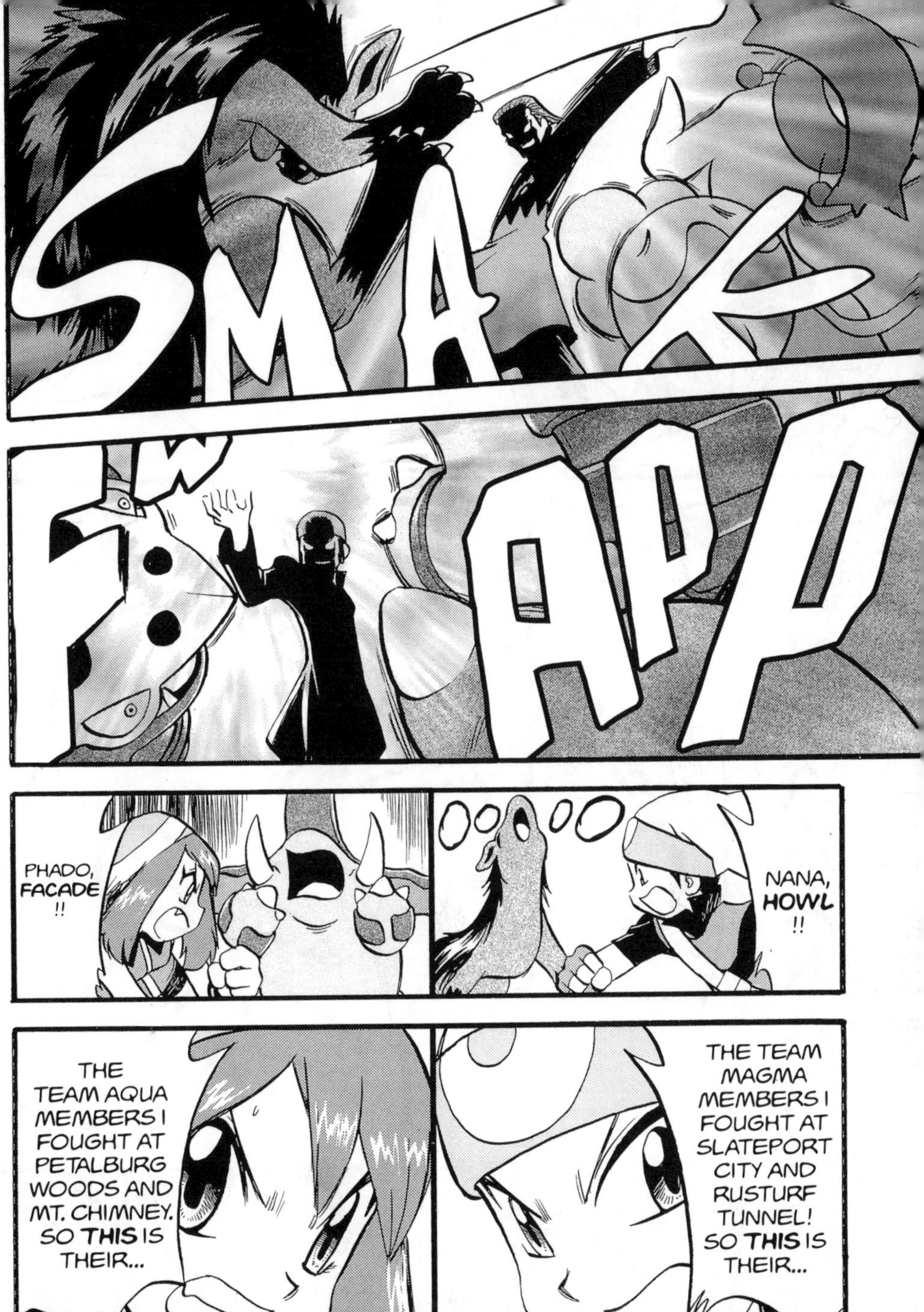
SMACK
FWAPP
NANA, HOWL !!
PHADO, FACADE !!
THE TEAM MAGMA MEMBERS I FOUGHT AT SLATEPORT CITY AND RUSTURF TUNNEL! SO THIS IS THEIR...
THE TEAM AQUA MEMBERS I FOUGHT AT PETALBURG WOODS AND MT. CHIMNEY. SO THIS IS THEIR...

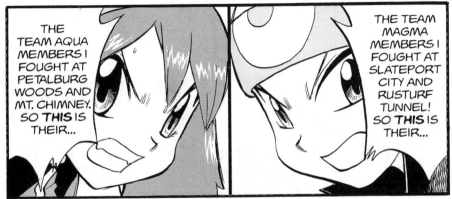

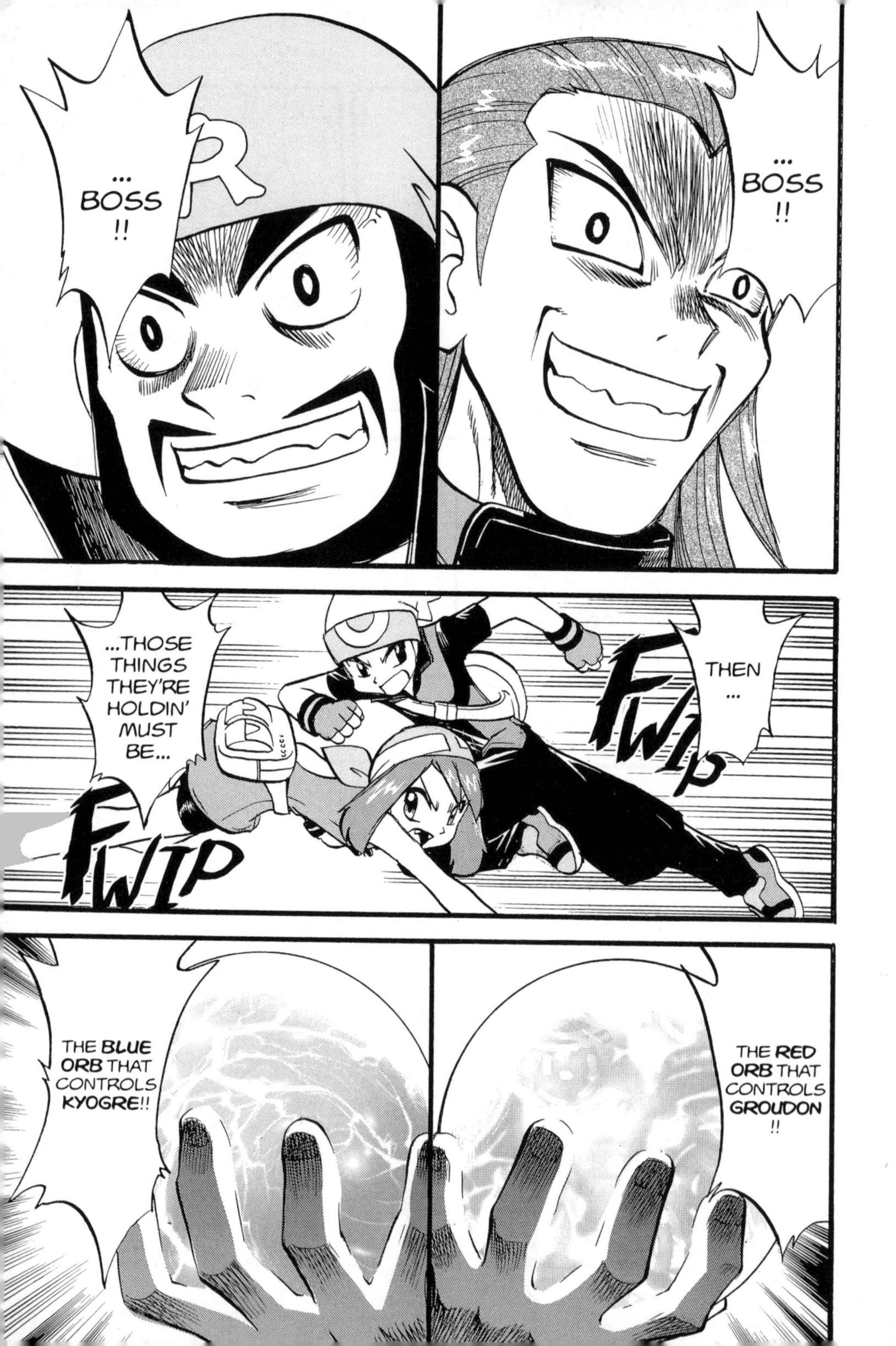
...BOSS!!
...BOSS!!
THEN...
FWIP
...THOSE THINGS THEY'RE HOLDIN' MUST BE...
FWIP
THE RED ORB THAT CONTROLS GROUDON!!
THE BLUE ORB THAT CONTROLS KYOGRE!!

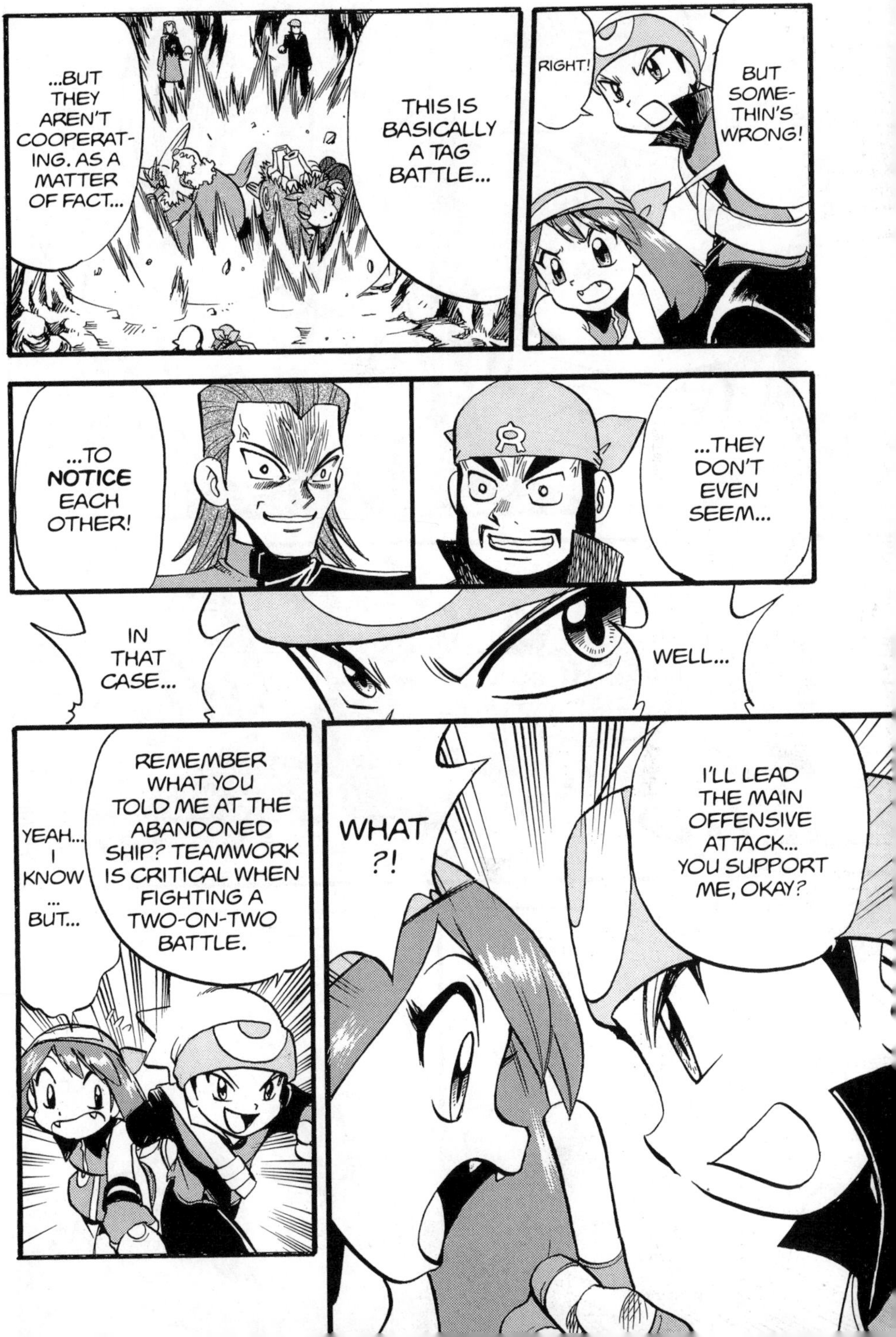
RIGHT!
BUT SOMETHIN'S WRONG!
THIS IS BASICALLY A TAG BATTLE...
...BUT THEY AREN'T COOPERATING. AS A MATTER OF FACT...
...THEY DON'T EVEN SEEM...
...TO **NOTICE** EACH OTHER!
WELL...
IN THAT CASE...
I'LL LEAD THE MAIN OFFENSIVE ATTACK... YOU SUPPORT ME, OKAY?
WHAT?!
REMEMBER WHAT YOU TOLD ME AT THE ABANDONED SHIP? TEAMWORK IS CRITICAL WHEN FIGHTING A TWO-ON-TWO BATTLE.
YEAH... I KNOW... BUT...

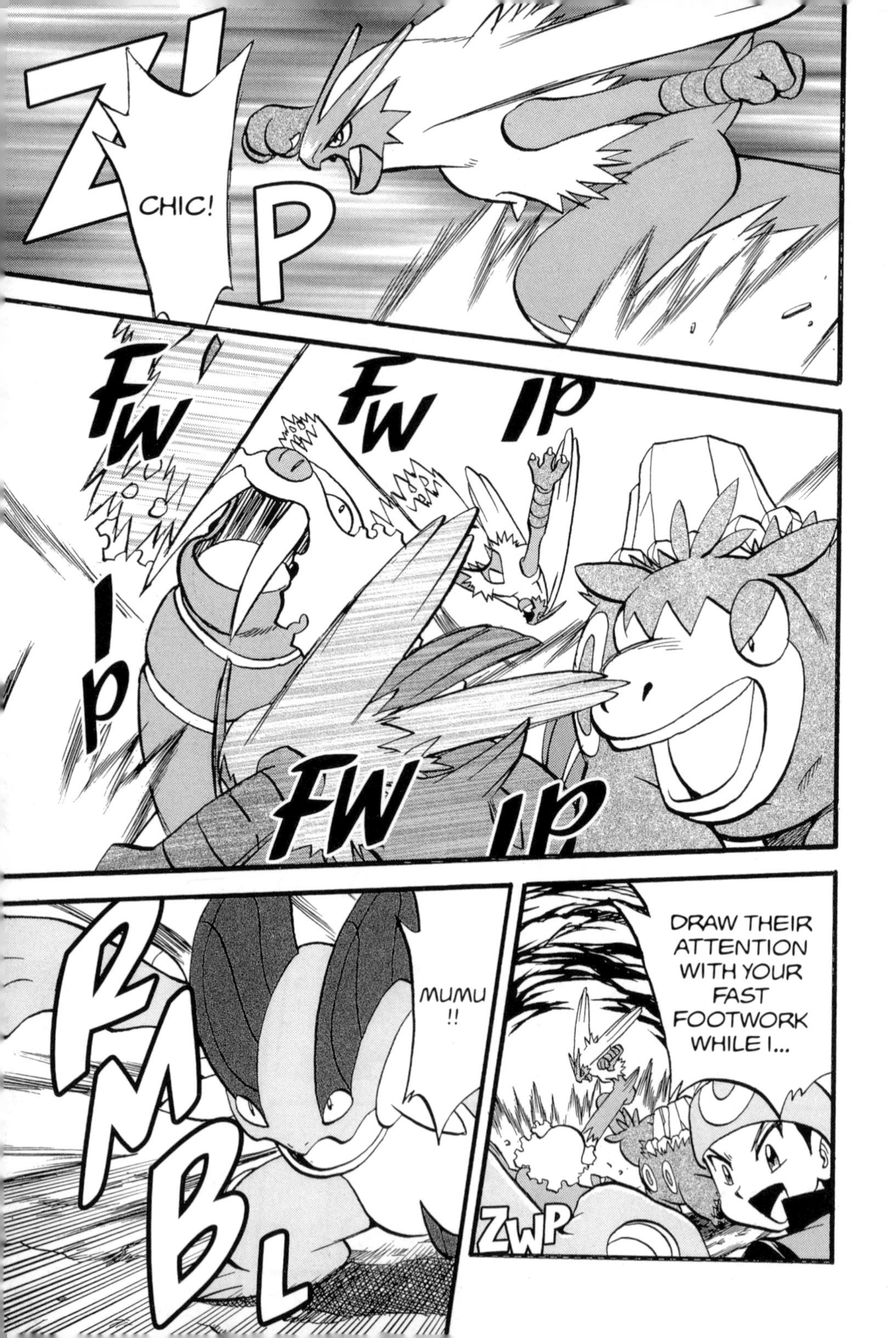
ZAP
CHIC!
FWIP
FWIP
FWIP
DRAW THEIR ATTENTION WITH YOUR FAST FOOTWORK WHILE I...
ZWP
MUMU !!
PMMBL

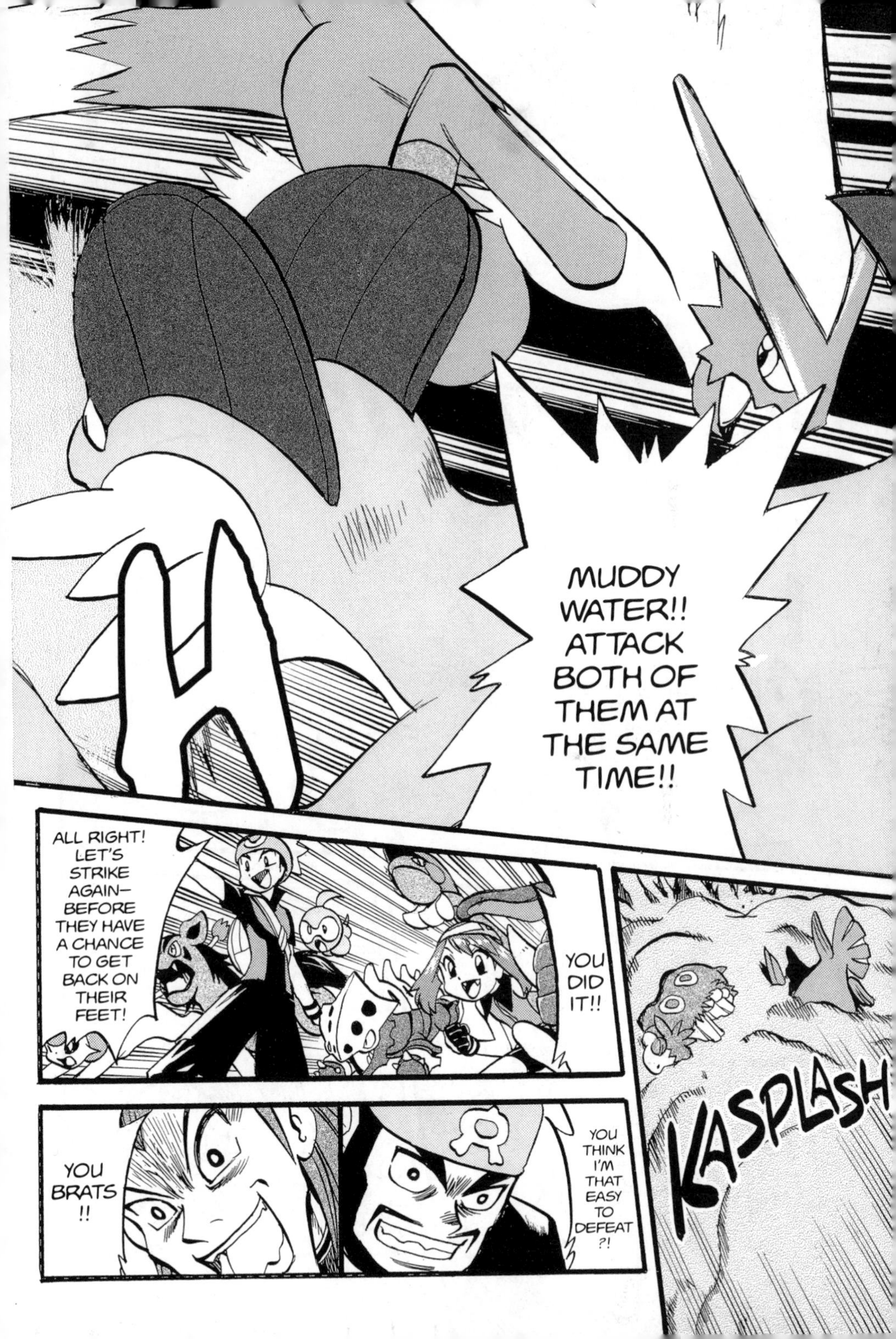
MUDDY WATER!! ATTACK BOTH OF THEM AT THE SAME TIME!!
KASPLASH
YOU DID IT!!
ALL RIGHT! LET'S STRIKE AGAIN— BEFORE THEY HAVE A CHANCE TO GET BACK ON THEIR FEET!
YOU THINK I'M THAT EASY TO DEFEAT ?!
YOU BRATS !!

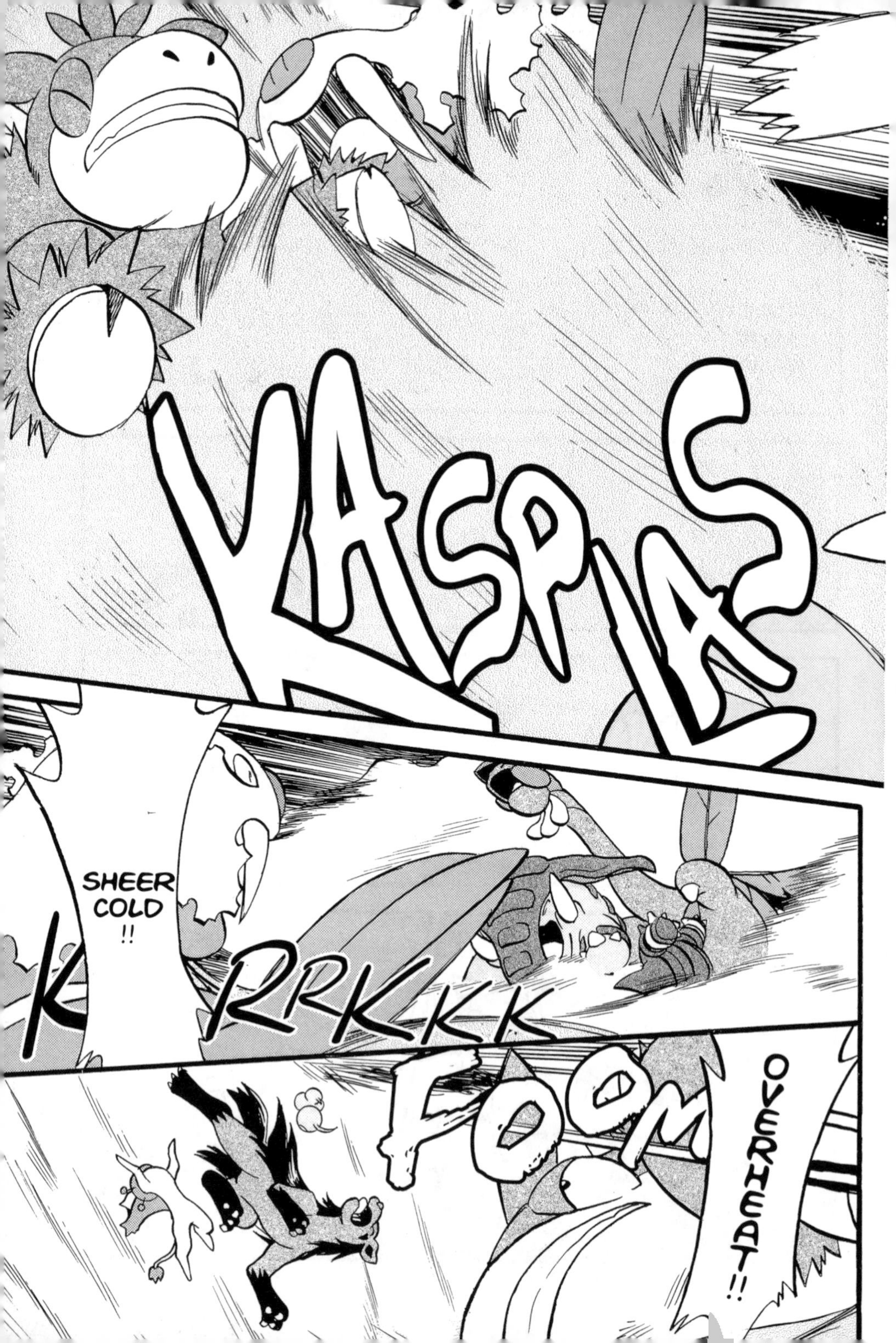
KASPIAS
SHEER COLD!!
KRRKKK
OVERHEAT!!
FOOM

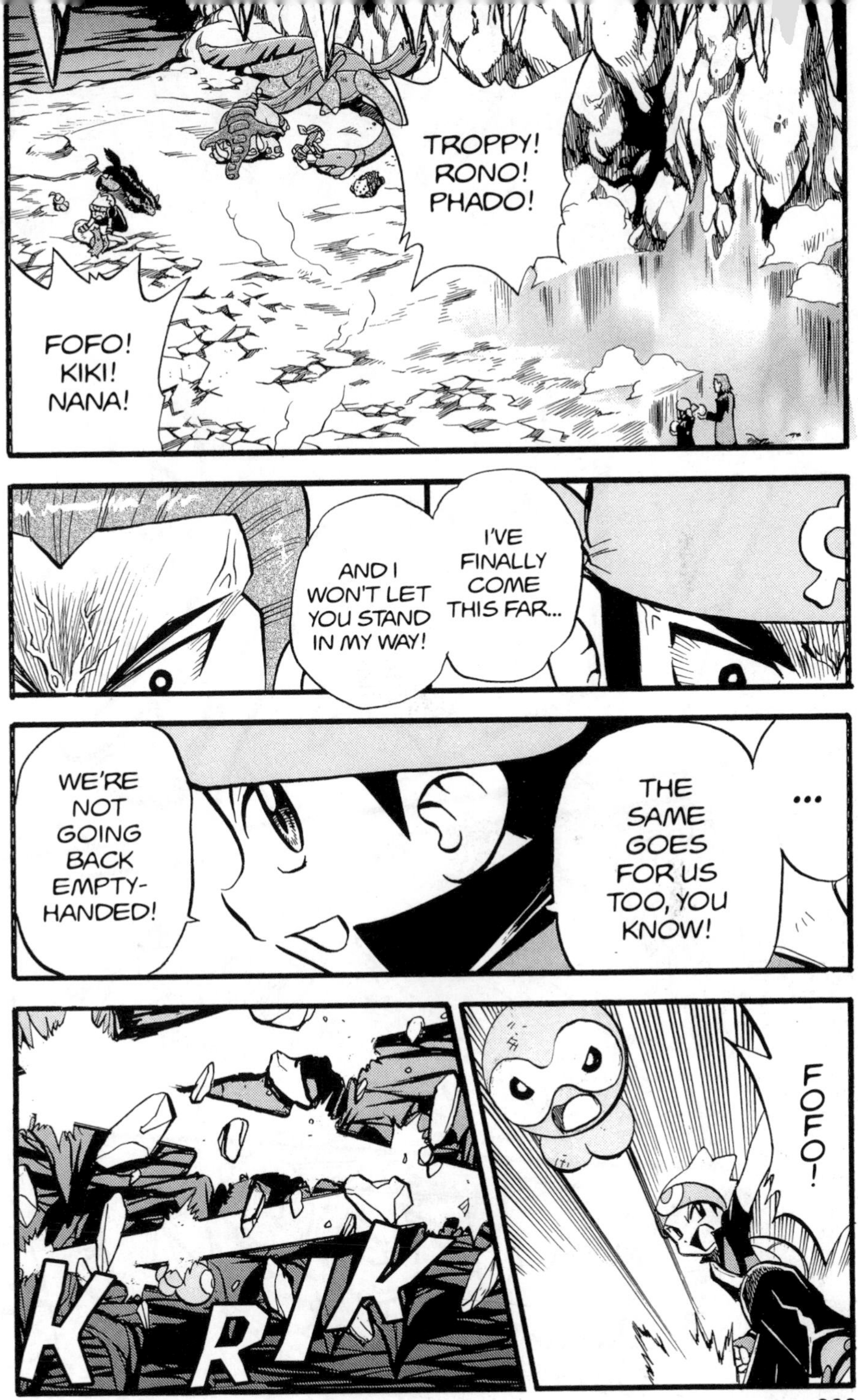
TROPPY! RONO! PHADO!
FOFO! KIKI! NANA!
I'VE FINALLY COME THIS FAR...
AND I WON'T LET YOU STAND IN MY WAY!
...
THE SAME GOES FOR US TOO, YOU KNOW!
WE'RE NOT GOING BACK EMPTY-HANDED!
FOFO!
KRIK

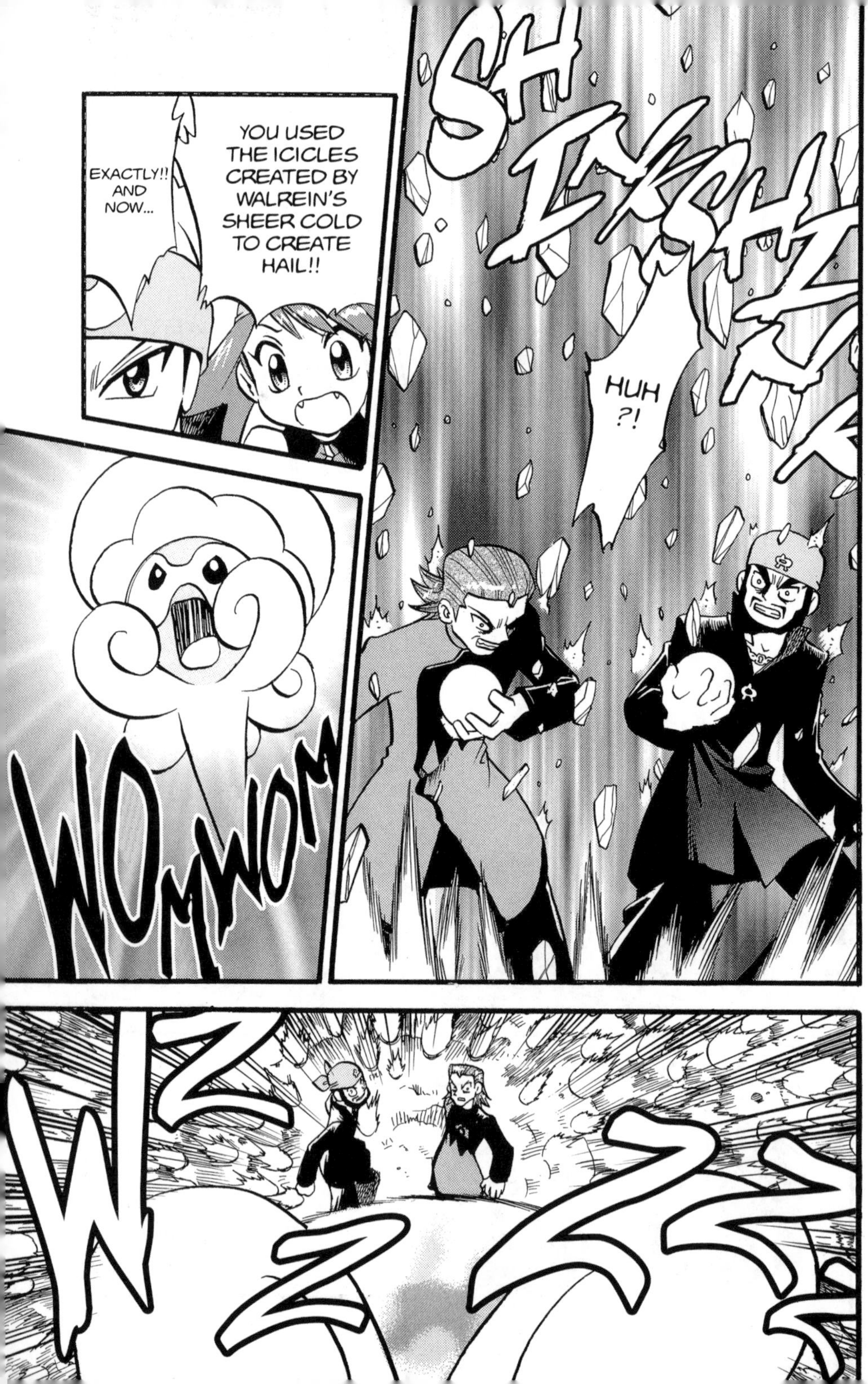
HUH ?!
YOU USED THE ICICLES CREATED BY WALREIN'S SHEER COLD TO CREATE HAIL!!
EXACTLY!! AND NOW...
WOMWOM

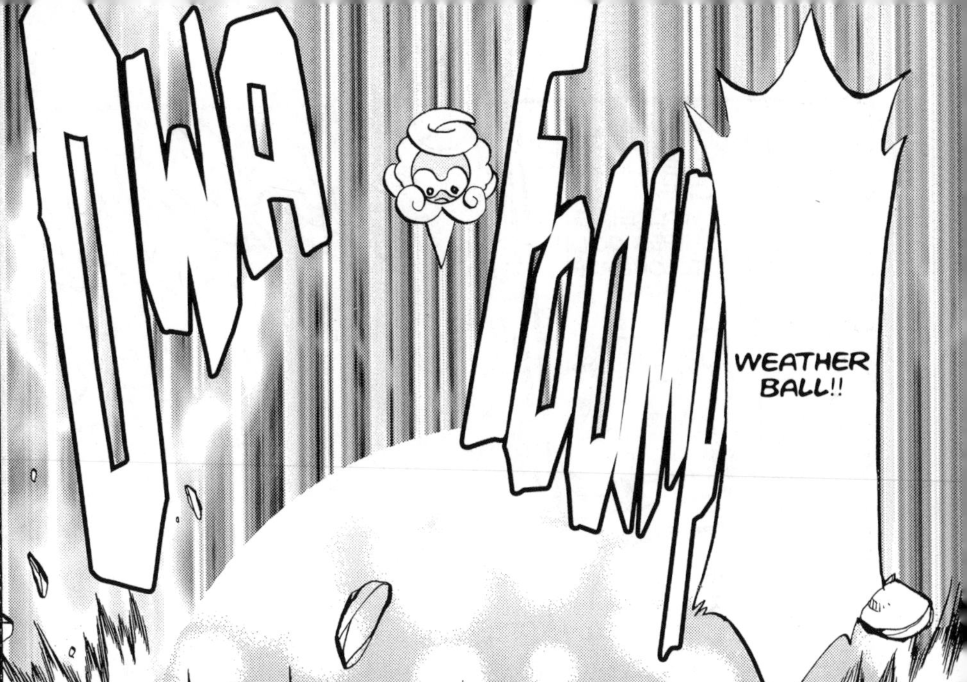
WEATHER BALL!!

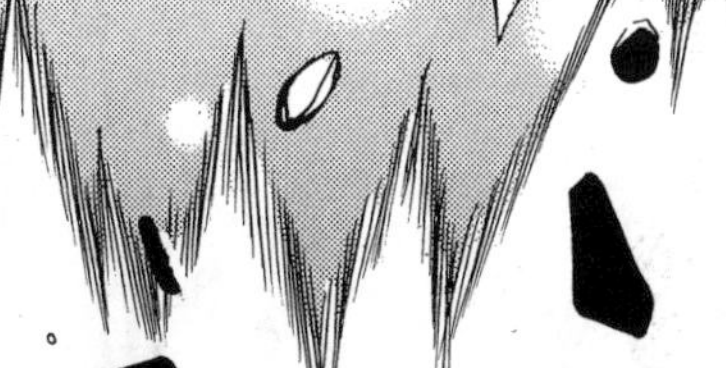

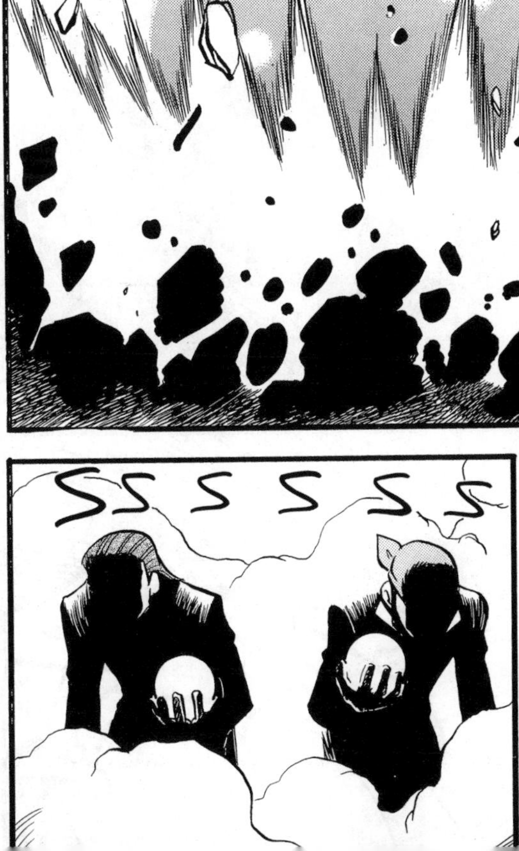
SSSSSS

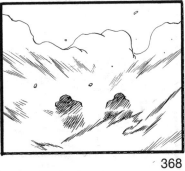

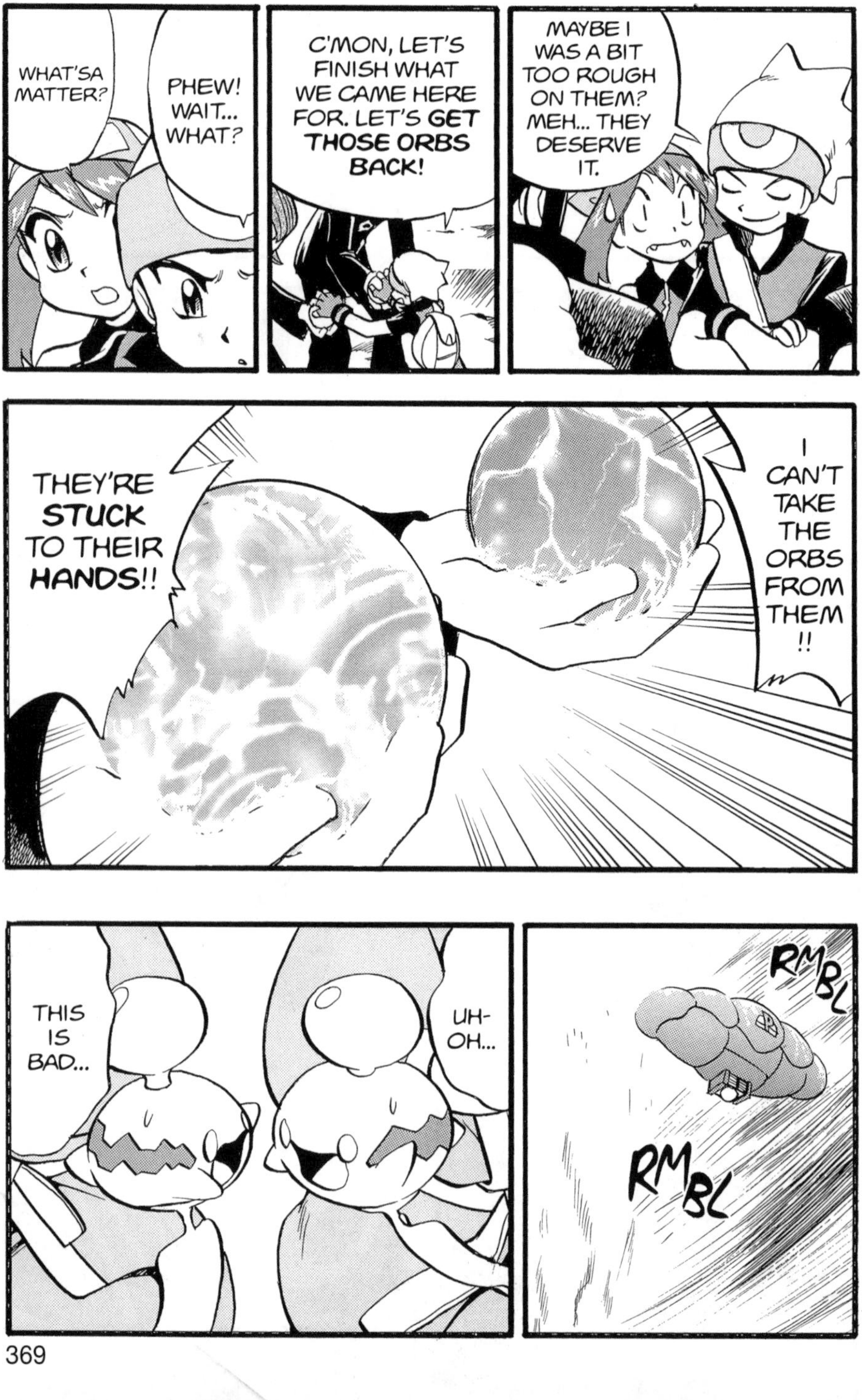
MAYBE I WAS A BIT TOO ROUGH ON THEM? MEH... THEY DESERVE IT.
C'MON, LET'S FINISH WHAT WE CAME HERE FOR. LET'S **GET THOSE ORBS BACK**!
PHEW! WAIT... WHAT?
WHAT'SA MATTER?
I CAN'T TAKE THE ORBS FROM THEM!!
THEY'RE **STUCK** TO THEIR **HANDS**!!
RMBL
RMBL
UH-OH...
THIS IS BAD...

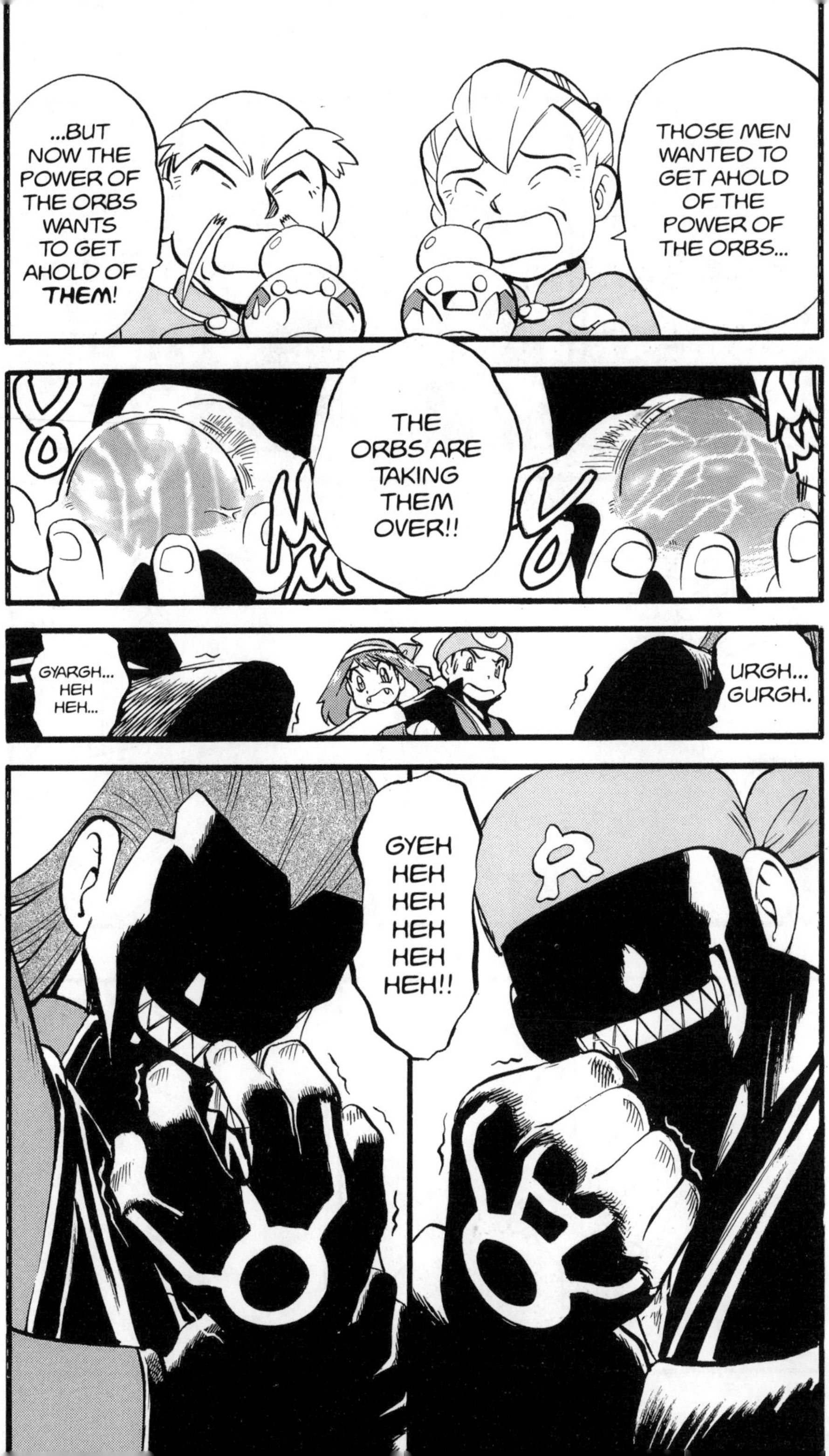
THOSE MEN WANTED TO GET AHOLD OF THE POWER OF THE ORBS...
...BUT NOW THE POWER OF THE ORBS WANTS TO GET AHOLD OF THEM!
THE ORBS ARE TAKING THEM OVER!!
URGH... GURGH.
GYARGH... HEH HEH...
GYEH HEH HEH HEH HEH HEH!!

● Adventure 249 ●

The Beginning of the End with Kyogre and Groudon, Part 11

Pokémon™ Adventures Ruby & Sapphire

The Fourth Chapter

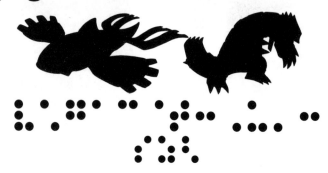

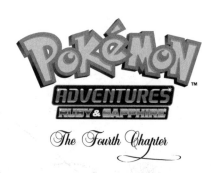

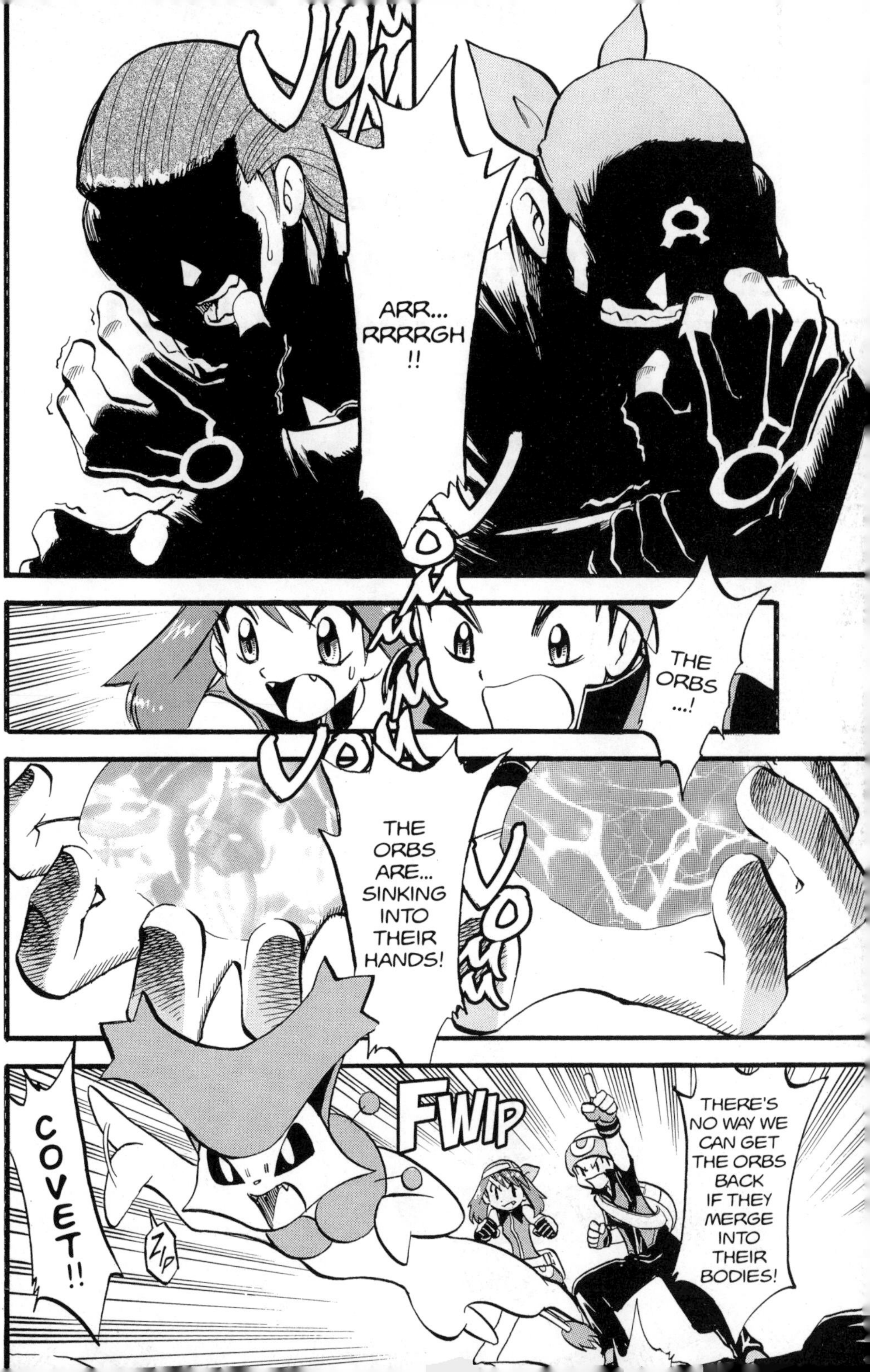
ARR... RRRRGH !!
THE ORBS ...!
THE ORBS ARE... SINKING INTO THEIR HANDS!
VOM
THERE'S NO WAY WE CAN GET THE ORBS BACK IF THEY MERGE INTO THEIR BODIES!
FWIP
ZIP
COVET!!

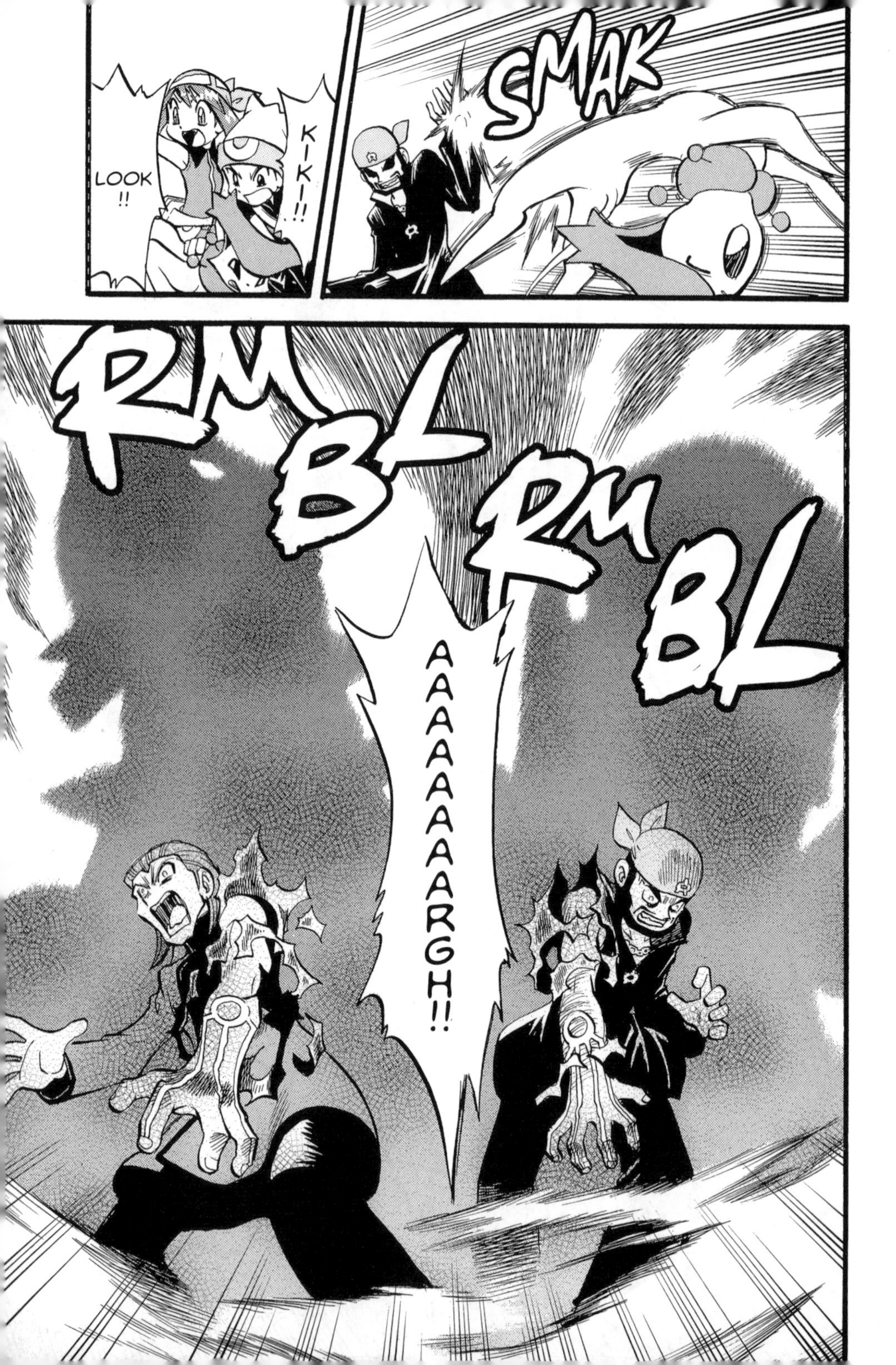
SMAK
KIKI!!
LOOK!!
RMBL RMBL
AAAAAAAARGH!!

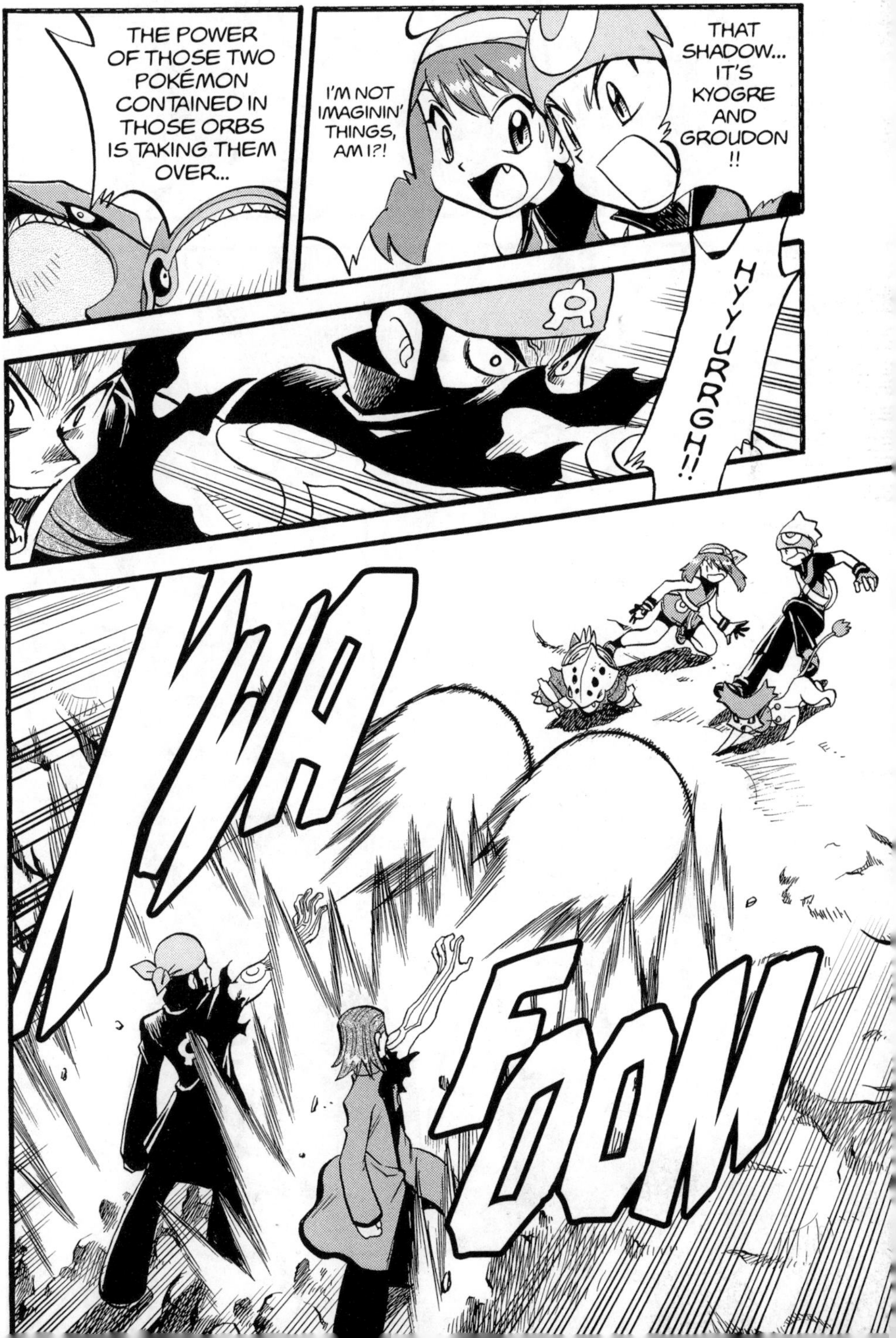
THAT SHADOW... IT'S KYOGRE AND GROUDON !!
I'M NOT IMAGININ' THINGS, AM I?!
THE POWER OF THOSE TWO POKéMON CONTAINED IN THOSE ORBS IS TAKING THEM OVER...
HYYURRGH!!
FOOM

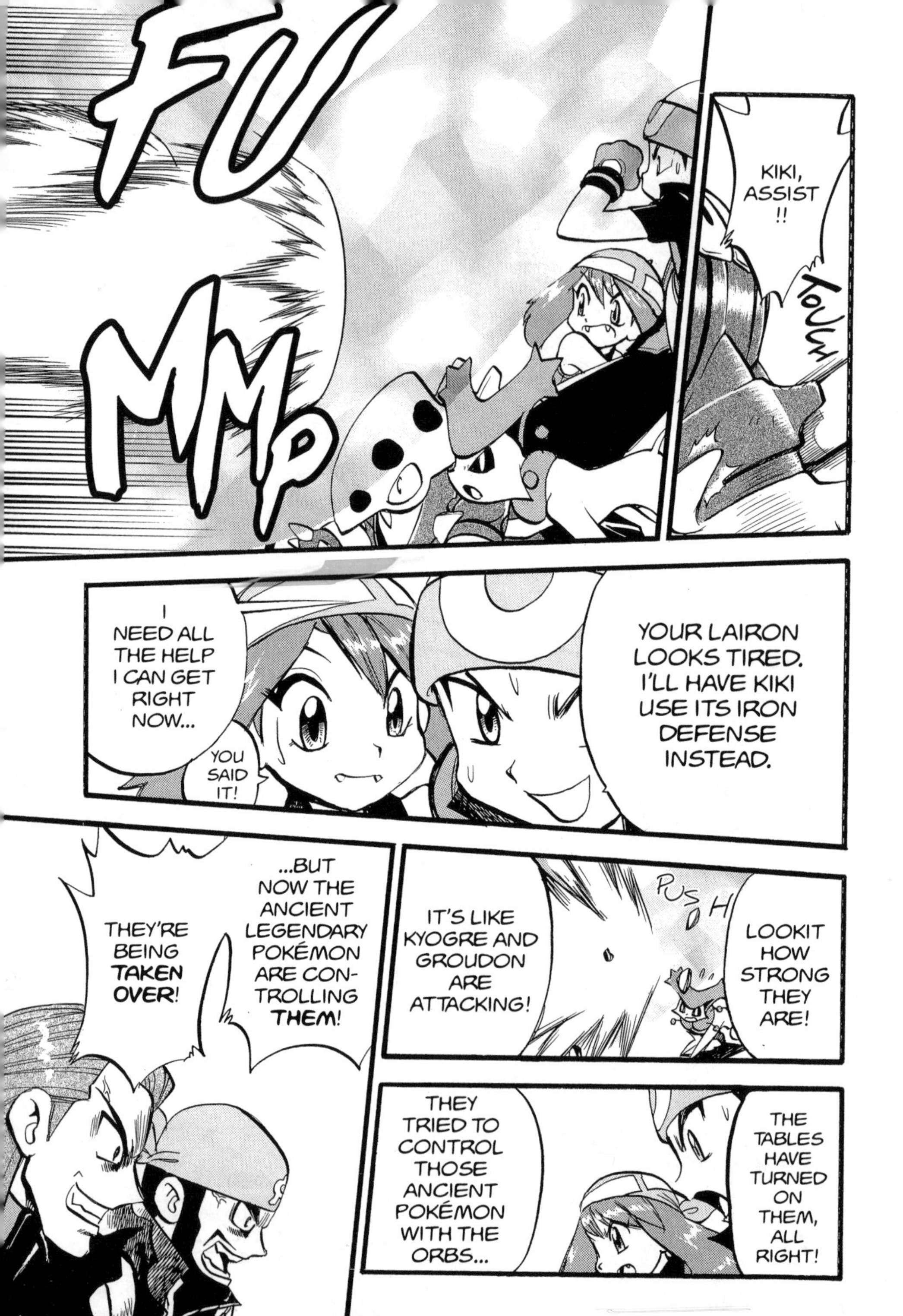
KIKI, ASSIST !!
TOUUN
FU
MMP
YOUR LAIRON LOOKS TIRED. I'LL HAVE KIKI USE ITS IRON DEFENSE INSTEAD.
I NEED ALL THE HELP I CAN GET RIGHT NOW...
YOU SAID IT!
LOOKIT HOW STRONG THEY ARE!
PUSH
IT'S LIKE KYOGRE AND GROUDON ARE ATTACKING!
THE TABLES HAVE TURNED ON THEM, ALL RIGHT!
THEY TRIED TO CONTROL THOSE ANCIENT POKÉMON WITH THE ORBS...
...BUT NOW THE ANCIENT LEGENDARY POKÉMON ARE CONTROLLING THEM!
THEY'RE BEING TAKEN OVER!

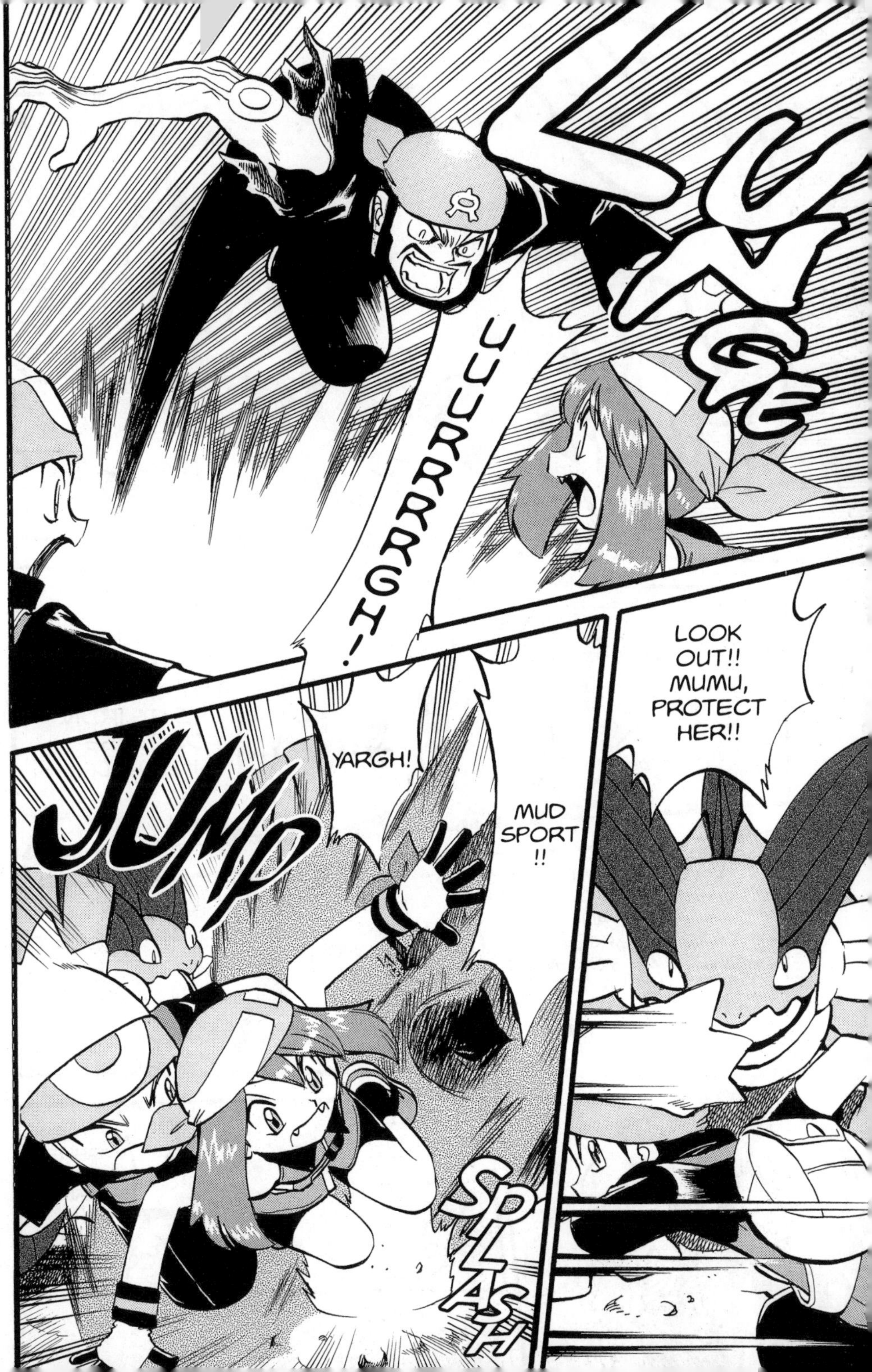
LUNGE
UUURRRRGH!
LOOK OUT!! MUMU, PROTECT HER!!
MUD SPORT!!
YARGH!
JUMP
SPLASH

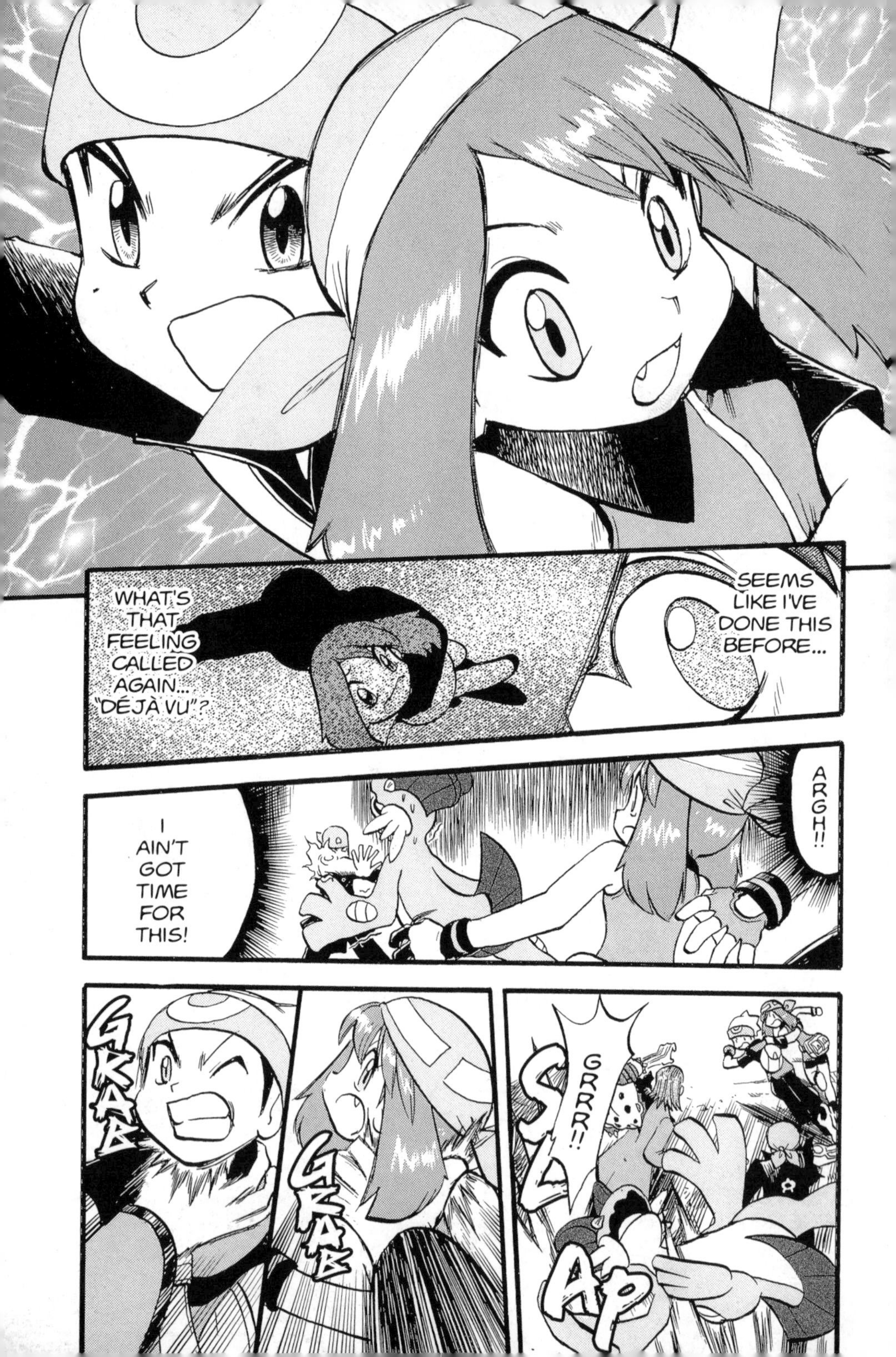
SEEMS LIKE I'VE DONE THIS BEFORE...
WHAT'S THAT FEELING CALLED AGAIN... "DÉJÀ VU"?
ARGH!!
I AIN'T GOT TIME FOR THIS!
GRRR!!
SLAP
GRAB
GRAB

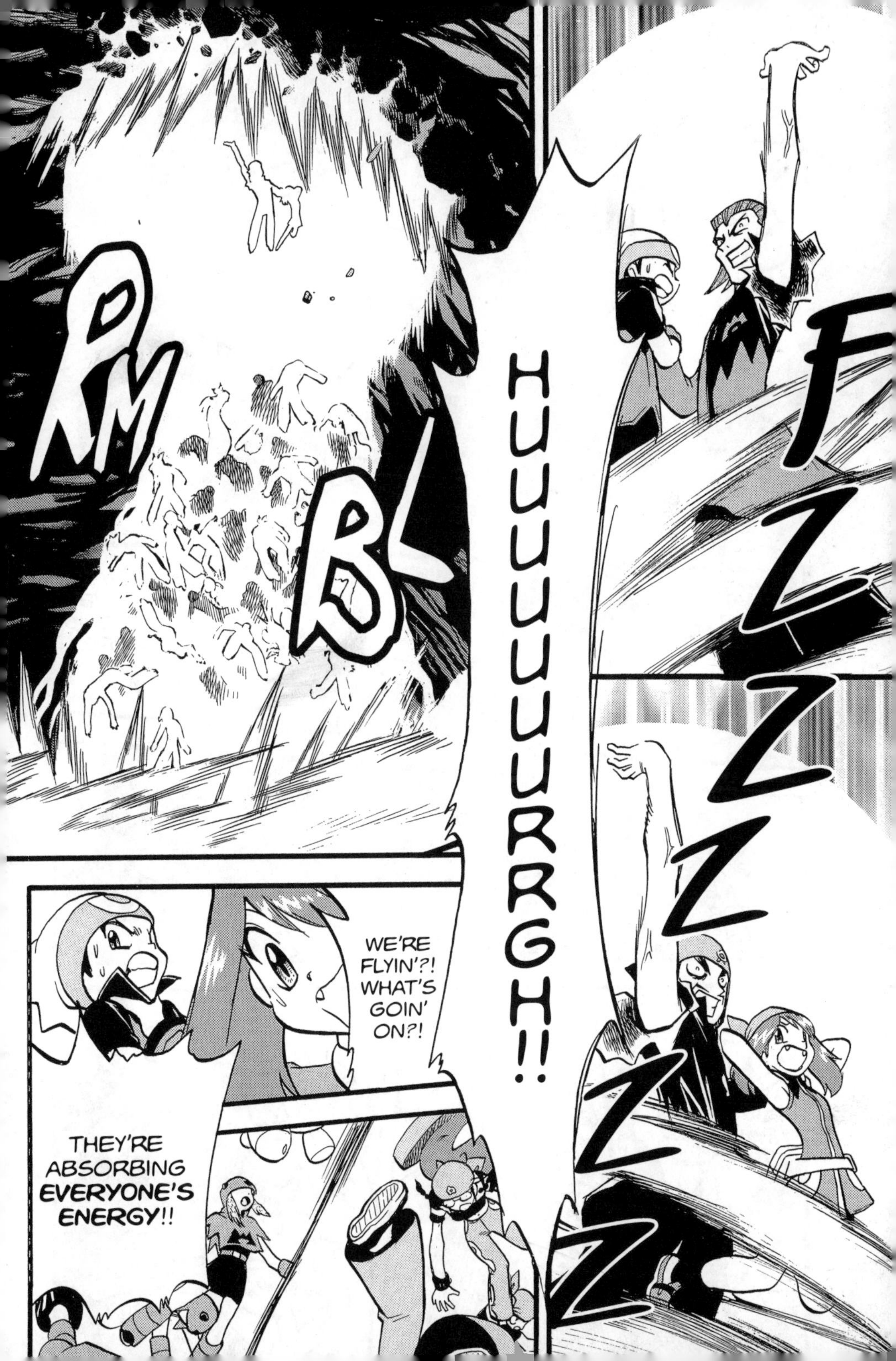
FZZZZZ
HUUUUUUURRGH!!
RMBL
WE'RE FLYIN'?! WHAT'S GOIN' ON?!
THEY'RE ABSORBING EVERYONE'S ENERGY!!

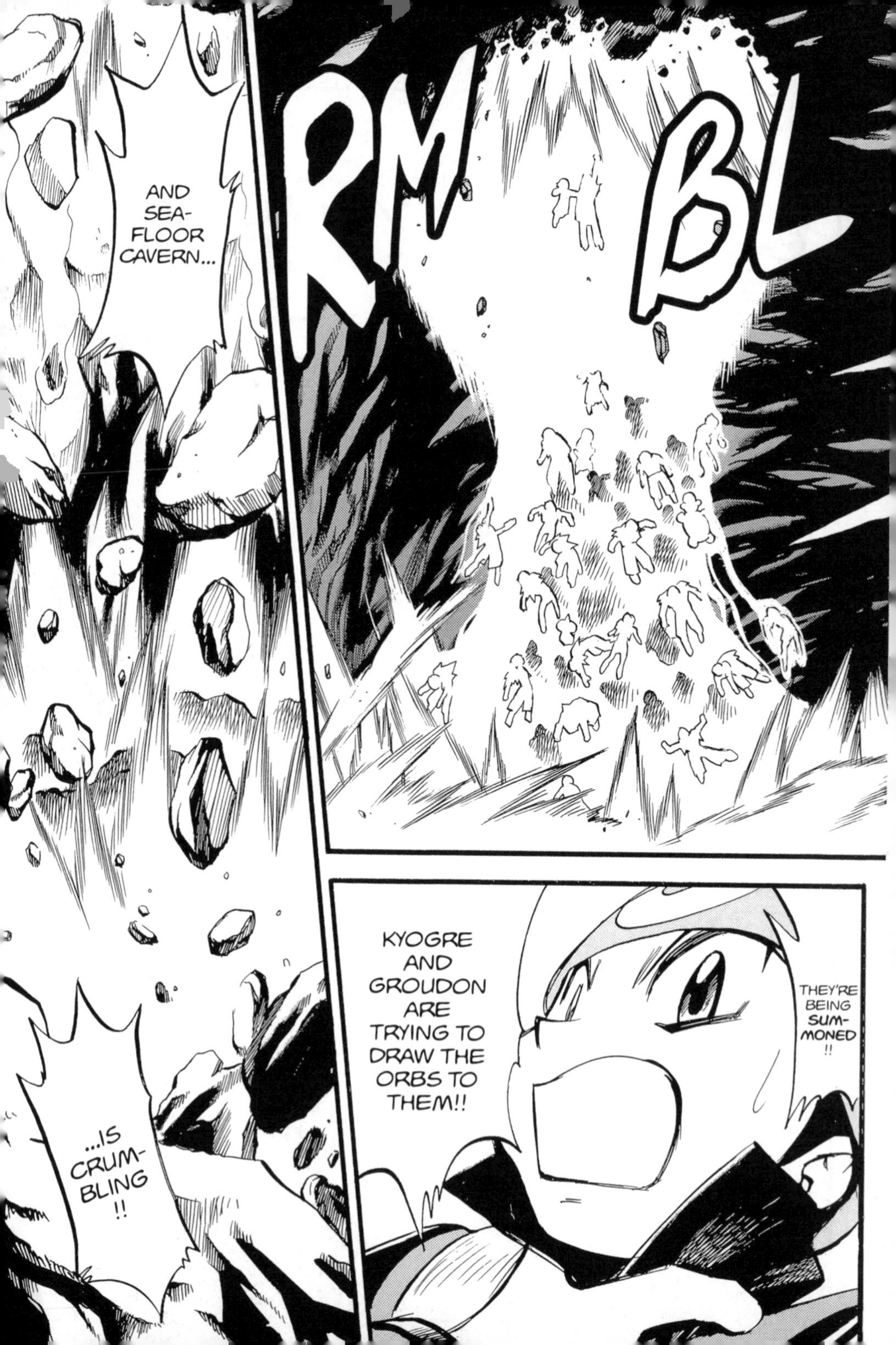
RMBL
THEY'RE BEING SUMMONED!!
KYOGRE AND GROUDON ARE TRYING TO DRAW THE ORBS TO THEM!!
AND SEA-FLOOR CAVERN...
...IS CRUMBLING!!

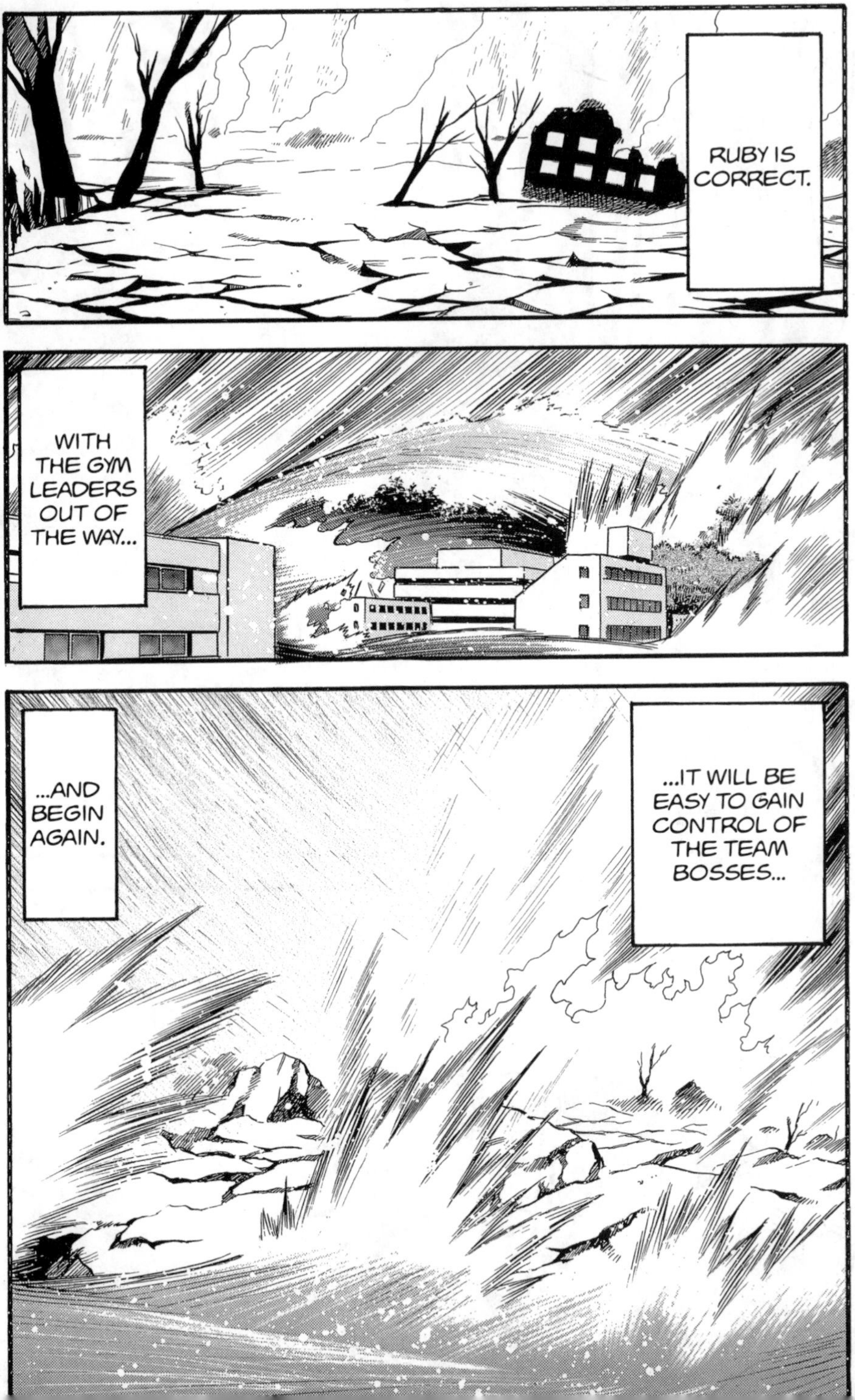
RUBY IS CORRECT.
WITH THE GYM LEADERS OUT OF THE WAY...
...IT WILL BE EASY TO GAIN CONTROL OF THE TEAM BOSSES...
...AND BEGIN AGAIN.

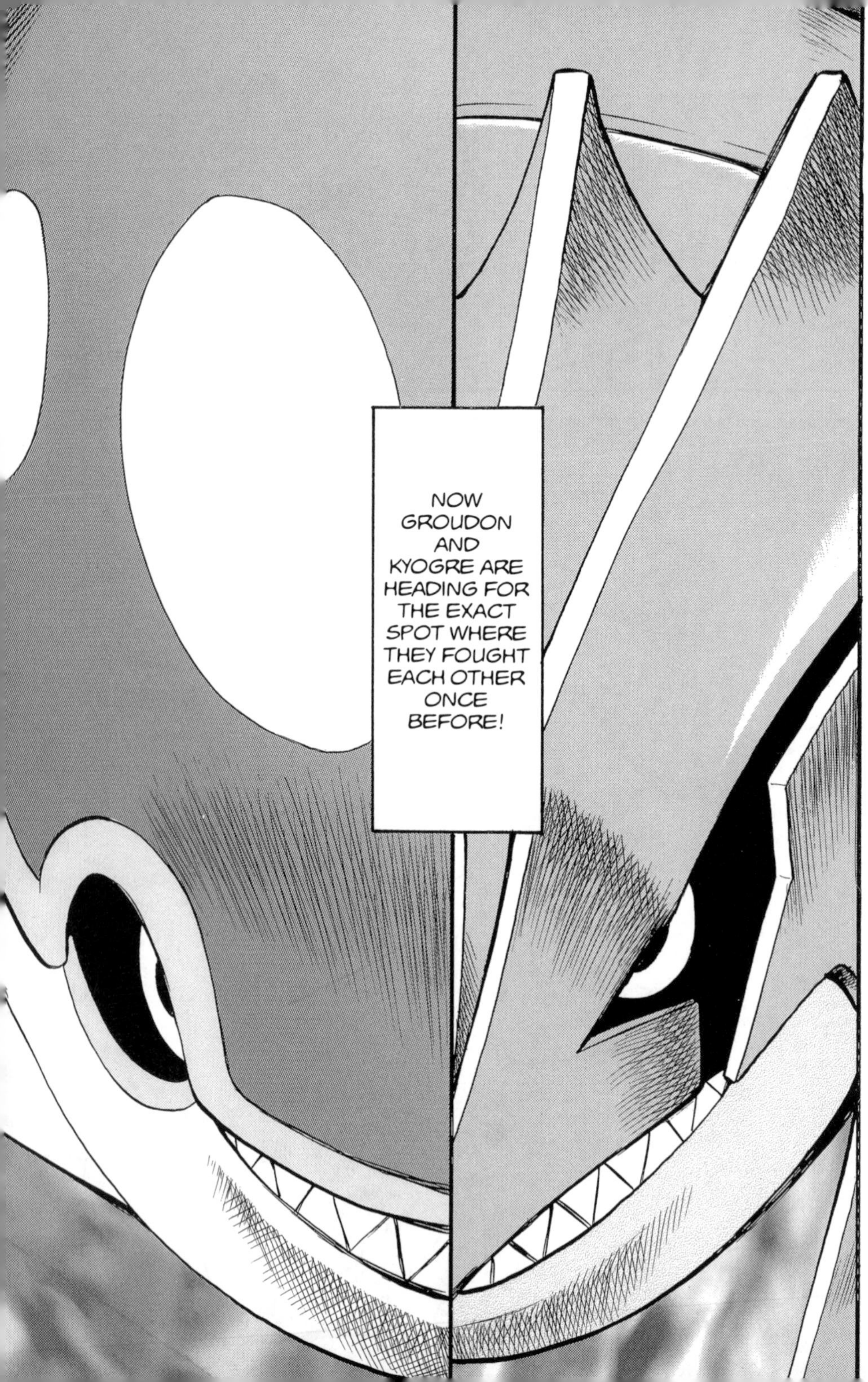
NOW GROUDON AND KYOGRE ARE HEADING FOR THE EXACT SPOT WHERE THEY FOUGHT EACH OTHER ONCE BEFORE!

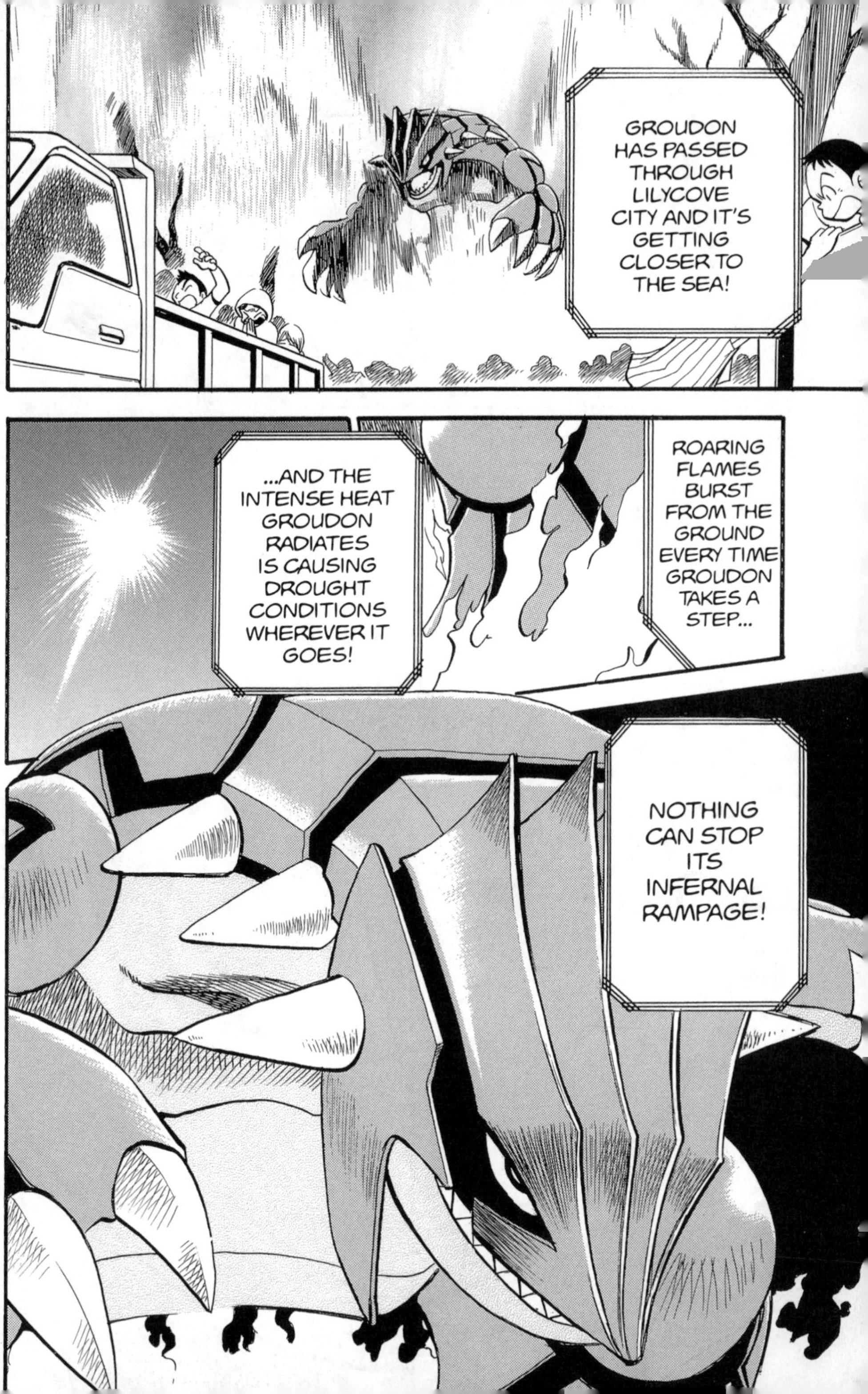
GROUDON HAS PASSED THROUGH LILYCOVE CITY AND IT'S GETTING CLOSER TO THE SEA!
ROARING FLAMES BURST FROM THE GROUND EVERY TIME GROUDON TAKES A STEP...
...AND THE INTENSE HEAT GROUDON RADIATES IS CAUSING DROUGHT CONDITIONS WHEREVER IT GOES!
NOTHING CAN STOP ITS INFERNAL RAMPAGE!

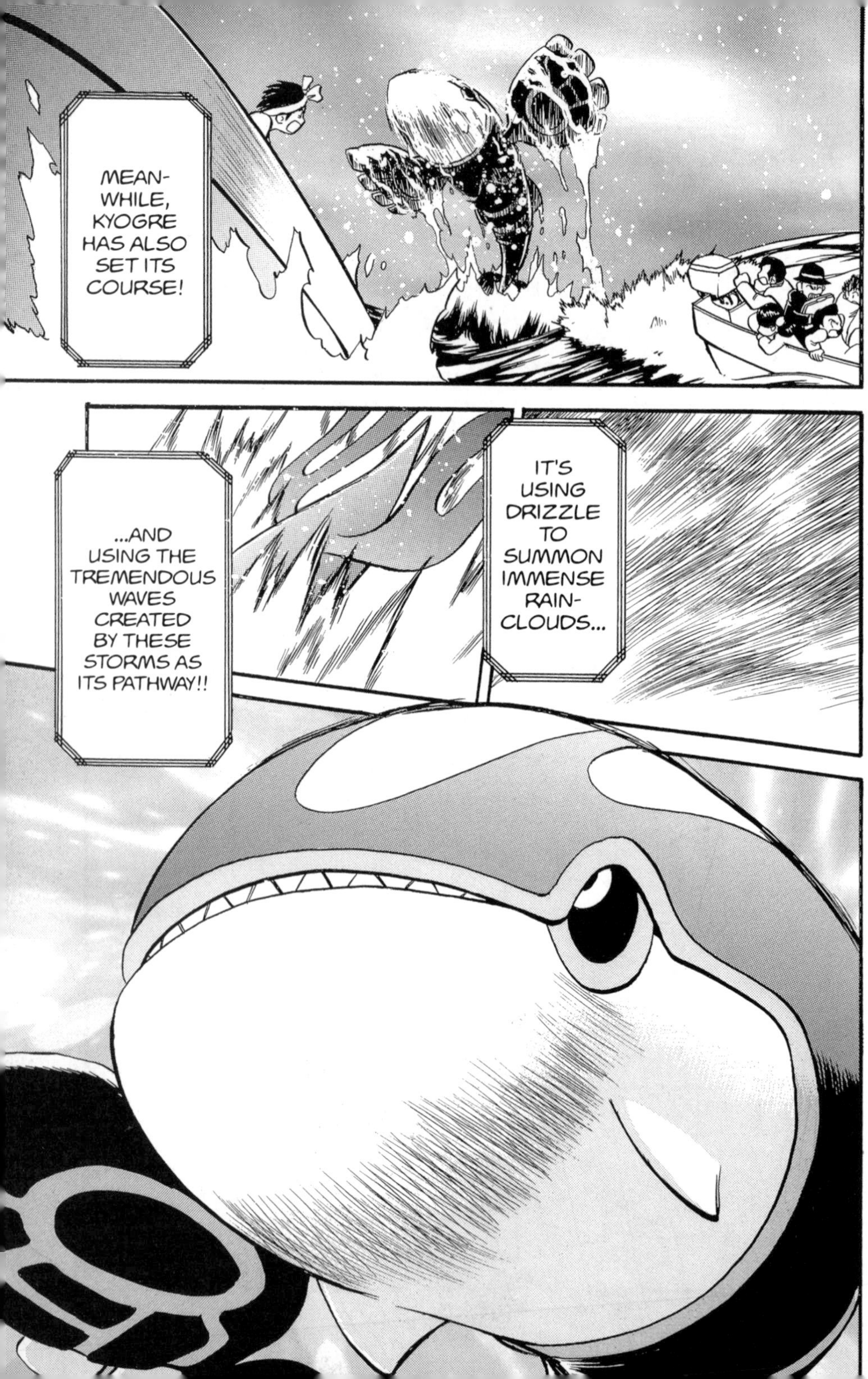
MEAN-WHILE, KYOGRE HAS ALSO SET ITS COURSE!
IT'S USING DRIZZLE TO SUMMON IMMENSE RAIN-CLOUDS...
...AND USING THE TREMENDOUS WAVES CREATED BY THESE STORMS AS ITS PATHWAY!!

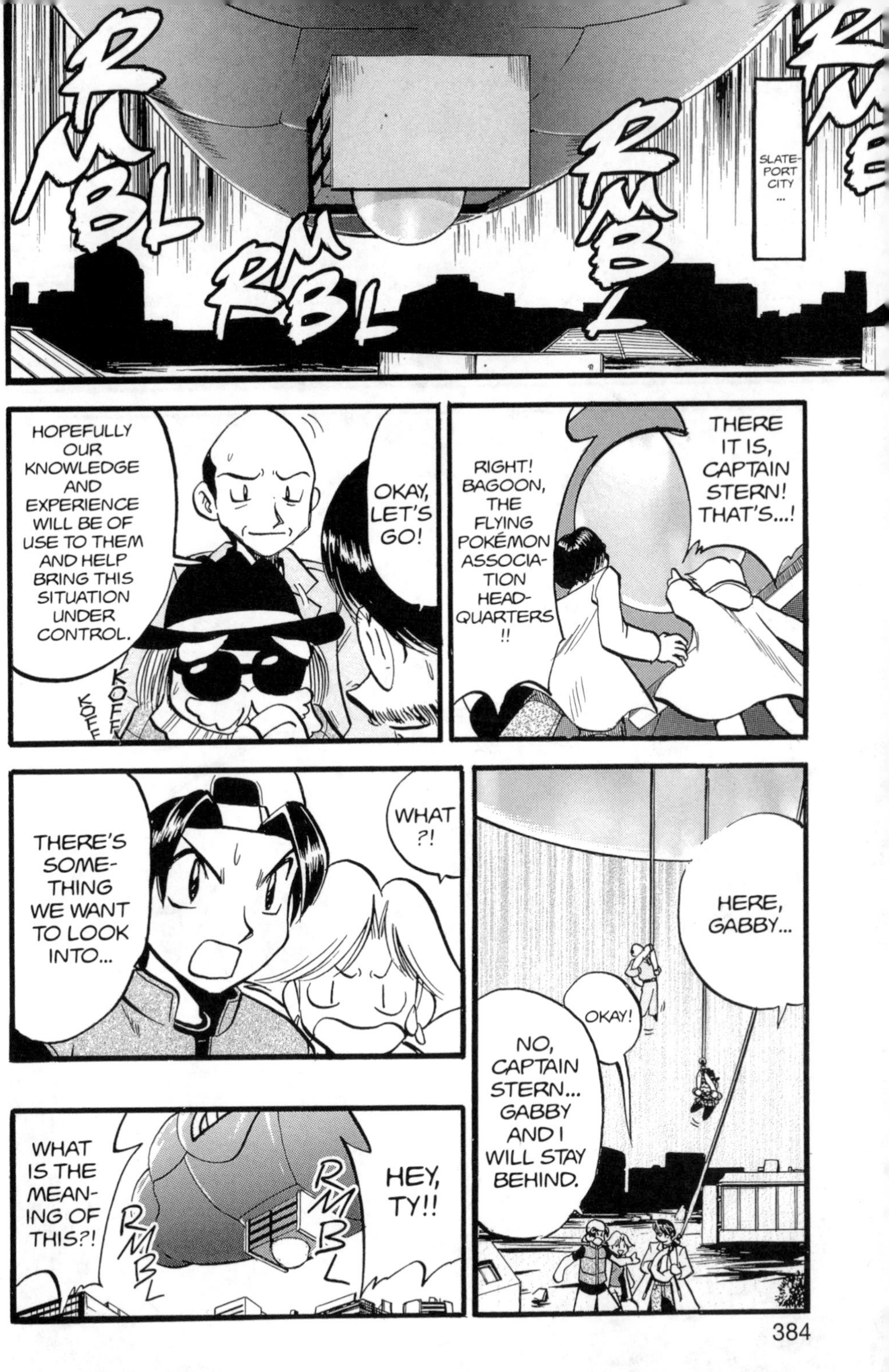
SLATEPORT CITY ...
RMBL
RMBL
RMBL
THERE IT IS, CAPTAIN STERN! THAT'S...!
RIGHT! BAGOON, THE FLYING POKÉMON ASSOCIATION HEADQUARTERS!!
OKAY, LET'S GO!
HOPEFULLY OUR KNOWLEDGE AND EXPERIENCE WILL BE OF USE TO THEM AND HELP BRING THIS SITUATION UNDER CONTROL.
KOFF KOFF
HERE, GABBY...
OKAY!
NO, CAPTAIN STERN... GABBY AND I WILL STAY BEHIND.
WHAT?!
THERE'S SOMETHING WE WANT TO LOOK INTO...
HEY, TY!!
RMBL
WHAT IS THE MEANING OF THIS?!
RMBL

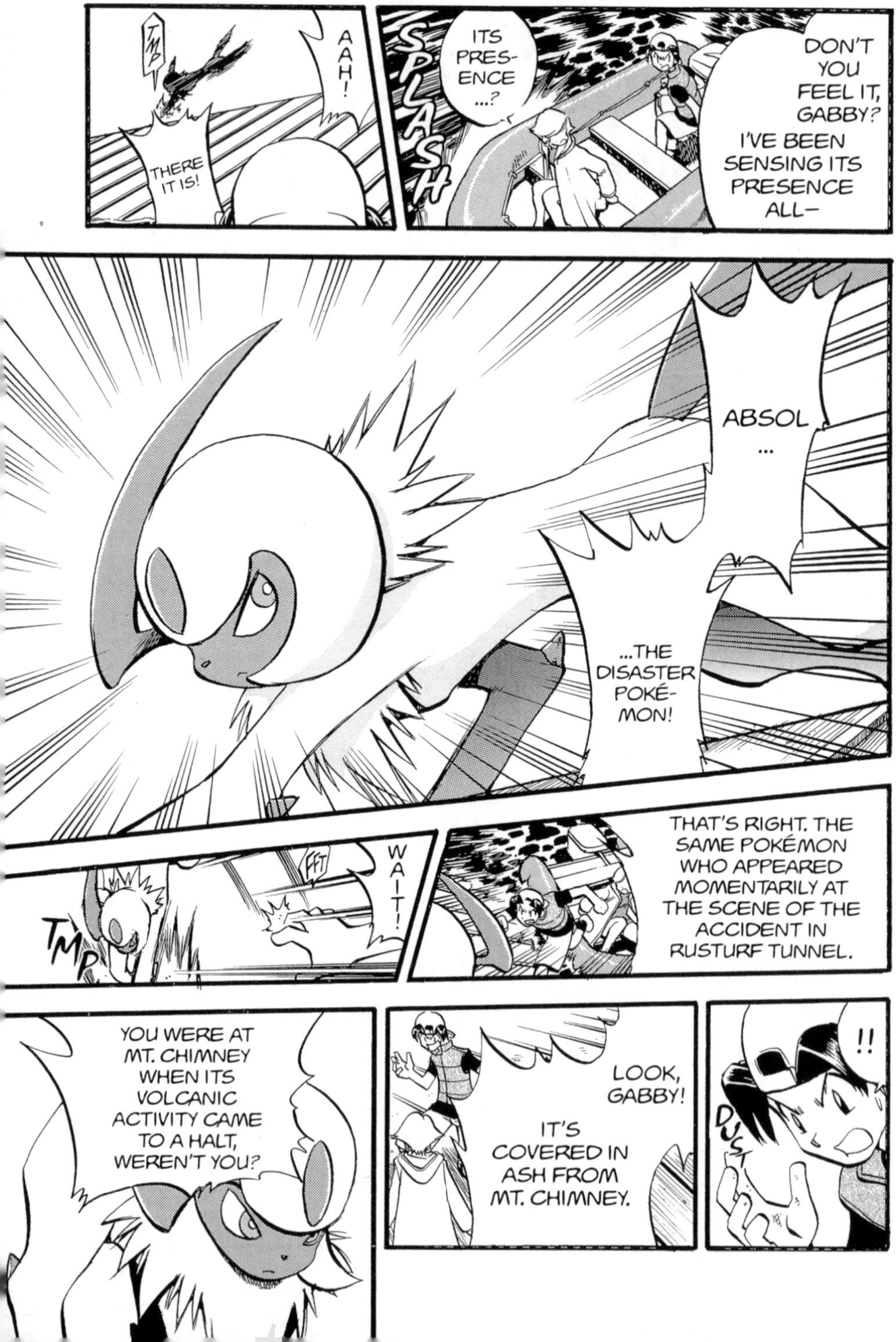
DON'T YOU FEEL IT, GABBY?
I'VE BEEN SENSING ITS PRESENCE ALL—
ITS PRESENCE...?
SPLASH
AAH!
TMP
THERE IT IS!
ABSOL ...
...THE DISASTER POKÉMON!
THAT'S RIGHT. THE SAME POKÉMON WHO APPEARED MOMENTARILY AT THE SCENE OF THE ACCIDENT IN RUSTURF TUNNEL.
WAIT!
FFT
TMP
!!
DUST
LOOK, GABBY!
IT'S COVERED IN ASH FROM MT. CHIMNEY.
YOU WERE AT MT. CHIMNEY WHEN ITS VOLCANIC ACTIVITY CAME TO A HALT, WEREN'T YOU?

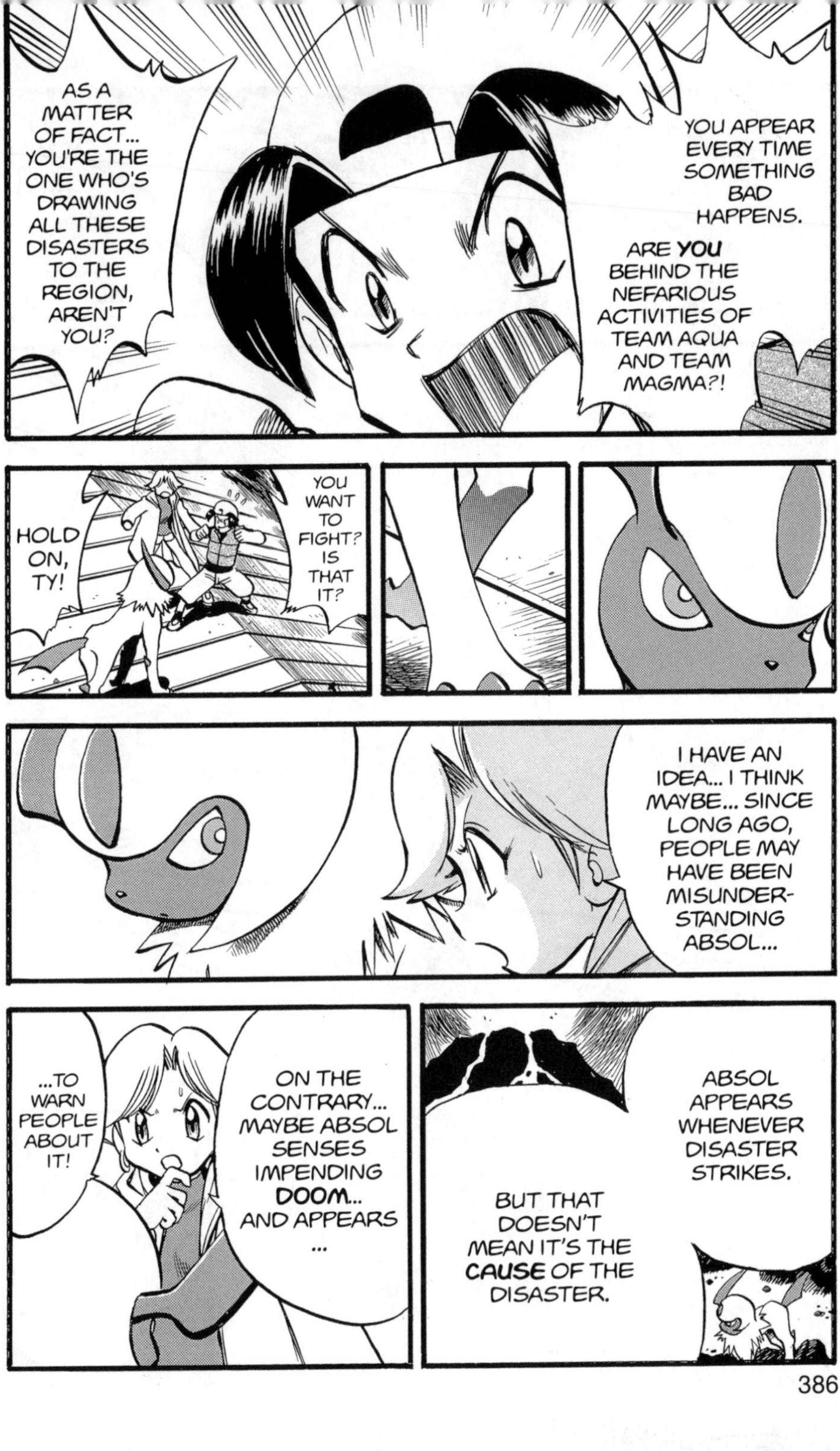
YOU APPEAR EVERY TIME SOMETHING BAD HAPPENS.
ARE **YOU** BEHIND THE NEFARIOUS ACTIVITIES OF TEAM AQUA AND TEAM MAGMA?!
AS A MATTER OF FACT... YOU'RE THE ONE WHO'S DRAWING ALL THESE DISASTERS TO THE REGION, AREN'T YOU?
YOU WANT TO FIGHT? IS THAT IT?
HOLD ON, TY!
I HAVE AN IDEA... I THINK MAYBE... SINCE LONG AGO, PEOPLE MAY HAVE BEEN MISUNDER-STANDING ABSOL...
ABSOL APPEARS WHENEVER DISASTER STRIKES.
BUT THAT DOESN'T MEAN IT'S THE **CAUSE** OF THE DISASTER.
ON THE CONTRARY... MAYBE ABSOL SENSES IMPENDING **DOOM**... AND APPEARS ...
...TO WARN PEOPLE ABOUT IT!

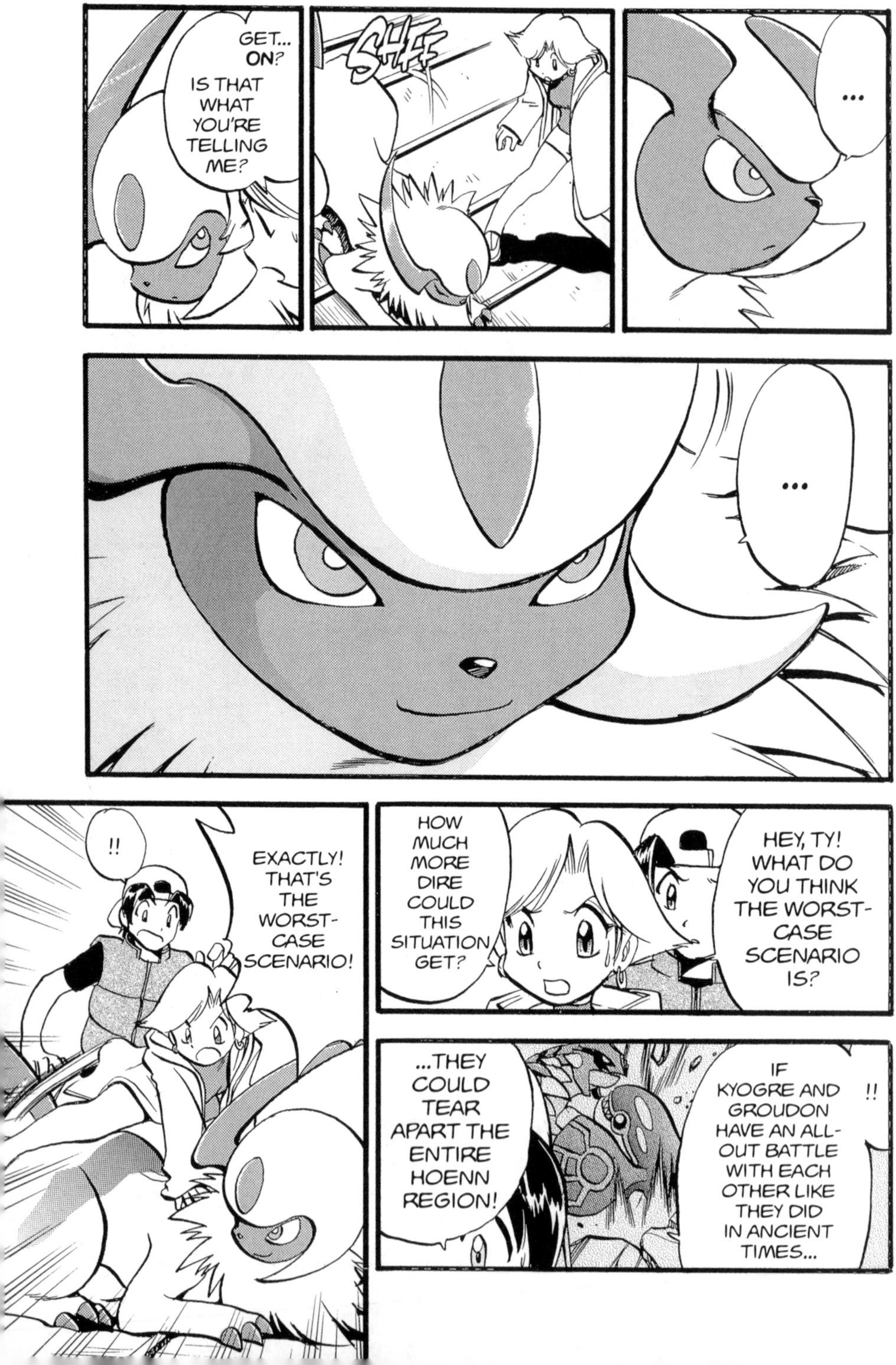
...
SHFF
GET... **ON**? IS THAT WHAT YOU'RE TELLING ME?
...
HEY, TY! WHAT DO YOU THINK THE WORST-CASE SCENARIO IS?
HOW MUCH MORE DIRE COULD THIS SITUATION GET?
!!
IF KYOGRE AND GROUDON HAVE AN ALL-OUT BATTLE WITH EACH OTHER LIKE THEY DID IN ANCIENT TIMES...
...THEY COULD TEAR APART THE ENTIRE HOENN REGION!
!!
EXACTLY! THAT'S THE WORST-CASE SCENARIO!

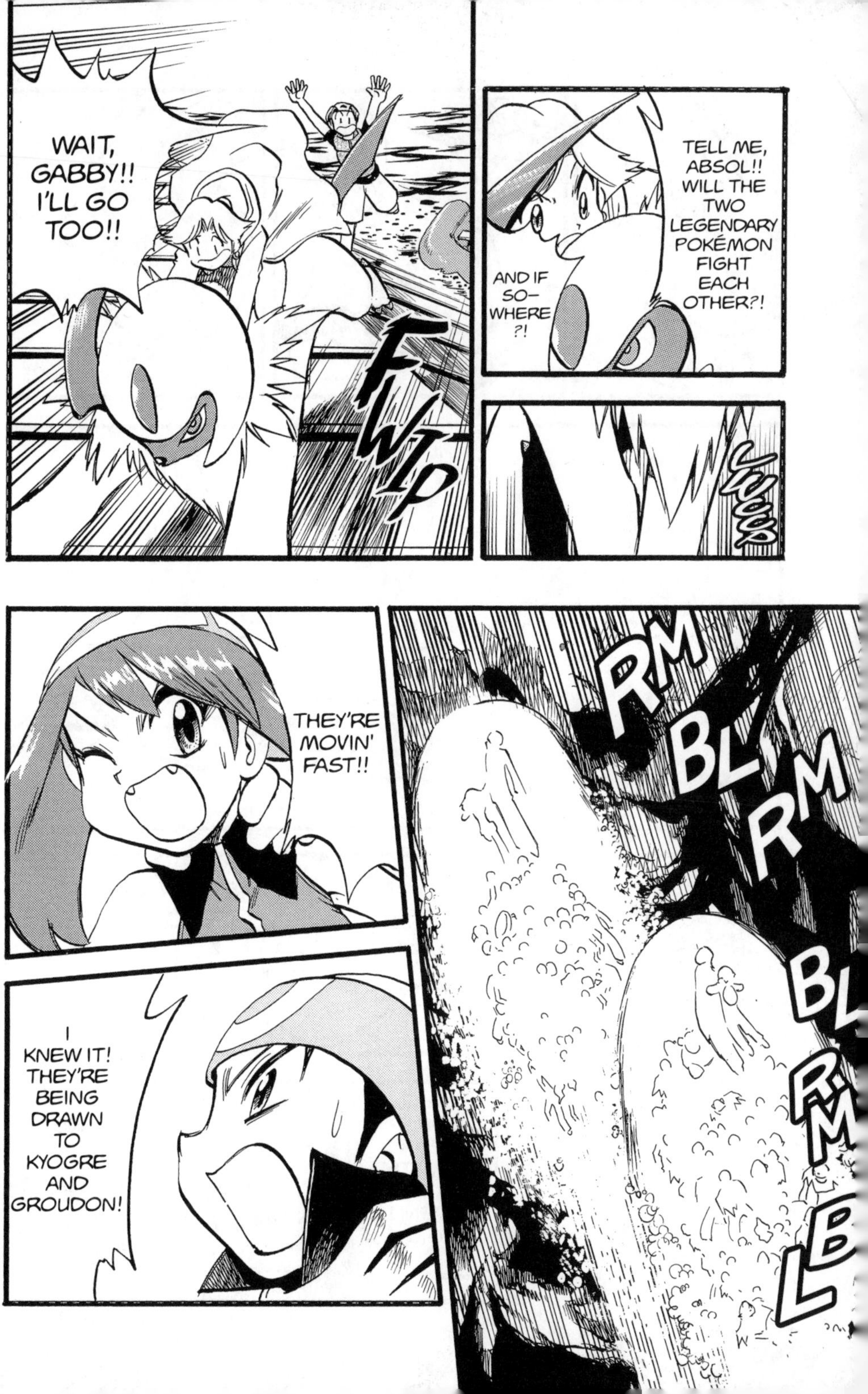

TELL ME, ABSOL!! WILL THE TWO LEGENDARY POKéMON FIGHT EACH OTHER?!
AND IF SO— WHERE?!
WAIT, GABBY!! I'LL GO TOO!!
FWIP
RM
BL
RM
RM
BL
RM
RM
BL
THEY'RE MOVIN' FAST!!
I KNEW IT! THEY'RE BEING DRAWN TO KYOGRE AND GROUDON!

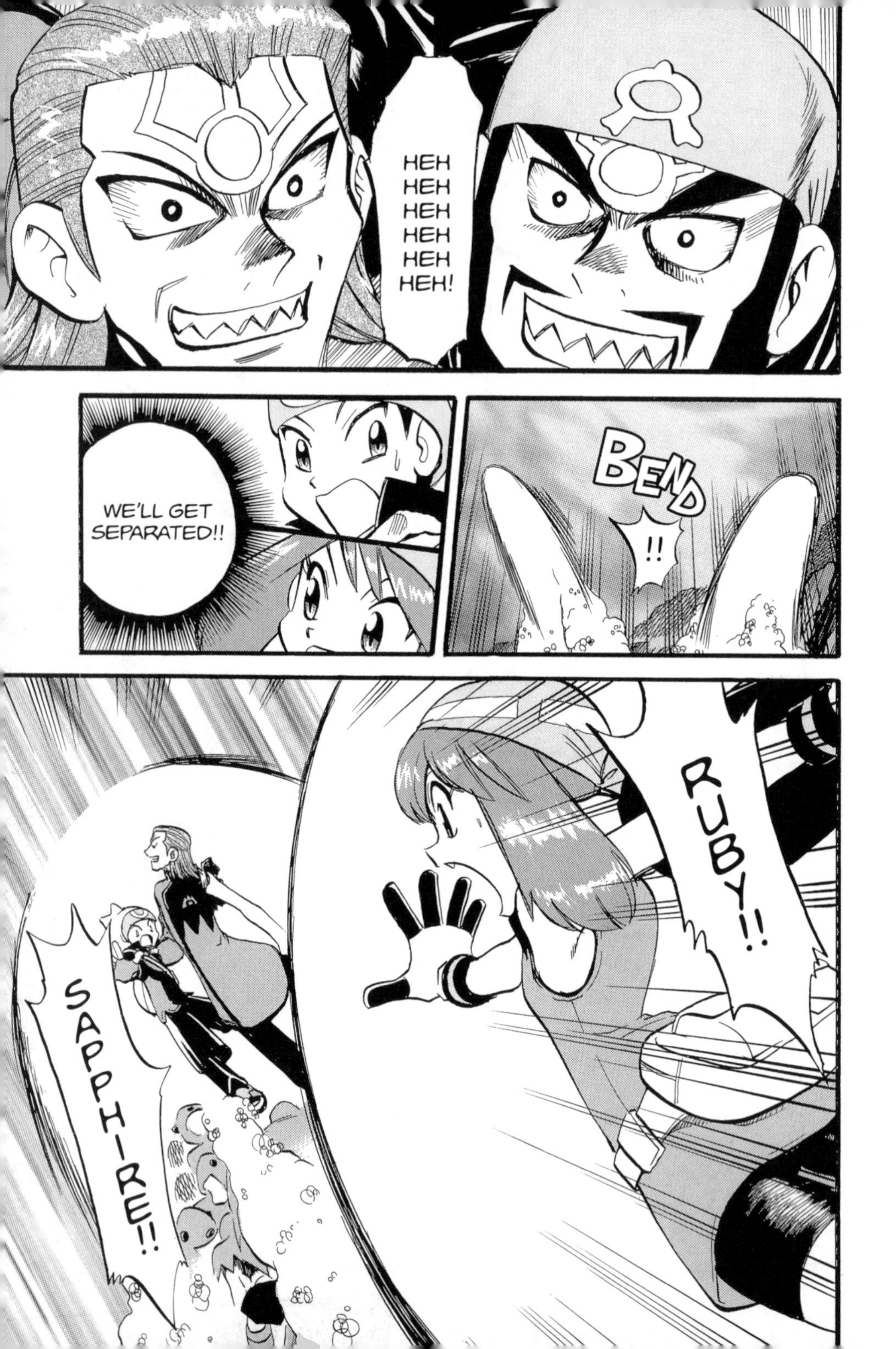
HEH HEH HEH HEH HEH HEH!
BEND
!!
WE'LL GET SEPARATED!!
RUBY!!
SAPPHIRE!!

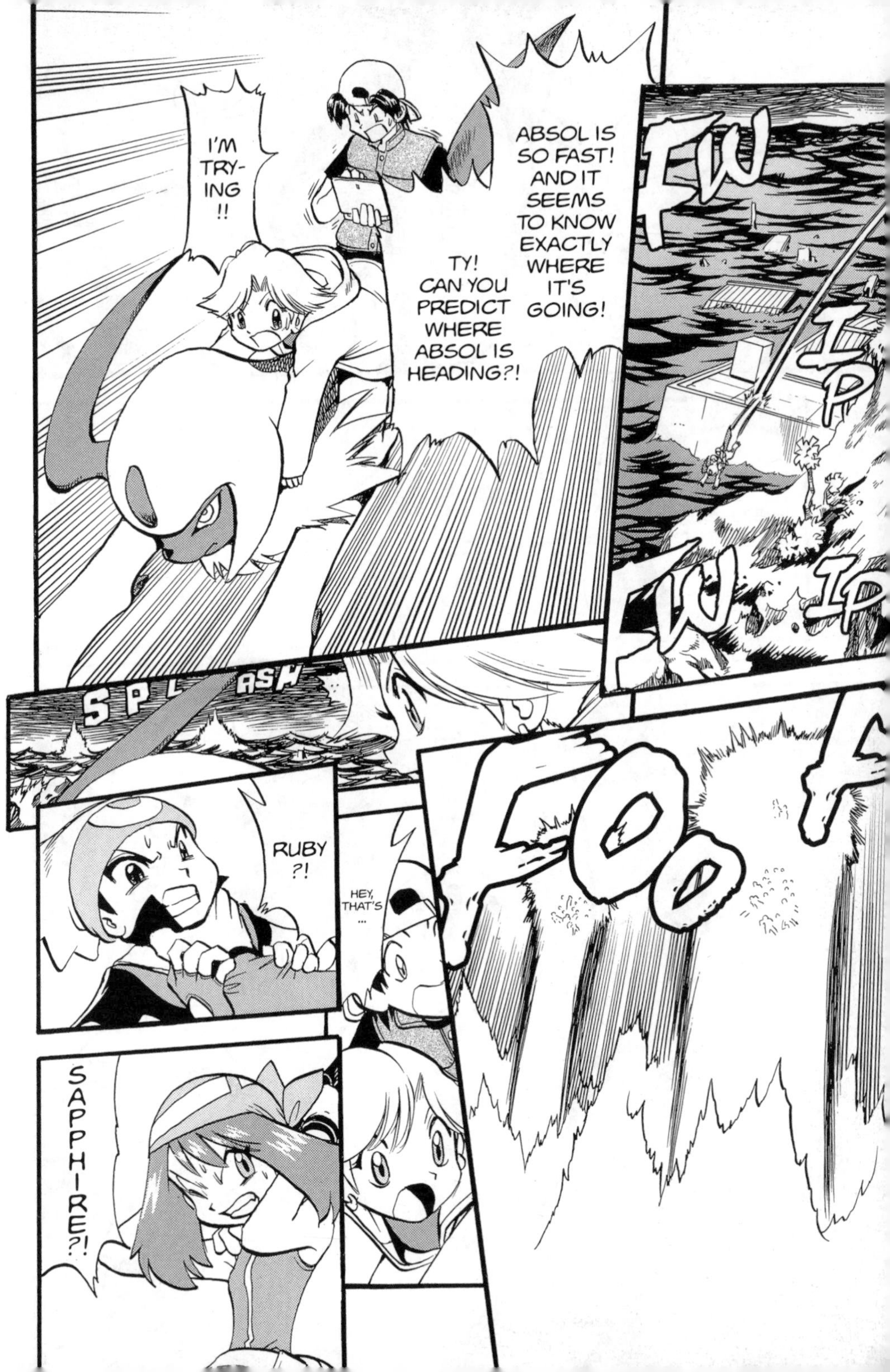

FWIP
FWIP
ABSOL IS SO FAST! AND IT SEEMS TO KNOW EXACTLY WHERE IT'S GOING!
TY! CAN YOU PREDICT WHERE ABSOL IS HEADING?!
I'M TRY-ING!!
SPLASH
FOO
RUBY?!
HEY, THAT'S ...
SAPPHIRE?!

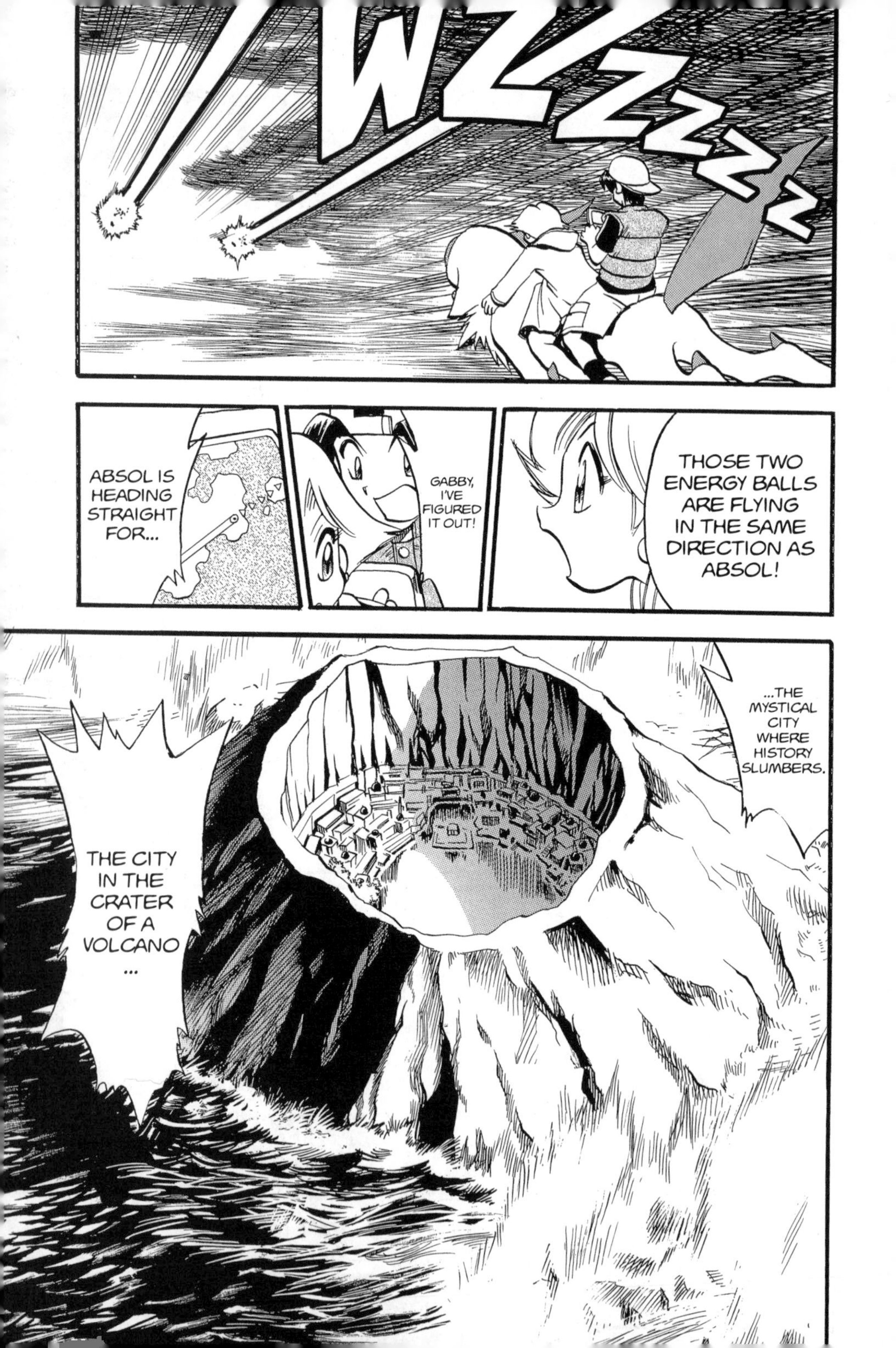
WZZZZZ
THOSE TWO ENERGY BALLS ARE FLYING IN THE SAME DIRECTION AS ABSOL!
GABBY, I'VE FIGURED IT OUT!
ABSOL IS HEADING STRAIGHT FOR...
...THE MYSTICAL CITY WHERE HISTORY SLUMBERS.
THE CITY IN THE CRATER OF A VOLCANO ...

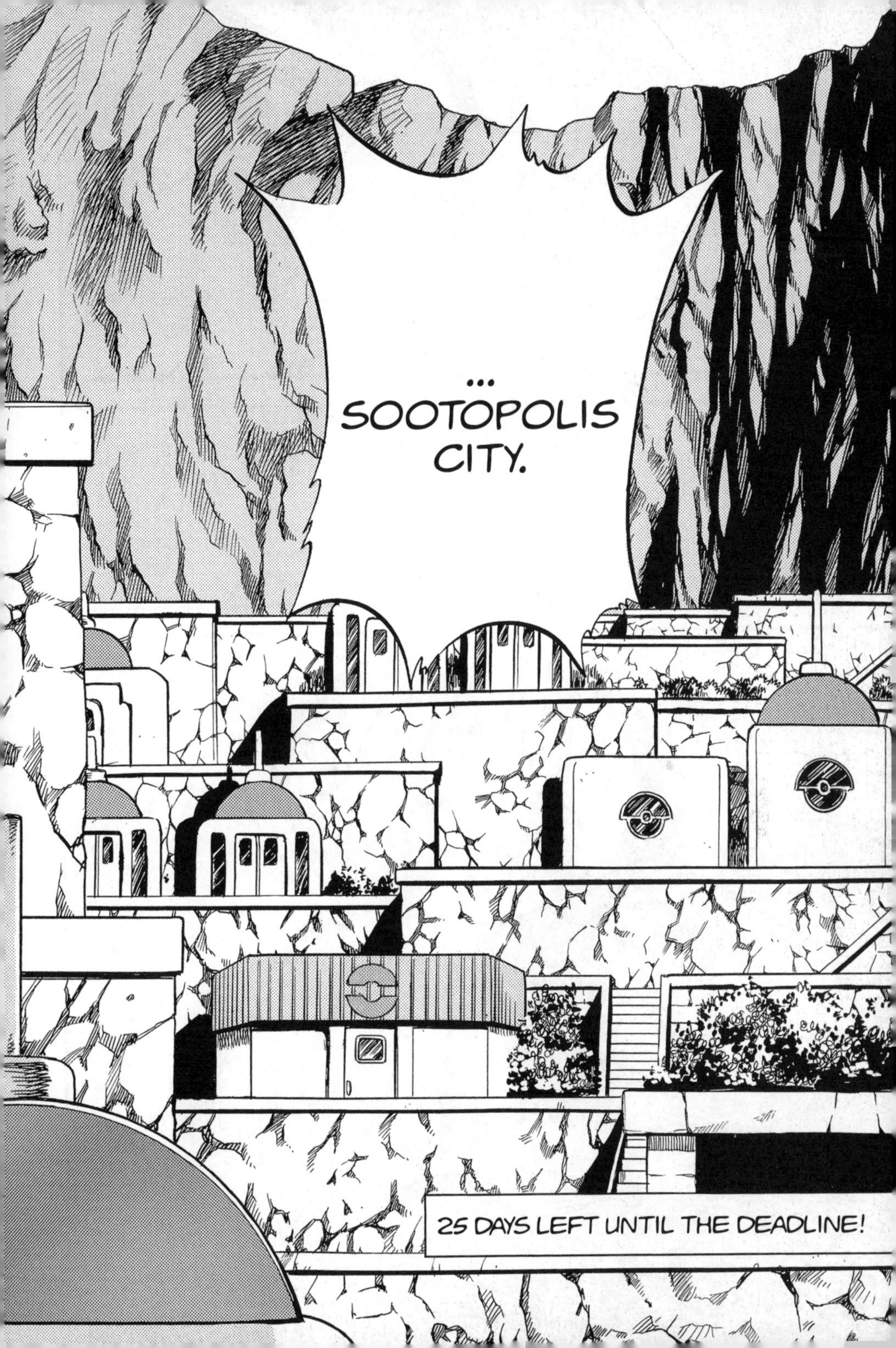
...SOOTOPOLIS CITY.
25 DAYS LEFT UNTIL THE DEADLINE!

Message from

Hidenori Kusaka

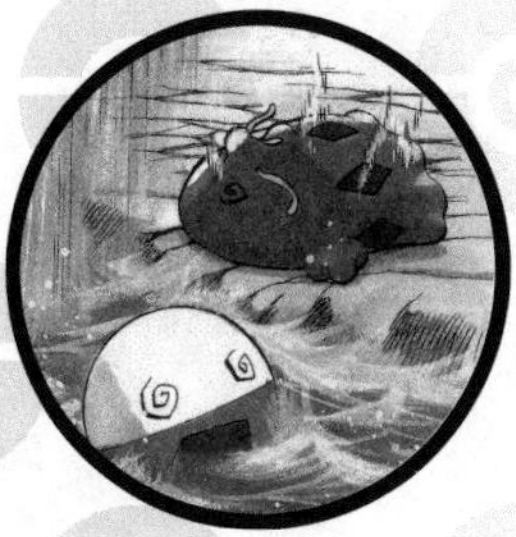

The Ruby and Sapphire story arc will be completed in the next two volumes, 21 and 22. Since it's the end of this story, I had Satoshi Yamamoto draw an illustration of Sapphire's complete team for the cover of volume 21 and Ruby's complete team for the cover of volume 22. Also, these two illustrations are drawn as a pair and connect at the top! Put the covers of the two volumes together and see for yourselves. This is the climax of the adventure set in the Hoenn region... I hope you enjoy finding out how our heroes fulfill their destiny!

–2006

Message from

Satoshi Yamamoto

Sorry to keep you waiting!! I now bring you...volume 21! The story is building up to the climax. This volume is filled with all sorts of major events, such as the appearance of the Elite Four and the Legendary Pokémon. It's packed with even more excitement than the last volume! Also, you'll learn about Ruby and Sapphire's past. I drew the scenes with passion in hopes of knocking your socks off, so please be careful not to get motion sickness as you read the scenes. (LOL)

–2006

● Adventure 250 ●

The Beginning of the End with Kyogre and Groudon, Part 12

Pokémon™ Adventures Ruby & Sapphire

The Fourth Chapter

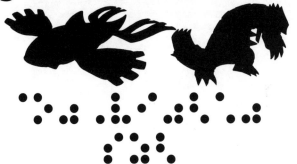

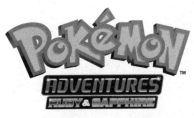

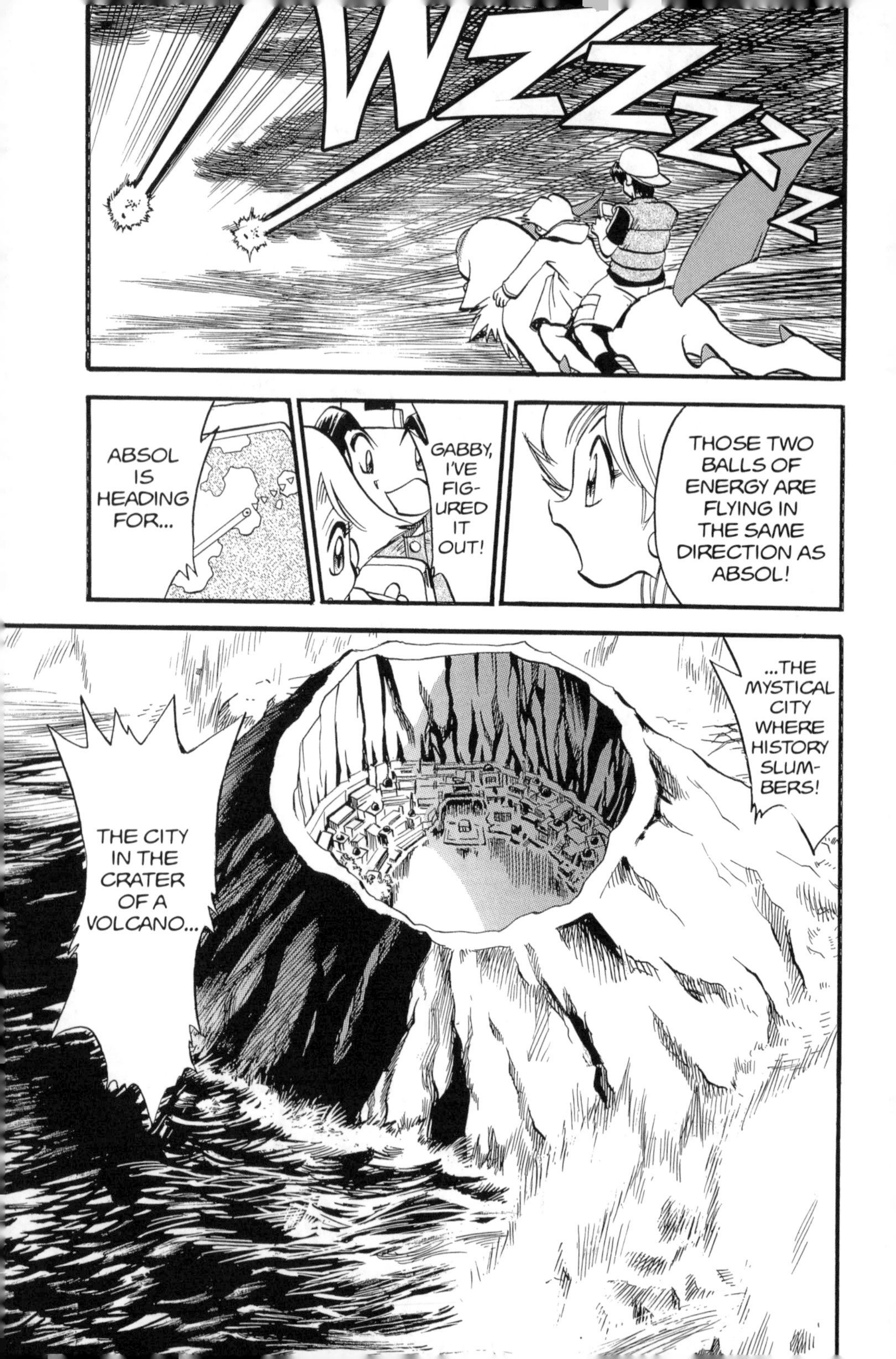
WZZZZZ
THOSE TWO BALLS OF ENERGY ARE FLYING IN THE SAME DIRECTION AS ABSOL!
GABBY, I'VE FIG-URED IT OUT!
ABSOL IS HEADING FOR...
...THE MYSTICAL CITY WHERE HISTORY SLUM-BERS!
THE CITY IN THE CRATER OF A VOLCANO...

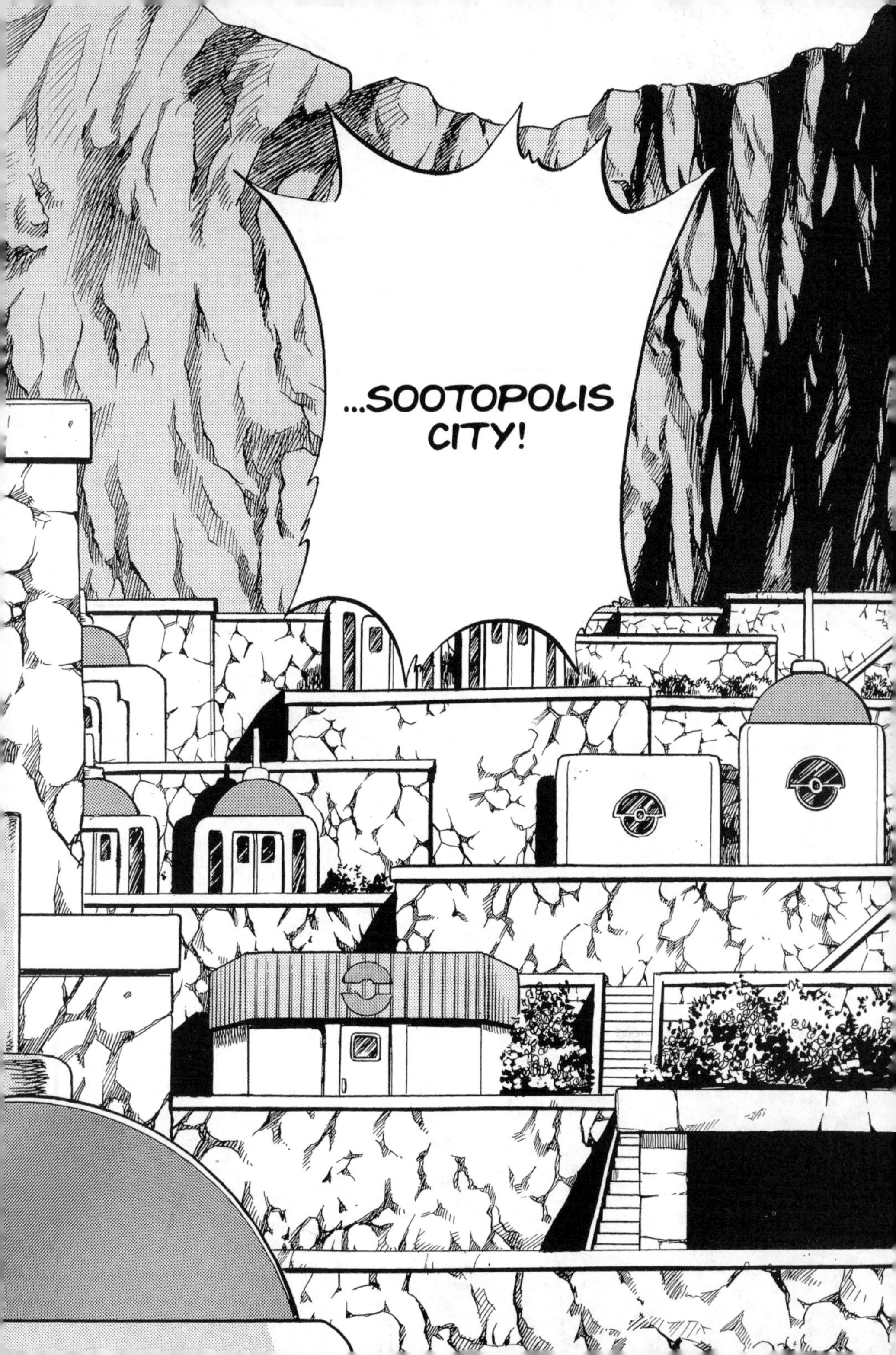
...SOOTOPOLIS CITY!

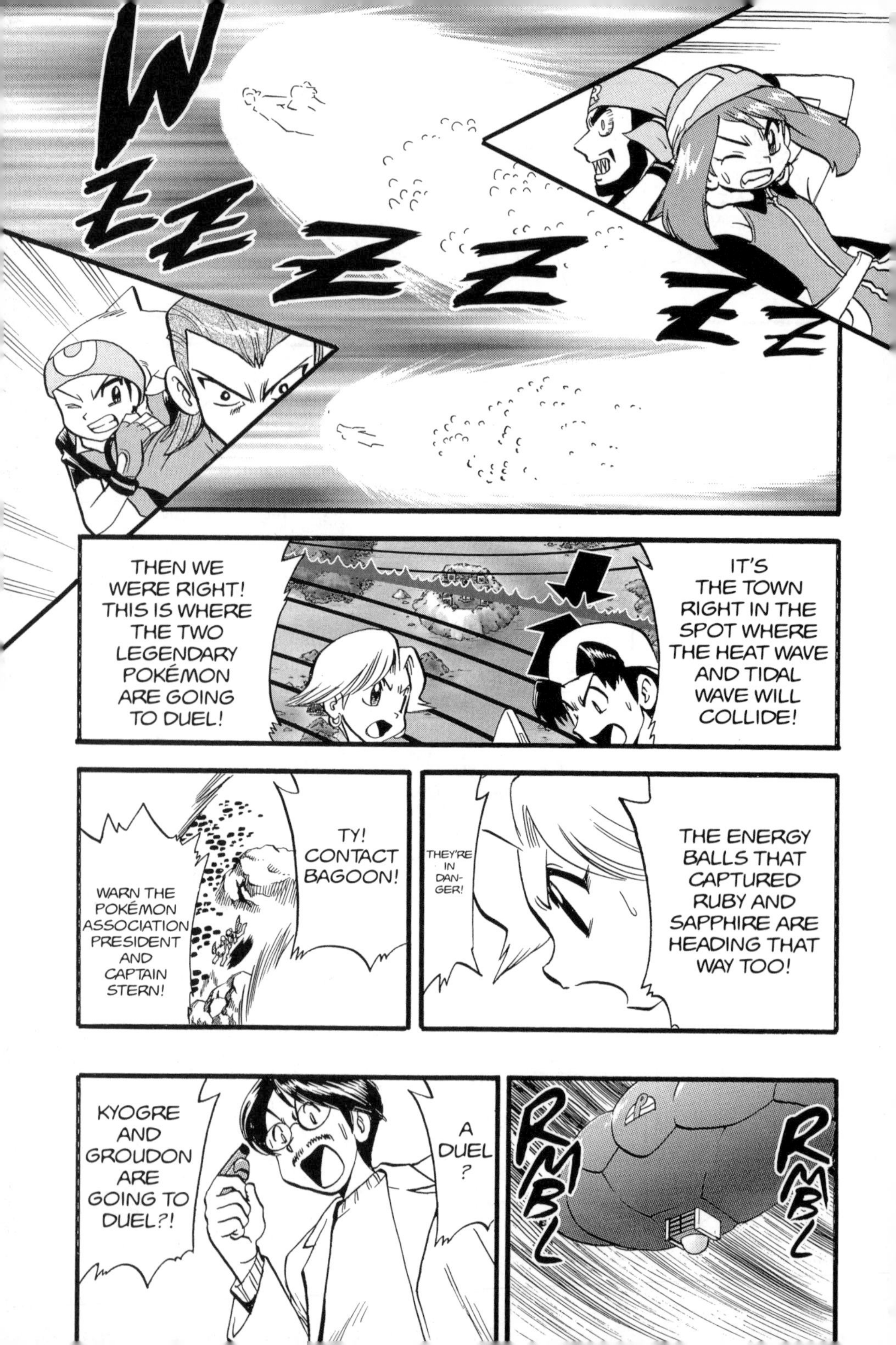
WZZZZZZZ
IT'S THE TOWN RIGHT IN THE SPOT WHERE THE HEAT WAVE AND TIDAL WAVE WILL COLLIDE!
THEN WE WERE RIGHT! THIS IS WHERE THE TWO LEGENDARY POKÉMON ARE GOING TO DUEL!
THE ENERGY BALLS THAT CAPTURED RUBY AND SAPPHIRE ARE HEADING THAT WAY TOO!
THEY'RE IN DAN-GER!
TY! CONTACT BAGOON!
WARN THE POKÉMON ASSOCIATION PRESIDENT AND CAPTAIN STERN!
RMBL
RMBL
A DUEL?
KYOGRE AND GROUDON ARE GOING TO DUEL?!

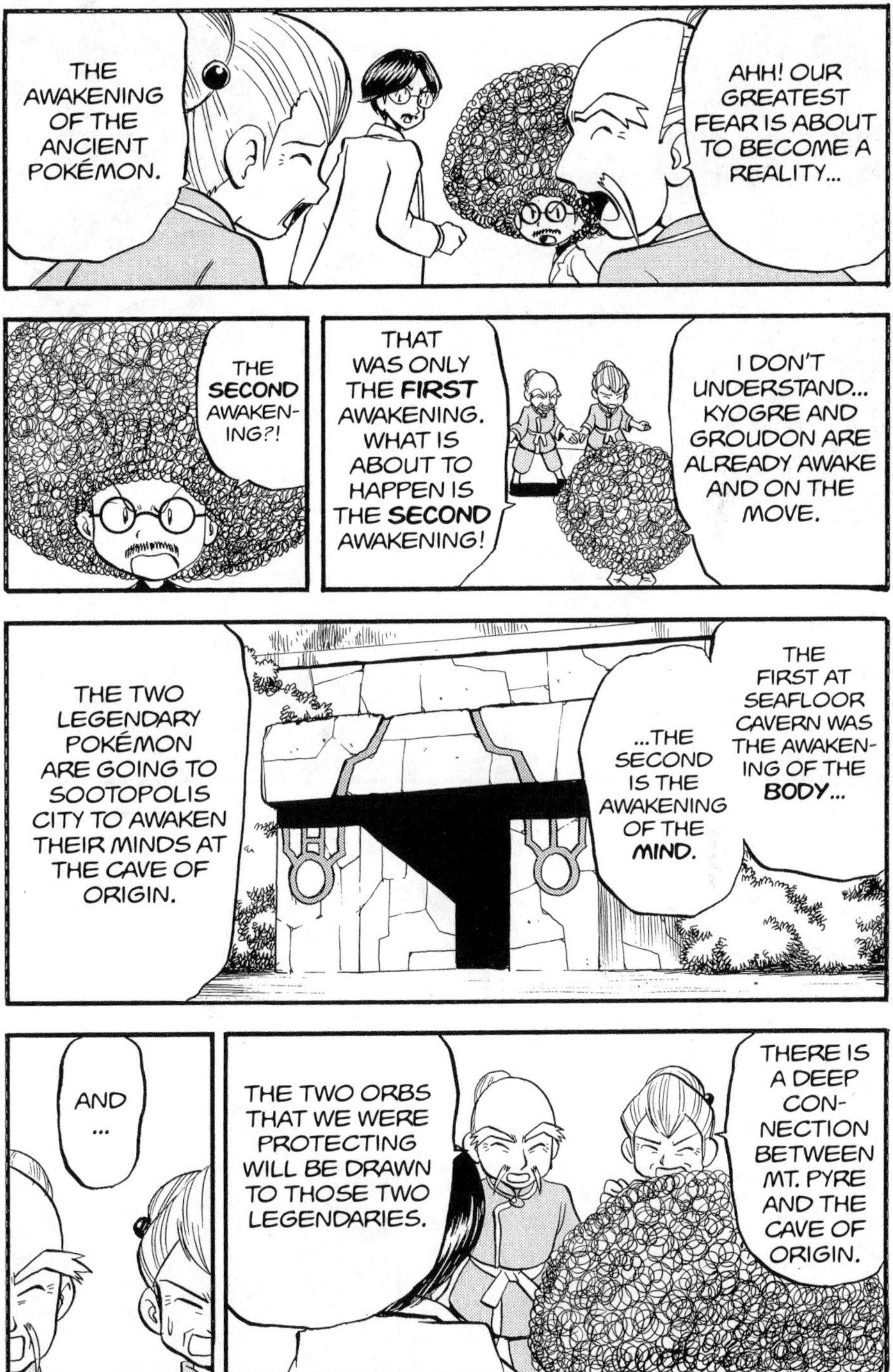
AHH! OUR GREATEST FEAR IS ABOUT TO BECOME A REALITY...
THE AWAKENING OF THE ANCIENT POKéMON.
I DON'T UNDERSTAND... KYOGRE AND GROUDON ARE ALREADY AWAKE AND ON THE MOVE.
THAT WAS ONLY THE **FIRST** AWAKENING. WHAT IS ABOUT TO HAPPEN IS THE **SECOND** AWAKENING!
THE **SECOND** AWAKENING?!
THE FIRST AT SEAFLOOR CAVERN WAS THE AWAKENING OF THE **BODY**...
...THE SECOND IS THE AWAKENING OF THE **MIND**.
THE TWO LEGENDARY POKéMON ARE GOING TO SOOTOPOLIS CITY TO AWAKEN THEIR MINDS AT THE CAVE OF ORIGIN.
THERE IS A DEEP CONNECTION BETWEEN MT. PYRE AND THE CAVE OF ORIGIN.
THE TWO ORBS THAT WE WERE PROTECTING WILL BE DRAWN TO THOSE TWO LEGENDARIES.
AND ...

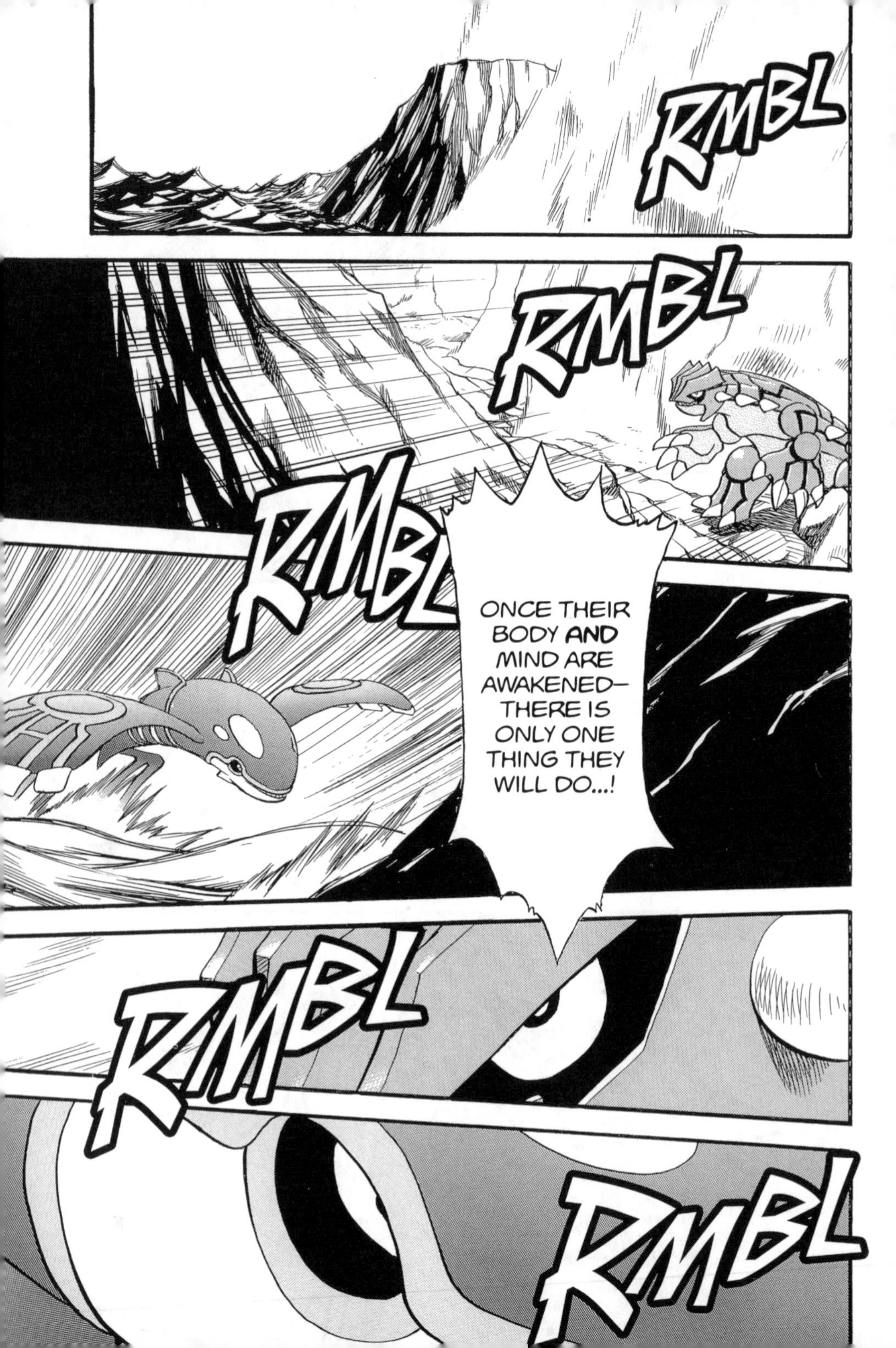
RMBL
RMBL
RMBL
ONCE THEIR BODY AND MIND ARE AWAKENED—THERE IS ONLY ONE THING THEY WILL DO...!
RMBL
RMBL

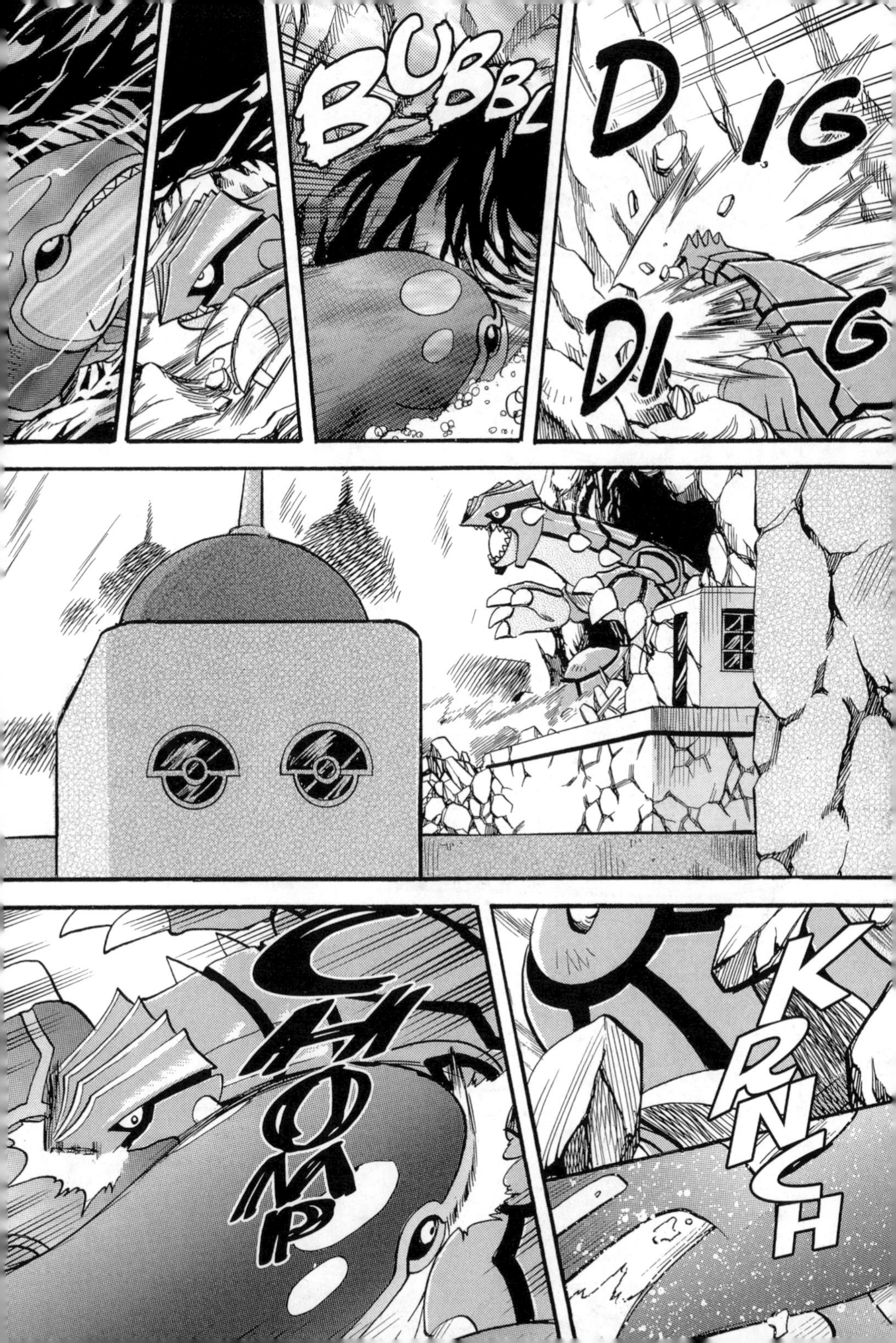
DIG
DIG
BUBBL
KRNCH
CHOMP

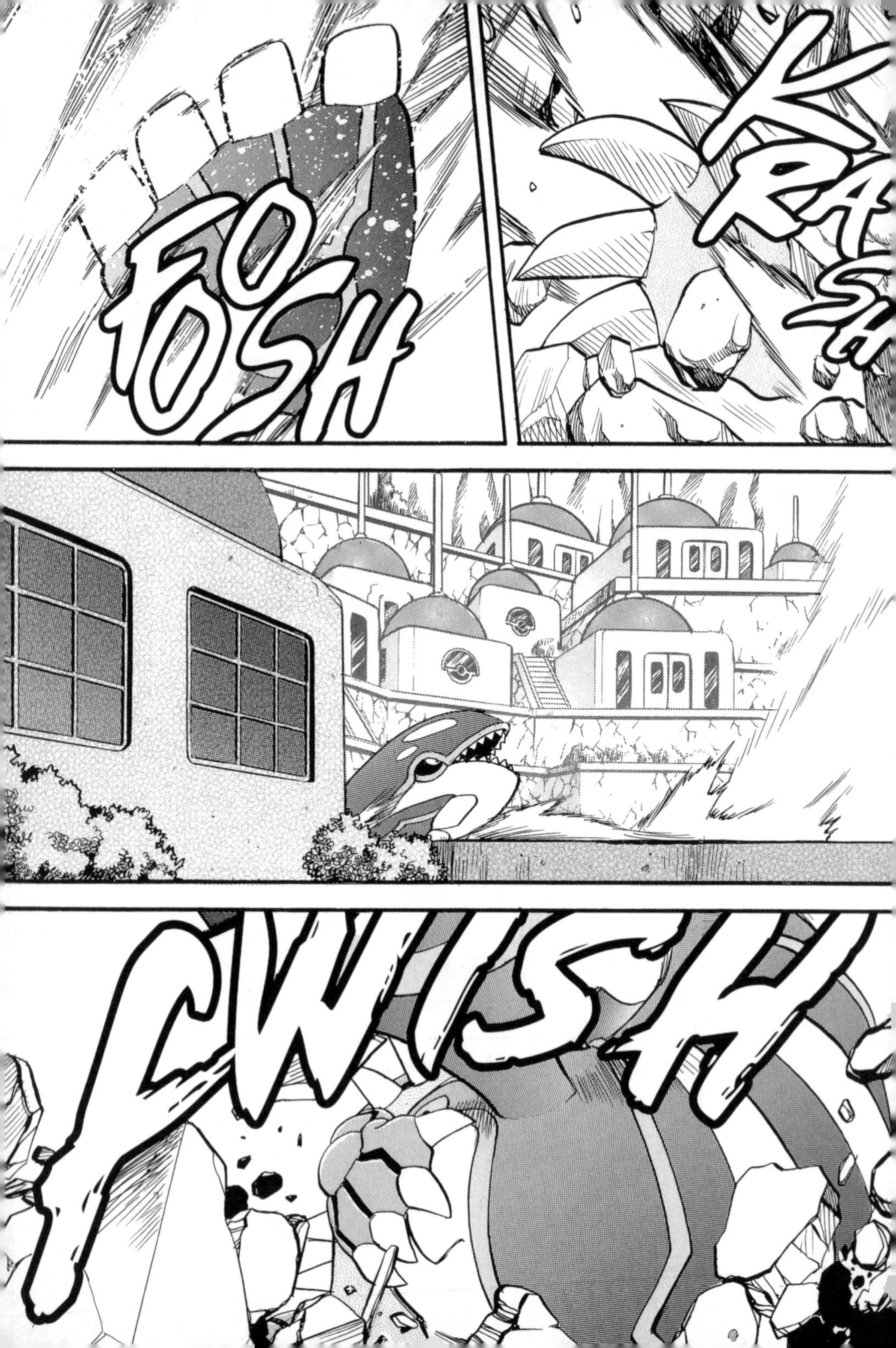
KRASH
FOOSH
CWISH

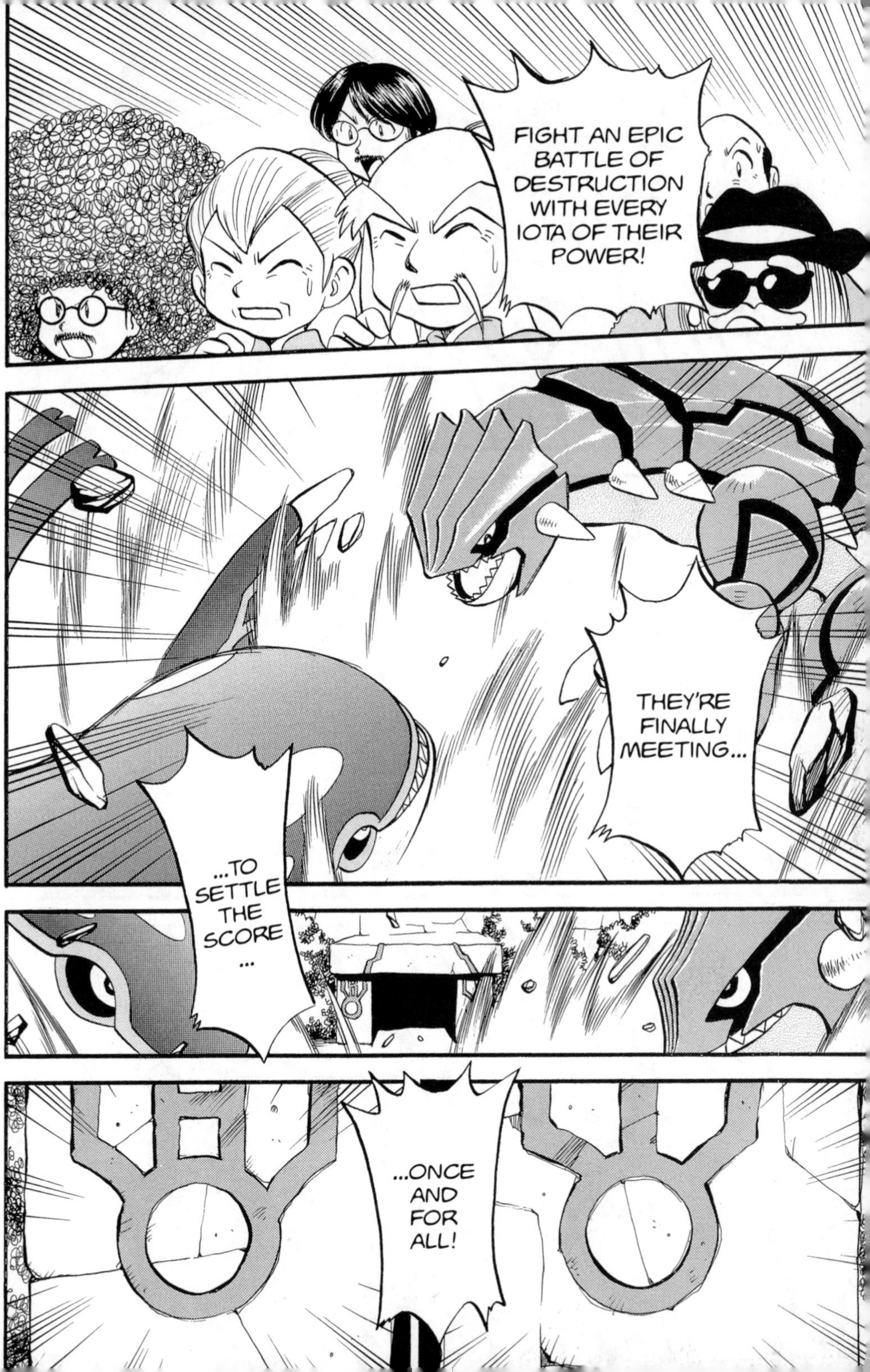
FIGHT AN EPIC BATTLE OF DESTRUCTION WITH EVERY IOTA OF THEIR POWER!
THEY'RE FINALLY MEETING...
...TO SETTLE THE SCORE ...
...ONCE AND FOR ALL!

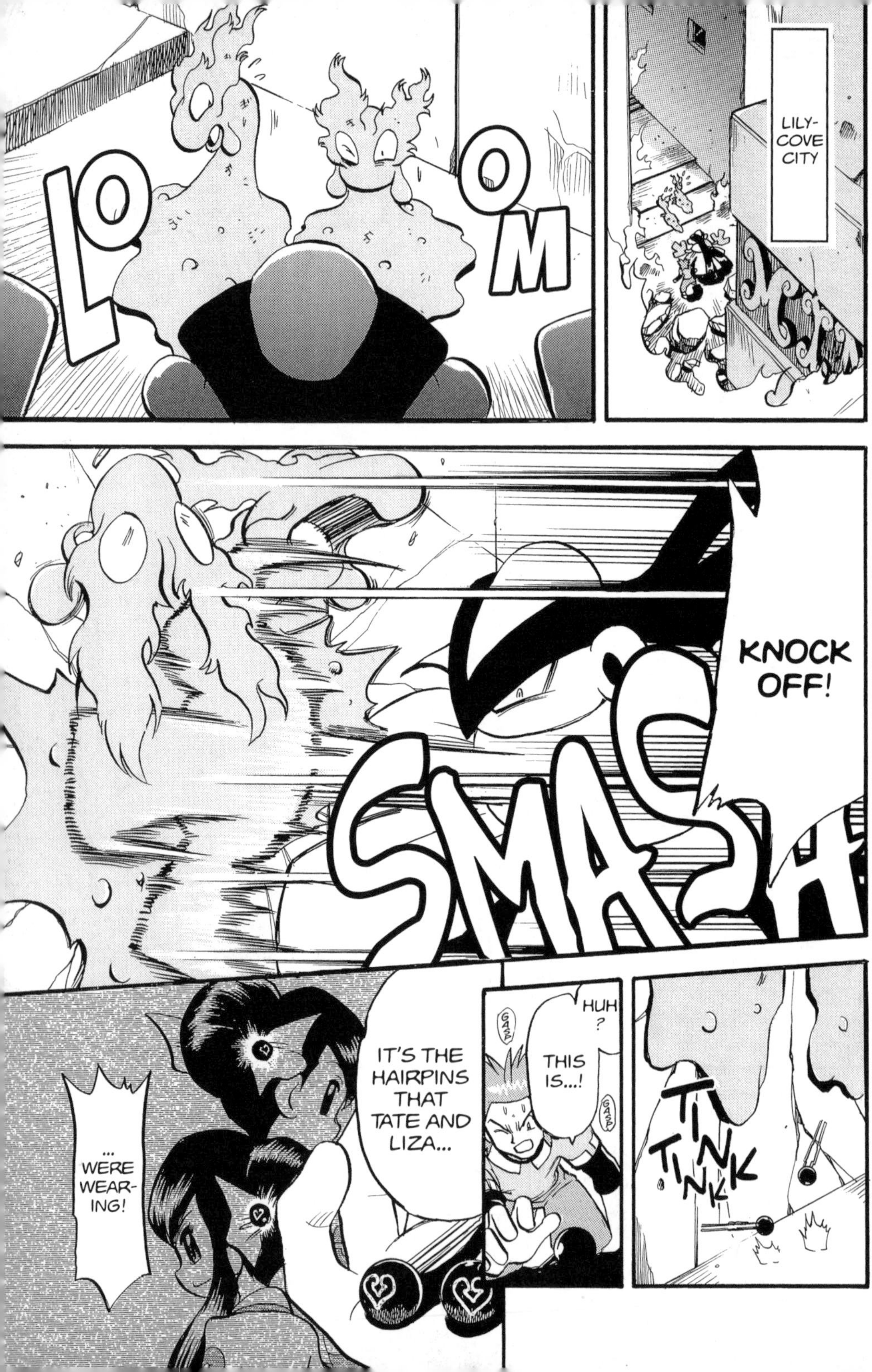
LILY-COVE CITY
LOOM
KNOCK OFF!
SMASH
TINK TINK
HUH?
GASP
THIS IS...!
GASP
IT'S THE HAIRPINS THAT TATE AND LIZA...
...WERE WEARING!

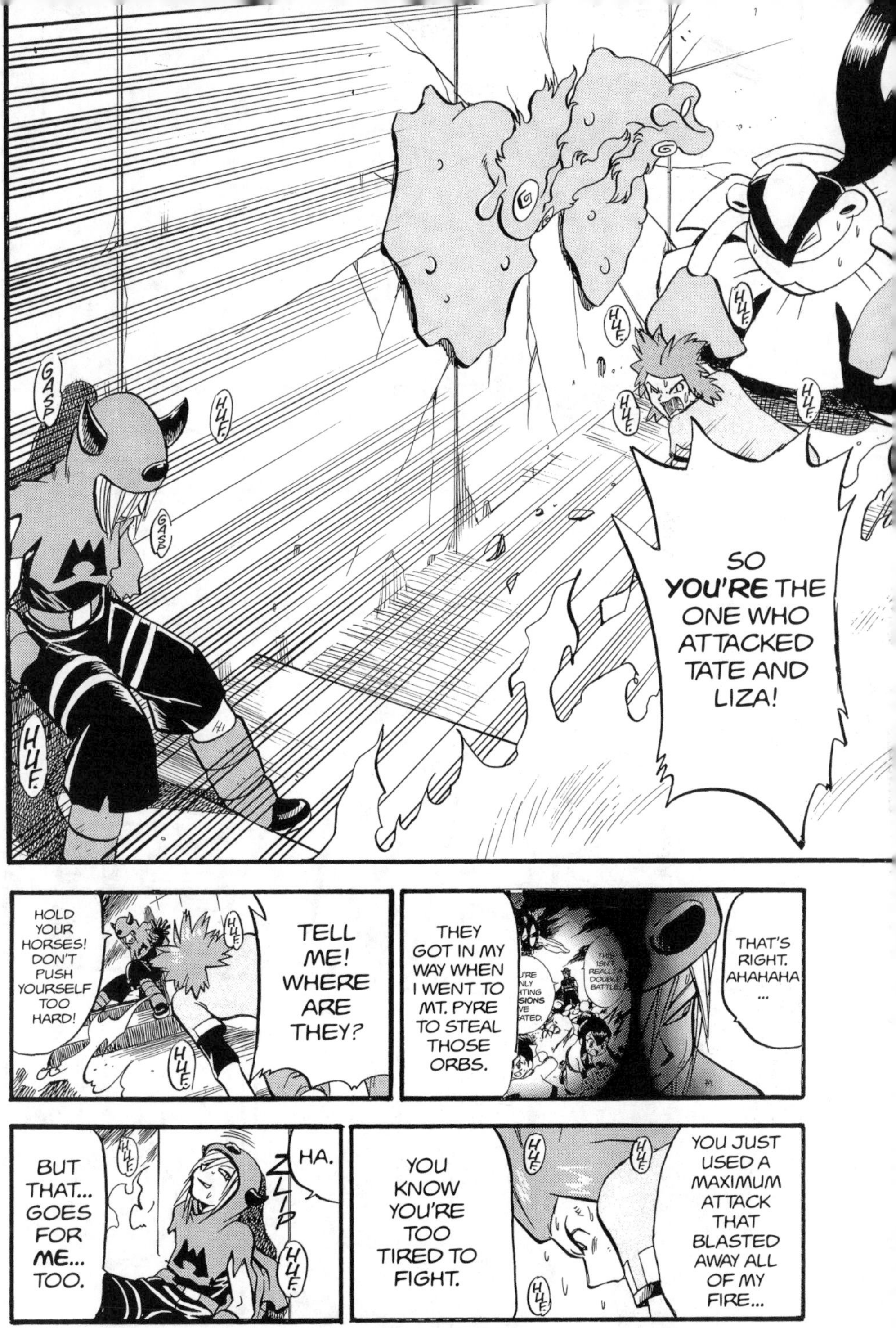
HUF.
HUF.
HUF.
SO YOU'RE THE ONE WHO ATTACKED TATE AND LIZA!
GASP
HUF.
GASP
HUF.
THAT'S RIGHT. AHAHAHA ...
THIS ISN'T REALLY A DOUBLE BATTLE.
THEY GOT IN MY WAY WHEN I WENT TO MT. PYRE TO STEAL THOSE ORBS.
TELL ME! WHERE ARE THEY?
HUF.
HOLD YOUR HORSES! DON'T PUSH YOURSELF TOO HARD!
HUF.
YOU JUST USED A MAXIMUM ATTACK THAT BLASTED AWAY ALL OF MY FIRE...
HUF.
HUF.
HUF.
YOU KNOW YOU'RE TOO TIRED TO FIGHT.
HA.
ZLIP
HUF.
HUF.
BUT THAT... GOES FOR ME... TOO.

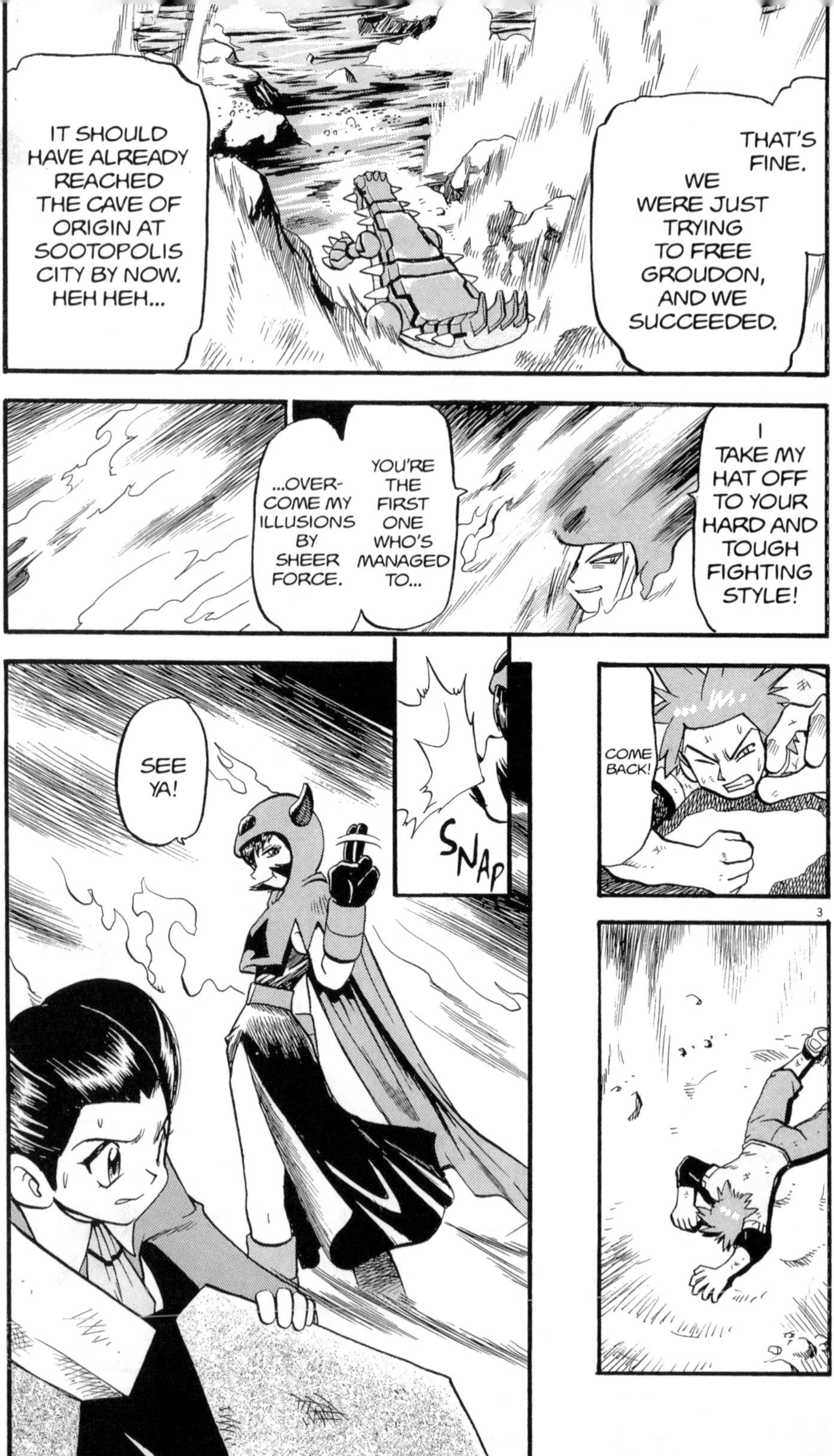
THAT'S FINE. WE WERE JUST TRYING TO FREE GROUDON, AND WE SUCCEEDED.
IT SHOULD HAVE ALREADY REACHED THE CAVE OF ORIGIN AT SOOTOPOLIS CITY BY NOW. HEH HEH...
I TAKE MY HAT OFF TO YOUR HARD AND TOUGH FIGHTING STYLE!
YOU'RE THE FIRST ONE WHO'S MANAGED TO...
...OVER-COME MY ILLUSIONS BY SHEER FORCE.
COME BACK!
SNAP
SEE YA!

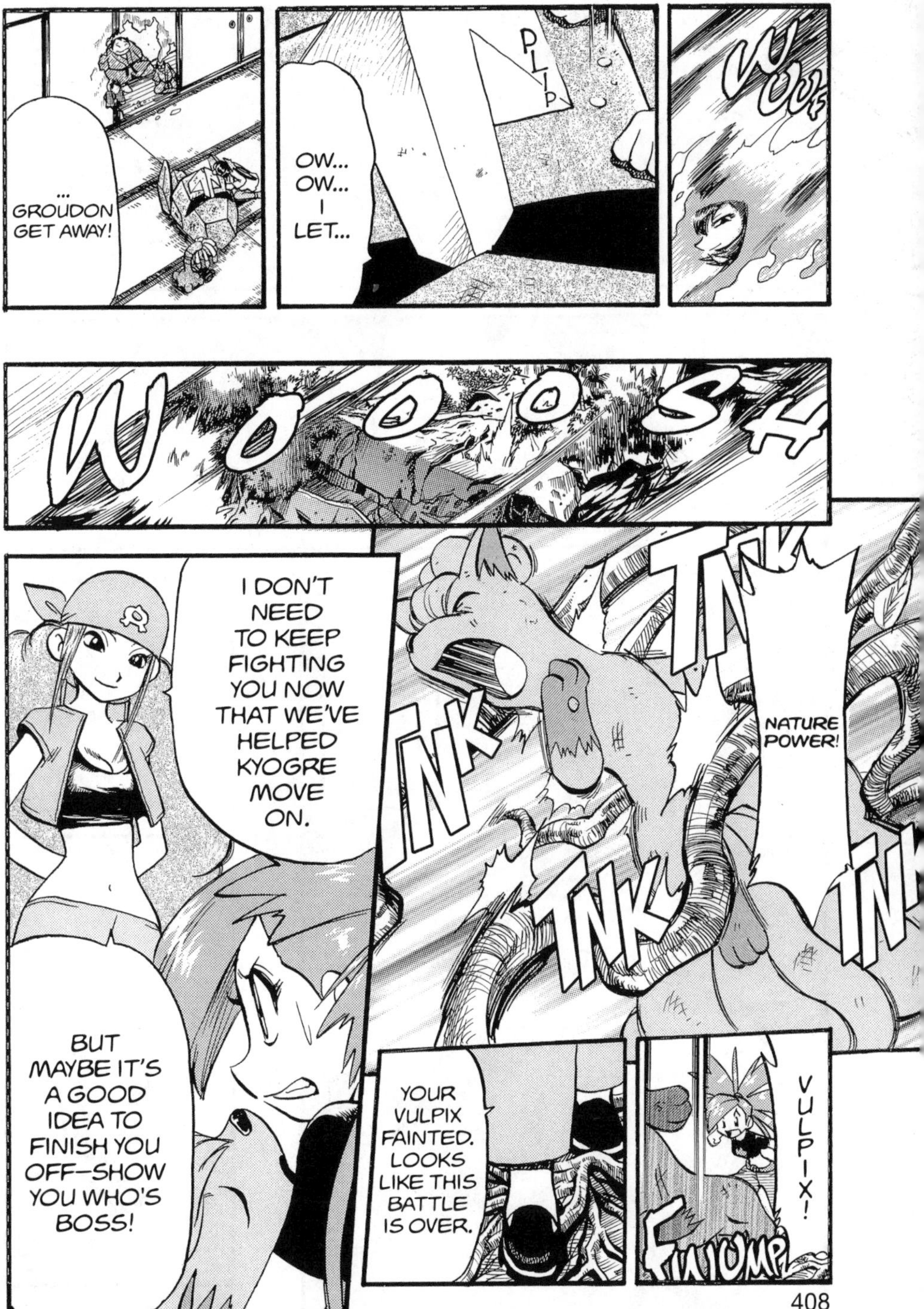
DLIP
OW... OW... I LET...
... GROUDON GET AWAY!
WOOOSH
TNK
TNK
NATURE POWER!
TNK
TNK
VULPIX!
YOUR VULPIX FAINTED. LOOKS LIKE THIS BATTLE IS OVER.
I DON'T NEED TO KEEP FIGHTING YOU NOW THAT WE'VE HELPED KYOGRE MOVE ON.
BUT MAYBE IT'S A GOOD IDEA TO FINISH YOU OFF—SHOW YOU WHO'S BOSS!

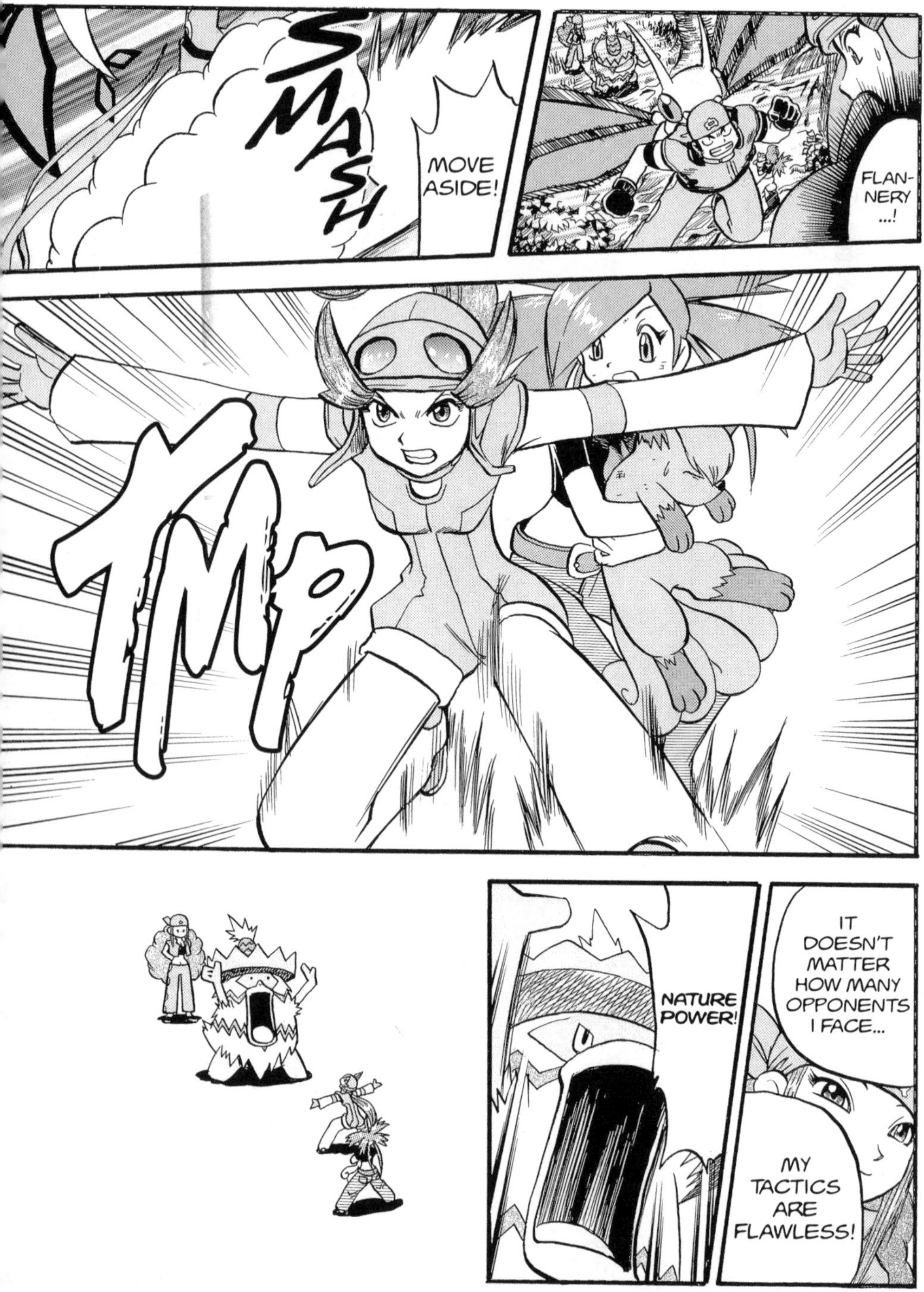
FLAN-
NERY
...!
MOVE
ASIDE!
SMASH
TMP
IT
DOESN'T
MATTER
HOW MANY
OPPONENTS
I FACE...
MY
TACTICS
ARE
FLAWLESS!
NATURE
POWER!

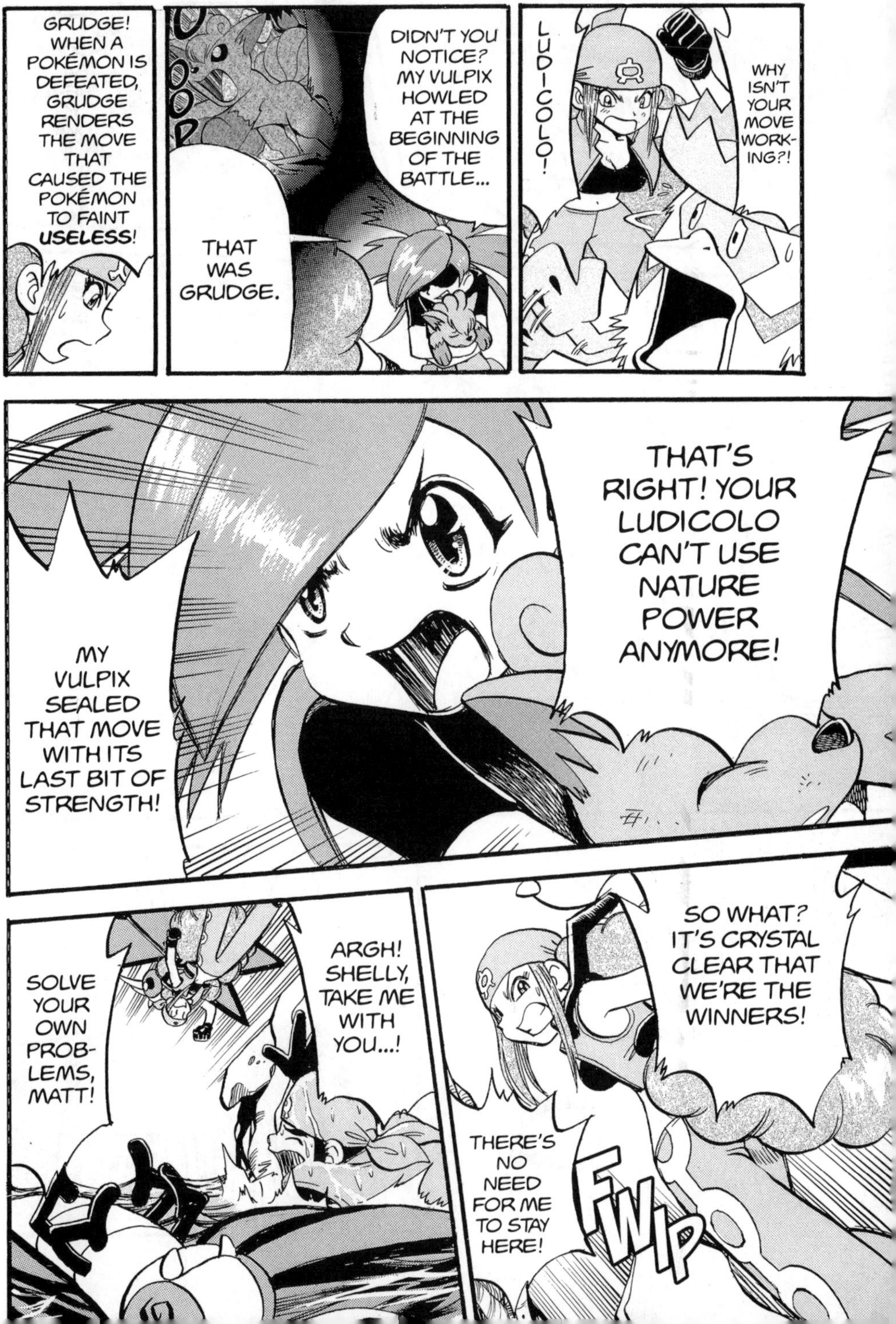
LUDICOLO!
WHY ISN'T YOUR MOVE WORKING?!
DIDN'T YOU NOTICE? MY VULPIX HOWLED AT THE BEGINNING OF THE BATTLE...
THAT WAS GRUDGE.
GRUDGE! WHEN A POKÉMON IS DEFEATED, GRUDGE RENDERS THE MOVE THAT CAUSED THE POKÉMON TO FAINT **USELESS**!
THAT'S RIGHT! YOUR LUDICOLO CAN'T USE NATURE POWER ANYMORE!
MY VULPIX SEALED THAT MOVE WITH ITS LAST BIT OF STRENGTH!
SO WHAT? IT'S CRYSTAL CLEAR THAT WE'RE THE WINNERS!
THERE'S NO NEED FOR ME TO STAY HERE!
FWIP
ARGH! SHELLY, TAKE ME WITH YOU...!
SOLVE YOUR OWN PROB-LEMS, MATT!

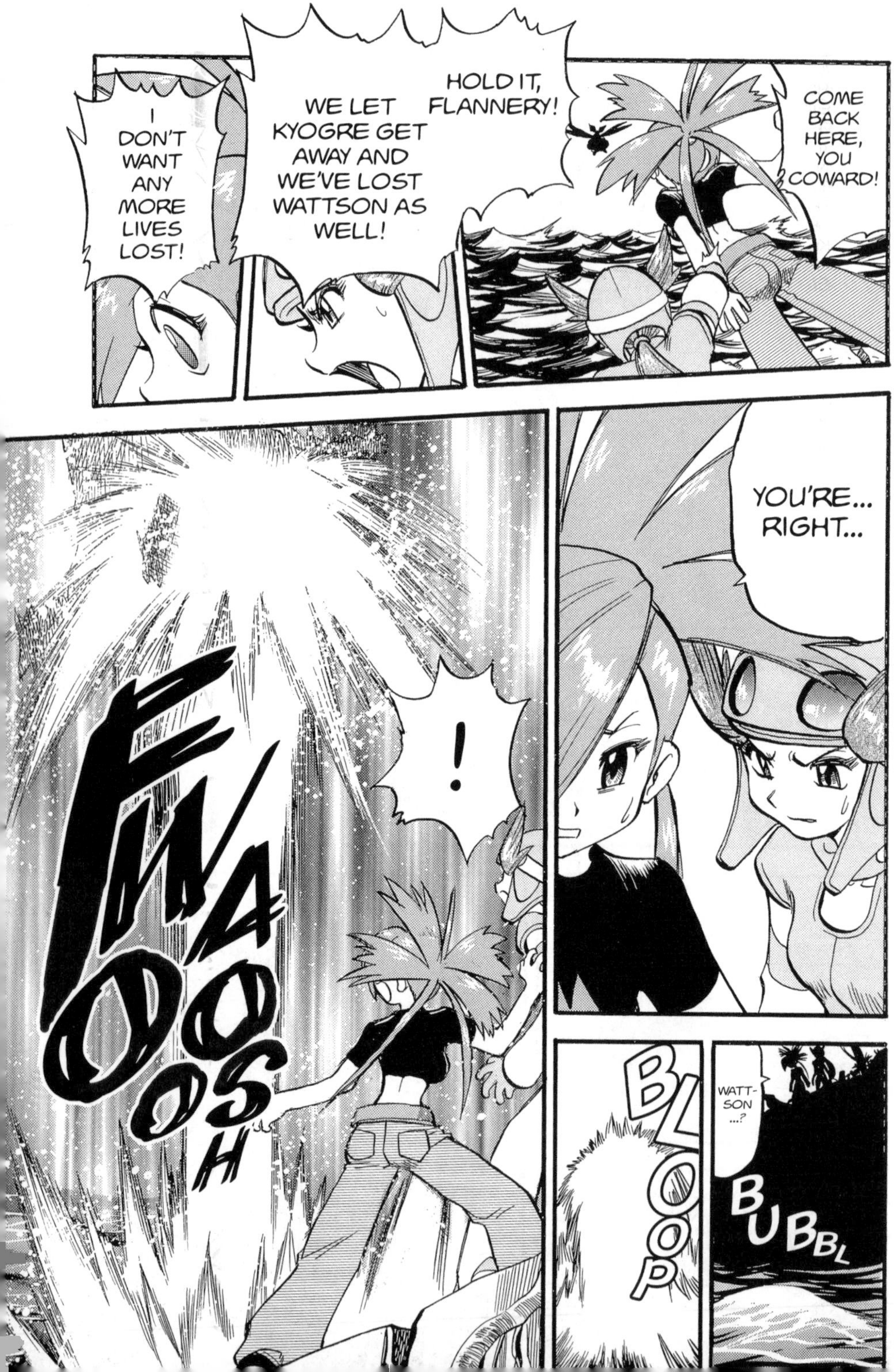
COME BACK HERE, YOU COWARD!
HOLD IT, FLANNERY!
WE LET KYOGRE GET AWAY AND WE'VE LOST WATTSON AS WELL!
I DON'T WANT ANY MORE LIVES LOST!
YOU'RE... RIGHT...
WATT-SON ...?
BUBBL
BLOOP
!
FWOOOOSH

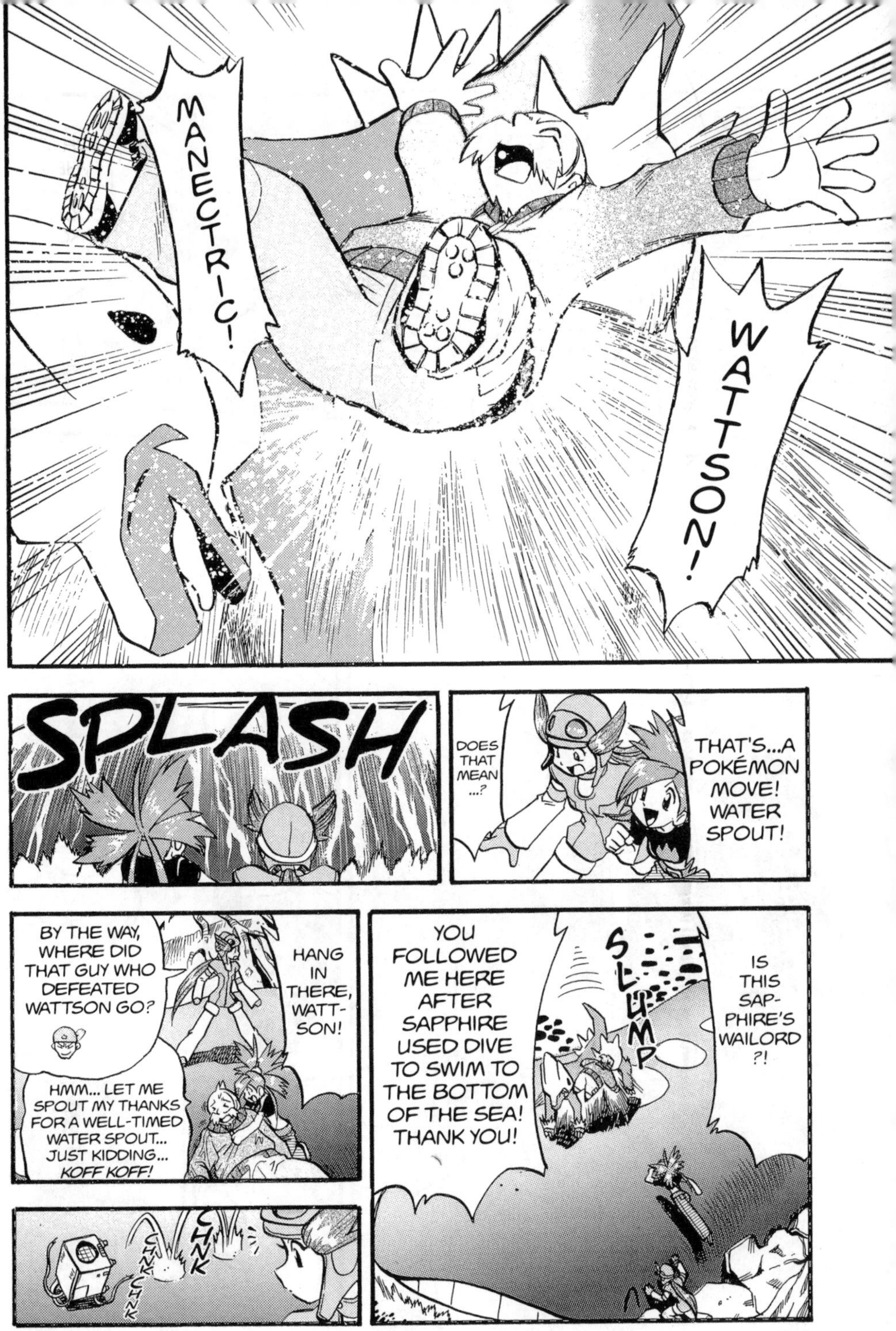
WATTSON!
MANECTRIC!
THAT'S...A POKÉMON MOVE! WATER SPOUT!
DOES THAT MEAN ...?
SPLASH
IS THIS SAP-PHIRE'S WAILORD ?!
SLUMP
YOU FOLLOWED ME HERE AFTER SAPPHIRE USED DIVE TO SWIM TO THE BOTTOM OF THE SEA! THANK YOU!
HANG IN THERE, WATT-SON!
BY THE WAY, WHERE DID THAT GUY WHO DEFEATED WATTSON GO?
HMM... LET ME SPOUT MY THANKS FOR A WELL-TIMED WATER SPOUT... JUST KIDDING... *KOFF KOFF!*
CHNK
CHNK CHNK

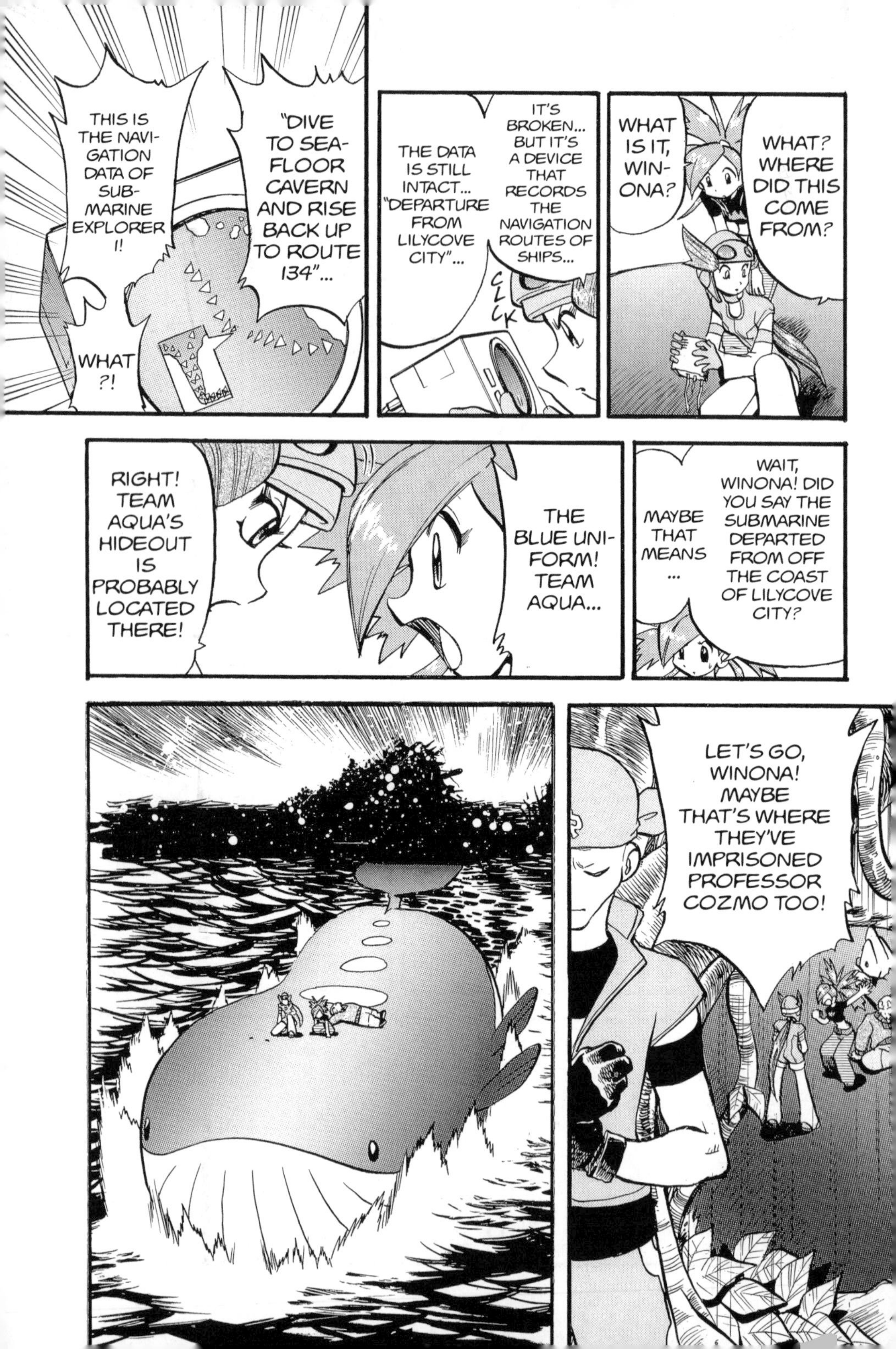
WHAT? WHERE DID THIS COME FROM?
WHAT IS IT, WINONA?
IT'S BROKEN... BUT IT'S A DEVICE THAT RECORDS THE NAVIGATION ROUTES OF SHIPS...
THE DATA IS STILL INTACT... "DEPARTURE FROM LILYCOVE CITY"...
CLICK
"DIVE TO SEAFLOOR CAVERN AND RISE BACK UP TO ROUTE 134"...
THIS IS THE NAVIGATION DATA OF SUBMARINE EXPLORER 1!
WHAT?!
WAIT, WINONA! DID YOU SAY THE SUBMARINE DEPARTED FROM OFF THE COAST OF LILYCOVE CITY?
MAYBE THAT MEANS...
THE BLUE UNIFORM! TEAM AQUA...
RIGHT! TEAM AQUA'S HIDEOUT IS PROBABLY LOCATED THERE!
LET'S GO, WINONA! MAYBE THAT'S WHERE THEY'VE IMPRISONED PROFESSOR COZMO TOO!

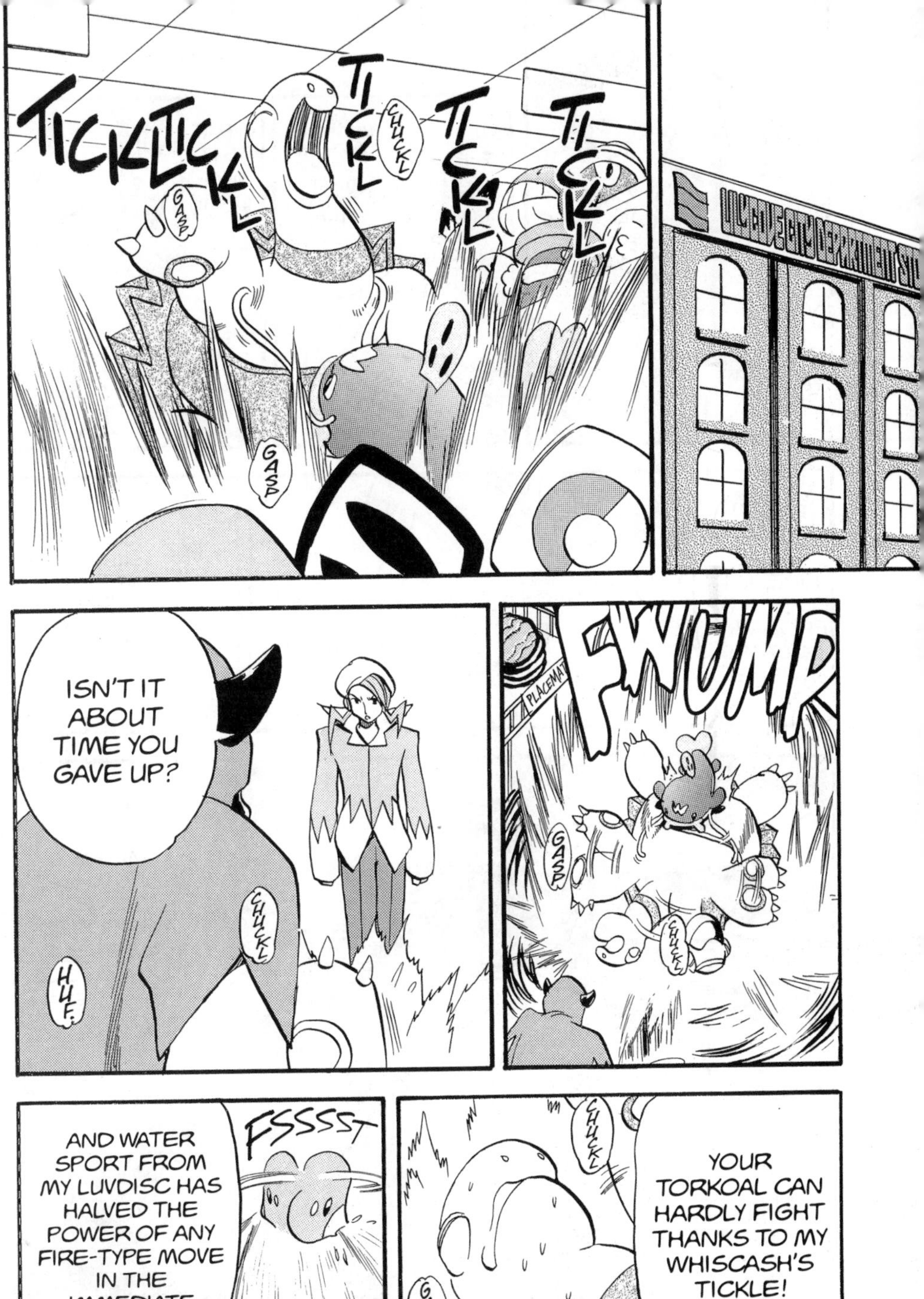
TICKL
TICKL
TICKL
CHUCKL
TICKL
TICKL
GASP
GASP
FWUMP
PLACEMAT
GASP
CHUCKL
ISN'T IT ABOUT TIME YOU GAVE UP?
CHUCKL
HUF.
YOUR TORKOAL CAN HARDLY FIGHT THANKS TO MY WHISCASH'S TICKLE!
CHUCKL
GASP
FSSSST
AND WATER SPORT FROM MY LUVDISC HAS HALVED THE POWER OF ANY FIRE-TYPE MOVE IN THE IMMEDIATE VICINITY.

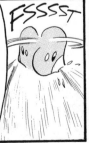

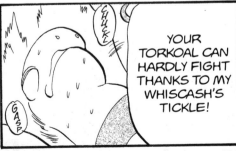

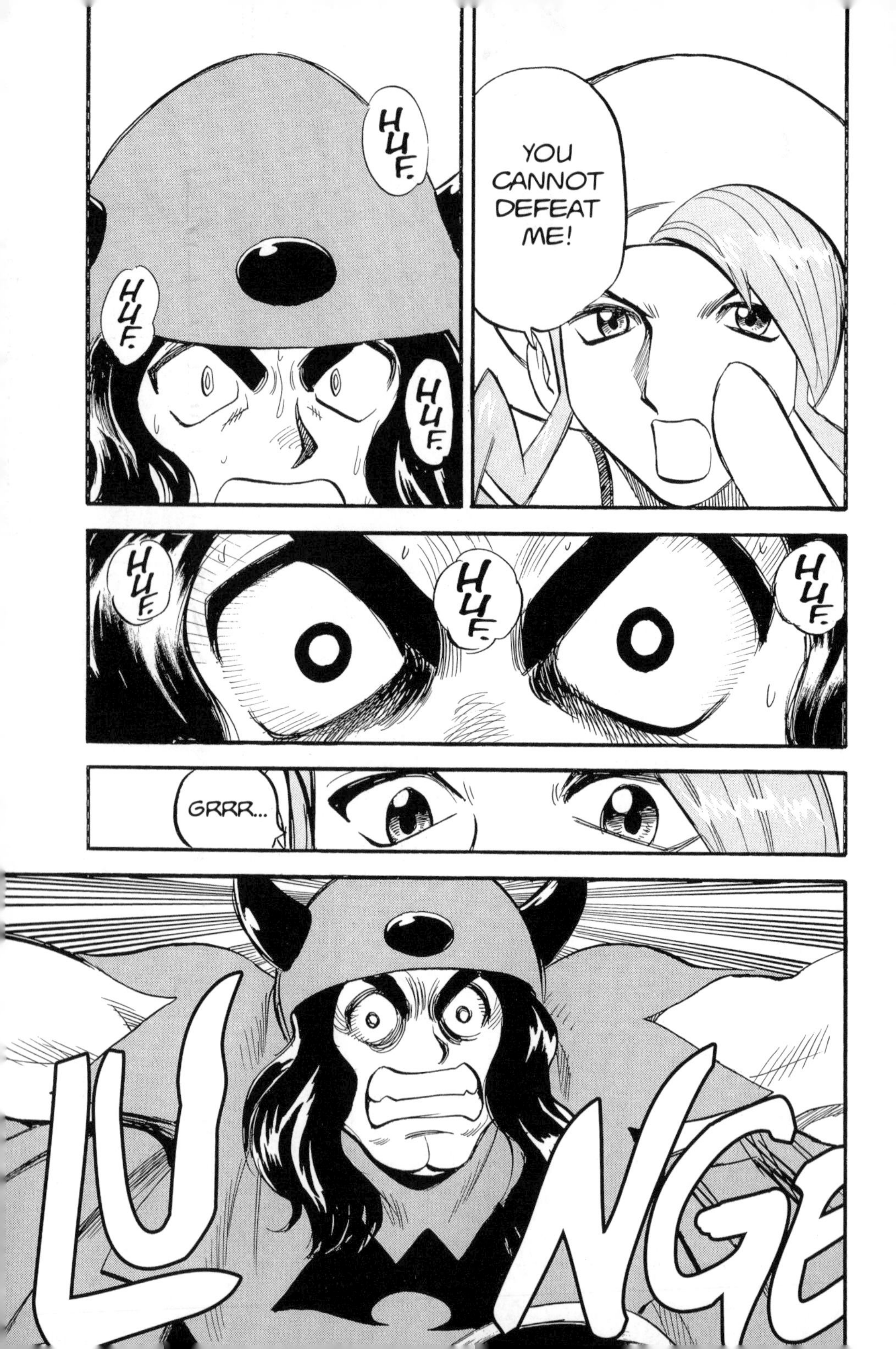
YOU CANNOT DEFEAT ME!
HUF.
HUF.
HUF.
HUF.
HUF.
HUF.
GRRR...
LUNGE

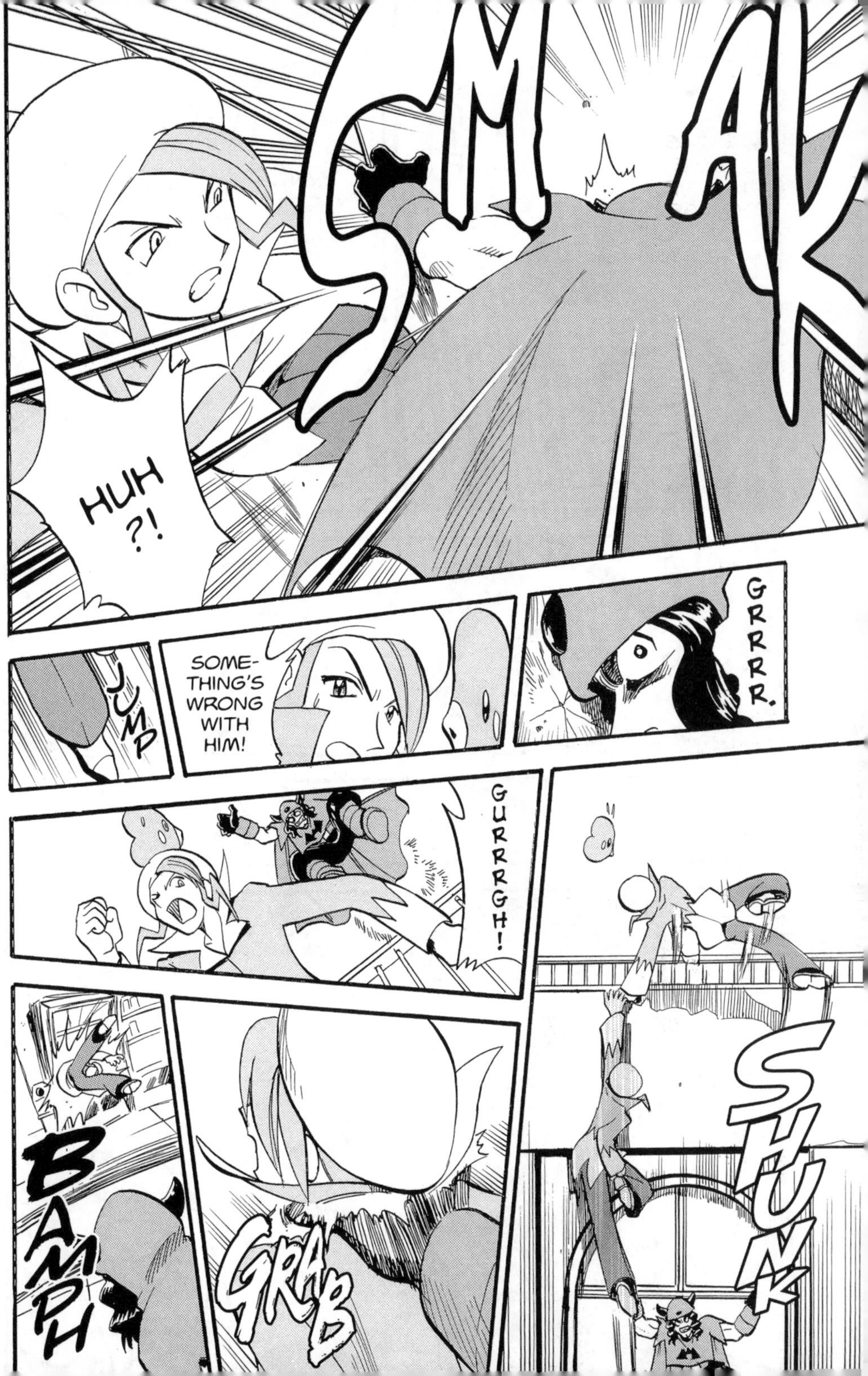
SMACK
HUH?!
GRRRR.
SOME-THING'S WRONG WITH HIM!
JUMP
SHUNK
GURRRGH!
GRAB
BAMPH

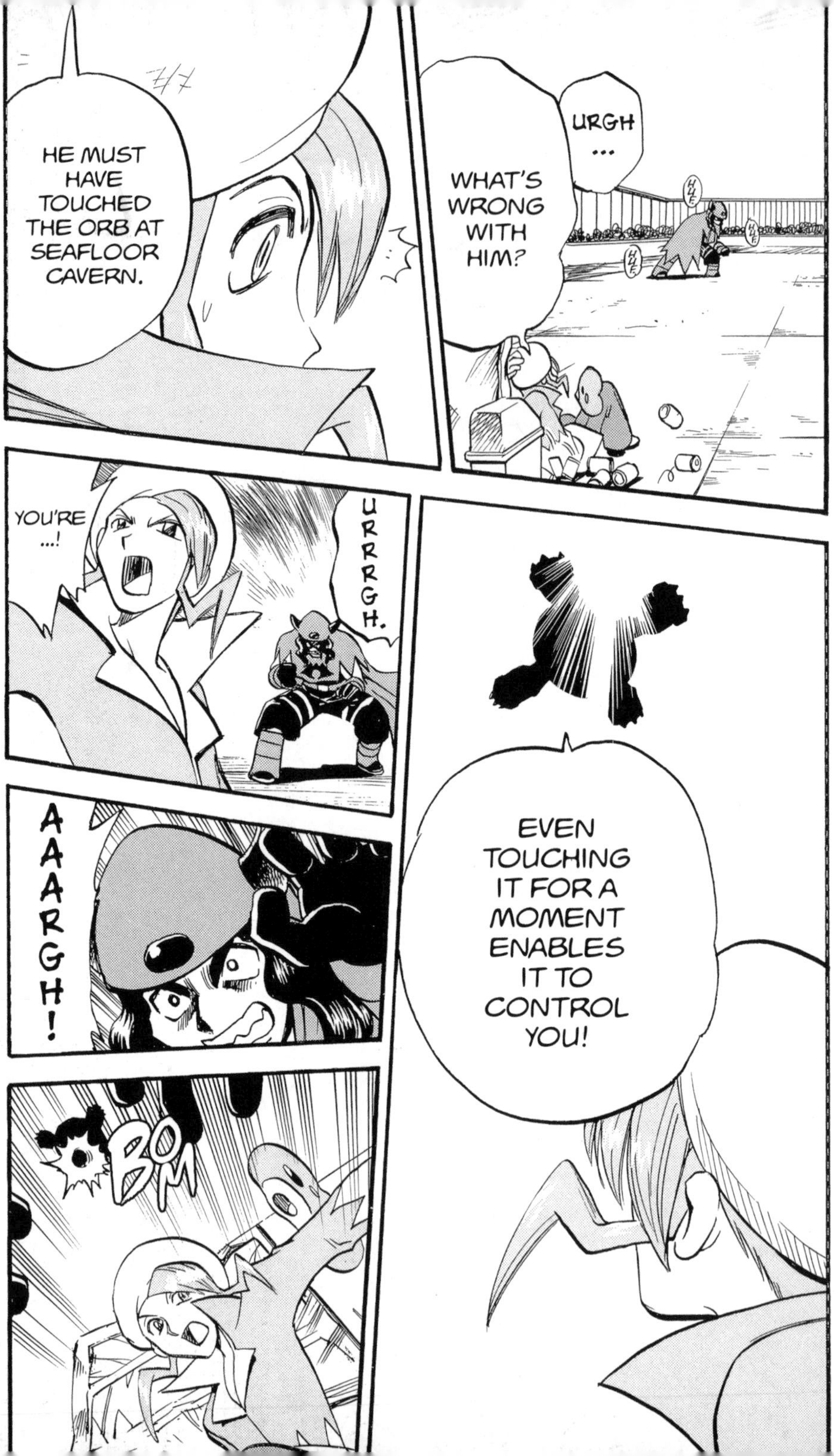
URGH ...
WHAT'S WRONG WITH HIM?
HE MUST HAVE TOUCHED THE ORB AT SEAFLOOR CAVERN.
EVEN TOUCHING IT FOR A MOMENT ENABLES IT TO CONTROL YOU!
YOU'RE ...!
URRRGH.
AAAARGH!
BOOM

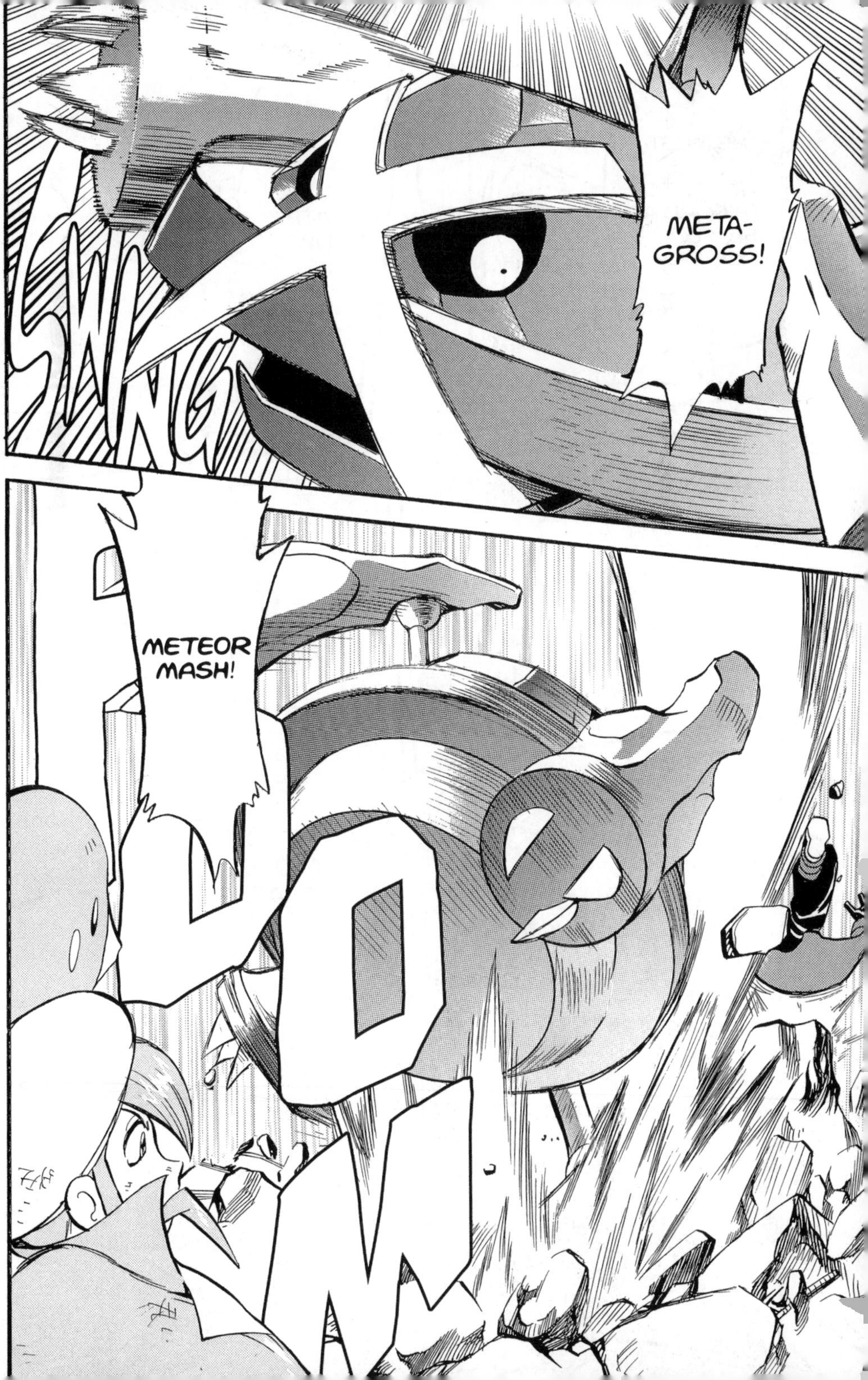
META-GROSS!
SWING
METEOR MASH!

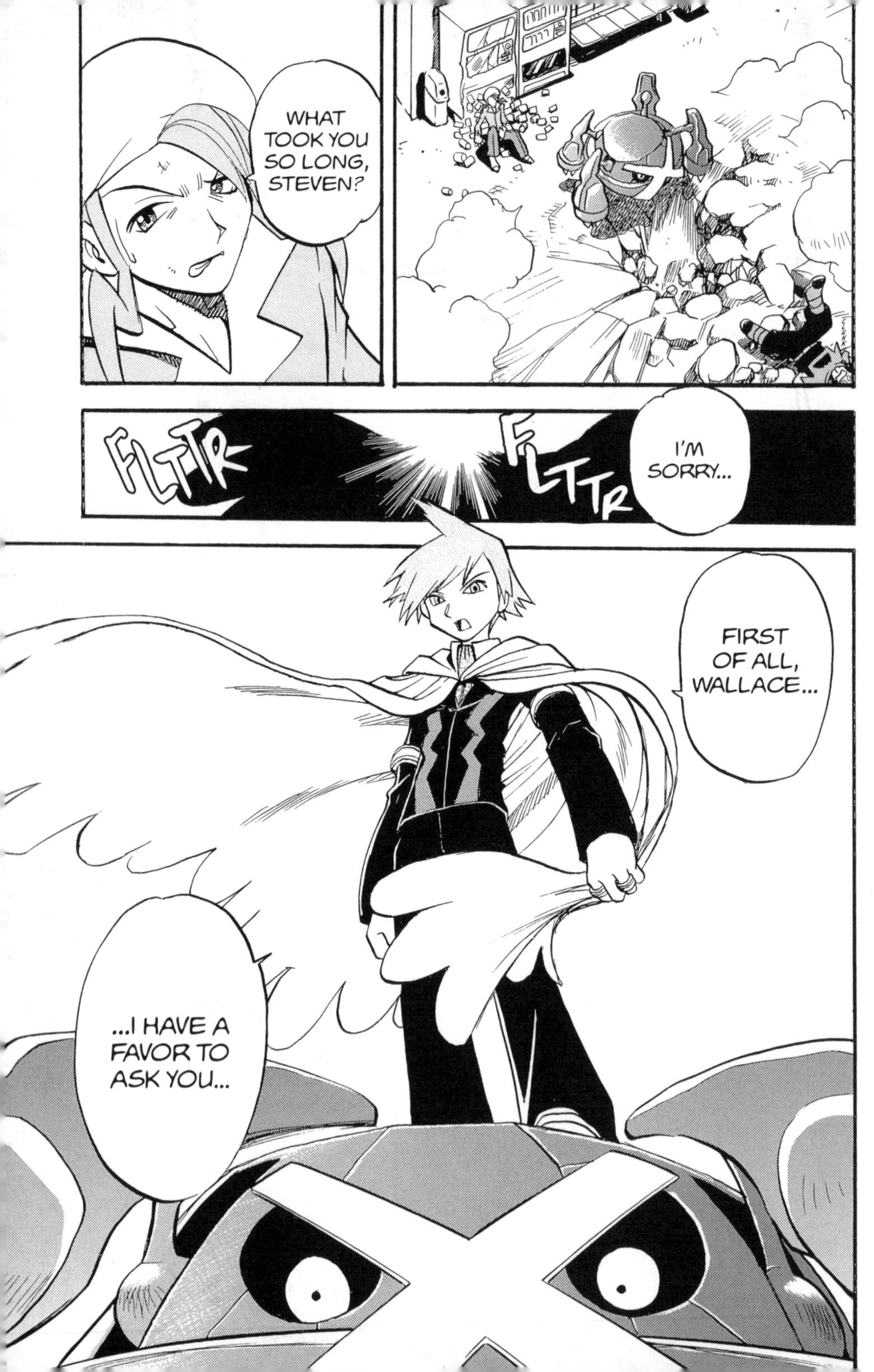
WHAT TOOK YOU SO LONG, STEVEN?
I'M SORRY...
FLTTR
FLTTR
FIRST OF ALL, WALLACE...
...I HAVE A FAVOR TO ASK YOU...

● Adventure 251 ●
The Beginning of the End with Kyogre and Groudon, Part 13

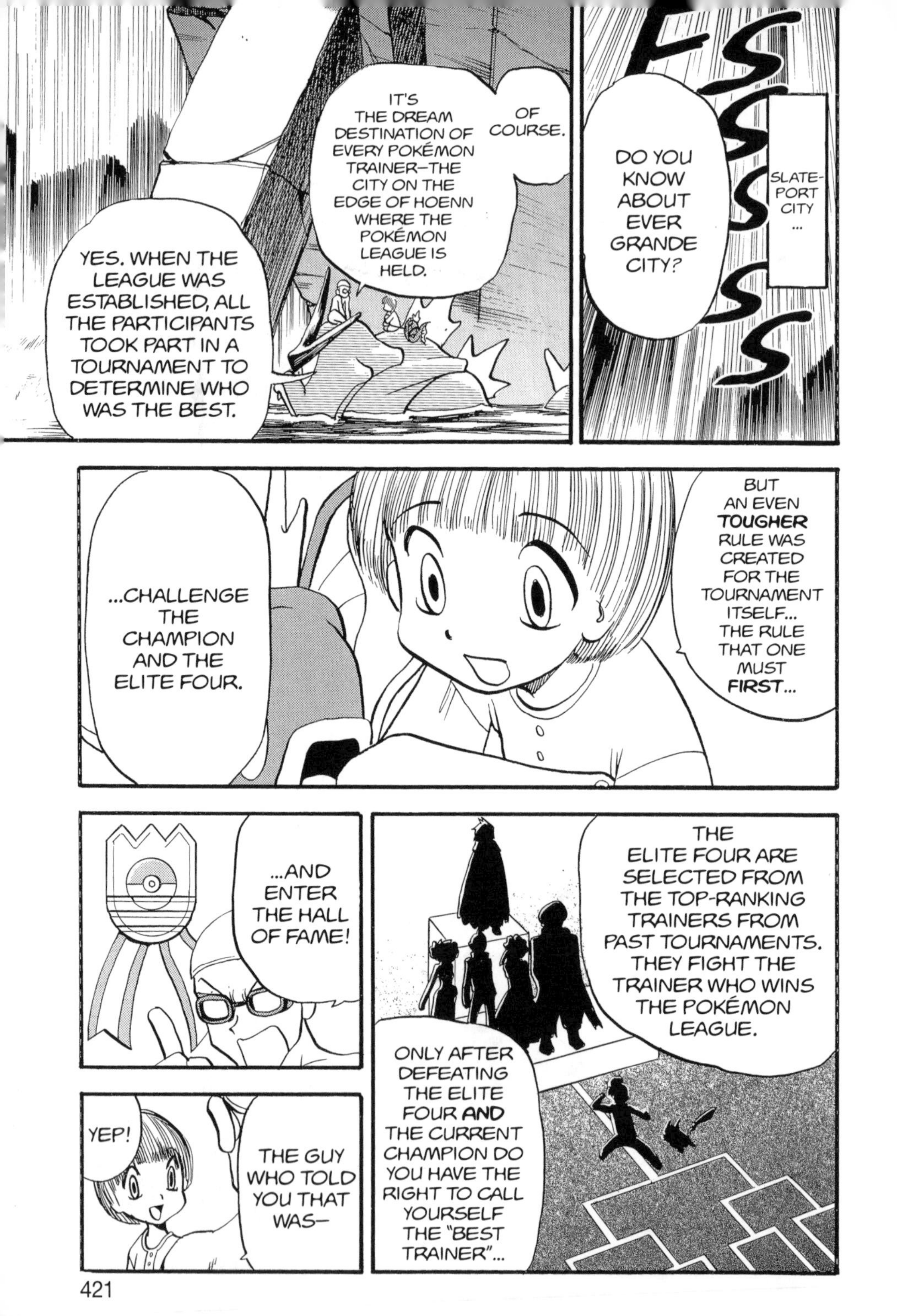

SLATEPORT CITY...
FSSSSS
DO YOU KNOW ABOUT EVER GRANDE CITY?
OF COURSE.
IT'S THE DREAM DESTINATION OF EVERY POKÉMON TRAINER—THE CITY ON THE EDGE OF HOENN WHERE THE POKÉMON LEAGUE IS HELD.
YES. WHEN THE LEAGUE WAS ESTABLISHED, ALL THE PARTICIPANTS TOOK PART IN A TOURNAMENT TO DETERMINE WHO WAS THE BEST.
BUT AN EVEN **TOUGHER** RULE WAS CREATED FOR THE TOURNAMENT ITSELF... THE RULE THAT ONE MUST **FIRST**...
...CHALLENGE THE CHAMPION AND THE ELITE FOUR.
THE ELITE FOUR ARE SELECTED FROM THE TOP-RANKING TRAINERS FROM PAST TOURNAMENTS. THEY FIGHT THE TRAINER WHO WINS THE POKÉMON LEAGUE.
ONLY AFTER DEFEATING THE ELITE FOUR **AND** THE CURRENT CHAMPION DO YOU HAVE THE RIGHT TO CALL YOURSELF THE "BEST TRAINER"...
...AND ENTER THE HALL OF FAME!
YEP!
THE GUY WHO TOLD YOU THAT WAS—

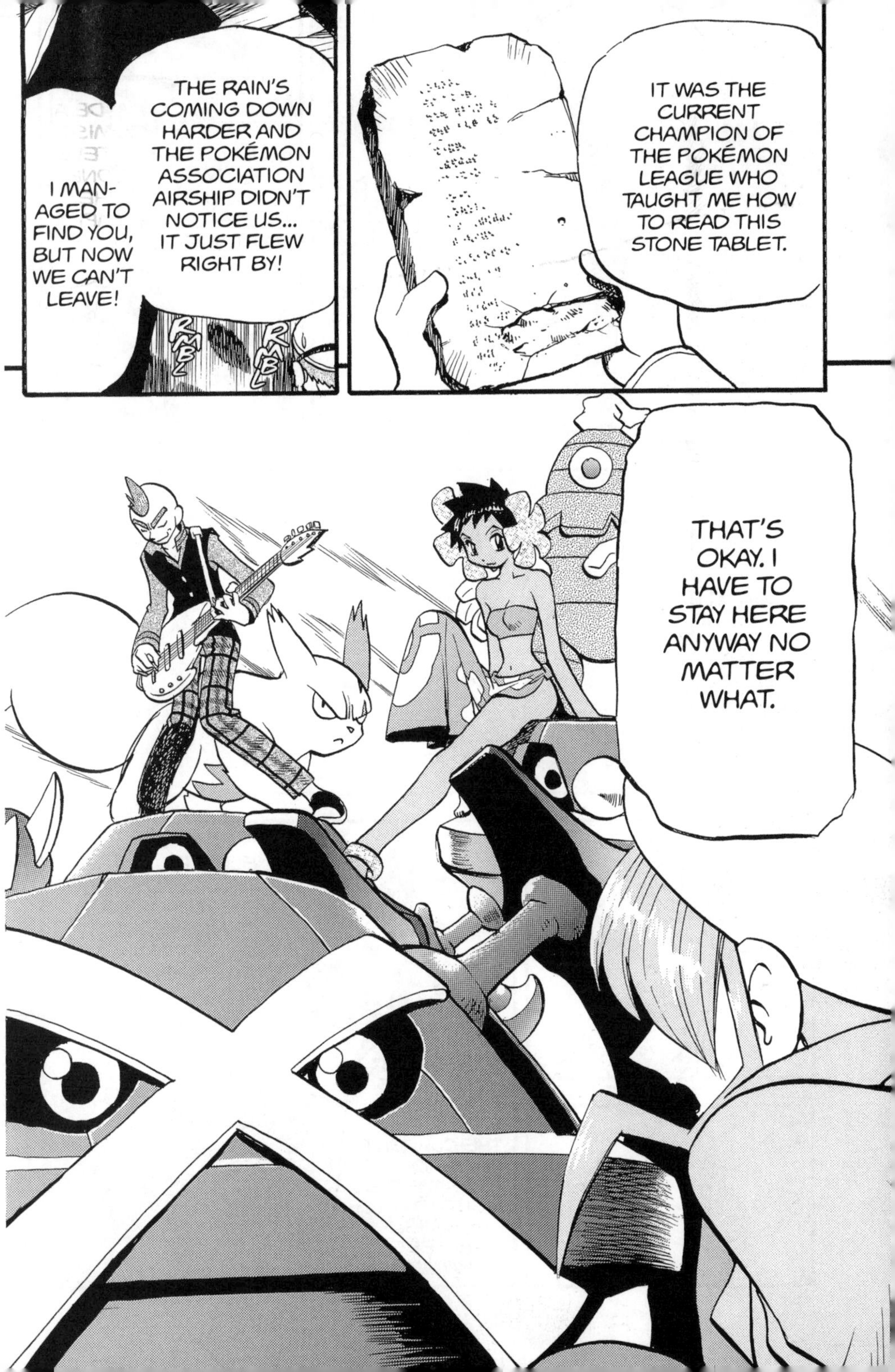
IT WAS THE CURRENT CHAMPION OF THE POKÉMON LEAGUE WHO TAUGHT ME HOW TO READ THIS STONE TABLET.
THE RAIN'S COMING DOWN HARDER AND THE POKÉMON ASSOCIATION AIRSHIP DIDN'T NOTICE US... IT JUST FLEW RIGHT BY!
I MAN-AGED TO FIND YOU, BUT NOW WE CAN'T LEAVE!
RMBL
RMBL
THAT'S OKAY. I HAVE TO STAY HERE ANYWAY NO MATTER WHAT.

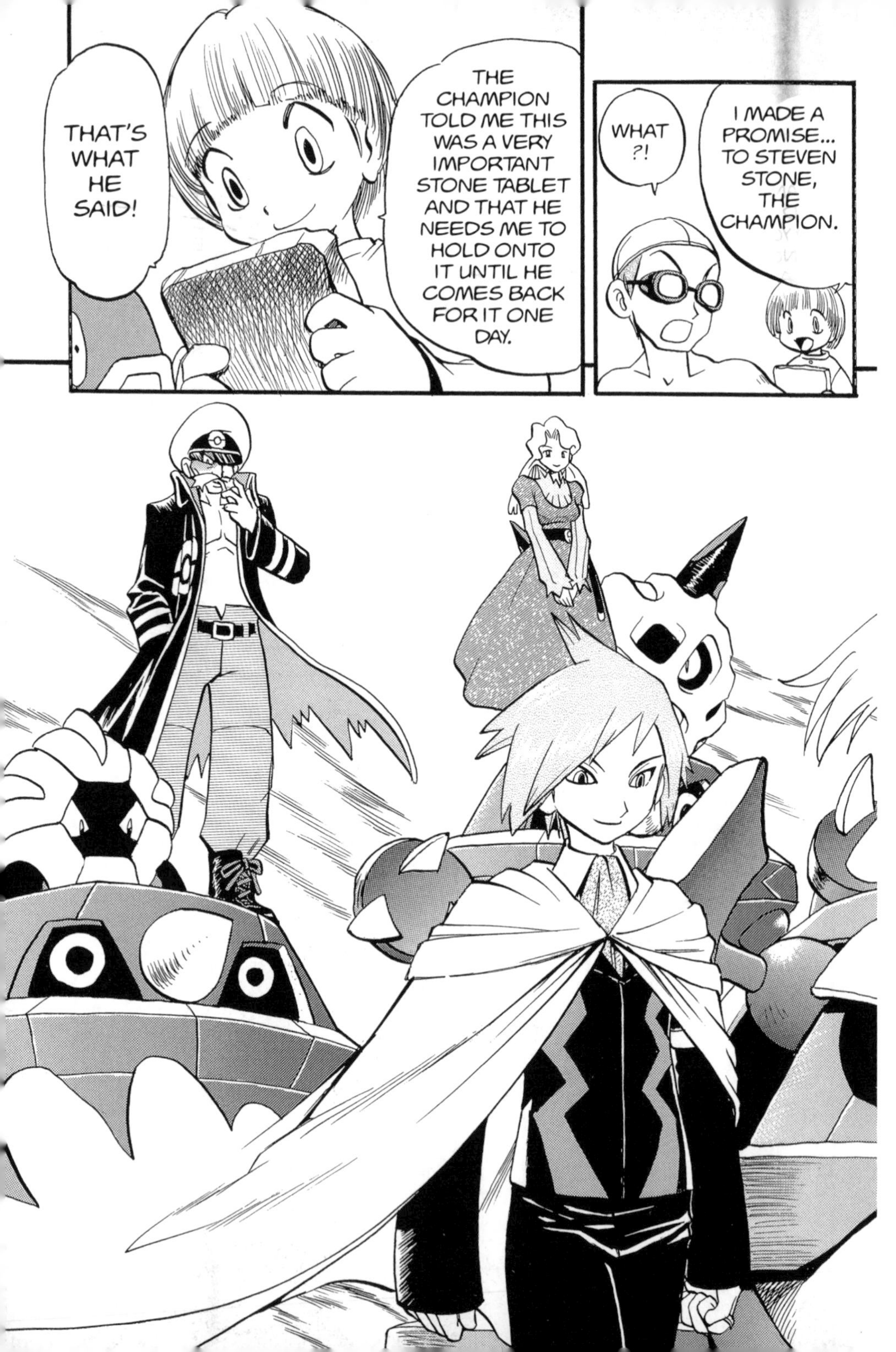
I MADE A PROMISE... TO STEVEN STONE, THE CHAMPION.
WHAT?!
THE CHAMPION TOLD ME THIS WAS A VERY IMPORTANT STONE TABLET AND THAT HE NEEDS ME TO HOLD ONTO IT UNTIL HE COMES BACK FOR IT ONE DAY.
THAT'S WHAT HE SAID!

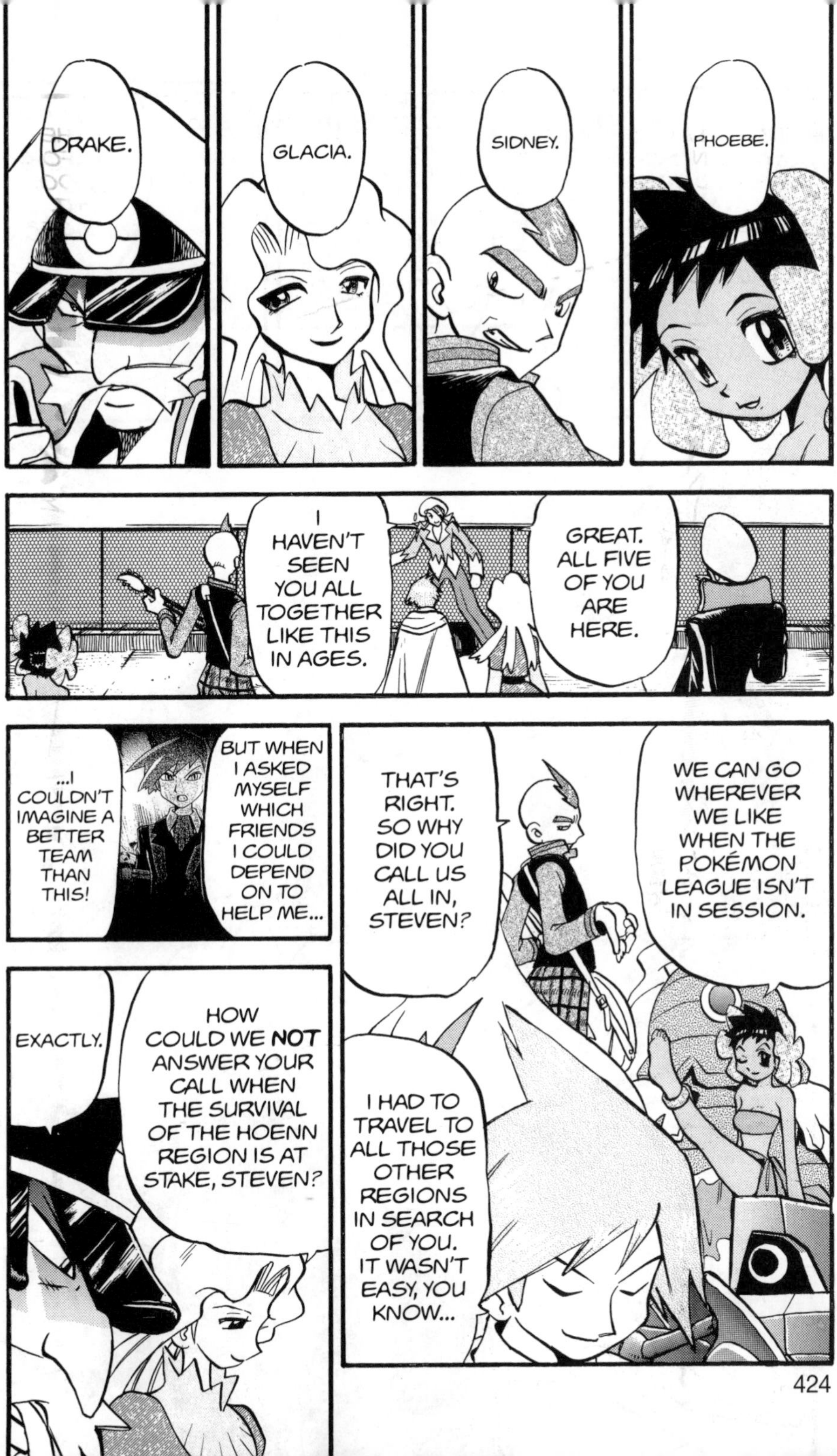
PHOEBE.
SIDNEY.
GLACIA.
DRAKE.
GREAT. ALL FIVE OF YOU ARE HERE.
I HAVEN'T SEEN YOU ALL TOGETHER LIKE THIS IN AGES.
WE CAN GO WHEREVER WE LIKE WHEN THE POKÉMON LEAGUE ISN'T IN SESSION.
THAT'S RIGHT. SO WHY DID YOU CALL US ALL IN, STEVEN?
I HAD TO TRAVEL TO ALL THOSE OTHER REGIONS IN SEARCH OF YOU. IT WASN'T EASY, YOU KNOW...
BUT WHEN I ASKED MYSELF WHICH FRIENDS I COULD DEPEND ON TO HELP ME...
...I COULDN'T IMAGINE A BETTER TEAM THAN THIS!
HOW COULD WE **NOT** ANSWER YOUR CALL WHEN THE SURVIVAL OF THE HOENN REGION IS AT STAKE, STEVEN?
EXACTLY.

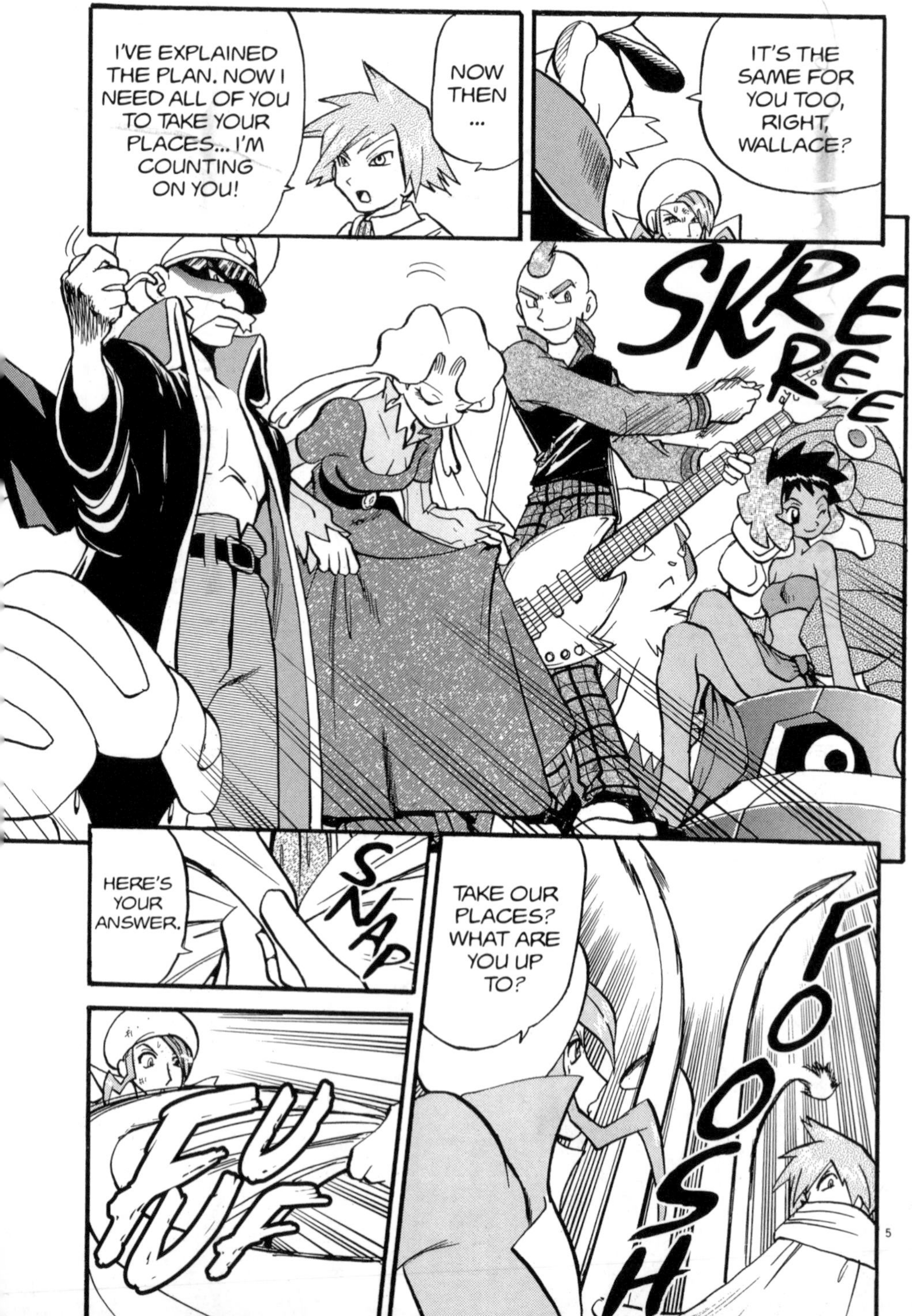
IT'S THE SAME FOR YOU TOO, RIGHT, WALLACE?
NOW THEN ...
I'VE EXPLAINED THE PLAN. NOW I NEED ALL OF YOU TO TAKE YOUR PLACES... I'M COUNTING ON YOU!
SKRE REEE
TAKE OUR PLACES? WHAT ARE YOU UP TO?
FOOOSH
HERE'S YOUR ANSWER.
SNAP

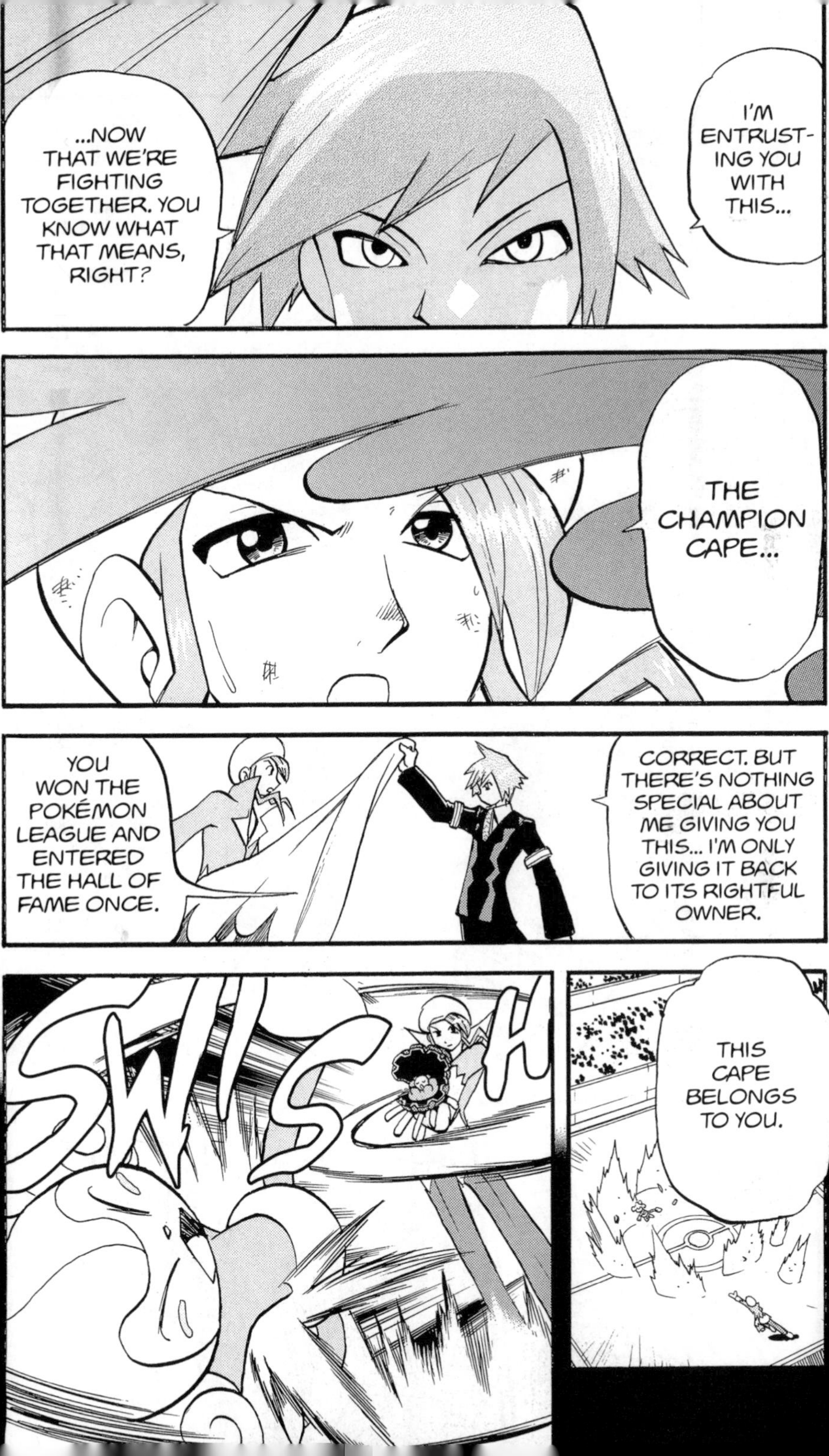
I'M ENTRUSTING YOU WITH THIS...
...NOW THAT WE'RE FIGHTING TOGETHER. YOU KNOW WHAT THAT MEANS, RIGHT?
THE CHAMPION CAPE...
CORRECT. BUT THERE'S NOTHING SPECIAL ABOUT ME GIVING YOU THIS... I'M ONLY GIVING IT BACK TO ITS RIGHTFUL OWNER.
YOU WON THE POKÉMON LEAGUE AND ENTERED THE HALL OF FAME ONCE.
THIS CAPE BELONGS TO YOU.
SWISH

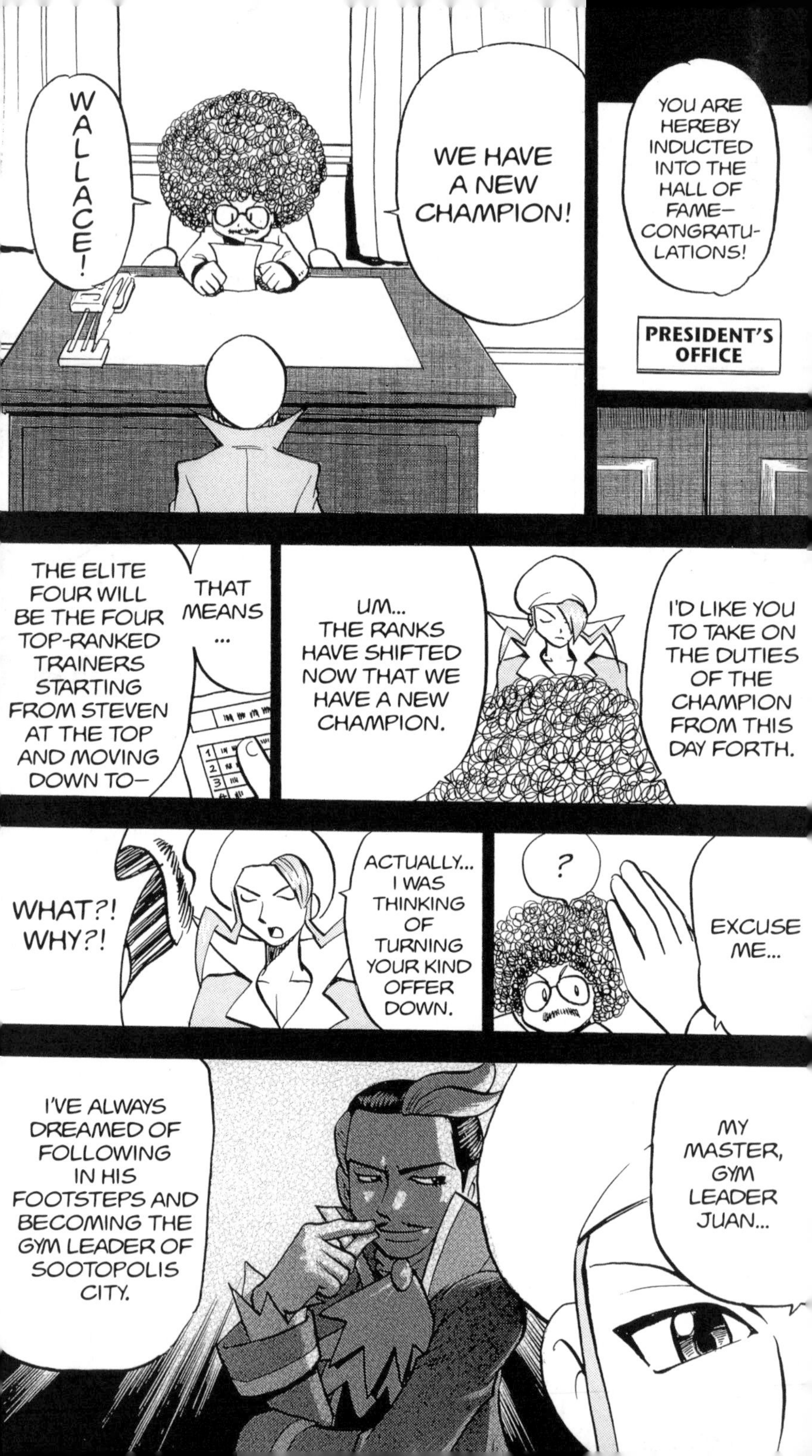
YOU ARE HEREBY INDUCTED INTO THE HALL OF FAME—CONGRATULATIONS!
PRESIDENT'S OFFICE
WE HAVE A NEW CHAMPION!
WALLACE!
I'D LIKE YOU TO TAKE ON THE DUTIES OF THE CHAMPION FROM THIS DAY FORTH.
UM... THE RANKS HAVE SHIFTED NOW THAT WE HAVE A NEW CHAMPION.
THAT MEANS...
THE ELITE FOUR WILL BE THE FOUR TOP-RANKED TRAINERS STARTING FROM STEVEN AT THE TOP AND MOVING DOWN TO—
EXCUSE ME...
?
ACTUALLY... I WAS THINKING OF TURNING YOUR KIND OFFER DOWN.
WHAT?! WHY?!
MY MASTER, GYM LEADER JUAN...
I'VE ALWAYS DREAMED OF FOLLOWING IN HIS FOOTSTEPS AND BECOMING THE GYM LEADER OF SOOTOPOLIS CITY.

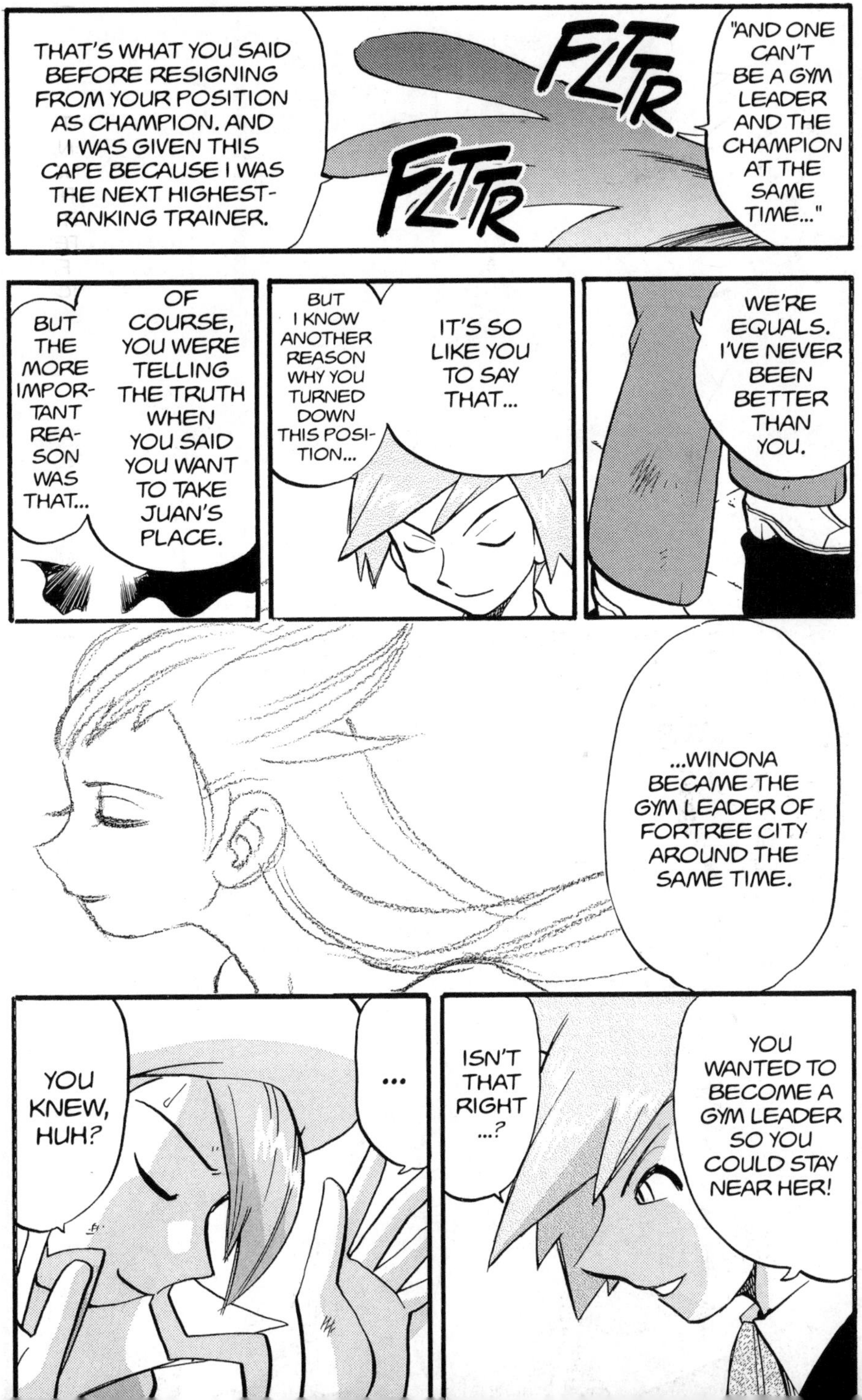
"AND ONE CAN'T BE A GYM LEADER AND THE CHAMPION AT THE SAME TIME..."
FLTTR
FLTTR
THAT'S WHAT YOU SAID BEFORE RESIGNING FROM YOUR POSITION AS CHAMPION. AND I WAS GIVEN THIS CAPE BECAUSE I WAS THE NEXT HIGHEST-RANKING TRAINER.
WE'RE EQUALS. I'VE NEVER BEEN BETTER THAN YOU.
IT'S SO LIKE YOU TO SAY THAT...
BUT I KNOW ANOTHER REASON WHY YOU TURNED DOWN THIS POSITION...
OF COURSE, YOU WERE TELLING THE TRUTH WHEN YOU SAID YOU WANT TO TAKE JUAN'S PLACE.
BUT THE MORE IMPORTANT REASON WAS THAT...
...WINONA BECAME THE GYM LEADER OF FORTREE CITY AROUND THE SAME TIME.
YOU WANTED TO BECOME A GYM LEADER SO YOU COULD STAY NEAR HER!
ISN'T THAT RIGHT ...?
...
YOU KNEW, HUH?

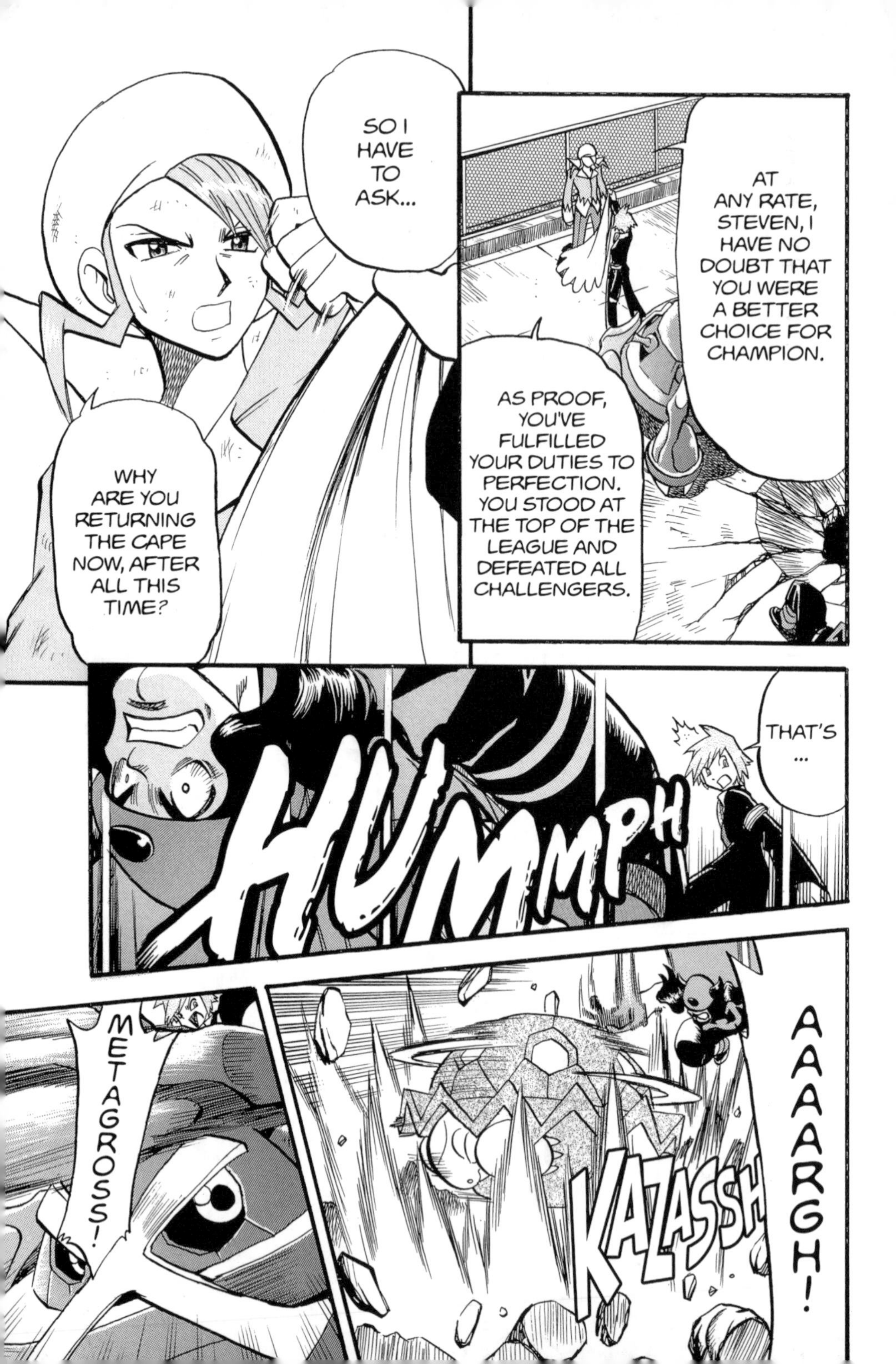
AT ANY RATE, STEVEN, I HAVE NO DOUBT THAT YOU WERE A BETTER CHOICE FOR CHAMPION.
AS PROOF, YOU'VE FULFILLED YOUR DUTIES TO PERFECTION. YOU STOOD AT THE TOP OF THE LEAGUE AND DEFEATED ALL CHALLENGERS.
SO I HAVE TO ASK...
WHY ARE YOU RETURNING THE CAPE NOW, AFTER ALL THIS TIME?
THAT'S ...
HUMMPH
AAAARGH!
KAZASSH
METAGROSS!

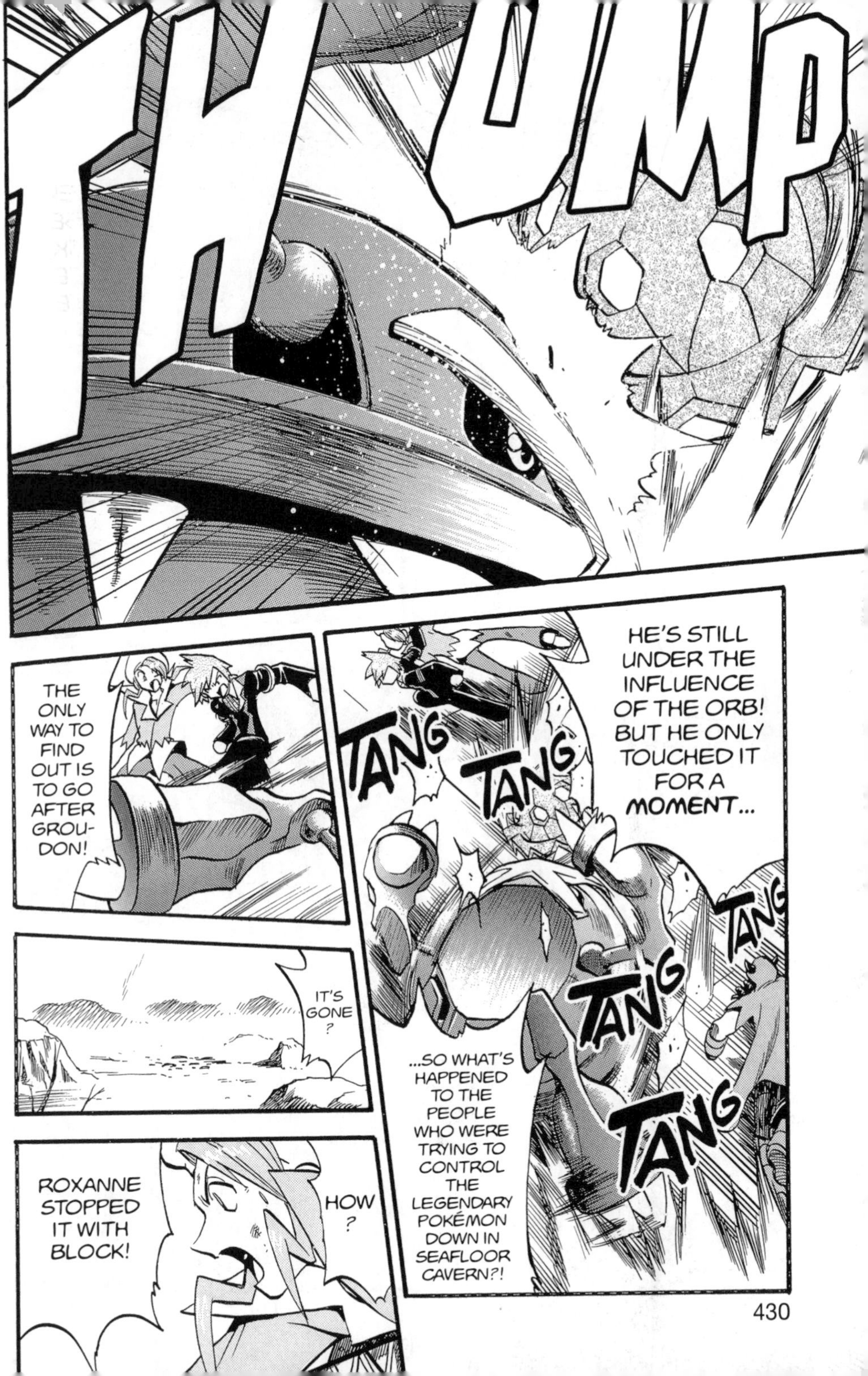
THUMP
HE'S STILL UNDER THE INFLUENCE OF THE ORB! BUT HE ONLY TOUCHED IT FOR A MOMENT...
TANG
TANG
TANG
TANG
TANG
...SO WHAT'S HAPPENED TO THE PEOPLE WHO WERE TRYING TO CONTROL THE LEGENDARY POKÉMON DOWN IN SEAFLOOR CAVERN?!
THE ONLY WAY TO FIND OUT IS TO GO AFTER GROU-DON!
IT'S GONE?
HOW?
ROXANNE STOPPED IT WITH BLOCK!

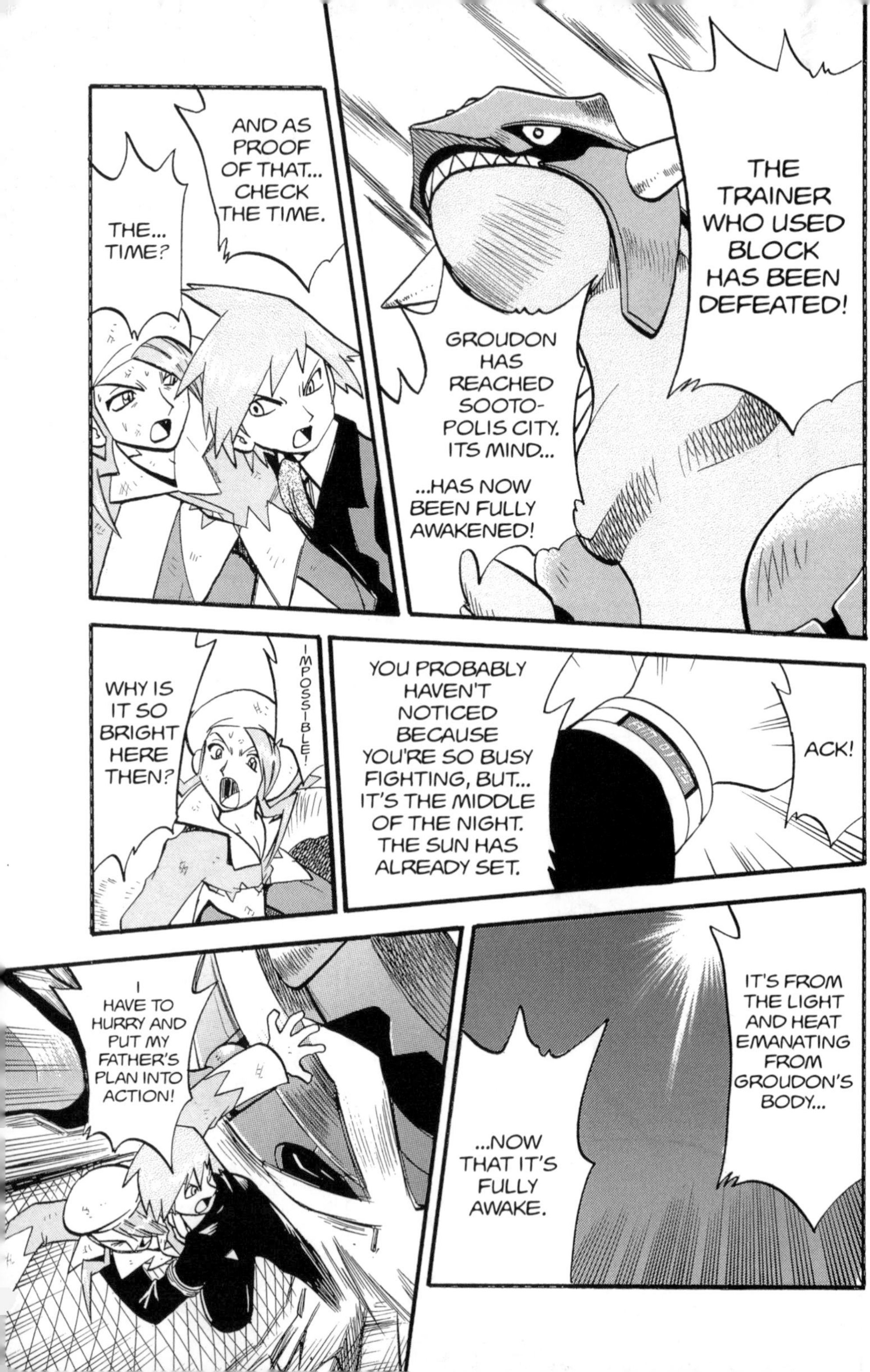
THE TRAINER WHO USED BLOCK HAS BEEN DEFEATED!
GROUDON HAS REACHED SOOTO-POLIS CITY. ITS MIND...
...HAS NOW BEEN FULLY AWAKENED!
AND AS PROOF OF THAT... CHECK THE TIME.
THE... TIME?
ACK!
YOU PROBABLY HAVEN'T NOTICED BECAUSE YOU'RE SO BUSY FIGHTING, BUT... IT'S THE MIDDLE OF THE NIGHT. THE SUN HAS ALREADY SET.
IMPOSSIBLE!
WHY IS IT SO BRIGHT HERE THEN?
IT'S FROM THE LIGHT AND HEAT EMANATING FROM GROUDON'S BODY...
...NOW THAT IT'S FULLY AWAKE.
I HAVE TO HURRY AND PUT MY FATHER'S PLAN INTO ACTION!

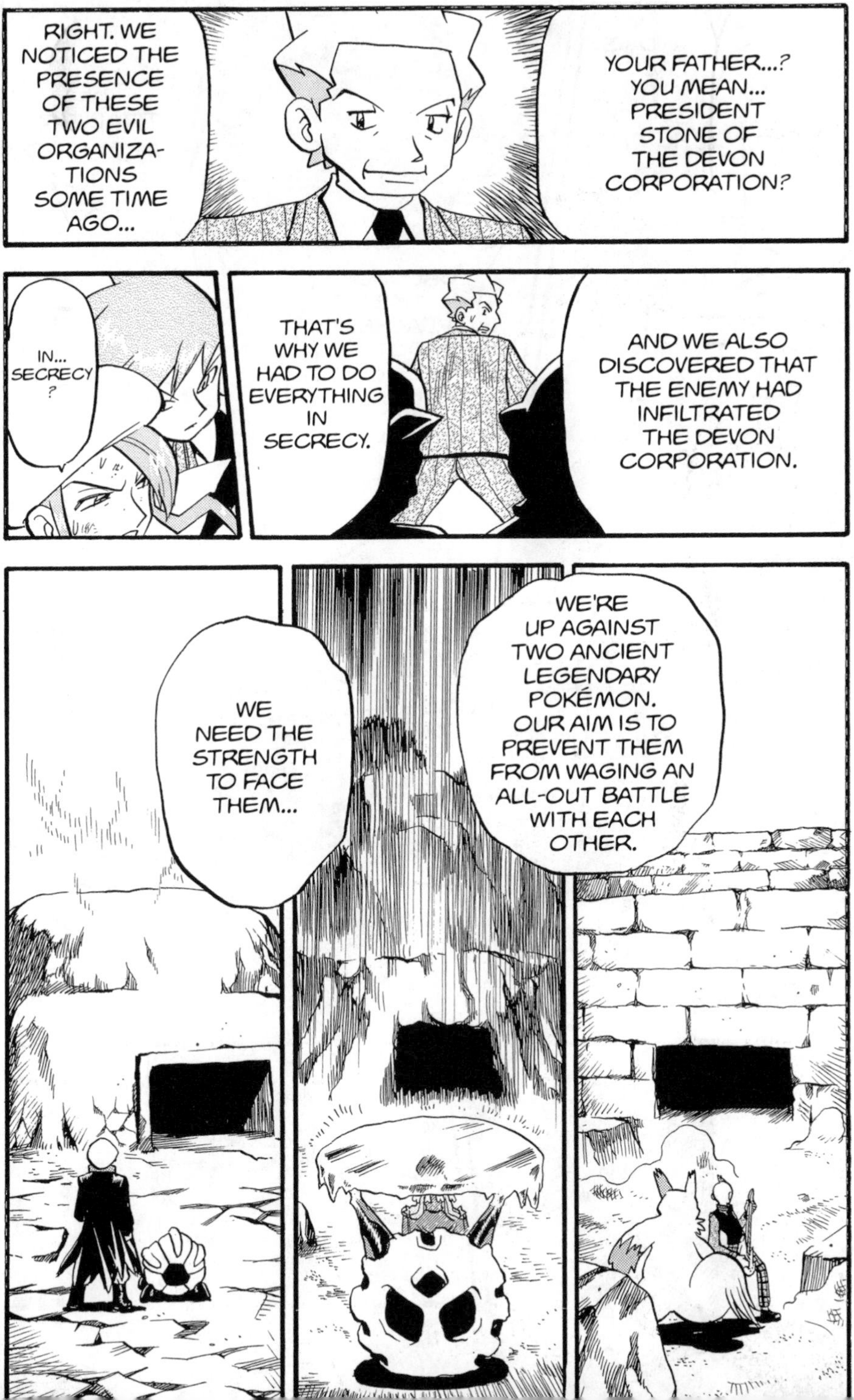
YOUR FATHER...? YOU MEAN... PRESIDENT STONE OF THE DEVON CORPORATION?
RIGHT. WE NOTICED THE PRESENCE OF THESE TWO EVIL ORGANIZA-TIONS SOME TIME AGO...
AND WE ALSO DISCOVERED THAT THE ENEMY HAD INFILTRATED THE DEVON CORPORATION.
THAT'S WHY WE HAD TO DO EVERYTHING IN SECRECY.
IN... SECRECY?
WE'RE UP AGAINST TWO ANCIENT LEGENDARY POKéMON. OUR AIM IS TO PREVENT THEM FROM WAGING AN ALL-OUT BATTLE WITH EACH OTHER.
WE NEED THE STRENGTH TO FACE THEM...

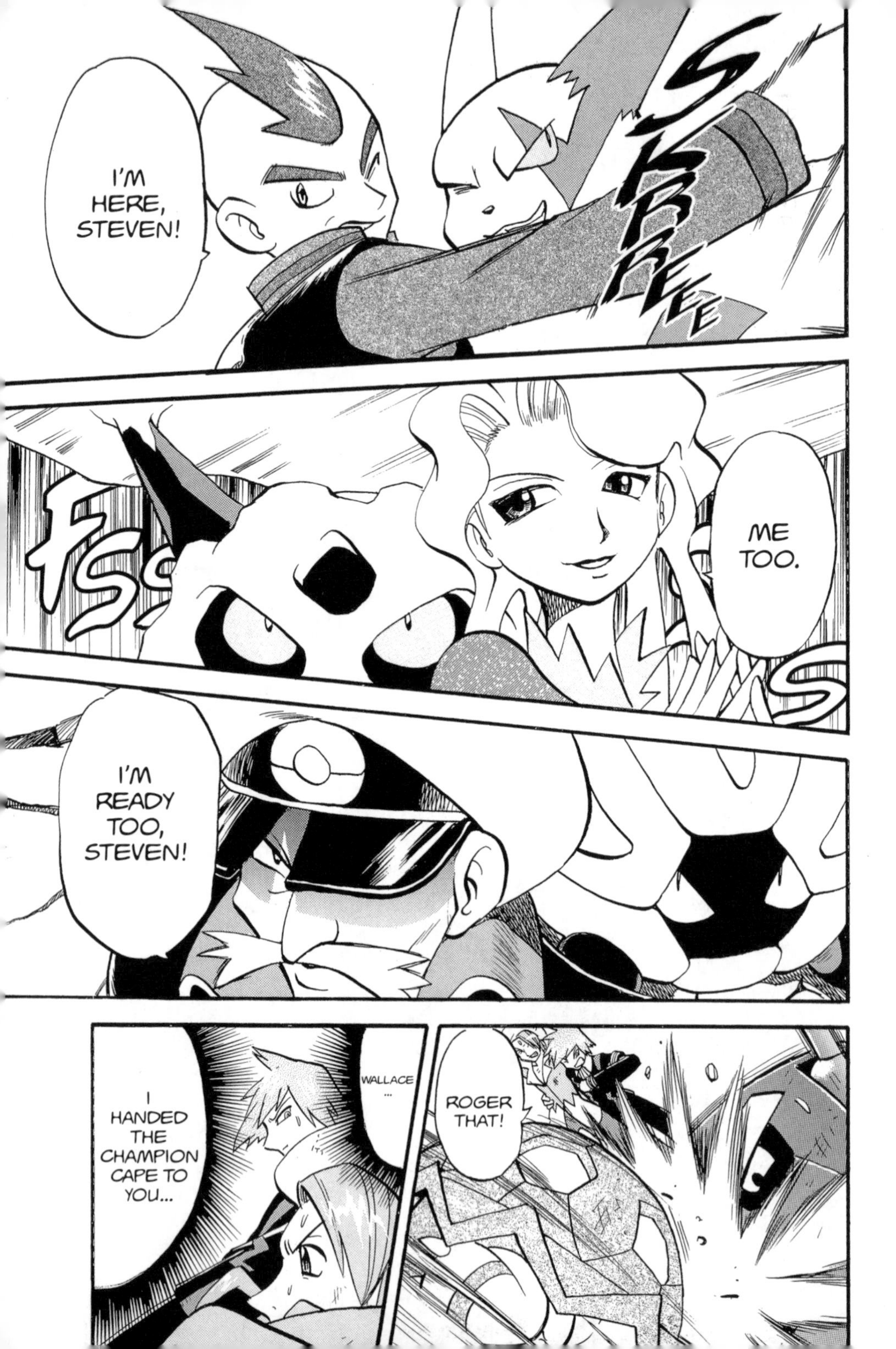
I'M HERE, STEVEN!
ME TOO.
I'M READY TOO, STEVEN!
ROGER THAT!
WALLACE...
I HANDED THE CHAMPION CAPE TO YOU...

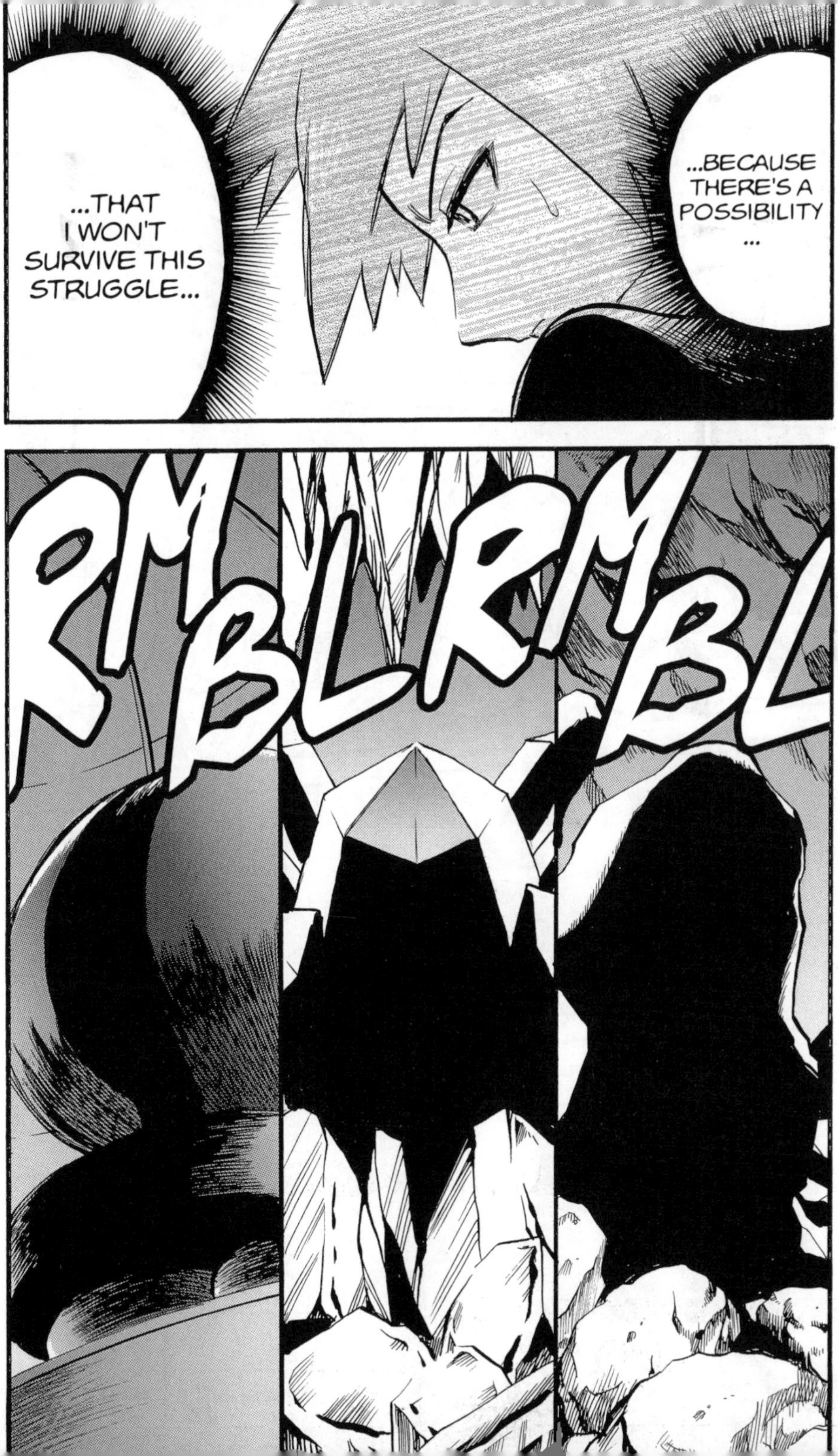
...BECAUSE THERE'S A POSSIBILITY ...
...THAT I WON'T SURVIVE THIS STRUGGLE...
RM BLRM BL

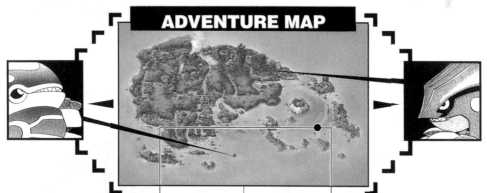

ADVENTURE MAP

SAPPHIRE

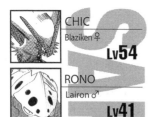

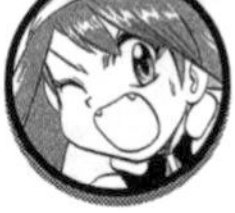

- CHIC — Blaziken ♀ — Lv54
- RONO — Lairon ♂ — Lv41
- RELLY — Relicanth ♂ — Lv55
- PHADO — Donphan ♂ — Lv56
- TROPPY — Tropius ♂ — Lv53
- LORRY — Wailord ♂ — Lv53

RUBY

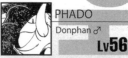

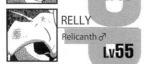

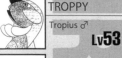

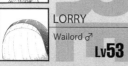

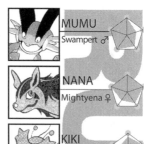

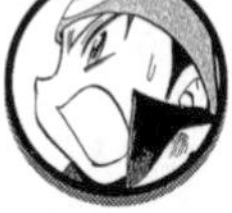

- MUMU — Swampert ♂
- NANA — Mightyena ♀
- KIKI — Delcatty ♀
- FOFO — Castform ♀

Route 126
▼
Seafloor Cavern
▼
Sootopolis City

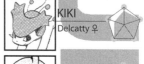

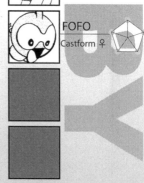

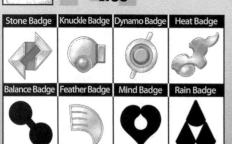

Stone Badge	Knuckle Badge	Dynamo Badge	Heat Badge
Balance Badge	**Feather Badge**	**Mind Badge**	**Rain Badge**

	Coolness	Beauty	Cuteness	Cleverness	Toughness
Normal					
Super					
Hyper					
Master					

● Adventure 252 ●

The Beginning of the End with Kyogre and Groudon, Part 14

Pokémon™ Adventures Ruby & Sapphire

The Fourth Chapter

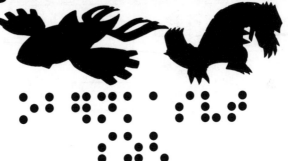

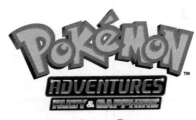

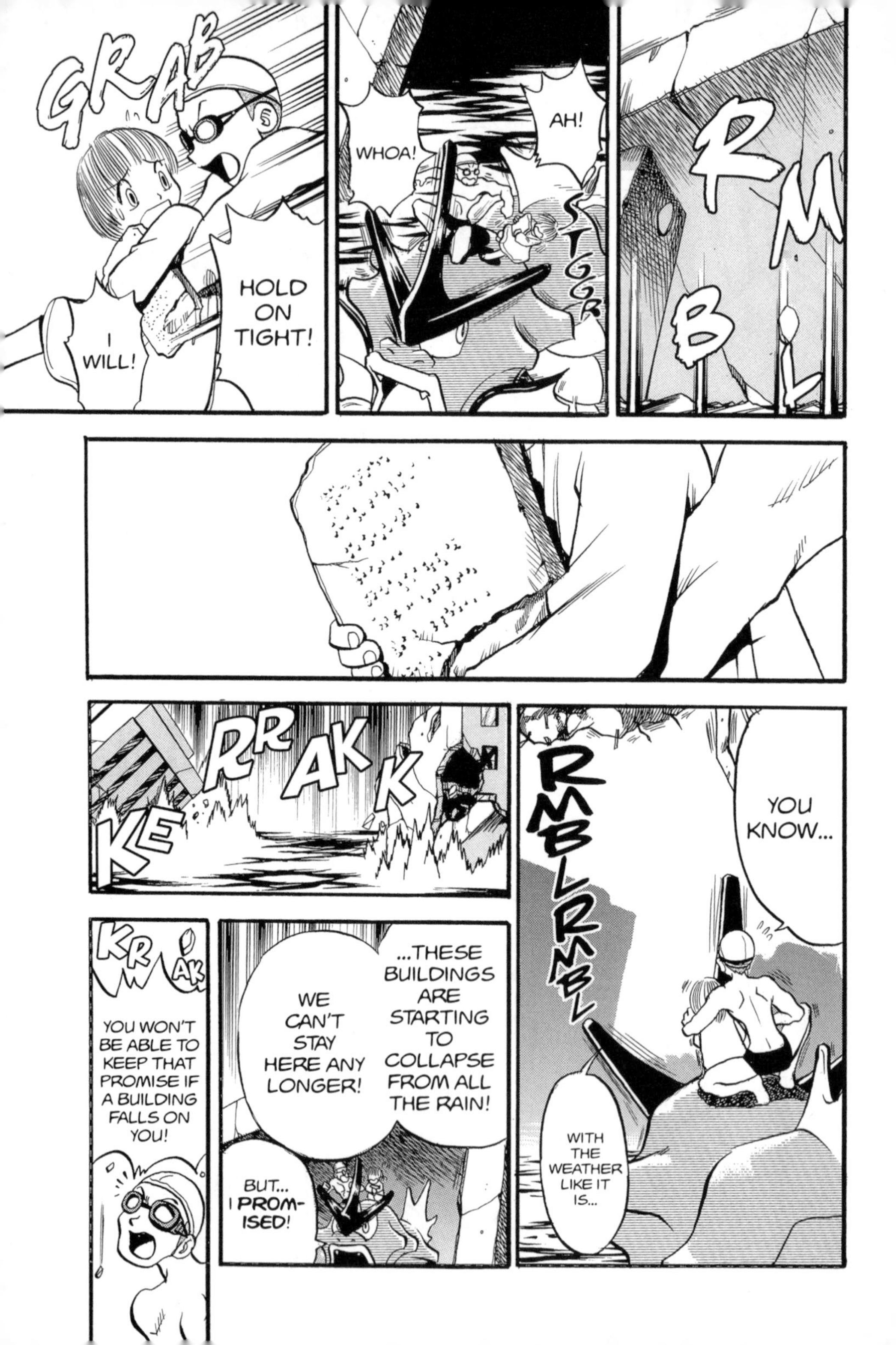
RMBL
AH!
WHOA!
STGGR
GRAB
HOLD ON TIGHT!
I WILL!
YOU KNOW...
RMBLRMBL
WITH THE WEATHER LIKE IT IS...
KERRAKK
...THESE BUILDINGS ARE STARTING TO COLLAPSE FROM ALL THE RAIN!
WE CAN'T STAY HERE ANY LONGER!
BUT... I PROMISED!
KRAK
YOU WON'T BE ABLE TO KEEP THAT PROMISE IF A BUILDING FALLS ON YOU!

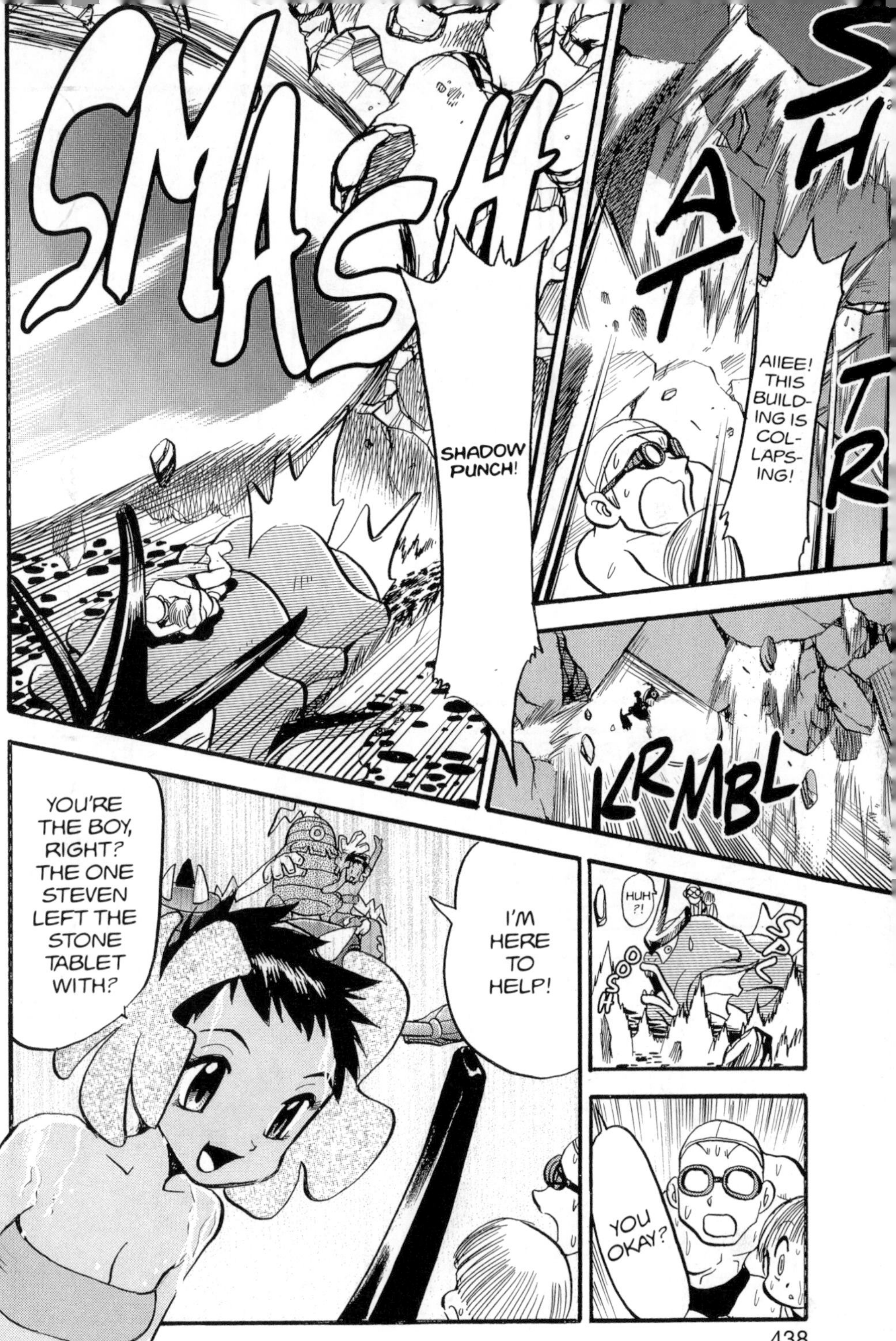
SHATTR
AIIEE! THIS BUILD-ING IS COL-LAPS-ING!
KRMBL
SMASH
SHADOW PUNCH!
HUH ?!
SPL
YOU OKAY?
I'M HERE TO HELP!
YOU'RE THE BOY, RIGHT? THE ONE STEVEN LEFT THE STONE TABLET WITH?

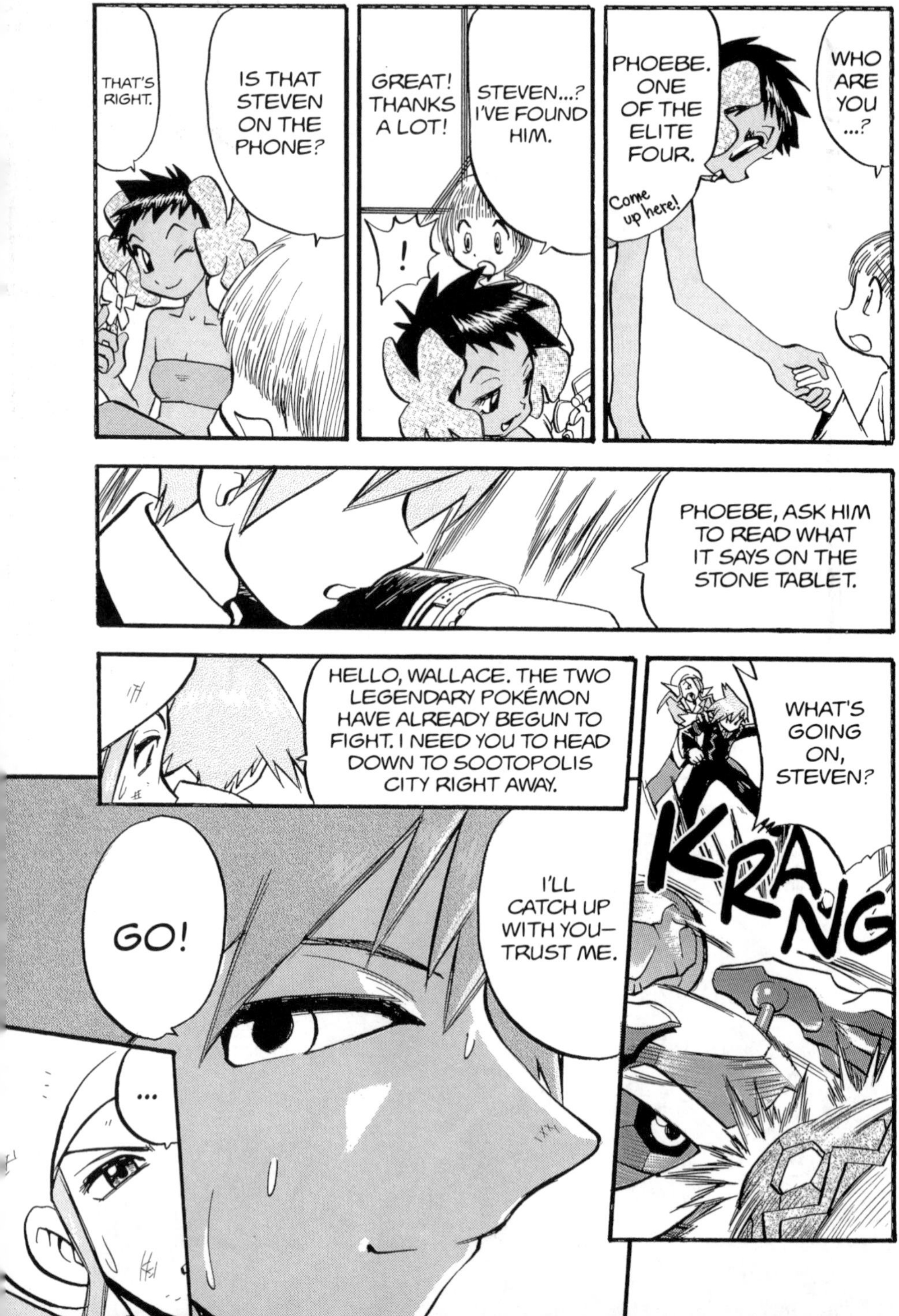
WHO ARE YOU ...?
PHOEBE. ONE OF THE ELITE FOUR.
Come up here!
STEVEN...? I'VE FOUND HIM.
GREAT! THANKS A LOT!
!
IS THAT STEVEN ON THE PHONE?
THAT'S RIGHT.
PHOEBE, ASK HIM TO READ WHAT IT SAYS ON THE STONE TABLET.
WHAT'S GOING ON, STEVEN?
KRANG
HELLO, WALLACE. THE TWO LEGENDARY POKéMON HAVE ALREADY BEGUN TO FIGHT. I NEED YOU TO HEAD DOWN TO SOOTOPOLIS CITY RIGHT AWAY.
I'LL CATCH UP WITH YOU—TRUST ME.
GO!
...

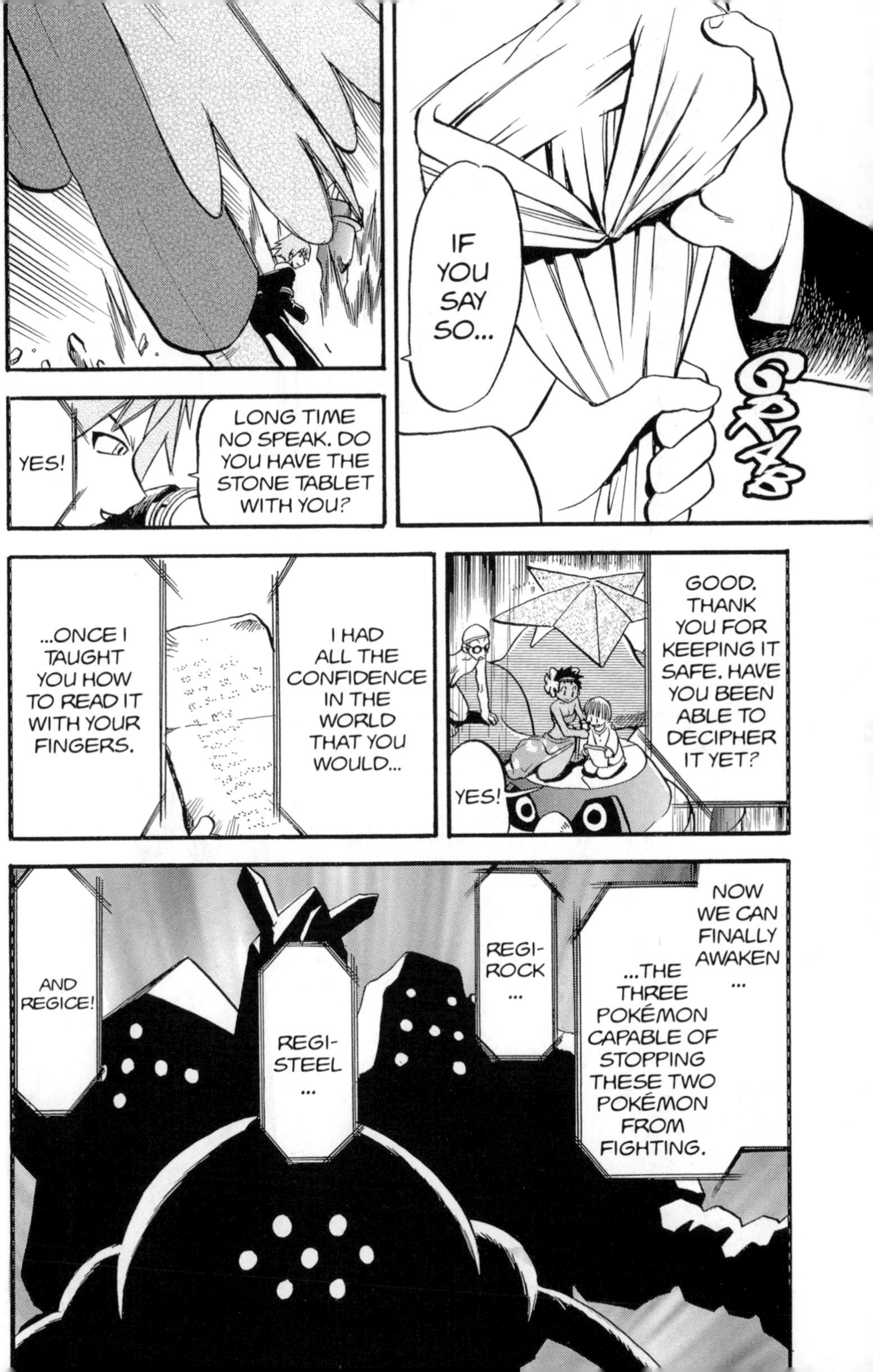
IF YOU SAY SO...
GRAB
LONG TIME NO SPEAK. DO YOU HAVE THE STONE TABLET WITH YOU?
YES!
GOOD. THANK YOU FOR KEEPING IT SAFE. HAVE YOU BEEN ABLE TO DECIPHER IT YET?
YES!
I HAD ALL THE CONFIDENCE IN THE WORLD THAT YOU WOULD...
...ONCE I TAUGHT YOU HOW TO READ IT WITH YOUR FINGERS.
NOW WE CAN FINALLY AWAKEN...
...THE THREE POKÉMON CAPABLE OF STOPPING THESE TWO POKÉMON FROM FIGHTING.
REGI-ROCK...
REGI-STEEL...
AND REGICE!

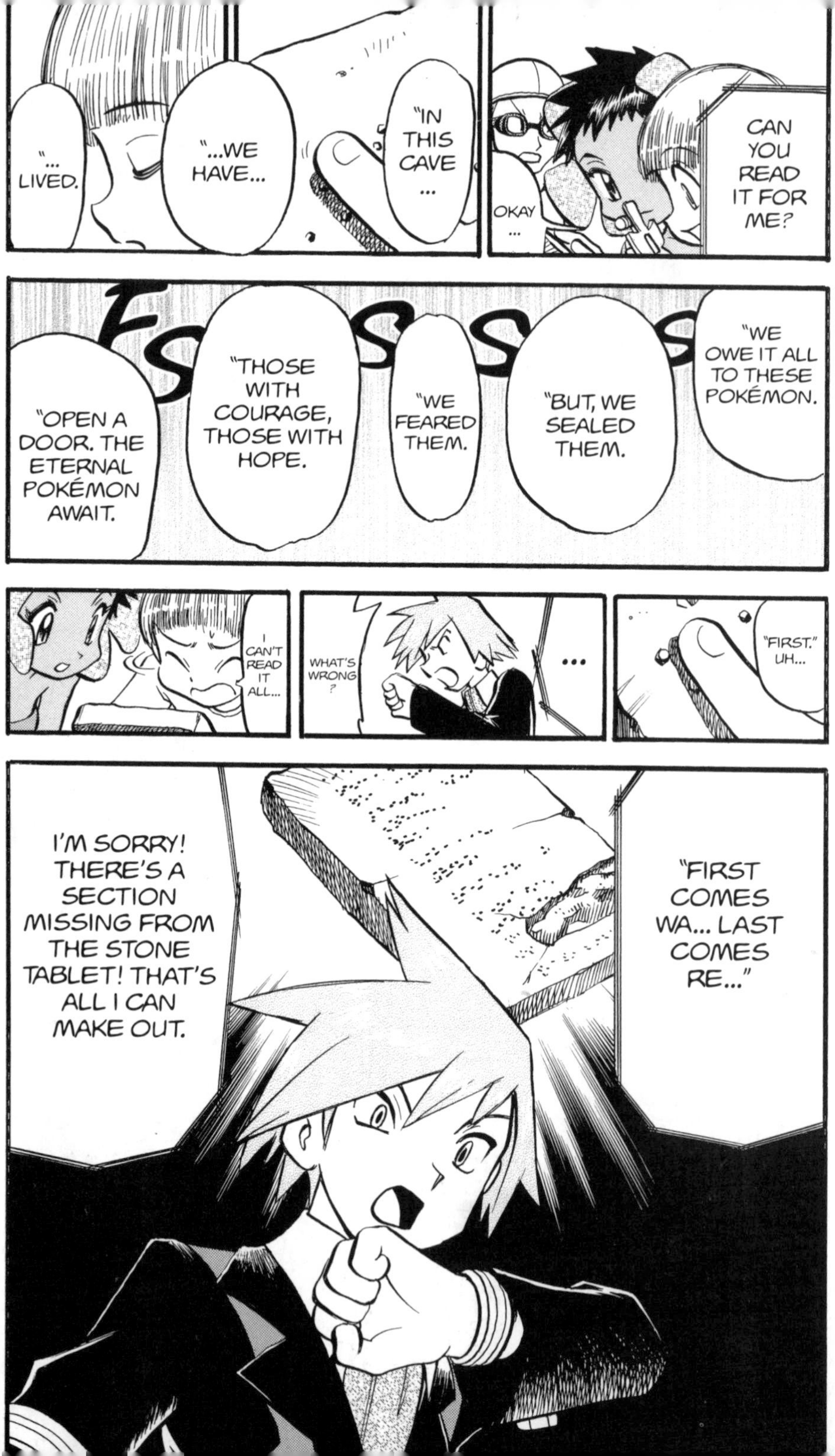
CAN YOU READ IT FOR ME?
OKAY ...
"IN THIS CAVE ...
"...WE HAVE...
"... LIVED.
FSSSS
"WE OWE IT ALL TO THESE POKÉMON.
"BUT, WE SEALED THEM.
"WE FEARED THEM.
"THOSE WITH COURAGE, THOSE WITH HOPE.
"OPEN A DOOR. THE ETERNAL POKÉMON AWAIT.
"FIRST." UH...
...
WHAT'S WRONG?
I CAN'T READ IT ALL...
"FIRST COMES WA... LAST COMES RE..."
I'M SORRY! THERE'S A SECTION MISSING FROM THE STONE TABLET! THAT'S ALL I CAN MAKE OUT.

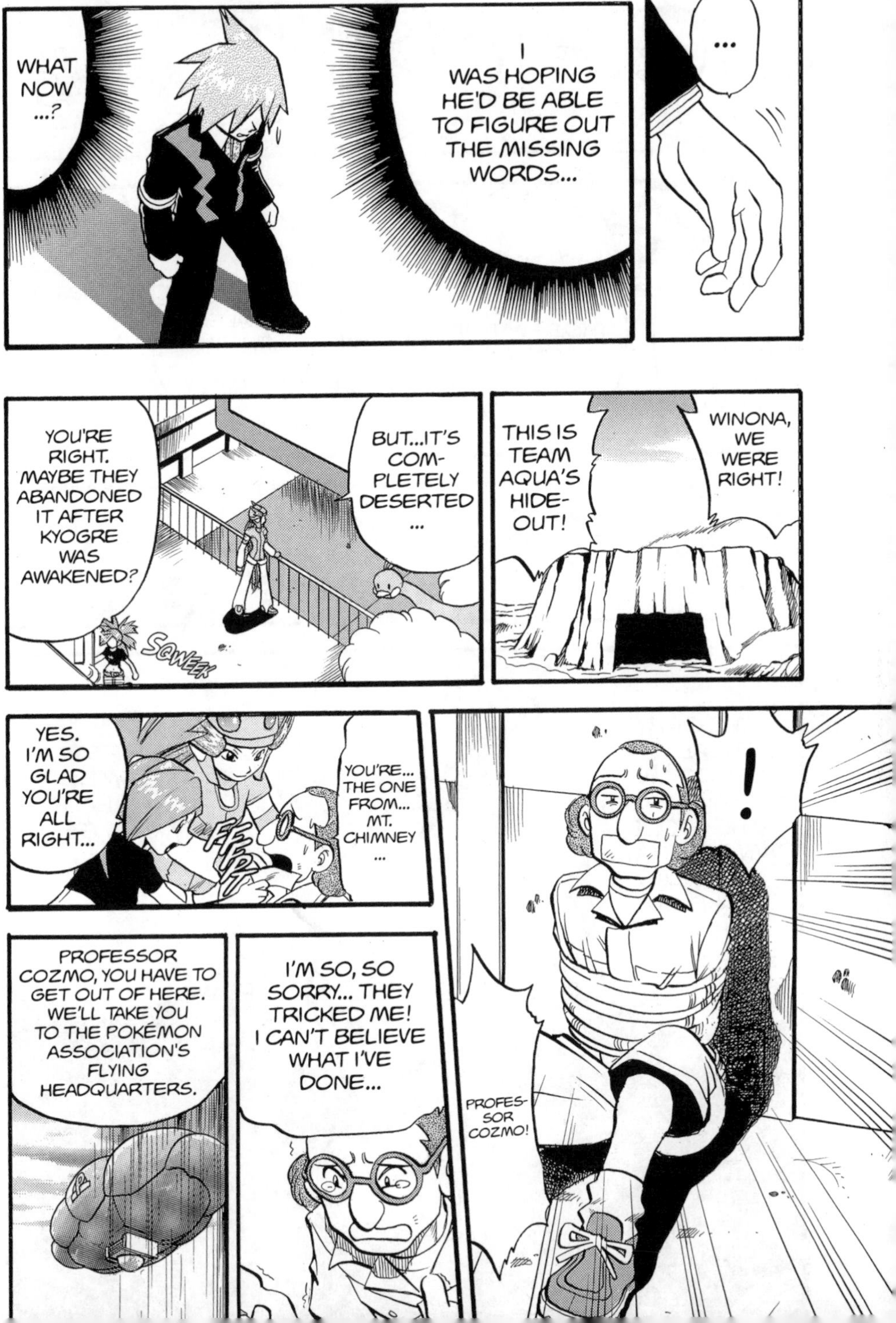
...
I WAS HOPING HE'D BE ABLE TO FIGURE OUT THE MISSING WORDS...
WHAT NOW ...?
WINONA, WE WERE RIGHT!
THIS IS TEAM AQUA'S HIDE-OUT!
BUT...IT'S COM-PLETELY DESERTED ...
YOU'RE RIGHT. MAYBE THEY ABANDONED IT AFTER KYOGRE WAS AWAKENED?
SQWEEK
!
PROFES-SOR COZMO!
YOU'RE... THE ONE FROM... MT. CHIMNEY ...
YES. I'M SO GLAD YOU'RE ALL RIGHT...
I'M SO, SO SORRY... THEY TRICKED ME! I CAN'T BELIEVE WHAT I'VE DONE...
PROFESSOR COZMO, YOU HAVE TO GET OUT OF HERE. WE'LL TAKE YOU TO THE POKÉMON ASSOCIATION'S FLYING HEADQUARTERS.

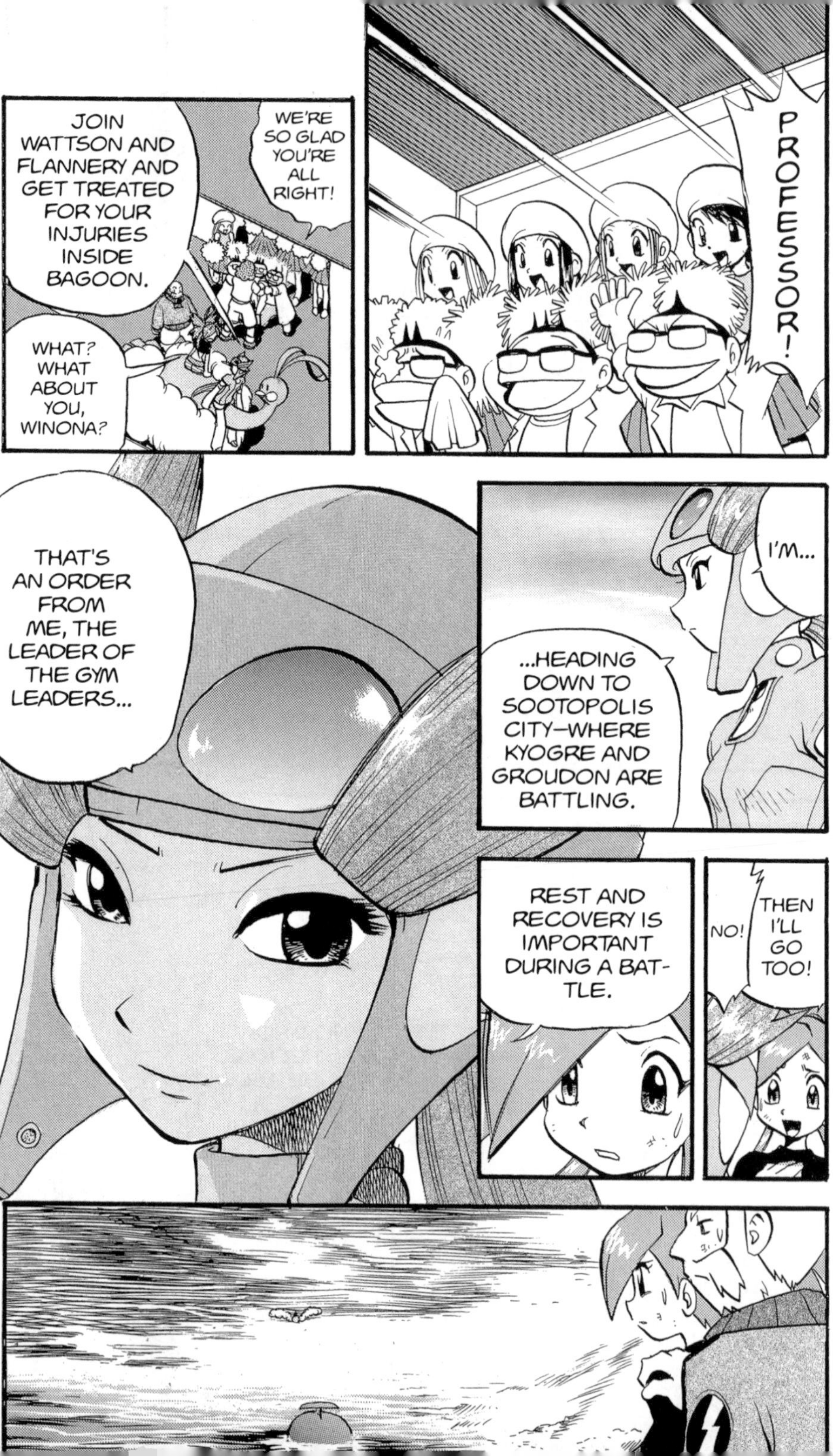
PROFESSOR!
WE'RE SO GLAD YOU'RE ALL RIGHT!
JOIN WATTSON AND FLANNERY AND GET TREATED FOR YOUR INJURIES INSIDE BAGOON.
WHAT? WHAT ABOUT YOU, WINONA?
I'M...
...HEADING DOWN TO SOOTOPOLIS CITY—WHERE KYOGRE AND GROUDON ARE BATTLING.
THEN I'LL GO TOO!
NO!
REST AND RECOVERY IS IMPORTANT DURING A BAT-TLE.
THAT'S AN ORDER FROM ME, THE LEADER OF THE GYM LEADERS...

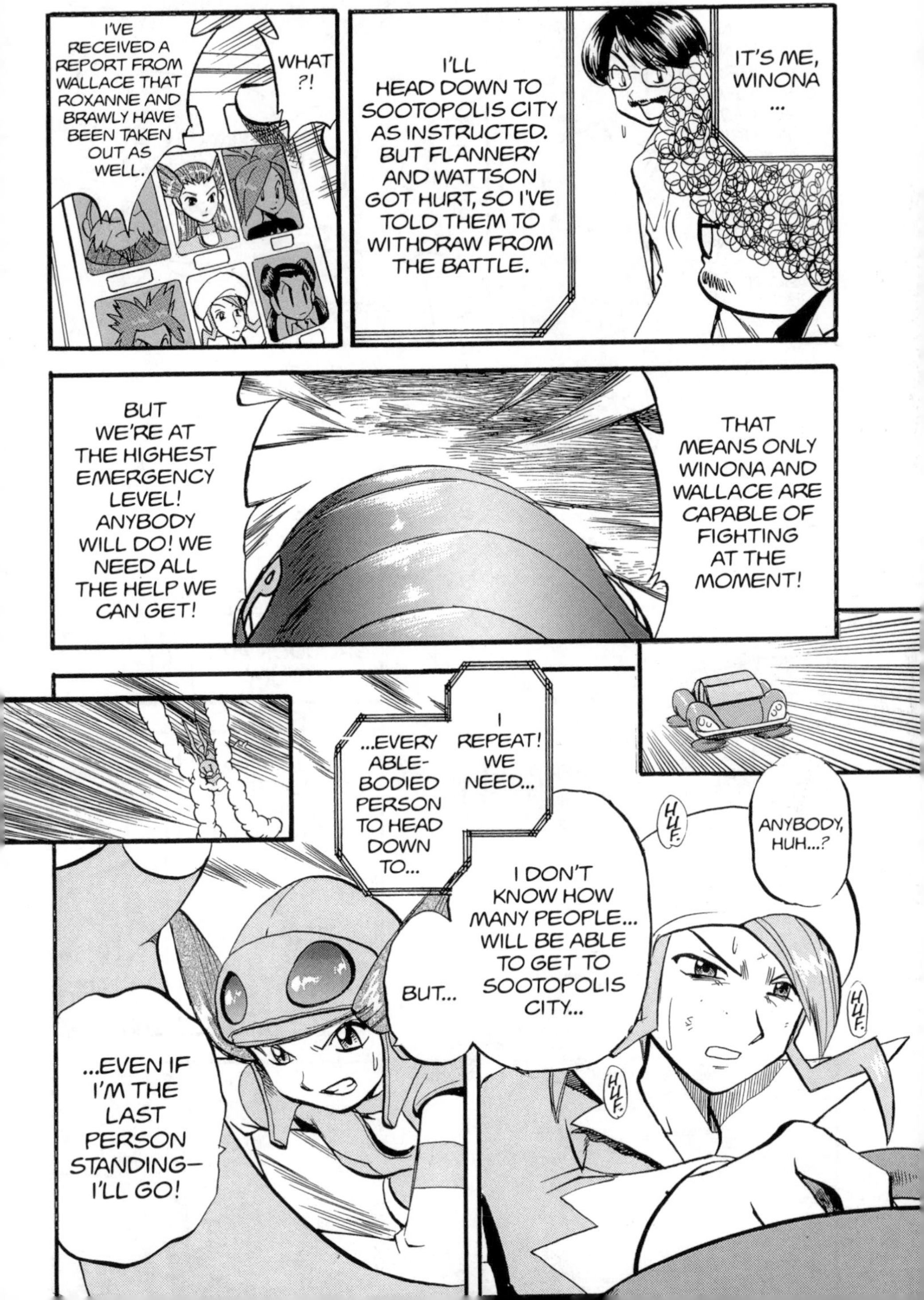
IT'S ME, WINONA ...
I'LL HEAD DOWN TO SOOTOPOLIS CITY AS INSTRUCTED. BUT FLANNERY AND WATTSON GOT HURT, SO I'VE TOLD THEM TO WITHDRAW FROM THE BATTLE.
WHAT ?!
I'VE RECEIVED A REPORT FROM WALLACE THAT ROXANNE AND BRAWLY HAVE BEEN TAKEN OUT AS WELL.
THAT MEANS ONLY WINONA AND WALLACE ARE CAPABLE OF FIGHTING AT THE MOMENT!
BUT WE'RE AT THE HIGHEST EMERGENCY LEVEL! ANYBODY WILL DO! WE NEED ALL THE HELP WE CAN GET!
I REPEAT! WE NEED...
...EVERY ABLE-BODIED PERSON TO HEAD DOWN TO...
ANYBODY, HUH...?
HUFF.
I DON'T KNOW HOW MANY PEOPLE... WILL BE ABLE TO GET TO SOOTOPOLIS CITY...
HUFF.
HUFF.
BUT...
...EVEN IF I'M THE LAST PERSON STANDING— I'LL GO!

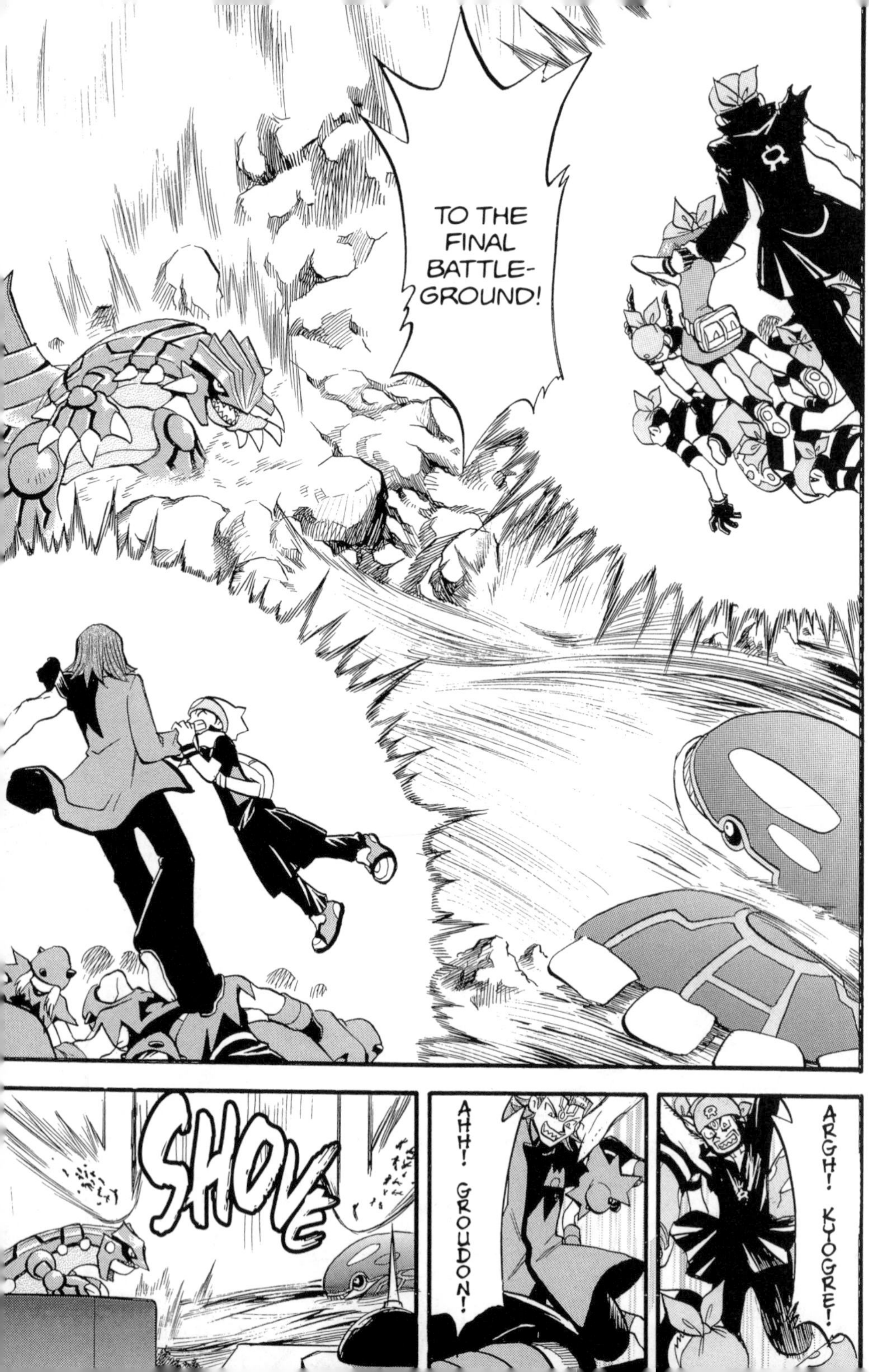
TO THE FINAL BATTLE-GROUND!
ARGH! KYOGRE!
AHH! GROUDON!
SHOVE

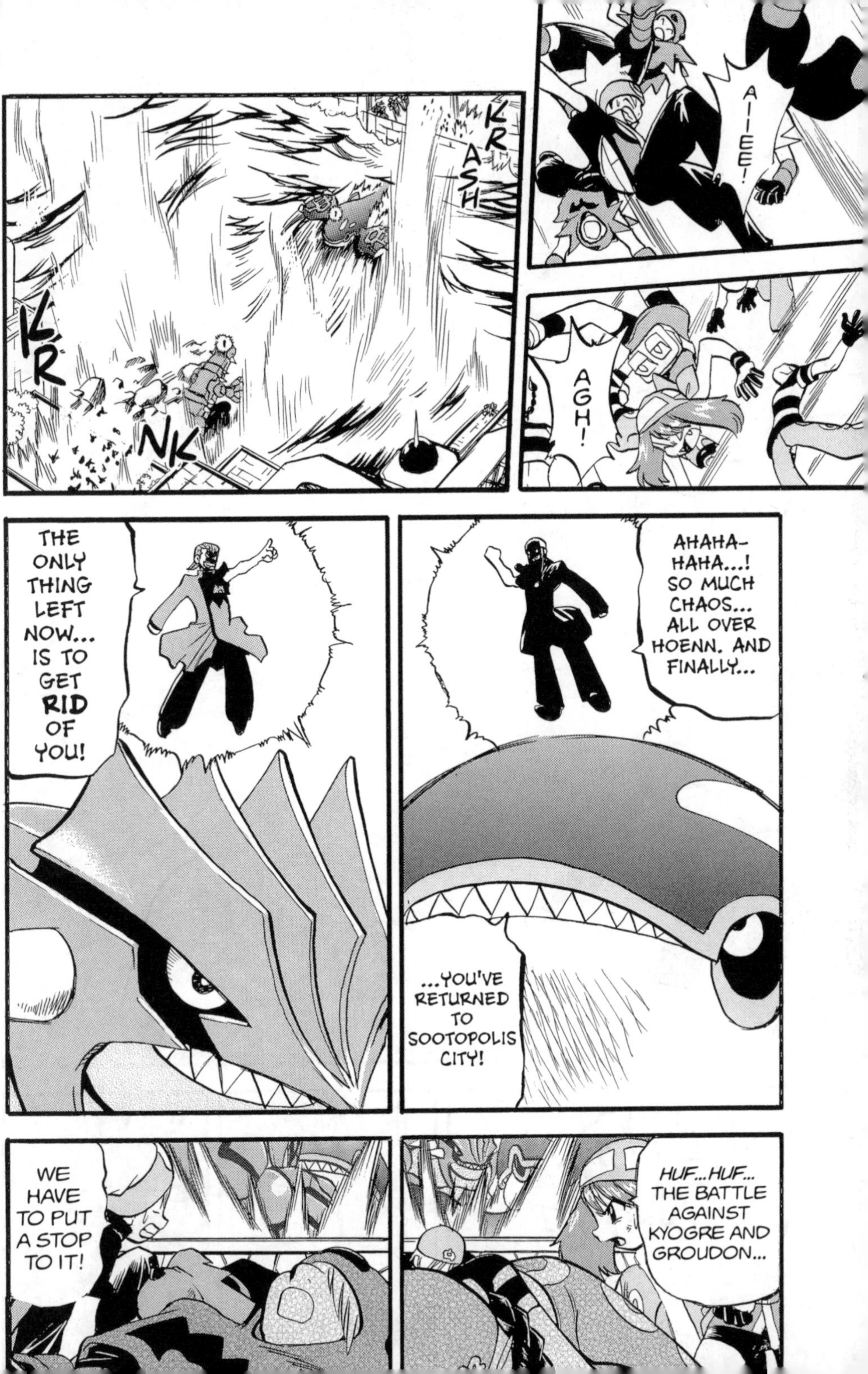
AIEEE!
AGH!
KRASH
KRNK
AHAHA-HAHA...! SO MUCH CHAOS... ALL OVER HOENN. AND FINALLY...
...YOU'VE RETURNED TO SOOTOPOLIS CITY!
THE ONLY THING LEFT NOW... IS TO GET RID OF YOU!
HUF... HUF... THE BATTLE AGAINST KYOGRE AND GROUDON...
WE HAVE TO PUT A STOP TO IT!

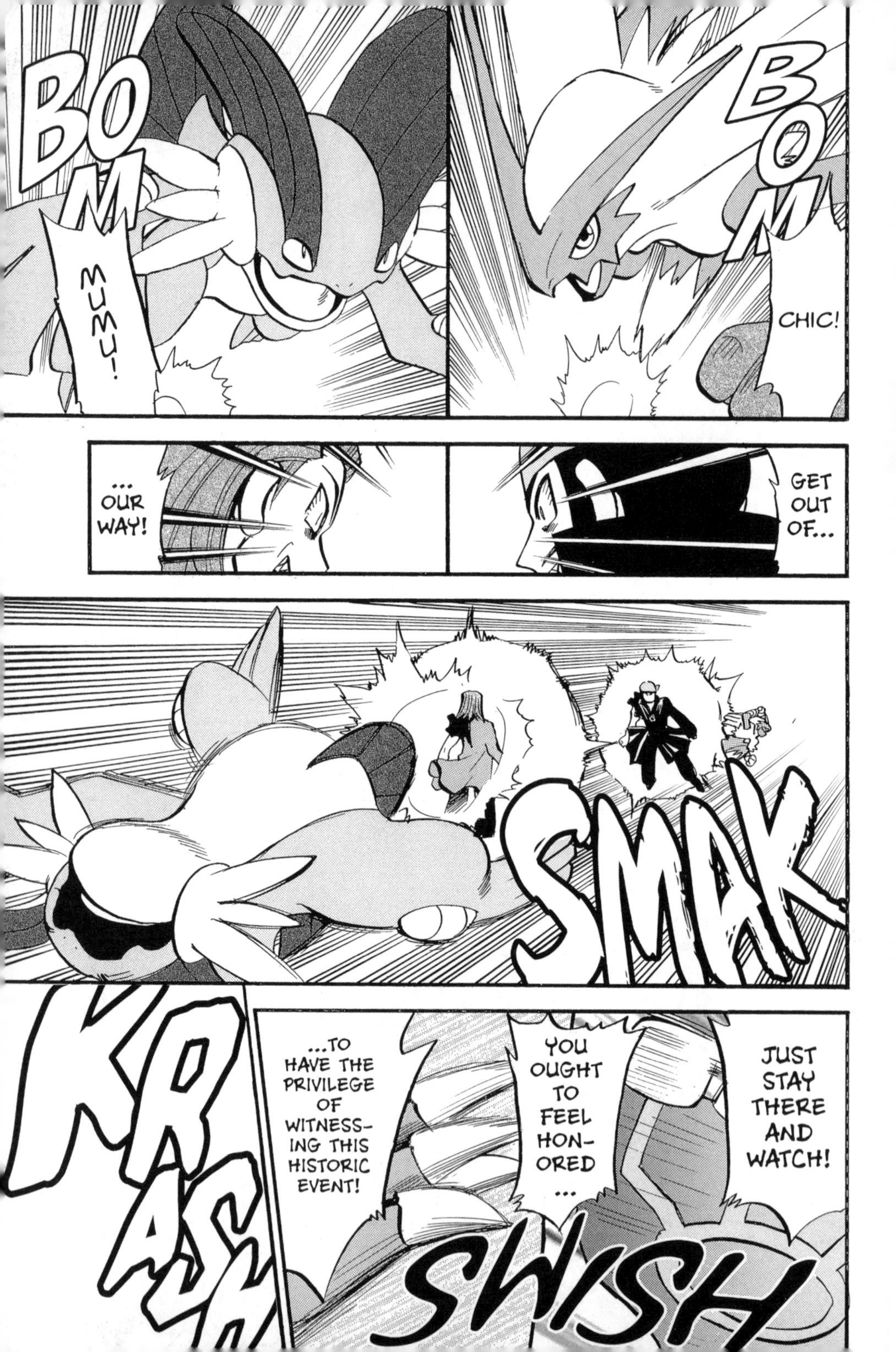
BOM
CHIC!
BOM
MUMU!
GET OUT OF...
...OUR WAY!
SMAK
JUST STAY THERE AND WATCH!
YOU OUGHT TO FEEL HON-ORED...
...TO HAVE THE PRIVILEGE OF WITNESS-ING THIS HISTORIC EVENT!
SWISH
KRASH

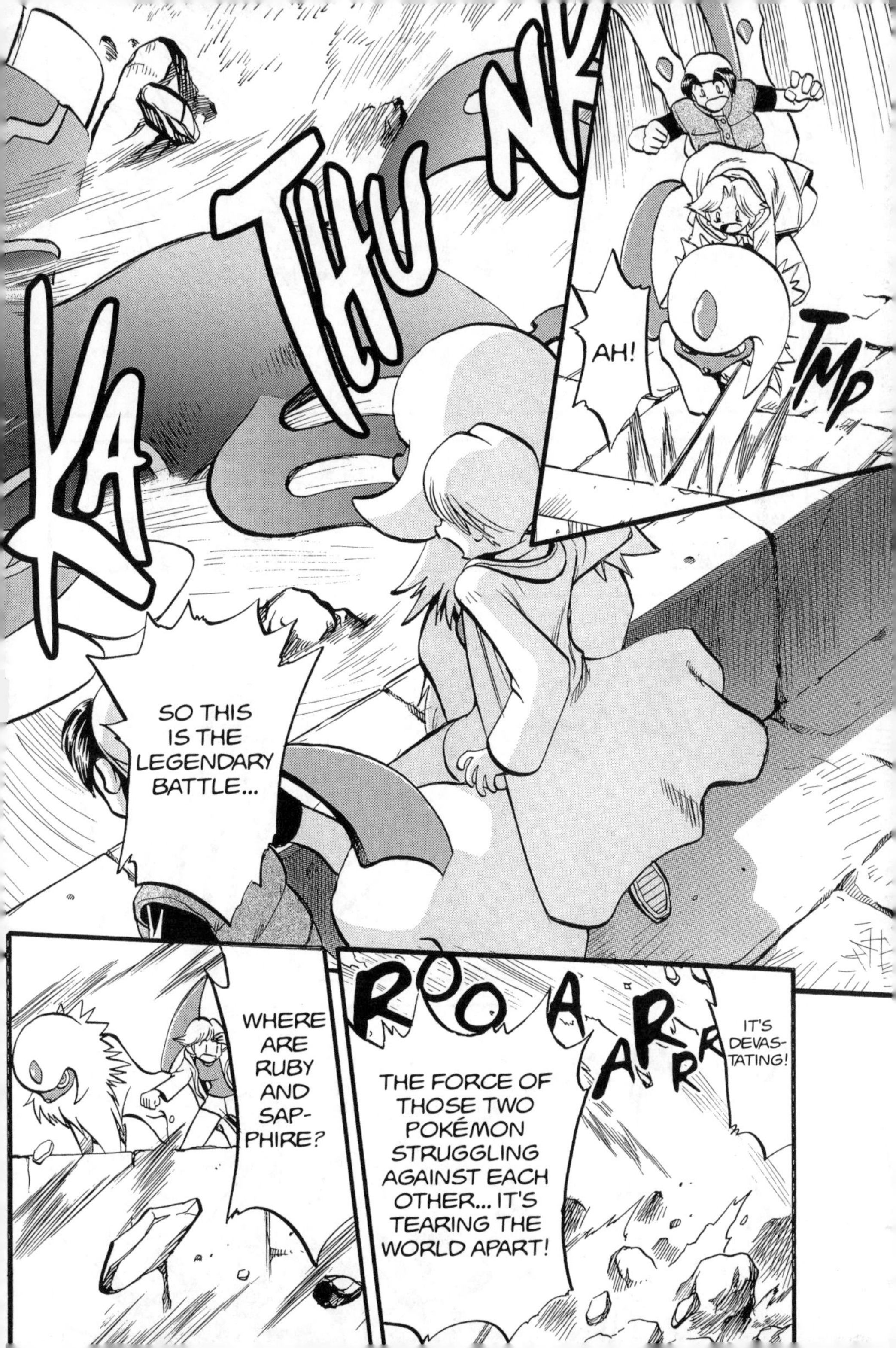
AH!
TMP
KA THUNK
SO THIS IS THE LEGENDARY BATTLE...
IT'S DEVAS-TATING!
ROOAARRR
THE FORCE OF THOSE TWO POKÉMON STRUGGLING AGAINST EACH OTHER... IT'S TEARING THE WORLD APART!
WHERE ARE RUBY AND SAP-PHIRE?

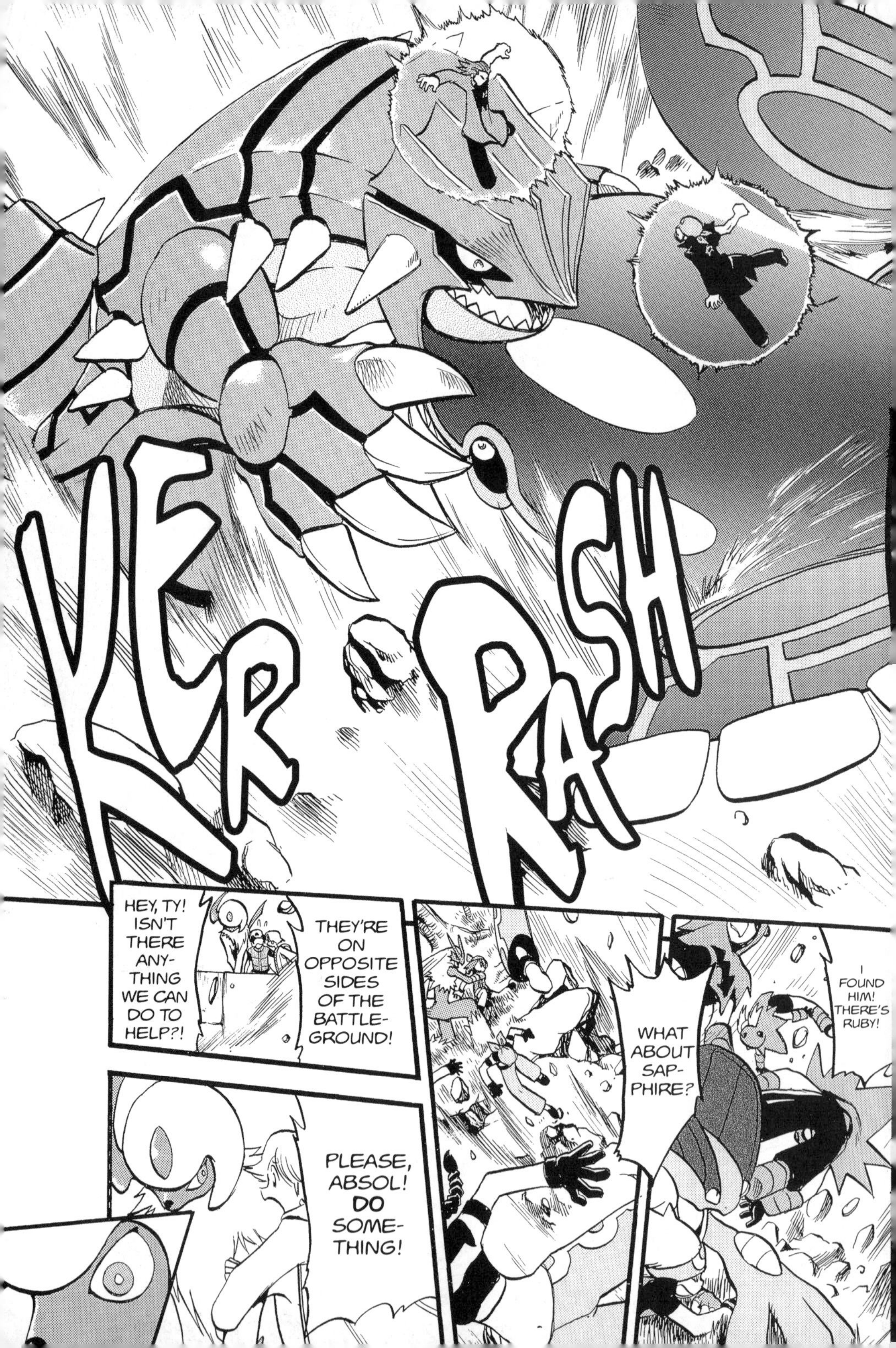
KERRASH--
I FOUND HIM! THERE'S RUBY!
WHAT ABOUT SAPPHIRE?
HEY, TY! ISN'T THERE ANYTHING WE CAN DO TO HELP?!
THEY'RE ON OPPOSITE SIDES OF THE BATTLEGROUND!
PLEASE, ABSOL! **DO** SOMETHING!

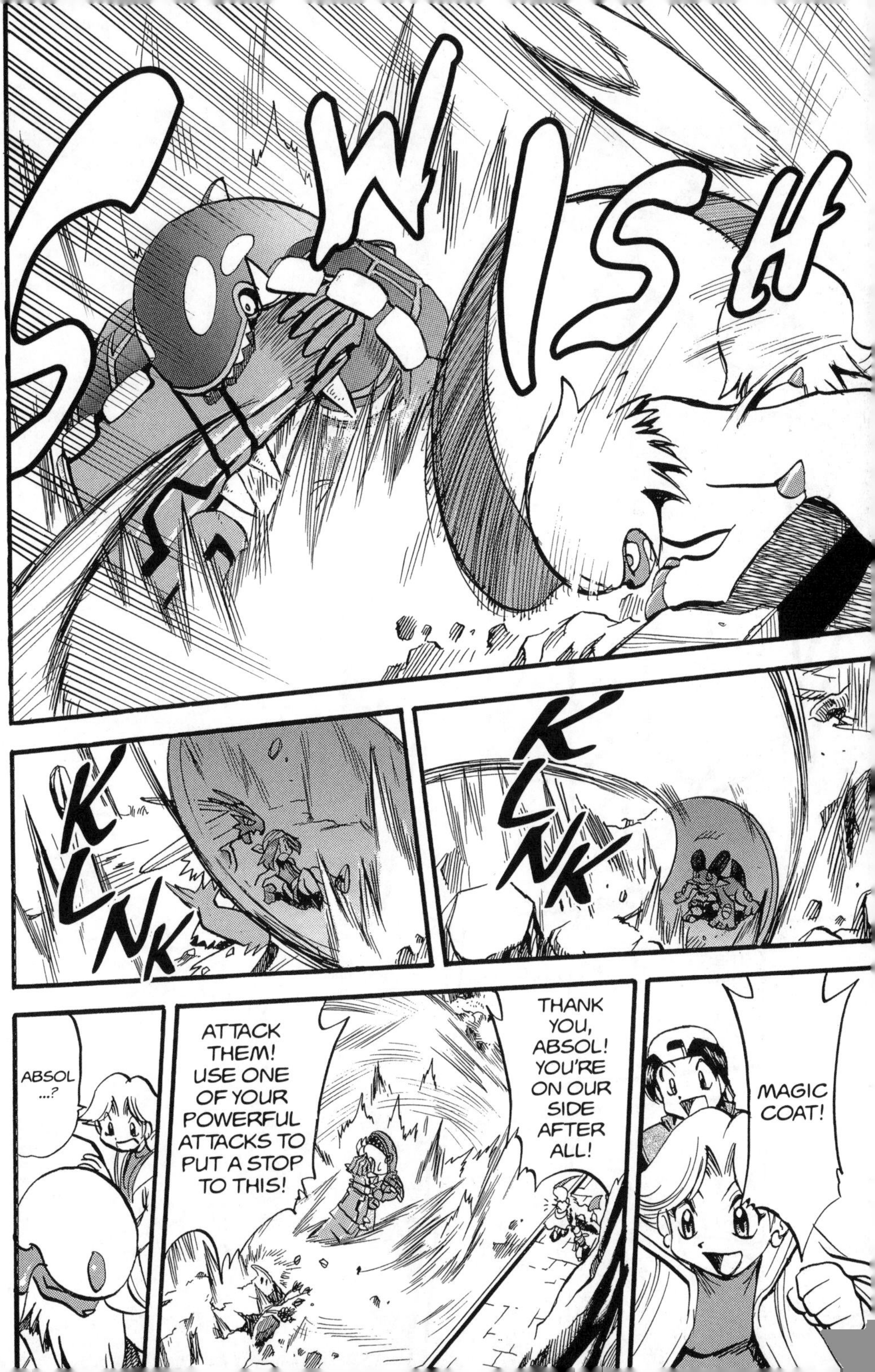
SWISH
KLNK
KLNK
MAGIC COAT!
THANK YOU, ABSOL! YOU'RE ON OUR SIDE AFTER ALL!
ATTACK THEM! USE ONE OF YOUR POWERFUL ATTACKS TO PUT A STOP TO THIS!
ABSOL ...?

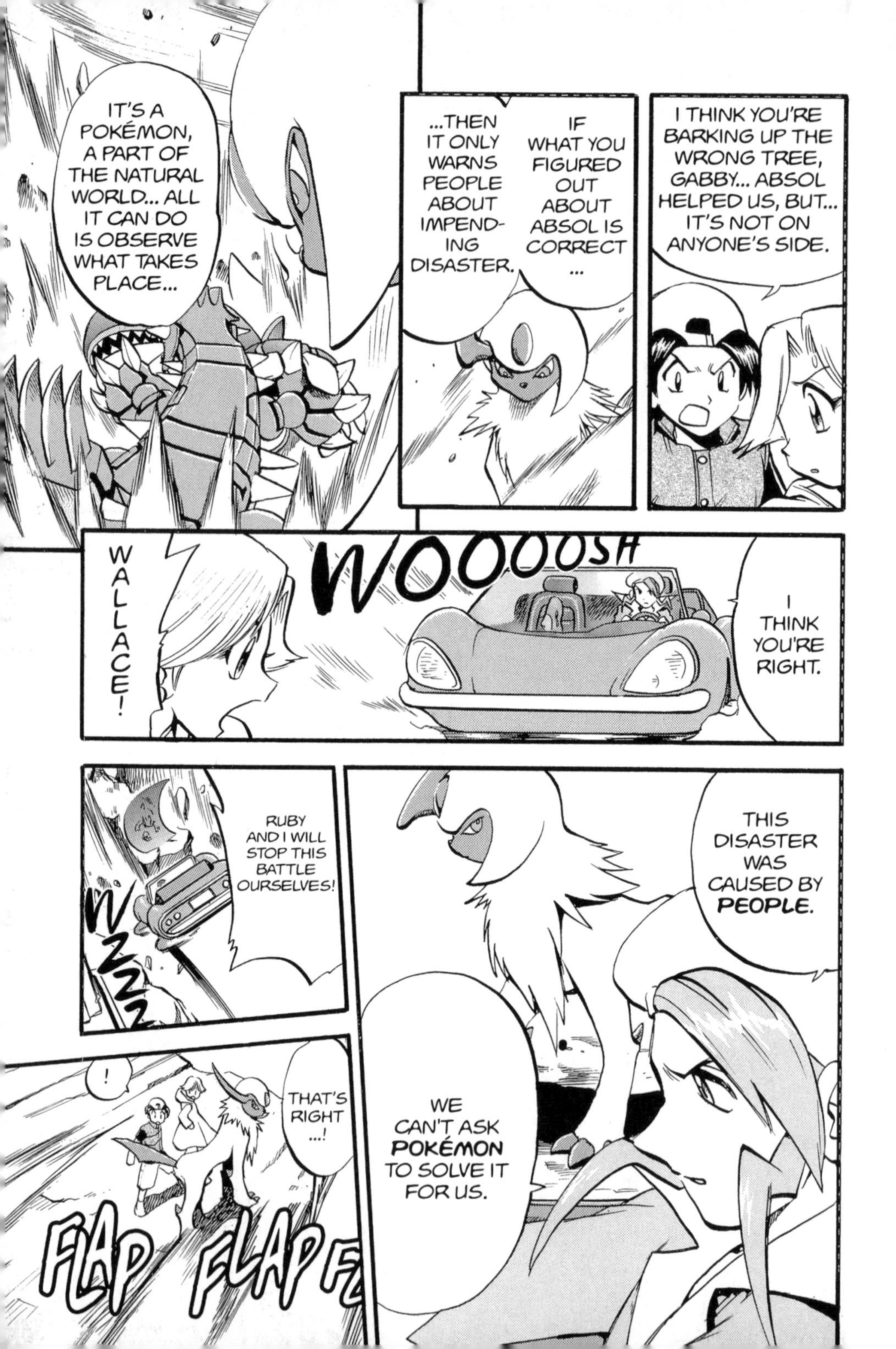
I THINK YOU'RE BARKING UP THE WRONG TREE, GABBY... ABSOL HELPED US, BUT... IT'S NOT ON ANYONE'S SIDE.
IF WHAT YOU FIGURED OUT ABOUT ABSOL IS CORRECT ...
...THEN IT ONLY WARNS PEOPLE ABOUT IMPEND-ING DISASTER.
IT'S A POKÉMON, A PART OF THE NATURAL WORLD... ALL IT CAN DO IS OBSERVE WHAT TAKES PLACE...
I THINK YOU'RE RIGHT.
WOOOOSH
WALLACE!
THIS DISASTER WAS CAUSED BY **PEOPLE**.
WE CAN'T ASK **POKÉMON** TO SOLVE IT FOR US.
RUBY AND I WILL STOP THIS BATTLE OURSELVES!
WZZZ
THAT'S RIGHT ...!
!
FLAP FLAP FL

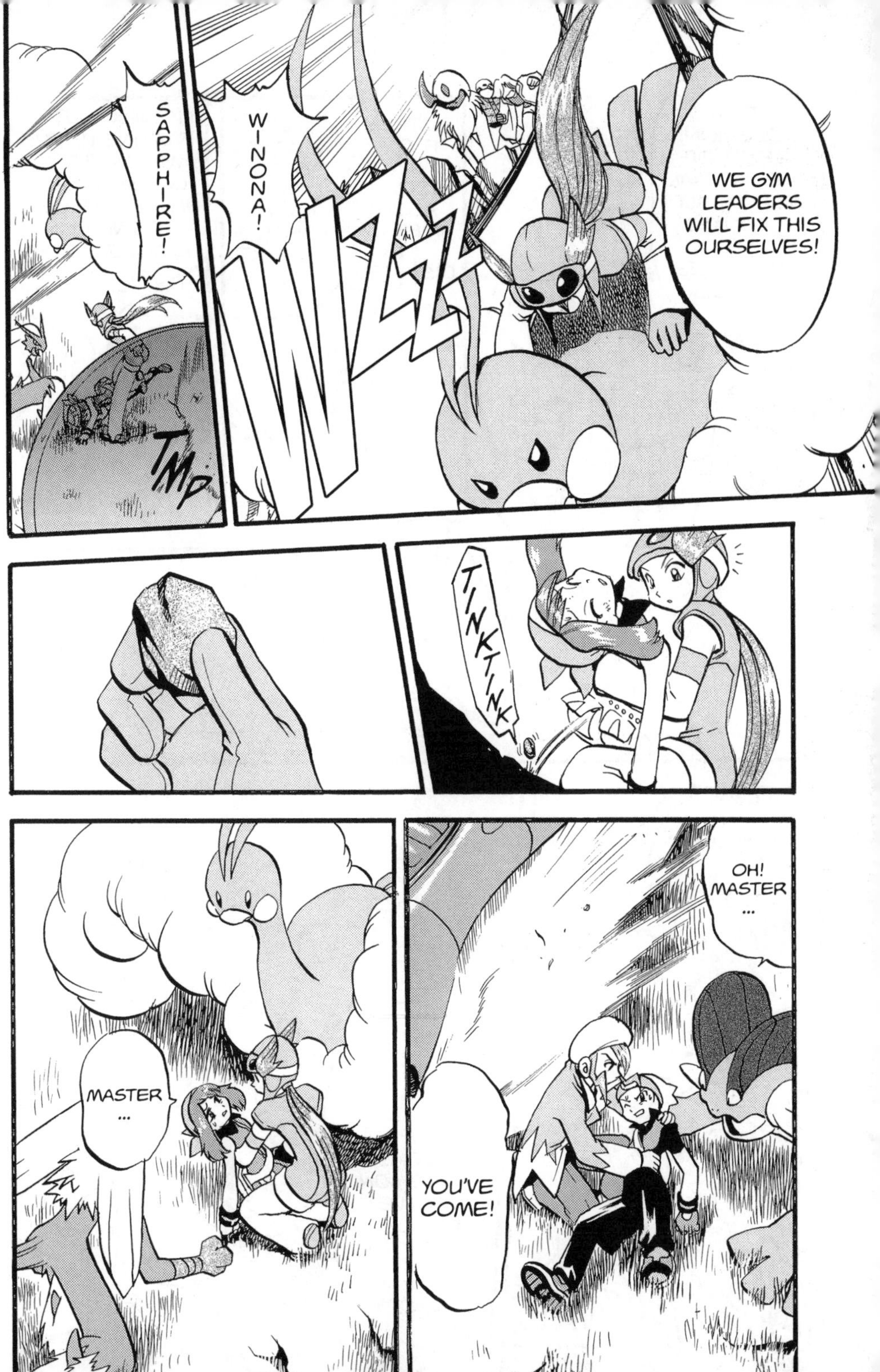
WE GYM LEADERS WILL FIX THIS OURSELVES!
WINONA!
WZZZ
SAPPHIRE!
TMP
TINKTINK
OH! MASTER ...
YOU'VE COME!
MASTER ...

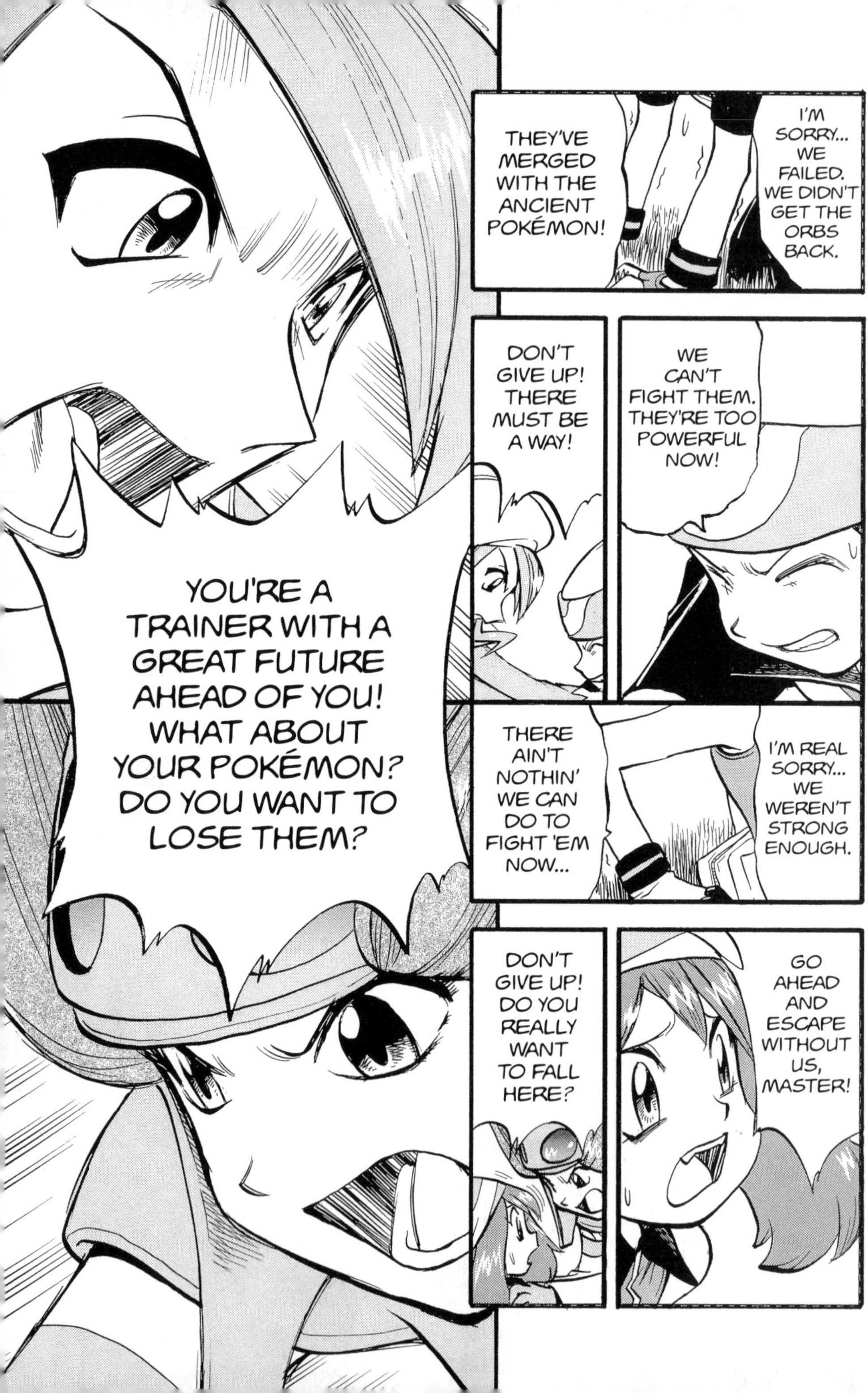
I'M SORRY... WE FAILED. WE DIDN'T GET THE ORBS BACK.
THEY'VE MERGED WITH THE ANCIENT POKÉMON!
WE CAN'T FIGHT THEM. THEY'RE TOO POWERFUL NOW!
DON'T GIVE UP! THERE MUST BE A WAY!
I'M REAL SORRY... WE WEREN'T STRONG ENOUGH.
THERE AIN'T NOTHIN' WE CAN DO TO FIGHT 'EM NOW...
GO AHEAD AND ESCAPE WITHOUT US, MASTER!
DON'T GIVE UP! DO YOU REALLY WANT TO FALL HERE?
YOU'RE A TRAINER WITH A GREAT FUTURE AHEAD OF YOU! WHAT ABOUT YOUR POKÉMON? DO YOU WANT TO LOSE THEM?

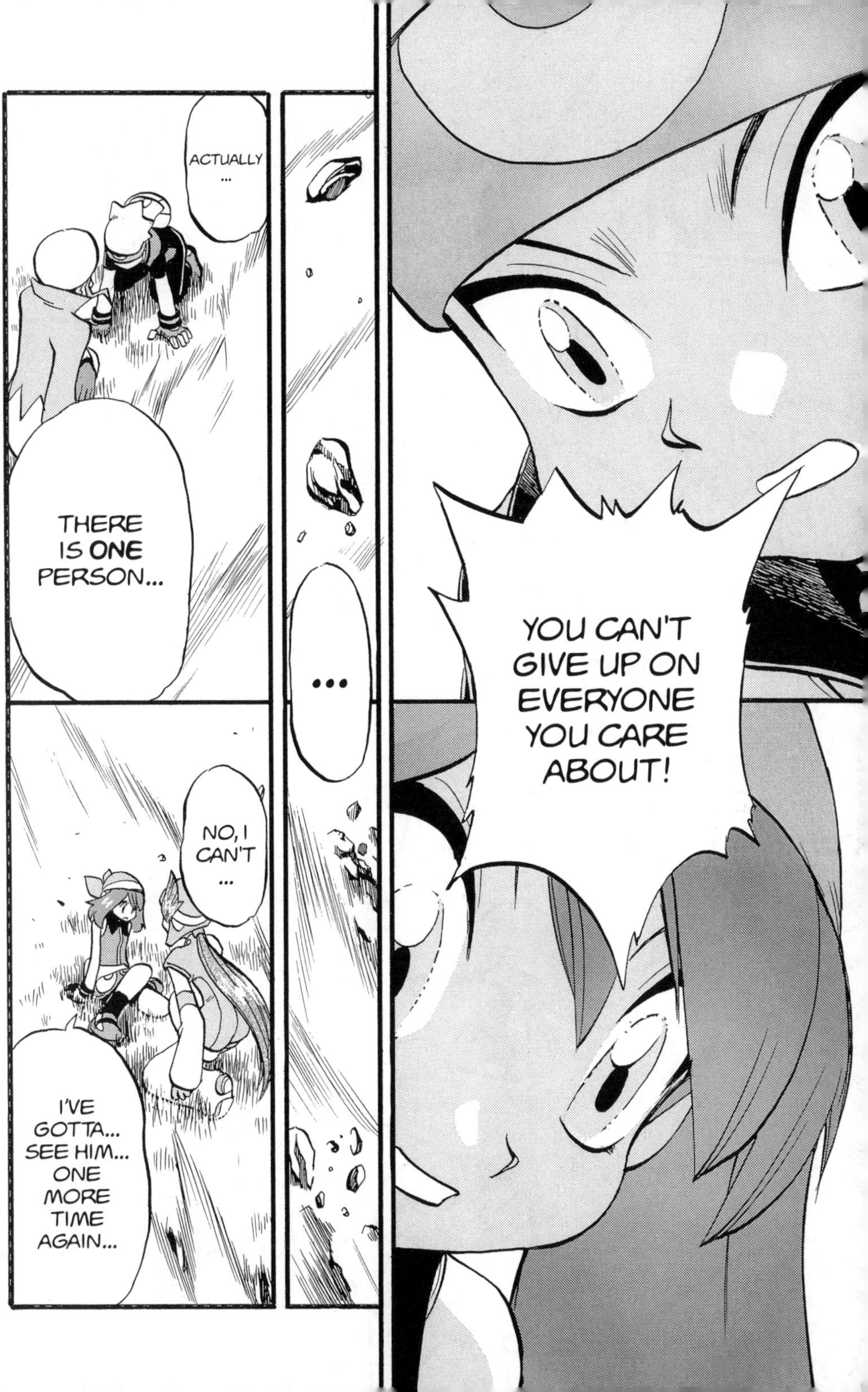
YOU CAN'T GIVE UP ON EVERYONE YOU CARE ABOUT!
...
ACTUALLY ...
THERE IS **ONE** PERSON...
NO, I CAN'T ...
I'VE GOTTA... SEE HIM... ONE MORE TIME AGAIN...

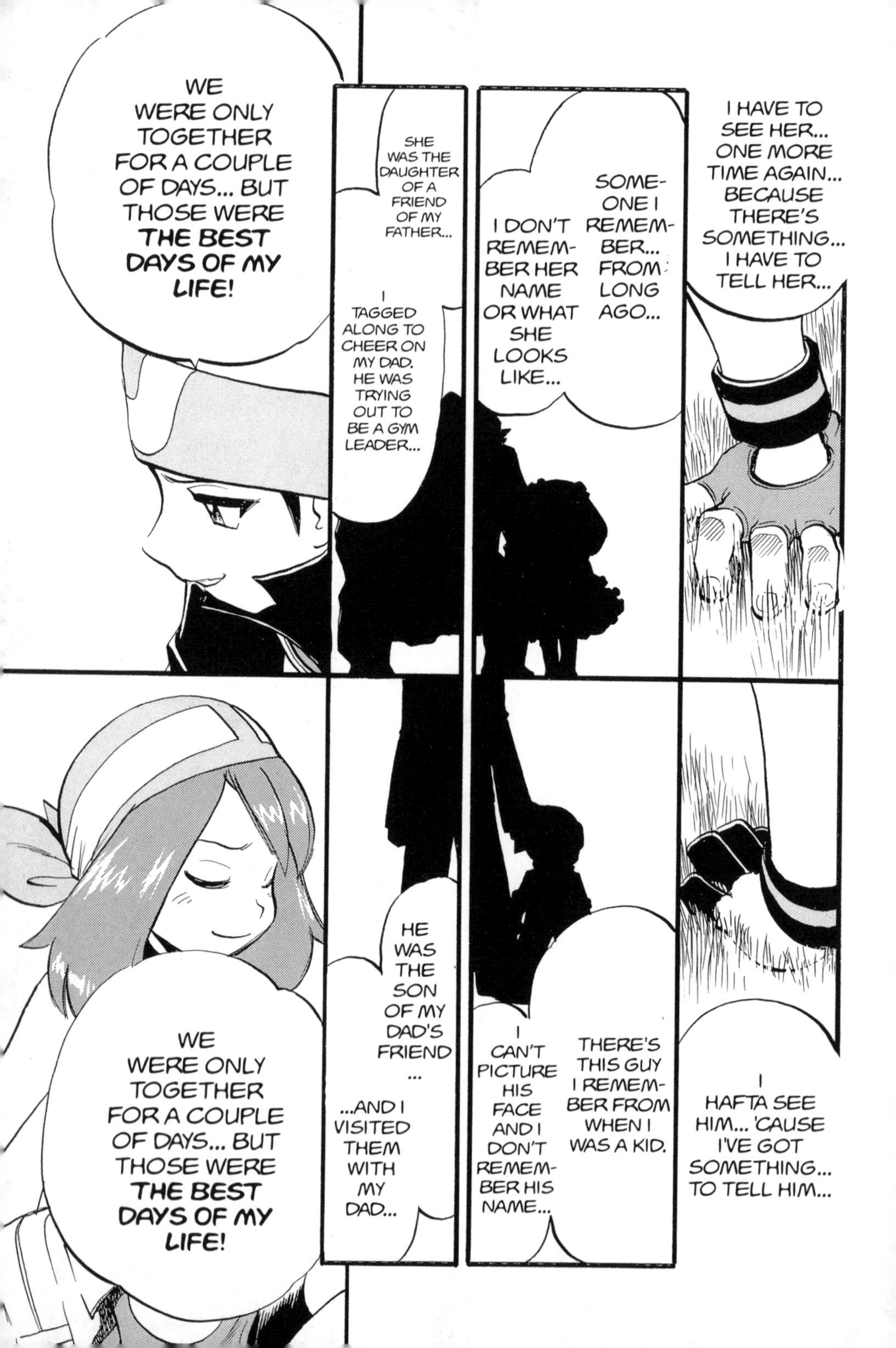
I HAVE TO SEE HER... ONE MORE TIME AGAIN... BECAUSE THERE'S SOMETHING... I HAVE TO TELL HER...
SOMEONE I REMEMBER... FROM LONG AGO...
I DON'T REMEMBER HER NAME OR WHAT SHE LOOKS LIKE...
SHE WAS THE DAUGHTER OF A FRIEND OF MY FATHER...
I TAGGED ALONG TO CHEER ON MY DAD. HE WAS TRYING OUT TO BE A GYM LEADER...
WE WERE ONLY TOGETHER FOR A COUPLE OF DAYS... BUT THOSE WERE **THE BEST DAYS OF MY LIFE!**
I HAFTA SEE HIM... 'CAUSE I'VE GOT SOMETHING... TO TELL HIM...
THERE'S THIS GUY I REMEMBER FROM WHEN I WAS A KID.
I CAN'T PICTURE HIS FACE AND I DON'T REMEMBER HIS NAME...
HE WAS THE SON OF MY DAD'S FRIEND...
...AND I VISITED THEM WITH MY DAD...
WE WERE ONLY TOGETHER FOR A COUPLE OF DAYS... BUT THOSE WERE **THE BEST DAYS OF MY LIFE!**

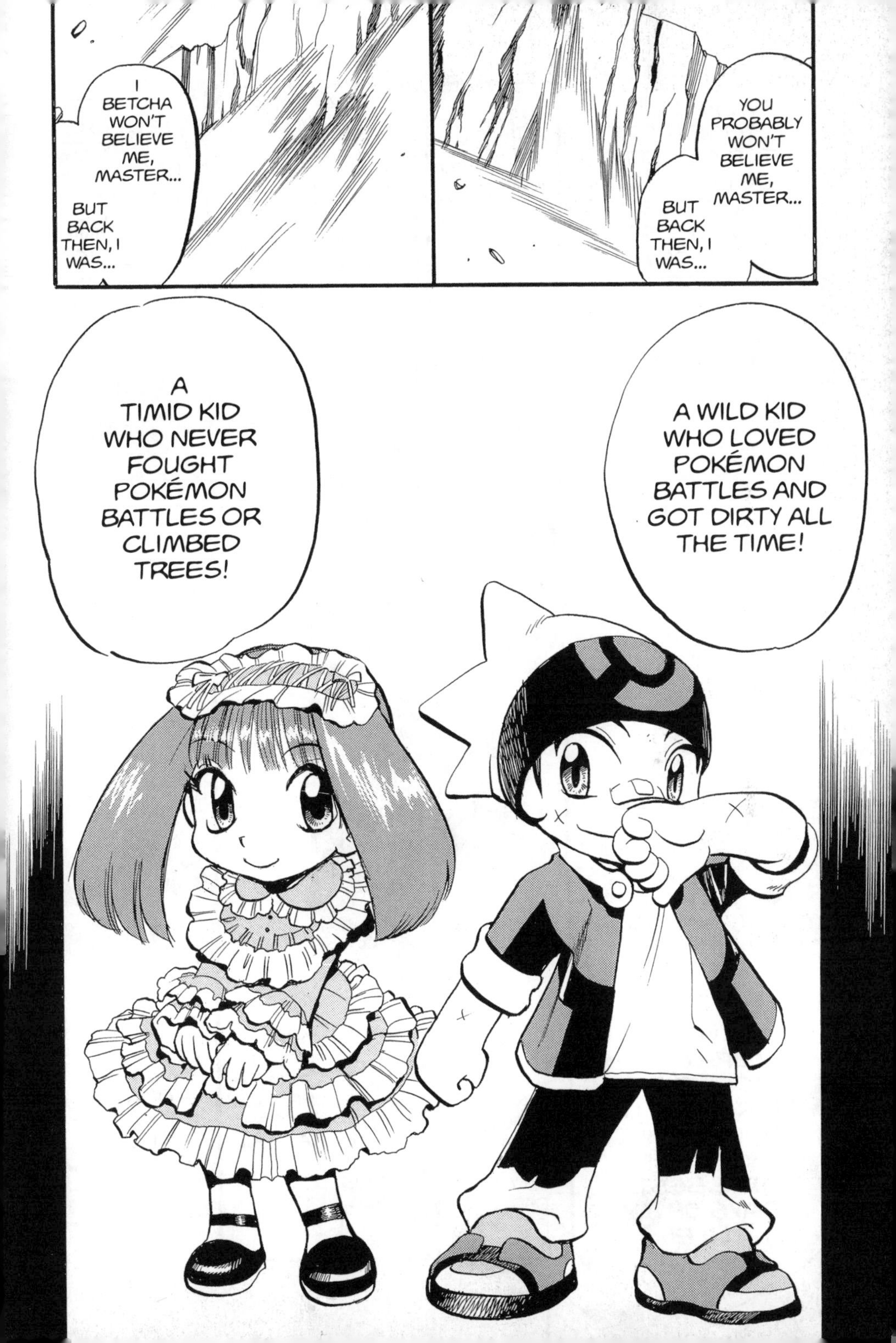
YOU PROBABLY WON'T BELIEVE ME, MASTER...
BUT BACK THEN, I WAS...
I BETCHA WON'T BELIEVE ME, MASTER...
BUT BACK THEN, I WAS...
A WILD KID WHO LOVED POKÉMON BATTLES AND GOT DIRTY ALL THE TIME!
A TIMID KID WHO NEVER FOUGHT POKÉMON BATTLES OR CLIMBED TREES!

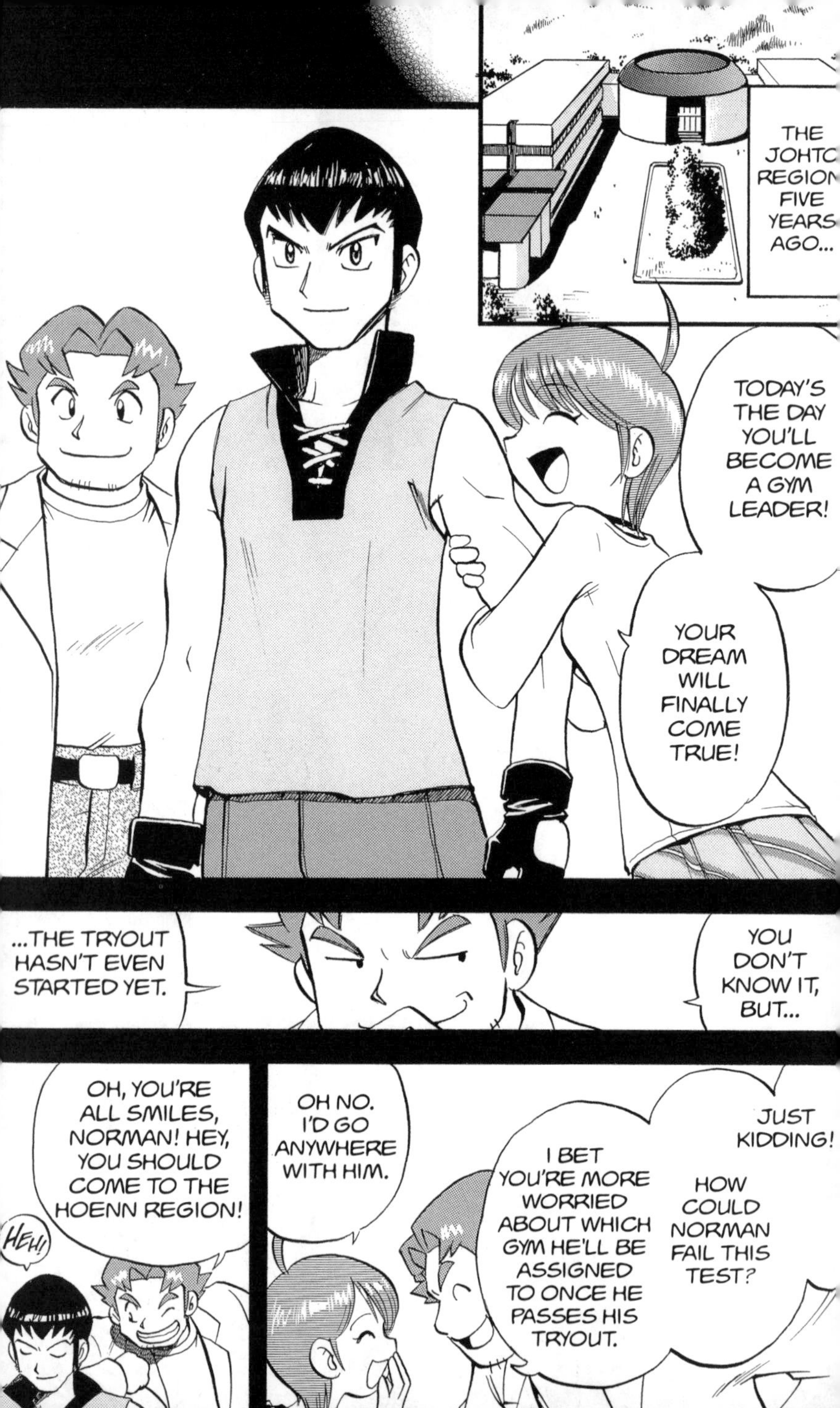
THE JOHTO REGION FIVE YEARS AGO...
TODAY'S THE DAY YOU'LL BECOME A GYM LEADER!
YOUR DREAM WILL FINALLY COME TRUE!
YOU DON'T KNOW IT, BUT...
...THE TRYOUT HASN'T EVEN STARTED YET.
JUST KIDDING!
HOW COULD NORMAN FAIL THIS TEST?
I BET YOU'RE MORE WORRIED ABOUT WHICH GYM HE'LL BE ASSIGNED TO ONCE HE PASSES HIS TRYOUT.
OH NO. I'D GO ANYWHERE WITH HIM.
OH, YOU'RE ALL SMILES, NORMAN! HEY, YOU SHOULD COME TO THE HOENN REGION!
HEH!

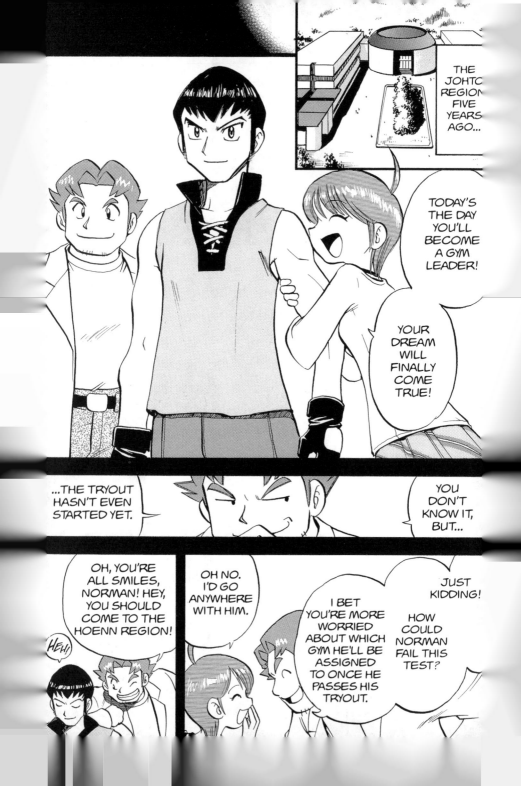

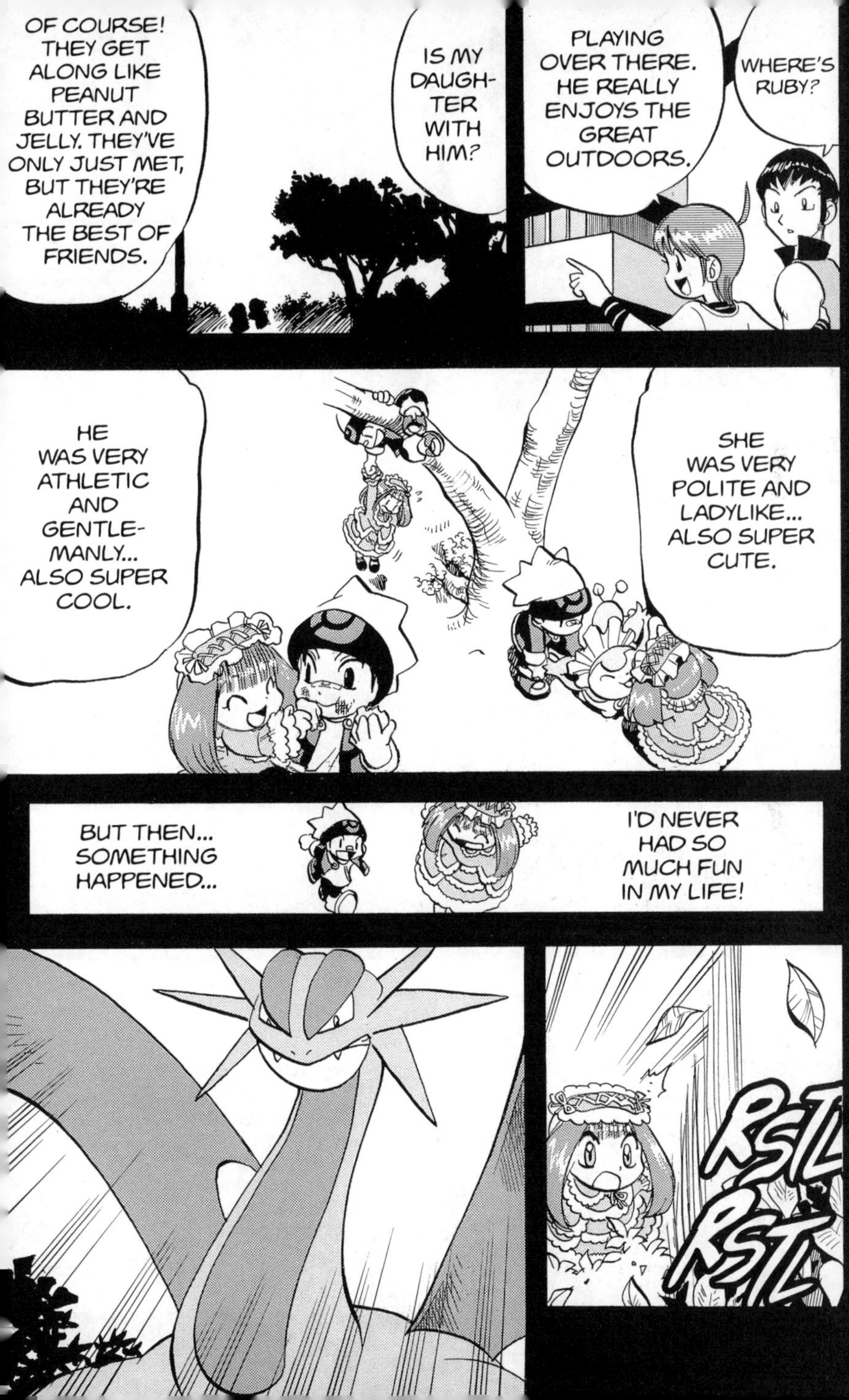
WHERE'S RUBY?
PLAYING OVER THERE. HE REALLY ENJOYS THE GREAT OUTDOORS.
IS MY DAUGH-TER WITH HIM?
OF COURSE! THEY GET ALONG LIKE PEANUT BUTTER AND JELLY. THEY'VE ONLY JUST MET, BUT THEY'RE ALREADY THE BEST OF FRIENDS.
SHE WAS VERY POLITE AND LADYLIKE... ALSO SUPER CUTE.
HE WAS VERY ATHLETIC AND GENTLE-MANLY... ALSO SUPER COOL.
I'D NEVER HAD SO MUCH FUN IN MY LIFE!
BUT THEN... SOMETHING HAPPENED...
RSTL
RSTL

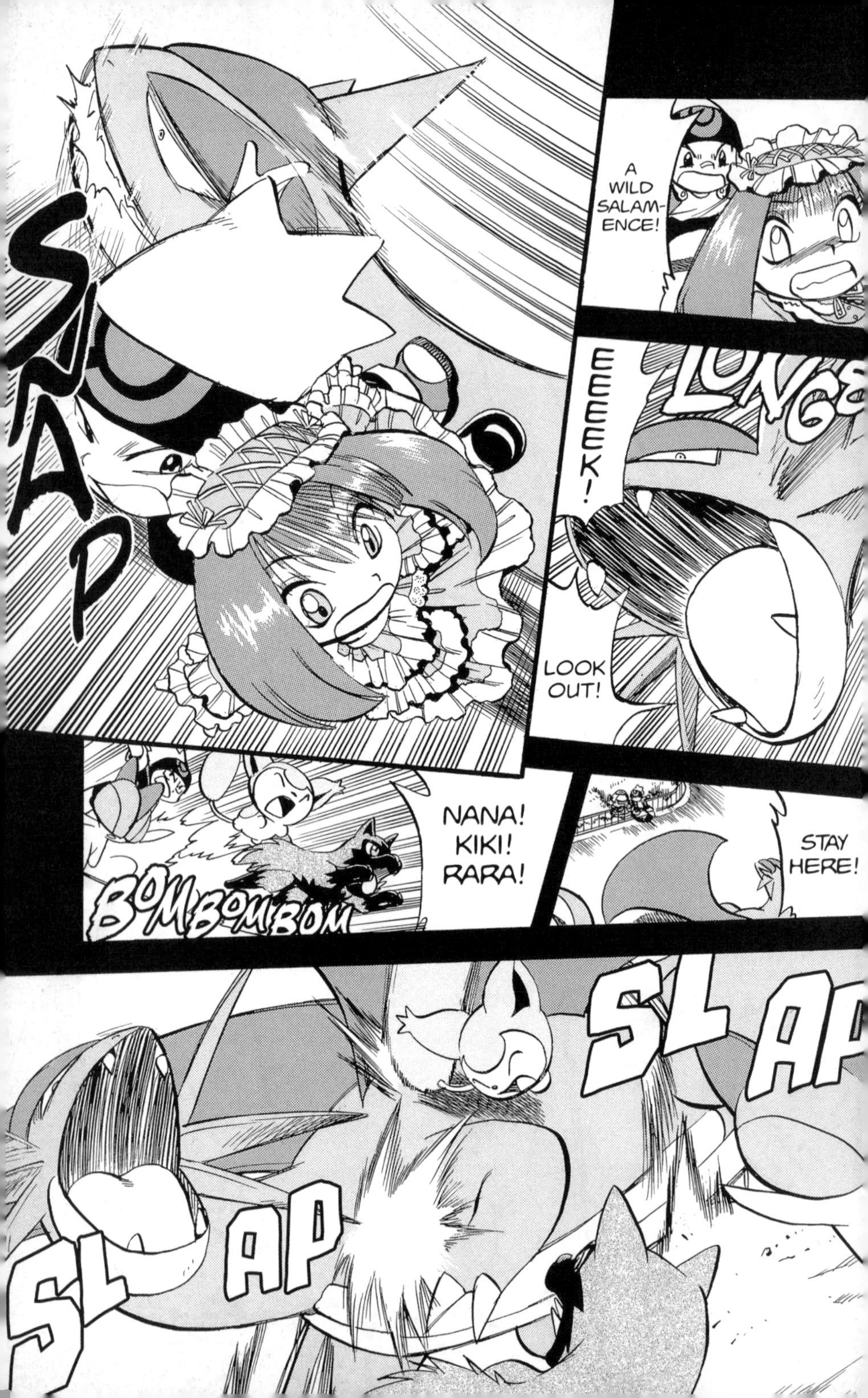
A WILD SALAMENCE!
LUNGE
EEEEEK!
LOOK OUT!
SLAP
STAY HERE!
NANA! KIKI! RARA!
BOMBOMBOM
SLAP
SLAP

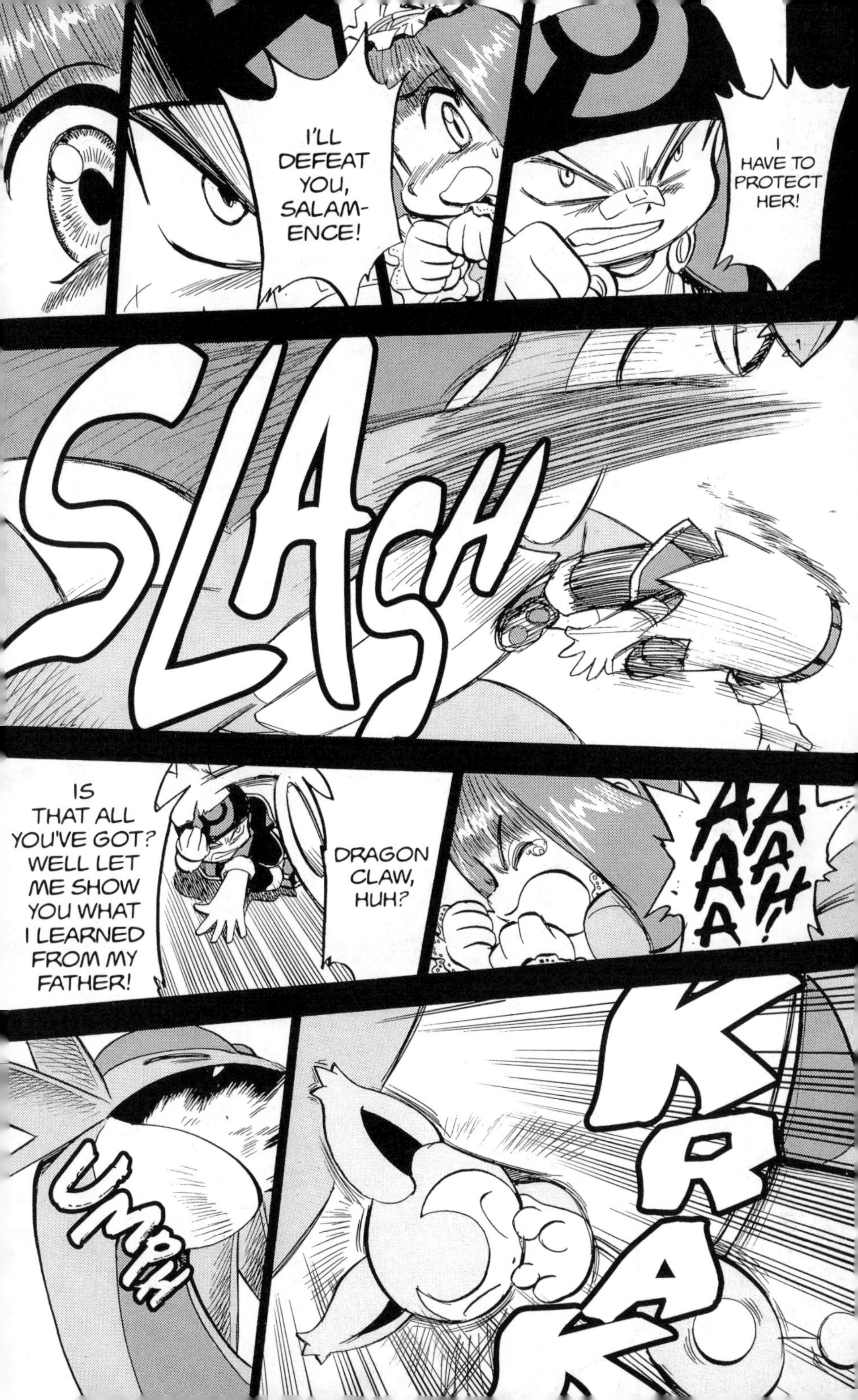
I HAVE TO PROTECT HER!
I'LL DEFEAT YOU, SALAMENCE!
SLASH
AAAAAH!
DRAGON CLAW, HUH?
IS THAT ALL YOU'VE GOT? WELL LET ME SHOW YOU WHAT I LEARNED FROM MY FATHER!
KRAK
UMPH

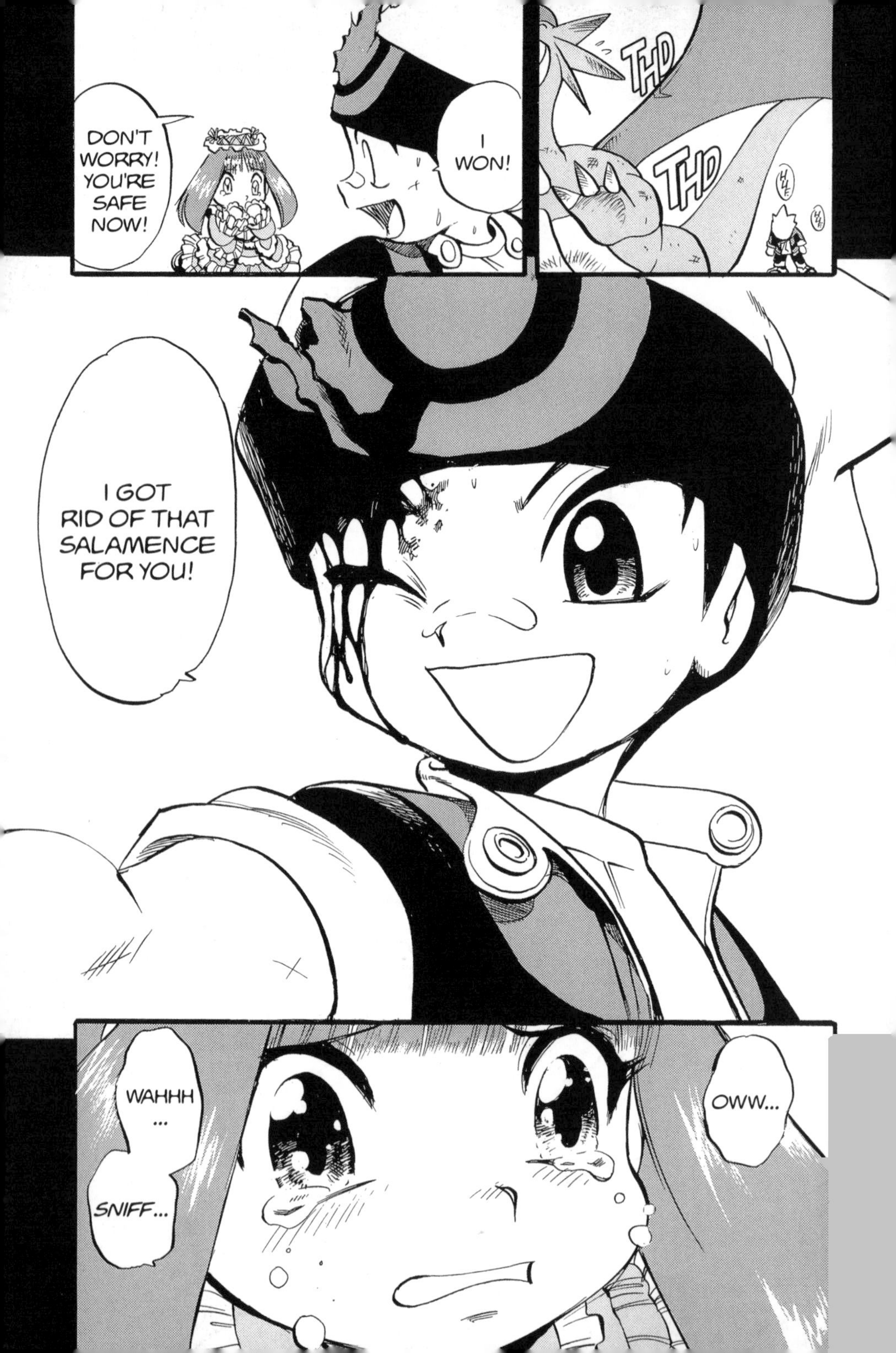
THD
THD
HUF
HUF
I WON!
DON'T WORRY! YOU'RE SAFE NOW!
I GOT RID OF THAT SALAMENCE FOR YOU!
OWW...
WAHHH...
SNIFF...

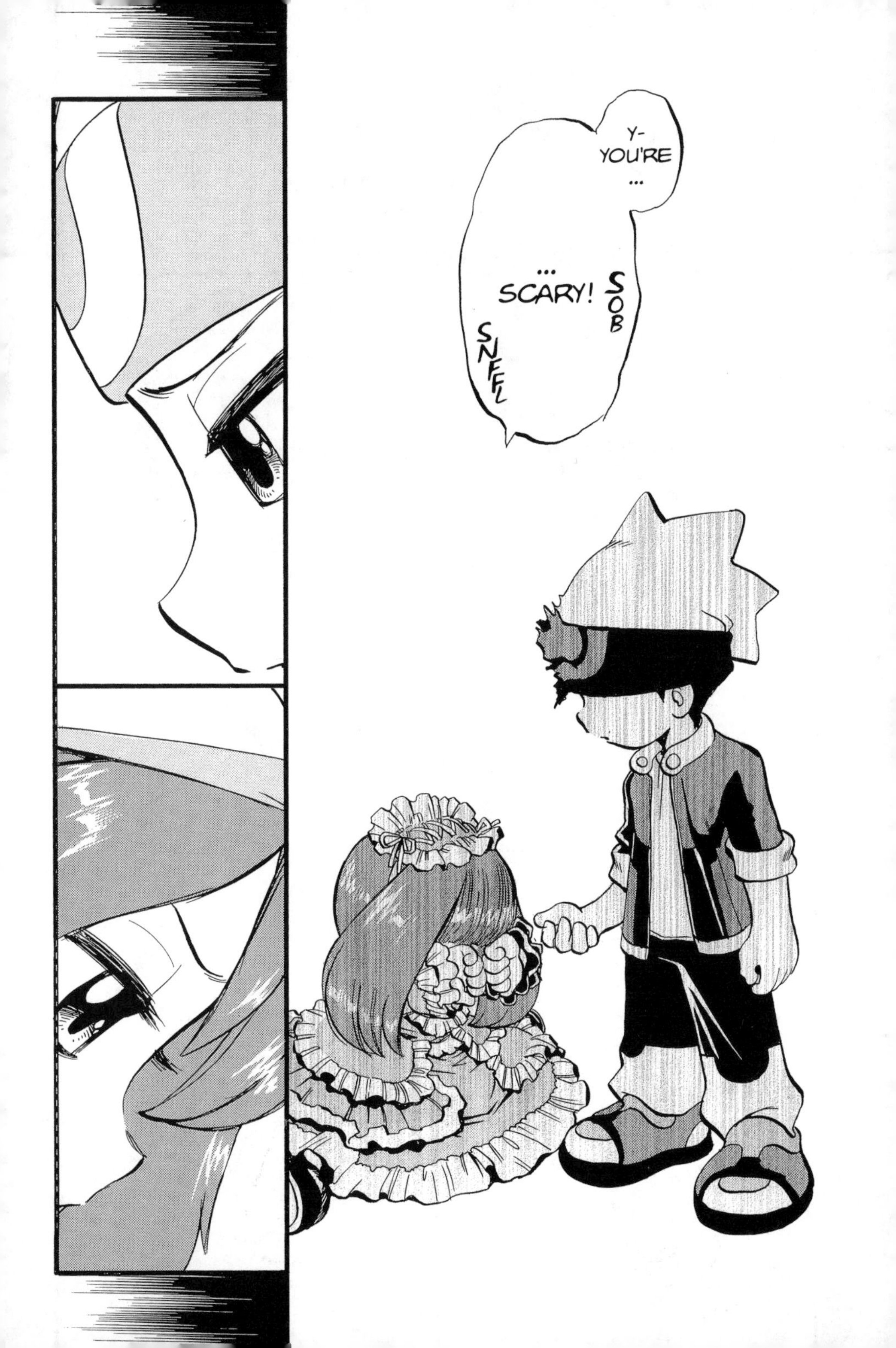
Y-YOU'RE ... ...SCARY!
SOB
SNFFL

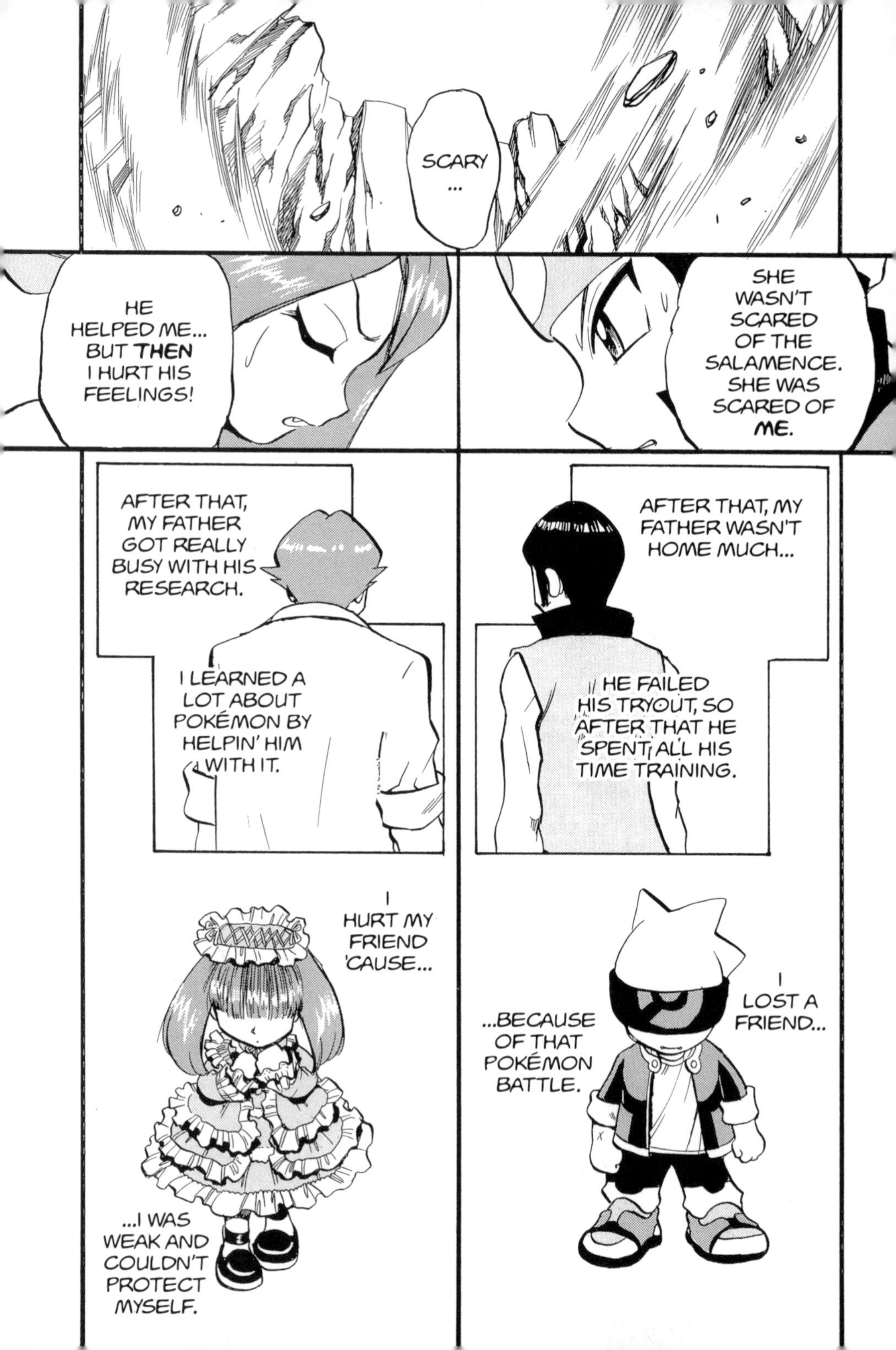
SCARY ...
SHE WASN'T SCARED OF THE SALAMENCE. SHE WAS SCARED OF **ME.**
HE HELPED ME... BUT **THEN** I HURT HIS FEELINGS!
AFTER THAT, MY FATHER WASN'T HOME MUCH...
HE FAILED HIS TRYOUT, SO AFTER THAT HE SPENT ALL HIS TIME TRAINING.
AFTER THAT, MY FATHER GOT REALLY BUSY WITH HIS RESEARCH.
I LEARNED A LOT ABOUT POKÉMON BY HELPIN' HIM WITH IT.
I LOST A FRIEND...
...BECAUSE OF THAT POKÉMON BATTLE.
I HURT MY FRIEND 'CAUSE...
...I WAS WEAK AND COULDN'T PROTECT MYSELF.

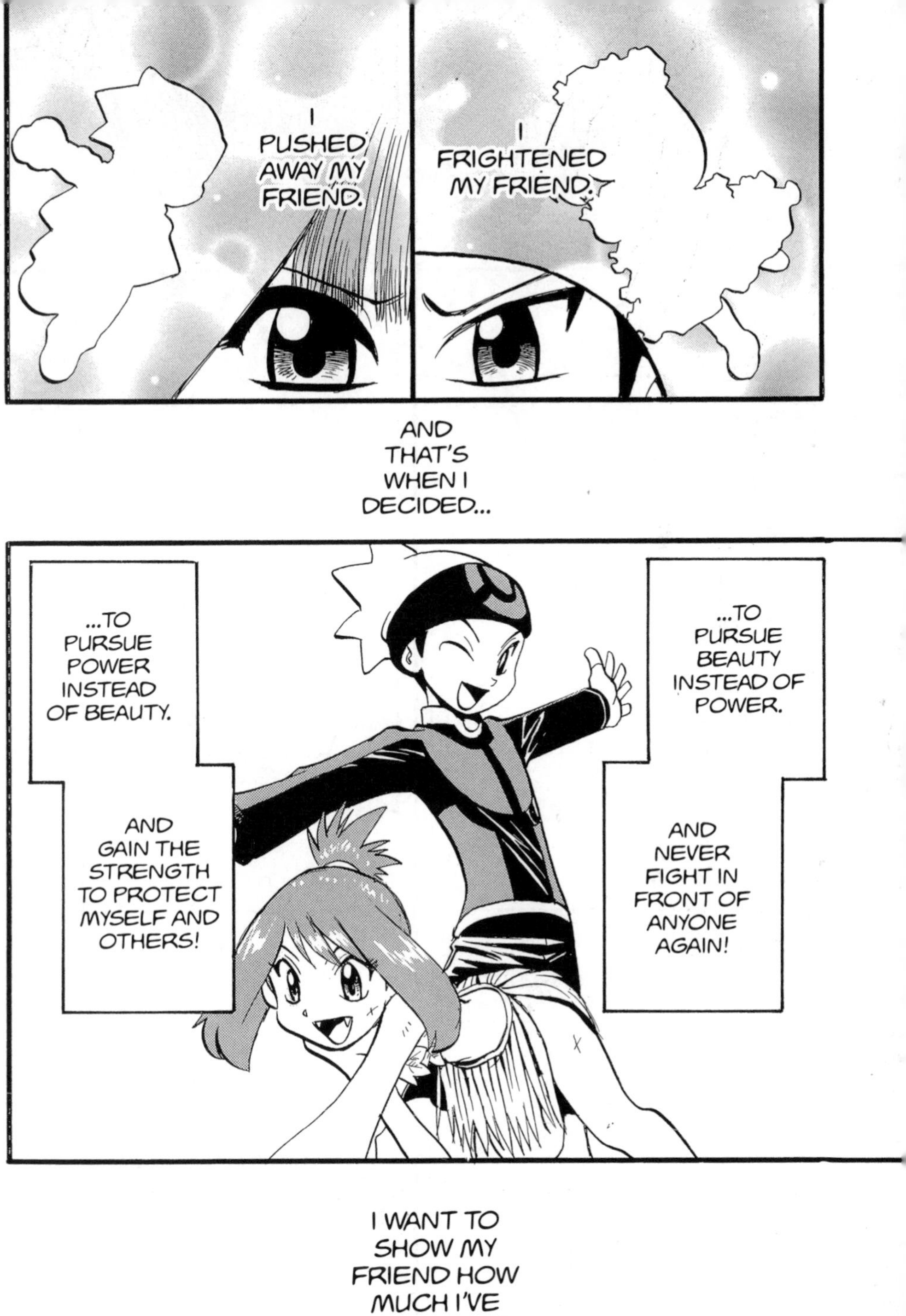
I FRIGHTENED MY FRIEND.
I PUSHED AWAY MY FRIEND.
AND THAT'S WHEN I DECIDED...
...TO PURSUE BEAUTY INSTEAD OF POWER.
AND NEVER FIGHT IN FRONT OF ANYONE AGAIN!
...TO PURSUE POWER INSTEAD OF BEAUTY.
AND GAIN THE STRENGTH TO PROTECT MYSELF AND OTHERS!
I WANT TO SHOW MY FRIEND HOW MUCH I'VE CHANGED!

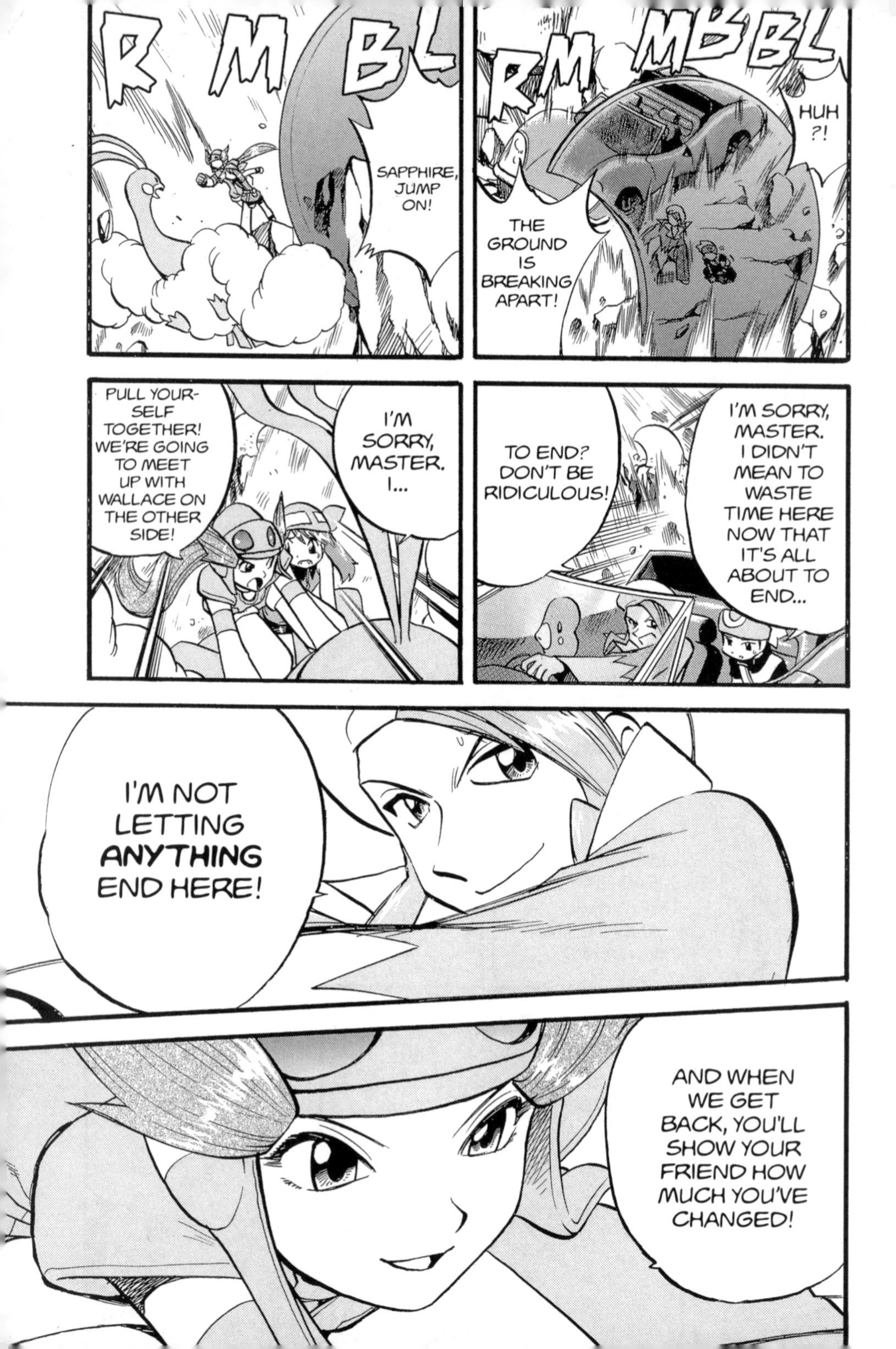
RM MBBL
HUH ?!
THE GROUND IS BREAKING APART!
R M BL
SAPPHIRE, JUMP ON!
I'M SORRY, MASTER. I DIDN'T MEAN TO WASTE TIME HERE NOW THAT IT'S ALL ABOUT TO END...
TO END? DON'T BE RIDICULOUS!
I'M SORRY, MASTER. I...
PULL YOURSELF TOGETHER! WE'RE GOING TO MEET UP WITH WALLACE ON THE OTHER SIDE!
I'M NOT LETTING **ANYTHING** END HERE!
AND WHEN WE GET BACK, YOU'LL SHOW YOUR FRIEND HOW MUCH YOU'VE CHANGED!

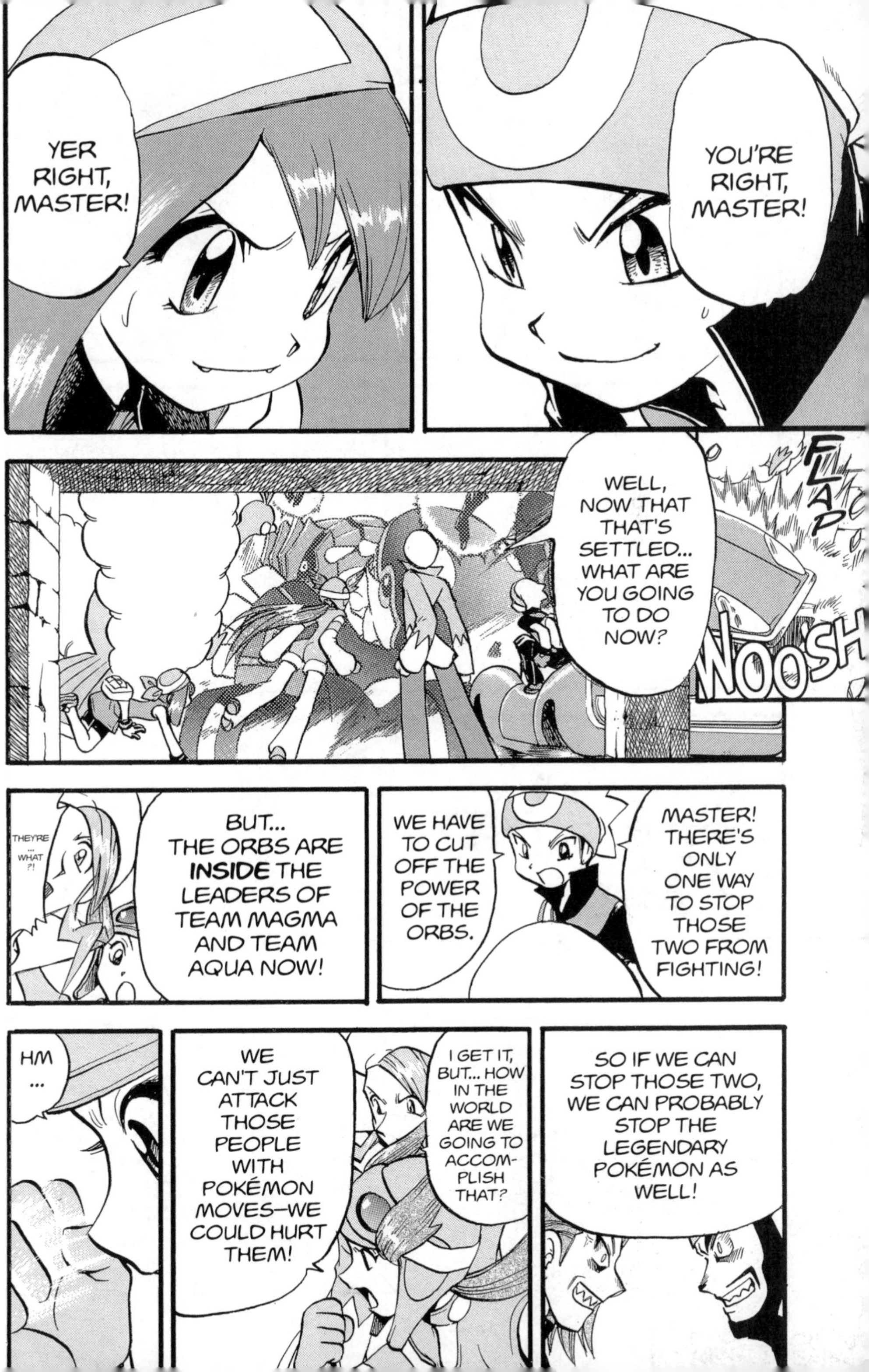
YOU'RE RIGHT, MASTER!
YER RIGHT, MASTER!
FLAP
WELL, NOW THAT THAT'S SETTLED... WHAT ARE YOU GOING TO DO NOW?
WOOSH
MASTER! THERE'S ONLY ONE WAY TO STOP THOSE TWO FROM FIGHTING!
WE HAVE TO CUT OFF THE POWER OF THE ORBS.
BUT... THE ORBS ARE **INSIDE** THE LEADERS OF TEAM MAGMA AND TEAM AQUA NOW!
THEY'RE ... WHAT ?!
SO IF WE CAN STOP THOSE TWO, WE CAN PROBABLY STOP THE LEGENDARY POKÉMON AS WELL!
I GET IT, BUT... HOW IN THE WORLD ARE WE GOING TO ACCOMPLISH THAT?
WE CAN'T JUST ATTACK THOSE PEOPLE WITH POKÉMON MOVES—WE COULD HURT THEM!
HM ...

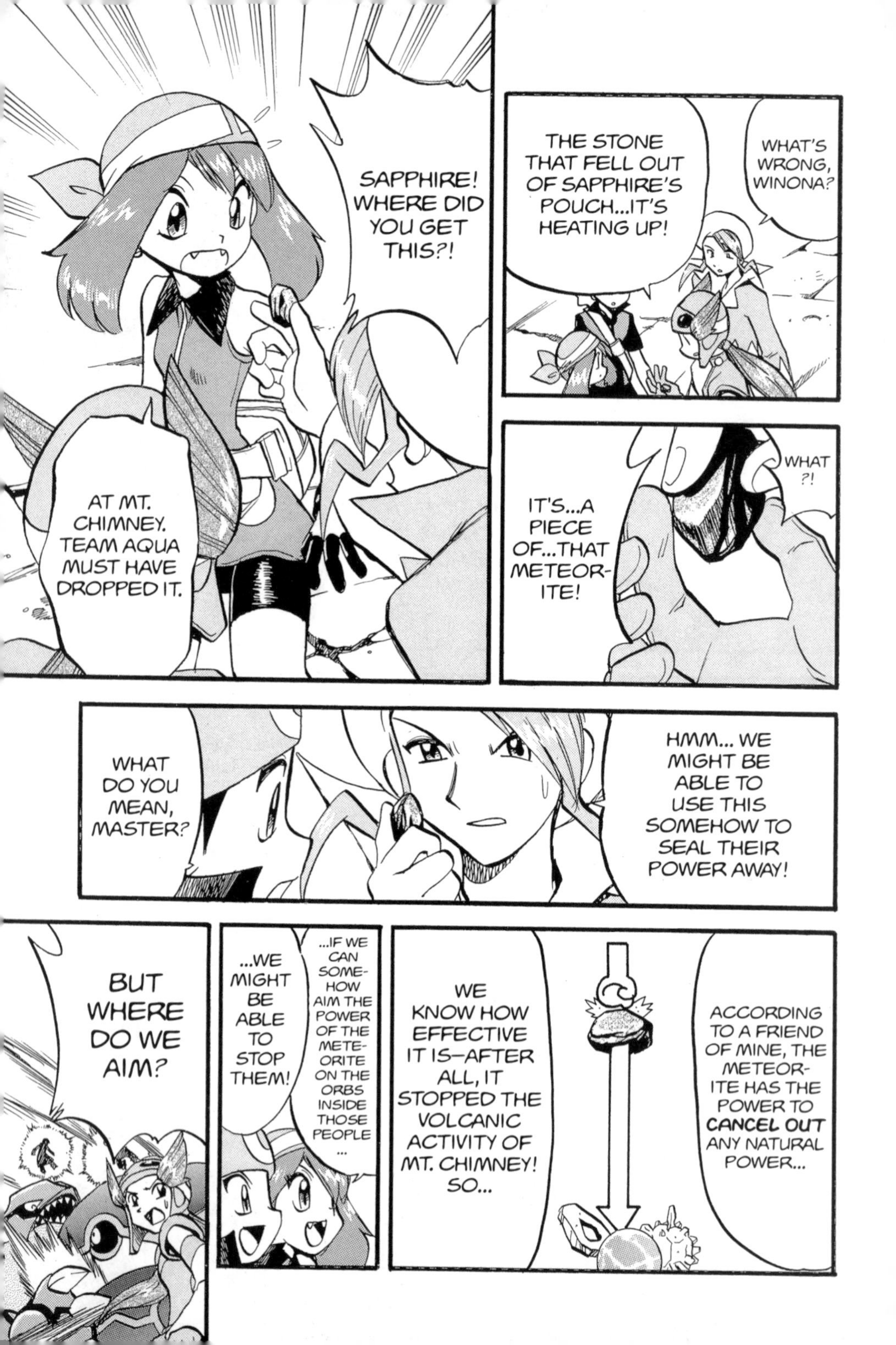
WHAT'S WRONG, WINONA?
THE STONE THAT FELL OUT OF SAPPHIRE'S POUCH...IT'S HEATING UP!
WHAT ?!
IT'S...A PIECE OF...THAT METEOR-ITE!
SAPPHIRE! WHERE DID YOU GET THIS?!
AT MT. CHIMNEY. TEAM AQUA MUST HAVE DROPPED IT.
HMM... WE MIGHT BE ABLE TO USE THIS SOMEHOW TO SEAL THEIR POWER AWAY!
WHAT DO YOU MEAN, MASTER?
ACCORDING TO A FRIEND OF MINE, THE METEOR-ITE HAS THE POWER TO **CANCEL OUT** ANY NATURAL POWER...
WE KNOW HOW EFFECTIVE IT IS—AFTER ALL, IT STOPPED THE VOLCANIC ACTIVITY OF MT. CHIMNEY! SO...
...IF WE CAN SOME-HOW AIM THE POWER OF THE METE-ORITE ON THE ORBS INSIDE THOSE PEOPLE ...
...WE MIGHT BE ABLE TO STOP THEM!
BUT WHERE DO WE AIM?

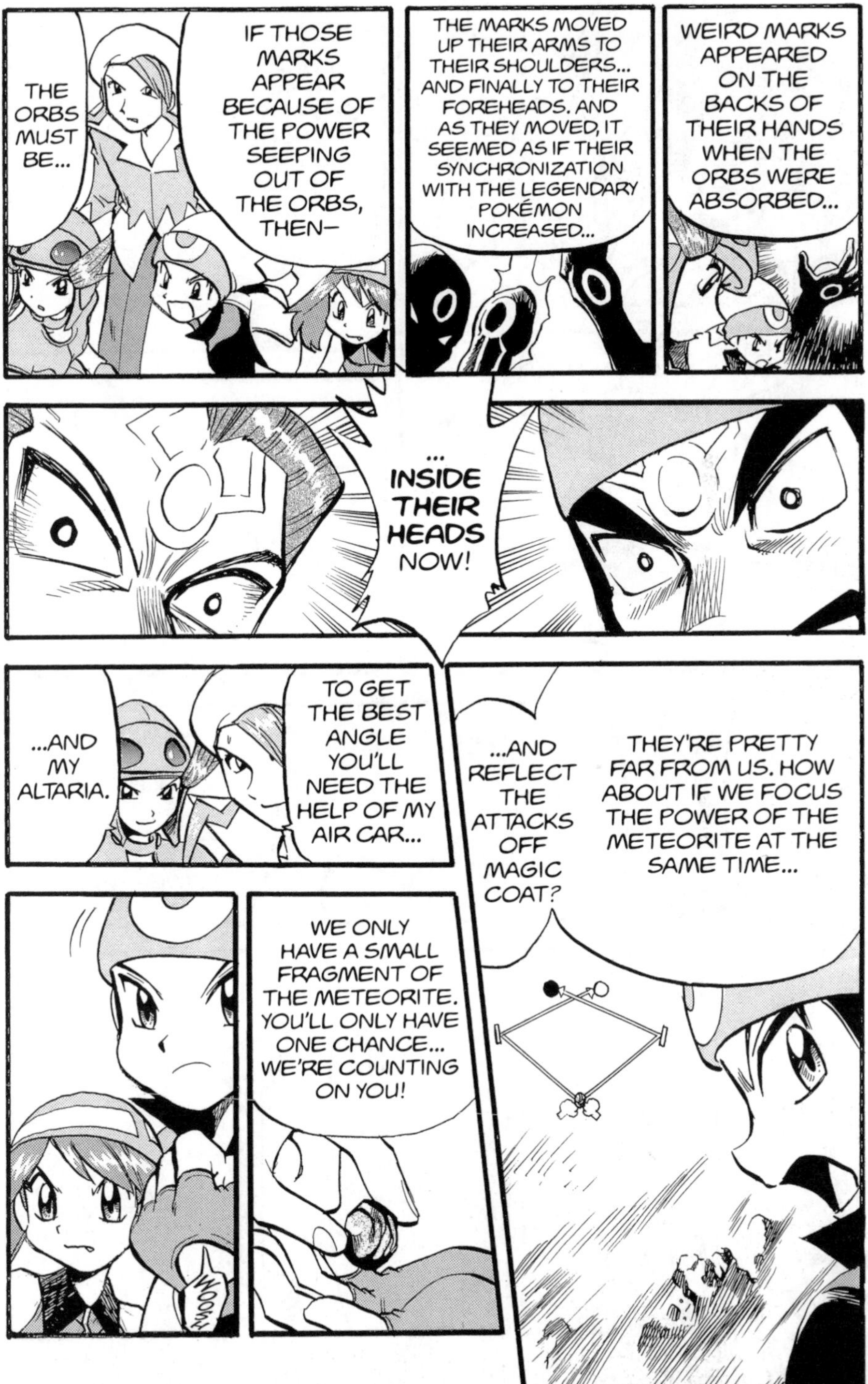
WEIRD MARKS APPEARED ON THE BACKS OF THEIR HANDS WHEN THE ORBS WERE ABSORBED...
THE MARKS MOVED UP THEIR ARMS TO THEIR SHOULDERS... AND FINALLY TO THEIR FOREHEADS. AND AS THEY MOVED, IT SEEMED AS IF THEIR SYNCHRONIZATION WITH THE LEGENDARY POKÉMON INCREASED...
IF THOSE MARKS APPEAR BECAUSE OF THE POWER SEEPING OUT OF THE ORBS, THEN–
THE ORBS MUST BE...
... INSIDE THEIR HEADS NOW!
THEY'RE PRETTY FAR FROM US. HOW ABOUT IF WE FOCUS THE POWER OF THE METEORITE AT THE SAME TIME...
...AND REFLECT THE ATTACKS OFF MAGIC COAT?
TO GET THE BEST ANGLE YOU'LL NEED THE HELP OF MY AIR CAR...
...AND MY ALTARIA.
WE ONLY HAVE A SMALL FRAGMENT OF THE METEORITE. YOU'LL ONLY HAVE ONE CHANCE... WE'RE COUNTING ON YOU!
WOOSH

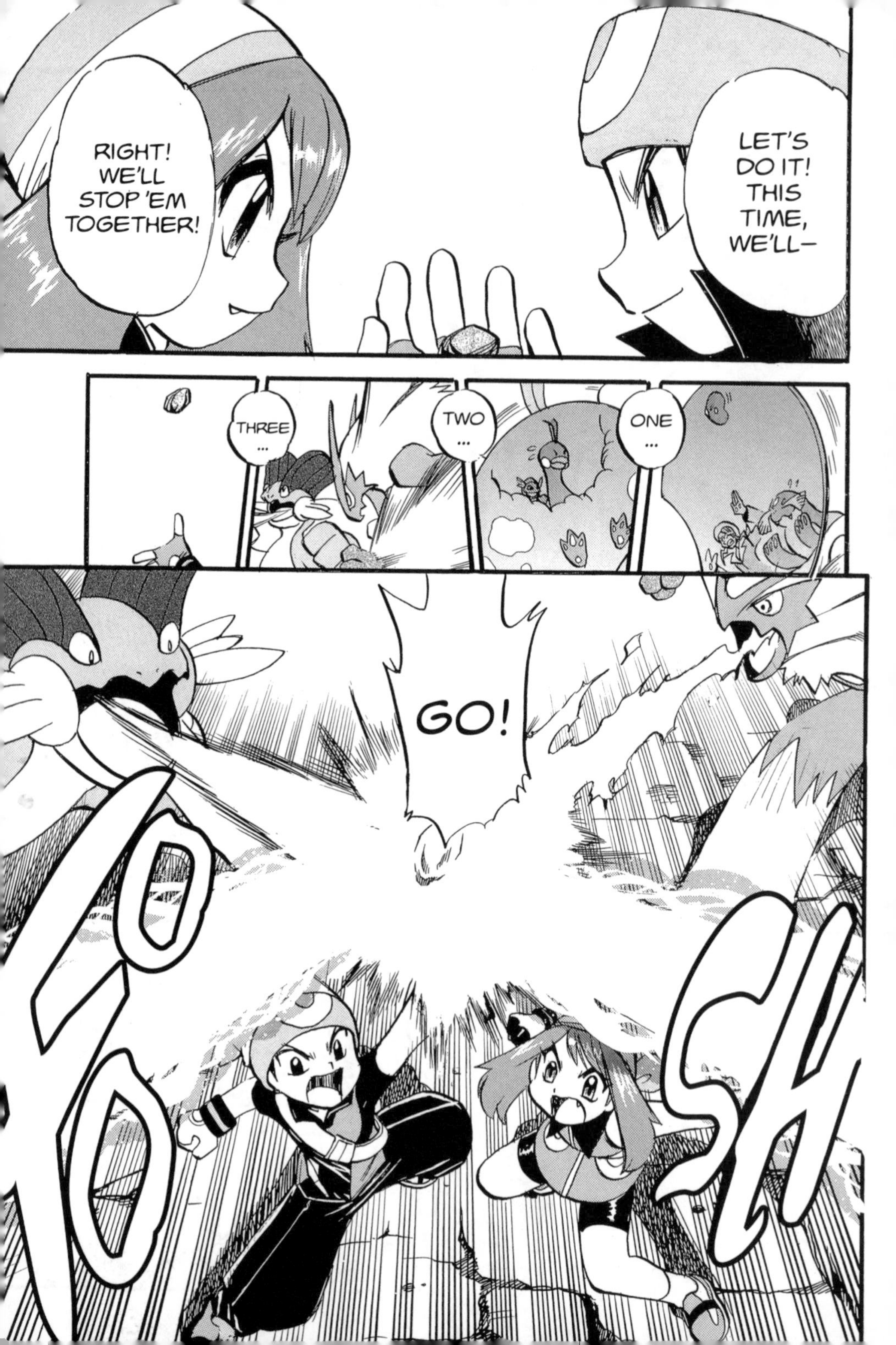
RIGHT! WE'LL STOP 'EM TOGETHER!
LET'S DO IT! THIS TIME, WE'LL–
THREE ...
TWO ...
ONE ...
GO!
FOOSH

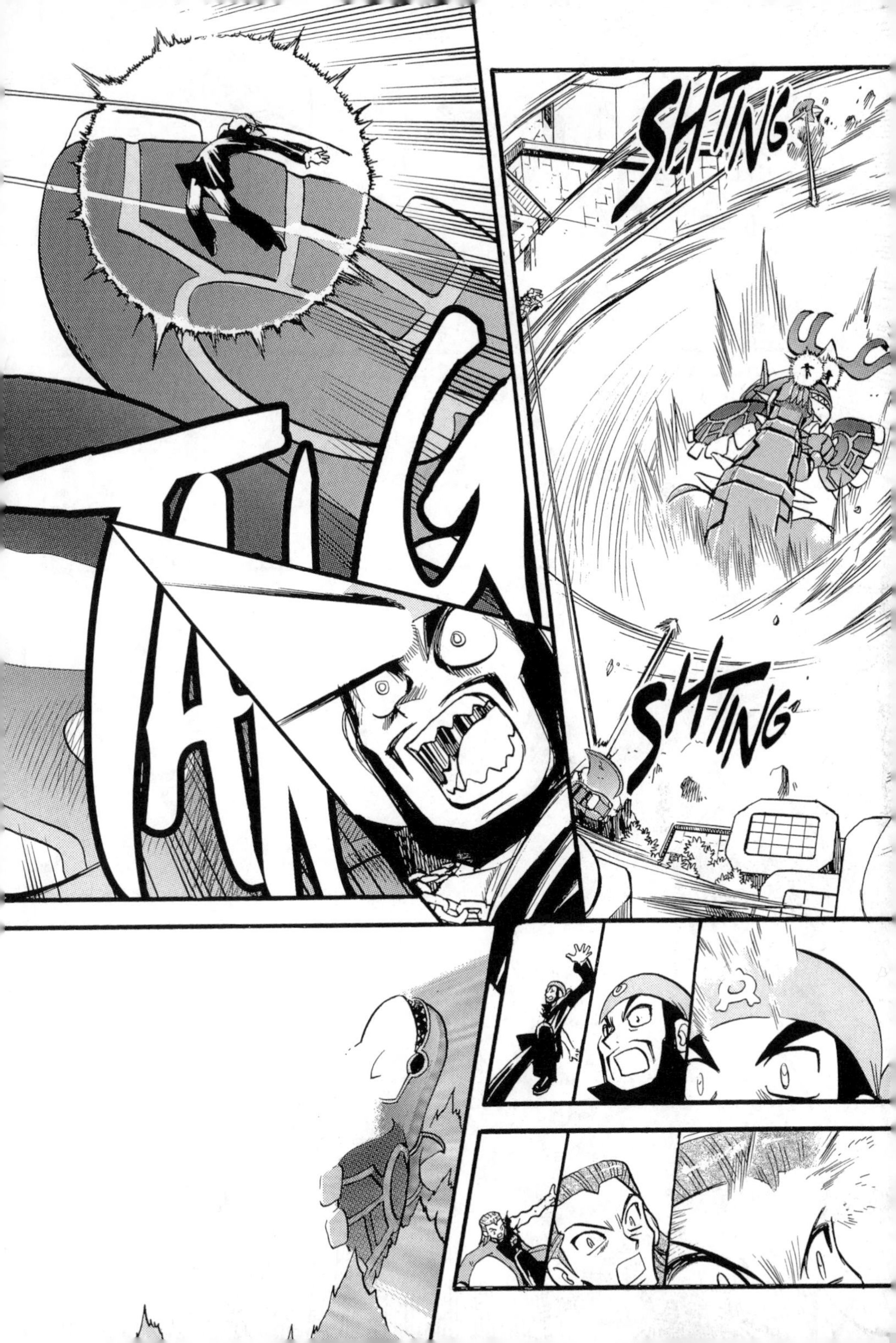
SHING
SHING

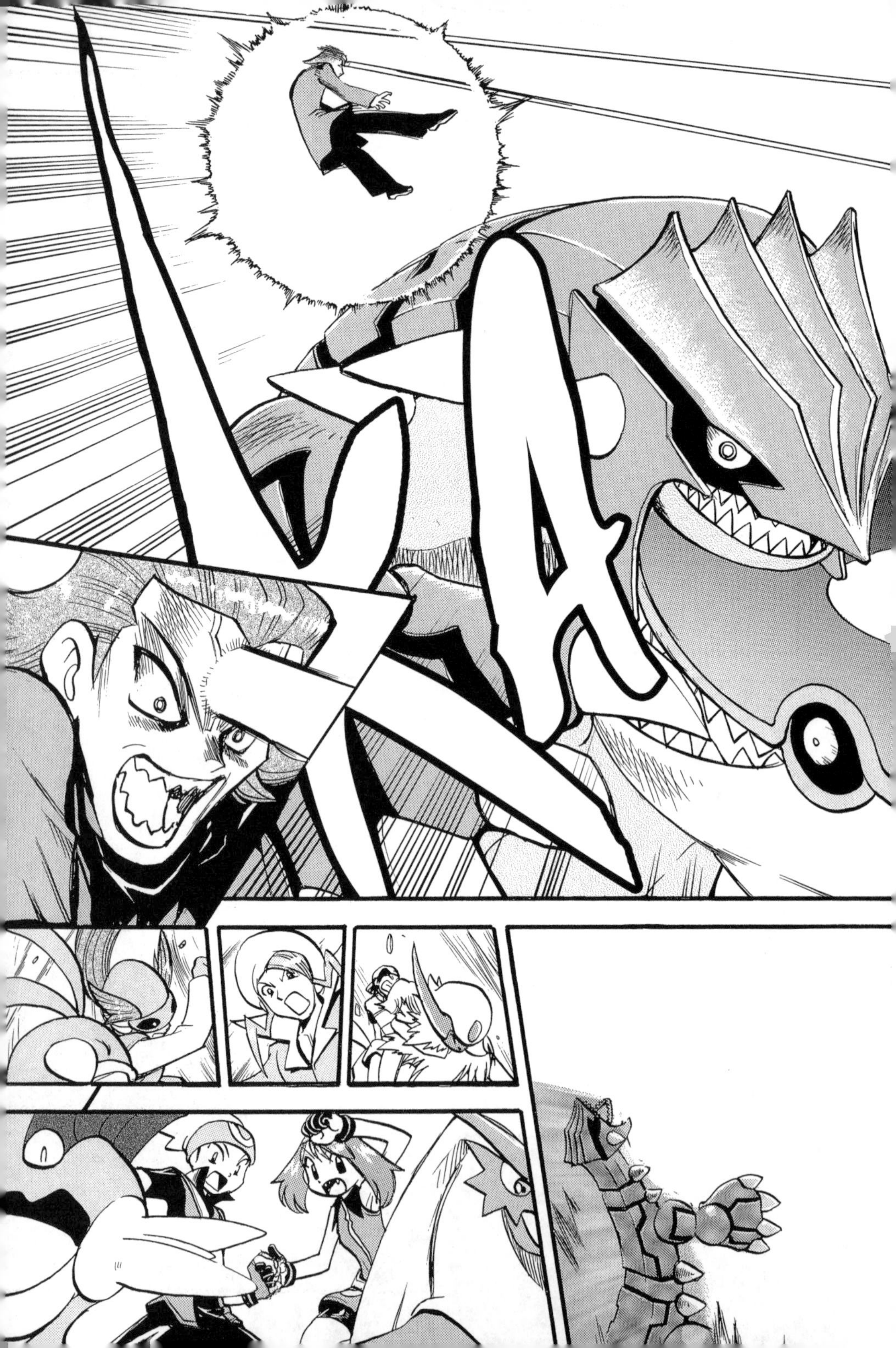

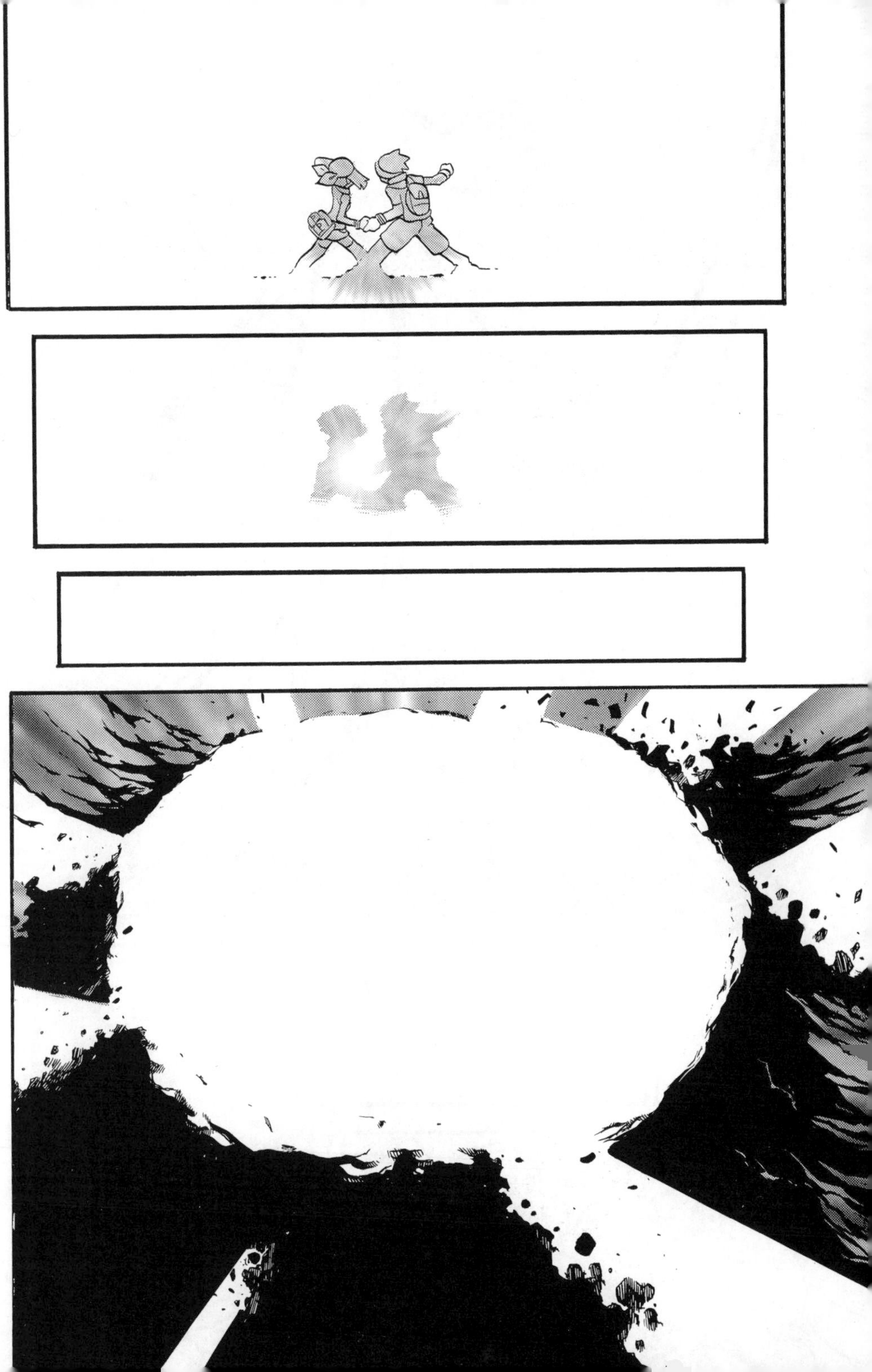

● Adventure 253 ●
A Royal Rumble with Regirock, Regice and Registeel, Part 1

Pokémon Adventures Ruby & Sapphire

The Fourth Chapter

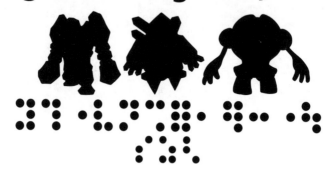

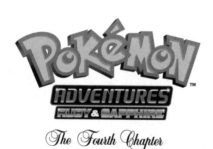

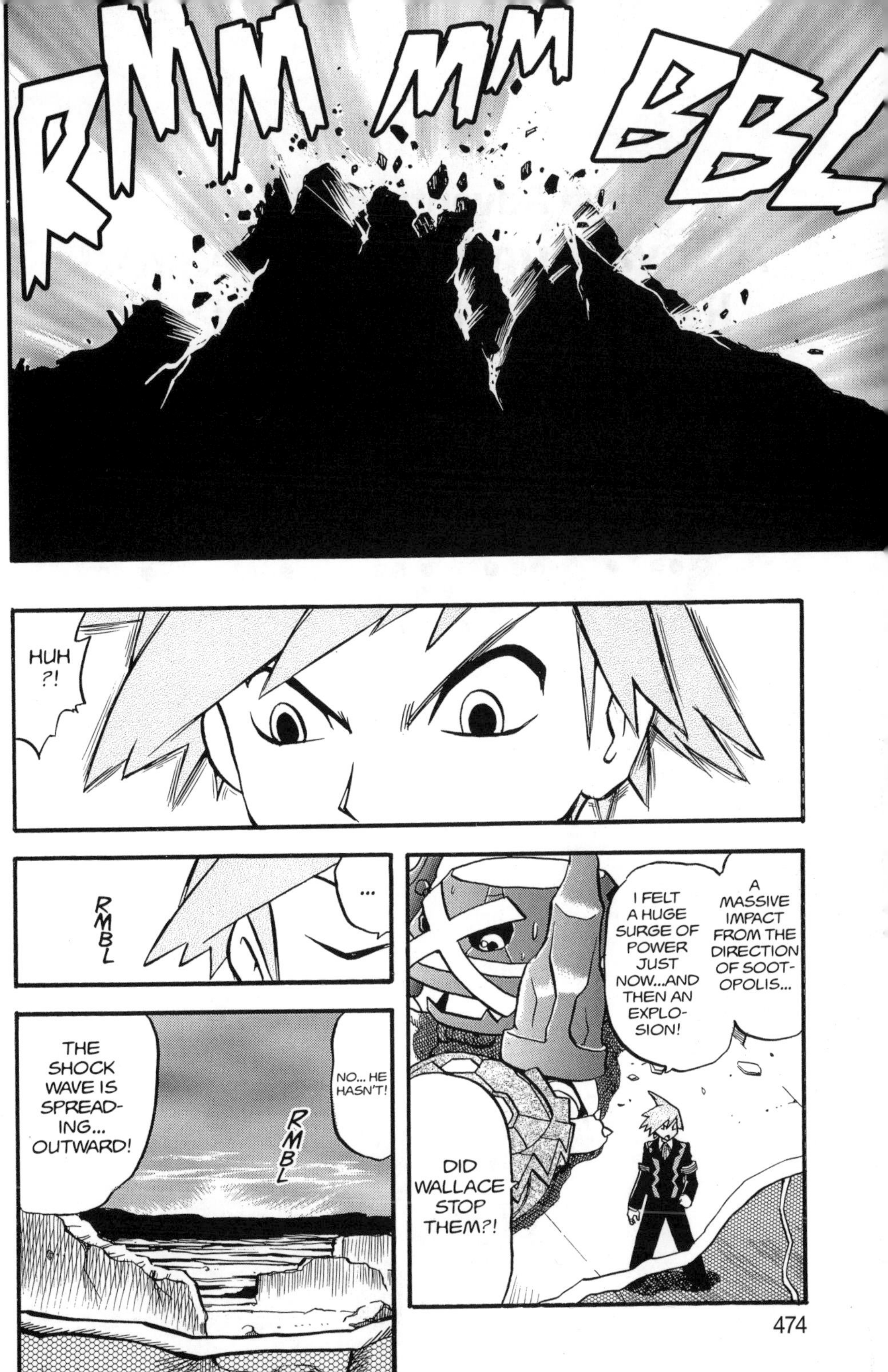
RMMMMMBBL
HUH ?!
A MASSIVE IMPACT FROM THE DIRECTION OF SOOT-OPOLIS...
I FELT A HUGE SURGE OF POWER JUST NOW...AND THEN AN EXPLOSION!
DID WALLACE STOP THEM?!
...
RMBL
NO... HE HASN'T!
RMBL
THE SHOCK WAVE IS SPREADING... OUTWARD!

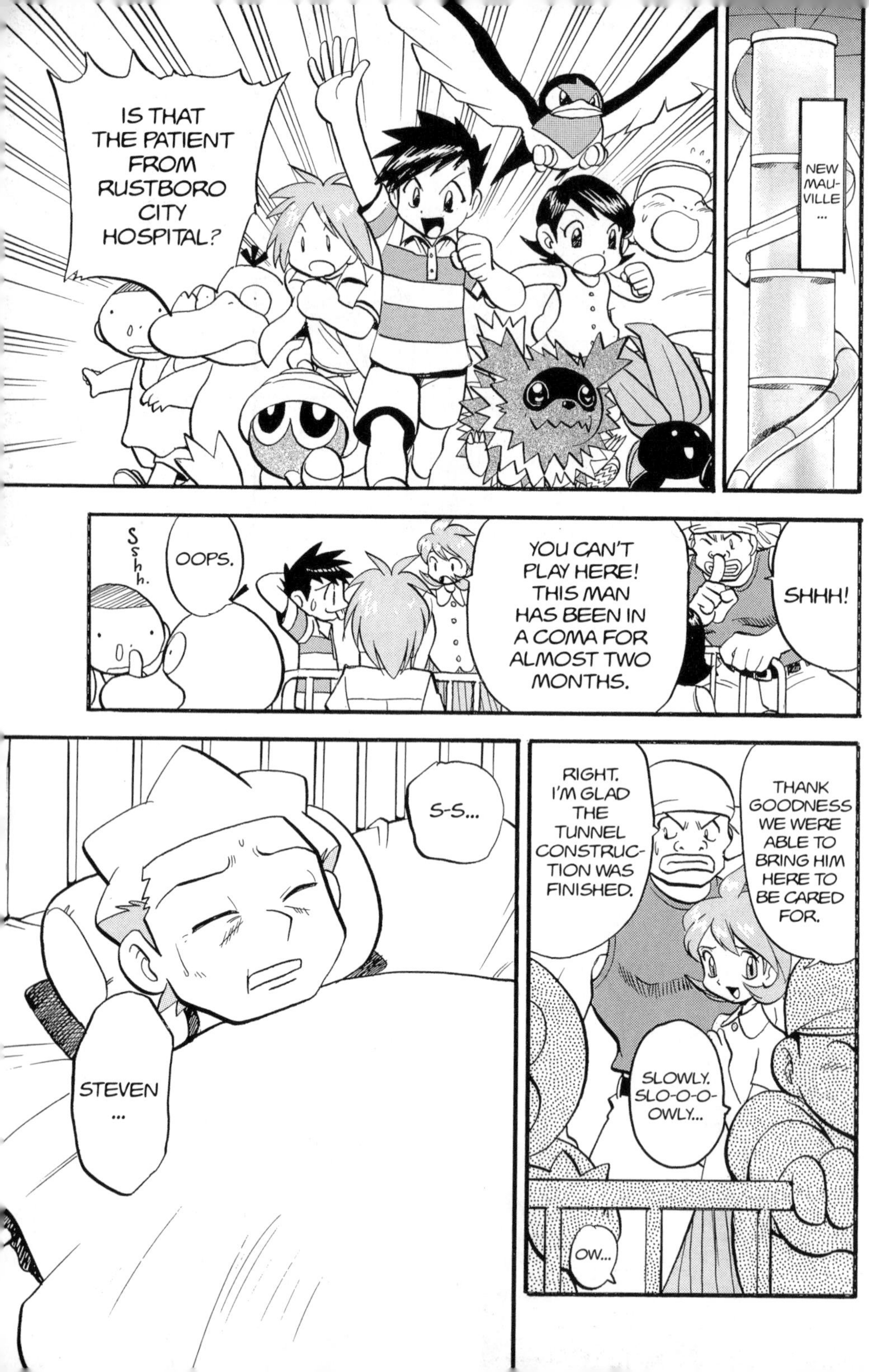
NEW MAUVILLE ...
IS THAT THE PATIENT FROM RUSTBORO CITY HOSPITAL?
SHHH!
YOU CAN'T PLAY HERE! THIS MAN HAS BEEN IN A COMA FOR ALMOST TWO MONTHS.
OOPS.
Sshh.
THANK GOODNESS WE WERE ABLE TO BRING HIM HERE TO BE CARED FOR.
RIGHT. I'M GLAD THE TUNNEL CONSTRUCTION WAS FINISHED.
SLOWLY. SLO-O-O-OWLY...
OW...
S-S...
STEVEN ...

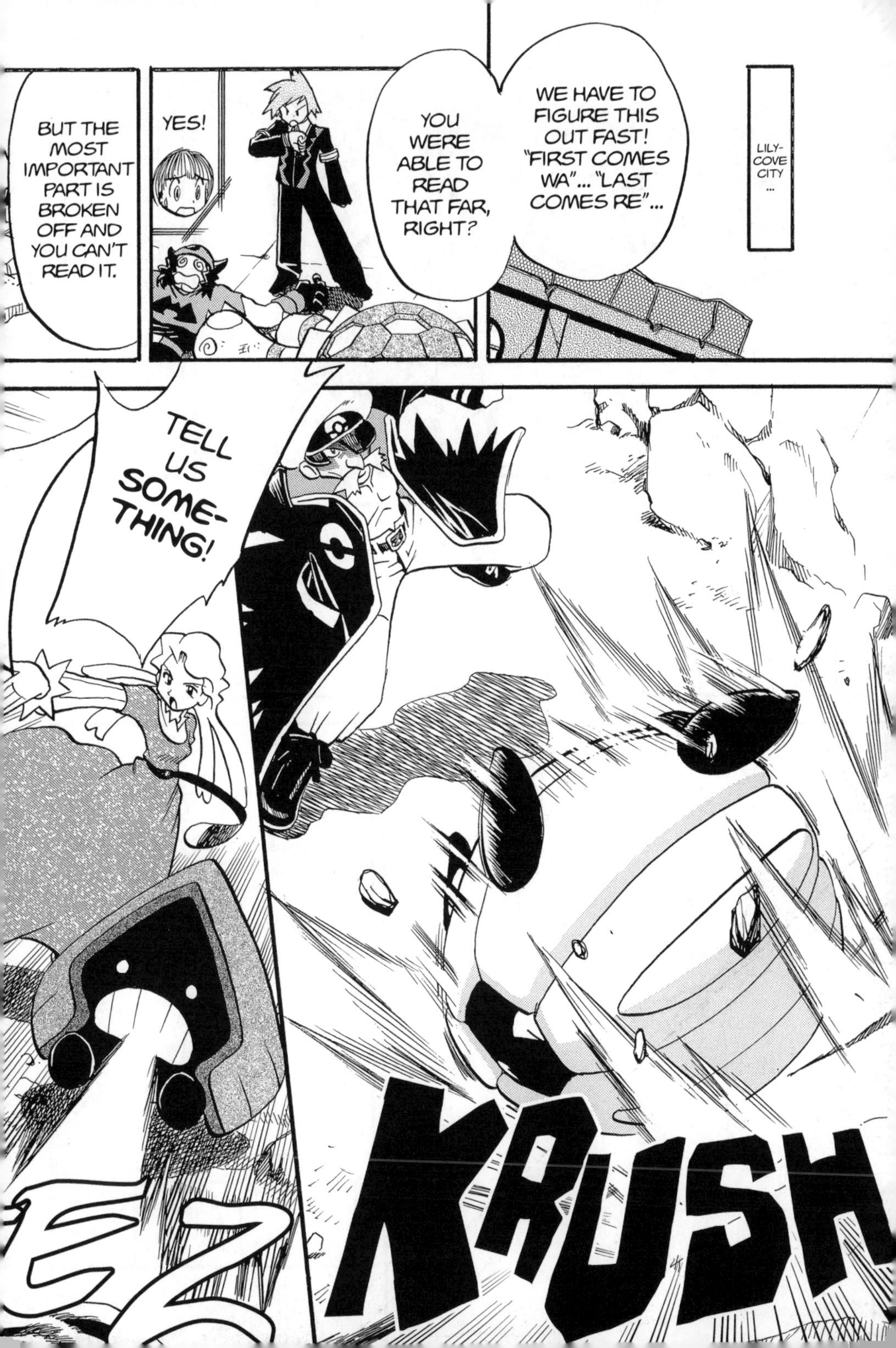
LILY-COVE CITY...
WE HAVE TO FIGURE THIS OUT FAST! "FIRST COMES WA"... "LAST COMES RE"...
YOU WERE ABLE TO READ THAT FAR, RIGHT?
YES!
BUT THE MOST IMPORTANT PART IS BROKEN OFF AND YOU CAN'T READ IT.
TELL US SOME-THING!
KRUSH

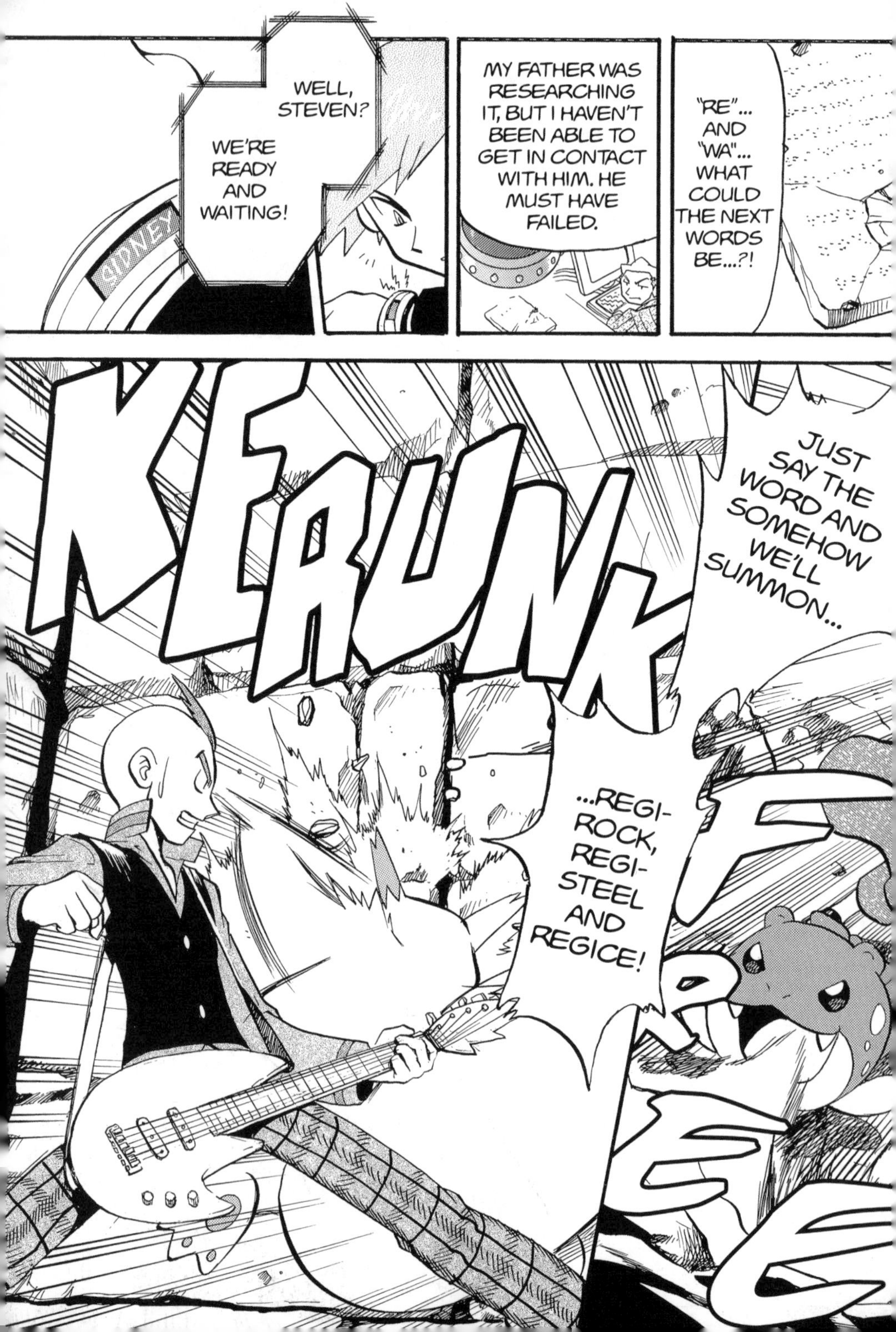
"RE"... AND "WA"... WHAT COULD THE NEXT WORDS BE...?!
MY FATHER WAS RESEARCHING IT, BUT I HAVEN'T BEEN ABLE TO GET IN CONTACT WITH HIM. HE MUST HAVE FAILED.
WELL, STEVEN?
WE'RE READY AND WAITING!
SIDNEY
KERUNK
JUST SAY THE WORD AND SOMEHOW WE'LL SUMMON...
...REGIROCK, REGISTEEL AND REGICE!

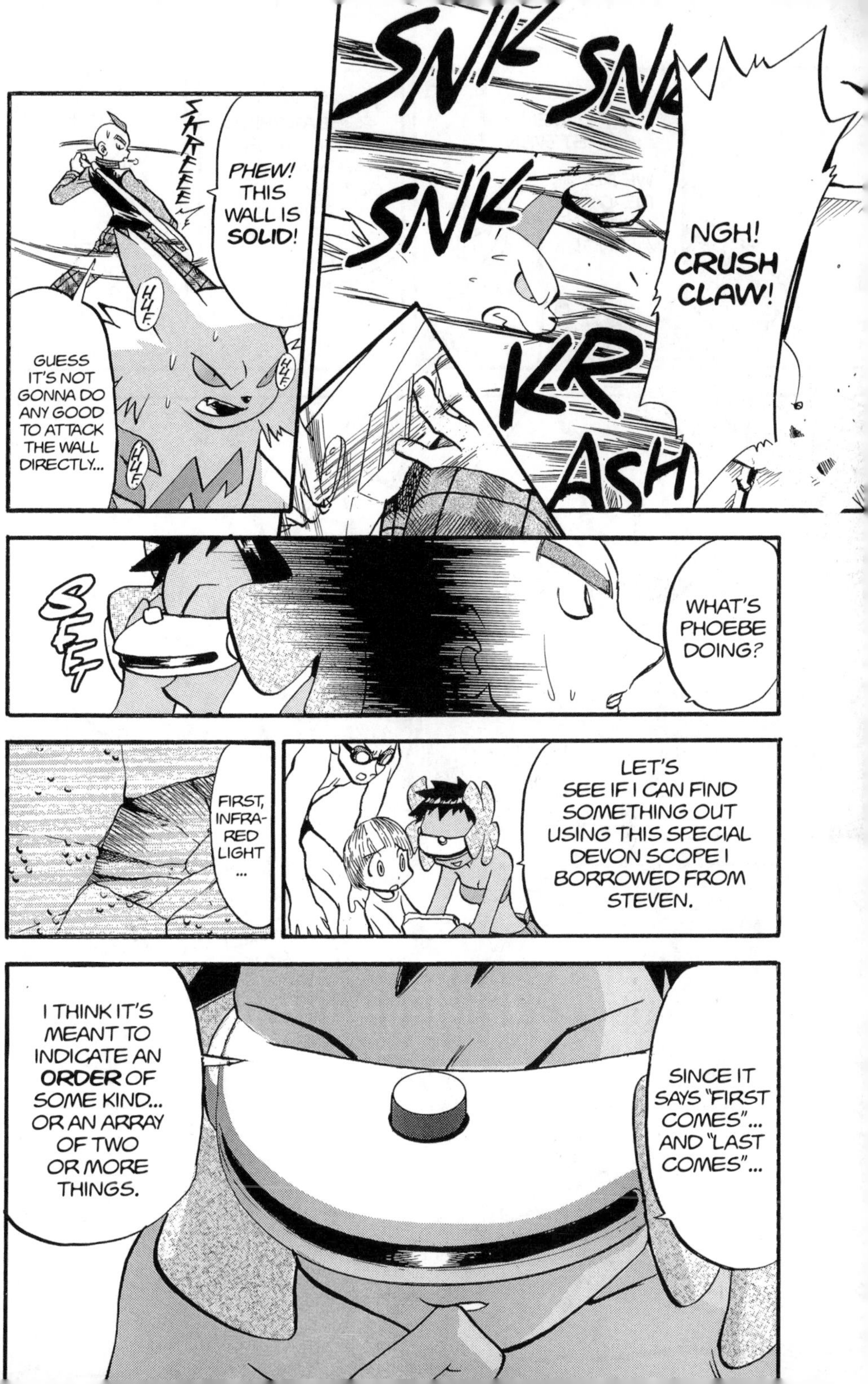
SNK SNK
SNK
NGH! CRUSH CLAW!
KRASH
SKREEEE
PHEW! THIS WALL IS SOLID!
HUF. HUF. HUF. HUF.
GUESS IT'S NOT GONNA DO ANY GOOD TO ATTACK THE WALL DIRECTLY...
WHAT'S PHOEBE DOING?
SFFT
LET'S SEE IF I CAN FIND SOMETHING OUT USING THIS SPECIAL DEVON SCOPE I BORROWED FROM STEVEN.
FIRST, INFRARED LIGHT ...
SINCE IT SAYS "FIRST COMES"... AND "LAST COMES"...
I THINK IT'S MEANT TO INDICATE AN ORDER OF SOME KIND... OR AN ARRAY OF TWO OR MORE THINGS.

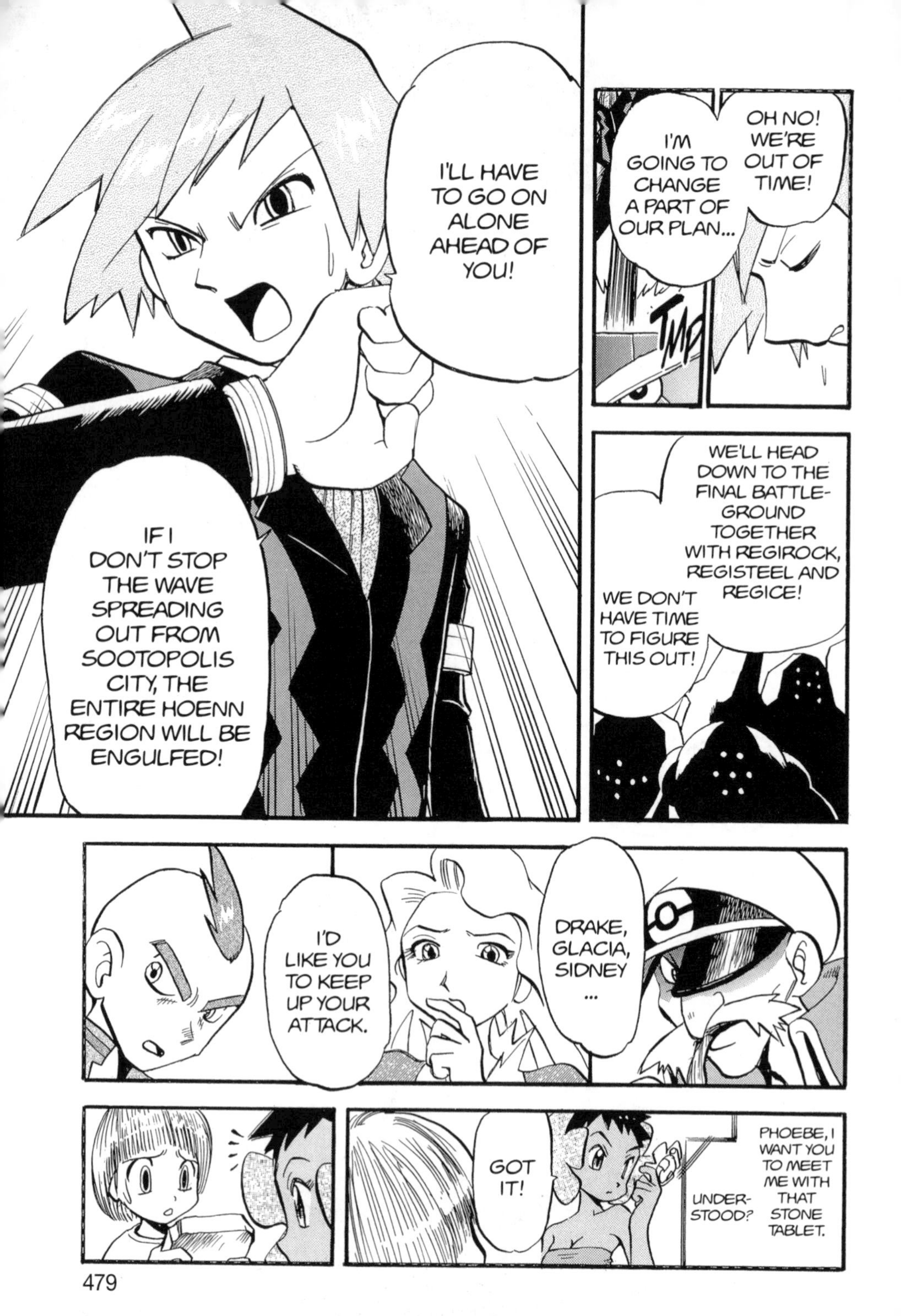
OH NO! WE'RE OUT OF TIME!
I'M GOING TO CHANGE A PART OF OUR PLAN...
TMP
WE'LL HEAD DOWN TO THE FINAL BATTLE-GROUND TOGETHER WITH REGIROCK, REGISTEEL AND REGICE!
WE DON'T HAVE TIME TO FIGURE THIS OUT!
I'LL HAVE TO GO ON ALONE AHEAD OF YOU!
IF I DON'T STOP THE WAVE SPREADING OUT FROM SOOTOPOLIS CITY, THE ENTIRE HOENN REGION WILL BE ENGULFED!
DRAKE, GLACIA, SIDNEY ...
I'D LIKE YOU TO KEEP UP YOUR ATTACK.
PHOEBE, I WANT YOU TO MEET ME WITH THAT STONE TABLET.
UNDER-STOOD?
GOT IT!

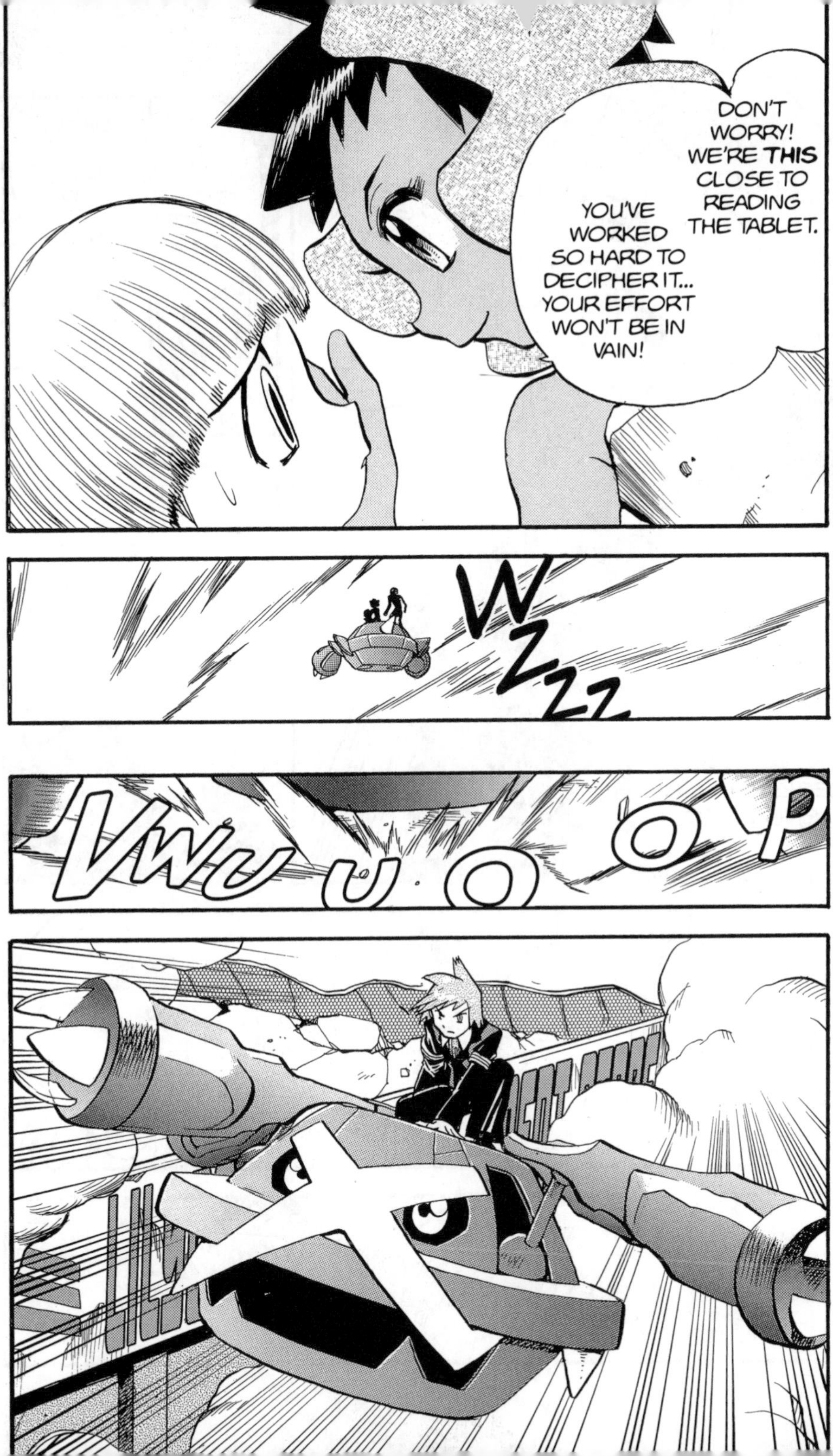
DON'T WORRY! WE'RE **THIS** CLOSE TO READING THE TABLET.
YOU'VE WORKED SO HARD TO DECIPHER IT... YOUR EFFORT WON'T BE IN VAIN!
WZZZ
VWUUOOOP

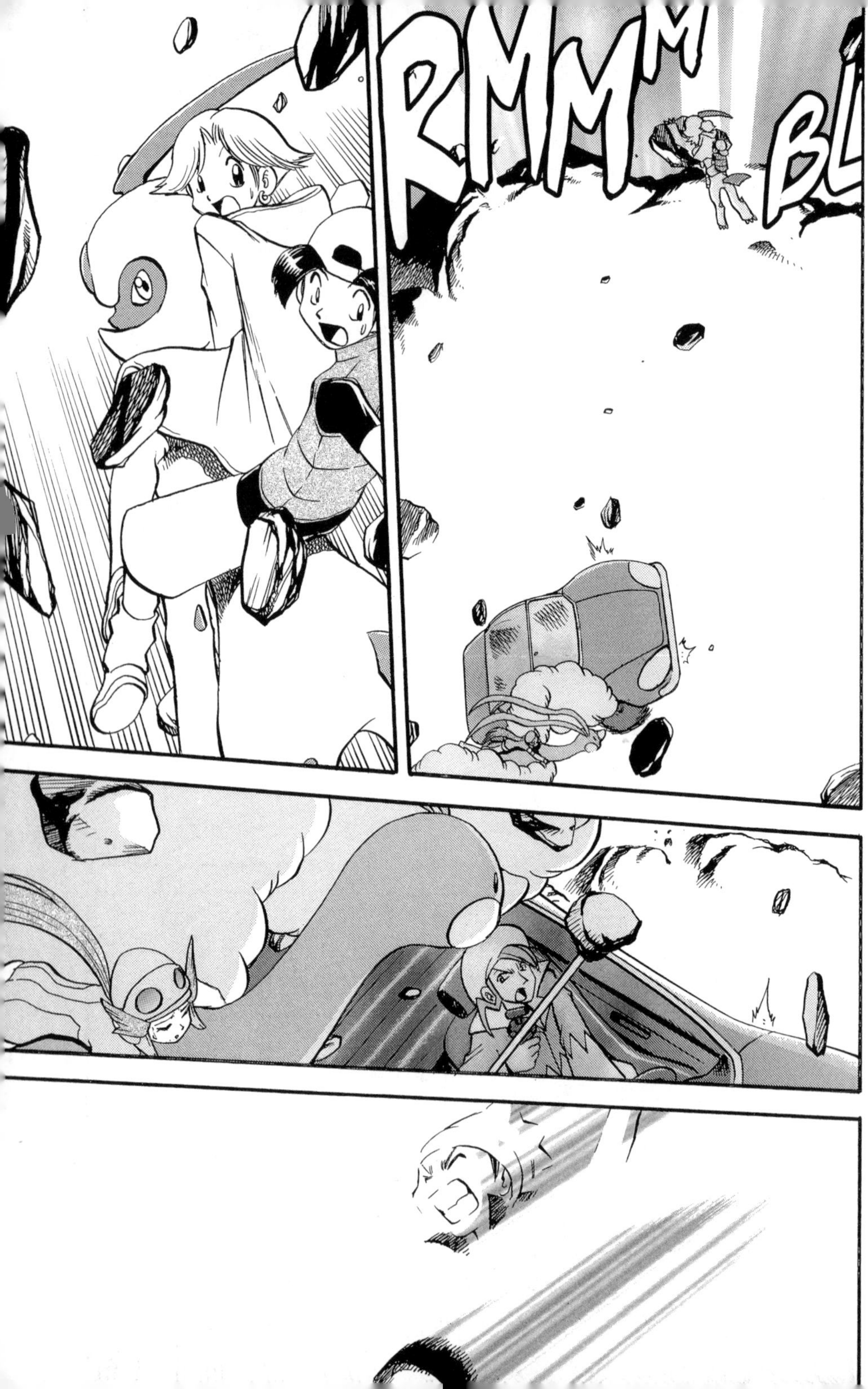
RMMM
BL

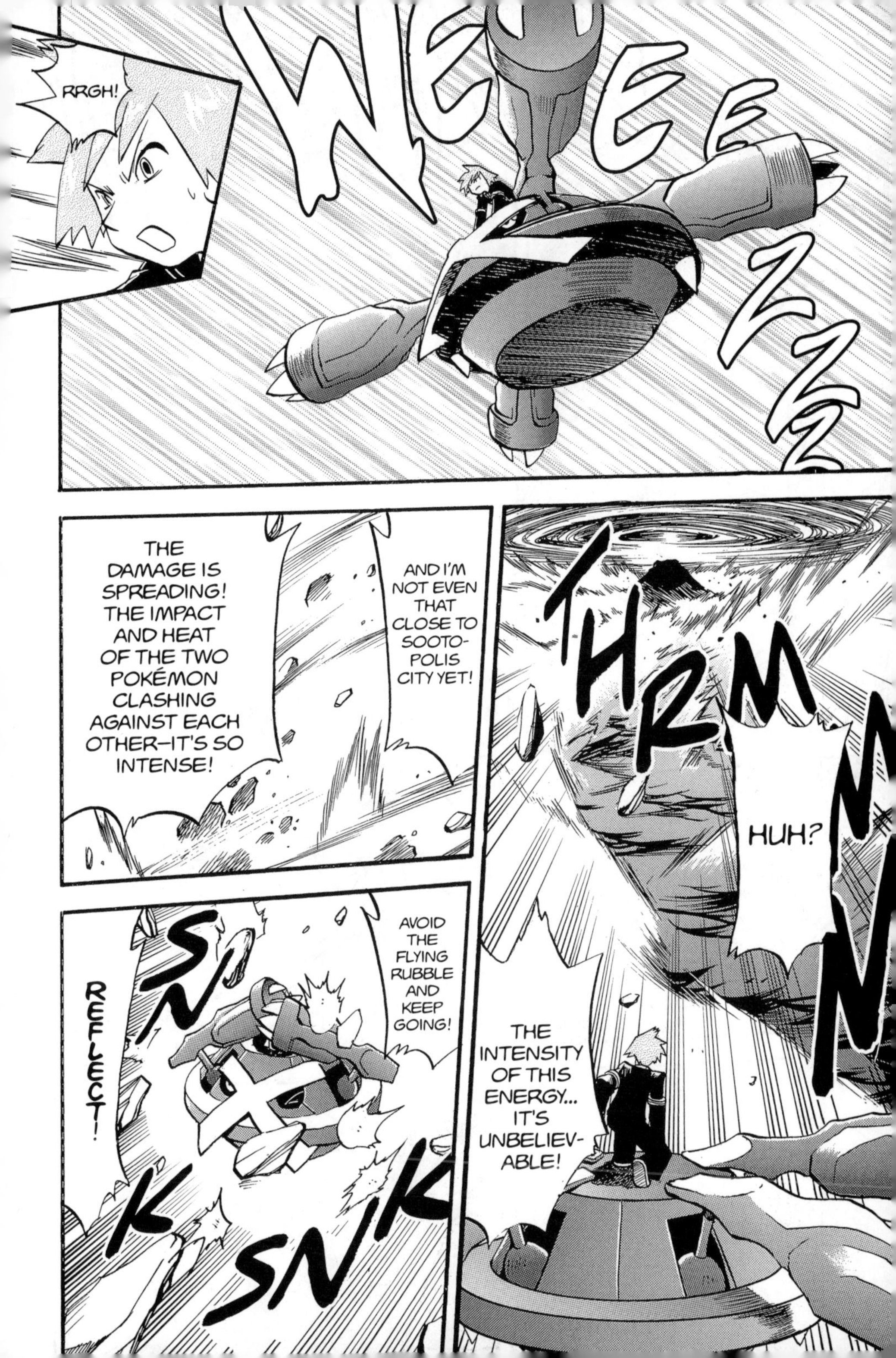
WEEEZZZZ
RRGH!
THRMMMM
HUH?
THE INTENSITY OF THIS ENERGY... IT'S UNBELIEV-ABLE!
AND I'M NOT EVEN THAT CLOSE TO SOOTO-POLIS CITY YET!
THE DAMAGE IS SPREADING! THE IMPACT AND HEAT OF THE TWO POKÉMON CLASHING AGAINST EACH OTHER—IT'S SO INTENSE!
AVOID THE FLYING RUBBLE AND KEEP GOING!
SNK
REFLECT!
SNK SNK

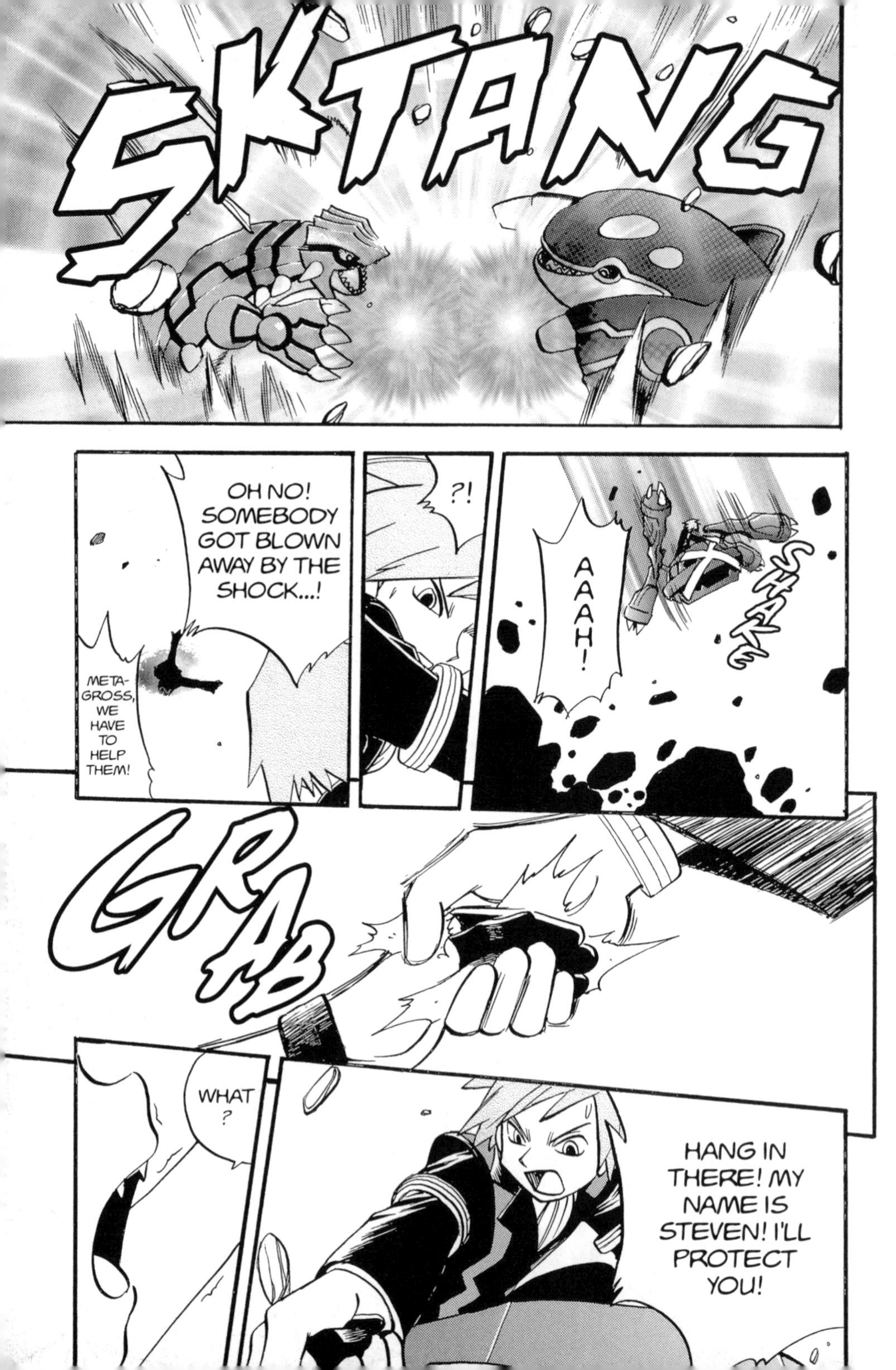
SKTANG
AAAAH!
SHAKE
?!
OH NO! SOMEBODY GOT BLOWN AWAY BY THE SHOCK...!
META-GROSS, WE HAVE TO HELP THEM!
GRAB
HANG IN THERE! MY NAME IS STEVEN! I'LL PROTECT YOU!
WHAT?

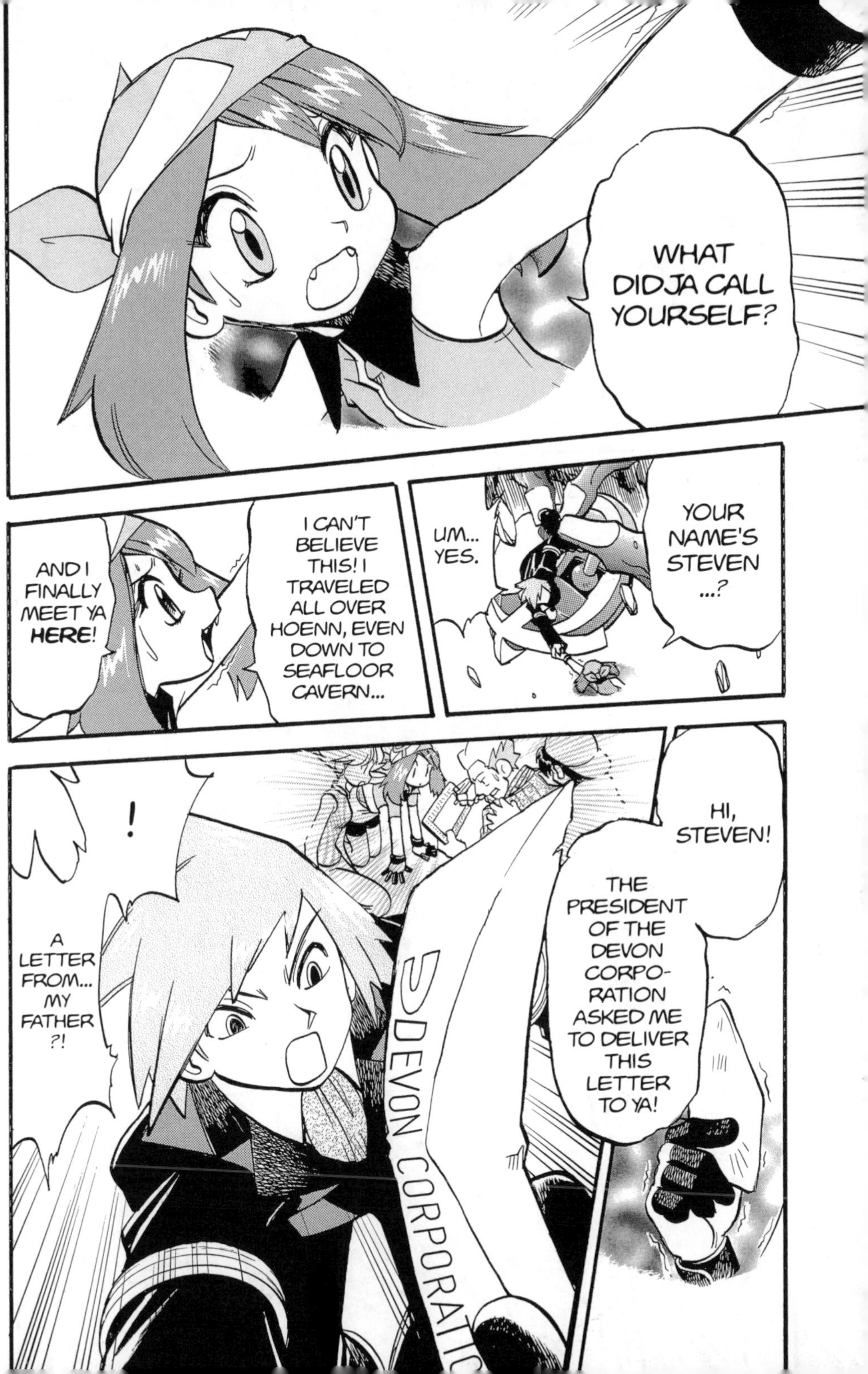
WHAT DIDJA CALL YOURSELF?
YOUR NAME'S STEVEN ...?
UM... YES.
I CAN'T BELIEVE THIS! I TRAVELED ALL OVER HOENN, EVEN DOWN TO SEAFLOOR CAVERN...
AND I FINALLY MEET YA **HERE**!
HI, STEVEN!
THE PRESIDENT OF THE DEVON CORPORATION ASKED ME TO DELIVER THIS LETTER TO YA!
DEVON CORPORATIO
!
A LETTER FROM... MY FATHER ?!

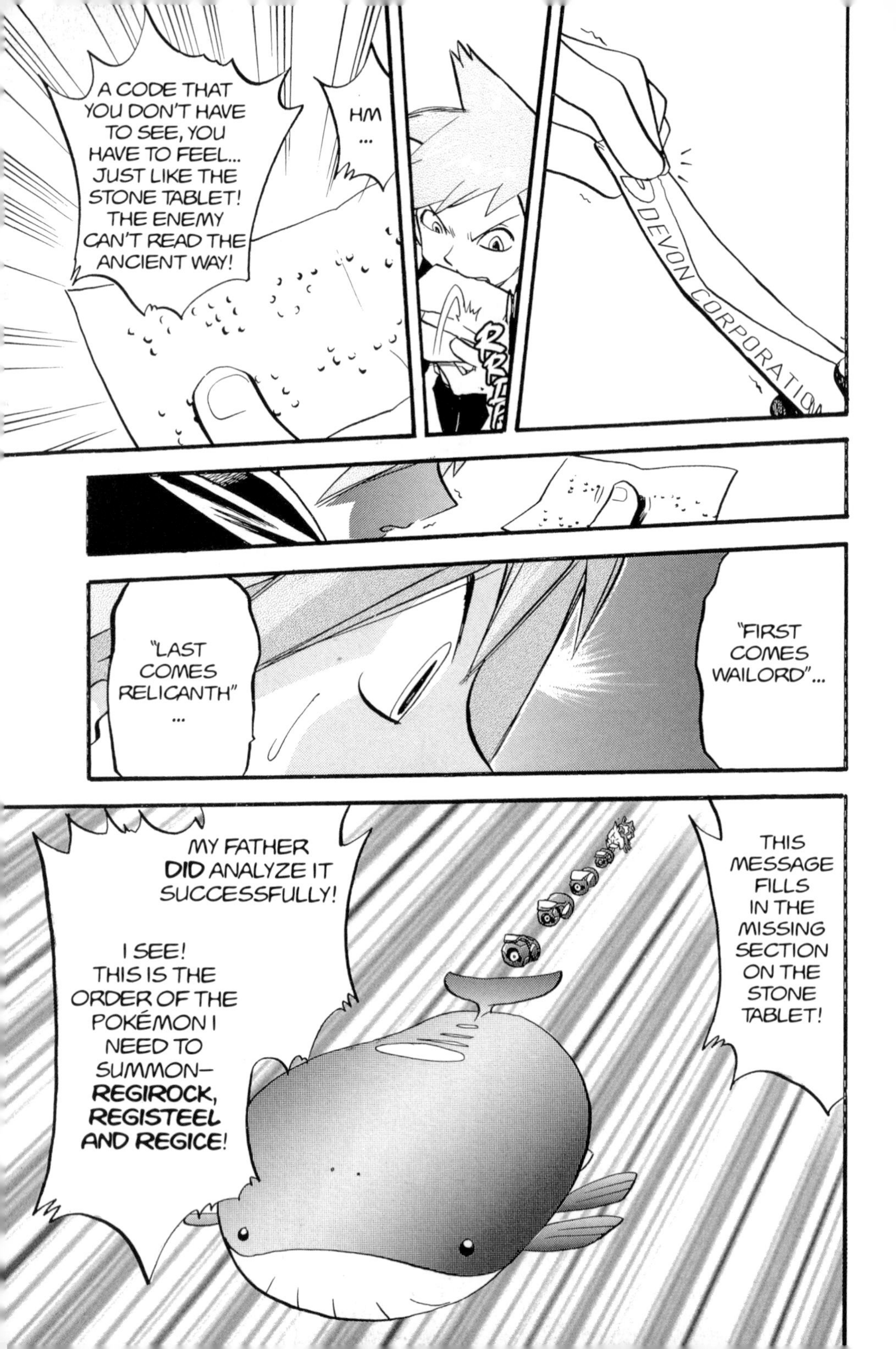
DEVON CORPORATION
HM ...
A CODE THAT YOU DON'T HAVE TO SEE, YOU HAVE TO FEEL... JUST LIKE THE STONE TABLET! THE ENEMY CAN'T READ THE ANCIENT WAY!
"FIRST COMES WAILORD"...
"LAST COMES RELICANTH" ...
THIS MESSAGE FILLS IN THE MISSING SECTION ON THE STONE TABLET!
MY FATHER **DID** ANALYZE IT SUCCESSFULLY!
I SEE! THIS IS THE ORDER OF THE POKÉMON I NEED TO SUMMON— **REGIROCK, REGISTEEL AND REGICE**!

● Adventure 254 ●
A Royal Rumble with Regirock, Regice and Registeel, Part 2

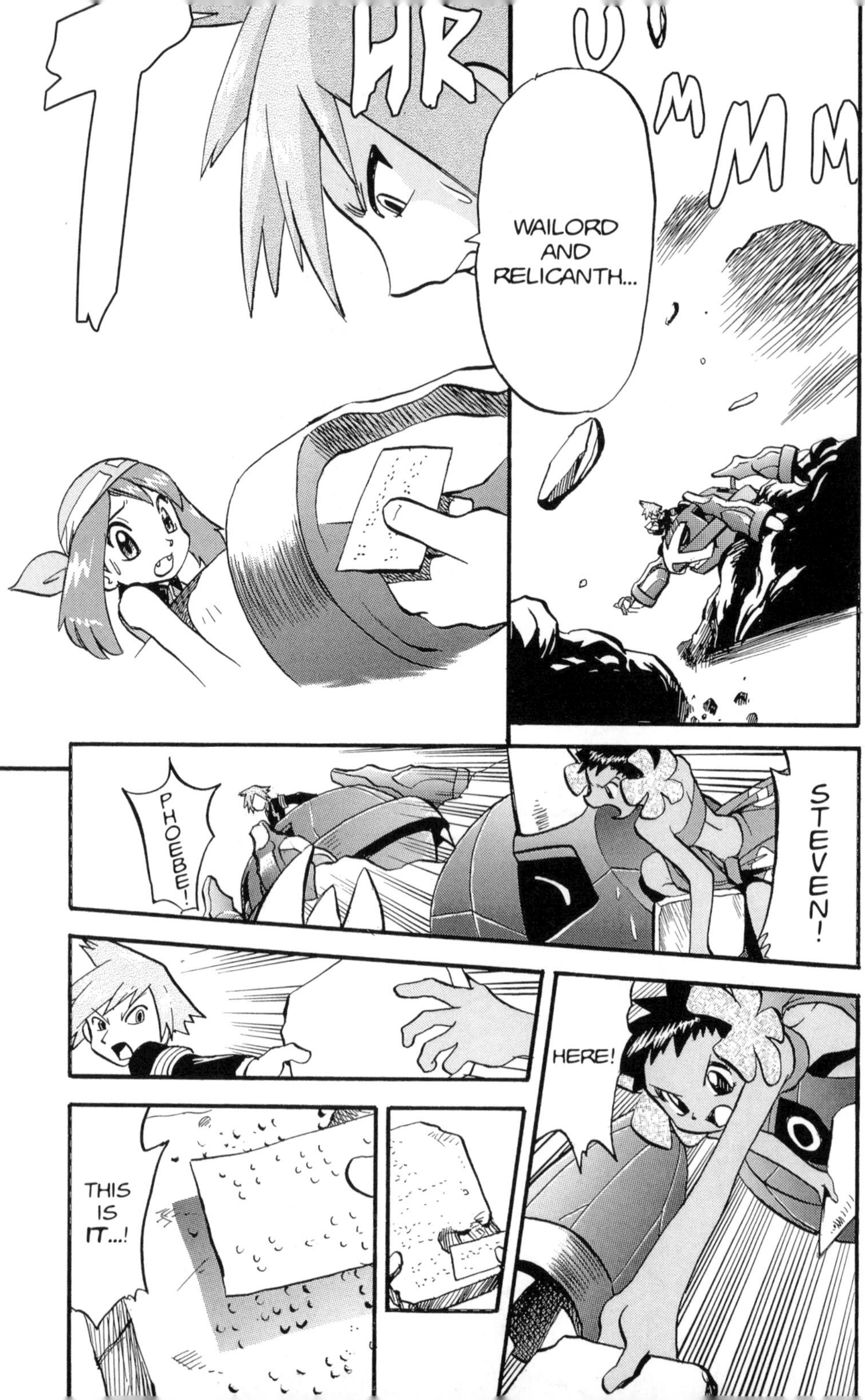
HRUMMMM
WAILORD AND RELICANTH...
STEVEN!
PHOEBE!
HERE!
THIS IS IT...!

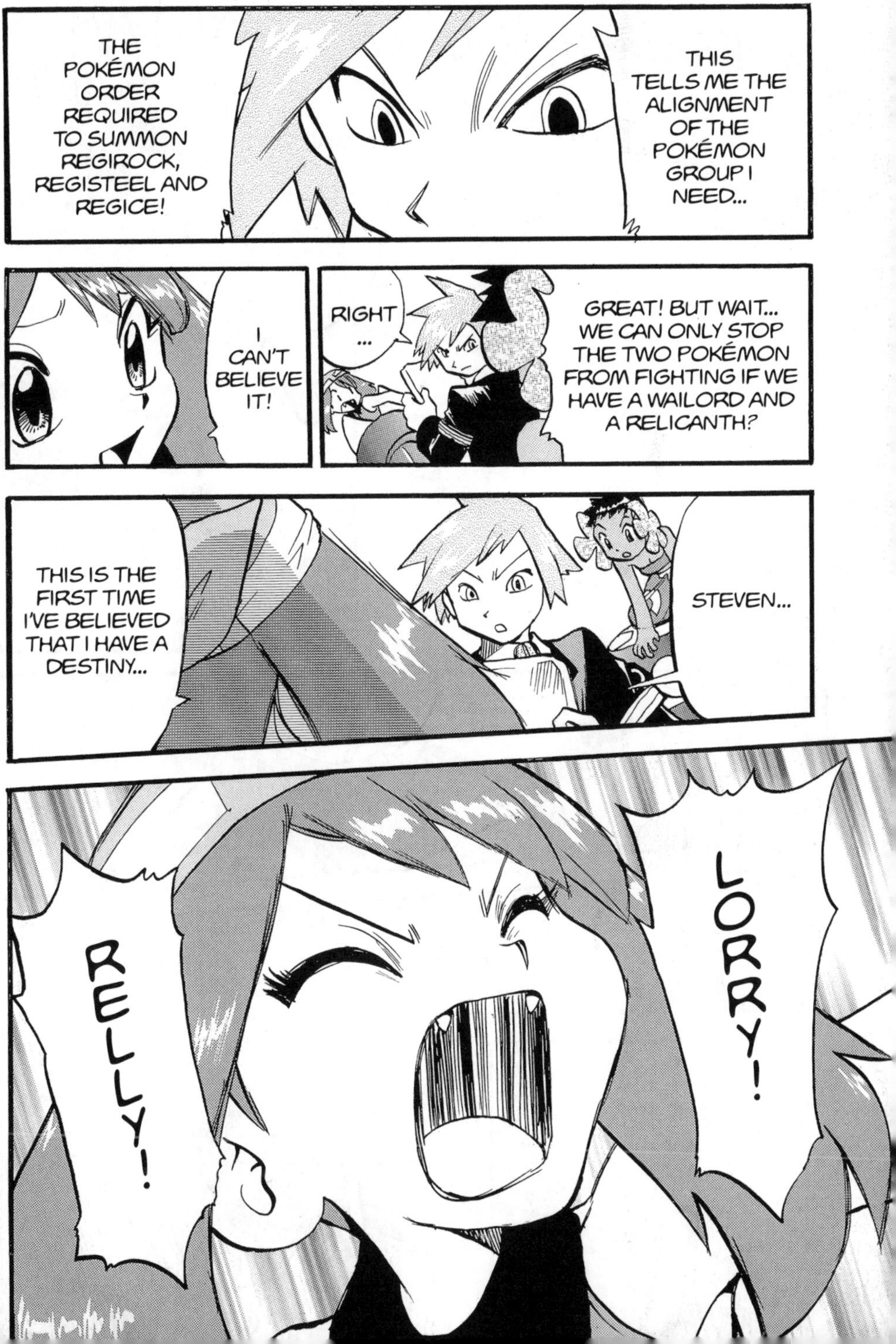
THIS TELLS ME THE ALIGNMENT OF THE POKÉMON GROUP I NEED...
THE POKÉMON ORDER REQUIRED TO SUMMON REGIROCK, REGISTEEL AND REGICE!
GREAT! BUT WAIT... WE CAN ONLY STOP THE TWO POKÉMON FROM FIGHTING IF WE HAVE A WAILORD AND A RELICANTH?
RIGHT ...
I CAN'T BELIEVE IT!
STEVEN...
THIS IS THE FIRST TIME I'VE BELIEVED THAT I HAVE A DESTINY...
LORRY!
RELLY!

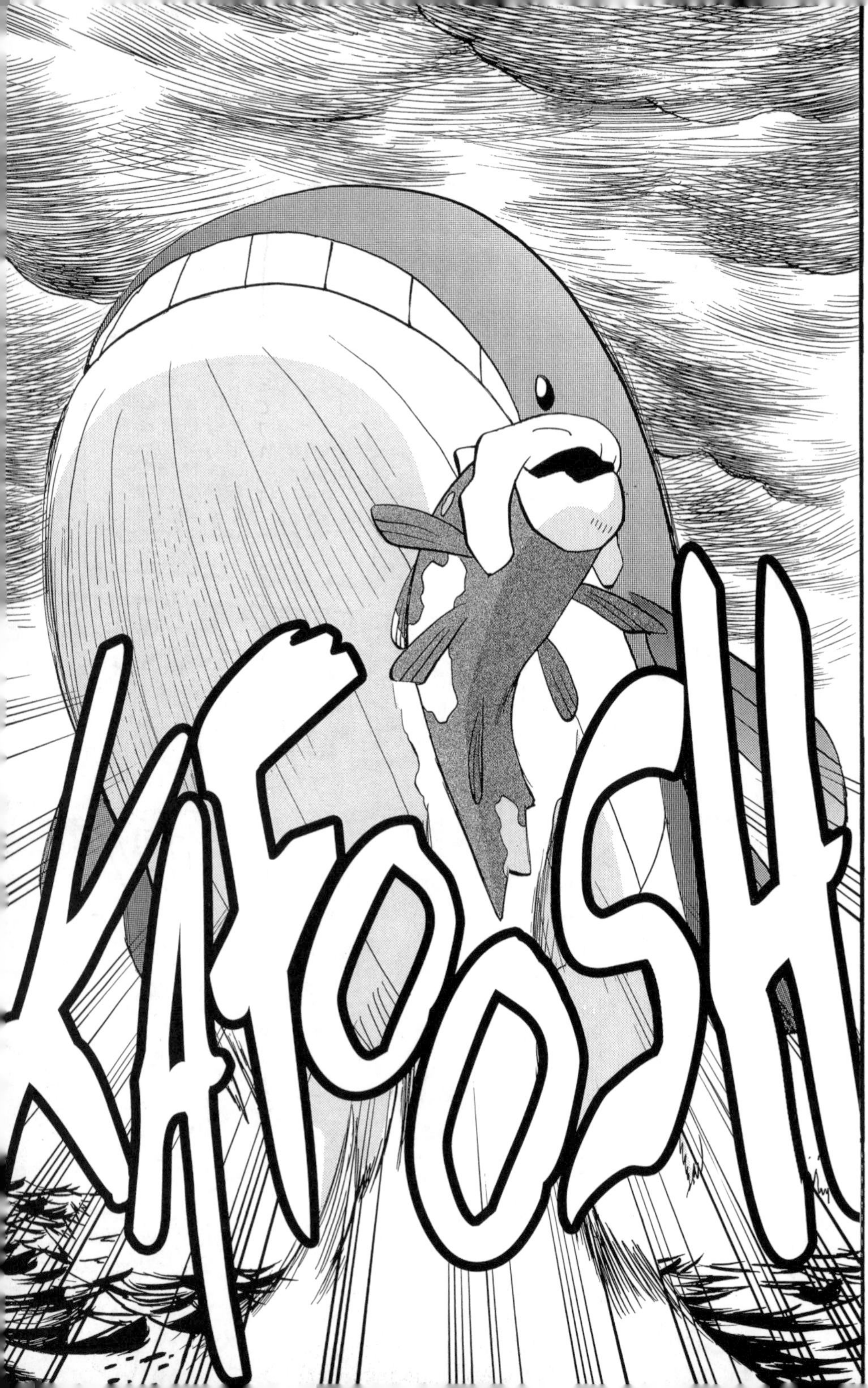
KAFOOSH

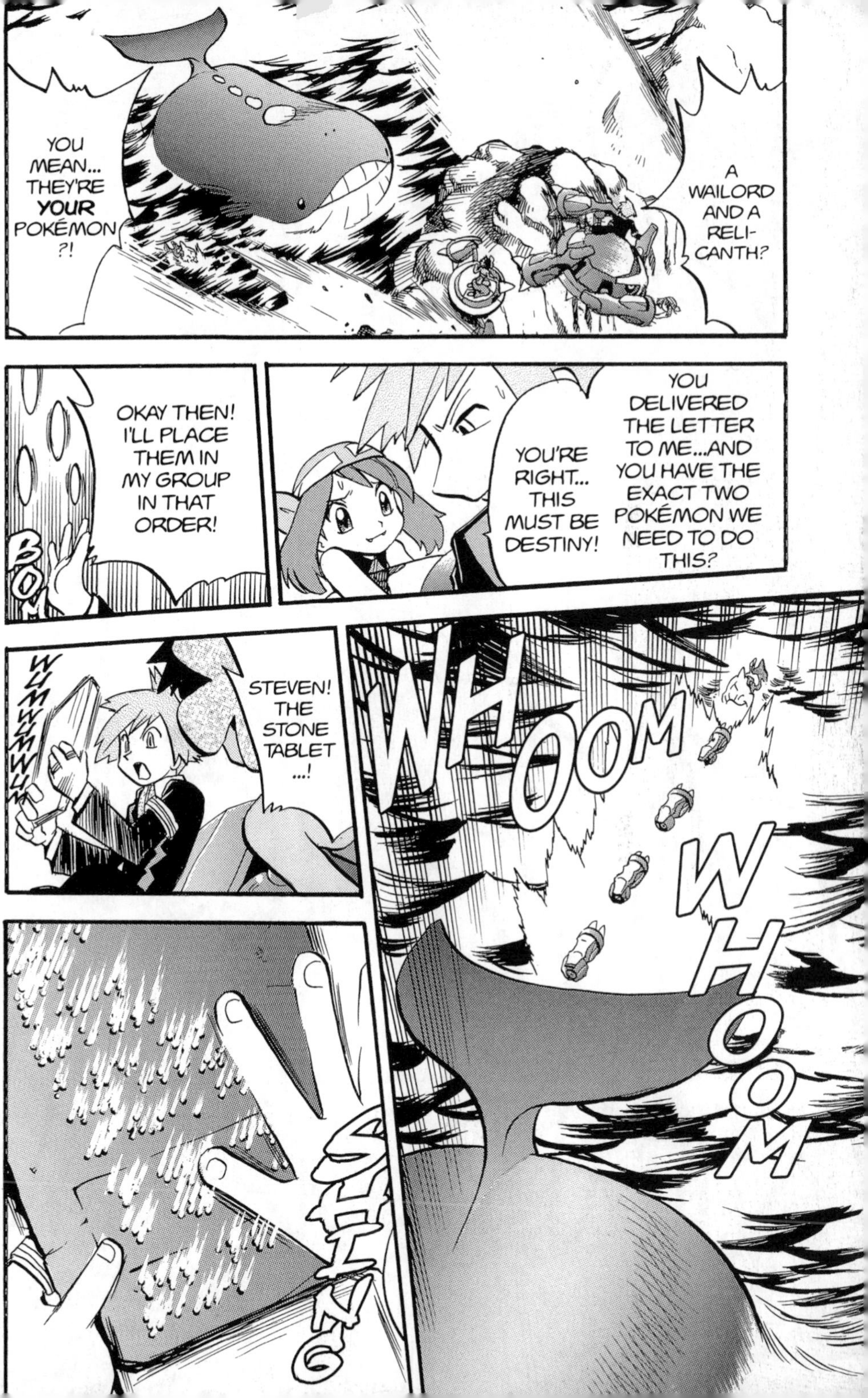
A WAILORD AND A RELI-CANTH?
YOU MEAN... THEY'RE **YOUR** POKÉMON?!
YOU DELIVERED THE LETTER TO ME...AND YOU HAVE THE EXACT TWO POKÉMON WE NEED TO DO THIS?
YOU'RE RIGHT... THIS MUST BE DESTINY!
OKAY THEN! I'LL PLACE THEM IN MY GROUP IN THAT ORDER!
BOM
WHOOM
WHOOM
STEVEN! THE STONE TABLET...!
WUMWUMWUM
SHING

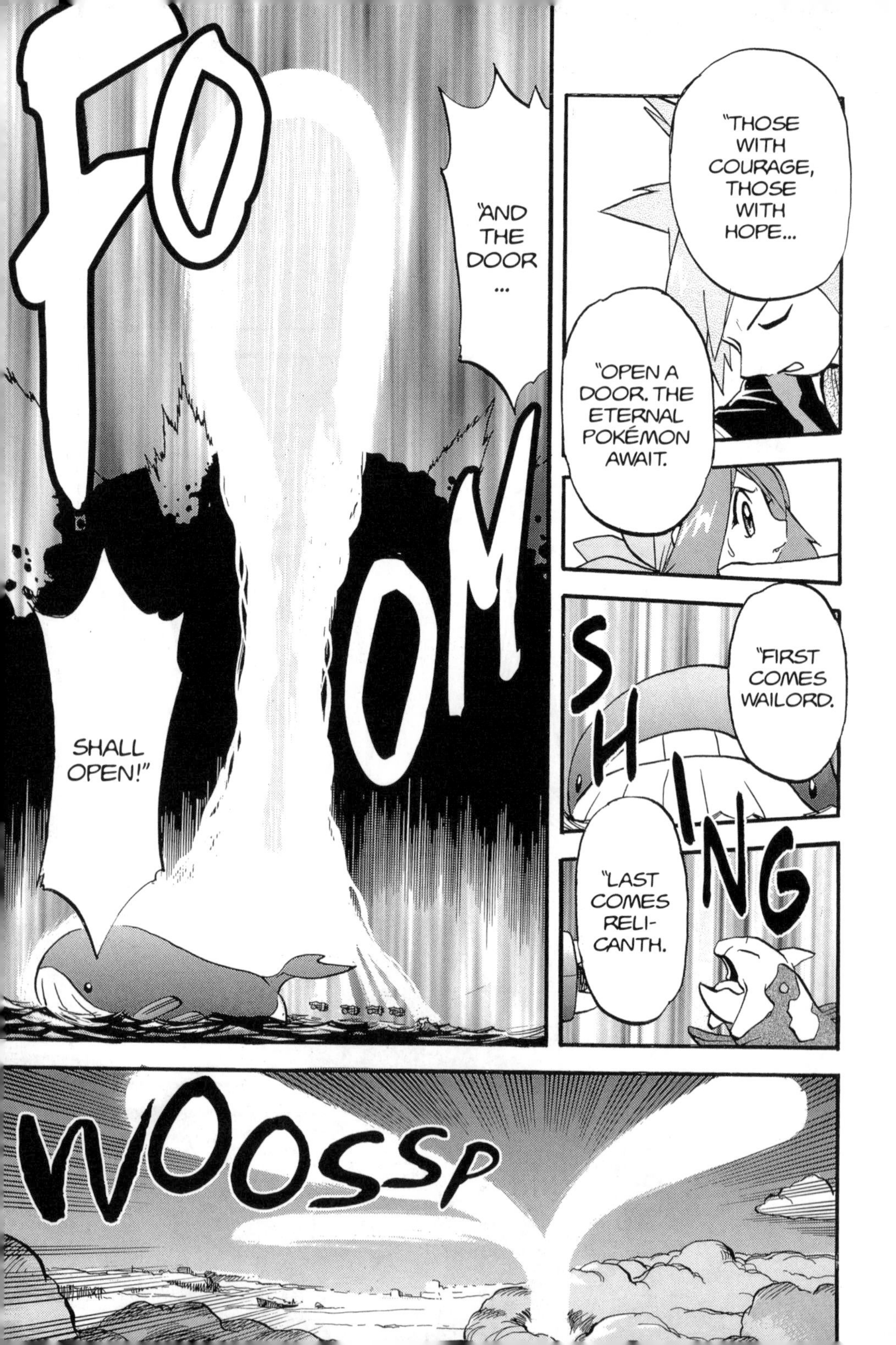
"THOSE WITH COURAGE, THOSE WITH HOPE...
"OPEN A DOOR. THE ETERNAL POKÉMON AWAIT.
"FIRST COMES WAILORD.
SHING
"LAST COMES RELI-CANTH.
"AND THE DOOR ...
FOOM
SHALL OPEN!"
WOOSSP

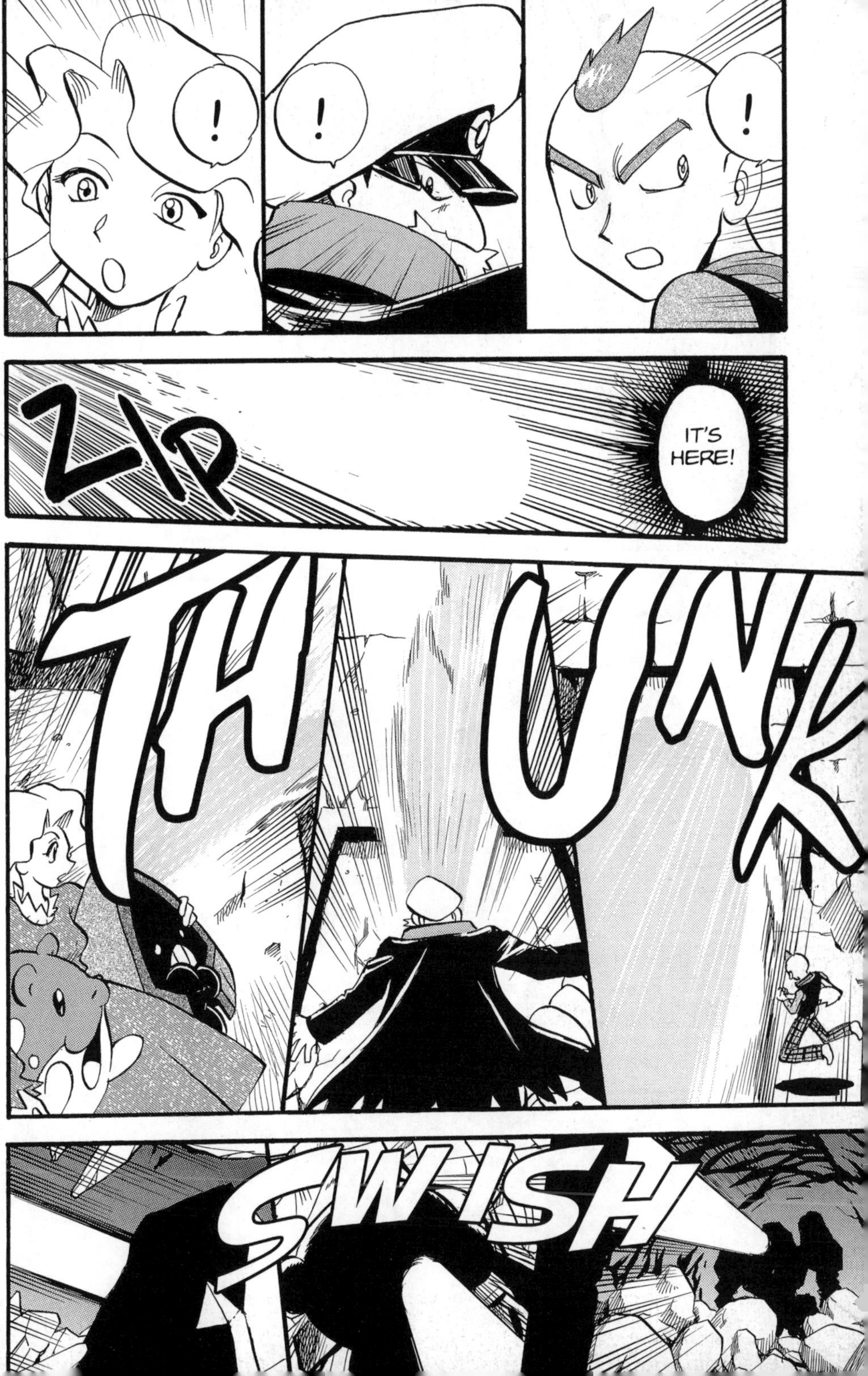
!
!
!
IT'S HERE!
ZIP
THUNK
SWISH

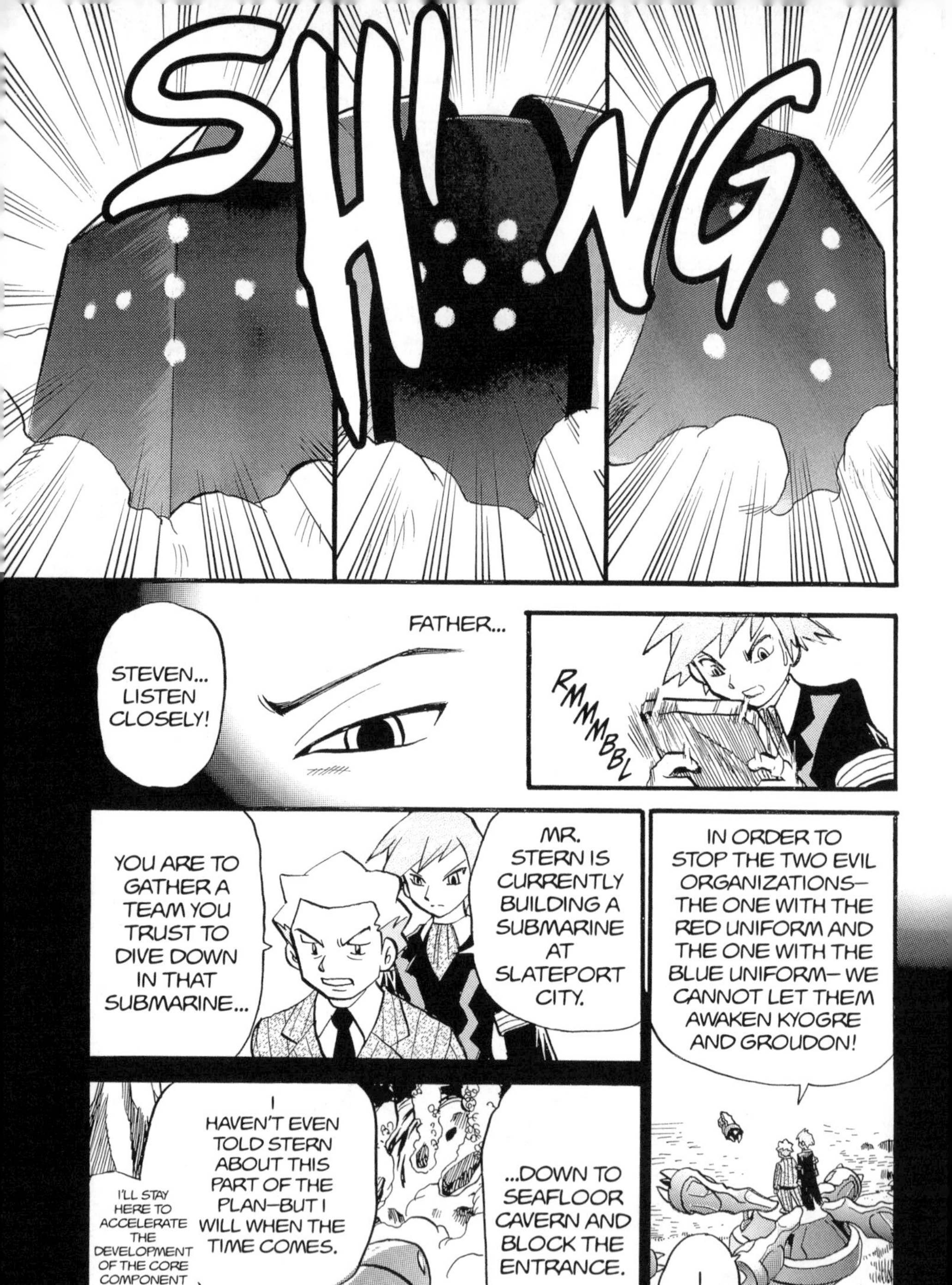
SHING
RMMMBBL
FATHER...
STEVEN... LISTEN CLOSELY!
IN ORDER TO STOP THE TWO EVIL ORGANIZATIONS—THE ONE WITH THE RED UNIFORM AND THE ONE WITH THE BLUE UNIFORM—WE CANNOT LET THEM AWAKEN KYOGRE AND GROUDON!
MR. STERN IS CURRENTLY BUILDING A SUBMARINE AT SLATEPORT CITY.
YOU ARE TO GATHER A TEAM YOU TRUST TO DIVE DOWN IN THAT SUBMARINE...
I SEE.
...DOWN TO SEAFLOOR CAVERN AND BLOCK THE ENTRANCE.
I HAVEN'T EVEN TOLD STERN ABOUT THIS PART OF THE PLAN—BUT I WILL WHEN THE TIME COMES.
I'LL STAY HERE TO ACCELERATE THE DEVELOPMENT OF THE CORE COMPONENT OF THE SUBMARINE. YOU'LL NEED IT TO DIVE THAT FAR DOWN.

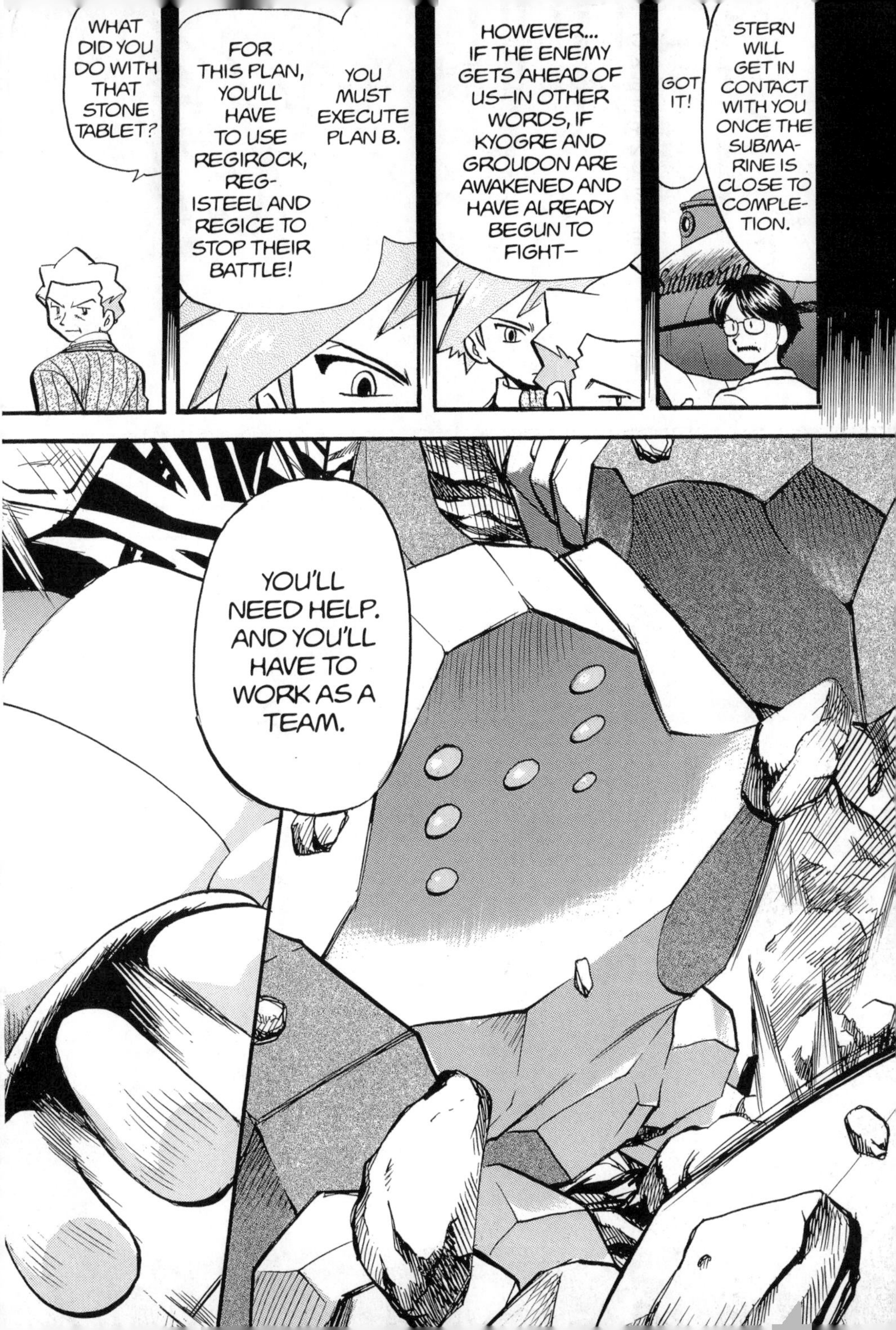
STERN WILL GET IN CONTACT WITH YOU ONCE THE SUBMARINE IS CLOSE TO COMPLETION.
GOT IT!
HOWEVER... IF THE ENEMY GETS AHEAD OF US—IN OTHER WORDS, IF KYOGRE AND GROUDON ARE AWAKENED AND HAVE ALREADY BEGUN TO FIGHT—
YOU MUST EXECUTE PLAN B.
FOR THIS PLAN, YOU'LL HAVE TO USE REGIROCK, REGISTEEL AND REGICE TO STOP THEIR BATTLE!
WHAT DID YOU DO WITH THAT STONE TABLET?
YOU'LL NEED HELP. AND YOU'LL HAVE TO WORK AS A TEAM.

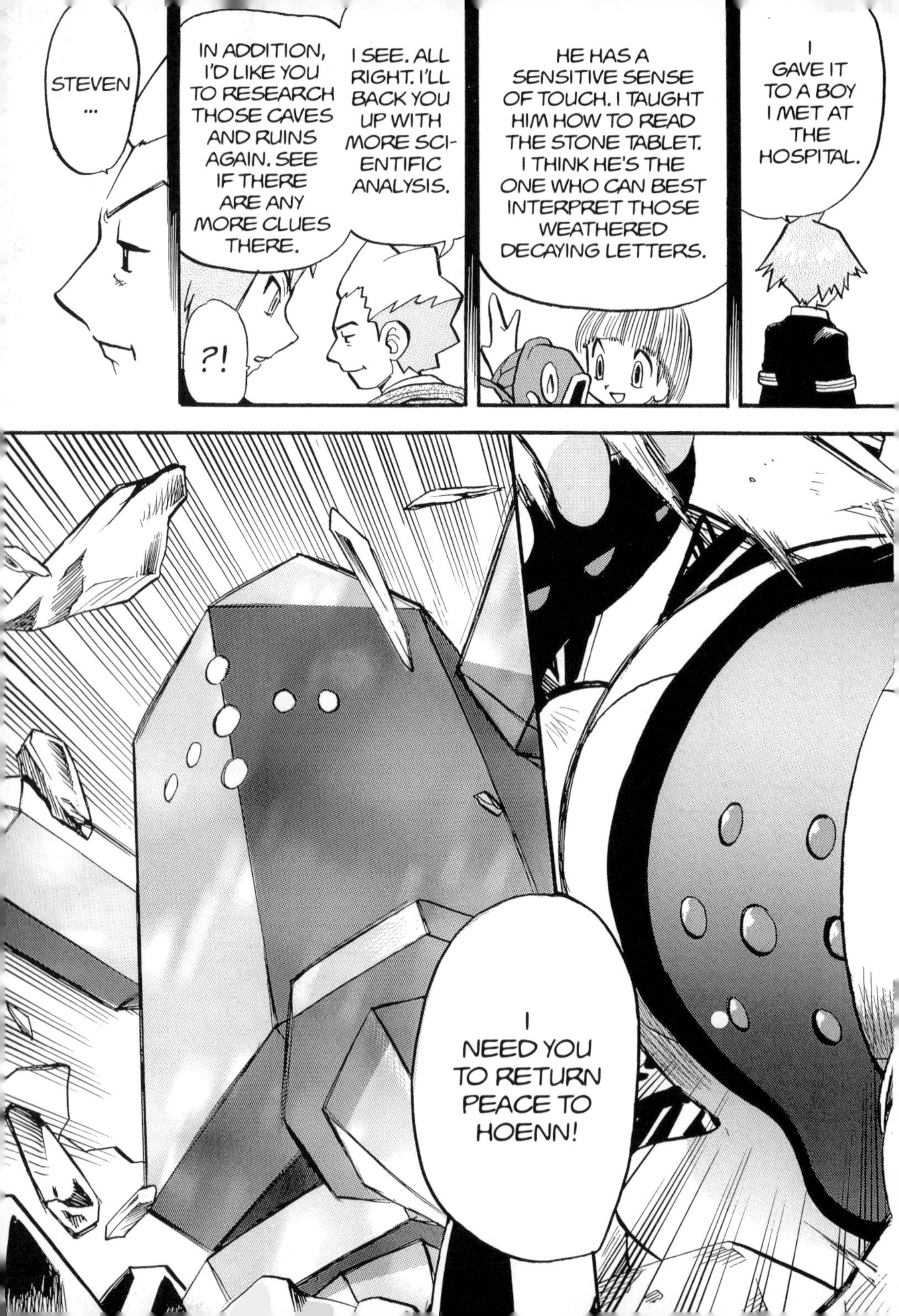
I GAVE IT TO A BOY I MET AT THE HOSPITAL.
HE HAS A SENSITIVE SENSE OF TOUCH. I TAUGHT HIM HOW TO READ THE STONE TABLET. I THINK HE'S THE ONE WHO CAN BEST INTERPRET THOSE WEATHERED DECAYING LETTERS.
IN ADDITION, I'D LIKE YOU TO RESEARCH THOSE CAVES AND RUINS AGAIN. SEE IF THERE ARE ANY MORE CLUES THERE.
I SEE. ALL RIGHT. I'LL BACK YOU UP WITH MORE SCI-ENTIFIC ANALYSIS.
?!
STEVEN...
I NEED YOU TO RETURN PEACE TO HOENN!

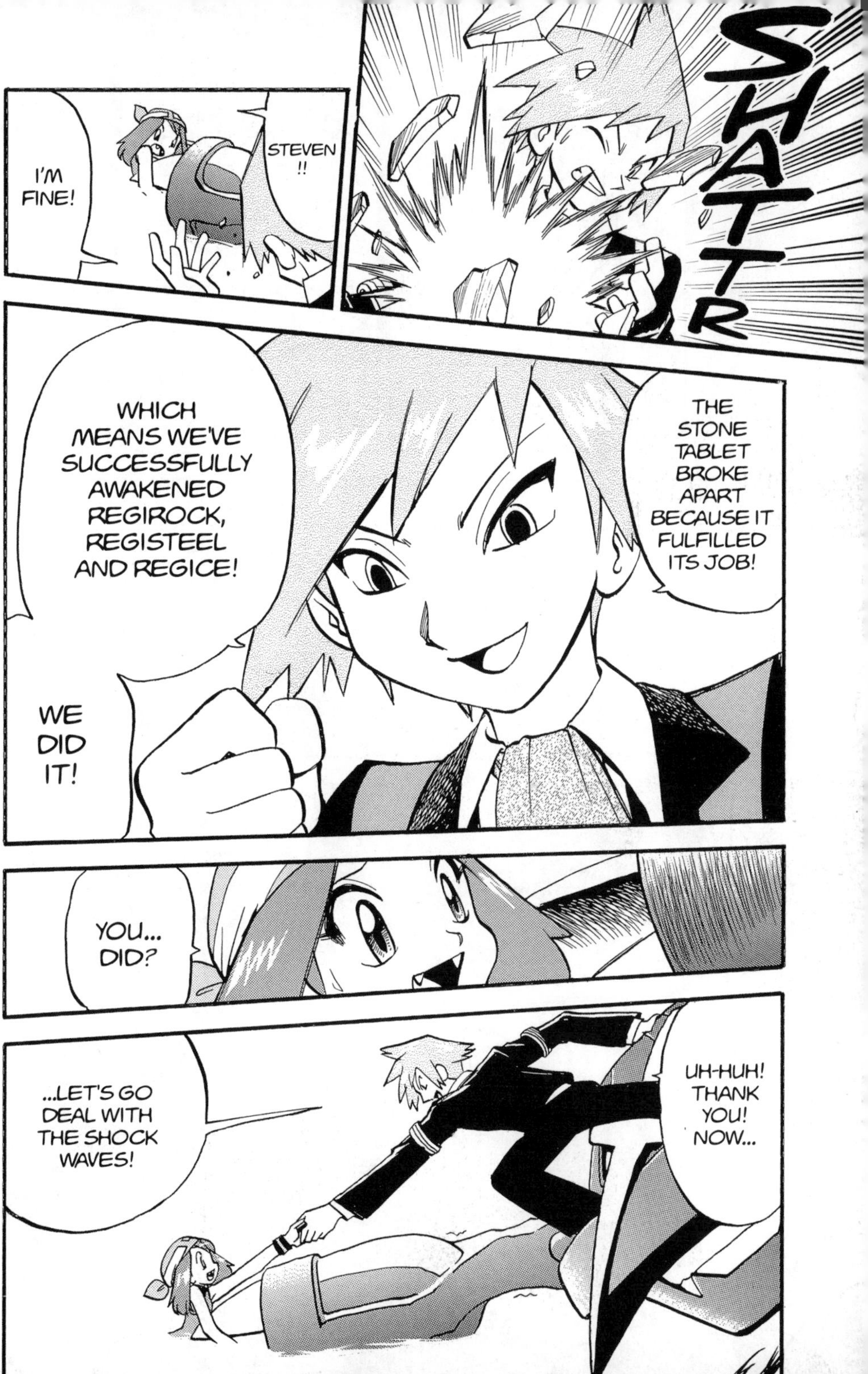
SHATTR
STEVEN !!
I'M FINE!
THE STONE TABLET BROKE APART BECAUSE IT FULFILLED ITS JOB!
WHICH MEANS WE'VE SUCCESSFULLY AWAKENED REGIROCK, REGISTEEL AND REGICE!
WE DID IT!
YOU... DID?
UH-HUH! THANK YOU! NOW...
...LET'S GO DEAL WITH THE SHOCK WAVES!

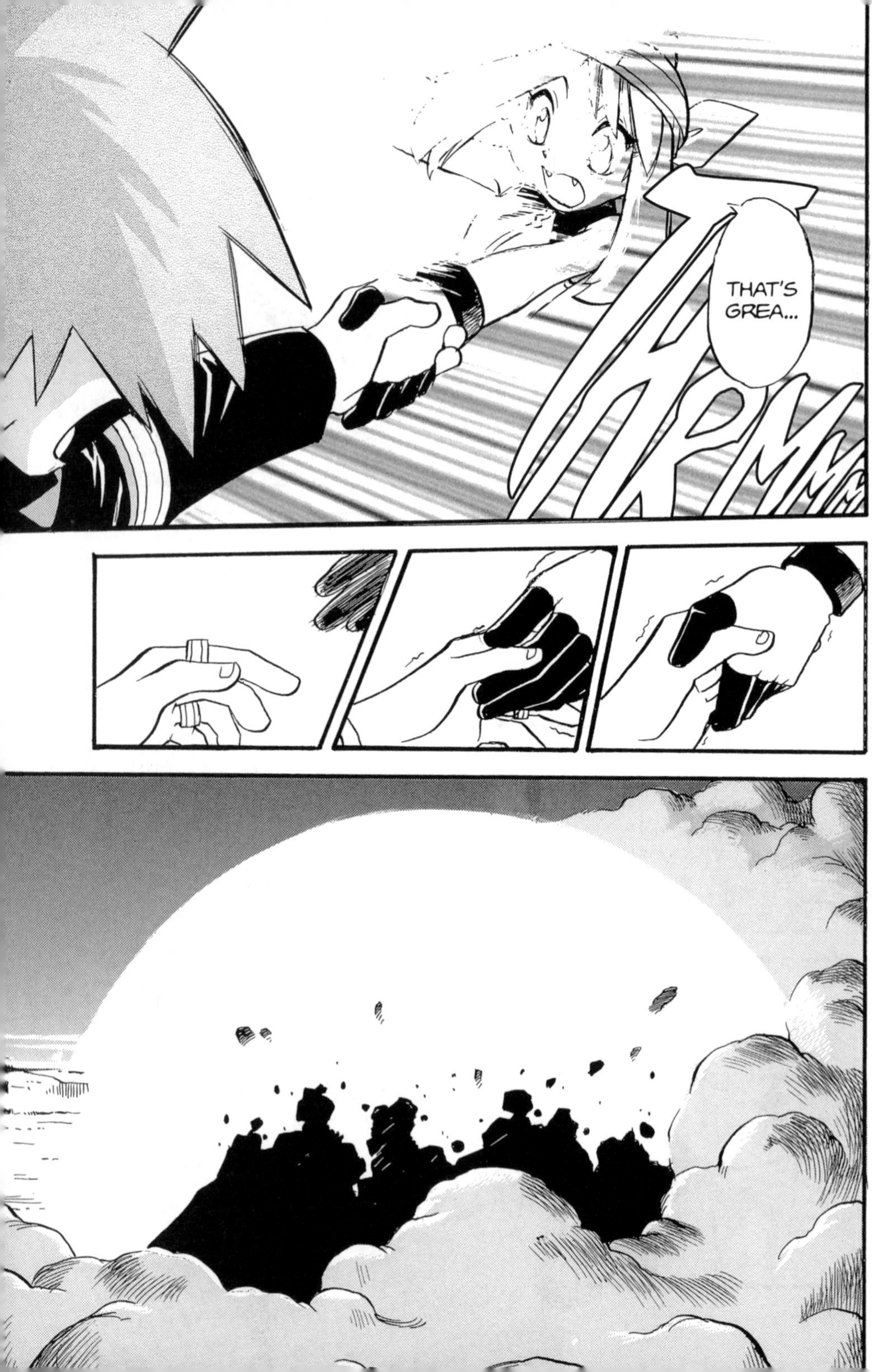
THAT'S GREA...

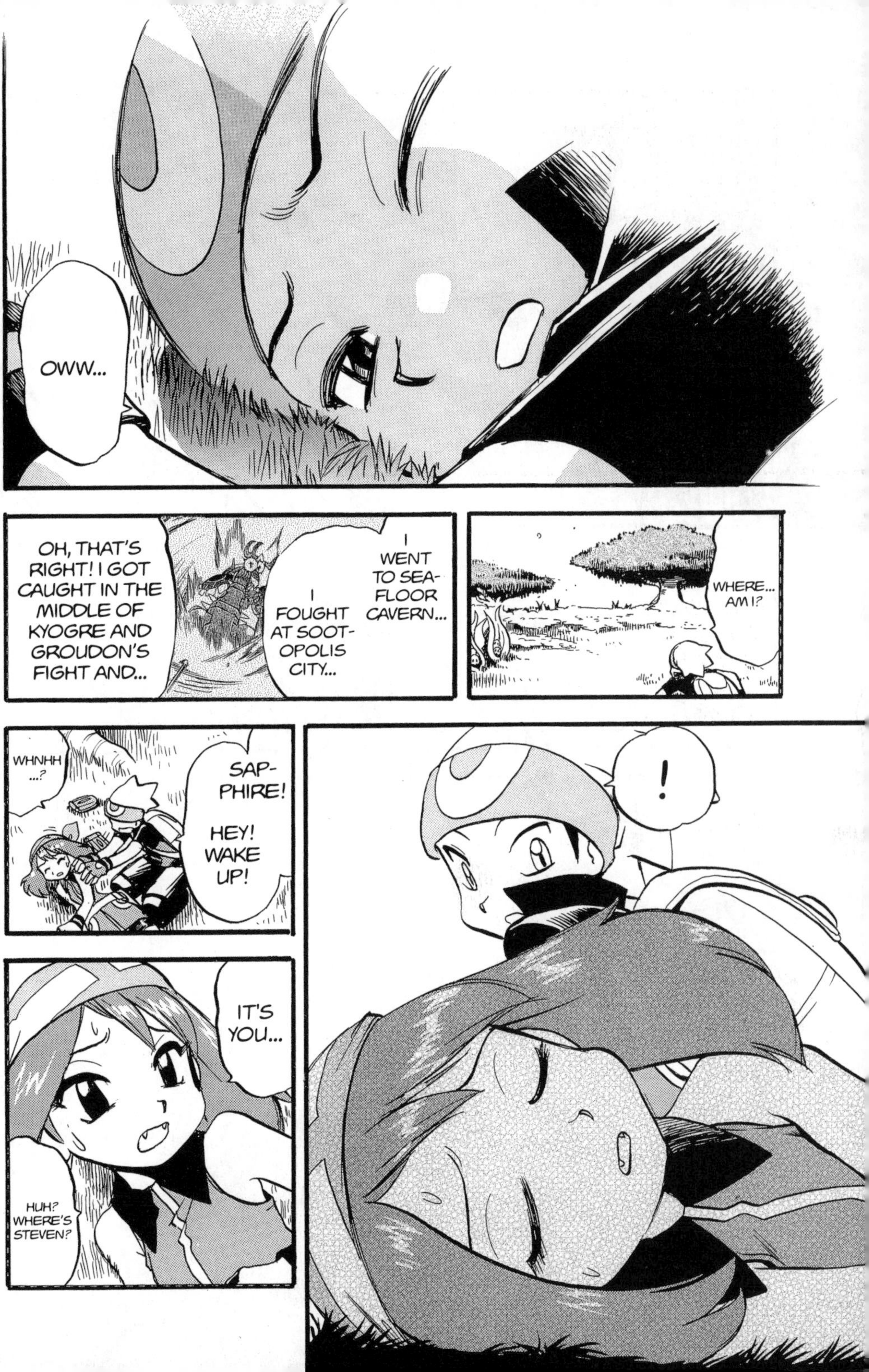
OWW...
WHERE... AM I?
I WENT TO SEA-FLOOR CAVERN...
I FOUGHT AT SOOT-OPOLIS CITY...
OH, THAT'S RIGHT! I GOT CAUGHT IN THE MIDDLE OF KYOGRE AND GROUDON'S FIGHT AND...
!
SAP-PHIRE!
HEY! WAKE UP!
WHNHH ...?
IT'S YOU...
HUH? WHERE'S STEVEN?

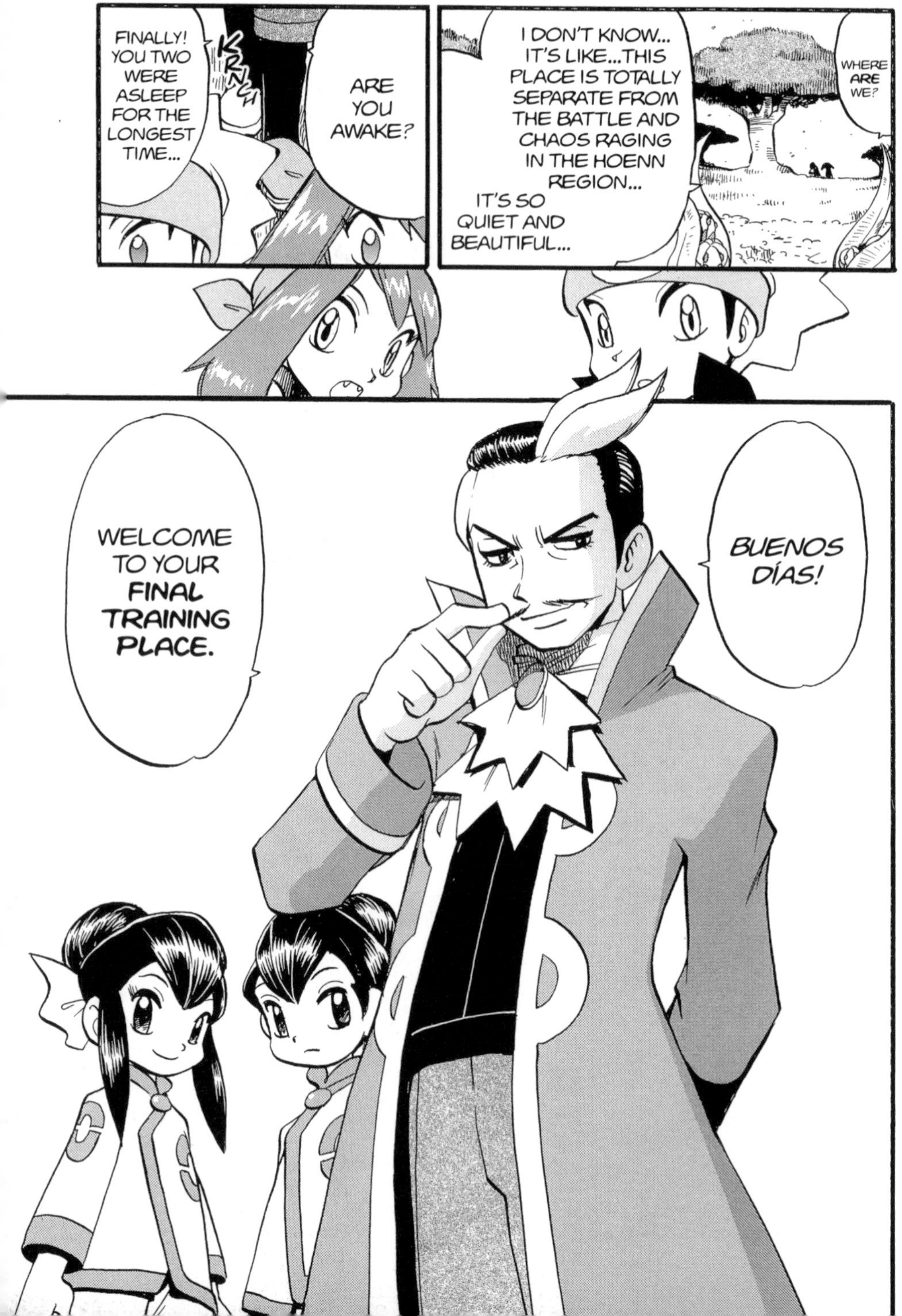
WHERE ARE WE?
I DON'T KNOW... IT'S LIKE...THIS PLACE IS TOTALLY SEPARATE FROM THE BATTLE AND CHAOS RAGING IN THE HOENN REGION...
IT'S SO QUIET AND BEAUTIFUL...
ARE YOU AWAKE?
KRNCH
FINALLY! YOU TWO WERE ASLEEP FOR THE LONGEST TIME...
BUENOS DÍAS!
WELCOME TO YOUR FINAL TRAINING PLACE.

● Adventure 255 ●
With a Spoink in Your Step, Part 1

Pokémon™ Adventures Ruby & Sapphire
The Fourth Chapter

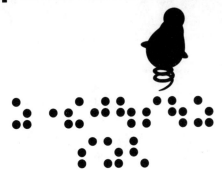

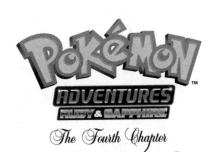

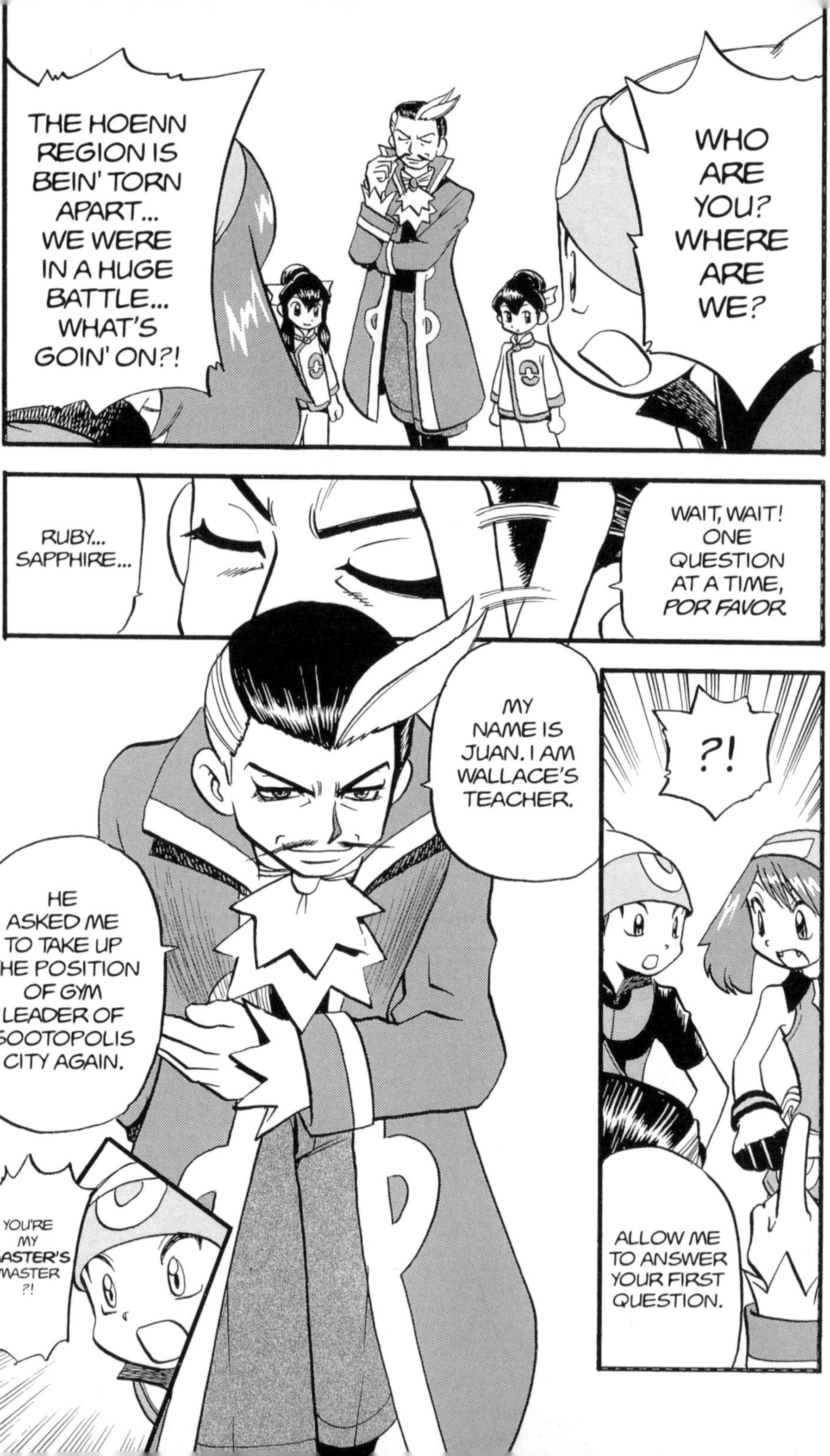
WHO ARE YOU? WHERE ARE WE?
THE HOENN REGION IS BEIN' TORN APART... WE WERE IN A HUGE BATTLE... WHAT'S GOIN' ON?!
WAIT, WAIT! ONE QUESTION AT A TIME, *POR FAVOR.*
RUBY... SAPPHIRE...
?!
ALLOW ME TO ANSWER YOUR FIRST QUESTION.
MY NAME IS JUAN. I AM WALLACE'S TEACHER.
HE ASKED ME TO TAKE UP THE POSITION OF GYM LEADER OF SOOTOPOLIS CITY AGAIN.
YOU'RE MY **MASTER'S** MASTER?!

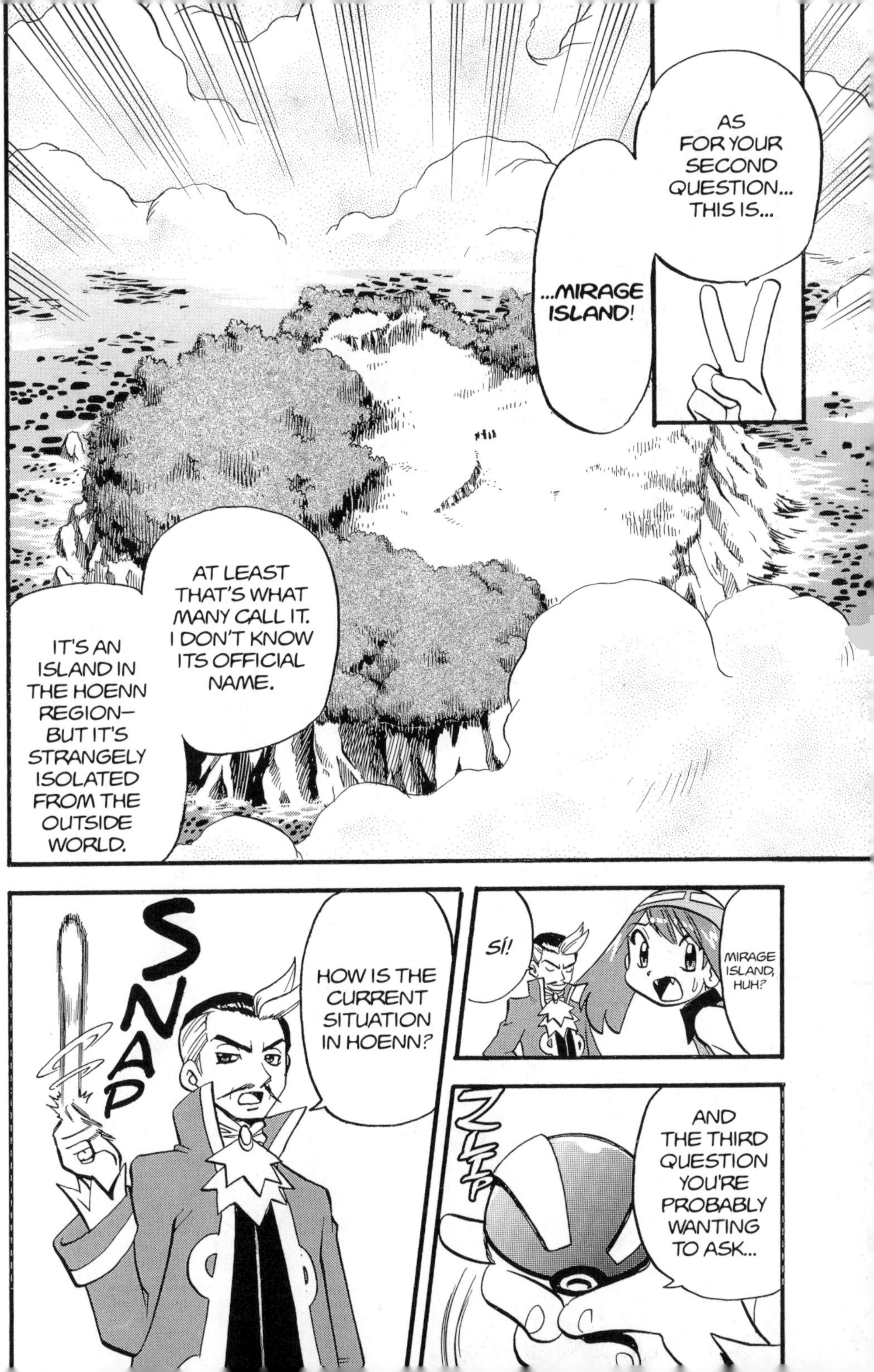
AS FOR YOUR SECOND QUESTION... THIS IS...
...MIRAGE ISLAND!
AT LEAST THAT'S WHAT MANY CALL IT. I DON'T KNOW ITS OFFICIAL NAME.
IT'S AN ISLAND IN THE HOENN REGION— BUT IT'S STRANGELY ISOLATED FROM THE OUTSIDE WORLD.
MIRAGE ISLAND, HUH?
SÍ!
ZLIP
AND THE THIRD QUESTION YOU'RE PROBABLY WANTING TO ASK...
SNAP
HOW IS THE CURRENT SITUATION IN HOENN?

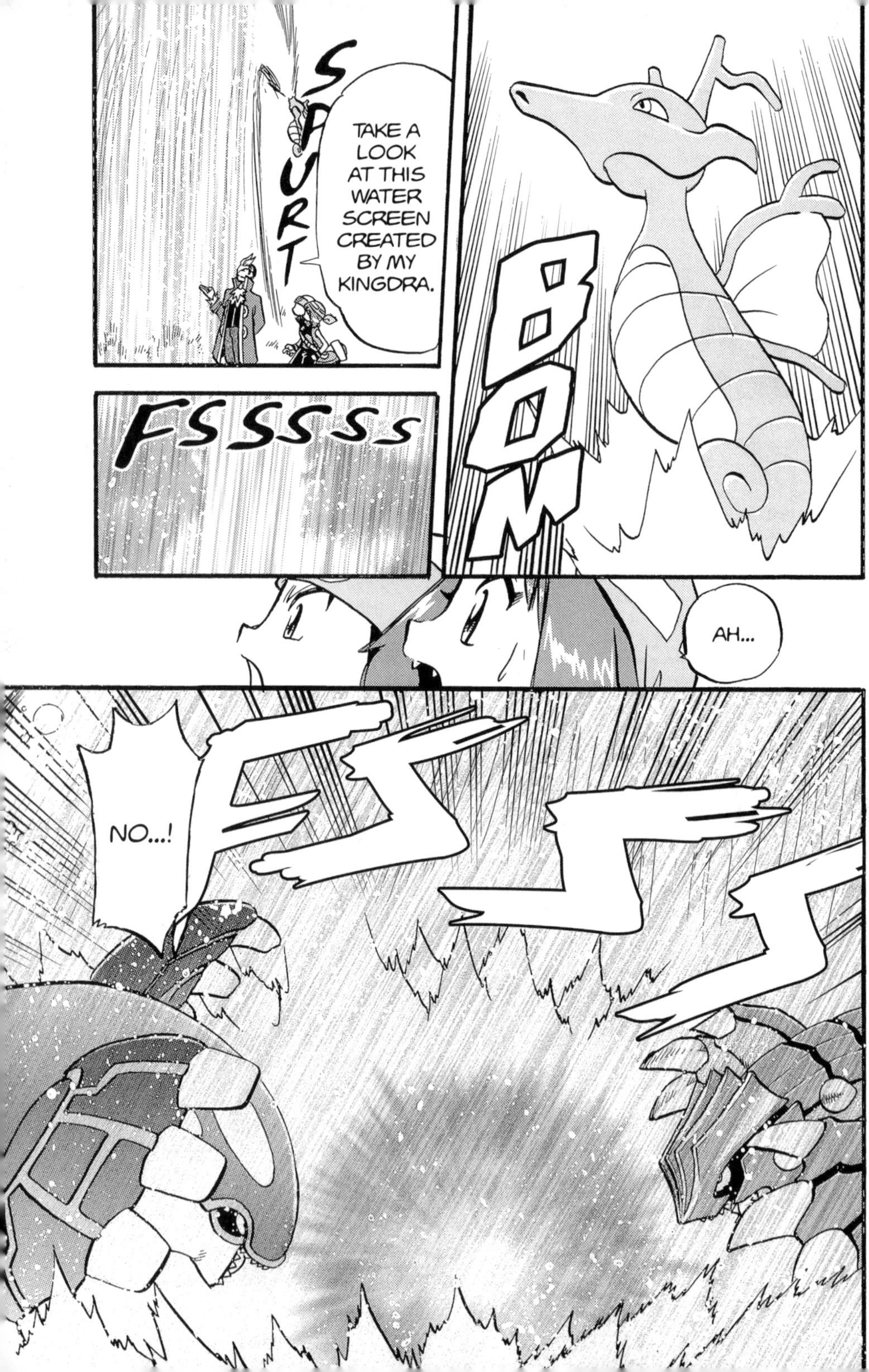
BOOM
SPURT
TAKE A LOOK AT THIS WATER SCREEN CREATED BY MY KINGDRA.
FSSSSS
AH...
FSSS
NO...!

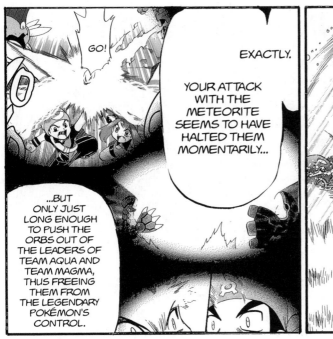

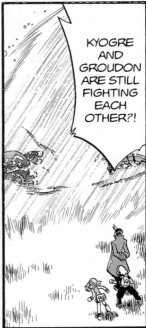

KYOGRE AND GROUDON ARE STILL FIGHTING EACH OTHER?!
EXACTLY.
YOUR ATTACK WITH THE METEORITE SEEMS TO HAVE HALTED THEM MOMENTARILY...
GO!
...BUT ONLY JUST LONG ENOUGH TO PUSH THE ORBS OUT OF THE LEADERS OF TEAM AQUA AND TEAM MAGMA, THUS FREEING THEM FROM THE LEGENDARY POKÉMON'S CONTROL.
THE TWO OF YOU WERE BLASTED AWAY BY THE IMPACT. I BROUGHT YOU HERE TO RECOVER.
...
SLUMP
WHAT'S ALARMING IS THAT THE TWO ARE COMPLETELY EQUALLY MATCHED NOW.
IT'S A STALEMATE. AT FIRST GLANCE, IT APPEARS AS IF THEY'VE STOPPED MOVING...

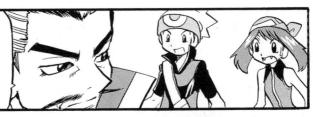

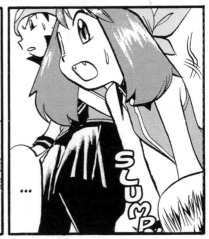

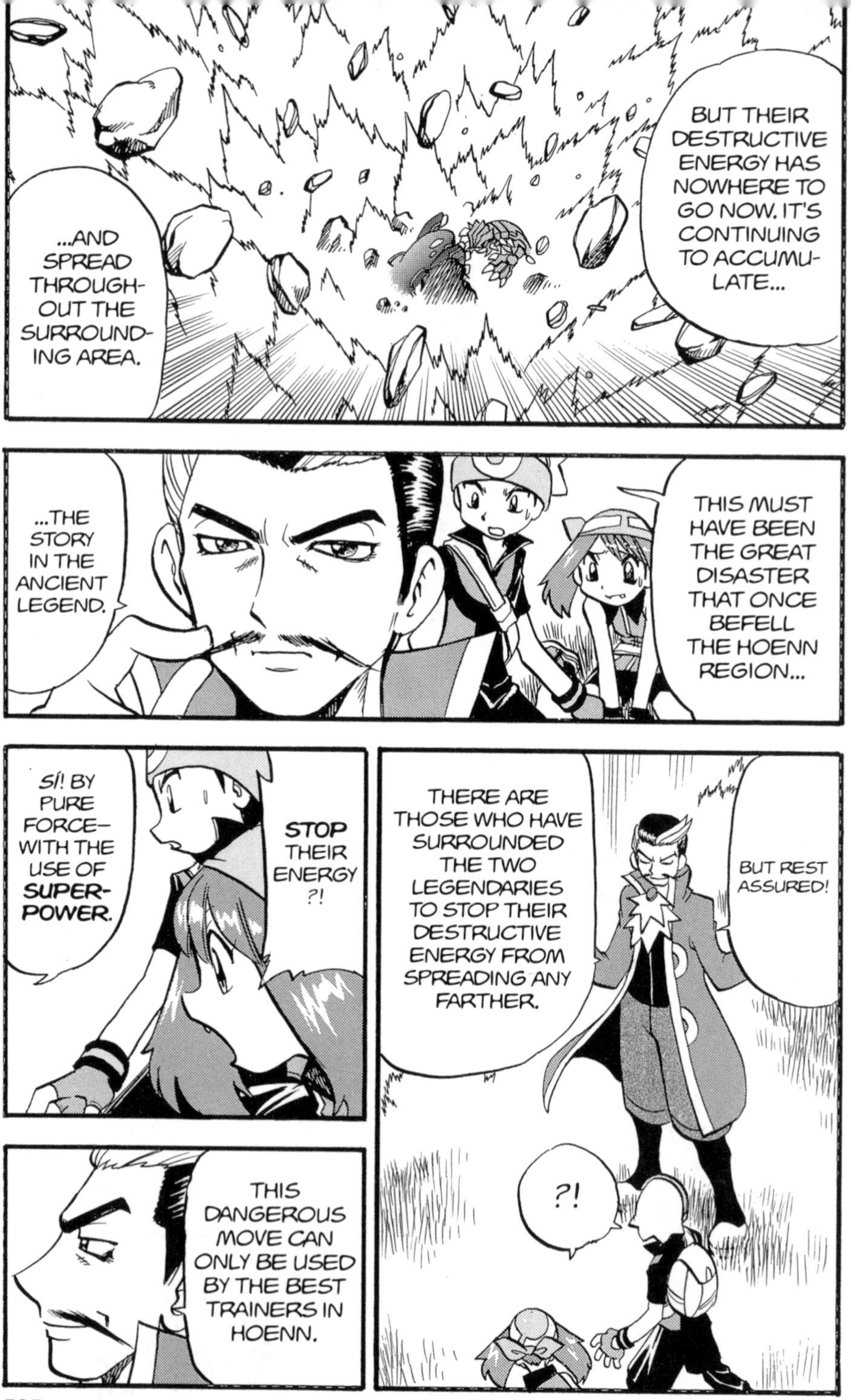
BUT THEIR DESTRUCTIVE ENERGY HAS NOWHERE TO GO NOW. IT'S CONTINUING TO ACCUMULATE...
...AND SPREAD THROUGHOUT THE SURROUNDING AREA.
THIS MUST HAVE BEEN THE GREAT DISASTER THAT ONCE BEFELL THE HOENN REGION...
...THE STORY IN THE ANCIENT LEGEND.
BUT REST ASSURED!
THERE ARE THOSE WHO HAVE SURROUNDED THE TWO LEGENDARIES TO STOP THEIR DESTRUCTIVE ENERGY FROM SPREADING ANY FARTHER.
?!
STOP THEIR ENERGY ?!
SÍ! BY PURE FORCE—WITH THE USE OF **SUPERPOWER**.
THIS DANGEROUS MOVE CAN ONLY BE USED BY THE BEST TRAINERS IN HOENN.

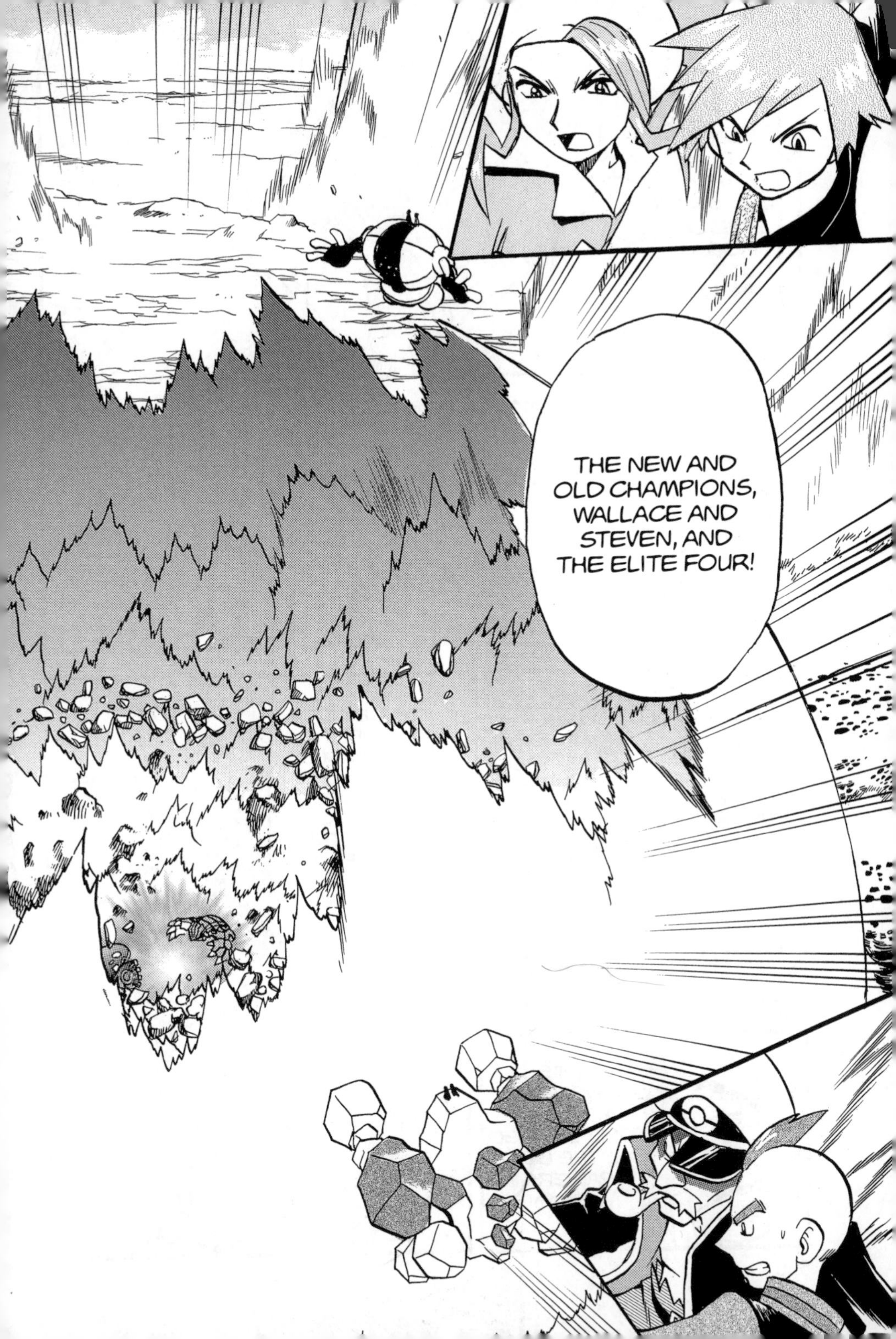
THE NEW AND OLD CHAMPIONS, WALLACE AND STEVEN, AND THE ELITE FOUR!

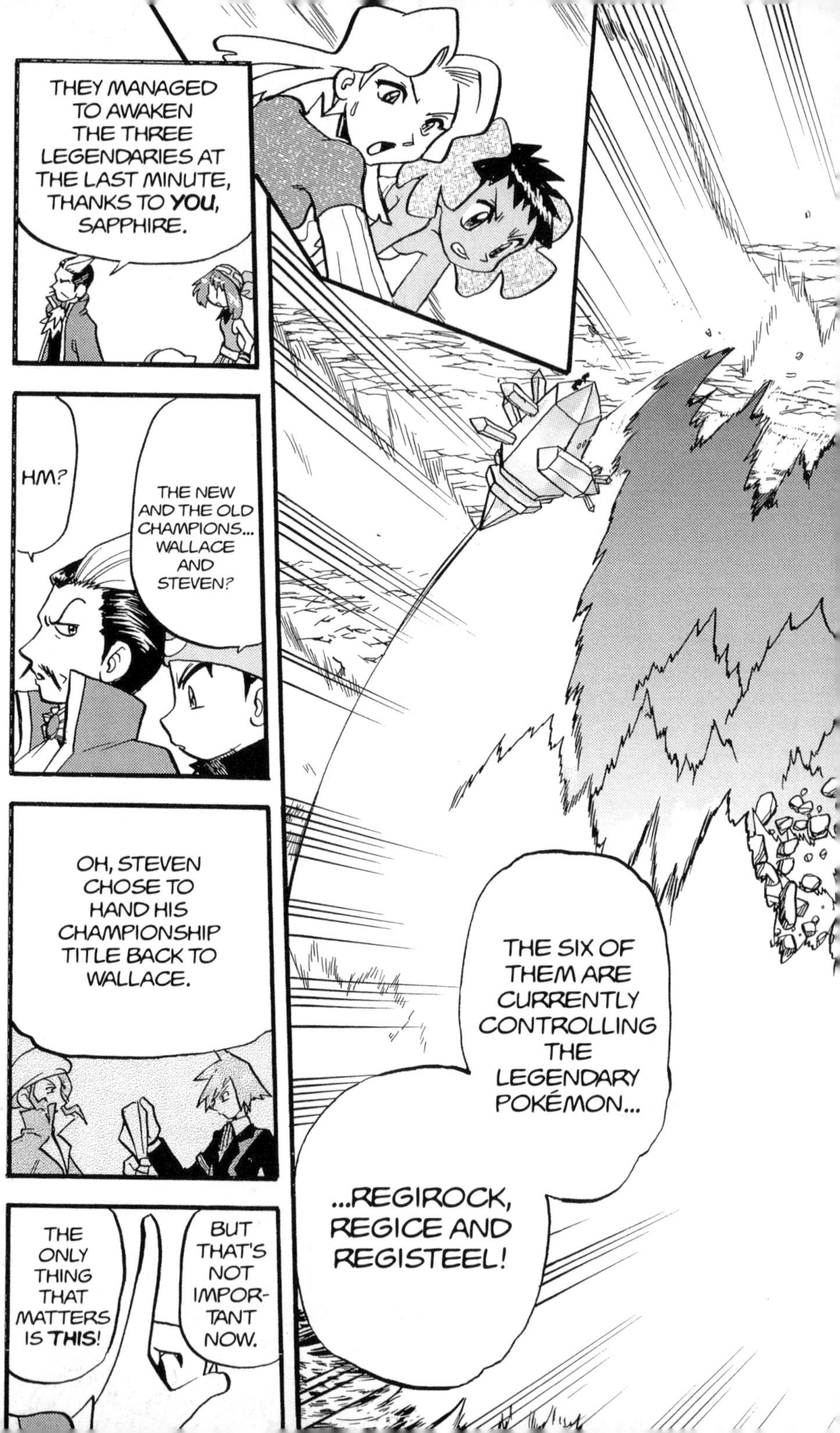
THE SIX OF THEM ARE CURRENTLY CONTROLLING THE LEGENDARY POKÉMON...
...REGIROCK, REGICE AND REGISTEEL!
THEY MANAGED TO AWAKEN THE THREE LEGENDARIES AT THE LAST MINUTE, THANKS TO **YOU**, SAPPHIRE.
THE NEW AND THE OLD CHAMPIONS... WALLACE AND STEVEN?
HM?
OH, STEVEN CHOSE TO HAND HIS CHAMPIONSHIP TITLE BACK TO WALLACE.
BUT THAT'S NOT IMPOR-TANT NOW.
THE ONLY THING THAT MATTERS IS **THIS**!

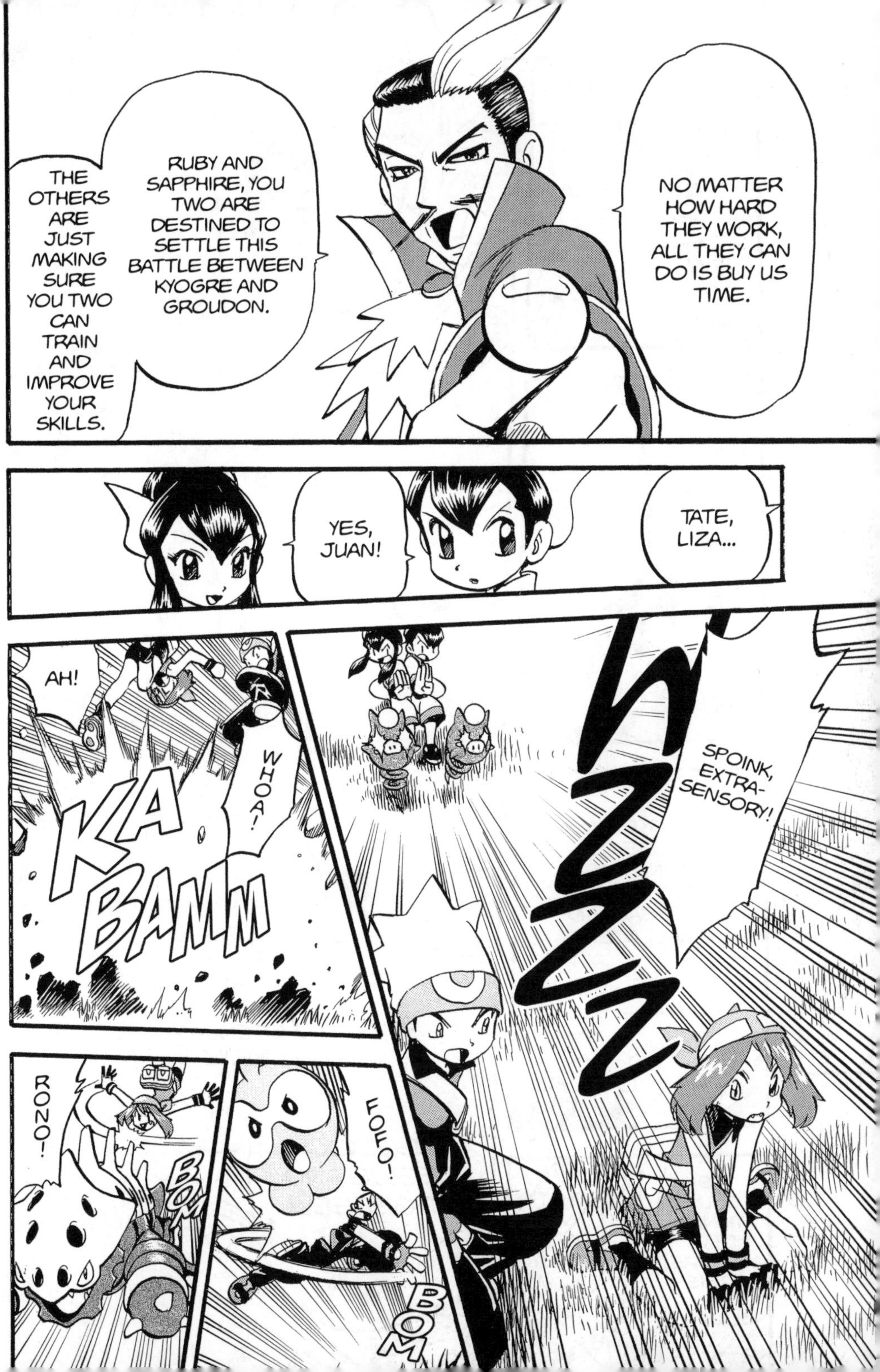
NO MATTER HOW HARD THEY WORK, ALL THEY CAN DO IS BUY US TIME.
RUBY AND SAPPHIRE, YOU TWO ARE DESTINED TO SETTLE THIS BATTLE BETWEEN KYOGRE AND GROUDON.
THE OTHERS ARE JUST MAKING SURE YOU TWO CAN TRAIN AND IMPROVE YOUR SKILLS.
TATE, LIZA...
YES, JUAN!
SPOINK, EXTRA-SENSORY!
WHOA!
AH!
KA BAMM
FOFO!
BOM BOM
RONO!
BOM

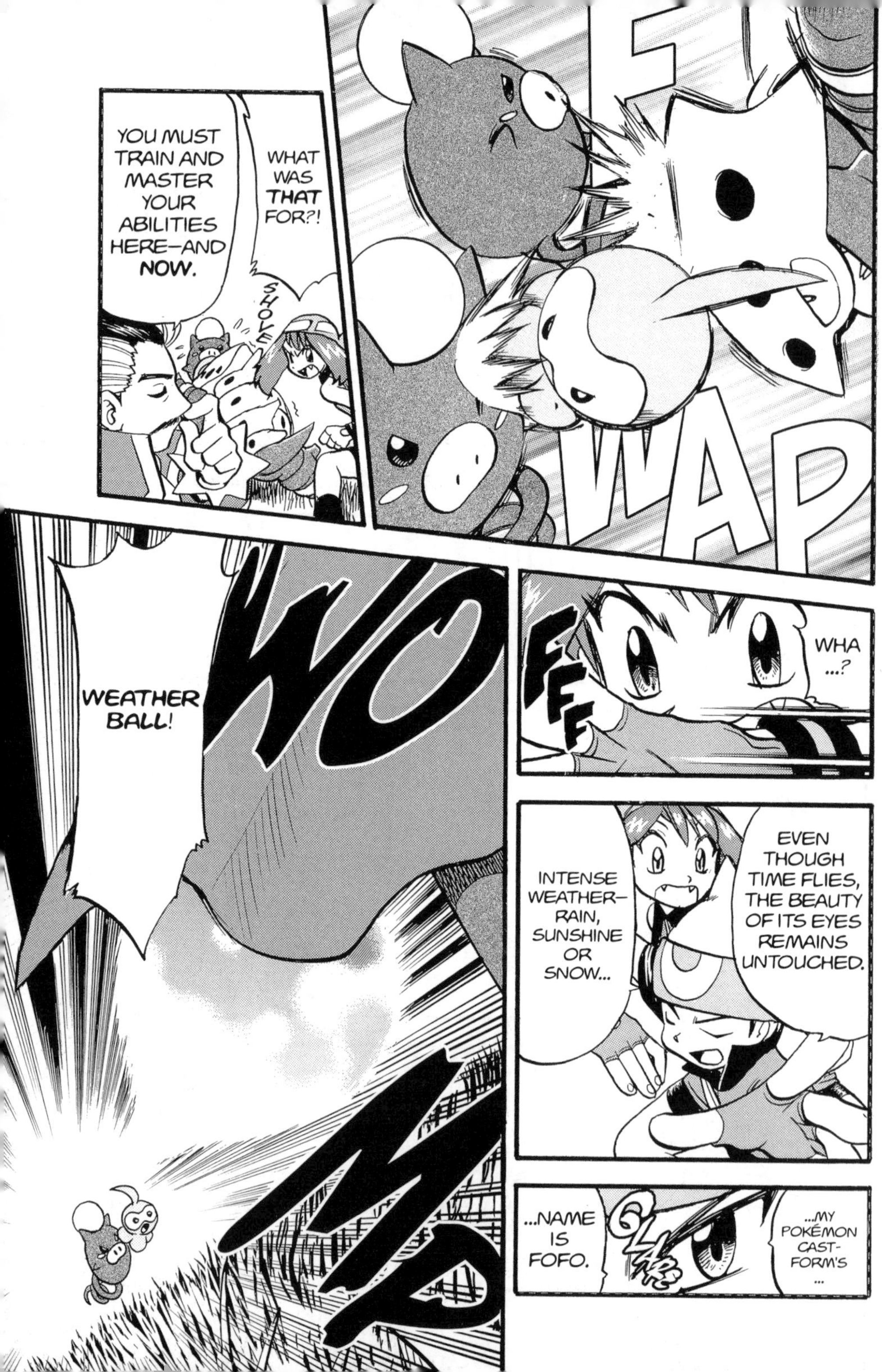
WAP
WHAT WAS THAT FOR?!
SHOVE
YOU MUST TRAIN AND MASTER YOUR ABILITIES HERE—AND NOW.
WHA ...?
FFF
EVEN THOUGH TIME FLIES, THE BEAUTY OF ITS EYES REMAINS UNTOUCHED.
INTENSE WEATHER—RAIN, SUNSHINE OR SNOW...
...MY POKÉMON CAST-FORM'S ...
CLAP
...NAME IS FOFO.
WEATHER BALL!
WOMP

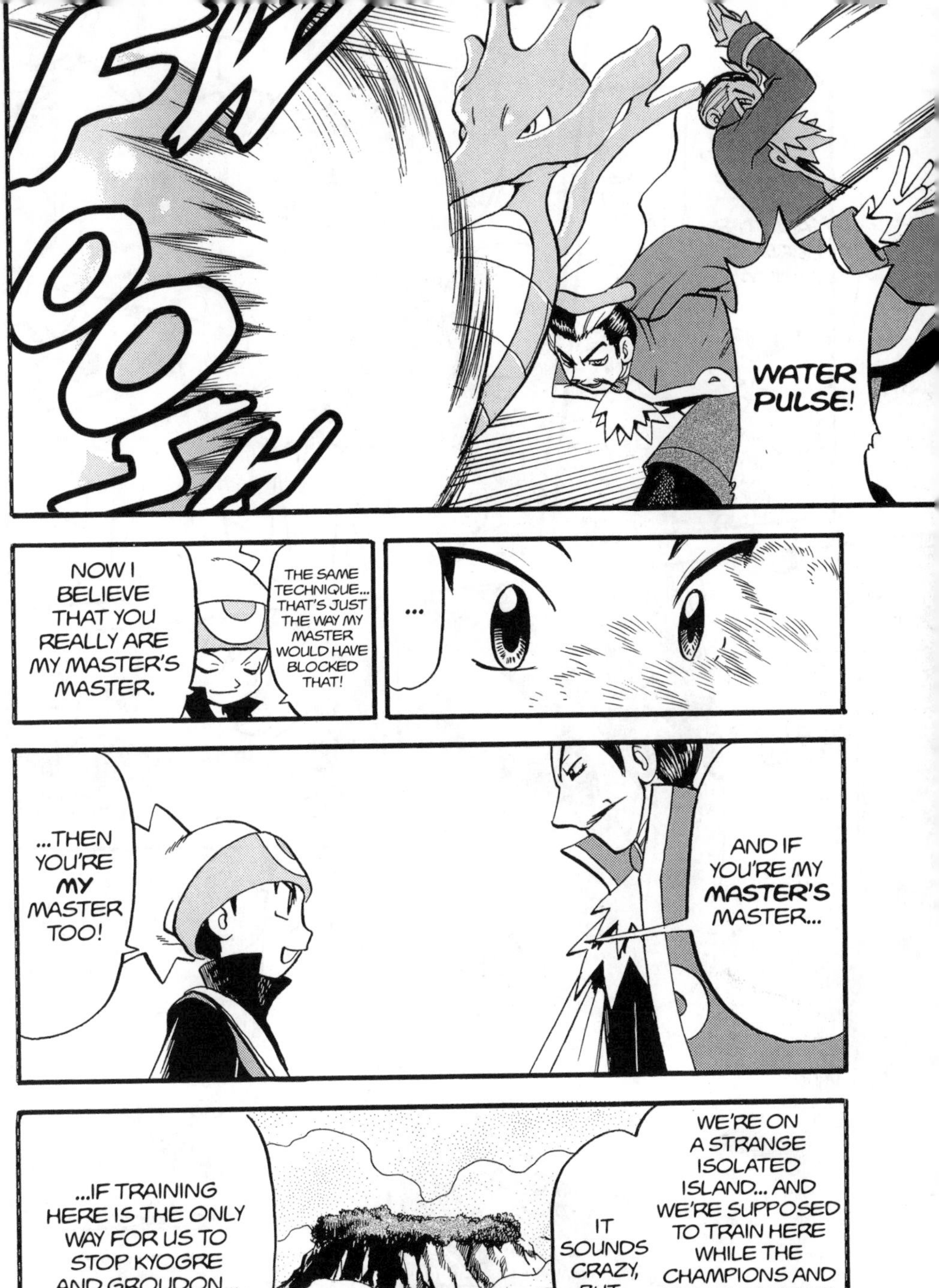
WATER PULSE!
FWOOOSH
...
THE SAME TECHNIQUE... THAT'S JUST THE WAY MY MASTER WOULD HAVE BLOCKED THAT!
NOW I BELIEVE THAT YOU REALLY ARE MY MASTER'S MASTER.
AND IF YOU'RE MY **MASTER'S** MASTER...
...THEN YOU'RE **MY** MASTER TOO!
WE'RE ON A STRANGE ISOLATED ISLAND... AND WE'RE SUPPOSED TO TRAIN HERE WHILE THE CHAMPIONS AND THE ELITE FOUR BUY US TIME...
IT SOUNDS CRAZY, BUT...
...IF TRAINING HERE IS THE ONLY WAY FOR US TO STOP KYOGRE AND GROUDON...

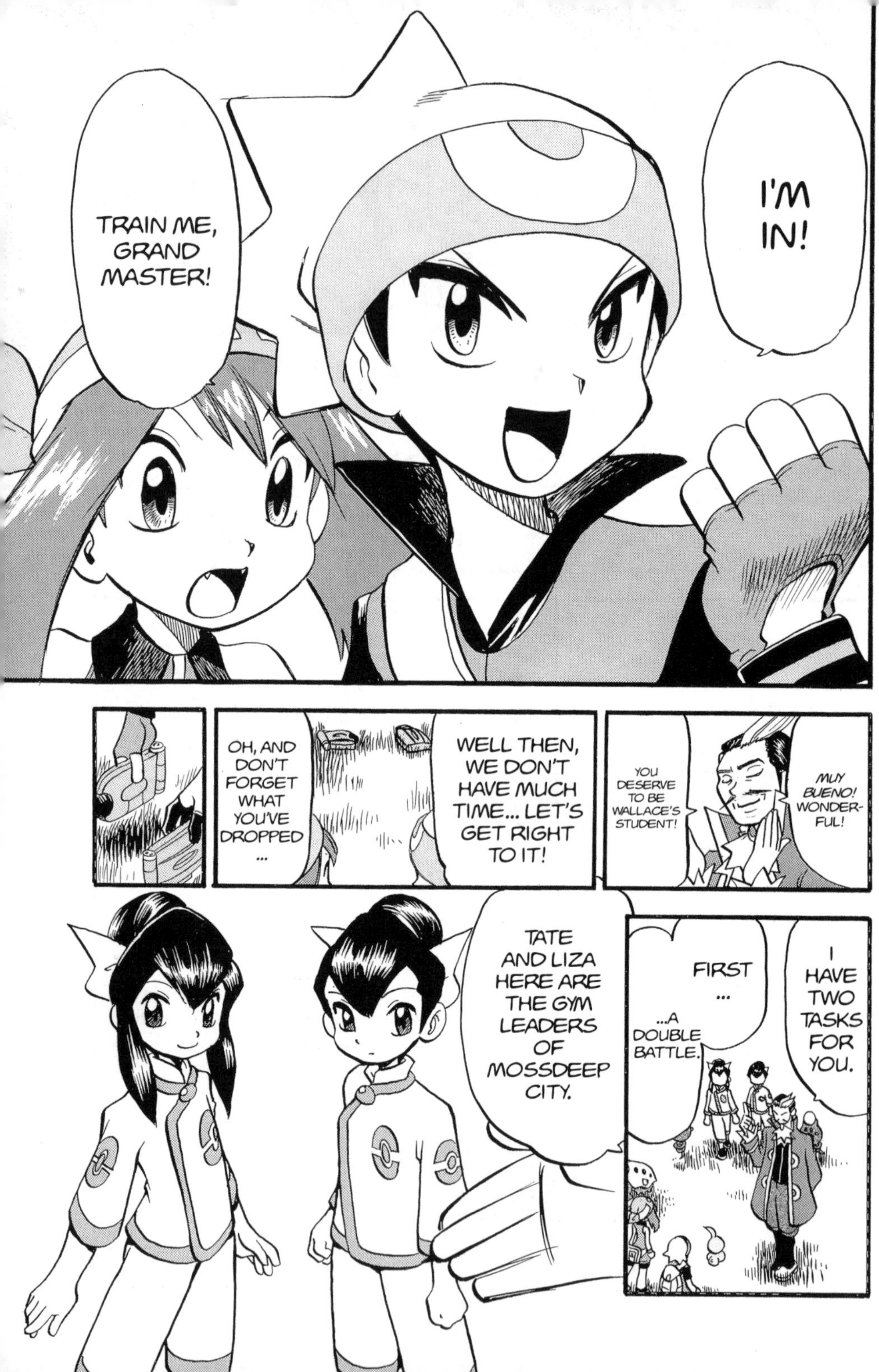
I'M IN!
TRAIN ME, GRAND MASTER!
MUY BUENO! WONDERFUL!
YOU DESERVE TO BE WALLACE'S STUDENT!
WELL THEN, WE DON'T HAVE MUCH TIME... LET'S GET RIGHT TO IT!
OH, AND DON'T FORGET WHAT YOU'VE DROPPED ...
I HAVE TWO TASKS FOR YOU.
FIRST ...
...A DOUBLE BATTLE.
TATE AND LIZA HERE ARE THE GYM LEADERS OF MOSSDEEP CITY.

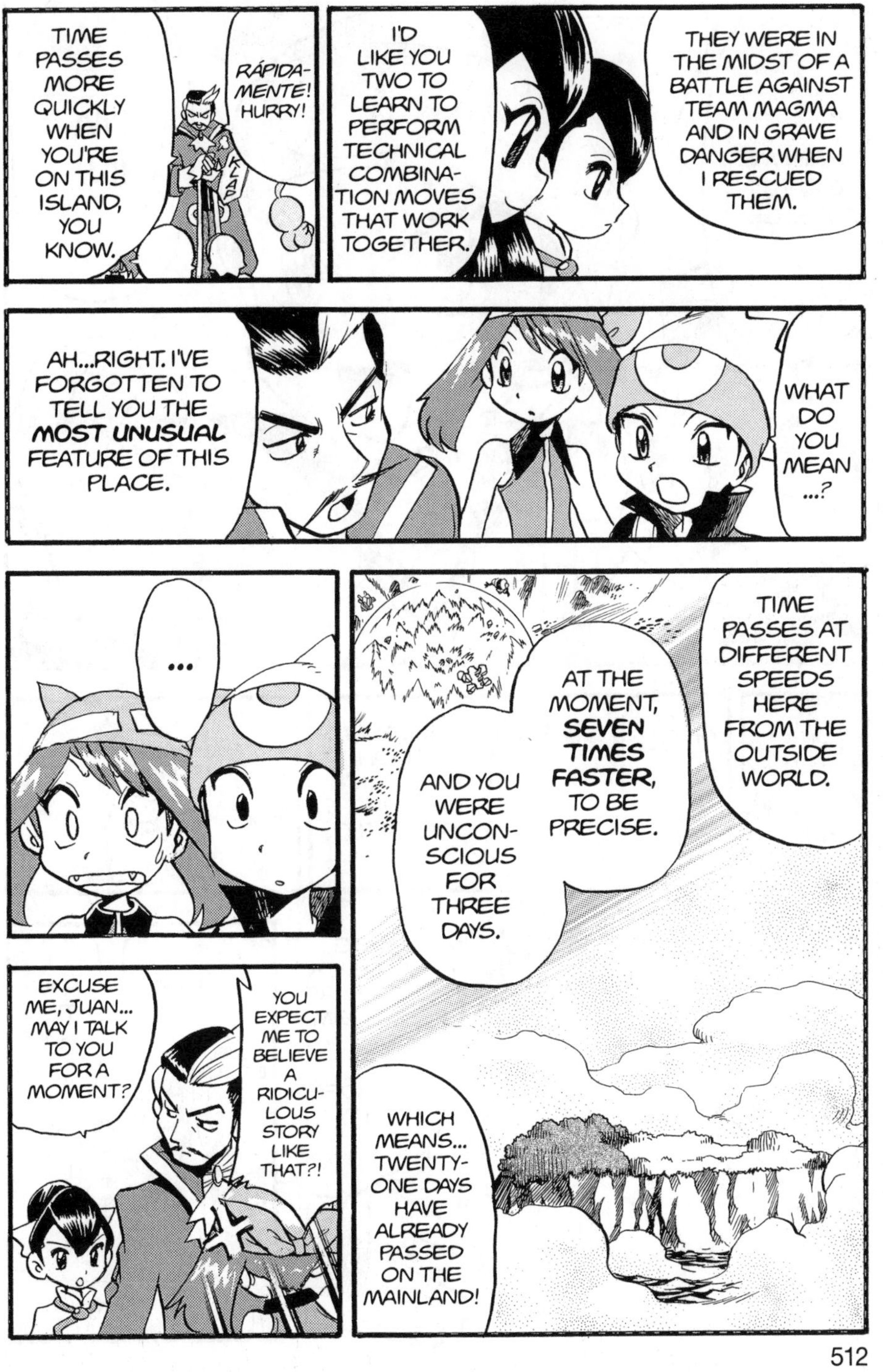
THEY WERE IN THE MIDST OF A BATTLE AGAINST TEAM MAGMA AND IN GRAVE DANGER WHEN I RESCUED THEM.
I'D LIKE YOU TWO TO LEARN TO PERFORM TECHNICAL COMBINATION MOVES THAT WORK TOGETHER.
RÁPIDAMENTE! HURRY!
KLAP
TIME PASSES MORE QUICKLY WHEN YOU'RE ON THIS ISLAND, YOU KNOW.
WHAT DO YOU MEAN ...?
AH...RIGHT. I'VE FORGOTTEN TO TELL YOU THE **MOST UNUSUAL** FEATURE OF THIS PLACE.
TIME PASSES AT DIFFERENT SPEEDS HERE FROM THE OUTSIDE WORLD.
AT THE MOMENT, **SEVEN TIMES FASTER**, TO BE PRECISE.
AND YOU WERE UNCONSCIOUS FOR THREE DAYS.
WHICH MEANS... TWENTY-ONE DAYS HAVE ALREADY PASSED ON THE MAINLAND!
...
YOU EXPECT ME TO BELIEVE A RIDICULOUS STORY LIKE THAT?!
EXCUSE ME, JUAN... MAY I TALK TO YOU FOR A MOMENT?

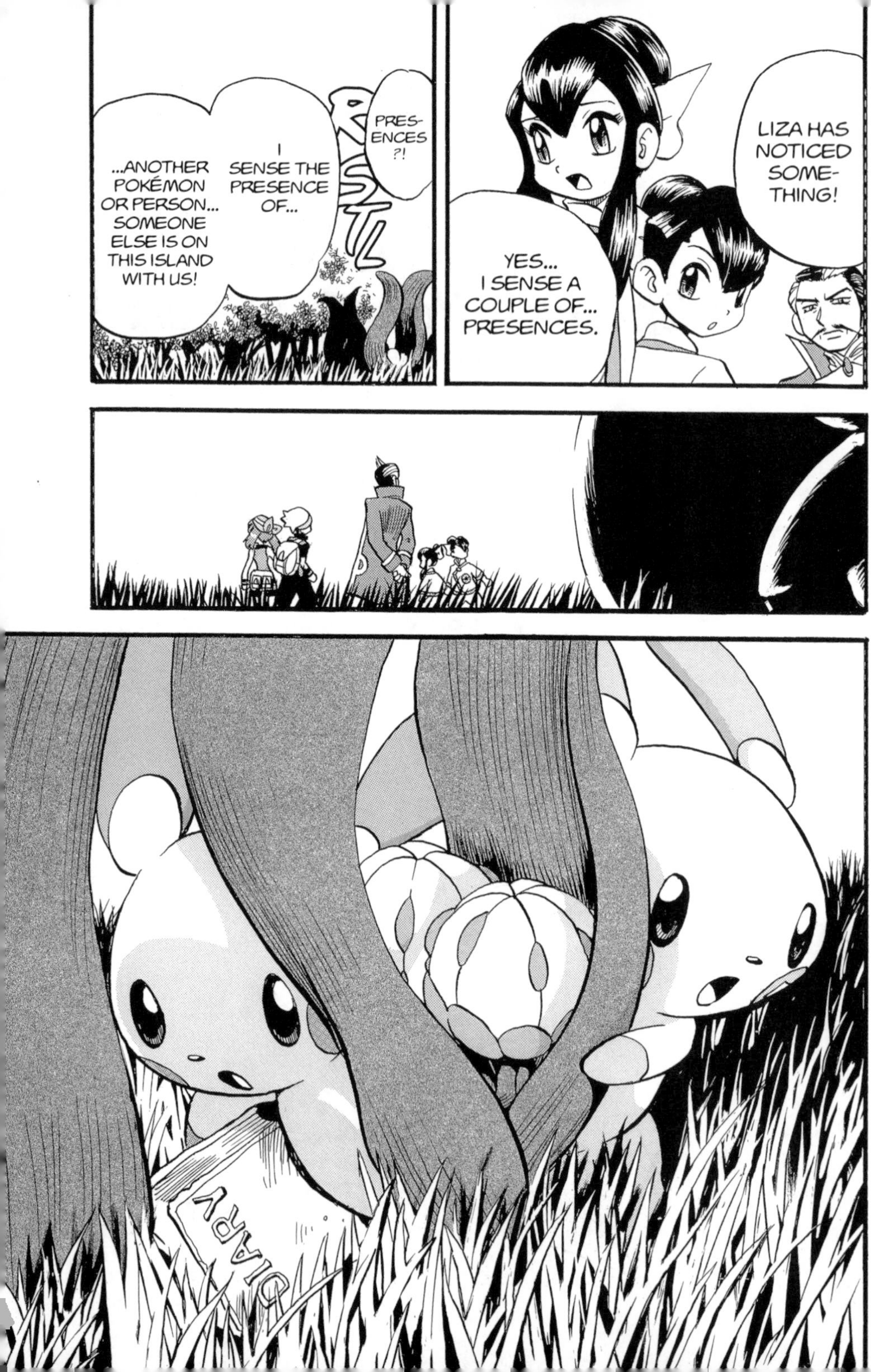
LIZA HAS NOTICED SOME-THING!
YES... I SENSE A COUPLE OF... PRESENCES.
PRES-ENCES?!
RUSTL
I SENSE THE PRESENCE OF...
...ANOTHER POKÉMON OR PERSON... SOMEONE ELSE IS ON THIS ISLAND WITH US!
DIARY

● Adventure 256 ●
With a Spoink in Your Step, Part 2

Pokémon™ Adventures Ruby & Sapphire

The Fourth Chapter

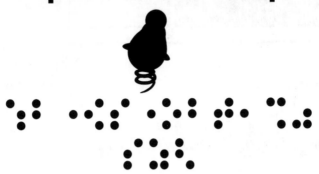

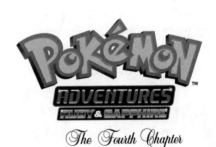

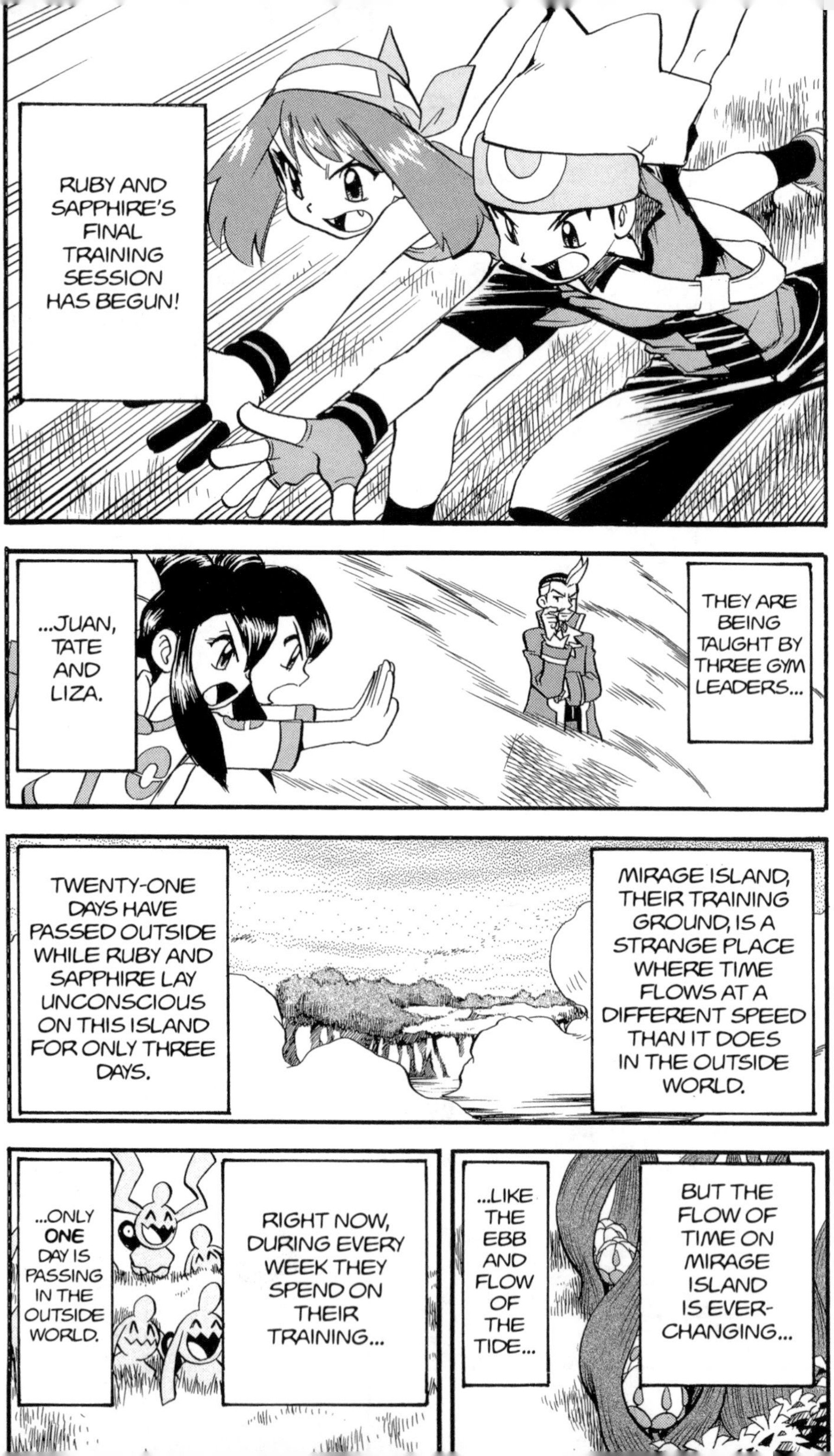
RUBY AND SAPPHIRE'S FINAL TRAINING SESSION HAS BEGUN!
THEY ARE BEING TAUGHT BY THREE GYM LEADERS...
...JUAN, TATE AND LIZA.
MIRAGE ISLAND, THEIR TRAINING GROUND, IS A STRANGE PLACE WHERE TIME FLOWS AT A DIFFERENT SPEED THAN IT DOES IN THE OUTSIDE WORLD.
TWENTY-ONE DAYS HAVE PASSED OUTSIDE WHILE RUBY AND SAPPHIRE LAY UNCONSCIOUS ON THIS ISLAND FOR ONLY THREE DAYS.
BUT THE FLOW OF TIME ON MIRAGE ISLAND IS EVER-CHANGING...
...LIKE THE EBB AND FLOW OF THE TIDE...
RIGHT NOW, DURING EVERY WEEK THEY SPEND ON THEIR TRAINING...
...ONLY **ONE** DAY IS PASSING IN THE OUTSIDE WORLD.

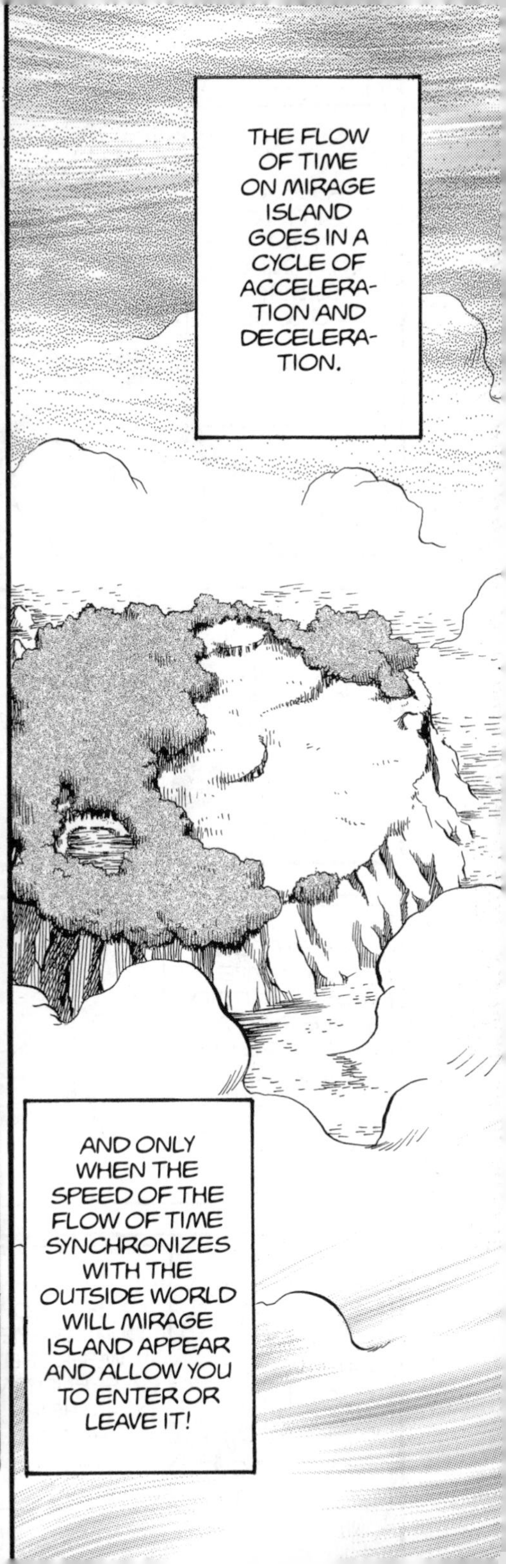
THE FLOW OF TIME ON MIRAGE ISLAND GOES IN A CYCLE OF ACCELERATION AND DECELERATION.
AND ONLY WHEN THE SPEED OF THE FLOW OF TIME SYNCHRONIZES WITH THE OUTSIDE WORLD WILL MIRAGE ISLAND APPEAR AND ALLOW YOU TO ENTER OR LEAVE IT!
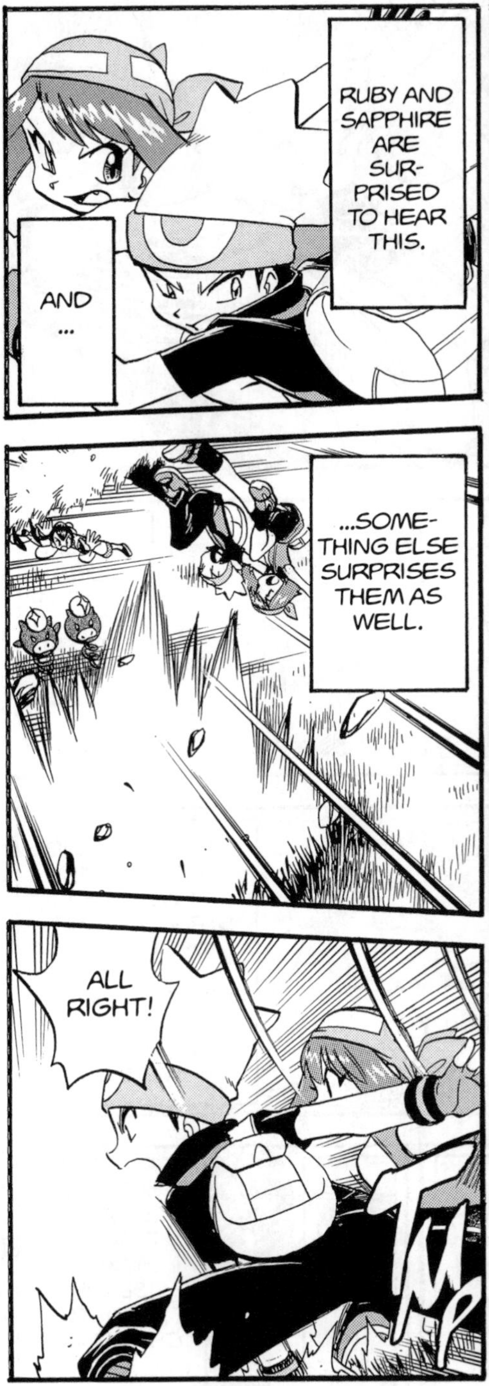
RUBY AND SAPPHIRE ARE SURPRISED TO HEAR THIS.
AND ...
...SOMETHING ELSE SURPRISES THEM AS WELL.
ALL RIGHT!

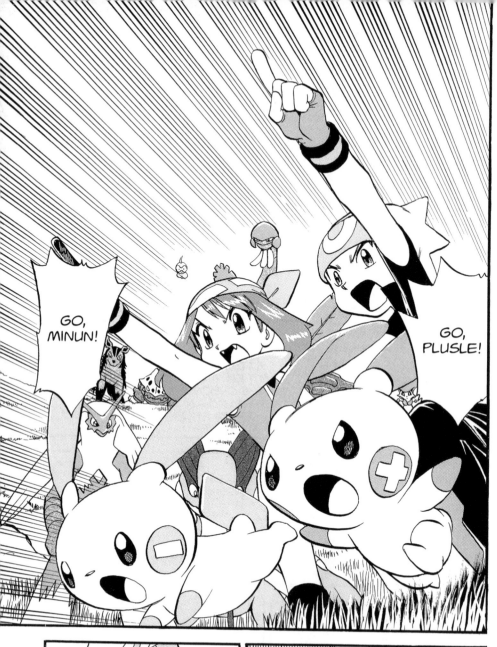

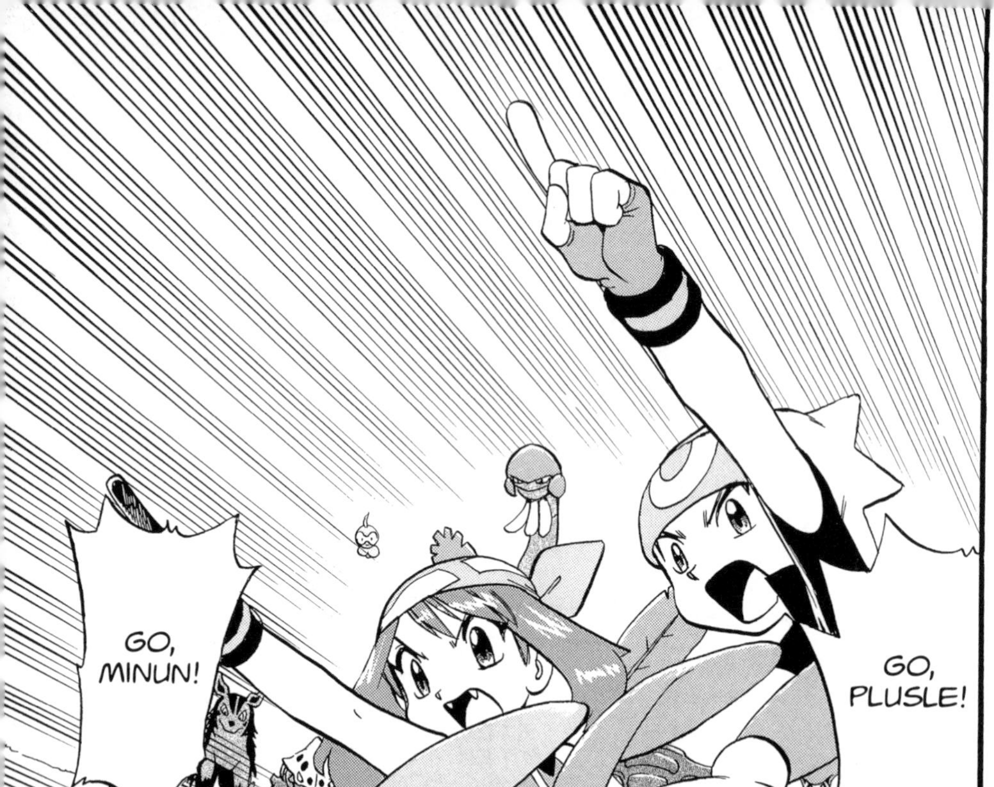
GO, PLUSLE!
GO, MINUN!

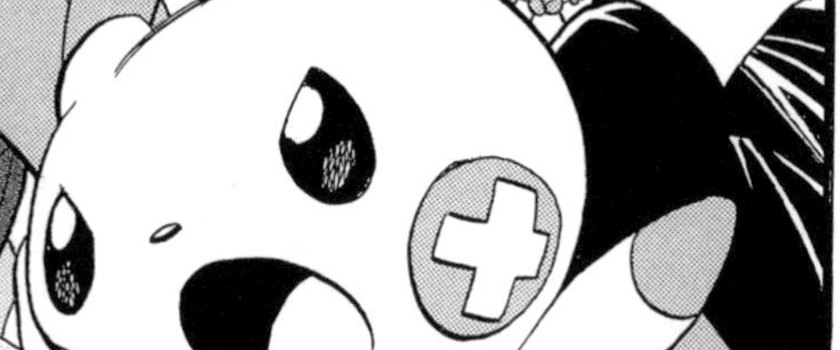
AWWW
PLUSLE, FAKE TEARS!

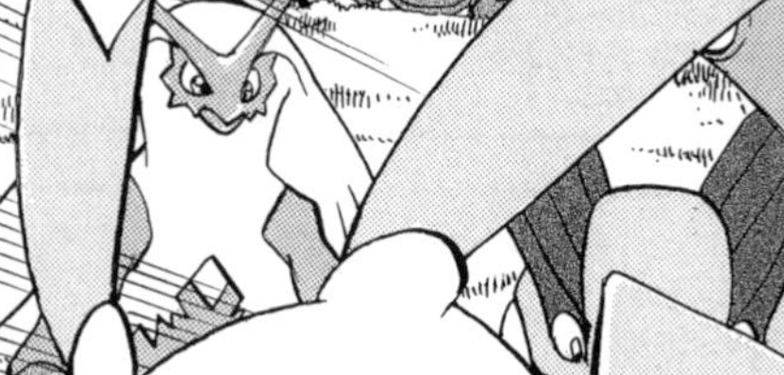
SPOINK'S SPECIAL DEFENSE HAS DECREASED!
NOW'S YER CHANCE, MINUN!

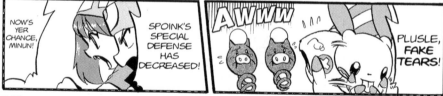

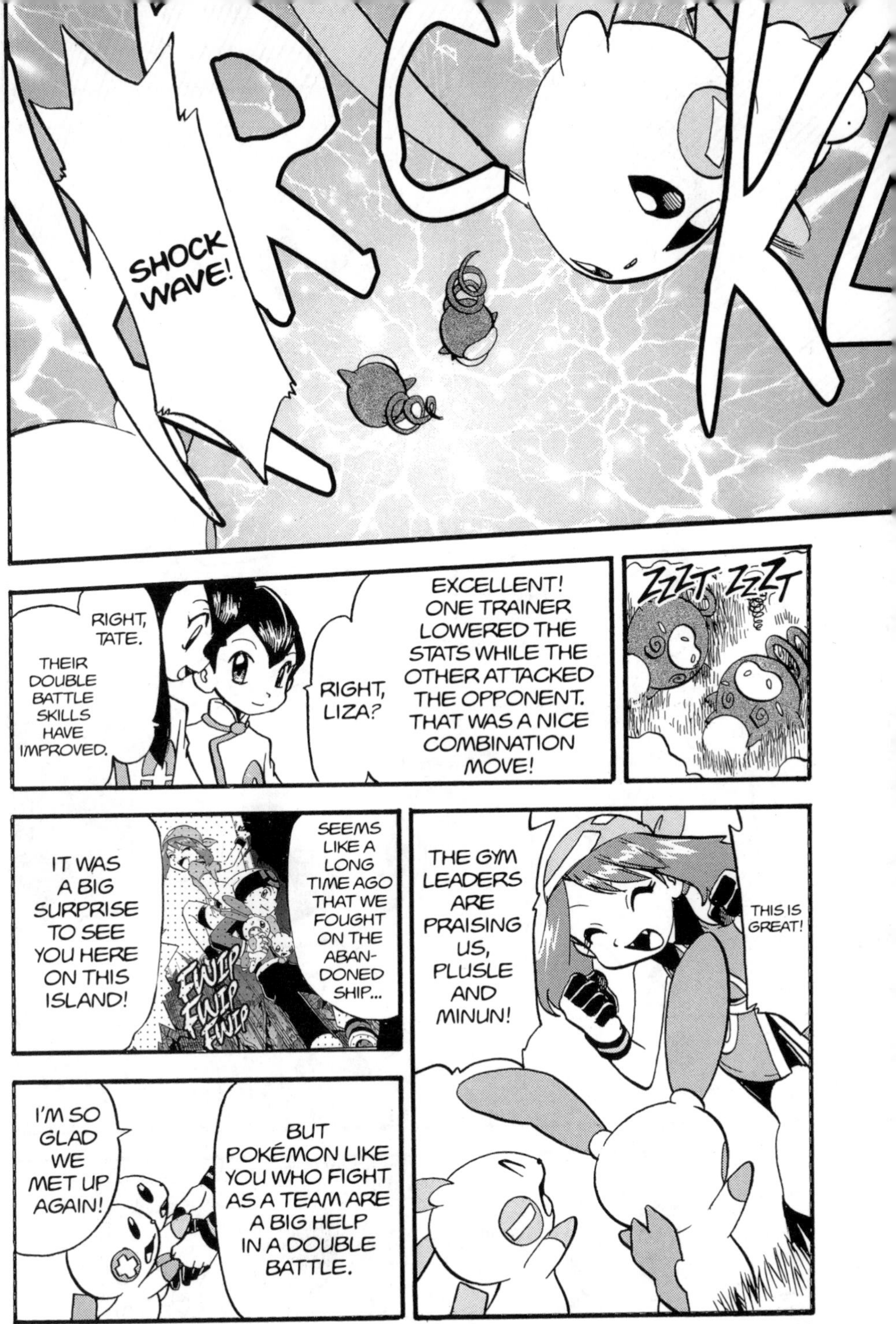
SHOCK WAVE!
ZZZT ZZZT
EXCELLENT! ONE TRAINER LOWERED THE STATS WHILE THE OTHER ATTACKED THE OPPONENT. THAT WAS A NICE COMBINATION MOVE!
RIGHT, LIZA?
RIGHT, TATE.
THEIR DOUBLE BATTLE SKILLS HAVE IMPROVED.
THIS IS GREAT!
THE GYM LEADERS ARE PRAISING US, PLUSLE AND MINUN!
SEEMS LIKE A LONG TIME AGO THAT WE FOUGHT ON THE ABANDONED SHIP...
FWIP FWIP FWIP
IT WAS A BIG SURPRISE TO SEE YOU HERE ON THIS ISLAND!
BUT POKÉMON LIKE YOU WHO FIGHT AS A TEAM ARE A BIG HELP IN A DOUBLE BATTLE.
I'M SO GLAD WE MET UP AGAIN!

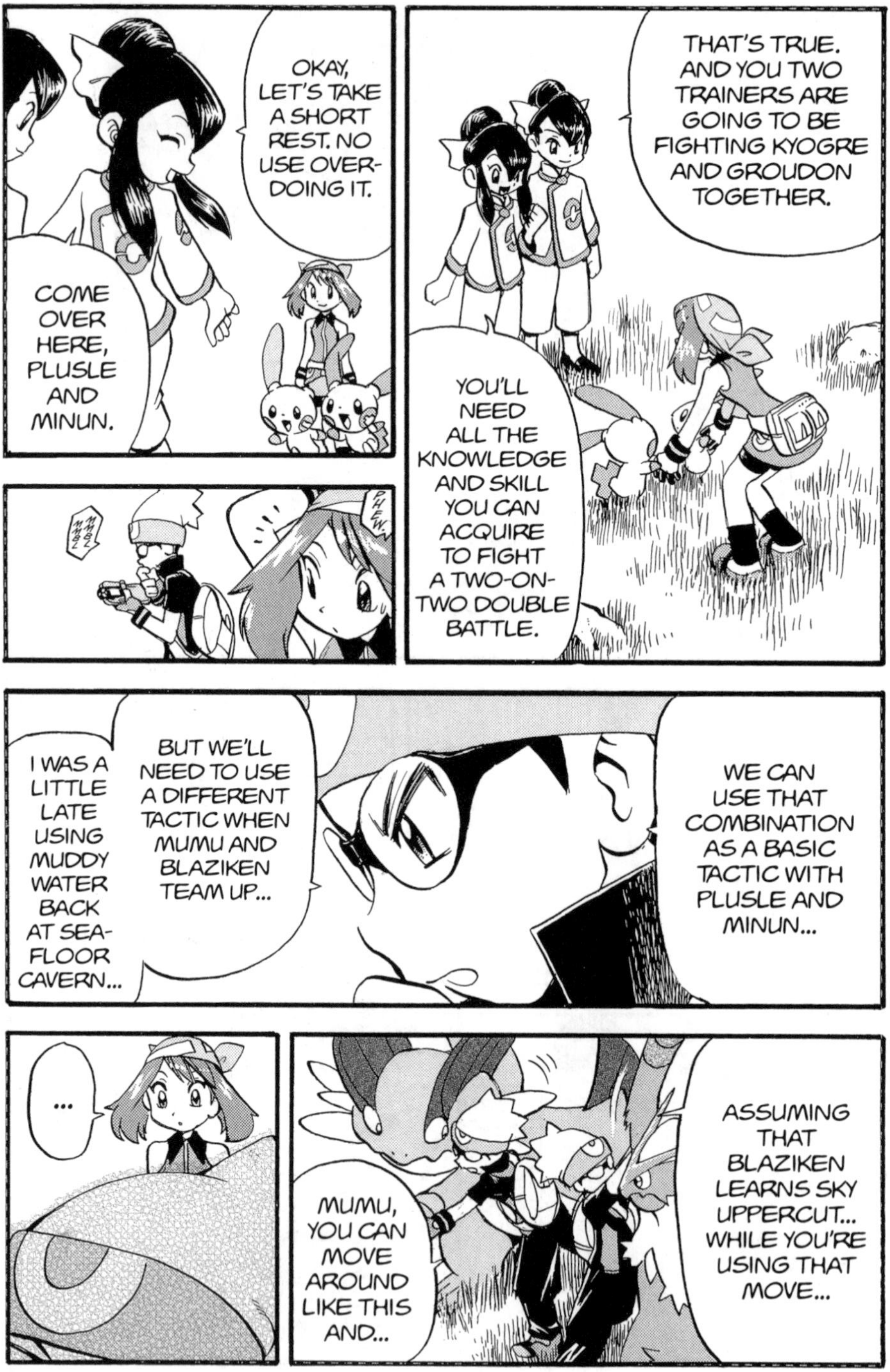
THAT'S TRUE. AND YOU TWO TRAINERS ARE GOING TO BE FIGHTING KYOGRE AND GROUDON TOGETHER.
YOU'LL NEED ALL THE KNOWLEDGE AND SKILL YOU CAN ACQUIRE TO FIGHT A TWO-ON-TWO DOUBLE BATTLE.
OKAY, LET'S TAKE A SHORT REST. NO USE OVER-DOING IT.
COME OVER HERE, PLUSLE AND MINUN.
PHEW.
MMBL MMBL
WE CAN USE THAT COMBINATION AS A BASIC TACTIC WITH PLUSLE AND MINUN...
BUT WE'LL NEED TO USE A DIFFERENT TACTIC WHEN MUMU AND BLAZIKEN TEAM UP...
I WAS A LITTLE LATE USING MUDDY WATER BACK AT SEA-FLOOR CAVERN...
ASSUMING THAT BLAZIKEN LEARNS SKY UPPERCUT... WHILE YOU'RE USING THAT MOVE...
MUMU, YOU CAN MOVE AROUND LIKE THIS AND...
...

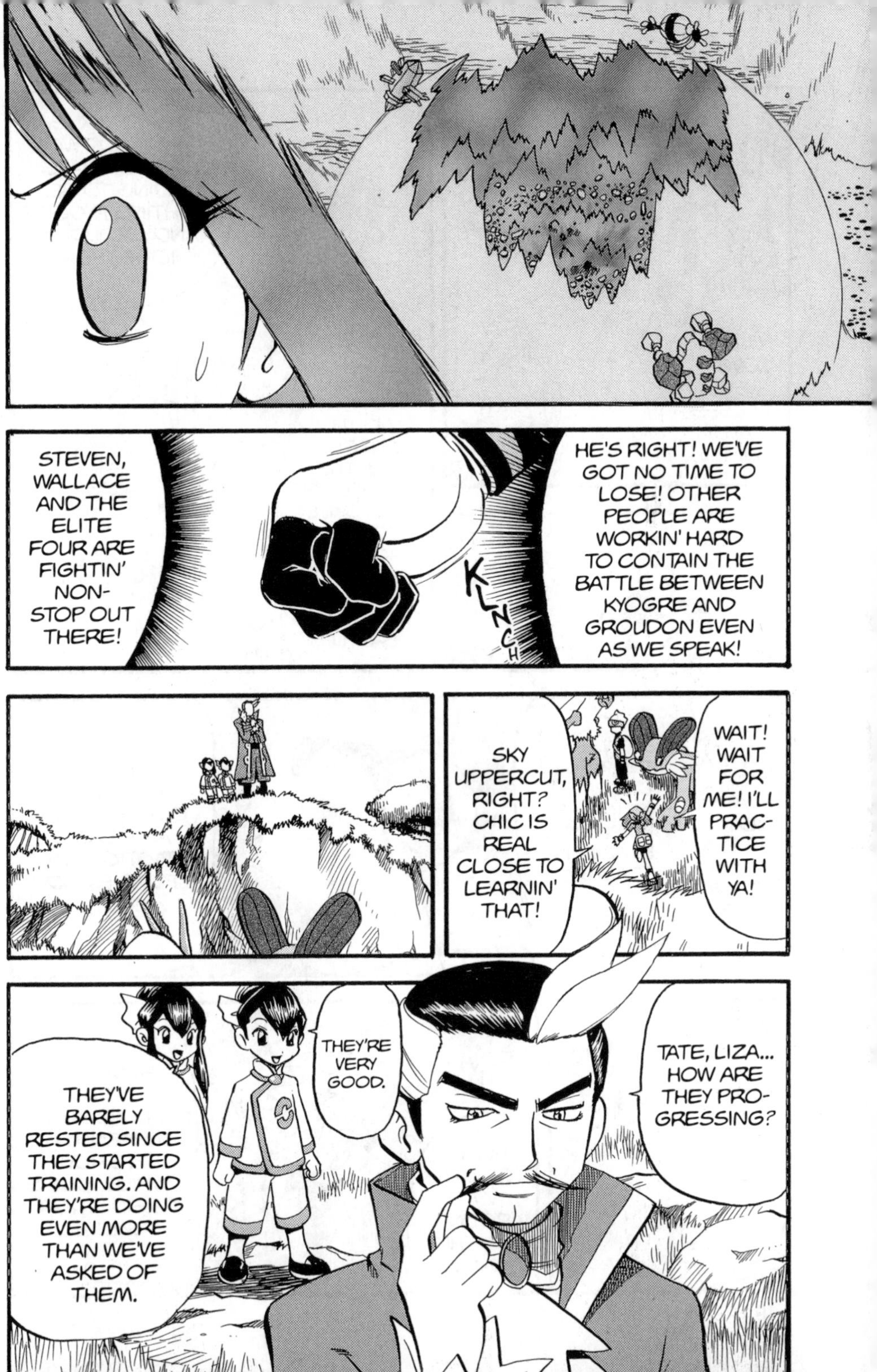

HE'S RIGHT! WE'VE GOT NO TIME TO LOSE! OTHER PEOPLE ARE WORKIN' HARD TO CONTAIN THE BATTLE BETWEEN KYOGRE AND GROUDON EVEN AS WE SPEAK!
KLNCH
STEVEN, WALLACE AND THE ELITE FOUR ARE FIGHTIN' NON-STOP OUT THERE!
WAIT! WAIT FOR ME! I'LL PRACTICE WITH YA!
SKY UPPERCUT, RIGHT? CHIC IS REAL CLOSE TO LEARNIN' THAT!
TATE, LIZA... HOW ARE THEY PROGRESSING?
THEY'RE VERY GOOD.
THEY'VE BARELY RESTED SINCE THEY STARTED TRAINING. AND THEY'RE DOING EVEN MORE THAN WE'VE ASKED OF THEM.

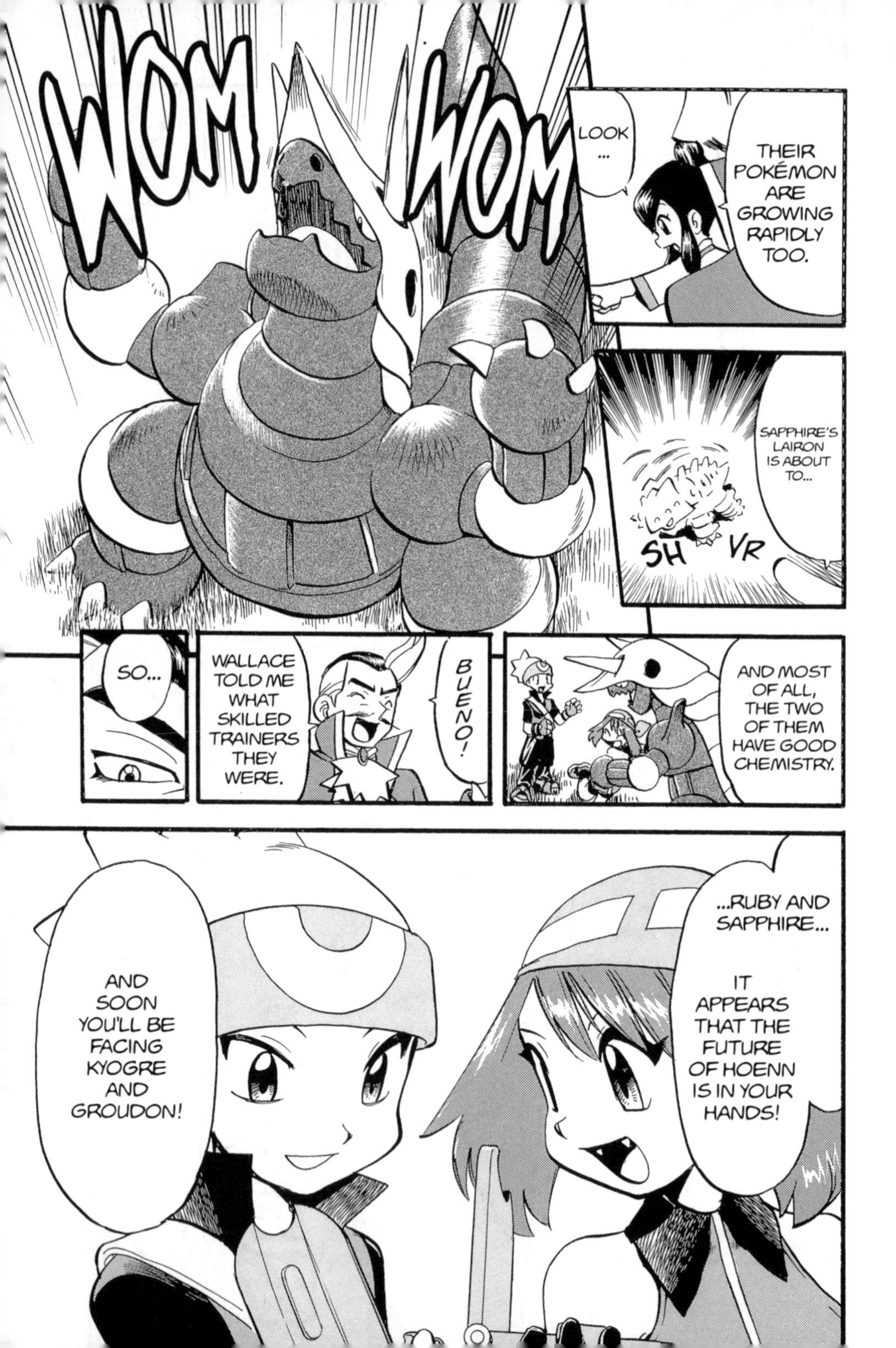
THEIR POKÉMON ARE GROWING RAPIDLY TOO.
LOOK...
SAPPHIRE'S LAIRON IS ABOUT TO...
SH VR
WOM WOM
AND MOST OF ALL, THE TWO OF THEM HAVE GOOD CHEMISTRY.
BUENO!
WALLACE TOLD ME WHAT SKILLED TRAINERS THEY WERE.
SO...
...RUBY AND SAPPHIRE...
IT APPEARS THAT THE FUTURE OF HOENN IS IN YOUR HANDS!
AND SOON YOU'LL BE FACING KYOGRE AND GROUDON!

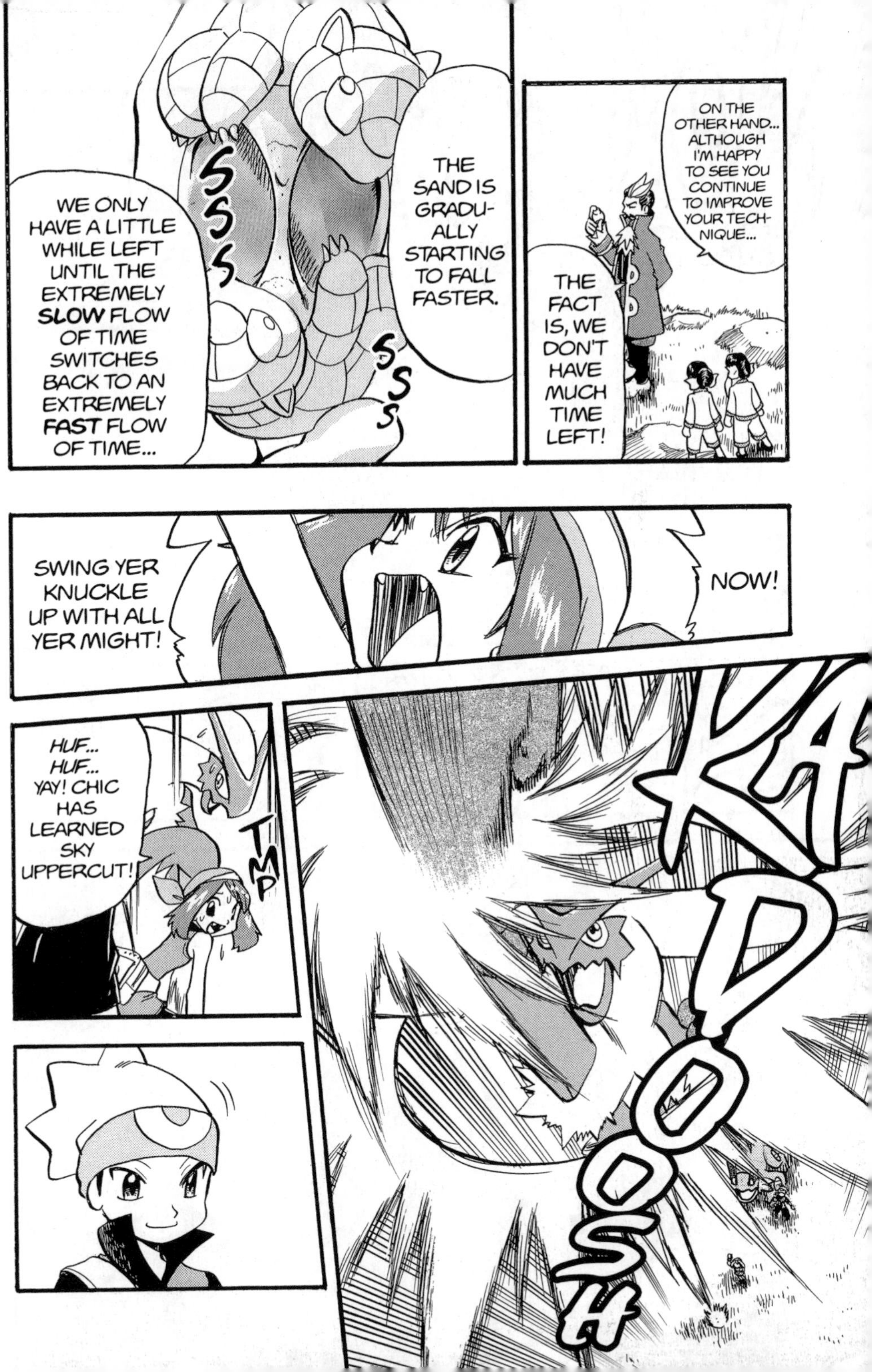
ON THE OTHER HAND... ALTHOUGH I'M HAPPY TO SEE YOU CONTINUE TO IMPROVE YOUR TECH-NIQUE...
THE FACT IS, WE DON'T HAVE MUCH TIME LEFT!
THE SAND IS GRADU-ALLY STARTING TO FALL FASTER.
SSS
WE ONLY HAVE A LITTLE WHILE LEFT UNTIL THE EXTREMELY **SLOW** FLOW OF TIME SWITCHES BACK TO AN EXTREMELY **FAST** FLOW OF TIME...
SSS
SWING YER KNUCKLE UP WITH ALL YER MIGHT!
NOW!
KADOOOSH
HUF... HUF... YAY! CHIC HAS LEARNED SKY UPPERCUT!
TMP

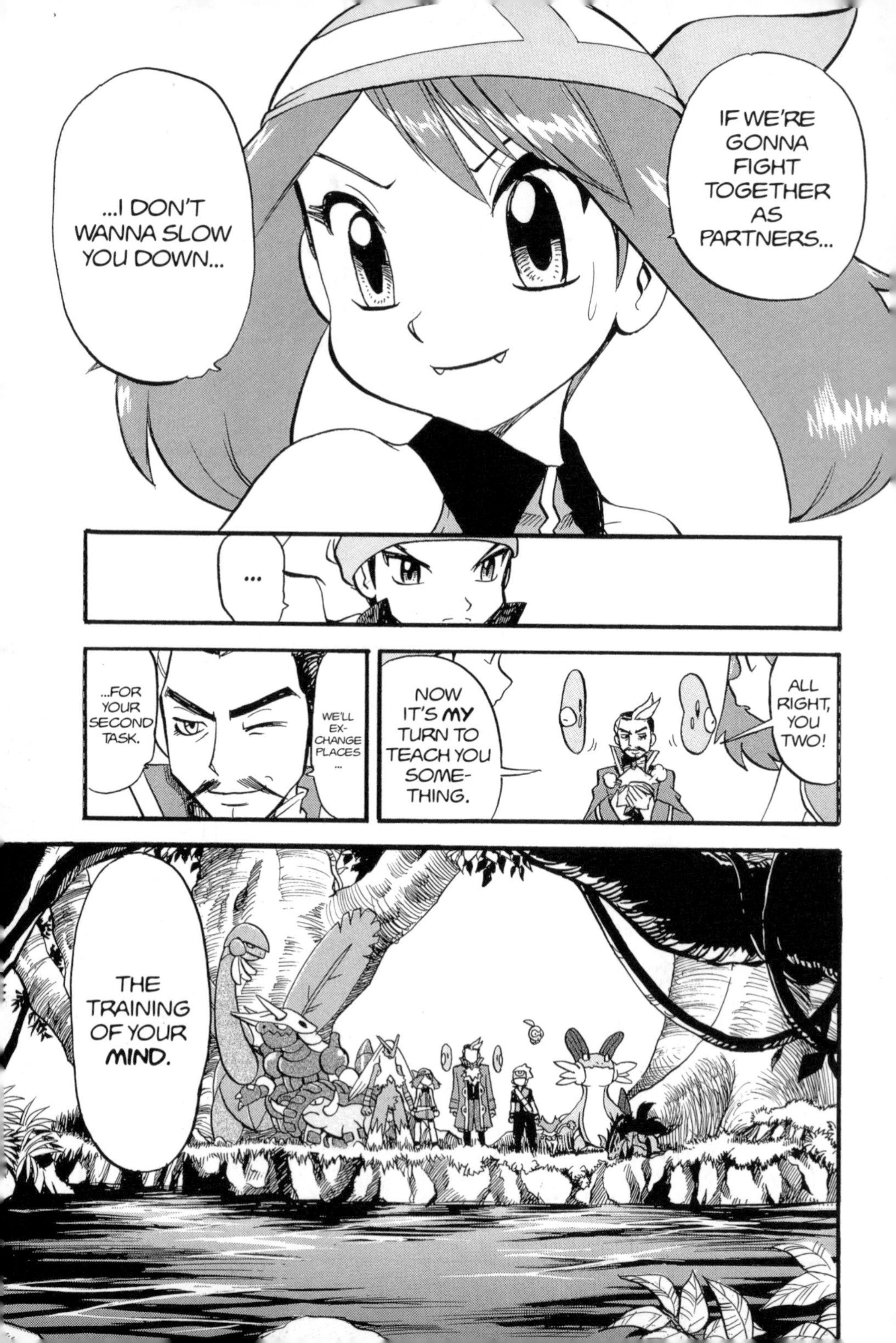
IF WE'RE GONNA FIGHT TOGETHER AS PARTNERS...
...I DON'T WANNA SLOW YOU DOWN...
...
ALL RIGHT, YOU TWO!
NOW IT'S **MY** TURN TO TEACH YOU SOME-THING.
WE'LL EX-CHANGE PLACES ...
...FOR YOUR SECOND TASK.
THE TRAINING OF YOUR **MIND**.

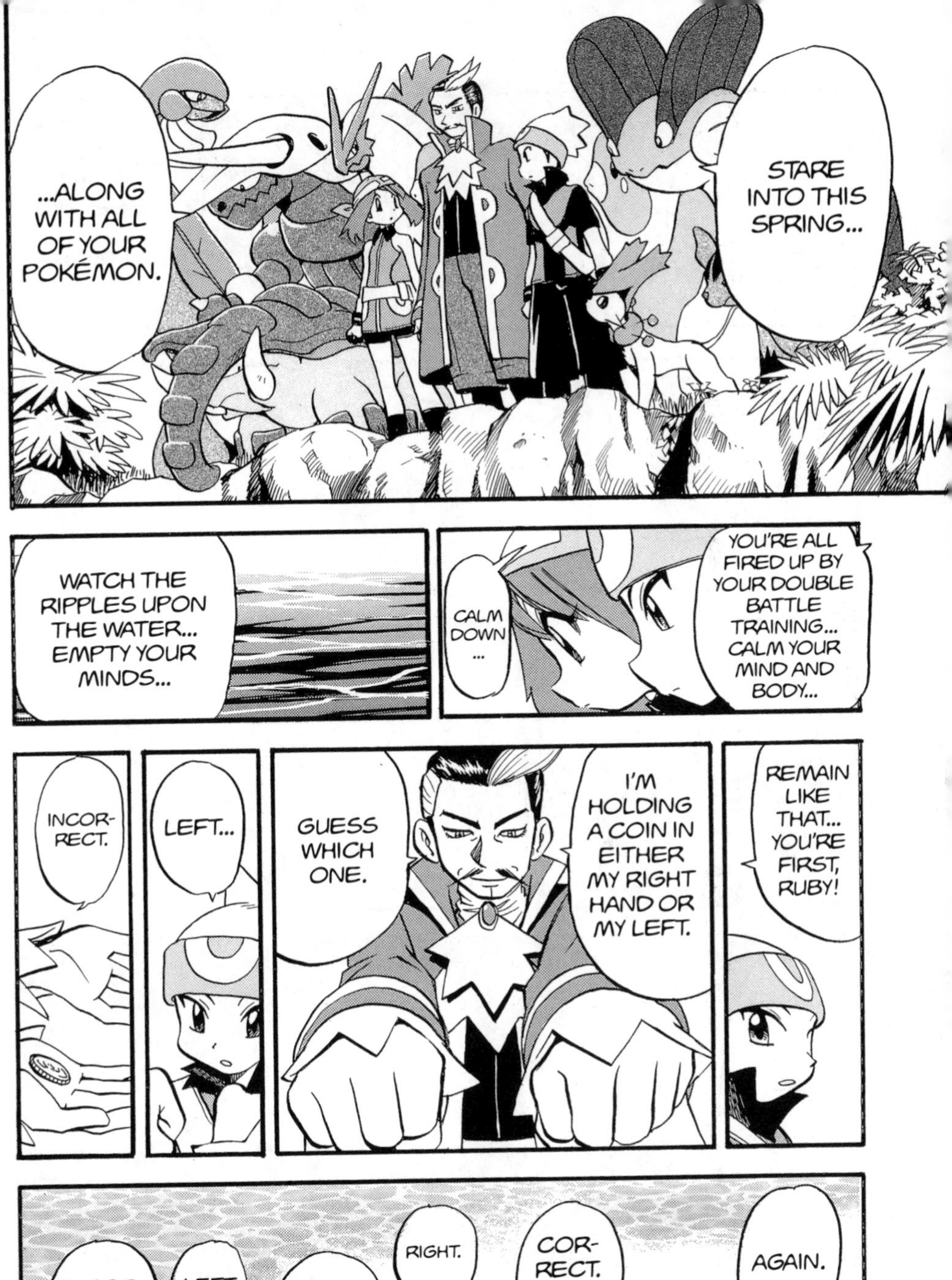
STARE INTO THIS SPRING...
...ALONG WITH ALL OF YOUR POKÉMON.
YOU'RE ALL FIRED UP BY YOUR DOUBLE BATTLE TRAINING... CALM YOUR MIND AND BODY...
CALM DOWN ...
WATCH THE RIPPLES UPON THE WATER... EMPTY YOUR MINDS...
REMAIN LIKE THAT... YOU'RE FIRST, RUBY!
I'M HOLDING A COIN IN EITHER MY RIGHT HAND OR MY LEFT.
GUESS WHICH ONE.
LEFT...
INCOR-RECT.
AGAIN.
RIGHT.
COR-RECT. AGAIN.
RIGHT.
INCOR-RECT. AGAIN.
LEFT.
INCOR-RECT. AGAIN.

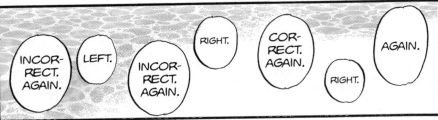

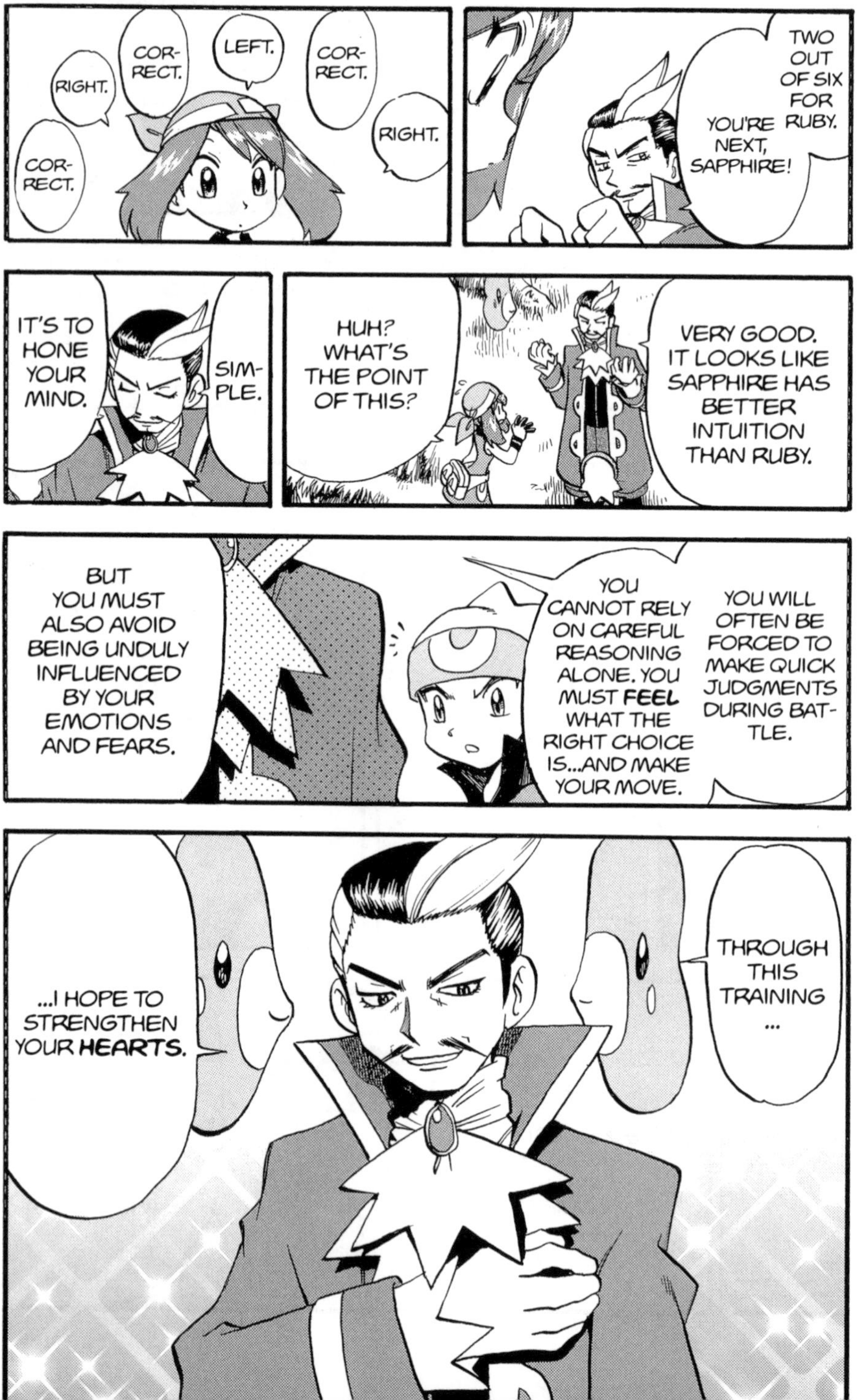
TWO OUT OF SIX FOR RUBY.
YOU'RE NEXT, SAPPHIRE!
RIGHT.
COR-RECT.
LEFT.
COR-RECT.
RIGHT.
COR-RECT.
VERY GOOD. IT LOOKS LIKE SAPPHIRE HAS BETTER INTUITION THAN RUBY.
HUH? WHAT'S THE POINT OF THIS?
SIM-PLE.
IT'S TO HONE YOUR MIND.
YOU WILL OFTEN BE FORCED TO MAKE QUICK JUDGMENTS DURING BAT-TLE.
YOU CANNOT RELY ON CAREFUL REASONING ALONE. YOU MUST **FEEL** WHAT THE RIGHT CHOICE IS...AND MAKE YOUR MOVE.
BUT YOU MUST ALSO AVOID BEING UNDULY INFLUENCED BY YOUR EMOTIONS AND FEARS.
THROUGH THIS TRAINING ...
...I HOPE TO STRENGTHEN YOUR **HEARTS**.

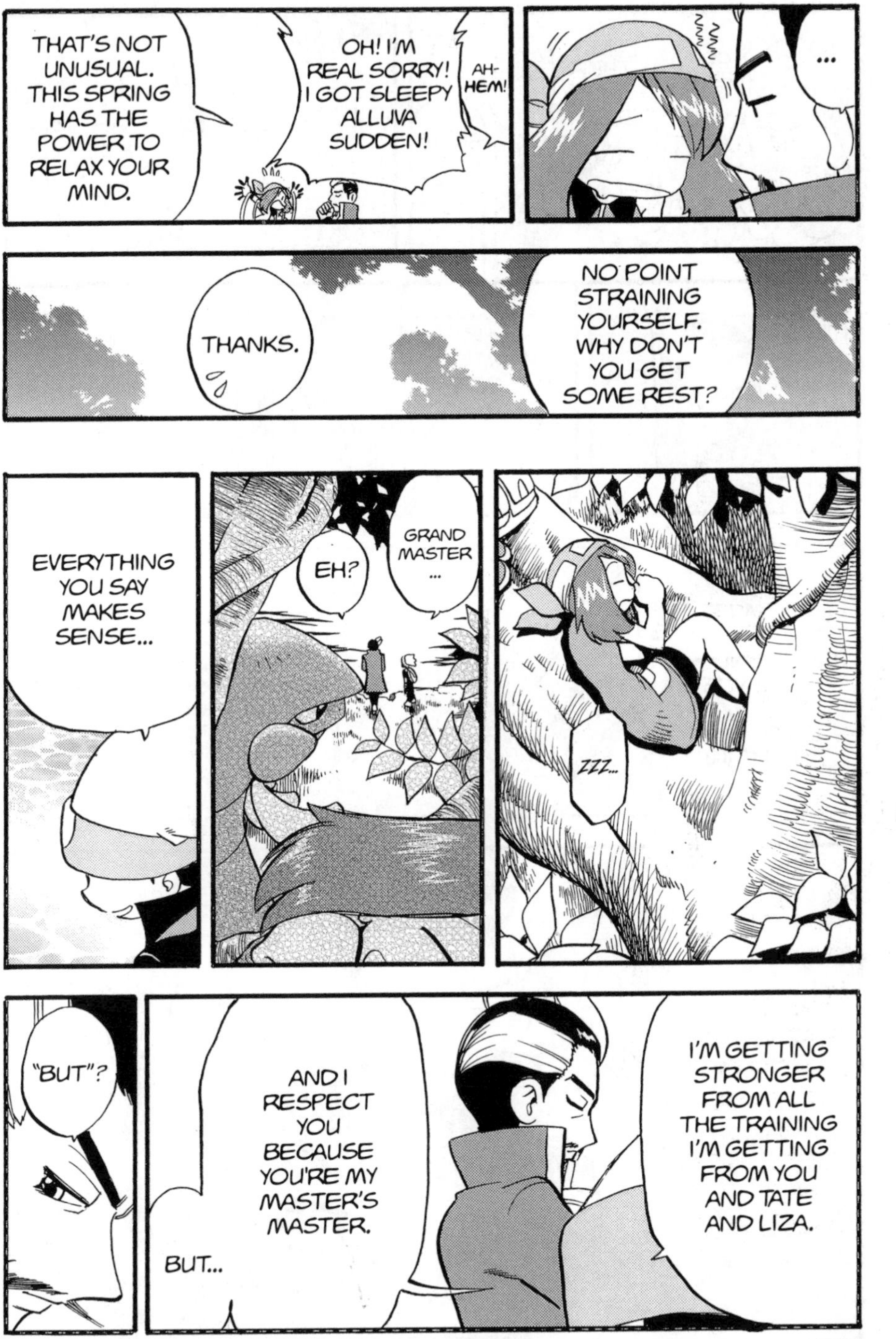
...
AH-HEM!
OH! I'M REAL SORRY! I GOT SLEEPY ALLUVA SUDDEN!
THAT'S NOT UNUSUAL. THIS SPRING HAS THE POWER TO RELAX YOUR MIND.
NO POINT STRAINING YOURSELF. WHY DON'T YOU GET SOME REST?
THANKS.
ZZZ...
GRAND MASTER ...
EH?
EVERYTHING YOU SAY MAKES SENSE...
I'M GETTING STRONGER FROM ALL THE TRAINING I'M GETTING FROM YOU AND TATE AND LIZA.
AND I RESPECT YOU BECAUSE YOU'RE MY MASTER'S MASTER.
BUT...
"BUT"?

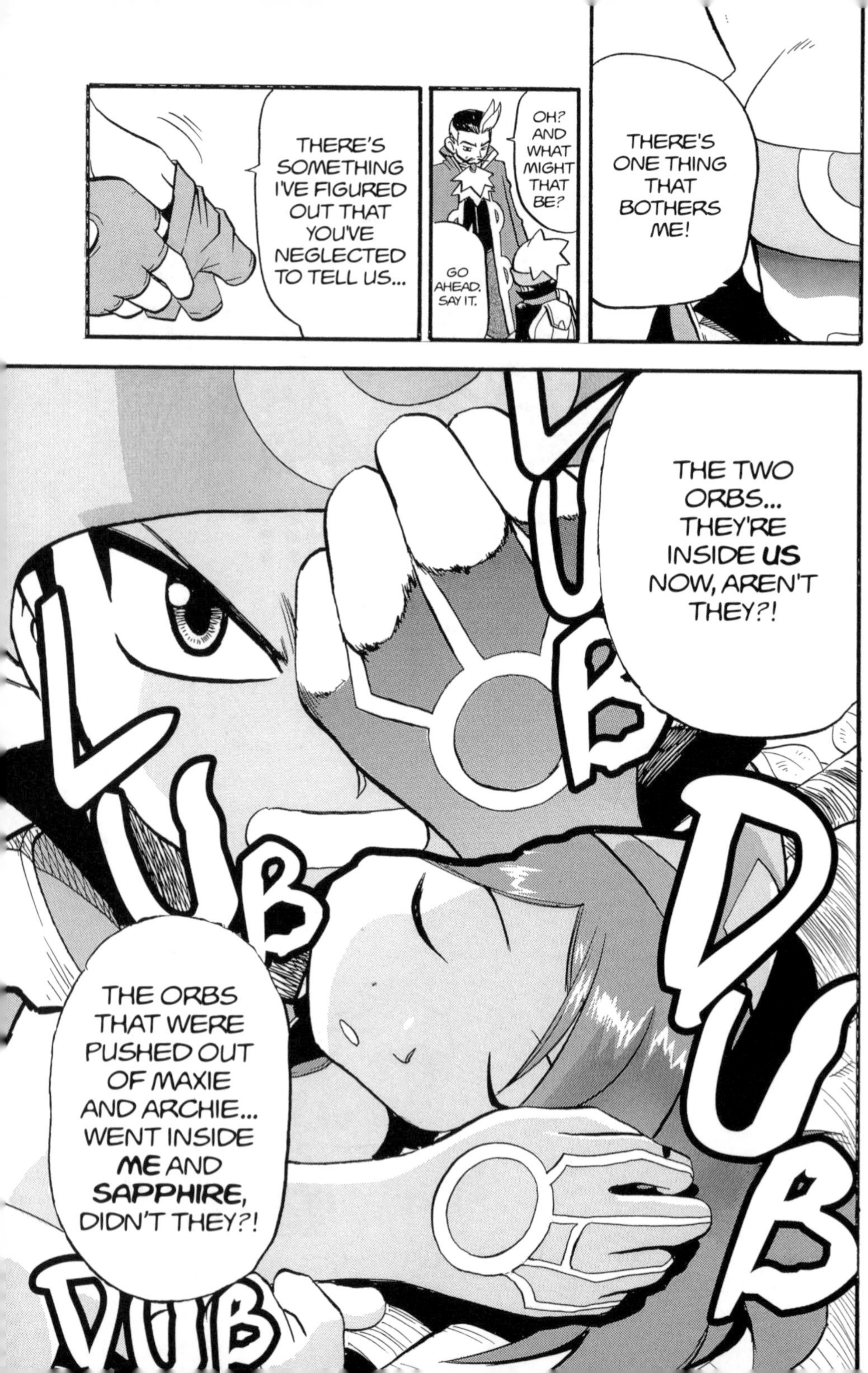
THERE'S ONE THING THAT BOTHERS ME!
OH? AND WHAT MIGHT THAT BE?
GO AHEAD. SAY IT.
THERE'S SOMETHING I'VE FIGURED OUT THAT YOU'VE NEGLECTED TO TELL US...
LUB
THE TWO ORBS... THEY'RE INSIDE **US** NOW, AREN'T THEY?!
DUB
LUB
THE ORBS THAT WERE PUSHED OUT OF MAXIE AND ARCHIE... WENT INSIDE **ME** AND **SAPPHIRE**, DIDN'T THEY?!
DUB

● Adventure 257 ●
The Beginning of the End with Kyogre and Groudon, Part 15

The Fourth Chapter

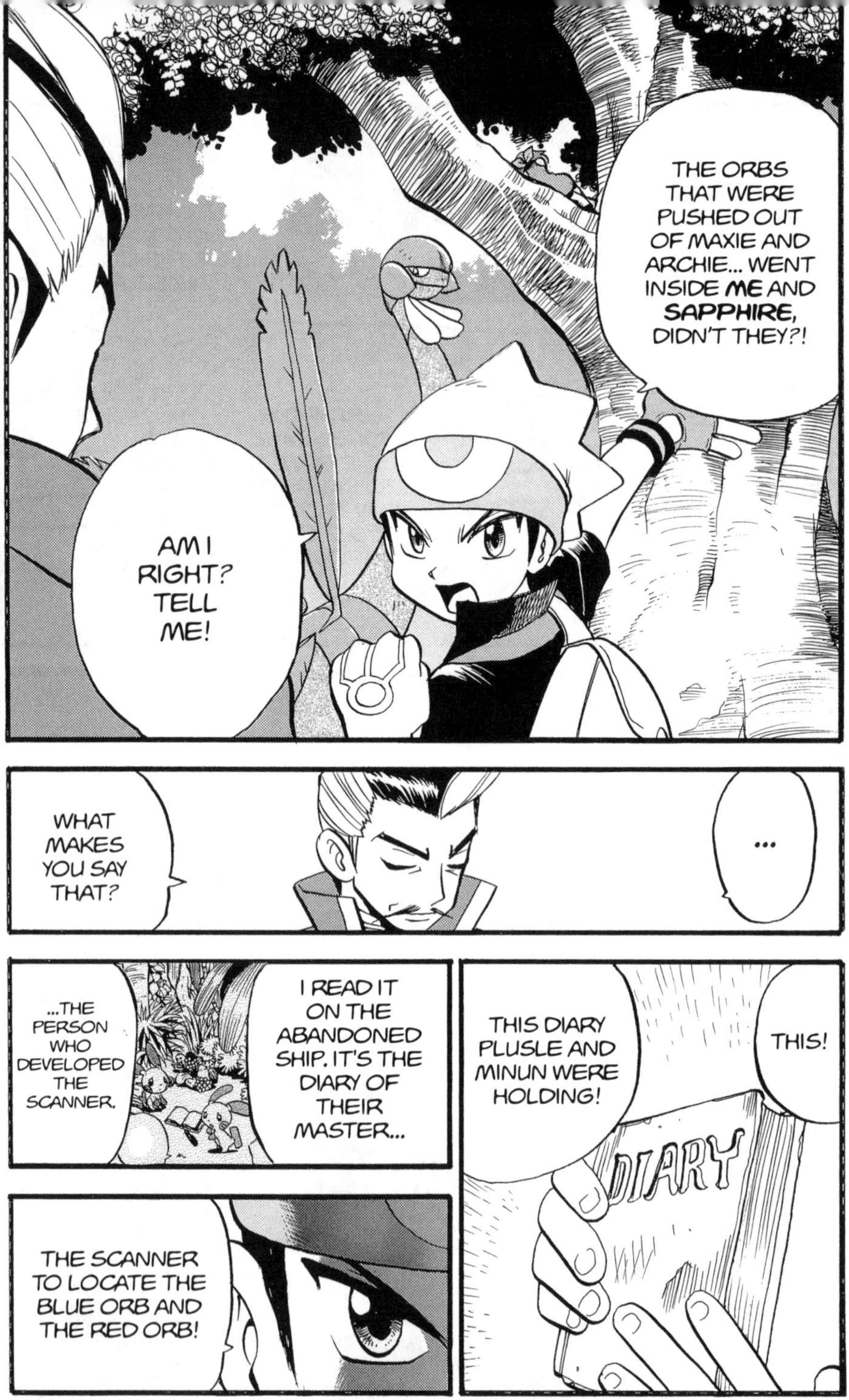
THE ORBS THAT WERE PUSHED OUT OF MAXIE AND ARCHIE... WENT INSIDE **ME** AND **SAPPHIRE,** DIDN'T THEY?!
AM I RIGHT? TELL ME!
...
WHAT MAKES YOU SAY THAT?
THIS!
THIS DIARY PLUSLE AND MINUN WERE HOLDING!
I READ IT ON THE ABANDONED SHIP. IT'S THE DIARY OF THEIR MASTER...
...THE PERSON WHO DEVELOPED THE SCANNER.
THE SCANNER TO LOCATE THE BLUE ORB AND THE RED ORB!
DIARY

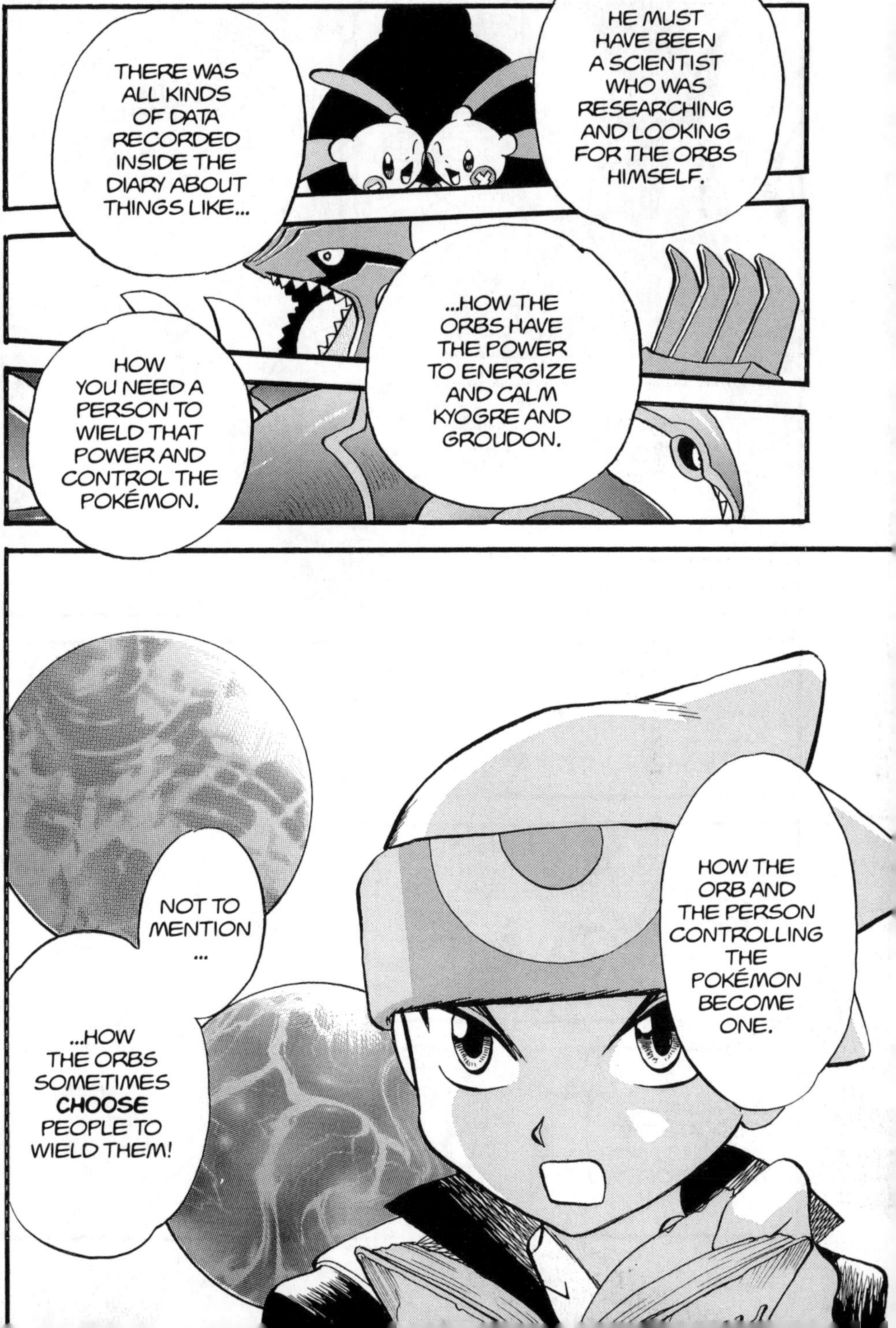
HE MUST HAVE BEEN A SCIENTIST WHO WAS RESEARCHING AND LOOKING FOR THE ORBS HIMSELF.
THERE WAS ALL KINDS OF DATA RECORDED INSIDE THE DIARY ABOUT THINGS LIKE...
...HOW THE ORBS HAVE THE POWER TO ENERGIZE AND CALM KYOGRE AND GROUDON.
HOW YOU NEED A PERSON TO WIELD THAT POWER AND CONTROL THE POKÉMON.
HOW THE ORB AND THE PERSON CONTROLLING THE POKÉMON BECOME ONE.
NOT TO MENTION ...
...HOW THE ORBS SOMETIMES **CHOOSE** PEOPLE TO WIELD THEM!

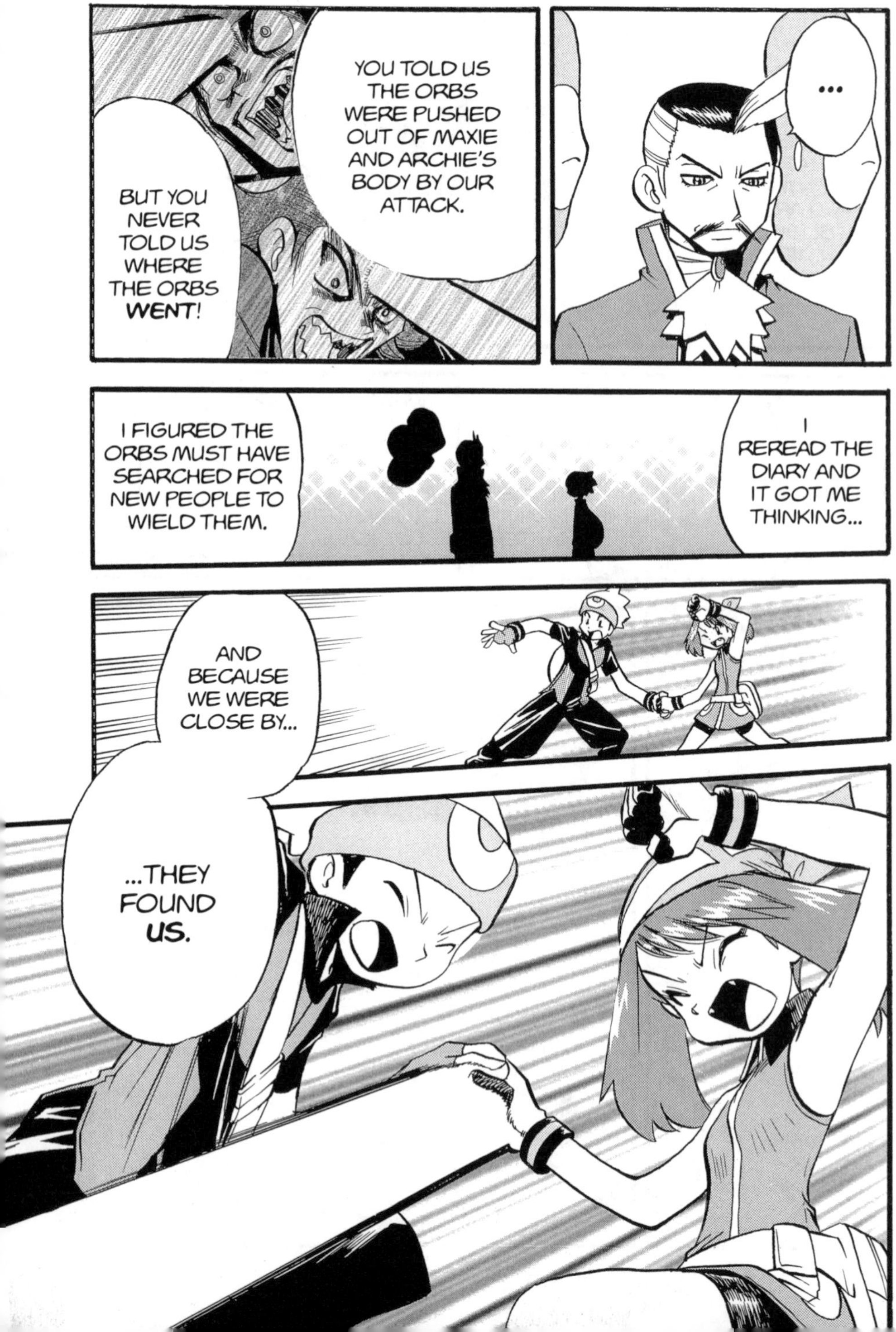
...
YOU TOLD US THE ORBS WERE PUSHED OUT OF MAXIE AND ARCHIE'S BODY BY OUR ATTACK.
BUT YOU NEVER TOLD US WHERE THE ORBS **WENT**!
I REREAD THE DIARY AND IT GOT ME THINKING...
I FIGURED THE ORBS MUST HAVE SEARCHED FOR NEW PEOPLE TO WIELD THEM.
AND BECAUSE WE WERE CLOSE BY...
...THEY FOUND **US.**

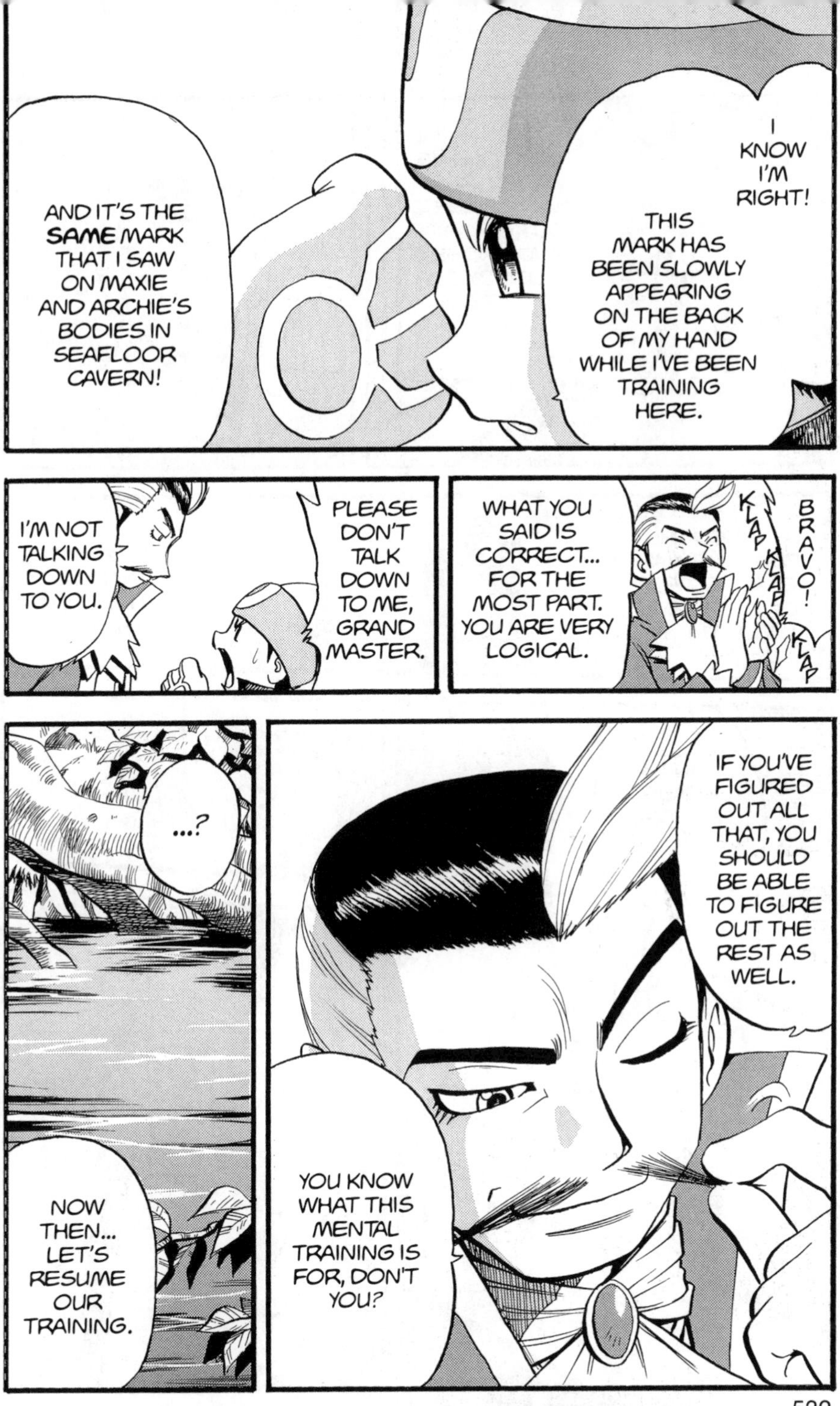

I KNOW I'M RIGHT!
THIS MARK HAS BEEN SLOWLY APPEARING ON THE BACK OF MY HAND WHILE I'VE BEEN TRAINING HERE.
AND IT'S THE **SAME** MARK THAT I SAW ON MAXIE AND ARCHIE'S BODIES IN SEAFLOOR CAVERN!
BRAVO!
KLAP KLAP KLAP KLAP
WHAT YOU SAID IS CORRECT... FOR THE MOST PART. YOU ARE VERY LOGICAL.
PLEASE DON'T TALK DOWN TO ME, GRAND MASTER.
I'M NOT TALKING DOWN TO YOU.
IF YOU'VE FIGURED OUT ALL THAT, YOU SHOULD BE ABLE TO FIGURE OUT THE REST AS WELL.
YOU KNOW WHAT THIS MENTAL TRAINING IS FOR, DON'T YOU?
...?
NOW THEN... LET'S RESUME OUR TRAINING.

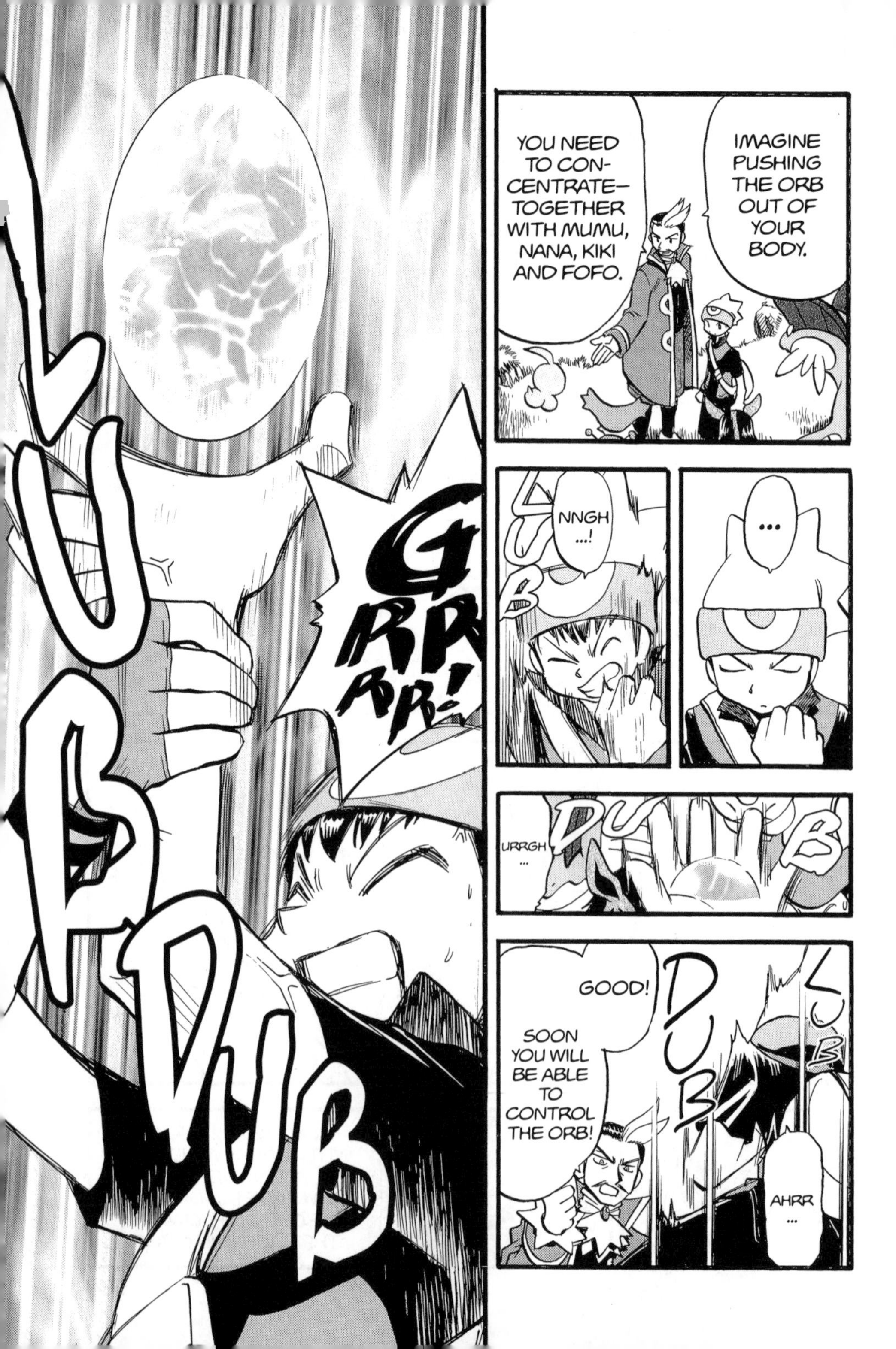
IMAGINE PUSHING THE ORB OUT OF YOUR BODY.
YOU NEED TO CONCENTRATE—TOGETHER WITH MUMU, NANA, KIKI AND FOFO.
...
NNGH ...!
LUB
DUB
URRGH ...
LUB
DUB
AHRR ...
GOOD!
SOON YOU WILL BE ABLE TO CONTROL THE ORB!
GRRRRR!
LUB
DUB

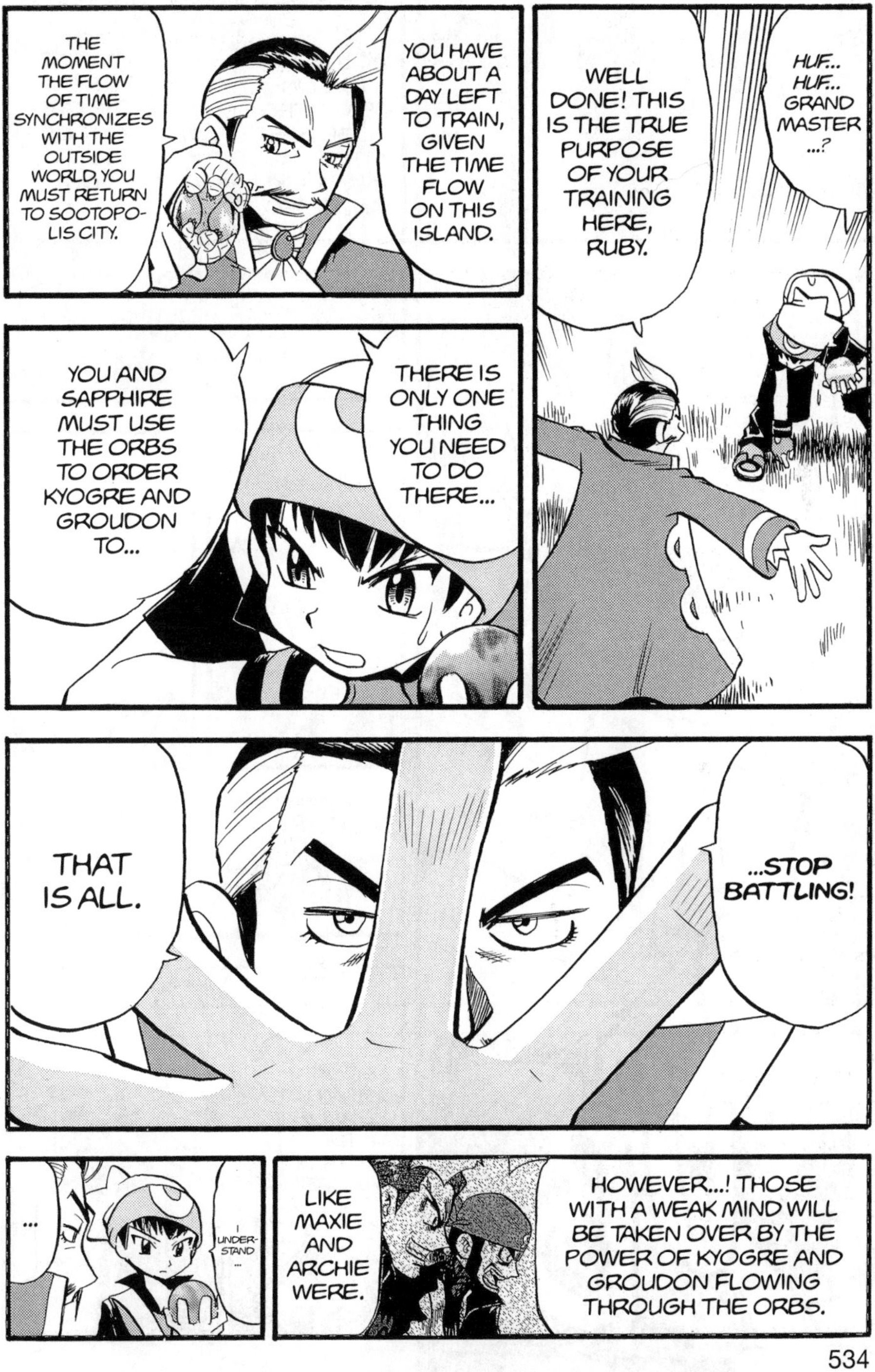
HUF... HUF... GRAND MASTER ...?
WELL DONE! THIS IS THE TRUE PURPOSE OF YOUR TRAINING HERE, RUBY.
YOU HAVE ABOUT A DAY LEFT TO TRAIN, GIVEN THE TIME FLOW ON THIS ISLAND.
THE MOMENT THE FLOW OF TIME SYNCHRONIZES WITH THE OUTSIDE WORLD, YOU MUST RETURN TO SOOTOPO-LIS CITY.
THERE IS ONLY ONE THING YOU NEED TO DO THERE...
YOU AND SAPPHIRE MUST USE THE ORBS TO ORDER KYOGRE AND GROUDON TO...
...STOP BATTLING!
THAT IS ALL.
HOWEVER...! THOSE WITH A WEAK MIND WILL BE TAKEN OVER BY THE POWER OF KYOGRE AND GROUDON FLOWING THROUGH THE ORBS.
LIKE MAXIE AND ARCHIE WERE.
I UNDER-STAND ...
...

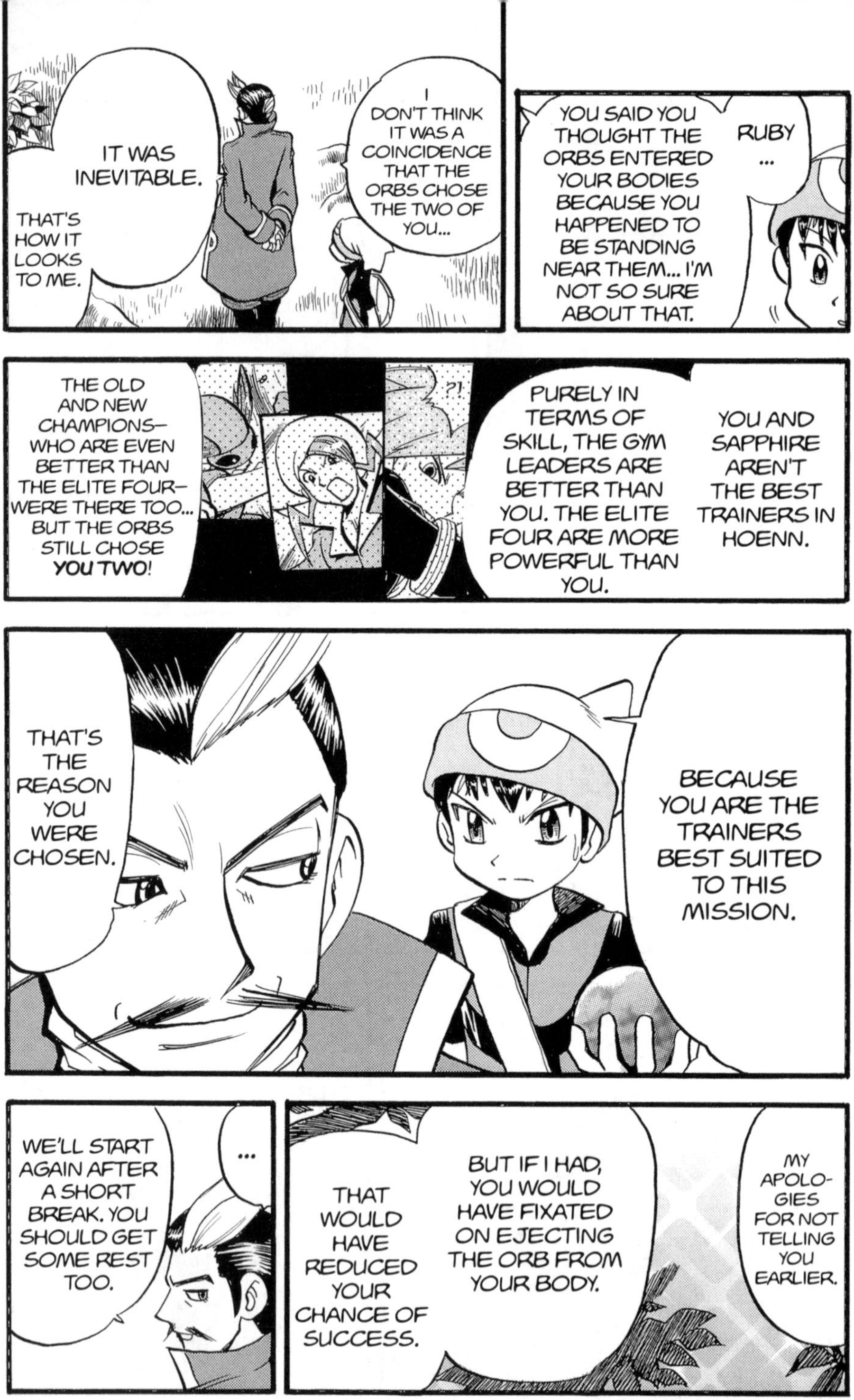
RUBY ...
YOU SAID YOU THOUGHT THE ORBS ENTERED YOUR BODIES BECAUSE YOU HAPPENED TO BE STANDING NEAR THEM... I'M NOT SO SURE ABOUT THAT.
I DON'T THINK IT WAS A COINCIDENCE THAT THE ORBS CHOSE THE TWO OF YOU...
IT WAS INEVITABLE.
THAT'S HOW IT LOOKS TO ME.
YOU AND SAPPHIRE AREN'T THE BEST TRAINERS IN HOENN.
PURELY IN TERMS OF SKILL, THE GYM LEADERS ARE BETTER THAN YOU. THE ELITE FOUR ARE MORE POWERFUL THAN YOU.
?!
THE OLD AND NEW CHAMPIONS—WHO ARE EVEN BETTER THAN THE ELITE FOUR—WERE THERE TOO... BUT THE ORBS STILL CHOSE **YOU TWO**!
BECAUSE YOU ARE THE TRAINERS BEST SUITED TO THIS MISSION.
THAT'S THE REASON YOU WERE CHOSEN.
MY APOLOGIES FOR NOT TELLING YOU EARLIER.
BUT IF I HAD, YOU WOULD HAVE FIXATED ON EJECTING THE ORB FROM YOUR BODY.
THAT WOULD HAVE REDUCED YOUR CHANCE OF SUCCESS.
...
WE'LL START AGAIN AFTER A SHORT BREAK. YOU SHOULD GET SOME REST TOO.

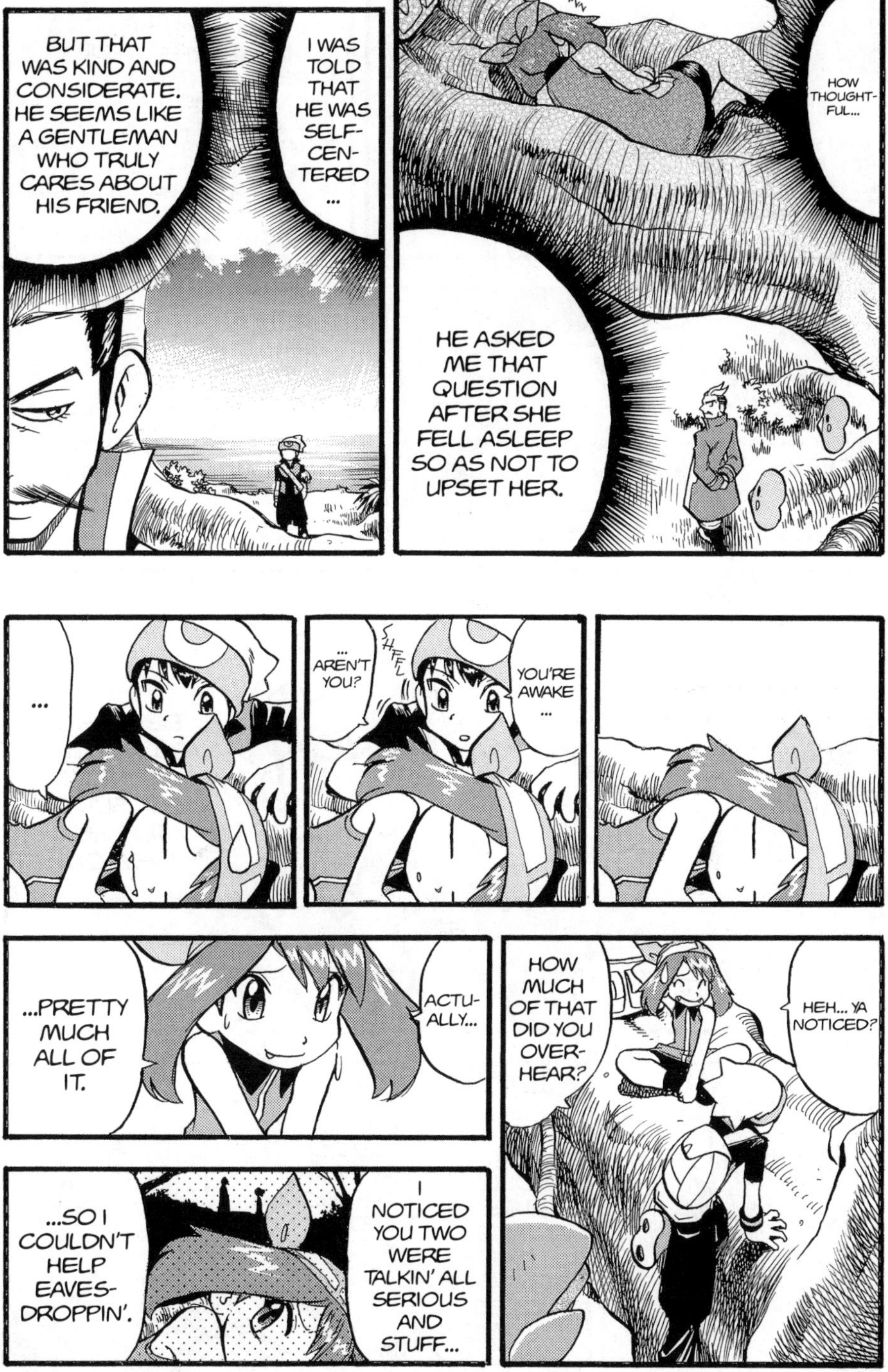
HOW THOUGHTFUL...
HE ASKED ME THAT QUESTION AFTER SHE FELL ASLEEP SO AS NOT TO UPSET HER.
I WAS TOLD THAT HE WAS SELF-CENTERED ...
BUT THAT WAS KIND AND CONSIDERATE. HE SEEMS LIKE A GENTLEMAN WHO TRULY CARES ABOUT HIS FRIEND.
YOU'RE AWAKE ...
SHFFL
... AREN'T YOU?
...
HEH... YA NOTICED?
HOW MUCH OF THAT DID YOU OVER-HEAR?
ACTU-ALLY...
...PRETTY MUCH ALL OF IT.
I NOTICED YOU TWO WERE TALKIN' ALL SERIOUS AND STUFF...
...SO I COULDN'T HELP EAVES-DROPPIN'.

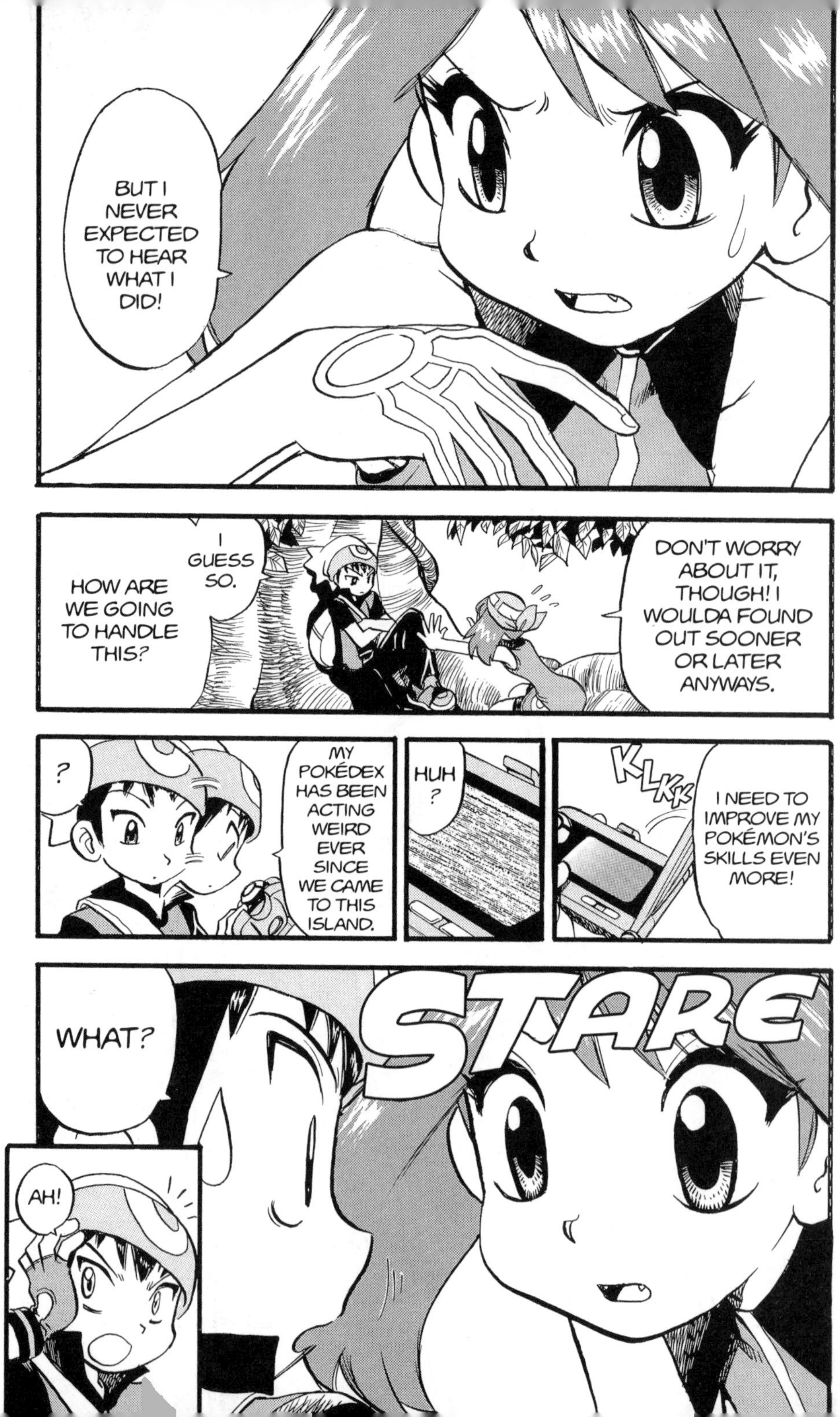
BUT I NEVER EXPECTED TO HEAR WHAT I DID!
DON'T WORRY ABOUT IT, THOUGH! I WOULDA FOUND OUT SOONER OR LATER ANYWAYS.
I GUESS SO.
HOW ARE WE GOING TO HANDLE THIS?
KLKK
I NEED TO IMPROVE MY POKÉMON'S SKILLS EVEN MORE!
HUH?
MY POKÉDEX HAS BEEN ACTING WEIRD EVER SINCE WE CAME TO THIS ISLAND.
?
STARE
WHAT?
AH!

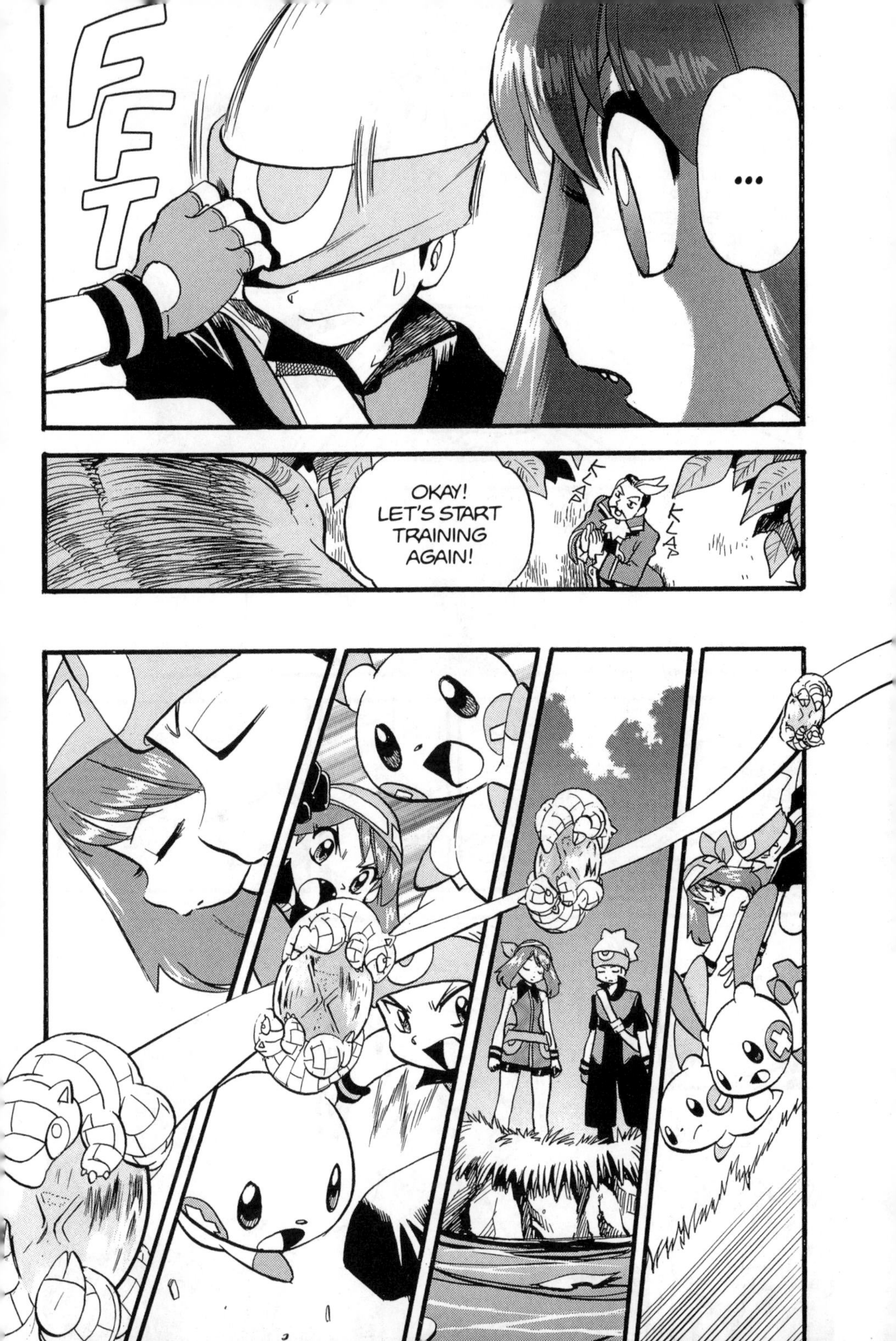
...
FFT
KLAP
KLAP
OKAY! LET'S START TRAINING AGAIN!

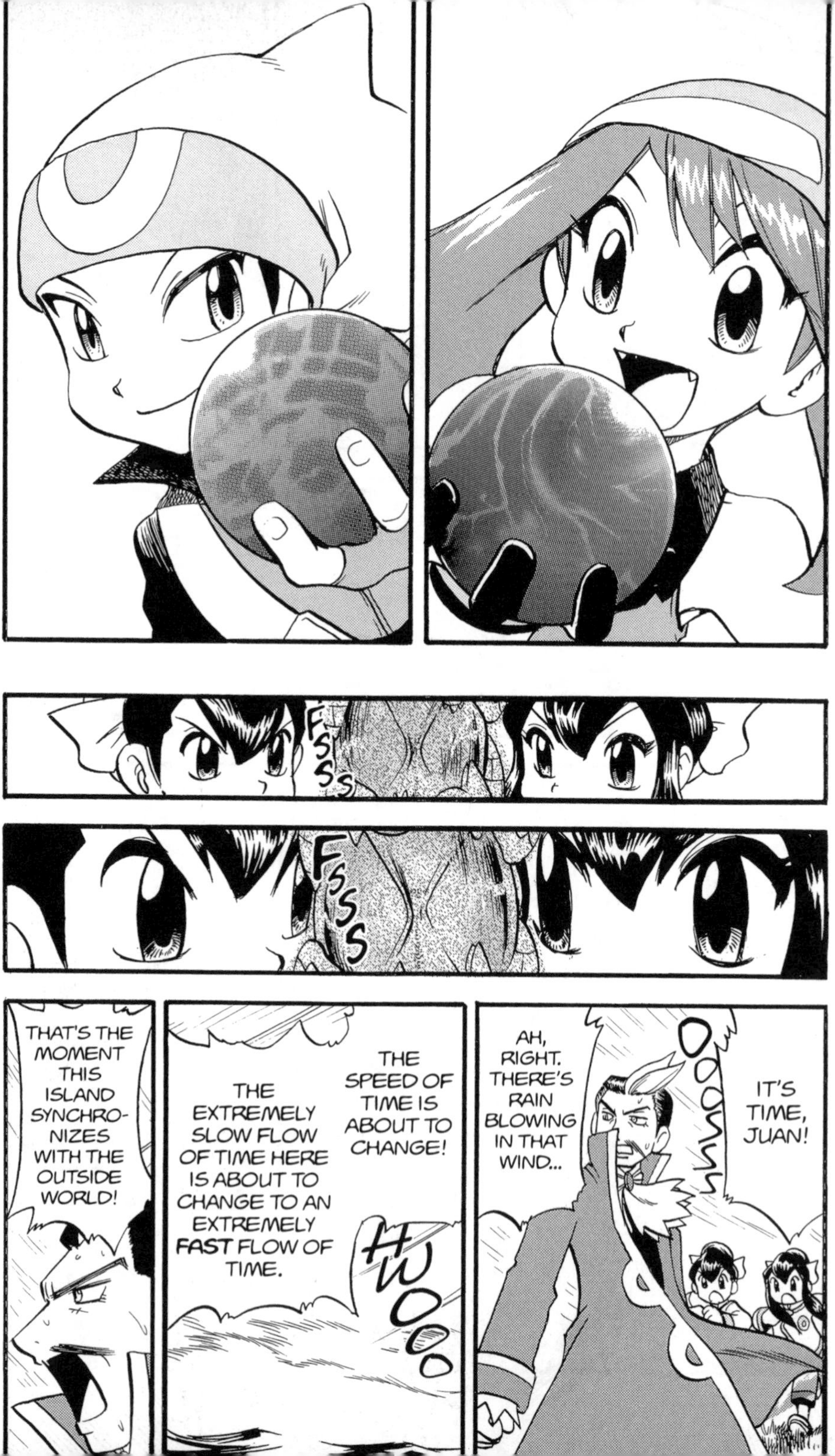
FSSS
FSSS
IT'S TIME, JUAN!
HWOOOO
AH, RIGHT. THERE'S RAIN BLOWING IN THAT WIND...
THE SPEED OF TIME IS ABOUT TO CHANGE!
THE EXTREMELY SLOW FLOW OF TIME HERE IS ABOUT TO CHANGE TO AN EXTREMELY **FAST** FLOW OF TIME.
HWOOOO
THAT'S THE MOMENT THIS ISLAND SYNCHRO-NIZES WITH THE OUTSIDE WORLD!

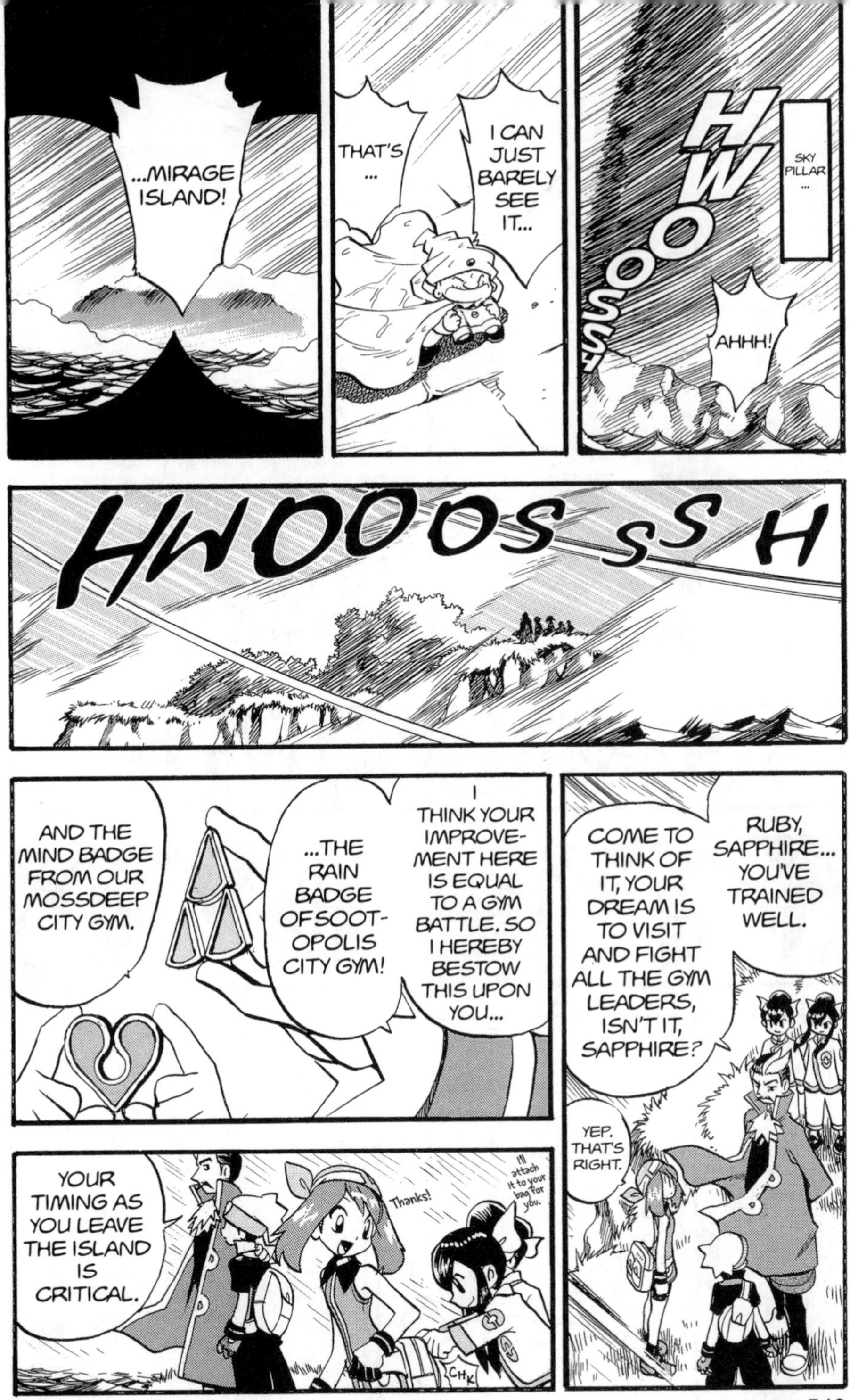
SKY PILLAR...
HWOOSSH
AHHH!
I CAN JUST BARELY SEE IT...
THAT'S...
...MIRAGE ISLAND!
HWOOOSSSH
RUBY, SAPPHIRE... YOU'VE TRAINED WELL.
COME TO THINK OF IT, YOUR DREAM IS TO VISIT AND FIGHT ALL THE GYM LEADERS, ISN'T IT, SAPPHIRE?
YEP. THAT'S RIGHT.
I THINK YOUR IMPROVEMENT HERE IS EQUAL TO A GYM BATTLE. SO I HEREBY BESTOW THIS UPON YOU...
...THE RAIN BADGE OF SOOTOPOLIS CITY GYM!
AND THE MIND BADGE FROM OUR MOSSDEEP CITY GYM.
I'll attach it to your bag for you.
Thanks!
YOUR TIMING AS YOU LEAVE THE ISLAND IS CRITICAL.
CHK

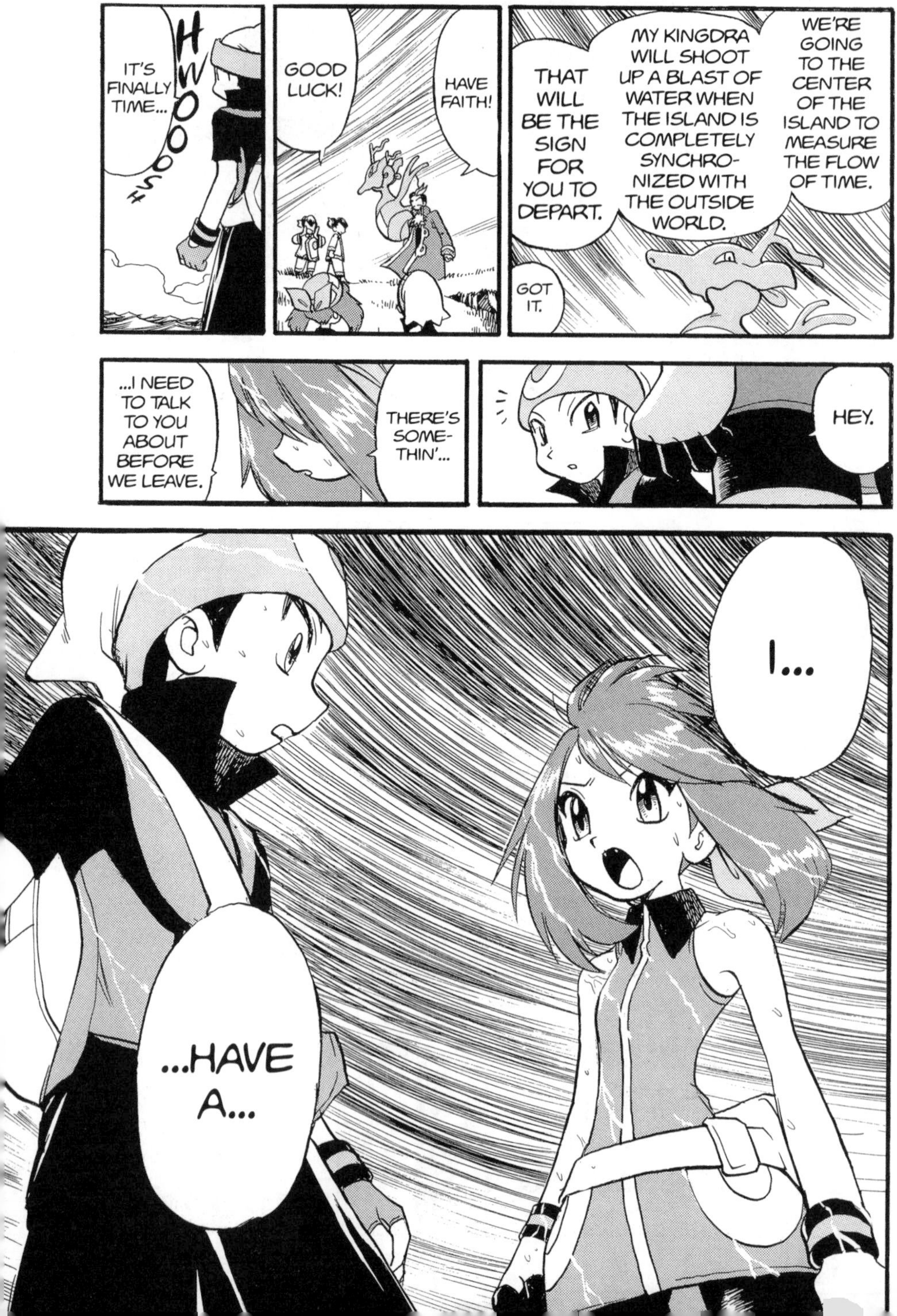
WE'RE GOING TO THE CENTER OF THE ISLAND TO MEASURE THE FLOW OF TIME.
MY KINGDRA WILL SHOOT UP A BLAST OF WATER WHEN THE ISLAND IS COMPLETELY SYNCHRO-NIZED WITH THE OUTSIDE WORLD.
THAT WILL BE THE SIGN FOR YOU TO DEPART.
GOT IT.
HAVE FAITH!
GOOD LUCK!
HWOOOOSH
IT'S FINALLY TIME...
HEY.
THERE'S SOME-THIN'...
...I NEED TO TALK TO YOU ABOUT BEFORE WE LEAVE.
I...
...HAVE A...

ADVENTURE MAP

SAPPHIRE

RUBY

CHIC
Blaziken ♀
Lv59

RONO
Aggron ♂
Lv54

PHADO
Donphan ♂
Lv58

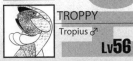

TROPPY
Tropius ♂
Lv56

MINUN
Minun ♀
Lv52

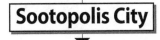

Route 126

▼

Seafloor Cavern

▼

Sootopolis City

▼▼

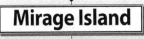

Mirage Island

MUMU
Swampert ♂

NANA
Mightyena ♀

KIKI
Delcatty ♀

FOFO
Castform ♀

PLUSLE
Plusle ♂

Stone Badge	Knuckle Badge	Dynamo Badge	Heat Badge
Balance Badge	Feather Badge	Mind Badge	Rain Badge

	Coolness	Beauty	Cuteness	Cleverness	Toughness
Normal					
Super					
Hyper					
Master					

● Adventure 258 ●

Rayquaza Redemption, Part 1

Pokémon Adventures Ruby & Sapphire

The Fourth Chapter

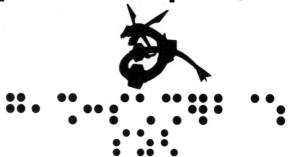

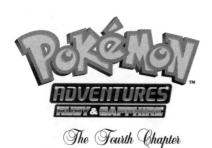

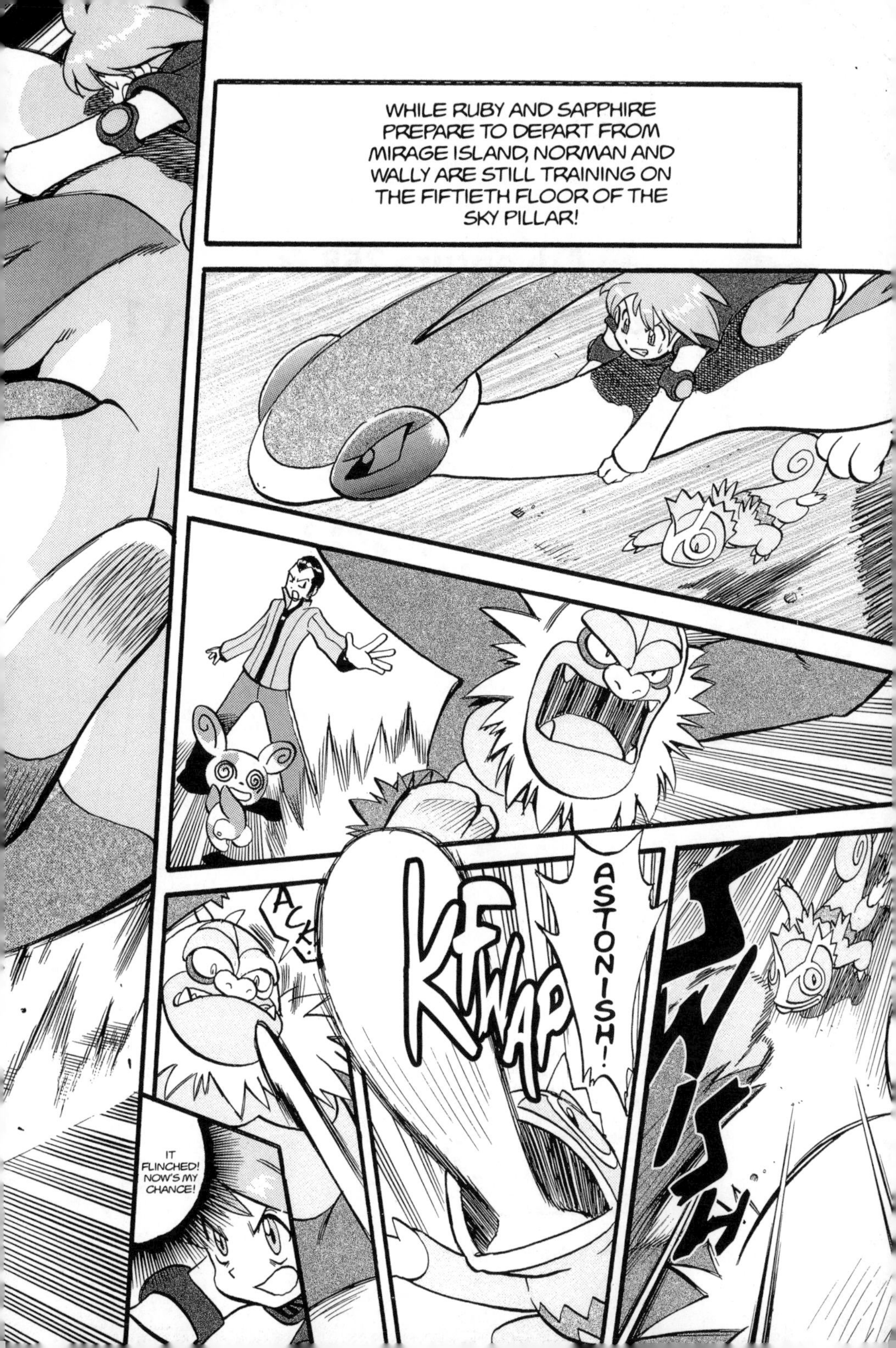
WHILE RUBY AND SAPPHIRE PREPARE TO DEPART FROM MIRAGE ISLAND, NORMAN AND WALLY ARE STILL TRAINING ON THE FIFTIETH FLOOR OF THE SKY PILLAR!
WHISH
ASTONISH!
KFWAP
ACK!
IT FLINCHED! NOW'S MY CHANCE!

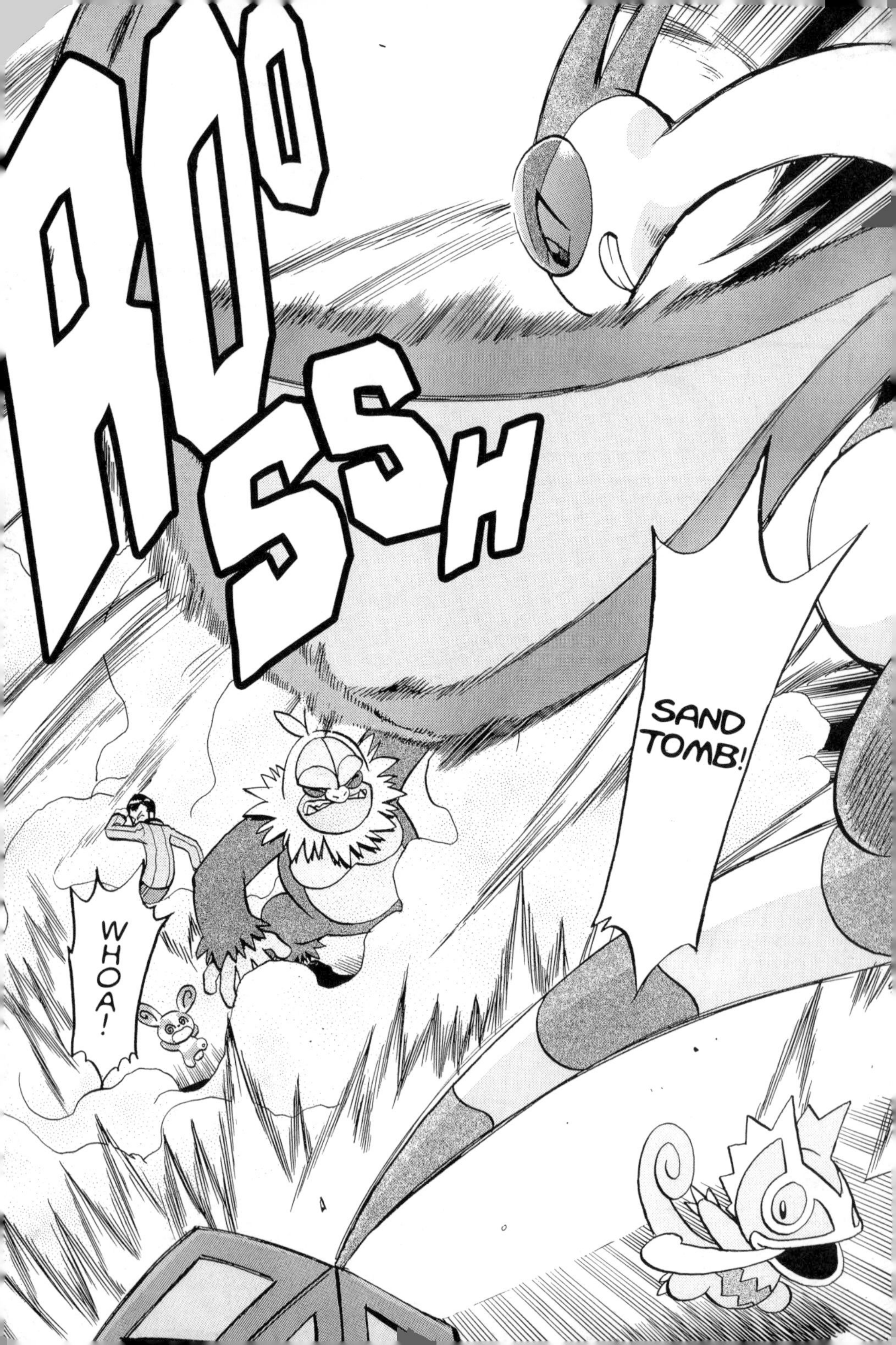
SAND TOMB!
FWOOSSH
WHOA!

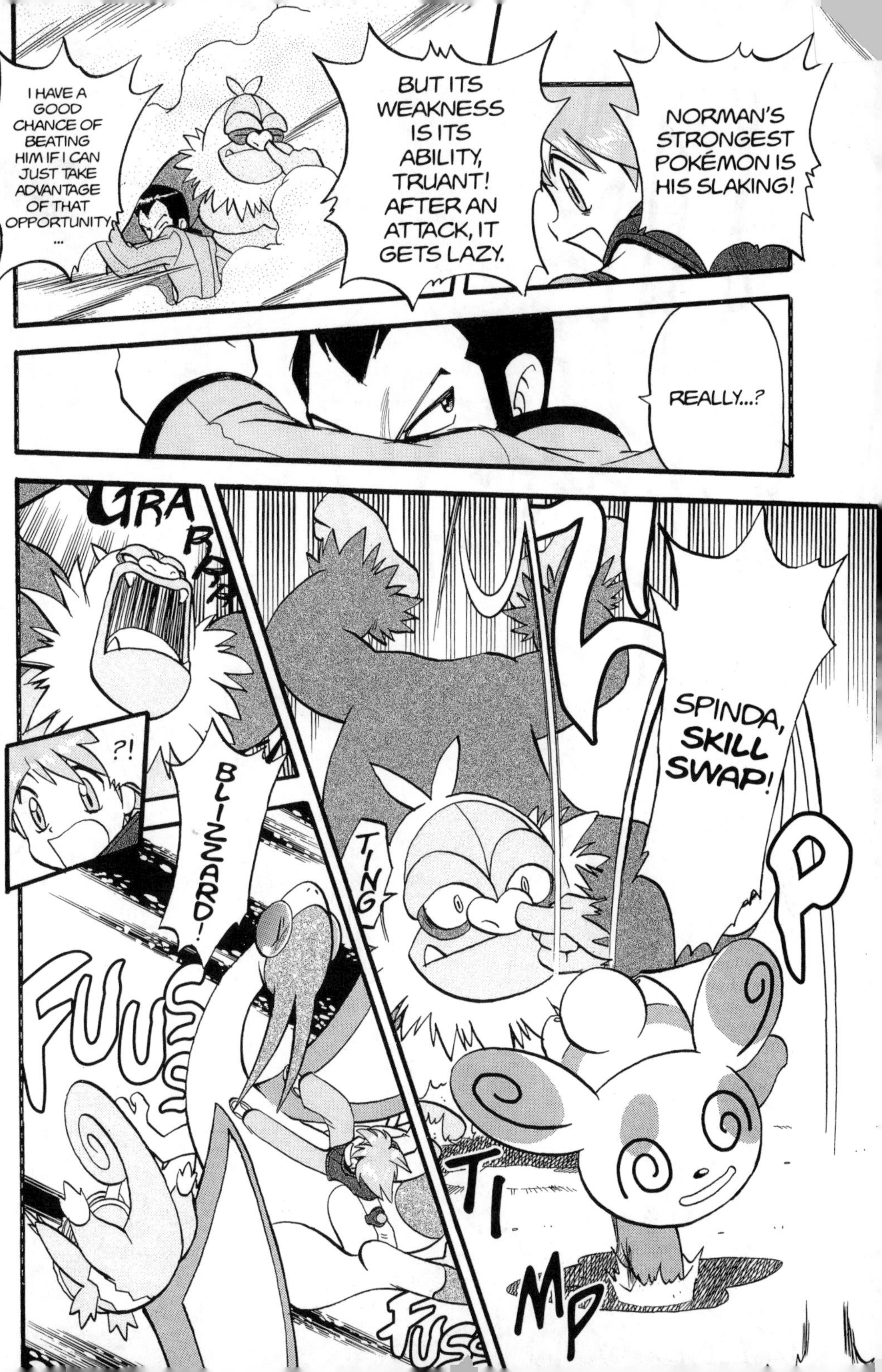
NORMAN'S STRONGEST POKÉMON IS HIS SLAKING!
BUT ITS WEAKNESS IS ITS ABILITY, TRUANT! AFTER AN ATTACK, IT GETS LAZY.
I HAVE A GOOD CHANCE OF BEATING HIM IF I CAN JUST TAKE ADVANTAGE OF THAT OPPORTUNITY...
REALLY...?
SPINDA, SKILL SWAP!
TING
TI
MP
GRARRR
?!
BLIZZARD!
FUUSS
FUSS

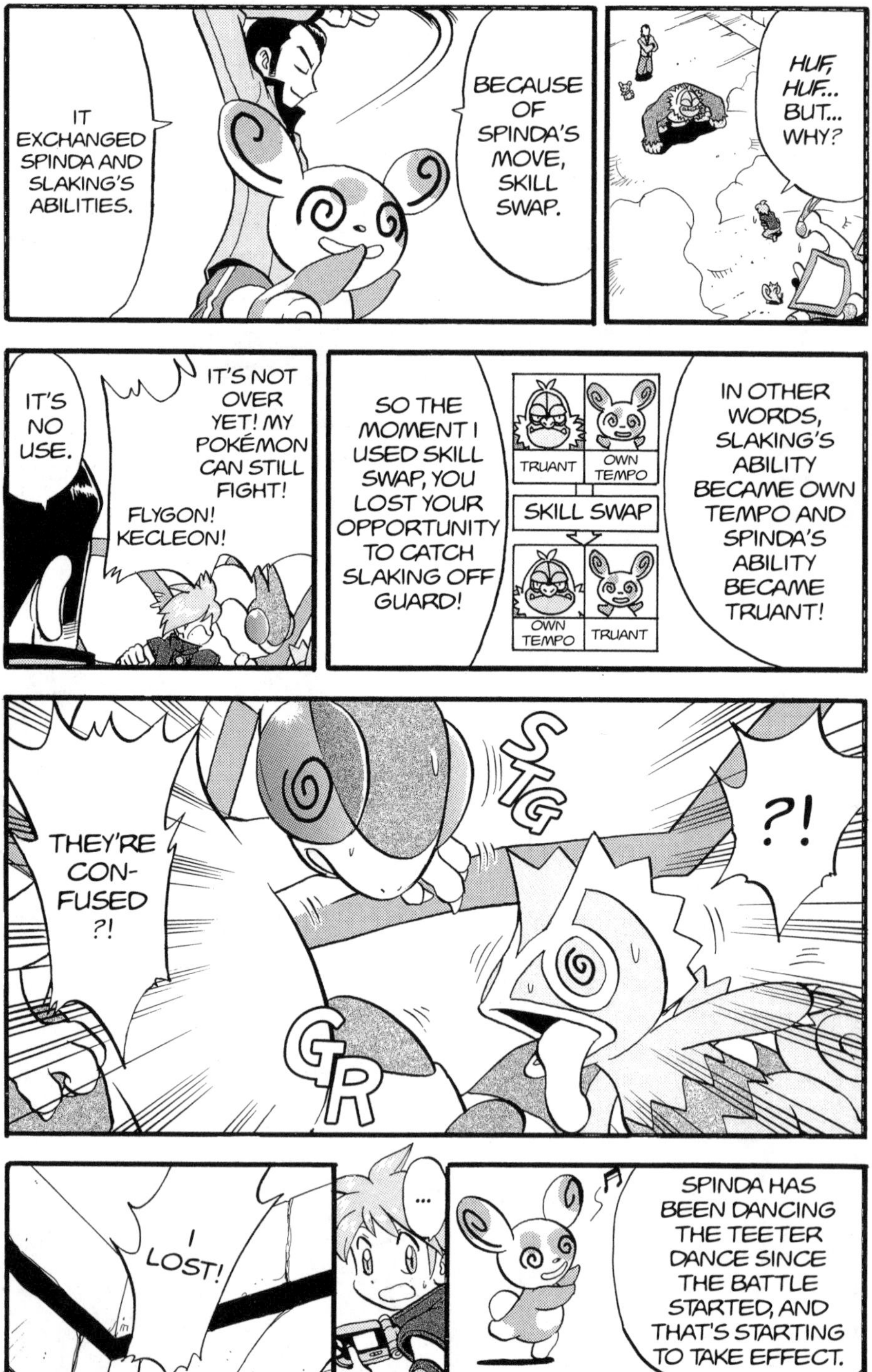
HUF, HUF... BUT... WHY?
BECAUSE OF SPINDA'S MOVE, SKILL SWAP.
IT EXCHANGED SPINDA AND SLAKING'S ABILITIES.
IN OTHER WORDS, SLAKING'S ABILITY BECAME OWN TEMPO AND SPINDA'S ABILITY BECAME TRUANT!
TRUANT
OWN TEMPO
SKILL SWAP
OWN TEMPO
TRUANT
SO THE MOMENT I USED SKILL SWAP, YOU LOST YOUR OPPORTUNITY TO CATCH SLAKING OFF GUARD!
IT'S NOT OVER YET! MY POKÉMON CAN STILL FIGHT!
FLYGON! KECLEON!
IT'S NO USE.
?!
STG
THEY'RE CON-FUSED ?!
GR
SPINDA HAS BEEN DANCING THE TEETER DANCE SINCE THE BATTLE STARTED, AND THAT'S STARTING TO TAKE EFFECT.
...
I LOST!

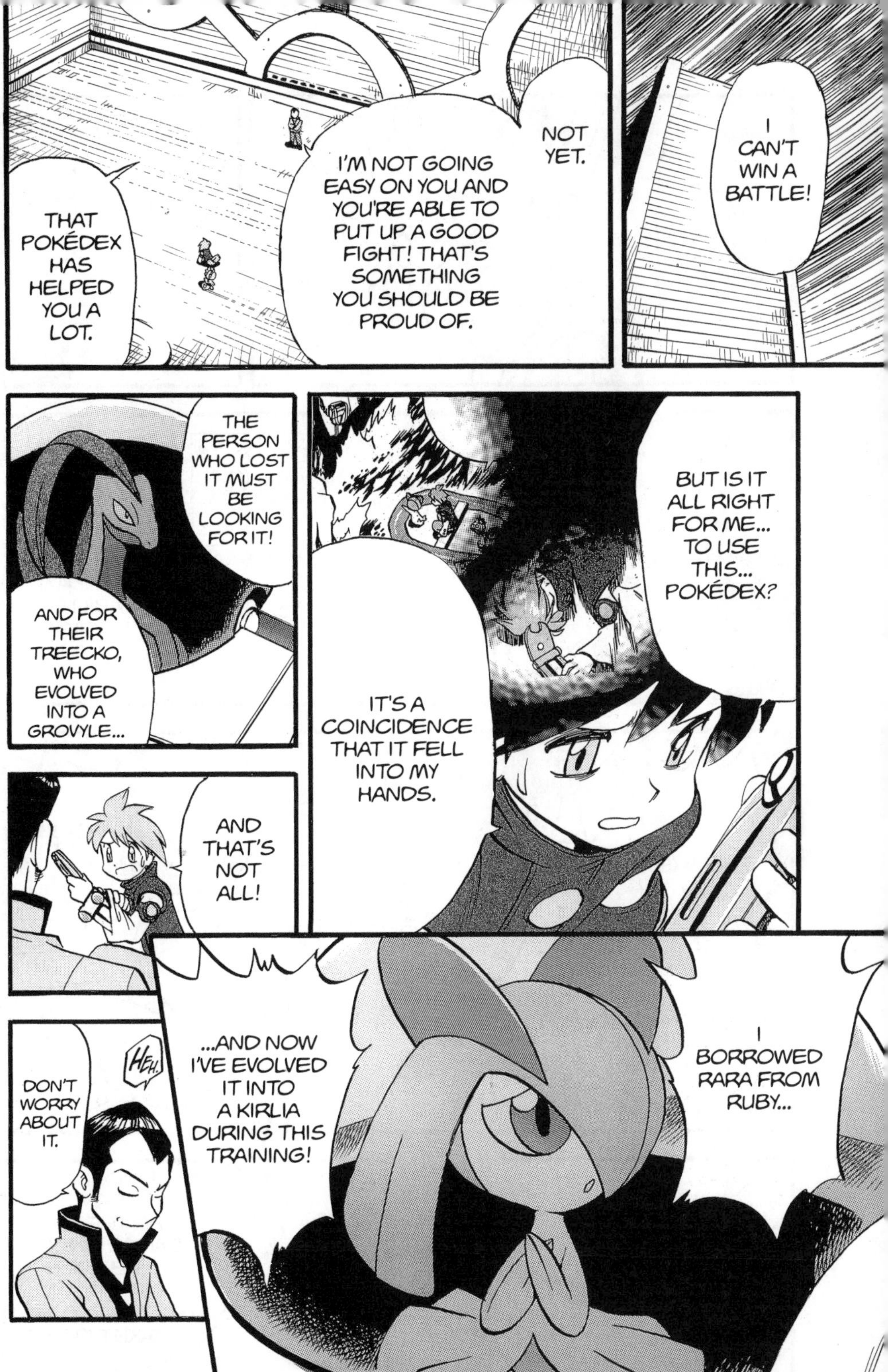
I CAN'T WIN A BATTLE!
NOT YET.
I'M NOT GOING EASY ON YOU AND YOU'RE ABLE TO PUT UP A GOOD FIGHT! THAT'S SOMETHING YOU SHOULD BE PROUD OF.
THAT POKÉDEX HAS HELPED YOU A LOT.
BUT IS IT ALL RIGHT FOR ME... TO USE THIS... POKÉDEX?
IT'S A COINCIDENCE THAT IT FELL INTO MY HANDS.
THE PERSON WHO LOST IT MUST BE LOOKING FOR IT!
AND FOR THEIR TREECKO, WHO EVOLVED INTO A GROVYLE...
AND THAT'S NOT ALL!
I BORROWED RARA FROM RUBY...
...AND NOW I'VE EVOLVED IT INTO A KIRLIA DURING THIS TRAINING!
HEH.
DON'T WORRY ABOUT IT.

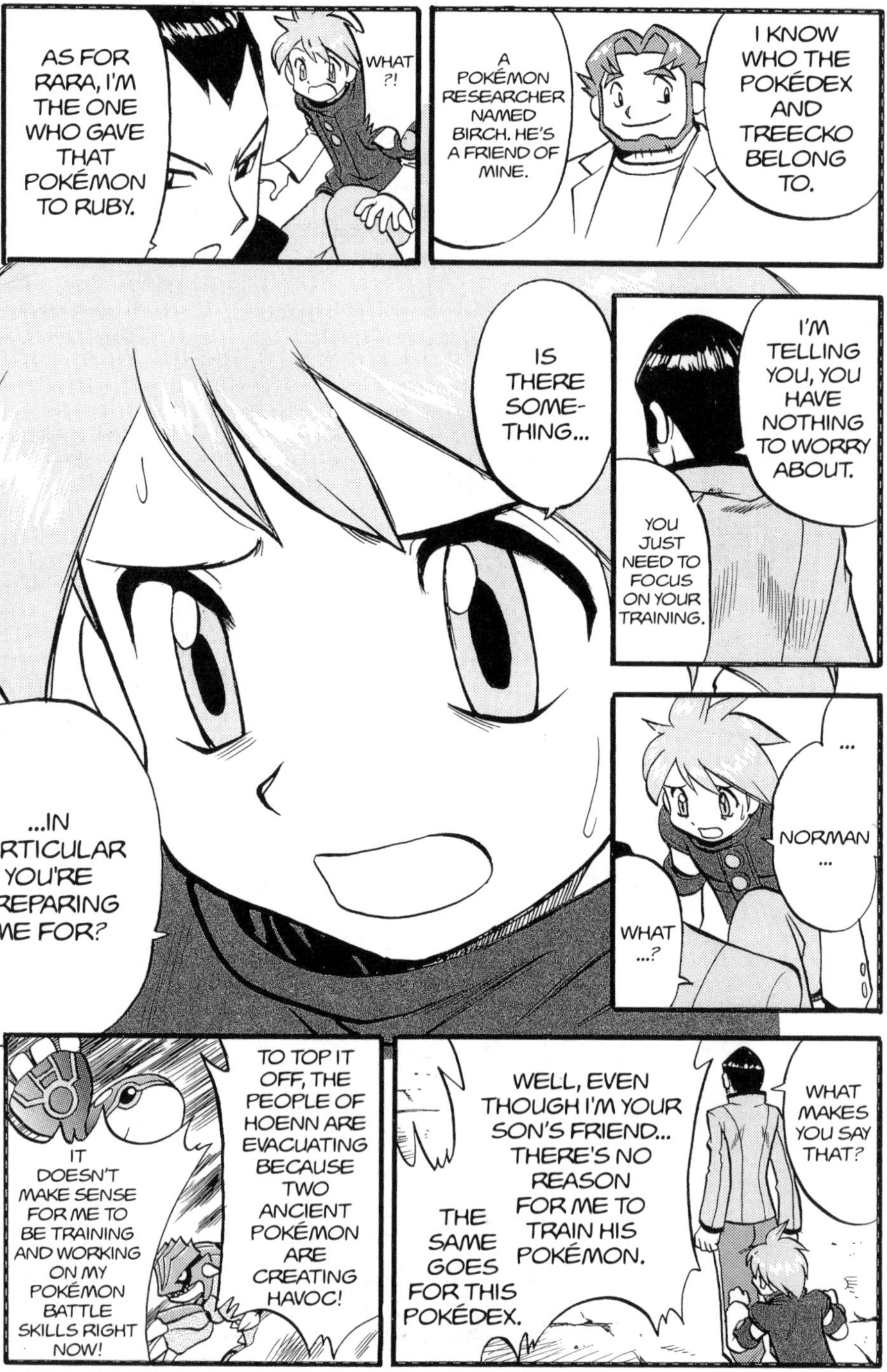
I KNOW WHO THE POKÉDEX AND TREECKO BELONG TO.
A POKÉMON RESEARCHER NAMED BIRCH. HE'S A FRIEND OF MINE.
AS FOR RARA, I'M THE ONE WHO GAVE THAT POKÉMON TO RUBY.
WHAT?!
I'M TELLING YOU, YOU HAVE NOTHING TO WORRY ABOUT.
YOU JUST NEED TO FOCUS ON YOUR TRAINING.
...
NORMAN...
WHAT...?
IS THERE SOME-THING...
...IN PARTICULAR YOU'RE PREPARING ME FOR?
WHAT MAKES YOU SAY THAT?
WELL, EVEN THOUGH I'M YOUR SON'S FRIEND... THERE'S NO REASON FOR ME TO TRAIN HIS POKÉMON.
THE SAME GOES FOR THIS POKÉDEX.
TO TOP IT OFF, THE PEOPLE OF HOENN ARE EVACUATING BECAUSE TWO ANCIENT POKÉMON ARE CREATING HAVOC!
IT DOESN'T MAKE SENSE FOR ME TO BE TRAINING AND WORKING ON MY POKÉMON BATTLE SKILLS RIGHT NOW!

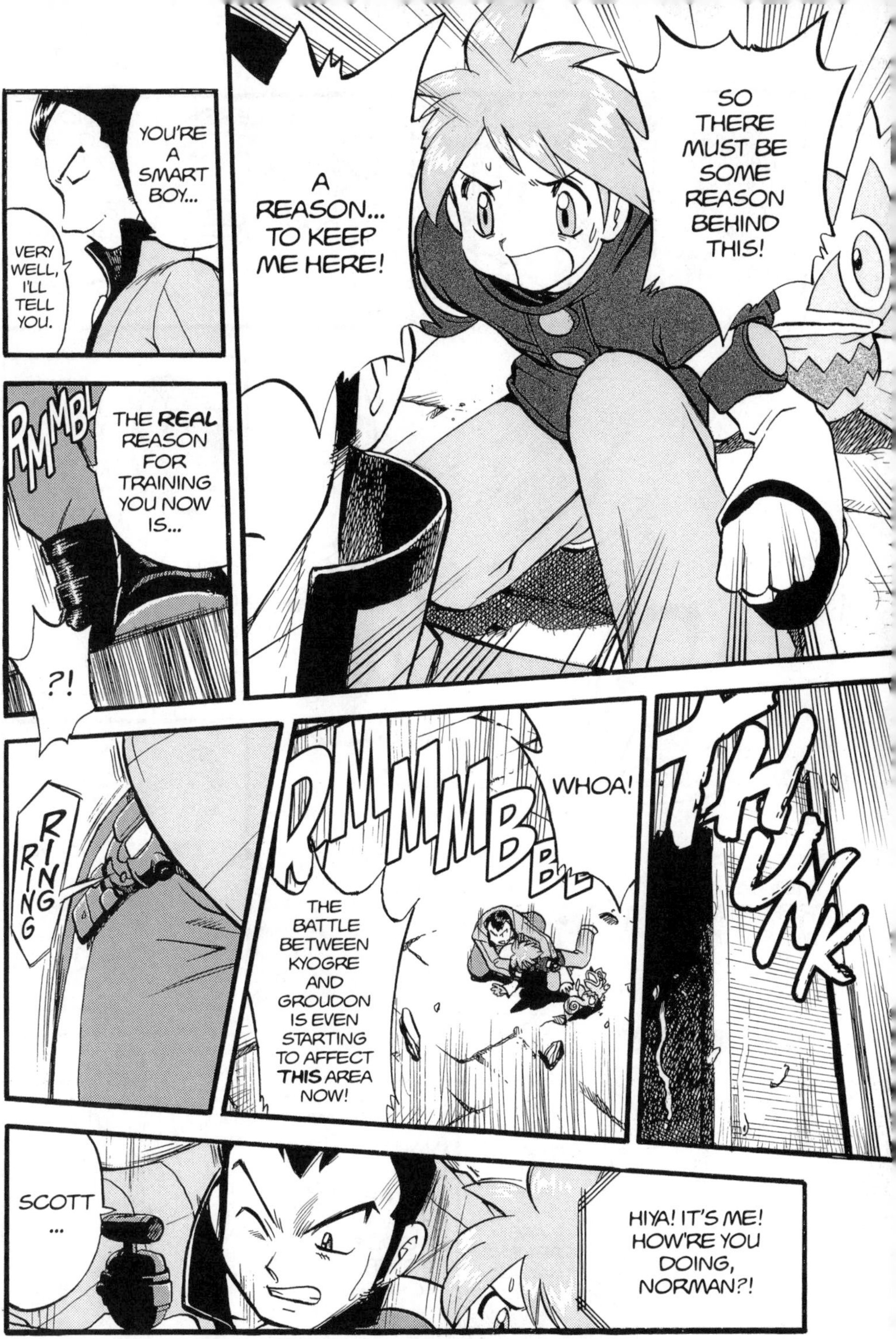
SO THERE MUST BE SOME REASON BEHIND THIS!
A REASON... TO KEEP ME HERE!
YOU'RE A SMART BOY...
VERY WELL, I'LL TELL YOU.
RMMBL
THE REAL REASON FOR TRAINING YOU NOW IS...
?!
THUNK
WHOA!
RMMMBBL
THE BATTLE BETWEEN KYOGRE AND GROUDON IS EVEN STARTING TO AFFECT THIS AREA NOW!
RING RING
HIYA! IT'S ME! HOW'RE YOU DOING, NORMAN?!
SCOTT ...

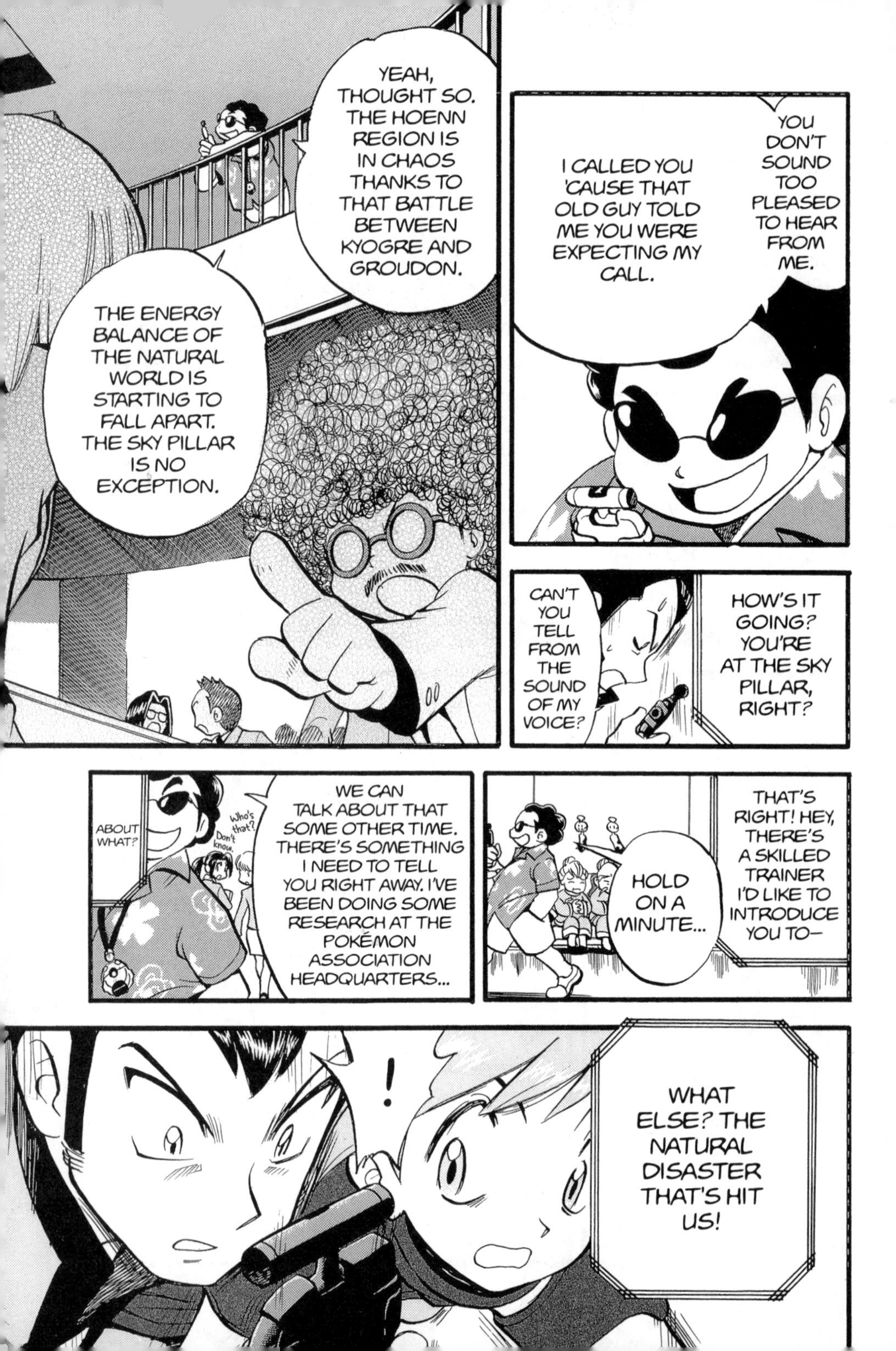
YOU DON'T SOUND TOO PLEASED TO HEAR FROM ME.
I CALLED YOU 'CAUSE THAT OLD GUY TOLD ME YOU WERE EXPECTING MY CALL.
HOW'S IT GOING? YOU'RE AT THE SKY PILLAR, RIGHT?
CAN'T YOU TELL FROM THE SOUND OF MY VOICE?
YEAH, THOUGHT SO. THE HOENN REGION IS IN CHAOS THANKS TO THAT BATTLE BETWEEN KYOGRE AND GROUDON.
THE ENERGY BALANCE OF THE NATURAL WORLD IS STARTING TO FALL APART. THE SKY PILLAR IS NO EXCEPTION.
THAT'S RIGHT! HEY, THERE'S A SKILLED TRAINER I'D LIKE TO INTRODUCE YOU TO—
HOLD ON A MINUTE...
WE CAN TALK ABOUT THAT SOME OTHER TIME. THERE'S SOMETHING I NEED TO TELL YOU RIGHT AWAY. I'VE BEEN DOING SOME RESEARCH AT THE POKÉMON ASSOCIATION HEADQUARTERS...
Who's that?
Don't know.
ABOUT WHAT?
WHAT ELSE? THE NATURAL DISASTER THAT'S HIT US!
!

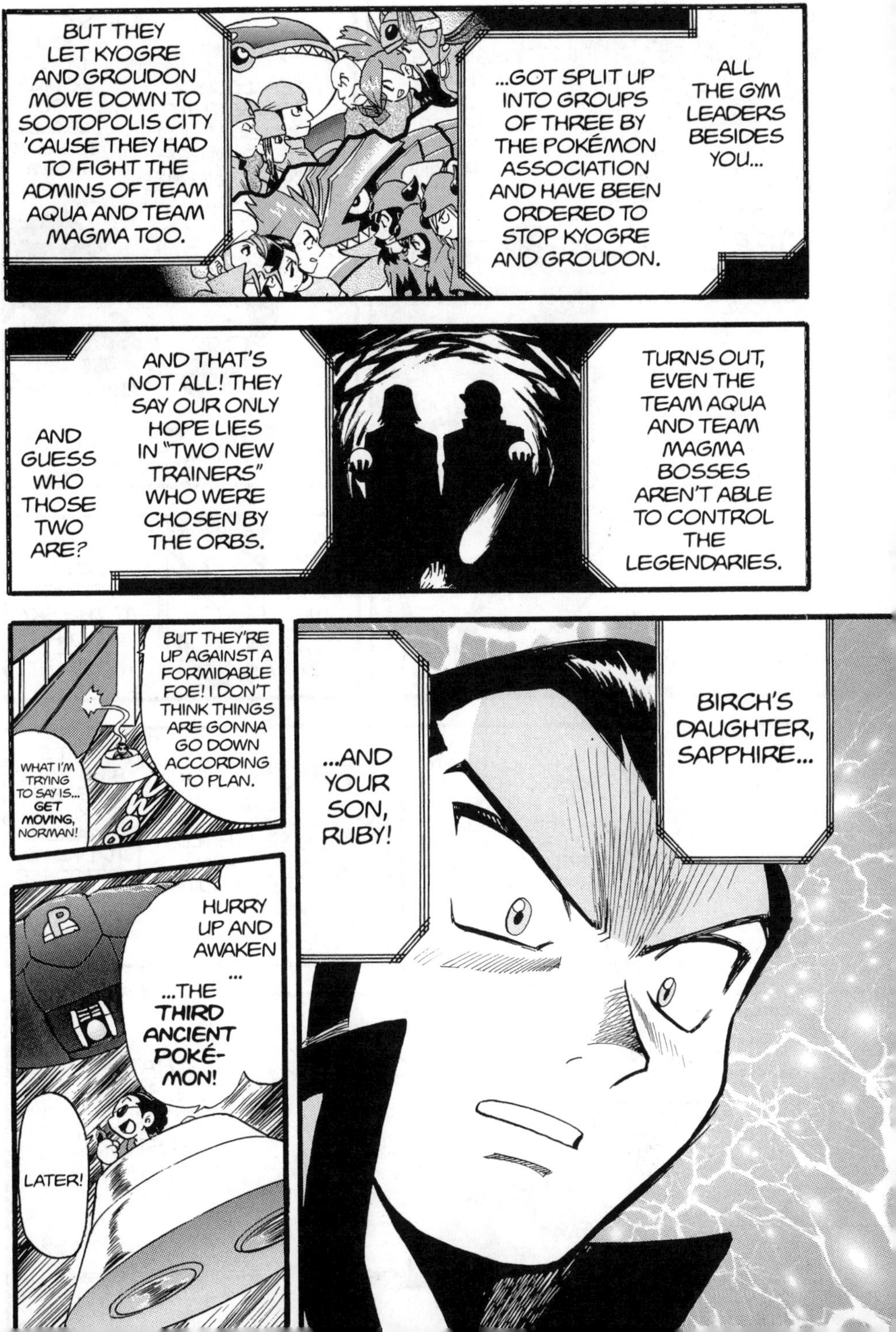
ALL THE GYM LEADERS BESIDES YOU...
...GOT SPLIT UP INTO GROUPS OF THREE BY THE POKÉMON ASSOCIATION AND HAVE BEEN ORDERED TO STOP KYOGRE AND GROUDON.
BUT THEY LET KYOGRE AND GROUDON MOVE DOWN TO SOOTOPOLIS CITY 'CAUSE THEY HAD TO FIGHT THE ADMINS OF TEAM AQUA AND TEAM MAGMA TOO.
TURNS OUT, EVEN THE TEAM AQUA AND TEAM MAGMA BOSSES AREN'T ABLE TO CONTROL THE LEGENDARIES.
AND THAT'S NOT ALL! THEY SAY OUR ONLY HOPE LIES IN "TWO NEW TRAINERS" WHO WERE CHOSEN BY THE ORBS.
AND GUESS WHO THOSE TWO ARE?
BIRCH'S DAUGHTER, SAPPHIRE...
...AND YOUR SON, RUBY!
BUT THEY'RE UP AGAINST A FORMIDABLE FOE! I DON'T THINK THINGS ARE GONNA GO DOWN ACCORDING TO PLAN.
WHAT I'M TRYING TO SAY IS... **GET MOVING,** NORMAN!
HURRY UP AND AWAKEN ...
...THE **THIRD ANCIENT POKÉ-MON!**
LATER!

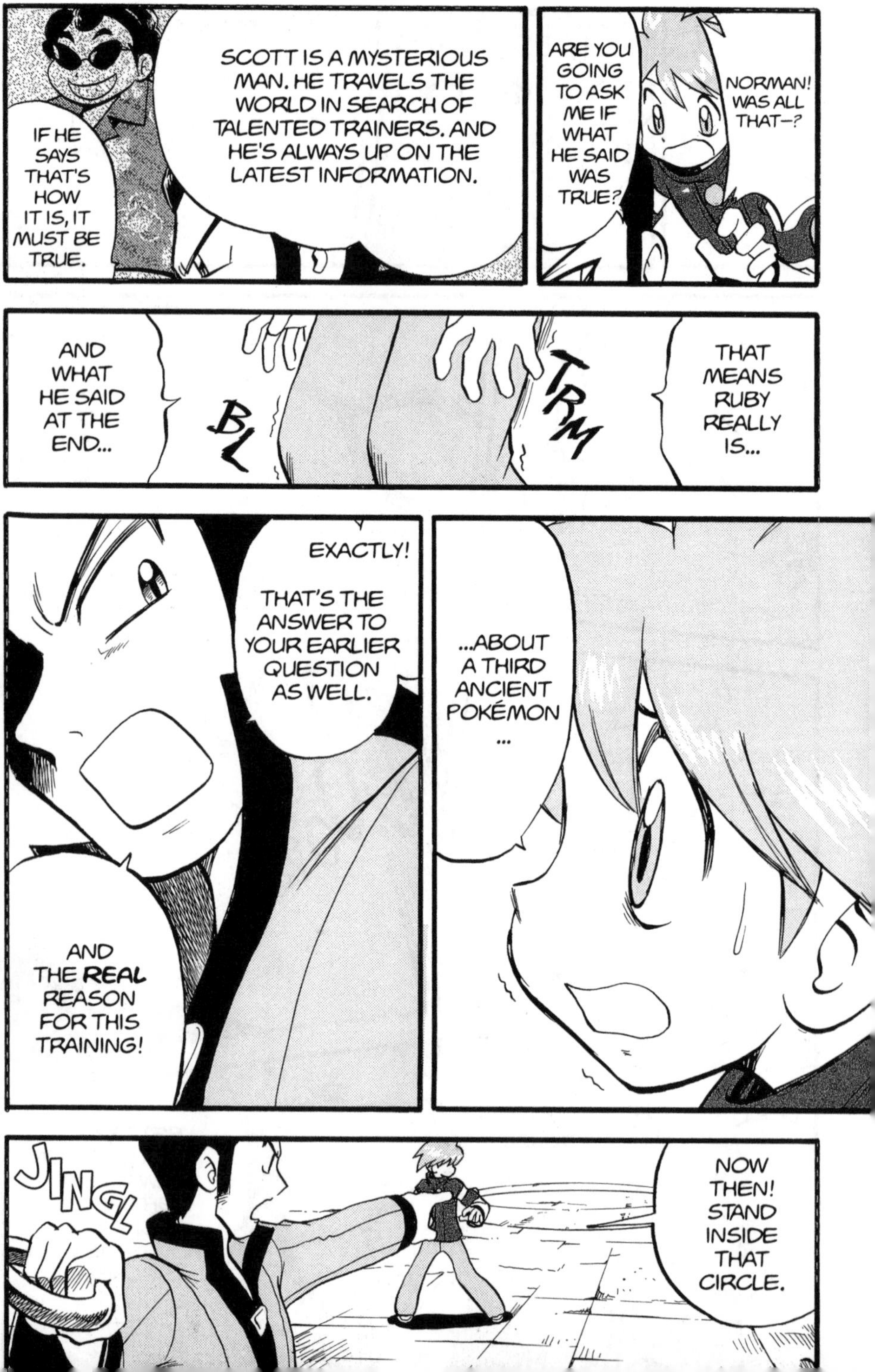
NORMAN! WAS ALL THAT—?
ARE YOU GOING TO ASK ME IF WHAT HE SAID WAS TRUE?
SCOTT IS A MYSTERIOUS MAN. HE TRAVELS THE WORLD IN SEARCH OF TALENTED TRAINERS. AND HE'S ALWAYS UP ON THE LATEST INFORMATION.
IF HE SAYS THAT'S HOW IT IS, IT MUST BE TRUE.
THAT MEANS RUBY REALLY IS...
TRM
BL
AND WHAT HE SAID AT THE END...
...ABOUT A THIRD ANCIENT POKÉMON ...
EXACTLY!
THAT'S THE ANSWER TO YOUR EARLIER QUESTION AS WELL.
AND THE **REAL** REASON FOR THIS TRAINING!
NOW THEN! STAND INSIDE THAT CIRCLE.
JINGL

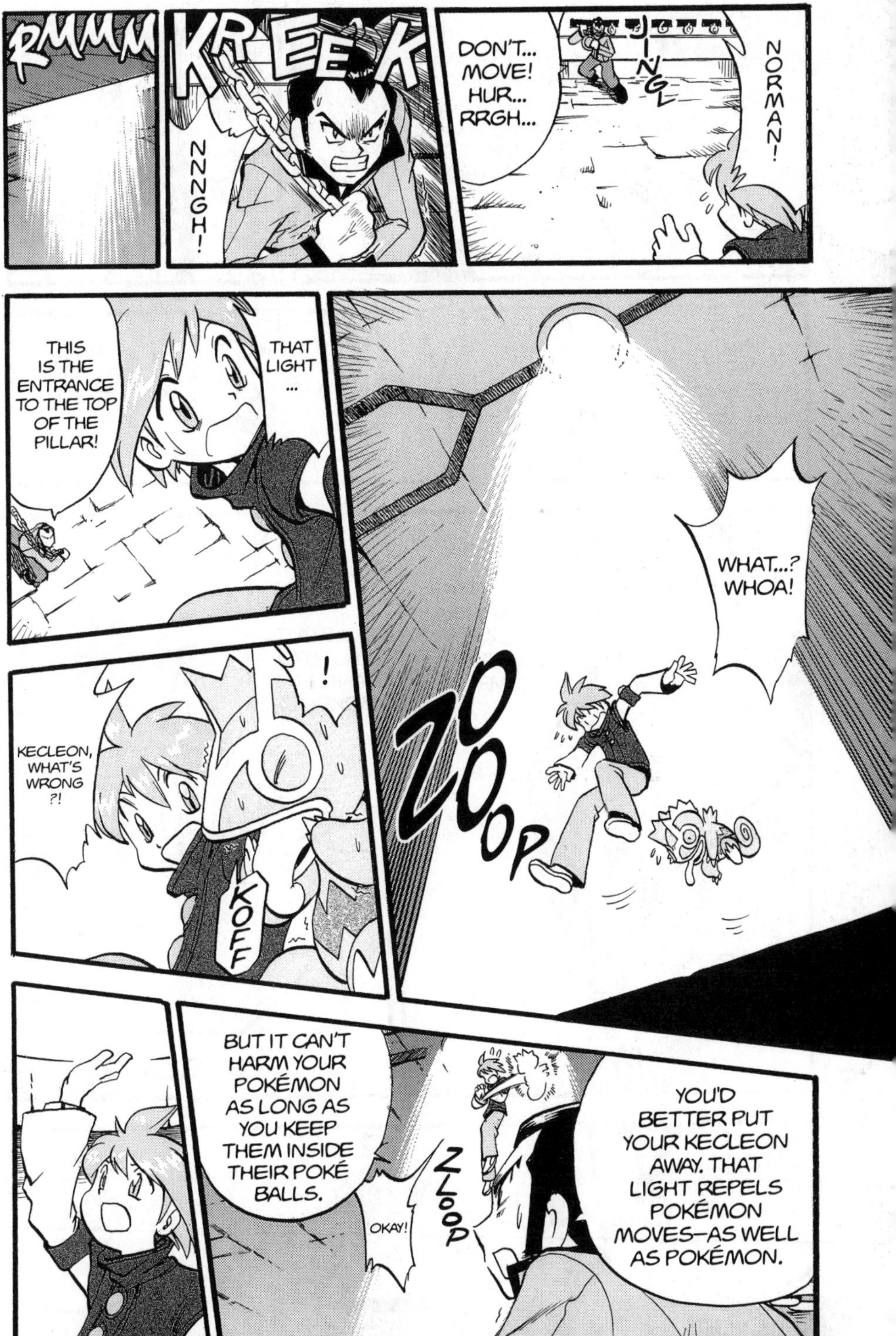
NORMAN!
JINGL
DON'T... MOVE! HUR... RRGH...
KREEK
NNNGH!
RMMM
WHAT...? WHOA!
ZOOOP
THAT LIGHT ...
THIS IS THE ENTRANCE TO THE TOP OF THE PILLAR!
!
KECLEON, WHAT'S WRONG ?!
KOFF
YOU'D BETTER PUT YOUR KECLEON AWAY. THAT LIGHT REPELS POKÉMON MOVES—AS WELL AS POKÉMON.
BUT IT CAN'T HARM YOUR POKÉMON AS LONG AS YOU KEEP THEM INSIDE THEIR POKÉ BALLS.
OKAY!
ZLOOP

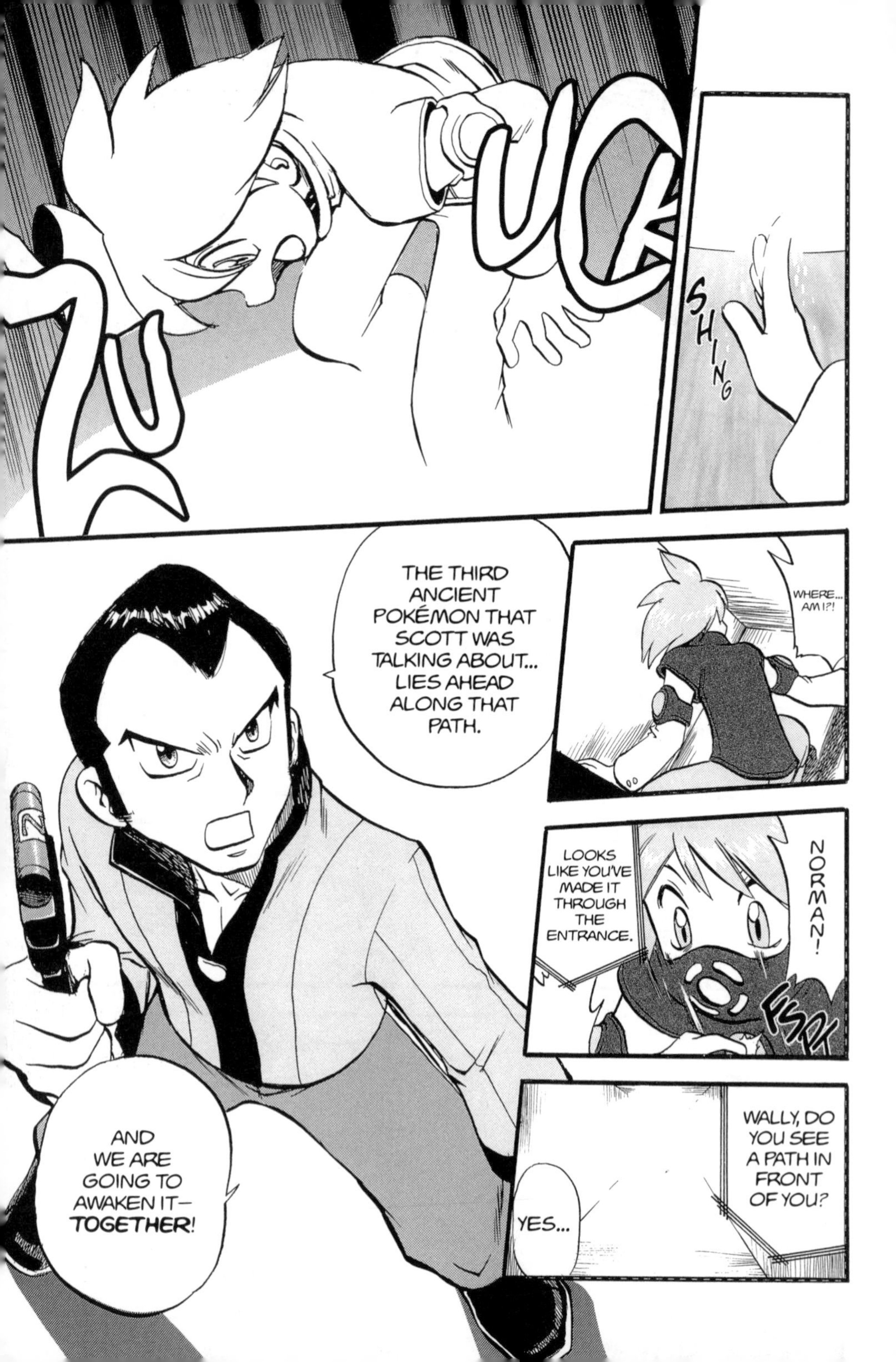
SHING
ZU
UCK
WHERE... AM I?!
NORMAN!
LOOKS LIKE YOU'VE MADE IT THROUGH THE ENTRANCE.
FSPK
WALLY, DO YOU SEE A PATH IN FRONT OF YOU?
YES...
THE THIRD ANCIENT POKÉMON THAT SCOTT WAS TALKING ABOUT... LIES AHEAD ALONG THAT PATH.
AND WE ARE GOING TO AWAKEN IT—**TOGETHER**!

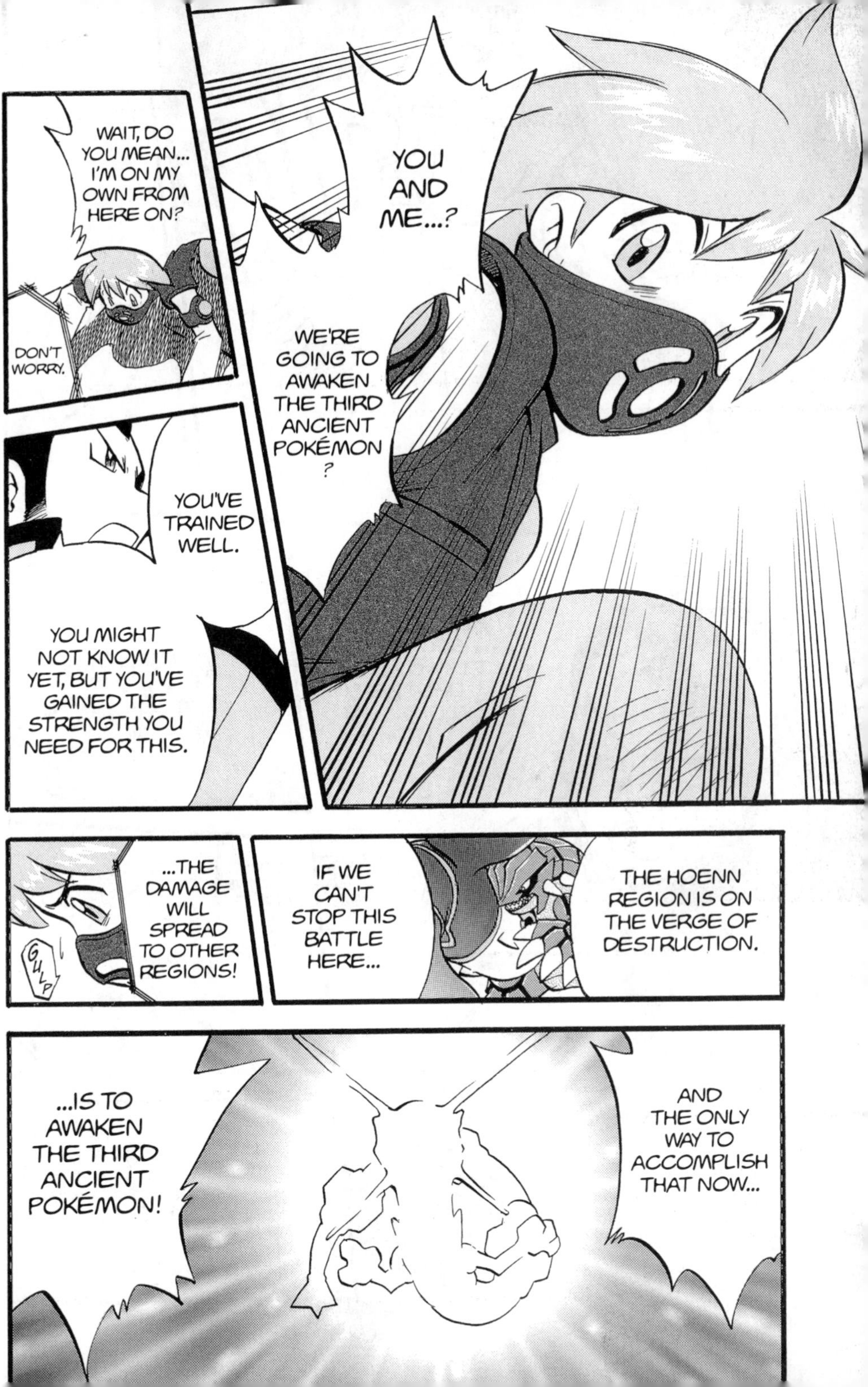
YOU AND ME...?
WE'RE GOING TO AWAKEN THE THIRD ANCIENT POKÉMON?
WAIT, DO YOU MEAN... I'M ON MY OWN FROM HERE ON?
DON'T WORRY.
YOU'VE TRAINED WELL.
YOU MIGHT NOT KNOW IT YET, BUT YOU'VE GAINED THE STRENGTH YOU NEED FOR THIS.
THE HOENN REGION IS ON THE VERGE OF DESTRUCTION.
IF WE CAN'T STOP THIS BATTLE HERE...
...THE DAMAGE WILL SPREAD TO OTHER REGIONS!
GULP
AND THE ONLY WAY TO ACCOMPLISH THAT NOW...
...IS TO AWAKEN THE THIRD ANCIENT POKÉMON!

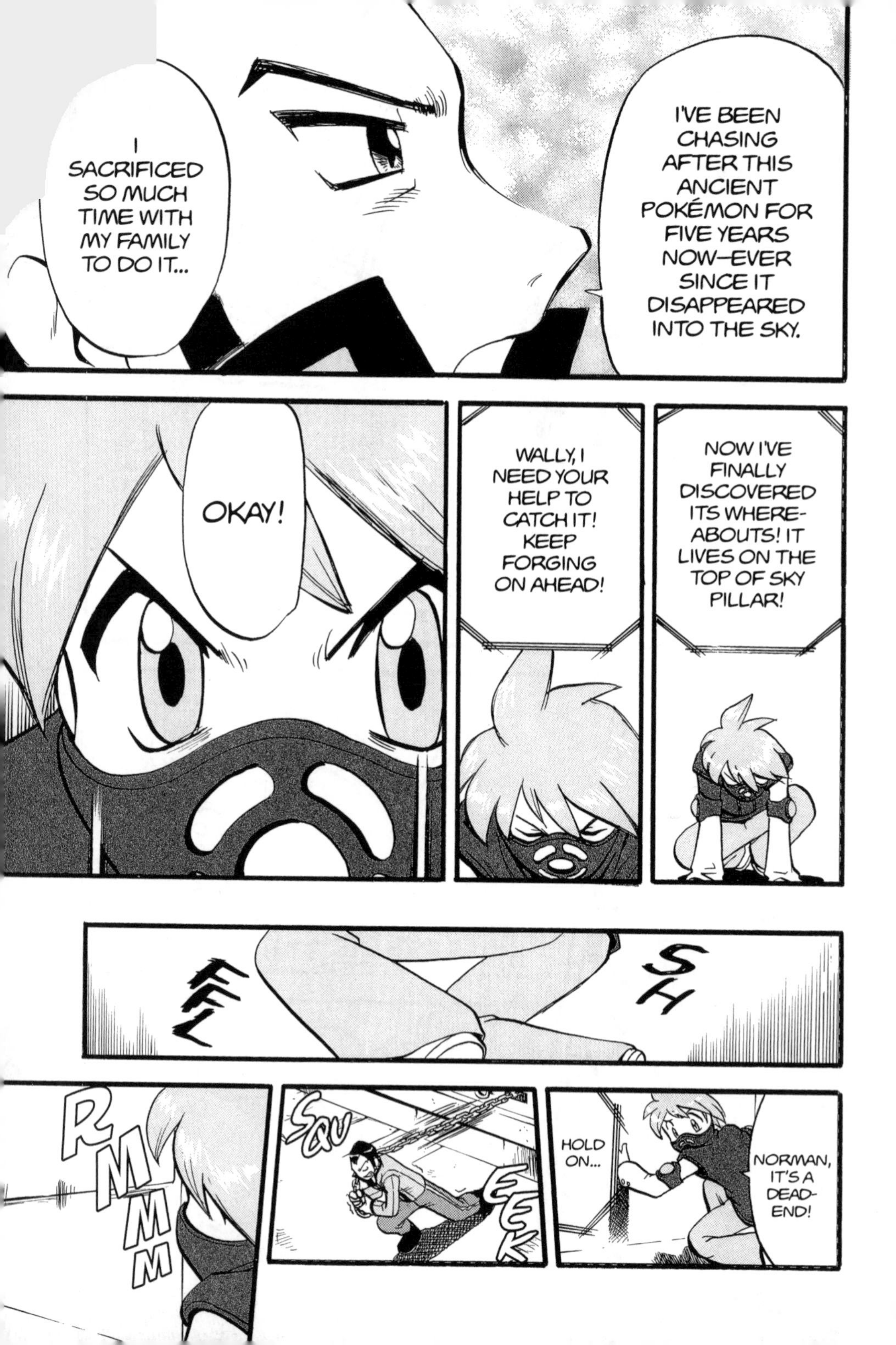
I'VE BEEN CHASING AFTER THIS ANCIENT POKÉMON FOR FIVE YEARS NOW—EVER SINCE IT DISAPPEARED INTO THE SKY.
I SACRIFICED SO MUCH TIME WITH MY FAMILY TO DO IT...
NOW I'VE FINALLY DISCOVERED ITS WHERE-ABOUTS! IT LIVES ON THE TOP OF SKY PILLAR!
WALLY, I NEED YOUR HELP TO CATCH IT! KEEP FORGING ON AHEAD!
OKAY!
SH
FFL
NORMAN, IT'S A DEAD-END!
HOLD ON...
SQU
EEK
RMMMM

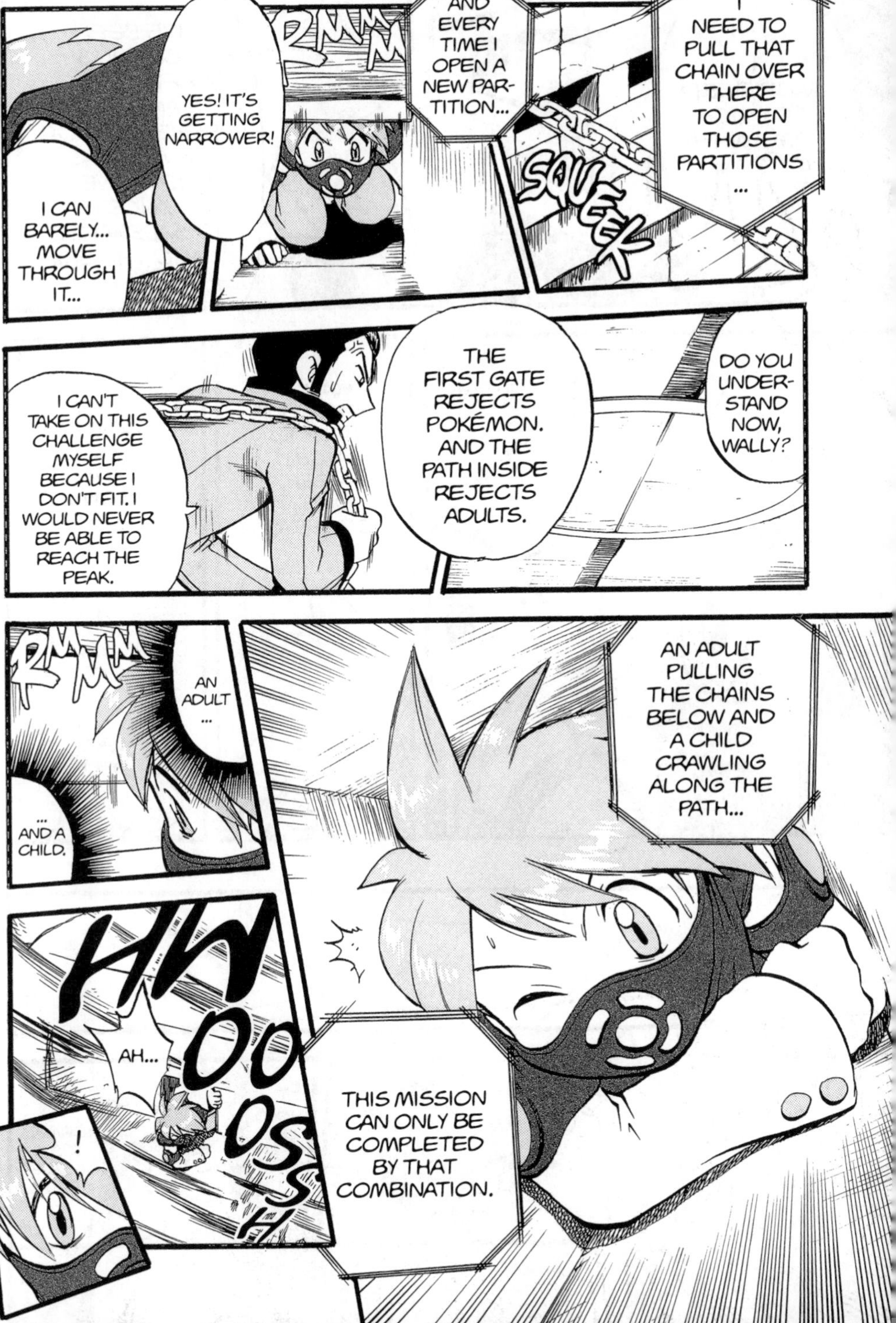
I NEED TO PULL THAT CHAIN OVER THERE TO OPEN THOSE PARTITIONS...
SQUEEK
AND EVERY TIME I OPEN A NEW PAR-TITION...
RMMMM
YES! IT'S GETTING NARROWER!
I CAN BARELY... MOVE THROUGH IT...
DO YOU UNDER-STAND NOW, WALLY?
THE FIRST GATE REJECTS POKÉMON. AND THE PATH INSIDE REJECTS ADULTS.
I CAN'T TAKE ON THIS CHALLENGE MYSELF BECAUSE I DON'T FIT. I WOULD NEVER BE ABLE TO REACH THE PEAK.
AN ADULT PULLING THE CHAINS BELOW AND A CHILD CRAWLING ALONG THE PATH...
THIS MISSION CAN ONLY BE COMPLETED BY THAT COMBINATION.
RMMMM
AN ADULT...
...AND A CHILD.
WHOOOSH
AH...
!

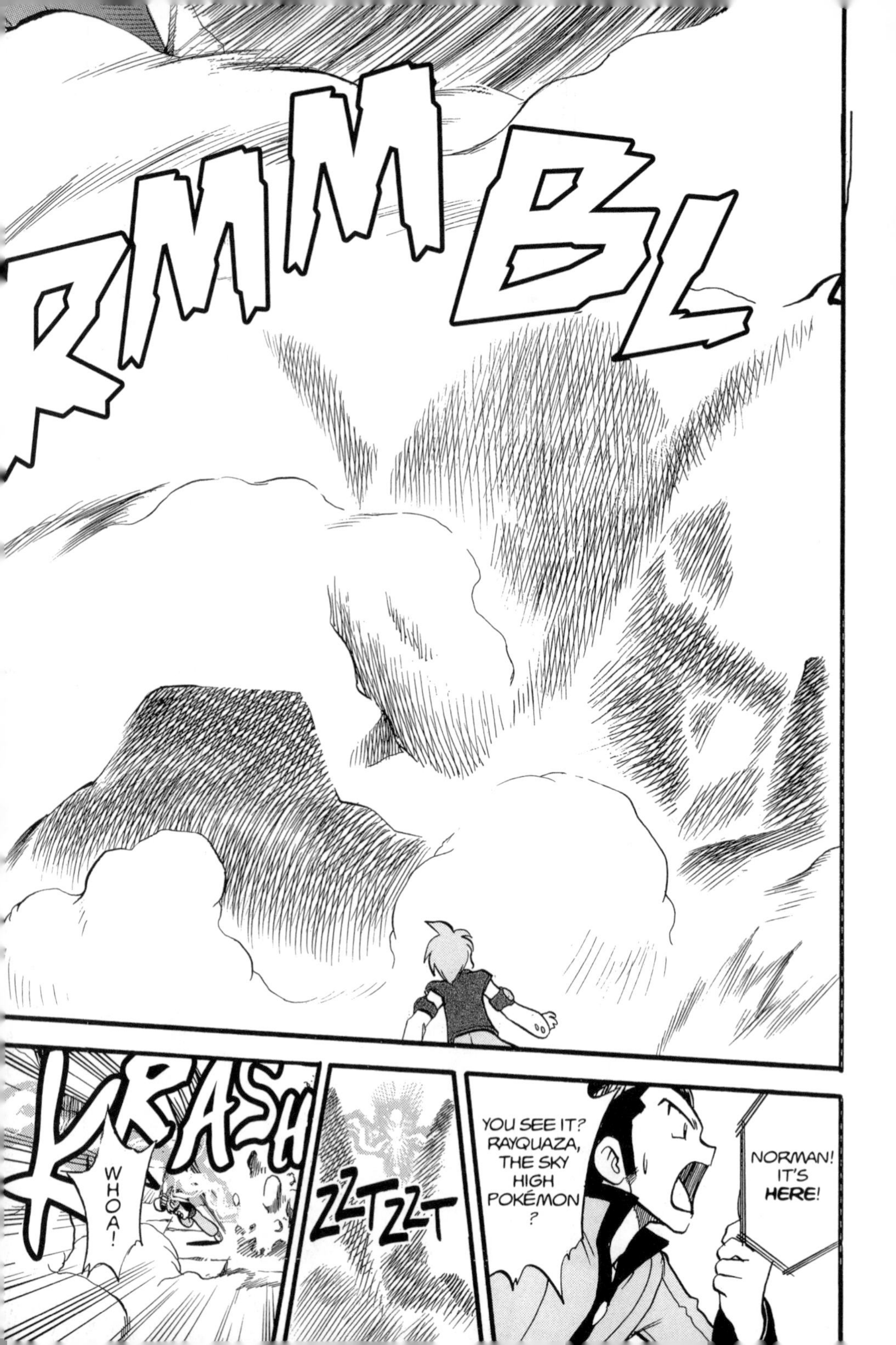
RMMBL
NORMAN! IT'S HERE!
YOU SEE IT? RAYQUAZA, THE SKY HIGH POKÉMON?
ZZTZZT
KRASH
WHOA!

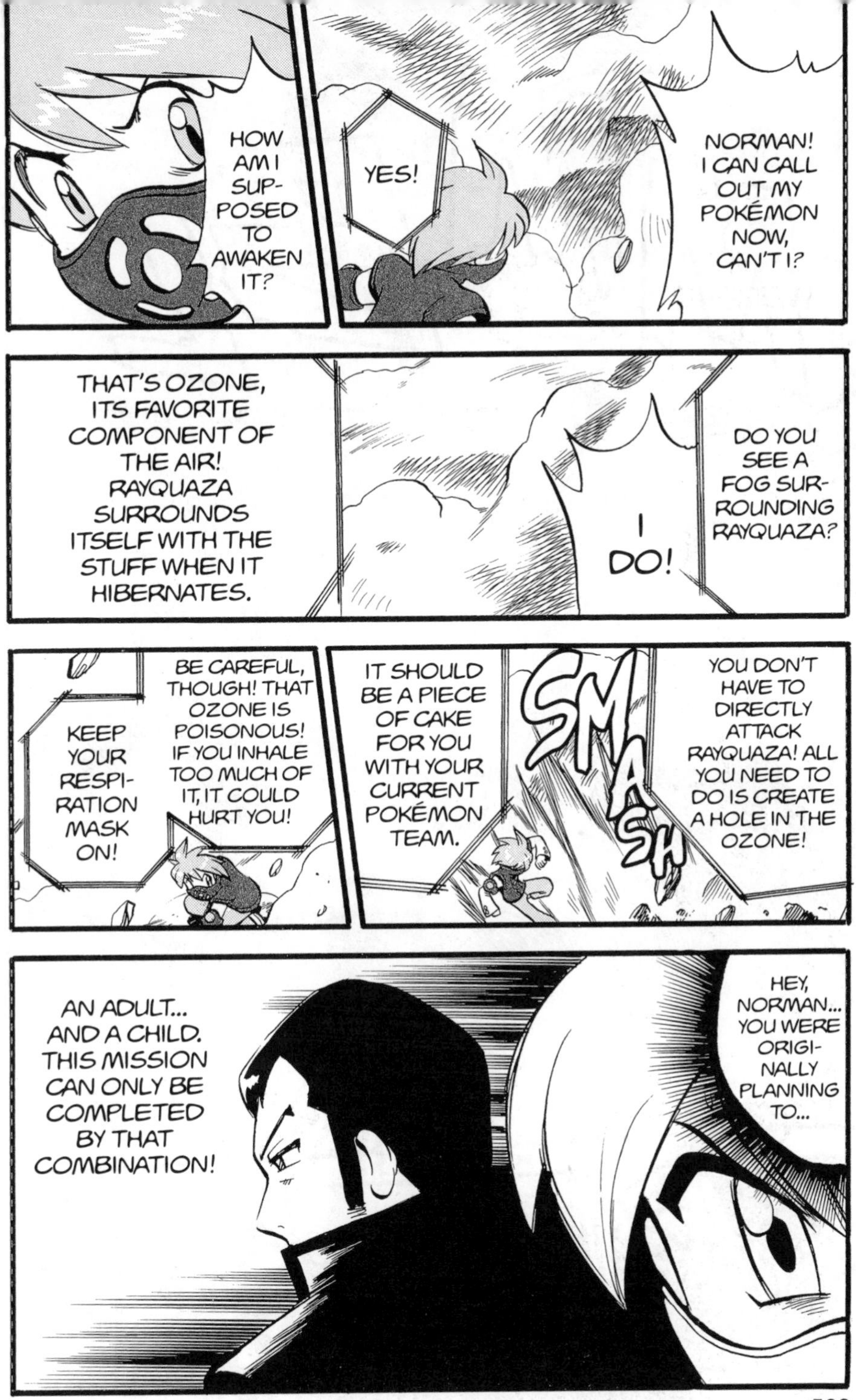
NORMAN! I CAN CALL OUT MY POKéMON NOW, CAN'T I?
YES!
HOW AM I SUPPOSED TO AWAKEN IT?
DO YOU SEE A FOG SURROUNDING RAYQUAZA?
I DO!
THAT'S OZONE, ITS FAVORITE COMPONENT OF THE AIR! RAYQUAZA SURROUNDS ITSELF WITH THE STUFF WHEN IT HIBERNATES.
YOU DON'T HAVE TO DIRECTLY ATTACK RAYQUAZA! ALL YOU NEED TO DO IS CREATE A HOLE IN THE OZONE!
SMASH
IT SHOULD BE A PIECE OF CAKE FOR YOU WITH YOUR CURRENT POKéMON TEAM.
BE CAREFUL, THOUGH! THAT OZONE IS POISONOUS! IF YOU INHALE TOO MUCH OF IT, IT COULD HURT YOU!
KEEP YOUR RESPIRATION MASK ON!
HEY, NORMAN... YOU WERE ORIGINALLY PLANNING TO...
AN ADULT... AND A CHILD. THIS MISSION CAN ONLY BE COMPLETED BY THAT COMBINATION!

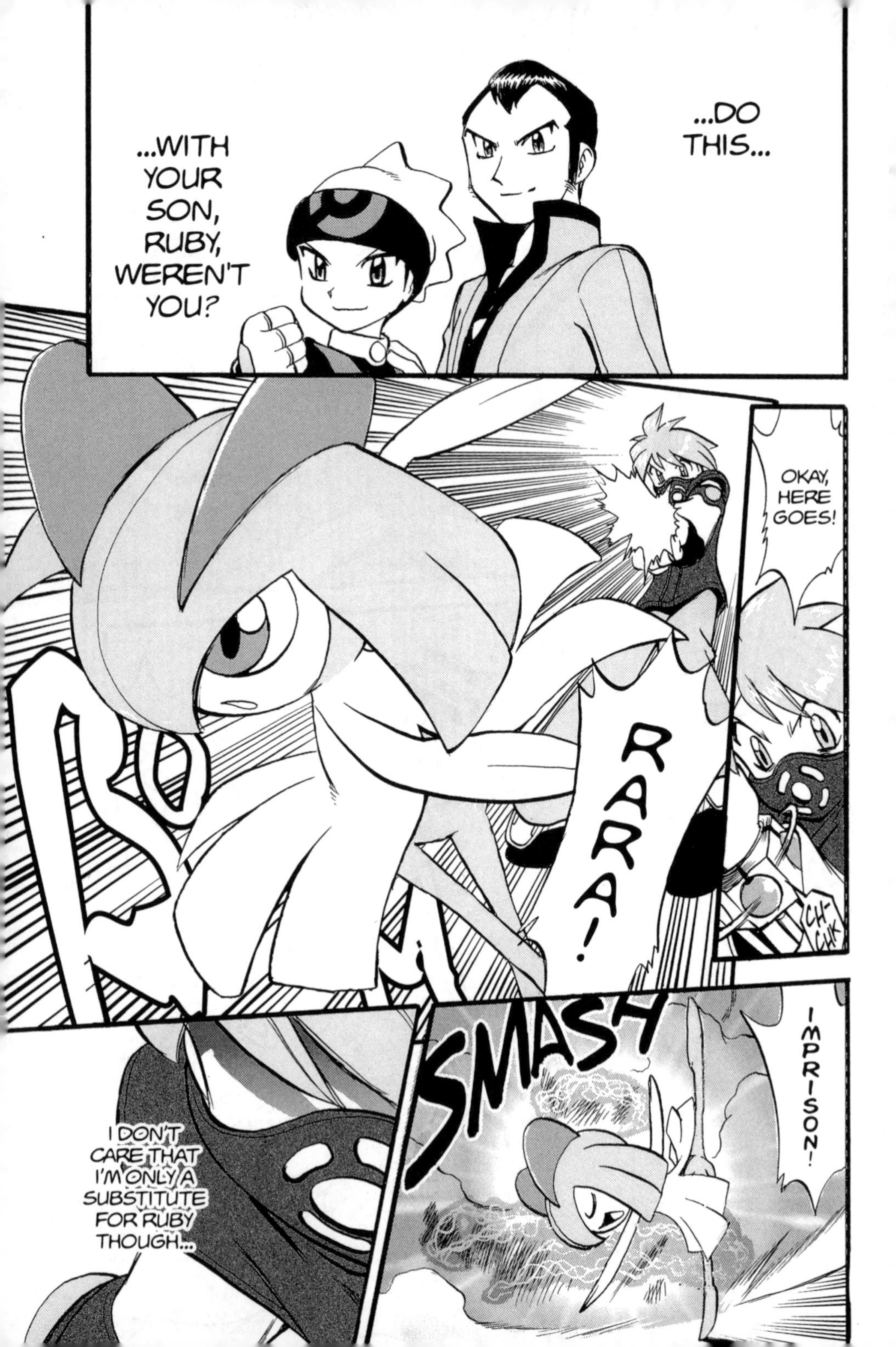
...DO THIS...
...WITH YOUR SON, RUBY, WEREN'T YOU?
OKAY, HERE GOES!
CH-CHK
RARA!
IMPRISON!
SMASH
I DON'T CARE THAT I'M ONLY A SUBSTITUTE FOR RUBY THOUGH...

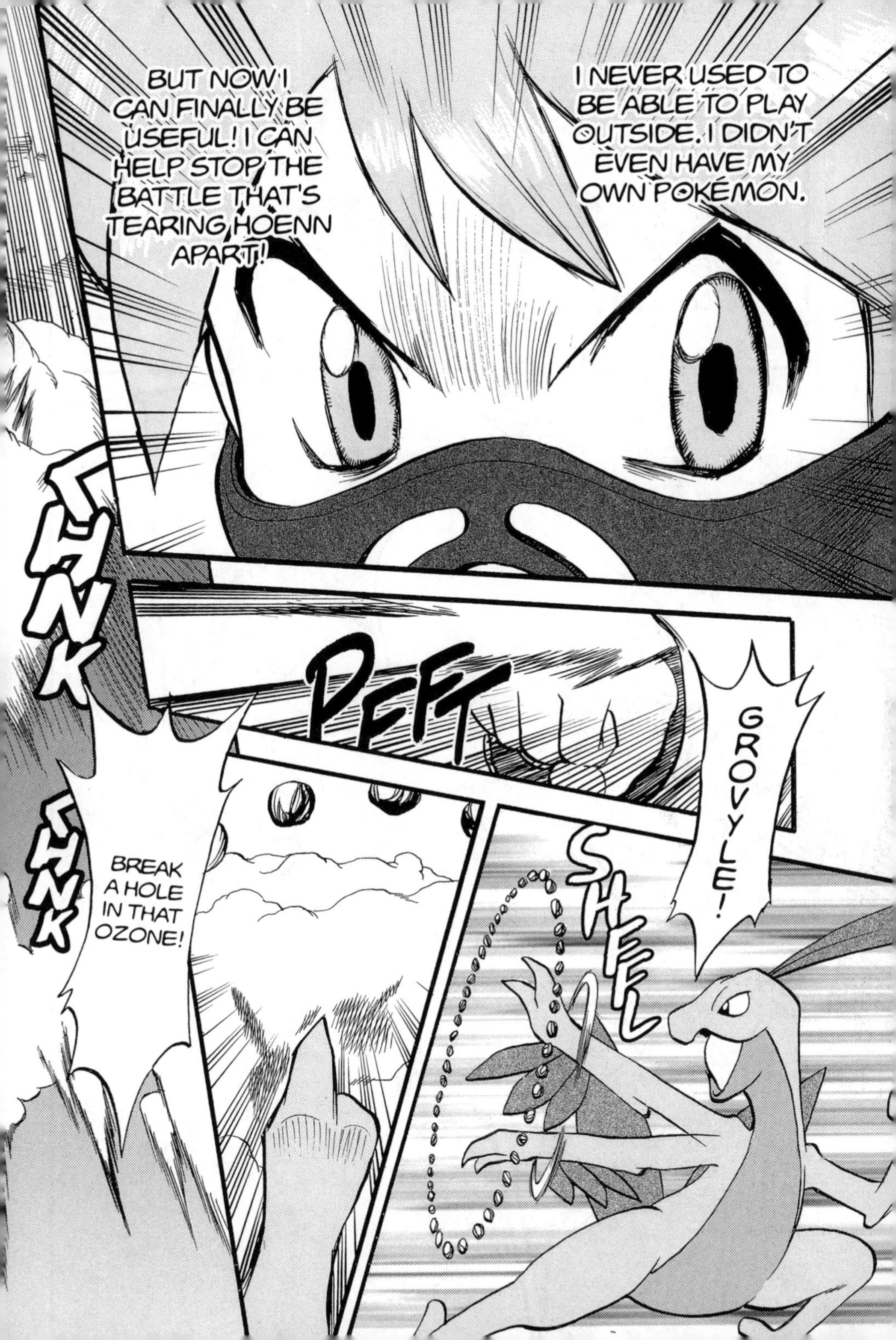
I NEVER USED TO BE ABLE TO PLAY OUTSIDE. I DIDN'T EVEN HAVE MY OWN POKÉMON.
BUT NOW I CAN FINALLY BE USEFUL! I CAN HELP STOP THE BATTLE THAT'S TEARING HOENN APART!
SHNK
PFFT
GROVYLE!
SHEEL
BREAK A HOLE IN THAT OZONE!
SHNK

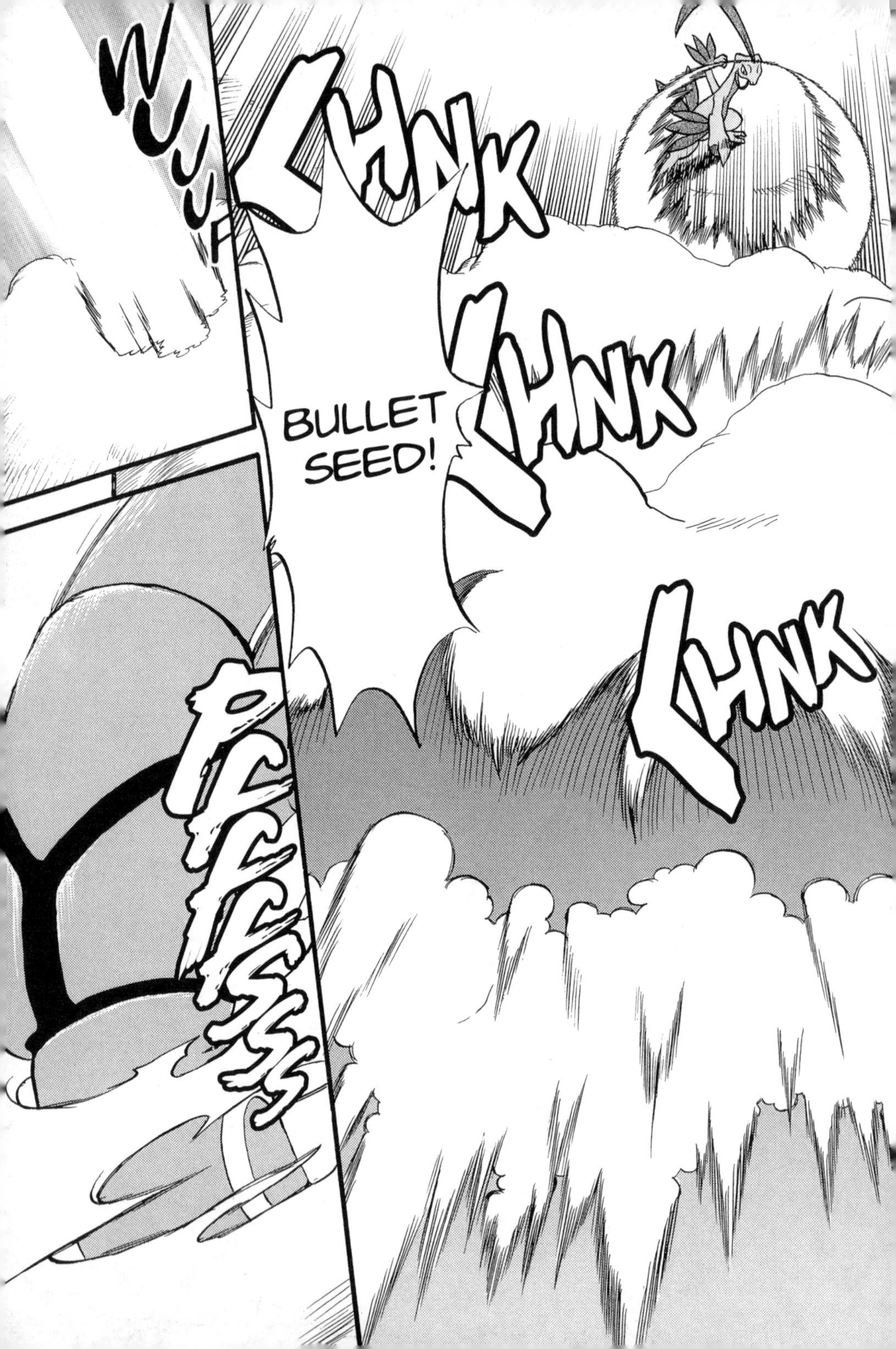
CHINK
BULLET SEED!
CHINK
CHINK
WUUUF
PSSSSSS

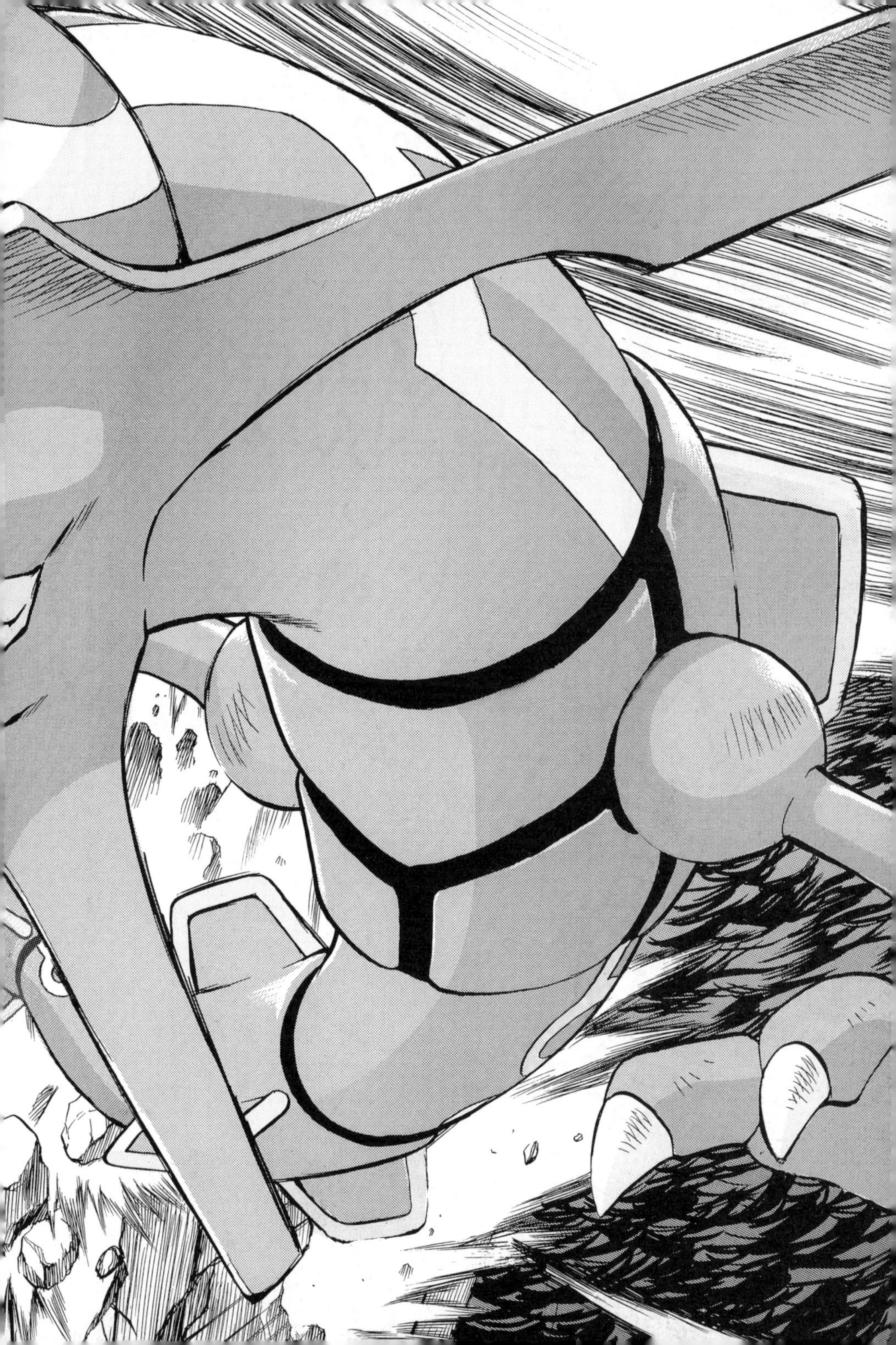

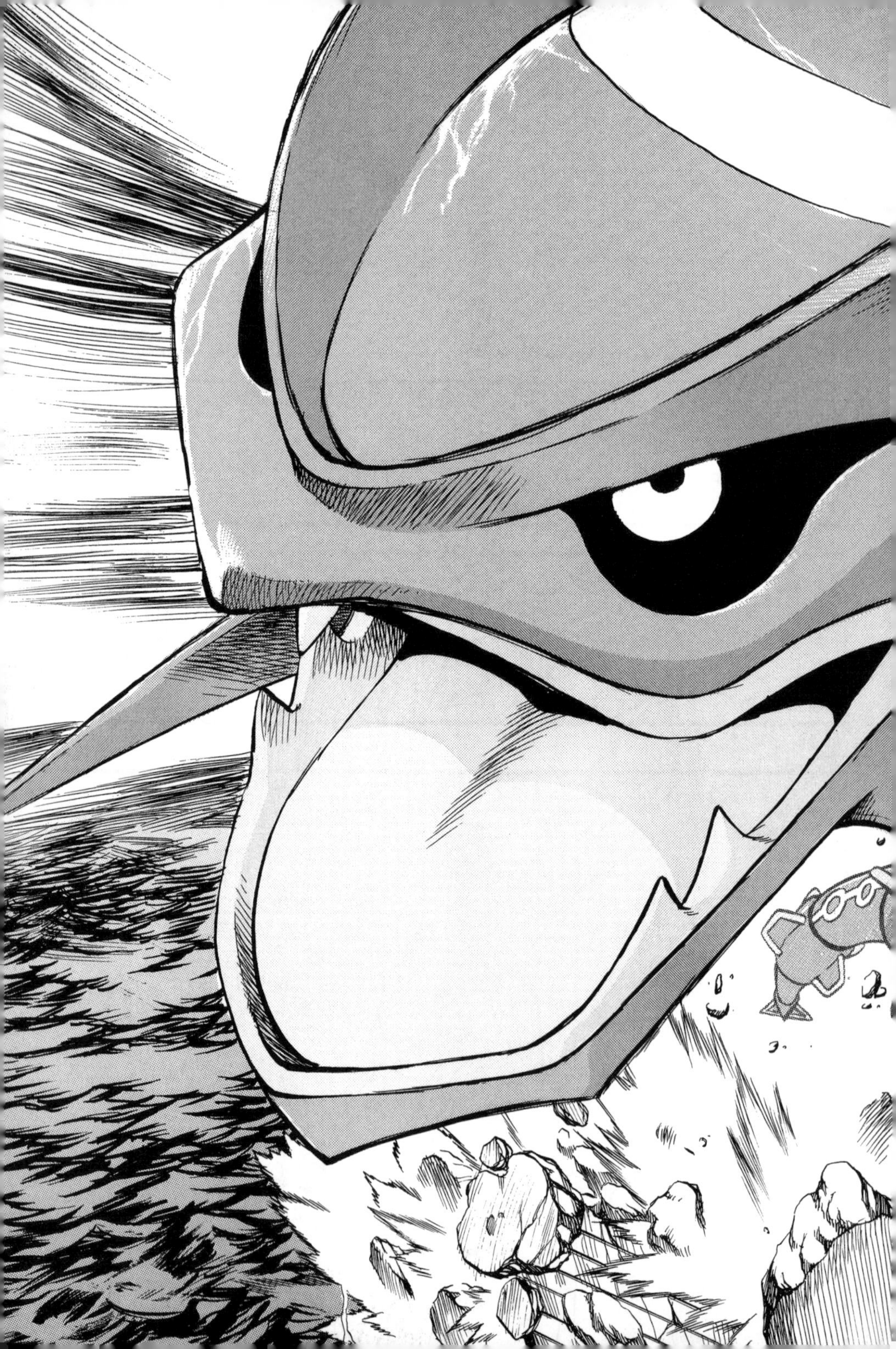

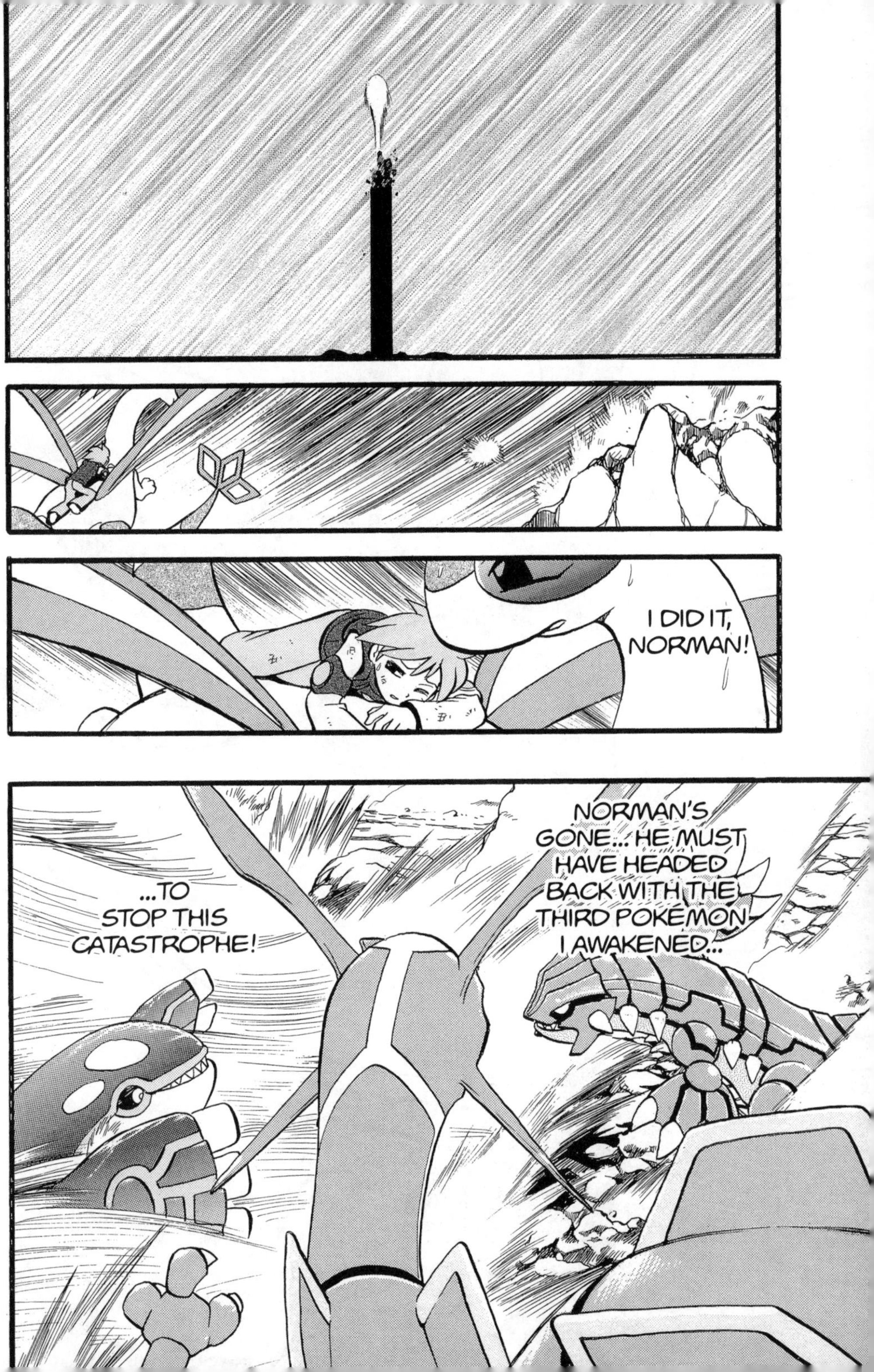
I DID IT, NORMAN!
NORMAN'S GONE... HE MUST HAVE HEADED BACK WITH THE THIRD POKéMON I AWAKENED...
...TO STOP THIS CATASTROPHE!

● Adventure 259 ●
Rayquaza Redemption, Part 2

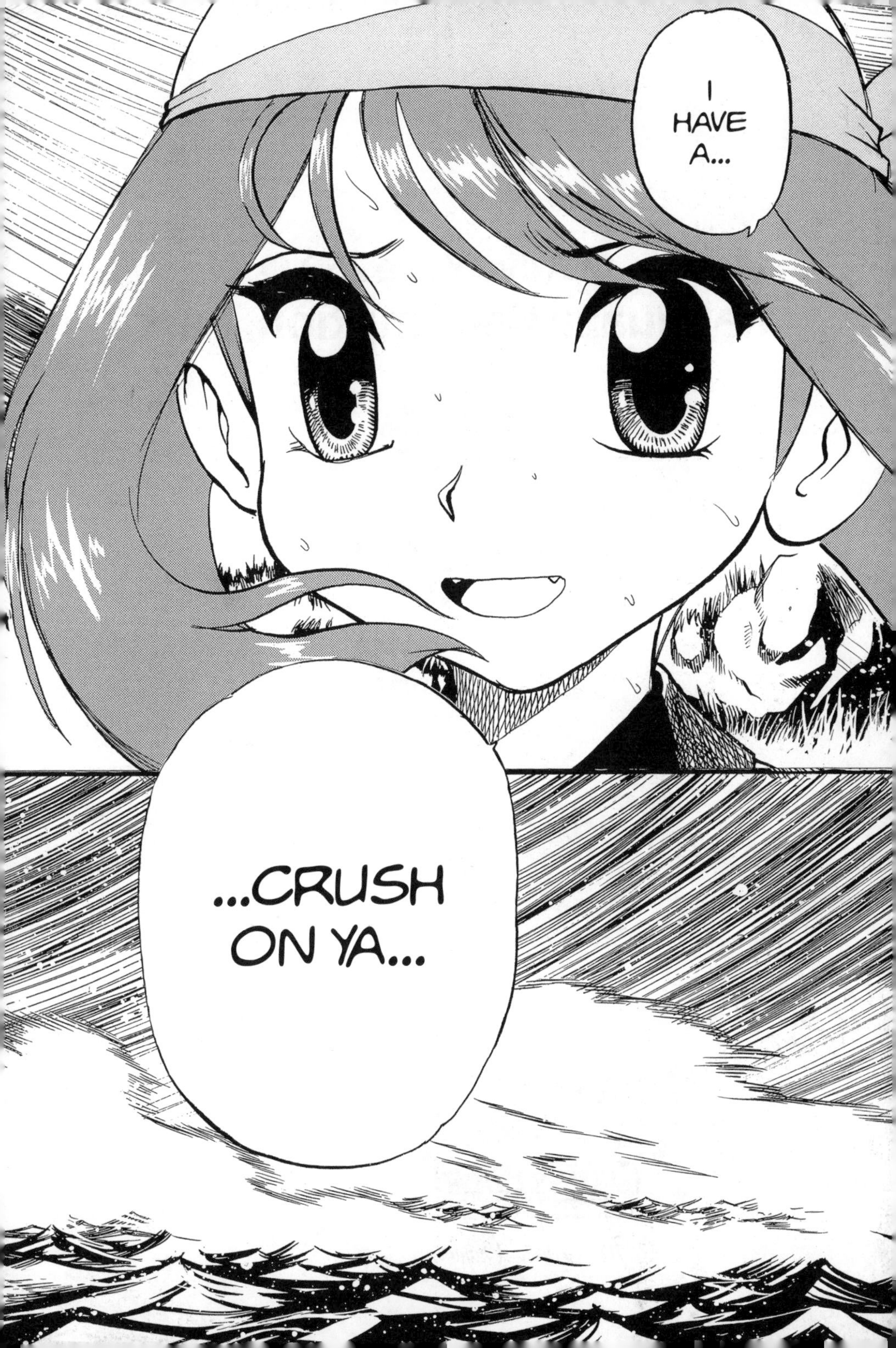
I HAVE A...
...CRUSH ON YA...

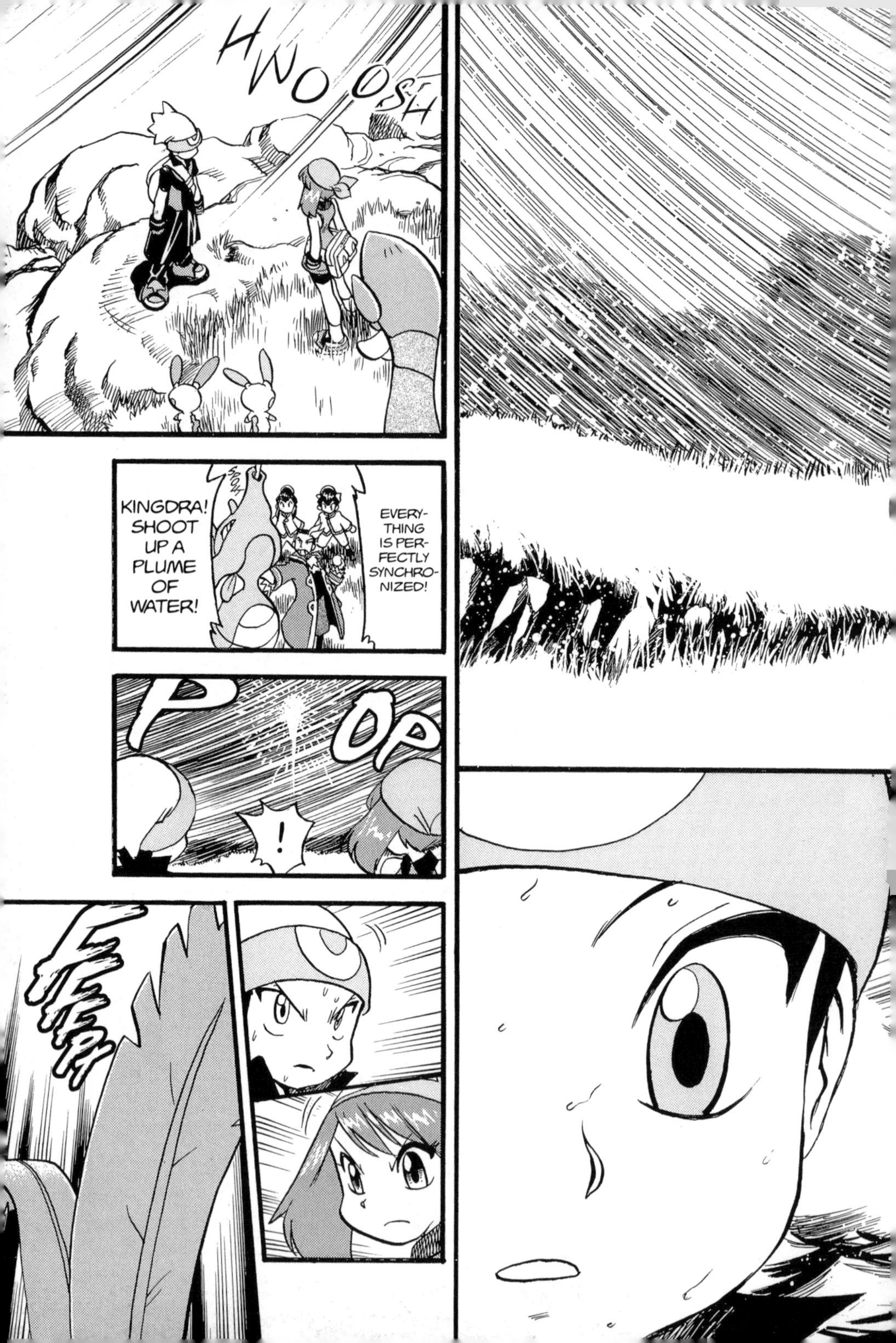
WHOOSH
EVERYTHING IS PERFECTLY SYNCHRONIZED!
KINGDRA! SHOOT UP A PLUME OF WATER!
POP
!

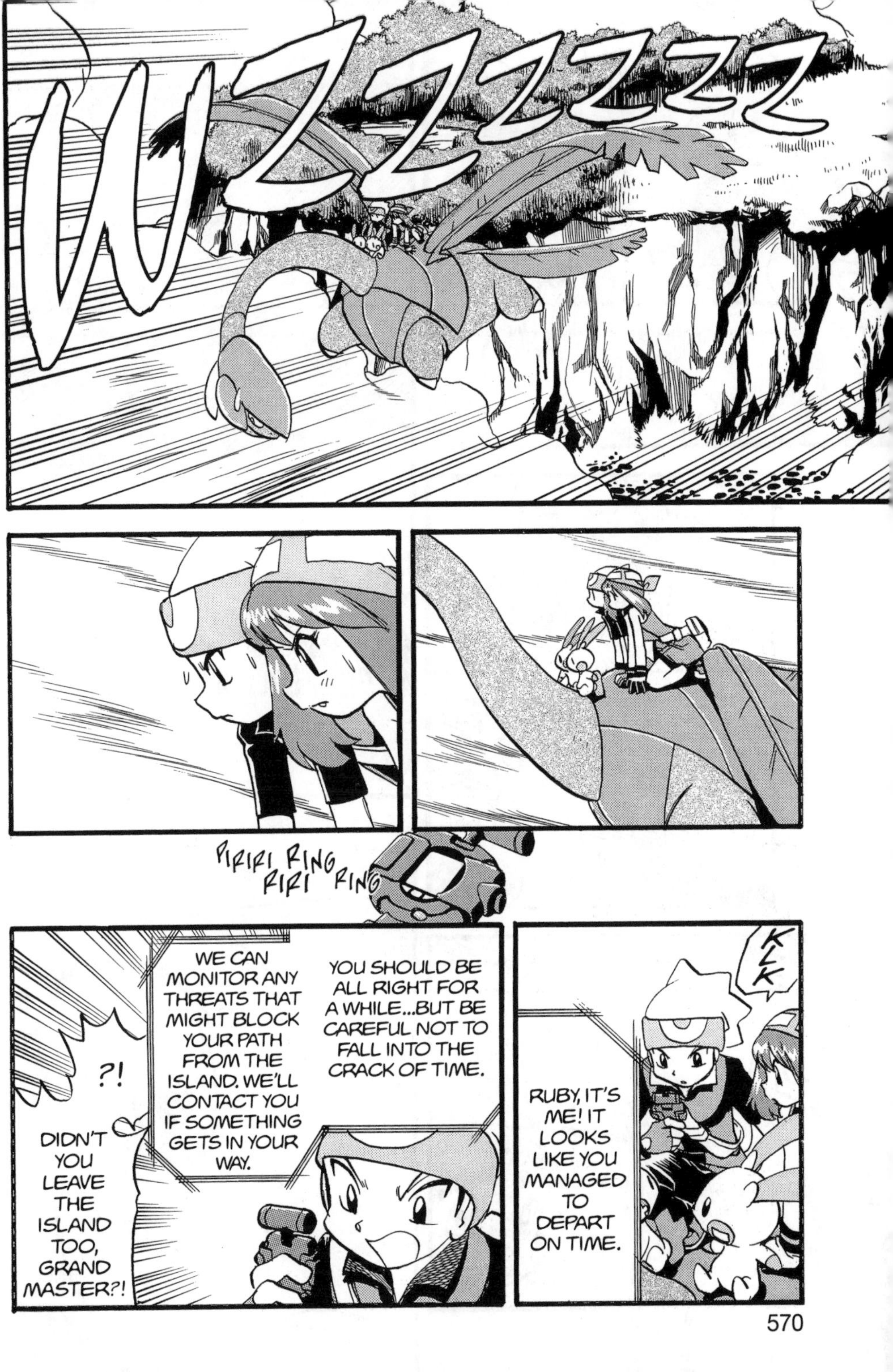
WZZZZZZ
PIRIRI RING RIRI RING
KLIK
RUBY, IT'S ME! IT LOOKS LIKE YOU MANAGED TO DEPART ON TIME.
YOU SHOULD BE ALL RIGHT FOR A WHILE...BUT BE CAREFUL NOT TO FALL INTO THE CRACK OF TIME.
WE CAN MONITOR ANY THREATS THAT MIGHT BLOCK YOUR PATH FROM THE ISLAND. WE'LL CONTACT YOU IF SOMETHING GETS IN YOUR WAY.
?!
DIDN'T YOU LEAVE THE ISLAND TOO, GRAND MASTER?!

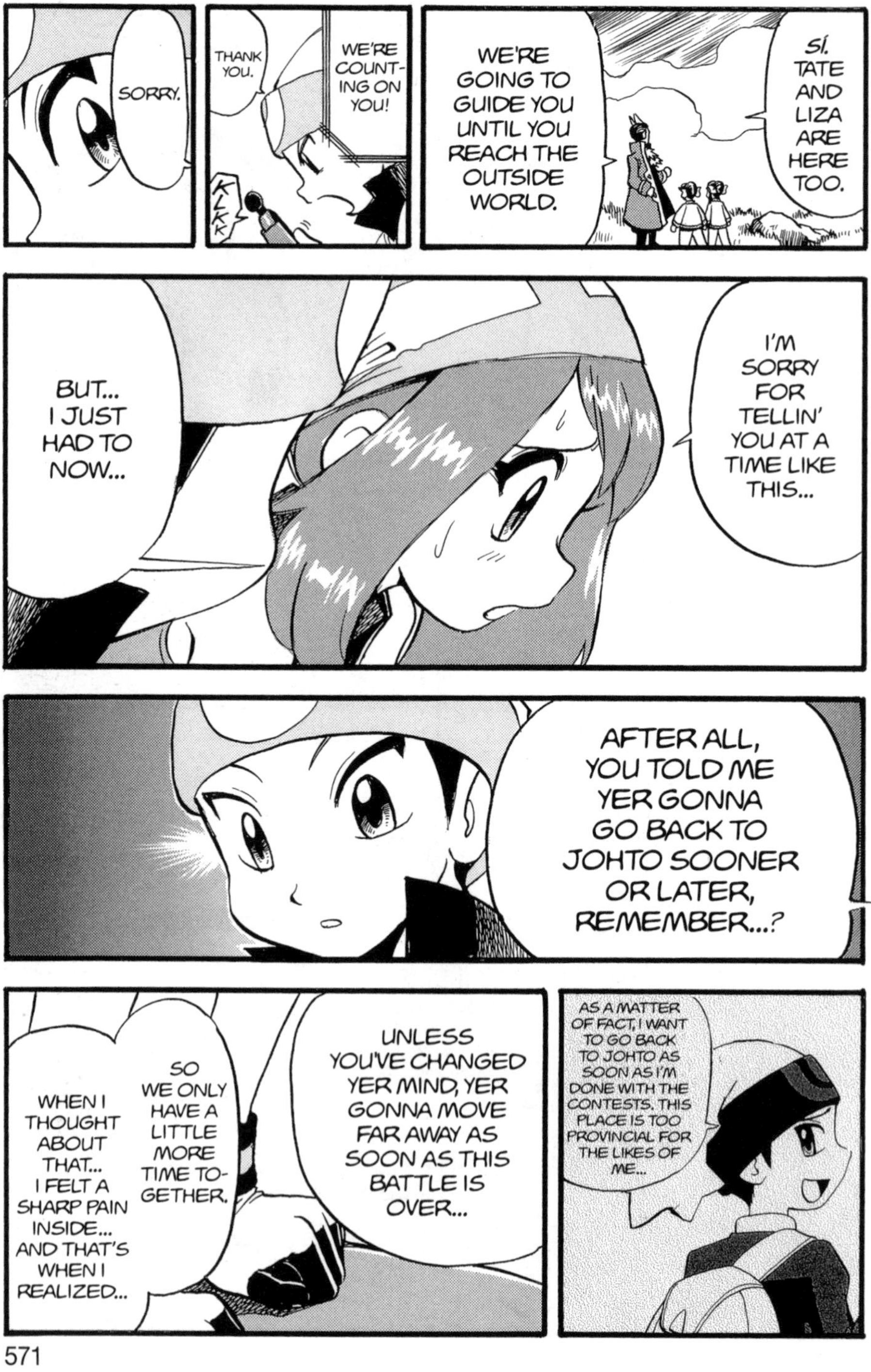
SÍ. TATE AND LIZA ARE HERE TOO.
WE'RE GOING TO GUIDE YOU UNTIL YOU REACH THE OUTSIDE WORLD.
WE'RE COUNTING ON YOU!
THANK YOU.
KLKK
SORRY.
I'M SORRY FOR TELLIN' YOU AT A TIME LIKE THIS...
BUT... I JUST HAD TO NOW...
AFTER ALL, YOU TOLD ME YER GONNA GO BACK TO JOHTO SOONER OR LATER, REMEMBER...?
AS A MATTER OF FACT, I WANT TO GO BACK TO JOHTO AS SOON AS I'M DONE WITH THE CONTESTS. THIS PLACE IS TOO PROVINCIAL FOR THE LIKES OF ME...
UNLESS YOU'VE CHANGED YER MIND, YER GONNA MOVE FAR AWAY AS SOON AS THIS BATTLE IS OVER...
SO WE ONLY HAVE A LITTLE MORE TIME TO-GETHER.
WHEN I THOUGHT ABOUT THAT... I FELT A SHARP PAIN INSIDE... AND THAT'S WHEN I REALIZED...

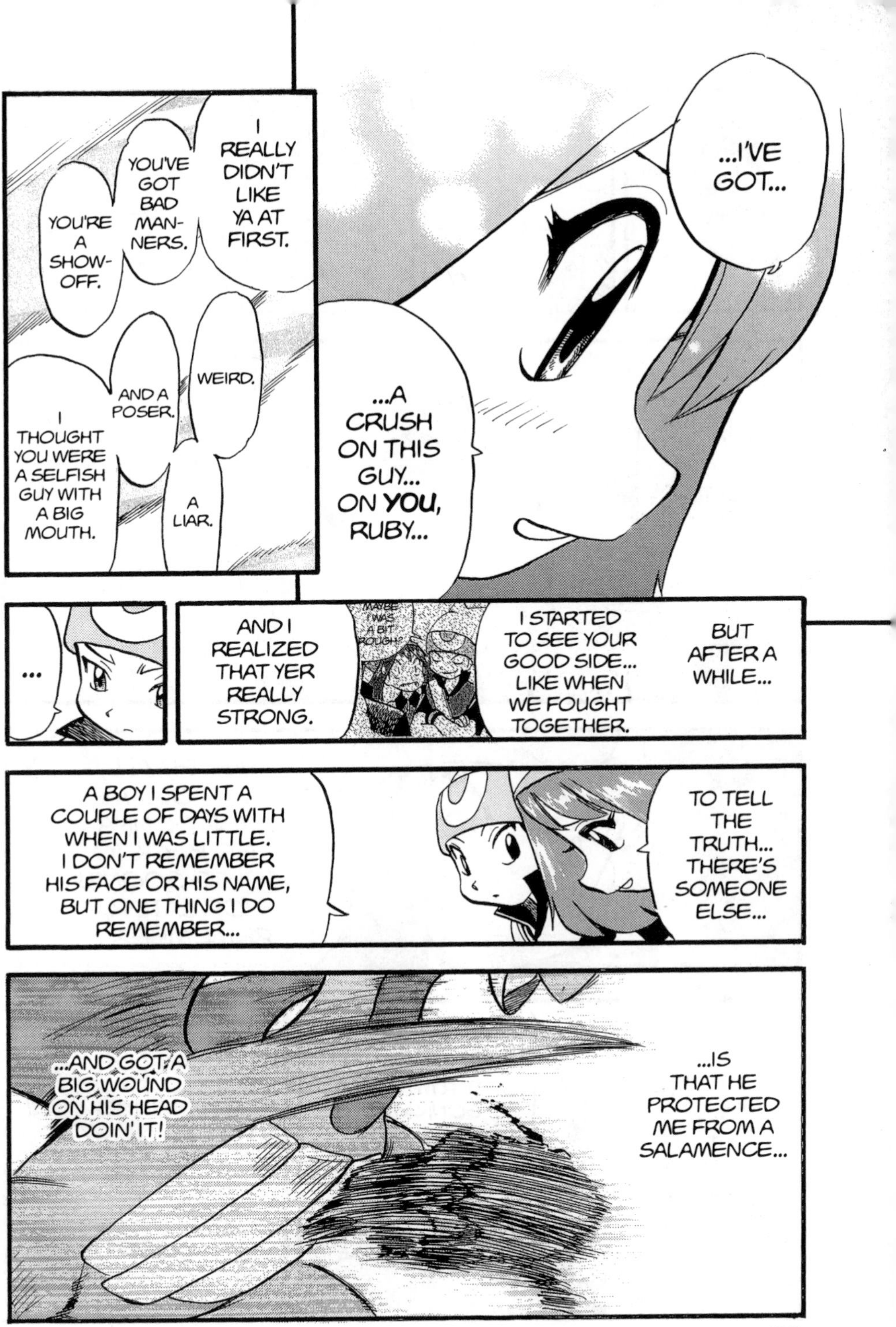
...I'VE GOT...
...A CRUSH ON THIS GUY... ON YOU, RUBY...
I REALLY DIDN'T LIKE YA AT FIRST.
YOU'VE GOT BAD MAN-NERS.
YOU'RE A SHOW-OFF.
WEIRD.
AND A POSER.
I THOUGHT YOU WERE A SELFISH GUY WITH A BIG MOUTH.
A LIAR.
BUT AFTER A WHILE...
I STARTED TO SEE YOUR GOOD SIDE... LIKE WHEN WE FOUGHT TOGETHER.
MAYBE I WAS A BIT ROUGH?
AND I REALIZED THAT YER REALLY STRONG.
...
TO TELL THE TRUTH... THERE'S SOMEONE ELSE...
A BOY I SPENT A COUPLE OF DAYS WITH WHEN I WAS LITTLE. I DON'T REMEMBER HIS FACE OR HIS NAME, BUT ONE THING I DO REMEMBER...
...IS THAT HE PROTECTED ME FROM A SALAMENCE...
...AND GOT A BIG WOUND ON HIS HEAD DOIN' IT!

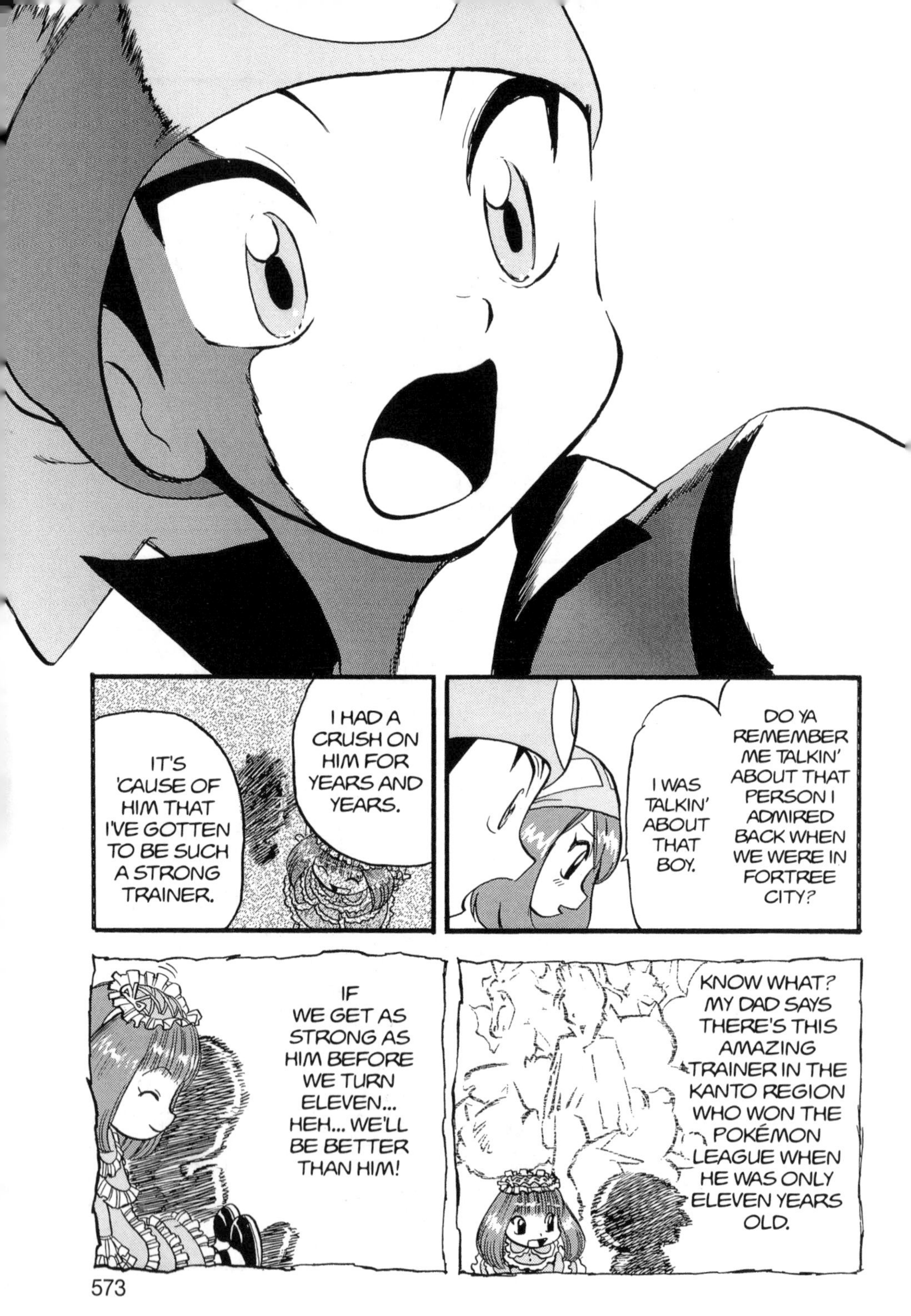
DO YA REMEMBER ME TALKIN' ABOUT THAT PERSON I ADMIRED BACK WHEN WE WERE IN FORTREE CITY?
I WAS TALKIN' ABOUT THAT BOY.
I HAD A CRUSH ON HIM FOR YEARS AND YEARS.
IT'S 'CAUSE OF HIM THAT I'VE GOTTEN TO BE SUCH A STRONG TRAINER.
KNOW WHAT? MY DAD SAYS THERE'S THIS AMAZING TRAINER IN THE KANTO REGION WHO WON THE POKéMON LEAGUE WHEN HE WAS ONLY ELEVEN YEARS OLD.
IF WE GET AS STRONG AS HIM BEFORE WE TURN ELEVEN... HEH... WE'LL BE BETTER THAN HIM!

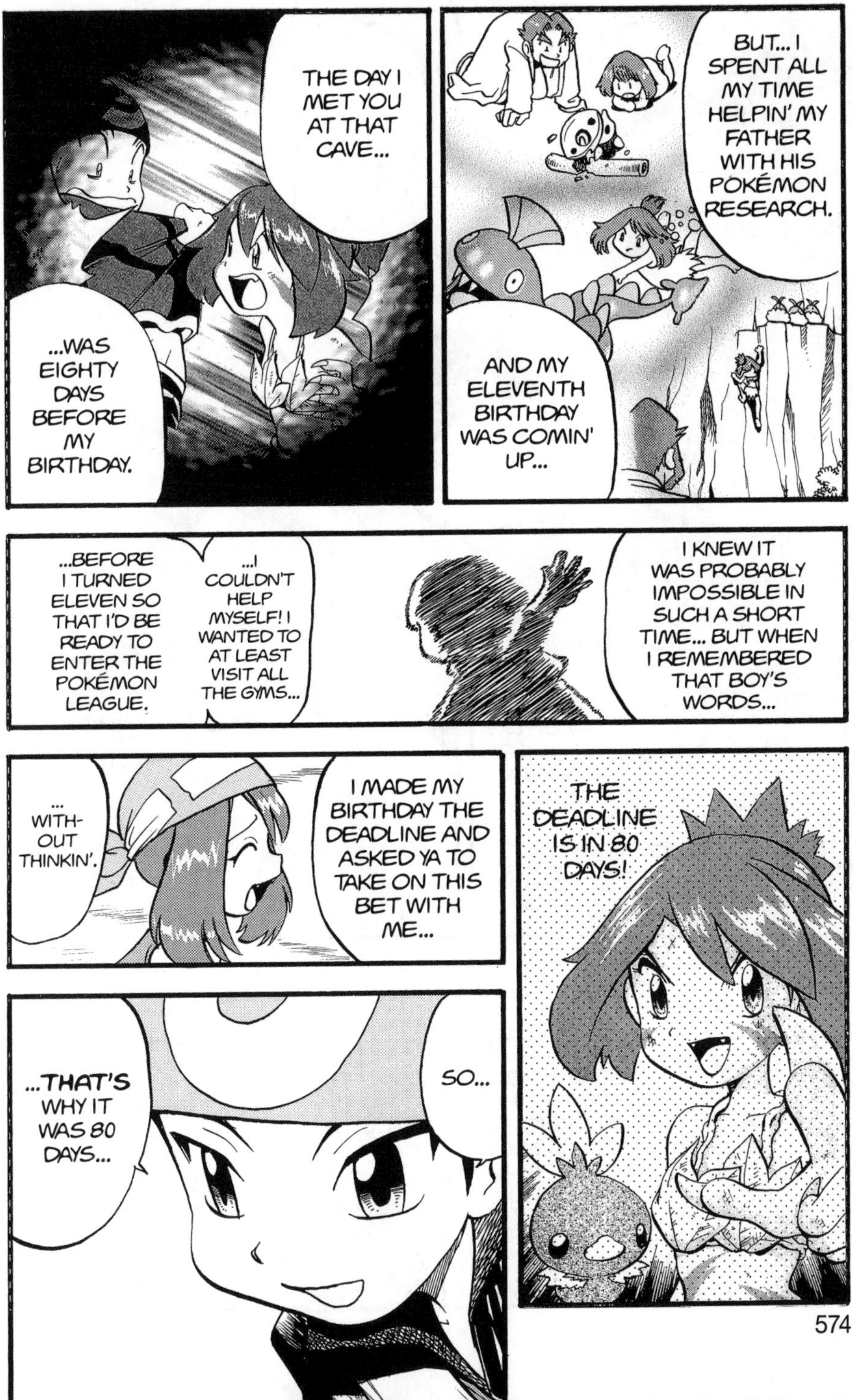
BUT... I SPENT ALL MY TIME HELPIN' MY FATHER WITH HIS POKÉMON RESEARCH.
AND MY ELEVENTH BIRTHDAY WAS COMIN' UP...
THE DAY I MET YOU AT THAT CAVE...
...WAS EIGHTY DAYS BEFORE MY BIRTHDAY.
I KNEW IT WAS PROBABLY IMPOSSIBLE IN SUCH A SHORT TIME... BUT WHEN I REMEMBERED THAT BOY'S WORDS...
...I COULDN'T HELP MYSELF! I WANTED TO AT LEAST VISIT ALL THE GYMS...
...BEFORE I TURNED ELEVEN SO THAT I'D BE READY TO ENTER THE POKÉMON LEAGUE.
THE DEADLINE IS IN 80 DAYS!
I MADE MY BIRTHDAY THE DEADLINE AND ASKED YA TO TAKE ON THIS BET WITH ME...
...WITH-OUT THINKIN'.
SO...
...THAT'S WHY IT WAS 80 DAYS...

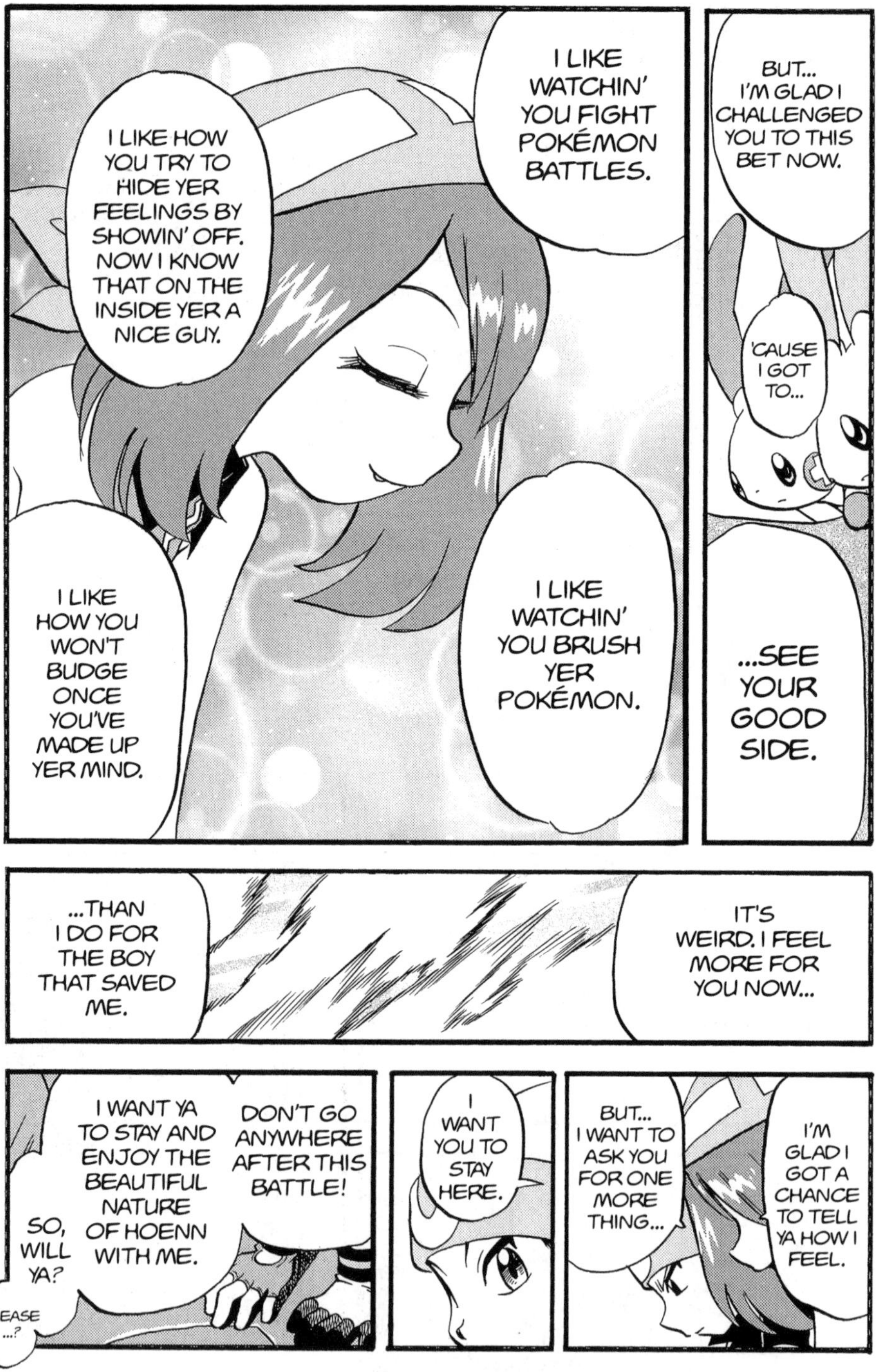
BUT... I'M GLAD I CHALLENGED YOU TO THIS BET NOW.
'CAUSE I GOT TO...
...SEE YOUR GOOD SIDE.
I LIKE WATCHIN' YOU FIGHT POKÉMON BATTLES.
I LIKE HOW YOU TRY TO HIDE YER FEELINGS BY SHOWIN' OFF. NOW I KNOW THAT ON THE INSIDE YER A NICE GUY.
I LIKE WATCHIN' YOU BRUSH YER POKÉMON.
I LIKE HOW YOU WON'T BUDGE ONCE YOU'VE MADE UP YER MIND.
IT'S WEIRD. I FEEL MORE FOR YOU NOW...
...THAN I DO FOR THE BOY THAT SAVED ME.
I'M GLAD I GOT A CHANCE TO TELL YA HOW I FEEL.
BUT... I WANT TO ASK YOU FOR ONE MORE THING...
I WANT YOU TO STAY HERE.
DON'T GO ANYWHERE AFTER THIS BATTLE!
I WANT YA TO STAY AND ENJOY THE BEAUTIFUL NATURE OF HOENN WITH ME.
SO, WILL YA?
PLEASE ...?

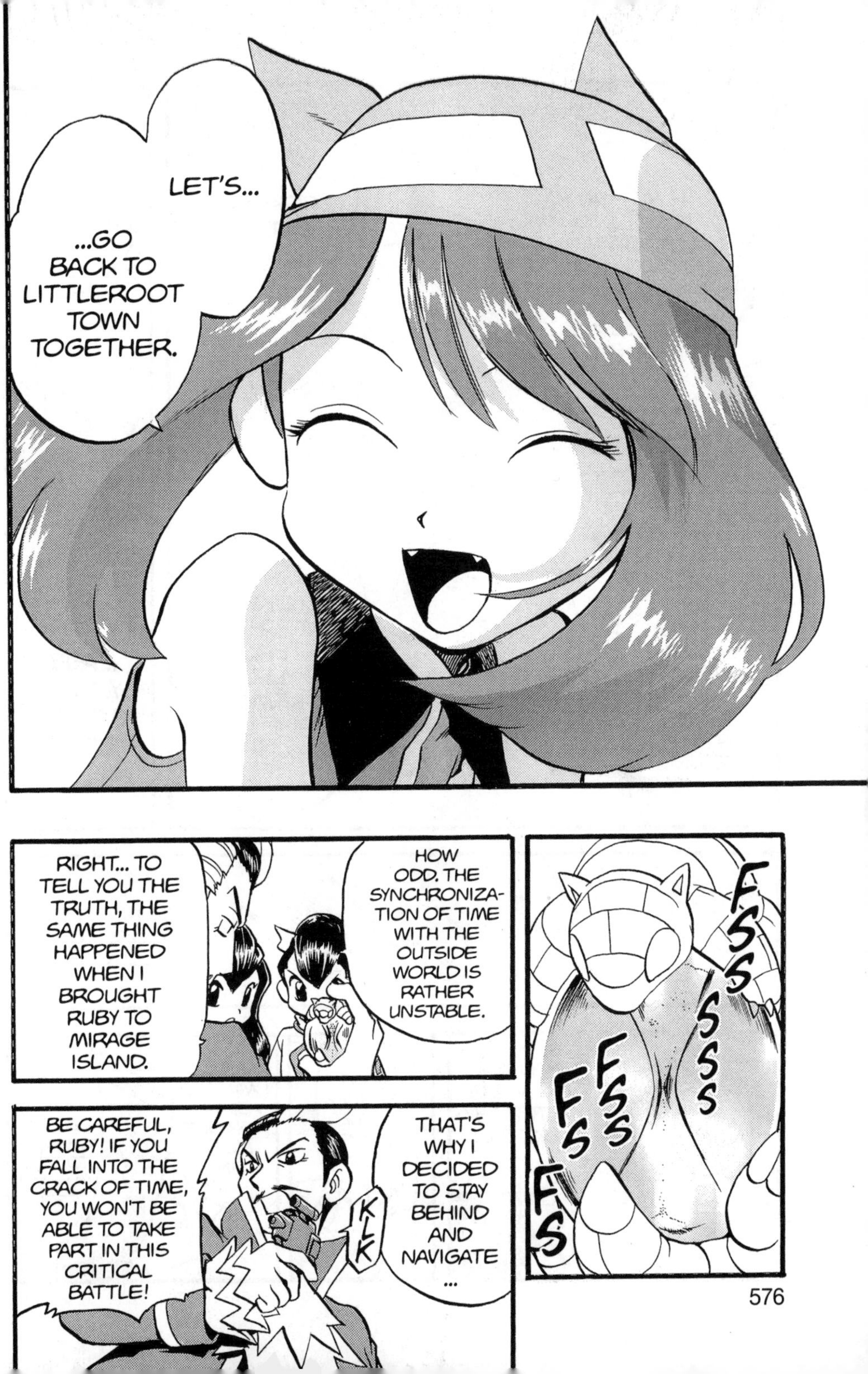
LET'S...
...GO BACK TO LITTLEROOT TOWN TOGETHER.
FSS SSS FSS FS FS
HOW ODD. THE SYNCHRONIZATION OF TIME WITH THE OUTSIDE WORLD IS RATHER UNSTABLE.
RIGHT... TO TELL YOU THE TRUTH, THE SAME THING HAPPENED WHEN I BROUGHT RUBY TO MIRAGE ISLAND.
THAT'S WHY I DECIDED TO STAY BEHIND AND NAVIGATE...
KLK
BE CAREFUL, RUBY! IF YOU FALL INTO THE CRACK OF TIME, YOU WON'T BE ABLE TO TAKE PART IN THIS CRITICAL BATTLE!

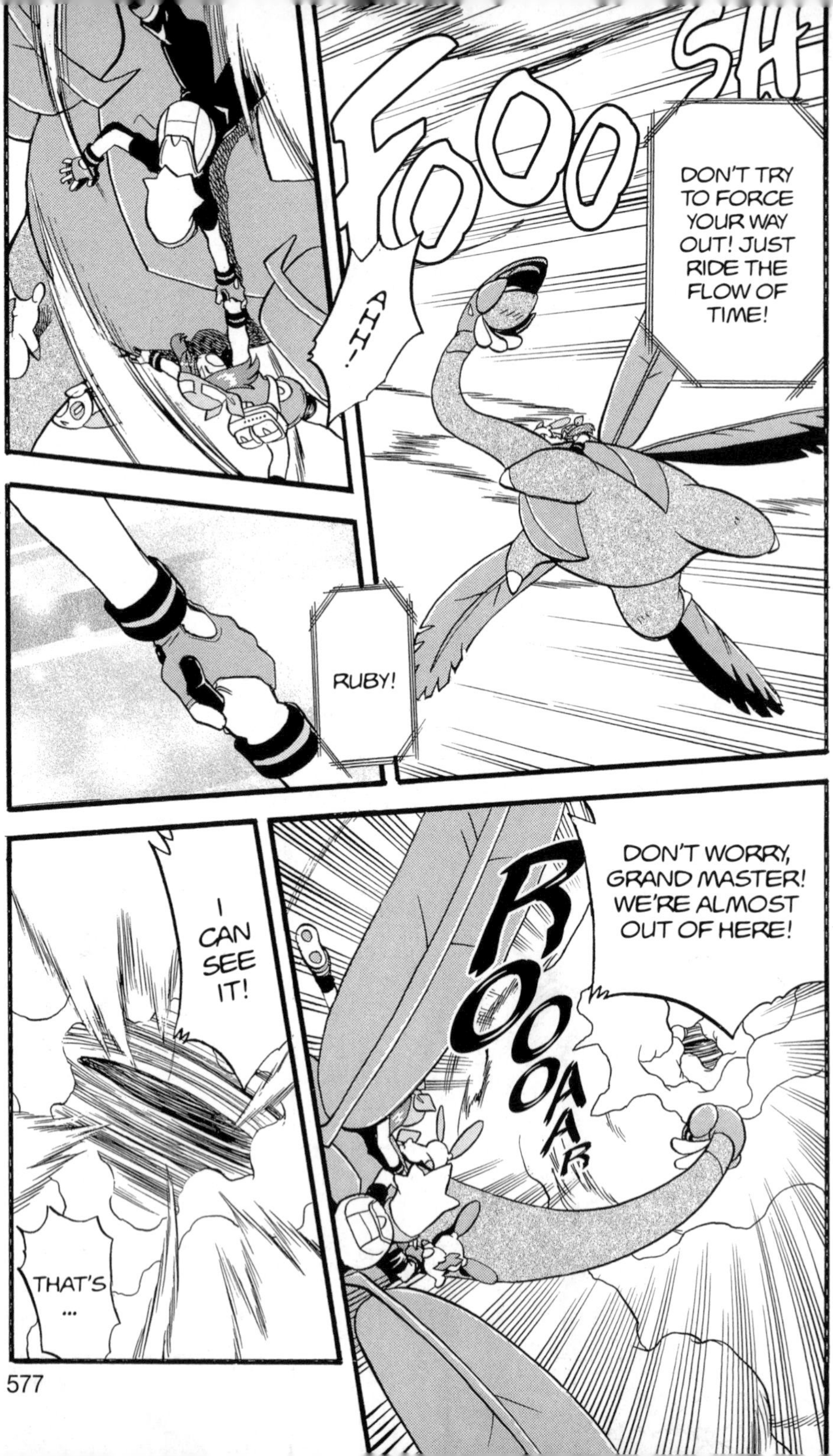
FOOOOSH
DON'T TRY TO FORCE YOUR WAY OUT! JUST RIDE THE FLOW OF TIME!
AHH!
RUBY!
DON'T WORRY, GRAND MASTER! WE'RE ALMOST OUT OF HERE!
ROOOAR
I CAN SEE IT!
THAT'S ...

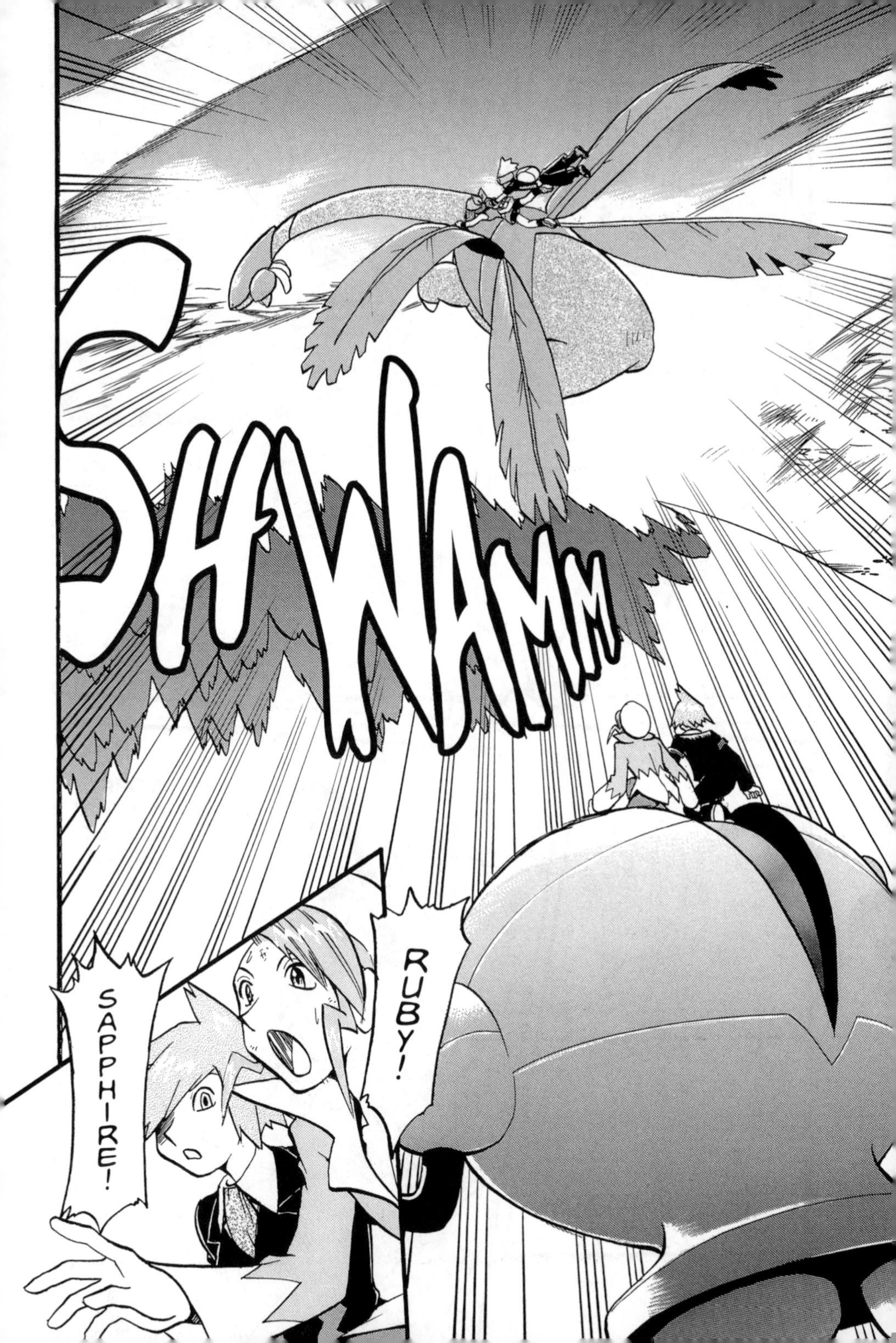
SHWAMM
RUBY!
SAPPHIRE!

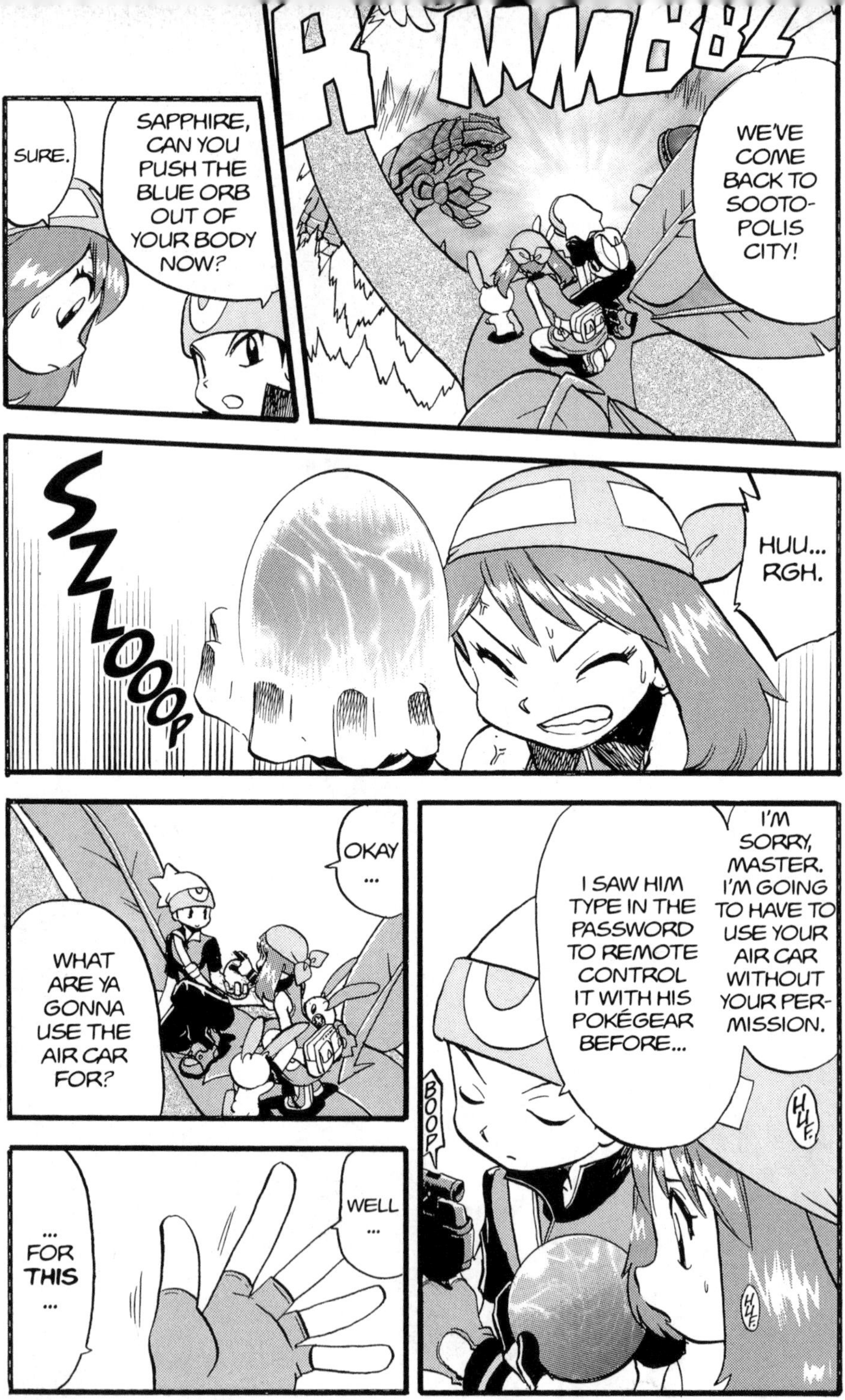
WE'VE COME BACK TO SOOTO-POLIS CITY!
SAPPHIRE, CAN YOU PUSH THE BLUE ORB OUT OF YOUR BODY NOW?
SURE.
HUU... RGH.
SZZLOOOP
I'M SORRY, MASTER. I'M GOING TO HAVE TO USE YOUR AIR CAR WITHOUT YOUR PER-MISSION.
I SAW HIM TYPE IN THE PASSWORD TO REMOTE CONTROL IT WITH HIS POKÉGEAR BEFORE...
BOOOP
HUF
HUF
OKAY ...
WHAT ARE YA GONNA USE THE AIR CAR FOR?
WELL ...
... FOR THIS ...

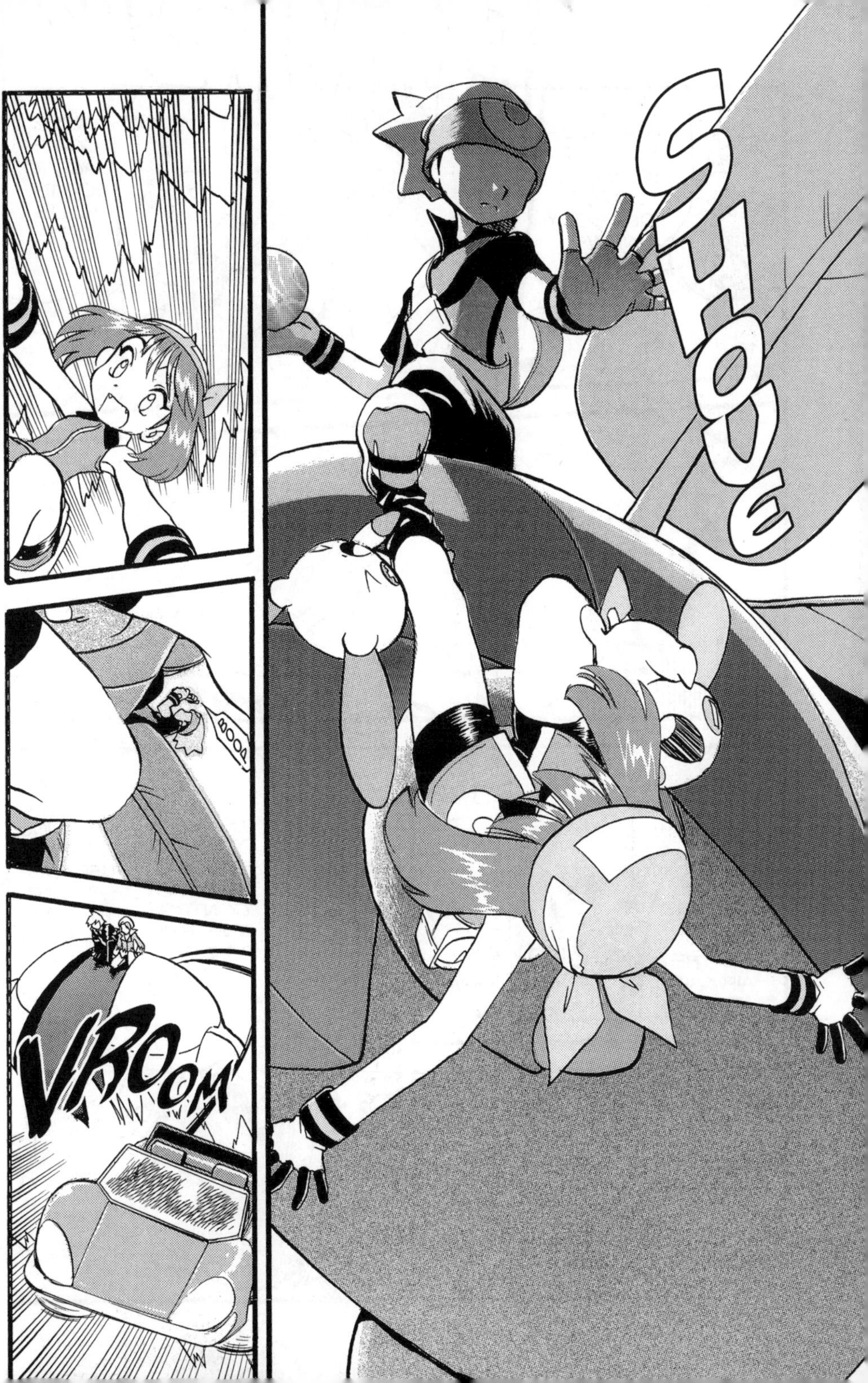
SHOVE
WOOA
VROOM

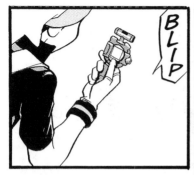

BLIP

FSSST

SMAK

WHY?!

WHY ARE YA DOIN' THIS?!

SMAK

SMAK

SMAK

I WANT TO THANK YOU. I'M GLAD I ACCEPTED THIS BET.

I REALLY AM.

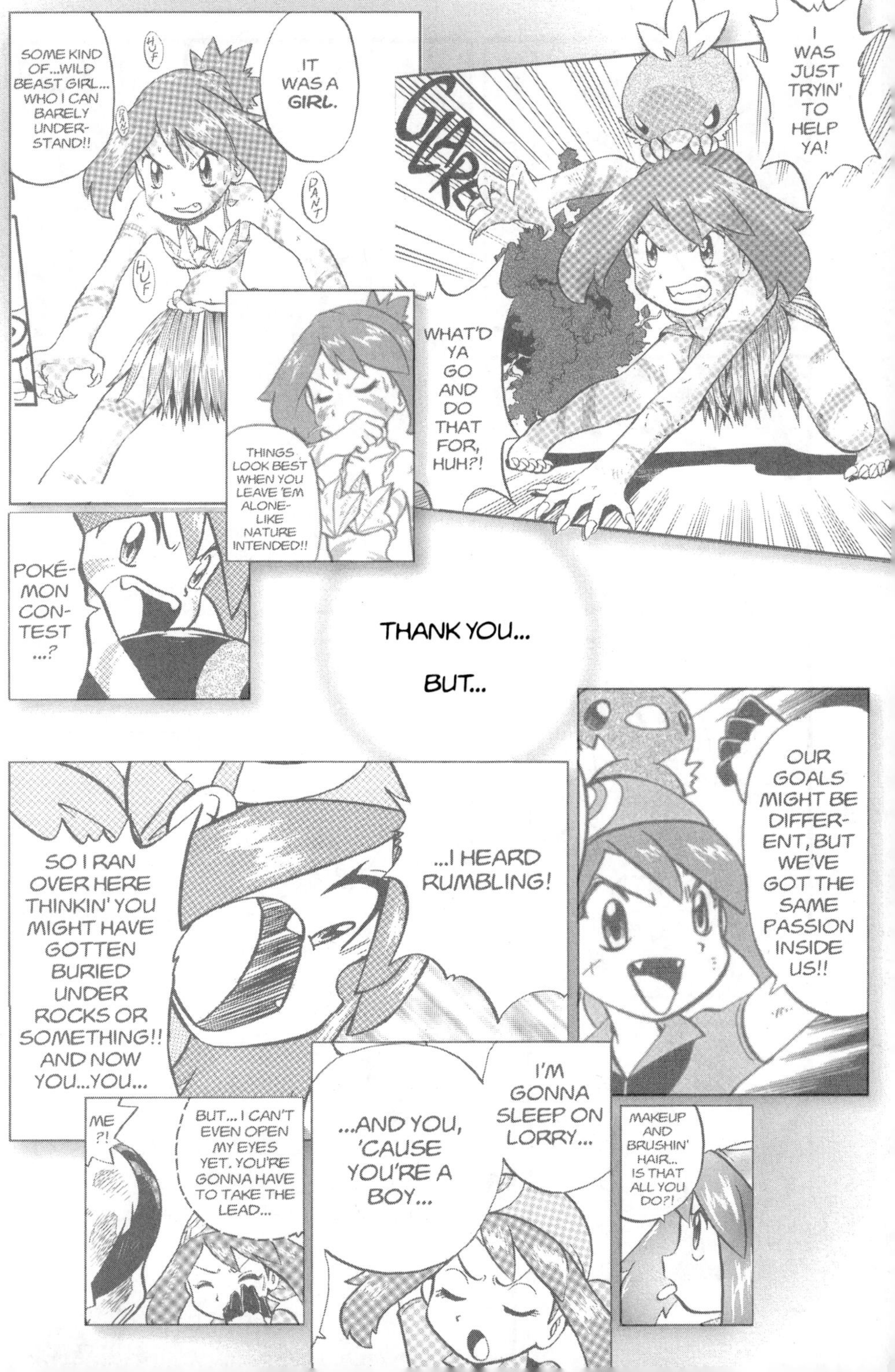
GLARE
I WAS JUST TRYIN' TO HELP YA!
WHAT'D YA GO AND DO THAT FOR, HUH?!
THINGS LOOK BEST WHEN YOU LEAVE 'EM ALONE- LIKE NATURE INTENDED!!
IT WAS A GIRL.
SOME KIND OF...WILD BEAST GIRL... WHO I CAN BARELY UNDER-STAND!!
HUF
PANT
PANT
HUF
POKÉ-MON CON-TEST ...?
THANK YOU...
BUT...
OUR GOALS MIGHT BE DIFFER-ENT, BUT WE'VE GOT THE SAME PASSION INSIDE US!!
...I HEARD RUMBLING!
SO I RAN OVER HERE THINKIN' YOU MIGHT HAVE GOTTEN BURIED UNDER ROCKS OR SOMETHING!! AND NOW YOU...YOU...
MAKEUP AND BRUSHIN' HAIR... IS THAT ALL YOU DO?!
I'M GONNA SLEEP ON LORRY...
...AND YOU, 'CAUSE YOU'RE A BOY...
BUT... I CAN'T EVEN OPEN MY EYES YET. YOU'RE GONNA HAVE TO TAKE THE LEAD...
ME ?!

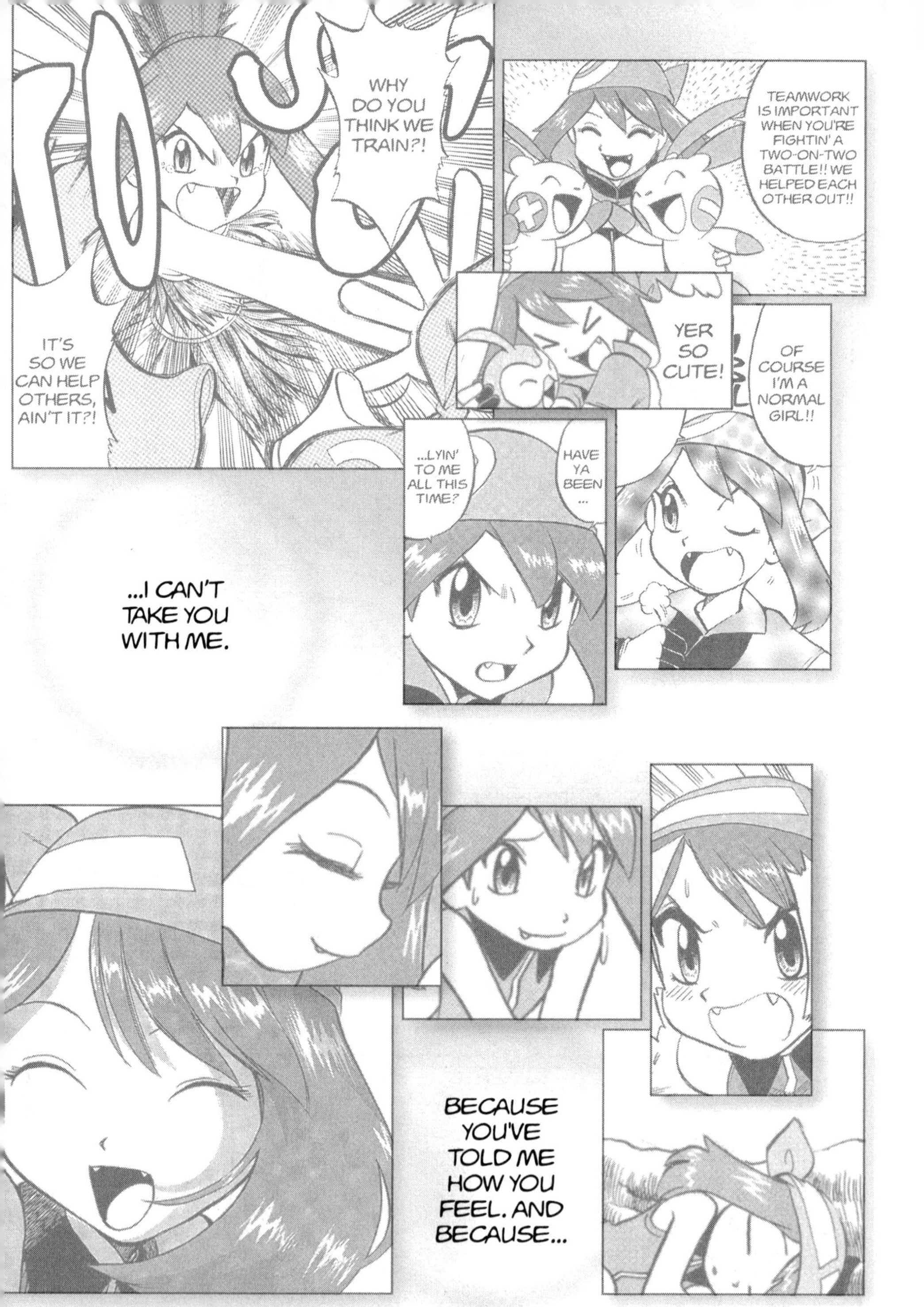
TEAMWORK IS IMPORTANT WHEN YOU'RE FIGHTIN' A TWO-ON-TWO BATTLE!! WE HELPED EACH OTHER OUT!!
YER SO CUTE!
OF COURSE I'M A NORMAL GIRL!!
HAVE YA BEEN...
...LYIN' TO ME ALL THIS TIME?
WHY DO YOU THINK WE TRAIN?!
IT'S SO WE CAN HELP OTHERS, AIN'T IT?!
...I CAN'T TAKE YOU WITH ME.
BECAUSE YOU'VE TOLD ME HOW YOU FEEL. AND BECAUSE...

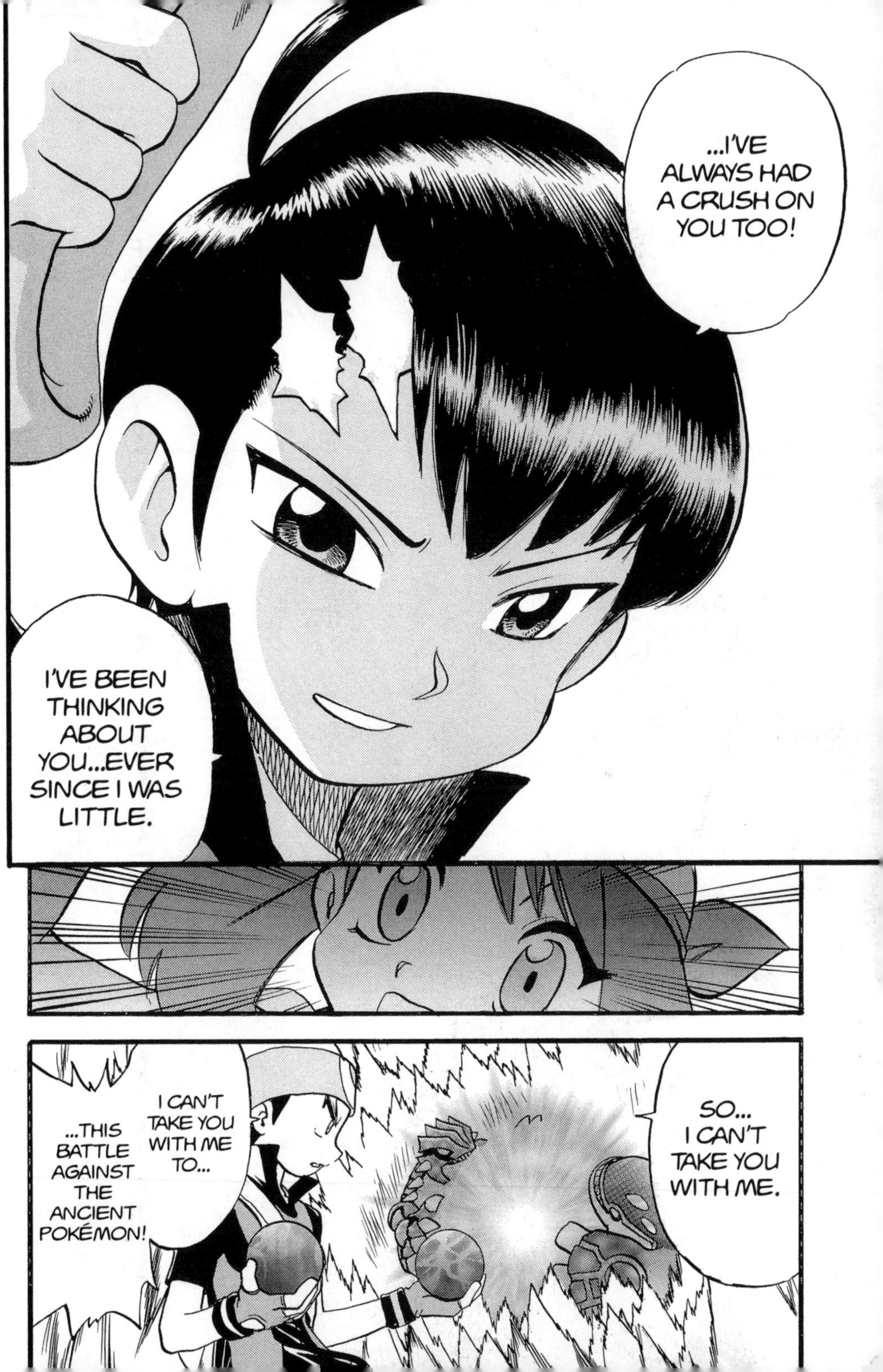
...I'VE ALWAYS HAD A CRUSH ON YOU TOO!
I'VE BEEN THINKING ABOUT YOU...EVER SINCE I WAS LITTLE.
SO... I CAN'T TAKE YOU WITH ME.
I CAN'T TAKE YOU WITH ME TO...
...THIS BATTLE AGAINST THE ANCIENT POKÉMON!

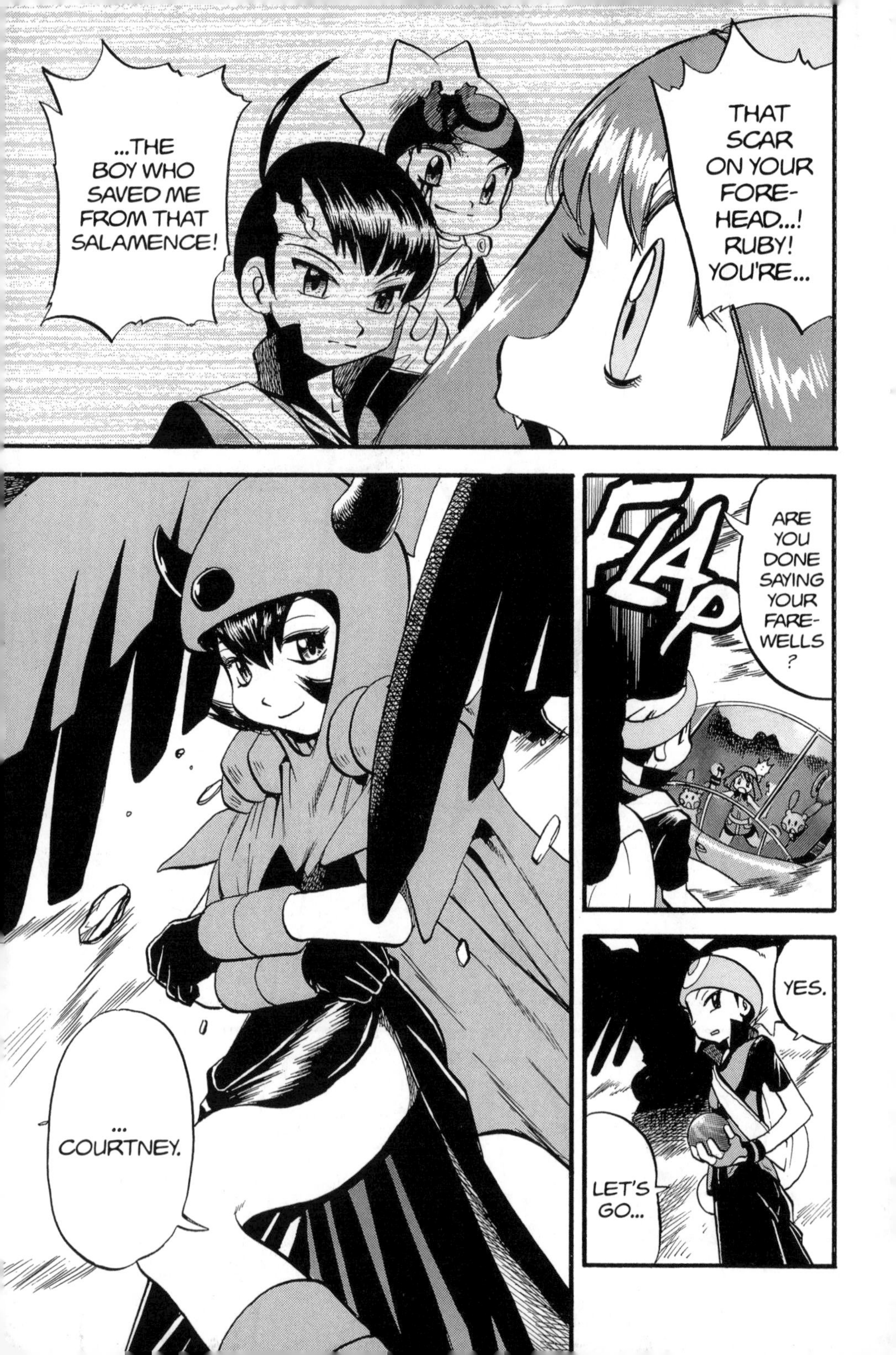
THAT SCAR ON YOUR FORE-HEAD...! RUBY! YOU'RE...
...THE BOY WHO SAVED ME FROM THAT SALAMENCE!
ARE YOU DONE SAYING YOUR FARE-WELLS?
FLAP
YES.
LET'S GO...
...COURTNEY.

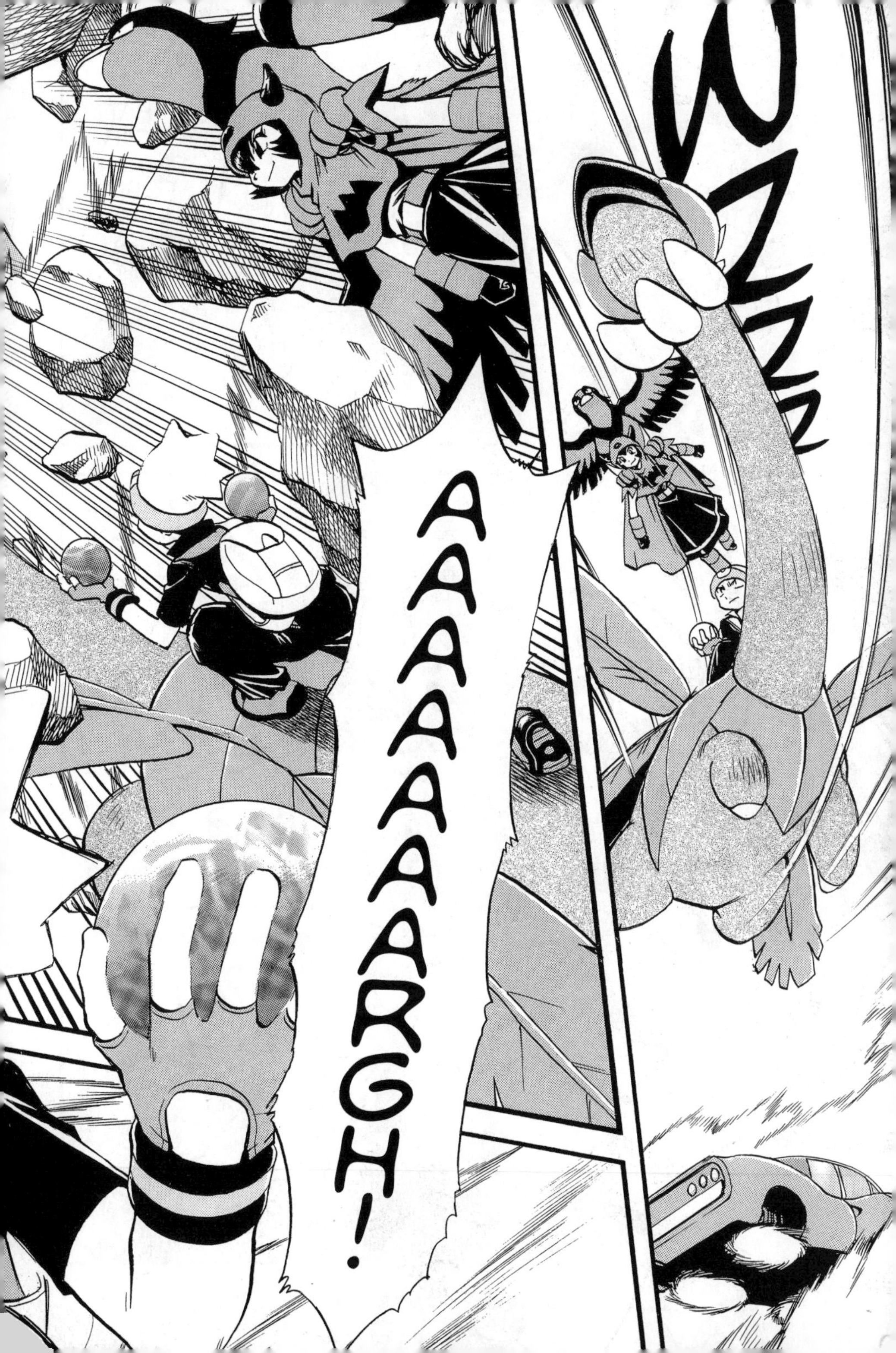
WAAAAAAAAAAARGH!

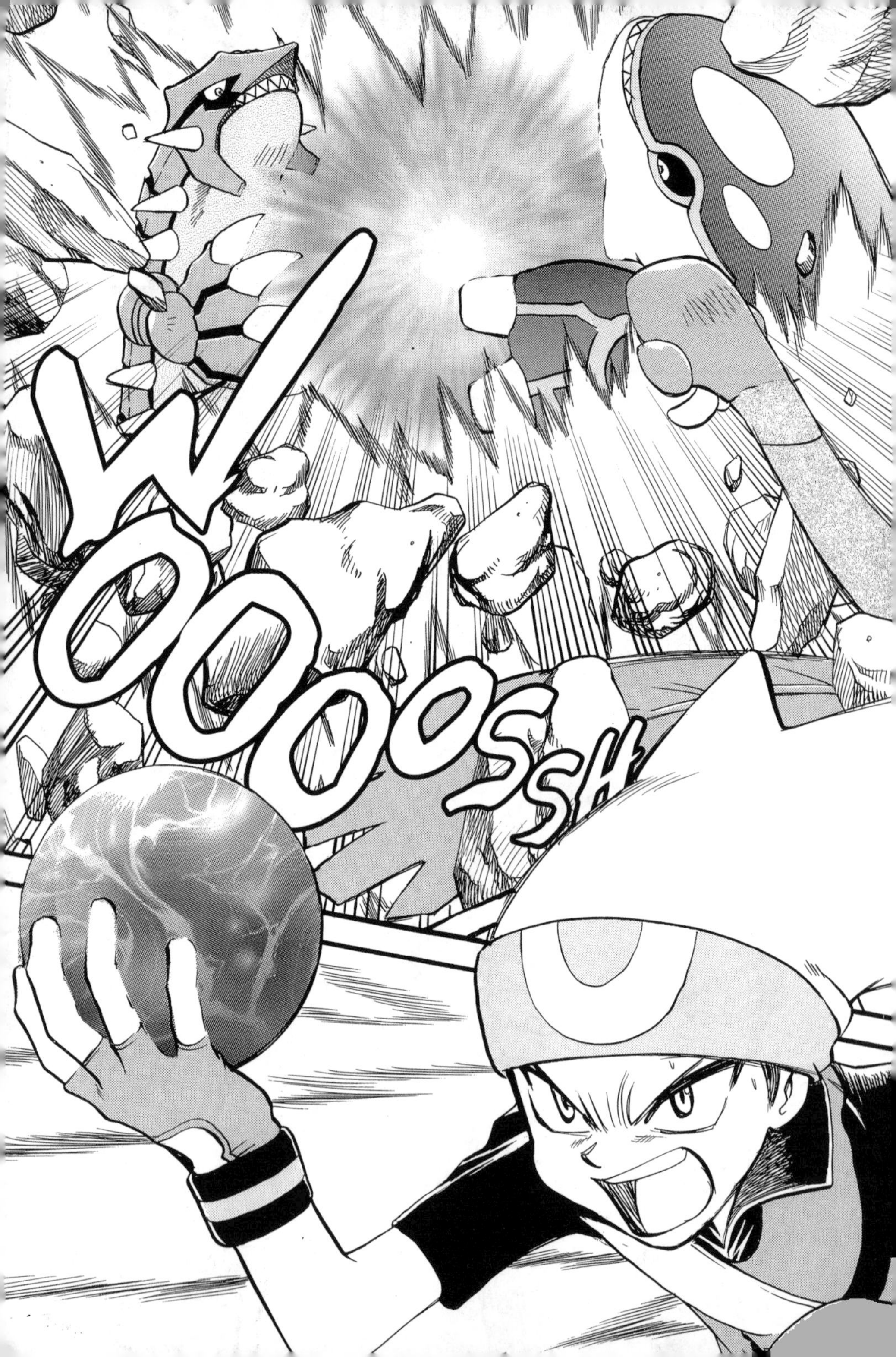
WOOOOSSH

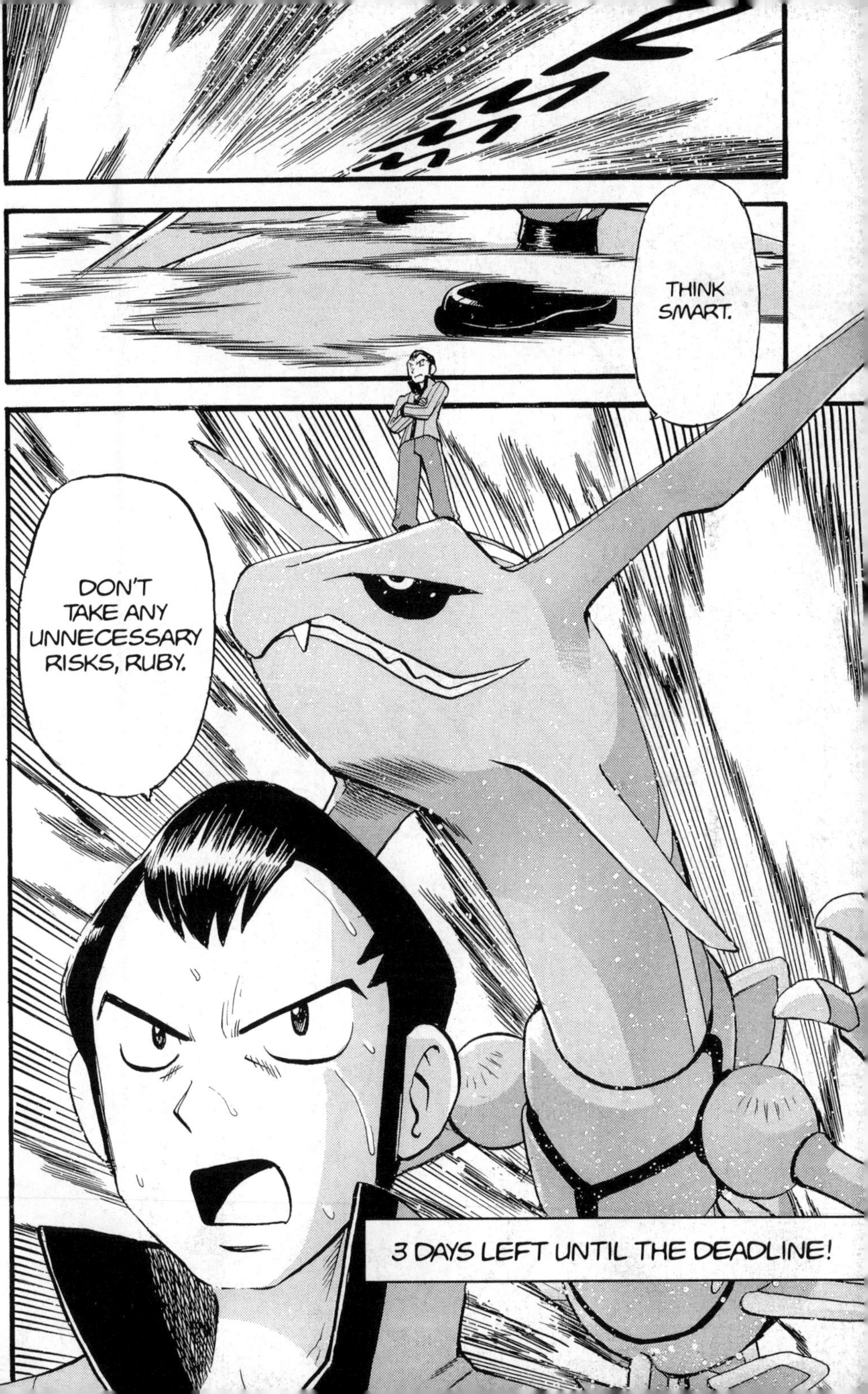
THINK SMART.
DON'T TAKE ANY UNNECESSARY RISKS, RUBY.
3 DAYS LEFT UNTIL THE DEADLINE!

Check out the moves of the Gym Leaders who are trying to stop the natural disasters that are splitting the Hoenn Region in two...

GROUDON

GROUDON RISES BACK UP ONTO THE LAND.

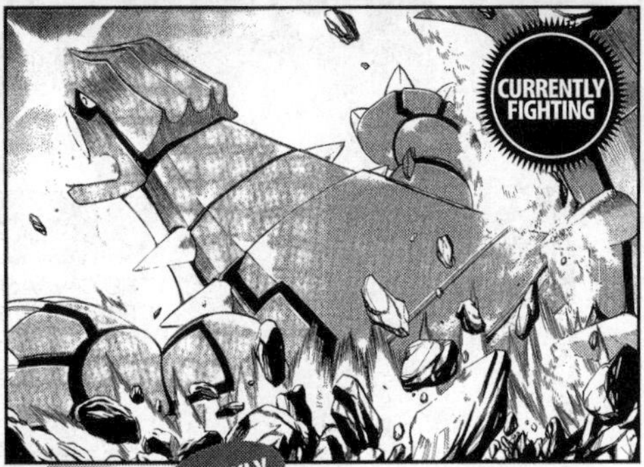
CURRENTLY FIGHTING

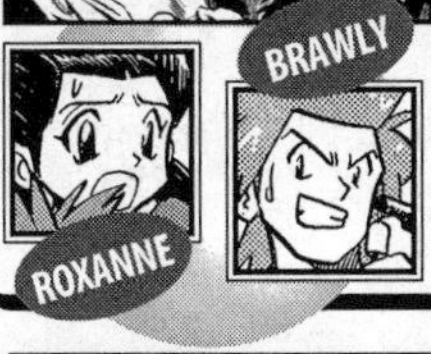
BRAWLY
ROXANNE

GROUDON HAS APPEARED NEAR FORTREE CITY! ROXANNE AND BRAWLY TRY TO HOLD OUT AGAINST ITS OVERWHELMING ATTACKS BUT...

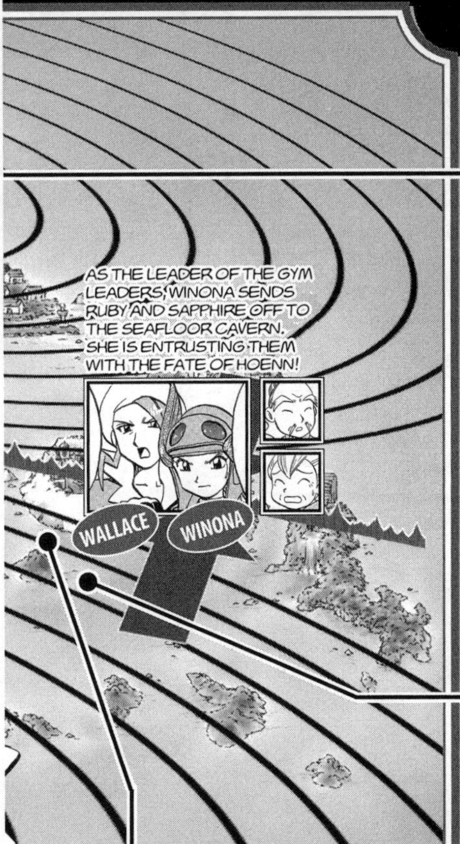
AS THE LEADER OF THE GYM LEADERS, WINONA SENDS RUBY AND SAPPHIRE OFF TO THE SEAFLOOR CAVERN. SHE IS ENTRUSTING THEM WITH THE FATE OF HOENN!
WALLACE
WINONA

TEAM MAGMA & TEAM AQUA

SEAFLOOR CAVERN

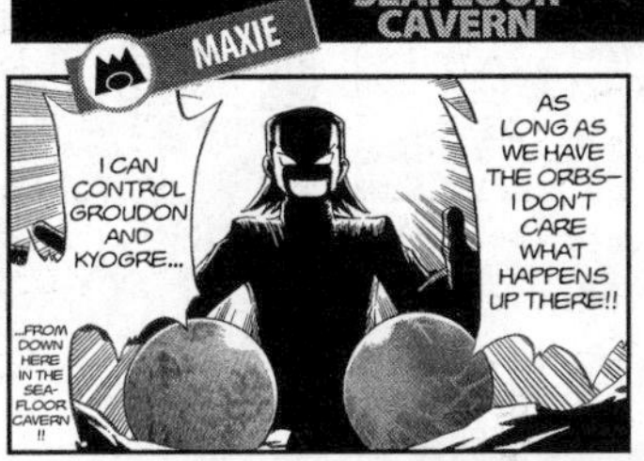
MAXIE
AS LONG AS WE HAVE THE ORBS— I DON'T CARE WHAT HAPPENS UP THERE!!
I CAN CONTROL GROUDON AND KYOGRE...
...FROM DOWN HERE IN THE SEAFLOOR CAVERN!!

◀ TEAM MAGMA HAS GOTTEN HOLD OF THE ORBS THAT ALLOW THEM TO CONTROL THE TWO ANCIENT POKÉMON. WILL THEY BEAT TEAM AQUA TO THE PUNCH?!

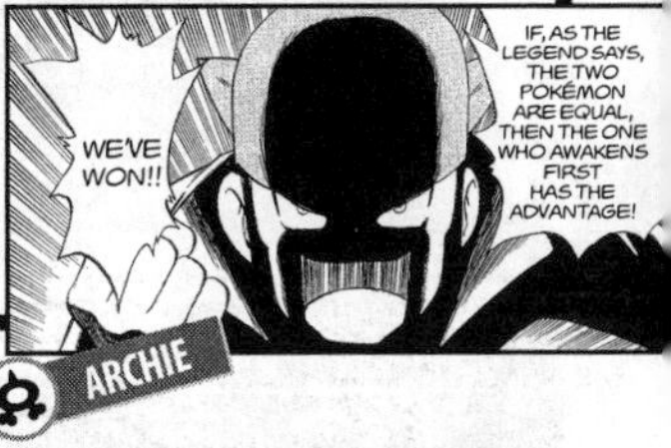
IF, AS THE LEGEND SAYS, THE TWO POKÉMON ARE EQUAL, THEN THE ONE WHO AWAKENS FIRST HAS THE ADVANTAGE!
WE'VE WON!!
ARCHIE

▶ ARCHIE BELIEVES HE'S WON BECAUSE TEAM AQUA BROUGHT KYOGRE BACK BEFORE TEAM MAGMA. BUT HE DOESN'T KNOW ABOUT THE ORBS. WILL THE ORBS ALTER THE BALANCE OF POWER?!

RUBY & SAPPHIRE

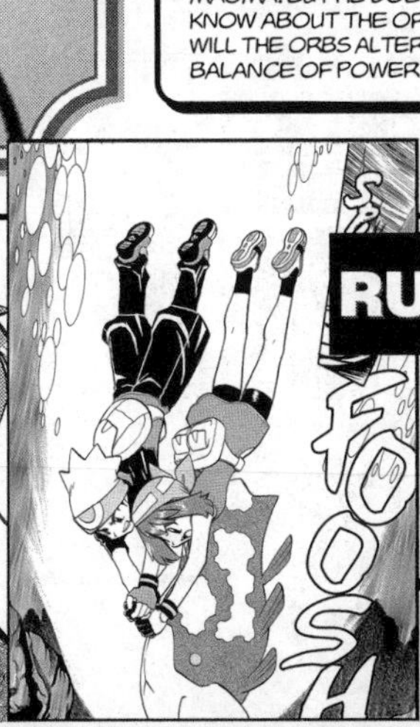
FOOOSH

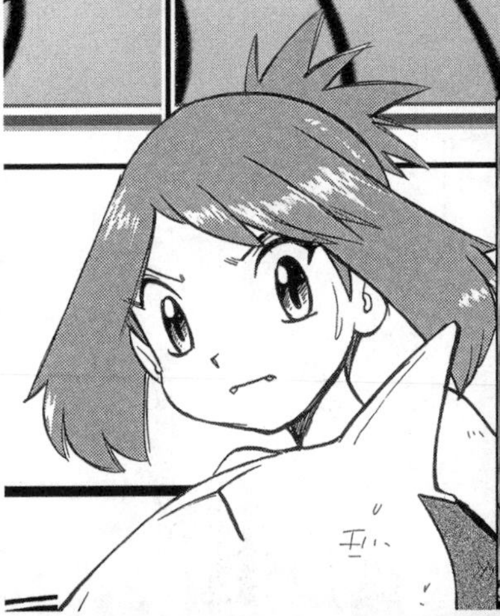

◀ THE TWO USE RELICANTH'S MOVE, DIVE, TO TRAVEL DOWN TO SEAFLOOR CAVERN, WHERE THEY PLAN TO CONFRONT THE MASTERMIND CONTROLLING THE LEGENDARY POKÉMON. THE FATE OF HOENN IS IN THEIR HANDS.

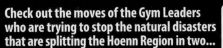

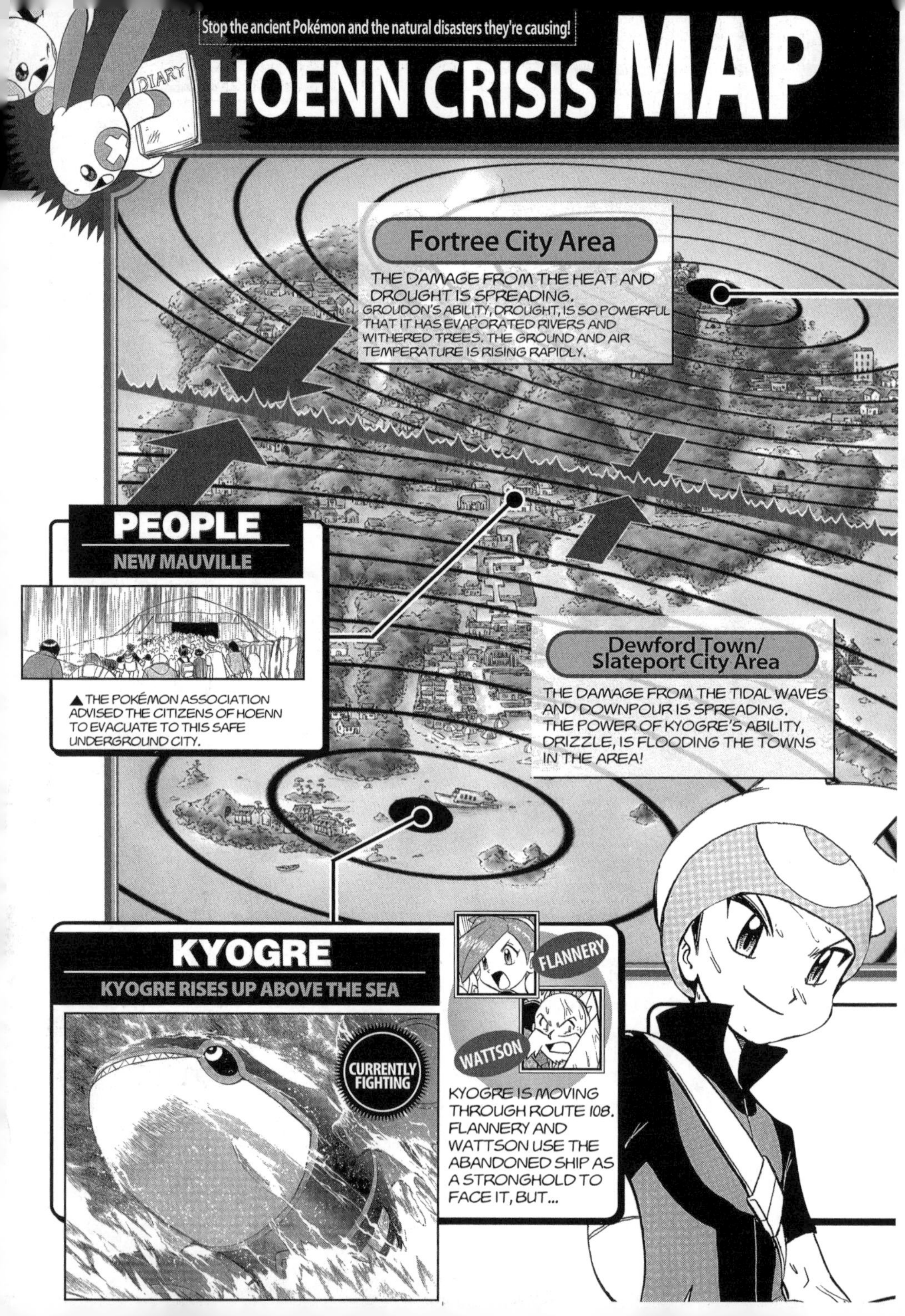
Stop the ancient Pokémon and the natural disasters they're causing!
HOENN CRISIS MAP
DIARY
Fortree City Area
THE DAMAGE FROM THE HEAT AND DROUGHT IS SPREADING.
GROUDON'S ABILITY, DROUGHT, IS SO POWERFUL THAT IT HAS EVAPORATED RIVERS AND WITHERED TREES. THE GROUND AND AIR TEMPERATURE IS RISING RAPIDLY.
PEOPLE
NEW MAUVILLE
▲THE POKÉMON ASSOCIATION ADVISED THE CITIZENS OF HOENN TO EVACUATE TO THIS SAFE UNDERGROUND CITY.
Dewford Town/ Slateport City Area
THE DAMAGE FROM THE TIDAL WAVES AND DOWNPOUR IS SPREADING. THE POWER OF KYOGRE'S ABILITY, DRIZZLE, IS FLOODING THE TOWNS IN THE AREA!
KYOGRE
KYOGRE RISES UP ABOVE THE SEA
CURRENTLY FIGHTING
FLANNERY
WATTSON
KYOGRE IS MOVING THROUGH ROUTE 108. FLANNERY AND WATTSON USE THE ABANDONED SHIP AS A STRONGHOLD TO FACE IT, BUT...

ILLUSTRATION GALLERY

PRESENTING ILLUSTRATIONS DRAWN FOR SOME OF THE PREVIOUS CHAPTERS
UPON FIRST PUBLICATION IN JAPANESE CHILDREN'S MAGAZINES.

Title
New Year's, First Fight?!

Date Drawn
Around October, 2003

First Appearance
January issue of *Shogaku Rokunensei*, 2004

Send Fan Mail to:

Pokémon
c/o VIZ Media
P.O. Box 77010
San Francisco, CA 94107

Title

Pair & Pair

Date Drawn

Around October, 2004

First Appearance

December issue of *Shogaku Yonensei*, 2004. Illustration for the 2005 New Year's greeting card.

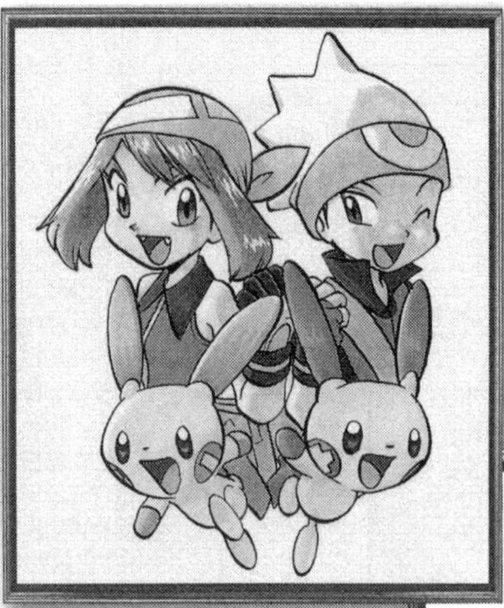

Title

Go! Go!

Date Drawn

Around December, 2003

First Appearance

March issue of *Shogaku Gonensei*, 2004

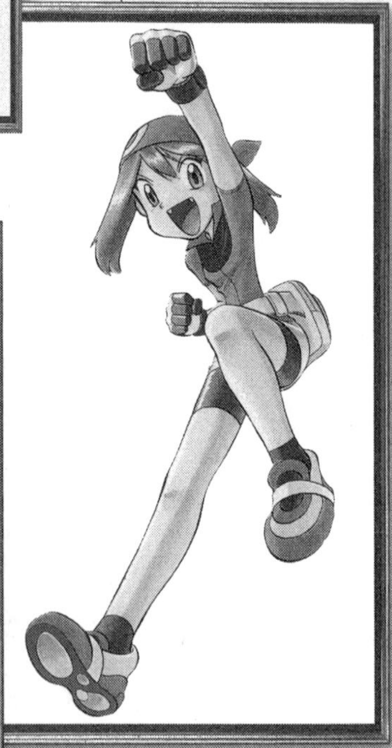

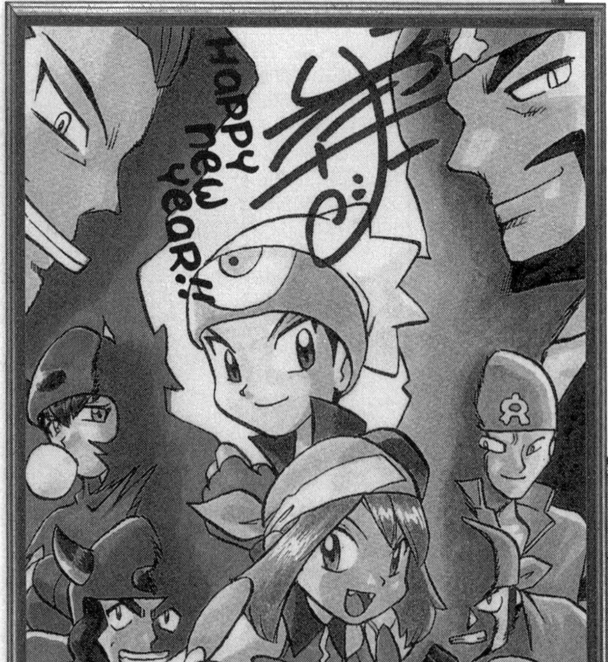
HAPPY new yeAR!!

Title

Defeat The Powerful Enemy!!

Date Drawn

Around October, 2004

First Appearance

December issue of *Shogaku Gonensei*, 2004. Illustration for the 2005 New Year's greeting card.

Special Feature: The Source of the Cosmic Power!

THE MYSTERY OF THE MYSTICAL ORBS AND STONES

The Orbs and Stones hold the key to this battle... Let's take a look at the incredible power hidden inside them.

ORBS AND STONES ARE VALUED AS WORKS OF ART IN THE HOENN REGION. THE TYPE OF ENERGY EMANATING FROM THE ORBS AND STONES IS STILL A COMPLETE MYSTERY. BUT SINCE THEY ARE DEEPLY CONNECTED TO ANCIENT POKÉMON AND THE CURRENT ENVIRONMENTAL CATASTROPHE, IT IS OF THE UTMOST IMPORTANCE TO UNDERSTAND THEIR SECRET.

ORBS

CAN BE USED TO CONTROL LEGENDARY POKÉMON'S BEHAVIOR.

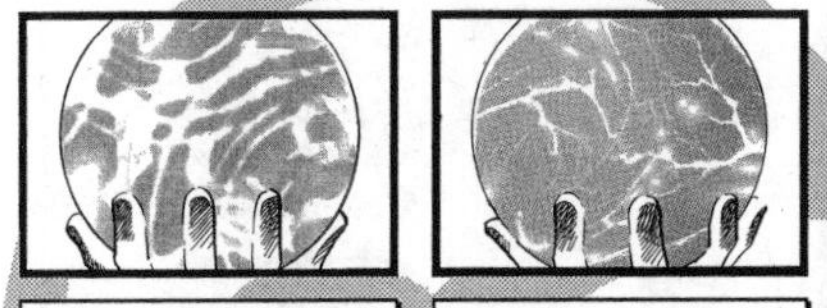

RED ORB

BLUE ORB

THE RED AND BLUE ORBS CONTROL KYOGRE AND GROUDON—AT A PRICE. THE ORBS TAKE OVER THE MINDS OF THOSE WHO WIELD THEM AND ABSORB THEIR LIFE ENERGY!

STONES

THESE SPECIAL STONES INFLUENCE POKÉMON EVOLUTION.

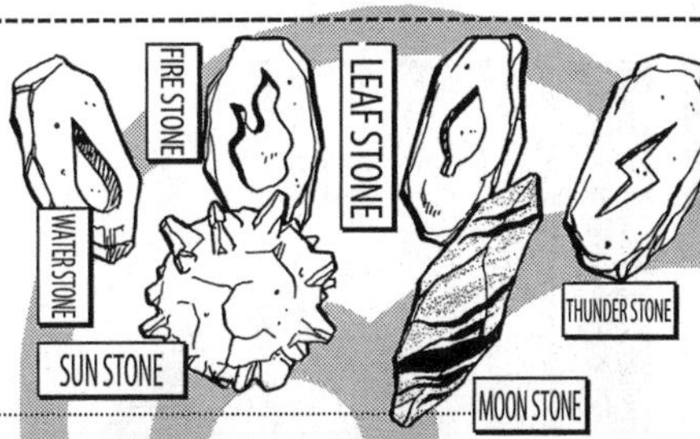
THUNDER STONE
LEAF STONE
FIRE STONE
WATER STONE
MOON STONE
SUN STONE

IT'S WIDELY KNOWN THAT THE STONES EXCAVATED THROUGHOUT THE HOENN REGION ARE CONNECTED TO POKÉMON TYPES, SUCH AS FIRE AND WATER, AND INFLUENCE POKÉMON EVOLUTION. CONVERSELY, A STONE CALLED THE EVERSTONE INHIBITS POKÉMON EVOLUTION.

METEORITE

A ROCK FULL OF MYSTICAL ENERGY THAT FELL FROM SPACE.

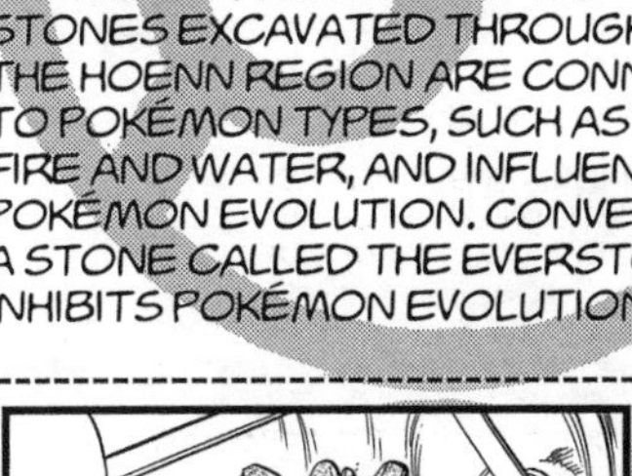
SO THIS IS...
KLUNK

METEORITE

ALTHOUGH SMALL IN STATURE, THIS METEORITE IS POWERFUL ENOUGH TO HALT THE ACTIVITY OF A VOLCANO. THE SOURCE OF ITS POWER IS THOUGHT TO BE SOME KIND OF SPECIAL ENERGY IT ABSORBED IN ITS JOURNEY THROUGH OUTER SPACE. THE MYSTERIES OF SPACE ARE ENDLESS...

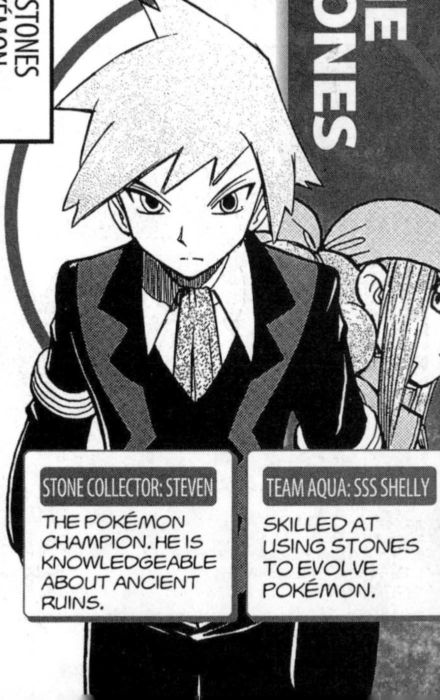

TEAM AQUA: SSS SHELLY

SKILLED AT USING STONES TO EVOLVE POKÉMON.

STONE COLLECTOR: STEVEN

THE POKÉMON CHAMPION. HE IS KNOWLEDGEABLE ABOUT ANCIENT RUINS.

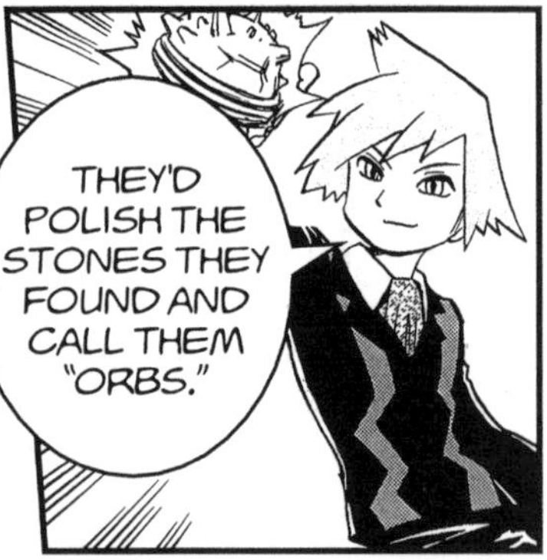
THEY'D POLISH THE STONES THEY FOUND AND CALL THEM "ORBS."

▲ THESE PRECIOUS ORBS WERE ORIGINALLY STONES.

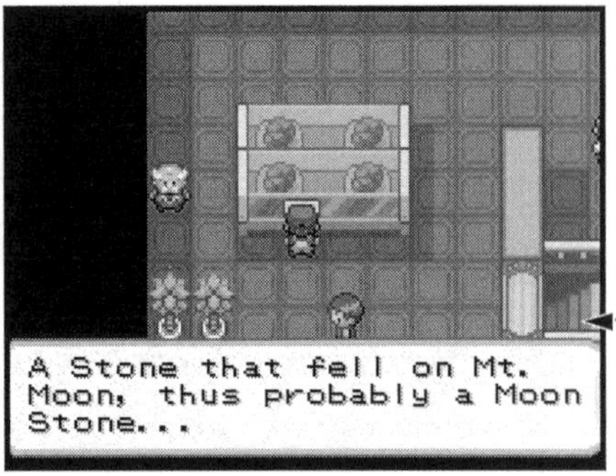
A Stone that fell on Mt. Moon, thus probably a Moon Stone...

▲ OF ALL THE STONES, ONLY THE MOON STONE HAS AN UNKNOWN DERIVATION. SOME THEORIZE THAT IT MIGHT BE A FRAGMENT OF A METEORITE THAT FELL FROM SPACE.

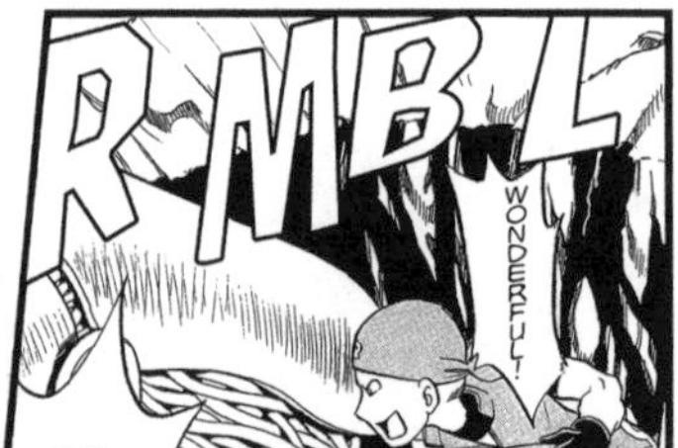
R-MB-L
WONDERFUL!
THE POWER OF THE METEORITE THAT FELL FROM SPACE IS INCREDIBLE!

▲ TEAM AQUA USED THE ENERGY OF THIS STONE TO ACCOMPLISH THEIR EVIL PLAN.

A HYPOTHESIS... DOES THE ROOT OF ALL THIS TROUBLE LIE IN...SPACE?!

THE SOURCE OF THE ORBS, STONES AND METEORITE IS ULTIMATELY LINKED TO OUTER SPACE. THERE ARE EVEN POKÉMON WHO ARE THOUGHT TO HAVE COME FROM THERE. MORE RESEARCH ON THEM IS CLEARLY CALLED FOR.

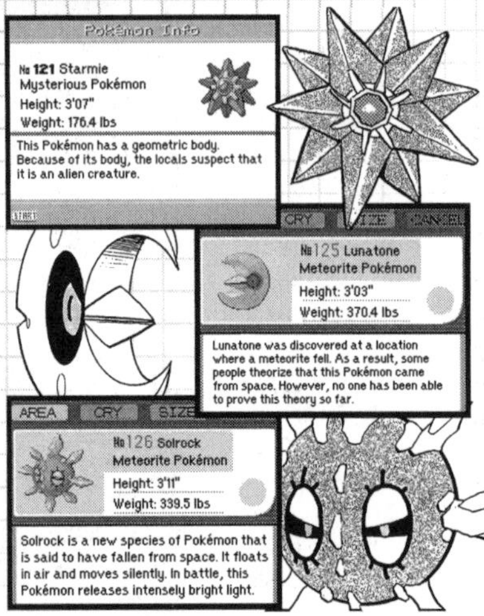
Pokémon Info
№121 Starmie
Mysterious Pokémon
Height: 3'07"
Weight: 176.4 lbs
This Pokémon has a geometric body. Because of its body, the locals suspect that it is an alien creature.
CRY
SIZE
CANCEL
№125 Lunatone
Meteorite Pokémon
Height: 3'03"
Weight: 370.4 lbs
Lunatone was discovered at a location where a meteorite fell. As a result, some people theorize that this Pokémon came from space. However, no one has been able to prove this theory so far.
AREA
CRY
SIZE
№126 Solrock
Meteorite Pokémon
Height: 3'11"
Weight: 339.5 lbs
Solrock is a new species of Pokémon that is said to have fallen from space. It floats in air and moves silently. In battle, this Pokémon releases intensely bright light.

▲ THREE POKÉMON THAT COULD BE CALLED SPACE POKÉMON. ARE THERE MORE OF THEM OUT THERE...?

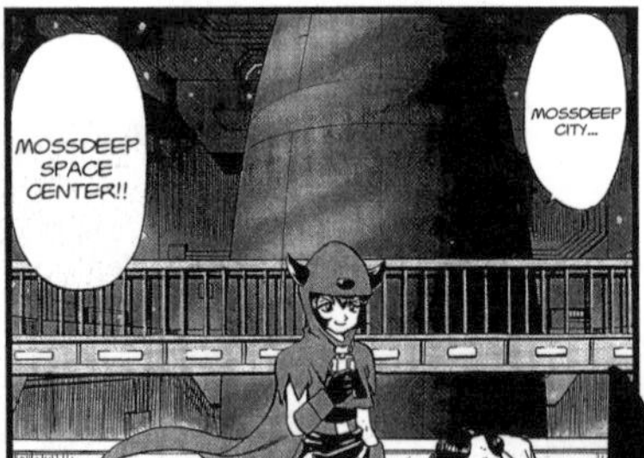
MOSSDEEP CITY...
MOSSDEEP SPACE CENTER!!

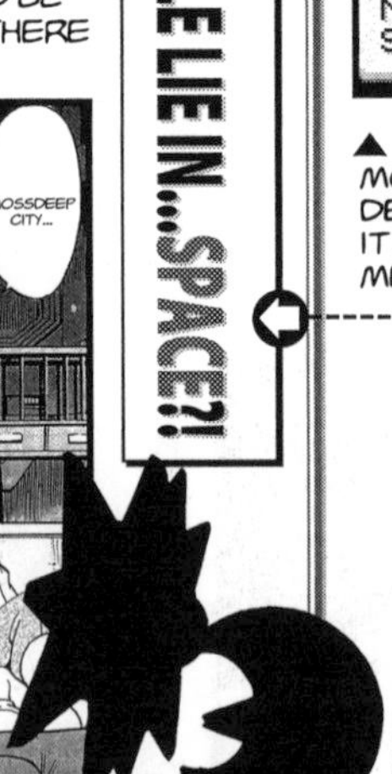

▲ HOENN IS FAMOUS FOR ITS DEVELOPMENT OF SPACE TECHNOLOGY. WILL THE ROCKET AT MOSSDEEP BE USED FOR FURTHER RESEARCH ON EXTRATERRESTRIAL LIFE FORMS?

COLLECTOR'S EDITION

Volume 7

Story by **HIDENORI KUSAKA**
Art by **SATOSHI YAMAMOTO**

Translation/Tetsuichiro Miyaki
English Adaptation/Bryant Turnage
Lettering/Annaliese "Ace" Christman
Original Series Design/Shawn Carrico
Original Series Editor/Annette Roman
Collector's Edition Production Artist/Christy Medellin
Collector's Edition Design/Julian [JR] Robinson
Collector's Edition Editor/Joel Enos

Published by VIZ Media, LLC
P.O. Box 77010
San Francisco, CA 94107

10 9 8 7 6 5 4 3 2 1
First printing, April 2021

PARENTAL ADVISORY
POKÉMON ADVENTURES is rated A
and is suitable for readers of all ages.

viz.com

HIS IS THE LAST PAGE.

THIS BOOK READS RIGHT TO LEFT.

D1513757